Enthusiastic applause for April Christofferson

Clinical Trial

"[A] deftly woven thriller . . . Substantial and intriguing."
—*Library Journal*

"Guaranteed to make any reader late for dinner, or even breakfast."
—*Booklist*

"Christofferson's smooth plotting and prose show the dexterity of a novelist coming into her own. She's especially good with her large cast of Blackfoot characters."
—*Publishers Weekly*

"Powerful."
—*Midwest Book Review*

"A well-crafted thriller."
—*Sullivan County Democrat*

"A good bit of tension—romantic as well as medical—keeps readers surging forward in this credible medical thriller. . . . And the medical insights offered by Christofferson make for good late-night reading."
—*Knight Ridder News Service*

The Protocol

"Christofferson is a writer you will become addicted to."
—*Ann Rule*

"Christofferson's second novel leaves us eagerly awaiting the third."
—*Booklist*

"Michael Chrichton-like. . . . This debut thriller is expertly paced and tautly woven. . . . Christofferson's narrative moves briskly. . . . The novel offers a rapid pace, high body count and well-rounded characters that combine to make the story a suspenseful success."
—*Publishers Weekly*

ALSO BY APRIL CHRISTOFFERSON

Clinical
Trial

April
Christofferson

A TOM DOHERTY ASSOCIATES BOOK
NEW YORK

This is a work of fiction. All the characters and events portrayed in this book are either products of the author's imagination or are used fictitiously.

CLINICAL TRIAL

Copyright © 2000 by April Christofferson

All rights reserved, including the right to reproduce this book, or portions thereof, in any form.

A Forge Book
Published by Tom Doherty Associates, LLC
175 Fifth Avenue
New York, NY 10010

www.tor.com

Forge® is a registered trademark of Tom Doherty Associates, LLC.

ISBN: 0-812-57468-0

First edition: October 2000
First mass market edition: December 2001

Printed in the United States of America

0 9 8 7 6 5 4 3 2 1

This book is dedicated to
Isabel, Jane, and Ruth,
for their courage, grace, and compassion,
And, of course,
Dad.

ACKNOWLEDGMENTS

Recently, I was standing, holding my horse while two veterinarians—my longstanding vet and another specialist he called in—examined her. After about ten minutes, the new vet turned to my regular vet and said (about me), "Does she always ask this many questions?" I realized then how many doctors, veterinarians, professional friends, and colleagues have patiently, thoughtfully, answered the never-ending questions I have plied them with over the years. Many of their answers have worked their way into my books, this one in particular. I'd like to thank Dr. Bill Schneble, Nancy Schneble, Dr. John Giesen, Dr. Dan Kennedy, Sally Teeters, Dr. Tina Ellenbogen, Dr. George Ihrke, Dr. Robert Lewis, and Joe Skovron.

A special thanks to Dr. Kit Bowerman, Susan Dos Pasos Fontaine, and Dr. Art Fontaine, who read my manuscript and provided valuable suggestions.

In Natalia Aponte, I have a terrific editor, whose vision is imprinted on every page of this book. The people at Forge are simply the best. And to my friend and agent Julie Castiglia, thank you.

Finally, to Steve, Mike, Crystal, and Ashley. You are my lifeblood. None of this would be possible without you. With you, everything is.

You must speak straight
so that your words may go as sunlight into our hearts

—Cochise, Chiracahua Apache (1812–1874)

PROLOGUE

ASI ASKGYZ CONSIDERED herself blessed. She had been born in the same modest two-room shack that now served as home to her, her beloved husband, Gorik, and their three-week-old son. The house sat near the shores of Lake Issyk-Kul, in the central Asian nation of Kyrgyzstan, and each morning Asi walked the short distance to the lake, where she drew water for tea.

This morning was especially lovely. Inside the house, her family still slept, and the spring sun made Asi feel younger than she had in months—since before she'd become pregnant and awkward in movement. She'd decided to forego the babushka that she wore daily out of respect for her Russian heritage, allowing her dark hair to fall free on her shoulders, and giving her a sense of freedom and exhilaration.

The air was so crisp and clear that the peaks of the Tyen-Shan mountains on the other side of the lake looked near enough for Asi to reach out and touch, though in reality more than thirty miles separated them.

The only thing that kept the moment from being absolutely perfect was a strange scent in the air. Asi had noticed it as soon as she stepped outside. It was light and bitter; it reminded Asi of almonds. It wasn't really unpleasant, she decided quickly, just unusual.

Soon, Asi thought, Issyk-Kul would live up to its name—"Hot Lake"—and she would bring the baby down to begin teaching him to swim. But today she simply waded in to her knees, gathering her long skirt in one hand to keep it dry.

Because of its alpine origin and considerable depth, Issyk-Kul's waters were among the cleanest natural waters in the world, and Asi had grown to love their slightly salty taste. Switching the bucket into the hand still clutching her skirt, she cupped the other hand and scooped into the coolness, drinking greedily.

After filling the bucket and gazing appreciatively out across Issyk-Kul's brilliant aquamarine expanse, Asi lifted the bucket to her lips and took another long sip. Then she turned, eager to return to her sleeping baby.

The first muscle tremors hit before she'd reached the front gate. Alarmed, Asi dropped the bucket and began to run, but her breathing had become so labored and rapid that the added effort left her clinging to the handle of the house's front door, gasping for air. She tried calling for Gorik, but her voice had deserted her.

She made it through the door, then collapsed on the floor.

As if sensing his mother's distress, the baby awoke from his sleep and began crying. At first short, birdlike bursts, the infant's sobs quickly grew to one continuous wail as Asi lay there, unable to respond.

Didn't Gorik hear their son? Frantic, Asi called upon all her strength to roll slowly over. She had to get to her baby. Rising onto her knees, she tried to lift her head. As the wailing grew louder, she managed to lift her forehead an inch or two off the floor.

Finally, just before the convulsions took hold of Asi and carried her away, she heard the shuffle of Gorik's feet. The baby quieted some for several seconds, but then his cries reached a new height.

He was hungry now. Asi recognized the cry.

But she was helpless to go to him.

•   •   •

JON LECOQUE, the fifty-seven-year-old CEO of World Resources, Inc., stood at the head of the enormous mahogany conference table, white-knuckled and trembling with rage.

"Do you mean to tell me that our truck spilled two thousand kilograms of cyanide into the Barskoon River and you actually reported it to the local authorities?"

"I wasn't even aware of the spill until yesterday afternoon. I'd been in Guyana, at the Essiquibo mine."

"One of the drivers reported it?"

"No, no sir." Pedor Oliver's frightened voice came through the speaker at the center of the conference table. "Some of the townspeople. The accident was witnessed by several fishermen."

LeCoque pounded his fist on the table, making it tremble.

"This is a disaster," said Pierre Sabin, the portly company attorney sitting to LeCoque's right.

There was a collective moan from the group assembled in Vancouver.

Jon LeCoque surveyed those assembled around him.

"It gets worse," LeCoque said. "Continue, Pedor."

"Well, people have been getting sick. One of the fishermen who was standing in the water. And now a young woman has died. They say it's because she drank from Issyk-Kul."

"The lake?" Sabin asked.

"Yes. The Barskoon runs into it."

"Is that possible, Eleanor?" Sabin turned to the stone-faced Asian woman sitting at the end of the table opposite LeCoque.

"No," Eleanor Nguyen said. Nguyen headed up WRI's environmental compliance department. "Lake Issyk-Kul is several miles downstream from the accident. By the time the cyanide reached the lake, it would have been so diluted that . . ."

"You're wrong, Eleanor. It's definitely possible," Tony Wilderman spoke up. Wilderman served as WRI's top exploratory geologist. The wild, rusty curls that formed a semicircle around his balding head and the only blue jeans in the room set him apart from the rest gathered there, who, despite the fact that it was Sunday morning, looked to have spent every bit as much time grooming themselves to come into the office this morning as they did every other day. "It's just what happened in Guyana. As soon as the cyanide hit the water, it formed a poisonous mass that would have moved downstream. The town of Barskoon gets its drinking water from the river. Those slugs tend to stay intact for a while. Eventually it would have reached the lake. Plenty of time to poison people."

Eleanor Nguyen shot Wilderman a look of contempt.

"Did the fisherman drink out of the river?" Sabin wanted to know from Pedor.

"Didn't have to," Wilderman cut in. "Cyanide enters the body through inhalation of the gas, absorption through the skin, or ingestion. If he was standing in the water that close to the spill, chances are the fisherman both inhaled *and* absorbed it. What's his condition? Do we know?"

"I talked to a doctor at the hospital," Pedor said. "He's severely ill. Has an enlarged liver. But the doctor thinks he'll pull through."

There was a moment of silence as all present began to process the ramifications of the information presented by Pedor.

"Anything in the papers?" Mike Lane, vice president of public relations, asked Pedor.

"Front page. Headlines."

"Thank you, Pedor," said LeCoque disgustedly. "We'll get back to you once we formulate a plan. Stand by."

Impatiently, he punched a button on the phone's panel, ending the call.

"This spill has the potential to be devastating to WRI, people. Damage control is essential. Let's hear suggestions."

Eleanor Nguyen, hoping to redeem herself after being contradicted by Wilderman, spoke up.

"We could send a team over there. Check for cyanide in the lake and soil. By the time we get there, it's likely the readings will have dropped to a level that's insignificant."

"What else?" LeCoque said.

"I think we need to get on the phone with the chief of police," Mike Lane said. "Tell him we regret the actions of the drivers, their failure to report the accident. Tell him we've fired the men involved and we're initiating an internal investigation."

"That's a dangerous route. It can be tantamount to an admission of guilt," Pierre Sabin said. "If people are getting sick, even dying, the last thing we want to do is start expressing regret."

The room fell silent.

"Okay," LeCoque said. "Eleanor, you get over there and conduct those tests. Mike, once Eleanor has readings for you, call the local paper. Tell them there's no chance the spill caused that woman's death. That WRI accepts full responsibility for the accident itself, but that what's happened since is a result of hysteria. Tell them that we will consider taking legal action if their irresponsible reporting does not stop. And that WRI may have to reassess its presence in Kyrgyzstan."

"The Kamton is our richest deposit," Tony Wilderman said, scowling.

"Exactly," LeCoque agreed. "That's why we can't afford to let one accident screw things up for us."

No one in the room dared to mention the fact that this accident made two, in two years.

"That mine contributes almost twenty-five percent to Kyrgyzstan's gross domestic product," LeCoque continued. "They're not about to let us leave over something this trivial. We just need to let a little time pass. This whole thing will blow over."

Suddenly, the shrill ring of the phone in the middle of the table pierced the air.

LeCoque signaled Mike Lane to pick it up.

Lane answered. He pressed the hold button and turned to his boss.

"It's the Vancouver *Herald*. They've picked up a story on the wire service about the spill. Are we prepared to comment?"

CHAPTER

ONE

ARLO IRON HEART wasn't exactly living up to his name. This would be Dr. Isabel McLain's second attempt to draw the blood required for a blood sugar test. In the three months that Isabel had been running the Blackfeet reservation clinic in Browning, Montana, Arlo had made, then failed to show up for, no fewer than three appointments. Finally, today, he'd arrived at the clinic without one.

His timing was rotten—Isabel was already running behind—but, as he'd been instructed to do when he made the earlier appointments, upon his arrival this morning Arlo had proudly announced that he'd fasted for the previous twelve hours. Knowing that if she sent him away she might never see him again, Isabel worked him in.

Arlo presented classic diabetes symptoms: unexplained weight loss, frequent urination, and increased thirst.

"Mr. Iron Heart, every time you look at the needle, you jerk your arm away and I have to start over. I'd suggest you either close your eyes or focus on something besides what I'm trying to do here."

"Can't help it," the old, braided Indian groused through a puckered mouth that drew down at either end. "Shoulda never come here in the first place."

When she first came to the reservation clinic, Isabel had tried an approach intended to soothe and calm patients like Arlo, offering condescendingly simplified explanations for what she was doing. When that only seemed to create more distrust, and her patience grew thin, she'd dropped any attempt at a bedside manner.

"Do you want me to help you or not? Because I can do that, help you feel better. But I can't do it until I'm sure what the problem is, and I'm not about to fight you for the ridiculously small amount of blood I need for this test."

She pushed back, ready to go on to her next patient.

The bluff worked. Iron Heart held his arm in front of him and closed his eyes.

"Be quick about it," he ordered.

With a sigh, Isabel inserted the needle. Iron Heart's blood had almost filled the tube when the door opened and her assistant, Suzanne Featherhart, appeared.

At the sound of the door opening, Iron Heart startled and jerked his arm away, spraying blood across the front of Isabel's white lab coat.

Reflexively, Isabel reached for the old man's elbow, pressing her gloved forefinger against the entry site. By now, Iron Heart looked easily as pale as the fair-skinned Isabel.

Exasperated, Isabel looked up at Suzanne.

"What is it?"

"I have to leave early for lunch," Suzanne said. Suzanne had a wild head of black, spiked hair and enormous, dark eyes, but sometimes all Isabel saw when she looked at her assistant was the cherry-red lipstick she wore day in and out. "And I won't be back 'til later."

"How much later?"

Suzanne shrugged her rounded shoulders.

"Don't really know. Depends on how long the meeting takes."

"What kind of meeting?"

"Tribal business. My Aunt Mary wants me to go with her."

"And you just found out about it now? You know how busy today's going to be."

Suzanne pushed the door farther open, enabling Isabel to see someone standing behind her in the poorly lit hallway.

"That's why I asked Joe to come."

Joe Winged Foot stepped forward, out of Suzanne's shadow.

Shaking her head wearily, Isabel looked down at the tube of blood she'd withdrawn from Arlo.

"That should be enough for the test." She nodded at Suzanne. "Take over here, will you? Clean him up before you leave. And be sure to pull the charts for this afternoon."

"Already did."

Clutching his arm dramatically, Arlo Iron Heart eyed Isabel's lab coat in disgust.

"Mr. Iron Heart, these tests should be done by Friday. Please make another appointment to see me then."

Finally, Isabel turned to Joe Winged Foot and smiled. She was always glad to see Joe.

"Come with me," she told him. "I need to change into a clean lab coat."

As Joe followed her into her office, Isabel glanced at her watch. Eleven forty-five.

"How'd you manage to get out of school so early?"

"Suzanne wrote me a note." Joe grinned, sliding his lanky form through the door and flopping like a rag doll into the chair next to Isabel's desk. "Besides, graduation's only a coupla weeks off. No one's payin' attention anymore. Mrs. Andrews, she likes that I come to visit you so much. She says I can learn a lot here."

As he spoke, Joe's basketball sneakers drummed a staccato beat on the linoleum flooring. Despite his height—just five feet nine inches—Joe served as the point guard and star of the Blackfeet high school team that had lost in overtime to a Missoula team in the state championship. He took great pride in his basketball skills and his team's successful season, frequently, like today, wearing his championship jersey layered over another T-shirt. Isabel thought all the Blackfeet youngsters a pleasure to look at, but Joe's lively brown eyes, perfectly etched nose, and ready grin made him unusually appealing.

Isabel crossed the cramped room to the closet and grabbed a white lab coat fresh from the dry cleaner.

"You and Suzanne set me up, didn't you?" she said, turning to eye Joe good-naturedly.

Despite her chagrin at her assistant, Isabel found Joe's broad smile infectious. Still, today it seemed just a tad less blinding than usual.

"You feeling okay?"

"Sure. Just a little tired from a late pickup game last night. You gonna let me give some shots today?"

Isabel slipped into the fresh lab coat as she ushered Joe back out into the hallway.

" 'Fraid not. But I might let you take a temperature or two."

Grinning, Joe continued down the hall to the reception area to find Isabel's next patient. Watching Joe, Isabel could not dispell the impression that he seemed somehow subdued. She made a mental note to question him further.

Joe reappeared moments later with Eli Walker.

"Jason Little Turtle just showed up without an appointment," Joe told Isabel. "Thinks he's got the flu."

"There you go." Isabel smiled. "Why don't you take Jason into the other exam room and get his temperature?"

When Joe hesitated, Isabel added, "The thermometer's in a glass container on the counter, but you need to put a disposable shield over it first. They're in the drawer next to the sink. Think you can handle that?"

" 'Course," he answered none too certainly, turning back toward the waiting room.

Isabel ushered Eli into the exam room.

"How's that leg doing, Eli?" she asked.

Eli had recently been hospitalized for a deep venous thrombosis—a large blood clot in his right femoral vein.

"Still sore some," Eli answered, eyes glued to the floor. "But I don't see why I gotta come in here so much."

"I told you," Isabel said. "The anticoagulant the doctors in Cutbank put you on will keep you from getting more clots, but we have to monitor it. We don't want your blood getting too thin."

Isabel pricked the tip of Eli's index finger and directed two drops of falling blood onto the protime monitor. Within seconds, a number indicating the time it took his blood to clot flashed on a small screen.

"Eleven. That's high." Isabel had been standing in front of a seated Eli, but now she lowered herself to his eye level.

"You look like crap, Eli. Have you been drinking?"

The stale odor of alcohol wafted to her nostrils from Eli's person and clothing.

Eli did not raise his gaze to meet hers.

"Mebbe a little," he mumbled to the floor.

Isabel straightened up and placed her hand on her right hip.

"What am I going to do with you? Don't you realize that alcohol plays havoc with the anticoagulant you're taking? We need to get you within the acceptable protime range and keep it there. Right now, you could bleed to death over something as insignificant as a bump on the head. Just how much did you have to drink?"

Eli shrugged his shoulders.

Isabel felt like shaking some sense into him, but instead she reached out and touched Eli under the chin.

"Look at me, Eli." When he finally raised heavily lidded eyes to hers, she continued. "Be honest with me. Is there a chance in hell that you can stop drinking for the six months you'll be on the anticoagulant?"

A blank stare gave her her answer, but Eli also managed a weak, "Not really."

"Okay, then. How about this? You keep it to two drinks

a day. Understand? But you have to be consistent. You have to drink those two drinks *every single day*."

For the first time, Eli perked up.

"Ya mean you *want* me to drink every day?"

"No, that's not what I said. But I can't get your coagulation levels steady if you can only manage to abstain a couple days before going on another binge. It would be better to have you drink a moderate amount consistently. At least that way I have half a chance of adjusting your medication to keep you within an acceptable range."

"What about three drinks?" Eli said hopefully. "Or four?"

"Two. That's the deal. Take it or leave it."

Eli fell silent for a moment as he appeared to study the floor.

"Didja mean that? That I could bleed to death?"

"We've already been over this, Eli. Yes, I do mean it. Right now your blood's about as thin as the chicken soup they serve down at Sandy's Diner. Blood that's too thin is almost as dangerous as blood that can throw a clot. In some ways, more. But I can fix that. If you'll just cooperate with me. What do you say?"

" 'Spose two drinks a day's better than none," he finally muttered. "Or bleedin' to death . . ."

"You bet it is. Now listen to me closely. I want you to skip your regular dose of anticoagulant for the next two days. Then come back in here for another reading. Do you have any questions? Two days without your medicine, two drinks a day, then come back in and we'll see if your protime's back where we want it."

After getting a mumbled acknowledgment from Eli, Isabel moved on to the next room, where Jason Little Turtle sat on the exam table with a thermometer sticking out of his tightly clenched mouth.

Jason and Arlo turned out to be the first of four unscheduled patients that afternoon. Isabel and Joe moved quickly from one room to another, with Joe ushering patients in, then cleaning up the rooms between visits. There was little time for small talk.

FINALLY, AROUND THREE-THIRTY, just as Isabel finished her exam of a four-year-old girl who'd suffered an asthma attack the night before, Suzanne reappeared.

"I'm back," she announced, crossing the room to help the wide-eyed child down from the exam table while the young mother bounced her wailing two-year-old brother on her knee.

"Good," Isabel answered. "Did you let Joe know that he can leave when he wants?"

"He's already gone."

"Oh."

The rest of the afternoon proved even more chaotic than the morning had been—too chaotic to worry about Joe. Late in the day, when she went into the storage closet and opened a supply cupboard, Isabel almost had a heart attack when a furry projectile shot straight out, as if aimed squarely at her face.

A mouse.

Luckily it fell short.

She sent Suzanne down to Standing Bear Hardware for traps, then raced off from her last patient to her quarterly meeting with the tribal council, leaving Suzanne to bait the traps with peanut butter, as instructed by Dan Standing Bear.

It was much later—almost midnight—before Isabel had time to give serious consideration to the fact that Joe had left the clinic without saying goodbye. When she dropped into bed, completely and utterly exhausted, it was the first thing to come to mind.

It was so unlike Joe to leave today without saying goodbye.

She would make a point of taking time to visit with him

tomorrow—surely he'd drop by after school—to make sure that everything was all right.

She was so fond of Joe, had such great hopes for him, as did everyone else in the town. Joe Winged Foot was the Blackfeets' shining light—college bound, intelligent, determined to make something of himself. He had recently told Isabel he might become a doctor, come back to the reservation and take care of his people. After he "got done playing in the NBA."

Nagged with a vague, unsettling worry about Joe, Isabel had difficulty getting to sleep. But finally exhaustion set in and she fell into a deep, profound slumber.

THE TRIBAL HEADQUARTERS business offices were located within a three-square-block area on the north side of Browning, half a mile from the clinic.

Suzanne and her Aunt Mary lived together in a trailer just off Highway 2, seven miles southeast of town. Mary had arranged for a neighbor to pick her up and drop her off at the Blackfeet Health and Safety Corps building, where the meeting was taking place. As Suzanne approached the dark brown, U-shaped log structure, she could see her frail aunt huddled outside on a bench next to a colorful sign that featured a large turquoise circle around a white, block-style cross. Overlaid upon the cross were an American flag, a turquoise star, and, in bold black letters, BHSC.

"Why are you sitting out here?" Suzanne scolded as she walked across the wet grass from the parking lot. "It's cold and wet."

"I was just waiting for you," Mary Talking Horse answered quietly. It had stopped raining but her thin powder blue sweatshirt offered little protection from the wind and fifty-degree temperature.

"But you could have waited inside."

With Suzanne holding one arm, Mary used her other hand

to cling tightly to the iron railing as the two women climbed half a dozen cement steps to the building's front door. Inside, several familiar faces lingered in the hallway. Suzanne nodded at Sumner Willow and his daughter, Ann. A large hand-lettered cardboard sign read TRUST AFFAIRS MEETING and pointed down the hallway.

As they approached an open door two-thirds of the way down the corridor, Suzanne heard voices. She steered Mary inside, where at least a dozen tribal members sat on folding chairs arranged in four rows.

"Here's Mary Talking Horse now," a strong, resonant baritone announced from the front of the room. "And Suzanne."

Both Suzanne and Mary turned toward the speaker. In three long strides, Monty Four Bear crossed the room to greet them.

When Suzanne heard that Monty would be chairing today's meeting, her aunt's request that she accompany her became all the more palatable. She'd known the handsome lawyer since they were children.

"Thanks for coming," Monty said. He placed a hand on Mary's bony shoulder and nodded to Suzanne over Mary's gray head of hair.

"Hey."

"Hey," Suzanne replied.

As Suzanne directed her aunt to a chair, both she and Mary nodded respectfully at Sky Thomas, who was seated dead center in the front row.

Sky was the oldest living member of the Blackfeet tribe. She lived in a two-room wood frame house just off Main Street and, at ninety-three, still walked to tribal functions and meetings in town—even those, like the one today, that did not pertain directly to her. Sky was widely believed to have visionary powers. Age had not dulled her good mind, and she enjoyed great respect from her Blackfeet family.

As Monty returned to the front of the room, Sumner and Ann Willow slipped into the room, coffee cups in hand.

"I think everyone's here now," Monty said, grabbing an empty chair. "We might as well get started."

Turning the chair backward, he eased himself, saddle-style, onto it. Six feet tall and lean, Suzanne couldn't help but notice that Monty still moved with the grace of the track star he'd once been. In faded blue jeans and well-scuffed cowboy boots, his long black hair parted neatly in the middle and pushed behind both ears, the sight of him stirred memories of the girlhood crush she'd had on him when she was twelve and he was eighteen.

"I think I've had one-on-one conversations with just about everyone in this room before today," Monty began. "Lester Wolf Spirit first came to me about the problems he was having getting information on his trust account over two years ago. After I looked into it for Lester, I guess word got out, and pretty soon more of you started coming to me. Before long, I kind of became a poster boy for this thing. Unfortunately, I haven't had much success—for Lester, or the rest of you."

"At least them people at the Bureau, they listen more to you than they do to us," Wolf Spirit called from the last row. "After you started callin' 'em, they sent me a letter. There wasn't no money with it, but it's the first time I got anything on paper from them in the forty years since my father died and passed that land on to me."

"I get statements a couple times a year, but I don't trust what they put on there anyway," Sumner Willow huffed from where he and Ann had settled. "I know damn well that the B and N is payin' somebody to run trains across my property. But I haven't seen a penny of it."

Suzanne felt her aunt's body stiffen. Usually quiet and much too shy to talk in public, Mary surprised her by standing.

"I get a check here and there from the Bureau," she said, slowly straightening into her usual erect posture. "Most of you know of my great-grandfather Black Bull. When the government divided the land up, Black Bull and his brother got a hundred-sixty acres. That's been passed down to me. I know that land is producing money 'cause every once and again I get a little check from the Bureau. It's never much. Usually just enough for me and Suzanne to splurge a little, buy some groceries so we can get a break from commodity food. Or maybe take a trip into Kalispell."

When she paused, the group remained silent and attentive.

"Back a couple years ago," she continued, "when my husband Charlie got so sick and I needed money to go back and forth to Cutbank for dialysis, I figured if I could find this land of Black Bull's, I could see for myself what was goin' on on it. Far as I know they could be pumpin' oil out of the ground. I heard stories like that, Indians living with their windows all boarded up 'cause they can't afford to fix them, while just outside—if they had glass in there, they'd be able to see it—trucks are hauling oil off their property by the barrel. Same thing could be happening to any one of us here. My family hasn't actually lived on Black Bull's land for generations. My mama forgot just where it was. So I tried calling the Bureau to get some information on it. 'Course we all know how that is, trying to get someone to talk to you on the phone. They got this thing they call . . ." She turned to Suzanne, a scowl creasing her already deeply lined brow, and Suzanne whispered, "Voice mail."

"Voice mail. They call it voice mail. Well, it made me half glad I couldn't afford a phone back then 'cause if that's what you get when you call for help, I don't need it. I got dizzy tryin' to figure out what they were tellin' me, which button to press and so on. Anyway, I never did talk to a real live person and I never heard from anyone after I left a message.

"You all know Charlie finally died. Suzanne here, she moved in to help me out and now at least the bills get paid and we got a phone. But it's no life for a young girl like Suzanne. If I got a little more money from that land, on a regular basis, she could move out and have a life of her own."

Suzanne stared at the old woman. She had no idea Mary considered herself a burden. It was the Blackfeet way for family to take care of family. Mary was Suzanne's deceased mother's only sister, and when Uncle Charlie died there had never been any question in Suzanne's mind that she would move in with Mary. She would have preferred Mary to come live with her in her apartment in town, but Mary refused to leave the trailer she'd called home for four decades. And so Suzanne had moved to the trailer, where she slept in the living room, a curtain hung between it and the kitchen for privacy.

After that one time, the situation was never discussed again.

Suzanne grabbed her aunt's hand to help her back into her seat. It was cold, and it shook.

"What I wanna know is what're we gonna do about it," Wolf Spirit said. "Can you help us, Monty? 'Cause you're about the only one of us who knows how to deal with this kind of stuff."

Heads nodded around the room.

"We can always count on Monty," Mary Talking Horse murmured.

Monty had remained silent, monitoring the mood in the room.

"It's obviously not an easy situation to correct," he finally offered. "Everyone knows how long this has been going on. For over a century. And while it's become politically correct to voice concern about how our people have been treated, no one's really stepped up to the plate to make any kind of changes. At least none that really make a difference. And even if they were to make them now, even if they correct things from here on out, there's still the matter of the money that was rightly due all of you in the past. There's only one way I know to recover that." His eyes measured each of the room's occupants. "And that's sue."

"We can do that? We can sue them?" Ann Willow asked.

"There's been talk for a while now among many tribes about a class action suit, for mismanagement of Indian assets. Maybe even fraud. I think we've taken this long enough. It's time to make them listen. I believe a class action suit will do that."

"Let's sue," Wolf Spirit grunted.

"You bet," Sumner Willow called out. "Sue them bastards."

Excited chatter broke out across the room, but when Sky Thomas lifted her thick cane and brought it down hard on the wood floor, not once, but twice, the room grew completely still.

" 'Course we deserve what we got comin' to us," she said in a croak of a voice. "Monty here, he does a good job of looking out for us, and if he thinks we should sue, most the time I'd be right behind him." She'd twisted her aged body to get a look at the others. "But trouble's coming."

Next to Suzanne, Mary Talking Horse drew in a short, sharp breath and pressed a hand to her heart. Sky's pronouncement caused a number of raised eyebrows as well, even among the usually stoic men.

"What kind of trouble, Sky?" Monty asked. There was no hint of skepticism or disrespect in his tone.

"I can't tell you that," the old woman answered grumpily. "I just know it's comin'. And I've seen what happens when our people try to fight too many battles at once. You gotta choose your battles. That's all I'm tryin' to say."

She turned back around to face the front of the room.

The room fell silent again as Monty studied the faces turned toward him, looking for answers.

"A lot of preparation goes into a lawsuit," he finally said. "Especially a class action. There's no need to rush the actual filing. I can get started with some of the groundwork, and then we can meet again, let's say in six months, to re-evaluate. How does that sound?"

"That sounds like a good plan," Suzanne said.

"We better just wait 'til we see what the heck Sky's talkin' about," Sumner agreed hesitantly.

CHAPTER

TWO

WHAT DO YOU mean you cayn't find it?"

A product of Louisiana's Cajun country, Alistair Bott's carefully honed Northwestern accent sometimes slipped when he was caught off guard.

Bott had been so engrossed in the discussion taking place in the online chat room that he'd ignored the phone the first two times it rang. But when it became apparent the caller would not give up, he'd finally picked up.

The sound of fear in Mary Pelandini's voice was most unwelcome.

"I expected it to be in that stack of faxes you took from your office at home," she explained. "But I've been through those papers a dozen times. It's not there."

"You mean to tell me you still haven't shredded all of those documents?"

"I didn't want to shred them until I rounded up all the originals and matched them up to be sure both the originals and any copies were destroyed. You said you didn't want any mix-ups, any loose documents out there that could come back to haunt us."

"And that's taken three months?"

"What took time was purging all the files at the clinic. That was a huge job—we're talking hundreds of boxes full of files. I had to go through every word on every page of every file, tear out pages, remove charts, you name it." Alistair could hear Mary's anxiety turning to exasperation. "Without one bit of help from you or anybody else, I might add."

"And you did a wonderful job, darlin'," Alistair cooed. "I hope you know how much I 'preciate it. Listen, I've been meaning to tell you something. It's very good news. Remember I said I have a friend who works for the FDA? Well, he's been keeping his eyes and ears open, and he says the word so far is that they didn't find anything in the audit. Which is exactly what I told you would happen. Isn't it? Hell, those files had already passed the scrutiny of dozens of monitors."

On the other end, Mary let out a short, caustic laugh.

"You doctors really do live in la-la land, don't you? So incredibly out of touch with what goes on in the world of us mere mortals." She took a deep breath, signaling her impatience. "Monitors only look at data, you know that. They don't look any deeper. They're not gonna find a damn thing. These auditors, they're another story."

Alistair swallowed hard, biting back his impulse to take Mary to task. How dare she speak to him with such disrespect? His employees always, always treated him with the utmost deference. Or they simply did not remain employees for long. But right now he needed Mary. He could not afford to alienate her.

"That may be the case, darlin', but still, from what I heard from my contact, we're in fine shape. However, according to my friend, the investigation won't be formally concluded for a while yet. Maybe even another month or two. We just have to hang tight 'til then."

"Did your friend tell you that an investigator's been snooping around Harborview?" Mary asked.

Reluctant to miss out on the chatroom give-and-take, Alistair's eyes had begun straying back to the computer screen, but with these words, they snapped back to attention. His grip on the phone tightened.

"What do you mean they're snooping around Harborview?"

"Just what I said. Ariana called to say they'd been over there, talking to people. She's getting real nervous."

"What did they ask her?"

"They haven't talked to her yet. She was off on the day the guy came around."

This was not good news at all.

"Can Ariana be trusted?"

"Definitely," Mary answered. "She gave me her file with all the information she's given us. She wanted it out of there. Ariana's raising four kids alone. No way she can afford to lose her job."

"The list was there, in her file?"

"The original was there. And I found a copy of it in my files, too."

"Then that's probably all there ever was," Alistair said emphatically. "We've had this conversation too many times now, Mary. I know Ariana told you she remembered faxing it to me, but I also told you, I never got it. She must have given the list directly to you. I must say, dear girl, you are startin' to exhibit signs of paranoia, and it's not especially attractive."

His grip had relaxed a bit. The only weak link, as he now saw it, was Ariana. If she was cooperating, they would be okay.

"Maybe it's not so much that I'm paranoid as it is you thinking you're goddamned invincible. All you doctors are the same. Think you're omnipotent. For your information, there's a problem with your safe little assumption that Ariana never faxed the list to you."

"What kind of problem?"

"There was another sheet attached to that original."

"Jesus H. Christ, Mary. Will you just get to the point? What're you tryin' to say?"

"It was a transmission report. It indicated the transmission had been successful. The number the fax was sent to," she hesitated, perhaps for effect, "is *yours*. It's the fax number at your house."

Alistair's free hand closed around the phone cord and balled into a tight fist.

"Then you better keep looking," he ordered. "It has to be there somewhere."

"Unless *she* took it."

"If she took it, she'd have turned it over to that bull dyke attorney of hers and the authorities would've been swarming over us like gnats on roadkill by now. She can't possibly have it. It has to be somewhere. *Find it.*"

He hung up the phone, his interest in the goings-on online extinguished.

This was not good news at all. After his last conversation with Robin Getty—his med school roommate who'd turned to the bureaucracy of the FDA when he couldn't hack it in private practice—Alistair had congratulated himself.

Nobody was going to bring Alistair Bott down, least of all his estranged wife.

Not after all he'd been through to get where he was today.

The only son of a mean-spirited alcoholic from the back-woods of Louisiana. Lazy, temperamental son of a bitch unable to stay sober long enough to hold down a job for more than a few months at a time, which meant that after Alistair's mother died—her income as a housekeeper was meager, but steady—Stanley Bott would take off for days, sometimes weeks at a time, telling his young son he was looking for work, leaving Alistair alone, from the age of ten on, to fend for himself and, at times, literally forage for food to fuel him through the school day.

School. It had been Alistair's salvation. His safe haven,

where, by working hard and playing upon the sympathy of his teachers, he learned what it took to garner attention and praise. He vowed as a young child to leave Louisiana the first opportunity that presented itself, and when he graduated from high school at the top of his class—a feat aided considerably by the copies he'd stolen of his calculus and chemistry final exams—that opportunity finally came, in the form of a scholarship to Gonzaga University in Spokane, Washington.

With each success, each move, Alistair managed to put a little more distance—not just geographical—between himself and his backwoods past, cultivating a gentleman's demeanor, an intellect, a mystique. He became something of a chameleon, able to adapt quickly. His charm and golden-haired good looks earned him instant popularity with the girls, but he was never as successful with the male population, who regarded him with suspicion—as something of a freak, with his silky southern accent, lack of interest in sports or beer, and his courtly demeanor with the coeds. Determined to overcome the frail, sickly image he had as a child, the long hours that Alistair spent in front of a mirror in the gym did nothing to further his popularity with his male colleagues, but his cover boy physique made a big impression on coeds.

With a 4.0 grade point and biology degree in hand, Alistair made the move across the Cascades to Seattle, to attend med school at the University of Washington, where he met Isabel McLain, the exotic loner in his first-year anatomy class.

In med school, study groups were just an analogue for small, tight-knit cliques. They formed instantly, like drops of oil hitting water, and had just as strong a tendency to cling together. Like him, Isabel was one of the few students who studied alone, who didn't really fit in. The difference, however, was clear to Alistair from the start—something about Isabel made her *choose* to be on the outside, while Alistair's need to be looked up to, admired, and envied, had tugged at every fiber of his being for so very long that he would have sold his soul to fit in.

Leggy, with long, thick black hair—usually tied back, which accentuated a face all angles and lips and eyes—all the guys in med school had a thing for Isabel. Alistair watched for two years, sat back with amusement, as Isabel politely but unequivocally rejected one after another, which, of course, only increased her allure, the entire male population's fascination with her. And only upped Alistair's determination to have her.

From the start, Isabel represented triumph to Alistair—triumph over his father's predictions that his son would end up just like the old man. Triumph over the poverty and hopelessness of the redneck hill country he'd grown up in. Triumph over all those arrogant sons of bitches who thought they were better than Alistair Bott.

And—the icing on the cake—Isabel also happened to turn him on like no other woman he'd ever known. Ever *had*. And he'd had plenty.

Isabel McLain would have nothing to do with the other guys, but eventually—perhaps out of pity for his outsider status, for he was not above using that to his advantage—she agreed to go out with him. He'd observed her, studied her for two years by that time, and he knew all the buttons to push. Environmentalist, openly disdainful of social status and wealth—yet still eager to please a father she clearly adored.

On their first date, he took her to a Sierra Club fund-raiser, feigning ignorance of the fact that her father was on the board of directors. Alistair had spent years hiding his past, but something told him that with Isabel, it could prove useful. For the first time since creating a new life for himself, he disclosed the hardships he'd endured as a child. He shared with her the fears and insecurities. The hunger and loneliness.

This took place at her apartment, as they shared a bottle

of wine. That night, drawn into those eyes that were like deep, warm pools, he'd actually fallen in love with Isabel McLain.

Amazingly, she'd made love to him that very night, and he'd discovered that under that cool-as-cucumber facade that kept everyone at arm's length resided a woman of incredible appetite and passion.

Once she trusted him—which, with some additional "confessions" regarding his childhood, took only a few more dates—there was little Isabel would not do, would not allow him to do to her. Making love to her was like riding the highest and wildest of roller coasters—the anticipation building time and again, with one exhilarating ride, one wildly frightening climax after another.

In all their years together, there was only one place that Isabel drew the line, and that was when he suggested videotaping their love sessions. Alistair already knew by then that when Isabel said no, she meant it, and no amount of pleading or cajoling could succeed in budging her. And so he did the only thing he could do. He installed a video camera in the ceiling fan above their bed.

And in the light fixture in the Jacuzzi room.

WHEN SHE LEFT him, those tapes became his salvation. He played and replayed them, night after night. And then he'd decided to share them.

She deserved it, after all.

She'd betrayed him, tried to take him down. But there was no way, no way he would allow Isabel McLain to take him down. Not after all the muck, all the maggot-infested shit, he'd crawled through to get where he was.

Which is why Robin Getty's recent news had been so welcome.

This—Mary's news that investigators were still digging

around—was not good. And what about that fucking fax she kept insisting he'd received?

It had been a long time now since Alistair had had any contact with Isabel. A long time since he'd laid eyes on her. Maybe it was time to instill a little fear, a little respect, in her.

The thought turned him on—just as everything about Isabel had always turned him on. Even now, after all she'd done to him, he could get an erection simply thinking about her.

And so, with all his other problems pushed temporarily out of mind, Alistair Bott turned back to the Internet.

"THIS THING HAS become a public relations nightmare," Mike Lane told the group of WRI execs assembled around him. "Four thousand have fled Barskoon. It's virtually a ghost town. Pedor tells me that families have grouped together. They send one of the men back for two days at a time to guard their homes, then rotate every other day because they don't want to endanger anyone by allowing them to stay for more than forty-eight hours."

"That's *bullshit*," Jon LeCoque answered, slamming his fist on the table. "Total bullshit. Our scientists checked for cyanide in the lake and river, even in the soil around Barskoon. It's safe there now."

Eleanor Nguyen nodded her bobbed hair in agreement. "Even Health Canada agrees. In fact, they've backed our contention that the level of cyanide received was never high enough to account for the problems they're alleging."

Her eyes made sure to seek out Tony Wilderman when she delivered this last bit of information.

"Still," LeCoque warned, "we can't be too careful about this. WRI's future is heavily dependent upon that mine. When's that lease up for renewal?" He turned to the company attorney. "Pierre?"

Pierre Sabin opened a file sitting in front of him and rifled through a half-inch thick document.

"Two-thousand-two," Sabin said. "Same year as the Essiquibo site."

"We can't let this incident become another Essiquibo," LeCoque said.

Heads around the table nodded.

Two years earlier, a dam holding toxic millings from WRI's Essiquibo mine in Guyana had ruptured, spilling 3.2 billion liters of cyanide-laced water into the Essiquibo River, which runs almost the length of the country of Guyana and happens to be one of its busiest waterways. The river had since been dubbed the "Cyanide River" and WRI was now drowning in a quagmire of lawsuits, especially after an independent engineer from the United States had reported that the dam, as designed and constructed, was "bound to fail." Fishermen had sued for loss of income. Loggers, miners, and those living or working on or around the river had soon joined in. Environmental groups, three at last count, had also sued. WRI had once been a popular presence in Guyana, but the public tide had turned, and there was little doubt among those in the room that the lease allowing WRI to continue its gold mining operations would not be renewed in 2002.

"I'm not ready to make any grand gestures at this point," LeCoque said. "But we can't afford more publicity or litigation. Pierre, I expect you to stay on top of this."

"Will do."

Tony Wilderman cleared his throat.

"Listen," he said, his voice coming out in a deep rattle, "this company has too much riding on those two mines. Especially if we're in danger of losing the Kyrgyzstan lease."

"What did you have in mind?" LeCoque asked.

"We should step up exploratory efforts," he said.

LeCoque lifted one of his bushy, gray eyebrows.

"Exploration's costly."

"Damn straight," Wilderman replied. "That's why we've

had it on hold these past couple years. But we lose either of those two mines and we're in trouble."

"Those fucking foreigners," LeCoque fumed. "They're going to ruin this company."

Wilderman reached into the back pocket of his blue jeans and pulled out a flat, round can of Copenhagen. He lifted the lid, extracted a pinch of pungent, brown tobacco leaves, and then, to Eleanor Nguyen's chagrin, held it in front of him as he ran his tongue along his upper teeth.

"That's just what *I've* been thinking," the geologist said, opening his mouth and pressing the wad inside. "But what I have in mind this time is a little closer to home."

CHAPTER

THREE

WE GOT TWO more," Suzanne called out, holding the door open while Isabel made the dash from her Jeep to the clinic.

A gale force wind sent the heavy spring rain flying sideways, rendering the visor of the Mariners hat that Isabel pulled low over her eyes nearly useless.

For the past three mornings, Suzanne had begun each day with a report on their project to rid the clinic of deer mice. So far they were batting a thousand—each morning both traps held lifeless victims.

"There might still be more," Isabel said, shaking the rain off her parka and ball cap as she stepped inside the waiting room. She shrugged out of the parka, revealing her usual attire—blue jeans, long-sleeved T-shirt, and hiking boots—

and threw both the parka and hat onto the rickety coat tree that stood in the corner of the newly wallpapered waiting room.

"Could be."

"Guess we better set them again tonight."

"Guess so," Suzanne echoed.

Isabel returned to the front door, her eyes scanning outside.

"No dogs this morning," she said.

When she first came to the reservation, Isabel had been struck by the sight of packs of dogs roaming Browning's streets, scavenging for food. So skilled were they that an odd metal contraption adorned the streets in front of each of Browning's small, mostly dilapidated houses: a post—once shiny aluminum but rusted now by years of exposure to the relentless elements—with a horizontal platform that held garbage cans three feet off the ground.

Isabel had taken to feeding the dogs that hung around the clinic. Most mornings now a group waited for her to arrive.

"Even those dogs're smart enough to stay outta this weather."

Isabel had turned and started down the hallway to her office when Suzanne's next words brought her to a complete standstill.

"You know some guy with a Southern accent?"

She twirled to face Suzanne.

"Why do you ask?"

Suzanne shrugged. She was always shrugging.

"Some guy was waiting outside last night. In this nice car. When I came out from puttin' the traps out."

"What did he want?"

"He asked for you. Wanted to know where you lived."

"Did he give his name?"

"Nope."

"What did he look like?"

"I dunno. White. Slick. Lucy picked me up last night. She

got a better look at him than I did. She thought he was pretty good lookin', but Lucy likes white guys. The only white guy does anything for me is that actor, Vince Vaughn. Did you see that movie *Clay Pigeons*? He's so hot it's hard to believe he's . . ."

"*Suzanne,* describe the man to me, will you?"

"I wasn't payin' that much attention. He was sittin' in his car. Skinny. Kinda curly hair."

It couldn't be.

Only one person Isabel knew fit Suzanne's description—the person Isabel least wanted to find her.

"What did you tell him?"

"Nothin'. The guy gave me the creeps. I didn't tell him a thing."

"But you said he asked where I lived."

"Yeah. He wanted to know how to find your cabin."

"He said that? He called it a cabin?"

"That's what he called it. I told him I didn't know where you lived. And . . ."

"And what?"

"And I lied to him. I told him you were out of town. I told you, the guy creeped me out. I hope that's okay."

Isabel stared at Suzanne, lost momentarily in her past.

"Yes. It is."

The rest of the day, Isabel felt troubled and distracted by Suzanne's news. Driving home that night, after helping Suzanne set out the mouse traps again, Isabel went back over everything Suzanne told her. After asking to see her, her unnamed visitor had apparently asked Suzanne how to find Isabel's cabin. Thank God Suzanne had kept her mouth shut, had even lied and told him Isabel was out of town.

He must have believed her since he did not show up again today. Still, that was little comfort. Just a short reprieve, at best.

How did Alistair find out that Isabel had moved to Browning? And who told him that she lived in a cabin? Someone had been loose-lipped with information that was supposed to have been kept secret.

The first thing Isabel would do when she got home was make a telephone call.

Because she had a hunch just who that someone might be.

"MOTHER, PICK UP the phone. Please."

Isabel paced back and forth across the wood planked floor in the kitchen of her log cabin as she waited for Nada McLain to come on the line. Normally Isabel started a fire in the wood stove the moment she got home from work. Even now, in late spring, the evening temperatures could plummet below freezing. But tonight she'd gone directly to the phone.

"This is important, Mother. I need to talk to you."

She knew from experience that she had to continue talking or her mother's answering machine would cut her off.

"It's six o'clock. I'll be up for several hours. Please call me, it's very impor—"

"Hello, dear."

Despite her seventy-two years and fragile health, Nada McLain still had the deep, silky voice of the stage actress she had once been.

"I hate it when you screen calls like that."

"I don't screen calls, Isabel. I was simply engrossed in the news. You know how much I enjoy Tom Brokaw."

Tom Brokaw was one of the few things they agreed upon.

"Mother, I need to know something. Have you seen or talked to Alistair?"

The pause on the other end of the line gave Isabel her answer.

"So it was you who told him?"

"Told him what, dear?"

"Where I work. Where I live."

"I did not tell him where you live."

"But you told him I moved to the reservation. You told him about the clinic. And that I live in a cabin."

"You were married to the man for three years. Now you don't even want him to know where you live?"

"I asked you to keep that information secret. My lawyer won't even give him that information. How could you have betrayed me?"

"Betrayed you?" Nada's voice rose in indignation. "I'm your mother. I would never betray you."

"Then what do you call it?"

"I don't understand you, Isabel. You were crazy about Alistair once."

"That was long ago, Mother. A different lifetime. A different Alistair."

"What's so wrong with him now? He's a successful doctor. And so handsome. And he *loved* you. He still does, dear."

"Where in the hell did you get that?"

"There's no need to swear, Isabel. He just about came out and said so."

"You still can't see through him, can you?"

Nada chose to ignore Isabel's comment.

"You could still come back, dear. I just know Alistair would take you back. You could get off that godforsaken reservation and move back in to your lovely home . . ."

"Mother, stop. That's not going to happen. Ever. How many times have I told you? I like my life here. I feel I'm making a difference." Then, without thinking, she added, "Just like Dad did."

The bitterness of Nada McLain's laughter should not have stung Isabel so. After all, around Nada the family had *always* avoided the subject of Tom McLain's year on the Flathead reservation, just one hundred and thirty miles southwest of the Blackfeet nation's home. Burdened by med school loans at a time when he and Nada were newlyweds planning to start a family, Tom had jumped at the government's offer to

forgive his debt in exchange for a year of service on one of
many North American reservations desperately in need of
medical personnel. The Flathead reservation had been the
closest to home. Despite the fact that Nada chose to stay
behind to perform in the Seattle Repertory Theatre, her
mother's resentment of Tom's service in Montana never
dimmed over the years. When Isabel was a child, it was only
when she and her father were alone that her father talked to
her, with great fondness, telling Isabel stories about the Salish and Kootenai who shared the vast reservation, about
their gentle spirit and way of life, their tragedy.

Those stories had planted a seed of fascination—even
envy—within Isabel's heart, her soul. A sense of longing that
ran beneath the surface, impossible to identify. Later, as Isabel grew up and began asking more probing questions, even
Tom seemed uncomfortable discussing that time. Eventually
it seemed that everyone wanted to forget it, put it out of their
minds. Everyone, that is, but Isabel.

"Just like your father," Nada huffed now. "Out to save the
world. At the expense of those you claim to love."

"Let's not do this to each other, Mother," Isabel said,
hands shaking with anger. "I'm going to hang up now. I'll
call you again soon."

A sense of unnamed dread washed over Isabel as she replaced the phone.

Maybe she should have been more honest with her mother
when she left Alistair. But despite the bitterness that had at
times strained her parents' marriage, even after the passage
of two years, Nada continued to reel from Tom McLain's
death. And despite Isabel and Nada's own differences, Isabel
felt a protectiveness toward her irksome mother. A mother
who placed undue emphasis on good looks and social status.

Nada McLain had always cherished her position in Seattle
society as a prominent surgeon's wife. Had she known the
truth about Alistair, her shame would have been tenfold what
Isabel felt. Isabel had wanted to spare Nada that. And she

could only thank God that her father—her pure of heart, generous-spirited father—hadn't lived to see this day.

Chilled inside and out, Isabel headed out to the porch for an armload of the tamarack Gus had split for her weeks earlier and stacked neatly under the overhang.

She should have known Alistair would eventually find her. Nothing stopped him once he'd made up his mind. If her mother hadn't handed him the information on a silver platter, he would have found another way to get it.

But the question is, why had he come looking for her?

As Isabel balanced several lengths of firewood in her arms, her eyes involuntarily swept the gravel road leading to her driveway. Then they turned to the open meadow that began at the cabin's front door and flowed to the road, where it picked back up on the other side until it reached a stand of white birch and poplar.

Her cabin was remote. It would be impossible for Alistair to find it without help. And no one, besides Suzanne and Gus, her landlord, knew exactly where she lived.

Still, the simple knowledge that Alistair had been there, on the reservation, that he'd seen the clinic where she worked, made Isabel feel violated.

Instead of starting the wood stove up, she decided to use the tamarack for a fire in the fireplace. Sleep would not come easy tonight. A fire might help her relax.

Half an hour later, after checking all the locks on the cabin's doors and windows and eating a peanut butter and jelly sandwich, she sat staring into the fire, propped against a pillow in front of the hearth, sipping wine from one of the canning jars she'd found in the empty cupboard when she'd first moved in. She pushed her feet against the rusted metal firescreen, savoring the heat that burned through her heavy gray wool socks.

Alistair had told her she would pay for what she'd done.

She'd passed along those words to K. T. Seinberg, her feisty attorney, who'd promptly headed to court for a restraining order. But the judge had decided that Alistair's threat, if it could be called that, was too vague for the court to act upon.

What difference would a restraining order make anyway?

As Isabel watched and listened to the flames spewing and spitting cinders skyward into the thin-aired Montana night, she knew better than to think that a piece of paper would protect her from her estranged husband.

CHAPTER

FOUR

J OE'S HERE . . ."

Phone pressed to ear as she listened to the Browning pharmacist's explanation for not being able to fill the prescription she'd just sent over with a patient, Isabel held up an index finger signaling Suzanne to wait.

"He don't look so good," Suzanne persisted.

Isabel's head jerked up, her eyes zeroing in on Suzanne.

"What do you mean?"

"I mean Joe's sick. Bad, I think."

Dropping the phone on her desk, Isabel rose immediately and followed Suzanne down the hallway.

If she hadn't been looking specifically for him, Isabel might not even have recognized Joe in the waiting room. The boy that sat hunched over, one arm clutching his chest while the other held the hand of a frantic-looking woman Isabel assumed to be his mother, might have been a stranger, had Isabel not known better. A stranger in deep distress.

"What is it, Joe?" Isabel asked, dropping to her knees in front of him.

His black eyes came up to meet hers.

"I can't breathe."

Isabel turned to the woman at Joe's side.

"Does he have asthma?"

"Don't think so."

"Anything like this ever happen before?"

The woman shook her head.

There was always the first time. Isabel reached out and touched Joe's forehead. Warm. A fever indicated they were dealing with an infection, not asthma.

"Come with me," she said, standing and grabbing one of Joe's elbows while his mother latched on to the other.

Suzanne had already displaced the patient who'd been waiting in the second exam room. Isabel went to help Joe up on the exam table, but he pushed her hand away gently and climbed up unassisted.

"When did this begin?" Isabel asked as she inserted a thermometer into Joe's mouth.

"Two or three days ago," his mother answered, her eyes glued nervously to her boy. "He started complaining about his shoulders aching. Then he got a fever. And he can't keep any food down. I thought it was the flu. But today he started this, like he can't get enough air."

Isabel took Joe's blood pressure. 122/83. Pulse 114. High—probably twice what it usually was. Respiratory rate was also elevated, to 27.

Joe's temperature—101.8—indicated an infection. Most likely pneumonia.

She lifted the stethoscope that hung from her neck to listen to Joe's lungs. She did not like what she heard. Bilateral rhonchi with coarse crackles indicated the presence of fluid.

"I want X rays," she said to Suzanne, who hovered nearby. "And let's draw blood."

A white cell count and an oxygen saturation test would be

helpful in making the diagnosis, but the clinic was not equipped to do either. She would have to send blood out and wait for results. Meanwhile, it was clear that Joe needed immediate treatment.

MINUTES LATER, ISABEL held the X ray films to the wall-mounted light. Bright white patches confirmed that Joe's lungs were filling with fluids. But why?

"Let's get him started on IV. He needs antibiotics, and he's dehydrated, probably from the vomiting."

The IV catheter went in easily. Intravenous fluids would ward off shock and help prevent Joe's blood pressure from dropping. Not knowing what she was dealing with—if it was pneumonia, she hoped it would turn out to be bacterial—she chose a broad spectrum antibiotic and also piggybacked IV droperidol, for nausea.

"I'd like to give your lungs a little help here, Joe. That means putting you on oxygen."

Joe managed a half smile.

"I'll take . . . any help . . . I can get."

His voice was little more than a whisper.

She administered oxygen for several minutes. But with every passing minute, the sense that something was wrong—that her efforts were futile—grew stronger. Joe's condition seemed to be deteriorating before her eyes. His chest heaved with each breath and he looked more and more frightened, as his mother stood by, stroking his back and telling him he would be okay.

"Check his blood pressure again," she told Suzanne as she returned to the X ray films for another look.

"Ninety-four over sixty."

A drop of almost thirty points. Isabel looked at the clock on the wall. *In less than an hour.*

At the same time, Joe's breathing had grown more labored

and rapid. A second respiratory reading showed his rate had increased to 39.

What the hell was she dealing with here?

Joe had been coughing intermittently, but suddenly, his entire being convulsed with his efforts to rid himself of the fluid accumulating in his lungs. As Joe's mother patted him futilely on the back, Isabel saw a drop of fluid fall from the hand he held to his mouth.

"Let me see, Joe," she said gently, pulling his hand down. A straw colored fluid coated his palm.

Serum.

Hantavirus. Adult respiratory distress syndrome—known in medical circles as ARDS—caused by exposure to aerosolized urine or feces from infected deer mice. The deadly disease had first surfaced in 1993, in the Four Corners region. It had claimed eleven lives that spring, most of them Native American.

Its victims drowned *in the serum* from their own blood.

Could Joe have contracted the deadly disease? Panic filled Isabel's every pore—a panic she had to keep hidden from Joe and his poor mother.

The coughing spasm had now passed and Isabel wrapped an arm around Joe's shoulders.

"I'll be right back. You hang in there, okay? We're going to take care of you."

Closing the door firmly behind her, Isabel ran at full speed to her office. En route, she debated about whether to call Harborview—which was a better equipped and staffed hospital, but was also five hundred miles away—or Missoula General. When she reached her office, she dialed Missoula General.

Immediately proclaiming the call an emergency, Isabel asked to be connected to the hospital's resident pulmonary specialist.

"I need a Life Flight. *Stat,*" she blurted into the phone when Dr. Lehman Morris, Missoula General's acute respiratory distress syndrome specialist, came on the line. "I have an eighteen-year-old male with ARDS. I suspect I'm dealing with hantavirus. What can you tell me?"

"Have you done chest films?"

"Yes. They indicate extensive interstitial and alveolar infiltrates. His respiratory rate has jumped from 27 to 39 in just one hour. I've drawn blood but don't have the facilities to run a WBC or O-two. I've initiated IV fluids, antibiotics, and oxygen—two liters per minute. What else should I be doing?"

"Sounds like you're doing everything right. If your diagnosis is correct, at this point, treatment is mainly supportive. You have a mechanical ventilator, don't you?"

The two things Isabel had ensured after accepting the job at the clinic were that she would have a portable X ray and ventilator. She'd had to raise the funds herself for the X ray, but the clinic already had an old ventilator that was in decent working condition.

"Yes."

"I suggest you be prepared for prophylactic intubation. This disease can progress at alarming speed. Let's hope you're wrong and it won't be necessary, but you may need to ventilate him until the medevac arrives. I'm dispatching a helicopter as we speak. I'll be on it."

FOR THE NEXT hour, Joe seemed to stabilize.

Isabel did not want to intubate him unless or until it became absolutely necessary, for intubation would require sedation. While she did not allow the thought to actually take form in her mind, deep down, there was the knowledge that, if her diagnosis was correct, these could be Joe's last hours with his mother. As long as he remained calm and was able to bear the discomfort, she didn't want to do anything to diminish the quality of their time together.

Guilt had already begun snaking its way into Isabel's subconscious.

She'd been worried about Joe earlier in the week when he stopped by. Why hadn't she probed further that day, or gone looking for him when he failed to show up at the clinic the past few days?

She'd been so busy. It had been easy to assume Joe was busy as well, with final exams, or graduation parties.

But why hadn't she checked in on him?

If she had, maybe they would have caught this earlier.

"'Copter's coming!"

Suzanne had been standing at the window, her eyes glued to the skies, which, ironically, after months of rain (which Isabel would later learn had brought about an increase in the vegetation that led to a surge in the deer mice population), were a brilliant blue.

After a quick assessment that Joe was still stable, Isabel hurried outside and stood in front of the clinic, buffeted by the winds and dust as the helicopter settled nicely in the empty lot next door. Before the blades had stopped turning, the door flew open and a man jumped down, wearing a blue uniform with the Life Flight logo on the pockets. Immediately behind him a tall, dark-skinned man dressed in a physician's coat followed suit. He was so tall that he had to stay hunched over until he'd cleared the helicopter's blades.

"Dr. McLain?" he yelled over their din.

"Yes."

"I'm Dr. Morris."

"Thank you so much for coming," Isabel said, relieved to have the specialist there.

At a run, Isabel led them to the exam room where she'd left Joe. But in the mere minutes she'd been absent, Joe's condition had changed.

He clutched frantically at his chest and then the horrible spasms overtook him again.

"We'll need to intubate here," Morris said.

The medic administered a sedative via the IV catheter. In another minute, a second medic appeared with a wheeled cart. Slowly, as the sedative kicked in, Joe stopped thrashing. With a medic positioning Joe's head, Isabel used a laryngoscope to pass the endotracheal tube into Joe's airway while Dr. Morris placed him on the ventilator, using positive and expiratory pressure to maximize oxygenation.

"Blood pressure's down to 60 over 40," one of the medics suddenly called.

At this, Mrs. Winged Foot began to wail. Isabel nodded at Suzanne to move the distraught mother into the corridor.

She heard Suzanne say, "Do it for Joey, Anna."

It was the first time Isabel had heard the woman's name and it brought a lump to her throat.

As she turned the IV wide open to stem the rapidly falling blood pressure, one of the medics hooked Joe up to a heart monitor.

"We obviously can't transport him now," Isabel said softly, though by now Joe appeared to be unconscious. Then, the dreaded words she'd never expected to say, "Do you have paddles in there?" She nodded toward the cart the second medic had wheeled in.

At that very instant, as if her words were prescient, an alarm pierced the air. All faces turned toward the heart monitor.

Joe's heart had stopped.

Isabel began CPR, pounding on Joe's breastbone, but with each push, a column of blood-tinged fluid rose from his lungs through the tubing coming from his mouth. Just as the article had described, Joe Winged Foot was drowning, before all their eyes, in his own serum.

"Ready to defib?" Dr. Morris called out.

"Ready."

Isabel moved aside, as Dr. Morris applied the defibrillator paddles to Joe's chest. A sickening *zzzzt* filled the room as

Joe's legs flew into the air, then dropped heavily back to the table.

When Joe remained unresponsive, they defibrillated him again.

"Let's try some atropine," Morris said without looking up.

Isabel injected atropine directly into the pericardium, then epinephrine, then more atropine. But Joe did not respond, and soon the EKG appeared agonal.

"I think he's gone," one of the medics—Isabel couldn't tell which, since her eyes were glued to Joe—said.

"*No,*" Isabel responded defiantly, angrily. "One more time."

Dr. Morris complied, but Joe was gone now, and even Isabel knew it.

Resuscitation efforts ended at 3:15. Barely four hours after Joe had entered the clinic.

Isabel thanked Dr. Morris and the medics for their efforts, and, after crossing Joe's arms over his chest, pulled a sheet up to cover the burns left by the defibrillator. She could not break down now, for she had to go out and face Anna Winged Foot.

She had to give her the news.

NOTHING ISABEL COULD say would keep Anna Winged Foot away from her son. Wild-eyed in disbelief, clutching her grief like a pillow to her chest, Anna insisted on being alone with Joe in the examination room.

Anna's wails filled the clinic. Isabel did not try to shut them out. She wanted—more than she'd ever wanted anything in her entire life—to join Anna. She, too, wanted to hold that lifeless body and scream her anguish and anger. Instead, as she waited for the coroner's office to arrive with the sealed, leakproof body bag that would carry Joe to the morgue, Isabel sat, numb, in the clinic's empty waiting room.

It did not take long for other family members to arrive,

each stone-faced as they approached the front door of the clinic, each pleading to be allowed inside with Anna and Joe. When Isabel turned them away, warning them of the danger, they would join the growing group of tribal members who had gathered outside, and the wailing would begin anew.

Isabel did not realize at first that Suzanne was gone, that she had joined the other Blackfeet gathered to show their support for the Winged Foot family. Instinctively, the tribe had come together, to draw strength from one another and suffer through the incomprehensible pain together.

As afternoon shadows inched their way across the waiting room floor, the rhythmic chanting from outside grew louder. Isabel sat, silent and alone, listening to the grief pouring out around her, her terror building with each passing second.

It would take several days to get the official results of Joe's autopsy, yet deep within her heart, she had little doubt regarding its outcome. She tried, in vain, to deny the similarities between the initial outbreak of hantavirus in 1993, where one of the first lives claimed was that of a healthy, young Indian male—that time, a Navajo—and an exceptional athlete.

Just like Joe.

That outbreak went on to claim thirteen members of the Navajo nation.

If, indeed, the autopsy results confirmed Isabel's worst fears—that Joe had died of the deadly hantavirus—what was in store for the Blackfeet, for Isabel's patients, in the coming weeks?

Despite the fact that it was growing too dark to read, Isabel's eyes strayed to the sheet of paper she'd held, clutched in her hands, ever since scrawling on it as she began her wait for the coroner. It was a list. Isabel had already read it so many times that she no longer needed light to make out the names on it.

Eli Walker
Jason Little Turtle

Sally Hawkeye and her two children, *Sam and Laurie*

It went on. Over a dozen names in total. Isabel had them all memorized now.

They were the names of the patients she'd seen earlier in the week. The day Joe filled in for Suzanne.

Names that until today held no more meaning for Isabel than those of hundreds of other patients. But now they were etched in her mind, along with each face.

For if the coroner confirmed Isabel's worst fear—that Joe's death had been caused by hantavirus—*would one of those names be its next victim?*

CHAPTER

FIVE

TONY WILDERMAN'S PASSION for his work could be traced to his childhood in Butte, Montana. His Dutch father, Henry, worked in the dangerously deep Anaconda mines until the 1950s, when his employer, the world's biggest producer of copper, moved from labor-intensive underground mining to open pit mining.

Tony could still remember the small yellow frame house on Butte's east side where he was born. He still remembered the day it was leveled, bulldozed flat as a pancake along with hundreds of other homes, to make way for the Berkely Pit—an ugly, mile-long blight on the land that eventually grew to a depth of over 1,800 feet. By the time the company switched to truck-operated open mining, the years spent underground had taken their toll on Henry's health; however, as a proven employee, Henry earned a coveted position driving one of dozens of trucks that hauled tons of sedimentary rock from the bottom of the vast pit to the mounds growing on its perimeter. On occasion, Henry would bring his son to work with him, entertaining a young and impressionable Tony with stories of mining catastrophes and terror half a mile below the earth's surface, explaining the mining process to him.

To many of Tony's classmates, "The Pit" symbolized everything they hated about Butte. Most left town as soon as they graduated from high school, some even sooner. But Tony loved The Pit and the time he spent there with his father. He loved the camaraderie of the mining community. Tony's carrot-colored hair and freckled skin, inherited from his mother, who had immigrated from Dublin the same year she met and married Henry Wilderman, made him a favorite of the droves of Irish who flocked to Butte in the 1930s and '40s to work in the mine. St. Patrick's Day celebrations were raucous and the highlight of the year for Tony.

Tony would gladly have remained in Butte and followed in his father's footsteps, but Henry Wilderman refused to entertain the possibility. He insisted that Tony get an education. At the University of Montana, Tony found a way to both placate his father and indulge his fascination with mining. He studied geology, earning first a B.S., then his master's and doctorate.

In the last three decades, Tony's keen mind and passion for his work had earned him a reputation as one of the mining industry's top exploratory geologists and one of the few WRI employees frequently consulted by its CEO. Like LeCoque, Tony considered the development of mineral resources essential; to Canada's, and the world's, future economic health. Also like LeCoque, he had little empathy or patience for the environmentalists that so often complicated their mission and their lives.

"I hear you've been back to your old stomping grounds." LeCoque had called this meeting the first day Wilderman returned from his most recent exploratory trip. "You still have family in Butte?"

"No," Tony answered, shaking a halo of rust colored curls. "After my father died, my mother moved to Los Angeles to live with my sister. I still like to swing through there once in a while, though it's a damn depressing sight anymore. But I didn't make it quite that far east this trip."

"Tell me about this trip."

Wilderman pushed back, elbows braced on either arm of his chair. When he lowered his jaw, his chin blended into fleshy jowls.

"Hell, Jon. You know I've always thought we oughta explore closer to home. Between the cost of doing business overseas and the growth of these goddamn environmental groups over there, watchdoggin' our every move, we can't win. I had a couple sites I'd been wanting to check out, one in particular. It—the one I'm referring to—could just solve a lot of our problems."

"Go on."

"Well, I visited four states in the Northwest. Idaho, Oregon, Washington, in that order, then finished up in Montana. Had some interesting meetings with folks from the USGS, and did extensive field evaluations in all four."

"And?"

"A couple interesting possibilities. The Owyhee region in southeastern Oregon for one. A team consisting of USGS scientists, university people, and Oregon state geologists has been evaluating the area. Geologic mapping shows a major gold deposit at Grassy Mountain."

"Volcanism?"

"Volcanism and basin development. The region has a bilateral symmetry along the Idaho-Oregon border, with older Miocene volcanic rock on the east and west, younger Miocene volcanic and volcaniclastic rocks."

"How big's the deposit?"

Wilderman shook his head. "Don't know. But we may be

too late on this one anyway. Apparently Hudson Bay is close to tying up rights."

"How close?"

"I'd say it's pretty much a done deal. We'd have to jump in there pretty damn quick if we're serious. No time for us to do our own exploration. It'd be a wild card."

"We can't afford any wild cards."

"That's what I figured."

"What about Washington?" LeCoque pressed. "Find anything there?"

Wilderman's brows came together in reflection.

"It would take quite a bit more exploring to come up with anything definitive. Cannon Mine at Wenatchee's still the biggest producer in the state. It's possible there are other veins in that area. And granitic bodies scattered along the eastern Cascades indicate the possibility of copper and molybdenum. The deposit at Holden's pretty much depleted. But maybe it's worth a closer look."

"Hell, Tony, I expected to hear something more promising than *maybe it's worth a closer look.*"

Wilderman's thin lips disappeared in a smile. "Hold your horses, will you?" He leaned forward, his green Irish eyes flickering with excitement. "There is something more promising. In Montana, along the eastern slope of the Rockies. This may be the find of my lifetime."

Wilderman knew words like these tended to do powerful things to LeCoque. He could feel the CEO watching closely as he withdrew a folded sheet of paper from his briefcase.

Holding up a map, Wilderman's finger traced over a short yellow line he'd drawn earlier with a magic marker. It started at a point about a hundred miles east of the Montana-Idaho border and just below the Canadian border.

"This K-Spar zone cuts downsection and to the southeast. I'm convinced that it's gold-bearing. It consists of siltite beds. Fine-grained Middle Proterozoic metasedimentary rocks between twelve hundred and fifteen hundred years old. The gold should be widely distributed."

"What did your samples show?"

"Values ranging from point-fifteen ppm in disseminated sites to forty-one in veinlets."

Excitement flickered in LeCoque's usually steely gaze.

"Go on."

"The deposits shallow upward from basin plain to subtidal. Episodic submarine volcanism mixed with sediment during transport away from eruptive centers and resulted in turbidite hosted deposits along this entire region. Your classic basin growth faults."

"What's the land use now? Ranching?"

"Not really. There are a couple small operations, nothing of consequence. We're basically looking at a couple hundred thousand acres of bluffs, plateaus, and ragged mountains."

"State?" LeCoque asked. "Or federal?"

Wilderman's smile broadened, exposing a row of teeth that were perfectly shaped, but stained by years of chewing tobacco and a pot-a-day coffee habit.

"Indian. The deposit's on a reservation. That's the kicker."

A slow grin spread across LeCoque's face.

"What tribe?"

"Blackfeet."

"How bad off are they?"

"Plenty bad off."

LeCoque stared at Wilderman's map, momentarily lost in thought.

"EPA doesn't have jurisdiction over Indian lands, does it?"

Wilderman shook his head.

"No, sir."

"Tell me about the Blackfeet."

"They're one of the United States's poorest tribes. A couple other tribes with more resources have set up their own EPA-type agency, which, as far as I'm concerned, could end up a bigger pain in the ass than the EPA. But there's nothing like that there. There's nothing there at all. Just a pencil factory. Unemployment's close to sixty percent.

"But I gotta warn you," Wilderman went on. "I wasn't exactly a welcome figure down there. Got chased away half a dozen times when I was scoutin' around. One time I thought I was a goner. Didn't know I'd stumbled upon a sacred site until I found human bones. At a place called Ghost Ridge Lake. I guess hundreds of Blackfeet starved and froze to death there when the government didn't get supplies to them, so they're a little touchy about strangers up there. Fella ran me off with a shotgun. And that was just one of the problems I had to deal with. Never seen anything like it."

"What else?"

"I'll tell you what else. Nothing on that damn reservation is mapped. I mean rivers and lakes aren't named or even marked on maps. Half the roads that *are* mapped peter out into impassable tracks up a butte. And with the exception of one old timer I ran into at the gas station, I met with nothing but hostility when I tried to get any answers in town. So what I'm tryin' to say is, we may not be dealin' with the United States government and their fuckin' EPA, but this won't be any picnic either."

"But you felt you were on to something there? Something with the potential to be big?"

"There's gold there. Plenty of it. I can feel it."

LeCoque stared at the yellow slash on the map, which Wilderman had placed face-up on his desk.

"We could practically reach out and touch that land," he murmured.

Wilderman beamed.

"You got that right."

CHAPTER

SIX

REMEMBER, LYDIA," ISABEL said, as she walked her elderly heart patient back to the waiting room, where the woman's husband sat, stiff as a board and staring straight ahead, "you mustn't forget to take your Lasix. Twice a day. That's the only way you're going to get rid of that swelling in your . . ."

A loud thud from the front of the clinic drew Isabel's attention. In the next instant, a young Blackfeet woman stumbled through the door, her cough deep and violent, her eyes filled with terror—a terror Isabel recognized immediately. She had seen it just two days earlier.

"Get Dr. Morris on the phone," she yelled at Suzanne, who simply stared wide-eyed, paralyzed with fear. "Have them send the Life Flight."

One step inside the clinic, the woman froze, hunched over, one hand covering her eyes, the other pressed against her chest. All eyes in the waiting room fixed on her in horror. Isabel ran to her, grabbing hold of her elbow and supporting her, trying to hurry her through.

As she passed Suzanne, Isabel lowered her voice.

"Clear this place out. *Now.*"

Halfway down the hallway to the exam room, the woman doubled over, her body spasming with ugly, wrenching coughs. Isabel's heart sank. Fluid in the lungs. Was she dealing with end-stage hantavirus, like Joe's? Stiffening her arm to support the young woman, Isabel turned her head away, toward the wall, as the frail frame convulsed with the young woman's attempts to clear her lungs.

In its early stages, hantavirus—at least the strain known to the United States—had not been found to be contagious. But near the end, as the disease progressed, the virus could aerosolize, making it deadly to simply share the same air. Isabel's first priority was getting the woman back to an exam room, away from the other patients.

Behind her, she could hear Suzanne ushering the patients who had been waiting to see Isabel outside. Though the fear in the air was palpable, the evacuation took place in near silence.

"In here," Isabel said, half lifting the woman's limp form, as she directed her to the exam room that had just been vacated.

With no time to spare, Isabel began her questions before they reached the table.

"When did you start feeling sick?"

"Last week," the young woman answered, expelling precious air.

Isabel wanted to scream at her, to ask her why she'd waited this long to come to the clinic.

Perhaps she didn't know about Joe. At this point Isabel hoped that she did not. The fear in the eyes of the poor child—she couldn't be more than twenty years old—told Isabel that she knew very well how serious her condition was.

"Up here," Isabel said, helping her on to the examination table. "Can you tell me your name?"

"Dolores . . ." The breaths were shallow and painful. ". . . Birdsong."

"Okay, Dolores. I'm going to hook you up to an IV and start you on an antibiotic. Do you understand?"

Pressing her eyes closed, Dolores nodded and swallowed against the liquid drowning her.

Isabel stepped away momentarily to slip on a mask and rubber gloves. The full protective gear she'd ordered for both her and Suzanne the day after Joe's death had not yet arrived. However, just that morning something precious had. A shipment of ribavirin had been delivered, courtesy of Dr. Morris. The antiviral drug was extremely difficult to obtain. Its therapeutic value in the treatment of hantavirus was still in question, but Morris was convinced of its efficacy. He'd confessed to having stockpiled some of it and offered to send some to Isabel.

After inserting the IV into Dolores's arm, Isabel drew the ribavirin into a syringe. Lehman Morris's words came back to her.

"Let's just pray you don't need it."

Isabel was reaching for the IV tubing, the syringe full of ribavirin poised in the air, when Dolores Birdsong went into another convulsion of coughing. This time she could not stop. The same pinkish sputum that Isabel had seen on Joe Winged Foot's hands dribbled from the corners of Dolores's mouth as she sucked the room's air, desperately trying to inflate her compromised lungs.

Standard procedure would have been for Isabel to take an X ray, draw blood for a CBC and blood chemistry, but there was no time for that now.

When the spasms had passed and Dolores had grown still, Isabel hurriedly injected the ribavirin into the IV tubing. As she did so, a slender hand grabbed hold of her forearm and, with what little strength remained, squeezed. Dolores's eyes came up to Isabel's and held them, pleading.

Isabel recognized that the situation was becoming more critical by the minute.

"Listen to me, Dolores," she said, forcing a smile, willing herself to remain calm. "I would like to help you breathe. I think you need that. I want to put you on a mechanical ventilator. It will breathe for you, help you get oxygen."

Dolores's huge eyes never strayed from Isabel's, never blinked.

"But in order to do that, I'm going to have to give you something to put you to sleep."

The eyes grew even larger.

"Do you understand?"

A nod of the head. Talking was simply too difficult.

"A team of specialists from Missoula is on its way *right this minute* to help us out," Isabel continued, praying her words were true. "I will be by your side all the way. Do you understand? I will be here with you." She absolutely could not bear to see the terror in those innocent young eyes a moment longer and so she did the one thing she'd always vowed she would never do to a patient. She lied. "You're going to be just fine."

A flicker of relief flowed, wavelike, across Dolores's face.

"I'm not gonna . . . die?" she whispered. "Like . . . Joe?"

Isabel's eyes widened. Dolores knew about Joe.

"Not if I have anything to do with it," she said.

Isabel had hoped to avoid bringing Suzanne into the room, hoped to avoid exposing her assistant to the hantavirus again. After Joe's death, she had advised Suzanne that if another hantavirus patient arrived, Suzanne was to keep her distance. But she needed help to insert the inch-wide endotracheal tube that would allow the machine to breath for Dolores until the helicopter arrived.

Isabel squeezed Dolores's hand, then turned toward the door to call Suzanne.

She did not see that Dolores's eyes flickered open one last time.

All Isabel heard, all that she would remember, was Dolores's voice, no bigger than a shaky whisper.

"Please save me."

EARLY MORNING SUN reflected blindingly off the waters of the Willamette River in southwest Portland, but instead of appreciating the rare treat, Ken MacStirling, senior scientist at ImmuVac, rose and lowered the blinds in his office to eliminate the glare on his computer screen. On a clear day like this one, MacStirling usually took time to stand and gaze appreciatively at the splendor of snow-covered Mount Hood in the distance. As a child in Glasgow, hours of watching American Westerns had instilled in him an awe of the West's mountains, and he usually relished the days when the almost mystical Mount Hood was not obscured by Portland's dismal weather.

But today, Ken eagerly hurried back to the medical article he'd just happened onto while scanning the Web sites he'd bookmarked.

He reached for his telephone and punched a four-digit extension.

"Chris?" he said, a note of urgency lacing his Scottish tongue. "I've got to talk to Dr. Lyons. Is he in yet?"

Chris Finch, administrative assistant to James Lyons, founder and CEO of ImmuVac, announced that her boss was, indeed, in the office and placed MacStirling on hold.

The next instant, Lyons's characteristically abrupt voice came on the line.

"Ken. What's up?"

"Say, James," MacStirling began. "Are you aware of the hantavirus outbreak over there in Montana?"

Lyons's pause was not a good sign.

"No."

"It's on an Indian reservation," MacStirling continued. "Northwest Montana. Three confirmed deaths so far. In less than one week."

"Three deaths doesn't change the situation, Ken. You know that."

MacStirling swallowed against the disappointment rising in his throat.

"This disease is not going to just disappear, James. I implore you. Let me proceed with my vaccine."

"I thought we agreed that you were to focus on your AIDS research," Lyons snapped.

"My AIDS work is progressing quite nicely. Blount can attest to that. I assure you I have not been ignoring it. But when you hired me, James, you promised to support my work on the HantaVac."

"Dammit, Ken, when I hired you, we had big hopes pinned on HV 4230. If the Phase III trials had gone as we expected, there would have been plenty of money to fund HantaVac trials. But you know as well as I do that that's not how things panned out. How do you think this company can afford to sink a million bucks into a clinical trial for a product that's unlikely to ever break even when we had to scrub our public offering just two months ago?"

"I shouldn't think it would run so high as a million, James. Maybe half that."

Lyons issued a snort of frustration.

"You're missing the point. This company has to focus where we can attract funding. That means AIDS and cancer. Can't you get that into your head?"

Without waiting for a response, Lyons hung up.

"Arsehole," MacStirling muttered angrily as he replaced the phone.

He pushed back from his desk and returned to the window. Raising the blinds he'd closed just minutes earlier, his eyes finally surveyed the view from his office window, but in his disappointment, the magnificence of the morning escaped him.

My vaccine could have saved those people's lives.

Lyons thought MacStirling didn't understand the situation, but that wasn't true. The biotech industry was one big crap shoot. Companies like ImmuVac often staked their entire future—hundreds of millions of dollars—on one or two products. Disastrous clinical trial results, like their recent Phase III on a cancer treatment for which they'd already invested upwards of fifty million, could easily take a whole company down, and all its promising products with it. MacStirling didn't want that to happen any more than Lyons did. They had some promising therapies in R&D, drugs that MacStirling had to admit would save many more lives than a vaccine for the hantavirus. The AIDS vaccine ImmuVac had in development was one of them.

But it made MacStirling bloody crazy to think that corporate profit more often than not dictated what disease was worth eradicating, what human life worth saving.

Isn't there anything in this industry, this entire country, that matters more than money?

CHAPTER

SEVEN

ISABEL DROVE SO fast that on the final curve of the dusty one-lane road her balding tires sent her skidding off into the scrubweed that ran along the side.

Suzanne's aunt Mary had warned her about that curve. She'd told Isabel to look for the trailer immediately after rounding it.

There, ahead, she saw it. Blue. With Suzanne's champagne-colored Dynasty sitting outside.

Unlike many of the mobile homes populating Browning, this one was freshly painted, with a perfectly maintained white picket fence surrounding its tiny yard.

As Isabel hurried up the stone path to the front door, she noticed a small garden, with handwritten tags—peas, strawberries, carrots—clipped with clothespins to sticks protruding from the fresh dirt at the head of each row.

A frail, gray-haired woman met her at the door.

"Mary?" Isabel asked.

The woman nodded.

"Thank you for coming. Please, come in."

"I'm just glad you called," Isabel answered.

Isabel stepped inside. To her left was a well-scrubbed kitchen. Beyond that, through a short hallway, she could see a room with a bed. It was empty.

A brightly colored floral shower curtain obscured most of the room to her right, but when Mary pushed it aside, Isabel saw that it was a living room.

On the couch lay Suzanne.

"You shouldna come all the way out here," Suzanne said. "I'm just comin' down with a little cold."

Isabel crossed to the couch and pressed her hand to Suzanne's forehead.

It felt warm.

As Isabel removed a thermometer and stethoscope from her brown leather bag, her eyes surveyed her assistant head to toe.

"Any headache?" she asked.

"Just a little bit, but I always get them with a cold."

"Cough?"

"Some."

"Shortness of breath? Dizziness?"

Suzanne did not answer.

"She's been complainin that it's hard to breathe," Mary said.

Then the elderly woman turned to Suzanne.

"You tell her everything, you hear?" she scolded, her eyes filled with concern.

Isabel sat down on the couch, hip pushed up against Suzanne's. She laid the thermometer and the stethoscope in her lap.

"Please," she said, her eyes grabbing hold of Suzanne's.

"Your aunt's right. You know better than to take chances. Tell me everything."

Suzanne took a deep breath before answering.

"I dunno . . . ," she said hesitantly. "Sometimes I feel like I'm havin' a hard time taking a deep breath. And I've had some dizzy spells."

"What else? Muscle pain?"

Suzanne nodded. As she did, her eyes welled with tears.

"In my shoulders."

Isabel reached up and brushed Suzanne's bangs off her face.

"You're going to be all right," she said, fighting back her own tears.

"That's what you told Dolores."

"You heard that?"

Suzanne nodded.

"Listen to me," Isabel said. "I lied to Dolores. I knew when I said it that it would probably end up being a lie. But I had to give her hope. I had to ease her fear. Please forgive me for that."

Suzanne's eyes were a mixture of suspicion, fear, and an intense need to reach out for help.

"But if this is hantavirus," Isabel went on, "we're catching it early. Very early. Much earlier than with Joe or Dolores. And I never even got to see Will Echohawk before he died."

"Do you think that will make a difference?" Suzanne asked weakly.

"It does make a difference. I know that. That's what I've been trying to tell you and everybody else. You have to come in early—the moment the first symptoms show up. Now, let me listen to your lungs."

Isabel's hands trembled as she helped Suzanne sit up. She lifted the yellow flannel nightgown and placed the stethoscope over her ribcage, instructing her to take a deep breath. She listened intently, then moved to Suzanne's back.

Just the slightest crackle. If indeed this was hantavirus, it was early stage.

They had a chance. Finally.

Isabel looked at Mary, who hovered nearby, her hands clutching the sides of her thin, blue-floral housedress. Red Converse hightops stuck out from underneath its hem.

"I'd like you to get together a few things for Suzanne," she said. "A small overnight bag."

Suzanne had fallen back to the pillow, but at this, she bolted upright.

"Wait a minute. I'm not going anywhere."

"Yes, you are," Isabel said. "You're going to the hospital in Missoula. I'm driving you myself. Right now."

"Hell you are."

Suzanne jumped to her feet, but immediately reached for the back of a chair for support.

"Take it easy, Suzanne. Please. Sit back down."

But Suzanne shook her head and remained standing.

"Treat me *here*," she said. "Right here. If I'm going to die, I'm doing it here, in my own house. My own bed."

"You are not going to die." Isabel practically shouted. "I won't let you."

Suzanne studied her, a glint of surprise in her eyes.

"Then make me well here. Save me here. In my home."

"Why? *Why are you willing to take such a chance?*" Isabel hadn't even realized that tears had sprung to her eyes. "I haven't been able to save *anyone*."

Suzanne turned her eyes downward, seemingly embarrassed by Isabel's tears. Then she lowered herself back to the couch and reached for the thermometer that Isabel had placed on the table.

Before inserting it in her mouth, Suzanne looked back up, into Isabel's eyes.

"Then save *me*."

•   •   •

"IT'S BEEN FORTY-EIGHT hours now," Isabel said into the phone. "The most recent radiographs show interstitial edema but no bibasilar or perihilar airspace. Surely that's a good sign."

Isabel's conversations with Lehman Morris had become her lifeline the past ten days, especially since Suzanne came down sick. As luck would have it—just when she'd begun believing there was no such thing as luck—the first person she'd called for help when Joe fell ill turned out to be the Northwest's most revered expert on HPS—hantavirus pulmonary syndrome. With Suzanne's life hanging in the balance, Isabel did not make a move now without consulting Morris.

"It's definitely a good sign," Morris answered. There was a pause before he continued. "But it's not conclusive. Why don't you overnight me those films so I can take a look at them? Meanwhile, don't get your hopes too high."

"She's going to make it, dammit," Isabel declared. "She has to. We started her on the ribavirin early. You said that could make a big difference."

"Yes. I told you. Ribavirin didn't seem to reduce fatality in the ninety-three outbreak, but it's been my theory all along that that was because the patients were too far along in their disease course for the antiviral to turn them around. You got Suzanne started early, and that may well make the difference. I suspect it already has. Typically, two thirds of the patients show extensive bibasilar or perihilar involvement within forty-eight hours of onset. The fact that Suzanne doesn't is definitely encouraging."

"Think there's any chance we're not dealing with hantavirus this time?"

"No. I'm convinced it's hantavirus. The interstitial changes in those first X rays you sent to me are classic indicators of early hantavirus."

"Also the Kerley B lines," Isabel added. She had done little but study this hideous disease—its symptoms, progression, treatment—ever since that day Joe Winged Foot walked into her office. Kerley B lines—the short linear opacities running perpendicular to the pleural surfaces in lung radiographs of patients with HPS—were not part of her vocabulary just two weeks ago. But they were now. As were Kerley A lines, longer lines radiating from the lung hilum.

"That's right. Now the question is, how did each of these victims contract it?"

Isabel rubbed her tired eyes. That was the sixty-four-thousand-dollar question that had haunted her night and day. Sleep was a thing of the past.

"The CDC investigator is due in town today," she said, "but I've been doing some investigating on my own in the meantime. Anna Winged Foot can't think of anything that might have exposed Joe. They haven't had any rodent infestation in the house, nor, from what I've been able to determine, at school. Joe'd been spending most of his evenings outside, playing basketball with his friends. Right now it's anyone's guess how he contracted the virus."

"That might explain it."

"What?"

"Playing ball outside. If those courts are anything like the ones I played on as a kid, and I suspect they are, the surface is like one big field of popcorn. A bad hop could send the ball flying into the weeds and dirt. Hantavirus isn't easy to catch outdoors, but say it's a still night, no wind. Joe bends over, stirs up the weeds and dirt trying to pick the ball up, gets a good whiff. It's possible. Not likely, but definitely possible."

"Why aren't I surprised to hear you played basketball?" Isabel asked, suddenly overcome by a desperate need to be distracted from this awful disease that had taken over her life, her very being. The image of Lehman Morris bending his six-foot-five frame to stay clear of the Life Flight copter's blades came back to her.

Morris chuckled.

"How else do you think a kid from the projects in Chicago ended up in Montana? Back in my day, someone my size could actually play center. That was my position here, at the university. These days, a center's gotta be seven feet. I tell you, I was really looking forward to watching that Winged Foot boy play for the Grizzlies."

"You knew Joe played basketball?"

"I saw him in the state championship. Hell of a player. Scrappy, and fast. It's such a shame, that boy dying like that. He had a chance. A chance to get out. To make something of himself."

The empathy in Morris's voice was as thick and clear as the Midwestern accent he'd yet to lose, even after two decades in the West.

It was no wonder. For the first time Isabel realized the strong similarities between Joe Winged Foot and Lehman Morris. Both talented young men for whom basketball had represented a way out of the poverty and despair that would eventually swallow most of their peers. But it was clear that Morris had long ago learned there was nothing to be gained by dwelling upon the inequities of being born poor and black.

"What about the others?" Morris asked. "What have you come up with for them?"

"About two weeks before she died Dolores Birdsong cleaned out an old pickup truck that had been sitting behind her house for years. She needed some cash and hoped to sell it now that the weather's turned nice."

"Classic scenario. The deer mice found a hole in the truck and have been wintering there, maybe for years, and she gets in there and starts stirring up dust containing dried feces and urine. What about Suzanne?"

"I think Suzanne was exposed here, at the clinic. She'd been complaining about mice. I asked her to set out traps. She found dead mice in them several days in a row." There was a hitch in Isabel's voice as she continued. "She picked them up. Threw them away, in the Dumpster outside. It never even occurred to me to warn her . . ."

"Listen to me, young lady . . ."

As far as Isabel could tell, Lehman Morris was no more than five or six years her senior, yet he often spoke to her as if generations separated them. Many of Isabel's male colleagues over the years had demonstrated condescenscion toward her and other women doctors. With them, Isabel simply refused to tolerate it. But intuitively, she knew that arrogance was not in Lehman Morris's makeup. His words were a genuine reflection of his concern.

"We've not had a single case of hantavirus in Montana prior to these," he went on. "You had no reason to think that extra precautions were necessary. You cannot blame yourself."

Isabel did not respond.

"Now tell me," Morris continued. "What was your exposure to these mice? Please say you didn't handle them too."

A brief silence ensued before Isabel answered.

"I had an encounter with one in the supply cabinet. Afterward, I cleaned up pellets."

"You may very well have exposed yourself."

"I've been thinking that's a possibility."

"How long ago was that?"

"Exactly thirteen days."

"Then you're not out of the woods yet. And neither is your patient. I'd feel much better if Suzanne would let us send the helicopter to pick her up. Any chance she'll change her mind?"

"Not for now. Suzanne's adamant about staying home."

"You've got her isolated? It's unlikely she'd be able to transmit the disease now, but if the virus progresses . . ."

"Aside from coming into the clinic twice now for X rays, she's stayed out at her trailer. There's no one out there but Suzanne and her aunt, and the aunt is as stubborn as Suzanne. But I did finally worm a promise out of Suzanne. That if her condition worsens, she'll reconsider going to Missoula General. That—the risk of infecting her aunt—was the only way I got that promise, by the way. That assistant of mine is so damn stubborn . . ." Isabel's voice rose in anger, then began to crack. She was furious with Suzanne for taking such a chance, insisting on staying home. And, if the truth be known, Isabel was terrified. She visited her newest patient each day, sometimes twice, to check in and make sure Suzanne and Mary were adhering strictly to the instructions Isabel gave them.

"Hey, you okay?"

Isabel swallowed against the flood of emotion threatening to choke her.

"I'm fine," she said. "Just tired."

"I imagine the clinic's keeping you busy," Morris said. "Usually one case of hantavirus sends everyone within fifty miles running to the doctor with the slightest ache or sniffle. It can create a real paranoia."

For the first time in days, Isabel let out a laugh.

"Well, that's certainly not a problem here," she said. "This place is like a morgue." She laughed again, a humorless laugh. "Forgive my choice of words. What I'm trying to say is either the residents of Browning have suddenly all acquired perfect health, or they've decided I, personally, am killing my patients."

"That bad, huh?"

"That bad. Hell, can you blame them? Joe, Dolores Birdsong, Will Echohawk. All dead."

"You never even saw Will Echohawk, did you?"

"No. When he came down with the same symptoms Joe had, his mother refused to bring him here. She said I hadn't been able to save Joe. Instead of bringing him in to the clinic, she had a doctoring ceremony performed by a traditional healer. A sweat lodge ceremony where they sprinkled herbs into the fire. By morning the poor kid was dead."

"You can't blame yourself, Isabel. Their suspicions are, in

many ways, well founded. And they run deep. You can't come in there and in a matter of months undo attitudes that took decades, over a century, to form."

"Maybe if I'd been able to save Joe . . ."

"Some of them, most likely Will Echohawk, would have stayed away anyway. They'll come back. It'll just take a little time."

"I hope you're right. In the meantime, I hear the native healers are keeping busy." She tried to sound lighthearted, but failed.

"Lehman," Isabel said, "I *have* to save Suzanne. I just have to."

ALISTAIR STEERED THE sleek sportscar around the curve of the Montlake exit. His mood matched the day. Gloomy, oppressive. Already regretting having agreed to meet Mary—his patience with the hand-holding she'd been demanding was growing paper thin—the sight of the long line of cars, at a dead stop in university traffic, made him consider turning around and heading back home. But he'd already merged onto Montlake and now found himself trapped in a sea of cars. He inched forward in the logjam that *Money* magazine had recently declared the nation's third worst. It was always bad this time of day, but today's nasty downpour only compounded it.

Fucking Seattle.

It took almost twenty minutes to travel the two miles from the Evergreen Floating Bridge to the clinic. The rain came in sheets, making it hard to see any distance at all, which is why he didn't notice all the official looking vehicles until after he'd already pulled into the left-turn-only lane that deposited cars directly into the parking lot for the clinic.

Stunned by the sight before him, he counted four, no five, generic white vans with official-looking seals on their doors. He had just slowed at the parking lot's mouth when a wave of wind and water washed over him, sending new shock waves through him. He turned to see a wet and frantic Mary Pelandini climbing in through the opened passenger door.

"*Back out,*" Mary wailed. "*Now,* no one's coming. Get out of here before they see you."

Alistair glanced briefly over his right shoulder to look for oncoming traffic. He could not see any cars, but then he couldn't really see at all. He slid the gear shift into reverse and punched the gas pedal.

The moment he did so, a horn, followed instantaneously by the sound of rubber screeching against pavement, announced that he'd pulled into someone's path.

"Mother of God!" Mary screamed, but the oncoming red Durango whizzed by, missing them by inches, as its driver vented her fury with a fist held to the horn.

Alistair shifted into drive and accelerated, heading west.

"What the fuck's goin' on?" he asked, eyeing Mary, who'd begun shaking and crying.

"They're raiding us," she sobbed. "They showed up just after we hung up. Like a SWAT team or something."

"Who're they?"

"They called themselves federal agents. There must be a dozen of them. They were watching me. I couldn't call you to tell you not to come. I asked to go to the bathroom, then snuck out the back door so I could warn you."

"This is unreal. What're they looking for?"

"Everything!" Mary cried. "They have a search warrant. It gives them the right to take everything. They're going through every drawer, every file, and packing it all in boxes."

"But they've already been through it once. That's what you told me."

"Now they're back. And this time they're taking everything with them. They even . . ." the sobs returned, ". . . they even videotaped me. Why would they do that? Why would they make me stand there while they videotaped me?"

Alistair could see it coming. Mary was about to crack. She

could end up spilling her guts. If he didn't watch it.

"They're just trying to intimidate you," he said, struggling to sound self-assured. "That's all. It's all for show, darlin'. All of it. There's not a goddamn thing there. Not a thing that can hurt us." He reached out and placed his hand on her thigh. Immediately, his touch seemed to calm her. "Now, darlin', I better get you back there. I'm gonna swing around Thirty-second and drop you in the lot of the office park next to ours. You sneak back in there. Tell them you were so shaken you stepped outside for some air. You can't let them rattle you, darlin'. Remember what my friend said? We're practically home free."

"But what about Ariana's fax?"

"You still haven't found that?"

"No."

"Then it doesn't exist."

Alistair had made three consecutive right turns and now approached the office complex adjacent to and north of the clinic.

"What if they start questioning me?" Mary whimpered, reaching for the door handle. "Should I call my lawyer?"

"Absolutely not," Alistair declared. "That just makes it look like you've got something to hide. You don't want that."

He didn't add that any lawyer worth his or her salt would work an immunity deal in exchange for Mary's cooperation in hanging Alistair.

"You have nothing to fear, Mary." He reached for her hand as the car came to a stop and squeezed reassuringly. "Nothing at all. What we've done is nothin' out of the ordin'ry, nothin' that others aren't doin' every single day. Remember that."

Mary gave him a weak smile.

The fear clenching at Alistair's throat relaxed its hold a bit. Mary would be all right. All it took was a little TLC, some attention from Alistair. But he would have to keep a close eye on her.

Alistair did not linger. He was back on Montlake within minutes, this time more preoccupied with his own troubles than with traffic.

Federal agents. No doubt called by the FDA's criminal division. Was this just some kind of bluff? A mind game designed to make someone talk? Alistair strongly suspected that to be the case.

But there was another explanation, and this one was far more difficult to dismiss. This one absolutely had to be explored.

Had somebody been feeding them information?

THE MESSAGE WAS so short, so maddeningly lacking in information, but the note of urgency in Mary Talking Horse's voice was unmistakeable.

"It's Suzanne. Please come."

For the past week, with Suzanne gone, Isabel had formulated her own routine before opening the clinic for the day.

Feed the dogs. With spring came bountiful rodent hunting on the reservation. Most of the pack she'd nourished through the winter had disappeared, but two—the mangy mutt and one of his female friends—continued to be waiting for her each morning. She'd taken to putting bowls of food out for them, out of sight, near the back door of the clinic.

Play back messages on the answering machine. If the message light blinked, she would press the playback button, then listen as she walked around the office turning on lights and checking the appointment book for the day's schedule.

Before this past week, Suzanne had complained routinely of having to wade through too many messages each morning. Today the machine had announced there were only two.

The first was from the CDC investigator who was in town

and wanted to schedule an appointment to speak with her.

The second had been Mary Talking Horse's.

Isabel had grabbed the bag she'd just deposited on the counter behind Suzanne's cluttered desk, rummaging frantically for the keys to relock the clinic's front door. There was no time to spare. She would call Mary from her cell phone and, if need be, contact Missoula General to have them dispatch a Life Flight team immediately.

As she sped out of town, Isabel punched Suzanne and Mary's telephone number into her cell phone. No response. She punched the redial button, then pressed the phone back to her ear. Nothing. She tried it again, then raised the phone to look at it. The screen flashed NO SVC.

No service.

Damn. Her cell phone worked just fine between her cabin near East Glacier and Browning, but she'd never tried to use it south or east of town.

She had a decision to make. Turn the car around and find a pay phone, or continue to Suzanne's.

Turning around would cost her at least five minutes.

She'd already learned that with hantavirus, five minutes could cost a life.

She had an ironclad grip on the steering wheel as she pulled off Highway 2. Still, her hands shook as she roared up the nameless gravel road leading toward the trailer.

Isabel realized that she'd done the unthinkable. She'd let herself become too involved. Suzanne's recovery, her survival, had become the only thing that mattered to Isabel. It had caused her to lose good judgment. She should never have agreed to treat Suzanne at home. Perhaps if she had refused, Suzanne would have been forced to do the prudent thing and go either to Cutbank or Missoula, where an entire hospital staff would be available to minister to her. But Isabel had been too afraid to call Suzanne's bluff and so she had acquiesced.

And now this.

Oblivious to the purple lupines dotting the meadows and the hawk circling lazily overhead, catching a light breeze in the cloudless morning sky, Isabel tore down the unmaintained road, the car shaking so violently as the ruts grew deeper and more frequent that her medical bag vibrated back and forth on the seat beside her, giving the appearance of riding on a cushion of air.

A long cloud of dust announcing its approach before the Jeep actually came into sight, Isabel finally rounded the last curve. She saw cars—at least three of them—outside the trailer. One was Suzanne's. As she drew near, she recognized another immediately. It belonged to Father McGrath, the parish priest.

Her anguish literally choking her, Isabel roared up to the white picket fence and approached the trailer door at a run.

It opened before she reached the steps.

Father McGrath, a compact, white-haired Irishman with a smile so benevolent Isabel suspected that it had dictated its owner's destiny, stood in its frame.

Only Father McGrath would smile at a time like this.

"Come in, my dear," he said.

"Am I too . . ." Isabel began, stepping inside, but the air she met stopped her mid-sentence. The unmistakable aroma of just-brewed coffee and baked goods fresh from the oven enveloped her. Not the air of illness or death.

Father McGrath's grin widened as he nodded toward the living room, where a small group had gathered.

Mary Talking Horse. Another elderly Blackfeet woman whom Isabel did not know.

And Suzanne.

Suzanne. Sitting up, fully dressed, a cup of tea in her hand, a big, jubilant grin—the most beautiful grin Isabel had ever seen—taking over her entire face. And, for the first time in days, cherry-red lipstick.

With legs of rubber, Isabel went to her and dropped to her knees, her medical bag falling thickly to the floor beside her.

"What . . . ?" Isabel stammered. "When?"

Suzanne's laughter reached out and enveloped her.

"You did it," she beamed. "You healed me."

"I don't understand. Just yesterday, you'd begun vomiting . . ."

Suzanne placed a hand on Isabel's shoulder.

"I don't understand any more than you. But last night, I could feel it. That the sickness was leaving my body. It was like my body was purging itself of it yesterday, when I couldn't keep anything down. I didn't want to call you and get your hopes up, but I knew. I knew I'd be well again this morning. And when I woke up, I was."

"It's a miracle," Isabel said softly.

The smile left Suzanne's face.

"*No*. It's no miracle. *You* did it. You saved me." She looked at the others in the room. "I owe my life to her. She came to me every day, twice, three times sometimes. She got me through this. She saved me."

Heads nodded all around.

Isabel grabbed Suzanne's wrist and felt for her pulse. Strong, steady. No sign of the tachycardia she'd noticed every other day.

She checked Suzanne's lungs. Clear.

Oxygenation, ninety-eight.

Suzanne had shown improvement in days three and four, fueling Isabel's optimism. But yesterday's nausea and vomiting had sent Isabel's spirits spiraling into the gutter. Now, overnight, her patient had recovered.

Lehman Morris had told her that those hantavirus patients who survived recovered almost as fast as the others died. But never, in her wildest dreams, had she dared hope for this.

"Now I can come back to work." Suzanne grinned as Isabel retracted the stethoscope.

"Not so fast," Isabel said, finally allowing the relief, the laughter that had been bubbling up inside her, to surface.

"You're staying right here. At home and in bed. Another couple days at the very least."

"Aw, come on. I'm bored to death out here." Suzanne turned to her aunt. "No offense, Mary. But next time I get so sick I almost die, I'm gonna demand a satellite dish. We're the only ones on the rez without one."

Isabel accepted the tea and fresh fry bread brought in celebration of Suzanne's recovery by Mary's elderly friend Rose, then she stood.

"I should get back to the clinic," she said.

"I'm sorry if we made you miss appointments," Mary Talking Horse said softly. "We just wanted you to see Suzanne for yourself. We thought you deserved that."

"Thank you. And no apology necessary. I haven't exactly been busy recently."

"That's what we heard." Suzanne's expression reflected both concern and embarrassment. "But that's gonna change now. You wait and see."

Isabel's smile was wide. And genuine.

"I hope so. But for now, I'm just happy to see you looking so well. Don't you push yourself too hard, you hear?"

After getting Suzanne and Mary's promise that Suzanne would take it easy for several more days, Isabel took her leave.

The lupines and hawk—now perched on top of a telephone post—that she'd missed on the way out gave Isabel great pleasure on her return trip. As did the blue columbine and the fiery Indian paintbrush dotting the meadows on either side of the road. The sense of relief that she felt surged through her like adrenaline, sharpening the blue of the morning sky. The morning air, still chilled from thirty-degree nights, never felt so pure and crisp as it did now, rushing through her open window. She could not get enough of it. Or of the heady sensation.

Suzanne did not die.

Just once they had beat this dreaded, loathsome disease.

Pulling up to the clinic, Isabel's mood lifted higher still to see two figures waiting outside. *Patients.* Had word of Suzanne's recovery already spread, or were there still some who did not blame her for Joe and Dolores's deaths?

Right now it didn't really matter.

Isabel flashed both patients, Eli Walker and a middle-aged woman whose face was unfamiliar, a smile of greeting. Eli looked clean and sober.

"I'm so sorry to keep you waiting outside like this," she said. She'd never felt so eager to treat a patient, so full of hope.

As she fingered her keys, searching for the one that opened the clinic's front door, she noticed it.

The package, small, thin, rectangular, leaning up against the locked door.

"You just missed UPS," Eli Walker said.

Without looking at its address label, Isabel picked up the package, which was the size and shape of a videocassette, unlocked the door, and ushered her two patients inside.

Then she dropped the package on top of Suzanne's desk and went to work.

CHAPTER

EIGHT

W HEN AN ENTIRE month passed with no new cases of hantavirus, then six weeks, Isabel finally began to breathe more easily.

The CDC investigator had confirmed Isabel's conclusion: that Dolores Birdsong contracted the virus while cleaning out the broken-down truck in her yard. Deer mice caught in Will Echohawk's house were sent for tests and came back confirmed carriers of the hantavirus. Since Suzanne had disposed of the mice caught in the clinic, there was no way to prove that her exposure originated there, but the final report labeled the clinic mice as "the probable source of exposure."

It was never determined how Joe contracted the virus. Anna Winged Foot's house was spotless and free of any signs of rodent infestation. There was no reason to think Joe had been exposed at school, especially in light of the fact that none of the other students at Browning High became ill.

Though Isabel could not control the thoughts that tormented her in the quiet of each night, during the day, she wasn't given that chance. Suzanne's recovery—accompanied by tales of Isabel's dedication—had spread like wildfire across the reservation. Isabel strongly suspected that her assistant had mounted a one-woman campaign from her trailer in the week between her recovery and the day Isabel allowed her to come back to work on a part-time basis. Whatever the explanation, Isabel suddenly found her patient load dramatically increased. Blackfeet residents who had suffered from a condition or ailment silently for years were filtering in to see what the new doctor could do to help. And the fear of hantavirus brought many in for sniffles or aches and pains that once would have been ignored.

The relief and gratification Isabel felt was immense. She relished the hard work, relished the exhaustion at the end of a twelve- or fourteen-hour day, for it represented her only hope for a few hours of mindless, merciful sleep.

This day, like the three before it, had started before dawn and was now ending well after the sun had dropped into the mountains. As Isabel approached the side door to her cabin, she could hear the telephone ringing inside. Flinging the door to the kitchen wide, she groped the wall blindly for the light switch. She told herself she'd start leaving a light on each morning when she left for work.

Dropping her medical bag on the dusty wood floor, she used both hands. After the fourth ring, the answering machine came on. As she heard her voice asking the caller to leave a message, Isabel continued groping the wall impatiently. There, at last, she found it. The kitchen sprang to light just as the caller began to speak.

Isabel's hand froze on the light switch.

"Nice to hear your voice, darlin'," her caller said. "But not nearly so nice as it was seein' your picture in this month's *Journal*." The words came out in the slow, silky drawl that he usually managed to keep more in check but that alcohol inevitably exposed, with long pauses between. "Ah see you're still crusadin' for the underdog. A regular Florence Nightingale."

The bitterness, even filtered through an answering machine, cut through the cabin's cold air like a knife. An irrational fear caused Isabel to stop breathing, for fear that he would hear her and realize that she stood just feet away from the telephone.

"Such a shame that you weren't able to save those young boys. Ah'm sure that's weighing heavy on your mind. Ah 'magine that it's pretty hard to sleep . . . out there in the wilderness."

His snicker ran through her like a current of electricity.

"You know . . ." He was breathing heavily into the phone, and in that moment, Isabel knew what he was doing on the other end. "Ah haven't forgotten what turns you on. How to make you moan. Ah could help you to sleep . . ."

More heavy breathing, and all Isabel could do was stand, a prisoner, and listen.

"Do you remember, Is? What it was like? It's been a long time . . . such a long time . . ."

Isabel pressed her hands to her ears and began breathing again, long deep inhales and exhales, focusing only on her breathing, shutting everything else out, until finally, what seemed an eternity later, she thought she heard the beep that signaled the end of the message.

But she was wrong. He was still talking.

"Did you get the video, darlin'?" In the background she heard the familiar note of Alistair's grandfather clock marking the half hour. "Ah hope you enjoyed it. It's just a little reminder for you. You know, in case you were thinkin' of causing me any more trouble. You looked so beautiful. Ah've been thinkin it's a shame not to share that much beauty . . ."

Dropping her hands, Isabel continued to stand, staring at the phone as if it were alive.

Finally, at last, he hung up.

Isabel crossed the room, grabbed the answering machine, and, holding it first at arm's length—as if it contained something deadly, something even worse than the killer hantavirus—flung it with a savage grunt against the wall. It bounced off a log, clattering noisily to the floor, where she kicked it irrationally, again and again, until it lay shattered in several pieces.

What did he mean about a video?

Isabel's mind spun wildly, dizzily. She reached for the back of a chair and once more forced deep breaths in and out of her lungs.

She'd known Alistair would eventually call. Still, the horror of hearing his voice, the images she was now battling to cleanse from her mind. And what video was he talking about?

His first comment she understood. The article she'd written for the *Journal of the American Medical Association* must have come out. Even now, five months after she'd left him, Alistair was still managing to spoil things for Isabel. No wonder he'd chosen tonight to call. He knew a simple call from him could ruin what little pleasure, or satisfaction, or hope, she might take from the fact that the article had been published.

If Alistair had seen *JAMA*, her copy may have arrived too. Isabel walked into the room off the kitchen. Years ago it had served as a pantry, but she had no need for extra storage—the few cupboards the kitchen provided were practically always bare anyway. She yanked on the metal chain hanging from a lightbulb over the desk she and Gus had found at a garage sale in Ennis.

Envelopes and files littered the desk's surface, but there was no sign of the monthly *JAMA*. How long had it been since she picked up the mail?

Pulling tight her wool sweater, Isabel stepped back into the night and headed down the long gravel road toward her mailbox. The moon, poised above Little Chief Mountain, was almost full. The jagged peaks, maybe even more magnificent in this light than at dawn, were silhouetted against an indigo blue sky. The sight usually sent shivers down Isabel's spine, but tonight she barely noticed, keeping a keen eye instead on the road.

As she approached the end of the driveway, the stand of cottonwoods across from the mailbox caught a headlight. She started, but then remembered the grandfather clock she'd just heard in the background. Alistair had called her from home. Within seconds she recognized another distinctive sound—the muffler on Gus Dearing's pickup. Only Gus was familiar enough with the winding roads to drive at night with such speed.

Gus was Isabel's landlord. His family had homesteaded in East Glacier, just across the reservation boundary, at the turn of the century. Real estate prices on that side of the line and that close to Glacier National Park had made him a wealthy man. Before Isabel came along, he'd had numerous offers to buy or rent the little log cabin where Gus's great-grand-daddy was born. He'd turned them all down. But something about Isabel caused him to reconsider, and they'd since become close friends. Gus lived up the road half a mile in a sprawling log home overlooking the Two Medicine River.

He could afford to drive any car he wanted, but he loved tooling around in his old green pickup.

He roared past, coming within a couple feet of Isabel, then, suddenly, gravel flew as the pickup screeched to a halt.

Gus was rolling down his window when Isabel approached his side of the truck.

"Damn, Isabel," he cursed, his bushy white eyebrows coming together in consternation. "I hardly saw you. You oughta carry a flashlight with you so you don't get run down."

"Sorry about that, Gus. I didn't mean to scare you."

Gus's moonlit, weathered face suddenly disappeared behind a mass of moving, golden fur.

"Hey there, Grunt," Isabel said, reaching to stroke the head of the big yellow Lab whose enthusiastic greeting for his friend shook the truck's cab and fogged its windows.

"Get the hell off my lap, will you?" Gus growled. But he simply craned his neck to see over the dog, which stayed put at the window, straddling Gus's legs. "You finally pickin' up your mail?"

Isabel tried for a laugh, but it came out a weak imitation. In Montana, nothing was private.

"Yes. I suppose Benny's been complaining again?"

"He's always got somethin' to whine about. Says if he keeps having so much trouble stuffing mail into your box, the post office'll stop making deliveries. You'll have to start picking it up in Browning."

"Well, tell Benny I'll try harder. Okay?"

Grunt's wet nose pushed at the hand she'd placed on Gus's half-opened window. For a brief moment, Isabel debated asking whether she could borrow Grunt for the night. Alistair's call had shaken her to the core. Even with the knowledge that he was four hundred miles away, she did not relish the thought of spending the night alone.

"You okay, Izzie?" Gus said.

"Of course."

If she told Gus something was bothering her, he would

insist that she come stay with him. As appealing a prospect as that now seemed, it was not a solution. She'd never before spoken to Gus about Alistair and right now the last thing she wanted to do was get into it.

"Seems like somethin"'s bothering you."

"No, Gus, really. I'm fine. Just tired, that's all. I've been awfully busy. Flu season, you know."

"No more cases of hantavirus?"

"No, thank God. It seemed to disappear as quickly as it showed up."

"Well, I'm glad for that. Drop by to see us one of these days."

"I will, Gus," Isabel said. "I promise."

She waved as Gus and Grunt resumed their way to Gus's ranch, then crossed to the mailbox. True to Benny-the-mailman's complaints, the box was crammed so full that Isabel had to use both arms, cradlelike, to carry its contents back to the cabin. Once inside, she dumped all the mail on top of the layer of papers already obscuring her desk and grabbed the newly delivered *JAMA*.

Before settling down to read, Isabel walked around the cabin, checking to be certain all the windows and doors were locked and curtains drawn. Finally, she went to the closet and from the back of the top shelf, pulled out a thirty-eight-caliber revolver given to her by Gus when she first moved in. He'd insisted that she keep it. In order to avoid an argument, she'd finally acquiesced, but had immediately tucked it away at the back of the closet.

The cardboard box containing the bullets he'd given her had never been opened. She opened it now and withdrew several cartridges, which she slid, one by one, into place in the gun's chamber.

Then, laying it on the bedside table so that it pointed toward the wall, she changed into the sweats and long-sleeved T-shirt she routinely slept in and climbed into bed. She reached to turn on the small lamp next to the bed and, falling back onto her pillows, turned to the *Journal*'s table of contents.

Two-thirds of the way down the page, under "Commentary," she saw it:

Hantavirus vaccine: not possible, or not profitable? by *Isabel McLain, M.D., page 1848.*

She turned to page 1848.

Then, with the loaded gun beside her, Isabel began to read.

IT DID NOT come to her until the middle of the night.

She awoke, AMA journal still resting on her chest. The lamp was still on.

The video. There had been a package that appeared to be a video delivered to the clinic that day that she locked up to go out to Suzanne's. It had been resting against the door. Eli Walker said he'd seen UPS deliver it.

What ever happened to it?

Isabel vaguely recalled dropping the package on Suzanne's desk, but things had been so hectic that day, and in the ensuing days and weeks. While she was away, a mound of mail and forms had grown on every available surface in Suzanne's office. Isabel had never seen or thought of the package that had been delivered that morning again.

Until now. Until Alistair's call.

She tried to go back to sleep. She would ask Suzanne about it in the morning. Suzanne had probably put it away somewhere.

It was nothing, nothing, she told herself.

Still, she could not sleep.

SOME DAYS IT felt as though she'd fully recovered from her terrifying bout with the hantavirus. Others, like today, Suzanne could still feel the aftereffects. Shortness of breath, tendency to tire easily. And then of course there were the nightmares. She'd watched Joe Winged Foot die of the hantavirus. For all practical purposes, Dolores Birdsong too—though Dolores hadn't actually died, gone flatline, until she was in the helicopter.

Suzanne felt kind of ashamed for the relief she felt about that. That they'd gotten Dolores on the helicopter before she actually died. It seemed a lot worse somehow, to die up there in the air, with her connection to their sacred Earth Mother severed. But Suzanne just didn't think she could've gone through another ordeal like the one with Joe.

'Course she didn't know Dolores all that well. Like she knew Joe.

All she knew, after seein' what she'd seen, watchin' Joe's dying heart go into ventricular fibrillation, then seein' his beautiful body just about jump off the table from them damn paddles—sizzle, sizzle, crankin' the dial up, then sizzle again—was that if she was gonna die of the hantavirus, she'd do it on her own. At home. No paddles for her. No medic squeezing air into the bladder connected to the endotracheal tube that they'd inserted into her lungs. No siree. That wasn't the way Suzanne was gonna go.

But in her dreams, in her nightmares, that's the way it went. Just like Joe and Dolores.

She didn't know why she'd been spared. Who to give the credit.

Isabel?

Maybe. The ribavirin Dr. McLain gave Suzanne might just have saved her life. And no question she received good care from her. Hell, seemed like those dark, pain-filled eyes were peering down at Suzanne every time she came to from one of those awful dreams.

She'd had a few doubts about Isabel before. They'd never quite hit it off. But she was learning—fast—that there was a whole lot more to Dr. McLain than Suzanne ever knew before. And a person'd have to be pretty damn ornery and heartless not to be touched by how hard that woman tried to get Suzanne better.

But Suzanne wasn't ruling out the Black-Tailed Deer Dance either. Mary had wanted to take Suzanne up to Badger Creek, to one of the sweat lodges that Mary's husband, Charlie, used to go to when he was real sick. Suzanne didn't want to hurt Mary's feelings by pointing out the fact that Charlie had died anyway—he was buried up there on the sacred grounds somewhere—so she just told Mary the truth. That she was too sick for the long drive. So instead Mary and her old friend Rose and a couple of the elders conducted kind of a scaled down Black-Tailed Deer Dance where they consecrated the sweetgrass and prayed for Suzanne's recovery. The ceremonies and dancing and midnight feast kept Suzanne up most of that night, but when she did sleep, a deer came to her, just like was supposed to happen. It didn't actually give her instructions about how to get well, like was supposed to happen, but she definitely saw a deer in her dream that night.

Suzanne made Mary and Rose and the two others promise to keep the ceremony a secret. It wasn't that she was ashamed to be callin' on the old ways, not at all. She actually liked the idea, felt like she was covering both bases this way. But if word got out that they'd had the ceremony, everybody on the rez was gonna think *that's* what healed Suzanne, and not Dr. McLain. And both because Suzanne felt a new tenderness toward her boss and because she knew her people—knew that they'd all but give up on Dr. McLain and the clinic if they found out, and that wasn't good—she made everyone promise to keep the ceremony a secret and she made sure to get the word out that Dr. McLain had saved her.

Besides, what was she gonna do if everybody stopped comin' to the clinic? It was her job, after all.

This morning she was surprised to see Dr. McLain's dirty Jeep when she pulled up to the clinic. Suzanne always beat Dr. McLain in, even now.

She was even more surprised at what she saw when she stepped into her office. Dr. McLain, on hands and knees, rummaging through the cupboard that ran below the counter that separated the waiting room and Suzanne's desk. Several of the file drawers had been opened, but not shut fully.

"Whatcha lookin for?"

Isabel McLain's head snapped up.

"Suzanne," she said. She'd been looking a lot more rested recently, but today dark circles framed Dr. McLain's eyes. "I didn't hear you come in."

"Can I help you find something?"

Isabel rocked back to sit on her heels and rested a hand on top of each thigh.

"You haven't by any chance seen a video that was sent here for me?"

Suzanne maintained a blank expression.

"A video?" she echoed.

"Yes. On the day you called me out to your house to celebrate your recovery, UPS delivered something that looked like it could have been a video. It was resting outside, against the locked door. I thought I put it on your desk. Then I just forgot about it."

"Gee, there was a ton of stuff on my desk when I got back to work. But I don't remember any video."

When a flicker of relief seemed to cross Isabel's features, Suzanne couldn't resist pressing for more information.

"Was it somethin' you were looking for? Something you might've ordered?"

Isabel shook her thick head of ebony hair—hair Suzanne had always thought looked every bit as Indian as that on any head on the rez—and snorted a caustic laugh.

"No. Definitely not."

" 'Cause I'll keep an eye out for it, if you're expecting somethin'."

This seemed to startle Isabel.

"Why don't you just put any mail you get for me on my desk?" she said, averting her eyes from Suzanne's stare.

"You still want me to open it for you?"

Isabel tried a light smile.

"You've got so much to do. Why don't you just leave that to me from now on?"

"Whatever you say."

If Suzanne had had any doubts about her actions before, she did not now. It was clear that the video for which Dr. McLain searched so frantically was about as welcome as a case of head lice.

Suzanne had had to trust her instincts when she'd opened that package. She knew right away somethin' wasn't right. After all, there was no return address on it and nobody sends somethin' of any value without putting a return address on it. Unless they don't want the person receiving it to know who it's from.

She'd actually thought it might be some kind of threat to her boss. After Joe and Dolores died, she'd heard talk that a few of the more radical Blackfeet were thinkin' about how they could run Isabel out of town. That's why Suzanne had taken it home, 'cause after all she'd been through recently, Suzanne didn't think Dr. McLain needed anything else to worry about. The lack of return address had made Suzanne suspicious right from the start.

But all Suzanne had to do was watch a couple minutes of the video to figure out who'd sent it. That it had to have come from the guy in it. The same guy who dropped by the clinic tryin' to find out where Isabel lived. No wonder Isabel had flipped out when Suzanne told her he'd been there askin' about her. I mean, this guy . . . There was no question in Suzanne's mind that he'd filmed the two of them in bed without Isabel's knowledge. It was the look in his eye—his awareness of the camera. He played to it like you do when you see your reflection in a store window and you suddenly lift your shoulders, suck your gut in, or when you look in the mirror.

Isabel didn't have that look. Good thing, 'cause what Suzanne saw was enough of a surprise about her boss without thinkin' that she was deliberately putting on a show for the camera.

Suzanne didn't think white women had it in them to make love like that.

Then there was the final clue. If she had any doubts that Isabel didn't know she was being filmed, the one line scrawled along the label of the video itself, where you usually write the date and whatever it is you've taped, was enough to dispel them.

Let this be a warning.

That's all it said. But the meaning had been pretty clear.

This guy was somehow tryin' to blackmail or threaten Isabel. And Suzanne had made the decision, all on her own, that Isabel had had enough to deal with without some slimeball with a southern accent adding to her troubles. She hadn't realized that she had it—that sense of loyalty to her employer. But hell if she was gonna stand by and let that sleazebag make her miserable.

And so Suzanne had destroyed the tape. Not just thrown it out, into the Dumpster. Guys were goin' through those Dumpsters all the time lookin' for drugs and such.

No, she'd pulled the guts out of the thing, the cassette, and ruined it good. Then she'd thrown it all in the trash.

CHAPTER

NINE

PULLING INTO THE Outlaw Inn, Isabel scanned the parking lot for out-of-state plates. When she'd heard Dr. MacStirling planned to drive all the way from Portland, she'd offered to meet him in Kalispell. The only information he'd been willing to offer her over the phone was that he had a "proposal" he'd like her to hear. She'd received several similar calls since her article appeared in *JAMA*. One from a graduate student at Duke who informed her that thanks to her article, he planned to apply for an NIH grant to study the hantavirus; another from a Native American candidate for the state legislature in Arizona who, if elected, planned to propose a bill sponsoring funding for hantavirus research; and one from an investigative reporter who claimed Joe's, Dolores's, and Will's deaths were actually the result of a biological weapons accident in Utah. Her initial elation at the fact that the article had drawn attention to the disease and stirred interest had now ebbed to a cynicism occasioned by the reality that no one with a serious chance of changing things had yet stepped up to the plate.

Isabel had no idea what to expect at today's meeting, but at the very least, she saw it as an opportunity to get out of town for a few hours. Some new scenery would do her good.

MacStirling had been happy to accept her offer to meet him in Kalispell.

"Lovely," he'd proclaimed in a brogue that had a musical ring to it. "That will give me a chance to wander about Glacier National Park while I'm up that way."

A tan Land Cruiser with flashy gold trim and a pricey-looking bicycle mounted on its back stood out among the rows of older-model cars and pickups. Oregon plates. That had to be it. Isabel pulled in next to the Land Cruiser, then got out, taking care not to brush up against her own vehicle, which had its usual coating of dried mud.

The motel's coffee shop had already emptied of the breakfast crowd. A lone man sat in a booth near the back of the restaurant. He stood and strode her way.

"Dr. McLain." He smiled, extending a hand. He was tall with longish, sandy hair that curled over the collar of his Patagonia jacket. Isabel recognized the accent right away as belonging to Ken MacStirling. "I'm Dr. MacStirling. It's a pleasure to meet you."

He escorted her back to his table, where a waitress with big hair was delivering steaming mugs.

"I hope you don't mind," MacStirling said now. "I took the liberty of ordering you a latte."

"Thanks," Isabel said, settling in to the booth.

There was a moment's awkward silence while both sipped at their drinks.

"That was some article you wrote for *JAMA*," MacStirling said. Just as she'd thought, MacStirling's call had to do with her article. "Some of my coworkers were a mite offended by it."

"Coworkers?"

"Yes. I work for a biotech company called ImmuVac. Our headquarters are in Portland."

"Are you an M.D. or a research scientist?"

"Ph.D. Immunology."

Isabel studied Ken MacStirling to see if he agreed with his coworkers' characterization of her article. She could not get a take on his expression.

"Hantavirus first appeared almost seven years ago," she answered, "and after all that time, we still don't have a vaccine. Or even an effective treatment."

"But to call the medical and pharmaceutical industries racist because they haven't poured millions of dollars into hantavirus research . . . don't you think you're being a wee bit hysterical?"

"Hysterical? If this disease had broken out in Manhattan, or Beverly Hills, or even Portland for that matter, we'd have a vaccine by now. My article merely told it like it is. I hardly think that equates with hysteria."

"You actually believe that no one cares about this disease because Native Americans have borne the brunt of it?"

"You're British, right?" Isabel asked.

"Scottish."

"Sorry. How long have you been in this country?"

"So you're implying I'm a bit naive about this country's treatment of its aboriginal peoples?"

"How else can you explain the fact that victims of this disease today have no better chance of surviving than they did seven years ago, when we first learned it existed? If the right people had died, you better believe that money would have been allocated for research."

MacStirling's rueful smile caught Isabel off guard.

"You find the subject amusing?"

"Well, I rather hate to disillusion you," MacStirling said. "But I've been working on a hantavirus vaccine for three years now."

"You . . . what?" Isabel fell back against the padded booth. "I did extensive research before I wrote that article. Bio-Screen was the only company at all interested in hantavirus. They'd developed a test to detect it in its earliest stages. But when someone put the numbers to it, they decided it wouldn't be profitable, so, of course, they dropped it." She directed a penetrating gaze at MacStirling. "Why doesn't anyone know about your work?"

"Probably because I haven't exactly had a lot of corporate backing. When I signed on with ImmuVac, it was to help develop an AIDS vaccine. But I managed to talk them into piggybacking my work on the hantavirus. The company's never really gotten behind it, but because they seem to think I've got something to contribute to the AIDS work, they've put up with the hantavirus research I've done on the side."

Isabel shifted forward, her palms flat on the table.

"How far along is your research on a vaccine?"

"It's been ready for clinical trials for over a year now."

"Let me guess. ImmuVac refuses to fund the trials."

"Correction. ImmuVac *refused* to fund a clinical trial. Thanks to your article, they've reconsidered."

"You mean ImmuVac is willing to invest in a clinical trial?" The disbelief in her voice was audible. "Because of my article?"

"Yes."

"That's incredible. Fantastic." Isabel paused. "I owe you an apology, don't I? And ImmuVac."

"Absolutely not. You had no way of knowing about my hantavirus work. If the truth be told, I'd about given up on it myself. ImmuVac has had plenty of opportunity to move forward with the clinical trials, but they chose not to. I couldn't be more pleased that that's changed now. And I have you to thank for that fact."

"But if my article swayed them, caused them to reconsider, ImmuVac is that rare company with a social conscience."

Ken MacStirling leaned across the table, bringing his narrow face within inches of Isabel's to speak in a conspiratorial tone.

"I'm going to level with you, lass. As moving as your article was, ImmuVac is not doing this to right a wrong. Or for the greater good of mankind. Your article seems to have stirred a great deal of interest in hantavirus. ImmuVac now sees the vaccine as a way to attract funding—you know, either larger pharmaceutical sponsors or maybe, if there's a good deal of positive publicity, a public offering."

"I don't really give a damn what their motivation is, so long as someone comes out with a vaccine. That's all that matters to me. That's why I wrote that article."

MacStirling eased back, studying her.

"I imagine writing it was a wee bit therapeutic too. I mean, your grief at the loss of your patients came through loud and clear."

MacStirling's observation was astute—a little too astute for Isabel's comfort.

"Tell me," she said, changing the subject. "When do you plan to begin the clinical trial? And where?"

"That depends."

"On?"

"On you."

Isabel drew back.

"On me? What do you mean?"

"We would like to conduct the clinical trial on the Blackfeet reservation. And we would like for you to head it up."

"You're kidding," Isabel said. "Aren't you?"

"No. I'm not. In fact, I couldn't be more serious."

"Well, then you're wasting your time and mine."

"Good God, girl, don't you want your patients protected?"

"Of course I do. But I'm not about to make guinea pigs of them. Now, if you'll excuse me."

Ken MacStirling reached out and grabbed her by the forearm.

"Please, hear me out. You owe me that much."

"I don't owe you anything!"

MacStirling reached into his briefcase, extracted something, and threw it down on the table.

"Then what was *this*?" Isabel's picture, alongside the *JAMA* article, stared up at her. "Some kind of a charade? How the devil can you write such an article then refuse the chance to participate in the process that will bring about the change you bloody claim to want? The change you say your patients need. Can you explain that?"

Isabel shook her arm free.

"I have nothing to explain. Find another study director," she said, standing so abruptly that coffee went flying.

She'd taken no more than two steps away from the table when she heard him say it.

"I should think I'd have trouble sleepin' if I were you."

She twirled, furious, and returned to the table. She stood above him, grasping the Formica edge as her anger erupted.

"Who do you think you are coming here like this and passing judgment on me?"

MacStirling studied her.

"Then please, explain it to me," he said. "As a professional courtesy if nothing else. How can you deny your patients—

bloody hell, the whole world—the chance to be protected from this disease?"

"Now if I've ever heard gross exaggeration, that's it. You're trying to tell me that my refusal to conduct the clinical trial for your vaccine is the equivalent of denying it to the world?"

"Unfortunately, that's just what I'm telling you. Because the simple truth is, if you don't agree to conduct this trial, ImmuVac will not proceed with the vaccine."

"*What?* That makes no sense, no sense at all . . . unless . . . *It's some kind of publicity ploy*," Isabel cried. "Doing the trial on a reservation. The media will eat it up. That's why you need me to be the study director."

MacStirling's gaze would not meet hers.

"You know what you and your company can do with your proposal?"

These words brought MacStirling's eyes back up to hers. They were angry, and anguished.

"Don't lump me in with the rest of your villains."

Isabel turned and stormed out of the restaurant.

IN ANOTHER RESTAURANT sixty miles away, inside East Glacier Lodge, a busload of Japanese tourists had disembarked their Greyhound and now made claim to all but two tables.

Tony Wilderman stood at the dining room's entrance and scanned the room. He hated crowds. But he was hungry, and it was a fifteen-minute drive into Browning.

The mere thought of eating in a Browning restaurant propelled him forward, into the dining room.

At one of the tables not occupied by the noisy tour group, a woman was spoon-feeding a toddler boy who sat on her lap. At the other, a lone man, nicely dressed, read a newspaper. Tony headed in his direction.

"Mind if I sit down?" Wilderman asked.

The man looked up from his paper, then surveyed the room, as if he were about to suggest that Tony go elsewhere.

"Be my guest," he drawled without expression, immediately looking back down at the paper.

Friendly sort, Tony thought to himself. When he spotted several sections of the *Seattle Times* strewn on the other side of the table—his tablemate was engrossed in the business section—he dared to speak up again.

"Sorry to bother you again, but mind if I borrow the sports section?"

"Help yourself."

"Where'd you find the Seattle paper? These Montana papers have the worst sports sections I've ever seen."

"Gift shop in the lodge here carries it."

"You a guest here?" Tony said. "So am I."

Without answering, the man went back to his article, just as a waitress showed up with a glass of iceless water and a menu which she placed in front of Tony.

"You're becoming a permanent fixture around here," she teased Tony good-naturedly as she eyed the other man. "I'll get you a cup of coffee while you decide what you want."

"Already know," Tony grinned back. "Western omelette, wheat toast. And a small juice. And coffee, as soon as it's convenient."

"That's easy enough," she said.

When she returned minutes later, she reached for the white ceramic mug in the upper right corner of the paper placemat that contained a map of Glacier National Park, then began to pour.

"So how's the prospecting going?" she asked.

"Now, that's highly confidential," Tony teased. "Suppose you were a spy for a rival mining company?"

"Do I look like a spy for a mining company?" Her laugh was easy and hearty.

"You never know." Tony held up a hand to stop her from

filling the cup to its brim. He needed plenty of room for cream. "Thanks. Actually, I'm encouraged by what I've found so far, out past Browning."

"On the reservation?"

"Yep."

"Good luck with that," she said. "Them Blackfeet don't like mines."

"I suspected as much," Tony answered as she turned to the next table.

It was then that Tony realized his tablemate had finally taken his nose out of the newspaper and now regarded him with considerably more interest than before.

"So," the man said, his tone much friendlier now, "you're a miner?"

"A geologist for World Resources, a Canadian mining company. I'm in charge of exploration."

"And you're planning to mine on the reservation?"

"Just doing some preliminary exploration."

Wilderman had just teased the waitress about being a spy. Had he accused the wrong person?

"My name is Alistair Bott," the man said, as he reached into his blazer pocket for his business card. It was gold embossed and stylish.

ALISTAIR BOTT, M.D. CARDIOVASCULAR SURGERY, it said. The address below was in Seattle.

"Tony Wilderman, Vancouver, B.C. Nice to meet you," Wilderman said, shaking the man's proffered hand.

A doctor. That explained the attitude. And expensive clothes.

"What's a heart surgeon from Seattle doing in these parts?"

"Just takin' a short vacation. I come up here from time to time."

"The park's really something, isn't it?" Tony said.

When Bott looked confused, he said, "Glacier National Park. It's something else. Don't you agree?"

How could this guy not know what he was talking about? Bott hesitated.

"Yes, yes it is. Actually, I've spent most of my time here."

"East Glacier? Not much in East Glacier besides fish. You a fly fisherman?"

"Yes," Bott said. "So you're doing a little exploration on the Indian reservation? That must be interesting."

"The reservation or the exploration? The reservation's downright depressing. You been over there at all?"

"Just a little. You're right. It's pretty bad. And none too friendly, I hear. How do they feel about someone like you snooping around?"

Wilderman snorted.

"Let's just say I watch my back. I've worked on other reservations, but something tells me this one's going to be a real challenge. Usually there's at least some faction of the community that welcomes me, that wants to cooperate because they know what mining can do for their economy. But if there's anybody like that up there in Browning, I haven't run into them yet."

"I suppose that means there's not much chance that you'll actually end up minin' there."

"Not necessarily. There are ways to get the approval we'd need. It just means it'll take more work on our part. A little more diplomacy. There's always a way, a button to push. You know much about mining?"

"Not really." Bott's smile was oddly amused. "But my ex-wife was one of those tree-hugger types. She hates minin' companies."

"She live in Seattle?"

"No. She moved away a few months ago," Bott said. Then, with a joviality that seemed misplaced, he lifted his glass of orange juice into the air.

"A toast to you, Mr. Wilderman. And World Resources. I wish you both the best of luck in your endeavor in Indian country."

•   •   •

KEN MACSTIRLING COULDN'T imagine who would be knocking at the door of his motel room. He'd just returned from dinner after an exhausting day in Glacier National Park, where he'd biked to the top of Going to the Sun Road.

The bathwater he'd been drawing to soak his aching limbs had drowned out his visitor's persistent rapping until he turned the faucet off and returned to the bedroom for a newspaper to read in the tub. Then its urgency could not be mistaken.

Grabbing the robe he'd thrown on the bed, he went to the door and, tying his sash, opened it.

Isabel McLain stood outside.

"May I come in?"

She seemed not to notice MacStirling's garb.

"Aye," he said.

Isabel entered the room, quickly assessed it, and settled into one of two overstuffed chairs under the window that looked out on to Kalispell's busy Highway 93.

MacStirling, his discomfort at hosting a visitor while wearing nothing but a robe overshadowed by immense curiosity, followed suit, settling in the other chair.

"How safe is your vaccine?" Isabel asked.

"Extremely safe. I have two years of animal studies to back it up." MacStirling stood and walked over to the bulging briefcase propped against the wall next to the bed. Extracting a three-inch-thick black binder, he returned and offered it to her. "Here, here's everything on the vaccine. Its mechanism of action. Tests to date. Everything. You can take it home with you. Keep it for as long as you like. Or I can go over it with you, page by page. You make the call."

Isabel took the binder and placed it on her lap. Despite her air of determination, she looked utterly miserable. And exhausted. The white lab coat with her name on it that she now wore over the same jeans and shirt she'd worn earlier that day indicated she must have driven back to Browning that morning after their meeting, put in a day's work, then returned to Kalispell to find him.

"Do you know how difficult this study will be to sell to the Blackfeet?" Isabel said.

"No. Tell me."

"They don't trust outsiders. They especially don't trust our medical establishment. They still remember the blankets given them by our government—blankets deliberately infected with smallpox. Like it was yesterday."

"But they trust you," MacStirling said, not unkindly.

Isabel raised her tortured eyes to his.

"Some do. And you're asking me to use that trust in a . . . a . . ." Her voice drifted off, as though she could not bring herself to say the words.

"A clinical trial. One that is without question the safest trial I've ever been involved with. A trial that will save lives. You wouldn't be back here tonight if you didn't believe this vaccine will help your patients. And many, many others."

Isabel remained silent.

"I admitted to you today what my company's motives are," MacStirling continued. "Maybe I shouldn't have done that. But surely you can't attribute the same motivation to me. I mean, I've worked on this vaccine for years now, without a reasonable expectation that it would ever be profitable."

"Why? Why did you choose hantavirus?"

"I don't know," he said, shaking his head. Then, finally, he smiled. "That's not true. I do know. It may sound silly. Westerns are very popular in Europe. I grew up watching *The Lone Ranger* and *Gunsmoke*. I always had empathy for the Indians, for the way they were portrayed, as either savage scalp-takers or straight men for the dashing cowboy hero. Those things you said today—when I called you hysterical— I had the exact same feelings that you described in your article after those people died in Four Corners back in ninety-three. Why isn't someone doing something to prevent this from happening again?" He'd been averting his eyes, embarrassed by sitting there practically naked, but now he raised them to find Isabel staring intently at him. "I decided to do something." He leaned forward, holding the lower half of his robe closed with one hand. "I give you my word that this vaccine is safe. I have already immunized myself. Three times. Over a period of two years. And I've never been healthier."

The silence that followed seemed to MacStirling to last forever.

"I don't know if I can convince them to take part in the study," Isabel McLain finally said softly.

MacStirling's hopes soared.

"If anyone can, it's you."

CHAPTER

TEN

HAVE YOU EVER stopped to think about how a society goes about stealing human rights?"

As usual, Monty Four Bear's lecture on Indian law was standing room only. Today's lecture was one of Monty's favorites. He sat with legs slung over the edge of the auditorium stage, facing his students. Bracing himself with his hands, he leaned toward them, his dark, piercing eyes roaming over his audience and drawing them in. His legs swung back and forth restlessly as the heels of his cowboy boots thudded rhythmically against the stage.

Ninety percent of the faces staring back at him were brown, like Monty's. Oftentimes when he looked out, Monty recognized faces from classes he'd taught in previous semesters—students who were back for more, auditing a course they'd already taken and, inevitably, passed. Sometimes it took a moment for Monty to recognize them, especially the young men who had worn their hair short when they started his class, but now—inspired by Monty's message of reclaiming their heritage—had returned with braids of their own.

"It's an interesting phenomenon, based on a simple principle." Monty shifted further forward. *"Wouldn't it be easier to steal someone's rights if you could do it with their cooperation?"*

He allowed the heavy silence that sometimes followed his remarks to settle over the hall.

"And how does one do that, get that cooperation? More specifically, how did the United States government gain the Indian's cooperation? Depending, of course, on your perspective, it's a thing of beauty. An art, really. *The art of stealing human rights.* And surprisingly, the United States can't even claim inventorship."

Monty reached into a back pocket of his jeans and withdrew a worn, folded sheet of paper.

"I'd like to read you something. These are extracts from a speech given by Gerry Gambill at a conference on human rights in New Brunswick in 1958. Just a couple years before I was born." This brought a titter from the class, especially the females. "Listen closely, and see if they sound familiar. I present to you the ABCs of the art of stealing human rights."

He began to read.

"Number one. Make him a non-person. Human rights are for people. Convince Indians their ancestors were savages, that they were pagan, that Indians were drunkards. Make them wards of the government. Make a legal distinction, as in the Indian Act, between Indians and persons. Write history books that tell half the story.

"Number two." He held two fingers up in a V. "Convince the Indian that he should be patient, that these things take time. Tell him that we are making progress, and that progress takes time.

"Number three. Make him believe that things are being done for his own good." He looked up from the paper, a smile twisting his mouth. "I love that one. Anyone want to cite an example?"

A hand shot up in the front row.

"Crystal?"

The girl stood. She was dressed in a plain white long-sleeved shirt that hung out over her khakis. Her black hair was tied in a tight ponytail. She was tall, with unusually regal bearing for someone so young. Her baggy trousers accentuated her thinness.

"The Dawes Act," she answered. "The federal government acted like they were doing us some kind of a favor by making Indians property owners."

"When they really wanted . . . ?"

"To divide us, break up our tribal unity."

"That's hogwash," another student called out from the back of the hall. "The Dawes Act gave your people a chance to be landowners. It gave you a chance to control your own destiny."

A husky, wheat-haired farmboy, one of only half a dozen whites in the class, rose in the last row.

Undeterred, Crystal shot back, "Your family's a perfect example of what was wrong with the Dawes Act. Thanks to the Dawes Act, our land ended up in white hands."

"We bought our acreage fair and square. My great grandfather didn't have to twist any arms to buy our ranch. He paid good money for it."

"How much?" Crystal demanded to know.

The boy's fair skin flushed.

"What we paid is beside the point anyway. One of your people wanted to sell and my great grandfather bought.

That's how our economy works. No law against that."

"But it's the reason most reservations today are more white than native," Crystal said. "Look at the Flathead."

"The Salish and Kootenai had the same deal you Blackfeet had. They made good money selling to whites."

"That's bullshit," the girl cried. Then glancing back at Monty, she said, "Sorry, Professor Four Bear. You know what the Dawes Act did for my family? I'll tell you. My grandfather worked his eighty acres for thirty years, then when he couldn't pay an eighty-seven dollar grocery bill, they took his land from him. Eighty acres for an eighty-seven dollar bill. He died penniless. We've been renting ever since."

She plunked back down into her seat, still visibly angry.

"Truth is, John," Monty said, "most Indians sold or lost the land they acquired through the Dawes Act. That's the reason the Flathead reservation has far more whites living on it today than natives. The only reason it didn't happen to as great a degree up here is that even the white men didn't want *this* land." The room filled with soft laughter, laughter that had a bitter edge to it. "I agree with Crystal. Though it was couched in the normal rhetoric about being for our good, the Dawes Act was intended to deal another blow to our culture and unity. And it worked."

"No disrespect intended, professor," John said, hands shoved angrily into the pockets of his carpenter pants, "but I'm not so sure you're objective about this kind of thing. I mean, you belong to AIM. That's a pretty radical organization . . ."

The room erupted in groans and angry name-calling.

Monty raised a hand, calling out calmly. "Let him speak." He held the hand high until the room fell silent again. "Go ahead, John."

It was obvious that the commotion he'd caused had started to unnerve John. But his feelings on the subject ran deep, just as deep as those of the Native American students surrounding him.

"I'm sick and tired of being made out to be the bad guy. We've been good neighbors here. Don't cause anyone problems. Go about our own business . . ."

"What's that got to do with AIM?" another male voice shouted.

John's face flushed a deeper shade.

"Nothin'. But anyone who thinks AIM is anything but a group of radicals trying to stir up trouble between your people and mine has a screw loose. They're just a bunch of troublemakers. They don't want us all to get along. What they want is to eliminate people like me."

"Sounds like a pretty good idea to me," one voice called out.

"What they want is fair treatment for Native Americans," Crystal said, rising again. "Right, Professor Four Bear?"

Monty waited for the uproar to die down.

"AIM is a lot of different things to different people. It certainly doesn't surprise me to hear John's perception of it. After the Pine Ridge shootout in 1973, the FBI, with considerable assistance from the media, I might add, succeeded in painting AIM members as radicals who preferred using violence over other means of achieving their objectives."

Monty jumped down from his perch on the stage and crossed the expanse before the first row of seats to stand within arm's distance of his students.

"But AIM is something entirely different to me. I spent three years as an attorney on the Wind River reservation in Wyoming, fighting for tribal water rights and environmental protections whose unpopularity with the ranchers and mining industry consistently resulted in defeat. Then I went over to the BIA. After two years there, I became convinced that I had about as much chance of changing things by working within the established bureaucratic framework as the buffalo did of ever roaming the plains free again.

"I see AIM as a positive force, a way of combating poverty and despair on the reservations. I like what Birgil Kills Straight calls AIM: 'the warrior class of this century.' He says AIM's business is *hope*. That's how I like to think of it."

It had taken a while for anyone to notice, for the students were rapt in their attention to Monty's words, but heads had begun to turn toward the back of the room, where a young woman stood, holding a piece of paper in the air to get Monty's attention.

"Excuse me for a moment," Monty said, waving her in and starting up the aisle to meet her.

"You had an emergency call," the young woman whispered, handing Monty the paper. "From someone named Leroy. Here's his number."

Monty looked down at the paper. He did not recognize the number. His father, Leroy, did not have a telephone, so he must have gone to a neighbor's to make the call.

Monty strode back to the front of the room and looked at his watch. He had another half hour to teach, but he knew Leroy wouldn't call if it wasn't important.

"I have to make a telephone call," Monty announced. "I'd like to ask you to sit quietly for ten minutes. If I'm not back by then, class is dismissed."

He jumped nimbly onto the stage, heading for the exit at its rear, then suddenly he turned, retraced his steps to the edge of the stage, and beckoned at a linebacker-sized youth in the front row.

Wearing a BCC Athletic Department sweatshirt, the crewcut-shorn Blackfeet approached without hesitation.

Bending at the waist, Monty spoke softly into his ear.

"Listen, Russell, I'd like you to keep the peace while I'm gone. Make sure no one hassles John Morris. Got it?"

"Got it," the youth said, clearly comfortable with the role of enforcer.

Monty turned and exited the auditorium through the back door.

Hurrying to his office—a windowless cube cluttered with books, stacks of newspapers and journals, with every square inch of wall space occupied by activist posters—Monty grabbed the phone and dialed. His father's voice, characteristically slurred, even at this hour of the day, greeted him.

" 'Lo?"

"It's me. Where are you? And what's going on?"

"I'm at Edna's." Edna was Edna Northrup, who lived about a quarter mile from his father's small frame house. "Luke's had an accident."

Luke was Monty's nephew.

"An accident? What happened?"

"On his bike. He's bleeding pretty bad. From the mouth. Think he lost a couple teeth. And he said he couldn't see right."

"Does Edna have a car?"

"It ain't running."

"I'll be right there."

"WE HAVE AN emergency," Suzanne Featherheart announced.

Isabel's head jerked up from the questionnaire she'd been drafting for participants in the ImmuVac study.

"What kind?"

"Eight-year-old boy. Rode his bike into a truck."

Isabel threw the yellow legal pad down and stepped into the hallway, almost colliding with a braided man who'd followed Suzanne down the hall. He was carrying a boy, cradle-like, in his arms.

"Where should I take him?" he asked.

Isabel stepped closer and checked to be sure the boy was breathing. Crushed or obstructed airways were always the first concern in a trauma situation. Once she ascertained that he was breathing on his own, she turned back in the direction she'd just come.

"Follow me."

She led the way to a room she'd termed the "shock room" and helped the man ease the boy onto the examination table in the center of the room.

Blood around the boy's mouth and nose had already dried. Isabel went to work, issuing the barrage of questions that had become second nature to her all those years working at Harborview's trauma center in Seattle.

"What's your name?" she asked, checking the boy's pulse.

"Luke."

"Luke, can you tell me what happened to you?"

"I rode my bike into a truck on my way home from school."

"What time was that, Luke?"

"I dunno. 'Bout three."

Isabel looked at the clock on the wall. It was almost four-thirty. How long had it taken them to bring this boy in?

"Was the truck moving?"

"No. It was parked. I just wasn't paying attention."

"That must have hurt. Listen to me, Luke, okay? I'm going to put this collar around your neck, to keep you from moving around until we've had a chance to take some X rays. Okay?"

"Okay."

Once the cervical collar was in place, Isabel began loosening Luke's shirt to inspect his torso.

"What hurts on you, Luke?"

"My head. And my shoulder."

"Tell me about your head. Did you black out when you hit the truck?"

"I don't think so."

"Are you dizzy now, lightheaded?"

"Maybe a little."

Isabel reached into the pocket of her lab coat and shone a

light in the boy's eyes. Just as she suspected, his pupillary response indicated he'd suffered a concussion.

"Were you wearing a helmet?"

Luke shook his head no.

"And what about your shoulder? Is it this one, your left side?

"Ouch, that hurts," Luke cried as she ran her hand along it.

"I'm sorry about that, Luke. I'll try not to hurt you, but I need to examine you to see where all you might have been injured. Did you hit the truck with this shoulder?"

"No, I think I landed on it, after I hit the truck."

"Does your neck hurt at all?"

"No."

"What about your belly? Does it hurt when I press on it like this?"

"No."

"That's good. Now I want you to take a deep breath for me."

Luke's chest rose.

"Good. Take another one. Look at me. Relax, you're fine. Relax for me. Deep breaths, okay Luke?"

Isabel was relieved with what she'd seen so far, but she suspected that Luke had fractured his left clavicle. If so, there was always the possibility of pneumothoraxis—the broken bone piercing the lung and causing it to collapse. Luke's respiration was a good sign that that hadn't happened, but an X ray would be necessary to rule it out altogether. And her greatest concern was that the boy might have fractured a cervical vertebrae when he hit the truck.

"Now Luke, I want you to lay perfectly still while we leave the room for just a few seconds to take a couple pictures of your neck and chest."

For the first time since their initial encounter, the man who had brought Luke in spoke up.

"I'll stay with him."

Isabel turned to face him.

"Are you Luke's father?"

"No. His uncle. My name's Monty Four Bear."

"Are Luke's parents nearby, where we can contact them?"

"My sister lives in Denver. Luke lives with my father, his grandfather. He called me to bring Luke in."

"Well, Mr. Four Bear, I'm afraid you'll have to step outside while we take the X rays. But you can rejoin Luke in just a few minutes."

By now Suzanne had arrived. She loaded the film and followed, her eyes on Monty, as Isabel and Four Bear stepped into the hallway.

Once in the hallway, Isabel turned to Monty again.

"We'll know the results of these X rays within a few minutes. But even if they're negative, one thing is certain. Your nephew has a concussion. I'd like to have you take him to the hospital in Cut Bank for a CAT scan."

"If all he has is a concussion, he doesn't need a hospital. Or more tests. I'll take him home and keep an eye on him. I know what to look for."

Startled, as much by the tone in which the words were spoken as by the words themselves, Isabel drew back and studied Monty.

What had she done to elicit such contempt? For wasn't that what she saw in his eyes?

"Are you Luke's guardian? Or should I be talking to his grandfather?"

"I'll have him give you a call. When he sobers up."

So that's what she was dealing with.

"If Luke's school ends around three o'clock can you explain to me why it took almost two hours to get him medical attention?"

If there had been any doubt before about the hostility in Monty Four Bear's eyes, the way he looked at her now left room for none.

"My father doesn't have a telephone. He had to walk to a

neighbor's to call me at work." That answer, it seemed to Isabel, would have sufficed. But Monty Four Bear had more to say. "Maybe you weren't aware of the fact that most the houses on the rez don't have phones."

Ignoring Four Bear's response, Isabel turned to Suzanne.

"Suzanne, please try to contact Luke's mother in Denver. I'd like to speak to her. Maybe Mr. Four Bear can help you."

After hearing the beep indicating the X ray had been taken, Isabel reopened the door to the shock room. She tried to pull it closed behind her, but Monty had grabbed the handle and stood in the doorway.

"I'll be right back, Luke," he said into the room. "I'm just down the hall. We're going to try to get ahold of your mom. Okay?"

Luke's big brown eyes stared past Isabel at his uncle. The only thing more clear than the close bond between the two of them was the little boy's absolute terror at being there.

"Promise?" he asked.

"Promise."

As the door closed behind him and Isabel turned back to her patient, she wondered just how it had come to pass that she felt like the villain in this whole scene.

"SORRY ABOUT LUKE," Suzanne said. "Try not to worry. He looks like he'll be fine."

"Sherry'll have Dad's hide if he's not," Monty answered. "And mine for good measure."

"You know her phone number, Monty?"

"I have it in my address book, but I rushed out so fast when Dad called that I left it in my office."

"I'll call information," Suzanne said. "Maybe you can start filling out these forms."

"Luke's been here before. That time he cut himself, remember?"

"New doctor, new forms. Dr. McLain's trying to get things organized here."

"Why doesn't that surprise me?" Monty said, half under his breath.

Suzanne smiled.

"She's a good doctor. Give her a chance."

Monty did not respond. His eyes had been drawn to a notice posted above the row of blue plastic chairs lining the opposite wall.

As Suzanne dialed directory assistance for Denver, he crossed the room to get a better look.

WOULD YOU LIKE TO SERVE
ON AN INSTITUTIONAL REVIEW BOARD?

ImmuVac Pharmaceutical Company has proposed a clinical trial on the Blackfeet Reservation. Participants will be vaccinated against the deadly hantavirus, a disease which recently struck three cherished members of the Blackfeet family. Would you like the honor of serving on the Institutional Review Board that has the grave responsibility of recommending FDA approval of this vaccination program? This is an opportunity to serve your community. Interested applicants should contact 1-800-334-4000.

When Monty returned to Suzanne, she appeared to be listening to an answering machine message. He held up the notice, which he'd ripped off the wall.

"What's this?"

Suzanne pointed a finger skyward, indicating she'd be right with him, then she began speaking into the phone.

"This is the Blackfeet reservation medical clinic. We're trying to reach Sherry Luster regarding her boy, Luke. If we've reached the right number, please contact us immediately at 406-444-1212. Thank you."

She hung up the phone and turned to Monty.

"They're gonna do a study here on a vaccine for the hantavirus. Isn't that great?"

"I heard about you being so sick," Monty said. "I was praying for you."

"Thanks, Monty."

"I was happy to hear you were okay," he continued, "but even after what happened, they can't just come in here and begin vaccinating people."

"You're right. First the review board's gotta say it's okay. That's what that piece of paper is all about."

"Mind if I keep this?"

"No, but if you're interested in being on the board, it's too late. They've already picked it. In fact, they're meeting here tomorrow night to learn all about the vaccine."

For the first time since he'd arrived, a half grin played at the corners of Monty's mouth.

"You know me better than that," he said. "What time's the meeting?"

Suzanne looked down and flipped a page on the appointment book on her desk.

"Looks like seven o'clock."

CHAPTER

ELEVEN

MONTY HATED CALLING class off, but after he'd stood by his refusal to take Luke to the hospital yesterday, the lady doctor had given him explicit instructions that his nephew was to be monitored closely for the next twenty-four hours. That meant missing today's lecture, for Monty wasn't about to leave Luke in Leroy's charge. Leroy had promised he'd stay sober, but when it came to Luke's well being, Monty wasn't taking chances.

Like many of his people, Monty had developed an attitude that fell somewhere between a reluctant acceptance of modern medicine and clinging to traditional native beliefs about healing. The difference between Monty and the others, however, was that while most of his people had spent their entire lives on the reservation and based their distrust more on a superstitious fear of the unknown, Monty had lived in the outside world. He'd gone to college in Missoula, law school in Seattle, and, during his stint with the BIA, lived in Washington, D.C. Monty was educated and knowledgeable—and *still* distrustful. In fact, the more he learned—medicine was one of many topics on which he strove to keep his knowledge current—the more his distrust grew, in direct proportion to his respect for spiritual healing.

Monty turned to modern medicine, especially modern medicine practiced by non-Indians, only out of absolute necessity. Many an Indian had recovered from a blow to the head without the aid of white doctors and their machines. The way he saw it, sending Luke to the hospital for a CAT scan represented more risk than keeping a close eye on him at home. It was time to give nature a chance to heal Luke.

Edna, his father's neighbor, had agreed to stay with Luke when she got home from work so that Monty could attend the meeting at the clinic. Driving into Browning after dropping Leroy off at a friend's—Edna made it clear she didn't want to have to baby-sit *both* Luke and Leroy—Monty found himself thinking that if it hadn't been for Luke needing him to stay home that morning, he would have been able to let his students know what was going on. No doubt some of them would have shown up tonight too. Of course, if it weren't for Luke getting injured, he wouldn't even know about this insane plan in the first place.

How had something like this slipped by him? Slipped by everyone?

The meeting had already begun when Monty stepped into the waiting room. Six chairs had been arranged in a semicircle, in the middle of which stood a tall, skinny white guy wearing a blue denim shirt and khakis. Acknowledging Monty's arrival, he nodded in a friendly manner, causing those seated in the semicircle to turn.

Monty recognized Father McGrath, a Jesuit priest from the mission; Ann Garity, a Blackfeet and science professor from the University of Montana; John Turnbull, a tribal elder; and the lady doctor from the day before. One man, African American, was a complete stranger, and the last person, a middle-aged woman, looked vaguely familiar to him. Seated behind the semicircle and now turned his way, Suzanne Featherheart grinned at him.

"Please, come in," the man said. "I'm Dr. Ken MacStirling. I'm with ImmuVac and I was just explaining the responsibilities these ladies and gentlemen have assumed in volunteering to serve on this board."

Monty nodded in response and slipped quietly into the only empty seat in the room, right next to Suzanne.

"As I was saying," Ken MacStirling continued, "the FDA requires the consent of an institutional review board any time human subjects are involved in research, which, of course, is what we have here.

"It's the job of the IRB to evaluate the research based on several criteria. The first is the risk involved to the subjects. Having developed the hantavirus vaccine myself, I can assure you that there is minimal risk involved. This vaccine has already been tested on animals. The results of that research were presented in the package given you upon your selection to the IRB. The compilation of data on pages seven through twelve shows that adverse reactions were practically nonexistent.

"A clinical trial like this is conducted in three phases.

Phase I is generally pretty small. Thirty to forty subjects, max. The primary objective of Phase I is to test safety. Once the FDA reviews the data, we move into Phase II. Because it is so safe, I'm confident we'll be able to move quickly to Phase II, which is just like Phase I, only on a bigger scale. In Phase III, large numbers of subjects, in this case thousands, will be injected. All three phases will take place here, on the reservation. Our goal is to vaccinate every resident. Now, all of you must have questions."

John Turnbull cleared his throat.

"What if this vaccine gives us the disease? What if it gives it to everyone on the reservation? The papers you gave us say it was tested on mice and rats. Well, we already know that the hantavirus doesn't kill them. Doesn't even make them sick. So how do we know it won't kill us?"

"That's a good question, but it's impossible for this vaccine to actually transmit the disease. You see, in the past, most vaccines actually consisted of whole microorganisms, alive or killed, of the disease they were intended to prevent. A flu shot, for example, actually works by introducing minute amounts of the virus into your system. This enables your body to produce natural antibodies, which build up and then protect you against the virus later when you're exposed to it. But that's not how this vaccine was made. This vaccine does not actually contain hantavirus. Instead, it contains a canary-pox virus that has been genetically engineered to be so similar to the hantavirus—without causing any of the same effects of the disease itself—that it will produce antibodies that will actually work against hantavirus. So you see, there's no chance that subjects who get the vaccine will be infected with the hantavirus."

Turnbull made a *hmmpf*like sound.

Ken MacStirling continued gamely.

"At most, subjects might have a little irritation at the injection site. The truth is, the worst part for most subjects will be having to give blood. As the protocol you have states, blood will be drawn at three points. Once before the vaccine, once one week after vaccination, and again at three weeks."

"Lotta blood," John Turnbull grumbled.

This caused Monty to smile. He noticed Suzanne Featherheart grinning too.

"The next criteria that you as a board should take into consideration in reviewing the proposed clinical trial is the anticipated benefits to the subjects and others." Ken MacStirling's eyes swept the panel. "I know I don't have to tell you about hantavirus. It is a very deadly disease—one of the deadliest in the world. As you've found out, its victims are often young and healthy and they literally drown in serum from their own blood. It is an experience that no human being should ever have to go through. Especially if there's a way to prevent it. Before now, there has been no way to prevent this terrible disease and once it strikes, very little that medical professionals could do to stop its course. But this vaccine will change all that."

The room had fallen still. Joe Winged Foot, Will EchoHawk, and Dolores Birdsong had been known by most of those present. Their memories hung heavily in the air.

"At what cost?"

Monty's words—spoken with that voice that had proven capable of mesmerizing students and causing young women to fall in love on the spot—broke through the silence with such force that several of the panel members actually startled in their seats.

All heads turned to Monty.

"At what cost?" he repeated, rising from his seat.

"I know what you're all thinking. I didn't know Will or Dolores very well, but I knew Joe from the time he was a little kid. He used to follow me on that bike of his, make a pest of himself. Always hanging around me and my friends, begging us to let him in our pickup games. Then I left the rez and when I came back, Joe was all grown up. The last couple years, the highlight of my winters has been watching

Joe's games, seeing him kick ass out there on the court. I was already planning my trips to Missoula to watch him play at the U next year."

Monty was in his element now. He had the full attention of everyone in the room. He zeroed in on each person in the room as he spoke, finally allowing his eyes to fall upon the one face he'd not been able to place before. It belonged to a middle-aged Blackfeet woman. Her eyes were those of someone in great pain. It wasn't until that very moment that he realized who she was. Anna Winged Foot. Joe's mother.

"But this vaccine won't bring Joe back," he said, quietly now, out of respect for Anna. "If it could, I'd be the first in line. We *all* grieved when we lost Joe. He belonged to all of us. He represented the best of us. We're all still grieving. But don't let those emotions color your rational thoughts. Don't make an impulsive decision out of grief. Or guilt."

"Excuse me." It was Ken MacStirling again. "Would you like to introduce yourself?"

"My name is Monty Four Bear."

"And you are . . . ?" The scientist was clearly taken off-guard by Monty's speech.

"I am a Blackfeet," was all Monty answered.

"Monty don't need to be introduced," John Turnbull piped up.

"Mr. Four Bear, what exactly are your concerns about this vaccine?"

Several heads nodded. They all wanted to know. Monty noted that the doctor, Isabel McLain, simply stared at him, blank faced. It was too bad she was the enemy because even Monty would admit she was pretty.

"Yes," Turnbull said, "tell us your concerns. And wouldja move to where we don't have to break our necks to see you?"

A twitter of laughter broke the tension in the room, as Monty stepped out to the side of the assembled chairs. He could have joined MacStirling at the center, but he wanted to maintain the distance between them.

"A friend of mine from college served in the Gulf War. In 1991, the government gave the troops experimental vaccines. My buddy, who's a Lakota, tried to refuse the vaccine. He didn't like the idea of being a guinea pig. But he was told he'd be court martialed if he refused. So he let them vaccinate him. He had headaches and dizziness for years afterwards. He's just been diagnosed with lupus. Can't work, can hardly play with his kids. All because he tried to serve his country."

"With all due respect, Mr. Four Bear," the man sitting next to Isabel McLain interrupted. "Your friend can't prove there's any connection between his problems and the vaccine he received."

"How do you know he can't? What makes you an authority?"

"My name is Lehman Morris. I'm a pulmonary specialist from Missoula. Dr. McLain asked me to serve on the review board. And I just happen to have an interest in what's known as the Gulf War Syndrome."

"You actually believe that thousands of vets like my friend are making these symptoms up? That there's no connection between the Gulf War and the fact that many of them can no longer live a normal life?"

"I'm just saying that as of yet, no direct connection has been established."

Monty shook his head.

"What's it going to take for someone to admit that it's not just a coincidence that all these people who got vaccinated ended up sick? You know what the government wants them to believe? That it's in their heads. They want the problem to go away so they won't have to take responsibility."

These words—condemnation of the federal government—seemed to strike a chord within some members of the group, who nodded or murmured under their breath. Ken MacStirling seemed well aware of the fact that things could easily get out of hand if Monty weren't neutralized.

"Mr. Four Bear," MacStirling said, "I don't feel knowledgeable enough to deal with your friend's situation. I would encourage him to continue his efforts to determine whether there could be a connection between the vaccine and his current health. But surely you wouldn't advocate abolition of all vaccines?"

"Don't be so sure."

"What about polio? Measles? Rubella? Many of us wouldn't be sitting here today if it weren't for vaccines. They've saved millions and millions of lives. That is an indisputable fact. Even if there is some truth to your friend's allegations, you can't let one—or even several—unfortunate results with vaccines taint all of them, across the board. That's the purpose of the FDA regulations. Of this panel. To provide safeguards. To ensure that every vaccine that's put on the market is safe, that its benefits have been established and that the risks presented are minimal."

"But just who is being used here to determine whether the risks exist?" Monty countered, his voice rising in anger. "*Our* people. When the vaccine is out on the market, maybe then some of us will choose to use it. I, for one, will not. But until then, let someone else be the guinea pig."

"So that more of your people can die in the meantime? Is that what you want?"

A new voice had entered the fray.

Isabel McLain stood, facing Monty. If her expression had seemed blank before, it was anything but now. She looked equal parts hostile and, oddly, shaken.

"I had some of the same thoughts." Before Monty even had time to respond, Isabel McLain continued. "Why not wait, until the vaccine has been tested? But Dr. MacStirling pointed something out to me. We're talking years, *years*, before this product is on the market. In the meantime, how many more lives will this despicable disease claim? Even if the answer is only one, that's one too many. I will do everything in my power," her voice weakened momentarily,

". . . *everything*, to make sure that what happened to Joe and Will and Dolores doesn't happen again. Not here. Not on this reservation."

"Let me ask you something," Monty jumped in. "Are you being paid by the patient? Because I read this morning that that's how it's done. An investigator gets paid a certain amount for each patient he or she enrolls in the study."

"See here," Ken MacStirling said, starting toward Monty as though he intended to throw him out. "That's totally uncalled for."

"No." Isabel held her hand up. "It's okay. Let him ask his questions."

She turned back to Monty.

"The answer is no. ImmuVac offered to pay me, but I refused. I know it would be a lot easier to sway everyone here if you could show this is all about money, but it's not. In fact, if you think ImmuVac stands to make big money from this vaccine, you're wrong. I'm sorry to disappoint you."

Monty realized, too late, that he'd gone too far. Even John Turnbull was shooting concerned glances Dr. McLain's way. Monty had to give her credit. He knew he'd shaken her up, but she'd held her own against him.

"Are there any other questions? Or comments?"

Anna Winged Foot raised a hand.

"I would like to say something." She spoke softly and slowly, choosing her words carefully. "Joey was a good boy. He loved his mother, and he loved all of you. He was a good boy. He always wanted to help people. And maybe this is his way. The way he can help. Maybe because Joey died other people won't have to.

"And there's one more thing. And no disrespect intended, Monty, cause we all know you're a good man. But maybe it's time we stop blaming everything on the government. They done us wrong. Everybody knows that. And they still do us wrong a lot of the time. But we have to look out for other people. Not just Indian people. Everyone. Maybe if we show we want to do this to help everyone, it will start something. You know what I mean? Maybe things can still change. Joey would have liked that."

The vote for approval was 5 to 0 in favor of endorsing the clinical trial. John Turnbull abstained.

AS MONTY WALKED out to his pickup, he felt a tug at his sleeve.

"You were pretty tough on her."

It was John Turnbull.

"She's a good doc, you know. She's been good for us here."

Monty offered Turnbull a ride home, but he'd already made arrangements with Anna Winged Foot. Monty sat in the truck, revving its engine a few times to warm it. The battery had been giving him trouble recently. Tomorrow he planned to drop it off at Lester's gas station and have it charged.

After two or three minutes, Monty backed the pickup up, turning the headlights on as he did so. Crossing the parking lot to a lone Jeep that Monty had parked next to, Isabel McLain stepped into their glare.

She lifted her hand in a thanks to the driver for waiting for her, then recognized Monty behind the wheel and dropped it. For a moment she froze, then she approached Monty's side of the truck.

Monty rolled his window down. Now what?

"How's Luke?"

"Fine. Much better in fact."

"Good."

She hesitated, and Monty could almost see the struggle taking place inside her over whether to give him a piece of her mind.

He'd failed in his mission to turn the IRB against the proposed study, but he'd definitely succeeded in getting under Isabel McLain's skin. Especially when he implied that her support for the study might have been related to payments from ImmuVac. He'd probably hit below the belt with that one, but he'd consider it payback for her inference yesterday that he'd been negligent in taking so long to bring Luke into the clinic. Plus, he'd long ago had to buy into the maxim that—at least where his people's welfare was concerned—the end justified the means. He had to keep focused on the mission. He mustn't let the fact that Isabel McLain had taken good care of Luke, the fact that his nephew had later told him he liked the "white lady doctor," interfere with that, with his mission. Nor the fact that, standing in the half-lit parking lot glaring at him, she looked so damn good.

Abruptly, Isabel McLain turned away.

Monty rolled his window up and watched as she walked to the old Jeep.

He waited until she was safely inside. Then he pulled onto Highway 2 and headed toward home.

CHAPTER

TWELVE

ARE YOU ABSOLUTELY certain I can only give forty vaccinations?" Isabel's eyes fell to the stack of papers in her hands. "There must be two hundred applications here."

"Forty is *it*," MacStirling replied decisively. "I told you before, Phase I is always small."

"It's going to be so hard to decide who gets the vaccine and who doesn't."

MacStirling reached across the Formica surface for the applications. They'd taken to meeting at the same table at the Outlaw Inn. MacStirling's visits had become a weekly event, as the initiation of Phase I of the HantaVac study drew near. "May I?"

Isabel pushed the stack his way.

"Be my guest."

While MacStirling perused the applications, Isabel dove in to her breakfast. Usually she grabbed a piece of fruit on the way out the cabin's door, then followed it up with Suzanne's leadlike coffee at the clinic. Hash browns and an omelette were a rare treat. At least she got a decent meal out of these meetings with MacStirling.

Halfway through her omelette, Isabel realized that as he reviewed each application, MacStirling placed it in one of two piles he'd formed in front of him on the table.

"What are you doing?"

"You said you wanted help deciding who to include in Phase I."

Isabel grabbed the pile to MacStirling's left.

"No, I didn't. I just said I wasn't sure how I'd make that decision."

"Well, I'm just helping you."

She recognized several names in the pile she'd grabbed. Jean White, a fifty-year-old patient who had undergone a mastectomy five years earlier but had been cancer-free ever since. Robbie Hill, a fortyish father of five and recovering alcoholic, who at first forbade his wife from bringing the children into the clinic, but who now dropped by himself—never with an appointment—when he wasn't feeling well. Also included in this pile was the application of Arlo Iron Heart.

"Is this your yes or no pile?"

"I'd exclude those applicants, at least from the first two phases of the trial and perhaps altogether," MacStirling answered. He pushed the other pile her way. "*These* are good candidates."

Isabel felt the blood rushing to her face. She'd been so pleased when Robbie had come in one day and asked for an application for the HantaVac study. And after her brush with cancer, Jean White enthusiastically embraced the trial as another means of ensuring her continued good health.

"Why? What's wrong with these applicants?

"Their histories. While I'm confident the vaccine doesn't present any increased risk to them, their complicating factors could skew the results."

"*Skew the results?* What is that—lab-speak?" Isabel cried. "The people who will ultimately get this vaccine will be *real* people with *real* problems. People like Robbie Hill and Jean White. Let me tell you something, Dr. MacStirling, I will not be part of some carefully manipulated scam to produce results simply to make your vaccine look good. This isn't about data and numbers for me. It's about my patients."

MacStirling looked surprised by the venomous response.

"Now let me tell you something, Dr. McLain," he said, anger twitching his jaw. "I'm a scientist. That's what we do—conduct systematic studies in which we collect and analyze data. I suppose you think I should apologize for that, but if it weren't for people like me, people like you would be a whole lot less effective in saving the world."

Isabel grabbed both piles, placing one on top of the other in clear disregard of MacStirling's attempt to order them.

"I'll take another look at these later," she said.

"We need a definitive list by tomorrow."

"That won't be a problem."

"Good," MacStirling said, using a mellower tone, as if he'd decided that nothing would be served by getting into a shouting match with her. "Then we can begin vaccinations. The pilot lot of the vaccine will be shipped directly to you at the clinic. It will arrive by the end of the week. You can either draw blood prior to the vaccine, in which case I'd suggest you get started as soon as you determine the participants, or you can make life simpler by doing both the same day."

"I've already decided to make it a two-step process," Isabel said civilly, following MacStirling's lead. "It would be easier to draw blood and administer the vaccine in one visit, but I think the study participants might find a single visit too intimidating. I'll use the first visit to draw the control sample of blood and to give them another opportunity to ask questions."

"Suit yourself. You'll be receiving all your supplies, including sterile kits and mailing cartons for the blood samples, within the next few days. Of course, I'll be in regular contact with you."

"Of course."

"There's one other thing." MacStirling shifted uncomfortably in the booth. "ImmuVac's CEO, Dr. Lyons, plans to arrange for a reporter from the Portland papers to be on hand at the inception of Phase I."

Isabel could do nothing but stare, disbelieving, at MacStirling.

"I realize," he said tentatively, "that the participants may not like it, but now that we have their consent, I can't really imagine anyone backing out simply because the trial is being observed by an outsider. They don't even have to know he's a reporter."

Isabel drew a deep breath.

"If a reporter shows his or her face, I will walk away from this study. Is that clear?"

"I think we've already had this conversation. You can't claim to have no knowledge of ImmuVac's desire for some good press for this study. I made that known to you from the start."

"I'm warning you. Publicity can only harm this study."

MacStirling's eyes narrowed on her.

"How so?"

"I've been hearing that there might be organized resistance. Remember Monty Four Bear, from the first IRB meeting? I've heard rumblings that he made the clinical trial a topic of one of his college classes. He apparently compared it to the Tuskegee experiments. I don't really think ImmuVac would benefit much from having *that* reported. Could have the opposite effect you're hoping for. Might actually scare investors off."

"Why haven't you said something?" MacStirling said, clearly agitated. "It sounds like I'd better plan to be there."

"That's why I haven't. Because I can handle this alone. In fact, I'm confident that if there *is* any resistance, your presence would only exacerbate the situation." She leaned MacStirling's way and leveled her brown eyes on his. "This entire experience is something very new to these people. New and frightening. It's taken me a while, but finally, many of them—almost all who've submitted applications—trust me. They are just beginning to see me as one of them. If you're there, I suddenly lose that. I become associated in their minds with you. With a world they've learned not to trust. Faced with Monty Four Bear and any support he's drummed up, it becomes us against them."

MacStirling studied Isabel silently.

"Maybe the reporter's not such a good idea," he said. "But do you promise to let me know if things with this Four Bear fellow get out of hand?"

Monty Four Bear could stage an armed takeover of the clinic and Isabel would still not call MacStirling for help. The mere notion struck her as ludicrous.

"I promise."

THAT NIGHT, ON her way home, Isabel made a turn at the fork leading to Gus's ranch. A full moon dominated the sky, mesmerizing Isabel as she crept down Gus's long drive. Many a night she'd lain awake observing the moon through the bedroom skylight in the house she and Alistair shared in Seattle, but never had she seen anything like the humbling sight of a full moon in Big Sky country.

Lights were on in the house, but Grunt's barks turned Isabel's attention to the barn where she saw Gus's silhouette. He was shoveling out a stall. Grunt ran halfway across the corral toward the driveway, barking a greeting at Isabel, then stopped and looked back at Gus, torn between the two.

Isabel entered the barn. Years ago all the stalls lining either side had been occupied, but now Gus was down to a single horse. Isabel walked the barn's length, then stepped out into the corral. Gus was pushing the wheelbarrow he'd just emptied back across the corral, toward where Isabel stood. Bessie, Gus's sorrel mare, followed close behind, her muzzle at Gus's shoulder.

"Hey, there," Isabel called. "What are you doing out here in the dark?"

"Full moon," Gus answered. "Plenty of light. Just thought I'd come keep Bessie here company."

"But it's freezing. I think you're losing it, Gus."

"Not cold if you keep moving."

"Well, I don't have enough energy to start shoveling manure with you, so how about taking a break and offering your neighbor some hot chocolate?"

The moonlight enabled her to see the twinkle of delight in Gus's eye.

"I was about to do that, if you'd just give an old man some time."

"Old man, huh! I only hope I'm as spry as you when *I'm* eighty."

Isabel had helped Gus celebrate his seventy-fifth birthday in April.

Gus glared at her.

"You better watch it. I never signed any papers when you moved into that cabin. Keep on insulting me and you might just end up out in the cold."

Isabel stood on tiptoe and pecked Gus on the cheek.

"How's that?"

"Much better."

When he smiled, Gus's eyes disappeared into folds of leathery skin.

After they'd locked Bessie in her stall for the night, they crossed the driveway. Grunt, tail wagging and nose to the ground, led the way.

"How's he doing?" Isabel asked.

"He's a tough old bugger," Gus said, laughing. "Limps a little bit in the morning but it doesn't slow him down none."

"Good. Maybe we can start running again one of these days." For months, Isabel had been in the habit of borrowing Grunt to keep her company on the runs she took several mornings each week. She didn't tell Gus that the reason she'd stopped was fear that Alistair could be nosing around the area and see her. "I've missed it."

"Haven't seen much of you recently. Clinic must be keeping you busy. I heard you got some kind of an experimental vaccine you're gonna be givin' out there."

Isabel shook her head and laughed. "Moccasin telegraph?"

It was what they called the lightning-quick wire through which gossip spread on the reservation. Even though Gus's property bordered the tribal lands, she hadn't expected the moccasin telegraph to extend that far.

"Yep."

Heated by a fire in the massive stone fireplace that dominated an entire wall, Gus's house felt warm and cozy. Isabel followed Gus to the kitchen, pulling a big can of powdered cocoa from the cupboard as he put milk on the stove to warm.

"Marshmallows?" Isabel asked. Gus loved to smother his hot chocolate in them.

"In the fridge."

Standing beside Gus at the stove, watching him stir the

milk that didn't require stirring, Isabel felt a sudden sense of peace. Her first two months in the cabin, she'd spent several evenings like this. Those first months had been difficult in so many ways, struggling for acceptance—struggling to get patients to come to the clinic—but it had given her a great gift in Gus. It had been too long since she'd dropped by to see her dear friend.

When they'd settled in front of the fire, Isabel listened as Gus rambled on about the neighboring rancher's poor fence-mending practices. Seems Gus and Bessie had to round up stray cattle on his property every other day or so. Isabel suspected that it didn't bother Gus half as much as he let on, that it gave him something to do with his time. A decade earlier, Gus had run two hundred head of cattle on his property. It always seemed to her that idle time was Gus's worst enemy.

An hour later, the fire and cocoa had taken effect, and Isabel found herself fighting back sleep.

"I'd better head on home," she said, rubbing her sore back as she rose from the sofa. Then she remembered one of the reasons she'd come. "Oh, yeah. I have something for you."

She reached into the back pocket of her army-green cargo pants and withdrew a sheet of paper.

"What's that?"

"It's an application for the vaccine program," she said, handing it to Gus. "I think it's important that you be vaccinated."

"I thought it was just for the Blackfeet."

"Technically, it is. But you just happen to have some pull with the lead investigator."

Gus's withered hand pushed the paper gently away.

"Thanks, but no thanks," he said.

"Why, Gus? I think this is important. You know I wouldn't suggest this if I didn't."

"I know," Gus said. "And I appreciate what you're trying

to do. You're a good girl, Izzie. But I don't want any part in some experimental program."

"Gus, what are you talking about?"

"Just what I said. You weren't around back then, but back in the fifties, all of us were given the polio vaccine."

"Yes, and thank God for it."

"Did you know it was contaminated? That they made it from some kind of monkey blood or something . . ."

"The rhesus monkey."

"That's it. Anyway, turns out the monkey had this virus."

"SV 40."

Isabel found herself tensing as Gus continued his explanation.

"That sounds about right. Anyway, they changed the kind of monkeys they used, but not before plenty of people had been given the bad vaccine. They say folks are getting cancer now from that vaccine. No, I'm steering clear of them. Don't even get a flu shot."

Isabel tried to hide the knee-jerk reaction Gus's words gave rise to.

"Gus, you're the last person on earth I expected to hear such paranoia from." The rise in her voice gave away her indignation. "Do you actually think I'd be involved with a vaccine that could be dangerous?"

"Hold on, there, Izzie. I'm not accusing you of anything."

"I certainly hope not."

Gus stared in confusion at Isabel, then at the application grasped so tightly in her clenched fist that it looked like it had gone through the washing machine.

"What's got into you, girl?"

Isabel dropped her hand to her side.

"Nothing, Gus. I apologize. It's just a touchy subject for me, that's all."

"I thought this study you're doin' was somethin' you're happy about."

For an old man with whom she had little in common, Gus possessed an uncanny ability to read her.

"Of course I'm happy about it, Gus," she insisted. "Why wouldn't I be?"

CHAPTER

THIRTEEN

ONE BY ONE, at the appointed time, the cars and pickups filed into the parking lot.

Monty Four Bear was there to greet them. He approached the latest arrival, a bumperless red VW with numerous activist stickers on it. I SUPPORT THE BUFFALO NATION. NO NUKES. BLM = ENEMY.

"We're expecting one more," Monty said, his breath visible in the early October air. "You might as well wait in your car, then we'll all spend a few minutes together before we caravan over to the clinic."

"Want to climb in and warm up?" Waylon Eagleplume asked, a thick black braid falling out the window as he rolled it halfway down to stick his head out.

Waylon was one of Monty's repeat students. His mother didn't have money to send him to a four-year school so he'd been attending classes at the community college for four years, working part-time at the Browning Bowl to pay for tuition. As usual, his girlfriend, LuAnn, was with him. Monty would have preferred that Waylon come alone. LuAnn was painfully shy and ill suited to today's task. But for as long as he'd known them, the two were inseparable, and Monty respected their commitment to each other.

"Thanks, but I'm fine. Good to see you again, LuAnn. Here's the literature we'll be handing out at the clinic. It's pretty much the same stuff we went over in class."

"Gotcha," Waylon said, his angular face bisected by a crooked smile.

"Here's Clyde now," Monty said as a newer-model Ford Bronco pulled up. "Give me a little blast on your horn, will you?"

Eagleplume obliged cheerfully as Monty waved all the vehicles' occupants over for a meeting.

They were a scraggly lot, mostly college students, with the exception of Clyde Birdseye, who posed as a cousin of Monty's from Denver but was, in reality, a fellow AIM member. They'd learned early on that if both men were known to be members of AIM, any activity they took part in together would inevitably be classified as AIM sponsored, which tended to close doors and minds.

Monty and Clyde had met at an AIM protest years earlier and formed a close friendship, fueled by the intensity of their shared ideology. Clyde had grown up on the Big Piney reservation. Like Monty, he was in his early forties and had abandoned a professional career, as a reporter for a Denver paper, to devote himself to AIM.

"Okay, listen up everyone," Monty said. "I'm glad to see you. We'll be heading over to the clinic in a few minutes, but I wanted to go over some ground rules first."

"To start with, no physical force is to be used today. These are our people, we're not there to intimidate or scare them. We're there because we care about their welfare, remember that. Keep that first and foremost in your mind. We're there to educate them. If you see someone you know, approach them first. As a friend. There's a good chance that at least one of us will know every participant in this study.

"If the police show up, I don't want to see any resistance. Everyone understand? There are situations where that's called for—any of you who accompanied me to Ward Valley know that—but this isn't one of them.

"I'm handing out literature for you to share with the study participants."

He passed the stapled sheets around, nodding and occasionally smiling through the cloud of crystallized breath billowing forth from each of the nine faces surrounding him.

"Any questions?"

"None here."

"No, sir."

Several nods.

It seemed they were all anxious to do what they'd come there to do.

"Okay," said Monty then. *"Let's go!"*

ISABEL'S STOMACH PICKED the worst time to complain about not having been fed. She'd been too nervous this morning for food, and in too big a hurry for lunch. Now, as she arranged chairs in the waiting room, she regretted not taking time to eat. Once the study group arrived, though, she was certain eating would be the last thing on her mind.

They were due within the next half hour.

After spending three days drawing blood for the control sample, she'd decided to split the study group in two and administer all the vaccinations during two consecutive afternoon sessions. She'd been generous in the time she'd given each participant when he or she came in for the blood sample, had patiently answered their questions and gone back over the protocol and scientific data supplied by ImmuVac. Now she felt that the most efficient way to conduct the vaccinations would be in two groups. That way, each group would have one last opportunity to ask questions before receiving the vaccine. Another big factor in her decision to handle it this way was that she hoped that seeing the other study participants would have a calming effect on each person. Though for the most part each applicant she'd chosen seemed pleased to be included, under the surface, she sensed more than a little bit of nervousness, too.

She was just trying to decide how to arrange the chairs, when she heard Suzanne mutter an uh-oh.

Isabel looked up to see the receptionist staring out the clinic's front door.

"You better come take a look," she said.

"What is it?" Isabel approached Suzanne, her gaze following that of the younger woman's.

A caravan of cars and trucks was pulling in to the clinic's parking lot. The lead pickup looked vaguely familiar. Then it hit her. The night of the IRB meeting. *Monty Four Bear.*

"Sweet Jesus," Isabel muttered, pushing through the front door.

Just as the last of the caravan pulled in from the east, she recognized the car of Arlo Iron Heart, whom she'd included in the Phase I group despite MacStirling's recommendation.

Isabel approached Monty Four Bear's truck. A tall, bony Indian with a hawkish nose, piercing eyes, and long straggly hair tied loosely at his neck stepped out of the passenger side and stared across the truck at her as she waited, with a twisted gut, for Monty to open his door.

"What are you doing here?" she asked when he did.

"Nice to see you again." Monty smiled.

"Answer me. What do you want?"

Monty turned to his companion and introduced him to Isabel over the truck's bed.

"This is my cousin, Clyde Birdseye. Clyde, this is Dr. Isabel McLain. She's the doctor I told you about, the one who's in charge of this study."

Clyde nodded and gave Isabel a half salute that was distinctly mocking.

By now, Arlo had pulled up to the spot nearest the clinic door and another member of Monty's caravan had approached him. Isabel glared at Monty, then rushed to Arlo's side in the hope of escorting him inside before something awful happened. But it was too late.

"Please, just read this literature," a round-faced young man with a shaved head was saying to Arlo. "This study could do you more harm than good."

Isabel grabbed the stapled pages the young man held in front of Arlo's face.

"What's *is* this?" she said.

The top sheet was entitled, in large bold print, HUMAN GUINEA PIGS.

Isabel groaned. By now, the kid had handed Arlo a second copy. Monty Four Bear and two other study participants had joined them.

Isabel turned on Monty.

"How dare you do this?"

Monty's eyes held hers momentarily, then he turned away and surveyed the group, which had grown with more arriving participants.

"We are not here to frighten you," he said. "Please, just give us a few minutes of your time. Let us share some important information with you before you decide to go inside."

Arlo Iron Heart had a look of sheer panic on his leathery face. The other participants appeared nervous and hesitant, but when Isabel opened the clinic door and pleaded with them to come in, no one budged.

"Please, just walk past them," she kept repeating.

"All we're asking," Monty Four Bear was saying to the group in a voice that Isabel found maddeningly reasoned, "is that you listen to us. Or read this." He raised the handout in the air. "These are facts. Actual statistics from sources like *The New York Times*. Or the Food and Drug Administration. Listen to this: The FDA issued a report that says that in the past year, one-point-five million Americans were hospitalized as a consequence of pharmaceutical drugs they were given to *cure* them. You can't assume this vaccine is safe, not when drugs already approved for commercial sale can harm you."

Isabel let go of the door and stepped forward angrily.

"Don't let him do this to you. He's just trying to confuse and frighten you. This vaccine is not a drug intended to cure you—it is meant to protect you from contracting a very dangerous virus. That FDA statistic means nothing in this context. *Nothing.* We're talking about a vaccine here."

"Okay, if you want to talk about vaccines," Monty broke in, "read this." He shook a copy of the pamphlet above his head. "How many of you knew that it is a proven fact—one admitted by the government—that the polio vaccine had been contaminated with a serious virus?"

Isabel groaned inwardly.

Had Gus and Monty Four Bear just read the same article?

"That was almost fifty years ago!" she cried. "It was a terrible accident that the government has admitted." She swept her eyes over their audience, which was growing by the minute. "Many of you might not be here today if it weren't for that vaccine. Please, all of you study participants, come inside. Ignore them."

Her voice fell on deaf ears. It was as if the only words actually ingested by the group were those coming from the mouth of Monty Four Bear. Until Clyde Birdseye opened his.

"Why do you suppose we've been selected to be the subjects of this noble gesture?" Birdseye asked. His voice did not have the lyrical quality to it that Monty's had, but it was strong and angry and could not be ignored. "You've all heard of the Tuskegee Institute experiments, haven't you? Where black men were deprived of treatment for syphilis for thirty-eight years?"

Even Arlo Iron Heart's head nodded in response.

Isabel could take no more.

"That's not why this reservation was chosen for this study

and you know it. We were chosen because hantavirus struck here. Because I wrote an article . . ."

"An article that condemned the medical establishment," Clyde shot back. "Called it racist. And now you're trying to deny that this type of thing happens. This one talks out of both sides of her mouth. Don't trust her."

"Don't you twist my words." Isabel gave Birdseye a withering glare. "There's one big difference between all those situations you described and this. A *huge* difference. The tragedy, the *crime,* in all those situations was that the patients were not informed. If what this man says is true," she turned back to the rest of the group, "and I don't for one moment buy into it, that alone should alleviate your concerns. You are protected here. There has been full disclosure. No one is forcing you to participate in this study. In fact, there were far more applicants than we could accommodate during this phase. This vaccine will save lives. It may well save each of *your* lives."

"I've heard it was some kind of vaccine that caused AIDS."

It was a statement that sounded more like a question, coming from one of the study participants, a young woman whom Isabel had first met just two days earlier. She'd directed it to Monty.

Monty nodded. "Some people believe the AIDS virus was caused by a contaminated hepatitis B vaccine given to gay men."

"Could that happen here?" The woman's eyes grew wider. "Could this vaccine be contaminated with something like AIDS?"

"Of course not," Isabel answered, but her words were drowned out by Monty's.

"Anything's possible when there's no independent testing to make sure the vaccine's pure."

"Nobody's tested this vaccine?" Arlo Iron Heart asked. "How can they tell us it's safe then?"

Isabel's flush gave away her flustered state.

"Mr. Four Bear is correct in stating that the FDA does not test each vaccine for purity. Quality assurance is the responsibility of the vaccine manufacturer. All of you received detailed information, results of tests and page after page of data, which demonstrates this vaccine's safety."

"I dunno," Arlo said softly. "Sounds a little risky to me."

"I've got two babies to feed. I ain't takin' chances with somethin' that's not even been tested," the same woman said, turning back toward the parking lot.

Isabel reflexively clenched her fists and set her jaw as she noticed two of Monty Four Bear's companions exchanging a high five at the back of the crowd.

"YOU WHAT?"

"I agreed to send the vaccine out to an independent lab for testing."

Ken MacStirling's breathing, which Isabel could usually hear over the telephone, ceased.

"Are you out of your mind?"

"No, I most certainly am not. It was the only way I could salvage this study. I told you, I was faced with an army of opposition. An *armed* army. They came well supplied with data and information. If I hadn't agreed to the independent testing, we'd have lost every volunteer there. And the more I thought about it, I decided it was a reasonable request."

"I knew I should have been there," MacStirling huffed. "I would never have allowed this to happen. This is insane. Lyons will have my head for this."

"I don't understand what the problem is. Unless you think the testing might turn something up."

"I've never seen anything like it."

"Like what?"

"A study investigator so paranoid about a study. I don't understand you. You write this article demanding that the pharmaceutical industry come up with a vaccine for hanta-virus, then put up roadblocks every step of the way."

"All this independent testing costs us is a little time," Isabel answered defensively, "and I'd rather lose time than lives. In the long run, this will give the study that much more credibility. I could tell it made an impression on them, our being willing to send the vaccine for testing."

"*Our* being willing? This was a decision you made unilaterally. I don't want any part of it. In fact, you can't just send the vaccine out. You signed a confidentiality agreement. That vaccine is proprietary to ImmuVac."

"I have to have my patients' trust. I will not participate in this study without it."

"Is that another threat?"

"It's not intended to be. It's merely a statement of fact."

"Well, I'll keep that in mind."

There was a long silence.

"Will you grant me permission to send it out?" Isabel pressed. "In writing?"

"I want your word that you will not disclose the lab results before I've had a chance to adequately address any adverse findings—which, of course, I don't anticipate."

Isabel hesitated for a moment.

"The full report has to be released to the study participants, regardless of the findings. As long as you agree to that, I'm agreeable to giving you whatever time you need to address it first. After all, I want this to put to rest, once and for all, any concerns that anyone—my patients *or* that damn Monty Four Bear—have."

"*Amen.*" Ken MacStirling sighed.

FOURTEEN

SOPHIA WHITE THUNDER winced as the needle penetrated the skin of her fleshy upper arm.

"I told you not to contract your muscles," Isabel scolded.

"Couldn't help it." Sophia smiled.

Isabel massaged the injection site for a moment before placing a piece of gauze and tape over it.

"Now don't forget to keep a journal of any reactions you have to the vaccine," Isabel said as she walked Sophia to the door. "Even if it doesn't seem related—if you're just tired, or achy—I want you to make note of it. Okay?"

"Sure, Dr. McLain. I'll do it. And thanks for letting me in the study. I know you had more people wanting in than you could vaccinate."

"We'll get them in Phase II and III." Isabel smiled.

When Suzanne came into the exam room a couple minutes later, she found Isabel lying on the exam table. She lifted her head and grinned at her assistant.

"What a day it's been."

"Ever give that many shots in one day before?"

Isabel laughed. The independent laboratory had confirmed the purity of the HantaVac, and she had just completed Phase I.

"No. Can't say that I have. Thirty-nine's a record for me. I just wish Arlo had shown up, but Monty Four Bear must have scared him off. It's a wonder more of the study participants didn't back out after seeing all that propaganda Four Bear and his group handed out."

"Dolores and those boys dying, that really scared everyone. Besides, they trust you. You wouldn't be doing this study if it wasn't a good thing for us."

Isabel had heard that same sentiment repeated throughout the day. Her patients trusted her, trusted that this study would safeguard them from what had happened to the others, that Isabel and ImmuVac had their best interests at heart.

The only flack she'd taken all day long had come from Lester Clay, a wiry, crewcut Blackfeet in his early thirties, whose ambivalence at participating in the clinical trial came through loud and clear.

"Probably shoulda listened to Monty and the others," he'd told Isabel.

"You're still welcome to change your mind, Mr. Clay," Isabel had responded, feeling somewhat guilty, for she knew that if it had been another of her patients, she would have done more to assuage any lingering concerns.

"Didn't say I wanted to change my mind. Did I?" Clay snapped. "What I want to know is if you're giving *yourself* the shot."

"I'm not allowed to participate."

"Why the hell not? Too dangerous?" he'd snickered.

But after he left, Isabel found herself regretting that she hadn't insisted on receiving the vaccination herself. She'd raised the issue once with MacStirling, and he'd told her it was forbidden, that for the study investigator to also participate in the trial would constitute a conflict of interest. He'd even pointed out that there was a limited amount of vaccine and that her participation would only deprive one of the Blackfeet of the protection it offered.

Isabel had to concede that there were probably situations in which the conflict of interest rule made sense, but surely this was not one of them. How could she ask these people to put their trust in her without subjecting herself to the same risks—if any existed—that she was exposing them to? Isabel had never believed in following rules that made no sense. And there was another consideration. Despite the explicit instructions she'd given each study participant, she knew that her patients had spent a lifetime ignoring symptoms—waiting, hoping to ride out an illness without having to resort to doctors and clinics. It was their nature to make light of aches and pains. Could they be counted on to report every symptom, even those they might be inclined to deem insignificant, that might or might not be related to the vaccine?

Suzanne had joined her, hoisting herself up on the edge of the exam table.

"Guess we can call it a day," she said. "Want me to help you clean up in here?"

"No, you go ahead. I can take care of the exam rooms. You go on home. I shouldn't have let you work such a long day. You're still recovering."

"I'm fine now. It was important to me to be here."

"I can see why it would be. Thank you. I couldn't have done it without your help, but go now. Before that sky opens up."

It had been threatening rain all day, but with the evening temperatures dropping in to the mid-twenties, snow was a distinct possibility now.

"Winter's almost here, enit?"

Isabel nodded.

"Drive carefully."

"You too."

Isabel waited for the sound of the deadbolt turning in the clinic's front door. Then she stood and walked to the small refrigerator which sat atop the exam room's counter.

She opened the door. The refrigerator was empty save for the bottom half of a cardboard carton labeled IMMUVAC HANTAVIRUS VACCINE: FOR CLINICAL TRIAL USE ONLY.

A single vial sat in the grid that earlier in the day held forty. A vial intended for Arlo Iron Heart. Isabel reached for the small glass container, which held three millimeters of clear fluid.

She shook it, then reflexively rolled it back and forth briskly between her palms as she had the other thirty-nine vials, letting friction warm its contents to minimize discomfort when it was injected.

She'd been deeply disappointed when Arlo Iron Heart failed to show up for his four-fifteen appointment, but maybe it was a good thing after all that he had changed his mind.

She'd seen the fear in each of the study participants' eyes as they watched her pierce the rubber dam at the end of the tiny vial and draw its contents into a syringe. What must each have been thinking? An experimental drug, never before tested on a human being. Created by outsiders who belonged to a people who had systemicatically gone about killing and torturing their ancestors, who to this day showed neither remorse nor concern for the likes of Suzanne Featherheart, or Joe Winged Foot, or the countless other gentle and destitute souls living on godforsaken reservations across the country.

She hadn't realized until just that moment the extent of the courage and trust each of the participants had demonstrated in casting aside those fears, overcoming the terror that surely had resulted from Monty Four Bear's campaign of warnings—for Isabel belonged to the "chosen" class, was herself a medical doctor, and even *she* entertained a fleeting fear as she rolled up her left sleeve.

What if, just what if, this vaccine had unanticipated side effects? What if, in protecting its recipients from the deadly hantavirus, it exposed them to other, potentially dangerous consequences?

Nonsense. What was she thinking? Surely she hadn't let Gus's or Monty Four Bear's paranoia get to her.

Dabbing her upper arm with an alcohol-soaked cotton ball, Isabel reached for the syringe and, feeling like a contortionist, twisted her left bicep as far forward as possible to enable her to see the meatiest portion of her arm.

She was just lifting the syringe when a sound stopped her right hand in midair.

What was *that*?

She listened, thinking it had probably been her imagination, but when it occurred again, there was no mistaking the fact. Someone was banging on the clinic door.

Setting the syringe down, Isabel walked to the door and stepped into the corridor. Suzanne had flipped the clinic's outside lights on before leaving, which enabled Isabel to make out the identity of this late visitor, who stood pounding the glass with the heel of one hand.

With mixed emotions, Isabel walked down the long hallway and let Arlo Iron Heart in for his vaccination.

"THE MUNICIPALITY OF Barskoon has filed suit," Pierre Sabin said. "They're asking for twenty-five million dollars and an injunction. They want all activity at the mine shut down until after trial. And from what I'm hearing, this is just the first of several suits. The family of the dead woman has retained an attorney. And GreenEarth is in the area, so we can expect them to jump on the bandwagon."

Jon LeCoque swiveled in his chair, turning away from the company attorney and toward the blue expanse below his window. This was just what he feared, the last thing WRI needed right now, with all the bad press they'd received over Essiquibo.

Twelve stories below, LeCoque could see activity on *Chesire*. He anchored the yacht in Vancouver harbor and often chose to spend the night there instead of returning home to his wife of thirty years. He would have to remember to call the steward and ensure that the liquor cabinet had been restocked, as he had the feeling that tonight would find him sleeping in *Chesire*'s state room. He turned back to Sabin.

"What's happened to the fucking moron who drove the truck into the river?"

"We let him go."

"Let him go? We should have him thrown in jail. He's the one responsible, not WRI."

"Jon, you know the law. He was working for us at the time. According to the suit they filed, the truckers routinely drove that route at excessive speeds. The police have records of complaints from citizens, and meetings with mining supervisors."

"I want names."

"Pardon me?"

"I want the names of any supervisors who were aware of the fact that the imbecilic drivers were speeding. That just proves my point, it was the driver's fault."

"There's no doubt that the driver was at fault. But ultimately the liability will be WRI's, especially if they can show that mining supervisors had been warned about the speeding."

"Have you talked to any of the supervisors involved?"

"Yes. One. He verified having received a warning."

"Then why the fuck didn't he do something about it?"

"He claims to have given the drivers a stern warning. He also faxed a request to fund a security officer to accompany the drivers up and down the mountain."

"Who'd he fax it to? I want answers and I want them now."

"He faxed it directly to your office. On June sixteenth." Sabin slid a sheet of paper across the desk. "Here it is."

LeCoque snatched it up and stared at it. It looked vaguely familiar.

"Never saw it before."

Sabin, looking as though he'd rather be anywhere on earth but sitting across from WRI's CEO, slid another paper LeCoque's way.

"Here's your response."

Omar operation is already over budget. I suggest you

worry more about output than finding more ways to spend
money. Request denied.

At the bottom, in his oversized scrawl, was LeCoque's
signature.

"How the hell can I keep track of every request that comes
through this office? If the supervisor knew about the problem
he's responsible, along with the driver."

"This shows we were put on notice. It's very damning.
Even without it, agency law would make WRI responsible."

"Have you researched this? Who's to say Kyrgyzstan has
the same laws as we do?"

"They've petitioned the Canadian courts to hear this case.
If their petition is granted, Canadian law will apply. WRI
will be responsible."

"What are the chances the court will grant the petition?"

"It would be a first. But that's not necessarily good. Because it would have such far-reaching consequences—every
company that does business on an international basis, from
mining companies to Nike, will be nervous as all hell about
the prospect of being held accountable at home—the whole
world will be watching to see what the court holds. So in
that sense, even if the court denies the petition, we lose because of the bad press we're sure to receive. And, of course,
then we face litigation in Kyrgyzstan."

LeCoque turned back to the window. He hated attorneys
and their fucking negativity. Just once he'd like someone to
come to him and say, "Jon, you've got a problem, but I can
solve it." Just once. Instead all he ever got were dire predictions. He was sick to death of Sabin and his doomsaying.

Without taking his eyes off the uniformed man scrubbing
the decks of the *Chesire*, LeCoque delivered his dictum.

"You're in charge of legal affairs. Take care of this
damned thing. Make it disappear. And don't come back to
me until you do."

CHAPTER

FIFTEEN

SERGEI KIROV COULD inevitably be found hunched over his lab table, bifocals in danger of sliding off a nose that looked like it had been lopped off two-thirds of the way down, wild, prematurely gray hair stabbing the air. Despite the comfortable temperature, his lab coat invariably bulged and gathered over the sweater he'd worn back home, working in a now-defunct Soviet lab.

Kirov had once served as director at the State Research Center of Virology and Biotechnology in Vector. But with the collapse of the Soviet Union, Kirov's position, along with most of the 70,000 scientists and technicians employed in the secret Soviet germ weapons program, had been eliminated. When James Lyons contacted him, he'd been working in a lab with neither heat nor electricity, oftentimes going without pay for months at a time. The sweater, it seemed, was a remnant of those days and just one of several things that set him apart from his coworkers.

Sergei and his coworkers were an odd lot. In the laboratories at ImmuVac, white-coated scientists routinely went about their business in a focused manner. The social atmosphere contrasted sharply with the friendly atmosphere common to most small companies, where camaraderie and team spirit usually flourished and most employees started with one basic common bond—the fact that they were local people working for a local company. The culture in the labs of small biotech firms reflected a transient, disparate grouping of employees. Talent was recruited from other countries and other labs. Scientists came and left with such frequency that bonding with other employees was a concept given little to no consideration. Fully half of the employees at ImmuVac were in the country on temporary working visas. The rest had been imported from the National Institutes of Health or any number of other ground-breaking research institutions, most of them concentrated in the East. Scientists followed funding. Period. It made for little stability. Those friendships that did form were based on nationality or previous institutional affiliations.

As the only Russian at ImmuVac, Sergei had no friends. That was okay with Kirov. He was just trying to survive, hoping the checks he sent home to his wife and children, who had been denied passports in an effort to lure Sergei back to the country, would ensure their survival as well.

Tonight, as the lab emptied of ImmuVac employees, not one of the departing scientists or technicians looked Kirov's way when calling out their farewells. Everyone had grown used to Kirov being the last to leave for the day. After all, he did not have a family waiting for him at home. If Kirov noticed the fact that he was regarded as little more than a piece of furniture, he did not let on or seem to care.

This was actually his favorite time of day, when he had the labs to himself. Which is why, thirty minutes after the last employee had departed, the sound of footsteps brought a scowl to his round features.

"Thought I'd find you still here."

Kirov looked up to see James Lyons, CEO of ImmuVac, towering over him. Sergei's contact with Lyons was minimal, which—to Sergei's way of thinking—was just as well. Lyons had lured him to ImmuVac with promises of big money in support of Sergei's immunization research. The promises had proved hollow from the start, and recent developments at ImmuVac had so angered Sergei that he'd begun thinking of returning to his homeland.

Sergei pushed back his lab stool and stood, but even then the short, stocky Russian found himself eyeballing Lyons's prominent chin.

"Yes, well," he stammered, taken aback from this unexpected visit, "I like the—what is it you call it?—solitary of working alone at night?"

"Solitude."

"Yes, solitude."

"May I pull up a chair?" Lyons said, already reaching for the lab stool at the next table.

"Of course."

Kirov settled back onto his own stool as Lyons noisily dragged the metal perch across the linoleum floor and plunked down on it.

"I understand your 2453 work is going well."

"Yes." It was about time Lyons paid some attention to his work. "By incorporating extracts from the mice's own tumors, the vaccine stimulates their immune system, teaching it to attack cancer cells. Sixty percent of subjects demonstrate reductions in tumor size."

"Impressive results," said Lyons. "But what concerns me is AngioGenics. They're about to complete Phase III, and I hear the study's going well."

"The mechanism of AngioGenics's vaccine is much different than mine. Theirs reacts against sugar molecules on the outside of the cancerous cells. Mine stimulates heat shock proteins, which serve as natural stimulants of the immune system."

"Isn't GeneFactor working on the same principle?"

"Yes. But their Phase I results were disappointing. I assure you, our clinical trials will not prove disappointing."

Lyons stroked his mustache.

"I'm afraid we're not in a position financially to be rushing into clinical trials of 2453. That's what I came here to discuss."

Sergei drew a deep, shaky breath. Americans were all the same. Liars who could not be trusted.

"I came to the United States to escape this . . . this . . . handcuff of finances. If money is in such short supply, why is ImmuVac conducting clinical trials on Dr. MacStirling's hantavirus vaccine? It is a comedy, putting resources into a vaccine like that. How many deaths have there been in this country from hantavirus? Not even a hundred." He stood, slamming his hand down angrily on the desk. He was shouting now. "*Cancer*. I am working on a way to prevent cancer! And you tell me my research must take a backseat to this ridiculous study being conducted on savages somewhere in . . . in . . ."

He stood there, face flushed with anger, his heart battering his rib cage ferociously. Lyons seemed undisturbed by this display.

"Montana," Lyons finished for him. "Browning, Montana. On the Blackfeet reservation." He studied Sergei, who now felt foolish standing but could not bring himself to be seated again either. "I didn't realize you felt so strongly about MacStirling's vaccine."

"I'll tell you how strongly I feel about it. I will not stay where my work is not appreciated. I would return first to my homeland, return to the labs without electricity or heat. At least there I am close to my family."

"But how will you feed your family if you return?"

Sergei had no answer.

"Listen, Sergei," Lyons said, "you may not approve of ImmuVac funding Ken MacStirling's hantavirus vaccine, but we believe it makes good business sense. And that's what I came here tonight to discuss with you. Another idea I've had. One that involves your work, and that I believe could make even more sense than the hantavirus vaccine. Will you please sit down and listen to me?"

Lyons had piqued Kirov's curiosity. For a man who had once enjoyed status and special privileges in Russia as a member of the scientific elite—as director of Vector, Sergei had lived in a spacious, well-appointed apartment and been invited to the most important state functions—ImmuVac's failure to showcase his considerable talents had been hugely disappointing. Maybe that was about to change. He lowered himself back onto his stool.

"Go on."

"I'm curious about something," Lyons began. "In your work at Vector, you were involved in developing and testing biological agents, weren't you? Anthrax, plague, smallpox. That's true, isn't it? How about the Marburg virus?"

Sergei had never seen his boss like this before, so attentive, so eager.

"Russian scientists studied many biological agents that had the ability to be used as weapons," Kirov spoke slowly and precisely, the subject matter exaggerating his usual need to think through his choice of English words.

"And this work went on even after the 1972 treaty banning the development of germ weapons. Didn't it?"

Since coming to America, Sergei had never discussed this secret past life of his, despite the fact that he took great pride in his accomplishments. This pride now overcame his natural reticence about the subject.

"It actually escalated after the treaty. In secret, of course. Different centers specialized in different diseases. At Obolensk, lethal bacteria. At Kazakhstan, anthrax. We made and studied several different viruses at Vector. But our specialty was smallpox."

Lyons's usually dull eyes were bright now with excitement.

"Smallpox," he echoed. "How many strains?"

There was a long pause.

"Maybe fifteen thousand."

"Fifteen *thousand* different strains?"

Kirov nodded.

"And how many of those were deadly? How many could have been considered for the warfare program?"

"Maybe one hundred had potential as weapons. Ten, maybe twelve had already been targeted."

"What happened to them? Were they all destroyed?"

"Officially, yes."

Lyons leaned closer, his arm pressing into Kirov's. It was one of those moments where you had to trust your instincts. Kirov could have lied to his boss. He had been conditioned to lie, for the good of his homeland. But something told him that this was a moment for honesty.

"What about *unofficially*?"

"Unofficially?" Kirov replied, the wariness cultivated by years of secrecy giving way to a sense of inexplicable anticipation. "That's another story."

WINTER IN THE Pacific Northwest was a miserable affair. Today's torrential rains were accompanied by winds gusting to sixty mph. Though sheltered in the harbor, *Chesire* rocked furiously, causing the steward to steady himself with a hand on the cherry dining table before depositing an appetizer of oysters on the half shell in front of his boss, Jon LeCoque, and WRI's attorney, Pierre Sabin. The plate delivered, the stately server topped off LeCoque's and Sabin's wine, then disappeared back into the ship's kitchen.

"Not ideal conditions for dining onboard *Chessie*," LeCoque apologized, "but I wanted to have our conversation in private."

"No problem," Sabin said, reaching for a shell.

They ate a dozen oysters in silence. LeCoque was a man of few passions, but food happened to be one. Discussion of WRI's legal problems would come later. He would not allow it to sully the meal he'd ordered prepared.

As Sabin downed the last oyster, the steward appeared again to clear their plates.

"May I open a new wine to accompany your main course?"

LeCoque nodded.

"Let's try that Beringer cabernet."

Impressed with its bouquet, LeCoque had purchased half a dozen bottles of the 1994 Private Reserve from Napa Valley at a recent wine tasting arranged by his wife. It was one of the few things the two did as a couple anymore. Two years earlier, they'd toured Northern California's wine country. When they returned home, they'd hired a contractor to convert their basement into a wine cellar. Stocking it had become an activity that gave both LeCoque and his wife pleasure.

The men ate the meal served them—lamb tagine with lemon and olives, couscous, and green beans—with gusto; however, midway through, Sabin began to look somewhat green, the yacht's rocking having grown more violent. The wind's roar and rain pelting against the windows added to the sensation of being caught in a squall at sea, but LeCoque rather enjoyed it. The previous year on a voyage to Kauai, he had piloted *Chesire* through forty-foot waves. On a subconscious level, LeCoque's lack of fear at crossing oceans compensated for his paranoia about flying.

With dinner over, LeCoque pushed back from the table.

"Well, I think we've delayed the inevitable long enough," he said. "Why don't you tell me about the proposed settlement?"

Sabin pulled the green linen napkin from his lap, wiped his mouth, and stood, heading for the briefcase he'd left on a chair.

"*Sit,*" LeCoque barked. "Just give me the basics. I don't need all the legalese."

Sabin cleared his throat.

"Basics. Okay. I received a written offer of settlement today from the City of Barskoon and the dead woman's family. The city will settle now for twenty million, Canadian. The woman's family wants two."

"What about the fucking environmentalists?"

"They haven't filed suit yet."

"But they will."

"I believe they will; however, the terms of settlement with the city may be enough to placate them."

"How so?"

"One of the conditions of settlement is that the lease will not be renewed in 2002."

"Those bastards. If we don't find another deposit, that could kill us."

"I thought Wilderman is on to something in the States. Montana."

"He is. But turns out it's on an Indian reservation. We have to go through the tribe for approval to do more exploration."

"When's that happening? Maybe I should be there."

"Next week. Tony can handle it. I want you to stay focused on this Kyrgyzstan thing. Now, what about resumption of operations? I suppose they're gonna fight to keep that injunction in place."

"Actually, no. They're amenable to resumption of operations, provided some safeguards are put in place."

"You know why that is, don't you? Because the fucking economy over there depends on that mine. Shut it down and their people start going hungry. What kind of morons would cut off their nose to spite their face like this?"

"Morons worried about their environment and their health, I guess."

"Twenty-two million is an outrage."

"It's a lot of money. But Zellman-Tusky settled out of court for thirty-eight million for their cyanide leaks in Montana. And North Country fought all the way, only to end up paying a seventy million dollar judgment." North Country

Mining Corporation was a Saskatchewan mining company sued when a sealed drainage tunnel at a tailings pit at their Pomater Mine in the Philippines collapsed, sending cyanide-laced tailings into the Boac River. "And I have to tell you, the damage alleged from the Philippines accident was considerably less than what we saw in Kyrgyzstan. Plus there were no deaths linked directly with it."

"That doesn't mean *we* can't win," LeCoque said. "I'm not sure I wouldn't take the odds. Seventy million or walk away free, versus a guaranteed hit for twenty-two million. A betting man would go for the chance to walk away. Or file for bankruptcy protection like Zellman-Tusky did."

"It's my legal opinion that WRI would not walk away free," Sabin said. "And there's the publicity to consider. As I told you before, if the Canadian courts approve their request to hear this, it will be a first. It's already getting a lot of press. Settling now nips that in the bud."

LeCoque was sick and tired of running scared from environmentalists and lawsuit-happy opportunists.

"You fucking lawyers are all alike. No balls."

"Balls?" Sabin repeated. "Okay. You want to talk balls? Well, how about this? The Philippines government filed criminal charges against four of North Country's top executives."

This news hit LeCoque precisely in the body part they'd been discussing.

"Reckless imprudence, violation of the Mining Act, Water Code, and Pollution Control Law," Sabin continued. "They could each get up to eighteen years in a Philippines prison. And to my knowledge, they hadn't received any warnings prior to the accident. We did. We received several warnings.

"Do you have the guts . . . er, excuse me . . . to use *your* term, the *balls*, to risk the same thing happening to you in Kyrgyzstan? Or would prudence dictate that we settle and move on. Turn our focus elsewhere?"

•   •   •

"WHAT'S THIS ABOUT Sergei going overseas?"

Bob Blount, head of medical research and a lifelong friend of Lyons's, had dropped by James Lyons's office unannounced.

Lyons looked up from the patent application that legal had sent over for him to review.

"What part don't you understand?" he said.

"Well, he made this sound like a company trip."

Lyons hesitated. Kirov's work would be highly secretive. Still, if his mission proved successful, it would probably be impossible to set up a new lab without some assistance. And of all the people in research, not only did Bob Blount stand to be the most helpful, he was also the one person Lyons felt he could trust.

"Sit down," he said.

When Blount had settled into a chair, Lyons continued.

"I've sent Sergei over to the Middle East, where he plans to meet with some of his former Soviet associates."

"You have Sergei recruiting for us now?" Blount's voice had risen an octave, signaling his indignation at the thought that Lyons had turned to one of his underlings for help in finding new research talent. "I thought we were looking at downsizing, not hiring."

"He won't be bringing back other scientists."

"James, do me a favor, will you? Stop playing games with me. As head of research, I feel entitled to know what this is about."

"You're right. But this is a very sensitive issue, one in which you would eventually have become involved. I was just waiting to see how things pan out."

Lyons stood and walked to the door. He looked into the outer office, but his secretary was nowhere to be seen, which explained why Blount's arrival had gone unannounced. He closed the door and returned to his desk.

"Ever since the disappointing Phase III results on our cancer vaccine, I've been wracking my brain, trying to come up with some new path for ImmuVac. A golden egg. I knew it had to fit two requirements: It couldn't cost too much and it couldn't take too long."

"I thought that's why we decided to proceed with the clinical trial for the HantaVac. To attract a new partnership, bolster the stock by getting some good press."

"It is. But there are no guarantees that strategy will pay. We all know there's no money to be made in the HantaVac vaccine, but it does stand to draw attention. And since MacStirling had already done the work, it satisfied both of my requirements, the cost and time factor."

"You're not thinking of abandoning it, are you?"

"Absolutely not. But I've never believed it was *the* answer. It would be foolhardy for us to put all our eggs in that basket. I've spent days going over our finances. We can continue operating, on a shoestring, less than two years."

"Define shoestring."

"Everybody but research and absolutely essential support staff gets laid off. Hopefully, within that time frame, the hantavirus vaccine will have attracted another partner, someone with deep enough pockets to fund our other therapeutics in development."

"But if it doesn't?"

"If it doesn't, then we'll have to close down shop. That is, unless we come up with a new product, one that fits those two criteria *and*, unlike the hantavirus vaccine, has strong commercial potential." Lyons leaned forward, lowering his voice and locking eyes with Blount. "That's what I believe I've finally come up with. *Listen to this. A smallpox vaccine.*"

Blount's head snapped to attention at these last two words.

"This is some kind of joke, right?"

"I couldn't be more serious."

"Smallpox was eradicated in the 1980s. The World Health

Organization's planning to destroy the last stock. The disease has vanished from the wild."

"It may have vanished from the wild, but there's still plenty of it out there. And the World Health Organization's never going to destroy the last official stock held by the United States and Russia."

"But that's the plan."

"That may be the official line they've handed out these past two years, but even the United States has backed down from it. We know, it's an established fact, that Russia continued to work with the smallpox virus after the Biological Weapons Convention treaty in 1972. Hell, Sergei himself admits it, as have a number of Russian scientists who've defected to the United States. Smallpox was their number one biological weapon. They grew it by the ton. There've been rumors for years of it being passed from country to country. After the Russians closed the Biopreparat institutes, a lot of scientists had to choose between going hungry and selling the only thing of value they had. Their knowledge. That's why the United States has been pouring money into Soviet labs and cooperative ventures. To stop what they call the brain drain. To give unemployed scientists an alternative to leaving their country, to going to work for Iran, Iraq, North Korea. That's how we got Sergei. Because the situation in Russia became desperate. And you can be sure there were some scientists smart enough and desperate enough to smuggle the biowarfare agents they'd been working on out of the labs. And out of the country."

"You're saying smallpox is already in the hands of bioterrorists."

"Exactly. And someone, somewhere is eventually going to use it. We read about it every day—the threat of bioterrorism. So far it's just been that. Pretty much a threat. Mostly hoaxes. But if smallpox is out there and in the hands of terrorists, it's not a matter of 'if'. It's a matter of 'when'. And since we long ago stopped vaccinating for smallpox, there's a damn good chance that no one will have any protection. Those of us who were vaccinated twenty-five years ago probably don't have any immunity left. Which means that a ready-made vaccine will be a thing of *considerable* value. Priceless, really."

"What if the government is already working on a vaccine, as we speak?"

"You know how the government operates. With the efficiency of a slug. And we have something the government doesn't. Sergei. No one knows this virus better than he does. Who are you going to bet on in a race to develop a vaccine for the inevitable day that bioterrorists unleash this on us: a government scientist, or the man who led the Russian smallpox program?"

"Do you mean to tell me you sent Sergei to get the virus?" Blount asked, incredulous. "He'll be bringing smallpox back with him?"

Lyons nodded. "If he succeeds."

"It's no wonder you've been secretive. This is insane. Not to mention highly illegal."

"We'll be setting up a separate lab. Level Four. No one but Sergei will have access. As far as the rest of the company is concerned, we'll tell everyone Sergei decided to stay in his homeland."

The room fell silent. Lyons studied Blount for his reaction.

"Well, what do you think?"

When Blount reached to straighten his glasses, his hands were shaking.

"I told you. I think it's insane," he said. "But it might work."

Both men grew silent again.

"What if Sergei gets caught with it? At the airport?"

"That won't happen. Once we began discussing this, I learned a great deal about Sergei. He's thrilled by the prospect of resuming the work he'd been doing in Russia. And, of course, I promised he'd be rewarded handsomely if this all works out."

In reality, Kirov's enthusiasm had erased any doubts Lyons had about the proposed project. The Russian had assured him that his earlier work would speed the creation of a vaccine. In addition, during their conversation it had become clear that Kirov had no doubt that smallpox had, indeed, fallen into the hands of terrorists and that he fully expected it to be used.

All the elements that Lyons needed to put WRI in a position to come to the world's rescue—and reap the resultant acclaim and profit—existed. He only needed to make them fall together.

"Everything hinges on whether he can get his hands on the virus," he said, his thoughts returning, as they had so many times these past days, to Sergei's words. "If he does, we're in business."

CHAPTER

SIXTEEN

I REALLY *HAVE* to get going," Suzanne declared, energetically scrubbing the counter of the exam room. The scent of isopropyl alcohol lingered as she paused in the doorway.

It was almost six-thirty. Isabel had miscalculated how long it would take to do the follow-up and blood work on the twenty study participants she'd scheduled to come in today.

"How many more are waiting out there?" Isabel asked.

"Just Sophia."

Isabel wiped a stray wisp of hair from her forehead. Tucking it behind her ear, she noticed for the first time how nice Suzanne looked. She wore a long denim dress and an exquisite turquoise pendant.

"That necklace is gorgeous."

"Thanks. It was passed down from my grandmother."

"Got a date?"

"No. Tribal council meeting at seven, and I want to grab a bite to eat first."

"Since when do you attend council meetings?"

"The council's thinking about leasing reservation land to some mining outfit. I'm sick of them leasing out our land cause nobody on the rez ever makes any money from it."

"Mining *here*? On the Blackfeet reservation?"

"Yep."

"That's appalling. What kind of mine?"

"Gold. My cousin lives on the Alamosa River in Colorado. Few years back a cyanide spill there poisoned seventy miles of the river. Same thing could happen here. They'll come in, ruin the land and water, take all the money, then leave us to deal with the whole mess."

"Why haven't I heard anything about this mine?"

"I dunno. I heard about it from Monty. He wants all of us to be there." Suzanne headed out the door, then turned back and said, "You ought to come."

"*Me?*" Isabel asked.

It was the first time she'd been invited to a meeting of the Blackfeet, and it took her by surprise.

Isabel put the council meeting out of mind while she finished up with her last appointment. But after she'd closed the clinic down and climbed into the Jeep for the half-hour ride home, Suzanne's words just kept pricking at her.

Suzanne had heard about the meeting from Monty.

Who the hell was this Monty Four Bear? Did he just go around looking for causes, people to blame and hate and strike out at? I mean, the guy seemed to be everywhere. He shows up at the clinic on the night of the IRB meeting. He's there the first day vaccinations were scheduled. And now he's rallying the troops for tonight's tribal council meeting. He obviously had a chip on his shoulder the size of a small planet.

Still, news that the Blackfeet reservation could end up mined disturbed Isabel tremendously. Her father had always been an ardent environmentalist. He used to rail against mining companies. Even as a small child, Isabel could remember him ranting about their environmental impact. It had always made her proud of him, for none of the other adults that inhabited the world in which she'd grown up seemed to care much about anything that didn't directly affect their everyday creature comforts.

"Once we destroy this earth," he used to tell her, "we won't be able to bring it back."

It used to scare Isabel—the mere proposition that the earth was capable of destruction. But if her mother overheard such remarks, she'd be sure to bring some levity to the situation, saying something like, "Oh, Tom, don't be so dramatic. Honey, your father's just a bleeding heart who wants to save the whole world."

She always said it like it was some kind of disease, but Isabel had been proud of her dad's passion.

She never could understand how two people as different as Nada and Tom McLain ended up together. Or stayed together for all these years.

Taillights on the highway ahead cut Isabel's reflection short. She braked. The right turn signal of the vehicle in front of her indicated it planned to turn into the drive of the Blackfeet tribal headquarters, but even from where her Jeep now sat, waiting for the car to turn off the highway, Isabel could see the lot was full.

When the car in front of her spurted forward, then took a quick left into the parking lot of the Dairy Queen, which also appeared near capacity, Isabel surprised herself by following suit.

•   •   •

TONY WILDERMAN HAD been there, done that. Nothing surprised him anymore, not even the packed meeting hall where the Blackfeet tribal council held its meetings.

It had been a real challenge to find out when the monthly meeting was held so that he could get WRI on the agenda. Hell, he'd even had trouble finding the tribal headquarters. No one in town wanted to give him any information. Word had apparently gotten out about who he was and why he was there, and everyone appeared to have made a pact to provide as little cooperation as possible. But finally he'd stumbled on to the building on the outskirts of Browning. A GONE FOR LUNCH sign had resulted in his sitting outside in his vehicle—appropriately, a Ford Explorer—almost ninety minutes, but finally, when she returned, the receptionist had given him Thomas Rose's phone number. Rose, tribal president, had been reserved but polite.

"If you want to talk to the council, I can't stop you," he'd said. His final words—"Guess I'd better not plan on getting much else done that night"—were his way of acknowledging the uproar the inclusion of WRI on the agenda would give rise to.

Now as the six council members, five men and one woman, settled behind the long table at the head of the room, Wilderman walked purposefully through the maze of gathering Blackfeet and seated himself in the front row of seats intended for the audience. He debated briefly about introducing himself to the council, but several of its members had looked his way, then averted their eyes when he tried to make eye contact.

The meeting was scheduled for seven P.M. At thirteen minutes past, one of the council members—a rangy, sharp-nosed man wearing a flannel shirt and jeans with a turquoise-studded belt buckle—pushed back his chair, stood, and banged a wooden gavel on the table three times.

"This meeting will come to order."

Wilderman recognized Thomas Rose's voice from their phone conversation. The leathery skin and salt-and-pepper hair put Rose's age in the late fifties or maybe even early sixties, but in other respects he appeared decades younger—broad shoulders and a flat stomach, and the posture and movement of a man whose daily activities kept him in excellent condition.

Those who had been standing seated themselves immediately, and the room fell silent.

"Been a while since we've seen this much interest in anything the council was doing," Rose said. "I guess most of you are here to hear what the mining company has to say, but before we get into that, Penny's going to read the minutes from the last meeting."

The lone female member of the board stood. Her charcoal hair was pulled back in a tight bun, showcasing high cheekbones and large, almond-shaped eyes. The size of the group seemed to make her nervous, but she read slowly in a strong, low voice that had a musical, rhythmical quality.

"The first item on the agenda last month was funding for a new elementary school," she started. "The council invited Susan Giles, the principal of Browning Elementary to speak about the condition of the school. Mrs. Giles reported that several windows are broken, the lunchroom has a leak in it, and some of the equipment on the playground is dangerous. She also said that a lot of classes don't have enough books for students, the computer's broken, and two of the teachers have given notice that they plan to quit at the end of the year. The council told Mrs. Giles that they'd have the windows and roof fixed but that there isn't enough money in the budget for new equipment or a new school. There was a unanimous vote to begin efforts to fund a new school. Thomas will talk with the tribal bank. The council agreed that this should be its top priority but they informed Mrs. Giles that there's not a very good chance she'll get a new school.

They'll try to borrow enough to at least get a new computer and new books for next year. And someone's gonna take a look at the playground equipment and remove anything that's dangerous.

"The next item on the agenda was complaints about road maintenance."

At this, laughter broke out across the room.

"What road maintenance?" someone called out.

Penny cracked a tight smile and continued.

"There've been several complaints about potholes and such. The council decided there wasn't enough money to do anything about most of them, but Arnie Holmsby says on some of the side streets the holes are so bad they're ruining his truck and he won't keep pickin' up garbage if we don't do somethin about it, so the council voted five to one to fill some of the biggest holes with gravel." She looked up. "I'm in charge of arrangin' that.

"Ann Beam asked if we could keep the tribal headquarters open on Saturdays so that members who worked off the rez during the week could use the copier and typewriter. The council decided it's our responsibility to support everyone's efforts to find a job, or maybe a job closer to home, which would be hard to do without a typed résumé, so Ann's request was approved. The Ping-Pong table and rec room will stay open too."

She looked at Thomas Rose.

"That's about it," she said.

Rose, still seated, asked for a motion to approve the minutes. The motion was made and accepted.

Finally, Thomas Rose slowly unfolded his lanky form again and stood to introduce Tony Wilderman.

"Everyone already knows that one of the speakers tonight is someone from a Canadian mining company called World Resources. Now, I know this isn't going to be a popular subject for a lot of you, but let's hear what Mr. Wilderman has to say before we go getting all stirred up. Mr. Wilderman, please come on up and tell us what's on your mind."

With that less than enthusiastic introduction, Wilderman strode to the front of the room. Seeing no podium from which to speak, he positioned himself to one side of the long table, where both the audience and council members could see him. He'd decided against bringing any visual materials along, as experience had told him that in situations where his reception could be counted on to be chilly, the more low-key he played it, the better.

"Good evening," he said in a tone that avoided being overly friendly—over the years, he'd also learned that being too solicitous only caused the level of suspicion to rise. "I appreciate this opportunity to speak to you tonight. As Mr. Rose explained, I'm here as a representative of WRI—World Resources, Inc. We are a Canadian mining company, but as the name implies, we operate worldwide. Our primary emphasis is on the production and exploration of gold, but we also mine uranium, which is used by electric utilities in the generation of electric power.

"Our interest in your reservation is based on our belief that minable gold may exist in the northwest corner of the reservation, between the North Fork and the South Fork of the Milk River. WRI would like to take a closer look at that region, conduct further exploration. We'd get set up over the winter, then, depending on the weather, begin next spring."

At that, a strikingly good-looking, braided man who'd been standing at the back of the room, stepped forward and interrupted him.

"What do you mean *further* exploration? That would indicate you'd already done some preliminary exploration, and if that's the case, what authority did you have?"

Though he fully expected to be under a magnifying glass tonight, the question and the manner in which it was presented took Wilderman aback somewhat. Intuitively, he knew to proceed with caution, that his interrogator was not someone to take lightly. Before he could respond, another member of the audience rose to his feet from the belly of the audience.

"He's been nosing all over the rez," this older and grizzled man, with a head of hair that had never seen a barber, said. "I seen him up there, near Duck Lake, coupla times. He was even nosin' up around Ghost Ridge."

Wilderman recognized the second speaker. The only thing missing was the shotgun that he'd aimed that day at Wilderman's back.

"My understanding is that Ghost Ridge is public property," Wilderman said politely. "If I strayed on to private property last time I was up here, I apologize. It's entirely possible, considering the fact that the only maps of the reservation I could get my hands on were pretty sketchy."

"They got *maps* of the *rez?*" someone called out in an incredulous tone, causing widespread laughter.

Thomas Rose banged the gavel.

"Now I told you, let Mr. Wilderman talk. Then we can ask him questions."

Wilderman nodded Rose's way.

"Thank you. I would be happy to answer your questions. But first I'd like to give you an idea of just what we have in mind when I say WRI wants to do more exploration.

"WRI would conduct an airborne magnetic and electromagnetic survey over the property involved. This, plus detailed mapping, soil geochemistry, and ground geophysics, would enable us to locate drill targets. Somewhere between six and eight diamond drillholes totalling twenty-five hundred to three thousand meters would be drilled. The drillholes enable us to test the down-dip extensions of the zone in which we expect to find gold and to test soil geochemical anomalies to the east and west of the zone."

Looking out, Wilderman couldn't tell whether he'd lost his audience or whether they were just waiting to pounce. The response to his next comment provided his answer.

"WRI would be looking at spending almost half a million

dollars for this exploration program. That's a lot of money. Money we'd be investing in your reservation."

"Investing in our reservation?" It was "the interrogator" again, angry now. "You make it sound like some kind of investment *on our tribe's behalf!* Companies like yours think they can come onto sacred native lands, lease them for a fraction of what they're worth, make millions, then leave the land scarred and so full of dangerous chemicals and pollutants that our cattle and our kids start getting sick. And you try to make it sound like it's some financial plan you're putting in effect for our benefit."

Several "Right-on"s and "Go get him"s could be heard, as across the room heads nodded defiantly and eyes pierced the distance between Wilderman and his audience, which seemed to grow shorter by the moment. Any trace of humor in the meeting hall's air had evaporated.

Wilderman looked to Thomas Rose for order, but Rose simply stared back at him.

"I'm not saying all of those things haven't occurred. They have. And the mining industry is responsible. But WRI doesn't operate that way. Our policy is to have ongoing field surveillance and auditing throughout the mining process." It was a bold lie, but a necessary one. He would deal with it later. "We would work hand in hand with your Environmental Protection Agency to ensure . . ."

Mention of the EPA brought another strong reaction, this time from the man standing to the interrogator's right. He stood several inches taller than the interrogator and looked much meaner.

"All we natives can count on from the EPA is institutional racism. As some of you know, I am a Cheyenne. Northern Cheyenne. We Cheyenne fought for ten years to get the EPA to acknowledge that the tribe is a government, that the Cheyenne have a right to establish their own Tribal Air Quality Implementation Plan." His sharp eyes scanned the group and Wilderman recognized that in both men, he was up against skilled orators. "If we let him tell us that the EPA is going to look out for us and our reservations, we're going to become the proverbial sheep being led to slaughter. We learned long ago that as a people, we have few allies. The EPA certainly isn't one of them."

Between the two men at the back of the room, it was clear the crowd was becoming agitated.

"What about Duck Lake?" someone called out. "And all the rivers? Mining'll kill all the fish. Poison all the wildlife. We'll all go hungry."

Another voice jumped in.

"My ancestors are buried up in that area. I don't want anybody messin' up there."

Wilderman knew it was a pivotal moment. He was about to lose them altogether.

"Please," he said, lifting his hand in the air like a cop stopping traffic. "Let's reason together. I *hear* what you're saying. I'm not unaware of this industry's track record. And I know the EPA has let many Native Americans down. But does that mean that change is impossible?"

"Unlikely," someone opined loudly.

"Unlikely and impossible are two different things. Change is not only possible, but in this situation, we realize it's *essential*. All I'm asking is for you to hear me out. We have some basic facts here that I think we need to lay out. Give me a few more minutes of your time. They could turn out to be the most wisely spent minutes of your collective lives."

Without giving anyone time to object, he continued.

"Fact number one. The world, this nation in particular, is heavily dependent upon gold. It's used as currency and as a basis for international monetary transactions. It's used in coins and jewelry, photography, dentistry, and now, it's even being used in biological research and the treatment of cancer. I know what you're thinking: Why do we care, because chances are none of these uses are high on any of your priority lists."

For the first time, Wilderman saw that he'd managed to elicit a smile or two.

"Here's why you care: because of fact number two. A fact that the minutes from the last meeting illustrated quite painfully. Your tribe needs money. Your children desperately need a new school. You all need better road maintenance. And at the risk of being impertinent, I'd say you could also use a new facility for your headquarters."

He could see he was beginning to get their attention now.

"The discovery and mining of gold on your reservation can give you all that. Your new school. Better roads, better health care and facilities. The fact is, my company will continue mining gold. If it's not here, it will be somewhere else. Why shouldn't you be the ones to benefit? Along with WRI, of course. There's no doubt we will reap benefits—that's our business. But there's enough to go around. We can address your concerns. Each and every one of them. But why turn your backs on what could be a winning situation for both parties?"

"Bullshit," one of the men from the back of the room— the one without braids—cried out. "He's full of shit. Don't you see?"

Wilderman felt a dash of satisfaction, and hope, at seeing one of his adversaries step off his intellectual soapbox and resort to the use of profanity. Both emotion and reasoning could be powerful tools with a group like this, but the expressions on most the faces in front of him told Wilderman that, with a little luck, calm logic and reasoning might just have a chance of winning the day.

Seeming to sense the peril, the braided man placed a restraining hand on the speaker's arm and stepped forward.

"Clyde's right. This is classic manipulation, textbook. Promises of wealth, enough money to fix all our problems. It's a technique these companies have used for over a century. *We must not let ourselves be fooled by it.* Listen to what he's promising. Then look back at our history. Since when have the promises made to our people been kept? Each and every one of you in this room knows all about promises. We can't even trust our trustee—the federal government—to keep its promises. That's why we're filing a class action suit against the BIA. We're suing them for a billion dollars."

The room erupted in cheers at this announcement.

Monty lifted a fist into the air, then continued, "It's time we get what's coming to us. Whenever we've leased our lands to companies like WRI, we never see the money we're promised anyway. The only ones getting rich from reservation lands are non-Indians. But that's all going to change with this lawsuit. We're going to teach the rest of the world what it costs to cheat us. Millions, maybe billions, of dollars. In the meantime, we can't keep repeating our mistakes."

More cheers resulted in three loud *thwacks* of Thomas Rose's gavel.

As the room quieted, the low rumble of a throat being cleared turned Wilderman's head back to the front of the room.

It had come from a wide-faced, portly man seated at the end of the council member's table opposite where Wilderman stood.

He "hrumphed" again loudly, waiting for the complete attention of everyone in the room.

"Seems to me we're puttin' the cart in front of the horse here," he said.

MONTY FELT THINGS were going well until old Rock Peacock opened his mouth.

"How's that, Rock?" Thomas Rose wanted to know.

"Well, we're all getting into some kind of a frenzy over something we don't rightly know for sure yet." Rock squinted in the direction of the audience. "Whether there's even gold on the reservation."

He turned and measured Wilderman with his large brown eyes.

"Let me ask you something. How much damage does that drilling you were talking about a few minutes ago do? And don't go getting tricky with me cause you can bet that we're gonna do some looking into all of this. We want honest answers here."

"Where are you coming from, Rock?" Monty could hardly contain himself. *What the hell was Rock trying to do?* "That's what all this is about. We don't *want* them drilling on our land. Period. Aren't you listening to what's been said here tonight?"

"Do me a favor, Monty. Let me ask my question. You're the one who teaches our kids about what our rights are. And I know damn well I have the right to ask this man any question I please. It's time to let someone else do some talking." He paused, as if waiting for more grief from Monty. When none came, he continued. "Here's how I see it. It's the council's job to take care of our tribe. That takes money. More than we have now. That means that we have a responsibility to give serious consideration to any financial opportunities that come our way. I'd say maybe we're shirking our duty if we don't even take this thing to a level where we find out if there *is* any gold to be fighting about."

"It's the council's responsibility to listen to the people," Monty declared from the back of the room.

"What's your problem, Monty? Now shut that big trap of yours up for a couple minutes and let me finish. We're only talking about a couple of holes here. No one's even *thinking* about letting them actually start mining. If and when that happened, it'd be down the road some. I don't see the harm of finding out just what the facts are. *If,* that is, this man can tell us this exploration plan of theirs wouldn't harm our land."

Wilderman jumped quickly on the life raft tossed him.

"The environmental impact of the tests we'd be conducting, including the drilling, would be negligible. I can bring you photos of other sites where we've done the same thing, put you in contact with people who can verify what I'm saying."

"If that's true," Rock said, "what's wrong with finding out just what we're sitting on? Good God, we all know we need some way to produce income on this rez. I'm as concerned as any of you about taking care of our Mother Earth—she is sacred to all of us. But we've been trying to find a way of bringing industry up here. The tribally owned bank is a great idea, something we're all proud of. But the truth is, we don't know if it's gonna even make it, and if it *does* make an impact financially, it's gonna take a while. We got no jobs to speak of, other than the pencil plant and the seasonal stuff during the summer. I mean, how can we afford not to at least take a look at this?"

Monty could literally see the tension in Clyde Birdseye's body as he stepped forward to respond.

"The Cheyenne have sacrificed many things to protect our homelands. We, too, would like new schools and better housing. If you think *this* is the answer, think again. Many years ago, the BIA, the same trustee you Blackfeet would be dealing with, leased over half our land to coal companies for stripmining. They sold the coal for eleven cents a ton. No environmental safeguards were put in the leases. We spent the next fifteen years fighting to get those leases voided. And during that time, conditions on our reservation did not improve, I can assure you. But we have decided that we would rather live without roads or indoor plumbing than allow any more desecration of our lands."

"This is Blackfeet territory," a voice called out, "not Cheyenne."

Monty had cautioned Clyde not to bring too much attention to the fact that he was not a Blackfeet. He should have known Clyde would find it impossible to keep his mouth shut.

"The Cheyenne are our brothers," Monty said calmly. "And Clyde here is my cousin. That gives him an interest in what we do here. If we Indians don't stand together, if we let the white man divide us on the basis of where we live or what tribe we belong to, we'll never have a chance to change things."

A young woman rose from the front row.

"I know this won't make me a whole lot of friends, but I have three kids at home. The oldest starts school next year. And I want them to have a better life than me. I never finished high school. Got pregnant and started havin' babies. That's not what I want for my kids. I want them to go to a good school, one that will help them make somethin' of themselves. If a gold mine on the reservation can do that for my kids, I'm all for it."

"Maybe you oughta just move off the rez, then," someone called out.

Another bang of the gavel indicated Thomas Rose had decided it was time to take back control of the meeting.

"Now all of you were welcome here tonight. You're always welcome at our council meetings. But the council will make this decision. We've heard your input. Now it's time to put this thing to a vote."

"No way, Thomas." Monty was halfway down the aisle before Rose had finished proclaiming his intention to put the drilling to a council vote. "This is too important to the whole tribe for the council to handle it alone. I demand a tribal referendum."

"Another word from you, Monty, and you're out of here. Understand?"

"The six of you have no right to make this decision alone." It was Clyde, right behind Monty.

Pandemonium was beginning to break out and Thomas Rose knew it.

"Where's the sheriff?" he called, scanning the room.

An imposing figure, clad in brown police uniform, stepped

out from the shadow of the back corner of the room.

"Okay, Monty," Bud Wolfkill said, approaching Monty and Clyde. Bud had been a linebacker in high school, and a friend for most of Monty's life. Still, it was apparent he was about to put duty ahead of friendship. "You two are outta here."

Clyde twirled around to face Bud, raising his fists as though ready to put up a fight.

"Cool it," Monty told him. "You don't want to mess with Bud."

The last thing Monty heard, before being ushered out of the hall, was Thomas Rose telling the rest of the group that the next person who opened his mouth would end up out on the sidewalk.

With Monty and Clyde.

THE MEETING HAD already started when Isabel slipped into the back of the packed hall. Jim Robinson, a patient, turned to see Isabel standing just inside the doorway and rose from the last row of chairs, insisting that she take his seat. Isabel noticed Monty Four Bear, standing along the back wall, in conversation with the same loathsome companion he'd had at the clinic the day of their protest, and felt grateful when he didn't notice her.

The number of Blackfeet in attendance surprised Isabel. Years ago, at her father's urging, she'd attended a similar public hearing in Wenatchee. Of course the proposed mining site that time had not been located on a reservation. Only a handful of locals had shown up to hear the proposal. With the exception of the objections raised by her father and two of his friends from the Sierra Club who had accompanied them, it went through without a hitch. Yuppies, she'd decided, had better things to worry about than driving a hundred miles across the Cascades to express concern over the environment.

Within minutes of watching Tony Wilderman at work, Isabel came to the conclusion that WRI had sent their best man for the job of negotiating with the Blackfeet. Wilderman was slick, playing on the economic poverty on the reservation, making clear what WRI's mine could do to turn life around for the reservation's inhabitants. Isabel took an instant dislike to the man and what he stood for.

Monty Four Bear was equally reprehensible. But at least this time she shared his passion for protecting the reservation from the decimation of WRI's mining.

Had the same kind of passion driven Monty to try to stop the clinical trial? For the first time, the possibility that Monty was someone truly driven by the desire to protect his people and culture entered Isabel's consciousness.

Monty and Clyde's ouster from the meeting had broken the backbone of the opposition. In near silence, the audience watched as the council approved WRI's proposed exploration by a four-to-two vote. Attached to the approval were two criteria required by the tribal council: that an agent designated by the council have access at all times to the drill sites, and that the approval could be withdrawn at any time and for any reason.

Wilderman had in turn insisted upon only one condition. In consideration for its investment, WRI wanted a right of first refusal in the event the tribe did, indeed, decide to proceed with mining. WRI did not want another mining company coming in and out-negotiating them for a lease after they'd spent half a million dollars finding the gold.

"Seems fair enough to me," Thomas Rose said. "What do the rest of you think?"

Anxious to dispose of the mining issue altogether and adjourn for the night, the rest of the members had agreed and the meeting was about to come to an end when Isabel's eyes settled upon the back of a head in the second row.

How could she have missed it—the sandy hiccup in row after row of black locks? But the man to whom the precisely styled waves belonged sat at the end, near the wall, and Isabel's attention had been focused ahead, on the speakers.

Thomas Rose had barely begun to announce the results of the vote when Isabel jumped up and began excusing herself, stepping on several toes in the process, but not stopping to apologize. Panicked, she pushed open the door at the back of the room, rushed down the hallway to the exit, and, stepping outside, came face to face with Monty Four Bear and Clyde Birdseye.

"You," Birdseye said. It was an accusation.

Monty stepped forward. "What happened in there?"

Isabel glanced over her back nervously.

"The council approved the exploration proposal," she said breathlessly, without stopping, but as she passed, Birdseye grabbed her by the arm.

"That probably pleases you, doesn't it?"

"Let me go," Isabel said.

Monty grabbed Birdseye's forearm and jerked it off Isabel's.

People had begun filing out the door. Without another word, Isabel turned and ran across the parking lot. She was so shaken that when she started to cross the two-lane highway to the Dairy Queen, she nearly stepped into the path of an oncoming car.

"Watch where you're going," its occupant screamed at her, swerving into the next lane, which, fortunately, was empty. As the older model Dodge retreated, through its back window Isabel saw a hand raised in an obscene gesture.

TOO RATTLED TO go home, Isabel stopped by Gus's.

It was obvious from his disheveled hair and shirt and the way he blinked at the light above the front door that she'd awakened him from a nap in front of the fireplace.

"I didn't mean to disturb you."

"Aw, nonsense," Gus said. "I can sleep anytime. Me and

Grunt would love some company, wouldn't we Grunt?"

Grunt pushed a wet nose into Isabel's hand, his body nearly convulsing with excitement at her arrival. She crouched down and threw her arms around the dog's thick neck. Deep folds of extra skin around his forehead and neck gave Grunt a Sharpei-ish look. Isabel buried her face in his warm fur.

She stayed that way—unable to face Gus, for she could no longer hide her emotions—until she felt the old man's hand on her shoulder.

"Okay, girl. You been lookin' like a scared rabbit lately. It's time you told me what's goin' on."

Isabel looked up into Gus's kind eyes and fought back tears.

"It's a long story, Gus."

"Well how 'bout I get each of us a glass of wine and you can tell it to me?"

They settled on either end of the long leather couch with Grunt in between them, his head taking up all of Isabel's lap. She stroked it as she told Gus the entire story, starting with when she first met Alistair, in med school.

For the most part, Gus maintained an expression that was difficult to read. But half an hour later, when Isabel reached the final days of her marriage—the events that led to her packing her bags and leaving town—he did not attempt to hide his shock.

"Someone shoulda beat the livin' daylights out of the son of a bitch," he huffed. "And you mean to tell me he's tracked you down now?"

"Yes. With the help of my mother."

"Some mother."

Isabel managed a half smile.

"She doesn't know much about what happened, Gus. I never told her."

She wondered what she saw in Gus's eyes now, which

studied her. Pity? Disapproval? She could not bear to let him down.

"So go on. What happened tonight to bring you to my door?"

"Let me backtrack a little first. Remember that night I saw you out by the mailbox? When you told me the mailman's mad at me?"

Gus nodded.

"Well, he'd called me that night. He was just leaving a message when I came in from work. He made it sound like he knew where I lived, but I was pretty sure he was just playing one of his sick games."

"I remember that night. I *knew* somethin' was wrong. But you wouldn't come clean."

"I guess I thought that if I ignored it, it might just go away."

"But it didn't."

"No. It didn't." Isabel thought back to the shock that had run through her entire body just thirty minutes earlier. "He was there tonight, Gus. At the tribal council meeting." The wine in Isabel's glass jumped with her shaky hands. "I saw him."

"Did he see you?"

"No. I'm sure he didn't. I got out of there the minute I recognized him."

"You're sure it was him?"

"I only saw the back of his head, but, yes, I'm sure."

Gus watched her closely, his brow furrowed into three deep folds, as she stroked Grunt.

"Why would he go to a tribal meeting? You think it has something to do with what happened between you?"

Isabel shook her head.

"I have no idea. That's what I keep asking myself. What's he up to now?"

"Well, one thing's for damn sure. You're staying here tonight. With me and Grunt."

"I really don't think that's necessary, Gus. Alistair can't know where I live. If he did, he'd have shown up at the cabin by now. And I've got that gun you gave me. I've had it loaded ever since that night."

"You listen to me, Isabel McLain. You ain't goin' nowhere tonight. You hear? And in the morning, I'm gonna find that SOB and send him packing."

"Good God, Gus, I don't want to drag you into this. Promise you won't do anything foolish."

He smiled at her then, easing her worries, and placed his misshapen hand on top of where hers rested, on Grunt's back.

"Don't you worry. How much trouble can an arthritic old man get into anyhow?"

"Knowing you, plenty."

This comment clearly pleased Gus. The gleam in his eyes erased a decade, and Isabel had a momentary glimpse of a younger man full of righteousness, piss, and vinegar.

"You're really something, Gus Dearing," she said. "You know that?"

"In my day maybe," he chuckled. "Now, how about a little more wine?"

Thanksgiving was three days away and they made plans to spend it together. Isabel had invited Gus and Grunt to dinner at her cabin. They were in the middle of planning the menu when Isabel closed her eyes to rest them for just a few seconds.

Sometime after midnight, she awoke to find herself still on Gus's couch. The fire had burned down to a crimson glow of smoldering embers. Grunt, stretched out the length of the couch, which had been vacated by Gus, snored loudly. Before going to bed, Gus had covered Isabel with a lambswool Pendleton blanket.

Shaking her head to clear it, Isabel stretched and stood, then folded the blanket. Then, tiptoeing to keep from waking Gus, she went to the kitchen where she scribbled a note:

Gus, Went home. Promise I'll be fine. Please don't worry. Love, Is

She left it on the kitchen table, then stepped into the cold night air and turned the key in her Jeep's ignition.

Maybe it was because she was there, at Gus's house, that his earlier warning came to her just then.

"Those tires of yours are gettin' bald," he'd told her the other day when she'd run into him in town. "You better get your studs on. Winter's gonna hit any day now and you'll be in a heap of trouble trying to get up to your cabin with those."

"I know. My snow tires are stored in the shed. I've been meaning to bring them into town with me and have them put on," Isabel had answered.

As she eased the car out of the driveway, she hoped that Gus was sleeping soundly. If he heard her leaving, he'd jump up and try to make her wait 'til morning.

That thought undoubtedly explained why Gus's words of warning had sprung to mind.

Or maybe Isabel simply had a premonition.

CHAPTER

SEVENTEEN

THE ROAD BETWEEN Gus and Isabel's houses hugged the shores of the Two Medicine River, and while it provided spectacular views during the day, Isabel knew to exercise caution at night. Montana's lack of guardrails along roadways that dropped off steeply had shocked her when she'd first moved to the reservation, but like everything else, she'd long since grown accustomed to the status quo.

Since she still felt sleepy and there was no moon to supplement her headlights tonight, Isabel proceeded even more tentatively than usual, her Jeep kicking up gravel as it began the long climb up the last ridge before the turnoff to her cabin. She hadn't warmed the car up, so its interior was frigid, and for a moment she regretted leaving the warmth of Grunt's company and Gus's couch. The fear prompted by seeing Alistair had shrunk to a manageable size. For the first time, she admitted to herself that it was just possible she'd been mistaken. After all, she'd only seen the back of a head. Maybe if she hadn't rushed out of the half crazy, she'd have discovered it was someone else. Alistair wasn't the only man with curly blond hair. She was even beginning to feel a bit silly for reacting so irrationally. She could hardly wait to get home and climb under her down comforter.

She became aware of the presence of a car behind her when, rounding the first of a series of S curves, she glanced in the rearview mirror. Had she imagined it, or was that a flash of light? She looked again. Her rearview mirror reflected a near total blackness outside. But then it happened again, and with a start, Isabel made out the outline of another vehicle, following dangerously close behind her. Something, perhaps her taillights as she rounded the curve, or a break in the cloud cover, had reflected off its front window.

At the realization that the vehicle was traveling without lights—an act of pure insanity on this road at night—her heart began to pound so ferociously that she fleetingly wondered which presented more danger: cardiac arrest, or this inexplicable company?

The answer to the question became clear momentarily, when Isabel slowed to round the next curve. A jolt, shockingly rough and unexpected, threw her entire body violently forward, into the razorlike restraints of the Jeep's frayed seatbelt.

Now that the vehicle had announced its presence by ramming her, its lights—blinding in their proximity and the mirror's reflection—ignited, making it impossible for Isabel to see her pursuer and even difficult for her to see the road in front of her.

Keep your head. Keep your head.

The isolation and solitude of her chosen home, which had previously held such allure to Isabel, now meant that there was nowhere to turn for help.

Pushing down on the accelerator, Isabel managed to put several car lengths between them. But just as she crested the hill, the increasing intensity of the glare in the rearview mirror warned her that her pursuer was about to ram her again.

Isabel tensed.

The hit sent the Jeep skyward. Isabel's grasp on the steering wheel became viselike. She could not allow herself to lose control. This time, prepared, she managed to ride with it. As the Jeep thudded back to earth, Isabel gunned it again. Her only hope was to outrun her anonymous predator.

In the next few seconds, it seemed she was gaining ground. The pursuing vehicle's lights receded, first just a couple car lengths, then more, as much as the length of a basketball court. Were they playing with her? Giving her a false sense of hope? Or did her old Jeep actually have enough life left to outrun the other vehicle? Choosing to believe the latter, Isabel began to formulate a plan. Ahead, several miles past the turnoff to her cabin, there was a ranch-house. If she could beat them there, she would arrive with horn blasting, drive through the fencing surrounding the corral if she had to to get their attention.

But suddenly, Isabel recognized her precise location on the dangerous switchback road. As that realization hit, instantaneously, she lifted the foot she'd pressed to the accelerator and slammed it down, hard, on the brake pedal.

They were racing toward a hairpin turn.

The realization had come too late. Her bald tires spun wildly, failing to gain purchase on the pebble-strewn road, and Isabel's Jeep began sliding sideways into the turn. Isabel knew this section of the road well, had even pulled over one gorgeous August morning and gotten out of the Jeep to pick flowers and walk the dozen steps to the precipice, so spectacular was the view.

It was just ahead that she'd stood, the pinnacle of the road that separated her house from Gus's, to gaze down at the frothing waters of the Two Medicine, two hundred feet below. She'd marveled that day at the fact that such a perilous section of the roadway, which ran so dangerously close to the steep dropoff, was not protected by guardrails.

Behind her, the oncoming vehicle had also slowed.

Heart pounding, her breath held, Isabel brought her full weight and strength to bear on the brake pedal. As if in slow motion, the Jeep, moving sideways now, continued its slide. When it reached the hairpin, the smooth ride across the roadway gave way to a shock of bumps. The Jeep was on the shoulder now, crossing the stretch where, throughout the summer, wildflowers had enchanted Isabel on her way to work.

And then a miracle occurred. Just as Isabel reached for the door handle to try to jump free, the Jeep came to a standstill. Snapping her head forward, Isabel saw that the headlights pierced nothing but the blackness of night. They illuminated not a single object.

The Jeep had stopped its uncontrolled slide at the very edge of the dropoff.

So terrified was she of the impending freefall, that Isabel had momentarily forgotten about her pursuer.

But a nudge, softer this time than the previous two, changed that.

And with the door partially open and Isabel grasping frantically for the release on her seat belt, the Jeep toppled over the rocky edge to the rushing waters below.

● ● ●

WHEN ISABEL CLOSED the front door behind her, a disappointed Grunt padded down the hallway to Gus's bedroom. Nudging the partially closed door with his nose, Grunt entered the room and took a flying leap onto Gus's big bed, where the big dog routinely slept alongside his beloved master.

"Settle down now," Gus groused sleepily.

Then he heard the car door slam. Jumping up, Gus hobbled to the window in time to see Isabel's Jeep backing out of his driveway. His creaky, arthritic knees would not allow him time to stop her, so Gus stood watching his friend back from the driveway onto the road.

Isabel had just disappeared down the road, heading north toward her cabin, and Gus was about to turn away when the floodlight on the arch over the mouth of the driveway picked up a surprising sight: a car—some kind of sport utility vehicle—following a short distance behind Isabel's Jeep. What startled Gus was the fact that it did not have its lights on, though once it passed, he could see brakelights, indicating the driver was deliberately hanging back.

It usually took a good thirty minutes for Gus to shake the early morning kinks and aches out of his bones, but now he moved quickly.

"Come on, Grunt," he called, grabbing a rifle from the antique oak gun cabinet that filled one wall along the foyer.

Holding the door open for Grunt, Gus climbed into his pickup and punched the gas pedal, shooting backward down his long drive. In his entire life, Gus had never had a car accident. He prided himself in his driving skills. Last time he went in to renew his license, old Esther Robank, who'd had a crush on him for as long as Gus could remember, winked as she told him his record was so spotless that she'd reissue the new license without requiring Gus to take the test all seniors over the age of seventy were required to take.

But adrenalin and age now combined to distort his reflexes, and by the time Gus realized he'd turned the wheel just a smattering too far to the right, it was too late to stop the truck from going off the drive and into soft, damp earth, where it lodged.

"Damn it to hell," he cried, rocking the truck between first and reverse, time and again. This only served to deepen the rut Gus had created. As soon as he realized the pickup was there to stay, he jumped out and half hobbled, half ran into the house for the keys to what he affectionately called his "beater"—a 1963 International Harvester Traveler.

The Harvester fired up on Gus's first try.

Frustrated by the delay, Gus tried to make up time as he followed in the direction of Isabel's cabin, taking curves faster than he'd ever dared before.

It was when he was approaching the last switchback to Isabel's turnoff that Gus came upon the bizarre sight of a beam of light shooting skyward. It originated beyond the cliff and lit up several tree tops along the cottonwoods lining a portion of the ridge.

As Gus pulled the Harvester over to the side of the road and jumped out, his sense of apprehension soared.

Grunt disappeared over the edge before Gus could stop him.

When Gus reached the spot of Grunt's descent, a slippery, steeply sloped and rocky section that, under other circumstances, Gus would never get near, it was with a sense of absolute terror that he recognized Isabel's Jeep, twenty to thirty feet below.

It had rolled onto its roof, and now lay wedged between the rocky surface of the hill—a thirty degree slope—and a stand of three medium-size cottonwoods, its front end pointing toward where Gus stood, the lights piercing the sky.

"Oh my God, Izzie."

Gus could hear Grunt's whines as he nosed around the car, which looked to be perched none too securely against the trees—which themselves looked none too sturdy.

Gus started down, but loose rocks immediately took his

feet out from under him. He grabbed the bare branch of a thistleweed to stop his descent. He would never be able to negotiate the steep terrain without help.

"Isabel," he yelled, cupping his mouth with the free hand. *"Isabel!"*

Grunt had by now reappeared at his side, and as the devoted dog hovered nearby, Gus managed to climb back to safety by pushing himself along the rocky ground on his rear end. Once back on solid ground, Gus rushed to the Harvester and opened the back door. The backseat and floor were strewn with trademarks of the ranching life—empty cans of chewing tobacco, worn out leather gloves, boots, used tubes of worming meds, a horse pick, several used shoes, newspapers. Gus rummaged frantically through it all until finally, hidden deep, on the floor, he found what he was looking for. A coil of rope.

Now the question was: Would it be long enough?

Gus started up the Harvester, backed onto the road, eased it forward, then backed it on to the shoulder again, leaning out the open door to watch his progress. He would need every inch of that rope to reach Isabel. That meant he had to back the Harvester as close as he dared to the edge of the precipice. When the ground illuminated by his taillights broke away into blank space, he stopped and pulled hard on the old vehicle's emergency brake. He tried not to think about the fact that for years, he'd been meaning to replace the brakes—one of those things that he'd just never gotten around to.

One thing a rancher learns just about as well as the rest of the world learns such basic tasks as buttoning a shirt is the art of tying knots. Luckily, like everything else littering the backseat of the Harvester, this rope had seen plenty of use, which made working with it easier. Deftly, Gus formed a slip-knot and looped it over the trailer hitch, then he snaked his hands to the other end of the coil and knotted it around his waist. He realized then that he'd forgotten something. Straddling the rope as he walked, he returned to the backseat and grabbed two mismatched gloves.

He gathered the loose length of the rope and coiled it as best he could, then, shooing Grunt out of the way, Gus began his descent. His weight supported by the rope, he leaned into the void behind him and slowly walked his way backward, down toward where Isabel lay in her Jeep.

If you're listening to me up there, please give me enough rope to reach Izzie.

The prayer almost worked. The rope ran out less than two yards from the overturned Jeep.

"*Izzie!*" Gus yelled.

Grunt whined and pawed at the vehicle.

"*Izzie.*" Gus dropped onto his rear end, bracing himself against gravity with his feet, and cursed as his damn fingers made untying the knot around his midsection difficult. But soon he was free, and as he inched his way to the Jeep, scooting on his rear end, he finally heard it. A soft cry.

"Gus?"

He covered the last yard of ground in a heartbeat.

"Izzie. I'm here. Don't move. Do you hear?"

The cottonwoods against which the Jeep was braced were leaning at close to ninety degree angles from the hillside, so strained were they by the weight. Gus surveyed the situation. The driver's side was wedged against the trees. He would have to get to Isabel through the passenger door.

The roots of the trees had formed something of a woven platform filled with loose soil as they'd grown. Gus kneeled on it as he struggled to get the Jeep's door open. But it was lodged tight against rocks and exposed roots.

"Turn your head, Izzie," he said. "I've got to kick this window out. Try to cover your face, do you hear me?"

"Yes. Go ahead, Gus. Just get me out of here."

Relief flooded Gus at hearing her speak. She was conscious, and understandably terrified.

Standing, he kicked out the window with his boot, then

stamped along its lower edge—the upper edge, were it up-right—trying to eliminate any shards. He would have to pull Isabel out through it.

When he dropped back to his knees, he stuck his head in the window and finally saw her.

"Good God, Isabel," he cried at the sight of her hanging upside down. He was inside now, crawling to her across the inside surface of the roof. "Can you find your seat belt? I'm here, I'll catch you."

He reached up to help her, but then heard her say, "I've got it. *Here I go.*"

She tumbled into his outstretched arms and as she did so, they both heard it. The unmistakable crack as one of the trees snapped—their movement, and Gus's added weight, had strained the slender trees to their limit.

CHAPTER

EIGHTEEN

GRUNT BEGAN BARKING, and as Gus inched back out the broken window he could feel canine teeth on his pant leg, pulling.

"Hold still," he whispered to Isabel, as though raising their voices might be enough to send the Jeep toppling down the hillside.

Isabel slung an arm around Gus's neck and began using her feet to propel herself in the direction of the open window.

Gus had one knee out of the Jeep and on the rocky ground, when the roof began to lift under them.

Pulling her free of the car, Gus fell back with Isabel in his arms. They both lay still, in horror, watching as the Jeep swayed once, twice—its weight supported now by just two trees and the remainder of the one that had broken. Then it grew still.

"Let's get you out of here," Gus said, turning to look for the rope.

QUESTIONS OF JURISDICTION were nothing new to Bud Wolfkill. When the call came in, he'd known the incident occurred just beyond the boundaries of the reservation. Other members of the tribal police force might have used that as an excuse to kick back and let the county sheriff's deputies respond, but not Bud. East Glacier County was understaffed, over one hundred miles long and eighty miles wide. Chances of a sheriff's deputy being in the vicinity were remote.

"You're sure you don't need to go to the hospital in Cutbank?" he asked the lady doctor. He'd heard plenty about Isabel McLain, and had seen her earlier that evening at the tribal council meeting, but this was the first time he'd actually met her.

"I'm sure. After all, I am a doctor. I'll be sore for a couple days, but I don't have any broken bones or internal injuries."

"Well, from what Gus here's told me, it's a miracle you don't. Soon as we're done, I'll head on up the road to see for myself."

"By now, that old Jeep might be floatin' down the river," Gus said.

Wolfkill grunted, *"Hrrmphf."*

"You're sure it was deliberate? That someone forced you off the road?"

"Absolutely. As I told you, he came up behind me with the lights out. Then he rammed me hard. Twice."

"I can vouch for the lights being out," Gus interjected again. "That's what really spooked me about it. Drivin' around in town, you might not know you forgot to put your lights on, but out here at night? Nobody *forgets* to turn 'em on."

"Wouldn't think so," Wolfkill said. He turned his dark, sleepy eyes back to Isabel. "So go on. You were trying to outrun them when you reached that hairpin." He looked back at Gus. "We used to call it Suicide Elbow."

"Yes. I'd slammed on the brakes when I realized I was approaching the turn, but it was too late—my car kept sliding toward the edge. But then, finally, it stopped and I thought I was safe. Next thing I knew, he'd driven up over the shoulder behind me and he was nudging me over the edge. I tried to jump out of the Jeep, but I couldn't get my seat belt undone. That's the last thing I remember."

Wolfkill scribbled a word here and there on a notepad, more to give himself time to think than anything else. He didn't know that many white women. Most those he did weren't to be trusted, 'cept of course Allison Becker, his son's fifth-grade teacher. But Ms. Becker was the exception to the rule. He'd seen too many white women who came on to the reservation to drink and look for good-looking Indian men to get laid by. Maybe it wasn't fair to judge them all by the ones he'd come in contact with. This Dr. McLain didn't seem like the hysterical type. And just about everyone who went to the clinic had good things to say about her.

Still her story was pretty hard to believe. Bud had never seen anything like that in all his years on the reservation. Over the years, he'd responded to more than his share of incidents of violence. Hell, violent crime rates, even murder, were almost twice the national average on the rez, but they were always the result of personal relationships, too much booze, emotions getting out of hand, that kind of stuff. This kind of faceless violence, well, it was something entirely different.

"You keep saying 'he.' Did you get a look at who was driving this car?"

"No."

"Have any idea who might do something like this to you? Enemies, patients who might be mad at you, something like that? Pretty hard to believe this was something random."

"It's not random . . ." Gus said, eyeing Isabel. "Tell him."

"Tell me *what*?" Wolfkill wanted to know.

Gus had fixed his gaze on Isabel.

"Tell him what you told me earlier tonight. About your ex-husband."

Wolfkill put the paper down on his knee and turned his complete attention on Isabel.

"Tell me about this ex-husband of yours."

The subject appeared to cause the lady doctor distress.

"We're not divorced yet. He's been showing up here, on the reservation. A couple times recently. I saw him tonight, at the council meeting."

"Has he contacted you? Threatened you in some way?"

"No."

"Do you have a restraining order against him?"

"No."

"Recognize the car?"

"*No,*" Isabel cried. "I did *not* recognize the car. But don't you think it's a bit of a coincidence that the same night he shows up at the meeting, I end up pushed over the fucking cliff?"

Wolfkill saw that he'd pushed some sensitive buttons with this line of questioning.

"Ma'am, I can understand how frightening that must have been for you. And it's apparent you're not very happy about this ex-husband of yours showing up here on the rez, which I can also understand, but I can't arrest a man based on coincidence."

"You can look for him," Gus interjected, "can't you? Find out what the hell he's doing here in Browning."

"I certainly can do that. And I will. But it's a free country. If she doesn't have a restraining order against him and he's not breaking the law, he's entitled to be here. All I'm saying is we'd need a lot more evidence than that to bring him in."

"Well then why don't you deputize me," Gus huffed, shifting impatiently in his chair, "and I'll get you that evidence?"

Wolfkill stifled the urge to smile.

"Now, Gus, I doubt this lady wants you goin' gettin' yourself in trouble on her account. You leave this matter to the sheriff's office."

Isabel McLain, who'd paced back and forth during the interview, stopped and placed her hand on Gus's shoulder.

"He's right, Gus. I need you right here."

Gus's arthritic fingers, balled into fists, looked ready to strike out. He glanced from Isabel to Wolfkill.

"You find the SOB who did this to her, you hear?"

"I'll do my best," Wolfkill answered.

CHAPTER

NINETEEN

BUD WOLFKILL WAS clearly ill at ease. It wasn't just that his large frame dwarfed the metal folding chair in which he now sat, the lack of leg space between the chair and Isabel's desk forcing his knees up at unnatural angles. He also just happened to be someone who was not comfortable sitting still. Especially when he had nothing worthwhile to report and his constituent was clearly not happy with him.

"But it's been almost a month," Isabel said, frustration echoing in her voice.

"I know that, Dr. McLain, but we still haven't come up with any evidence that it was your ex-husband who tried to run you off Suicide Elbow that night. Two officers from the police department over there in Seattle questioned him. He admitted being on the reservation that day. Going to the tribal council meeting. But he says he drove straight back to the lodge in East Glacier after the meeting."

"What about his car? Did they check his car?"

"It was a rental. He couldn't produce the rental records. All he could tell them was that he picked it up at one of the rental counters at the Kalispell airport. I've sent a guy over there to try to track the car down and see if there's any evidence indicating it could have been the car that rammed your Jeep, but you said it was a sport utility vehicle. Most of them have bumpers like steel tanks. Wouldn't do much damage to give your Jeep a little bump."

"It was more than a *little bump.*"

"Sorry. Poor choice of words." Wolfkill pushed a hand through his head of thick black hair, as if stalling for time. "Unfortunately, your ex also has an alibi for later that night, the time you and Gus said the accident took place."

It didn't escape Isabel's attention that Bud was now calling it an "accident."

"An alibi? Like what?"

Wolfkill cleared his throat.

"Umm, a lady friend. Someone who works there at the lodge. She's apparently willing to vouch for him. Says she spent the whole night with him. I talked to her myself."

Wolfkill looked startled when Isabel let loose with a laugh.

"Classic," was all she said.

Wolfkill lumbered to his feet, nervously fingering his brown felt uniform hat.

"I want you to know that we'll keep looking for whoever did this to you. We're not giving up. We'll track down the car he was driving that night, and if there's anything suspicious, we'll bring him in. And his lady friend."

Suddenly his eyes jumped up and to the left, to the half-opened door behind Isabel.

Isabel swiveled in her chair to see Ken MacStirling standing in the hallway.

"Dr. MacStirling," she said, taking a quick glance at her watch. "You're early."

"Sorry about that," MacStirling said. "When I flew in and saw the snow, I decided to give myself plenty of time to drive up from Kalispell—I guess maybe I gave myself a wee bit too much." He eyed Wolfkill. "I can come back in a while, if you'd like."

Wolfkill moved quickly toward the door.

"I'm on my way out," he said. Nodding at Isabel, he added, "We'll get back to you if we find anything else about Dr. Bott."

"Thank you, Officer Wolfkill," Isabel said. "Not just for your work, but for coming here to talk to me in person."

Her words of appreciation seemed to surprise Wolfkill.

"You're welcome, ma'am. And you can call me Bud. Everybody else does."

Ken MacStirling had stepped aside for Wolfkill's passage, but even now, after the brown uniform had disappeared down the hall, MacStirling did not move.

"Please, come in," Isabel said.

MacStirling entered Isabel's office looking confused and took up the seat just vacated by Wolfkill.

"Bott?" he finally blurted out when he could contain himself no more. "*Alistair* Bott?"

"Were you standing out there listening?" Isabel's eyes narrowed in accusation.

"Of course not. All I heard was what that officer just said. That he'd let you know if they found out anything about Dr. Bott. Did he mean Alistair Bott, the cardiologist from Seattle?"

"Dr. MacStirling, the meeting between Officer Wolfkill and myself dealt with private personal business."

"Listen here now, this is my clinical trial," said Mac-

Stirling, furious. "Anything that might affect it *is* bloody well my business."

Suddenly the realization of what MacStirling had to be thinking came to Isabel and she let out a soft groan. He was right. She had no choice but to tell him.

"What?" MacStirling said, his gaze boring through her. "What is it?"

Every ounce of air went out of her as Isabel raised her eyes to meet MacStirling's scrutiny.

"Alistair Bott was my husband," she said softly. "Correction, he still is—until our divorce becomes final."

"Your husband? How can this be? How could I not know this?" MacStirling said, wild eyed.

"Why *would* you?"

"Well, for starters, you should have told me," MacStirling said indignantly.

"I DON'T SEE what my soon-to-be-ex-husband's identity has to do with my heading up the HantaVac study."

"Under ordinary circumstances," MacStirling said, "that might be true. But not when your husband was accused of being paid millions of dollars for studies for which he faked results . . . I heard he even listed patients that had died as study participants! You don't think that's relevant here? That it merits mention?" He shook his head incredulously. "Please tell me he's had nothing to do with the HantaVac study. Is that why the police were here? Something to do with my study?"

"Calm down, Dr. MacStirling. This has nothing to do with *your* study."

"Then what? Why was that officer just here?"

Isabel had always refused to worry about what anyone thought of her. And she guarded her privacy fiercely. But in this instance, she felt a duty to breach both longstanding rules. In all fairness, she couldn't blame MacStirling for his reaction. A scandal like Alistair's could ruin a career. She'd known that all along. But she hadn't let it stop her.

With years of research and the HantaVac study at stake, MacStirling deserved to know the truth.

"Just before Thanksgiving," Isabel began, "a car ran me off the road. Actually, over the cliff. I reported it to the police. I also told them that I believed it was Alistair behind the wheel of that car. Officer Wolfkill was here today to report to me on his investigation."

MacStirling looked even more confused than he had when he first entered the office.

"Why? Even if you're divorcing him, why would your husband want to harm you?"

"Because he blames me for everything that happened."

MacStirling's spine went stiff.

"You mean the clinical trials? *You* were involved? Bott holds you responsible?"

"In a sense, yes."

"Oh my God."

MacStirling dropped his head into his hands, and began rocking back and forth slowly.

Isabel reached over and gently squeezed his shoulder.

"Ken. Listen to me, will you?"

MacStirling raised weary eyes to hers.

"There's a reason my husband blames me for what happened."

The memory was still so fresh, so disturbing. Still something she didn't want to talk about. But now she must.

"He blames me," Isabel continued, with a sigh of resignation, "because I'm the one who turned him in."

CHAPTER

TWENTY

ISABEL HAD KNOWN for some time that something was not right. Alistair was devoting more and more time to conducting clinical drug trials and less to his lucrative surgical practice, yet the new cars, expensive clothes, and high-tech gadgetry—one state-of-the-art laptop was not enough; Alistair had recently come home with two—indicated that money had never flowed more freely. When Alistair called from his car, ten minutes away from their house, and announced he'd just purchased oceanfront property in the Cayman Islands, Isabel's suspicions had driven her upstairs, to the third floor office loft where Alistair was spending more and more time.

"When was the last time you operated on a patient?"

The pleased-with-himself grin he'd worn into the house disappeared as Alistair threw the FedEx package containing the signed real-estate documents for the Cayman property onto the hall table.

"What the hell is that supposed to mean?"

"Just answer my question. When was the last time you did a bypass? Or even *saw* a cardiology patient? I mean, that's what you are, isn't it? A cardiovascular surgeon? Or have you given that up altogether now, to conduct drug studies?"

"Do you ever get tired of riding that moral high horse you're always on?" Alistair said. They were standing in the foyer of their million-dollar home. Isabel had been waiting for him to come in from the garage. "You don't know how easy you have it, working in the ER. Insurance companies aren't tyin' your hands every fuckin' step you try to take. Hell, it was getting to where I couldn't even perform the tests I needed to make a diagnosis."

"That's such a bullshit cop-out," Isabel cried. "I know how maddening managed care has become. I sympathized with you, but that doesn't mean you just quit. That you give up saving lives with those incredible hands of yours—hands that performed miracles—and just sell out to any greedy drug company that comes along and asks you to run a trial for them. Look at this. It just came through on your fax machine. *Read it*," Isabel found herself practically screaming as she shoved a sheet of paper under his nose.

Improve Your Cash Flow
Discover the secret for obtaining more funded studies. List with our service and your name will go out to hundreds of pharmaceutical companies looking for doctors to test their products. Investigator grants average $48,000 per study. Top recruiters can earn as much as $1 million a year.
SO GET BUSY!!

Alistair glanced at the fax, then threw it down with the FedEx.

"Calm down, Isabel. How do you manage to turn every fucking move I make into some loaded issue? How do you think your ER patients would do without drugs? I mean, some guy comes in with a smashed face and you don't have anything to kill the pain. How would that go over? Or a diabetic in shock? And just how do you think those drugs are made possible? Because of studies, that's how. Because of people like me, who conduct them."

"For money." Isabel's chest heaved with each angry breath. "*Bonuses*. There's another fax in there. It says Warner-Bick will increase the four thousand dollars they're already paying you for some diabetes study you're doing to five thousand for every new participant you enroll in the next thirty days. Have you seen that one? It's hard to keep track of them. There's a stack of faxes an inch high. How many of these studies are you doing?"

She'd heard that some doctors were turning away from their private practices to conduct lucrative clinical trials, but she'd had no idea how much money an investigator stood to make. Nor that Alistair had become so heavily involved.

"Pharmaceutical companies are a business. And time is money. They provide incentives to enroll patients as quickly as possible."

"Just what are you doing conducting a study on a diabetes drug anyway? You're a cardiologist. What do you know about diabetes?"

"I could do a diabetes study blindfolded," Alistair answered with undisguised disdain. Then he turned on her. "What are you doing in my office anyway, snooping around my fax machine?"

"Your office? Since when is it your office? We always said that it would be both of ours. But it just so happens my *medical practice,*" she couldn't help but goad him, "doesn't give me time to spend in it."

"That's it. That's why this all gets to you. You resent my success. It drives you crazy to see how well I'm doing." His expression mellowed just enough to test the waters. "I've told you, Is, you can get in on it. All you have to do is start referring your patients to me. Most of these pharmaceutical companies will pay you five hundred dollars just for the referral."

Isabel simply stared at him.

"You've turned patients into a commodity. Money machines."

Disgusted, Alistair stormed up the stairs, into his office, and slammed the door.

They didn't talk for two days after that, which actually

wasn't all that big a jump from their usual state of affairs. Over the past few months, they'd almost made a concerted effort to steer clear of one another.

After that day, when Alistair was out of the house, Isabel began exploring his office, reading the faxes that came through, sometimes dozens in a single day. Her busy work schedule usually meant taking only a twenty-minute lunch at a deli near the hospital, but now she found herself running home for lunch to see what had come in over the fax machine.

Many of the faxes were generic solicitations from drug companies wanting doctors to head new studies or recruit patients for existing studies. Without question, the majority, however, came from the same fax number, and a person named Mary, who Isabel soon surmised to be Alistair's study coordinator for the clinical trials he was already conducting. From what Isabel could see, it appeared that Alistair was involved in no fewer than a dozen trials. He was testing products ranging from angina medications to acne treatments to prostate cancer therapies.

During one such lunch hour, when she was up in Alistair's office, the telephone rang. Isabel picked it up before the third ring, but heard only a dial tone. Thinking the caller must have changed his mind at the last minute or realized he had the wrong number, Isabel hung the phone back up, but then, on an impulse, she picked it up again and this time, heard the interrupted signal that indicated a message had been received. She dialed the access number she always used and punched in her four digit password, but was informed by a mechanical sounding voice that she had no messages.

That couldn't be true—the dial tone clearly indicated they had messages.

Isabel took a closer look at the phone. It wasn't until then that she realized that the phone number written on the plastic-covered plate differed from the number for the rest of the phones in the house. Alistair had apparently installed a separate line into his office without telling her.

She dialed the number written on the plate and immediately, after just one ring, Alistair's voice came on the line.

"This is Dr. Alistair Bott. If you are calling regarding a clinical trial, please feel free to leave a message. If this is a medical emergency, please contact my study coordinator, Mary Pelandini, at 206-282-1789."

Before the beep sounded, Isabel pressed "zero" and was instructed to punch in her password. She tried Alistair's birthdate, 12/14, and was told by the same mechanized voice to try again. Their anniversary, 09/21, received a similar response.

Then she tried 1962, the year Alistair was born, and was immediately informed there was one new message:

"Alistair, this is Mary. Mrs. Hougham's blood pressure keeps rising, ever since she started the study drug. She was already on an antihypertensive when she entered the study, and I added that other one you told me to try, but they're not working either. She's complaining about dizziness. I know she's the last patient we needed to complete this study and get final payment, but I'm wondering whether you want me to drop her. Will you call me back immediately?" There was a pause. "Oh yeah, I also wanted to let you know that I've signed James Burgdorff up for the asthma inhaler study." She chuckled, then added, "Good old James."

Isabel hung up the phone, stunned.

Could they be talking about Bernice Hougham? Bernice was an especially sweet elderly patient Isabel had treated just two months earlier at the hospital emergency room. She'd come in complaining of chest pains. Isabel had run an EKG on her and determined that she was not in danger of imminent cardiac arrest, but her blood pressure had been on the high end, and she'd urged Bernice to see a specialist.

She had not referred Bernice specifically to Alistair. Despite the fact that Isabel considered Alistair one of the city's best cardiovascular specialists, she never referred patients to him, deeming it a conflict of interest. If, however, a patient or coworker enquired about Alistair, Isabel felt confident and comfortable recommending him.

Could the Mrs. Hougham this Mary was talking about be the Bernice Hougham Isabel had treated? She thought back to the evening Bernice had been brought by ambulance to the hospital.

With a sick dread in the pit of her stomach, Isabel grabbed the stack of faxes that Alistair had allowed to pile up on the machine and began perusing them.

It had become clear that Mary routinely faxed new information, primarily study data, to Alistair. Isabel began running her finger down lists of names of study participants. On a sheet labeled Warmer-Bick Pharmaceuticals, a study for a drug to treat hypertension, she ran across the name of James Burgdorff, but no Hougham.

Another study, this one for a drug called TriGlys, listed almost a hundred participants. Near the top, she again came across the name Burgdorff.

Many of the names sounded vaguely familiar to her. Perhaps because Alistair had mentioned them as patients.

By the time she was done going through every sheet in the stack, she'd found James Burgdorff listed on four study lists. But she never found a reference to Mrs. Hougham.

Ariana Pitts, the regular admissions clerk, was not on duty the next day. Isabel asked one of the other clerks on duty to pull the records on a Mrs. Hougham. Later, the clerk handed her a sheet of paper. *Bernice Hougham*, it said.

Isabel subscribed to the belief that there are few coincidences in life. This was not one of them.

She'd planned to call Bernice Hougham that day, under the guise of following up on her visit to Harborview's ER. But she'd never had a moment's rest at work, and that night, Alistair seemed so determined to make amends for the strain between them that she'd not been able to sneak away from him to make the call.

It had almost seemed as though he were courting her again. But later, in bed, despite the wine, which he'd poured liberally, Isabel had turned away from him. They had once shared a passionate love life, but increasingly Alistair had displayed an appetite for sexual practices that Isabel found disturbing, and when he touched her now, she could barely refrain from pulling back in revulsion.

The next morning, when Isabel awoke—later than usual from the wine—Alistair was nowhere to be seen. She tiptoed up the stairs to the third floor office, reached for its door, and found it locked.

Furious—her instincts telling her she'd been had—she began pounding.

"Alistair? Are you in there?"

When he failed to answer, Isabel ran down both flights of stairs, flung open the garage door, and saw that his Jaguar was gone.

Stopping in the kitchen for a steak knife, she raced back to the office and jabbed at the keyhole, jiggling the knob repeatedly. She hadn't even realized the door had a lock on it. In fact, when she thought about it, she knew that it had not. Not until now.

She was about ready to give up trying to jimmy the door open when it occurred to her.

There was a small ledge that ran outside the third floor bathroom and the office.

In the bathroom, she climbed on top of the toilet, opened the window, and, her bare foot groping for purchase on the rain-slicked composition roof, stepped out, keeping a tight grip on the windowsill. Her nightgown lifted with the breeze off Elliott Bay.

The ledge was only three feet wide, and sloped gradually. Don't look down, she told herself.

The distance between the bathroom window and the first

of three office windows was no more than two yards. Midway between, there was a decorative column of tan shingles. Isabel tugged on one of the shingles. When it held, she let go of the windowsill. Changing hands and shingles, she inched her way through the galeish wind to the first of the paned office windows. She breathed a sigh of relief to see it was unlocked. Still grasping hold of a shingle, she used her free hand to force the window up and, moments later, lowered herself inside the office.

She turned and immediately saw something missing—the stack of papers on the fax machine. The phone light blinked. She picked it up and dialed the number on its plate, then again punched the four digits of Alistair's birth year, but this time was told that she'd selected an incorrect password.

Every file drawer she tried to open proved locked, and a search through the desk yielded no keys.

Now she understood the previous evening—why Alistair had been so attentive, why he'd insisted they open the bottle of Duckhorn merlot they'd been saving. He must have come up to the office during the night, cleaned it of any information regarding the clinical trials, and changed his password to his voice mail.

But why? And why last night?

SHE'D DRESSED IN record time, rushing so much that as she climbed into her car she realized she'd left the information the clerk had given her yesterday in the lab coat that she'd thrown into the dirty clothes. She ran back into the house and retrieved the sheet of paper from a pocket.

She had only asked for Ms. Hougham's first name and telephone number. Fortunately, the clerk had also jotted down her address.

601 Summit, Apt 2.

Isabel steered her Jeep across the Magnolia Bridge, then

followed Denny Avenue along the waters of Elliott Bay before it curved east, toward Capitol Hill.

She climbed over Interstate 5, then, at Summit, turned left and slowed, watching for the 600 block. Six-oh-one was a three-story frame house, with a recent coat of yellow paint and turquoise trim. Ignoring the warning signs, Isabel parked in front of a fire hydrant and climbed the four steps to the porch, where three metal mailboxes were aligned. Each one had its own buzzer.

Above each box was a unit number and name, two handwritten—Gilbert and Ochoa—and a third, this one typed. MacNaughton.

Isabel took three steps back to recheck the numerals on the column at the top step.

601.

She pressed the buzzer to apartment two. No one answered.

She pressed again.

Still no answer.

Then, through the glass panes of the front door, she saw a head pop out of a door just inside the hall. A slender woman, her red hair in tight pigtails, stepped into the foyer and opened the heavy walnut door.

"Are you trying to get into Bernie's apartment?" she asked. "I heard you buzz."

"Yes. Do you know if she's home?"

"Are you family?"

"No. A friend. Actually, I'm a doctor. I treated her a couple months ago at Harborview's emergency room."

"She told me about you," the girl said, finally smiling. But Isabel thought it an oddly melancholy smile. "She said you were so nice."

"That's always good to hear. Listen, I'd like to talk to her, if you think she's home."

The girl's eyes suddenly filled with tears.

"You didn't know?" she said, swiping at them with the

sleeves of her gray sweatshirt, which was inscribed with the letters PAWS over a gigantic pawprint.

"Bernie died," she sniffed. "Yesterday."

ISABEL WAS PACKING the last of three suitcases when the front door of the house slammed shut so violently that the framed Bev Doolittle over the bed she and Alistair had shared the night before threatened to fall off its mounting.

Alistair appeared in the doorway moments later.

"Are you out of your mind?" he screamed at her.

Isabel did not turn to face him. Instead, she continued transferring clothes and personal items—a photo album, birthday cards she'd saved over the years, hair clips and pins—from the dresser to the suitcase.

Seconds later, he was on her, grabbing her by the shoulders and jerking her around to face him.

"Look at me," he bellowed. "Are you out of your fucking mind? You called Warmer-Bick? Told them I'd killed a patient in my study?"

The veins in his neck looked like slender blue snakes leading to his face, which was the color of a fiery sky just before sunset. Isabel refused to flinch under his glare, or from the force with which his hands squeezed both shoulders.

"How did you get to her?" she hissed at him. "How did you get Bernice Hougham to join your study?"

"I don't know what you're talking about. I've never even heard of her."

"You're a liar! She was my ER patient that night you picked me up at the ER for the Fred Hutch dinner. Someone named Mary left you a message about her just the other day, told you she was having problems with Warmer-Bick's hypertensive."

One of Alistair's hands let go of her shoulder and slapped her across the face so forcefully that she felt, and heard, a distinctive *pop* in the back of her neck.

"You bitch! You listened to my messages. *What have you done?*"

She had seen many ugly emotions in her husband's eyes. Greed, anger. But now she saw something she had never before seen. Terror. And hatred.

"If what you're saying is true, if your patient was enrolled in my study, they'll think it was *you* who enrolled her. I'll make sure they do. I'll bring you down with me. You'll never be able to practice medicine again."

"I didn't just call Warmer-Bick. I called LaRouche too," Isabel said. "And Angiogenics. I told all of them that you had the same person enrolled in four different studies."

Alistair released his grip on her other shoulder as he fell back.

"You'll never be able to prove any of it."

"The attending physician at Swedish said Bernice Hougham's heart attack was caused by the antihypertensives. She was on three of them. You killed her."

"I told you, I don't know what you're talking about. I meet the patients who enroll in my studies once. Do you actually think I remember all of their names? If this woman was one of your patients, you must have referred her to me."

"That's a lie."

"Who's to say?" Alistair smiled.

Then, suddenly, his face transformed.

"Don't you see what you've done, Isabel? Don't you?" They stood facing each other.

"You've just made the biggest mistake of your life."

CHAPTER

TWENTY-ONE

ISABEL KNEW THE moment she awoke that something was different. She lay cocooned in her down comforter, trying to figure out what it was. And then it came to her.

Silence. The absolute lack of sound, inside or outside her cabin.

Turtlelike, she inched her head out from under her comforter. The cabin's frigid morning air condensed each breath into a short billowing cloud. She inhaled, pursed her lips, and exhaled in a silent whistle, sending a stream toward the ceiling, where it quickly drifted into oblivion.

Dreading getting up to build a fire, Isabel briefly entertained the idea of staying in bed all morning, but then she remembered what day it was. Almost simultaneously, she heard the first sounds of the morning.

A man's muffled voice, then a *woof*.

Isabel jumped up and hurried to the window. Pulling open the curtain, she drew in her breath at the sight that met her eyes.

Outside, the world had been transformed overnight. Huge, soft flakes drifted lazily from a ceiling of low clouds. A solid, undisturbed white velvet blanket spread as far as Isabel could see, silencing the world, covering even the trees, whose branches hung low with their weight. The only thing breaking the moonlike expanse were two narrow ribbons created by the horse-drawn wagon approaching the cabin.

Urged on by Gus, who wore a fringed jacket and Daniel

Boone–style cap, Bessie plodded forward, unfazed by the weight of the sleigh, tossing her head occasionally, while Grunt balanced uncertainly on the seat beside his master.

Scurrying back to the bed for her comforter, Isabel wrapped it around her shoulders and ran through the kitchen, where she threw open the door and stood watching her friends in childlike glee from the doorway.

"Merry Christmas!" she called as Gus stepped down into thigh-high snow.

Grunt jumped off the sled and, running toward her, porpoised his nose in and out of the snow. Once under the shelter of the porch, the exuberant dog executed a shake that started at his head and traveled, wavelike, down his back, sending snow flying into Isabel's eyelashes and bangs.

As Gus literally climbed his way to Isabel through two and a half feet of fresh fluff, the mini-icicles that had formed on the longer strands of hair protruding from his cap and at either end of his mustache became visible to Isabel. Gus clapped his gloved hands together and began scolding her even before he reached the first step.

"I don't see any smoke coming out that chimney. How do you propose to entertain Christmas guests?"

Isabel's laughter drifted like a bell across the morning stillness.

"Mercy, Gus. I slept so soundly I let the fire go out. And I don't even have coffee to offer you. Grab a handful of kindling and let's get the woodstove going again."

"I'll start it up, but just so's the pipes don't freeze while you're gone. You get yourself dressed and we'll head on over to my place. I already got a big old fire going. I'll cook us a rancher's breakfast that'll knock your socks off."

"I was planning to put the turkey on here this morning, then bring it over in time for dinner."

"Even with that fancy new truck of yours, you're not going to make it anywhere until the plows come by. Bessie was itchin' to get out in this stuff. Let's just pack up the whole kit and kaboodle and put it on at my place."

Nothing sounded better to Isabel right now than a day spent in front of Gus's fireplace, and cooking in his spacious kitchen.

"You got yourself a deal," she said, giving Gus a big hug as he stepped inside the kitchen. "But I *have* to have a cup of coffee before I venture out."

"I'll make the coffee," he said firmly. "You get dressed."

When Isabel returned minutes later, dressed in blue jeans and thermal T-shirt, over which she'd slipped a red wool sweater, the woodstove was spitting and crackling and Gus was spooning instant coffee into two mugs.

He gave her a mischievous smile, then reached inside his jacket and extracted a pint-sized pewter flask.

"This'll warm you up for the ride," he said, unscrewing its cap.

"Why not?" Isabel laughed, watching as he poured watery brown liquid into both mugs. "Whoa, Gus, go light on mine!"

She'd begun bagging the groceries she'd bought the day before for their Christmas dinner when the phone rang. Isabel froze and turned anxious eyes toward Gus. The caller would not be her mother. She'd already had a long talk with her the night before.

"Want me to get it?" Gus asked.

"Would you mind?"

Gus's "hello" was decidedly more gruff than Isabel had ever heard before. He listened briefly then placed his calloused palm over the mouthpiece.

"Some guy named Ken MacStirling," he said. "Want me to tell him to get lost?"

"I'll take it."

Isabel grabbed the phone from Gus.

"Hello?"

"Merry Christmas," MacStirling said. Isabel could hear children's voices in the background.

"Same to you. I certainly didn't expect a Christmas call from you."

"Well, I've been wanting to apologize for the other day. What better day to do it?"

"I don't blame you for anything you said or felt, Ken. I should probably have told you about Alistair, but it's not . . ."

"Please, no," MacStirling interrupted her. "I didn't call for explanations. The more I've thought about what you did, turning your own husband in, the more impressed I am. Now I understand your reluctance to get involved with the HantaVac study."

"Well, don't be too impressed. My attorney tells me there's a good chance that Alistair will get away with little more than a slap on the wrist. The pharmaceutical companies don't want any of this making the news. She's heard they're prepared to make the whole thing go away. They've pulled Alistair off most of their studies, but they're saying they don't have proof of intentional wrongdoing, that it can all be attributed to sloppy paperwork."

Bud Wolfkill's words came back to her then. *We haven't come up with any evidence that it was your ex-husband who tried to run you off Suicide Elbow that night.*

Alistair was an expert at eliminating proof of his misdeeds.

"I should think the FDA would get involved. It would be terrible if Bott isn't made to pay," MacStirling said. "Still, if you think your actions were wasted, you're wrong. I can tell you, that whole incident opened plenty o' eyes. It spread through the industry like wildfire. Truth is, there'd been a lot more of that goin' on than anyone wanted to say. Let's hope what happened to that coof you had the misfortune of being married to changes all that. If it doesn't, people like him are going to end up ruining things for important trials, like the HantaVac study.

"But listen, no need to get so serious on such a joyous

day. I also received some good news and wanted to share it with you. Thought it might add to your holiday cheer."

"What's that?"

"We'll be getting on with Phase II. Following the holidays. Lyons gave me the go ahead yesterday. I tried callin' you last night, but your line was busy."

"That *is* great news. I already have the Phase II participants signed up. I was just waiting for the go-ahead."

"Well, now you have it. You can start drawing blood immediately. The new vaccine lot will be shipped to you the first of the new year. Things are going so well, we should be into Phase III by late spring, early summer. Aye, I almost forgot. ImmuVac got more good news yesterday. One of the biggest pharmaceutical companies in the nation, Pfister, is interested in a partnership. Thanks to our study."

Isabel couldn't help but smile—it was back to being "our" study again.

"Congratulations. Sounds like you have a lot to celebrate."

Gus had handed her a mug and now Isabel took a long sip from it. The old man's throaty laughter rattled through the kitchen as he watched Isabel's expression when the whiskey burned its way down her throat.

"We both do," MacStirling said. "I have the feeling it's going to be a very good year for both of us."

WHEN SHE WAS a child, Christmas day often left Isabel with an emptiness that stacks of presents and plates piled high did not touch. There were always invitations from other physicians and family friends, but early on, Nada made it a rule that the three of them—Nada, Tom, and Isabel—spend the day alone together, as a family. Isabel had always secretly hoped that they'd accept one of those invitations.

While she couldn't put a name to it when she was young, later she decided that the joy at her household on Christmas Day always seemed particularly forced. Nada McLain seemed determined to create an atmosphere of gaiety and celebration with lavish gifts. Isabel's father, who did not have a materialistic bone in his body, never complained—throughout their marriage, Isabel had never heard him criticize Nada—but Isabel sometimes sensed he escaped times like that by going somewhere far away in his mind, which only made Isabel more lonely.

Christmas Day with Gus turned out to be the simplest Christmas Isabel ever spent. Just Isabel and Gus in front of the fire, exchanging modest but thoughtfully selected gifts—a leather-bound world atlas for Gus, handmade moccasins for Isabel. They'd feasted on turkey and stuffing, potatoes and green beans, then worked some of it off outside, shoveling Gus's driveway, then grooming Bessie and mucking out her stall. Afterward, Gus produced a mammoth pumpkin pie that he'd bought at Sandy's Diner, for which Isabel whipped real cream.

Gus also broke out his homemade Irish cream, which they drank straight at first. Then, after downing a third of the bottle, they added it to the coffee Isabel brewed.

"What a magical day it's been, Gus," Isabel said, smiling at him across the dinner table, her face flushed with alcohol, heat from the fire, and happiness.

"Hell, Is, I would've thought today was a disappointment for you."

"How can you say that?"

"Well, Grunt and me here have been celebratin' Christmas alone for a long time. Having a little company's a real treat for us. But I would've thought you'd be used to a lot more excitement than this."

"No, Gus, I'm not. This has been perfect."

They both grew thoughtful, sipping their creamy coffees.

"Gus?"

"Yep?"

"Would I be a busybody if I asked you about your wife?"

The smile that graced Gus's eyes was slow and sweet.

"Hell, no. What'd you want to know?"

"Anything. Everything."

"Well, let's see. Her name was Marian." A tenderness and warmth laced Gus's words. "She died two weeks short of our forty-third anniversary. And there wasn't a single day in all those forty-three years that I didn't thank my lucky stars for her."

Isabel felt a catch in her throat. What would it feel like to be loved like that?

"What was she like?"

Gus grew thoughtful.

"Patient. Marian was a patient woman. She just kinda rolled with the flow, which is a good way for a rancher's wife to be. And she didn't mind bein' alone. Course she had so damn many critters that I had to fight for my spot on the bed every night. That woman just loved animals. Which is a good thing, 'cause many a night they were about all the company she had."

"You were gone a lot?"

"I traveled some, but it wasn't that so much. The weather and cattle, they don't pay much attention to a clock. Runnin' a ranch is a twenty-four-hour proposition. Marian accepted that. Hell, she'd always have a warm meal waitin' for me, no matter what time of day or night I was called out to tend to things."

"How did you meet her?"

"Marian grew up on the Flathead reservation."

"She was Indian?"

"No. But her grandfather bought eighty acres 'bout the time of the Dawes Act and then he just kept buyin' up the stuff around him as it became available. I used to drive down there for my alfalfa. That's how I met Marian. I bought hay from her old man . . . What is it, Isabel? You look like you've just seen a ghost. Did I say somethin'?"

Isabel's voice grew soft and tentative.

"Did I ever tell you my father was a doctor on the Flathead

reservation? That he spent a year there just before I was born?"

Gus's eyes widened to the size of silver dollars.

"What was his name?"

"Tom. Tom McLain."

"Holy Toledo. *Dr. Tom.* I can't believe I didn't make the connection. But then it's been so long, and the only name I ever really heard him go by was Dr. Tom."

Isabel's entire body went taut.

"You knew him?"

It was an odd thing, Isabel would recall later. Watching Gus at that moment. His initial surprise seemed to transform itself into something else. Something Isabel couldn't quite put a finger on.

"Well, no. I never actually met him."

"How'd you remember him then?"

"Well, Marian had this friend." Gus's words seemed measured somehow. "Her name was Hattie Bay. The two of them grew up together. They went to school together, on the reservation. It was Hattie who knew your father."

It struck Isabel as strange that Gus would remember a man who had only lived on the Flathead reservation for one year, and whom he'd only heard about because his wife's friend had known him. Still, Isabel couldn't hold back the excitement that she felt building inside.

"Did she work with my father at the clinic? Was she a nurse?"

"No. I think Hattie was just a patient of his."

"Hattie's Indian?"

Gus nodded. "Yup. Salish."

"Do you suppose I could find her, Gus? It'd be so incredible to meet her and talk to her about my dad. That time meant so much to him, but it wasn't exactly a popular subject around our house. I'd just love to meet her."

"Hattie died, Isabel. A long time ago."

Isabel's heart dropped back into her chest, where it belonged.

"Were they friends? Hattie and my father?"

Gus pushed back from the table so suddenly, and with such force, that it actually startled Isabel.

"You know, that's about all I remember on the subject. It was a long time ago." He stood. "Now, I better hitch Bessie back up and see you home, girl, before I pass out from all that good food and drink."

SOMETHING WAS AMISS. She first noticed it when she went into the bathroom. The wall just to the right of the toilet had a small, old-fashioned window that opened outward, to the back of the cabin. When Isabel moved in, she'd replaced the cheap steel rings intended to hold towels with a long brass rod that she'd positioned directly beneath the window. On warm summer days, she liked opening the window so that her towels could absorb the scents of the mountain air and flowers.

It was that—a towel—that tipped Isabel off. She'd done laundry yesterday, and last night, before going to bed, she'd folded a fresh towel over the rod. Just as Isabel had a thing about installing toilet paper so the paper always rolled off the top of the roll, not the bottom, she was fastidious in the way she folded towels. Lengthwise in thirds, not halves. It was one of those little, admittedly anal idiosyncrasies.

But as Isabel reached for the forest green towel to dry her face, her hands froze in midair.

The towel was folded in half. Not thirds.

And there was no way, no way at all, that she had folded it like that.

Immediately, her eyes went to the window, which was secured with a latch that rotated its way clear of the locking position.

She'd kept it locked all winter. But it was not locked now.

Lowering the lid to the toilet, Isabel stepped onto it and pushed the window out, a blast of cold air immediately turning her breaths into clouds.

Snow, falling thickly, made it difficult to see far. The square of light from the small window illuminated a patch of snow below.

It afforded Isabel just enough light to make out the imprint of a boot in the snow beneath the window. She watched, momentarily transfixed, as it filled with snow.

"YOU HAVE TO report it."

Isabel had waited until morning to call her attorney in Seattle with her discovery.

"I'm telling you, K. T., it won't do any good. Look what happened when he tried to push me into the Two Medicine." Anger seized Isabel's chest and tightened around her throat, giving her voice an ugly edge. "I've turned him in to the authorities twice now. It just makes it worse when they come back and tell me they can't find any evidence against him. I can practically feel him mocking me, taunting me. And that just makes me crazy."

K. T. Seinberg sounded just as disturbed as her client.

"I don't agree with you, but it's your decision. Okay, then. What's missing? What did he take?"

"Nothing. At least nothing that I can tell. But it's clear he was looking for something. He turned my entire office upside down."

K. T.'s silence indicated she was deep in thought.

"He obviously knows where I live now," Isabel continued. "If he wanted to hurt me, he could have."

"Don't count on that. My guess is Alistair would have no problem with hurting you. But he's too smart to break into your cabin and harm you. He knows he'd be the prime suspect. But there has to be a reason he won't leave you alone." She mulled this over for several seconds. "He's either trying to frighten you, or he's actually looking for something."

"I agree. But what?"

"I don't know. Remember all those documents you found in his office, on his fax machine?"

"Yes."

"You never kept any of them, right?"

"No. I've told you that. I could kick myself, but he locked me out of there before I became suspicious enough to actually do something."

"Which is why, from what I've heard, they haven't been able to prove any serious wrongdoing. The agent I talked to said it appeared that Alistair and his assistant had done a very thorough job of purging their files."

"If I'd only had the presence of mind to take them when I saw them," Isabel sighed. "I know those faxes would have led somewhere."

"That's it," Seinberg cried suddenly.

"What?"

"Alistair must think you *did* have the presence of mind. He must think you took something. Something that could hurt him."

Isabel mulled this over a moment before responding.

"That would make sense of his comment that night he left the message here for me . . ."

"That's right. What was it he said? That the video was a *reminder?*"

"Yes. He said something like 'in case you were thinking of doing me any more harm.' Something like that."

"You never did figure out what video he meant," Seinberg said. "Did you?"

"No. Never." Suzanne continued to claim that she never saw a video, despite Isabel's clear recollection of UPS delivering one that day. "Listen, K. T., isn't this enough to go after him in court again? Get a court order, a restraining order?"

"You still don't have any proof, Isabel. None. It's all too circumstantial. Any judge is going to see it that way. Unless you call the police and they can come up with something. Like fingerprints. Or even footprints."

"I really don't want to call the police. Besides, we're in

the middle of a blizzard. The footprints are long gone. And Alistair's too smart to have left fingerprints. We both know that. I just have to figure out what it is he's after."

"He's like a wounded animal," Seinberg mused. "And that's when they're most dangerous. When you shoot, you have to shoot to kill. You didn't do that. Turning Alistair in for the fraud you suspected him of just nicked him. Just made him that much more dangerous."

K. T. was right. Isabel had blown it. She'd naively assumed the drug companies would be eager to hear her suspicions about Alistair. Instead, all she'd succeeded in doing was giving him a warning, a chance to clean up his files, destroy any evidence of wrongdoing. But if K. T. was right, Alistair was still nervous about her. About Isabel's power to hurt him. And Isabel knew only too well what Alistair was capable of when his back was to the wall.

"Maybe if I find out what it is he's after," she said with more optimism than she felt, "I can finish him off. Bury him, once and for all."

"Let's hope you can," K. T. Seinberg, who never minced words, answered. "Because I have no doubt that he'd bury you in a heartbeat if he felt it could save his own sorry ass."

· CHAPTER
―――――

TWENTY-TWO

Y OU KNOW, MARY, darlin'," Alistair stared over Mary Pelandini's shoulder at a striking blonde who'd just entered Starbucks, "this hysteria of yours is becoming tiresome."

Mary's shock at Alistair's words, let alone his tone of voice, caused her fleshy jaw to drop.

"Hysteria? Do you understand what I'm telling you? They found at least six invoices from Laticia that were labeled *urine samples*."

"Who made those invoices? Whose handwriting were they in?"

"Mine," Mary practically screamed.

"How could you have the stupidity to label the invoices like that?"

Alistair thought Mary might pass out from shock at his behavior. But he'd had about enough of all this. And the fact that the invoices for the urine they'd routinely purchased from a former nurse at the clinic—urine with high levels of protein, which was a prerequisite to enrollment in the GenSci trial—were written by hand, *by Mary,* was really some of the best news he'd had in a long time. He could just hear himself now, telling the FDA investigators of his devastation upon realizing that his study coordinator had been commiting fraud of such unimaginable proportions.

But that would be a last resort. Mary knew so much. So very much. Who knew if, when told to destroy all the evidence against him, she'd held back something incriminatory? As annoyingly emotional as she was, she could also be cunning. He had one final card to play before he would resort to that plan.

"Listen, darlin'," he said, eyes now making contact with the blonde, who had moved to the line waiting for drinks, "I think it's time we change tactics with my former wife." Isabel and Alistair's divorce had become final just that week. "I think it's time to throw the blame on her."

"What do you mean?"

"I mean, the investigators are so fucking hung up on the fact that some of our study participants were former patients of Isabel's. Aside from the invoices, which are an unfortunate new development, you did such a good job of cleaning up the files, that's about all they can hang their hat on. I think it's time we tell them that it was all Isabel's idea."

Mary drew back in shock.

"But the fax from Ariana. If she has that . . ."

"Will you please forget about that fucking fax? She doesn't have it. I've searched her cabin high and low for it. I've told you all along, it doesn't exist."

"You're absolutely certain?"

"Yes, I'm certain. Believe me, if Isabel had that fax, she'd have used it by now. Especially now."

"What do you mean, especially now?"

"Now that the divorce is final. Now that she undoubtedly realizes that I'm the one who broke into her cabin."

He didn't add the thought that was foremost in his mind. *Now that she's seen that video.*

He'd felt certain that the video was the one weapon that would guarantee Isabel's cooperation. But, to his amazement, he'd been wrong. He'd expected Isabel to come crawling to him after he sent it to her. Begging him to let her off the hook. He'd expected that video to really scare the bejesus out of her. After all, the one thing Isabel held dearest was her pride. And her goddamn arrogance. The threat of having their kinky lovefest broadcast to the wonderful world of online perverts . . . well, he was pretty sure she'd do just about anything to prevent that from happening. Instead, she'd ignored the damn video altogether and even had the nerve to send some fucking redskin cop to question him about breaking into her cabin. Which was, of course, a joke, since Alistair had been a little too smart to actually leave fingerprints that night. What did she think he was, a fucking idiot?

He glanced in the direction of the good-looking blonde, just in time to see her flash a giant smile at a broad-shouldered jock who had joined the line next to hers. The slob was dressed in sweats and a pitted-out jersey, wearing

his hat backward like some punk kid, but the blonde didn't
seem to mind. When her eyes swept across the tables moments later, they skipped right over Alistair, returning
quickly to the jock.

Alistair felt as if he would explode. Sorry bitches were all
alike.

"It's definitely time," he said, his anger growing as the
blonde's transgressions brought back thoughts of Isabel's refusal to fuck him that last night. She'd pretended to be
asleep, but Alistair knew it was an act. He knew she could
hear him, that she realized what he was doing next to her in
bed. He knew how disgusted it would make her.

Which was half the fun.

He realized then that Mary was staring at him.

"Time for what?" she said.

"I just told you, darlin'. Time to make Isabel pay."

CHAPTER

TWENTY-THREE

S HE WAS SO shaken and frazzled—the call had awakened her only two hours earlier—and she'd used every
spare minute in the early hours, before dawn, on the telephone, arranging for a Cutbank doctor to cover for her in
her absence. She hadn't had time to put on any makeup whatsoever, or do anything with her hair. She told herself she
regretted that fact only because she knew it would disturb
her mother to see Isabel dressed in jeans and looking like
she'd just rolled out of bed. It certainly wasn't because she
happened to run into Monty Four Bear.

What were the chances they'd both be on the first flight that morning from Kalispell to Spokane?

What were the chances that when she rushed out onto the tarmac to climb into the small Dash 8—the single flight attendant having held the door open for her, their last-minute passenger—the only remaining seat on the plane would be next to him?

Upon looking up to see his new seatmate—for whom the plane had been held a good ten minutes—Monty's expression signaled that he was no less chagrined at this development than Isabel.

"Figures," he muttered.

"Pardon me?"

"Figures you'd be the one who kept us waiting."

Furious, Isabel pursed her lip, ready to launch her defense. But then she realized just how near to tears she was over the news that her mother had had a heart attack. Too close to trust herself by trading barbs with Monty Four Bear right now. She would not allow him to see her cry. And so, buckling her seat belt, she refrained from answering.

Isabel had always been a nervous flyer. In fact, she'd steadfastly refused to fly in anything less than a full-sized jet. But the only way to get to Seattle before noon was the little Horizon puddle-jumper that was now taxiing out to the runway.

As the propellers kicked in gear and the plane began its takeoff, Isabel gripped the armrests on either side of her.

Monty Four Bear looked up momentarily from his newspaper. When his eyes stopped to rest on Isabel's white knuckles, she instructed her fingers to release her grip, but they refused to cooperate.

The ascent out of Kalispell went smoothly, and by the time the flight attendant came along, Isabel had finally let go of the armrests. Isabel had been surprised to see a flight attendant on such a small plane. This one, older than most and decidedly more cheerful, stopped at their row and bent over Isabel's shoulder.

"Are you doing okay?" she asked with concern that was unquestionably genuine.

Isabel startled.

"Why, yes," she answered. "I'm fine."

"Good. I'm so sorry about your mother." She gave Isabel's shoulder a light squeeze. "You just let me know if there's anything we can do for you."

When Isabel called the ticket counter from her car, pleading with them to hold the seven A.M. flight so that she could get to the hospital in Seattle, where her mother lay in critical condition, she hadn't expected that that information would be passed along to the crew.

"Thank you. And thank you for holding the plane."

Red-faced, Isabel reached for the *Horizon* magazine in the seat pocket in front of her and began flipping through it. She could feel Monty Four Bear's eyes drifting her way.

"Your mother's ill?" he finally asked.

Isabel did not meet his eyes.

"Yes. I just got word she had a heart attack."

"I'm sorry."

"Thank you."

There was a pause.

"I'm also sorry for my remark about making the plane wait."

Isabel's eyes drew upward, toward Monty's.

"That's all right," she said, smiling involuntarily.

The smile seemed to disarm Monty, whose own eyes dropped quickly back to his newspaper.

The flight attendant had just served beverages—water for Isabel, V8 for Monty—when the plane suddenly began to shudder. As the pilot came on the loudspeaker and warned them they might experience "a little turbulence," the plane suddenly dropped out from under them.

Seconds later, Isabel had a lap full of water and an ironclad hold on both armrests.

"He'll get us out of this in no time," she heard Monty say. She could only nod.

True to Monty's promise, the plane soon leveled out. As if possessed of eyes in the back of her head, the flight attendant showed up almost immediately with a stack of paper napkins.

"Here you go, dear," she said, offering them to Isabel.

Isabel, by this point emotionally numb, simply nodded and took them. She set about pressing them against the large wet spots on her blue jeans, and it was while she was doing that that the tears began. Not many, not the all-out good cry she needed, but several big drops from each eye. She was grateful she'd not tied her hair back, for it shielded her face from Monty and made it impossible for him to see her.

Suddenly his hand came into her field of vision. It held a red bandanna. The kind movie cowboys tied over their mouths on a cattle drive.

"Thank you," Isabel mumbled, taking it and wiping dry each eye. For the rest of the flight, she did not look at him. She could not.

When the plane rolled to a stop in Spokane, where Isabel was scheduled to switch to an Alaska Airlines flight, she gathered up her bag and finally, with no small amount of effort, glanced Monty's way.

Most of the passengers stood, but Monty remained seated, seat belt still buckled.

"Aren't you getting off?"

He shook his head.

"I'm going on. To Moscow."

Moscow. The University of Idaho. A touch of curiosity arose in Isabel.

"Oh," she said. "Listen, I'll get this back to you." She raised the fist still clutching the bandanna.

"No need," Monty Four Bear replied.

Isabel stepped in line and, keenly aware of Monty's eyes on her, inched her way toward the plane's exit.

STEPPING BACK INSIDE the corridors of Harborview Medical Center, corridors she'd walked for more than six years, Isabel's body and mind switched involuntarily, unreasonably, into fight-or-flight mode.

Silently, eyes cast downward—she was in no mood for reunions—she headed for the elevators. Cardiac ICU was on four.

If anyone should have been prepared for what she would see when she entered the large room housing four beds, four critically ill patients, it should have been Isabel. Patients fresh from surgery, with tubes running from nose and mouth, neck, arms, and any other exposed surface. Overworked nurses, one for every two patients, huddling over a semiconscious form, checking monitors, listening. Always listening, needing to distinguish that one cough or groan that signaled one of his or her charges was in trouble. Monitors everywhere, mounted in each corner of the room for easy visibility.

And the smell. Isabel remembered that smell.

Isabel knew to expect it all.

But knowing and being prepared turned out to be two entirely different matters. As she entered 4A and stepped around the first partially drawn curtain, it was a wonder she even recognized Nada McLain.

Nada lay unconscious, tubes extending from her nostrils, both arms, and protruding from under the groin area of her hospital gown. A ventilator stood nearby. Nada's white hair, usually perfectly coiffed, lay flattened against her head. In repose, her features seem sunken and frail, much more frail than Isabel remembered.

Isabel eyed the monitor above the bed. Nada's blood pressure was low: 94 over 55.

"What are you doing here?"

Isabel turned. A young nurse with perfectly drawn brown lips stood eyeing her warily.

"I'm her daughter," Isabel said. "Isabel McLain." She did not preface her name with "Dr." "How is she?"

"She's had a rough night. She was only sent up here from her angioplasty five or six hours ago. We're planning to keep her sedated most of the day. It's unlikely she'll even know you're here."

Isabel had long ago learned to quickly peg a nurse. She had the utmost respect for nurses, and sympathy. They did the real grunt work, especially in surgical wards. But all the credit went to the doctors. She'd found that those nurses who stayed in the profession for any length of time were in it because they truly cared about the patients, not about glory or gratitude. But there were some with an attitude.

"I see."

"Maybe no one told you, but visiting hours are quite restricted in ICU. You're only allowed to be here from . . ."

"Dr. McLain? Is that you?"

Both women turned to see an anesthesiology resident standing in the doorway.

"Dr. Arati." Isabel smiled. "How are you?"

The young man, a handsome East Indian, stepped forward, extending his hand, his face all toothy grin.

"It's so good to see you," Dr. Arati said. "Last I heard you were running a clinic in Montana. This doesn't mean you've decided to return to us here at Harborview, does it?"

Isabel felt a flush of satisfaction at his obvious pleasure at seeing her.

"No. I'm actually here on a personal matter. My mother had a heart attack last night."

Dr. Arati's eyes roamed to the bed where Nada McLain lay.

"Oh, I'm so very sorry. How is she doing?"

Isabel looked at the nurse, straining to read her name tag.

"I was just asking . . . Kathy that very question."

Kathy's jaw jutted out defiantly as if to say *How the hell was I supposed to know she's a doctor?*

"She's stable for now. I'll be keeping a close eye on her."

"As will I," said Isabel.

"I'll check in on her also," Dr. Arati said in his formal, clipped English. "I'll leave you alone with your mother now, but I would love to buy you a cup of coffee when you're ready for a break."

"Thank you."

When Dr. Arati had departed, Kathy attempted to get back on track with Isabel.

"There are a couple chairs at bed three. Let me grab one for you." When she returned, she deposited the chair near the foot of Nada's bed.

"Feel free to stay as long as you'd like."

NADA McLAIN CAME to only briefly, late in the evening. Isabel jumped up from her chair, bending low over her mother's shrunken form as she stroked her hair back off the shriveled forehead.

"Isabel?" Nada said weakly.

"Mother. I'm here. You just take it easy now. Okay?"

The corners of Nada McLain's thin lips lifted ever so slightly into a smile.

"You're a good girl, Isabel."

She mouthed it more than voiced it, but Isabel caught every word.

The new nurse on duty, Annette, whom Isabel took an immediate liking to, appeared instantly.

"I'm going to give her more sedative," she said. "Dr. Holmes wants her to stay as quiet as possible."

Isabel watched as she injected the clear liquid into the IV line running to Nada's elbow.

"You really should get some rest," Annette said to Isabel.

"She's not going to open those eyes again until morning."

"I suppose you're right," Isabel said, stifling a yawn. She hadn't eaten all day and felt ready to drop. "Maybe I'll head to my mother's house to catch a few hours. I won't be much good to her tomorrow if I don't."

BUT BACK AT the house in which she'd grown up, a house in which she had not slept for over half a decade, Isabel found herself too overcome by nostalgia to sleep. She ate a bowl of cereal, then padded from one room to another, taking everything in. Over the years, she'd visited Nada and Tom at this house, and then Nada alone, but now, with both absent, she took everything in as if it were the first time she'd returned since childhood. The fireplace mantel lined with photos of Isabel as a child, Isabel in her teens, Isabel's graduation from college. Isabel and Alistair's wedding. Photos, mainly of Isabel, lining the stairwell to the second floor. In Nada and Tom's bedroom, more photos still. They were everywhere. And with each new photo she discovered, as if for the first time, the pain in Isabel's chest grew sharper.

It was like a shrine to Isabel. A heartbreaking shrine.

And what had she done to deserve such adoration? True, she'd been, in some ways, the "perfect" daughter. Good student, popular. Active in school. The pictures were testaments to the pride Nada took in those accomplishments and Isabel took some satisfaction, some consolation in being reminded of that.

Isabel may even have married Alistair in large part to please her parents, for both Nada and Tom McLain had shown more enthusiasm for Alistair than just about any other man she'd ever dated.

Wasn't that enough? Hadn't Isabel done enough to please her parents? Why did she feel so unbelievably guilty right now?

It was because, when it came down to it, even while she

was achieving, and marrying, and becoming a doctor, just like her father, Isabel was rejecting her parents, her life with them. She resented it. Resented how wrong it all felt.

And finally, her actions had caught up with her innermost feelings and—despite the fact that she knew the effect it would have on Nada McLain—she had fled. Moved away. And not just away, but to a Montana reservation. Just as her father had done decades earlier.

How was that for gratitude? For making a statement?

Her bedroom looked exactly as it had the day she left for USC. Isabel took off her shoes and lay back on the pillows, studying the figurines Nada had collected for her—Lladro, which Isabel detested. There was a crack in the corner of the ceiling above her bed, where the plaster bubbled. The roof must be leaking.

Everything looked the same. Everything except the trunk sitting against the wall, underneath the window that looked out on Nada McLain's gardens, which were now overgrown.

Isabel rose and went to the trunk. She lifted its lid.

Inside were scrapbooks. She picked up the first one. The photos inside were all old and yellowed, but the scrapbook, like the trunk, was clearly new.

Nada McLain had been making scrapbooks of Isabel's life.

There were almost a dozen of them, along with yearbooks, programs from dance recitals, award certificates for good attendance. Letters Isabel had written home from camp.

What did Nada plan to do with all of it?

With a twinge of melancholy, the answer came to Isabel. Everything in the trunk related to Isabel. It was as if Nada knew that Isabel would never make the effort, never care enough to organize the mementos that symbolized her life.

The contents of the trunk represented hours of labor on Nada's part. It was as if Nada feared that once she was gone, Isabel's history, their life together, would just cease to exist.

Nada McLain was preparing to die.

Isabel spent hours going through the photo albums and

scrapbooks, one by one. Each one had been put together which such care, so much thought. Sitting on her bed, legs crossed, Isabel stepped back in time, and she realized something. That there had been good times. Many of them. For some reason, she'd thrown them away, like worthless trash, but now, before her eyes, she saw them. Relived them.

Finally drowsy, Isabel put the last of the scrapbooks back into the trunk. That's when she noticed it. Beneath all the scrapbooks and albums, a clear plastic file.

It contained documents of some sort.

Isabel could tell that much even before she lifted the flap and reached inside.

"I HEARD YOU were back in town," the voice cried from the hallway.

Isabel pulled her eyes off Nada McLain's pained features—even in her sleep, Isabel could tell her mother was in agonizing pain—and looked toward the door.

"Candace," she said, rising to give the director of human resources a hug.

"I'm sorry about your mother, Isabel," Candace said, throwing both arms around her. Isabel took a deep, shaky breath, inhaling Candace's perfume, which had always reminded Isabel of Nada's cherished rose gardens. "The whole staff is praying for her."

"Thank you," Isabel said, pulling back to face the disarmingly vivacious Candace.

"Is there anything we can do for you? Have you seen the chaplain?"

"Yes, he's been here. I think she's getting excellent care and I appreciate that." Isabel lowered her voice. "According to Dr. Holmes, her heart suffered massive damage. It may just be beyond repair."

Candace Abrahams reached out and squeezed Isabel's hand.

"Page me if you need anything. Anything at all."

"Okay," Isabel said, turning back to Nada, who had begun stirring.

"Isabel?"

The voice was cracked and dry, like Nada's poor lips, to which Isabel had gently been applying Vaseline.

Isabel lowered herself on to the bed next to Nada's tiny form and took her hand.

"Right here, Mom."

"I'm so happy you're here, honey." The words came slowly. "Thank you for coming."

Isabel swallowed against the lump in her throat.

"Of course I came, Mom. I love you."

Nada's fingers curled around Isabel's palm and squeezed.

"I want to tell you something, Isabel," she whispered.

"You just rest now, Mom. We can talk later."

"No," Nada's head rolled from side to side in protest. "This . . . has . . . to be . . . said."

A nameless terror gripped Isabel.

"You shouldn't strain yourself, Mother. I want you to relax now. Please."

"I loved you so much, but in some ways, I wasn't a very good mother."

The fear escalated when Isabel realized that Nada's voice came out in the thinnest of whispers as much by choice as necessity. She did not want the nurse to hear her.

"Stop that," she scolded. "You were. You were a wonderful mother."

"But I did you such a grave disservice, Isabel. I should have told you . . ."

Isabel could not bear to hear the words.

"Mother, you must stop this right now. You listen to me. I love you dearly. I could not have loved you more." Isabel's tears began falling freely, on to Isabel and Nada's clasped hands. "You gave me a wonderful life. You did what you thought was best for me. I'll be grateful to you forever for that."

As she studied her sobbing daughter, Nada McLain's eyes suddenly took on a clarity. And in that moment, Isabel knew her mother understood what Isabel was trying to tell her.

"I was afraid I'd lose you, like I lost your father," Nada's whisper was fading fast.

"You didn't lose Dad, Mother."

"Yes . . . I . . . did . . . long . . . ago."

Isabel could not stop the tears.

"Sleep now, Mother. Sleep."

As Nada McLain closed her eyes, Isabel leaned over to kiss her forehead. Then she whispered into Nada's ear.

"I love you, Mother. I love you so much."

A very small smile tilted Nada's once lovely mouth. She squeezed her little girl's hand.

And then she drifted peacefully away.

CHAPTER

TWENTY-FOUR

MORNING, BROTHER." CROUCHED in front of the fire, one hand raised over its flames for warmth while the other grasped a mug of steaming coffee, Monty Four Bear nodded at Clyde Birdseye as he emerged from the teepee.

His Cheyenne friend had slept in the blue jeans and flannel shirt in which he'd arrived the night before. A boldly striped blanket, wrapped around his shoulders, had since been added to the ensemble. Wild hair that had escaped its ponytail during the night, as well as only four hours of sleep, made Clyde look more ill-tempered than usual.

Monty studied him, imagining him as a warrior of years ago, awakening on the day of battle. The imagery worked.

"Pour yourself some coffee."

"Thanks," said Clyde, reaching for the blackened aluminum kettle perched on a rock at the edge of the fire. "*Shit.* Colder than a polar bear's toenails out here."

Monty grinned.

"Springtime in Montana."

Just the day before, the mountain passes had been closed and showers in the valley had come in the form of coin-sized snowflakes. Still, there had been several mild stretches of weather over the winter, enough for WRI to move in equipment and erect chain-link fencing around the first drill site.

Actually drilling two thousand feet into frozen earth would be another matter though. WRI's exploration in earnest had had to wait for spring. But despite outward appearances, spring had now come and today's date had been circled for a good long while on many a reservation calendar.

For this was the day that WRI's drilling was to begin.

Monty had also put the time since the tribal council meeting to good use. Lulled into a false sense of security by the lack of further visible opposition to the mine, WRI had never even given consideration to posting a guard at the site, which enabled last night's execution of Monty's months of planning to go off without a hitch. During the night, three teepees— two canvas and one buffalo hide—had been assembled in front of the fenced entrance to the drill site. Now, as Bobby Lighthouse's drum punctuated the predawn sky, the hardy souls who had slept in the teepees were beginning to stir.

"What time are the rest due?" Clyde asked, using his coffee mug to cover a toothy yawn.

"Soon," Monty answered, reaching for a stick. He poked at the coals on the perimeter of the firepit, rolling them back into the flames, while Clyde, fueled by caffeine, slowly came to life.

"So what's going on with that class action?"

Monty shook his head.

"Did I ever tell you about what Sky Thomas said at that meeting we had?"

"Who's Sky Thomas?"

"The oldest living Blackfeet. A visionary. Sky was at the trust affairs meeting. She told us trouble was coming. That we should hold off on the suit until the trouble passed."

"And you let her change your plans?" Birdseye snorted in amusement.

"When Sky talks, I listen. Wasn't long after that meeting that the hantavirus killed three of our people. Anyway, I've started some preliminary discovery. Maybe this summer, after we shut this baby down, I'll actually have time to get the suit filed."

"Hell, even if we get this thing shut down by then, there'll be another mine, or someone murdered, or *something* to keep you too busy to get to your lawsuit."

"You know the problem with you?" Monty said, tossing his stick at Clyde good-naturedly. "You're always so full of good cheer."

Birdseye chuckled.

"It's early. Wait 'til I warm up."

Suddenly a pair of lights drew both men's eyes to the horizon. A vehicle was approaching from the south. Soon several other vehicles followed. The two stood, watching the vehicles' progress in a silence punctuated by the drumbeat and increasing activity around the tents. As the first vehicle neared, they could see it was the bus Monty had arranged. It would be filled with students from Monty's classes.

"Just in time for the sunrise ceremony."

Several protesters had begun dancing around the fire to the beat of Bobby Lighthouse's drum. Monty and Clyde stepped in line, their feet stomping the ground slowly at first, gracefully, their heads bobbing with the rhythm. As bodies filed down from the bus and other arriving vehicles, the loosely formed circle grew.

In a low, strong voice, Clyde began to chant the words to the Cheyenne Sun Dance Song.

E ya ha we ... ye he ye ye
He ye ... ho we ... ye whi ye ye
E ya ha we ... ye he ye ye
He ye ... ho he we ... ye hai i yi hi ha

Monty could not help but thrill at the experience of gathering with his brothers and sisters, dancing rhythmically at the first light of day, as they prayed for the protection of their sacred lands. The rocks, water, and all living things. Sunrise was the most powerful time of day, a time when prayers would be most far-reaching. Monty prayed for wisdom and strength, for the ability to influence the day's outcome.

He ... yi ha i ... ya ha ya ya
Ha ai ya ha ai yo yu ai ye ye
Ha ai ya ho ho o ya
Ho ai ho ho ho ... o ya
He ye he a ya

The dancers continued for almost ninety minutes. As the sun began its climb up the distant slopes of the mountains, the ceremonial firekeeper, Victor Green, walked around the human circle, cleansing each participant with smoke from a sage bundle. Then he offered each a pinch of sacred tobacco.

A large crowd had by now assembled in the camp, with as many watching the dance as participating. There was a festive atmosphere, with food and drink passed around freely. Monty knew most of those present. Some had come from as far away as Nevada, where Monty had placed a call to the Shundahai network for support. Many of those faces were new to him.

As Monty took the tobacco given him by Victor and threw it into the fire, something drew his eye to where two non-Indians stood, several yards away from the circle, observing. There were other non-Indians—strangers—in the crowd that had come up from Nevada. But these two Monty recognized. He had seen the man before. An old rancher who'd lived in the valley forever. Monty couldn't remember the rancher's name right now, but he knew his ranch, just off the reservation, along the Two Medicine.

And his companion. He had not seen her since his trip to give a guest lecture on Indian activism at the University of Idaho.

Before he had a chance to look away, she'd caught sight of Monty, and for the briefest of moments, he found himself staring into the eyes of Isabel McLain.

ALL WINTER LONG, Tony Wilderman thought the silence too good to be true. Monty Four Bear and Clyde Birdseye— he'd made sure to familiarize himself with the names after the tribal council meeting—had impressed him as serious, perhaps even violent, activists. Too serious to let the proposed drilling go forward without further resistance.

Still, the sight that met Tony and his crew's eyes upon rounding the last bend in the gravel road leading to the drill site left Tony's fleshy jowls resting on his even fleshier neck.

"What the fuck?"

Tony, driving the lead truck, slowed to a crawl.

Ahead, the only part of the equipment he'd installed over the winter that was visible were the tops of the rigging poles. The fence, tractors, and red canvas lean-to had been swallowed by the crowd. There had to have been a hundred gathered there, directly in front of the only entrance to the drill site. Maybe more.

If Tony hadn't known better, he'd think he'd stumbled, uninvited, upon a party, so festive the scene appeared. But Tony knew better. And three teepees, plus the reaction of the crowd upon its recognition of WRI's vehicles, left little room for doubt as to the purpose of the gathering.

Two hundred yards from the group, Tony stopped his truck. The three vehicles behind him followed suit. Stepping out, his eyes trained on the scene in front of him, Tony could hear the approaching footsteps of his workers.

"We're not goin' in there, are we?" one asked.

"You told us those Indians approved the drilling," another added.

Tony peeled his eyes off the scene awaiting them and bore them instead into the men assembled behind him.

"Calm down," he ordered. "Do you hear? You sound like a bunch of old women."

The last of the crew, Rod Sokaski, a six-foot-three, broad-shouldered ex-hockey player from Calgary, had just approached the rest of them from the last truck. Rod had played for five years for the Vancouver Canucks. Now he was the star of Calgary's recreational league.

"It don't bother *me* to go in there," Rod said, spewing chewing tobacco through the gap in his front teeth that used to house his upper right canine. "I'll beat the shit out of anyone who tries to stop me."

The others, stung by Wilderman's rebuke, made half-hearted noises of agreement, although it was clear no one but Rod felt exhilarated by the sight of the protestors.

Reaching into the truck, Wilderman grabbed his cell phone and dialed 911.

"We've got trouble at the WRI drill site. You better get some of your people out here."

"What kind of trouble?" the operator wanted to know.

"Demonstrators blocking the site."

"Has there been any violence?"

"No."

"Has anyone threatened violence?"

"No."

"Are you certain this is an emergency?"

"It will be just as soon as we get back in our trucks and drive onto the site."

"Just where is the drill site located?"

Wilderman let out a sigh of exasperation.

"On the Blackfeet reservation. The tribal police know where. Get someone out here. *Now.*"

He threw the phone back into the truck and turned to assess the situation.

The road leading to the gate of the enclosed area was blocked, not only by protestors bearing banners, but a large teepee painted with murals had also been erected dead-center in the road. Several protesters were dressed in traditional Indian war bonnets. Upon seeing the WRI vehicles, the festivities had stopped and the group had begun forming a human chain around the fenced area. The fact that they'd succeeded in circling the entire site told Wilderman that, if anything, he'd underestimated their numbers.

From this distance it was impossible to identify any of them, but Wilderman knew he would find Monty Four Bear and Clyde Birdseye among them.

"Climb back in your trucks," Wilderman ordered.

"We're going in there?" one of the men said tentatively.

"You bet your sweet ass we are."

"All right," Rod Sokaski exclaimed.

With Wilderman's WRI-logoed truck in the lead, the convoy started back up.

The protesters, hand in hand, had begun chanting.

We . . . will . . . protect . . . our . . . land.

As Wilderman's truck inched forward, displaying no sign that its occupant would allow the human wall to deter him, reinforcements positioned themselves in front of the section of the human chain that blocked the road. In just seconds, Wilderman was making eye contact with them.

With only yards separating the protesters and the truck, Monty Four Bear stepped into the gap between them. Crossing his arms over his chest, Four Bear braced himself and glared at Wilderman, daring him to proceed.

Motherfuckin' Indian. I oughta just run you down and get rid of you once and for all.

Wilderman was considering doing just that when sirens filled the air. With the approaching tribal police car in his rearview mirror, Wilderman braked.

Wouldn't do to run someone over in front of the police.

Instead of toning things down, the arrival of the police and the proximity to Wilderman and his crew, who were all alighting from their vehicles, agitated the crowd.

Wilderman had just turned to yell instructions to his men when something large and wet hit him in the back of the head. His hand shot up to his scalp and came back full of smashed tomato.

Laughter and shouts rose from the crowd.

This was the final straw for Rod Sokaski, who charged into the crowd.

"I'll kill you sons of bitches."

Several of the WRI men had been holding back. One had even jumped back in his truck. But Rod's daring inspired two others, who followed, fists swinging, in Rod's path.

A free-for-all broke out, and the lone officer who'd responded to the 911 call seemed helpless to stop it. Wilderman saw him run back to his car to radio for reinforcements.

Wilderman kept his head down and plodded forward slowly through the crowd, keys to the gate in hand. Most of the attention seemed to be directed now toward Rod and his coworkers. Many of the activists were trying to stop those that had stepped into the fray, but passions ran high, and even if one protester was persuaded or physically restrained from striking out, another stepped in.

Rod Sokaski had taken on two and three Blackfeet at a time. Blood dripped from his nose and a gash above his left eye, but he showed no sign of surrender. Fueled by memories of many a ruckus on the hockey ice, Rod continued charging the crowd like a bull.

Wilderman could no longer see any of his other men, though waves of activity and shouts hinted that at least one had ended up on the ground.

Wilderman had one goal in mind.

Opening the gate to the drill site. No motherfucking Indian was gonna stop him from doing what he'd come here this morning to do.

Pushing his way through the outer perimeter of the crowd, he finally saw it. The chain lock on the gate. He'd just extended his hand to reach for it when someone jumped him from behind. His assailant on his back, Wilderman fell to the ground, where the two men twisted and grunted, his attacker clinging like a monkey to him, preventing Wilderman from being able to land a single blow. Maintaining a tight grasp on the ring that held the key to the lock, Wilderman had just managed to break his parasitic attacker's ironclad hold on him when a heavy boot came down on his wrist.

Wilderman's eyes followed the worn cowboy boot skyward to see Monty Four Bear's cold black eyes staring down at him.

"I'll take these," Four Bear said, bending to take the key ring.

At the tightening of Wilderman's grasp, Four Bear stomped down harder on the wrist, which felt to Wilderman like it might shatter. Reflexively, his fingers opened and Four Bear grabbed the keys.

At that moment, the first shot rang out.

BUD WOLFKILL AIMED his .45 skyward, away from the crowd and into the distance, and pulled the trigger. He'd just been clocking out at the station after another night shift when the call from Jason Prather came in. Prather needed reinforcements out at the WRI drill site.

By the time Bud arrived, a wild brawl—worthy of the reputations of both Montana and the Blackfeet reservation—was underway. Prather, fresh from the criminology program at the University of Montana, was so green he hadn't even broken up a good bar fight yet. He scuttled from one fisticuffs to the next, breaking protester from miner, but without assistance, he felt helpless to make any arrests.

The crowd barely noticed Bud's sirens as his squad car squealed to a halt, raising a cloud of dust.

But all heads turned at the blast of the .45.

"Next jackass that throws a punch gets a free ride to jail."

For a moment, the crowd seemed inclined to comply with Bud's command, but then a rock sailed overhead, shattering the windshield of a white truck bearing the WRI logo, and once again all hell broke loose.

Grabbing Officer Prather by the arm, Bud had to yell in his ear to be heard.

"Who the fuck started this?"

"Don't know," Prather, wild-eyed, answered.

"Indians or miners?"

"Far as I could see, they've both done their fair share."

Frustrated, Bud snapped, "Well, don't just stand there. Arrest someone."

He watched as Prather approached a miner who was on the ground, surrounded by protesters. Prather looked back, uncertain as to who Bud wanted him to arrest. Bud pointed at an Indian about to boot the downed miner in the rear end. Prather grabbed the offender by the elbow, jerking him around. The Blackfeet protester's fists came up, and in the instant before they connected with the fresh-faced officer's jaw, Bud fired another shot into the air.

"You don't wanna do that, Riley. Assaulting an officer, resisting arrest. Assault and battery on that fella you been kickin'. Be a long while 'fore you'd be back home with Tana and the kids."

Riley glared at Prather, then dropped his fists. Prather promptly snapped a pair of handcuffs on them.

The gunshots and arrest had finally succeeded in capturing the attention of the crowd.

"The rest of you," Bud roared, "I can fit three of you in my car, and three in Junior here's car. Who's next?"

More fists fell, as did one or two rocks. The WRI employee on the ground rose slowly, brushing dirt off his shirt sleeves and jeans.

Bud surveyed the crowd.

"Where you at, Monty?" he called.

"Here."

The voice came from the back of the gathering.

The protesters split as Wolfkill strode toward the fenced enclosure.

Bud found Wilderman and Monty Four Bear in front of the gate, standing side by side—though from the looks of Wilderman's clothes, he had recently spent a little time on the ground.

"What the hell's going on here?" Wolfkill demanded to know.

"We're just demonstrating our opposition to the mine, that's all," Monty said. "Nobody's breaking any laws."

"Since when's it legal to destroy property and break noses?"

"You're right. Destruction of property isn't legal. Trouble is, I don't know who threw that rock, and I doubt very much if you know either, Bud. And as for breaking noses, even demonstrators have the right to protect themselves."

Wilderman's face turned a bright red.

"That's the biggest crock of shit I ever heard."

Monty Four Bear smiled.

"Your gorilla threw the first punch. Everyone here saw it. What happened after that was self-defense."

Wilderman turned to Wolfkill.

"Are you gonna let this . . ." both Monty and Bud waited for the racial slur, but Wilderman came to his senses before continuing. "Are you gonna let *him* get by with this? This bullshit about self-defense? Me and my men were just trying to go to work. To do the job your tribal council gave us permission to do. And this is what we have to put up with."

Bud looked both men over, then answered in his usual unhurried manner.

"Monty's right about one thing. No law against demonstratin'. And this is reservation land, so there's been no trespass. If Monty's tellin' the truth and your man threw the first punch, I'm not sure any of his people broke the law."

"What about my truck's windshield?"

"You might have something there, if you could identify who threw that rock."

"You know damn well I can't identify who threw it. It came from the crowd."

"Pretty hard to arrest a whole crowd. Don't got enough cells to hold 'em."

Wolfkill turned to Monty.

"Monty, like it or not, you're gonna have to let these men get in there and do their job."

"We *can't* get in," Wilderman said. "Not without keys to my truck and the gate."

"Where's the keys?"

Wilderman glared at Monty Four Bear.

"*He* took them. Then he threw them back into the crowd."

Bud had to stifle a grin at this revelation.

He turned back to the crowd, a large section of which had gathered around the three men.

"Okay, who's got the keys?"

This inquiry was met with looks of surprise and shoulder shrugs that proclaimed innocent ignorance.

As Wolfkill stood waiting for someone to cough up the keys—or at least giving the appearance he was waiting for someone to cough up the keys, for in reality, he knew that the chances of that happening were somewhere between slim and none—his attention was drawn to a commotion near the center teepee.

Breaking back through the crowd, Bud approached the teepee, where a heated argument was taking place.

Isabel McLain was ministering to a big bloke of a man, who had blood spouting from a three-inch gash on his forehead. The man sat propped up against one of the teepee's support poles. Isabel's medical bag was open on the ground, next to her patient, while she rummaged through it.

Standing over them was a very angry Clyde Birdseye.

"What do you think you're doing?" he railed at Isabel. "What the hell are you doing helping him?"

At first, Isabel refused to acknowledge Clyde, but when he tried to grab the bandages she'd finally located, she flew into him.

"Get your hands off me." One errant strand of black hair hung over Isabel's dark eyes—which surprised Bud with the intensity of the hatred they bore for Birdseye. "Don't you dare interfere with my treating this man."

Clyde turned to face the protesters gathering around them.

"See. She's one of them. I knew it. Are you really going to trust this woman with your lives? Take your kids to her when they're sick? Allow her to vaccinate you as part of some perverted experiment on Indians?"

Bud could see Isabel's hands shaking as she stood to face her accuser.

"I came today to protest the mine," she said. "I don't want this mine on the reservation any more than you do. But that doesn't mean I will sit by and allow an injured man to go untreated. Now get out of my way before I ask Sheriff Wolfkill to arrest you."

Bud hadn't seen her until now. If he had, he'd have escorted her right to his car, out of harm's way. But as bodies parted at the frontline of the onlookers, a frail Sky Thomas, bent nearly double over her cane, stepped forward.

"What makes you think she's not one of us?" Sky barked angrily at Clyde Birdseye.

"*One of us?*" Clyde hooted. "You crazy old . . ."

Wolfkill grabbed his arm and stopped him.

"That's enough, Clyde," he said. "You show Sky some respect. And let this lady do her job. Now get out of here."

NOTHING COULD HAVE surprised Isabel more than the sight of a yellow taxicab sitting in the driveway of her cabin when she returned home from the protest. She hadn't even known there were cabs in Browning. One look at the door of this one and she saw it had come all the way from Kalispell.

As Isabel pulled into her driveway behind the cab, blocking it, a back door opened. A tall, dark woman with strong features and stylishly short hair emerged.

"K. T.," Isabel called, jumping out of her truck.

K. T. Seinberg didn't walk, she flowed. The effect was enhanced by her tendency to wear long, loose skirts that hid the fact that, with a sixty-hour work week, she spent more time lunching with clients than working out. The two women embraced.

"My God, Isabel, you told me you'd moved to the country, but this is ridiculous."

"How did you find me?"

K. T. lowered dark sunglasses to the tip of her nose and eyed Isabel over their frame.

"I practically had to bribe that damn assistant of yours. She wouldn't give me the time of day until I convinced her I was actually your attorney and that I was here to help you."

Isabel let out a brief laugh.

"Suzanne can be a force to reckon with. It's wonderful to see you, but I have to say, I'm more than a little surprised."

"Listen, dearie, this isn't a social call. Let's go inside. I have news for you."

"News that you didn't want to deliver over the telephone."

"That's right."

With a sense of dread, Isabel steered K. T. up the path to the cabin's front door. Isabel ignored the shock that registered on her attorney's face upon seeing the modest accommodations.

"Should I make us some tea?" she offered.

"Right about now I could use something a little stiffer than that."

"I think I have a cheap pinot."

"Let's open it."

Isabel had finally mastered the woodstove so that she could leave for the better part of the day without it burning completely out. Keenly aware of K. T.'s penetrating gaze, she opened its door, threw two pieces of wood on the bed of coals, unwound the damper to let it stoke up. Then she went to the cupboard above the sink and located the bottle of pinot noir.

"That's how you heat this place?" K. T. asked.

"That plus the fireplace."

"Who cuts the wood?"

"My landlord usually does, but if I'm home, I help him."

Isabel's curiosity was killing her, but still, she did not ask the question hanging in the air.

They each took a sip of the wine she'd poured.

"You ever miss Seattle? Or your old house?"

Isabel smiled.

"You're not doing a very good job of hiding your shock."

"I'm not trying to."

"No. I don't miss my old house at all. And for the most part, I don't miss Seattle either. In fact, the longer I'm here, the more I begin to suspect that I was never actually happy there. Even before Alistair."

"That's sad."

"Yes. It is." It was Isabel's turn to stare now. "But I am happy now, K. T. Truly happy. Not in some fairy tale kind of way, but in a very basic way. It's not something I can explain."

K. T. did not respond, instead she stared at the jelly jar holding her wine.

"As I said, I have news. News that I wanted to deliver in person." She raised her eyes to Isabel's. "You have become the subject of a criminal investigation by the FDA."

CHAPTER

TWENTY-FIVE

ISABEL'S HEAD SNAPPED back.

"For what?"

"Conspiracy to commit fraud in a number of clinical trials."

"This must be some kind of joke."

K. T. Seinberg reached across the table and grabbed Isabel's hand.

"I'm sorry, Isabel. But it's no joke. The drug companies were willing to turn their heads to what was going on with Alistair's trials, but the FDA came in. They've had half a dozen agents scrutinizing all of his records. It didn't take them long to see a pattern with the patients Alistair was enrolling in the different trials. Many of them had been patients of yours in the ER shortly before enrolling in his studies."

"You mean it wasn't just Bernice Hougham? There were more?"

K. T. nodded her head.

"Quite a few more."

"But how could he have known who my patients were? How is that even possible?"

"According to Alistair, you gave him that information. Routinely."

Isabel yanked her hand loose from K. T.'s, spilling her wine across the table as she did so.

"That's ridiculous. I was the one who turned him in. As soon as I learned about Bernice."

"That's what I've told them."

"You've been talking to them?"

"They came to me looking for you. Listen, Isabel, if you didn't give Alistair that information, he had to have gotten it some other way. How? How else could he have known your patients? I mean, he contacted most of them at home. He had their addresses. He wrote them a letter introducing himself as your husband. Saying you'd provided their names to him because you believed they stood to benefit from whatever clinical trial it was he was trying to get them to sign up for. How could he have gotten that information?"

Isabel had the childish urge to press her hands to her ears and scream gibberish, anything to block out what she was hearing.

"I don't know," she finally said. "I simply don't know."

"FANCY MEETING YOU here."

Tony Wilderman looked up from the fax he'd picked up at the front desk on his way down to breakfast. After yesterday's riot at the drill site, half the crew had requested reassignment. He'd called WRI's headquarters first thing this morning and asked to be faxed a complete list of all WRI field workers. He'd been going down the list of names and addresses, checking off those who'd requested transfers, and drawing stick-figure stars next to those who were already on the Blackfeet crew and willing to stay, and those men he knew personally from other crews around the world.

"Dr. Bott," he said. "I didn't expect to see you back here again so soon."

"I'm developing a bit of a fondness for this place, even if they don't serve grits," Alistair Bott grinned. "Mind if I join you?"

"Of course not. I could use some company."

As Bott settled in, he signaled the waitress.

"I heard about what happened yesterday," he said, "out at your drill site. Ugly business."

"You got that right. Fucking Indians. And the damnedest thing is that the tribal police say they've got a right to be there. They've been no help at all."

"What do you expect from their own people? Sounds like you're in a bit of a bind."

"Bit of a bind?" Wilderman scoffed. "It's a hell of a lot worse than a bind. WRI's had big expectations for that mine." He refrained from telling Bott that LeCoque, furious at yesterday's turn of events, had told Wilderman the company's future may well rest on the Montana deposit. "It just burns me up to think a bunch of Indian radicals might put an end to those plans."

"Surely you don't intend to capitulate?" Bott said, an expression of shocked disapproval on his face. "I mean, if it were me, I'd fight fire with fire."

The waitress had arrived with coffee and orange juice.

"Mornin', Alistair," she cooed, sliding a menu to him. "Be right back for your order."

"Fight fire with fire?" Wilderman repeated. "We tried that yesterday. I've got one real goon on the crew who went apeshit on those Indians. Used to be a hockey player on the Vancouver team. The rest of my men were scared shitless by the time all was said and done, but I swear to God, Rod got off on it. But all *that* did was turn the tribal police against us. They told us we were there as the Indians' guests. That the protesters had every right to be there too. And that if we used violence again, we'd be arrested and charged."

"Now, you obviously can't count on the local police." Bott's "police" came out POE-leece. "Maybe you just need to be a little more covert in dissuading these troublemakers."

"I'm not following you."

"Let me tell you something. As you may have guessed, I'm from the South. Now, my daddy, he wasn't exactly a role model, but I do have to give him credit for teaching me some things. Especially about getting by in the real world. You see, Daddy was a Klansman . . ."

"The Ku Klux Klan?" Wilderman made no attempt to disguise his shock.

"That's right. Nasty business, that Klan stuff. As I said, my daddy wasn't exactly my hero. But you have to give the Klan one thing. They knew how to silence their opponents. Some fire-breathin' liberals'd come to town, tryin to stir up trouble," as he talked, Bott seemed to slip back into time, into a lazier drawl, "and the Klan, they knew how to shut them right up. Those folks are all hot air. Daddy always said it just took findin' their weakness—he never said it, but I always knew what he meant, their wives, or kids—and they'd back down real quick-like."

Bott slipped back into the present and smiled. He could have been talking about the weather, so matter of fact was he over this disclosure about his past.

"You find the ring leaders, and give them a little of what they gave you and your men yesterday," he finished. "I promise you, you'll be back in business in no time."

Wilderman thought about what the doctor from Seattle seemed to be suggesting. When the waitress returned to take Bott's order, he studied him. He was an odd bird. Dressed to the nines all the time. Refined acting. Yet what he was suggesting was not only illegal, someone could easily end up getting hurt.

The waitress took Wilderman's empty plate and headed toward the kitchen with Bott's order.

"What did you say that ex–hockey player's name was?" Bott asked casually.

"I didn't say."

Bott laughed then.

"That's right. You didn't."

WHILE ISABEL, THROUGH K. T. Seinberg, had been the one to request the meeting, it soon became clear that it would only have been a matter of time before the FDA investigators came looking for Isabel.

K. T. had requested that the meeting be held away from Browning. They settled on Kalispell, where they rented a conference room at the Outlaw Inn.

Isabel and K. T. agreed to get together that morning, in K. T.'s room, to discuss what to expect. K. T. had ordered room service. With their breakfasts eaten, they finally got down to business.

"Here's how I see it," K. T. began, pacing back and forth as she spoke, while Isabel, seated near the open window, focused on staying calm. Isabel always sensed that her attorney hated seeing her clients in trouble but relished the actual battle. K. T.'s energy this morning declared her primed for their meeting.

"Ever since those congressional hearings last February got so much media attention—you know, the hearings called to look into deaths of patients in clinical trials—the FDA's been looking for a scapegoat. The pressure's on. Someone has to be held accountable. The NIH is blaming the FDA, and the FDA's blaming the NIH. The drug companies just want the whole thing to go away before it becomes impossible to recruit patients for their studies. Your ex-husband could hand them what they all want on a silver platter. A scapegoat. The villain who will take all the attention and pressure off the rest of this sorry lot."

"But what does that have to do with me?" Isabel replied.

"I'm as outraged by what I've been reading about those poor patients as anyone else. If Alistair did what they think he did—what I suspected him of doing—he *should* pay. I want that as much as they do." She laughed then, a short joyless laughter. "Probably more."

"That's the problem. We may learn otherwise today, but from what I see, almost everything they have on Alistair is circumstantial. They're desperate to change that."

They spent half an hour discussing K. T.'s expectations and strategy, then left the room, heading for the meeting.

"They need someone who can drive the stake through Alistair's heart," K. T. predicted as they approached the conference room. "And they think you're that someone."

"WE ARE LOOKING at research fraud of audacious proportions," the lead FDA investigator, a small, pinched man by the name of Earl Wittren, started out. His cohort, a humorless, oversized Dane named Hans Thomasen, sat by his side, making notes. "Cutting corners, inventing data, fictitious patients. Failure to report study deaths. You name it."

"But I had nothing to do with that," Isabel protested. "Nothing."

"Dr. McLain, we are conducting an extensive investigation into the clinical trials conducted under the supervision of your husband."

"*Former* husband," K. T. Seinberg inserted.

"Former husband," Wittren conceded. "A cross-check of your ER patients and Alistair Bott's study participants seems to contradict your statement that you had no involvement."

"I never gave my former husband a single patient's name for his trials. I didn't even know he was so heavily involved in them until a couple weeks before I called the drug companies and told them of my own concerns."

Wittren's sparse eyebrows shot up.

"You never mentioned your patients to Dr. Bott? Not even

in conversation? After all," he said in a conspiratorial, almost lascivious tone, "you were husband and wife."

Isabel thought back to the night Bernice Hougham came into the ER. Alistair had waited patiently for her to finish with Bernice. And then, in the car on the way to the fund-raising dinner, he'd questioned Isabel about her patient's condition. And Isabel had provided answers.

"You're right. On occasion I probably did mention my patients. But only in casual conversation. And it happened so rarely."

"One doctor sharing information with her spouse, who also happens to be a doctor, does not constitute a crime," K. T. Seinberg said. "If you've got something of substance, fellas, let's hear it. Otherwise, both my client and I have better things to do."

Isabel actually found herself trying to stifle a smile. Leave it to her feisty attorney to threaten to walk out on a meeting they had called.

"Were you aware that your husband enrolled patients for studies who were taking medications prohibited by the study protocols?" Wittren pressed on.

"No."

"Were you aware that records were falsified according to the requirements of a particular drug study? For example, if a certain blood pressure was required for a patient to partic-ipate in a hypertension study and your husband had a willing patient, but that patient's blood pressure was too low or too high, the records would be falsified?"

"No."

"What do you know about urine your husband routinely paid for because it contained high levels of proteins—just the level needed for patients to qualify for one of his studies? Urine that was then falsely attributed to study participants? We actually have invoices issued from your husband's office for these purchases."

Isabel jumped to her feet, clenching an angry fist.

"I have *never, ever* in my entire career deliberately misrepresented or fabricated patient data. Nor have I ever knowingly put a patient in a position of danger."

K. T. had risen too and now placed a steadying hand on Isabel's forearm.

"Take it easy," she said under her breath. "Don't let them bait you."

She turned to the investigators.

"Are you implying that my client was the source of this urine?"

"No."

"Because if you are, maybe we can just settle this matter once and for all. With a urine sample. Because I don't understand what the hell this has to do with my client if you're not planning to accuse her of either providing this extraordinarily valuable urine or buying it. And you've already told us the invoices were from Bott's office. They had nothing to do with my client. What will it be, gentlemen? Would you like my client to provide you with a sample? Here and now?"

Both men turned red-faced and appeared too startled to respond.

"Let's stick to matters that directly involve my client, gentlemen. Or else cut this meeting short."

Wittren cleared his throat and stared at Isabel, waiting for her to take her seat again.

Slowly, Isabel lowered herself into it.

"Do you recall an ER patient of yours by the name of Alice Richards?" he asked.

"The name isn't familiar, but you have to understand, I had dozens of patients each shift."

Wittren took the paper handed him by Thomasen and began to read.

"Mrs. Richards came to the clinic after injuring herself—her knee—in an adult soccer game."

"May I see that?" Isabel asked, reaching for the paper.

Wittren hesitated, then pushed the document across the desk to her.

It took only seconds for Isabel to remember.

"Yes. I remember this patient."

"What was the diagnosis?"

"A partial tear of the anterior cruciate ligament."

"What treatment did you render?"

"It's here, in the file. I took an X ray. Prescribed anti-inflammatories. I sent her home with instructions to alternate hot and cold compresses."

"Did you recommend surgery?"

"No. I told her she should consult with an orthopod. Sometimes a slight tear will heal on its own, without surgery. I wasn't qualified to make that recommendation."

"Did you relay—during casual conversation—any of this information to your husband?"

"*No.*"

"You're certain of that?"

"Absolutely."

He glanced knowingly at Thomasen, who handed him another paper from the same file.

"Here is a sworn affidavit from Mrs. Richards," Wittren said, making no attempt to hide his glee. "It states that your husband contacted her at home just two days after her visit to Harborview's ER. Dr. Bott told her that you had suggested that he contact Mrs. Richards, that if she were lucky, she might just be a candidate for a study he was conducting on a new product that could stave off arthritis. He asked her to come to his office for a meeting.

"When Mrs. Richards arrived at his office, she attests to feeling pressured by your husband. He told her that an injury like hers almost always resulted in arthritis, oftentimes so severe it ultimately impaired one's mobility. As a very athletic young woman, Mrs. Richards was very concerned. Still, she had some reservations about the study, but your husband rushed her, forced a decision that very day by telling her they had only one spot left in the study. That he couldn't hold it for her and that she'd regret her decision for the rest of her life if she didn't act right then. Needless to say, she signed up."

Again, he slid his "evidence" against Isabel across the table toward her and K. T.

"As you can see in the affidavit, in addition to being frightened by the prospect of developing arthritis in that knee, Mrs. Richards stated that she didn't want to make either you or your husband mad."

"That's outrageous," Isabel cried.

"We agree."

"Does Mrs. Richards's affidavit claim that she had any direct contact with my client? Other than her visit to the ER?" K. T. Seinberg cut in.

"No."

"That's because she did not. My client knew nothing of any of this. She had no way of knowing her husband was contacting her ER patients and using her name—and the relationship she'd already established with the patients—as an introduction. And you can't prove otherwise."

"No, Ms. Seinberg," he finally said, "we do not have unequivocal proof of your client's knowledge or involvement. But just how do you think Alistair Bott obtained such sensitive information as this? Mrs. Richards's case is just one of dozens. If Dr. McLain didn't supply this information to her husband, then who did?"

He was speaking to K. T. Seinberg, but his eyes were trained on Isabel.

"Dr. McLain. We are willing to work with you. We may even be able to strike a deal with you, let you off the hook, if you agree to provide us with the proof we need to convict your husband."

"*Let me off the hook?*" Isabel practically hissed. "Aren't you listening? I haven't done anything wrong. Nothing. I'm the one who turned my husband in."

"We've talked to Dr. Bott. According to him, that was simply a clever but desperate attempt on your part to distance yourself from these studies. Your husband claims that you're the mastermind behind the whole thing. That he wanted to report the death of Bernice Hougham, but you refused. That when Bernice died, you became frightened and turned on him. He says you initiated contact with the pharmaceutical companies to throw us off, to make it look as though you were innocent. He also suggests that we keep a close eye on the study you're currently involved with."

Isabel was so stunned and enraged by the lies Alistair had fed them that she found herself speechless. Wittren continued.

"Dr. McLain, I ask you: Without hard evidence, just who are we supposed to believe?"

CHAPTER

TWENTY-SIX

ON THE ELEVENTH day of what had become widely known across the reservation as the Encampment, Monty and the half dozen remaining protesters awoke to the deafening roar of a helicopter, flying low across the draw between the two ridges.

On several occasions over the past week, WRI employees had ventured near the protesters' occupation zone, each time coming a little closer to the protesters themselves. They would sit in their trucks in silence, observing, then retreat. There had been no further confrontations or violence of any sort, which was beginning to get on Monty's nerves, because he didn't believe for one moment that WRI had reversed its decision to proceed with the drilling. They were playing some kind of a waiting game.

And Monty was not a patient man.

With the exception of two trips to Browning for supplies, Monty had not left the site. The initial adrenalin rush of battle had long faded and even the solace he derived from the traditional customs the protesters had agreed to observe—daily sunrise ceremonies, storytelling, and songs of war and victory—had been wearing thin. Until last night.

The mescal religion was an ancient Indian faith that had in the past few decades been revived and adopted by younger Indians. Mescal, or peyote, came from the tip of a cactus. The disk-shaped button induced a druglike effect that produced feelings of lightness and visions of beauty. It had been used for centuries for pain relief.

Two of the protesters still remaining at the drill site belonged to the Shundahai network. They'd come to Montana from Nevada, bearing a precious gift from the Southwest for their fellow activists.

Mescal buttons.

On the previous night, as darkness fell, the six brothers and one sister—all Native American—had entered the center teepee, where a fire was kept burning all night. Sitting cross-legged and blanketed in a circle around the fire, Monty, Clyde, and the other protesters each solemnly ingested one of the buttons. Heads bowed, some with blankets drawn over their heads to enhance the imagery, throughout the night each person took turns singing. Most of the songs contained no words, simply sounds that invoked that the truths of the universe be revealed to the singer. A small buckskin drum was passed around from one person to the next.

Monty had experienced a sensation of release, as though he were floating above the earthly troubles that had been sitting, like a wounded buffalo, on his shoulders. The fatigue brought on by a week of sleeping on the ground dissipated, and the anger and sadness that had filled his soul gave way to joy at visions of spectacular sunsets, glorious mountains, brooks singing to him of the power to heal.

As it was intended to do, the mescal ceremony helped Monty to see the road before him, to see the truths of life and the spirit. It renewed his hope.

And then, just before dawn, it lulled Monty and his brothers and sister to sleep.

Now the roar of a helicopter bearing a WRI logo had shattered that peace, and Monty's anger exploded skyward.

Grabbing a rock from the fire pit, Monty heaved it skyward at the passing helicopter.

"Sons of bitches."

In a rare turn of events, the restraining hand on his shoulder turned out to belong to Clyde.

"No offense, bro, but you're no Joe Montana." He shouted over the helicopter's din, giving Monty's shoulder a short squeeze. "Don't let them rob you of the spirit, man."

Monty turned to face Clyde. The mescal ceremony still lingered on his prematurely lined face.

Monty ran both hands through hair that hung loose to his shoulders. The two stood watching the helicopter retreat.

"You're right," Monty said. "It's not like I thought they'd given up."

"No, we knew that wasn't gonna happen anytime soon. Looks like they've just decided to begin the aerial survey." Clyde paused. "Only way we'll stop that is firepower."

"No violence. We agreed."

"Not yet anyway."

They'd just finished breakfast—scrambled eggs, coffee, and toast, all cooked over the fire—when the patrol car pulled up.

Bud Wolfkill emerged slowly, an unusually serious expression on his round face. He approached the group, who were seated around the fire. It wasn't until he stopped in front of where Monty sat on a large rock, plate balanced on his knees, that Bud made eye contact.

"I've got some bad news, Monty," he said. "You better come with me."

THE HOSPITAL IN Cutbank was a nondescript brown brick affair that, at four stories, claimed honors as the highest building in town.

Monty followed Bud Wolfkill through the lobby and to the elevator. When it failed to come immediately, he scanned the corridor for an exit sign and, finding one, made a beeline for the stairwell.

"Meet you up there," he told Bud over his shoulder.

He took two and three stairs at a time.

A nurse had just left room 414 when he stepped into the hallway from the stairwell.

"How is he?" Monty called.

She turned his way. The nameplate identified her as Julie Watson, R.N. Up close, she looked too fresh-faced and young to be a full-fledged nurse. Maybe without the short bangs and pageboy cut of her chestnut hair.

"He's sleeping right now. We've got him on morphine. Are you a relative?"

"His son."

"You can go in, but please don't disturb him. Sleep is probably the most powerful medicine for him right now."

"When can I see the doctor?"

"I'll let him know you're here."

Slowly Monty pushed the door open. The first bed was unoccupied. A white cotton curtain had been pulled around the bed by the window.

Monty stepped around it.

Asleep, drugged, illuminated by the sunlight pouring through the window, Leroy Four Bear appeared to have shrunk to a fraction of his normal five-foot-eight self. His formerly straight and aristocratic nose—the feature of which he'd always been most proud—was, however, twice its former size and no longer traveled a steady course. His upper lip, in particular the left side, had also at least doubled in size. Over his right eyebrow, a three-inch gash had already been stitched.

Monty felt Bud Wolfkill's presence, but did not turn. It wasn't because he did not want Wolfkill to see his tears, but because he could not take his eyes from his father's beaten form.

He heard Wolfkill steal back out of the room, closing the door behind him.

Monty settled on to the window ledge, shading his father, and sat watching the clear liquid drip, one precise drop at a time, into the clear tubing that ran from the bag hanging over Leroy Four Bear's head to somewhere under the white sheet covering him. His father's breaths were short and shallow, like those of a small animal. He did not stir.

"Mr. Four Bear?"

Monty turned toward the door. A wiry, bald man with glasses, wearing a telltale white smock and stethoscope, gestured for him to follow.

Out in the hallway, Bud Wolfkill joined them.

"I'm Dr. Sharp. Your father is lucky to be alive. Aside from a broken nose and two fractured ribs, there are no broken bones. He was in a great deal of pain when he came in, which is why I've got him on morphine. Those injuries will just take time. I'm more concerned about internal injuries. And his concussion. The CAT scan shows a good-sized bruise on the brain. He sustained one hell of a blow. Or maybe a series of blows. But he was alert throughout his admission and the subsequent testing, so there's every reason to be hopeful that there's no permanent damage."

"You mentioned internal injury."

"Yes. Nothing showed up on the X rays or CAT scan, but there are a couple reasons I want to monitor him closely.

First, his abdominal region is extremely tender. Considering the beating he took, this fact alone might not have that much significance."

The beating.

Monty had assumed Wolfkill had come to the drill site to arrest him, that WRI had finally managed to force the tribal police into action.

But when they'd climbed into the squad car, Wolfkill had turned to him with the news.

"It's about Leroy, Monty."

Luke had awakened in the middle of the night to the sounds of Leroy's screams. He'd rushed to his grandfather's bedroom, where a "giant" of a man with the crushed and distorted features of a monster stood over Leroy's limp form on the ground.

Luke had rushed the giant, pummeling him with his fists.

"Leave my grandpa alone."

With one swat, the giant had sent Luke flying.

"Out of my way, kid."

He'd reached down, grabbed Leroy by the shirt collar— Leroy always fell into bed in his clothes from the previous day—and pulled the old Indian's face up to within inches of his.

"You tell your son to back off," he'd said.

"Or I'll be back."

He'd kicked Leroy in the ribs, which sent Luke flying onto his back.

"Fuckin' kid."

Luke rode him halfway down the hallway before being tossed into the wall. Shaken, but amazingly reasoned for what he'd just witnessed, Luke had returned to the bedroom to make certain Leroy was alive. When he determined he was, he'd run the quarter-mile to Edna's house to call 911.

"Where's Luke now?" Monty had demanded of Wolfkill. "How is he?"

"He wanted to go to school," Wolfkill had answered.

"Tough little guy. Edna offered to have him stay with her tonight."

"No, he'll stay with me."

"You sure that's a good idea?" Wolfkill had responded.

It took Monty a second to get Wolfkill's point. If Luke wasn't safe at Leroy's, he certainly wouldn't be safe at Monty's house.

Monty could not afford to lose control. Not when Luke and Leroy needed him. But now, standing in the glare of the harsh hospital lights, hearing a doctor describe the injuries sustained by his sixty-nine-year-old father—as a result of Monty's actions—the anger and guilt threatened to explode into a hurricane that would rattle even Monty Four Bear.

"But in addition to the tenderness," Dr. Sharp continued, "your father's blood work, the hemoglobin in particular, is borderline. We'll monitor it, and his urine and stool for signs of internal bleeding. We'll be keeping him on IVs for several days."

"And if there is bleeding?"

"Then we'll operate."

"Is he in any kind of condition for that? For surgery?"

"If there's bleeding, we'll have no choice."

A NEW NURSE, Julie Watson's replacement for the night shift, kicked Monty out at precisely eight P.M. She and Monty had already butted heads over the fact that earlier that day they'd brought another patient into the room.

"There are plenty of empty rooms," Monty had complained at the nurse's station after his father's roommate had been there two hours. "I've seen them. There's one right next door. This guy's gonna keep my father up all night with his coughing. And he's got that goddamn TV up so loud it's hard to think. I want him moved."

Nurse Ratchet, as Monty had quickly nicknamed Julie's fiftyish, brusque replacement, gave him a look designed to intimidate. With the shoulders of a linebacker and wiry gray

hair pulled back so tightly into a bun that her temples were
stretched like a rubber band, the look really wasn't that difficult for her to achieve.

"Take it up with the administration office tomorrow."

Case closed.

Now, at Monty's resistance to leaving his father's bedside,
she employed similar subtlety.

"Out."

Monty, still perched on the windowsill, looked at his father. Leroy had awakened several times during the day, usually when the nurses came in to take his blood pressure and
make sure he hadn't lost consciousness from the head blows.
Each time, he'd acknowledged Monty's presence with a
look, or a word or two, but for the most part, he'd slept. A
deep sleep—despite the short, shallow breaths, which Julie
Watson explained were the result of the broken ribs. Even
the simple act of breathing, she told Monty, would be painful
for Leroy for a while.

Now Leroy's eyes, the left lid still puffy, opened again.

"Go home," he said softly. It obviously hurt to talk too.
"I'm okay. Luke needs you."

"I just talked to him. He's at Edna's. He sounds okay."

"Go home. I'm juz gonna sleep. Come back tomorrow."

"You sure, Pop?"

" 'Course I'm sure."

Monty bent to kiss a leathery cheek. When was the last
time he'd kissed—or even hugged—his father? He'd spent
so much time these past few years—hell, most of his life—
being angry with Leroy for letting the family down. Giving
him a hard time about the booze. Wondering why he'd never
even tried to get a job.

Monty flushed with sudden shame.

All that mattered was that Leroy was still alive. Monty
would not take him for granted again.

"I love you," he said, standing there.

Leroy's eyes popped open again.

"Not gonna die on you, if that's what you're thinking."

The annoyance was feigned. Monty could tell the display of affection pleased his father.

Monty stopped in the lobby to telephone Edna and Luke again.

"I'm just leaving the hospital. Thought I'd stop by and check on Luke," he told Edna.

"Boy's already sleepin', Monty. I'd let him be."

"You'll call me if he needs me?"

"You bet."

"You got your doors locked, Edna?"

"We're locked in tight. And nobody gonna get within hundred feet of here with Grizz outside."

Grizz was Edna's rottweiler.

"Plus I've got that .45. Only good thing that no-good husband of mine left me. And I know how to use it."

"Okay, then. I'll stop by in the morning, take Luke to school."

"He'll like that."

The thirty miles to Browning passed in a blur. Monty's anger was beginning to take hold, get the best of him.

He mustn't let it. Intimidation of activists was not new to him. He even taught a short section on it in his lecture on activism. Telephone threats and harassment, arson, even violent assaults like the one on Leroy. He'd taught his students that they were a price an activist could end up paying. That they were intended to make advocates think twice before taking a public stand, or, as in this case, to force them to back down from a stance already taken.

It's not personal, he'd said. It's simply a political act committed by your opponents in an effort to silence you.

But Monty's father lying in a hospital bed was personal. Very personal.

When Monty pulled up to his small white frame house, two miles outside Browning, he sensed immediately that something was not right. It was dark by now, and hard to see the unlit house, but as he walked up the dirt path to its front door he put his finger on it.

The curtains in the living room had been drawn. Monty couldn't remember the last time he'd closed them.

Monty stood, silent, frozen on the cement stoop, listening. Nothing.

Slowly, he reached for the doorknob. It took only a light touch for the door to creak open. He'd left it locked.

He stepped inside the darkened living room.

When Monty was a boy, Leroy used to tell him he would have made a good Indian scout, so fine-tuned were his senses. Now these senses told Monty the house was empty.

He reached for the light switch on the wall.

And saw that a storm had swept through the living room, upending furniture, smashing framed photographs of Monty's deceased mother and grandmother. The little black-and-white TV that formerly occupied a table in the corner lay in pieces against the far wall.

Monty strode past all of it, through the tiny kitchen that he could see had not escaped the assault, into his bedroom. He stepped over a lamp on his way to his desk. The digital clock, untouched, shed enough light for him to see that the space usually taken by his laptop now sat empty. His feet slid on loose papers scattered over the floor.

He reached for the desk lamp, then, unable to find it, returned to the lamp he'd stepped over. Fumbling to locate the electrical outlet in the dark, he managed to plug it in, but the bulb had been broken.

He retreated to the kitchen, where he found a new bulb.

He was angry about the stolen computer, but he knew that it would be next to impossible for anyone to penetrate the AIM files it contained. His biggest fear, he realized as he retraced his steps to the bedroom, concerned his paper files. They contained everything from research he'd conducted on WRI and other mining companies with bad environmental records, to pamphlets he'd prepared, to names and addresses of other activists. It was these, the identities of other activists, plus plans for further disruption of WRI's activities, that he most feared falling into enemy hands.

The light revealed that his filing cabinet had been literally torn apart in a search. One drawer hung open, the other lay next to the bed on its side. Every file had been perused. Papers—those apparently holding little interest—had been flung across the floor.

It took just minutes to determine that while many files had been perused, then left behind, several were missing.

His WRI and ImmuVac files. And the entire file on the BIA lawsuit.

"HOW YOU DOING today, Pop?"

"Better," Leroy grunted, barely audible over the *oohs* and *aahs* emanating from the wall-mounted television. On its screen, above the subtitle "I used to be a geek but look at me now," a curvy brunette strutted to the applause of an appreciative audience. She embraced Sally Jesse Raphael before settling seductively into her seat of honor.

Monty drew the curtain between Leroy and his roommate's bed, eliminating Leroy's view of the TV but giving the two of them more privacy. He cracked the window open half an inch, then settled in his seat on the sill.

Leroy's color did look better today. And while he'd remained flat on his back all the day before, he could sit up now, at least at the thirty-degree angle his nurse had raised his bed. But his face still looked as though he'd walked in front of a train. And he was still hooked up to an IV. Monty would have to ask the doctor about that.

"How's Luke?"

"Luke's fine. He's just worried about you, that's all. Edna is taking good care of him."

"Tell him not to worry 'bout me. I'll be home 'fore he knows it. He oughta just enjoy Edna's fry bread while he can."

Monty chuckled.

"I had a piece this morning when I picked Luke up for school. Hot off the grill. Edna's fry bread's somethin'."

"Enit? Maybe you can bring me some."

"You bet, Pop. I'll bring you some tomorrow."

They settled into silence, listening to Sally Jesse Raphael, but not really paying much attention.

"So what you gonna do about this?" Leroy finally said, turning to study his son.

Monty's gaze met that of his father.

Monty shrugged.

"I'm not sure."

He did not mention the fact that his house had been ransacked, most likely by the same person who'd broken into Leroy's house and attacked him.

"Putting myself in danger's one thing. This happening to you . . . well, that's different."

"Don't let them bastards get away with this," Leroy said, his anger causing him to lean forward suddenly. "That's just how they want you to start thinkin'. *Don't do it.*" Involuntarily, Leroy took a deep breath, which caused him to grimace. He beckoned Monty closer with his index finger.

"Get your ass back out there at that drill site," he whispered, "and raise hell. You hear me?"

Monty put his hand on his father's shoulder and managed a sad half smile.

"I don't know if it's worth it. Endangering you. What if they go after Luke next?"

Leroy raised a withered hand and reached for the collar of Monty's blue flannel shirt. Latching on to it, he pulled his son closer.

"You listen to me, boy." His words came in short, breathy stretches. "That's our land you're trying to protect. Blackfeet land. Nothing's more important. *Nothing.* You send Luke to Denver, to his mama. Then you get back out there. You hear me?"

The old fingers shook with emotion.

Monty curled his own hand around that of his father's.

"You sure about this?" he asked.

"Damn right, I'm sure."

CHAPTER

TWENTY-SEVEN

ALL OF THE material had been packaged neatly in a cardboard filing box. Now he lifted the lid and withdrew the first of half a dozen files, the one labeled WRI.

Inside were personnel records, including employee names, phone numbers, addresses. A profile on Jon LeCoque gave the names of his wife, grown children, and two grandchildren. A picture of LeCoque's residence along with his yacht, *Chesire,* were even included, along with their addresses.

Tony Wilderman's impressive résumé included several awards garnered from the world and Canadian mining communities. Wilderman was credited with finding the company's two biggest money producers to date: the Krygyzstan mine and the Essiquibo mine. Wilderman's family history even included a special note about his Irish roots and his fondness for St. Patrick's Day.

He sat back momentarily, impressed. This clearly was not the product of one man working alone. Only a skilled and well-funded network could put this much information together.

He moved on to another file.

CLASS ACTION: BLACKFEET VS. BIA

Inside, lawyer names. Plaintiff's names. An unauthorized copy of something called the Morris Audit.

He thumbed through the twelve-page document, stopping

to read the last page, which contained a summary of the independent audit's findings. It concluded that the BIA's record-keeping was a joke. That the Indians had been cheated out of substantial amounts—perhaps even as much as $2.4 billion.

He let out a low whistle, then pushed the lawsuit file aside as another file caught his eye.

IMMUVAC STUDY

He reached for it.

The first page he opened to was a stapled document entitled HUMAN GUINEA PIGS. He began to read.

Vaccines couldn't be trusted, it proclaimed. Too many were contaminated: the polio vaccine, contaminated with a simian virus, had caused hundreds of thousands of deaths from cancer. Vaccines given to soldiers during the Gulf War resulted in Gulf War Syndrome. According to the literature in his hand, even AIDS was a result of a contaminated vaccine.

He flipped to the last paragraph of the second page.

This is a call to all Blackfeet, and to all our brothers and sisters. To participate in this study is suicide. To allow it to go forward could result in genocide, since ImmuVac plans to vaccinate every resident of the reservation against hantavirus. Did you know that? Every resident.

We must all stand together in opposing this insane, genocidal plan.

His heart beating harder and faster, he rifled quickly through the rest of the file. There was a notice for the formation of an Institutional Review Board. A list of Phase I and Phase II study participants. A profile on ImmuVac, the company sponsoring the study, and Dr. Ken MacStirling, the research scientist responsible for the HantaVac's development.

The identity of the study's lead investigator.

It was perfect. Almost too perfect.

•   •   •

AT THE APPOINTED time—midnight—Clyde Birdseye showed up at Monty's door. He was dressed in black, head to toe, as was Monty.

"All our people out of there?" Monty asked. Monty had had a brief meeting with Clyde after returning from the hospital in Cutbank, then he'd gone by Luke's school to pick him up. Clyde had agreed to oversee the speedy dismantling of the teepees and encampment while Monty drove Luke to the airport in Kalispell, where he put his nephew on an Alaska Airlines flight to Denver. Luke's mother would be waiting on the other end. Monty had only been home from Kalispell twenty minutes when headlights from Clyde's four-wheel-drive swept across the living room wall as it pulled into Monty's driveway.

"Yep. Everyone went home," Clyde answered, watching as Monty grabbed a dark ballcap from a coat tree standing near the door and pulled it down low over his thick hair. "Nobody put up much of a fight. They were all burned out. Tired of waiting for something to happen."

Monty snickered softly as he pulled the door shut behind them and stepped into the night.

CHAPTER

TWENTY-EIGHT

IT WAS WITHOUT doubt the most difficult telephone call she'd ever made. She had put it off until after her meeting with the FDA investigators. She had wanted to verify for herself what K. T. had told her before going to Ken Mac-Stirling with the news.

But Isabel left her meeting with the investigators from the FDA with little doubt. She was, indeed, a subject of investigation. And the stakes were high—much higher than she'd ever dreamed possible. It was time to talk to MacStirling.

Twice during the day she tried reaching him at his ImmuVac office. Finally, on her third try, she'd left a message saying it was urgent that she speak with him.

Still, she hadn't expected MacStirling to return her call at night, and somehow the simple act of discussing the sordid, awful business there, in the cabin she considered her refuge, only managed to magnify the situation.

"I'm sorry to be calling you so late," MacStirling began. "I had to make a quick day trip down to the San Diego area today. You'll like hearing this. I went down to take a look at a manufacturing facility down there. We've begun discussions on the commercial manufacture of HantaVac."

At any other time, this news would have produced the desired response in Isabel. But tonight it simply made things worse, if that was possible.

"Did you hear me?" MacStirling pressed. "ImmuVac is already planning for the manufacture of the vaccine? Isn't that brilliant?"

Isabel's sigh rose from the depths of her soul.

"Yes, Ken. It is. But I'm afraid I have some bad news for you. And it regards the HantaVac trial."

A stunned silence followed.

"What?" MacStirling finally said, his voice high and tight. "What news?"

"It's about me. I received word recently that I'm under investigation by the FDA. A criminal investigation for fraud in Alistair's clinical trials."

Isabel expected Ken MacStirling to fall apart at this news. What she hadn't expected was no reaction. No reaction at all.

"Ken? Are you there? Listen to me, I'm resigning from

my position as lead investigator. I'll do everything in my power to ensure that the HantaVac trial isn't prejudiced by this."

"You will not." MacStirling's voice was forbidding, and stiffly Scottish.

"I promise. I give you my word. I'll talk to the investigators, make sure they know that I've removed myself from ImmuVac's trial. I give you my word."

"No," MacStirling said. "I didn't mean it that way. What I meant is that you *will not* resign from this trial. I will not allow it."

"I don't understand. Didn't you hear me? I'm under investigation. For fraud involving numerous clinical trials. Don't you realize what this could do to the HantaVac study?"

"Not if you're cleared."

"But I may not be cleared. I had a meeting with the FDA just yesterday. It seems hopeless. Just hopeless."

MacStirling took a long breath before answering.

"I have a confession to make," he said. "I also had a meeting with the charming agents from the FDA."

"You met with them, with Wittren, and . . . and . . ."

"Thomasen. Charming laddies, aren't they? Yes. They came snooping around. Said your ex told them you were heading the HantaVac study. That he warned them to keep an eye on you."

Isabel could feel the crimson rush of blood to her cheeks. She felt grateful that this conversation was taking place over the telephone and not in person. All that she'd worked for, gone. Destroyed by Alistair's vengeful, twisted mind.

"Isabel? Isabel?" MacStirling chanted. "Isabel?"

"Yes."

"Aren't you interested in what I had to say? In what I told the self-righteous sons of bitches?"

"What?"

"I told them that they were pathetic. That it was obvious

they'd failed miserably in building a case against your husband and so, to save their own fat fannies, they'd targeted you. I told them that they could search high and low for the rest of their lives and they would never, ever come up with solid evidence against you because you, Isabel McLain, just happen to be a person of the highest integrity. I told them that I feel exceptionally honored and secure having you head the HantaVac trial, and that they are welcome to sit on my or your doorstep and hover over our every move, but that it will be time wasted, time when they could be pursing legitimate villains. Like your ex-husband. That, my dear, is what I told them."

Isabel took in a deep breath, filling her lungs.

"What makes some people so incredibly decent," she sighed, "and others so terribly depraved?"

MacStirling was quiet for a moment.

"I don't know the answer to that question," he said. "I don't know how a man fortunate enough to have you for a wife could want anything more from the universe."

Any other time, these words would have made Isabel uncomfortable. But tonight they repaired her damaged soul. Tonight they helped her sleep.

SHE'D ONLY BEEN asleep a short while when the cabin's walls shook with the pounding.

Groping blindly, Isabel smacked her hand down on her reading glasses, knocking them off the bedside table. Then her fingers found the gun.

She rose slowly, eyes glued to the front door, where the relentless pounding continued.

Isabel crept up to it.

"Is anybody home in there?"

The voice sounded vaguely familiar, but it did not belong to Alistair. She relaxed her grip on the gun.

She stepped to the window and pushed back the curtain. At first, in the darkness, she saw nothing. But when her eyes adjusted, she made out two figures, both male, standing on the wooden porch. The smaller of the two had an arm slung over the shoulder of the other, who stooped forward to accommodate the difference in height and provide support.

"Open up. He's hurt."

That voice. The peachfuzz hair at the nape of Isabel's scalp bristled. She froze, her professional instincts slowed by sudden recognition.

But any hesitation was fleeting. She was a doctor and someone needed help.

Placing the gun on the floor, she grabbed hold of the thick iron bolt that locked the door by sliding in place. She had to wrestle with it, for, over the years, the door had shifted in its frame and the bolt had rusted. That, plus the fact that it could only be locked from the inside, had prompted Isabel to mainly use the kitchen door, upon which Gus had installed a deadbolt.

Finally, with Isabel's grunt, the bolt gave way. She bent to retrieve the gun, flipped on the bare lightbulb above the door, then pulled the door open.

The taller of the two had raised his hand reflexively to shield his eyes from the light's glare. But Isabel had no trouble recognizing Clyde Birdseye.

Monty Four Bear, slouched against Clyde, did not bother covering his eyes, for they were closed. The front of Monty's blue flannel shirt, mostly its right side, was drenched in blood.

Momentarily stunned, Isabel squinted in disbelief at the sight before her.

"He's been shot," Birdseye said.

"Bring him in here."

"I will when you put that gun down."

Isabel placed the gun on the table under the front window,

then opened the door fully. She hurried ahead of Clyde, turning on lights as she directed him inside.

"On the bed."

Together they lowered Monty to the bed. He fell back, semiconscious.

Isabel had already begun unbuttoning Monty's shirt.

"Is this the only wound?"

"I think so, but I'm not sure."

"Go into the kitchen. Put some water on to boil," Isabel ordered.

Monty's semiconscious state troubled Isabel, but he was breathing spontaneously. Blood, however, continued to seep from the upper right quadrant of his chest, and the extent of the staining on his clothing indicated he'd lost a great deal—which most likely explained his lack of consciousness. Decreased circulating blood volume caused blood vessels to narrow, limiting the perfusion of blood to vital organs, such as the brain. If circulation wasn't restored, the brain could become starved for oxygen and hypoxia could develop.

Ultimately, uncorrected, all his organs would fail and Monty would die.

She unbuttoned his shirt, pushing it back off his chest on the left side. She would like to have removed the shirt covering the wound, which appeared to be just below his clavicle on the right side, for a better assessment, but the rule of thumb was never to remove dressings covering areas of active, heavy bleeding.

Eyeballing the bullet's entry point, she realized Monty was a lucky man—same position on the left and it would have punctured the heart. She was concerned, however, that, depending on its trajectory, the bullet might have penetrated the right lung.

Isabel rushed to grab her medical bag. Withdrawing the stethoscope, she moved quickly to place it over Monty's heart and lungs. Both normal. The bullet had missed the lung.

Hemorrhaging appeared to be the most immediate problem. A small stream of fresh blood continued to seep from the wound. Upon entry, the bullet had taken some of the shirt's material with it, imbedding it in Monty's tissue. When Isabel tried to peel the shirt back for a closer look, a surge of blood indicated she'd dislodged a partial clot.

Clyde had returned.

"Grab one of those white packets from my bag and put gloves on," Isabel said, reaching for one of her bed pillows. She ripped its case off and folded it into a neat square, which she placed over Monty's chest.

"I don't need gloves."

"Suit yourself. But throw me a pair. Then come over here and put pressure on this while I find some makeshift dressings."

"Don't we have to clean it first?"

"No. We have to stop the hemorrhaging before we do anything else."

She didn't add what she was thinking. *If we don't, he'll bleed to death.*

She ran to the built-in wooden cabinet along the wall beside the fireplace, pushed aside the floral curtains she'd hung there when she first moved in, and grabbed several hand towels.

The pillowcase was already soaked clear through by the time she returned to her bed. She replaced it with two towels, one stacked on top of the other.

"Harder, press harder. There, that's better. And keep your hand steady. We want a clot to form. Any movement at all could dislodge it."

It was a horrible place for a deep wound. An extremity could be tourniqueted. With a chest wound, short of surgery, pressure was the only means of stopping the bleeding. The question was: Would it be enough?

Monty moaned softly.

A blur of motion now, Isabel grabbed two pillows from

the couch and placed them under Monty's legs. Then she extracted her blood pressure cuff from her bag and took a reading.

108 over 55. For most patients, low. But Monty was young and fit. Another reading in a few minutes would be key.

Heart rate still at 73 beats per minute.

She ran her hand over Monty's shoulder, feeling for a fracture of the clavicle. She slid her hand under his right shoulder, looking for an exit wound, but found the shirt there intact and dry. The bullet had lodged somewhere in the upper right quadrant of Monty's chest.

"Okay, I'll take over now, but don't release the pressure until my hand's in place."

As Isabel placed her hand on top of Clyde's, she felt his entire body tense at her touch.

"Slowly," she cautioned.

As instructed, Clyde pulled his hand out from under Isabel's slowly and steadily. As he stepped back, Isabel said, "Now, go call 911. Tell them we'll be transporting him to the hospital in Cutbank. We'll need a surgeon on hand. And blood."

She looked down at Monty. The poor lighting in the cabin made it difficult to assess his color. How much blood had he already lost?

She called out after Clyde.

"How long ago did this happen?"

Suddenly she realized that Clyde still stood beside her.

"I told you to call 911," she snapped.

The look in Clyde's eyes spelled trouble.

"We can't do that."

"What do you mean? We have to. He's going to bleed to death if we don't."

"I'm not gonna bleed to death."

All eyes fell on Monty. His own had opened, only to narrow slits, but Isabel could see their pupils.

"Just clean . . . me up, then . . . we'll leave."

"You're out of your minds. Both of you. I'm calling for help."

In fewer than half a dozen long strides, Clyde reached the kitchen. Isabel watched as he jerked the phone away from the wall, severing the line.

"Nobody's calling for help," he said, returning to the bedside. He stared down at Monty. "You sure you're up to traveling?"

Monty nodded, closing his eyes again.

"He's not going anywhere," Isabel said. "This man needs medical treatment. Are you his friend, or are you *trying* to kill him?"

"Why do you think I brought him here?"

Monty appeared to slip into unconsciousness. Still leaning over him, applying pressure to his chest wound, Isabel glared at Birdseye.

"What's going on here? And don't bullshit me."

Birdseye studied her before answering.

"We had some trouble tonight. Out at the mine site."

Isabel's unflinching eyes bore down upon Birdseye, demanding further explanation.

"There was an explosion . . ."

"I thought you said this was a bullet, not shrapnel," Isabel cut him off.

"It *is* a bullet. There was a guard at the site," he continued. "We didn't realize it until it was too late. We exchanged gunfire. Monty was hit."

"And the guard?"

Clyde did not respond.

"The guard?"

Birdseye's black eyes, the coldest, hardest eyes Isabel had ever looked into, rose to meet hers.

"The guard's dead."

"You killed him? You murdered a man?"

"It was self-defense. He started the shooting. We didn't even know he was there. Son of a bitch was hiding in the brush. Ready to ambush us. He could have stopped us before we doused the site with gasoline, but he actually waited for us, then while we were standing there watching it burn, he opened fire."

"You expect me to believe that?"

Birdseye's contempt filled the air between them.

"Ordinarily, I wouldn't give a damn what you believe. But since you hold my friend's life in your hands, I'll humor you. Have you heard about Monty's father, about Leroy?"

Isabel nodded. Yes, she had heard about Leroy. For the past twenty-four hours, it had been all anyone talked about on the reservation.

"You heard who did that to him?"

"I heard it had to do with the mine."

What Isabel actually heard—though something, most likely their past history, prevented her from phrasing it this way—was that WRI had hired some goon to beat Leroy Four Bear to a pulp. That it had been done to force Monty to back down from the mining protest. Isabel refrained from saying all that. Just as she refrained from disclosing how deeply disturbed—in fact, downright crazy with anger and disbelief—the news had made her.

"So you tell me. Do you actually think someone who'll break into a home where a sixty-seven-year-old man and an eight-year-old boy are sleeping and beat the shit out of the old man, in front of the boy . . . you find it impossible to believe this same person would open fire on us after we'd just set fifty thousand bucks worth of equipment on fire?"

"But one of you *killed* him."

"Lady, when you're being shot at, you shoot back."

"Then tell that to the authorities. Tell them it was self-defense."

"Ever hear of Leonard Peltier?" Birdseye asked, his voice full of cynicism.

"Of course. He was convicted of murdering two FBI agents at Pine Ridge."

"Exactly. He's been in Leavenworth for more than twenty years. Problem is, he didn't do it."

"You don't have to lecture me about Leonard Peltier. I've written letters protesting the medical care he's received, demanding his clemency."

Birdseye snickered.

"You find that funny?" Isabel sneered right back at him. "Letters a bit too civilized for people like you? You'd rather use violence, wouldn't you? So that people like your friend here end up dying."

Clyde's hand came up, encircling Isabel's upper arm like a vise.

"You're not going to let him die."

"Take your hands off me."

Their eyes met over Monty's half-conscious form.

"I want you to go," she said. "Leave. Now."

"Get him ready to travel first."

Isabel placed a hand on Monty's forehead. His skin was diaphoretic, pale and cool to the touch.

The bleeding, however, appeared to have stopped. Maybe she could stabilize him here, without help. It wasn't ideal, but Monty had a whole lot better chance there at the cabin with her than traveling in his condition, on the run from authorities.

"I didn't mean the two of you," Isabel said. "I mean you. He stays. You go. If you take him now, in this condition, he'll die."

The way she saw it, she had no choice really. Monty Four Bear had come to her for help. She could not turn her back on him.

"You mean you'll take care of him?" Birdseye mumbled. "I don't get it."

Isabel raised her eyes to meet Birdseye's puzzled stare.

"I'd treat him either way, but I believe you. I believe that it was self-defense."

"And the explosion?"

"I don't agree with that. But destruction of property is a far cry from gunning a man down."

For the briefest of moments, Isabel thought she saw a flicker of relief in Clyde Birdseyes's expression. A brief respite from the disdain.

"They'll be looking for him. For both of us."

"I'll handle that. Now *go*."

WITH CLYDE GONE, Isabel turned all her attention back to Monty. Checking his blood pressure, she saw that the diastolic pressure had risen slightly.

Heart rate was up to 95, elevated from the last reading, which indicated Monty's heart was working overtime to compensate for the blood he'd lost.

The external bleeding had stopped. That didn't mean Isabel's work was done. Restoring circulating volume would be critical to averting hypovolemic shock.

Isabel prepared an intravenous catheter, choosing a large diameter tubing—the mini-drip or small-bore catheters didn't deliver fluid quickly enough for this situation. If she were at the hospital, she would have chosen a 0.9 percent sodium chloride solution—the only solution that was safe to run in the same IV line with blood products, which Monty would undoubtedly need. But her home supplies only contained lactated Ringer's solution. It would have to do.

Monty stirred as she inserted the needle into his right forearm.

"Where's Clyde?" he said, his voice weak, dry mouthed.

"Clyde's gone. I insisted that he leave you here with me."

"You *what*?" Despite the excruciating pain it had to have caused, he struggled to a sitting position. The movement jerked the needle, which Isabel had just begun taping to his forearm, out of his vein. It dangled, loose, from the tape stuck to his skin.

With a hand on his uninjured shoulder, Isabel tried to push him back down on to the bed.

"Lie still. Look what you've done to the IV."

Using his good left hand, Monty ripped the tape, with attached needle, off his right arm, which hung limp from the shoulder wound.

"To hell with an IV. I'm not staying here."

The way Isabel saw it, there was just so much she could do to force Monty's cooperation. Wrestling him back to bed was not an option. She watched as he pulled himself up off the bed. He stood, wobbling, the effort bringing beads of sweat to his brow.

"I suppose you're going to walk back to town," Isabel said. "Or hitchhike. Now *that's* a good idea. I don't suppose a wounded Indian hitchhiking would draw any attention."

Monty shot her a quizzical look.

"How much did Clyde tell you?"

"Everything. Or at least, enough. Enough for me to know he had to get out of here."

"Son of a bitch left me here," he said in disbelief, almost to himself. He reached out then for the headboard, steadying himself.

Isabel didn't know why she felt the sudden tug of sympathy for Monty. After all, he was a felon. Perhaps even a murderer.

"He'll be back. He made me promise to tell you that. He tried to tell you himself, but you were out cold."

"When? When will he be back?"

"When you're well enough to travel. He told me to tell you he'll be taking care of things. Whatever that means."

"I can catch up with him," Monty said, turning toward the cabin's front door. He stepped out away from the bed, but as he did so, a wave of intense dizziness crumpled him, taking him to his knees.

Isabel caught him before he doubled over.

"You're not going anywhere."

Ducking under his good arm—the left one—Isabel wrapped her right arm around Monty's waist. She tried to rise, lifting him, but his 180 pounds felt like twice that.

"Maybe you can help me a little here?"

"Loan . . . me . . ." his words came with short, shallow breaths, "your car."

"You're out of your mind. You're in no condition to drive, you . . ."

Suddenly she felt a slow, thick warmth wash over the index finger of her right hand.

Monty's shoulder wound had started hemorrhaging again.

At the same instant, Monty's entire form went limp as he once again slipped into unconsciousness.

Awkwardly, trying to support his head to prevent it from hitting the stone hearth in front of the fireplace, Isabel sank with Monty to the floor. Rolling him from his side onto his back, she spotted a gray sweatshirt on the floor and grabbed it. She pressed its soft fleece against Monty's grossly bloodied shirt, directly over the wound.

"Clot, damn you," she ordered.

The steady flow and dark red color she watched saturate the sweatshirt indicated venous bleeding. Had the bullet ruptured Monty's subclavian vein? Isabel chastised herself. Why hadn't she taped a compress over Monty's chest before starting the IV? Monty had been only half conscious, at best, while lying on the bed. She'd assumed he'd stay that way (which did not take into account his macho reaction to the news Clyde had left without him), and decided that building his circulatory fluids took precedence over dressing a wound that had already stopped bleeding.

Not a decision without a rational basis, but as every doctor did when a decision turned out to be the wrong one, Isabel's choice now anguished her. Monty had already lost so much blood. Time was running out. And there was just so much she could do with the supplies she routinely kept at home.

Luckily, the hemorrhaging this time proved easier to stay.

She kept steady pressure on it and once again elevated Monty's legs.

This time when she inserted the IV catheter into his forearm, Monty offered no resistance. In fact, he did not stir. Isabel would have been relieved if he had. But the night had taken its toll on him, and, for the first time, Isabel wondered whether the decisions she'd made since answering the door—especially the decision to go along with Clyde and Monty's insistence that no other medical personnel be called in for help—would wind up costing Monty his life.

She pulled the bloodied comforter off her bed and placed it across Monty's midsection, tucking it gently around his legs, then she secured the compress by wrapping elastic bandages around Monty's chest. Again, he did not stir.

Isabel had always managed to maintain her professional detachment with patients, but the intimacy of the moment unnerved her. Ministering to this proud man, whose passions and political beliefs forced him to don a demeanor of such anger and invincibility, especially in his current helpless state, gave rise to a sense that she was an intruder, trespassing on that part of Monty that was most sacred to him.

Each life she touched as a doctor had always weighed heavily on Isabel's mind and heart. Too heavily, Alistair had often declared. But never before had she experienced this, this tremendous sense of responsibility. A feeling that more, much more, than a single life was at stake here.

Did that explain why Monty's simple nearness unnerved her?

She pressed a hand to his forehead. His body temperature was subnormal. Once she was certain the IV flow was steady and adequate, Isabel wadded up a section of the previous Sunday's paper, stuffed it under a web of kindling she constructed hastily in the fireplace, and set it ablaze.

She returned to Monty's side, keeping a close eye on the IV, monitoring his pulse and, in between, staring into the flames.

What a bizarre evening it had been.

Monty and Clyde showing up at her door.

A WRI guard dead.

Too much to digest in one dose. Too much to sort out. Better to put her overactive mind on hold, focus on her patient.

When fire had swallowed most of the kindling, Isabel placed two pieces of tamarack into the heart of the flames, then settled back against the frame of the bed, wondering how the long night would end.

THE SIMPLE ACT of turning his head away from the blinding morning sunlight that had been creeping steadily across the cedar-planked floor toward where he lay gave rise to a razor-sharp arrow of pain that started at Monty's shoulder and radiated down the right side of his torso.

An involuntary shudder followed. This set Monty's entire body in motion, tensing in spasms of shivers, despite the fact that during the night he'd been wrapped, papooselike, in a down comforter. An unfamiliar tightness about his scalp caused him to pull his left arm free of his cocoon and touch his head. Instead of hair, his fingers met the coarse wool of a ski cap.

Inhaling, the faint smell of alcohol assaulted his nostrils and lungs, causing a wave of nausea to wash over him.

Monty opened his eyes.

With his awakening, the events of the past six or seven hours came back to him, all too real.

Less than a yard away, seated on the floor, her head tilted back at an awkward angle against the top of the mattress, Isabel McLain slept. Her hands lay clasped, prayerlike, on her lap. Her gray sweatshirt rose which each deep, slow breath. Monty spied the offending bottle of rubbing alcohol, minus its top, on the floor next to her. Several discarded white wrappers with writing his eyes could not yet focus to read and a roll of white medical tape also lay scattered within Isabel's reach.

Still groggily piecing together fragments of memories from last night's semiconscious state, Monty's eyes followed the clear plastic tube from his right forearm to a nearly empty bag of clear fluid hanging from a twisted wire coat hanger that had been looped over the post of the bed's headboard.

The sight immediately brought Leroy to mind.

How quickly would news of what had happened at the drill site reach Leroy? And what would his father make of the fact that neither Monty nor Clyde were anywhere to be found?

A loud sigh diverted Monty's attention away from that troubling thought.

Isabel, still deep in sleep, sat so close to him that if his right arm were any good, he could reach out and touch her.

His eyes came to rest on her hands. Long, slender fingers with nails unpolished and short. No jewelry.

Nothing of the city about her, especially now, dressed in a sweatshirt and loose-fitting, weathered Levis. Her feet were bare, their bottoms dirty from the dusty hardwood floor.

It took a moment for one oddity—a single concession to vanity or feminity or, perhaps, unpredictability—to register. Her toenails were painted a soft pink.

A single tendril of hair had escaped the knot at the nape of her neck. It dangled over one eye, floating in and out of her parted lips with each breath.

Despite the fact that she'd taken him in last night, as he studied her, Monty tried to work up his usual disdain.

Like Clyde, Monty had from the start categorized Isabel as one of those misguided do-gooders for whom he had no use. He'd worked with them before. Sympathy for the plight of Native Americans had become chic, the politically correct thing. He'd lumped Isabel into a category of people who moved through phases of do-gooding. This year it might be "righting" the wrongs done Native Americans, the next saving the tropical forests. All in an effort to make sense of their own sadly lacking, screwed-up lives.

Despite the courage demonstrated by her response last night, Isabel was no different from the others. And now he also blamed her for something else: Clyde's leaving him behind.

When Isabel began to stir, Monty chose to risk the pain caused by turning away rather than let her catch him studying her.

He closed his eyes, in order to delay interaction with her, but when Isabel's breathing resumed its steady rhythm, opened them again. The sun had climbed, creating a new pattern on the cabin's floor that allowed him to look around now free of its glare.

The cabin's furnishings were remarkably sparse. Just a rocking chair and a bed, a table under the front window, through which Little Chief Mountain declared its rule. On top of the table an assortment of framed photos provided the only personal touch of the cabin's inhabitant. Two were black and white—one of a white couple on their wedding day, both wearing forced smiles, and another of a toddler with hands clasped on her lap, much like Isabel's now. A built-in floor-to-ceiling bookshelf overflowed with volumes. Those books that couldn't fit upright had been laid sideways on top of the neatly ordered rows.

"Have you been awake long?"

Monty turned his head. Just a quarter turn, so he faced the ceiling, not Isabel.

"Couple minutes."

Out of the corner of his eye, he saw her stretch her arms out into the air, shake her head, as if trying to clear it of sleep, then push the errant lock behind an ear.

Then she bolted upright.

"I let the fire burn out."

She reached his way and placed her hand lightly across

his forehead. The effect—most likely the warmth—was remarkably soothing.

"Your temperature's fallen." She leaned forward, studying him. "You're shivering."

Isabel scrambled to her feet and flattened a hand on either side of a bag of fluid hanging from the bedpost.

"Damn. It's too cold. How long has that fire been out?" she said to herself. "I can't believe I let myself fall asleep."

Pushing aside the flowered curtain to shelving built into the wall, she grabbed a new bag from a cardboard box labeled LACTATED RINGERS, then headed into the kitchen. Monty watched her standing at the sink, running hot water over the bag, which she kept turning over and over.

"Here," she said as she went about replacing the old bag. "This solution will help warm you. I can't believe I fell asleep."

"Take it easy. I'm fine," Monty lied. In reality, he'd never felt so awful.

"You're *not* fine." Her hands worked quickly, first clamping shut the IV line, then substituting the warmed bag for the old one. "You need to go to the hospital. Immediately. I should have insisted last night. You could be bleeding internally. That could be another reason your temperature's dropped. Now I *do* insist."

Without thinking, Monty's right hand shot out, grabbing hold of Isabel's blue jean–clad ankle. The movement caused a bolt of searing pain, but he did not let go.

"You're not taking me anywhere."

Isabel glanced briefly down at him, her hand still poised on the clamp for the tubing. Then, ignoring his grasp on her leg, she slowly, deliberately released the clamp, until the warmed liquid filled the tube.

"Now," she said, turning her attention back to Monty, *"let go of me."*

Monty met her angry, determined stare with one of his own, but released his grasp.

Isabel sank to her knees on the floor beside him.

"Don't you see? I'm limited in what I can do for you here. You could die if we don't go for help."

"That's a decision for me to make, not you."

"Hell it is. You've pulled me into this drama of yours. I didn't ask for you and your buddy to show up at my door in the middle of the night. And you're not going to die here in my charge."

"That's really what this is all about, isn't it? Your ego. Your not wanting this kind of responsibility. I mean, a dead Indian, one running from the law, on your hands—pretty messy stuff, huh?" Each word exacted a price, but his face didn't betray that fact. He'd had a whole lifetime in which to learn the art of hiding his pain. "When it comes to actually taking risks—not just quitting a good job and moving to an uncivilized Indian reservation—*real* risks, you fall back on your middle-class-America rules to justify taking the easy way out."

Isabel simply stared at him as he delivered this blistering indictment.

"Don't worry, I'm leaving," Monty finished.

He began to rise, but the force with which Isabel pushed him back down flattened him.

"Don't you *dare* to think you know me, to patronize me with your Indian racism." She huddled over him wild-eyed and visibly exhausted. "Everything is about you, isn't it? The atrocities your people have suffered—they don't give you a blank check to step on the rest of us, mock our purpose or our dignity. Unless, of course, the only thing that matters to you is getting even. And if that's the case, then what makes you any better than the rest of us? In fact, if the truth be known . . ."

"*What?*"

Isabel stood there, staring at him angrily.

"Let's get you on the bed," she said. "This floor isn't help-ing the situation."

Monty had expended all his energy. He knew he wasn't going anywhere. He didn't have the strength. And Isabel McLain obviously knew it too.

Maybe he would, indeed, die without further treatment.

He did not want to die.

CHAPTER

TWENTY-NINE

JAMES LYONS PULLED absentmindedly on one end of his mustache, then the other, as he paced back and forth, waiting for Sergei Kirov. He was oblivious to the sound made by his loafers as they crunched across the crumb-littered linoleum. He had purchased this building—an abandoned schoolhouse in Gaston, a rural community twenty miles southwest of Portland—to ensure that Sergei's work would be conducted in secrecy. No one was supposed to know that Sergei was back in the Northwest. ImmuVac employees had been told that Kirov decided to stay in his homeland. The redbrick structure that formerly housed a school for Gaston's children was close enough for Lyons to visit on a weekly basis, but distant enough that no one from ImmuVac would inadvertently happen by. From outward appearances, the building looked as if it had been converted to a residence.

Lyons had called ahead from his car and asked Sergei to meet him on the first floor. He rarely entered the lab on the third floor when he visited. Didn't like having to struggle into the awkward self-contained, oxygenated suits imperative in Level IV labs. And not even an oxygen mask made him comfortable entering the room in which Sergei conducted his work with the deadly smallpox virus.

Finally, Lyons heard the soft slap-slap of the Russian's Nikes descending the wood stairs. Dressed in a crumpled white lab coat and baggy brown cords, Sergei carried a green plastic tray balancing two Styrofoam cups.

"Coffee?" Sergei extended the tray.

"No." Lyons would starve to death before accepting food or beverage offered by Sergei. "This place is a pigsty. When was the last time you swept the floors?"

"I am a scientist, not a janitor. If you want clean floors, hire someone to sweep them."

"You know we can't do that. We can't let anyone near this place."

"Then you'll have to stand on dirty floors when you visit. They don't bother me."

Motioning for Lyons to do likewise, Sergei settled in one of two ladderback chairs that faced a small table dominated by a TV with a built-in VCR. He placed the tray with the extra cup of coffee on the table, next to the TV. On the floor beneath the table lay two videos: *Armageddon* and *The Godfather*.

"How did you get those?" Lyons scowled, pointing an accusatory finger toward the floor.

"A little store in town rents them."

"We agreed you wouldn't go into town."

"It's just a little market. No one from Portland would have reason to go there."

"But I bought you several videos. I bring you supplies every week. You don't need to go into town. All you have to do is tell me what you want."

"Sometimes what I want is to go to town."

"Listen here, Sergei. You knew damn well what you were getting into when you signed on to this project. All it takes is one ImmuVac employee to spot you and this whole thing could come tumbling down on both of us."

The Russian placed his cup on the tray, rose from his chair, and zeroed in on Lyons.

"You come here, in your fancy car, and drop off supplies like I'm some kind of slave. Or animal. Doing your dirty work. I came to this country to be treated like I deserve to be treated, not to be hiding out, forbidden to leave my lab."

"Well then, maybe it's time we call it quits," Lyons said. "Between what I read in the papers this morning and Pfister Pharmaceuticals, maybe this project should be shut down."

"Pfister Pharmaceuticals?"

"Yes. They're very enthused about our HantaVac study. Thanks to Dr. MacStirling's work, it looks like they may be interested in a partnership."

Lyons could see the effect this information had on the Russian. Sergei's jaw jutted forward while he let loose with an animated stream of Russian. The only word Lyons recognized was "MacStirling."

He finally switched to English and continued his diatribe.

"Comparing MacStirling's vaccine to mine is like comparing a . . . a . . ." his sparse eyebrows furrowed into thin commas above intense, beady eyes, "*insect* to a magnificent Kodiak. My vaccine is *revolutionary*. The day will soon come when it will save millions. The world will call us saviors. Geniuses. Who will be saved by MacStirling's work? *Indians*. The same Indians your country shows such contempt for. Such stupidity would be unforgiveable."

The intensity of the Russian's bitterness forced Lyons back a step.

"Have you read today's papers?"

"How am I to obtain a newspaper when I am forbidden to leave?"

Lyons ignored him and relayed the information he'd just read.

"Intelligence sources are reporting that Iraq and Russia have concealed large stockpiles of smallpox for military use. Apparently this was reported to the president and the Pentagon at the end of last year. The article I read this morning says the U.S. has already begun work on a vaccine." Lyons paused to let this news sink in. "If the government comes up with a vaccine, your work will be obsolete."

"We already knew that military or bioterrorist attacks utilizing smallpox are certain to occur. Long before your government spent millions of dollars to discover what the rest of the world has known."

"But that's the whole point. If the government develops a vaccine in preparation for military or civilian defense, ours loses all its value."

The faintest trace of a smile lifted the corners of the Russian's mouth.

"The government's vaccine will be for the vaccinia strain of vareola. I've told you there are many, many deadly strains."

"You may not have much respect for our government scientists, but you can be sure they're working on several different vaccines. Or a single vaccine that's effective against multistrains."

"That assumes that they've been able to acquire all the different strains. That's a big assumption."

"I agree. But you're not the only former Soviet scientist to emigrate to the United States. You can bet others have been willing to sell samples to the government."

"Even if they have, you have nothing to fear. Any vaccines they develop will be ineffective."

Lyons knew Sergei would be difficult to reason with.

"You're talking nonsense. Smallpox vaccines aren't like trying to develop a vaccine for AIDS. We perfected them years ago."

Sergei locked eyes with Lyons.

"Tell me, years ago, staphylococcus infection was a simple thing to treat. Many different antibiotics were effective. Vancomycin was the—how do you say it?—the drug that always worked when others did not. How do you say that?"

"You mean the last resort?"

"Yes. That's it. The drug of last resort. It always worked. And then what happened? Now some patients with staph infections are not responding, even to vancomycin. Why is that? Tell me."

"Because the staph has mutated. The new superbugs have developed a resistance to all known antibiotics. Even vancomycin."

"Exactly. Now what if scientists created new strains of smallpox—strains that were genetically engineered to resist all known vaccines?"

"You mean . . . ?"

Sergei's chest lifted with pride.

"My Russian comrades have genetically engineered strains of smallpox that U.S. scientists have never seen, never even heard of. Mutant strains that will be resistant to any vaccine the government makes. It's like stapphylococcus. The only difference is that the smallpox mutations did not occur naturally. They've been manipulated, genetically engineered. Specificity will be absolutely essential in creating a vaccine that protects against these new strains. These strains were sold. They are now in the hands of the Iraqis. And North Koreans."

"How do you know this?"

"It was a theory I had proposed during Biopreparat. My pet project actually. I'd been looking at genetically engineering existing strains of smallpox with two goals in mind. The first was trying to target certain gene pools. I believed it possible to manipulate the vareola DNA to create a new strain that could be selective in who it infected."

"Like Hitler. Or Kosovo." Despite his repugnance, there was a note of admiration in Lyons's voice. "A way to wipe out the enemy, purify the population."

"Exactly. Of course, the Union collapsed and my research was never completed. But I told you my work was two-pronged. I'd also been exploring the possibility of creating the smallpox equivalent of the staph superbug. An entirely new strain, one that would be resistant to all known vaccines."

"An artificially contrived human pathogen?"

"After I left, two of my colleagues continued the work I'd begun. They extracted genes from *bacillus cereus* and inserted them into the DNA of existing vareola strains. They created an entirely new pathogen, with new capabilities. And then they took it with them to the Middle East.

"I can assure you, your government's vaccine will not be effective against these new strains. To create a vaccine against the new strain, even to develop a test to detect it, you'd need a supply of the new organism. The U.S. government can't possibly have that. And once there's an attack, millions will die or go blind in the months it will take to get enough vaccine produced."

"Why the hell didn't you tell me this before? If what you're telling me is true, *we* can't even create a vaccine for these new strains."

"That's where you're wrong. Follow me."

Sergei turned and headed for the stairs.

"I don't have time to suit up for the lab."

It was a lie, but Lyons did not want to go to the third floor.

"We're just going up to the kitchen."

The second floor hosted Sergei's bedroom and kitchen, as well as half a dozen former classrooms that had been boarded off.

Entering the kitchen, Sergei strode to the refrigerator and opened the door. When Lyons caught up with him, he could hardly believe his eyes. Milk cartons and juice, a jar of peanut butter, a carton of eggs, stood alongside culture dishes and test tubes. He had to stifle a gag at the thought that Sergei actually ate the food.

Sergei, either oblivious or indifferent to his boss's repulsion, reached inside to the back of the refrigerator. Very carefully, with the steady hands of a surgeon, he withdrew a small glass vial.

A clear liquid filled two thirds of the 10-mm tube.

"Voila," he beamed. "The newest strain of vareola. So new it hasn't even been named."

Lyons drew back in horror.

"Are you out of your fucking mind? Exposing me to some deadly virus?"

He began to turn and flee, but a sudden fear came to him. What if, just what if, the Russian were crazy enough to remove the plug, deliberately expose him to it?

"You didn't seem too concerned about me traveling across two continents with this in my briefcase," Sergei snapped.

"This is crazy. Put it back."

Sergei rotated the vial slowly, allowing the light from the window to filter through it.

"There's enough in there to wipe out half of the city of Portland. That's all it would take," he said gleefully. "Amazing, isn't it?"

"Put it back in there, goddamn it."

Lyons had begun backing out of the kitchen.

Sergei finally dropped his eyes from the vial and laughed.

"Okay," he said, "have it your way."

Turning, he replaced it in the refrigerator, using the same degree of caution with which he'd removed it.

Back downstairs, Lyons declined his offer, but Sergei insisted on walking him outside.

"I need to get some fresh air," he explained.

After what had just happened, Lyons was in no mood to argue. All he wanted was to put as much distance as possible between himself and the crazy Russian. As they crossed the front lawn to Lyons's green Range Rover, his heart thumped against his rib cage crazily.

"So you see," Sergei said as Lyons climbed into his car. "There's no need for you to worry. No need at all. I can do more for you than Pfister Pharmaceuticals. I can make you a champion. A visionary."

"I see that," Lyons mumbled as Sergei watched him go.

IN ORDER TO avoid suspicion, the driver of the dark blue Jaguar had driven right on by the red brick building when James Lyons's Range Rover pulled into its drive. It proceeded up the road a short distance, until, just out of sight of the building, it reached an opening, apparently a turnaround for the narrow two-lane road. The positioning was perfect. Still well within the range of the equipment he'd secured just the day before from a friend of a friend who now worked for the FBI.

He reached over and, using both thumbs, flipped open the latches on either side of the attache. Raising the lid to the digitized intelligence system, he mentally walked through the checklist given him by his friend: flicking the first switch to Operate, making certain the recorder switch was on Automatic, then pressing the Battery Test Button. As promised, everything checked out.

Switching the receiver switch to the on position, he turned up the volume. Then he turned his attention to the channel selector.

Initially, a blast of static assaulted his ears, but he adjusted to it quickly, and as he rolled the selector knob between thumb and forefinger, it did not take long to find just what he'd been looking for.

Voices. First the strong, fast clipped, typically American voice of a mature male. Anxious. Impatient.

Then another, even more distinctive, voice. This one much slower and deliberate. No note of panic in this one, only confidence.

He found himself straining, leaning closer to the speaker, trying to make out the words of the second voice. It wasn't that the reception was bad. It was, in fact, crystal clear.

No, the reason he was having such a difficult time understanding the second speaker wasn't the equipment, it was the speaker's thick accent. An accent that indicated its owner hadn't been in this country very long.

A heavy, Russian accent.

CHAPTER

THIRTY

Y OU SURE YOU'RE feelin' okay? Maybe you should've taken today off, too."

Suzanne Featherheart's big brown eyes peered at Isabel from over the pages of her month-old issue of *People* magazine.

"It's just the same flu that kept me home yesterday," Isabel answered. "I'm still not one hundred percent."

"Lucky thing then that today's so quiet. Just one more appointment. You'll be outta here in no time."

"That'd be nice. Seems kind of strange that we didn't have more walk-ins today. Especially since I missed yesterday, and today's Friday."

Patients often rode out an illness all week, but then, when Friday came along, panicked at the thought of the clinic being closed all weekend. Inevitably, some of them showed up Friday afternoon.

"Everybody's kind of spooked right now, what with the explosion and all. And Monty and Clyde missing. That kind of thing gets a person's mind off his own troubles."

Isabel tried not to register any sign of discomfort at the turn their conversation had taken.

"Any new news on what happened to them? To Monty and Clyde?"

"Nope. Bud Wolfkill came out to the trailer last night, wantin' to talk to Mary. Thought mebbe she'd know something. But Mary told him she didn't know a thing. It's not like Monty would've talked to Mary 'bout somethin like that. Bud's desperate to find Monty."

"Well, a man died. The authorities *have* to take it seriously."

"You ask me, WRI was askin' for trouble. I don't like seein' anyone get killed over all this, but what did they expect after beatin' poor Leroy like that? Only bad thing is that now Monty's in big trouble. And Monty's a good man. No way he shot that guard first. Monty would never do somethin' like that. Never."

"Did Bud say that? That Monty's in trouble?"

"Bud says everyone figures Monty lost his head over Leroy. The FBI says that the explosion was just a cover-up. That Monty murdered the guard, then blew things up to hide the evidence. He didn't say so, but I know that's the reason Bud's so desperate to find him. Cause he wants to find him before the FBI does."

"What if Monty shot the guard in self-defense?"

Suzanne's thick black eyebrows drew together in clear amazement that Isabel could be so naive.

"You really think that anyone but the tribal police would believe that? Would even listen? Now that the FBI's involved, Monty doesn't stand a chance. Which is too bad cuz Monty's the best thing this rez had going for it. I'll miss him—everybody will—but I hope he's long gone. Him and Clyde too."

Throughout Isabel's last appointment of the day—a two-year-old with an ear infection—Suzanne's words continued to echo through her mind.

Monty didn't stand a chance of fair treatment if he turned himself in, or if the authorities found him. And apparently

Bud Wolfkill was searching high and low, hoping to find Monty before federal agents did.

Isabel had just finished giving the toddler's mother two sample boxes of antibiotics that had been left recently by the pharmaceutical sales rep on one of her rare visits to the reservation, when Suzanne stuck her head in the exam room doorway.

"Sorry to disturb you, but did you want me to call for a pickup for this blood that was in the 'frigerator?"

Suzanne raised a half-full tube of blood in the air. It was the tube that Isabel had taken from Monty the morning before. She'd brought the sample in first thing in the morning, before Suzanne arrived, to type Monty's blood and pick up more supplies.

In her hurry to get out of the clinic before Suzanne arrived, Isabel accidentally left the tube in the refrigerator.

"Thanks, but no. That's actually an old sample."

"Should I toss it?"

"No," Isabel cried. Then, with forced casualness, she said, "Just stick it back in the fridge. I may decide to take another look."

Suzanne rotated the tube.

"No name on it."

"That's right. Forgot to label it. It's from . . . from . . . from my neighbor, Gus Dearing."

"Really? Never seen Gus in the clinic before."

"He hasn't been feeling well. I dropped by his place to check on him the other day and took a sample home with me."

"Oh." It was a statement but it sounded more like a question. "I'll label it for you."

"That'd be great."

"By the way, you get your phone fixed yet?"

The day before, when Isabel snuck into the clinic before it opened, she did some blood work on the sample she'd drawn from Monty, grabbed medical supplies to replenish what she had at home, and quickly jotted a note to Suzanne.

> *I drove in to get some meds and let you know I'm*
> *staying home today. I have a touch of the flu, noth-*
> *ing to worry about. Unfortunately, my phone's out*
> *of order, but I can either be reached on my cell*
> *phone, or if that doesn't work, through Gus Dearing*
> *in case of an emergency. And I'll be in tomorrow.*

She'd jotted down Gus's phone number, reminding herself
to recharge her cell phone so that it would not become necessary for Suzanne to try Gus.

"Not yet."

"Want me to call the phone company for you before I
leave?"

"No thanks. I've already talked to them. They'll be out
soon. In the next day or two."

WHEN SHE PULLED up to her cabin, the first thing Isabel
saw—the *only* thing she saw—was a beat-up green pickup
sitting outside.

Gus.

She'd stopped by Gus's house on the way home from the
clinic yesterday morning. Monty's condition, combined with
his status as a fugitive, made it impossible for her to call the
phone company out to repair the line Clyde had cut. But as
a doctor, she simply could not leave her patients with no
means of contacting her. Her decision to leave Gus's phone
number for Suzanne had been impulsive, but necessary. After
doing so, she had no choice but to drop by Gus's and inform
him.

"Line's just dead," she'd told Gus. "And I'm staying home
today, don't feel well, so I gave the clinic your number in
case there's an emergency. Hope you don't mind."

" 'Course not," Gus had answered. "You call the phone
company yet?"

"Yep. They'll get it fixed right away."

She was making decisions—and lying—right and left, and by the seat of her pants. She hoped no emergencies arose that would result in someone calling Gus, which would have sent him to the cabin to find her. If something did come up, she decided, she'd deal with it then.

Luckily, yesterday had passed without word from Gus that she was needed.

As an added precaution against his coming over to check on her while she was gone, she'd also stopped by Gus's house again this morning and told him she felt better and was heading in to work.

But there sat Gus's truck.

Her heart beating wildly, Isabel parked her own truck behind Gus's, then approached the kitchen door tentatively.

Monty was in no condition to put up much of a fight, but he was also a desperate man. Who knows how he had responded when Gus showed up.

Isabel had no idea what to expect when she opened the door. Certainly not the sight of Gus's long legs splayed across the kitchen floor.

"Gus!" she screamed.

Gus's head came up and peered at her from over an arm that held a screwdriver to the phone jack in the wall.

"You scared me to death," Isabel scolded. "What are you doing here?"

"Fixing the goddamn phone. What's it look like?"

"But . . ."

Lifting onto his elbow, he leveled his gaze on her. "You mighta told me you had company."

Isabel's eyes scanned to the living room. Monty looked exactly as he had when she left him that morning, still sleeping in her bed. She crossed to where he lay and placed a hand on his forehead.

He still had a slight temperature. The antibiotics she'd given him intravenously the day before, and again by injection this morning before leaving for work, had helped, but they hadn't succeeded in getting it down all the way.

Monty mumbled incoherently, but did not open his eyes.

"He don't look so good to me," Gus said over her shoulder.

"How long have you been here?"

"An hour or so."

"Was he awake when you got here?"

Gus snickered.

"You might say so. Damn fool started a wrestling match with me before he realized who I was. I'd used my key to let myself in and fix the phone. Once we had a little talk, and I assured him I wasn't gonna turn him in, he settled down. But I think that took it all out of him."

Isabel lifted the comforter and saw immediately that the dressing over Monty's chest was covered with fresh blood.

"I tried to change that," Gus said, following her eyes. "But he told me you wouldn't want me to. I just put pressure on it and it stopped soon enough."

"Thank God for that. He can't afford to lose any more blood. Not until I find a way to replace it."

"That why he's so darn weak?"

"That plus the fact that there's a bullet in his shoulder and his body's trying to reject it."

Isabel could feel Gus's eyes on her. She turned to face him.

"You sure you're doin' the right thing?" he asked.

"Sure? No. But I think I am." The exhaustion of the past two days swept over her suddenly, weakening her to near tears. "I just don't know if I can do enough, though, Gus. What if I can't save him? What if he dies here, when a trip to the hospital would save his life?"

"If that's how it turns out, you can't blame yourself. Monty made this decision. He told me that. He wouldn't want you to feel responsible."

"But it's my job to try to save his life, not to protect him from the law."

"Honey, a white man's dead. Believe me, one way or another, what you're doing could save his life."

"Not if I don't get my hands on some blood for him. I may have to drive to Missoula, Gus. Try to get a couple pints there. I think Lehman Morris might be willing to help. But I hesitate to put him in that position."

"If you have to go, I'll stay here while you're gone."

"Would you? I didn't want to leave him alone today, but he insisted. Said they'd send someone out here for sure if I missed another day of work, and he's probably right. And of course I have other patients who need me. I'd hoped I could make a couple calls from the clinic, get ahold of some AB-positive for him. From a friend in Seattle. The only one I have there who'd be willing to break the rules for me. But she's on vacation. She'll be gone another week." She shook her head, discouraged. "Wouldn't you know I'm rH negative. I'd been praying he'd turn out to be negative too. But of course, he's not."

"What does that mean?"

"You're either rH positive or negative. And then you're either A, B, AB, or O."

"And you gotta get an exact match for it to work?"

"Not necessarily. O-positive is a universal donor. It works for any rH-positive recipient."

Isabel could tell by the expression of concentration on his face that Gus had been paying close attention to her explanation.

"Maybe *I'm* a match. Or that universal type you just mentioned."

This simple, sweet gesture did it—unleashed the tears that Isabel had been holding back. She stepped toward Gus and threw her arms around him.

"You dear, dear man," she said, laying her head on his bony shoulder, her body trembling with exhaustion.

But it wasn't just exhaustion overcoming her. It was fear— fear for Monty's life, fear for what her actions could do to her career, fear from feeling her life so horribly out of control.

"There, now," Gus said, stroking her hair gruffly, like she'd seen him stroke Grunt dozens of times. "We gotta stay strong. We gotta take care of this young man here."

Isabel pulled back, locking eyes with Gus.

"You mean it, Gus? That you'd be willing to give Monty blood if you're a suitable donor?"

"Way I figure it, I'm an old geezer who isn't much use to anyone anymore. If a coupla pints of my blood can help save this young man, it's my opportunity to make a difference in this world."

"Okay, then," Isabel said, "let's go find out if you're a match."

CHAPTER

THIRTY-ONE

I SHOULD THINK Pfister's a wee bit pleased about this."
Ken MacStirling's eyes remained fixed on the CDC report. Lyons had received a preliminary copy of the report only an hour earlier. After reading it, he'd called MacStirling into his office.

"I haven't shared the information with them yet. I'll bring it to our meeting next week. I want to give it to them in person so I can see their reaction when they see these new statistics."

"By then," MacStirling said, "they'll probably already have seen it. Not that that's a bad thing. Our own marketing department couldn't come up with anything so brilliant."

Lyons laughed. Things were finally looking up and he felt good.

"You can say that again. But I still want to be the one to present this to Pfister. They won't have seen this yet. I have a close friend at the CDC who released the findings to me early. The official report won't be out for another month."

"I knew the hantavirus had spread and that the number of cases had increased, but this is just shocking," MacStirling said, shaking his head.

Lyons always marveled at Ken MacStirling's puritanical approach to what he did—his burning desire to wipe out disease contrasted sharply with the motivation of many of his colleagues, who often lost sight of that end somewhere along the way in their pursuit of acclaim and recognition.

"Thirty states have seen deaths from it now," Lyons said. "As you can see from that graph, the number of cases has climbed exponentially. And the pattern's changing. First couple of years, no one got sick until late spring. Now we're seeing it in February."

"The only thing that seems to be holding constant," MacStirling replied, "is the death rate. Still about forty percent."

"And did you read the CDC's plan?" Lyons sneered. "The report says the first priority should be to study mouse populations so they can learn how the virus is spread among the rodents."

MacStirling snorted his contempt.

"Not one word about funding a vaccine."

"Thank the Lord for that."

Pfister's interest in a long-term partnership with ImmuVac had only grown over the past few weeks. This report had the potential to seal the partnership deal.

"I assume you've been working on your presentation for next week's meeting."

"Yes," MacStirling answered. "As you know, I've already presented the results from Phase I to Pfister. Next week I'll present Phase II's results, which were better than I could have hoped for. And I'll lay out the plans for starting Phase III."

"Are we on target with Phase III?"

"Yes. Isabel McLain is enrolling subjects now. She's hoping to vaccinate ninety percent of the reservation population by the time we're through."

"I haven't heard tales of any opposition recently. What's happening on that front?"

MacStirling took a deep breath.

"Apparently this Canadian mining company came in right about the time Phase I was completed and began doing some exploration on the reservation. Monty Four Bear, the Jimmy who'd caused us so much trouble, turned all his attention to fighting the mine instead. Then things really got weird. There was some kind of explosion at the mine site where a guard was killed and Monty Four Bear disappeared, with another activist friend of his. Horrible mess, I guess. But at least we don't have to worry about him anymore."

"I guess that's what the son of a bitch gets for meddling in affairs that are none of his business."

"Funny thing is," MacStirling added, "Dr. McLain seems sympathetic to him when it comes to this mining situation."

"She's a strange one, if you ask me."

"I don't know. I quite admire her," MacStirling said defensively. "And I'll tell you one thing, without her, this study would never have succeeded."

"I hope you're keeping your relationship with Dr. McLain entirely professional."

MacStirling's fair cheeks flushed. "I don't appreciate that. When have I given you reason to question my professionalism?"

"You're right. I apologize." It wouldn't do to offend MacStirling right now. He needed him for these Pfister negotiations. "That was uncalled for. Now, tell me more about Phase III."

MacStirling hesitated. Then he cleared his throat.

"As I was saying, since the FDA's given us the go-ahead for Phase III, I'll begin production of the next batch of vaccine immediately. By the time Dr. McLain finishes enrollment, we should be ready to go."

"That's great. Let me know if you need any additional resources. I'd like to move this along as quickly as possible. Pfister is very eager to get this vaccine to market." He leaned toward MacStirling. "I want you to know I appreciate the job you've done for us on this one, Ken. If this Pfister partnership goes through, you'll have earned a promotion. How does director sound to you?"

"Thanks, James," MacStirling said, rising. "But you know I don't care about titles. Just keep funding my work."

As MacStirling left Lyons's office, Chris Finch slid by him.

"You have a call on two," she told Lyons.

"Who is it?"

"He wouldn't say."

"Why would you even waste my time then?" he chided, reaching for the Biotech Resource Library DVD on the corner of his desk. "You know I'm not going to talk to someone who won't even identify himself."

"I knew you'd say that, but . . . his voice sounded familiar. Maybe it's my imagination, but I think it could be Dr. Kirov."

Lyons's hands froze in midair.

"I'm sure you're mistaken," he said with a casual air that he hoped didn't sound forced. "But I'll take it. Close my door on your way out, will you?"

"WHAT THE HELL are you doing calling me here?"

"You're not answering your cell phone," Sergei accused. "Don't you pick up your messages?"

Lyons had, indeed, picked up his messages. There had

been two from Sergei, saying he needed to talk to Lyons. But Lyons hadn't yet decided the fate of Sergei's work. After the episode with the mutated vareola, he realized he had to think things through carefully before making any announcements to Sergei.

"I told you never to call me here at the office. My secretary recognized your voice."

"Tell her she was wrong."

"What do you want?"

"What have you decided?"

"Nothing. I told you. I won't have any decision made until I find out what happens with Pfister."

"I've been wondering what you plan to do with me if things work out with Pfister."

Lyons paused.

"We'll find something for you, you know that."

"But my work here?"

"Let's take one thing at a time. When we know about Pfister, we'll make that decision."

"When will you know?"

"MacStirling and I have a meeting with them in New York next week. Tuesday through Thursday. I'll have a better idea after that."

"That must mean you're proceeding with Phase III of the hantavirus vaccine."

"Yes. Of course. I told you when I was out there, the hantavirus vaccine is the main reason Pfister is interested in ImmuVac."

"When do you expect to begin Phase III?"

"Soon, goddammit," Lyons said. Then he hesitated. "Why do you care when we begin Phase III? That study has nothing to do with you."

"I'm only curious. That's all. How do you think it feels to be out here, cut off from everyone else? I just like to hear what ImmuVac is planning. After all, the partnership with

Pfister will mean more money for research, including mine. Didn't you just say that?"

Lyons felt Kirov was testing him somehow.

"Yes, of course," he said, trying to sound sincere.

"Well, then, tell your secretary that's why I called. Because I may be coming back before too long."

Lyons hadn't decided to pull the plug on the smallpox vaccine quite yet, but only because the Pfister deal hadn't been sewn up. Once it was, he'd be foolish to risk proceeding with Sergei's work.

One thing he *had* decided. Once he closed down the Gaston lab, there was no way in hell he'd hire Sergei Kirov back. He'd always thought Kirov a bit eccentric, but his last visit to Gaston left him convinced the Russian scientist's problems amounted to a lot more than eccentricity. He was dangerous. And—and this was the really scary thing about him—watching the scientist twirl the vial containing the modified smallpox in the air, Lyons had also realized that Sergei, at least when it came to the deadly vareola virus, was fearless.

A deadly combination.

THE FIVE MEMBERS of the Blackfeet tribal council mingled in the hallway outside the meeting room as they waited for Penny Runningwind to arrive. Penny had warned Thomas she might be late. She worked as a sales representative for an office supplier out of Helena, and when Thomas had called her the night before to tell her about this afternoon's impromptu meeting, she told him she'd have to drive up after a sales call in Polson.

"C'mon, Thomas," Rock groused, "let's get the show on the road."

Thomas looked at his watch. Five thirty-nine.

"Penny should be along any minute. I guess we can get started. Provided you're willing to take notes, Rock."

"Why me?" Rock grumbled.

" 'Cause you're the one in such an all-fired hurry, that's why."

"Ahright. Let's go."

The group of five men sauntered into the meeting room, arranging themselves in their usual positions around the long, battered pinewood table that had hosted many a tribal council meeting over the past two decades.

"What's up with the tie, Thomas?" Jimmy Schroeder, sitting to the tribal chief's left, wanted to know.

Thomas had abandoned his customary jeans and denim shirt and today wore nicely pressed black slacks, a white shirt, and a bolo tie. He ignored Jimmy and started the meeting.

"I called this meeting 'cause I've heard now from just about all of you—everyone but you, Rock, I guess—that you think it's time we re-evaluate the permission we gave WRI to drill for gold."

"Re-evaluate?" Jimmy echoed. "Hell, that's not what we said. We've already re-evaluated. What we want is to kick them off the rez, once and for all."

Murmurs of agreement rose from around the table.

"Now, I know everyone's pretty upset about what's happened this past week, and I'm not saying I haven't changed my mind on this thing, too, but I want to make sure we don't just react out of anger."

"How else do you expect us to react?" Dave Matthews asked. "I mean, look what they did to Leroy Four Bear. It's no wonder Monty and Clyde blew that equipment up. I'da done the exact same thing if Leroy was my dad."

"We don't know for sure that WRI had anything to do with what happened to Leroy," Rock Peacock said. "Bud Wolfkill says they're still investigating."

"Hell, Rock, you know damn well that's who did it," Matthews said. "The boy heard them threaten to come back if Monty didn't back off his opposition to the mine. What is it with you?"

"What it is with me is that I'm not going to make a rash decision that could end up hurting this reservation. That gold mine could be the answer to our prayers. Could pay for a new school, fix our roads, maybe even allow us to hire a couple emergency medical personnel. When the clinic's closed, someone could die of a heart attack while they waited for that lady doctor to drive into town."

"At least she's living here," Charlie Spencer piped up, "not just coming here twice a week like old Dr. Hammer did from Kalispell. That Dr. McLain's the best thing to happen to this reservation, if you ask me. Her and that vaccine. I got my whole family signed up to get it."

"Really?" Matthews asked. "I been thinkin' about it, but I don't know. Still have a bad feeling about it."

"I'd rather take my chances with the vaccine than risk dying of hantavirus," Penny Runningwind said as she settled in to her customary seat to Thomas Rose's right. "It's been over eight months since Phase I of the trial. Between Phase I and Phase II, almost two hundred Blackfeet have been vaccinated. And not one of them's gotten sick as far as I know."

Rock pushed the pad of paper he'd been scrawling on across the table to Penny.

"I'm signed up," he said.

"This meeting isn't about the clinical trial," Thomas Rose said testily. "Now let's get back to WRI. There's no doubt that the proposed mine's caused plenty of trouble here already. And I think we all have good reason to be concerned. But the question is—and it's a serious question that we have a responsibility to answer wisely—whether or not the mine still stands to be a benefit to our people, as Rock just said. I think we have to separate what happened to Leroy, and what happened out there the other night, from that question. Let law enforcement deal with the rest. We need to decide whether we want to let WRI continue to explore."

"You *can't* separate them, Thomas," Jimmy said. "Don't you see?"

"I don't know," Rose answered. "I just don't know. Maybe you're right."

"And as for letting law enforcement deal with the rest," Matthews chimed in, "do you really think that's how this whole mess should be resolved? With the FBI crawling all over the rez, do you think Monty and his cousin are gonna get a fair shake? We all know what happened out there the other night. Monty was mad, rightfully so if you ask me, about what they did to Leroy. And we all know Clyde was more than happy to help him get even by setting that equipment on fire. But no way Monty killed that guard without him firing first. No way. I'd stake my kids on that. This whole mess is WRI's fault, and letting them stay here will only make things worse."

"Get them off the rez," Jimmy echoed.

"I agree," Penny said, looking up from the notes she scribbled on the pad.

"Me, too," Charlie said. "And I also think we should kick the FBI off."

"That's not easy to do," Rock said.

"Everything that happened happened on reservation land. Far as I can see, that makes it a matter for the tribal police, not the feds."

"The way things stand," Penny said, "we'll never see Monty again."

Thomas Rose banged angrily on the table with his fist. "That's another matter entirely. We can take it up at another meeting. Will you people please stick to the subject here? Rock, you're the only one we haven't heard from. What's your vote on this thing? Do we kick WRI out, or let them stay?"

"You haven't voted yet yourself," Rock responded.

"Okay," Rose said. "I vote to rescind the permission we gave WRI to explore for gold on the reservation. Everyone in agreement, say aye."

A chorus of ayes greeted him.

"Anyone opposed say nay."

A single nay, from Rock, could be heard.

"The ayes have it," said Thomas. "I'll notify WRI to pack up."

CHAPTER

THIRTY-TWO

As HE'D DEVELOPED a habit of doing at the same time each day, Monty found himself glancing frequently at the old bell-shaped oak clock that dominated the mantel.

Four-forty. Isabel would be home soon.

Rolling onto his right side, he pushed himself up onto his elbow. He waited in that position until the dizziness passed. He'd learned from experience that if he stood too quickly, he might end up doing a face-plant on the floor—the position in which Isabel had found him two days earlier when she'd returned from the clinic.

Today he'd decided to demonstrate his improved condition by building a fire and greeting Isabel, not from her bed, but instead from the rocking chair. It wasn't just a matter of pride. *That*—his pride—had taken such a beating already that it was no longer salvageable. Sleeping in Isabel's bed while she slept next to him on the hard floor. Lying, shivering, wrapped in her comforter, wearing her wool ski cap, sipping lukewarm soup from a straw. Relying on Isabel to help him to the bathroom, where she stood just outside, listening in case he should fall—this, of course, only after the first few days where, after his absolute refusal to catheterization, Monty had urinated into a glass mayonnaise jar.

Glass so that Isabel could see it, examine it, to make sure that his urine did not contain blood.

It brought back memories of his mother, in the days before the cancer finally took her, decrying the fact that the blasted disease wasn't content to take just her life, that it first insisted on taking her dignity.

No. The simple act of building a fire could hardly restore his lost pride. But by demonstrating his improved condition, it might help him convince Isabel to drive him to Kalispell, where he could board a bus to Wyoming. He had to get to the Wind River reservation. He'd not heard from Clyde since he left, but Monty knew that's where his friend would have gone. Clyde and Monty both had ties there. Friends who could harbor them while they planned their next move. For they still had work to do. Monty and Clyde might not be able to maintain a visible presence in the fight against WRI's mine, but through their network, they could ensure that the disruptions to WRI's plans continued.

Shuffling slowly across the wood-planked floor, Monty crossed to the kitchen. He opened the door and stood there on its sill, breathing in the spring air dampened by a light mist of rain. That, the simple act of taking a normal breath, in itself showed progress.

He hungrily sucked the air deep into his lungs, savoring it.

Monty had always been able to smell the seasons, to distinguish each from the other by the texture and perfume of the air. Closing his eyes, he inhaled the honeysuckle and wild grasses, the blanket of deep blue wild Camas from the moist meadow in front of Isabel's cabin. There was a freshness to the scent, a newness, that he'd always loved. The season of rebirth. Rivers flush with winter runoff, fawns taking their first wobbly steps. Eagles and hawks and osprey focused only on feeding the gaping mouths awaiting them in their treetop nests.

He loved this land. This reservation.

Soon he would leave. He had no choice. Would he ever be able to return? Had his actions doomed him to become a permanent fugitive?

His wounded shoulder only allowed him to carry two pieces of wood at a time, so Monty shuffled back and forth between the fireplace and Isabel's winter supply of firewood—low now, no more than half a cord—which was stacked neatly at the far end of the porch that ran along the side of the house. After the second trip, on his way back for the last armload of split tamarack, he paused in the kitchen, leaning against the heavy table, exhausted by the effort.

The crunch of tires against gravel announced Isabel's arrival.

Damn, she was early.

He eyed the rocking chair in the living room. Judging he didn't have time to make it there, he decided to stay put.

Two booted footsteps on the porch, and Isabel appeared in the open doorway.

"You're up!"

Her hair, usually tied back, fell over the shoulders of her chamois jacket in a wild pattern. For the past week that he'd been there, Isabel's features had rarely altered from their reflection of her intense anxiety. Even in sleep, when he'd studied her, lying on the floor, her face lit by each night's dying fire, the worry had been there. But her eyes now were clear and bright and she approached him with a smile.

"I have good news." She placed a hand on his shoulder. "Please. Sit down."

Isabel pulled out one of the heavy wooden chairs for him, and Monty lowered himself into it. She positioned herself across from him then and placed both hands flat on the table's surface, as if she were trying to bridge the distance between them.

Monty had developed a level of comfort with the relationship they had forged in the past few days. A relationship where each kept to themselves; where, aside from a few angry exchanges over Isabel's refusal to help Monty leave the reservation, emotions were kept in check. He sometimes wondered if Isabel's concern for him had taken on a new dimension, felt that she had begun looking at him with different eyes; and, if the truth be known, the admiration and gratitude he felt for her had only grown as the days passed. But the expression of any such feelings had, until now, appeared as unthinkable to Isabel as it was to Monty. This— this display of enthusiasm—startled him.

"What is it?"

"The tribal council held a special meeting last night. They voted to rescind WRI's rights to drill on the reservation." Isabel's smile transformed the planes of her face, accentuating her high cheekbones. "You *did* it. There will be no mine on the reservation."

Overcome, Monty dropped his head into his hands and offered a silent prayer of thanks.

When he felt Isabel's grasp on his forearm, he lifted his eyes to hers.

"Congratulations," she half whispered.

"Thank you."

When he was promoting a cause, or teaching a lecture, Monty never lacked for the right words. But now he found himself unable to express the flood of emotions washing over him.

"What?" Isabel said, tightening her fingers around his wrist. "What are you thinking?"

He shook his head.

"I don't know. It's crazy. But I'm thinking maybe I should turn myself in."

Isabel drew back.

"You can't do that."

"We've accomplished what we set out to accomplish. If what you heard is true, our land won't be destroyed. I planned to run, to stay in hiding, so I could continue to fight the mine. Make sure that it never happened. Now that's been done." He paused. "Maybe I'm willing to spend some time in prison for what I did. After all, I broke the law. Destroyed property. If that's the price I had to pay to rid my people of the mine, if that's the price I have to pay to be able to return to my home one day, it would be worth it."

"But you could be convicted of murder."

"It was self-defense. We were fired on."

"I can't believe we're having this conversation," Isabel said angrily. "That now I'm the one sitting here telling you you're out of your mind if you think any court will buy that."

Monty stared at her.

"I would've thought you believed in our system of justice."

Isabel's laughter, bitter and caustic, shocked him.

"What is it?" he asked. He could see he had touched upon something very personal and painful for her. It was in her eyes, which she'd averted.

When she brought them up to meet his, he saw an entirely new side of Isabel. A bitterness he would not have thought her capable of.

"Have I told you I'm also the subject of a federal investigation?"

Monty managed to keep the shock from his face. He remained silent.

"You of all people should appreciate this," she said. "My ex-husband gave up his cardiology practice to conduct clinical trials. The drug companies were paying him lots of money, obscene amounts. I had no idea. And then one day I learned that a former emergency room patient I'd treated had been enrolled in one of his studies. She died. He'd given her three different medications, two of which were prohibited by the study. She should never have been in it in the first place. Her blood pressure was too high."

Isabel eyes focused on the wall, the table. Anything but Monty.

"I turned him in. That's when I left him. And now he's

sucked me into it. Turns out it wasn't just Bernice Hougham. He'd enrolled many of my former patients. I don't know how he did it. How he got the information. I would never have given him that, never have allowed it."

"Have you talked to them? Told the investigators?"

Isabel issued another short, harsh laugh.

"Oh yes. I certainly did. But they're convinced I provided him names and medical conditions. In fact, Alistair has them believing it was my idea to start with."

She tried to smile.

"How's that for justice? I may lose my license. In fact, I may end up in prison. Right next to you, if you insist on this foolishness. If you turn yourself in."

Slowly he reached for her, placing his hand, palm up, on the table in front of her. Isabel placed her own hand on his, wrapping her fingers around his.

"I'm sorry," he said softly.

"You can't do it, Monty. You can't turn yourself in."

"But if I run, I may never be able to come back."

They both heard it at the same time. A soft rumble coming up the road. It sent Isabel running to the door as Monty rose to retreat to Isabel's study. Since it was the only room without windows, they'd decided early on that he should hide there if anyone ever came to the door when Isabel was away.

"It's Gus."

Relieved, Monty remained at the table. But moments later, as Gus hobbled into the kitchen, the adrenaline rush returned.

"The FBI," Gus huffed. "They just left my house. They're heading this way."

"How do you know?" Isabel asked.

"They knew you lived up this way. Asked about how to get here. I steered them in the wrong direction. Told them to go up Carnation Creek, then cut over to the river road. I bought us some time. But not much."

"Quick," Isabel said, turning to Monty. "Get in my truck."

"No," Gus said. "I'll take him to my place. I think it's better if you stay here and talk to them."

"Excuse me, you two," Monty interrupted, "but would you mind if I had some say in all of this?"

"Not much time for that," Gus wheezed, "but go ahead."

"Gus, you've done enough for me. Giving me your blood was one thing, taking me in is another."

"So you're just gonna stay here and let yourself get caught? What about Isabel? You know how much trouble she'll be in when they find out she's been hiding you?"

Gus was right. He couldn't do that to Isabel.

He turned to her.

"Let me use your truck."

"No. Go with Gus, Monty. *Please.*"

WHEN GUS'S HARVESTER disappeared, with Monty lying, hidden by a blanket, on the backseat, Isabel tore through the small cabin, tossing any evidence of his having been there into a black plastic garbage bag. Rolls and pads of gauze, a prescription bottle of Keflex, betadine solution, syringes, IV bags, tubing, anything that hinted at her having treated an injury or illness—it all went into the bag, which she stuffed into the back of a shelf in her clothes closet.

Next she rolled up the sleeping bag she'd been using each night and shoved it under the bed. Hurriedly she straightened the bedding, and as she arranged an assortment of decorative pillows that had proved helpful in making Monty comfortable, she heard the car pull up.

A quick glance out the front window showed her a black sedan parked in the spot just vacated by Gus. When the door on the passenger side opened, she did not wait to see who disembarked, but instead ran to the kitchen, where she grabbed the roast she'd fixed two nights earlier, on Sunday, threw it into the oven and turned the heat on. At the same time, she turned the flame on under a pan of water.

It had to appear she was not expecting them.

Simultaneous with the knock on the front door, Isabel ripped open a package of pasta and dumped it into the water.

Her struggle to unlock the front door brought back thoughts of when she'd opened it a week earlier to find Monty and Clyde on the stoop. This time, however, the two men waiting outside were very clean cut, all business. And white.

"Dr. McLain?" The taller of the two stepped forward.

"Yes."

"We're from the FBI. I'm Agent Tierney and this is Agent Jacobs. May we come in?"

"Of course."

Agent Tierney, tall, slender, with a head of sandy waves and wire-rim glasses that gave him the appearance more of an accountant than an FBI agent, seemed to be the designated communicator. As he explained the purpose of their visit to Isabel, the other agent, Jacobs, stood to the side, out of her line of vision. Isabel suspected immediately that this positioning was designed to enable Jacobs to examine the room while Isabel's attention was focused on Tierney. It made her very nervous. Had she overlooked anything?

"So we've basically been going door to door," Tierney continued his explanation, "trying to find someone who might have seen either of these two men in the past week."

He opened his blue blazer and withdrew two photos from the inside chest pocket.

Isabel waved the photos away.

"There's no need," she said. "I'm familiar with both men. I'd recognize them if I saw them."

"And have you?" Tierney asked. "Seen them, that is?"

Isabel had never been a good liar, but she looked the agent straight in the eye when she answered.

"No. Not since the explosion."

Agent Jacobs had now moved in the direction of the

kitchen. Isabel could see him turning to peer inside her darkened study.

"When was the last time that you saw either Four Bear or Birdseye?"

"Let me see. I guess that would be at the rally out at the drill site. That was maybe two, two and a half weeks ago."

Tierney raised an eyebrow.

"You participated in the disturbance that day?"

"Disturbance? No. I participated in a rally. I oppose mining on the reservation and I went that day to lend my support. Along with maybe a hundred others, I might add. Ninety-nine percent of whom were peaceful."

"Just how involved were you in this movement?"

The FBI clearly characterize any protest against the mine as subversive.

"Movement? I'm not sure I'd call it a movement. I just attended the rally that day. Nothing more."

Jacobs had now taken two or three more steps toward the kitchen.

"Have you attended other meetings with Four Bear and Birdseye?"

"Yes. I have." Now Jacobs froze where he stood. Isabel was getting annoyed. "I attended the tribal council meeting where a vote was taken on whether to allow WRI to explore for gold."

"And?" Jacobs returned to Tierney's side, having now decided that Isabel's testimony was more interesting than the cabin.

"And I was also at a meeting of the Institutional Review Board that Monty Four Bear attended."

She had both agents' full attention.

"Go on," Jacobs said. "Tell us more about this meeting."

"I'd be happy to. It was a meeting to seek approval for a clinical trial being proposed for the reservation. Four Bear was there to oppose it."

The two men shot sideways glances at each other.

"Were there other protesters, besides you and Four Bear?"

Isabel laughed.

"You don't understand. I'm the lead investigator on the study. I was there that night to convince the IRB to go forward with the study. Monty," she'd slipped in using his first name, "he was there to try to stop the trial."

Now both men looked totally confused. So much so that for a moment neither one spoke.

"Gentlemen, with all due respect, anyone on the reservation can tell you that there is no love lost between Monty Four Bear, his cousin, and me. In fact, you'd have no trouble finding witnesses to the fact that the last time I saw the two of them, the day of the rally, Clyde Birdseye confronted me. He basically told me to go home. Get off the reservation. So if you think I may have some involvement in what happened the other night, you couldn't be more mistaken."

Agent Tierney cleared his throat.

"Of course not," he said. "If we'd suspected you might be involved, we'd have been out here long before now. As I already told you, these men are wanted for questioning on two very serious matters. The sabotage of WRI's mine site. And murder. It's our job to find them and bring them to justice. I'm sure you understand that."

Bring them to justice.

"Of course." Isabel should have known better, but the assumption of Monty and Clyde's guilt implicit in these words temporarily disabled any common sense. "By the way, are you also investigating the beating of Leroy Four Bear?"

"That's not a federal matter."

How she wanted to argue this response. Both Leroy's beating and the incident at the mine site took place on tribal land. Both allegedly involved one or more Blackfeet and WRI. Why the difference in treatment?

But she'd already said too much.

"Is there anything else I can do for you? Any further questions you'd like to ask? I'll be eating cinders if I don't see to my dinner."

"There is one question I'd like to ask," Jacobs said. Now that he'd entered the conversation, Isabel had her first opportunity to take a good look at him. He was an average kind of guy, not someone she'd ordinarily find menacing, but he had eyes that bored right through you. "We believe that one or both of the suspects were wounded in an exchange of gunfire at the mine site. There was a trail of blood that led to their vehicle. But there are no records of any gunshot wounds being treated at any of the hospitals in a four state region. Can a man who's lost that much blood survive without treatment?"

"It's impossible for me to answer that, Mr. Jacobs. Even if you were able to tell me exactly how much blood he'd lost, I'd have to know the nature of the injuries."

"But it would be difficult, would it not, for a man who'd lost enough blood to actually leave a trail behind, to travel, wouldn't it? I mean, the son of a bitch couldn't get far without help of some sort."

"Anything I say would be pure speculation."

"Go ahead," Jacobs challenged, "speculate."

"Okay. Assuming the hemorrhaging is external only, that it can be stopped before he literally bleeds to death and that there are no other life-threatening injuries, there's no reason to think he couldn't travel. Someone with elementary knowledge of first aid could apply a pressure compress, elevate his legs, force liquids. In theory, it would be quite possible to travel, despite the blood loss. Your suspect could easily be in Canada, Arizona, or even Mexico by now. Maybe you ought to consider widening the scope of your search."

"But alone? Could someone who'd lost a fair amount of blood travel alone?"

"I thought you said he had his cousin with him."

Jacobs's eyes never stopped roaming the room.

"Would you like to take a look around?" Isabel invited.

Before Jacobs could answer, Tierney nudged him with an elbow.

"Let's let the lady eat her dinner in peace. I'm hungry myself."

CHAPTER

THIRTY-THREE

WHEN THE FBI agents had been gone several minutes, Isabel reached for the phone to call Gus. She dialed the first three digits of his number then, suddenly, hung up.

Agent Jacobs had disappeared into the kitchen. Could he have planted a bug?

Turning off the oven and burner, she grabbed her jacket and hurried outside to her truck.

When she pulled into Gus's driveway, there was no sign of the Harvester. Gus had probably pulled it into the garage to make sure the coast was clear before Monty crossed from the garage to the house.

Was she being paranoid, thinking that the agents might have returned to Gus's, or perhaps even followed her there? Could they be watching? Playing it safe, she stifled her impulse to run to the front door and instead crossed Gus's front yard at a leisurely pace.

Gus had seen her coming, for the door opened before she reached for its knob.

"How is he?" she asked.

"Nervous, like you'd expect. But doesn't seem like he's any worse for the wear."

"He's probably running on adrenaline now. Like we all are."

With Grunt padding behind both of them, pushing a cool, wet nose against Isabel's hand, Gus ushered Isabel into a spare bedroom at the back of the house, where Monty sat braced by both arms on Gus's ornate brass bed. He looked surprisingly strong. And startlingly handsome. Isabel had grown so used to seeing Monty in the prone position, weak from loss of blood or a fever, bundled in ski cap and blankets, that the sight of him now, his long hair pulled back, exposing his strong jaw and classic profile, disarmed her momentarily.

"Are you alright?" Monty asked.

She nodded.

"I'm fine. They didn't stay long. One of them nosed around while the other asked me how I knew you and when I'd last seen you. They know you were wounded and asked me hypothetical questions about whether you could travel."

"What did you tell them?"

"That in theory, with basic first aid administered to you, you might have been up to traveling quite a ways. Then he wanted to know whether I thought you could go very far on your own."

"Sounds like someone caught sight of Clyde," Monty muttered.

"Could be," Gus said.

All three fell silent. Had Clyde been caught? Would Monty be next? And, if so, what price would Isabel and Gus pay for helping him?

"It's time for me to leave," Monty finally said. "Follow Clyde. I think I know where he is. All I need is a ride to Kalispell. I can take a bus from there."

"Don't you realize they'll be checking the bus stations?" Isabel said. "And airports? You can't go. Not now. Besides, you're still not strong enough to travel alone."

"You better listen to Izzie," Gus said. "She knows what

she's talking about. They'll have your picture plastered all over every bus depot and train station in the state."

"But I can't ask either of you to continue hiding me. You could be arrested because of me. I can't live with that."

"Son, the truth is, we've already committed some crimes and we know it. Running now just ups the risk that all of us *will* end up in jail. You need to stay put and think through what you want to do nice and slow. I agree with you on one count, though, and that's that Isabel shouldn't be involved anymore. You're welcome to stay here, and let her get her life back to normal."

"No. He's coming back to my place."

Isabel hadn't intended to raise her voice.

She could feel both men's eyes turn on her. Embarrassed, she continued.

"It makes no sense for you to stay here, Monty. You still need medical care. And Gus, you've done enough now."

If it weren't for Isabel, Gus would never have been put in this precarious position. She had to minimize the chance of his involvement being discovered by the authorities. She was doing this for Gus's sake.

"What if the agents come back to your house?" Monty asked.

"There's no more reason to think they'd come to my place than Gus's. Besides, I told them about the clinical trial. That we've been enemies from the start. If they ask around, everyone will tell them I'd be the last person you'd turn to for help."

"You're sure about this?" Gus asked. Isabel could see the concern in his eyes, but for some reason, he wasn't putting up his customary fight.

"Yes."

While they waited for darkness to descend upon the reservation, Isabel prepared a meal of venison burgers and fried potatoes. Gus hovered near her in the kitchen, quieter than usual, while Monty rested in the back room.

When Gus cleared his throat, Isabel knew that he had something important to say.

"I'm worried about you."

Isabel focused on the diced onions she was scraping into the skillet of potatoes.

"There's nothing to worry about, Gus. Things will be fine. I promise."

"You know you can't promise any such thing."

He grew quiet again and Isabel realized just how deep Gus's concern for her ran. She finished stirring the onions into the potatoes, flipping them to brown evenly, then rested the spatula in the skillet and turned to face him.

"Tell me," she said. "What is it you want to say?"

Rivers of bright red capillaries mapped the whites of Gus's tired eyes, but Isabel still thought them beautiful.

"I know what you said a while ago. What we both said. But do you really understand what you're getting yourself into?"

Isabel reached for Gus's hand.

"Yes. I do. And I'd be lying if I told you I wasn't frightened by what's happening. But it's as though I have no choice, Gus. I think you feel it, too, don't you?"

Gus drew a deep breath between front teeth stained by years of chewing tobacco.

"I think what you and I are feeling are two different things. They may have started out the same, but that's changed."

Isabel dropped her eyes momentarily, then raised them again to meet his.

"So what am I supposed to do?" she said softly.

Gus shook his head; whether in sadness or resignation, Isabel could only guess.

"Just be careful. You and he come from two different worlds. He's a good man, I'd be the first to admit it. But sometimes that's not enough."

•   •   •

WHEN ISABEL AND Monty arrived back at her cabin, she had him wait just inside the kitchen while she checked the rest of the cabin for anything that looked out of place.

"Okay," she finally called from the living room, turning on a lamp.

Monty walked slowly to the bed and sank onto it, falling onto his back, his legs hanging over the edge.

"Need some help?"

"No," he said, watching as she stacked kindling on the fireplace grate. "So much for my plans."

"Plans?"

"To have a roaring fire going by the time you came home from work."

Isabel smiled.

"Thanks for bringing more wood in. That's a big help."

After washing up and changing into a long flannel gown and robe, Isabel settled into the rocker, rocking softly and watching until the flames had swallowed the kindling. Then she rose and placed two of the lengths of tamarack Monty brought in earlier on the grate, six inches apart and parallel to each other. Moments later, she laid a third on top of and at right angles to the first two.

She watched for a few minutes, then scooted on hands and knees over to the bed where she pulled at the down sleeping bag she'd stuffed under it when the FBI agents arrived.

Monty had by now climbed under the covers. Isabel hadn't realized he lay watching her until he spoke.

"There's room for both of us," he said.

"What?"

"Here, on the bed. There's room for both of us."

"But your shoulder. You need plenty of space."

"I'm sleeping on my back these days. I'll take the right side. You take the left."

She stared at him, still crouched next to the bed, not knowing how to respond.

"Come on, Isabel."

It was the first time he'd used her first name.

"You've slept on the floor long enough. It's not much—just a good night's sleep in your own bed—but it's about all I can offer right now. Allow me that. Please."

After all they'd been through—from the shared danger to the intimacy forced by her tending to his injuries—sharing a bed seemed a harmless practicality. Monty was a proud man for whom she knew such invitations could not come easy.

She lay the sleeping bag down and rose. One by one, she turned out the lights in the cabin. Then, framed by the fire's light, she dropped her flannel robe to the floor and climbed under the covers.

She expected to be immensely uncomfortable, to have trouble falling asleep. But the truth was that it felt good to be in her bed again, under her down comforter.

Neither spoke, and in a matter of minutes, the sound of Monty's now familiar pattern of slow, deep breaths signaled he'd fallen asleep. It didn't take long after that for Isabel to drift off too, but she slept lightly, waking often. With the curtains shutting out any light, it was impossible to see him, but each time she awakened, the steady rhythm of Monty's breathing told her he was sleeping soundly. But just before dawn—in the darkness, the only indication of the hour was the song of a family of swallows nesting under the cabin's gutter—Monty had fallen silent.

That realization, however, did not hit Isabel immediately because of another, more alarming one—the fact that, in her sleep, she'd rolled onto her side and slung her leg across Monty's, as she once used to do with Alistair.

Praying that Monty was still sleeping, Isabel shifted her weight to lift her leg and move away. Immediately, a warm hand came down on her thigh.

"Don't leave," Monty murmured sleepily into her hair.

Isabel took a deep breath, aware for the first time of a scent other than the smells of sickness and medicines that had become familiar. This was musky, distinctively male.

She did not *want* to leave. And so, instead of doing so, she lifted her head and placed it on Monty's good shoulder.

"I didn't mean to wake you."

"Don't talk."

She could hear the smile, and the thrill, in his voice, because she felt both too.

Without thought, she lifted her mouth to him and in the next instant, his lips found hers.

The love they made was silent, and sweet, and gentle. Afterward, lying in his arms, she found herself wondering whether Monty was always so gentle a lover, or whether his injury made it a necessity this one time. She also wondered if she would ever have the opportunity to learn the answer to that question.

When they'd each exhausted the other with pleasure, Isabel at last fell into a deep sleep. The sleep of someone at peace.

HE WAS PROPPED up on his elbow and staring at her when she finally opened her eyes to the daylight that had filtered in around the perimeter of the curtains.

"Still think I'm the enemy?" he whispered.

She expected to see a teasing grin, not the serious eyes and turned-down lips.

"What do you mean?"

"You told those feds that we were enemies. Do you still feel that way?"

"No. Of course not."

He smiled then, and tilted his head to study her. During their lovemaking, he had tried to help her slip out of her nightgown, but with only one good arm, he'd been pretty much useless. In the end, Isabel had helped him out of the blue jeans he'd climbed into bed wearing. She lay next to him now, her eyes drinking him in, storing for future recall the pleasure of the moment.

"Are all Indians such gentle lovers?" she asked playfully.

"Just the wounded ones." His smile deepened the lines at his eyes.

Isabel could feel him studying her, his gaze lingering on her bare shoulders, covered only by strands of her long black hair.

"My turn," he said softly. "Do all white women look this good in the morning?"

She'd been holding back from him. Perhaps because she was still digesting the information herself. Perhaps because she'd feared that voicing it would make it more real, and in doing so, dishonor Nada in some way.

Or perhaps the real explanation was that she had not fully accepted the truth yet. Until now.

Her lips slipped into an uncertain smile.

"I think there's something you should know . . ."

CHAPTER

THIRTY-FOUR

SERGEI KIROV'S MOOD was downright jubilant as he steered his battered Dodge across the Ross Island Bridge, heading for the business district southwest of downtown Portland. He hadn't realized he actually missed Portland until this moment, nor that it would feel this good to return. And, of course, his mission tonight . . . well, how could he *not* feel a strong sense of anticipation?

He knew from his long nights in the ImmuVac labs that

at this hour, just past ten P.M., he would find the building empty. Lyons's news last week—that both he and Mac-Stirling would be out of town this night, on the East Coast, selling their souls to Pfister—had disposed of any serious concerns Sergei might otherwise have had about his ability to pull tonight off.

There was no reason to think his security passkeys would not get him inside both the building and the labs. While he was still working at ImmuVac, an employee had been caught downloading patent information from the legal department's computer network. She'd been promptly fired, and all locks and security codes throughout the building changed. For weeks, it had caused problems—employees locked out, a re-examination of who should have access where, which led to numerous disputes and ill feelings. In the end, the action, while necessary, had so irritated the rest of ImmuVac's employees that Sergei felt confident Lyons would not have made another change because of Sergei's departure. Besides, as Lyons told it, Sergei was out of the country. And, of course, Lyons supposedly trusted him. After all, he'd set him up in Gaston, doing work that could land them both in jail if either were to slip up.

Sergei also had an ace in the hole. While the property posted numerous signs boasting of twenty-four-hour security, he knew that the night guard, Vinh Dang, wasn't scheduled to arrive until eleven P.M. And in reality, Sergei also knew from the many nights he'd worked until early morning that Vinh Dang rarely arrived until midnight. The fact that Sergei had kept his mouth shut about these late arrivals had on several occasions prompted Vinh Dang to tell Sergei, "I owe you one." He could always wait until the guard showed up and talk himself inside if need be.

Still, in spite of his confidence, Sergei's pulse quickened as he pulled up to the ImmuVac parking garage. His passkey gained him immediate access.

When working at ImmuVac, his routine had been to travel

directly from the parking garage to the labs on the second floor, but tonight when he stepped into the elevator, he pressed the button for the fourth floor, which housed quality control and the manufacturing facilities, which were minimal.

Like most small biotech companies, ImmuVac was in many senses a virtual company. It farmed out a great deal of its work. When the grand day finally arrived that one of ImmuVac's products received FDA approval and went into commercial production, the job of manufacturing and packaging would be delegated to a large plant in the San Diego area. Federal regulation of the manufacture of commercial pharmaceuticals, especially vaccines, was so stringent that it made the cost of manufacturing prohibitive for small companies like ImmuVac.

In an effort to assure consistency, prevent errors, and avoid contamination, federal regulators closely reviewed manufacturing procedures to ensure compliance with what was known in the industry as GMP—good manufacturing processes. Commercial vaccines were manufactured in large lots. Prior to release, each lot was subjected to stringent testing for potency and lack of contamination. This drove the cost of manufacturing sky high, while giving the public good reason to feel confident about the safety of medications sold commercially.

But something the average person didn't realize was that these stringent regulatory safeguards did not apply to medical studies. The only regulations pertaining to medical studies involving humans had been adopted by the Department of Health and Human Services and the FDA in 1981—and these regulations applied only to those studies funded by the government. Private entities, such as drug companies, could, in theory at least, ignore the antiquated rules. These loopholes allowed small companies like ImmuVac to produce their own vaccine lots for clinical trials.

Sergei headed for the labs where the HantaVac lots would

be manufactured. Exiting the elevator on four, he hurried past a door marked QUALITY CONTROL, then stopped at the juncture of two corridors. He peered both ways, then turned left, down a poorly lit hallway.

At its end, a door declared MANUFACTURING, AUTHORIZED PERSONNEL ONLY. Sergei stopped in front of the small black box posted next to the entry. Raising his hand, he pressed his right thumb against the small screen, then waited, breath held.

Several seconds passed, then a familiar click and the flash of a small, pen-sized green light indicated he'd been authorized for entry.

Sergei pulled the door open, stepping inside a vast, semidark space filled with the hum of machinery. Walking quickly and surely along an aisle between rows of tables that contained computers, autoclaves, electron microscopes, electrophoresis apparatus, and row upon row of cultures and test tubes, Sergei headed for the annex off the main room.

Entry to the annex was strictly limited, for it was in the annex that ImmuVac manufactured and stored vaccines to be used in clinical trials. The purity of the vaccines, stored in large stainless steel vats, could not be compromised, as the success of the trial and safety of the participants rested on that basic assumption of purity.

In a small locker room outside the annex, Sergei found the oxygen-equipped suit he was looking for. The only two ImmuVac scientists who ever had occasion to use the suits had been Ken MacStirling and Sergei. He remembered the day the suits had arrived—any time new equipment arrived at ImmuVac, the scientists who stood to benefit most stayed close at hand to protect their interest in it. He and MacStirling had argued over the suits. One suit was a large, the other extra large. Both men had eyed the extra large, which allowed greater freedom of movement. But MacStirling, taller than Sergei, had prevailed, laying claim to the extra large. With Sergei out of the picture, it was likely the second suit now served as a backup in the event the bigger suit became punctured or developed problems with its oxygen. Knowing MacStirling would pick up on any change in the oxygen level, Sergei made sure he held the smaller of the two suits, then stepped clumsily into it

Only then did he raise the lid of the insulated cooler he'd carried with him. He'd bought it that morning at a convenience store in Gaston.

BUY TWO SIX PACKS OF BEER AND WE'LL THROW A MINI-COOLER IN FOR ONLY $3, a sign on the counter read.

Extracting the small glass vial from the crude stand he'd fashioned inside the cooler, Sergei retraced his steps to the annex.

CHAPTER

THIRTY-FIVE

That's right," Ken MacStirling said, "tomorrow. The first shipment of the vaccine for Phase Three should arrive by ten A.M. I'm sending shipments of one thousand vials at a time. You'll receive a new shipment every two weeks."

"Great," Isabel said. She'd been waiting for MacStirling's call to confirm the vaccine's arrival. "I've devoted two days a week for the rest of June and all of July to Phase III. I have off-site clinics set up in Heart Butte and East Glacier, and I've recruited drivers to pick up anyone who needs transportation. The first scheduled session in East Glacier is Friday. But if the vaccine arrives early enough tomorrow, maybe I'll get a few vaccinations in ahead of time, at the clinic."

MacStirling chuckled.

"I'm anxious to get started too, but I'd prefer you wait until Friday. Since I didn't make Phase I or Phase II, I very much want to be there for the kick-off of Phase III, and that's the earliest I can make it. I'm leaving Portland at seven."

Isabel knew she should act pleased, but a visit from MacStirling was the last thing she needed with everything else going on right now.

If he noticed her failure to respond, he chose to ignore it.

"That portable refrigeration unit we shipped you working out okay?"

"Yes. It's just what I need for the off-site clinics."

"Lovely. Now for the really brilliant news. Pfister has signed on. Thanks to your success with the first two phases, we now have a corporate partnership with one of the strongest, most aggressive pharmaceutical companies in the world."

"Congratulations. I know that's good news for ImmuVac, but what does it mean for the HantaVac?"

"With the resources Pfister has—not just capital, but a staff of attorneys and regulatory people experienced in rushing a drug through approval—it's realistic to think the vaccine will be available commercially within a year."

"That's wonderful. Really."

"Hey," MacStirling said, "you don't sound quite yourself. Everything okay out there?"

Okay?

In addition to her own legal troubles, Isabel was falling in love with a man who just happened to be the focus of an intense manhunt. A man who was leaning more and more toward turning himself in, despite Isabel's fierce opposition and the knowledge that if he did, he would undoubtedly be charged with a murder he did not commit.

"Sure. Everything's great," she said. "Listen, I wanted you to know that I plan to be the first vaccinated with the new lot. I know you discouraged me before, but there's certainly plenty of vaccine now." She had argued with Monty about this the night before and wasn't in the mood to argue with MacStirling. "It's a matter of principle for me, Ken. If I encourage my patients to participate in this study, I have to be able to demonstrate my own faith in it."

"Tell you what," MacStirling replied. "Go ahead. But let's not include your name in the data we turn in to the FDA. They won't like the investigator participating in the trials. You know that."

"What if I experience adverse effects? You'd expect me not to report them?"

"You are one determined lady. How about this? If you experience adverse effects, we include your data. If not, we leave you out. Can you live with that?"

"I suppose."

Funny, Isabel thought after she hung up the phone, during their discussions about her immunizing herself with HantaVac, both Monty and MacStirling had called her a "determined lady," as though women who stood firm when it came to their beliefs were somehow unreasonable. With MacStirling, she didn't care enough to let it bother her. But last night, when she and Monty had argued about it, she'd used his similar comment to turn on him.

"*I'm* determined," she'd practically shouted at him. "What about you and this insane idea of turning yourself in? What's crazier? Me taking a vaccine that could save my life, or your turning yourself in and ending up spending the rest of your life in prison for a crime you didn't commit?"

"Far as I'm concerned," he'd answered hotly, "they amount to the same thing. Both of us could be throwing our lives away."

"Why are you so damn paranoid about this vaccine?" she'd cried. "We've vaccinated two hundred people now and there hasn't been a single serious reaction to the vaccine. But come next spring, those same two hundred people will be protected against the virus that killed Joe Winged Foot, Will Echohawk, and Dolores Birdsong."

"You're right. We lost three, three too many. But that doesn't warrant risking the lives of an entire tribe."

She'd turned on him fiercely and reflexively.

"How *dare* you accuse me of jeopardizing lives?"

Monty had reached out and grabbed her arm.

"I understand why you're so senstive about this study, Isabel. I know you believe in it. But do you actually think you can be objective about it?"

"What the hell does that mean?"

"Only that maybe this study means too much to you. You're so damn determined to undo what happened with your husband."

"I never wanted to get involved with this study in the first place," she'd snapped, filled with indignation. How dare Monty imply that this study had anything to do with Alistair? "I only did it because it was the only way ImmuVac was going to proceed with the vaccine."

"Listen, it doesn't really matter what made you take on this study. You can't know for certain that this vaccine is safe. No one will know for a long time if that's true. I just don't want you taking the HantaVac."

"You don't want me taking it?" Isabel's voice had risen. "What are you thinking?"

Monty had dropped the hold he had on her arm.

"I'm thinking that a lot rides on this clinical trial of yours," he'd answered, his mouth tight with anger. "For my people. And for you."

THE CLOCK TOWER in the chapel across the street had just struck twelve when Suzanne's ashen face appeared in the doorway of Isabel's office.

"What is it?" Isabel asked.

"It's Leroy. He's dead."

The gasp that escaped Isabel was more the sound of a wounded animal.

"*How?* What happened?"

"They killed him. Those bastards." At this Suzanne began sobbing. "They broke into his house again last night and murdered him."

Isabel's world began spinning out of control. She had to get to Monty. Had to be there when he learned this horrific news about his father.

She pushed back from her desk and grabbed her bag, all but oblivious to Suzanne, who still stood sobbing in her doorway.

"Where are you going?" Suzanne asked, clearly startled by the strength of Isabel's reaction to her news.

"I don't know," Isabel said. "I just have to get out of here for a while. Have to get away."

Suzanne followed along at her side as Isabel half ran to her truck.

"You sure you're okay? What about the rest of your appointments?"

"Cancel them."

ISABEL DROVE WITHOUT caution, completely ignoring the yellow stripe that indicated a no-passing zone as she accelerated around a brown '72 Chevy laboring on its climb up one of the many hills leading to East Glacier. Morning clouds usually clung to Glacier's peaks and the surrounding foothills long after they'd burned off on the plains below. By the time Isabel approached the turn-off to her cabin, the sun had disappeared behind a veil of thick gray clouds.

Rounding the last bend to her cabin, she came within yards of hitting a cow meandering down the gravel road. Uncharacteristically, she laid on the horn, but the animal, unfazed, continued dead center down the road. She yanked the pickup's wheel hard to the right, relying on its four-wheel drive to maneuver her over the abrupt grassy shoulder, past the lazy Jersey.

Even from a distance she could tell that the figure sitting on the front steps of her cabin was not Monty. Drawing near, she saw that it was a Blackfeet woman. The woman barely moved when Isabel pulled into the driveway.

Isabel threw the truck into park and jumped out, rounding the pickup's front end to head for this unexpected visitor.

Who was she? And why had she shown up now, when all Isabel cared about was seeing Monty?

"Can I help you?"

Slowly, the woman got to her feet. Isabel had learned long ago that the age of Blackfeet women was a difficult thing to judge. Some looked far older than their years while with others, usually the stouter ones, like the woman before her, she'd often been surprised to learn they were years older than she'd guessed. This woman she would put in her late fifties. She was dressed in attire typical on the reservation—black stretch pants and an oversized, powder blue Coors T-shirt that, though generous, hugged rolls of flesh around her torso.

"Monty said that you might be able to give me a ride back home."

She had the same lyrical tone that typified Suzanne's speech. Her words—even this simple and surprising statement—seemed spoken to unwritten music.

"Monty? I don't understand."

Alarmed, Isabel stepped onto the porch and tried to look inside.

"He's gone," the woman said matter-of-factly. "I didn't think you'd want a stranger in your house, so I've been waitin' outside."

"What do you mean *gone*?" Isabel said. "Where? Where did he go? And who *are* you?"

"My name's Edna. Edna Northrup. I'm Leroy's neighbor. Leroy's dead." She delivered this news without expression. "I came out here to tell Monty."

"But how did you know where to find Monty?"

"Monty's been callin' me every coupla days, to check on Leroy. He wanted me to tell Leroy he's okay, so Leroy wouldn't be too worried about him." She shook her head slowly from side to side. "Now this."

"You mean Monty called you from here, from my house?"

"Coupla times. But I ain't told nobody. Monty told me to keep my mouth shut. And I have. He told me not to come out here ever, but I had to tell him . . ." Like Suzanne, the woman finally broke down as tears streamed down her cheeks. "I had to tell him about Leroy."

Isabel was usually a tremendously compassionate person, one who could not stand to see someone upset without trying to help, but her concern for Monty, her fear, now overpowered even her most deeply instilled instincts. Instead of trying to comfort Edna, she stooped to the other woman's height and pulled her hand away from her eyes.

"What happened?" she cried. "What did Monty say when you told him what had happened to Leroy?"

Edna sniffled loudly.

"He went after them. After the guys who killed Leroy. I gave him my car."

"You *what*?"

"I gave him my car. It might not get him very far, but it's better than nothin'."

"How long ago?"

"Oh, I dunno. Maybe two, two and a half hours."

Isabel collapsed onto the front steps. Stunned, she sat in silence. Shortly, Edna lowered herself next to her onto the step, and both women stared out at the peaks of East Glacier.

"You were Leroy's neighbor?" Isabel finally said, her voice softer now, as she thought about what Edna had been through.

"Yes. I been bringin' him meals since he got out of the hospital."

Isabel knew the Blackfeet did not like to discuss the dead. Nor did she want to hear the grisly details of how Leroy had died. But some questions needed to be asked.

"How would Monty know who did it? Was there a witness?"

"Those mining people are the only ones who woulda done that to Leroy."

"How can you be sure? How could Monty know that for sure?"

"Nobody on the rez would hurt Leroy. He's just an old man. A harmless old man."

"But how can Monty find who killed him? He can't possibly know who actually did it."

"I dunno. He seemed pretty sure 'bout it."

"Did he say who he was going after? Did he mention a name?"

"No." Edna grew quiet for a moment, her amazingly unlined brow furrowing. "He got awful upset. Punched his hand into your wall—don't think he hurt the wall none since it's logs, but his hand has to be hurtin' pretty bad. Then he asked me for my car. Said he couldn't take me home 'cause he was goin' the other way."

"Did he say anything about me? Did he want you to tell me anything?"

Edna squinted, thinking.

"Just that you might be willin' to give me a ride home."

CHAPTER

THIRTY-SIX

WHEN KEN MacSTIRLING realized that his schedule for Thursday was unusually light, he picked up the phone and called down to Frankie, ImmuVac's receptionist. He'd have Frankie change his reservations to Kalispell. Might as well go tomorrow instead of Friday morning. If she was free, maybe he could take Isabel to dinner. She'd sounded so strange when he talked to her. If they had some time together he might discover what was bothering her.

"Reception," an unfamiliar voice said.

"Hi. This is Ken MacStirling from research. I'm looking for Frankie."

"She's home sick today. I'm a temp filling in for her. Anything I can do to help you?"

MacStirling hesitated. He hated dealing with temps. They usually made a mess of things.

"I was just going to have her change an airline reservation she made for me earlier. But I might as well do it myself.

"Sure you don't want me to help?"

"Thanks, but I can handle it."

He picked up the phone and dialed directory assistance.

"The number for Rainy Day Travel," he asked the operator politely.

At the travel agency, a friendly voice, belonging to "Kim," answered.

"This is Dr. Ken MacStirling from ImmuVac. I believe you do all our corporate bookings for us. Our receptionist booked a flight for me, and I'd like to reschedule the outbound leg."

"What company did you say you're with?" the voice on the other end said. It was clear she hadn't been paying attention.

"ImmuVac."

"Janet usually handles those bookings, but she's at lunch right now. Let's see what I can find in the ImmuVac file . . ."

Batting oh for two—Frankie and now his regular travel agent—MacStirling waited patiently, picturing Kim on the other end running through computer screens to locate his reservation.

"Here we go. Did you say you're Dr. Kirov? A ticket for Leningrad?"

MacStirling couldn't help but laugh at the incompetency.

"You're a couple months off. Dr. Kirov's trip was this past spring."

"Not according to this entry. It says here he requested a ticket for Leningrad just two days ago."

"That can't be."

"Well, if you want to argue about it, you'll have to talk to Janet. Now, if you're not Dr. Kirov, what did you say your name is?"

"Dr. MacStirling. Ken MacStirling."

There was a pause.

"Okay, here we go. Now I've found you. Dr. Ken MacStirling. Round trip to Kalispell, leaving Friday at six A.M."

"That's more like it."

MacStirling made the change to Thursday, then hung up, thoroughly distracted by the information that Sergei Kirov had booked a trip to Russia. Lyons had told everyone at ImmuVac that the scientist returned to his homeland months ago.

It had to be some mistake—someone made an incorrect entry. That had to be it.

MacStirling had already put that thought out of mind when, later in the day, his own phone rang.

"Dr. MacStirling?" a female asked.

"Yes?"

"This is Hillary Gilbert calling from New York. I'm Pfister's director of quality control. I'm afraid I was out of the country last week when you and Dr. Lyons paid us a visit, so I missed the opportunity to meet both of you. I thought I'd call and introduce myself."

"How thoughtful of you," MacStirling said. "If I remember correctly, they told us you were in London."

"That's right. We're sponsoring a study at Cambridge. I try to get over there every three or four months."

"Well, I'm sorry we didn't get a chance to meet last week," MacStirling said, "but I'm sure we'll have another opportunity before long."

"Absolutely. I'll look forward to it. In the meantime, I wanted to check in with you on your hantavirus vaccine. It's my understanding that you're about to commence Phase III."

"That's right. In fact, the first lot was shipped yesterday. I'll be heading to Browning myself tomorrow to be there for the first of the Phase III vaccinations."

"Great. I'm glad to see you're a hands-on person. We encourage that at Pfister. You say you already shipped some of the Phase III vaccine. I'm assuming you kept a sampling for QC."

Who did she think she was dealing with? The question offended MacStirling, but he decided to keep his tone friendly.

"Of course," he said. "I keep a sample of each lot. We used the same lot for Phases I and II, but because of the size of the third phase—we expect to vaccinate up to seven thousand participants—of course we had to manufacture a new lot."

"You've run a YOYO dye on each lot then?"

MacStirling hoped Gilbert didn't notice his momentary hesitation.

"Yes," he lied. "The first lot was also tested by an independent laboratory, which verified its purity."

He did not offer the information that the third-party testing had been at the insistence of Isabel McLain.

"Did you have third-party testing of this most recent lot?"

"There was no need. I'm pretty much a one-man show. I prepared the lot. The formula didn't change."

"And the YOYOs? How do they compare for the two lots?"

"About as close to identical as possible."

"Great," Hillary Gilbert said. "I'll look forward to seeing the photos when I come to Portland."

"And will that be anytime soon?"

"You can count on it."

Damn. MacStirling hung up, the good mood occasioned by the start of Phase III and the prospect of dinner with Isabel dashed.

He hadn't expected to feel Pfister's heavy hand quite this soon. In his entire professional career, until now, he had never before lied to a colleague. But his pride, plus an earlier conversation with Lyons, caused him to this time.

ImmuVac had only acquired the new YOYO technology recently, and he knew that to admit as much to Gilbert would immediately label ImmuVac, in her eyes, as another minor-league biotech startup. A lightweight to be pushed around by its new, bigger, and more powerful partner.

MacStirling had, indeed, tested both lots for purity, but instead of using the newest technology, he'd run gels. For decades, scientists had used a method known as gel electrophoresis to determine the genetic fingerprint of DNA fragments. Gels were capable of detecting contaminants in vaccines and other medications. States linked by a national network of computers were able to share genetic profiles, derived from gels, of microbes causing outbreaks of food poisoning, which enabled epidemiologists to identify multistate outbreaks, trace their origin, and issue prompt public warnings.

But traditional gels were cumbersome. They could take as many as eleven steps, and several hours. More recent developments, such as YOYO dyes, saved scientists trouble and time.

YOYO dyes were state of the art, and standard equipment in research labs like those at Pfister. Solutions of DNA molecules were dyed with YOYO-1, then applied to a silicon-based mold lined with channels a few micrometers wide. Single dyed DNA molecules were drawn by capillary action into each of the channels, then illuminated with a laser. The flouresced dye revealed the size of the molecules. This process could be completed one hundred times faster than traditional gels, and remarkably, it used a million times less sample.

For months MacStirling had pleaded with Lyons to buy the new YOYO technology, to no avail. He'd run traditional gels on the single lot used for Phase I and Phase II of the hantavirus vaccine. Then, just before the trip to New York, when Lyons still had not acquiesced, he'd run a gel on the lot for Phase III. As he told Hillary Gilbert, the results from both lots were nearly identical.

Unbeknownst to him, however, Lyons had ordered a YOYO device earmarked specifically for him, in "celebration," as Lyons put it, of their new partnership. When they returned from New York, one had been waiting. Indeed, the ImmuVac CEO had splurged and purchased a multiplex device capable of sizing up to eight samples at once.

"If we want to hold our own with Pfister," Lyons had said, "we need to be cutting edge all the way. Gels are antiquated."

Since both techniques accomplished the same thing and he'd already gone to the trouble of running gels on both lots, MacStirling hadn't planned to use the YOYO device on the clinical trial lots of the hantavirus vaccine. But now that Hillary Gilbert expected to see them, he had no choice.

Glancing at his watch, he saw that he had exactly one hour before his four P.M. staff meeting. Just enough time to start the YOYOs. The staff meeting could be counted on to run late, after five. And he'd promised his wife he'd make it home before six for a dinner party she'd had planned for weeks. But he could start the dyes now, then come back later in the evening to check the results.

Maybe, with a little luck, he could still catch an afternoon flight tomorrow to Kalispell.

With a little luck.

CHAPTER

THIRTY-SEVEN

HE FELT LIKE a time bomb, each beat of the windshield wipers the ticking of its clock. The wipers had become necessary just before Snoqualmie Pass. The brutal desert sun that had caused him to pull over twice, first at the top of Ryegrass and again leaving Cle Elum, was now nowhere to be seen. Just rain. Dark, gray, matching his mood.

He liked the analogy. That of a time bomb. Each second that passed, his fuse grew shorter, the inevitable, welcome violence at its end closer. For only violence could put an end to the anger and guilt that filled every pore, infected every fiber of Monty Four Bear's being.

Two stops to give Edna's old Impala a chance to cool down had set Monty back over an hour. He'd pushed the car to its limits coming over the mountains, and finally, climbing I-90 out of the Columbia River Gorge near Ryegrass, it had overheated. Adding water and letting it sit awhile had done the trick, and before long, he'd been on his way again. But it happened again at Easton, just east of the pass. A Colville brother named Bob had pulled over to offer assistance that time. Good-natured and obviously in no hurry, Bob had watched Monty add more water, then waited with him to be sure the Impala started again. He'd followed Monty to North Bend, where he rolled down the window of his turquoise Toyota pickup and gave Monty a thumbs-up before turning off Interstate 90.

Before leaving Montana, Monty had considered crossing

the border into Canada just north of Whitefish, but he'd decided it was too close to home. Agents at the Montana and Idaho state lines would be much more likely to know about the explosion and be on the lookout for him. He was taking his chances here, too, but at this point in time there was no warrant for his arrest. Technically, he was only wanted for questioning. The number of individuals who fit that description heading north out of Seattle surely made keeping track of them unrealistic.

And the route he'd chosen—out of Missoula, I-90 all the way to I-5 in Seattle—also meant traveling high-speed interstates most of the way, which would save precious time. For every minute that Leroy's death went unavenged weighed like a boulder on Monty's grief-stricken heart.

Despite that fact, Monty welcomed the delay when he approached the Canadian border and saw the backup of vehicles beneath the Peace Arch—a downsized replica of the French Arc de Triomphe that symbolized the friendship between the two neighboring countries. It might cost a few extra minutes, but the long line of cars and RVs waiting to enter Canada would limit the amount of attention paid to Monty.

"Are you a U.S. citizen?" the guard asked now from his booth. His elevated seat gave him a good view into the car's interior, but aside from a plastic bag filled with flattened beer cans that Edna collected weekly from several East Glacier campgrounds, there was not much to see.

"Yes," Monty replied. "Montana."

"Where you heading?"

"Vancouver."

"How long you plan to be in Vancouver?" the guard wanted to know.

"One night, maybe two," Monty replied.

"Business?"

"Yeah. Business."

"May I see your driver's license?"

Monty reached for his wallet, grateful that Edna had run after him waving it in the air as he commandeered her car.

"Don'tcha need some money?" she'd yelled after him.

Poor Edna. He hadn't even given her a ride back to her house.

The guard took a quick look and handed the wallet back through the window.

"Have a safe trip."

Monty nodded, then shifted the rumbling car into drive and crossed into Canada.

A highway sign declared the distance to Vancouver forty kilometers. If only he still had those files on ImmuVac. It was long past quitting time at WRI. If he had the files, he could find LeCoque's house. Without them, he would be forced to wait until tomorrow. Maybe, just maybe, LeCoque's residence was listed in the phone book.

As soon as he entered the city, Monty pulled over at a phone booth in the parking lot of a gas station. He rifled through the tattered directory hanging from a chain attached to the booth.

There was no listing for a Jon LeCoque. He dialed directory assistance and was told the number was unlisted.

Next he turned to the Ws, and there he found what he was looking for: the address of WRI's corporate headquarters.

1515 W. Georgia.

Flipping to the front of the book, he found a city map. He ripped the page out and, stuffing it inside his shirt to protect it from the rain, returned to the car.

As the Impala inched its way through the congested streets of Vancouver, Monty found himself somewhat surprised by the sights. He'd expected a carbon copy of Seattle, but crossing Granville Bridge into the heart of the city, instead of Seattle's brisk, yuppie-friendly feeling, the pedestrians and shops struck him as decidedly slower and more sophisticated. Less crassly commercial than its American counterpart. And there were more people out at night, on the streets.

Georgia looked easy to find on the map, but a series of one-way streets forced Monty to circle around several times before finding 1515.

When he finally did find it, the sight of a giant WRI logo etched in the glass above the front double door hit Monty hard. Shaken, he pulled over across the street from the building and sat staring, pulse pounding, at the supersized letters. WRI.

The building gave the appearance of being made entirely of glass, city lights reflecting off its windows like dozens of mirrors. But its roofline set it apart from the others, sloping dramatically to the east, as if a giant hand had come along and lopped its top off at a forty-five degree angle.

It had taken a great deal of money to build such a monument to WRI's greed. How many people had paid the tab along the way?

DINNER WITH STELLA'S friends had been a long, drawn-out affair, made all the more grueling by MacStirling's impatience to get back to the lab and complete the YOYO dyes that evening.

When he'd finally made his escape, he'd found the ImmuVac building deserted. Carefully reading and rereading the instructions that came with the device, he'd added the YOYO dye to the DNA solution and, as directed, applied drops from each solution to adjoining grids, one for each lot.

Gels took hours, but since he'd already added the enzymes, which would slice the DNA molecules into small pieces, before leaving ImmuVac that afternoon, MacStirling only had to give the YOYO devices ten minutes to allow the capillary action to pull the dyed DNA molecules into the apparatus's channels.

Curious, but sure of what he would find—identical patterns in the side-by-side grids, indicating identical solutions for Lot One and Lot Two—MacStirling read through the material that had accompanied the device again, then he turned on the laser lights positioned above the grids and strode over to the light switch.

With gels, it took longer for larger pieces of DNA to travel the electric field of the gels than for the smaller pieces. Therefore, when the shortest molecules reached the end of the charged gel and the gel was illuminated under ultraviolet light, a pattern that looked somewhat like a bar code emerged, with shorter DNA pieces (having traveled farther) at the far end, and longer pieces closer to the starting point.

With the YOYO dye, single molecules of dyed DNA were pulled by capillary action into the grooved channels of the device. When the molecules were subsequently exposed to flourescent light, the larger molecules absorbed more and gave off more light. The size of the molecules could therefore be determined from the pattern of brightness.

Though MacStirling knew that the end result of the two processes would differ in appearance, he'd fully expected the pattern created in the two side-by-side grids of the YOYO multiplex device to be identical, just as the two gels he'd run on the solutions had been.

Flipping off the light switch, he'd hurried back to the counter where the equipment sat, his earlier irritation at having to run the tests suddenly replaced by an anticipation like that of a kid unwrapping a new toy. Ever since reading about the new technology, he'd been anxious to see firsthand how it worked.

The darkened room and laser light had heightened the sense of drama.

MacStirling leaned over to view the results of the YOYO tests.

"This can't be right."

Two very distinctive patterns glowed back at him in the dark.

His hands beginning to shake, MacStirling placed them on

either side of the device and folded his long torso closer to the table for a better look.

Upon closer examination, he saw that the two patterns had more in common than he'd first realized. The grid on the left, which represented Lot One, the vaccine used for both Phase I and II, was virtually mirrored in the grid on the right. He hadn't realized that at first because there was more, much more to the right grid. On the right side, DNA not seen in the other grid glowed so brightly that at first it had obscured the similarities of the two.

A contaminant.

The realization took the breath out of MacStirling.

The additional DNA in the righthand grid indicated that Lot Two contained material not found in Lot One. Additional, unwanted material. A contaminant.

But how? How could it possibly have happened?

Trying with little success to fight back the panic, Mac-Stirling's mind raced from one unpleasant thought to another. How would he tell Lyons? Phase III had already been scheduled. What would Pfister think if it now had to be delayed? And Isabel, how would she respond?

Would a new lot have to be manufactured?

Lyons had been calling him a hero, crediting him for the Pfister deal. What if they hadn't actually signed all the papers yet? Could Pfister still pull out of the partnership?

But despite the myriad other questions running through it, his mind kept returning to the first one.

How could this have happened?

He'd run the gel on Lot Two just before his trip to New York. It matched that of Lot One, confirming the purity and conformity of both lots.

Lot Two now contained an impurity. The contamination had to have occurred after he'd run the last gel.

But how?

CHAPTER

THIRTY-EIGHT

I HAVE TO have that address."

Ken MacStirling had waited in his car outside the Rainy Day Travel offices since seven A.M. At just past eight, a red Volvo finally pulled up. An attractive brunette slid out from behind the wheel and approached the office's front door. As she unlocked it, MacStirling had startled her.

"Kim?"

The woman had turned, reflexively pulling her purse into her body.

"No. I'm Janet. Kim comes in later. Around nine."

"Actually, you're the one I need to talk to," MacStirling said. "I'm Dr. MacStirling from ImmuVac."

Instinctively, this announcement caused the woman named Janet to relax. A smile finally broke her heavily made-up face.

"Oh, Dr. MacStirling. I'm sorry. You startled me. I'm always a little nervous about opening the office alone."

"I understand. And I'm sorry to surprise you like that. It's just that there's been a little emergency and I thought you might be able to help."

By now, Janet had unlocked the door. Holding it open, she said, "Please, come in. We can talk in here."

She directed him to her desk, where she deposited her bag on the floor and turned to give him her full attention.

"How can I help?"

"I need the address of another ImmuVac employee. His

name is Sergei Kirov. You booked a flight for him recently to Leningrad." He did not tell her that he'd obtained that information from her coworker. "He's on vacation and there's been an accident in his lab. It's imperative that I reach him. I have to have that address."

Janet's brow scrunched in puzzlement.

"Surely your personnel department can give it to you."

"That's the problem. Kirov moved recently. We all knew it, but apparently no one ever thought to get his new address or telephone number. I'd just booked my own flight to Kalispell yesterday. When I did, Kim verified my home phone and address. So it occurred to me that you'd have that same information on file for Sergei. I'm just hoping it's the updated information."

Janet's expression told MacStirling she clearly did not know what to do.

"I have to have that address," MacStirling reiterated. "One of our lab workers may have been exposed to a dangerous disease. Time is critical. If I have to, I'll go to the police and you'll be forced to provide it to them. But please don't make me do that. As I said, time is critical if our lab technician has indeed been exposed."

The lab worker angle seemed to sway her.

"How awful." She flipped a switch on her computer to boot it up. "It *is* highly unusual, but let me see what I can do for you."

Ten minutes later, Ken MacStirling walked out with an address. It was a rural route, in Gaston.

AFTER THE SCIENTIST from ImmuVac left, it occurred to Janet McIntosh.

Why hadn't they thought of it?

She had Sergei Kirov's telephone number right here in his electronic file. It seemed odd that that doctor from ImmuVac—MacStirling, wasn't that his name?—hadn't

even asked for it. Of course, she could see he was in a state
of panic. That, as much as anything, had convinced her that
the right thing to do was cooperate by giving him Dr. Kirov's
address. It probably also explained why he hadn't even
thought to ask for the phone number.

But since time was so critical, maybe she could help. Do
her good deed for the day.

The phone only rang once before being picked up.

"Dr. Kirov?"

"Yes."

"This is Janet McIntosh from Rainy Day Travel. I just
wanted to let you know that one of your colleagues was in
here a few minutes ago asking for your address. A Dr.
MacStirling, I believe. He said there'd been an accident at
your lab and that he needed to contact you immediately. After he left I couldn't believe neither of us had thought of
calling you. Anyway, he's on his way out there now. I
thought my calling ahead could save time."

"How wise of you," the Russian said. He sounded truly
appreciative. "I'll be on the lookout for Dr. MacStirling."

"THEY JUST DELIVERED the vaccine," Suzanne whispered
to Isabel as she entered the examination room to help placate
an uncooperative four-year-old whose ears Isabel suspected
were infected.

Isabel made brief eye contact with Suzanne and nodded.

"That's great," she said, returning to the exam table with
a rubber glove, which she handed to Suzanne. The child's
already large eyes grew even bigger at the sight of this new
person and the glove, but then, when Suzanne held the glove
to her mouth and began blowing air into it, creating a gro-
tesque version of a balloon, he erupted in giggles. Isabel used
the opportunity to insert the otoscope in his left ear and have
a good look. The inner surface of the outer ear bore multiple
blisters.

In reality, the news that the vials of vaccine had arrived, the realization that Phase III would commence the day after next, failed to make any impression on Isabel whatsoever. She was simply going through the motions. She'd been on autopilot since yesterday when she heard about Leroy. The only thing keeping her going was the knowledge that her patients needed her.

Her first instinct had been to follow Monty. She was still thinking about it, but had been held back by several concerns. First and foremost was the fact that Monty would not want her to follow. Of that, she was certain. The likelihood of actually finding him, if she did, was small. And she worried that her sudden disappearance could end up exposing not only her involvement with Monty, but possibly Gus's as well.

Edna seemed to have read her mind. When she'd driven her home—to a dark, brown planked structure with a single window on each side and one long, thin stovepipe sticking out from the low, barely angled roof—Edna had turned to her before climbing out of the pickup.

"You done a good thing helping Monty," she said. "But you gotta be careful. Monty's always drawn trouble. You're a good girl. And the people need you. Don't be doin' somethin' stupid like goin' after him. Ahright now?"

The evening had passed with no word from Monty. Only a call from Gus, making sure she was okay. He'd heard about Leroy. He didn't even seem surprised to hear Monty had taken off.

"I figured as much," was all he said. Then he, too, had warned her. "Don't you lose your head over this. Want to come spend the night here with me and Grunt?"

"No," Isabel answered. "Maybe he'll try to call."

But the phone had not rung again and the night had crept along at a slug's pace, with Isabel lying sleepless in the bed she and Monty had shared.

She wanted to feel angry with him for taking off on this mission for which the only possible outcome could be tragedy. But the only anger she felt was directed at WRI. The murder of Monty's father was cruel and senseless. She shared Monty's rage. Combined with the guilt he also had to be feeling—knowing Leroy had been sacrificed to exact revenge upon Monty—it was no wonder Monty had, as Edna put it, "gone a little bit crazy."

Isabel had always been a take-charge person. But now, when she most cared, she felt helpless.

"You still need me here?" Suzanne asked after Isabel had examined both the child's ears.

"Go ahead. I can handle it from here. Have you refrigerated the vials yet?"

Suzanne nodded.

"First thing. There's sure a lot of them. Just lookin' at how many made me realize how big a thing this is. Enit?"

"Yes. It is a big thing."

"You don't seem very excited about it anymore."

Isabel had the distinct feeling that Suzanne knew about her and Monty. She'd been trying to act as though everything was fine, but Suzanne knew her too well to believe that. Still, Suzanne did not pry and Isabel appreciated that.

"That's not true. I couldn't be more pleased with how things have gone. Still, we've got a big job ahead of us."

"We'll get it done."

"Yes, we will."

After the boy and his aunt left, Isabel walked down the hall to Suzanne's desk.

"When's my next appointment? I want to run down to Ben Franklin's and pick up something to read."

"You've got almost half an hour," Suzanne said. "After that you're done for the day. Maybe a good book will get your mind off everything."

Isabel decided not to pursue that line of discussion.

"Can I bring you anything?" she said instead.

"No, thanks."

Isabel drove the three blocks to TeePee Village. At a newspaper box in front of the Ben Franklin store, she bought a Kalispell *Daily Interlake*. Suzanne had no new information on Leroy's case. Perhaps the newspaper would.

She climbed back in her truck and scanned every page. The paper contained no mention whatsoever of Leroy's death. Apparently the annual "Art on the Green," featured on the front page, rated higher in importance than the death of an Indian on the Blackfeet reservation. Frustrated, Isabel threw the paper down on the seat next to her and sat staring across Browning's main street.

Two of the dogs she frequently gave handouts at the clinic wandered down from one of the side streets. They stopped every few feet to pick up the scent of earlier dogs and sniff at litter strewn everywhere, then slowly meandered across the empty street.

Isabel sat like that for some time, just looking out. She watched as the wind picked up a Subway wrapper and rolled it across the street. It was the first time she'd noticed that the 'P' was missing on the NAPA Auto Parts sign across the street. An elderly man, bone thin and dressed in a torn down jacket despite the seventy degree weather, leaned heavily on his crutch as he slowly made his way out of the liquor store and down the sidewalk, brown paper bag in hand.

So engulfed was Isabel in her own thoughts that when something rapped tersely on her window, she let out a sharp, startled gasp.

She turned her head to see an elderly Blackfeet woman holding a cane to the glass. Strands of wiry gray hair had escaped her colorful flowered scarf and blew across a face etched with almost a century of hard living.

Isabel realized that she'd seen the woman before. The day of the mining protest. She had called Clyde Birdseye to task that day.

Hurriedly rolling her window down, Isabel managed a flustered smile.

"Can I help you?"

"You're the lady doctor."

"Yes. I am."

"I saw you sitting here."

Isabel did not know what to say in response, but it did not seem to faze her visitor.

"Monty's in a lotta trouble," the old woman said. "He might not be back."

Isabel drew up, tensing. She leaned toward the woman, grasping the upper edge of the rolled down window with both hands.

"What have you heard?"

"Nothin'," the old woman said. "But I know."

"If you haven't heard anything, how do you know?"

The woman simply stared at Isabel, into her eyes, as if she did not hear her. Her eyes were small and sharp, like the eyes of a wizened crow. Isabel felt pierced by them, but she could not look away.

"You're one of us, aren't you?"

Isabel did not answer.

"It's hard for a child to grow up when they belong to two worlds," the woman said.

"But I didn't know when I was growing up. I only . . ."

The woman waved a knobby hand, cutting her off.

"I don't mean you," she said impatiently. "I don't mean you. Even if Monty don't come back, you should stay. The child belongs here."

"What child?" Isabel said.

But the old woman had already turned, pivoting on her cane, and begun hobbling toward the sidewalk.

"Wait a minute," Isabel cried. "What do you mean?"

The woman did not answer.

"What's your name?" Isabel called after her.

The wind was strong and the woman's voice so low that Isabel barely heard her response.

"Sky," she said, over her shoulder. "Sky Thomas."

ISABEL RETURNED TO the clinic and her last appointment of the day.

Afterward, she stopped in the supply room and opened the refrigerator sent to her by Ken MacStirling. She hadn't realized Suzanne was just steps behind her.

"See what I mean?" Suzanne said from over her shoulder. "There must be a thousand doses there."

"I think that's exactly how many Dr. MacStirling said he'd be sending. We'll get a new shipment every couple weeks. Would you mind handing me a three-cc syringe?" Isabel said over her shoulder as she grabbed a tiny glass vial from the refrigerator's top shelf.

"You finally talk Dr. MacStirling into letting you vaccinate yourself?"

"I didn't exactly give him an option this time."

"You shoulda just vaccinated yourself back in Phase I," Suzanne said. "Want me to give it to you?"

Isabel turned to look at Suzanne. According to Suzanne, the former clinic doctor, Dr. Hammer, used to let her give shots all the time. Suzanne had been very unhappy when, during her first weeks at the clinic, Isabel made it clear that practice would have to end.

"Would you mind?" Isabel said.

" 'Course not. I like giving shots."

CHAPTER

———

THIRTY-NINE

AT FIRST, KEN MacStirling passed right by the old red-brick building. Sergei Kirov had lived in an apartment building in Portland. MacStirling was looking for another multiplex or perhaps even a small house. The idea that Sergei could be inhabiting the old schoolhouse, which looked deserted, did not occur to him until he drove another two miles down the road and failed to find another building. Not even a turnoff.

Finally, he turned his Land Cruiser around and headed back down the two-lane road. He slowed at the old schoolhouse. The first time by he hadn't seen the numerals etched in the stone above the front door. He had to squint now to make them out. He looked at the numerals, then back to the piece of paper upon which Janet McIntosh had written Sergei Kirov's new address.

They matched.

MacStirling pulled into the gravel lot. He looked for a car, but found none. However, a narrow drive appeared to circle around the back of the building.

He approached the front door, hesitated, then knocked loudly three times. There was no answer.

He knocked again and waited.

Still, no answer.

If this was indeed where Sergei lived, he must not be home. Emboldened by his anger and panic at discovering the vaccine had been contaminated, MacStirling reached for the door knob and turned. It opened easily.

He pushed the door open and called inside.

"Hello?"

He was greeted by silence.

He stepped inside and found himself in what had obviously once been the lobby of a school building, but a television and chairs and a broken-down couch with several beer cans on the floor in front of it indicated someone now resided there.

MacStirling had left the front door open, perhaps subconsciously, as a safety precaution, and morning sun spilled in across the floor. The feathered inhabitants of the thickly forested area surrounding the building chattered so noisily just outside that MacStirling wished he'd shut the door so that he could better hear what, if anything, was going on inside. But still, as he walked back by the door on his way to the staircase, he refrained from pushing it shut.

Scattered lines of sawdust and the smell of newly milled pine indicated the stairs had recently been rebuilt.

MacStirling climbed them slowly, stopping several times to listen. He no longer felt comfortable calling out. He felt drawn upward, to the higher levels of the building, yet at the same time an inner voice told him to get out.

He continued up the stairs.

At the top, he could see where boards had been nailed across several doors opening off the long hallway. Another door was partially closed. At the very end, he could see what looked to be a kitchen. Slinking along, hugging close to the walls, as if doing so made him less visible, he approached it.

He found the kitchen empty. Dirty dishes sat in a sink. A coffee cup and partially eaten Hostess apple pie, its wrapper turned back like a rolled-up sleeve, sat on the table.

An open door revealed another flight of stairs, leading to the third floor.

MacStirling turned slowly around. Should he enter the stairwell? The sign above indicated it had once been an emergency exit for schoolchildren.

Tentatively, he placed a foot on the first step. The stairwell was not lighted, and a door at its top was closed. He had to feel his way up, running his hands along the wall for support. By the time he'd reached the top, his eyes had adjusted somewhat to the absence of light. He could see the door handle.

He reached for it and turned.

The door creaked open. MacStirling stepped through it, into a narrow corridor. This floor was well lit from large paned-glass windows on each end. Again, MacStirling saw no sign of life; however, a steady humming sound came from the other side of the wall facing him.

MacStirling crept down the hall, toward the first door on his left, the direction from which the sound of machinery seemed to emanate. Fifty-and one-hundred-mile bike rides every weekend normally kept his pulse in the low sixties, but he could feel it now, beating nearly out of control.

He could see the upper third of the door was dominated by a window. Reaching it, he kept his body to one side, then slowly peeked inside.

What he saw stunned him.

Laboratory equipment—an autoclave, a magnetic resonance machine, several microscopes, and a computer—filled one long table. In disbelief, MacStirling stepped closer, craning his neck to see the rest of the room.

"Would you like the grand tour?" a voice said from behind him.

He knew the owner of the voice before he turned.

"Sergei," he said. "What are you doing here?"

He found himself face-to-face with the Russian, who was wearing a blue blazer and tan slacks. A red handkerchief stuck out of the blazer's top pocket. It was the first time MacStirling had ever seen his colleague in anything other than a lab coat.

"Here?" Sergei answered. "As in the United States? Or *here,* as in his laboratory?"

"Both."

The Russian smiled slowly. MacStirling couldn't remember ever seeing Sergei's teeth before. They were straight, but disproportionately small, exposing a great deal of gum. MacStirling reflexively stepped back.

"In answer to your question," Sergei said, "I'm back to continue the work I started in the Soviet Union."

"Your work in the Soviet Union? I thought you were involved in Russia's biowarfare research."

"That's right."

This was crazy.

"Who are you working for now?"

"ImmuVac, of course."

"You're doing biowarfare research for ImmuVac?"

"No, not exactly. I'm actually helping our beloved leader, Dr. Lyons, by developing a vaccine that will be quite valuable when biowarfare does, indeed, break out."

MacStirling did not know what to think. None of this made sense. Why had James Lyons secreted Sergei out here in Gaston, while telling the rest of the ImmuVac employees the Russian had returned home?

"What kind of vaccine?"

Kirov giggled. Almost like a woman. The sound sickened MacStirling.

"Smallpox."

MacStirling stared at Kirov. The Russian was playing with him. But what was the game?

"Now," Kirov said, "to what do I owe the pleasure of this most unexpected visit?"

MacStirling momentarily wondered if he was going mad. The discovery that the HantaVac was contaminated. Sergei's lab in Gaston. It all had taken on a sense of the surreal.

He shook his head.

"I don't know," he said. "I just found out you might be back yesterday. It was an accident, the girl at the travel agency said something about your buying a ticket to Leningrad."

"Yes. I will be returning home. Shortly. But enough about me, how is your study going? The HantaVac trials?"

"Brilliant. Great. At least they were, until late last night when I discovered that the most recent lot had been contaminated."

"Contaminated? How dreadful."

"Dreadful hardly describes it. Phase III is scheduled to

begin tomorrow morning. The entire trial may be jeopardized."

"You can't mean that you've called off Phase III?"

Kirov's voice had risen now. His casual, almost teasing demeanor seemed to turn stiff as he stuck his hand into the pocket of his blazer.

"I haven't called it off yet. In fact, I haven't even told Lyons about the contamination. You know how he'll react. But you know as well as I do that we can't use a contaminated vaccine. Not until we identify the contaminant and establish it's harmless."

"Dr. Lyons doesn't know about this yet?"

"No." MacStirling studied Sergei. "I just told you I hadn't told him yet."

"Who *have* you told?"

"No one. I've told no one. I wanted to have some answers before I did. That's why I came here."

MacStirling didn't like the direction this conversation had taken. He'd come here to be the questioner, not the person being questioned.

It had occurred to him in the middle of the night. He'd returned from the lab in a state of near hysteria. Since Stella had locked him out of the bedroom, he'd literally paced the living room floor for hours, trying to imagine how a contamination could have occurred while he was out of town.

And then, at some point, after he'd worked through countless possibilities, none of which seemed even remotely possible, the words of the travel agent had come to him.

Here we go. Dr. Kirov? A ticket for Leningrad?

According to the travel agent, two days earlier Sergei Kirov had purchased a ticket to Leningrad. MacStirling had finally decided the girl was mistaken, that she was referring to the ticket purchased before Sergei took his long trip, the one that ended in Lyons's announcing Sergei had decided to stay in Russia. But as he paced the floor last night, MacStirling began to contemplate the possibility that Sergei had returned to Portland. That he had, indeed, purchased another ticket out of the country.

His going to Rainy Day Travel had been a shot in the dark. He hadn't really expected any cooperation, and even if anyone at the travel agency did agree to help, he'd expected to learn that the ticket had been purchased before Sergei disappeared.

But the new address given him for Sergei changed all that.

After the seed regarding Sergei had been planted last night, he'd come up with other damning evidence.

The only other person who ever seemed comfortable working in the maximum-containment annex at ImmuVac had been Sergei Kirov.

Sergei had shown clear resentment at having funds channeled into the hantavirus vaccine instead of to his own work.

If, indeed, the contamination was deliberate, Kirov would have been a logical suspect—if it weren't for the fact that he'd returned to Russia.

But now MacStirling knew that Kirov hadn't returned to Russia. He'd instead been set up in a lab that no one knew about, twenty miles outside Portland.

On his drive out to Gaston, MacStirling had tried to make sense of it all. He'd been furious. Furious to know Kirov still resided in the area. More furious still to think he may have been the one to contaminate Lot Two.

He'd planned to let Kirov have it with both barrels, but the eerie setting and discovery of the third floor lab had unsettled him.

And now he'd allowed Kirov to turn the tables on him and become the interrogator.

"Listen here, Sergei," MacStirling said, stepping forward again, into Kirov's face. "I came here to find out if you'd been in the maximum-containment facility."

Kirov's eyebrows rose.

"You think I am the one who contaminated your vaccine?"

"Right about now, I don't know what to think. But I know

that I need answers. Preferably before I go to James Lyons."

This time it was Sergei who stepped back. When he did, he simultaneously withdrew his hand from the pocket of his blazer. It held a small handgun.

"You won't be going to Lyons with anything," he said.

MacStirling's eyes darted from the gun to Sergei Kirov's expressionless face, his worst fears confirmed.

"It was you. You contaminated the vaccine, didn't you?"

Kirov displayed his gums once more.

"Of course it was me. No one else at ImmuVac is smart enough, or courageous enough, to do it."

"But why? Why would you do it?"

"Technically, I did it for money. I was paid to contaminate the vaccine. But the truth is, I've been wanting to destroy your precious trial ever since it started." He laughed then. "At first, I'd hoped to talk Lyons into calling it off. But now, now you see, I find myself in a position where I cannot allow that. Phase III must go forward. It's the only way I'll receive the money I've been promised. And then I will leave this godless country."

"Sergei, listen to me. You don't realize what you're doing. We can't allow a contaminated vaccine to be used. It could be dangerous. This is bigger than a petty rivalry between two scientists. People could be harmed by it."

"You are very correct about that," Sergei said. "There's no doubt. Most will die."

"What?"

"Most will die. I predict approximately ninety percent."

"What is it?" MacStirling shouted, ignoring the gun now as he grabbed Sergei by the collar. "What did you contaminate the vaccine with?"

Turning, he followed Sergei's smiling eyes through the window into the lab.

"No, God, please, tell me. Not smallpox. You didn't use smallpox, did you?"

He heard the click then and turned back to Kirov.

Only two inches separated his forehead from the barrel of the gun.

"You can't get away with this," MacStirling said, sweat running down his face and beading on the point of his chin. "Isabel's expecting me there tomorrow, at the start of Phase III. She won't begin it without me. Don't you see? You can't kill me."

Kirov hesitated just long enough to be sure MacStirling registered the last words he would ever hear.

"Oh, can't I?"

And then he pulled the trigger.

CHAPTER

FORTY

AFTER A SLEEPLESS night in Edna's Impala, Monty had used a gas station rest room to wash up and then, a little after nine, he'd strolled into the WRI building, his hand in the pocket of the hooded sweatshirt he'd taken from Isabel's closet, over the pistol Gus had given her.

The directory in the lobby listed the sixth floor for the executive offices. Never removing his hand from the pocket, he'd stepped onto the elevator with two well-dressed women, both of whom got off before six. When the doors opened on six, he'd stepped into a marble-floored reception area. A heavily made-up Asian woman drew back at the sight of him. When he'd asked for LeCoque, she'd told him WRI's CEO was out of town.

"When's he due back?"

"I'm not sure," she'd answered, though Monty knew that

she was sure. He saw her hand going for the phone, no doubt to call security.

Not wanting to wait around for security, Monty had turned and stepped back onto the elevator, which hadn't yet left the sixth floor. This time he pressed the button for four, which is where the directory said Wilderman's office was located.

The receptionist on four, more accustomed to crewmen visiting the office, was far more relaxed.

"Can I help you?" she'd said with a smile that indicated Monty's good looks were not wasted on her.

"I'm looking for Tony Wilderman," Monty said. "I'm a friend of his."

"Tony's out of town today, with Mr. LeCoque. He'll be in the office again first thing in the morning. Who should I tell him stopped by?"

"Thomas Rose," Monty answered.

"Well, you're welcome to come back tomorrow, Mr. Rose."

"Thanks. I'll do that."

Patience had never been Monty's strong suit and the idea of having to wait another day to confront LeCoque and Wilderman made him half crazy. Another night of sleeping in the car, counting the hours until he would avenge Leroy's death.

If only he had that file . . .

Suddenly a visual image of the Intelligence Gathering Unit sheet on Lyons came to him. It had stated his address, but there was something else. Something about a boat. A yacht that he kept harbored nearby, so close that he could see it from his office window. Monty had thought it silly and useless information when he'd first read it. He'd questioned IGU's use of time. But now it stood to be very valuable, and he had AIM's IGU to thank.

Finding itself all too often the target of government-backed intelligence investigations, years earlier AIM decided that its survival depended upon developing its own spies. The IGU had proven itself indispensable in alerting members to pending anti-AIM activities by the FBI and other governmental agencies.

Reports from IGU had also proven a valuable tool in the organization's many crusades. More and more of the report on Lyons came back to Monty now. LeCoque often slept aboard the vessel and he *liked to brag about being able to keep an eye on it from his high-rise office.*

Bingo.

JON LECOQUE HAD asked Tony Wilderman along for his meeting with Walt Lundgren of Global Finance. He and Wilderman had just returned from a trip to southeastern Oregon, where they'd been informed that Hudson Bay Mining had already secured rights to the Grassy Mountain deposit Wilderman had investigated earlier, on the same trip when he'd discovered the Blackfeet deposit. LeCoque wanted Lundgren to meet Wilderman. He felt that the geologist's assurances that WRI had several promising deposits under exploration could help convince Lundgren to provide the bridge financing WRI needed to survive.

They'd driven straight to the restaurant from the airport.

LeCoque and Lundgren had a history together. They'd both grown up dirt poor in a small town outside of Calgary, where they'd attended the same school. Both ended up heading large corporations in Vancouver and had been deemed "mavericks" by the press for their willingness to take risks. And, perhaps their greatest bond, they both understood the desperation occasioned by the prospect of losing the respect and power they'd fought so hard to obtain.

"Tell you what, Jon," Lundgren had told him over dinner at Rudy's Grill, "I told you I'd consider the loan if in the next six months you could show me where you'd have an active, productive mine by the year 2002. Based on our friendship and your excellent record with Global, I might just be willing to extend that time frame another year. You provide me with a solid lease on a solid deposit in the next eighteen months, and my original offer stands."

"You know I appreciate that, Walt," LeCoque had answered. "As you heard tonight from Tony, we're confident we can do just that. All we need is a little extra time."

One of Lundgren's bushy black eyebrows shot up.

"You got something up your sleeve?"

"Hell no. But Wilderman's the best damn exploratory geologist in the business. And we've still got the right of first refusal on that Blackfeet deposit."

"Too bad about that Blackfeet business. Good deposit, close to home. With that kind of P-and-L, it could've been a bonanza for WRI."

"Who knows? Still could be."

"You never know," Lundgren conceded. Then he broke into a grin. "Hey, remember that time we snuck that truckload of beer over the border and sold it on the reservation?" He turned his toothy grin on Wilderman. "We made about as much money in one trip as Ike Newman paid us the entire summer working at his Dairy Queen."

"I remember." LeCoque forced a laugh. He hated Lundgren's trips down memory lane. He'd spent a lifetime trying to forget where he came from. Lundgren, however, suffered from no such compunction and loved to dredge up their youths, which is why LeCoque avoided including other business associates in their meetings whenever possible.

"Listen, Walt," he'd finally said. "We'd better call it a night. I'm leaving for Ontario in the morning."

In the car, he invited Wilderman back to *Chesire* for an after-dinner drink.

"I've got Rod Sokaski meeting me there," he explained. "I thought the three of us might have a little chat. After finding out Hudson Bay's tied up rights to Grassy Mountain, I think it's even more important that we see if there's anything else we can do to salvage that Blackfeet deposit."

Wilderman had been glum all day, ever since learning

Hudson Bay had beat them to the Oregon deposit, but he brightened a bit at the suggestion.

"Can't hurt anything," he'd mused.

ARRIVING AT THE yacht club, LeCoque parked in his reserved stall, then the two men picked their way carefully down the rain-slickened walkway to the gated pier. A wrought iron gate prevented unwelcome visitors from proceeding further. LeCoque punched in the three-digit code and the gate swung open.

As a charter member of the yacht club, LeCoque had been given his choice of moorage. He'd chosen the end of the pier for its unobstructed view of the mountains and city. Approaching *Chesire,* LeCoque noticed that her cabin was cloaked in darkness. An automatic timer had been set to turn on a cabin light each evening at dusk. The bulb, he observed out loud to Wilderman, must have burned out.

LeCoque fumbled momentarily with the key to the cabin door, then stepped inside. Clutching the railing tightly, he descended the four stairs to the cabin, with Wilderman following on his heels.

"Blasted dark in here with that light burned out outside."

He placed his palm flat against the cabin wall and inched toward the light switch, irritated at the discomfort and sense of vulnerability caused by something so minor as a burned-out light bulb.

His hand finally made contact with the light switch, and as he flipped it, an inexplicable sense of foreboding raced through him. Simultaneous with the light flooding the room, LeCoque sensed the presence of someone besides Wilderman.

As he turned, he heard a distinctive click.

Above the barrel of a .38-caliber handgun, the wild eyes of a disheveled, dark-skinned man—unmistakably Indian, whether American or Canadian, it took LeCoque just seconds to learn—met his.

Expressionless, except for the glint in his black eyes, his visitor looked at home in LeCoque's favorite captain's chair, his feet planted squarely, legs splayed. He clutched his right arm close to the chest of his soggy flannel shirt.

"Monty Four Bear," Wilderman sputtered.

Four Bear simply stared at them. The sense of danger he exuded—his silence and steely demeanor—utterly terrified LeCoque. From the absence of sound or movement next to him, he knew that Wilderman was experiencing the same fear.

"What is it you want?" Wilderman asked. "You won already. Didn't you? Your tribal council kicked us out. What more could you want?"

Rising from the chair, the gun's aim never wavering, Four Bear took one step toward LeCoque and Wilderman.

"Who did it?" he said, his eyes trained now on Wilderman.

"Did what?" Wilderman cried.

"Who killed my father?" With each word, LeCoque's sense of dread grew. He was grateful, however, that Four Bear seemed more focused on Wilderman. "Who did you pay to pull the trigger?"

"I don't know what you're talking about."

Four Bear crossed the distance separating them in an instant. Backhanding Wilderman across the face with the gun, he exploded.

"Don't fuck with me!" he screamed. "Just tell me. I want a name. Who did it? Who killed my father?"

The blow threw Wilderman to the floor of the cabin. With Wilderman down, groaning in pain as he held his shattered jaw, Four Bear turned on LeCoque, the gun still raised threateningly.

"Please," LeCoque begged, "There's no need for that. I'll tell you. We had Sokaski beat him up . . ."

"Jon, *shut up*," Wilderman screamed from the floor.

"He's going to kill me," LeCoque snapped back. "Kill both of us." He turned pleading eyes on Monty. "Sokaski did it. He beat him up. It was his," he nodded his head toward Wilderman, on the floor, "*his* idea."

Another low groan, this one of dread, could be heard from the floor.

"Who killed him?"

LeCoque shook his head.

"We didn't have him killed. We just wanted to scare you, make you back down. I swear, we didn't kill him."

Just then, LeCoque's peripheral vision picked up movement behind Four Bear. The cabin door had opened and muddy brown construction boots silently began their descent of the stairs.

Thank God, Sokaski had arrived.

MONTY FELT HIS presence before he saw it.

Gun first, he spun around and recognized the man descending the stairs as the big-mouthed miner who'd been involved in the fight at the protest. Now he looked considerably milder, picking his way down carefully, both arms held high in the air. Behind the big miner, an even bigger man also descended slowly.

Bud Wolfkill. He held a gun to the miner's back.

"What are you doing here?" Monty asked.

Wolfkill's eyes quickly assessed the situation.

"Saving your ass, what else?" he answered. "Drop that, Monty. Do you know what a jurisdictional nightmare it would be if someone got hurt here?"

"Sorry, Bud, but you shouldn't have followed me. If you think I'm gonna let them go, you wasted your time. I'll die before I let that happen."

"You don't know who killed Leroy, Monty. But we'll find out. The legal way. Now drop that gun."

Ignoring him, Monty raised it instead, level with Sokaski's face.

"Drop the fuckin' gun, man," Sokaski said, sweat beginning to bead along his hairline and the stubble on his upper lip.

"You did it," Monty cursed. "You killed Leroy."

"I don't know what you're talking about."

"Play games with me and I'll blow that ugly face off."

Bud did not move from his position behind Sokaski, where his eyes roamed from one WRI man to another.

"They admitted you were the one who beat Leroy up," Monty said, closing the gap between him and Sokaski. "You killed him too."

Sokaski eyes went from LeCoque to Wilderman.

"You sons of bitches. You told him."

A new level of panic seized his features.

"Okay. I admit it. I beat him up. They paid me to." He hesitated. "But I'm not the one who killed your old man."

"You expect me to believe that?"

Deftly, with amazing quickness, Monty backhanded Sokaski across the face.

Reflexively, Sokaski's hands dropped to protect himself.

"Put 'em back up," Wolfkill ordered.

Slowly, the arms rose again.

"Okay. Okay," Sokaski said. "I told you. I just roughed the old guy up. I didn't kill him. But I can tell you who did."

Every eye in the room turned on Sokaski.

"It was this guy with this Southern accent," he declared, his eyes clearing of some of their panic. "That's who killed him. He called me. He wanted to hire me to kill some Russian dude outside Portland. *He's* the one who killed the old man. He told me he slit his throat while he was sleeping."

Monty had assumed Leroy was shot. The idea of someone using a knife . . .

Enraged, he lunged forward with a deep growl, tackling Sokaski.

"No one makes a move," he heard Wolfkill say from where he stood over Monty and Sokaski.

Seconds later, a sharp boot landed in Monty's back.

"Monty," Wolfkill bellowed, "in about two minutes the Canadian police are gonna be showing up. Do you want to hear what this asshole has to say about Leroy's killer, or do you want to leave the whole thing to the Canadians?"

Monty released his lopsided hold on Sokaski. He grabbed him by the collar and pulled him to a sitting position on the floor.

"Who is he?" he demanded. "The guy who called you."

Sokaski shook his big head.

"I dunno. He wouldn't give me his name. Only a phone number. It was from Seattle."

"Why did he want to kill the Russian?" Wolfkill broke in.

"Forget that," Monty snapped. "We're here about Leroy."

But Sokaski ignored Monty and looked up at Wolfkill.

"He said he wouldn't need the Russian after tomorrow. He wanted me to kill him to make certain he wouldn't talk."

"Talk about what?"

"Goddamn it, Bud," Monty barked, "let someone else deal with this fucking Russian. I want to know who this Southern guy is."

"I told you," Sokaski said, "I don't know. He never gave me his name. But he said he hated all you Blackfeet. Something about his wife being a traitor."

"I might be able to help," Wilderman offered from the floor.

"I think I know who he's talking about," he continued. "He's a doctor. I ran into him a couple times in East Glacier. A strange bird, really interested in the mine on the reservation. Beating Four Bear's father up was his idea. He's the one who suggested that it would scare you into backing down."

"You know where we can find this guy?" Wolfkill asked. "What his name is?"

Wilderman reached for his back pocket, then seeing Bud take aim on him, explained, "I've got his card in my wallet."

When Wilderman finally produced the business card, Wolfkill scanned it first, then passed it to Monty. But by then, Monty already knew what he'd see.

ALISTAIR BOTT, M.D. Isabel's ex-husband.

Monty's gut twisted at the sight. He snatched the card from Wilderman and turned a wary eye on Sokaski.

"Why would Bott want to kill Leroy?"

"I told you. He hates you Blackfeet. He said he was gonna take care of all of you once and for all. That he hired the Russian dude to do it for him. He wanted me to kill the Russian after tomorrow. Said he wouldn't need him after that. Told me I'd find fifty-thousand dollars on him. That was supposed to be my payment. But I told him I had to have money up front and he never sent it."

"Tomorrow's the big vaccination clinic on the rez," Bud Wolfkill said softly.

Monty's head jerked up to catch Wolfkill's eye.

"Could there be a connection?"

Wolfkill's expression was somber.

"We better find out." He turned back to Sokaski.

"What more can you tell us about this Russian?"

"Just that he lives in an old schoolhouse. In a town called Gaston."

WOLFKILL HAD CALLED the Royal Canadian Mounted Police before surprising Rod Sokaski outside the *Chesire*. When they showed up minutes later, they took Sokaski, Wilderman, and LeCoque into custody.

Monty and Bud sped to the airport, where Bud had landed only five hours earlier—after following his hunch that Monty could be found near LeCoque.

At the airport, they learned they would have to fly from Vancouver to Seattle, before changing planes for Kalispell.

While they waited, Wolfkill placed three calls.

The first was to the station in Browning, telling them to be on the lookout for Alistair Bott. The second, with identical instructions, was to the Seattle police.

The final call was to the local police in Gaston, Oregon.

"All I know," Bud stated into the phone, "is that this Russian lives in some old schoolhouse in your town. We need this man detained. It's urgent."

The officer on the other end knew right away what he was talking about.

"Must be the old elementary out on Ridge Road. Someone's living there now. I'll send an officer right out."

Before they boarded, Bud pulled out a pair of handcuffs and fastened first Monty's good arm, then the bad.

"Sorry about this, pal," he said. "But in the frame of mind you're in, you wouldn't think twice about makin' a fool outta me."

Monty glared at him. Neither man said a word to the other on either flight.

When Bud went to the pay phone at the Kalispell airport, his order that Monty stay at his side was unnecessary. Monty stood close enough to smell the gum on Wolfkill's breath, his eyes focused intensely on Bud, while Bud listened to a wild tale told by the chief of police in Gaston, who'd been called in to handle the city's first homicide in two decades.

"You mean to tell me it's too late? The Russian's already dead?" Wolfkill asked.

"The guy who died was British or Scottish," the Gaston chief of police reported, "not Russian. He was a scientist at a company nearby, in Portland. An outfit called ImmuVac."

Bud visibly stiffened at the familiar name. ImmuVac was the company sponsoring the HantaVac study on the reservation.

"What about the Russian? Where's he?"

"We don't know. Apparently he shot the guy we found out there at the old schoolhouse. The poor fella was near death, medevacs couldn't save him. But he could talk a little. I'm not sure he was all there though, if you know what I mean. Said some pretty bizarre things."

"Like what?"

"My officer said he was pretty hard to understand, but before he died, he kept mumbling something about 'phase three.' "

"*What?*" Wolfkill pressed. "What was it he said?"

"Something about a contamination. That the Russian who shot him had contaminated phase three—whatever *that* is."

Wolfkill's face had drained of color.

"Did he say what, what he'd contaminated it with?"

"My man swore he said it was smallpox."

BUD WOLFKILL LOOKED at the clock above the gate where they'd just disembarked. Nine A.M. One hour until the vaccinations were to start.

He went to the telephone and called the Browning clinic. A recording. They'd already left for East Glacier.

He couldn't waste any more time. He could make it to East Glacier in an hour. And he would radio ahead for reinforcements from the car.

He started to jog through Kalispell's sleepy airport. Monty kept pace with him, silent. When they reached the squad car, in the parking lot where Bud had left it the day before, Wolfkill climbed in and slid the key into the ignition.

Monty did not follow suit.

Wolfkill reached across the seat and opened the door.

"Get in, dammit," he said. "We can't afford to waste time."

Monty bent to look Wolfkill in the eye.

"I'm going after him, Bud. After Bott."

"Goddammit, Monty. You're under arrest. Get your ass in here, now."

"It only takes one of us to stop the clinical trial. You go to East Glacier. I have to do this, Bud. Can't you see? I have to be the one who brings the bastard in. If I go back with you now, I'll be taken into custody and he could go free."

Bud had never known Monty Four Bear to plead, but he was pleading now.

"He killed Leroy, Bud. And look what he's done to Isabel, and to our people. I give you my word. I'll be back. But first let me do what I have to do."

Wolfkill's fist came down hard on the steering wheel.

"Jesus Christ, Four Bear," he growled. He stared out at the cloudless sky for several seconds, then punched the steering wheel once again.

Finally he turned troubled eyes to Monty. "Nobody knew how Leroy died. We kept that quiet. Nobody knew. Except the murderer. The way I see it, that could still be Sokaski," he said. "Or it could be Bott."

He pulled the keys out of the ignition.

"Put your hands out."

Monty struggled to extend both hands, his injured shoulder not allowing full extension of the right arm.

Wolfkill stretched across the vehicle's front seat and inserted the key. The metal links dropped noisily to the seat.

"Now get out of here," he ordered.

CHAPTER

FORTY-ONE

WHILE SHE NO longer felt much of anything besides a gnawing grief and worry related to Monty's disappearance, Isabel could not help but feel grateful to see the sun shining this day.

The former shoe repair shop on the edge of the town of East Glacier, which had been offered as a site for the kickoff of Phase III, had a depressing air about it. Isabel had learned from Phases I and II that participants were jumpy enough about taking part in the clinical trial. They didn't need their sense of dread heightened by a damp, musky setting.

The sky had turned a soft, silky blue just before sunset the previous night, and Isabel had awakened this morning to near-blinding sunlight streaming through her windows. She'd closed her eyes, pressing the back of her hands to them, as if she could keep the tears away with sheer physical force.

Now, just after nine A.M., the temperature had climbed into the mid-seventies. A soft breeze promised to keep the day comfortable. She'd asked Suzanne to help her set up a table for the vaccinations outside, on the wooden porch.

A young Blackfeet mother with her two children in tow had arrived while they were setting up the table. She did not introduce herself to either Isabel or Suzanne, but instead went to sit on the edge of the long wood-planked boardwalk that ran the length of what was officially downtown East Glacier, watching as her children played in the weedy area between the abandoned shoe repair shop and a gas station that had closed years earlier.

"Good morning," Isabel said, approaching her.

"Mornin'," the woman returned softly.

"Are you here for the clinical trial?"

The young woman nodded.

"I'm Dr. McLain."

"I'm Lucy Freeman."

"Nice to meet you, Lucy. Since you're the first here, you'll be lucky enough to be the first done. I'll have Suzanne come over and talk to you about what to expect today." She looked at her watch. Nine-fifteen. She'd told MacStirling the trial was to begin at ten, but she could tell by how nervous Lucy appeared that that long a wait would be difficult for her and her children.

"The vaccinations aren't supposed to begin until ten."

"Ten? I heard nine." Isabel could see Lucy's anxiety level rising with the news that she and her children would have to wait.

"We're expecting Dr. MacStirling from ImmuVac to arrive any minute. Maybe we can get started a little early."

"I hope so," Lucy said softly.

More study participants, Isabel knew, would come straggling in over the next couple of hours, regardless of the appointment time that had been given them. Isabel had learned early on not to be a clock-watcher when it came to her Blackfeet patients. If they had an appointment, she could usually count on them eventually showing up.

Knowing Ken MacStirling, he would arrive early and they could send Lucy and her kids on their way. Just as that thought entered her mind, Isabel caught sight of a gold vehicle approaching from the west, on Highway 2. She stood watching, then as it slowed upon entering the town of East Glacier, she recognized Ken MacStirling's Land Cruiser and began waving.

But MacStirling cruised right on by, as if he didn't see her.

Isabel watched as the Land Cruiser slowed to a crawl, then pulled over at the sign she and Suzanne had made just that morning.

EAST GLACIER CLINICAL TRIAL SITE.

By the time she reached MacStirling's vehicle, the door on the driver's side had opened. Isabel stepped down off the sidewalk to greet him.

But the man who emerged was not Ken MacStirling.

Isabel took a step backward and looked at the license plate on the front of the Land Cruiser.

Oregon. She hadn't been mistaken. It was Ken MacStirling's vehicle.

By now, its driver had honed in on her and approached, right hand extended.

"Dr. McLain?" He spoke in a thick accent and looked woefully out of place in his blue blazer, with a silly red hankie poking out of the upper pocket.

Confused, Isabel nonetheless extended her hand and grasped his.

"Yes. Where's Dr. MacStirling?"

"I'm Dr. Kirov, an associate of Dr. MacStirling's. I'm afraid he's fallen ill. He asked me to take his place today."

"I hope it's nothing serious."

"Not at all. Just a touch of the flu. But it was important to him, to all of us, that a representative from ImmuVac be here on this important day. In fact, as you can see, Dr. MacStirling even loaned me his car."

"I'm surprised Dr. MacStirling didn't call me," Isabel said. After all, if Dr. Kirov had enough time to drive all the way to East Glacier from Portland, MacStirling had plenty of time to call Isabel and tell her he'd sent a substitute.

The comment seemed to throw Kirov off. He hesitated before responding.

"He can barely speak." Maybe she'd imagined it. "Laryngitis. I'm afraid it's my fault no one called you. Dr. MacStirling asked me to and I simply forgot."

Something about Dr. Kirov bothered Isabel. His formal attire and manner of speech were entirely out of place there, on the reservation. But it was more than that.

ImmuVac had every right to have a representative present at the start of Phase III; still, Isabel resented Kirov's presence, when she had so much to do. She'd understood MacStirling's desire to be there; but, technically, he had no role in the actual administration of the vaccine. Sending Dr. Kirov in his place was nonsense. She had enough on her mind without having to play host to some figurehead sent there as a symbolic gesture.

"I'm most eager to get started," Kirov said then, further annoying her.

"Well, we're not scheduled to begin for another forty-five minutes, but as you can see, people have already begun arriving." Two more cars had pulled up, alongside the Land Cruiser. "I was thinking we may actually want to begin a little early. Lucy Freeman, the young woman over there with the two cute kids, thought we started at nine. I'm afraid she may change her mind if we keep her waiting much longer."

"Then by all means, we should accommodate her."

Isabel looked around. There was no real harm in starting a little early. She should just be pleased to see the turnout they already had. It would be a shame to lose anyone who got nervous during their wait.

"Okay," she said. "Let's. Listen, you might as well take off your jacket. It's warming up and it's going to be a long day. I'll just have Suzanne help me set up, then after we introduce you, we can get started."

"There's no need to introduce me," Dr. Kirov said briskly. He made no move to take off his blazer, but stood stiffly, appearing overly anxious, even irritated, at any possible delay, however insignificant.

The arriving participants had begun shooting curious glances Kirov's way.

This is just what we need, thought Isabel. Many of her patients had grown used to seeing MacStirling around. And to give him credit, Ken did have a low-key manner about him. This Dr. Kirov, however, was another matter entirely. Isabel could see his presence made many of those gathering around the table uneasy.

She stepped closer to him and lowered her voice.

"Listen, Dr. Kirov, these people are somewhat uncomfortable with outsiders. Especially when it's related to this trial. I think it would be a good idea for you to either stand back some distance, where you'd be less visible, or take off your jacket, roll up your sleeves, and get busy. Would you like to assist me by drawing the vaccine while Suzanne does the paperwork?"

"I prefer to keep my jacket on. But of course I can help you with the vaccine."

Isabel decided to dispense with any formalities and get started, before Kirov's presence did too much harm. Besides, why bother introducing this pompous jerk?

She picked up the clipboard that had been sitting on the table. She and Suzanne had worked out a procedure for the large-scale Phase III clinics. Suzanne would have participants sign in as they arrived, then, once she verified that the signed application and consent forms were on file—they'd brought two portable filing boxes full of documents with them—she placed a red check mark after each name.

Isabel looked at the top of the list.

Lucy Freeman, then the names of her two children, Marcus and Nancy. A red check mark followed all three names.

"Mrs. Freeman?" Isabel called out.

Lucy Freeman approached slowly from her spot on the end of the sidewalk. On either side, a young, reluctant child held tight to her hand.

"Now," Isabel said with a reassuring smile, "who would like to be the first one vaccinated?"

Lucy Freeman bent at the waist to consult with her children. Isabel could just hear her.

"Would you guys like me to go first, or do you want to get your shots over with first?"

"You go first, Mama," the little girl said, still clutching Lucy's hand.

"No, I'll go first."

The boy stepped forward, toward Isabel.

Isabel looked to Lucy Freeman for a definitive answer.

"Let Marcus," Lucy said.

"Okay, Marcus," Isabel said, "let's go right over to the table. See that chair? All you have to do is take a seat there and roll up your left sleeve."

The crowd parted as all eyes followed Marcus, who

marched bravely to the chair. Isabel nodded at Dr. Kirov. He reached into a box labeled MONOJECT SYRINGES, then into a small cooler sitting next to it.

As Isabel helped Marcus roll up his sleeve, Kirov inserted the hypodermic needle he'd withdrawn from the box through the rubber seal of a vial he'd taken from the cooler. The vial contained two and a half cc's of clear liquid—the HantaVac vaccine. Pulling back on the syringe's stopper, Kirov drew the fluid into the syringe.

Then he handed it to Isabel. Isabel dabbed Marcus's upper arm with alcohol. Then, as Marcus winced, she inserted the needle and emptied the syringe's contents.

LUCY FREEMAN WAS next. But when it was her little girl's turn, the child began screaming and crying, her howls filling East Glacier's main street.

"Ms. Freeman," Isabel said, "maybe you should take Nancy on a little walk. See if she calms down a bit, and then you can come back."

Isabel could tell the child's howls were beginning to unnerve some of the dozen or more people who had arrived in the past few minutes.

"No," Kirov said, "we must vaccinate her now."

"Dr. Kirov," Isabel said, making a great effort to conceal her anger. "May I speak to you in private?"

When they'd stepped inside the former shoe repair shop, she let him have it.

"Do not contradict me in front of my patients. You are here as an observer. Nothing more."

Isabel was startled to see Kirov smile.

"Let me ask you, Dr. McLain. Have you received the vaccine yet?"

"Yes. Just yesterday."

"You did not participate in Phase I or Phase II?"

"No. Ken MacStirling asked me not to. But I insisted on being vaccinated now."

"A very wise decision," Kirov said. "I will behave myself, Dr. McLain. Please, let's proceed."

Back out on the sidewalk, things had calmed down. Isabel looked at her watch. Almost ten A.M.

"Okay," she said to Suzanne. "Who's next?"

"My aunt Mary," Suzanne answered, nodding toward the frail woman standing next to her.

"Hello, Mary," she said. "Why don't you make yourself comfortable over here, in this chair?"

The syringe containing the dose of HantaVac drawn for Nancy Freeman still lay on the table. Isabel reached for it as she swabbed Mary's bony upper arm.

As she raised the syringe, a sudden squeal of brakes, followed by the sound of gravel flying drew everyone's attention toward the road.

A Tribal Police car shuddered to a stop and the door flew open.

Why would Bud Wolfkill be here?

"Don't do it," Bud yelled to her. "Don't give her the shot."

Isabel hadn't realized that she still held the needle, poised above Mary's shoulder.

Bud Wolfkill had started forward, toward her.

"Don't come any closer," a voice from behind Isabel ordered.

She turned. Dr. Kirov no longer stood behind the table, where she'd last seen him. Instead, he had moved to Suzanne's side. A wash of adrenaline seized Isabel when she saw the gun he held to Suzanne's temple.

"Immunize her," Kirov said calmly. "Now."

"Don't do it, Isabel." It was Wolfkill again. "He contaminated the vaccine with smallpox."

Most of the crowd had scrambled upon seeing the guns, but the word "smallpox" brought gasps from several directions. Out of the corner of her eye, Isabel saw two men restraining Lucy Freeman. She could hear the young woman's sobs, mixed with the cries of her children.

Kirov's eyes jerked back and forth between Isabel and Wolfkill, who had frozen in his tracks. Wolfkill had pulled his gun and now held it in both hands, arms outstretched and directed at Kirov.

"Don't you move," Sergei Kirov ordered Mary Talking Horse.

Isabel placed a reassuring hand on Mary's shoulder and squeezed. She could push the woman to safety, then try to position herself in the line of fire between Kirov and her. But with Kirov holding the gun to Suzanne's head, any movement could have deadly repercussions.

"Immunize her," Kirov repeated. "Now."

"Don't do it," Suzanne said weakly.

"Dr. Kirov," Isabel said. "*Please,* lower your gun." She couldn't help herself. "It isn't true, is it?"

The sound that issued from Kirov's throat—laughter—could not possibly be human.

"Oh, but it is true," he said.

"But Dr. MacStirling . . ."

"Dr. MacStirling had nothing to do with it. In a way, it's a shame that he could not be here . . ."

It all suddenly made sense for Isabel. Nothing could keep Ken MacStirling away on this day.

"Oh my God. What did you do to him?"

Kirov's eyes were devoid of emotion.

"Vaccinate the woman. Or this one dies."

Suzanne closed her eyes as he touched the gun's barrel to her temple.

"Why?" Isabel was stalling for time. "Can you tell me that? Why does it matter if she's vaccinated?"

"Before I die, I want to see my life's work realized. I want the world to remember Sergei Kirov."

"But *I've* already received the vaccine," Isabel said. "I told you. So has Lucy Freeman, and Marcus. So you see, you *will* be remembered."

When Kirov did not respond, desperate, she kept trying.

"Why do you think you have to die, Dr. Kirov?"

"I would die before I would live with the scum your society puts in its prisons."

"Listen to me," Isabel said. "You can run. Take me as a hostage. Let Suzanne and Mary go. I'll go with you. To Canada. The border's less than fifty miles from here."

"Don't do it, Dr. McLain," Bud Wolfkill ordered.

"Let's go, Dr. Kirov. Take me with you."

"Dr. McLain," Bud Wolfkill called out, "leave this to the police."

"Mary doesn't need to receive the vaccine," Isabel said, locking eyes with Kirov. "Marcus and Lucy already have. And *I* have."

"How do I know you're telling me the truth?"

"Why do you think I'm willing to go with you now? It's because I have nothing to lose, do I? Not if that vaccine is contaminated with smallpox."

This reasoning seemed to make an impression on Kirov.

"Come here," he said.

Dropping the syringe, Isabel gave Mary a shove.

Quickly, as Mary scrambled to safety, Isabel moved toward Kirov. When she was within reach, he lifted the gun from Suzanne and redirected it to Isabel.

"Let's go," he said, reaching out and grabbing her roughly by the elbow.

"You're not taking her anywhere," Wolfkill protested, but Kirov seemed to know that he would not risk trying to stop them.

Sergei began maneuvering Isabel toward the Land Cruiser, the gun poking sharply against her spine.

"Drop your gun," he barked at Wolfkill.

Wolfkill did not move.

"Do as he says, Bud," Isabel pleaded.

"I can't do that. He's already killed Dr. MacStirling. If we let him go, he'll kill you too. And who knows how many others?"

Ever the man of reason, Kirov paused.

"I will make you a deal," he said. "You will allow us to leave now. And you will not alert the border patrol. If we make it safely inside Canada, I will release Dr. McLain and tell her where to find my smallpox vaccine. It's the only chance she has to survive the contaminated vaccine she received. But everything must go as I say. If not, one way or another, she will die."

"Let us go, Bud," Isabel coaxed. "That vaccine's our only chance."

As Bud lowered his weapon, Kirov smirked at Wolfkill and pushed Isabel forward. She stumbled, and in that instant, a shot rang out.

Without another sound, Sergei Kirov fell to the ground.

ALL HEADS TURNED in the direction of the gunfire.

Across the street, rifle poised across the bed of his green pickup, Gus Dearing straightened his old arthritic form.

Wolfkill dropped to the dirt, next to Sergei's lifeless form, and began shaking him.

"Don't die on me, you son of a bitch."

A pool of blood had already formed under Kirov's head. Wolfkill rolled him over and saw that the left side of his face no longer existed.

Isabel searched in vain for a pulse.

"He's dead," she said.

Dead. And their chances gone with him.

"Are you okay?"

The voice, clearly shaken, came from above where Wolfkill and Isabel knelt. Simultaneously, they looked up.

"Gus."

In his misguided attempt to save Isabel, Gus had robbed her of the chance to live.

CHAPTER

FORTY-TWO

MONTY SPENT A cold, damp night in the Toyota he'd rented at Kalispell Airport before moving into the house that Isabel had once occupied. He was waiting for Alistair Bott to return to his home in the Magnolia neighborhood Isabel had described so well. Ridiculously large houses, landscaped yards. Just the right cars parked out front. Sidewalks, as if pedestrians were welcome, yet he had to wonder how many friendly *hellos* a long-haired Indian might expect.

That first night, he had parked the Toyota at a remote corner of a lot that serviced the local marina and an assortment of restaurants, the smells from which tormented his empty stomach. The next day he broke into Bott's house and helped himself to the contents of the refrigerator. The food was fresh, indicating Bott had been there recently.

At night, under cover of darkness, he'd left his car and hiked up the steep hillside, to the top of the bluff overlooking Elliott Bay. After driving by it half a dozen times, he'd been able to recognize Bott's house—the house that Isabel had once lived in—from the back. It was just three-fourths of a mile and a dozen or so houses along the bluff. Keeping low, he skirted each yard and used the beef jerky he'd bought at a nearby 7-Eleven to buy passage from a couple of menacing dogs.

When Monty broke into the house, it immediately became clear that Alistair had skipped town suddenly. Clothes strewn everywhere in the bedroom, food left on the kitchen table, and the computer still on in an upstairs office. Monty jiggled the mouse to get rid of the screen saver—a picture of Isabel in hiking shorts, boots, a backpack, and a smile that stung Monty. A message box in the middle of the screen, overlaid across an adult Web site entitled "Candy Girl," indicated the Internet connection had been terminated due to inactivity, but Bott had clearly been enjoying the buxom blond's photo gallery until something pulled him away.

RECONNECT? a second box flashed.

Monty had hoped Bott would return—that in his haste he might have forgotten something important, important enough to risk coming back. But now, after two days, that seemed unlikely, and the waiting game was threatening to drive Monty mad. The downtime agreed with him physically—his shoulder was healing and he was regaining the strength he'd lost—but mentally, he was close to going over the edge.

He had absolutely no sense of where Bott had fled.

Returning to the reservation without him was not an option.

One person might be able to provide some answers, a lead. At least once each day, Monty would find himself staring at the telephone. Isabel might be able to help. But as hungry as he was for her voice, as desperate as he was to find Bott, he could not draw her into this. His plan for revenge. And who knows, by now her phone could be tapped. Even Bud Wolfkill had his limits. A call like that could bring Monty down.

He'd gone through every drawer in the house, hoping to find something that might indicate where Alistair had fled. Even a letter, perhaps from family or a friend, would have given him something, some kind of lead. But if Alistair Bott had friends or family with whom he maintained close ties, their existence was not in evidence in his home.

The night before, long after the lights in neighboring

houses had gone out, Monty had stolen outside, moving soundlessly along the cement wall that separated Bott from his neighbor to the west. There was a street lamp that made some exposure absolutely unavoidable, but Monty darted in and out of the lamp's arc like a light breeze. Within seconds, he'd removed the contents of the mailbox and returned to the shadows.

Back inside, a quick search through the mail provided some information, but ultimately proved disappointing. It appeared to have been sitting in the box for three or four days, which meant Alistair had skipped town the day before Monty showed up—the same day that Ken MacStirling's body had been discovered.

Monty pocketed a replacement MasterCard in Bott's name. He was running low on money.

Aside from bills and a copy of a final decree of divorce between Bott and Isabel, Monty found nothing. He soon came to realize that it was an impossible task, finding a man he knew so little about, who appeared to have so few ties to the rest of the world. He had to have help.

His search always returned to the third floor office, where, despite Alistair's absence, faxes came in daily. There was a stack of them. Monty had never seen anything like it. All solicitations from drug companies, trying to get Bott to either head up this study or that, or refer patients to an ongoing study.

Three thousand dollars per patient!
Enroll fourteen patients by September 1st and earn an additional $2,000.
Authorship of drug study (we hire the medical writer!)
Too busy to conduct a study? How about a $500 finder's fee?

Monty passed time on the computer. Accessing Bott's e-mail account could prove invaluable in providing some kind of clues. He spent hours making up passwords. But the task proved impossible. Time after time, after trying everything from the name of the street he lived on to Bott's middle name—Arnold, according to the divorce decree—he failed. It was while he was playing around with passwords that the hum of the fax machine kicked in, signaling a new arrival. It had become a diversion for him—almost a form of entertainment—to read the fucking things, though with each new scheme, Monty's contempt mounted.

Out of the corner of his eye, Monty watched another drug company logo make its appearance on the other side of the machine as he finished reading the online edition of the *Daily Interlake*'s account of the investigation into the death of a WRI guard in an explosion at the drill site on the Blackfeet reservation. Monty's name was not mentioned, but the article reported that "two men, one Blackfeet, one Cheyenne, with known ties to the AIM, are being sought. They are considered armed and dangerous."

Disgusted, Monty clicked off the article. He was surprised to see the fax still coming. All the previous solicitations were short and to the point—*Want money? We can help*—but this one apparently consisted of two pages.

As the second page inched its way onto a tray so full its contents had become level with the incoming transmission, it had begun pushing the preceding page forward, out of its way. With a soft swoosh, the first page disappeared.

Monty rose from the chair and went to explore. The fax had fallen into the small space between the end of the desk, where the fax machine was situated, and the filing cabinet.

He dropped to his knees. He could see the white page, within reach. He tried poking a finger into the space but there wasn't enough room. He reached for a pencil on top of the desk and used it to poke at the page, teasing it his way, until a corner protruded from between the two pieces of furniture. Grasping it between thumb and forefinger, Monty also grabbed the sheet that had just arrived and took both back to his desk.

He noticed immediately that the two sheets did not belong together.

The fax that had just come in was from a company named GenSearch. The last sentence at the bottom of the page was incomplete, confirming the fact that a second page would follow.

The page he'd just retrieved from between the desk and filing cabinet was from a company named VacRx. The date on the top indicated it had been sent months ago, some time in February.

Monty stood again and went back to the filing cabinet. Allowing his good arm to do most the work, he wrestled the heavy cabinet away from the desk.

What he discovered gave him some degree of pleasure. Several sheets of paper lay nested between the two pieces of furniture.

Perhaps one would provide a clue as to Bott's whereabouts.

If nothing else, at least he had some new reading material.

NEVER IN HER life had Isabel seen a face so full of grief and remorse as that of Gus Dearing.

Despite her admonitions, he came each day, roaring up the road to her cabin as if the place were on fire, Grunt's head hanging out the passenger window of the truck, tail wagging to beat the band.

Today, as she had the two days before, Isabel jumped up and closed the windows at which she'd taken to sitting for most of each day. Summer had finally arrived, and Isabel spent hours at a time coming to know the sparrows, barn swallows, and squirrels that visited the birdbath Gus had made for her. She had never known idle time before, not in her entire life, and despite the circumstances—or perhaps because of them—the summer breeze, carrying hints of fields of mountain flowers and songs of swallows and whippoorwills, soothed and comforted her.

Like Suzanne, she had already decided that if she were to die, she wanted to go right there, in her little cabin in the woods.

The recent change in weather had had a healing effect on Gus's old, arthritic body, and watching him now, walking toward her with just the slightest of limps, clad in denim head to toe, that fact pleased Isabel. She picked up the cordless telephone that he had brought her the first day and sat in her rocker, still now, waiting as the old-timer fumbled with the cell phone he'd purchased for himself at the same time.

It took a full two minutes, but finally the phone in her hand rang.

"Damned contraption," Gus growled.

"You know you shouldn't be here," she told Gus, their eyes meeting through the window and across the patch of wild grass that separated them. "You have to take this quarantine seriously, Gus. It's dangerous for you to come."

As usual, Gus ignored her scolding and launched right into his interrogation.

"Any temperature?" he asked.

"None."

"Rash? Any sign of a rash?"

On down his list.

To each Isabel answered the same: "No."

Finally, he paused, shaking a head of hair that overnight seemed to have grown more shockingly white.

"Damn, Iz. What have I done?"

"Stop that, Gus. You saved my life, that's what you did."

"But I killed the son of a bitch. And he had the only thing that could save you now."

She would smile when he made comments like that, and stand for him to see her.

"Look at me, Gus. I'm fine. Can't you see that? Who's to say I've contracted smallpox?"

Isabel did not dare tell him that a CDC immunologist had telephoned just yesterday, confirming Isabel's worst fear—that Lot Two of the HantaVac was, indeed, contaminated with live smallpox virus. Without emotion, he had informed her that the likelihood of her contracting the deadly disease was considerable. In his words, "greater than seventy percent." And that the onset of symptoms could be expected within ten days of exposure. He had strongly advised her to check herself in to the hospital in Missoula or Cutbank, and then, when she refused to discuss the matter, become threatening.

But K. T. had assured Isabel that she had the right to refuse, so long as she did not endanger others in the process.

Isabel did not think she could bear to see the pain in Gus's eyes if she told him about that call.

"How are Marcus and Lucy?" she asked instead, as she did each day. Marcus and Lucy Freeman had been taken to Cutbank Hospital's isolation unit. "Have you heard anything?"

Grunt had returned from his customary exploration with a thick branch protruding from either side of his mouth, which he dropped at Gus's feet. His eyes jumped eagerly from master to stick. Gus bent down, picked it up, and tossed it into the air.

"They're doing okay. So far anyway." The guilt was clearly there too. Sergei Kirov's smallpox vaccine might have saved Lucy and Marcus as well.

"Is there anything I can do for you, Iz?" Gus pleaded. "Anything at all?"

Isabel had thought about that, long and hard, these past couple of days.

"Yes, Gus. There is."

Gus's eyes brightened.

"What? You name it."

"You can tell me about Hattie."

THE COMPUTER HAD, in the end, been his salvation. Since arriving in Seattle, Monty had several times tried telephoning mutual friends of his and Clyde's on the Wind River reservation, hoping to find Clyde. But the numbers he had for them had been disconnected—a tactic often used by AIM members, who changed phone numbers regularly.

Then it had occurred to him—he remembered the e-mail address of one of them,

Richie Greyhorse: *runningpony@aol.com.*

Since his ongoing efforts to break into Bott's e-mail account had been fruitless, this recollection proved of little value until, on the third day, a banner at the top of the Yahoo Web site drew his attention.

Free e-mail, it flashed.

Monty clicked on the banner and opened an account in the name of Alistair Bott, using the address from one of Bott's bills. He typed with trembling fingers.

Runningpony:

Trouble, need to locate lost cousin. Do you have any information?

Blackfeet brother

The response had come quickly.

Dear Blackfeet brother,

Cousin is safe; how can we help?

Running Pony

Monty knew that AIM members' e-mails were sometimes monitored by the FBI and that the simple correspondence between them might already have put Richie, and perhaps Clyde, at risk. He thought long and hard about how to respond.

If my cousin remembers where the arrow pierced his heart, I will call you there.

Less than one minute later, the response:

He remembers. Call in one hour.

Monty's smile was his first since learning of Leroy's death.

When Monty and Clyde had worked together on the Wind River reservation, they frequented a hamburger joint. The Full Moon was owned by an old Arapahoe woman named June. Clyde had fallen in love with Lizzie, a pretty young Arapahoe waitress at Full Moon. They'd dated several times, but Lizzie disapproved of what she called the "troublemaking" side of Clyde and eventually, much to Clyde's anguish, ended their relationship. To Monty's knowledge, Clyde had never fallen for another woman as hard as he'd fallen for lovely, gentle Lizzie.

Now Monty was faced with a problem. His car was parked at the marina and it was broad daylight. Apparently on alert from Bud Wolfkill, the police were cruising by Bott's house regularly. Twice they had stopped and, to Monty's considerable amusement, pressed the doorbell. On the reservation, Bud would simply have broken in to see if Alistair was inside. In the end, Monty decided that walking to his car, in order to drive to a pay phone, would present more risk than using Bott's phone to place the call to the Full Moon.

He waited until fifty-five minutes had passed, then called directory assistance for Fort Washakie. There was a moment of panic when the operator claimed not to be able to find the restaurant's listing, but then, sounding irritated at having succeeded, she announced she had it.

Monty waited five more minutes, then dialed.

"H'lo?" It was a woman's voice.

"Is this June?" Monty asked.

"Yeah, it's June. Who's this?"

"An old friend. I'm looking for someone, a tall Cheyenne. He's supposed to be there with an Arapahoe named Richie Greyhorse."

"You mean Clyde?"

"Yes. Clyde."

"Hold on then."

Monty had been so void of any emotion besides unrelenting anger that the effect of hearing Clyde's voice left him momentarily speechless.

"Is that you?" Clyde said. "Hello?"

"Yeah, it's me. It's good to hear your voice, bro."

"Damn, it's good to hear yours. I hear you're off on some wild goose chase."

"You've talked to someone back home? Have you heard anything about Isabel?"

"You mean the lady doc?"

"Yes."

There was a pause.

"So that's what I get for leaving you there."

"Tell me, is she okay?"

"I don't really know, brother. I heard she was in isolation. That she took that vaccine."

No, God no.

"Hey, you still there?"

Monty drew in a breath.

"Yeah, I'm here," he said softly.

"Sorry 'bout that, man. Maybe she won't come down with it."

Monty would not have believed he was capable of more anger than that he'd already been feeling, but Clyde's words gave rise to an entirely new anger in him, one even more intense and violent. Any caution about whether it was safe to have this discussion on Bott's phone simply disappeared.

"You have to help me find the guy who did this to her. I'm sure he killed Leroy, too. His name is Alistair Bott."

"That's the name that was on that e-mail you sent Richie."

"Yeah. I'm using his computer."

"Let me talk to Richie. We'll contact the IGU. Call us back tomorrow, same time. Okay?"

"I don't want to wait that long," Monty snapped.

"Listen, brother, you gotta give us a little time. Hang tight, okay?"

CHAPTER

FORTY-THREE

GUS'S EYES SEARCHED for Isabel's, but they were too old, too farsighted to give him the answer he needed. He stepped closer, onto the porch and out of the glare.

"You know about Hattie?" he asked, his disbelief coming through loud and clear despite the crackle of his cell phone.

"Yes." Isabel nodded. "I know."

Gus stared at Isabel through the window, silent, for a good long while. Then, slowly, as if the arthritis had just returned, he took several short steps to the stack of firewood and lowered himself to the dusty porch, his back propped against the woodpile and his face to Isabel, his free arm slung over both bony, bent knees. But when Grunt ran up enthusiastically and dropped onto the porch beside him, Gus reflexively straightened one long leg out in front of him and Grunt's heavy head plopped down on the old man's thigh.

It was an odd sight. That cranky old man sitting there on the porch, stroking his sleeping dog's head as he spoke into the cell phone pressed to his ear.

"My wife Marian and Hattie Day were best friends," Gus started, "back at a time that nice white girls like my Marian weren't supposed to be runnin' around with Indian girls."

He looked up at Isabel to monitor her response, then continued.

"Hattie's father was a Cheyenne. Her mother was Salish. She never did know her father, but Marian always said her mother did a real good job of raising Hattie alone."

"What was her name?" Isabel asked.

"Whose?"

"Hattie's mother."

The hand on Grunt's back went still as Gus tried to remember.

"I don't rightly recall. She'd already died by the time I met Hattie. I think Marian said it was from polio."

"When was that? That you met Marian?"

"Back in 1943. That's when I fell in love. I'd just come home from the war and took over my grandfather's ranch here. We had an awful drought that year, none of the timothy was worth a damn and the cattle were near to starvin' to death. Marian's family ran a big spread down near Pablo, where the drought hadn't been so bad. I bought hay from them that summer to keep from losing any more cattle. Marian was about eighteen then. She helped her brothers load my truck. I'll always remember that, the first time I saw her. She did just as good a job as they did, only she was a helluva lot prettier."

Gus's initial wariness had faded.

"I started going down to Pablo on weekends after that, and during the week, if I could come up with a good excuse. That's when I met Hattie. Since she and Marian had always been schoolmates, Marian's family kind of took her under their wing when Hattie's mother died. She lived in the same little house in Pablo that she'd grown up in, but she was around the ranch a lot."

Isabel's breath seemed to leave her. They were discussing the young woman whose name she'd found in the trunk in Nada's house.

On her birth certificate.

"What was she like, Gus?" She struggled getting the words out.

Gus seemed to sense the emotional impact his recollections were having on Isabel, but intuitively, he knew he could no longer keep anything from her. She had come this far, she had to know everything now.

His face creased in a tender smile.

"She was a real nice young lady," he said. "Like you. She was quiet, but you always knew there was a lot goin' on inside her head." He was watching Isabel for her reaction. "And she was a real beauty. You have her eyes. And her nose."

Isabel did not know whether to laugh or cry. Her entire life, a piece of herself, of her very being, had been missing. She'd known it, felt it, always. And now, Gus was giving her that single, magical piece that enabled her, for the first time in her entire life, to truly know and understand who she was.

But the joy that this gift might once have given her was tainted now. She had so recently buried her own mother. The only mother she had ever known. The woman who had loved her so dearly. Obviously much more dearly than Hattie Day, who had given Isabel up.

"Marian and me got married in 'forty-six," he continued. "She moved up here on to the ranch, and after that, we'd see Hattie from time to time, but she and Marian both had busy lives. Hattie married an Indian fella—Kootenai I believe—and it seemed they were doin' pretty well with a garage he owned there in town. But then he died in a car wreck. And a little after that, your father arrived in Pablo to run the clinic there."

Again, a quick glance at Isabel.

"Go on," she urged.

"Well, Hattie was no mechanic, so she took to cleaning houses, and that's how she met your father. She cleaned house for him. The way Hattie told it to Marian—'cause this wasn't anything she was gonna share with me or anybody but her closest friend—the two of them just fell in love. Hattie knew he was married and she told Marian he tried to do the right thing, but neither one of 'em could help themselves. Your dad, he was only gonna be there a year, and the end of that year was comin' and Hattie turned up pregnant. According to Marian, your dad wanted to marry her. But Hattie was a good Christian and she wouldn't have any part of breaking up a marriage, so she sent him on his way. 'Bout near broke her heart, but she figured she'd always have the baby, even if she didn't have him.

"From all Marian could piece together, 'cause this wasn't stuff that anyone talked about in the open, your father went back home and told his wife that he'd fallen in love with an Indian girl. He told her he wanted to go back and live there with her, marry her. That him and Hattie were about to have a baby."

Even Gus seemed to find the discussion too painful now to meet Isabel's eyes. Instead he kept his gaze on Grunt, stroking him all the while he told his tale.

"You came early, Isabel. Your father hadn't returned to Hattie yet. He was still trying to smooth things over with your mother, I guess. Trying to make things right for her. They kept you in the hospital 'cause you were so tiny. And that's when it happened . . ."

His wrinkled hand grew still once more and his strikingly blue eyes finally came up to meet Isabel's.

"Hattie got herself killed drivin' out to Marian's family's place. She was gonna borrow the camera to take pictures of her new baby. Of you, Izzie. It wasn't her fault. Some drunken Indian crossed right into her lane and hit her head on."

Isabel's gasp shattered the stillness that had taken hold.

"You okay?"

Biting her lower lip, she nodded.

"Want me to stop?" Gus asked, his voice plaintive.

"No. Tell me everything."

"Well, there's not a whole lot more after that. When your father found out about Hattie, he showed up in Pablo right quick and took you back to Seattle with him." Gus's kind eyes fixed now on her face. "And we never knew what happened to you. Until now. It appears your mother was another good woman. She took you in and raised you as her own child. She did right by you, didn't she, Izzie?"

Isabel could only nod her head, so overcome was she by this tale, a tale she somehow always knew existed. A tale kept hidden from her her entire life.

And now, finally, she understood why.

"Gus?" she said, after several minutes of silence had passed between them.

"Yeah?"

"Do you know someone named Sky Thomas?"

"Sure. She's the oldest living Blackfeet. Has been for a long time. A lotta Blackfeet think Sky can tell the future."

A queasy, uneasy feeling moved lightly across Isabel's belly.

"Would she have known Hattie? Or my father?"

Gus scratched his head.

"Don't see how," he answered. "Never heard of Sky leaving the rez."

Just then, Grunt sprung up and bounded off the porch with a loud *arrff*, heading toward the road.

Both still reeling from their discussion, Isabel and Gus turned to see what had caught the dog's eye. At first, all they saw was a cloud of dust, but soon they could make out a patrol car, approaching at an even faster clip than Gus usually did.

What now? Isabel wondered. Could K. T. have been wrong? Were they coming to force her into the hospital? Or—worse yet, far worse—could something have happened to Monty?

The car came to a gravel-spraying halt behind Gus's truck. One second later, Bud Wolfkill emerged and came toward them with long, fast strides. His large brown hands carried a thick black binder.

A sense of foreboding paralyzed Isabel as she watched Bud approach.

"You know you're not supposed to be here," Bud said curtly to Gus. Then he surprised Isabel by following with, "But I'm glad you are."

The heels of his black boots thudded noisily as he stepped up onto the wooden porch.

"Give me that thing, will you?" he said, nodding toward the cell phone Gus still grasped.

Gus handed it over.

Bud Wolfkill cleared his throat, removed his sunglasses, and, finally, met Isabel's frightened eyes.

She picked up her own phone and pressed it to her ear.

"*What?*" she asked. "Is it Monty? Has something happened to Monty?"

"Still no word from him," Bud said. "I don't imagine there will be until he finishes what he set out to do. This is about you. I brought something for you." He raised the hand holding the binder. "I'm gonna put this up against your door, then Gus and me are gonna step back a ways while you pick it up. You only have a few minutes to read it and make a decision. I'm afraid that's all I can give you."

"I don't understand," Isabel said.

"You will when you see it."

Bud had already stepped toward the front door, where he gingerly placed the binder, leaning it against the frame.

"Come on now, Gus," he ordered. "Back away."

Turning to shoot Isabel a troubled glance over his shoulder, Gus complied, stepping down from the porch.

When Isabel opened the door, Grunt's wet nose poked through.

"Go away, Grunt," Isabel said, pushing him back.

The dog whined as she reached for the binder.

There were no markings on its cover. None. She took it

inside, to her seat by the window, and with trembling hands opened it.

The first page was written in Russian.

She turned to page two. It read:

PROTOCOL
VAREOLA VACCINE
STRAIN X

She began flipping through the following pages. Data, results, earlier research papers. Returning to the first page, it suddenly hit her. Sergei Kirov had been Russian.

Incredulous, she lifted her eyes to where Gus and Bud stood, leaning against Gus's truck.

Bud Wolfkill still had the phone pressed to his ear.

She lifted her phone again.

"It's the protocol for Kirov's smallpox vaccine," she said. "Isn't it?"

Bud nodded. Even from this distance, his posture, the tilt of his head, declared his excitement.

"That's right."

"How did you get this?"

"I found it. Hidden in the spare tire on the Land Cruiser Kirov was driving. He'd been planning to leave the country. There was fifty-thousand dollars in cash too. And his passport."

"The CDC must want this," Isabel said, confused.

"They certainly would, but they don't know it exists," Wolfkill said. "I haven't told them yet. I wanted you to see it first."

Isabel tried to read Bud's eyes, but from this distance, it was impossible.

"I don't understand," she said. "Why would you want me to see it?"

"So that you could decide whether it looked like the real thing."

Isabel stared at Bud, trying to make sense of it all.

"Yes. It does. It's just what I would expect from a scientist like Dr. Kirov."

Bud Wolfkill looked from Isabel to Gus, then back to Isabel.

"Then would you be willing to bet your life on it?" he finally asked.

SUDDENLY, WITH A terrible sense of disappointment—for without even realizing it, she had allowed the excitement in Bud's eyes to give her hope—Isabel realized what Bud was thinking.

"You don't understand, Bud," she said. "No one could duplicate this work in the amount of time left before . . ."

"Before you come down with smallpox?"

"Yes. It's a wonderful discovery, it could save lives. But not mine. Not Lucy or Marcus."

Bud seemed to falter at the mention of the Freemans.

"I don't know about Lucy and Marcus," he said, dropping his head momentarily in despair. Then he raised it again.

"But it might not be too late for you."

Isabel was getting angry.

"It's too late, Bud. Believe me."

Shaking his head, Wolfkill turned on his heel and headed back to his car. This time he went to the trunk, where he removed a small silver thermos.

As he returned to the porch, thermos carried like a communion chalice in front of him, Isabel could see the Starbucks logo on it.

Bud came directly to the window, so close that he could reach out and touch Isabel if the glass did not separate them. He held the thermos within fifteen inches of where she sat. Then, slowly, he rotated it. As the logo disappeared, a label on the opposite side rotated into view.

Confused, impatient, Isabel did not like this game Bud was playing with her.

The sharp cry she let out when Bud stopped rotating the thermos and pressed it up against the window for her to read the handwritten label did not require a telephone to be heard outside.

VAREOLA VACCINE

STRAIN X

Gus had followed Bud up to the porch.

"What, what is it?" he demanded to know when he heard Isabel cry out.

Ignoring Gus, Isabel lifted the telephone to her ear. Bud did likewise.

"Is it . . . ?" she stammered, her eyes searching his. "Is it really Dr. Kirov's vaccine?"

Bud Wolfkill didn't smile often, but the one he flashed now made up for that.

"It sure as hell appears to be," he said. "I found it in the wheel well, with the notebook. Now, the question is—and you don't have much time to decide—are you willing to take the chance that it is?"

CHAPTER

FORTY-FOUR

DID YOU KNOW your man has ties to antigovernment, survivalist-type groups?"

The next day when Monty called the Full Moon, Clyde had picked up on the first ring.

Monty's grasp on the receiver tightened. Finally, a lead.

"No."

"You know that e-mail you sent us from this dude's computer? Well IGU used it to trace his movements on the Internet."

"They can do that?" Monty asked.

"Something about cookies. They're like these little markers that they can trace to see what Web sites you're surfing. Seems your man was spending an awful lot of time at porn sites and in survivalist chat rooms. You know the kind— antitax, antigovernment, racist, preparing for Armageddon."

Monty had already discovered Bott's prurient side. But his interest in survivalist groups came as a surprise.

"Like the Freemen?"

"Exactly. In fact, one site he kept hitting time and again is this group up there in Byrd, Montana. You might want to check out their Web site. Pretty ugly stuff."

"Tell me about them."

"Well, IGU's investigated them before 'cause they've caused some trouble up in that area for some of the Kootenai from Bonners Ferry. They're heavily armed. In fact, IGU believes they actually use a gun shop there for a front. A place called Powder Keg. Could be your guy headed that way. They're no strangers to fugitives. But these aren't people you want to mess with, ya know?"

Monty had thanked Clyde and departed Seattle within minutes, using Bott's MasterCard to buy gas on the way to Montana.

Climbing the interstate after crossing the Columbia River, Monty had thrilled momentarily at the sight of a herd of wild horses before realizing they stood motionless, the lead horse rearing on hind legs made of brass. Metal sculptures.

At one time Monty might have felt disdain for the trickery, but today he took it as a sign from the spirits, encouraging him in his pursuit.

The summer sun beat mercilessly into the back window

as he drove east, crossing 250 miles of farmland, but by the time he pulled off Interstate 90 in Coeur d'Alene, Idaho, shadows had begun creeping across the rolling, lush green landscape.

He headed north on Interstate 95. The terrain felt more familiar to him now. The mountains in the distance did not compare to Montana's peaks, but there was more open space than in Seattle. He felt less confined by the dense growth everywhere, less claustrophobic. The closer to his native soil he came, the stronger, more confident he grew.

In Sandpoint, he stopped at a souvenir shop and bought a ball cap. He'd driven through Byrd before. An Indian with long hair would draw attention.

Driving further north, through Bonners Ferry, the sun finally disappeared into the foothills, which were becoming bigger and more spectacular the closer he got to the Canadian border. Two miles north of Bonners Ferry, Monty turned east, onto Highway 2.

In the dark, Monty negotiated the narrow highway with great care. It twisted and turned in corkscrews as it followed the course of the Kootenai River. The small white crosses on red poles that marked traffic fatalities and seemed every bit as abundant as the purple lupine lining the road sides kept Monty at a moderate speed. By the time he arrived, all the shops in Byrd would be closed. It would be another wasted night, spent in the car. No need to hurry, despite the sense of urgency that was eating him alive.

At Yaak Lookout, a sign announced Byrd was just four miles ahead. Ten minutes later, another sign welcomed him to Byrd, Montana, population 953.

Had that number recently increased by one?

As he'd expected, the shops had closed for the night. Most were completely darkened, while a few—the local mercantile and a drugstore—left lights burning inside.

The Powder Keg was easy to find. A two-story frame

structure on Byrd's main street, with a wood-planked porch, much like shops in Browning. No lights illuminated the shop's interior, but above the structure, a single bulb glowed in a room with an open, curtainless window.

Monty cruised through town twice. On the second go-round, a Byrd police car coming from the other direction slowed to take note of the Toyota.

It would not be wise to stay in town. He did not want to draw attention to himself.

Monty remembered seeing a sign for a snowmobile trail at Yaak Lookout. Turning the car around, he headed back the way he'd come, on Highway 2. At the side road marked snowmobile trail, he exited and parked in the forest service lot, where he rolled down one of the Toyota's front windows, climbed in the backseat. The familiar night sounds soothed him into a deep sleep.

At dawn, Monty climbed the steep trail up to Yaak Mountain Lookout, where the panoramas of gently rolling mountains, the smell of mossy branches of the old growth forest, revitalized him. He prayed to the Great Spirit for the survival of his people and gave thanks for his sacred bond with Mother Earth. He prayed that Leroy's spirit be at peace.

And then, slowly and with renewed strength and purpose, he descended the mountain.

BUD AND GUS watched helplessly from the front porch as Isabel administered the vaccine to herself, her hands trembling so wildly that it took two tries.

Was this really happening? Was the liquid in the thermos what its label claimed? Even if it were, Sergei Kirov's protocol was the work of only one man, manufactured illegally, without FDA oversight. Was it safe? Did it contain live virus that might actually increase Isabel's smallpox exposure?

Even if it were the smallpox vaccine that Sergei Kirov

claimed to have developed, even if it proved effective in protecting unexposed subjects against smallpox, could it do Isabel any good? Or was it too late now, three days after exposure?

All of those questions ran through Isabel's mind in the short window of time that she had to make her decision and act upon it. And in the end, none of the doubts mattered. What mattered is that Bud had just tossed her a possible lifeline. A reed-thin lifeline, but she grabbed hold of it with both hands.

"We have to get the vaccine to Marcus and Lucy," Isabel said. "The longer we wait, the less likely any vaccine will protect them."

A haunted look returned to Bud's eyes.

"I wish now that Lucy had been as stubborn as you about going to the hospital. You know as well as I do that none of those doctors are gonna take a chance on something I found in a car. Not with the CDC looking over their shoulders. That's why I brought it out here before I reported it. I figured I'd let you make your own mind up. 'Cause once I turn this stuff in, who knows what's gonna happen?"

With a sinking feeling, Isabel realized that Bud was right.

"I have to leave now, to turn these in," Bud said, nodding at the black plastic bundle in his hands. He'd brought along heavy-duty garbage bags, which he'd doubled over the thermos and notebook to retrieve them from Isabel's porch. "Maybe if I hurry there's still a chance."

Bud handed the phone over to Gus and turned away.

"Gus, please, put Bud back on," Isabel cried.

When Wolfkill pressed the phone to his ear again, he seemed reluctant to meet Isabel's gaze.

"How can I ever thank you?" Isabel asked.

A wisp of a smile returned to Bud Wolfkill's somber face.

"By staying alive," he answered. Then he turned and walked away.

CHAPTER

FORTY-FIVE

GUS HAD DEPARTED close on Bud's heels, leaving Isabel to ponder what had just taken place. The initial elation of Bud's discovery ebbed quickly as reality set in.

She had just injected a foreign substance, created by an obviously deranged man—a scientist who once headed a Russian biowarfare program—into her body.

Was she out of her mind? Or simply that desperate?

Time would tell.

Time. She was literally a prisoner of the passage of time right now. The waiting was growing intolerable. Days of waiting to see if she, Lucy, or Marcus developed a fever or rash, the first symptoms of smallpox.

Days, minutes, *seconds* waiting for word of Monty.

The seemingly endless wait for word regarding the FDA investigation into her involvement in Alistair's misdoings.

And now she could add another cliff-hanger to the list. Would the strain X vaccine she'd just bet her life on *save* her—or perhaps, if it wasn't what it seemed, kill her?

Her life had been put on hold, and Isabel had no idea whatsoever what it would be like when it was given back to her—if she was lucky enough to even survive.

Would Monty ever be part of it again? Would her license to practice medicine be revoked?

Was the life ahead of her one worth fighting for, or would it be stripped of everything that mattered to her?

She did not know if she could bear the guilt if Lucy or Marcus Freeman died. Lucy had entrusted Isabel not only with her own life but with those of her children. So many of the Blackfeet had trusted her. They had put aside their well-founded fears and distrust and voluntarily come forward to participate in the HantaVac clinical trial *because they trusted Isabel.*

And, as surely as if she'd been the one to come up with the hideous plot, as surely as if it had been her, and not Kirov, who actually tainted the vaccine, Isabel was now responsible for the fact that two of those who had trusted their lives to her could die.

For there was no escaping the cold, hard facts. Contaminating the HantaVac was Alistair's way to get back at Isabel. His ultimate revenge.

She was responsible. She was responsible.

When Gus's truck appeared later that evening, for the first time Isabel wished that her well-intentioned friend would just leave her alone. But the lopsided grin he emerged from the truck wearing managed to intrigue her.

Gus carried a large brown paper bag, which he plopped down on the porch while he fussed with the phone.

"Got a little present for you," he finally announced, reaching inside the bag for what turned out to be a binder. This one was a soft blue.

"What is it, Gus?"

"I thought you might want more time to look over those scientific documents that Bud found," he explained. "Bud had Suzanne meet us at the clinic so that we could sterilize the binder in that contraption . . ."

"The autoclave?"

"Yeah, the autoclave. Then I talked Bud into letting me borrow it while he called all the folks he had to call. Them gals at the Ben Franklin got an eyeful, tryin' to help me figure out that fancy Xerox machine they got there."

Gus looked like a new man now that there was reason to hope Isabel would survive the tainted HantaVac.

"You made a copy of Kirov's protocol?"

"Yup."

"Gus, you're brilliant."

He left the binder up against the door. Isabel was already reaching for it by the time the old green pickup disappeared down the road.

She must not give in to despair. For Gus's sake. For the sake of Lucy and Marcus Freeman.

Isabel settled back into her chair and began reading.

She read through the night. So much of the material was new to her. She had to go back over some sections several times to make certain she understood them.

Much of what she read horrified and repulsed her.

The strain of smallpox that had been used to contaminate Lot Two was no ordinary strain of smallpox. No, Sergei Kirov and his comrades had created a new strain of smallpox, one with a delayed onset.

It was right in the protocol, on page thirteen, the rationale behind developing a form of the disease whose onset was expected to be at least twice, perhaps even three times, as late as the natural strains of vareola:

Delayed onset considered desirable in that it allows a greater degree of inadvertent exposure during that period of incubation in which the patient is asymptomatic.

Isabel had reread that portion of the developmental history of Kirov's vaccine over and over again, for it took time for her to accept the truth behind the cryptic words: that Sergei and his comrades deliberately engineered a new strain of smallpox whose onset was delayed *so that a greater number of innocent victims could be infected.*

Since smallpox spread readily through the air, in a single day a person who didn't realize she was infected could un-

knowingly expose dozens more while she went about her
daily activities. The first symptom, fever, was not expected
to appear for at least two weeks after exposure. Whereas the
vaccinea strain the world had always known caused an eruption of telltale sores just two days after the onset of fever,
with strain X, it could be another week to ten days before
the sores allowed a definitive diagnosis. Thousands—perhaps
tens of thousands—more victims could die, be disfigured, or
be blinded, due to the delayed onset of symptoms.

It was a rationale so hideous and twisted that Isabel bolted
to the bathroom sink. She stood there, hanging over it, sweat
dripping from her chin to the white porcelain. She tried to
will herself to throw up, to rid herself of the poisonous information she'd just acquired, but as foul and poisoned as
she now felt, her body would not cooperate. She stood there,
hands shaking, holding tight to the cool, smooth surface.

But when she returned to her reading, Isabel soon learned
that the same subject matter that had just caused her such
distress might have a silver lining. As she read on, she realized that as depraved as the genesis of the delayed-onset
strain might be, that very characteristic of strain X stood to
give Isabel, Marcus and Lucy a better chance of surviving.
If the liquid in the thermos turned out to be Kirov's strain X
vaccine.

Isabel read on with renewed intensity.

Most vaccines were intended to be given before exposure
to a disease. However, with infectious organisms that mul-
tiplied slowly enough, such as rabies, post-exposure vaccination was known to succeed. The shorter the period between
exposure and the development of severe symptoms, the less
likely that a vaccine given after a person was exposed to a
disease would work. Dengue fever, ebola, and smallpox, with
its seven to seventeen day incubation, were typically considered not susceptible to post-exposure immunization.

Kirov's notes painstakingly explained that this was because immunizations produced two types of immune re-

sponse: humoral immunity (the production of antibodies) and cellular immunity due to activation of killer T lymphocytes. Antibodies generated in the humoral response often provided the needed immune response for an infectious organism free in the blood plasma. However, once an infectious organism made its way into a target cell—an essential step in order for viruses to multiply—the only effective immune response became a cellular one.

Achieving a therapeutic level of cellular immunity took longer than the humoral response. Therefore, in the event the smallpox contaminant in the Hanta Vac vaccine managed to penetrate Isabel's target cells, the delayed onset engineered into strain X would give the cellular immunity produced by Kirov's vaccine time to build, hopefully producing a level high enough to save Isabel's life.

Isabel threw down the binder and reached for the phone.

There was still time to save Marcus and Lucy Freeman.

If they acted fast enough.

The sky behind Little Chief's peaks had just begun to show the first pink trace of daylight when Lehman Morris's rich baritone came on the line.

"Thank God you're there." Isabel sighed. "I need your help."

THE CAMPGROUND EAST of Byrd had become a home of sorts to Monty. He'd been hanging around the area for six days now but still had not caught sight of Bott. Down to his last twenty dollars and a stolen credit card, he was living in large part off the land, which didn't create that big a problem as he'd been able to devise a fishing pole. It was a pathetic attempt, whittled from a branch of white birch, but the Kootenai's pure, cold water was home to an abundance of rainbow, brown, and cutthroat trout, so Monty ate well each evening over a campfire.

The credit card enabled him to buy gas, and he'd found a

Mini-Mart with a quick-swipe checkout. He'd used cash on his first visit and tipped the clerk, a pimply faced kid, two bucks—almost the amount of his purchase. It was money Monty could not spare, but it paid off. On several occasions after that, he used Bott's MasterCard for toiletries, beverages, and a daily newspaper. The kid, who worked afternoons, never asked to see an ID.

The biggest problem caused by the shortage of cash was the fact that without spending money Monty dared not hang around Byrd for long periods. He was pushing his luck already. He could feel Byrd's police eyeing him, but he took great pains to avoid giving them anything to hassle him about—no loitering, no speeding. Always polite to the locals. Yes, sir. No, sir. Thank you, ma'am.

The perfect visitor, only he knew that they suspected he wasn't another tourist.

Monty may not have seen Bott yet, but he'd become convinced he was there, in Byrd. And he was pretty certain he knew where.

Every night the light in the window above the Powder Keg went on at about the same time. It was always after the store had closed, after the redneck who Monty had pegged as the shop's owner left for the night.

Someone was living up there, no doubt about it. A man, slight of build. Monty had seen his back, just once, as he drove slowly down main street.

His frustration at not being able to stake out the place until he discovered whether the shadowy figure was indeed Bott led him to consider breaking in. He could wait until the shop closed and take his chances. But in reality he only had one chance at this. Monty knew that if it turned out not to be Bott up there, he'd have blown it. And the man who killed his father, the man who had put Isabel's life at risk, would go free.

He had to be patient. He had to be certain before he acted.

Besides, living outside sure as hell beat the jail cell he'd be going home to. He could take his time.

On the morning of the seventh day, Monty awoke to the sound of a visitor. He'd removed the backseat from the Toyota—which he'd been parking on a remote, no longer used logging road—and taken to sleeping on it on the ground in a stand of old growth cedars. Someone might be able to sneak up to the car with him sleeping inside, but no one could ambush Monty Four Bear out in the open.

But this morning, a white-tailed deer had done just that. This time of year most does her size were accompanied by a fawn or two, but this one foraged alone, just yards from where Monty lay. He watched the long-legged creature with no less appreciation, no less sense of awe than that he'd felt as a child on hunting trips with Leroy.

The day before, he'd hiked up above Kootenai Falls, then sat watching a herd of bighorn sheep, picking their way across the ledges and rocks high above the river. He'd also seen an eagle and several osprey along the river. All good signs.

Suddenly the deer sensed his presence. She stood, frozen, for several seconds, her nose high, picking up his scent. Then calmly, as if she knew that there was nothing to fear, she turned the cottony underside of her tail toward him and slowly disappeared into the dense underbrush.

That was when Monty knew.

Today would be the day.

HAIR TUCKED INTO the ball cap he'd purchased in Sandpoint, Monty entered the Three Rivers Diner and found an empty seat facing the window, with a good view of the Powder Keg, across the street and several storefronts down.

Heads turned, but after that the breakfast crowd showed only mild interest in the Indian, who did not seem to be a troublemaker. Down to his last three dollars, but clean-

shaven from his morning bath on the shores of the swollen
Kootenai, Monty ordered coffee and toast.

Across the street, shop owners and workers began arriving
to open up. The same yellow Dodge pickup that sat outside
the Powder Keg all day each day pulled up. A husky blond
man dressed in black T-shirt, camouflage pants, and army
boots emerged and went to the shop's door, where, with the
use of a key, he entered and flipped the cardboard sign hanging on the window from CLOSED to OPEN. Several other vehicles pulled up in the time Monty sat there observing, but
as had been true all week, none of the occupants resembled
the portrait back in Seattle.

Monty dragged out his coffee and toast until the red-haired
waitress, squeezed into a pink uniform two sizes too small,
returned for the fourth time and asked, "Maybe you want to
order something else? If not, I got some customers waiting
for a table."

Monty could not see anyone waiting, but it would serve
no purpose to make a scene. Tossing his three dollars on the
table, he detoured into the restroom before leaving the restaurant.

He'd parked at the end of town, on a side street, where he
hoped his car wouldn't draw attention. He crossed the street
and walked down the sidewalk in the direction of the Powder
Keg.

As he approached, the door opened and a tall, slender figure emerged.

Monty recognized him instantly.

Alistair.

The silk shirt and slacks from the portrait in Bott's living
room had been replaced by garb similar to that worn by the
man who opened the shop. The only thing that kept him from
fitting in with the other customers Monty had seen coming
and going all week was the hair—too neatly styled for these
parts.

It took all of Monty's resolve to keep walking. He could

not, however, stop himself from glancing into the eyes of the man he believed to be Leroy's killer. The man who, in some twisted way that Monty did not yet fully understand, had put Isabel in harm's way.

They were cold, disinterested eyes that looked right through Monty as they passed one another on the sidewalk. The restraint that it took to continue on was made possible only by Monty's resolve to do this right. He had been patient this long; now that he'd found Bott, that patience would soon pay off. Monty picked up his pace. When he got to the Toyota, he drove up Main Street and back down again looking for him, but Bott had vanished.

Not for long, however.

As the day progressed and town filled with traffic, both pedestrian and vehicle—folks coming in from the country and neighboring towns even smaller than Byrd—Monty felt safe parking the Toyota on the street, where he could keep track of the comings and goings at the Powder Keg.

Bott returned in midafternoon, in the company of a straggly looking redhead and a military type with shaved head. The threesome stayed inside for two hours, until closing at 5:30. Then the two who had accompanied Bott emerged, along with the driver of the yellow pickup. Reversing his routine of the morning, he reached in the shop, flipped the sign back to CLOSED, and, after several minutes' discussion on the sidewalk, bid the other two good-bye and climbed in the truck.

The remaining two sauntered down the street and entered the Three Rivers Diner. Bott, however, never reappeared.

As nightfall approached and the streets of Byrd emptied, Monty moved the Toyota to a residential side street that ran perpendicular to the back of the Powder Keg. On foot now, he stationed himself in the grassy alley between the pharmacy and a Western-wear shop.

Just before nine, he watched as the two men emerged from the diner. They strode back toward the gun shop. Their clumsy, lumbering gate indicated they'd been drinking. Both men climbed into a green Blazer with Montana plates, which cruised away, to the east, without headlights.

Monty watched as the same light he'd observed each night went on in the room directly above the shop.

CHAPTER

FORTY-SIX

DAY NUMBER NINE.
Still no temperature.

Still no news about Monty. Each day, Isabel spent hours poring over the trio of newspapers Gus brought her regularly—the Kalispell *Daily Interlake*, *USA Today*, and the *Seattle Times*, always a day old—searching for news connected to Leroy's or MacStirling's death, or the explosion at the mine site. Anything that might hint at Monty's whereabouts or fate. Aside from one sentence in *USA Today*'s "Across the Nation" section—"two Native Americans, believed to belong to the American Indian Movement, are being sought in connection with an explosion at the site of a proposed gold mine"—she'd found nothing. But this morning an article that she'd overlooked the day before had caught her eye.

ONTARIO COURTS ALLOW MINING SUIT
In a precedent-setting decision, a lawsuit filed against World Resources, Inc., a Canadian mining company, over the death of a Kyrgyzstan woman is to be heard in Canadian courts.

At first Isabel failed to make the connection. World Resources, Inc. *WRI.* According to the article, a young mother had died after drinking from a lake poisoned by an accident at WRI's Kyrgyzstn mining operation. An entire village's water supply had been contaminated and several other villagers had ended up hospitalized. WRI steadfastly refused responsibility, but the Ontario courts had decided the multimillion-dollar lawsuit against WRI had merit. They would allow the suit to be brought in Canada.

Isabel didn't know whether to attribute the dull ache in her chest to thoughts of the young woman and her baby, or to another day without word of Monty.

But Gus had called her last night, telling her that Bud wanted to talk to him. Maybe today she would finally hear something.

By the time Gus's pickup roared to a standstill outside her cabin, Isabel was already dialing.

Climbing out of the cab, Gus looked startled when the ring of the cell phone in his chest pocket pierced the balmy morning air.

"For Pete's sake, Izzie, what's the hurry?"

"Did you see Bud?"

Gus cleared his throat.

"I just came from there."

"You said you'd call me right away," she charged. They'd discussed it last night. Gus had promised to call her from town, right after he saw Bud.

"I thought I should tell you in person. It's not good news, Izzie."

"Tell me."

"Dammit to hell, Isabel, can't we just be happy you got that vaccine? And that your Dr. Morris talked them folks at the CDC into giving it to Marcus and Lucy too? Can't we just be happy about that for a while?"

All the joy, all the hope, suddenly drained from Isabel.

Gus's blue eyes finally came up to meet hers.

"Bud says the FBI's brought murder charges against Monty and Clyde."

"*No,*" Isabel cried. "How could they do that after all they've learned? Monty and Clyde didn't mean to hurt anyone. They only went out there to destroy the equipment, to get back at WRI for what they did to Leroy. My God, Gus, he was beaten. Then murdered."

Gus's thin lips tightened in a grimace.

"According to Bud, WRI admitted to having Leroy beaten up, but they swear they didn't kill him. Bud's told those FBI agents all that. He told them everything that happened that night he followed Monty to Vancouver, all the stuff they learned from those hooligans. But I guess the FBI doesn't think that changes what happened out at the drill site that night."

"*Where are the charges against WRI?* And if the FBI believes WRI didn't kill Leroy, what are they doing to find who did?" Isabel ranted. "Why, Gus? Why are they willing to believe someone who comes right out and admits to beating an old man, but not Monty and Clyde?"

Gus's eyes locked with hers.

"You know the answer to the question, Isabel. We both do."

THEY'D CRUISED THROUGH Byrd twice now, but no sign of Monty.

"It'd help if we knew what he was drivin'," Richie Greyhorse said.

Clyde had driven all the way from Fort Washakie to Missoula, then he'd turned the wheel of the Ford pickup over to Greyhorse.

Clyde had been scanning the sidewalks and streets for Monty, but now he glanced sideways at Greyhorse's striking profile. Richie Greyhorse's noble and perfectly formed features—high cheekbones, chiseled nose, and strong jaw—had earned him cameos in *Dances with Wolves* and a TNT epic on the history of the West. Richie had been told that if he'd moved to Hollywood, he could have a lucrative career. But Greyhorse only used his occasional acting jobs—if they could be called that—to fund another kind of life. That of an activist bent on helping his people.

"He left Browning in Edna's car," Clyde answered. "But he wouldn't be driving it now. Too bad. Edna's car'd be easy to spot."

"It's been what? Six days since you talked to him? I bet he's long gone by now."

"Probably," Birdseye answered. "But I figured Byrd was just about on our way to Calgary anyway. I gotta at least try to find him. Talk him into coming with us."

"You're right. Monty's gotta get out," Greyhorse concurred. "Fuckin' feds."

They continued down to the end of Byrd's main street in silence.

"Pull into that Mini-Mart," Clyde ordered. "I've gotta take a piss. And I'm hungry as hell."

The smell of burned popcorn greeted them as they stepped inside. A towheaded teenager sat at the counter, head buried in an old issue of *Snowboarding* magazine. He did not look up.

Clyde left Greyhorse to wander around while he went to the men's room. It stunk of urine. Wadded paper toweling littered the floor.

When he emerged, Greyhorse was standing at the counter, watching the kid scoop popcorn into a paper bag.

"That stuff's burnt," Clyde said. "Can't you smell it?"

"Smells good enough to me," Greyhorse answered, smiling.

"Anything else?" the kid asked, turning to hand the bag to Richie. Poor bastard, thought Clyde. At least Indian kids didn't get such bad acne.

"Yeah. I'll take one of those hot dogs. And a large Coke."

He reached over into Richie's bag and threw some popcorn into his mouth.

"We're looking for a buddy of ours," he said between crunches. "An Indian. He would've been here sometime this past week. Seen anyone like that?"

In one hand, the kid had a hot dog pinched between a pair of tongs. With the other he was reaching for a bun. He turned and looked over his shoulder.

"Some guy's been comin' in here every day this past week or so."

Simultaneously, Clyde and Greyhorse stopped crunching. "Yeah?"

"Yeah," the kid said, returning to where they stood, clutching a hot dog wrapped in waxed paper.

"What's this guy look like?" Greyhorse asked.

"Black hair. Braids. Thin."

"Know where we can find him?"

"He's camping in one of the campgrounds. I'm not sure which one. But he usually comes in here right about now. Buys some food, then takes off. Bet if you hang around, you'll see him."

Clyde paid for the food, then dropped a five-dollar bill in the prominently displayed tip jar.

The kids blue-green eyes lit up.

"Want me to tell him anything if he comes in?"

"Yeah," Clyde answered. "Tell him his cousin's looking for him."

THE NIGHT HAD always been Monty's friend. Even as a small child. Often, when Leroy had fallen asleep from too much wine, he'd sneak out of the house. He'd loved to roam the fields and woods surrounding the small frame house he grew up in, guided only by the stars, keenly aware of the other creatures keeping track of him.

Tonight's sky reminded him of those days. Those times—some good, many bad—with Leroy.

He'd left the .38 he'd taken from Isabel's cabin in the car. If he were stopped by police, carrying a gun would mean the difference between being arrested or merely sent on his way. But he did carry his knife, and before he headed for the back of the Powder Keg, he detoured to the city park. He'd formulated his plan days ago. An Indian from out of town couldn't walk into a hardware store and buy enough rope to commit a proper hanging, especially if all he had to make the purchase was a stolen credit card. Over the next few days, he'd scouted town for other options.

The children's play area in the park included climbing toys, a seesaw, and two swing sets, each housing three swings. Each rubber swing seat was suspended by a single length of rope that was threaded through the bottom of the seat and fixed on either end to the top of the swing set. Monty pulled out his knife, and with the speed of lightning, one swing fell. Then another. Then another.

Tying the ropes end to end, Monty headed back to Main Street. Hiding in the same alley, he coiled the final length of almost thirty feet over his shoulder, then, when no cars or pedestrians were in sight, he sprinted across the street and disappeared between the building that housed a row of shops, including the Powder Keg, and a barbershop that stood alone.

Back behind the building, the light from the room at the front of the second story filtered softly through the unlit room at the building's rear. It was warm tonight, and still. Like the one in front, the double-hung window stood open wide.

While the architecture and even the building materials varied from one to the next, the shops formed one continuous structure, all one story, with the exception of the gun shop. Scaling a giant oak tree whose branches brushed the far end of the single story roofline was child's play for Monty. He dropped onto the roof with little more than a dull thud, then moved with quiet grace toward the gun shop.

The night was still and quiet, with the exception of an occasional vehicle—mostly trucks—and intermittent blasts of raucousness when the doors to the diner were flung open. Monty took one long look skyward, then he stretched his arms high, reaching for the stars. For Leroy. At that moment, he could feel his father's presence, as real and powerful and comforting as the night sky. The glitter of Orion became Leroy's mischievous eyes, urging Monty on.

The gap between the single-story roofline and that of the two-story Powder Keg presented his first real challenge. Approaching the lower roof's edge, he dropped to his haunches and, cranelike, peered around the corner of the two-story section. The window he'd seen from the ground was beyond reach—perhaps twelve feet away. Through it, Monty heard welcome sounds—those of a television, coming from the room at the front.

He moved quickly, assessing his options. A rainspout ran from the roofline of the second floor to the first with thick dark cables, most likely telephone, running alongside it. Monty grabbed hold of the spout, testing it for stability. It gave some, but in combination with the cables, which were affixed to the building's siding with heavy-duty staples, it might just do. With the rope still slung over his shoulder, he grabbed hold of the rainspout and cables with his good hand and raised himself off the lower roof. Pain shot through him as his right arm reached up and grabbed, following suit. Slowly, lopsidedly, like an injured runner, he worked his way up, the rubber bottoms of his running shoes against the horizontally oriented siding making black tracks as he slid back down time and again.

Finally he reached the second-story roof and hoisted himself up and over its edge, landing softly on his belly.

Jumping to his feet, Monty tied one end of the rope around the building's chimney. Then he threw the remainder of the coil over the roof's edge and rappelled down its length, dangling over the side of the building, until his foot found the ledge of the open window.

The moment he lowered himself inside, the smell of gunpowder—thick and acidic—assaulted his nostrils.

The room had been filled with row upon row of boxes, stacked four and five high. Ammunition, guns, and survival gear. 3-D, Smith & Wesson, Colt. Handguns, rifles, night-vision goggles, and an open box of gas masks.

One corner of an NRA poster that had been taped to the wall flapped loose, doubling over on itself and partially obscuring the message:

Preserve Our Freedom

On a metal folding chair next to the door sat an ashtray overflowing with cigarette butts, and a spool of brown packaging twine. Empty or half-full beer bottles lay everywhere. Several well-used guns and rifles lay propped against walls and on top of boxes. It was clear the room housed meetings, as well as inventory.

Enough firepower, thought Monty, to stage an uprising. Far more than a shop that size needed.

Monty stole to the door and glanced across the narrow corridor.

After having seen Bott's portrait above the fireplace in his Magnolia home, and then the real thing that afternoon on the sidewalk, Monty recognized him instantly. Alistair Bott half reclined, half sat on a worn red couch, its upholstery torn and frayed, with filthy, once-white stuffing protruding everywhere. Propped against one arm of the couch, with his right leg extended to its other arm and the left resting on the floor, Bott faced the television, his back to the door. On the floor, next to his bare foot, lay a Glock automatic.

A sudden calm descended upon Monty as he crept forward, a length of twine stretched taut between his hands. He was completely unaware of his throbbing shoulder.

There was no fear in Monty at that moment. Only anticipation. And relief.

He stopped just inches from where Alistair sat, almost willing the other man to feel his presence.

And then, as if on cue, Bott's spine stiffened. Without turning to look, his arm shot out toward the floor, but Monty's hands had already swept down over the other man's face. They jerked back now, the twine cutting into Bott's neck as he gasped and struggled, clawing frantically at his throat and his attacker.

Monty kicked the gun, sending it spinning across the room. Expressionless, he watched Bott's terror. He took Bott just to the brink of passing out, then as his grasp on Monty's hands loosened and his head began to fall back, he let up just enough to keep his prey conscious.

Bott's head jerked sideways. At the sight of Monty, he tried to talk while gulping precious oxygen.

"My . . . wallet's . . . on . . . the . . . table."

"I don't want your fucking wallet."

The eyes grew wider, more confused. Breathing had become easier.

"Then the cash register . . . ah can open it. Ah know where Randy keeps the key."

A rage seized Monty. He jerked his hands back even more roughly this time.

Bott's fingers flew up again, wildly clutching at his neck, trying to work their way between the hemp and his flesh.

"Who are you?" he gasped. "What do you want?"

"A full confession. Nothing less. Do you hear?"

Nodding his head frantically, Bott mouthed through his spittle, "Yes, yes."

"I will kill you if you don't cooperate, do you understand?"

Again, a nod of blond curls.

And then, just as Monty relaxed his grip on the twine, the

cold, unforgiving barrel of a gun dug in to the back of his skull.

"My, my," a hearty, nameless voice chortled from behind him. "It looks like we got ourselves a little war party."

THE FAIR-HAIRED GOOD looks were grossly misleading. Monty knew immediately that with the arrival of the husky blond—the shop owner he'd seen closing up earlier that evening—he was up against one ugly soul.

Bott rolled off the couch onto his knees, still clutching his throat, then rose from the floor slowly.

"This fucker about killed me, Randy," he said, his eyes wild with disbelief.

The shopowner let out another hearty laugh.

"Hell, Alistair, he was only toyin' with you. You been leadin' the soft life a little too long."

"Toying with me? The son of a bitch was strangling me."

Gun still trained on Monty, the shop owner reached out and gave him a powerful push into the center of the room.

"What do you have to say for yourself, Indian boy?"

"Fuck you." Monty glared, turning to face his captors.

"Well, well. An Indian with an attitude. We don't take too kindly to *Injuns* with attitudes up here in this neck of the woods, do we, Alistair?"

Bott had fallen back on to the couch where he continued to massage his neck, all the while glowering at Monty.

" 'Course Alistair here is new to our fair town too." The shop owner went on, clearly used to being center stage and always wearing a big, mean grin. "But it wasn't much different back where we came from, was it, Alistair?"

"No," Bott answered. "It wasn't."

"Just what do you suppose our daddies and their buddies would've done back then if an Indian with an attitude showed up in southeast Lousiana?"

Bott did not answer.

"You know, that just gave me an idea." The blue-green eyes lit up like a Christmas tree. "I think we oughta just have ourselves a little party. How's about I go make a call to a couple of the guys, have them meet us out at Turner Road, where we can do this up right?" He handed his gun—an antique Colt .45—butt first to Bott. "I hope you haven't become too citified to use this. Keep him quiet 'til I get back."

Bott nodded and took the gun. He turned it around, training it on Monty.

Monty remained standing in the middle of the room. He might be able to wrestle the gun away from Bott if he dove at him. But there was probably just as good a chance Bott would get a shot off. Either way, the shop owner would hear the scuffle downstairs and be on him in no time.

And either way, it wouldn't get Monty what he'd come for. Answers.

"Why'd you kill my father?"

The question seemed to startle Bott. After a moment, recognition lit his green, catlike eyes.

"You're Four Bear."

"Why did you kill my father?"

Bott snickered.

"So that's what this is about."

"That and other things."

"Such as?"

"The contaminated hantavirus vaccine."

"Whew, you're good. You know that?" Bott studied Monty. "Didn't I hear you're an attorney? And some kind of professor?"

"Why?" Monty pressed. "Why did you kill my father?"

"I didn't."

This had obviously become more of Bott's kind of game. A contest more mental than physical. A challenge of sorts.

"Then who did?"

"Some anvil-headed hockey player. He works for the minin' company."

Rod Sokaski.

"He said *you* killed Leroy."

Bott shook his head, grinning now.

"Maybe he's not such an anvil-head after all. No, I didn't do it. Other than the pleasure of knowing there's one less of your kind, why would I?"

"That's what I've been trying to figure out," Monty said. His eyes narrowed on Bott. "Maybe because of Isabel and me."

Bott's eyebrows shot up.

"My wife? *You* and my wife?"

"She's not your wife. Not anymore."

The attitude of detached reason had evaporated. Bott rose from the couch, an expression of disbelief and rage distorting his already sharp features.

"Are you fucking her?"

Monty did not answer. As Bott closed the distance between them, he raised the gun even with Monty's face.

"You're fucking Isabel, aren't you?"

Without waiting for an answer, he pulled back on the hammer, cocking it. He was so close Monty could see the thin line of dirt under the otherwise perfectly manicured nail on his index finger. The hand shook with Bott's fury.

"Hold on there, Alistair." The shop owner had returned. His smile indicated great amusement at what he'd just overheard. "We'll save that for the little party the boys are putting together. We leave here in half an hour."

Grabbing the gun back from Bott, he said, "Give me that. So that fancy doctor wife of yours has been sleeping with an Indian, huh? Don't that beat all? Here you went and made somethin' of yourself, got a doctor's diploma, some big house in the city, a trophy wife, and she ends up taking up with scum like him. Go figure."

Bott had begun pacing back and forth, clasping and unclasping the fingers of both hands.

"Sounds to me like you need to teach that wife of yours

a lesson," Randy's goading continued. "I mean the woman's obviously a conniving slut. First she tries to destroy your career, then this. I know what I'd do if a woman of mine betrayed me like that."

The silence in the room was thick and filled with tension.

"He's already done that," Monty ventured, eyes still trained on Bott. "Haven't you? Isn't that why you contaminated the vaccine?"

Bott stopped his restless pacing and stepped face-to-face with Monty. For a moment he looked ready to throw a punch, but then, his eyes glimmering with a more powerful weapon, he began to speak.

"You want answers, do you? Why not? After all, you won't be doing much talkin' after tonight. Not after the party Randy has in mind. The same kind of parties our daddies used to throw when scum like you came through the town where we grew up. Randy's daddy here, he was an imperial wizard. Surely a liberal, educated fella like you knows what that means."

Bott's voice had slipped into a slow, backwoods drawl.

"You're right about the vaccine," he went on. "In fact, as a true gentleman, ah must give credit where credit is due. It was you who actually gave me the idea. All that material you had in your files, about how dangerous vaccines could be . . ."

"You're the one who broke into my house."

Bott chuckled now, almost a giggle.

"You thought it was WRI, didn't you? It was so perfect. Everything I did, including contaminating the vaccine with smallpox, would have been blamed on WRI. Who had a better reason to strike out at you, to want to kill all you people? They had a first right of refusal on that deposit. Kill off enough Blackfeet and it would have been theirs. If they were smart, they would have thought of it themselves.

"I'd been trying to decide how to get back at Isabel," he continued, clearly enjoying himself, "how to make her pay for what she did to me. And there it was, right in front of my eyes, in those files of yours. ImmuVac's hantavirus vaccine. What better way to make her suffer? Kill her beloved patients, and maybe, if I'm really lucky, her too."

His twisted smile indicated he knew the effect his words had on Monty, who fought to keep his expression neutral.

"It was brilliant, really. Surely you see the beauty of it. I mean, using a clinical trial to destroy her, bring her down, just like she brought me down. And wipe out you fucking redskins at the same time. And from what we've been hearing the past few days, it worked. Some of Randy's friends that live up that way say the word is that Isabel has come down with smallpox. She's dying, all alone, out in that disgusting little cabin of hers. And I have you to thank."

Something in Monty broke at that moment, but he did not flinch, did not look away. He would not give Bott the satisfaction.

"You're even sicker than she said you were," he said calmly. "I can see why you disgusted her. She told me she was repulsed by you."

"Shut the fuck up!" Bott screamed, suddenly lunging at Monty.

Monty let Bott wrestle him to the floor. It was almost like child's play. Bott knew how to use words as weapons, but he had no idea how to fight with his hands. His fists pummeled Monty without doing any damage, while above them, the smiling face of the shop owner hooted and chortled wildly.

Finally, a big, thick-wristed hand reached down and grabbed hold of Monty's hair, pulling his head sharply back. Before Monty knew what was coming, the barrel of Randy's antique gun had been shoved in his open mouth.

"I guess mebbe we don't actually have to wait for all the other fellas to start havin' ourselves a little fun," the shop owner said eagerly.

Monty saw them first, out of the corner of his eye. But

Bott and his buddy were too wrapped up in their perverted game. They were caught totally off guard.

"Make one move and we'll blow both your fucking heads off."

The grip on Monty's hair loosened as Randy swiveled toward the doorway.

In it stood Clyde Birdseye and Richie Greyhorse. They were armed to the teeth.

ALISTAIR BOTT ROSE from the floor with both hands held high.

"Don't shoot," he cried.

With Randy momentarily distracted, Monty fell back, one leg twisted under him, The gun, however, was still trained on him and when Randy turned his attention back to Monty, he lifted it dead even with Monty's forehead.

"Your buddy dies with me," he declared.

Birdseye and Greyhorse froze momentarily, but Monty's bent leg shot forward, connecting with Randy's knee. There was a loud grunt, simultaneous with a shot that rang out, nicking the skin on the upper edge of Monty's ear. And then the big form of the shop owner came crashing down under the weight of Birdseye's tackle.

The tackle had stunned Randy. Monty watched as Clyde lifted the other man's head in both hands and slammed it into the hardwood floor. Clyde was just as tall, but at least twenty pounds lighter. Still, he had one big advantage: a lifetime of anger to unleash. Randy put up a struggle, but Birdseye had more endurance, and more at stake. When the two rolled within reach of the Glock, Birdseye reached out and brought it down hard on the shop owner's skull. Instantly, the big man fell limp, lifeless.

"What the hell are you two doing here?" Monty finally asked as he watched Greyhorse grab hold of the bottom of the shop owner's boots and flip him onto his stomach.

Sitting on the floor, Clyde flashed a grin.

"Just passin' through."

"What do you mean, passing through?"

"On our way to Canada. I didn't know if you'd still be hanging around, but Byrd was practically on the way, so we figured we'd try. Looks like a good thing we did."

"You can say that again. But how'd you find me? I mean, here? tonight?"

"We got here this afternoon and started askin' around. Kid down at the convenience store said you were living out of your car somewhere but you came into town just about every afternoon. We hung around there all afternoon, but you never showed up, so we checked out all the campgrounds. Found your fire pit out there near the falls. Then we headed back into town. We knew that eventually you'd show up around the gun shop. When we went around back tonight and saw the rope hanging from the roof, we figured you were probably doing something stupid, like trying to take on an armed militia singlehanded."

Monty shook his head in wonder.

"Why do you suppose I'm always getting rescued by some big ugly Indian?"

Both Clyde and Richie Greyhorse looked at each other and grinned.

"Which one of us you callin' ugly?" Greyhorse asked.

They used the rope from the playground to hogtie the shop owner and a wild-eyed Bott, who maintained a frightened silence.

"We better get them out of here. Fast," Monty said. "They've got friends waiting for them outside of town. When they don't show up, they're sure to come looking."

"What're you gonna do?" Clyde asked, turning serious brown eyes on his friend.

"Take him back to Browning," Monty said, nodding toward where Bott lay.

"Come with me, bro, to Canada. We can drop them both somewhere, leave them in the trunk of the car you're driving and call Bud to tell him where to find them."

"Nope," Monty said. "I'm taking him back home with me. I gave Bud my word."

"Don't do it, man. The feds have filed murder charges against us. Did you know that? That's why I'm going over the border. You can't go back, Monty. Come with us. You've found your man now. Bud'll make sure he pays."

"But that's it," Monty said, shaking his head. "I still don't know who killed Leroy. I don't know if he's the one."

Clyde looked long and hard at his friend.

"If you haven't got the right man now, you never will. You go back and they'll put you behind bars." He turned away, clearly anguished, then once again drilled those big, dark eyes into Monty's. "It's her, isn't it? She's the reason you're willing to take that chance."

Monty looked around him. Two bound bodies. Two of his best friends on the run to Canada.

And back home, Isabel was dying.

Clyde was right. What was there to return to?

"Isabel's a big part of it. But not all. I *have* to go back. It's my home, man. My land. My people." His eyes searched Clyde's, and then Greyhorse's, for understanding. "It's all I really have."

CHAPTER

FORTY-SEVEN

THE BEST PART of Isabel's isolation took place while she slept.

The night Gus told her about the murder charges, she'd awakened in a sweat, thinking of Monty facing a future locked up in a cold, sterile jail cell. How could someone whose connection with the earth so defined his very being survive prison? She feared the answer to that question.

But ever since that night that she felt such deep despair, a miraculous thing had been happening. Isabel did not know where Monty's physical being might be, but when she was asleep, his spirit came to lie with her.

It had happened several times. He would stay with her while she drifted in and out of a dreamlike state. Don't leave me, she'd plead silently. But by morning, he'd be gone.

During her more conscious moments of the first night it happened, Isabel became frantic, thinking she'd developed a fever that had made her delirious. But the next morning she felt well, better than she had since going into quarantine, and she'd realized the visits were not her imagination, nor caused by febrile hallucinations.

After that she no longer feared the visits. In fact, her fear now focused on going a night without them.

This evening, Isabel finally drifted off, after watching the embers of the fire burn out, one by one.

Hours later, a wild chorus of yips and howls tugged at her consciousness, pulling her reluctantly from her sleep. Coyotes announcing a kill, calling their friends to a meal.

She hoped it wasn't the gimpy wild turkey she'd seen hopping across the meadow behind the cabin on one leg, the other dangling useless. Or a young fawn. She'd enjoyed watching several foraging in the meadow with their mothers, in the half light of each evening.

The sound, and the thoughts it evoked, made her feel terribly lonely and heartsick. She turned into her pillow, wanting to retreat back into sleep, wondering if she would ever look forward to awakening again.

"It's the full moon."

Isabel's eyes sprang open. She'd only *felt* Monty's presence during his previous nightly visits. She had never actually heard him. Or seen him. But now, the room washed by the light of the moon, she did. He was sitting on the side of her bed, smiling down at her, his hair long and loose, his face all angles in the light.

"It's just the full moon," he repeated. "They're just celebrating. Don't let it make you sad."

Isabel issued a single, heart-wrenching sob and reached for him. Half expecting to find nothing but air, another sob followed when she felt Monty's cool, rough hand cup the side of her face. She turned into it hungrily, pressing it to her lips and inhaling his familiar scent of trees and wind and dried sweat.

This was no dream.

"You're all right," Monty whispered over and over as he stroked her skin. "He told me you were dying. That you'd come down with . . ."

"Oh my God," Isabel cried suddenly, interrupting him. She bolted upright. "You can't be here. I'm quarantined."

Monty tried to pull her back.

"You don't have to worry."

"Of course I do. You have to leave, Monty. Now."

"It's okay, Izzie. I've been vaccinated."

"What?"

"Bud gave me the vaccine."

"How could he? He turned it over to the CDC."

"He didn't turn it all over. He kept some, in case they refused to give it to Lucy and Marcus Freeman. He was planning to sneak it in to them at the hospital. But the doctors approved giving them the vaccine, so Bud still had some. I vaccinated myself. Just before I came out here."

"But you . . . you've always said . . ."

Monty finally succeeded in pulling her down beside him. He lifted himself onto his elbow to see her better.

"I've said and done a lot of stupid things. Nothing would have kept me away from you tonight. Vaccine or no vaccine.

But I knew you wouldn't let me stay if I didn't take the shot." He smiled. He looked stronger, healthier. And peaceful. "It was a small price to pay."

"But we still don't know whether the vaccine will work."

"You haven't gotten sick yet, have you? Or Marcus and Lucy?"

"I hope you're right, but I don't want you exposed. You have to leave, Monty. We can't be certain that the vaccine protected me for another two weeks. I'll be quarantined that long."

"*We'll* be quarantined that long."

"They'll find you, Monty. The FBI will find you here. They've been here several times already, asking questions."

Monty laughed. A sound so pure and musical that Isabel's heart momentarily forgot its pain.

"They've dropped the charges, Is. Apparently WRI already has their hands full with another legal matter. A lawsuit over a cyanide spill. When they learned that their man killed Leroy, they did an about-face."

"Wait a minute. Someone from WRI killed Leroy? Bud said you went after Alistair because you thought *he* killed Leroy."

"Rod Sokaski killed him. It turned out the guard who died at the drill site that night was a good friend of Rod's. He killed Leroy to get back at me. Then he tried to make us believe Bott did it. When WRI learned the truth, they said they wanted to do the right thing. They urged the Feds not to bring charges. With all the attention their lawsuit's getting, I'm sure they decided they didn't need any more bad publicity. The guard's death and the explosion will be left to the tribal courts, Is."

"Alistair . . . ?"

"I found him."

"Is he . . . ?"

"He's in Bud's custody."

"Thank God."

Isabel had thought about it long and hard. She wanted Alistair brought to justice but she did not want him harmed. She would rather he live each day with the knowledge that he would never get his life back. That he would pay, each and every moment of each day, for the lives he had endangered. And those, like Bernice Hougham, who had died. She wanted him to pay for the fact that Isabel might be deprived of the one thing she believed she'd been born to do. Like her father before her. Practice medicine. Here, with the people she loved. A people she now belonged to.

If she was to lose that, she wanted Alistair to pay for it dearly.

Monty reached into the back pocket of his jeans.

"I have something for you," he said, producing a folded piece of paper. "A present."

Isabel took it and slowly unfolded it. The moonlight allowed her to see that it contained a list of some sort, but she could not read it. She reached for the lamp on the table next to the bed.

The light brought the document to life.

It was printed on Harborview Medical Center stationery. Isabel's first impression proved correct. It was a list.

Still squinting from the harshness of the light in the middle of the night, she pulled the paper closer.

At the top left, the column heading read: *Dr. McLain's ER patients.*

THE LIST WAS arranged in two columns. The first listed the name and date of birth of patients. Many of the names, including that of Bernice Hougham, looked familiar to Isabel. Underneath each name was an address and telephone number.

The second column contained notes.

Isabel clamped hold of it as she read the comments addressing each patient on the list.

After the name of one, a forty-eight-year-old man whom Isabel remembered treating for a severe asthma attack, it read: *Smoker, but otherwise fits profile for asthma inhaler study.*

The next patient's name was followed by a star: *No insurance. Good candidate for cholesterol lowering.*

Her eyes scanned downward. Many stars, always noting patients who'd come to the ER uninsured.

"My God," she whispered.

"What?"

"They deliberately went after patients without insurance."

"Why would they do that?"

"Because they're the most desperate, the ones who would be the most eager to participate in a study that promises free treatment."

"Even if the drug hasn't been shown to be safe." Monty scowled. "Or even effective."

"Exactly. From what I read in that affidavit the FDA investigators showed me, Alistair downplayed any risk and exaggerated any potential benefits. And look here, look at this one. It's Bernice Hougham, the woman who died of heart failure after they'd bombarded her body with antihypertensive drugs."

The comments after Bernice Hougham's name read: *Already on anti-hypertensive meds and bp too high, but Ms. Hougham would be easy to recruit.*

Isabel pressed her hand to her mouth.

"Do you know why that is?" she asked Monty. "Why someone wrote that? Because she was just such a sweet, trusting soul."

They were sitting on the side of the bed. Monty wrapped both arms around her and pressed his face up against hers.

"You did nothing wrong, Isabel. Don't you see? This proves it."

Isabel turned to him.

"It does, doesn't it?"

"Look at the bottom."

Isabel hadn't even noticed yet the words at the very bottom of the page. They were so faint and difficult to read. They'd been written by hand, a note from the sender. She raised the paper to the light, but Monty took it from her.

He did not have to strain to make out what it said. He'd already done that. Many times.

Dr. Bott, he read, *I've still not received payment for the last list. AP.*

"AP," Isabel mused. "AP . . . Ariana Pitts! She worked in admissions. I saw Alistair talking to her the night Mrs. Hougham came in. Ariana would have had access to all the records."

"There's your connection. The reason so many of your ER patients ended up in Bott's studies."

Isabel sat stunned.

"This is proof. Proof I had nothing to do with it. Proof that Alistair knew he was recruiting patients who didn't belong in the studies."

A slow smile spread across her face, half joyous, but equally sad.

"I won't lose my license," she said softly. "I'll be able to clear my name . . ."

"And complete Phase III of the HantaVac study," Monty finished.

Isabel turned to stare at him, at this man who had risen like a phoenix from the ashes, bringing with him everything she cherished. The life she'd thought she lost.

He looked so incredibly noble and handsome. Like one of those chiefs her father used to show her in history books. Books about Native Americans. *Her* people.

Letting the paper fall to the floor, she pulled his lips to hers. Their kiss was sweet and tentative. The kiss of two people afraid to believe the moment was real.

"Thank you," she whispered, moving her mouth to his ear,

then down his sinewy neck. Monty uttered a low groan and pulled her down on to the bed.

Isabel reached for the light, to turn it out, but his hand caught hers.

"Don't. *Please*. I need to see you."

THEY SLEPT WELL beyond sunrise, beyond the hour that Gus usually arrived to check in on Isabel. For some reason he hadn't come this day. Isabel suspected the moccasin telegraph had been on fire since Monty showed up at the police station, and that word of his return had reached Gus.

"Does the fact that the FBI dropped charges mean you'll go free?"

She had been perched on her elbow, watching Monty sleep, waiting for his eyes to open. Waiting to ask the question foremost on her mind.

Monty brushed the back of his hand across his dry mouth and squinted against the bright morning sun filtering through the cabin's curtains.

"No matter how you look at it," he said somberly, "I killed a man."

"But it was self-defense."

"I was in the act of committing a felony, Isabel. Self-defense may not cut it. Even in tribal courts."

"But they'll understand. They'll know that you were set up. They know what happened to Leroy and . . ."

He pressed a finger to her lips, silencing her.

"I'll accept whatever the tribal courts decide. You have to too. The whole world will be watching. The tribal court must issue a fair ruling. And that may mean I end up in prison."

Stifling a sob, Isabel pressed a hand against the fluttering that had become so familiar in her abdomen. Slowly, eyes wide, Monty reached out and placed his large hand on top of hers.

"I'll wait for you as long as I have to," she whispered through tears.

Monty drew in a deep breath of morning air. Regardless of his fate in tribal court, his eyes mirrored a peace, even joy. He studied Isabel for a good long while before speaking.

"Did I ever tell you where we got the name Four Bear?"

Even through her tears, Isabel couldn't help but laugh.

"Where did that come from?" she asked. Then she saw the serious expression on Monty's face and said, "No, you haven't."

"My grandfather," Monty began, "Leroy's father, went by the name Spoonhunter most his life. He was an amazing man, a spiritual leader for my people. He'd go up on the mountain and fast for days. This one time he was up there and he saw this grizzly mama. She comes up to him where he's sitting on this rock, and pretty soon her three little cubs come along. Three cubs. That's almost unheard of. Grandfather used to tell how they sat there with him all that night. That he spoke to them and learned from them. That they had entered his spirit and he theirs. They started calling him Four Bear after that."

Isabel searched Monty's somber eyes, trying to understand.

"Why are you telling me this now?"

"Because I was hoping you'd consider taking my name," he answered.

He reached out and ran his finger along the angle of her jaw.

"And I thought you might like to know."

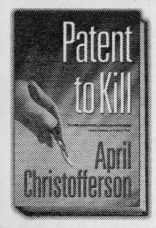

Deborah Har[...]ing author
of *A Discover*[...]e. A history
professor at the University of Southern California, Harkness has received
[...]bright, Guggenheim, and National Humanities Center fellowships.

[...]low Deborah on Twitter @DebHarkness and visit www.deborahharkness.
[...]m and www.facebook.com/AuthorDeborahHarkness.

Praise for Deborah Harkness:

'We literally fell head over stilettos in love with volume one in the
trilogy . . . If you loved *Twilight* but need to sink your teeth into a much
more meaty, intelligent and feisty story – with an addictive love thread to
boot – then read *A Discovery of Witches* quick' *Glamour*

'Gripping and impossible to put down, this is *Twilight* for grown ups – a
[...]nderful read!' Katie Fforde

'Romantic, erudite, and suspenseful' *O, The Oprah Magazine*

'One of the most exciting novels I've read in years . . . I fell in love with it
[...]om the very first page' Danielle Trussoni, author of *Angelology*

'This might just be a *Twilight* for the tweedy set' *Entertainment Weekly*

'A spellbinding saga . . . unputdownable' *Woman & Home*

'[...] vast, sexy, historical romp of a novel. There's no doubting Harkness's
[...]vid imagination' *Daily Mirror*

'[...]he perfect summer read' *Prima*

'[...] romp through magical academia' *Guardian*

For Lexie and Jake, and their bright futures

IT BEGINS WITH ABSENCE AND DESIRE.

IT BEGINS WITH BLOOD AND FEAR.

IT BEGINS WITH A DISCOVERY OF WITCHES.

CHAPTER 1

The leather-bound volume was nothing remarkable. To an ordinary historian, it would have looked no different from hundreds of other manuscripts in Oxford's Bodleian Library, ancient and worn. But I knew there was something odd about it from the moment I collected it.

Duke Humfrey's Reading Room was deserted on this late-September afternoon, and requests for library materials were filled quickly now that the summer crush of visiting scholars was over and the madness of the fall term had not yet begun. Even so, I was surprised when Sean stopped me at the call desk.

'Dr Bishop, your manuscripts are up,' he whispered, voice tinged with a touch of mischief. The front of his argyle sweater was streaked with the rusty traces of old leather bindings, and he brushed at it self-consciously. A lock of sandy hair tumbled over his forehead when he did.

'Thanks,' I said, flashing him a grateful smile. I was flagrantly disregarding the rules limiting the number of books a scholar could call in a single day. Sean, who'd shared many a drink with me in the pink-stuccoed pub across the street in our graduate-student days, had been filling my requests without complaint for more than a week. 'And stop calling me Dr Bishop. I always think you're talking to someone else.'

He grinned back and slid the manuscripts – all containing fine examples of alchemical illustrations from the Bodleian's collections – over his battered oak desk, each one tucked into a protective gray cardboard box. 'Oh, there's one more.' Sean disappeared into the cage for a moment and returned with a thick, quarto-size manuscript bound simply in mottled calfskin. He laid it on top of the pile and stooped to inspect it. The thin gold rims of his glasses sparked in the dim light provided by the old bronze reading lamp that was attached to a shelf. 'This one's not been called up for a while. I'll make a note that it needs to be boxed after you return it.'

'Do you want me to remind you?'

'No. Already made a note here.' Sean tapped his head with his fingertips.

'Your mind must be better organized than mine.' My smile widened.

Sean looked at me shyly and tugged on the call slip, but it remained where it was, lodged between the cover and the first pages. 'This one doesn't want to let go,' he commented.

Muffled voices chattered in my ear, intruding on the familiar hush of the room.

'Did you hear that?' I looked around, puzzled by the strange sounds.

'What?' Sean replied, looking up from the manuscript.

Traces of gilt shone along its edges and caught my eye. But those faded touches of gold could not account for a faint, iridescent shimmer that seemed to be escaping from between the pages. I blinked.

'Nothing.' I hastily drew the manuscript toward me, my skin prickling when it made contact with the leather. Sean's fingers were still holding the call slip, and now it slid easily out of the binding's grasp. I hoisted the volumes into my arms and tucked them under my chin, assailed by a whiff of the uncanny that drove away the library's familiar smell of pencil shavings and floor wax.

'Diana? Are you okay?' Sean asked with a concerned frown.

'Fine. Just a bit tired,' I replied, lowering the books away from my nose.

I walked quickly through the original, fifteenth-century part of the library, past the rows of Elizabethan reading desks with their three ascending bookshelves and scarred writing surfaces. Between them, Gothic windows directed the reader's attention up to the coffered ceilings, where bright paint and gilding picked out the details of the university's crest of three crowns and open book and where its motto, 'God is my illumination,' was proclaimed repeatedly from on high.

Another American academic, Gillian Chamberlain, was my sole companion in the library on this Friday night. A classicist who taught at Bryn Mawr, Gillian spent her time poring over scraps of papyrus sandwiched between sheets of glass. I sped past her, trying to avoid eye contact, but the creaking of the old floor gave me away.

My skin tingled as it always did when another witch looked at me.

'Diana?' she called from the gloom. I smothered a sigh and stopped.

'Hi, Gillian.' Unaccountably possessive of my hoard of manuscripts, I remained as far from the witch as possible and angled my body so they weren't in her line of sight.

'What are you doing for Mabon?' Gillian was always stopping by my desk to ask me to spend time with my 'sisters' while I was in town. With the Wiccan celebrations of the autumn equinox just days away, she was redoubling her efforts to bring me into the Oxford coven.

'Working,' I said promptly.

'There are some very nice witches here, you know,' Gillian said with prim disapproval. 'You really should join us on Monday.'

'Thanks. I'll think about it,' I said, already moving in the direction of the Selden End, the airy seventeenth-century addition that ran perpendicular to the main axis of Duke Humfrey's. 'I'm working on a conference paper, though, so don't count on it.' My aunt Sarah had always warned me it wasn't possible for one witch to lie to another, but that hadn't stopped me from trying.

Gillian made a sympathetic noise, but her eyes followed me.

Back at my familiar seat facing the arched, leaded windows, I resisted the temptation to dump the manuscripts on the table and wipe my hands. Instead, mindful of their age, I lowered the stack carefully.

The manuscript that had appeared to tug on its call slip lay on top of the pile. Stamped in gilt on the spine was a coat of arms belonging to Elias Ashmole, a seventeenth-century book collector and alchemist whose books and papers had come to the Bodleian from the Ashmolean Museum in the nineteenth century, along with the number 782. I reached out, touching the brown leather.

A mild shock made me withdraw my fingers quickly, but not quickly enough. The tingling traveled up my arms, lifting my skin into tiny goose pimples, then spread across my shoulders, tensing the muscles in my back and neck. These sensations quickly receded, but they left behind a hollow feeling of unmet desire. Shaken by my response, I stepped away from the library table.

Even at a safe distance, this manuscript was challenging me — threatening the walls I'd erected to separate my career as a scholar from my birthright as the last of the Bishop witches. Here, with my hard-earned doctorate, tenure, and promotions in hand and my career beginning to blossom, I'd renounced my family's heritage and created a life that depended on reason and scholarly abilities, not inexplicable hunches and spells. I was in Oxford to complete a research project. Upon its conclusion, my findings would be published, substantiated with extensive analysis and footnotes, and presented to human colleagues, leaving no room for mysteries and no place in my work for what could be known only through a witch's sixth sense.

But — albeit unwittingly — I had called up an alchemical manuscript that I needed for my research and that also seemed to possess an otherworldly power that was impossible to ignore. My fingers itched to open it and learn more. Yet an even stronger impulse held me back: Was my curiosity intellectual, related to my scholarship? Or did it have to do with my family's connection to witchcraft?

I drew the library's familiar air into my lungs and shut my eyes, hoping that would bring clarity. The Bodleian had always been a sanctuary to me, a place unassociated with the Bishops. Tucking my shaking hands under my elbows, I stared at Ashmole 782 in the growing twilight and wondered what to do.

My mother would instinctively have known the answer, had she been standing in my place. Most members of the Bishop family were talented witches, but my mother, Rebecca, was special. Everyone said so. Her supernatural abilities had manifested early, and by the time she was in grade school, she could outmagic most of the senior witches in the local coven with her intuitive understanding of spells, startling foresight, and uncanny knack for seeing beneath the surface of people and events. My mother's younger sister, my Aunt Sarah, was a skilled witch, too, but her talents were more mainstream: a deft hand with potions and a perfect command of witchcraft's traditional lore of spells and charms.

My fellow historians didn't know about the family, of course, but everyone in Madison, the remote town in upstate New York where I'd lived with Sarah since the age of seven, knew all about the Bishops. My ancestors had moved from Massachusetts after the Revolutionary War. By then more than a century had passed since Bridget Bishop was executed at Salem. Even so, rumors and gossip followed them to their new home. After pulling up stakes and resettling in Madison, the Bishops worked hard to demonstrate how useful it could be to have witchy neighbors for healing the sick and predicting the weather. In time the family set down roots in the community deep enough to withstand the inevitable outbreaks of superstition and human fear.

But my mother had a curiosity about the world that led her beyond the safety of Madison. She went first to Harvard, where she met a young wizard named Stephen Proctor. He also had a long magical lineage and a desire to experience life outside the scope of his family's New England history and influence. Rebecca Bishop and Stephen Proctor were a charming couple, my mother's all-American frankness a counterpoint to my father's more formal, old-fashioned ways. They became anthropologists, immersing themselves in foreign cultures and beliefs, sharing their intellectual passions along with their deep devotion to each other. After securing positions on the faculty in area schools – my mother at her alma mater, my father at Wellesley – they made research trips abroad and made a home for their new family in Cambridge.

I have few memories of my childhood, but each one is vivid and surprisingly clear. All feature my parents: the feel of corduroy on my father's elbows, the lily of the valley that scented my mother's perfume, the clink of their wineglasses on Friday nights when they'd put me to bed and dine together by candlelight. My mother told me bedtime stories, and my father's brown briefcase clattered when he dropped it by the front door. These memories would strike a familiar chord with most people.

Other recollections of my parents would not. My mother never seemed to do laundry, but my clothes were always clean and neatly folded. Forgotten permission slips for field trips to the zoo appeared in my desk when the teacher came to collect them. And no matter what condition my father's study was in when I went in for a goodnight kiss (and it usually looked as if something had exploded), it was always perfectly orderly the next morning. In kindergarten I'd asked my friend Amanda's mother why she bothered washing the dishes with soap and water when all you needed to do was stack them in the sink, snap your fingers, and whisper a few words. Mrs Schmidt laughed at my strange idea of housework, but confusion had clouded her eyes.

That night my parents told me we had to be careful about how we spoke about magic and with whom we discussed it. Humans outnumbered us and found our power frightening, my mother explained, and fear was the strongest force on earth. I hadn't confessed at the time that magic – my mother's especially – frightened me, too.

By day my mother looked like every other kid's mother in Cambridge: slightly unkempt, a bit disorganized, and perpetually harassed by the pressures of home and office. Her blond hair was fashionably tousled even though the clothes she wore remained stuck in 1977 – long billowy skirts, oversize pants and shirts, and men's vests and blazers she picked up in thrift stores the length and breadth of Boston in imitation of Annie Hall. Nothing would have made you look twice if you passed her in the street or stood behind her in the supermarket.

In the privacy of our home, with the curtains drawn and the door locked, my mother became someone else. Her movements were confident and sure, not rushed and hectic. Sometimes she even seemed to float. As she went around the house, singing and picking up stuffed animals and books, her face slowly transformed into something otherworldly and beautiful. When my mother was lit up with magic, you couldn't tear your eyes away from her.

'Mommy's got a firecracker inside her,' was the way my father explained it with his wide, indulgent grin. But firecrackers, I learned, were not simply bright and lively. They were unpredictable, and they could startle and frighten you, too.

My father was at a lecture one night when my mother decided to clean the silver and became mesmerized by a bowl of water she'd set on the dining-room table. As she stared at the glassy surface, it became covered with a fog that twisted itself into tiny, ghostly shapes. I gasped with delight as they grew, filling the room with fantastic beings. Soon they were crawling up the drapes and clinging to the ceiling. I cried out for my mother's help, but she remained intent on the water. Her concentration didn't waver until something half human and half animal crept near and pinched my arm. That brought her out of her reveries, and she exploded into a shower of angry red light that beat back the wraiths and left an odor of singed feathers in the house. My father noticed the strange smell the moment he returned, his alarm evident. He found us huddled in bed together. At the sight of him, my mother burst into apologetic tears. I never felt entirely safe in the dining room again.

Any remaining sense of security evaporated after I turned seven, when my mother and father went to Africa and didn't come back alive.

I shook myself and focused again on the dilemma that faced me. The manuscript sat on the library table in a pool of lamplight. Its magic pulled on something dark and knotted inside me. My fingers returned to the smooth leather. This time the prickling sensation felt familiar. I vaguely remembered experiencing something like it once before, looking through some papers on the desk in my father's study.

Turning resolutely away from the leather-bound volume, I occupied myself with something more rational: searching for the list of alchemical texts I'd generated before leaving New Haven. It was on my desk, hidden among the loose papers, book call slips, receipts, pencils, pens, and library maps, neatly arranged by collection and then by the number assigned to each text by a library clerk when it had entered into the Bodleian. Since arriving a few weeks ago, I had been working through the list methodically. The copied-out catalog description for Ashmole 782 read, '*Anthropologia, or a treatis containing a short description of Man in two parts: the first Anatomical, the second Psychological.*' As with most of the works I studied, there was no telling what the contents were from the title.

My fingers might be able to tell me about the book without even cracking open the covers. Aunt Sarah always used her fingers to figure out what was in the mail before she opened it, in case the envelope contained a bill she didn't want to pay. That way she could plead ignorance when it turned out she owed the electric company money.

The gilt numbers on the spine winked.

I sat down and considered the options.

Ignore the magic, open the manuscript, and try to read it like a human scholar?

Push the bewitched volume aside and walk away?

Sarah would chortle with delight if she knew my predicament. She had always maintained that my efforts to keep magic at arm's length were futile. But I'd been doing so ever since my parents' funeral. There the witches among the guests had scrutinized me for signs that the Bishop and Proctor blood was in my veins, all the while patting me encouragingly and predicting it was only a matter of time before I took my mother's place in the local coven. Some had whispered their doubts about the wisdom of my parents' decision to marry.

'Too much power,' they muttered when they thought I wasn't listening. 'They were bound to attract attention – even without studying ancient ceremonial religion.'

This was enough to make me blame my parents' death on the supernatural power they wielded and to search for a different way of life. Turning my back on anything to do with magic, I buried myself in the stuff of human adolescence – horses and boys and romantic novels – and tried to disappear among the town's ordinary residents. At puberty I had problems with depression and anxiety. It was all very normal, the kindly human doctor assured my aunt.

Sarah didn't tell him about the voices, about my habit of picking up the phone a good minute before it rang, or that she had to enchant the doors and windows when there was a full moon to keep me from wandering into the woods in my sleep. Nor did she mention that when I was angry the chairs in the house rearranged themselves into a precarious pyramid before crashing to the floor once my mood lifted.

When I turned thirteen, my aunt decided it was time for me to channel some of my power into learning the basics of witchcraft. Lighting candles with a few whispered words or hiding pimples with a time-tested potion – these were a teenage witch's habitual first steps. But I was unable to master even the simplest spell, burned every potion my aunt taught me, and stubbornly refused to submit to her tests to see if I'd inherited my mother's uncannily accurate second sight.

The voices, the fires, and other unexpected eruptions lessened as my hormones quieted, but my unwillingness to learn the family business remained. It made my aunt anxious to have an untrained witch in the house, and it was with some relief that Sarah sent me off to a college in Maine. Except for the magic, it was a typical coming-of-age story.

What got me away from Madison was my intellect. It had always been precocious, leading me to talk and read before other children my age. Aided by a prodigious, photographic memory – which made it easy for me to recall the layouts of textbooks and spit out the required information on tests – my schoolwork was soon established as a place where my family's magical legacy was irrelevant. I'd skipped my final years of high school and started college at sixteen.

There I'd first tried to carve out a place for myself in the theater department, my imagination drawn to the spectacle and the costumes

— and my mind fascinated by how completely a playwright's words could conjure up other places and times. My first few performances were heralded by my professors as extraordinary examples of the way good acting could transform an ordinary college student into someone else. The first indication that these metamorphoses might not have been the result of theatrical talent came while I was playing Ophelia in *Hamlet*. As soon as I was cast in the role, my hair started growing at an unnatural rate, tumbling down from shoulders to waist. I sat for hours beside the college's lake, irresistibly drawn to its shining surface, with my new hair streaming all around me. The boy playing Hamlet became caught up in the illusion, and we had a passionate though dangerously volatile affair. Slowly I was dissolving into Ophelia's madness, taking the rest of the cast with me.

The result might have been a riveting performance, but each new role brought fresh challenges. In my sophomore year, the situation became impossible when I was cast as Annabella in John Ford's *'Tis Pity She's a Whore*. Like the character, I attracted a string of devoted suitors — not all of them human — who followed me around campus. When they refused to leave me alone after the final curtain fell, it was clear that whatever had been unleashed couldn't be controlled. I wasn't sure how magic had crept into my acting, and I didn't want to find out. I cut my hair short. I stopped wearing flowing skirts and layered tops in favor of the black turtlenecks, khaki trousers, and loafers that the solid, ambitious prelaw students were wearing. My excess energy went into athletics.

After leaving the theater department, I attempted several more majors, looking for a field so rational that it would never yield a square inch to magic. I lacked the precision and patience for mathematics, and my efforts at biology were a disaster of failed quizzes and unfinished laboratory experiments.

At the end of my sophomore year, the registrar demanded I choose a major or face a fifth year in college. A summer study program in England offered me the opportunity to get even farther from all things Bishop. I fell in love with Oxford, the quiet glow of its morning streets. My history courses covered the exploits of kings and queens, and the only voices in my head were those that whispered from books penned in the sixteenth and seventeenth centuries. This was entirely attributable to great literature. Best of all, no one in this university town knew me, and if there were witches in the city that summer, they stayed well away. I returned home, declared a major in history, took all the required courses in record time, and graduated with honors before I turned twenty.

When I decided to pursue my doctorate, Oxford was my first choice among the possible programs. My specialty was the history of science, and my research focused on the period when science supplanted magic – the age when astrology and witch-hunts yielded to Newton and universal laws. The search for a rational order in nature, rather than a supernatural one, mirrored my own efforts to stay away from what was hidden. The lines I'd already drawn between what went on in my mind and what I carried in my blood grew more distinct.

My Aunt Sarah had snorted when she heard of my decision to specialize in seventeenth-century chemistry. Her bright red hair was an outward sign of her quick temper and sharp tongue. She was a plain-speaking, no-nonsense witch who commanded a room as soon as she entered it. A pillar of the Madison community, Sarah was often called in to manage things when there was a crisis, large or small, in town. We were on much better terms now that I wasn't subjected to a daily dose of her keen observations on human frailty and inconsistency.

Though we were separated by hundreds of miles, Sarah thought my latest attempts to avoid magic were laughable – and told me so. 'We used to call that alchemy,' she said. 'There's a lot of magic in it.'

'No, there's not,' I protested hotly. The whole point of my work was to show how scientific this pursuit really was. 'Alchemy tells us about the growth of experimentation, not the search for a magical elixir that turns lead into gold and makes people immortal.'

'If you say so,' Sarah said doubtfully. 'But it's a pretty strange subject to choose if you're trying to pass as human.'

After earning my degree, I fought fiercely for a spot on the faculty at Yale, the only place that was more English than England. Colleagues warned that I had little chance of being granted tenure. I churned out two books, won a handful of prizes, and collected some research grants. Then I received tenure and proved everyone wrong.

More important, my life was now my own. No one in my department, not even the historians of early America, connected my last name with that of the first Salem woman executed for witchcraft in 1692. To preserve my hard-won autonomy, I continued to keep any hint of magic or witchcraft out of my life. Of course there were exceptions, like the time I'd drawn on one of Sarah's spells when the washing machine wouldn't stop filling with water and threatened to flood my small apartment on Wooster Square. Nobody's perfect.

Now, taking note of this current lapse, I held my breath, grasped the manuscript with both hands, and placed it in one of the wedge-shaped cradles the library provided to protect its rare books. I had made my decision: to behave as a serious scholar and treat Ashmole 782 like an ordinary manuscript. I'd ignore my burning fingertips, the book's strange smell, and simply describe its contents. Then I'd decide – with professional detachment – whether it was promising enough for a longer look. My fingers trembled when I loosened the small brass clasps nevertheless.

The manuscript let out a soft sigh.

A quick glance over my shoulder assured me that the room was still empty. The only other sound was the loud ticking of the reading room's clock.

Deciding not to record 'Book sighed,' I turned to my laptop and opened up a new file. This familiar task – one that I'd done hundreds if not thousands of times before – was as comforting as my list's neat checkmarks. I typed the manuscript name and number and copied the title from the catalog description. I eyed its size and binding, describing both in detail.

The only thing left to do was open the manuscript.

It was difficult to lift the cover, despite the loosened clasps, as if it were stuck to the pages below. I swore under my breath and rested my hand flat on the leather for a moment, hoping that Ashmole 782 simply needed a chance to know me. It wasn't magic, exactly, to put your hand on top of a book. My palm tingled, much as my skin tingled when a witch looked at me, and the tension left the manuscript. After that, it was easy to lift the cover.

The first page was rough paper. On the second sheet, which was parchment, were the words '*Anthropologia, or a treatis containing a short description of Man,*' in Ashmole's handwriting. The neat, round curves were almost as familiar to me as my own cursive script. The second part of the title – '*in two parts: the first Anatomical, the second Psychological*' – was written in a later hand, in pencil. It was familiar, too, but I couldn't place it. Touching the writing might give me some clue, but it was against the library's rules and it would be impossible to document the information that my fingers might gather. Instead I made notes in the computer file regarding the use of ink and pencil, the two different hands, and the possible dates of the inscriptions.

As I turned the first page, the parchment felt abnormally heavy and revealed itself as the source of the manuscript's strange smell. It wasn't simply ancient. It was something more – a combination of must and musk that had no name. And I noticed immediately that three leaves had been cut neatly out of the binding.

Here, at last, was something easy to describe. My fingers flew over the keys: '*At least three folios removed, by straightedge or razor.*' I peered into the valley of the manuscript's spine but couldn't tell whether any other pages were missing. The closer the parchment to my nose, the more the manuscript's power and odd smell distracted me.

I turned my attention to the illustration that faced the gap where the missing pages should be. It showed a tiny baby girl floating in a clear glass vessel. The baby held a silver rose in one hand, a golden rose in the other. On its feet were tiny wings, and drops of red liquid showered down on the baby's long black hair. Underneath the image was a label written in thick black ink indicating that it was a depiction of the philosophical child – an allegorical representation of a crucial step in creating the philosopher's stone, the chemical substance that promised to make its owner healthy, wealthy, and wise.

The colors were luminous and strikingly well preserved. Artists had once mixed crushed stone and gems into their paints to produce such powerful colors. And the image itself had been drawn by someone with real artistic skill. I had to sit on my hands to keep them from trying to learn more from a touch here and there.

But the illuminator, for all his obvious talent, had the details all wrong. The glass vessel was supposed to point up, not down. The baby was supposed to be half black and half white, to show that it was a hermaphrodite. It should have had male genitalia and female breasts – or two heads, at the very least.

Alchemical imagery was allegorical, and notoriously tricky. That's why I was studying it, searching for patterns that would reveal a systematic, logical approach to chemical transformation in the days before the periodic table of the elements. Images of the moon were almost always representations of silver, for example, while images of the sun referred to gold. When the two were combined chemically, the process was represented as a wedding. In time the pictures had been replaced by words. Those words, in turn, became the grammar of chemistry.

But this manuscript put my belief in the alchemists' logic to the test. Each illustration had at least one fundamental flaw, and there was no accompanying text to help make sense of it.

I searched for something – anything – that would agree with my knowledge of alchemy. In the softening light, faint traces of hand-writing appeared on one of the pages. I slanted the desk lamp so that it shone more brightly.

There was nothing there.

Slowly I turned the page as if it were a fragile leaf.

Words shimmered and moved across its surface – hundreds of words – invisible unless the angle of light and the viewer's perspective were just right.

I stifled a cry of surprise.

Ashmole 782 was a palimpsest – a manuscript within a manuscript. When parchment was scarce, scribes carefully washed the ink from old books and then wrote new text on the blank sheets. Over time the former writing often reappeared underneath as a textual ghost, discernible with the help of ultraviolet light, which could see under ink stains and bring faded text back to life.

There was no ultraviolet light strong enough to reveal these traces, though. This was not an ordinary palimpsest. The writing hadn't been washed away — it had been hidden with some sort of spell. But why would anyone go to the trouble of bewitching the text in an alchemical book? Even experts had trouble puzzling out the obscure language and fanciful imagery the authors used.

Dragging my attention from the faint letters that were moving too quickly for me to read, I focused instead on writing a synopsis of the manuscript's contents. '*Puzzling*,' I typed. '*Textual captions from the fifteenth to seventeenth centuries, images mainly fifteenth century. Image sources possibly older? Mixture of paper and vellum. Colored and black inks, the former of unusually high quality. Illustrations are well executed, but details are incorrect, missing. Depicts the creation of the philosopher's stone, alchemical birth/creation, death, resurrection, and transformation. A confused copy of an earlier manuscript? A strange book, full of anomalies.*'

My fingers hesitated above the keys.

Scholars do one of two things when they discover information that doesn't fit what they already know. Either they sweep it aside so it doesn't bring their cherished theories into question or they focus on it with laserlike intensity and try to get to the bottom of the mystery. If this book hadn't been under a spell, I might have been tempted to do the latter. Because it was bewitched, I was strongly inclined toward the former.

And when in doubt, scholars usually postpone a decision.

I typed an ambivalent final line: '*Needs more time? Possibly recall later?*'

Holding my breath, I fastened the cover with a gentle tug. Currents of magic still thrummed through the manuscript, especially fierce around the clasps.

Relieved that it was closed, I stared at Ashmole 782 for a few more moments. My fingers wanted to stray back and touch the brown leather. But this time I resisted, just as I had resisted touching the inscriptions and illustrations to learn more than a human historian could legitimately claim to know.

Aunt Sarah had always told me that magic was a gift. If it was, it had strings attached that bound me to all the Bishop witches who had come before me. There was a price to be paid for using this inherited magical power and for working the spells and charms that made up the witches' carefully guarded craft. By opening Ashmole 782, I'd breached the wall that divided my magic from my scholarship. But back on the right side of it again, I was more determined than ever to remain there.

I packed up my computer and notes and picked up the stack of manuscripts, carefully putting Ashmole 782 on the bottom. Mercifully, Gillian wasn't at her desk, though her papers were still strewn around. She must be planning on working late and was off for a cup of coffee.

'Finished?' Sean asked when I reached the call desk.

'Not quite. I'd like to reserve the top three for Monday.'

'And the fourth?'

'I'm done with it,' I blurted, pushing the manuscripts toward him. 'You can send it back to the stacks.'

Sean put it on top of a pile of returns he had already gathered. He walked with me as far as the staircase, said good-bye, and disappeared behind a swinging door. The conveyor belt that would whisk Ashmole 782 back into the bowels of the library clanged into action.

I almost turned and stopped him but let it go.

My hand was raised to push open the door on the ground floor when the air around me constricted, as if the library were squeezing me tight. The air shimmered for a split second, just as the pages of the manuscript had shimmered on Sean's desk, causing me to shiver involuntarily and raising the tiny hairs on my arms.

Something had just happened. Something magical.

My face turned back toward Duke Humfrey's, and my feet threatened to follow.

It's nothing, I thought, resolutely walking out of the library.

Are you sure? whispered a long-ignored voice.

CHAPTER 2

Oxford's bells chimed seven times. Night didn't follow twilight as slowly as it would have a few months ago, but the transformation was still lingering. The library staff had turned on the lamps only thirty minutes before, casting small pools of gold in the gray light.

It was the twenty-first day of September. All over the world, witches were sharing a meal on the eve of the autumn equinox to celebrate Mabon and greet the impending darkness of winter. But the witches of Oxford would have to do without me. I was slated to give the keynote address at an important conference next month. My ideas were still unformed, and I was getting anxious.

At the thought of what my fellow witches might be eating somewhere in Oxford, my stomach rumbled. I'd been in the library since half past nine that morning, with only a short break for lunch.

Sean had taken the day off, and the person working at the call desk was new. She'd given me some trouble when I requested one crumbling item and tried to convince me to use microfilm instead. The reading room's supervisor, Mr Johnson, overheard and came out of his office to intervene.

'My apologies, Dr Bishop,' he'd said hurriedly, pushing his heavy, dark-rimmed glasses over the bridge of his nose. 'If you need to consult this manuscript for your research, we will be happy to oblige.' He disappeared to fetch the restricted item and delivered it with more apologies about the inconvenience and the new staff. Gratified that my scholarly credentials had done the trick, I spent the afternoon happily reading.

I pulled two coiled weights from the upper corners of the manuscript and closed it carefully, pleased at the amount of work I'd completed. After encountering the bewitched manuscript on Friday, I'd devoted the weekend to routine tasks rather than alchemy in order to restore a sense of normalcy. I filled out financial-reimbursement forms, paid bills, wrote letters of recommendation, and even finished a book review. These chores were interspersed with more homely rituals like doing laundry, drinking copious amounts of tea, and trying recipes from the BBC's cooking programs.

After an early start this morning, I'd spent the day trying to focus on the work at hand, rather than dwelling on my recollections of Ashmole 782's strange illustrations and mysterious palimpsest. I eyed the short list of to-dos jotted down over the course of the day. Of the four questions on my follow-up list, the third was easiest to resolve. The answer was in an arcane periodical, *Notes and Queries*, which was shelved on one of the bookcases that stretched up toward the room's high ceilings. I pushed back my chair and decided to tick one item off my list before leaving.

The upper shelves of the section of Duke Humfrey's known as the Selden End were reachable by means of a worn set of stairs to a gallery that looked over the reading desks. I climbed the twisting treads to where the old buckram-covered books sat in neat chrono-logical rows on wooden shelves. No one but me and an ancient literature don from Magdalen College seemed to use them. I located the volume and swore softly under my breath. It was on the top shelf, just out of reach.

A low chuckle startled me. I turned my head to see who was sitting at the desk at the far end of the gallery, but no one was there. I was hearing things again. Oxford was still a ghost town, and anyone who belonged to the university had left over an hour earlier to down a glass of free sherry in their college's senior common room before dinner. Given the Wiccan holiday, even Gillian had left in the late afternoon, after extending one final invitation and glancing at my pile of reading material with narrowed eyes.

I searched for the gallery's stepstool, which was missing.

The Bodleian was notoriously short on such items, and it would easily take fifteen minutes to locate one in the library and haul it upstairs so that I could retrieve the volume. I hesitated. Even though I'd held a bewitched book, I'd resisted considerable temptations to work further magic on Friday. Besides, no one would see.

Despite my rationalizations, my skin prickled with anxiety. I didn't break my rules very often, and I kept mental accounts of the situations that had spurred me to turn to my magic for assistance. This was the fifth time this year, including putting the spell on the malfunctioning washing machine and touching Ashmole 782. Not too bad for the end of September, but not a personal best either.

I took a deep breath, held up my hand, and imagined the book in it.

Volume 19 of *Notes and Queries* slid backward four inches, tipped at an angle as if an invisible hand were pulling it down, and fell into my open palm with a soft thwack. Once there, it flopped open to the page I needed.

It had taken all of three seconds. I let out another breath to exhale some of my guilt. Suddenly two icy patches bloomed between my shoulder blades.

I had been seen, and not by an ordinary human observer.

When one witch studies another, the touch of their eyes tingles. Witches aren't the only creatures sharing the world with humans, however. There are also daemons – creative, artistic creatures who walk a tightrope between madness and genius. 'Rock stars and serial killers' was how my aunt described these strange, perplexing beings. And there are vampires, ancient and beautiful, who feed on blood and will charm you utterly if they don't kill you first.

When a daemon takes a look, I feel the slight, unnerving pressure of a kiss.

But when a vampire stares, it feels cold, focused, and dangerous.

I mentally shuffled through the readers in Duke Humfrey's. There had been one vampire, a cherubic monk who pored over medieval missals and prayer books like a lover. But vampires aren't often found in rare-book rooms. Occasionally one succumbed to vanity and nostalgia and came in to reminisce, but it wasn't common.

Witches and daemons were far more typical in libraries. Gillian Chamberlain had been in today, studying her papyri with a magnifying glass. And there were definitely two daemons in the music reference room. They'd looked up, dazed, as I walked by on the way to Blackwell's for tea. One told me to bring him back a latte, which was some indication of how immersed he was in whatever madness gripped him at the moment.

No, it was a vampire who watched me now.

I'd happened upon a few vampires, since I worked in a field that put me in touch with scientists, and there were vampires aplenty in laboratories around the world. Science rewards long study and patience. And thanks to their solitary work habits, scientists were unlikely to be recognized by anyone except their closest co-workers. It made a life that spanned centuries rather than decades much easier to negotiate.

These days vampires gravitated toward particle accelerators, projects to decode the genome, and molecular biology. Once they had flocked to alchemy, anatomy, and electricity. If it went bang, involved blood, or promised to unlock the secrets of the universe, there was sure to be a vampire around.

I clutched my ill-gotten copy of *Notes and Queries* and turned to face the witness. He was in the shadows on the opposite side of the room in front of the paleography reference books, lounging against one of the graceful wooden pillars that held up the gallery. An open copy of Janet Roberts's *Guide to Scripts Used in English Handwriting Up to 1500* was balanced in his hands.

I had never seen this vampire before — but I was fairly certain he didn't need pointers on how to decipher old penmanship.

Anyone who has read paperback bestsellers or even watched television knows that vampires are breathtaking, but nothing prepares you to actually see one. Their bone structures are so well honed that they seem chiseled by an expert sculptor. Then they move, or speak, and your mind can't begin to absorb what you're seeing. Every movement is graceful; every word is musical. And their eyes are arresting, which is precisely how they catch their prey. One long look, a few quiet words, a touch: once you're caught in a vampire's snare you don't stand a chance.

Staring down at this vampire, I realized with a sinking feeling that my knowledge on the subject was, alas, largely theoretical. Little of it seemed useful now that I was facing one in the Bodleian Library.

The only vampire with whom I had more than a passing acquaintance worked at the nuclear particle accelerator in Switzerland. Jeremy was slight and gorgeous, with bright blond hair, blue eyes, and an infectious laugh. He'd slept with most of the women in the canton of Geneva and was now working his way through the city of Lausanne. What he did after he seduced them I had never wanted to inquire into too closely, and I'd turned down his persistent invitations to go out for a drink. I'd always figured that Jeremy was representative of the breed. But in comparison to the one who stood before me now, he seemed raw-boned, gawky, and very, very young.

This one was tall – well over six feet even accounting for the problems of perspective associated with looking down on him from the gallery. And he definitely was not slight. Broad shoulders narrowed into slender hips, which flowed into lean, muscular legs. His hands were strikingly long and agile, a mark of physiological delicacy that made your eyes drift back to them to figure out how they could belong to such a large man.

As my eyes swept over him, his own were fixed on me. From across the room, they seemed black as night, staring up under thick, equally black eyebrows, one of them lifted in a curve that suggested a question mark. His face was indeed striking – all distinct planes and surfaces, with high-angled cheekbones meeting brows that shielded and shadowed his eyes. Above his chin was one of the few places where there was room for softness – his wide mouth, which, like his long hands, didn't seem to make sense.

But the most unnerving thing about him was not his physical perfection. It was his feral combination of strength, agility, and keen intelligence that was palpable across the room. In his black trousers and soft gray sweater, with a shock of black hair swept back from his forehead and cropped close to the nape of his neck, he looked like a panther that could strike at any moment but was in no rush to do so.

He smiled. It was a small, polite smile that didn't reveal his teeth. I was intensely aware of them anyway, sitting in perfectly straight, sharp rows behind his pale lips.

The mere thought of *teeth* sent an instinctive rush of adrenaline through my body, setting my fingers tingling. Suddenly all I could think was, *Get out of this room NOW*.

The staircase seemed farther away than the four steps it took to reach it. I raced down to the floor below, stumbled on the last step, and pitched straight into the vampire's waiting arms.

Of course he had beaten me to the bottom of the stairs.

His fingers were cool, and his arms felt steelier than flesh and bone. The scent of clove, cinnamon, and something that reminded me of incense filled the air. He set me on my feet, picked *Notes and Queries* off the floor, and handed it to me with a small bow. 'Dr Bishop, I presume?'

Shaking from head to toe, I nodded.

The long, pale fingers of his right hand dipped into a pocket and pulled out a blue-and-white business card. He extended it. 'Matthew Clairmont.'

I gripped the edge of the card, careful not to touch his fingers in the process. Oxford University's familiar logo, with the three crowns and open book, was perched next to Clairmont's name, followed by a string of initials indicating he had already been made a member of the Royal Society.

Not bad for someone who appeared to be in his mid- to late thirties, though I imagined that his actual age was at least ten times that.

As for his research specialty, it came as no surprise that the vampire was a professor of biochemistry and affiliated with Oxford Neuroscience at the John Radcliffe Hospital. Blood and anatomy — two vampire favorites. The card bore three different laboratory numbers in addition to an office number and an e-mail address. I might not have seen him before, but he was certainly not unreachable.

'Professor Clairmont.' I squeaked it out before the words caught in the back of my throat, and I quieted the urge to run screaming toward the exit.

'We've not met,' he continued in an oddly accented voice. It was mostly Oxbridge but had a touch of softness that I couldn't place. His eyes, which never left my face, were not actually dark at all, I discovered, but dominated by dilated pupils bordered with a gray-green sliver of iris. Their pull was insistent, and I found myself unable to look away.

The vampire's mouth was moving again. 'I'm a great admirer of your work.'

My eyes widened. It was not impossible that a professor of bio-chemistry would be interested in seventeenth-century alchemy, but it seemed highly unlikely. I picked at the collar of my white shirt and scanned the room. We were the only two in it. There was no one at the old oak card file or at the nearby banks of computers. Whoever was at the collection desk was too far away to come to my aid.

'I found your article on the color symbolism of alchemical trans-formation fascinating, and your work on Robert Boyle's approach to the problems of expansion and contraction was quite persuasive,' Clairmont continued smoothly, as if he were used to being the only active participant in a conversation. 'I've not yet finished your latest book on alchemical apprenticeship and education, but I'm enjoying it a great deal.'

'Thank you,' I whispered. His gaze shifted from my eyes to my throat.

I stopped picking at the buttons around my neck.

His unnatural eyes floated back to mine. 'You have a marvelous way of evoking the past for your readers.' I took that as a compliment, since a vampire would know if it was wrong. Clairmont paused for a moment. 'Might I buy you dinner?'

My mouth dropped open. Dinner? I might not be able to escape from him in the library, but there was no reason to linger over a meal – especially one he would not be sharing, given his dietary preferences.

'I have plans,' I said abruptly, unable to formulate a reasonable explanation of what those plans might involve. Matthew Clairmont must know I was a witch, and I was clearly not celebrating Mabon.

'That's too bad,' he murmured, a touch of a smile on his lips. 'Another time, perhaps. You are in Oxford for the year, aren't you?'

Being around a vampire was always unnerving, and Clairmont's clove scent brought back the strange smell of Ashmole 782. Unable to think straight, I resorted to nodding. It was safer.

'I thought so,' said Clairmont. 'I'm sure our paths will cross again. Oxford is such a small town.'

'Very small,' I agreed, wishing I had taken leave in London instead.

'Until then, Dr Bishop. It has been a pleasure.' Clairmont extended his hand. With the exception of their brief excursion to my collar, his eyes had not drifted once from mine. I didn't think he had blinked either. I steeled myself not to be the first to look away.

My hand went forward, hesitating for a moment before clasping his. There was a fleeting pressure before he withdrew. He stepped backward, smiled, then disappeared into the darkness of the oldest part of the library.

I stood still until my chilled hands could move freely again, then walked back to my desk and switched off my computer. *Notes and Queries* asked me accusingly why I had bothered to go and get it if I wasn't even going to look at it; my to-do list was equally full of reproach. I ripped it off the top of the pad, crumpled it up, and tossed it into the wicker basket under the desk.

' "*Sufficient unto the day is the evil thereof*," ' I muttered under my breath.

The reading room's night proctor glanced down at his watch when I returned my manuscripts. 'Leaving early, Dr Bishop?'

I nodded, my lips closed tightly to keep myself from asking whether he knew there had been a vampire in the paleography reference section.

He picked up the stack of gray cardboard boxes that held the manuscripts. 'Will you need these tomorrow?'

'Yes,' I whispered. 'Tomorrow.'

Having observed the last scholarly propriety of exiting the library, I was free. My feet clattered against the linoleum floors and echoed against the stone walls as I sped through the reading room's lattice gate, past the books guarded with velvet ropes to keep them from curious fingers, down the worn wooden stairs, and into the enclosed quadrangle on the ground floor. I leaned against the iron railings surrounding the bronze statue of William Herbert and sucked the chilly air into my lungs, struggling to get the vestiges of clove and cinnamon out of my nostrils.

There were always things that went bump in the night in Oxford, I told myself sternly. So there was one more vampire in town.

No matter what I told myself in the quadrangle, my walk home was faster than usual. The gloom of New College Lane was a spooky proposition at the best of times. I ran my card through the reader at New College's back gate and felt some of the tension leave my body when the gate clicked shut behind me, as if every door and wall I put between me and the library somehow kept me safe. I skirted under the chapel windows and through the narrow passage into the quad that had views of Oxford's only surviving medieval garden, complete with the traditional mound that had once offered a green prospect for students to look upon and contemplate the mysteries of God and nature. Tonight the college's spires and archways seemed especially Gothic, and I was eager to get inside.

When the door of my apartment closed behind me, I let out a sigh of relief. I was living at the top of one of the college's faculty staircases, in lodgings reserved for visiting former members. My rooms, which included a bedroom, a sitting room with a round table for dining, and a decent if small kitchen, were decorated with old prints and warm wainscoting. All the furniture looked as if it had been culled from previous incarnations of the senior common room and the master's house, with down-at-the-heels late-nineteenth-century design predominant.

In the kitchen I put two slices of bread in the toaster and poured myself a cold glass of water. Gulping it down, I opened the window to let cool air into the stuffy rooms.

Carrying my snack back into the sitting room, I kicked off my shoes and turned on the small stereo. The pure tones of Mozart filled the air. When I sat on one of the maroon upholstered sofas, it was with the intention to rest for a few moments, then take a bath and go over my notes from the day.

At half past three in the morning, I woke with a pounding heart, a stiff neck, and the strong taste of cloves in my mouth.

I got a fresh glass of water and closed the kitchen window. It was chilly, and I shivered at the touch of the damp air.

After a glance at my watch and some quick calculations, I decided to call home. It was only ten-thirty there, and Sarah and Em were as nocturnal as bats. Slipping around the rooms, I turned off all the lights except the one in my bedroom and picked up my mobile. I was out of my grimy clothes in a matter of minutes – how do you get so filthy in a library? – and into a pair of old yoga pants and a black sweater with a stretched-out neck. They were more comfortable than any pajamas.

The bed felt welcoming and firm underneath me, comforting me enough that I almost convinced myself a phone call home was unnecessary. But the water had not been able to remove the vestiges of cloves from my tongue, and I dialed the number.

'We've been waiting for your call,' were the first words I heard.

Witches.

I sighed. 'Sarah, I'm fine.'

'All signs to the contrary.' As usual, my mother's younger sister was not going to pull any punches. 'Tabitha has been skittish all evening, Em got a very clear picture of you lost in the woods at night, and I haven't been able to eat anything since breakfast.'

The real problem was that damn cat. Tabitha was Sarah's baby and picked up any tension within the family with uncanny precision. 'I'm *fine*. I had an unexpected encounter in the library tonight, that's all.'

A click told me that Em had picked up the extension. 'Why aren't you celebrating Mabon?' she asked.

Emily Mather had been a fixture in my life for as long as I could remember. She and Rebecca Bishop had met as high-school students working in the summer at Plimoth Plantation, where they dug holes and pushed wheelbarrows for the archaeologists. They became best friends, then devoted pen pals when Emily went to Vassar and my mother to Harvard. Later the two reconnected in Cambridge when Em became a children's librarian. After my parents' death, Em's long weekends in Madison soon led to a new job in the local elementary school. She and Sarah became inseparable partners, even though Em had maintained her own apartment in town and the two of them had made a big deal of never being seen heading into a bedroom together while I was growing up. This didn't fool me, the neighbors, or anyone else living in town. Everybody treated them like the couple they were, regardless of where they slept. When I moved out of the Bishop house, Em moved in and had been there ever since. Like my mother and my aunt, Em came from a long line of witches.

'I was invited to the coven's party but worked instead.'

'Did the witch from Bryn Mawr ask you to go?' Em was interested in the classicist, mostly (it had turned out over a fair amount of wine one summer night) because she'd once dated Gillian's mother. 'It was the sixties,' was all Em would say.

'Yes.' I sounded harassed. The two of them were convinced I was going to see the light and begin taking my magic seriously now that I was safely tenured. Nothing cast any doubt on this wishful prognostication, and they were always thrilled when I had any contact with a witch. 'But I spent the evening with Elias Ashmole instead.'

'Who's he?' Em asked Sarah.

'You know, that dead guy who collected alchemy books,' was Sarah's muffled reply.

'Still here, you two,' I called into the phone.

'So who rattled your cage?' Sarah asked.

Given that both were witches, there was no point in trying to hide anything. 'I met a vampire in the library. One I've never seen before, named Matthew Clairmont.'

There was silence on Em's end as she flipped through her mental card file of notable creatures. Sarah was quiet for a moment, too, deciding whether or not to explode.

'I hope he's easier to get rid of than the daemons you have a habit of attracting,' she said sharply.

'Daemons haven't bothered me since I stopped acting.'

'No, there was that daemon who followed you into the Beinecke Library when you first started working at Yale, too,' Em corrected me. 'He was just wandering down the street and came looking for you.'

'He was mentally unstable,' I protested. Like using witchcraft on the washing machine, the fact that I'd somehow caught the attention of a single, curious daemon shouldn't count against me.

'You draw creatures like flowers draw bees, Diana. But daemons aren't half as dangerous as vampires. Stay away from him,' Sarah said tightly.

'I have no reason to seek him out.' My hands traveled to my neck again. 'We have nothing in common.'

'That's not the point,' Sarah said, voice rising. 'Witches, vampires, and daemons aren't supposed to mix. You know that. Humans are more likely to notice us when we do. No daemon or vampire is worth the risk.' The only creatures in the world that Sarah took seriously were other witches. Humans struck her as unfortunate little beings blind to the world around them. Daemons were perpetual teenagers who couldn't be trusted. Vampires were well below cats and at least one step below mutts within her hierarchy of creatures.

'You've told me the rules before, Sarah.'

'Not everyone obeys the rules, honey,' Em observed. 'What did he want?'

'He said he was interested in my work. But he's a scientist, so that's hard to believe.' My fingers fiddled with the duvet cover on the bed. 'He invited me to dinner.'

'To *dinner*?' Sarah was incredulous.

Em just laughed. 'There's not much on a restaurant menu that would appeal to a vampire.'

'I'm sure I won't see him again. He's running three labs from the look of his business card, and he holds two faculty positions.'

'Typical,' Sarah muttered. 'That's what happens when you have too much time on your hands. And stop picking at that quilt – you'll put a hole in it.' She'd switched on her witch's radar full blast and was now seeing as well as hearing me.

'It's not as if he's stealing money from old ladies and squandering other people's fortunes on the stock market,' I countered. The fact that vampires were reputed to be fabulously wealthy was a sore spot with Sarah. 'He's a biochemist and a physician of some sort, interested in the brain.'

'I'm sure that's fascinating, Diana, but what did he *want*?' Sarah matched my irritation with impatience – the one-two punch mastered by all Bishop women.

'Not dinner,' Em said with certainty.

Sarah snorted. 'He wanted something. Vampires and witches don't go on dates. Unless he was planning to dine on *you*, of course. They love nothing more than the taste of a witch's blood.'

'Maybe he was just curious. Or maybe he does like your work.' Em said it with such doubt that I had to laugh.

'We wouldn't be having this conversation at all if you'd just take some elementary precautions,' Sarah said tartly. 'A protection spell, some use of your abilities as a seer, and – '

'I'm not using magic or witchcraft to figure out why a vampire asked me to dinner,' I said firmly. 'Not negotiable, Sarah.'

'Then don't call us looking for answers when you don't want to hear them,' Sarah said, her notoriously short temper flaring. She hung up before I could think of a response.

'Sarah does worry about you, you know,' Em said apologetically. 'And she doesn't understand why you won't use your gifts, not even to protect yourself.'

Because the gifts had strings attached, as I'd explained before. I tried again.

'It's a slippery slope, Em. I protect myself from a vampire in the library today, and tomorrow I protect myself from a hard question at a lecture. Soon I'll be picking research topics based on knowing how they'll turn out and applying for grants that I'm sure to win. It's important to me that I've made my reputation on my own. If I start using magic, nothing would belong entirely to me. I don't want to be the next Bishop witch.' I opened my mouth to tell Em about Ashmole 782, but something made me close it again.

'I know, I know, honey.' Em's voice was soothing. 'I do understand. But Sarah can't help worrying about your safety. You're all the family she has now.'

My fingers slid through my hair and came to rest at my temples. Conversations like this always led back to my mother and father. I hesitated, reluctant to mention my one lingering concern.

'What is it?' Em asked, her sixth sense picking up on my discomfort.

'He knew my name. I've never seen him before, but he knew who I was.'

Em considered the possibilities. 'Your picture's on the inside of your latest book cover, isn't it?'

My breath, which I hadn't been aware I was holding, came out with a soft whoosh. 'Yes. That must be it. I'm just being silly. Can you give Sarah a kiss from me?'

'You bet. And, Diana? Be careful. English vampires may not be as well behaved around witches as the American ones are.'

I smiled, thinking of Matthew Clairmont's formal bow. 'I will. But don't worry. I probably won't see him again.'

Em was quiet.

'Em?' I prompted.

'Time will tell.'

Em wasn't as good at seeing the future as my mother was reputed to have been, but something was niggling at her. Convincing a witch to share a vague premonition was almost impossible. She wasn't going to tell me what worried her about Matthew Clairmont. Not yet.

CHAPTER 3

The vampire sat in the shadows on the curved expanse of the bridge that spanned New College Lane and connected two parts of Hertford College, his back resting against the worn stone of one of the college's newer buildings and his feet propped up on the bridge's roof.

The witch appeared, moving surprisingly surely across the uneven stones of the sidewalk outside the Bodleian. She passed underneath him, her pace quickening. Her nervousness made her look younger than she was and accentuated her vulnerability.

So that's the formidable historian, he thought wryly, mentally going over her vita. Even after looking at her picture, Matthew expected Bishop to be older, given her professional accomplishments.

Diana Bishop's back was straight and her shoulders square, in spite of her apparent agitation. Perhaps she would not be as easy to intimidate as he had hoped. Her behavior in the library had suggested as much. She'd met his eyes without a trace of the fear that Matthew had grown to rely upon from those who weren't vampires — and many of those who were.

When Bishop rounded the corner, Matthew crept along the rooflines until he reached the New College wall. He slipped silently down into its boundaries. The vampire knew the college's layout and had anticipated where her rooms would be. He was already tucked into a doorway opposite her staircase when she began her climb.

Matthew's eyes followed her around the apartment as she moved from room to room, turning on the lights. She pushed the kitchen window open, left it ajar, disappeared.

That will save me from me breaking the window or picking her lock, he thought.

Matthew darted across the open space and scaled her building, his feet and hands finding sure holds in the old mortar with the help of a copper downspout and some robust vines. From his new vantage point, he could detect the witch's distinctive scent and a rustle of turning pages. He craned his neck to peer into the window.

Bishop was reading. In repose her face looked different, he reflected. It was as if her skin fit the underlying bones properly. Her head bobbed slowly, and she slid against the cushions with a soft sigh of exhaustion. Soon the sound of regular breathing told Matthew she was asleep.

He swung out from the wall and kicked his feet up and through the witch's kitchen window. It had been a very long time since the vampire had climbed into a woman's rooms. Even then the occasions were rare and usually linked to moments when he was in the grip of infatuation. This time there was a far different reason. Nonetheless, if someone caught him, he'd have a hell of a time explaining what it was.

Matthew had to know if Ashmole 782 was still in Bishop's possession. He hadn't been able to search her desk at the library, but a quick glance had suggested that it wasn't among the manuscripts she'd been consulting today. Still, there was no chance that a witch – a Bishop – would have let the volume slip through her fingers. With inaudible steps he traveled through the small set of rooms. The manuscript wasn't in the witch's bathroom or her bedroom. He crept quietly past the couch where she lay sleeping.

The witch's eyelids were twitching as if she were watching a movie only she could see. One of her hands was drawn into a fist, and every now and then her legs danced. Bishop's face was serene, however, unperturbed by whatever the rest of her body thought it was doing.

Something wasn't right. He'd sensed it from the first moment he saw Bishop in the library. Matthew crossed his arms and studied her, but he still couldn't figure out what it was. This witch didn't give off the usual scents — henbane, sulfur, and sage. *She's hiding something*, the vampire thought, *something more than the lost manuscript.*

Matthew turned away, seeking out the table she was using as a desk. It was easy to spot, littered with books and papers. That was the likeliest place for her to have put the smuggled volume. As he took a step toward it, he smelled electricity and froze.

Light was seeping from Diana Bishop's body — all around the edges, escaping from her pores. The light was a blue so pale it was almost white, and at first it formed a cloudlike shroud that clung to her for a few seconds. For a moment she seemed to shimmer. Matthew shook his head in disbelief. It was impossible. It had been centuries since he'd seen such a luminous outpouring from a witch.

But other, more urgent matters beckoned, and Matthew resumed the hunt for the manuscript, hurriedly searching through the items on her desk. He ran his fingers through his hair in frustration. The witch's scent was everywhere, distracting him. Matthew's eyes returned to the couch. Bishop was stirring and shifting again, her knees creeping toward her chest. Once more, luminosity pulsed to the surface, shimmered for a moment, retreated.

Matthew frowned, puzzled at the discrepancy between what he'd overheard last night and what he was witnessing with his own eyes. Two witches had been gossiping about Ashmole 782 and the witch who'd called it. One had suggested that the American historian didn't use her magical power. But Matthew had seen it in the Bodleian — and now watched it wash through her with evident intensity. He suspected she used magic in her scholarship, too. Many of the men she wrote about had been friends of his — Cornelius Drebbel, Andreas Libavius, Isaac Newton. She'd captured their quirks and obsessions perfectly. Without magic how could a modern woman understand men who had lived so long ago? Fleetingly, Matthew wondered if Bishop would be able to understand him with the same uncanny accuracy.

The clocks struck three, startling him. His throat felt parched. He realized he'd been standing for several hours, motionless, watching the witch dream while her power rose and fell in waves. He briefly considered slaking his thirst with this witch's blood. A taste of it might reveal the location of the missing volume and indicate what secrets the witch was keeping. But he restrained himself. It was only his desire to find Ashmole 782 that made him linger with the enigmatic Diana Bishop.

If the manuscript wasn't in the witch's rooms, then it was still in the library.

He padded to the kitchen, slid out the window, and melted into the night.

CHAPTER 4

Four hours later I woke up on top of the duvet, clutching the phone. At some point I'd kicked off my right slipper, leaving my foot trailing over the edge of the bed. I looked at the clock and groaned. There was no time for my usual trip to the river, or even for a run.

Cutting my morning ritual short, I showered and then drank a scalding cup of tea while drying my hair. It was straw blond and unruly, despite the ministrations of a hairbrush. Like most witches, I had a problem getting the shoulder-length strands to stay put. Sarah blamed it on pent-up magic and promised that the regular use of my power would keep the static electricity from building and make my hair more obedient.

After brushing my teeth, I slipped on a pair of jeans, a fresh white blouse, and a black jacket. It was a familiar routine, and this was my habitual outfit, but neither proved comforting today. My clothes seemed confining, and I felt self-conscious in them. I jerked on the jacket to see if that would make it fit any better, but it was too much to expect from inferior tailoring.

When I looked into the mirror, my mother's face stared back. I could no longer remember when I'd developed this strong resemblance to her. Sometime in college, perhaps? No one had commented on it until I came home for Thanksgiving break during freshman year. Since then it was the first thing I heard from those who had known Rebecca Bishop.

Today's check in the mirror also revealed that my skin was pale from lack of sleep. This made my freckles, which I'd inherited from my father, stand out in apparent alarm, and the dark blue circles under my eyes made them appear lighter than usual. Fatigue also managed to lengthen my nose and render my chin more pronounced. I thought of the immaculate Professor Clairmont and wondered what *he* looked like first thing in the morning. Probably just as pristine as he had last night, I decided – the beast. I grimaced at my reflection.

On my way out the door, I stopped and surveyed my rooms. Something niggled at me – a forgotten appointment, a deadline. There was something I was missing that was important. The sense of unease wrapped around my stomach, squeezed, then let go. After checking my datebook and the stacks of mail on my desk, I wrote it off as hunger and went downstairs. The obliging ladies in the kitchen offered me toast when I passed by. They remembered me as a graduate student and still tried to force-feed me custard and apple pie when I looked stressed.

Munching on toast and slipping along the cobblestones of New College Lane was enough to convince me that last night had been a dream. My hair swung against my collar, and my breath showed in the crisp air. Oxford is quintessentially normal in the morning, with the delivery vans pulled up to college kitchens, the aromas of burned coffee and damp pavement, and fresh rays of sunlight slanting through the mist. It was not a place that seemed likely to harbor vampires.

The Bodleian's blue-jacketed attendant went through his usual routine of scrutinizing my reader's card as if he had never seen me before and suspected I might be a master book thief. Finally he waved me through. I deposited my bag in the cubbyholes by the door after first removing my wallet, computer, and notes, and then I headed up to the twisting wooden stairs to the third floor.

The smell of the library always lifted my spirits – that peculiar combination of old stone, dust, woodworm, and paper made properly from rags. Sun streamed through the windows on the staircase landings, illuminating the dust motes flying through the air and shining bars of light on the ancient walls. There the sun highlighted the curling announcements for last term's lecture series. New posters had yet to go up, but it would only be a matter of days before the floodgates opened and a wave of undergraduates arrived to disrupt the city's tranquillity.

Humming quietly to myself, I nodded to the busts of Thomas Bodley and King Charles I that flanked the arched entrance to Duke Humfrey's and pushed through the swinging gate by the call desk.

'We'll have to set him up in the Selden End today,' the supervisor was saying with a touch of exasperation.

The library had been open for just a few minutes, but Mr Johnson and his staff were already in a flap. I'd seen this kind of behavior before, but only when the most distinguished scholars were expected.

'He's already put in his requests, and he's waiting down there.' The unfamiliar female attendant from yesterday scowled at me and shifted the stack of books in her arms. 'These are his, too. He had them sent up from the New Bodleian Reading Room.'

That's where they kept the East Asia books. It wasn't my field, and I quickly lost interest.

'Get those to him now, and tell him we'll bring the manuscripts down within the hour.' The supervisor sounded harassed as he returned to his office.

Sean rolled his eyes heavenward as I approached the collection desk. 'Hi, Diana. Do you want the manuscripts you put on reserve?'

'Thanks,' I whispered, thinking of my waiting stack with relish. 'Big day, huh?'

'Apparently,' he said drily, before disappearing into the locked cage that held the manuscripts overnight. He returned with my stack of treasures. 'Here you go. Seat number?'

'A4.' It's where I always sat, in the far southeastern corner of the Selden End, where the natural light was best.

Mr Johnson came scurrying toward me. 'Ah, Dr Bishop, we've put Professor Clairmont in A3. You might prefer to sit in A1 or A6.' He shifted nervously from one foot to the other and pushed his glasses up, blinking at me through the thick glass.

I stared at him. 'Professor *Clairmont*?'

'Yes. He's working on the Needham papers and requested good light and room to spread out.'

'Joseph Needham, the historian of Chinese science?' Somewhere around my solar plexus, my blood started to seethe.

'Yes. He was a biochemist, too, of course – hence Professor Clairmont's interest,' Mr Johnson explained, looking more flustered by the moment. 'Would you like to sit in A1?'

'I'll take A6.' The thought of sitting next to a vampire, even with an empty seat between us, was deeply unsettling. Sitting across from one in A4 was unthinkable, however. How could I concentrate, wondering what those strange eyes were seeing? Had the desks in the medieval wing been more comfortable, I would have parked myself under one of the gargoyles that guarded the narrow windows and braved Gillian Chamberlain's prim disapproval instead.

'Oh, that's splendid. Thank you for understanding.' Mr Johnson sighed with relief.

As I came into the light of the Selden End, my eyes narrowed. Clairmont looked immaculate and rested, his pale skin startling against his dark hair. This time his open-necked gray sweater had flecks of green, and his collar stood up slightly in the back. A peek under the table revealed charcoal gray trousers, matching socks, and black shoes that surely cost more than the average academic's entire wardrobe.

The unsettled feeling returned. What was Clairmont doing in the library? Why wasn't he in his lab?

Making no effort to muffle my footsteps, I strode in the vampire's direction. Clairmont, seated diagonally across from me at the far end of the cluster of desks and seemingly oblivious to my approach, continued reading. I dumped my plastic bag and manuscripts onto the space marked A5, staking out the outer edges of my territory.

He looked up, brows arching in apparent surprise. 'Dr Bishop. Good morning.'

'Professor Clairmont.' It occurred to me that he'd overheard everything said about him at the reading room's entrance, given that he had the hearing of a bat. I refused to meet his eyes and started pulling individual items out of my bag, building a small fortification of desk supplies between me and the vampire. Clairmont watched until I ran out of equipment, then lowered his eyebrows in concentration and returned to his reading.

I took out the cord for my computer and disappeared under the desk to shove it into the power strip. When I righted myself, he was still reading but was also trying not to smile.

'Surely you'd be more comfortable in the northern end,' I grumbled under my breath, rooting around for my list of manuscripts.

Clairmont looked up, dilating pupils making his eyes suddenly dark. 'Am I bothering you, Dr Bishop?'

'Of course not,' I said hastily, my throat closing at the sudden, sharp aroma of cloves that accompanied his words, 'but I'm surprised you find a southern exposure comfortable.'

'You don't believe everything you read, do you?' One of his thick, black eyebrows rose into the shape of a question mark.

'If you're asking whether I think you're going to burst into flames the moment the sunlight hits you, the answer is no.' Vampires didn't burn at the touch of sunlight, nor did they have fangs. These were human myths. 'But I've never met . . . *someone like you* who liked to bask in its glow either.'

Clairmont's body remained still, but I could have sworn he was repressing a laugh. 'How much direct experience have you had, Dr Bishop, with "someone like me"?'

How did he know I hadn't had much experience with vampires? Vampires had preternatural senses and abilities – but no supernatural ones, like mind reading or precognition. Those belonged to witches and, on rare occasions, could sometimes crop up in daemons, too. This was the natural order, or so my aunt had explained when I was a child and couldn't sleep for fear that a vampire would steal my thoughts and fly out the window with them.

I studied him closely. 'Somehow, Professor Clairmont, I don't think years of experience would tell me what I need to know right now.'

'I'd be happy to answer your question, if I can,' he said, closing his book and placing it on the desk. He waited with the patience of a teacher listening to a belligerent and not very bright student.

'What is it that *you* want?'

Clairmont sat back in his chair, his hands resting easily on the arms. 'I want to examine Dr Needham's papers and study the evolution of his ideas on morphogenesis.'

'Morphogenesis?'

'The changes to embryonic cells that result in differentiation—'

'I know what morphogenesis is, Professor Clairmont. That's not what I'm asking.'

His mouth twitched. I crossed my arms protectively across my chest.

'I see.' He tented his long fingers, resting his elbows on the chair. 'I came into Bodley's Library last night to request some manuscripts. Once inside, I decided to look around a bit – I like to know my environment, you understand, and don't often spend time here. There you were in the gallery. And of course what I saw after that was quite unexpected.' His mouth twitched again.

I flushed at the memory of how I'd used magic just to get a book. And I tried not to be disarmed by his old-fashioned use of 'Bodley's Library' but was not entirely successful.

Careful, Diana, I warned myself. *He's trying to charm you.*

'So your story is that this has just been a set of odd coincidences, culminating in a vampire and a witch sitting across from each other and examining manuscripts like two ordinary readers?'

'I don't think anyone who took the time to examine me carefully would think I was ordinary, do you?' Clairmont's already quiet voice dropped to a mocking whisper, and he tilted forward in his chair. His pale skin caught the light and seemed to glow. 'But otherwise, yes. It's just a series of coincidences, easily explained.'

'I thought scientists didn't believe in coincidences anymore.'

He laughed softly. 'Some have to believe in them.'

Clairmont kept staring at me, which was unnerving in the extreme. The female attendant rolled the reading room's ancient wooden cart up to the vampire's elbow, boxes of manuscripts neatly arrayed on the trolley's shelves.

The vampire dragged his eyes from my face. 'Thank you, Valerie. I appreciate your assistance.'

'Of course, Professor Clairmont,' Valerie said, gazing at him raptly and turning pink. The vampire had charmed her with no more than a thank-you. I snorted. 'Do let us know if you need anything else,' she said, returning to her bolt-hole by the entrance.

Clairmont picked up the first box, undid the string with his long fingers, and glanced across the table. 'I don't want to keep you from your work.'

Matthew Clairmont had taken the upper hand. I'd had enough dealings with senior colleagues to recognize the signs and to know that any response would only make the situation worse. I opened my computer, punched the power button with more force than necessary, and picked up the first of my manuscripts. Once the box was unfastened, I placed its leather-bound contents on the cradle in front of me.

Over the next hour and a half, I read the first pages at least thirty times. I started at the beginning, reading familiar lines of poetry attributed to George Ripley that promised to reveal the secrets of the philosopher's stone. Given the surprises of the morning, the poem's descriptions of how to make the Green Lion, create the Black Dragon, and concoct a mystical blood from chemical ingredients were even more opaque than usual.

Clairmont, however, got a prodigious amount done, covering pages of creamy paper with rapid strokes of his Montblanc Meisterstück mechanical pencil. Every now and again, he'd turn over a sheet with a rustle that set my teeth on edge and begin once more.

Occasionally Mr Johnson drifted through the room, making sure no one was defacing the books. The vampire kept writing. I glared at both of them.

At 10:45, there was a familiar tingle when Gillian Chamberlain bustled into the Selden End. She started toward me – no doubt to tell me what a splendid time she'd had at the Mabon dinner. Then she saw the vampire and dropped her plastic bag full of pencils and paper. He looked up and stared until she scampered back to the medieval wing.

At 11:10, I felt the insidious pressure of a kiss on my neck. It was the confused, caffeine-addicted daemon from the music reference room. He was repeatedly twirling a set of white plastic headphones around his fingers, then unwinding them to send them spinning through the air. The daemon saw me, nodded at Matthew, and sat at one of the computers in the center of the room. A sign was taped to the screen: OUT OF ORDER. TECHNICIAN CALLED. He remained there for the next several hours, glancing over his shoulder and then at the ceiling periodically as if trying to figure out where he was and how he'd gotten there.

I returned my attention to George Ripley, Clairmont's eyes cold on the top of my head.

At 11:40, icy patches bloomed between my shoulder blades.

This was the last straw. Sarah always said that one in ten beings was a creature, but in Duke Humfrey's this morning the creatures outnumbered humans five to one. Where had they all come from?

I stood abruptly and whirled around, frightening a cherubic, tonsured vampire with an armful of medieval missals just as he was lowering himself into a chair that was much too small for him. He let out a squeak at the sudden, unwanted attention. At the sight of Clairmont, he turned a whiter shade than I thought was possible, even for a vampire. With an apologetic bow, he scuttled off to the library's dimmer recesses.

Over the course of the afternoon, a few humans and three more creatures entered the Selden End.

Two unfamiliar female vampires who appeared to be sisters glided past Clairmont and came to a stop among the local-history shelves under the window, picking up volumes about the early settlement of Bedfordshire and Dorset and writing notes back and forth on a single pad of paper. One of them whispered something, and Clairmont's head swiveled so fast it would have snapped the neck of a lesser being. He made a soft hissing sound that ruffled the hair on my own neck. The two exchanged looks and departed as quietly as they had appeared.

The third creature was an elderly man who stood in a full beam of sunlight and stared raptly at the leaded windows before turning his eyes to me. He was dressed in familiar academic garb – brown tweed jacket with suede elbow patches, corduroy pants in a slightly jarring tone of green, and a cotton shirt with a button-down collar and ink stains on the pocket – and I was ready to dismiss him as just another Oxford scholar before my skin tingled to tell me that he was a witch. Still, he was a stranger, and I returned my attention to my manuscript.

A gentle sensation of pressure on the back of my skull made it impossible to keep reading, however. The pressure flitted to my ears, growing in intensity as it wrapped around my forehead, and my stomach clenched in panic. This was no longer a silent greeting, but a threat. Why, though, would he be threatening me?

The wizard strolled toward my desk with apparent casualness. As he approached, a voice whispered in my now-throbbing head. It was too faint to distinguish the words. I was sure it was coming from this male witch, but who on earth was he?

My breath became shallow. *Get the hell out of my head*, I said fiercely if silently, touching my forehead.

Clairmont moved so quickly I didn't see him round the desks. In an instant he was standing with one hand on the back of my chair and the other resting on the surface in front of me. His broad shoulders were curved around me like the wings of a falcon shielding his prey.

'Are you all right?' he asked.

'I'm fine,' I replied with a shaking voice, utterly confused as to why a vampire would need to protect me from another witch.

In the gallery above us, a reader craned her neck to see what all the fuss was about. She stood, her brow creased. Two witches and a vampire were impossible for a human to ignore.

'Leave me alone. The humans have noticed us,' I said between clenched teeth.

Clairmont straightened to his full height but kept his back to the witch and his body angled between us like an avenging angel.

'Ah, my mistake,' the witch murmured from behind Clairmont. 'I thought this seat was available. Excuse me.' Soft steps retreated into the distance, and the pressure on my head gradually subsided.

A slight breeze stirred as the vampire's cold hand reached toward my shoulder, stopped, and returned to the back of the chair. Clairmont leaned over. 'You look quite pale,' he said in his soft, low voice. 'Would you like me to take you home?'

'No.' I shook my head, hoping he would go sit down and let me gather my composure. In the gallery the human reader kept a wary eye on us.

'Dr Bishop, I really think you should let me take you home.'

'No!' My voice was louder than I intended. It dropped to a whisper. 'I am not being driven out of this library – not by you, not by anyone.'

Clairmont's face was disconcertingly close. He took a slow breath in, and once again there was a powerful aroma of cinnamon and cloves. Something in my eyes convinced him I was serious, and he drew away. His mouth flattened into a severe line, and he returned to his seat.

We spent the remainder of the afternoon in a state of détente. I tried to read beyond the second folio of my first manuscript, and Clairmont leafed through scraps of paper and closely written note-books with the attention of a judge deciding on a capital case.

By three o'clock my nerves were so frayed that I could no longer concentrate. The day was lost.

I gathered my scattered belongings and returned the manuscript to its box.

Clairmont looked up. 'Going home, Dr Bishop?' His tone was mild, but his eyes glittered.

'Yes,' I snapped.

The vampire's face went carefully blank.

Every creature in the library watched me on my way out – the threatening wizard, Gillian, the vampire monk, even the daemon.

The afternoon attendant at the collection desk was a stranger to me, because I never left at this time of day. Mr Johnson pushed his chair back slightly, saw it was me, and looked at his watch in surprise.

In the quadrangle I pushed the glass doors of the library open and drank in the fresh air. It would take more than fresh air, though, to turn the day around.

Fifteen minutes later I was in a pair of fitted, calf-length pants that stretched in six different directions, a faded New College Boat Club tank, and a fleece pullover. After tying on my sneakers I set off for the river at a run.

When I reached it, some of my tension had already abated. 'Adrenaline poisoning,' one of my doctors had called these surges of anxiety that had troubled me since childhood. The doctors explained that, for reasons they could not understand, my body seemed to think it was in a constant state of danger. One of the specialists my aunt consulted explained earnestly that it was a biochemical leftover from hunter-gatherer days. I'd be all right so long as I rid my bloodstream of the adrenaline load by running, just as a frightened ibex would run from a lion.

Unfortunately for that doctor, I'd gone to the Serengeti with my parents as a child and had witnessed such a pursuit. The ibex lost. It had made quite an impression on me.

Since then I'd tried medication and meditation, but nothing was better for keeping panic at bay than physical activity. In Oxford it was rowing each morning before the college crews turned the narrow river into a thoroughfare. But the university was not yet in session, and the river would be clear this afternoon.

My feet crunched against the crushed gravel paths that led to the boathouses. I waved at Pete, the boatman who prowled around with wrenches and tubs of grease, trying to put right what the under-graduates mangled in the course of their training. I stopped at the seventh boathouse and bent over to ease the stitch in my side before retrieving the key from the top of the light outside the boathouse doors.

Racks of white and yellow boats greeted me inside. There were big, eight-seated boats for the first men's crew, slightly leaner boats for the women, and other boats of decreasing quality and size. A sign hung from the bow of one shiny new boat that hadn't been rigged yet, instructing visitors that NO ONE MAY TAKE THE FRENCH LIEUTENANT'S WOMAN OUT OF THIS HOUSE WITHOUT THE PERMISSION OF THE NCBC PRESIDENT. The boat's name was freshly stenciled on its side in a Victorian-style script, in homage to the New College graduate who had created the character.

At the back of the boathouse, a whisper of a boat under twelve inches wide and more than twenty-five feet long rested in a set of slings positioned at hip level. *God bless Pete*, I thought. He'd taken to leaving the scull on the floor of the boathouse. A note resting on the seat read, '*College training next Monday. Boat will be back in racks.*'

I kicked off my sneakers, picked two oars with curving blades from the stash near the doors, and carried them down to the dock. Then I went back for the boat.

I plopped the scull gently into the water and put one foot on the seat to keep it from floating away while I threaded the oars into the oarlocks. Holding both oars in one hand like a pair of oversize chopsticks, I carefully stepped into the boat and pushed the dock with my left hand. The scull floated out onto the river.

Rowing was a religion for me, composed of a set of rituals and movements repeated until they became a meditation. The rituals began the moment I touched the equipment, but its real magic came from the combination of precision, rhythm, and strength that rowing required. Since my undergraduate days, rowing had instilled a sense of tranquillity in me like nothing else.

My oars dipped into the water and skimmed along the surface. I picked up the pace, powering through each stroke with my legs and feeling the water when my blade swept back and slipped under the waves. The wind was cold and sharp, cutting through my clothes with every stroke.

As my movements flowed into a seamless cadence, it felt as though I were flying. During these blissful moments, I was suspended in time and space, nothing but a weightless body on a moving river.

My swift little boat darted along, and I swung in perfect unison with the boat and its oars. I closed my eyes and smiled, the events of the day fading in significance.

The sky darkened behind my closed lids, and the booming sound of traffic overhead indicated that I'd passed underneath the Donnington Bridge. Coming through into the sunlight on the other side, I opened my eyes – and felt the cold touch of a vampire's gaze on my sternum.

A figure stood on the bridge, his long coat flapping around his knees. Though I couldn't see his face clearly, the vampire's considerable height and bulk suggested that it was Matthew Clairmont. Again.

I swore and nearly dropped one oar. The City of Oxford dock was nearby. The notion of pulling an illegal maneuver and crossing the river so that I could smack the vampire upside his beautiful head with whatever piece of boat equipment was handy was very tempting. While formulating my plan, I spotted a slight woman standing on the dock wearing paint-stained overalls. She was smoking a cigarette and talking into a mobile phone.

This was not a typical sight for the City of Oxford boathouse.

She looked up, her eyes nudging my skin. A daemon. She twisted her mouth into a wolfish smile and said something into the phone.

This was just too weird. First Clairmont and now a host of creatures appearing whenever he did? Abandoning my plan, I poured my unease into my rowing.

I managed to get down the river, but the serenity of the outing had evaporated. Turning the boat in front of the Isis Tavern, I spotted Clairmont standing beside one of the pub's tables. He'd managed to get there from the Donnington Bridge – on foot – in less time than I'd done it in a racing scull.

Pulling hard on both oars, I lifted them two feet off the water like the wings of an enormous bird and glided straight into the tavern's rickety wooden dock. By the time I'd climbed out, Clairmont had crossed the twenty-odd feet of grass lying between us. His weight pushed the floating platform down slightly in the water, and the boat wiggled in adjustment.

'What the hell do you think you're doing?' I demanded, stepping clear of the blade and across the rough planks to where the vampire now stood. My breath was ragged from exertion, my cheeks flushed. 'Are you and your friends *stalking* me?'

Clairmont frowned. 'They aren't my friends, Dr Bishop.'

'No? I haven't seen so many vampires, witches, and daemons in one place since my aunts dragged me to a pagan summer festival when I was thirteen. If they're not your friends, why are they always hanging around you?' I wiped the back of my hand across my forehead and pushed the damp hair away from my face.

'Good God,' the vampire murmured incredulously. 'The rumors are true.'

'What rumors?' I said impatiently.

'You think these . . . *things* want to spend time with me?' Clairmont's voice dripped with contempt and something that sounded like surprise. 'Unbelievable.'

I worked my fleece pullover up above my shoulders and yanked it off. Clairmont's eyes flickered to my collarbones, over my bare arms, and down to my fingertips. I felt uncharacteristically naked in my familiar rowing clothes.

'Yes,' I snapped. 'I've lived in Oxford. I visit every year. The only thing that's been different this time is *you*. Since you showed up last night, I've been pushed out of my seat in the library, stared at by strange vampires and daemons, and threatened by unfamiliar witches.'

Clairmont's arms rose slightly, as if he were going to take me by the shoulders and shake me. Though I was by no means short at just under five-seven, he was so tall that my neck had to bend sharply so I could make eye contact. Acutely aware of his size and strength relative to my own, I stepped back and crossed my arms, calling upon my professional persona to steel my nerves.

'They're not interested in me, Dr Bishop. They're interested in *you*.'

'Why? What could they possibly want from me?'

'Do you really not know why every daemon, witch, and vampire south of the Midlands is following you?' There was a note of disbelief in his voice, and the vampire's expression suggested he was seeing me for the first time.

'No,' I said, my eyes on two men enjoying their afternoon pint at a nearby table. Thankfully, they were absorbed in their own conversation. 'I've done nothing in Oxford except read old manuscripts, row on the river, prepare for my conference, and keep to myself. It's all I've ever done here. There's no reason for any creature to pay this kind of attention to me.'

'Think, Diana.' Clairmont's voice was intense. A ripple of something that wasn't fear passed across my skin when he said my first name. 'What have you been reading?'

His eyelids dropped over his strange eyes, but not before I'd seen their avid expression.

My aunts had warned me that Matthew Clairmont wanted something. They were right.

He fixed his odd, gray-rimmed black eyes on me once more. 'They're following you because they believe you've found something lost many years ago,' he said reluctantly. 'They want it back, and they think you can get it for them.'

I thought about the manuscripts I'd consulted over the past few days. My heart sank. There was only one likely candidate for all this attention.

'If they're not your friends, how do you know what they want?'

'I hear things, Dr Bishop. I have very good hearing,' he said patiently, reverting to his characteristic formality. 'I'm also fairly observant. At a concert on Sunday evening, two witches were talking about an American – a fellow witch – who found a book in Bodley's Library that had been given up for lost. Since then I've noticed many new faces in Oxford, and they make me uneasy.'

'It's Mabon. That explains why the witches are in Oxford.' I was trying to match his patient tone, though he hadn't answered my last question.

Smiling sardonically, Clairmont shook his head. 'No, it's not the equinox. It's the manuscript.'

'What do you know about Ashmole 782?' I asked quietly.

'Less than you do,' said Clairmont, his eyes narrowing to slits. It made him look even more like a large, lethal beast. 'I've never seen it. You've held it in your hands. Where is it now, Dr Bishop? You weren't so foolish as to leave it in your room?'

I was aghast. 'You think I *stole* it? From the Bodleian? How dare you suggest such a thing!'

'You didn't have it Monday night,' he said. 'And it wasn't on your desk today either.'

'You *are* observant,' I said sharply, 'if you could see all that from where you were sitting. I returned it Friday, if you must know.' It occurred to me, belatedly, that he might have rifled through the things on my desk. 'What's so special about the manuscript that you'd snoop through a colleague's work?'

He winced slightly, but my triumph at catching him doing something so inappropriate was blunted by a twinge of fear that this vampire was following me as closely as he obviously was.

'Simple curiosity,' he said, baring his teeth. Sarah had not misled me – vampires don't have fangs.

'I hope you don't expect me to believe that.'

'I don't care what you believe, Dr Bishop. But you should be on your guard. These creatures are serious. And when they come to understand what an unusual witch you are?' Clairmont shook his head.

'What do you mean?' All the blood drained from my head, leaving me dizzy.

'It's uncommon these days for a witch to have so much . . . potential.' Clairmont's voice dropped to a purr that vibrated in the back of his throat. 'Not everyone can see it – yet – but I can. You shimmer with it when you concentrate. When you're angry, too. Surely the daemons in the library will sense it soon, if they haven't already.'

'I appreciate the warning. But I don't need your help.' I prepared to stalk away, but his hand shot out and gripped my upper arm, stopping me in my tracks.

'Don't be too sure of that. Be careful. Please.' Clairmont hesitated, his face shaken out of its perfect lines as he wrestled with something. 'Especially if you see that wizard again.'

I stared fixedly at the hand on my arm. Clairmont released me. His lids dropped, shuttering his eyes.

My row back to the boathouse was slow and steady, but the repetitive movements weren't able to carry away my lingering confusion and unease. Every now and again, there was a gray blur on the towpath, but nothing else caught my attention except for people bicycling home from work and a very ordinary human walking her dog.

After returning the equipment and locking the boathouse, I set off down the towpath at a measured jog.

Matthew Clairmont was standing across the river in front of the University Boat House.

I began to run, and when I looked back over my shoulder, he was gone.

CHAPTER 5

After dinner I sat down on the sofa by the sitting room's dormant fireplace and switched on my laptop. Why would a scientist of Clairmont's caliber want to see an alchemical manuscript – even one under a spell – so much that he'd sit at the Bodleian all day, across from a witch, and read through old notes on morphogenesis? His business card was tucked into one of the pockets of my bag. I fished it out, propping it up against the screen.

On the Internet, below an unrelated link to a murder mystery and the unavoidable hits from social-networking sites, a string of biographical listings looked promising: his faculty Web page, a Wikipedia article, and links to the current fellows of the Royal Society.

I clicked on the faculty Web page and snorted. Matthew Clairmont was one of those faculty members who didn't like to post any information – even academic information – on the Net. On Yale's Web site, a visitor could get contact information and a complete vita for practically every member of the faculty. Oxford clearly had a different attitude toward privacy. No wonder a vampire taught here.

There hadn't been a hit for Clairmont at the hospital, though the affiliation was on his card. I typed '*John Radcliffe Neurosciences*' into the search box and was led to an overview of the department's services. There wasn't a single reference to a physician, however, only a lengthy list of research interests. Clicking systematically through the terms, I finally found him on a page dedicated to the 'frontal lobe,' though there was no additional information.

The Wikipedia article was no help at all, and the Royal Society's site was no better. Anything useful hinted at on the main pages was hidden behind passwords. I had no luck imagining what Clairmont's user name and password might be and was refused access to anything at all after my sixth incorrect guess.

Frustrated, I entered the vampire's name into the search engines for scientific journals.

'Yes.' I sat back in satisfaction.

Matthew Clairmont might not have much of a presence on the Internet, but he was certainly active in the scholarly literature. After clicking a box to sort the results by date, I was provided with a snapshot of his intellectual history.

My initial sense of triumph faded. He didn't have one intellectual history. He had four.

The first began with the brain. Much of it was beyond me, but Clairmont seemed to have made a scientific and medical reputation at the same time by studying how the brain's frontal lobe processes urges and cravings. He'd made several major breakthroughs related to the role that neural mechanisms play in delayed-gratification responses, all of which involved the prefrontal cortex. I opened a new browser window to view an anatomical diagram and locate which bit of the brain was at issue.

Some argued that all scholarship is thinly veiled autobiography. My pulse jumped. Given that Clairmont was a vampire, I sincerely hoped delayed gratification was something he was good at.

My next few clicks showed that Clairmont's work took a surprising turn away from the brain and toward wolves – Norwegian wolves, to be precise. He must have spent a considerable amount of time in the Scandinavian nights in the course of his research – which posed no problem for a vampire, considering their body temperature and ability to see in the dark. I tried to imagine him in a parka and grubby clothes with a notepad in the snow – and failed.

After that, the first references to blood appeared.

While the vampire was with the wolves in Norway, he'd started analyzing their blood to determine family groups and inheritance patterns. Clairmont had isolated four clans among the Norwegian wolves, three of which were indigenous. The fourth he traced back to a wolf that had arrived in Norway from Sweden or Finland. There was, he concluded, a surprising amount of mating across packs, leading to an exchange of genetic material that influenced species evolution.

Now he was tracing inherited traits among other animal species as well as in humans. Many of his most recent publications were technical – methods for staining tissue samples and processes for handling particularly old and fragile DNA.

I grabbed a fistful of my hair and held tight, hoping the pressure would increase blood circulation and get my tired synapses firing again. This made no sense. No scientist could produce this much work in so many different subdisciplines. Acquiring the skills alone would take more than a lifetime – *a human lifetime, that is.*

A vampire might well pull it off, if he had been working on problems like this over the span of decades. Just how old was Matthew Clairmont behind that thirty-something face?

I got up and made a fresh cup of tea. With the mug steaming in one hand, I rooted through my bag until I found my mobile and punched in a number with my thumb.

One of the best things about scientists was that they always had their phones. They answered them on the second ring, too.

'Christopher Roberts.'

'Chris, it's Diana Bishop.'

'Diana!' Chris's voice was warm, and there was music blaring in the background. 'I heard you won another prize for your book. Congratulations!'

'Thanks,' I said, shifting in my seat. 'It was quite unexpected.'

'Not to me. Speaking of which, how's the research going? Have you finished writing your keynote?'

'Nowhere near,' I said. That's what I *should* be doing, not tracking down vampires on the Internet. 'Listen, I'm sorry to bother you in the lab. Do you have a minute?'

'Sure.' He shouted for someone to turn down the noise.

It remained at the same volume. 'Hold on.' There were muffled sounds, then quiet. 'That's better,' he said sheepishly. 'The new kids are pretty high energy at the beginning of the semester.'

'Grad students are always high energy, Chris.' I felt a tiny pang at missing the rush of new classes and new students.

'You know it. But what about you? What do you need?'

Chris and I had taken up our faculty positions at Yale in the same year, and he wasn't supposed to get tenure either. He'd beaten me to it by a year, picking up a MacArthur Fellowship along the way for his brilliant work as a molecular biologist.

He didn't behave like an aloof genius when I cold-called him to ask why an alchemist might describe two substances heated in an alembic as growing branches like a tree. Nobody else in the chemistry department had been interested in helping me, but Chris sent two PhD students to get the materials necessary to re-create the experiment, then insisted I come straight to the lab. We'd watched through the walls of a glass beaker while a lump of gray sludge underwent a glorious evolution into a red tree with hundreds of branches. We'd been friends ever since.

I took a deep breath. 'I met someone the other day.'

Chris whooped. He'd been introducing me to men he'd met at the gym for years.

'There's no romance,' I said hastily. 'He's a scientist.'

'A gorgeous scientist is exactly what you need. You need a challenge – and a life.'

'Look who's talking. What time did you leave the lab yesterday? Besides, there's already one gorgeous scientist in my life,' I teased.

'No changing the subject.'

'Oxford is such a small town, I'm bound to keep running into him. And he seems to be a big deal around here.' Not strictly true, I thought, crossing my fingers, but close enough. 'I've looked up his work and can understand some of it, but I must be missing something, because it doesn't seem to fit together.'

'Tell me he's not an astrophysicist,' Chris said. 'You know I'm weak on physics.'

'You're supposed to be a genius.'

'I am,' he said promptly. 'But my genius doesn't extend to card games or physics. Name, please.' Chris tried to be patient, but no one's brain moved fast enough for him.

'Matthew Clairmont.' His name caught in the back of my throat, just as the scent of cloves had the night before.

Chris whistled. 'The elusive, reclusive Professor Clairmont.' Gooseflesh rose on my arms. 'What did you do, put him under a spell with those eyes of yours?'

Since Chris didn't know I was a witch, his use of the word 'spell' was entirely accidental. 'He admires my work on Boyle.'

'Right,' Chris scoffed. 'You turned those crazy blue-and-gold starbursts on him and he was thinking about Boyle's law? He's a scientist, Diana, not a monk. And he is a big deal, incidentally.'

'Really?' I said faintly.

'Really. He was a phenom, just like you, and started publishing while he was still a grad student. Good stuff, not crap – work you'd be happy to have your name on if you managed to produce it over the course of a career.'

I scanned my notes, scratched out on a yellow legal pad. 'This was his study of neural mechanisms and the prefrontal cortex?'

'You've done your homework,' he said approvingly. 'I didn't follow much of Clairmont's early work – his chemistry is what interests me – but his publications on wolves caused a lot of excitement.'

'How come?'

'He had amazing instincts – why the wolves picked certain places to live, how they formed social groups, how they mated. It was almost like he was a wolf, too.'

'Maybe he is.' I tried to keep my voice light, but something bitter and envious bloomed in my mouth and it came out harshly instead.

Matthew Clairmont didn't have a problem using his preter-natural abilities and thirst for blood to advance his career. If the vampire had been making the decisions about Ashmole 782 on Friday night, he would have touched the manuscript's illustrations. I was sure of it.

'It would have been easier to explain the quality of his work if he *were* a wolf,' Chris said patiently, ignoring my tone. 'Since he isn't, you just have to admit he's very good. He was elected to the Royal Society on the basis of it, after they published his findings. People were calling him the next Attenborough. After that, he dropped out of sight for a while.'

I'll bet he did. 'Then he popped up again, doing evolution and chemistry?'

'Yeah, but his interest in evolution was a natural progression from the wolves.'

'So what is it about his chemistry that interests you?'

Chris's voice got tentative. 'Well, he's behaving like a scientist does when he's discovered something big.'

'I don't understand.' I frowned.

'We get jumpy and weird. We hide in our labs and don't go to conferences for fear we might say something and help someone else have a breakthrough.'

'You behave like wolves.' I now knew a great deal about wolves. The possessive, guarded behaviors Chris described fit the Norwegian wolf nicely.

'Exactly.' Chris laughed. 'He hasn't bitten anyone or been caught howling at the moon?'

'Not that I'm aware of,' I murmured. 'Has Clairmont always been so reclusive?'

'I'm the wrong person to ask,' Chris admitted. 'He does have a medical degree, and must have seen patients, although he never had any reputation as a clinician. And the wolves liked him. But he hasn't been at any of the obvious conferences in the past three years.' He paused. 'Wait a minute, though, there was something a few years back.'

'What?'

'He gave a paper — I can't remember the particulars — and a woman asked him a question. It was a smart question, but he was dismissive. She was persistent. He got irritated and then mad. A friend who was there said he'd never seen anybody go from courteous to furious so fast.'

I was already typing, trying to find information about the controversy. 'Dr Jekyll and Mr Hyde, huh? There's no sign of the ruckus online.'

'I'm not surprised. Chemists don't air their dirty laundry in public. It hurts all of us at grant time. We don't want the bureaucrats thinking we're high-strung megalomaniacs. We leave that to the physicists.'

'Does Clairmont get grants?'

'Oho. Yes. He's funded up to his eyeballs. Don't you worry about Professor Clairmont's career. He may have a reputation for being contemptuous of women, but it hasn't dried up the money. His work is too good for that.'

'Have you ever met him?' I asked, hoping to get Chris's judgment of Clairmont's character.

'No. You probably couldn't find more than a few dozen people who could claim they had. He doesn't teach. There are lots of stories, though – he doesn't like women, he's an intellectual snob, he doesn't answer his mail, he doesn't take on research students.'

'Sounds like you think that's all nonsense.'

'Not nonsense,' Chris said thoughtfully. 'I'm just not sure it matters, given that he might be the one to unlock the secrets of evolution or cure Parkinson's disease.'

'You make him sound like a cross between Salk and Darwin.'

'Not a bad analogy, actually.'

'He's that good?' I thought of Clairmont studying the Needham papers with ferocious concentration and suspected he was better than good.

'Yes.' Chris dropped his voice. 'If I were a betting man, I'd put down a hundred dollars that he'll win a Nobel before he dies.'

Chris was a genius, but he didn't know that Matthew Clairmont was a vampire. There would be no Nobel – the vampire would see to that, to preserve his anonymity. Nobel Prize winners have their photos taken.

'It's a bet,' I said with a laugh.

'You should start saving up, Diana, because you're going to lose this one.' Chris chuckled.

He'd lost our last wager. I'd bet him fifty dollars that he'd be tenured before I was. His money was stuck inside the same frame that held his picture, taken the morning the MacArthur Foundation had called. In it, Chris was dragging his hands over his tight black curls, a sheepish smile lighting his dark face. His tenure had followed nine months later.

'Thanks, Chris. You've been a big help,' I said sincerely. 'You should get back to the kids. They've probably blown something up by now.'

'Yeah, I should check on them. The fire alarms haven't gone off, which is a good sign.' He hesitated. ''Fess up, Diana. You're not worried about saying the wrong thing if you see Matthew Clairmont at a cocktail party. This is how you behave when you're working on a research problem. What is it about him that's hooked your imagination?'

Sometimes Chris seemed to suspect I was different. But there was no way to tell him the truth.

'I have a weakness for smart men.'

He sighed. 'Okay, don't tell me. You're a terrible liar, you know. But be careful. If he breaks your heart, I'll have to kick his ass, and this is a busy semester for me.'

'Matthew Clairmont isn't going to break my heart,' I insisted. 'He's a colleague – one with broad reading interests, that's all.'

'For someone so smart, you really are clueless. I bet you ten dollars he asks you out before the week is over.'

I laughed. 'Are you ever going to learn? Ten dollars, then – or the equivalent in British sterling – when I win.'

We said our good-byes. I still didn't know much about Matthew Clairmont – but I had a better sense of the questions that remained, most important among them being why someone working on a breakthrough in evolution would be interested in seventeenth-century alchemy.

I surfed the Internet until my eyes were too tired to continue. When the clocks struck midnight, I was surrounded by notes on wolves and genetics but was no closer to unraveling the mystery of Matthew Clairmont's interest in Ashmole 782.

CHAPTER 6

The next morning was gray and much more typical of early autumn. All I wanted to do was cocoon myself in layers of sweaters and stay in my rooms.

One glance at the heavy weather convinced me not to return to the river. I set out for a run instead, waving at the night porter in the lodge, who gave me an incredulous look followed by an encouraging thumbs-up.

With each slap of my feet on the sidewalk, some stiffness left my body. By the time they reached the gravel paths of the University Parks, I was breathing deeply and felt relaxed and ready for a long day in the library — no matter how many creatures were gathered there.

When I got back, the porter stopped me. 'Dr Bishop?'

'Yes?'

'I'm sorry about turning your friend away last night, but it's college policy. Next time you're having guests, let us know and we'll send them straight up.'

The clearheadedness from my run evaporated.

'Was it a man or a woman?' I asked sharply.

'A woman.'

My shoulders floated down from around my ears.

'She seemed perfectly nice, and I always like Australians. They're friendly without being, you know . . .' The porter trailed off, but his meaning was clear. Australians were like Americans — but not so pushy. 'We did call up to your rooms.'

I frowned. I'd switched off the phone's ringer, because Sarah never calculated the time difference between Madison and Oxford correctly and was always calling in the middle of the night. That explained it.

'Thank you for letting me know. I'll be sure to tell you about any future visitors,' I promised.

Back in my rooms, I flipped on the bathroom light and saw that the past two days had taken a toll. The circles that had appeared under my eyes yesterday had now blossomed into something resembling bruises. I checked my arm for bruises, too, and was surprised not to find any. The vampire's grip had been so strong that I was sure Clairmont had broken the blood vessels under the skin.

I showered and dressed in loose trousers and a turtleneck. Their unalleviated black accentuated my height and minimized my athletic build, but it also made me resemble a corpse, so I tied a soft periwinkle sweater around my shoulders. That made the circles under my eyes look bluer, but at least I no longer looked dead. My hair threatened to stand straight up from my head and crackled every time I moved. The only solution for it was to scrape it back into a messy knot at the nape of my neck.

Clairmont's trolley had been stuffed with manuscripts, and I was resigned to seeing him in Duke Humfrey's Reading Room. I approached the call desk with shoulders squared.

Once again the supervisor and both attendants were flapping around like nervous birds. This time their activity was focused on the triangle between the call desk, the manuscript card catalogs, and the supervisor's office. They carried stacks of boxes and pushed carts loaded with manuscripts under the watchful eyes of the gargoyles and into the first three bays of ancient desks.

'Thank you, Sean.' Clairmont's deep, courteous voice floated from their depths.

The good news was that I would no longer have to share a desk with a vampire.

The bad news was that I couldn't enter or leave the library – or call a book or manuscript – without Clairmont's tracking my every move. And today he had backup.

A diminutive girl was stacking up papers and file folders in the second alcove. She was dressed in a long, baggy brown sweater that reached almost to her knees. When she turned, I was startled to see a full-grown adult. Her eyes were amber and black, and as cold as frostbite.

Even without their touch, her luminous, pale skin and unnaturally thick, glossy hair gave her away as a vampire. Snaky waves of it undulated around her face and over her shoulders. She took a step toward me, making no effort to disguise the swift, sure movements, and gave me a withering glance. This was clearly not where she wanted to be, and she blamed me.

'Miriam,' Clairmont called softly, walking out into the center aisle. He stopped short, and a polite smile shaped his lips. 'Dr Bishop. Good morning.' He raked his fingers through his hair, which only made it look more artfully tousled. I patted my own hair self-consciously and tucked a stray strand behind my ear.

'Good morning, Professor Clairmont. Back again, I see.'

'Yes. But today I won't be joining you in the Selden End. They've been able to accommodate us here, where we won't disturb anyone.'

The female vampire rapped a stack of papers sharply against the top of the desk.

Clairmont smiled. 'May I introduce my research colleague, Dr Miriam Shephard. Miriam, this is Dr Diana Bishop.'

'Dr Bishop,' Miriam said coolly, extending her hand in my direction. I took it and felt a shock at the contrast between her tiny, cold hand and my own larger, warmer one. I began to draw back, but her grip grew firmer, crushing the bones together. When she finally let go, I had to resist the urge to shake out my hand.

'Dr Shephard.' The three of us stood awkwardly. What were you supposed to ask a vampire first thing in the morning? I fell back on human platitudes. 'I should really get to work.'

'Have a productive day,' Clairmont said, his nod as cool as Miriam's greeting.

Mr Johnson appeared at my elbow, my small stack of gray boxes waiting in his arms.

'We've got you in A4 today, Dr Bishop,' he said with a pleased puff of his cheeks. 'I'll just carry these back for you.' Clairmont's shoulders were so broad that I couldn't see around him to tell if there were bound manuscripts on his desk. I stifled my curiosity and followed the reading-room supervisor to my familiar seat in the Selden End.

Even without Clairmont sitting across from me, I was acutely aware of him as I took out my pencils and turned on my computer. My back to the empty room, I picked up the first box, pulled out the leather-bound manuscript, and placed it in the cradle.

The familiar task of reading and taking notes soon absorbed my attention, and I finished with the first manuscript in less than two hours. My watch revealed that it was not yet eleven. There was still time for another before lunch.

The manuscript inside the next box was smaller than the last, but it contained interesting sketches of alchemical apparatus and snippets of chemical procedures that read like some unholy combination of *Joy of Cooking* and a poisoner's notebook. '*Take your pot of mercury and seethe it over a flame for three hours*,' began one set of instructions, '*and when it has joined with the Philosophical Child take it and let it putrefy until the Black Crow carries it away to its death.*' My fingers flew over the keyboard, picking up momentum as the minutes ticked by.

I had prepared myself to be stared at today by every creature imaginable. But when the clocks chimed one, I was still virtually alone in the Selden End. The only other reader was a graduate student wearing a red-, white-, and blue-striped Keble College scarf. He stared morosely at a stack of rare books without reading them and bit his nails with occasional loud clicks.

After filling out two new request slips and packing up my manuscripts, I left my seat for lunch, satisfied with the morning's accomplishments. Gillian Chamberlain stared at me malevolently from an uncomfortable-looking seat near the ancient clock as I passed by, the two female vampires from yesterday drove icicles into my skin, and the daemon from the music reference room had picked up two other daemons. The three of them were dismantling a microfilm reader, the parts scattered all around them and a roll of film unspooling, unnoticed, on the floor at their feet.

Clairmont and his vampire assistant were still stationed near the reading room's call desk. The vampire claimed that the creatures were flocking to me, not to him. But their behavior today suggested otherwise, I thought with triumph.

While I was returning my manuscripts, Matthew Clairmont eyed me coldly. It took a considerable effort, but I refrained from acknowledging him.

'All done with these?' Sean asked.

'Yes. There are still two more at my desk. If I could have these as well, that would be great.' I handed over the slips. 'Do you want to join me for lunch?'

'Valerie just stepped out. I'm stuck here for a while, I'm afraid,' he said with regret.

'Next time.' Gripping my wallet, I turned to leave.

Clairmont's low voice stopped me in my tracks. 'Miriam, it's lunchtime.'

'I'm not hungry,' she said in a clear, melodic soprano that contained a rumble of anger.

'The fresh air will improve your concentration.' The note of command in Clairmont's voice was indisputable. Miriam sighed loudly, snapped her pencil onto her desk, and emerged from the shadows to follow me.

My usual meal consisted of a twenty-minute break in the nearby bookstore's second-floor café. I smiled at the thought of Miriam occupying herself during that time, trapped in Blackwell's where the tourists congregated to look at postcards, smack between the Oxford guidebooks and the true-crime section.

I secured a sandwich and some tea and squeezed into the farthest corner of the crowded room between a vaguely familiar member of the history faculty who was reading the paper and an undergraduate dividing his attention between a music player, a mobile phone, and a computer.

After finishing my sandwich, I cupped the tea in my hands and glanced out the windows. I frowned. One of the unfamiliar daemons from Duke Humfrey's was lounging against the library gates and looking up at Blackwell's windows.

Two nudges pressed against my cheekbones, as gentle and fleeting as a kiss. I looked up into the face of another daemon. She was beautiful, with arresting, contradictory features – her mouth too wide for her delicate face, her chocolate brown eyes too close together given their enormous size, her hair too fair for skin the color of honey.

'Dr Bishop?' The woman's Australian accent sent cold fingers moving around the base of my spine.

'Yes,' I whispered, glancing at the stairs. Miriam's dark head failed to emerge from below. 'I'm Diana Bishop.'

She smiled. 'I'm Agatha Wilson. And your friend downstairs doesn't know I'm here.'

It was an incongruously old-fashioned name for someone who was only about ten years older than I was, and far more stylish. Her name was familiar, though, and I dimly remembered seeing it in a fashion magazine.

'May I sit down?' she asked, gesturing at the seat just vacated by the historian.

'Of course,' I murmured.

On Monday I'd met a vampire. On Tuesday a witch tried to worm his way into my head. Wednesday, it would appear, was daemon day.

Even though they'd followed me around college, I knew even less about daemons than I did about vampires. Few seemed to understand the creatures, and Sarah had never been able to answer my questions about them. Based on her accounts, daemons constituted a criminal underclass. Their superabundance of cleverness and creativity led them to lie, steal, cheat, and even kill, because they felt they could get away with it. Even more troublesome, as far as Sarah was concerned, were the conditions of their birth. There was no telling where or when a daemon would crop up, since they were typically born to human parents. To my aunt this only compounded their already marginal position in the hierarchy of beings. She valued a witch's family traditions and bloodlines, and she didn't approve of daemonic unpredictability.

Agatha Wilson was content to sit next to me quietly at first, watching me hold my tea. Then she started to talk in a bewildering swirl of words. Sarah always said that conversations with daemons were impossible, because they began in the middle.

'So much energy is bound to attract us,' she said matter-of-factly, as if I'd asked her a question. 'The witches were in Oxford for Mabon, and chattering as if the world weren't full of vampires who hear *everything*.' She fell silent. 'We weren't sure we'd ever see it again.'

'See what?' I said softly.

'The book,' she confided in a low voice.

'The book,' I repeated, my voice flat.

'Yes. After what the witches did to it, we didn't think we'd catch a glimpse of it again.'

The daemon's eyes were focused on a spot in the middle of the room. 'Of course, you're a witch, too. Perhaps it's wrong to talk to you. I would have thought you of all witches would be able to figure out how they did it, though. And now there's this,' she said sadly, picking up the abandoned newspaper and handing it to me.

The sensational headline immediately caught my attention: VAMPIRE ON THE LOOSE IN LONDON. I hurriedly read the story.

Metropolitan Police have no new leads in the puzzling murder of two men in Westminster. The bodies of Daniel Bennett, 22, and Jason Enright, 26, were found in an alley behind the White Hart pub on St Alban's Street early Sunday morning by the pub's owner, Reg Scott. Both men had severed carotid arteries and multiple lacerations on the neck, arms, and torso. Forensic tests revealed that massive loss of blood was the cause of death, although no blood evidence was found at the scene.

Authorities investigating the 'vampire murders,' as they were dubbed by local residents, sought the advice of Peter

Knox. The author of bestselling books on modern occultism, including *Dark Matters: The Devil in Modern Times* and *Magic Rising: The Need for Mystery in the Age of Science*, Knox has been consulted by agencies around the world in cases of suspected satanic and serial killings.

'There is no evidence that these are ritual murders,' Knox told reporters at a news conference. 'Nor does it seem that this is the work of a serial killer,' he concluded, in spite of the similar murders of Christiana Nilsson in Copenhagen last summer and Sergei Morozov in St Petersburg in the autumn of 2007. When pressed, Knox conceded that the London case may involve a copycat killer or killers.

Concerned residents have instituted a public watch, and local police have launched a door-to-door safety campaign to answer questions and provide support and guidance. Officials urge London residents to take extra precautions for their safety, especially at night.

'That's just the work of a newspaper editor in search of a story,' I said, handing the paper back to the daemon. 'The press is preying on human fears.'

'Are they?' she asked, glancing around the room. 'I'm not so sure. I think it's much more than that. One never knows with vampires. They're only a step away from animals.' Agatha Wilson's mouth drew tight in a sour expression. 'And you think *we're* the unstable ones. Still, it's dangerous for any of us to catch human attention.'

This was too much talk of witches and vampires for a public place. The undergraduate still had his earphones in, however, and all the other patrons were deep into their own thoughts or had their heads close to their lunch companions'.

'I don't know anything about the manuscript or what the witches did to it, Ms Wilson. I don't have it either,' I said hastily, in case she, too, thought I might have stolen it.

'You must call me Agatha.' She focused on the pattern of the carpet. 'The library has it now. Did they tell you to send it back?'

Did she mean witches? Vampires? The librarians? I picked the likeliest culprits.

'Witches?' I whispered.

Agatha nodded, her eyes drifting around the room.

'No. When I was done with it, I simply returned it to the stacks.'

'Ah, the stacks,' Agatha said knowingly. 'Everybody thinks the library is just a building, but it isn't.'

Once again I remembered the eerie constriction I'd felt after Sean had put the manuscript on the conveyor belt.

'The library is whatever the witches want it to be,' she went on. 'But the book doesn't belong to you. Witches shouldn't get to decide where it's kept and who sees it.'

'What's so special about this manuscript?'

'The book explains why we're here,' she said, her voice betraying a hint of desperation. 'It tells our story – beginning, middle, even the end. We daemons need to understand our place in the world. Our need is greater than that of the witches or vampires.' There was nothing addled about her now. She was like a camera that had been chronically out of focus until someone came by and twisted the lenses into alignment.

'You know your place in the world,' I began. 'There are four kinds of creatures – humans, daemons, vampires, and witches.'

'And where do daemons come from? How are we made? Why are we here?' Her brown eyes snapped. 'Do you know where *your* power comes from? Do you?'

'No,' I whispered, shaking my head.

'Nobody knows,' she said wistfully. 'Every day we wonder. Humans thought daemons were guardian angels at first. Then they believed we were gods, bound to the earth and victims of our own passions. Humans hated us because we were different and abandoned their children if they turned out to be daemons. They accused us of possessing their souls and making them insane. Daemons are brilliant, but we're not vicious – not like the vampires.' Her voice was clearly angry now, though it never lifted above a murmur. 'We would never make someone insane. Even more than witches, we're victims of human fear and envy.'

'Witches have their share of nasty legends to contend with,' I said, thinking of the witch-hunts and the executions that followed.

'Witches are born to witches. Vampires make other vampires. You have family stories and memories to comfort you when you're lonely or confused. We have nothing but tales told to us by humans. It's no wonder so many daemons are broken in spirit. Our only hope lies in brushing against other daemons one day and knowing we're like them. My son was one of the lucky ones. Nathaniel had a daemon for a mother, someone who saw the signs and could help him understand.' She looked away for a moment, regaining her composure. When her eyes again met mine, they were sad. 'Maybe the humans are right. Maybe we are possessed. I see things, Diana. Things I shouldn't.'

Daemons could be visionaries. No one knew if their visions were reliable, like the visions that witches had.

'I see blood and fear. I see you,' she said, her eyes losing focus again. 'Sometimes I see the vampire. He's wanted this book for a very long time. Instead he's found you. Curious.'

'Why does Matthew Clairmont want the book?'

Agatha shrugged. 'Vampires and witches don't share their thoughts with us. Not even your vampire tells us what he knows, though he's fonder of daemons than most of his kind. So many secrets, and so many clever humans these days. They'll figure it out if we're not careful. Humans like power — secrets, too.'

'He's not *my* vampire.' I flushed.

'Are you sure?' she asked, staring into the chrome on the espresso machine as if it were a magic mirror.

'Yes,' I said tightly.

'A little book can hold a big secret — one that might change the world. You're a witch. You know words have power. And if your vampire knew the secret, he wouldn't need you.' Agatha's brown eyes were now melting and warm.

'Matthew Clairmont can call the manuscript himself if he wants it so badly.' The idea that he might be doing so now was unaccountably chilling.

'When you get it back,' she said urgently, grabbing my arm, 'promise me you'll remember that you aren't the only ones who need to know its secrets. Daemons are part of the story, too. Promise me.'

I felt a flicker of panic at her touch, felt suddenly aware of the heat of the room and the press of people in it. Instinctively I searched for the nearest exit while focusing on my breathing, trying to curb the beginnings of a fight-or-flight response.

'I promise,' I murmured hesitantly, not sure what it was I was agreeing to.

'Good,' she said absently, dropping my arm. Her eyes drifted away. 'It was good of you to speak with me.' Agatha was staring at the carpet once more. 'We'll see each other again. Remember, some promises matter more than others.'

I dropped my teapot and cup into the gray plastic tub on top of the trash and threw away the bag from my sandwich. When I glanced over my shoulder, Agatha was reading the sports section of the historian's discarded London daily.

On my way out of Blackwell's, I didn't see Miriam, but I could feel her eyes.

The Selden End had filled with ordinary human beings while I was gone, all of them busy with their own work and completely oblivious to the creature convention around them. Envious of their ignorance, I took up a manuscript, determined to concentrate, but instead found myself reviewing my conversation in Blackwell's and the events of the past few days. On an immediate level, the illustrations in Ashmole 782 didn't seem related to what Agatha Wilson had said the book was about. And if Matthew Clairmont and the daemon were so interested in the manuscript, why didn't they request it?

I closed my eyes, recalling the details of my encounter with the manuscript and trying to make some pattern of the events of the past few days by emptying my mind and imagining the problem as a jigsaw puzzle sitting on a white table, then rearranging the colorful shapes. But no matter where they were placed, no clear picture emerged. Frustrated, I pushed my chair away from my desk and walked toward the exit.

'Any requests?' Sean asked as he took the manuscripts from my arms. I handed him a bunch of freshly filled-out call slips. He smiled at the stack's thickness but didn't say a word.

Before leaving, I needed to do two things. The first was a matter of simple courtesy. I wasn't sure how they'd done it, but the vampires had kept me from being distracted by an endless stream of creatures in the Selden End. Witches and vampires didn't often have occasion to thank one another, but Clairmont had protected me twice in two days. I was determined not to be ungrateful, or bigoted like Sarah and her friends in the Madison coven.

'Professor Clairmont?'

The vampire looked up.

'Thank you,' I said simply, meeting his gaze and holding it until he looked away.

'You're welcome,' he murmured, a note of surprise in his voice.

The second was more calculated. If Matthew Clairmont needed me, I needed him, too. I wanted him to tell me why Ashmole 782 was attracting so much attention.

'Perhaps you should call me Diana,' I said quickly, before I lost my nerve.

Matthew Clairmont smiled.

My heart stopped beating for a fraction of a second. This was not the small, polite smile with which I was now familiar. His lips curved toward his eyes, making his whole face sparkle. God, he was beautiful, I thought again, slightly dazzled.

'All right,' he said softly, 'but then you must call me Matthew.'

I nodded in agreement, my heart still beating in erratic syncopation. Something spread through my body, loosening the vestiges of anxiety that remained after the unexpected meeting with Agatha Wilson.

Matthew's nose flared delicately. His smile grew a bit wider. Whatever my body was doing, he had smelled it. What's more, he seemed to have identified it.

I flushed.

'Have a pleasant evening, Diana.' His voice lingered on my name, making it sound exotic and strange.

'Good night, Matthew,' I replied, beating a hasty retreat.

That evening, rowing on the quiet river as sunset turned to dusk, I saw an occasional smoky smudge on the towpath, always slightly ahead of me, like a dark star guiding me home.

CHAPTER 7

At two-fifteen I was ripped from sleep by a terrible sensation of drowning. Flailing my way out from under the covers, transformed into heavy, wet seaweed by the power of the dream, I moved toward the lighter water above me. Just when I was making progress, something grabbed me by the ankle and pulled me down deeper.

As usual with nightmares, I awoke with a start before finding out who had caught me. For several minutes I lay disoriented, my body drenched with sweat and my heart sounding a staccato beat that reverberated through my rib cage. Gingerly, I sat up.

A white face stared at me from the window with dark, hollow eyes.

Too late I realized that it was just my reflection in the glass. I barely made it to the bathroom before being sick. Then I spent the next thirty minutes curled into a ball on the cold tile floor, blaming Matthew Clairmont and the other, gathering creatures for my unease. Finally I crawled back into bed and slept for a few hours. At dawn I dragged myself into rowing gear.

When I got to the lodge, the porter gave me an amazed look. 'You're not going out at this hour in the fog, Dr Bishop? You look like you've been burning the candle at both ends, if you don't mind me saying so. Wouldn't a nice lie-in be a better idea? The river will still be there tomorrow.'

After considering Fred's advice, I shook my head. 'No, I'll feel better for it.' He looked doubtful. 'And the students are back this weekend.'

The pavement was slick with moisture, so I ran more slowly than usual to make allowances for the weather as well as my fatigue. My familiar route took me past Oriel College and to the tall, black iron gates between Merton and Corpus Christi. They were locked from dusk until dawn to keep people out of the meadows that bordered the river, but the first thing you learned when you rowed at Oxford was how to scale them. I climbed them with ease.

The familiar ritual of putting the boat in the water did its work. By the time it slipped away from the dock and into the fog, I felt almost normal.

When it's foggy, rowing feels even more like flying. The air muffles the normal sounds of birds and automobiles and amplifies the soft thwack of oars in the water and the swoosh of the boat seats. With no shorelines and familiar landmarks to orient you, there's nothing to steer by but your instincts.

I fell into an easy, swinging rhythm in the scull, my ears and eyes tuned to the slightest change in the sound of my oars that would tell me I was getting too close to the banks or a shadow that would indicate the approach of another boat. The fog was so thick that I considered turning back, but the prospect of a long, straight stretch of river was too enticing.

Just shy of the tavern, I carefully turned the boat. Two rowers were downstream, engaged in a heated discussion about competing strategies for winning the idiosyncratic Oxbridge style of racing known as 'bumps'.

'Do you want to go ahead of me?' I called.

'Sure!' came the quick response. The pair shot past, never breaking their stroke.

The sound of their oars faded. I decided to row back to the boathouse and call it quits. It was a short workout, but the stiffness from my third consecutive night of little sleep had lessened.

The equipment put away, I locked the boathouse and walked slowly along the path toward town. It was so quiet in the early-morning mist that time and place receded. I closed my eyes, imagining that I was nowhere – not in Oxford, nor anywhere that had a name.

When I opened them, a dark outline had risen up in front of me. I gasped in fear. The shape shot toward me, and my hands instinctively warded off the danger.

'Diana, I'm so sorry. I thought you had seen me.' It was Matthew Clairmont, his face creased with concern.

'I was walking with my eyes closed.' I grabbed at the neck of my fleece, and he backed away slightly. I propped myself against a tree until my breathing slowed.

'Can you tell me something?' Clairmont asked once my heart stopped pounding.

'Not if you plan to ask why I'm out on the river in the fog when there are vampires and daemons and witches following me.' I wasn't up for a lecture – not this morning.

'No' – his voice held a touch of acid – 'although that's an excellent question. I was going to ask why you walk with your eyes closed.'

I laughed. 'What – you don't?'

Matthew shook his head. 'Vampires have only five senses. We find it best to use all of them,' he said sardonically.

'There's nothing magical about it, Matthew. It's a game I've played since I was a child. It made my aunt crazy. I was always coming home with bruised legs and scratches from running into bushes and trees.'

The vampire looked thoughtful. He shoved his hands into his slate gray trouser pockets and gazed off into the fog. Today he was wearing a blue-gray sweater that made his hair appear darker, but no coat. It was a striking omission, given the weather. Suddenly feeling unkempt, I wished my rowing tights didn't have a hole in the back of the left thigh from catching on the boat's rigging.

'How was your row this morning?' Clairmont asked finally, as if he didn't already know. He wasn't out for a morning stroll.

'Good,' I said shortly.

'There aren't many people here this early.'

'No, but I like it when the river isn't crowded.'

'Isn't it risky to row in this kind of weather, when so few people are out?' His tone was mild, and had he not been a vampire watching my every move, I might have taken his inquiry for an awkward attempt at conversation.

'Risky how?'

'If something were to happen, it's possible nobody would see it.'

I'd never been afraid before on the river, but he had a point. Nevertheless, I shrugged it off. 'The students will be here on Monday. I'm enjoying the peace while it lasts.'

'Does term really start next week?' Clairmont sounded genuinely surprised.

'You *are* on the faculty, aren't you?' I laughed.

'Technically, but I don't really see students. I'm here in more of a research capacity.' His mouth tightened. He didn't like being laughed at.

'Must be nice.' I thought of my three-hundred-seat introductory lecture class and all those anxious freshmen.

'It's quiet. My laboratory equipment doesn't ask questions about my long hours. And I have Dr Shephard and another assistant, Dr Whitmore, so I'm not entirely alone.'

It was damp, and I was cold. Besides, there was something unnatural about exchanging pleasantries with a vampire in the pea-soup gloom. 'I really should go home.'

'Would you like a ride?'

Four days ago I wouldn't have accepted a ride home from a vampire, but this morning it seemed like an excellent idea. Besides, it gave me an opportunity to ask why a biochemist might be interested in a seventeenth-century alchemical manuscript.

'Sure,' I said.

Clairmont's shy, pleased look was utterly disarming. 'My car's parked nearby,' he said, gesturing in the direction of Christ Church College. We walked in silence for a few minutes, wrapped up in the gray fog and the strangeness of being alone, witch and vampire. He deliberately shortened his stride to keep in step with me, and he seemed more relaxed outdoors than he had in the library.

'Is this your college?'

'No, I've never been a member here.' The way he phrased it

made me wonder what colleges he *had* been a member of. Then I began to consider how long his life had been. Sometimes he seemed as old as Oxford itself.

'Diana?' Clairmont had stopped.

'Hmm?' I'd started to wander off toward the college's parking area.

'It's this way,' he said, pointing in the opposite direction.

Matthew led me to a tiny walled enclave. A low-slung black Jaguar was parked under a bright yellow sign that proclaimed POSITIVELY NO PARKING HERE. The car had a John Radcliffe Hospital permit hanging from the rearview mirror.

'I see,' I said, putting my hands on my hips. 'You park pretty much wherever you want.'

'Normally I'm a good citizen when it comes to parking, but this morning's weather suggested that an exception might be made,' Matthew said defensively. He reached a long arm around me to unlock the door. The Jaguar was an older model, without the latest technology of keyless entries and navigation systems, but it looked as if it had just rolled off the showroom floor. He pulled the door open, and I climbed in, the caramel-colored leather upholstery fitting itself to my body.

I'd never been in a car so luxurious. Sarah's worst suspicions about vampires would be confirmed if she knew they drove Jaguars while she drove a broken-down purple Honda Civic that had oxidized to the brownish lavender of roasted eggplant.

Clairmont rolled along the drive to the gates of Christ Church, where he waited for an opening in the early-morning traffic dominated by delivery trucks, buses, and bicycles. 'Would you like some breakfast before I take you home?' he asked casually, gripping the polished steering wheel. 'You must be hungry after all that exercise.'

This was the second meal Clairmont had invited me to (not) share with him. Was this a vampire thing? Did they like to watch other people eat?

The combination of vampires and eating turned my mind to the vampire's dietary habits. Everyone on the planet knew that vampires fed on human blood. But was that all they ate? No longer sure that driving around in a car with a vampire was a good idea, I zipped up the neck of my fleece pullover and moved an inch closer to the door.

'Diana?' he prompted.

'I could eat,' I admitted hesitantly, 'and I'd kill for some tea.'

He nodded, his eyes back on the traffic. 'I know just the place.'

Clairmont steered up the hill and took a right down the High Street. We passed the statue of George II's wife standing under the cupola at The Queen's College, then headed toward Oxford's botanical gardens. The hushed confines of the car made Oxford seem even more other-worldly than usual, its spires and towers appearing suddenly out of the quiet and fog.

We didn't talk, and his stillness made me realize how much I moved, constantly blinking, breathing, and rearranging myself. Not Clairmont. He never blinked and seldom breathed, and his every turn of the steering wheel or push of the pedals was as small and efficient as possible, as if his long life required him to conserve energy. I wondered again how old Matthew Clairmont was.

The vampire darted down a side street, pulling up in front of a tiny café that was packed with locals bolting down plates of food. Some were reading the newspaper; others were chatting with their neighbors at adjoining tables. All of them, I noted with pleasure, were drinking huge mugs of tea.

'I didn't know about this place,' I said.

'It's a well-kept secret,' he said mischievously. 'They don't want university dons ruining the atmosphere.'

I automatically turned to open my car door, but before I could touch the handle, Clairmont was there, opening it for me.

'How did you get here so fast?' I grumbled.

'Magic,' he replied through pursed lips. Apparently Clairmont did not approve of women who opened their own car doors any more than he reportedly approved of women who argued with him.

'I am capable of opening my own door,' I said, getting out of the car.

'Why do today's women think it's important to open a door

themselves?' he said sharply. 'Do you believe it's a testament to your physical power?'

'No, but it is a sign of our independence.' I stood with my arms crossed, daring him to contradict me and remembering what Chris had said about Clairmont's behavior toward a woman who'd asked too many questions at a conference.

Wordlessly he closed the car's door behind me and opened the café door. I stood resolutely in place, waiting for him to enter. A gust of warm, humid air carried the smell of bacon fat and toasted bread. My mouth started to water.

'You're impossibly old-fashioned,' I said with a sigh, deciding not to fight it. He could open doors for me this morning so long as he was prepared to buy me a hot breakfast.

'After you,' he murmured.

Once inside, we wended our way through the crowded tables. Clairmont's skin, which had looked almost normal in the fog, was conspicuously pale under the café's stark overhead lighting. A couple of humans stared as we passed. The vampire stiffened.

This wasn't a good idea, I thought uneasily as more human eyes studied us.

'Hiya, Matthew,' a cheerful female voice called from behind the counter. 'Two for breakfast?'

His face lightened. 'Two, Mary. How's Dan?'

'Well enough to complain that he's fed up being in bed. I'd say he's definitely on the mend.'

'That's wonderful news,' Clairmont said. 'Can you get this lady some tea when you have a chance? She's threatened to kill for it.'

'Won't be necessary, dearie,' Mary told me with a smile. 'We serve tea without bloodshed.' She eased her ample body out from behind the Formica counter and led us to a table tucked into the far corner next to the kitchen door. Two plastic-covered menus hit the table with a slap. 'You'll be out of the way here, Matthew. I'll send Steph around with the tea. Stay as long as you like.'

Clairmont made a point of settling me with my back to the wall.

He sat opposite, between me and the rest of the room, curling the laminated menu into a tube and letting it gently unfurl in his fingers, visibly bristling. In the presence of others, the vampire was restless and prickly, just as he had been in the library. He was much more comfortable when the two of us were alone.

I recognized the significance of this behavior thanks to my new knowledge of the Norwegian wolf. He was protecting me.

'Just who do you think poses a threat, Matthew? I told you I could take care of myself.' My voice came out a little more tartly than I had intended.

'Yes, I'm sure you can,' he said doubtfully.

'Look,' I said, trying to keep my tone even, 'you've managed to keep . . . them away from me so I could get some work done.' The tables were too close together for me to include any more details. 'I'm grateful for that. But this café is full of humans. The only danger now would come from your drawing their attention. You're officially off duty.'

Clairmont cocked his head in the direction of the cash register. 'That man over there told his friend that you looked "tasty." ' He was trying to make light of it, but his face darkened. I smothered a laugh.

'I don't think he's going to bite me,' I said.

The vampire's skin took on a grayish hue.

'From what I understand of modern British slang, "tasty" is a compliment, not a threat.'

Clairmont continued to glower.

'If you don't like what you're hearing, stop listening in on other people's conversations,' I offered, impatient with his male posturing.

'That's easier said than done,' he pronounced, picking up a jar of Marmite.

A younger, slightly svelter version of Mary came up with an enormous brown stoneware teapot and two mugs. 'Milk and sugar are on the table, Matthew,' she said, eyeing me with curiosity.

Matthew made the necessary introductions. 'Steph, this is Diana. She's visiting from America.'

'Really? Do you live in California? I'm dying to get to California.'

'No, I live in Connecticut,' I said regretfully.

'That's one of the little states, isn't it?' Steph was clearly disappointed.

'Yes. And it snows.'

'I fancy palm trees and sunshine, myself.' At the mention of snow, she'd lost interest in me entirely. 'What'll it be?'

'I'm really hungry,' I said apologetically, ordering two scrambled eggs, four pieces of toast, and several rashers of bacon.

Steph, who had clearly heard far worse, wrote down the order without comment and picked up our menus. 'Just tea for you, Matthew?'

He nodded.

Once Steph was out of earshot, I leaned across the table. 'Do they know about you?'

Clairmont tilted forward, his face a foot away from mine. This morning he smelled sweeter, like a freshly picked carnation. I inhaled deeply.

'They know I'm a little different. Mary may suspect I'm more than a little different, but she's convinced that I saved Dan's life, so she's decided it doesn't matter.'

'How did you save her husband?' Vampires were supposed to take human lives, not save them.

'I saw him on a rotation at the Radcliffe when they were short staffed. Mary had seen a program that described the symptoms of stroke, and she recognized them when her husband began to struggle. Without her he'd be dead or seriously incapacitated.'

'But she thinks you saved Dan?' The vampire's spiciness was making me dizzy. I lifted the lid from the teapot, replacing the aroma of carnations with the tannic smell of black tea.

'Mary saved him the first time, but after he was admitted into hospital he had a terrible reaction to his medication. I told you she's observant. When she took her concerns to one of the physicians, he brushed them aside. I . . . overheard – and intervened.'

'Do you often see patients?' I poured each of us a steaming mug of tea so strong you could stand a spoon up in it. My hands trembled slightly at the idea of a vampire prowling the wards at the John Radcliffe among the sick and injured.

'No,' he said, toying with the sugar jar, 'only when they have an emergency.'

Pushing one of the mugs toward him, I fixed my eyes on the sugar. He handed it to me. I put precisely half a teaspoon of sugar and half a cup of milk into my tea. This was just how I liked it – black as tar, a hint of sugar to cut the edge off the bitterness, then enough milk to make it look less like stew. This done, I stirred the concoction clockwise. As soon as experience told me it wouldn't burn my tongue, I took a sip. Perfect.

The vampire was smiling.

'What?' I asked.

'I've never seen anyone approach tea with that much attentiveness to detail.'

'You must not spend much time with serious tea drinkers. It's all about being able to gauge the strength before you put the sugar and milk in it.' His steaming mug sat untouched in front of him. 'You like yours black, I see.'

'Tea's not really my drink,' he said, his voice dropping slightly.

'What *is* your drink?' The minute the question was out of my mouth, I wished I could call it back. His mood went from amusement to tight-lipped fury.

'You have to ask?' he said scathingly. 'Even humans know the answer to that question.'

'I'm sorry. I shouldn't have.' I gripped the mug, trying to steady myself.

'No, you shouldn't.'

I drank my tea in silence. We both looked up when Steph approached with a toast rack full of grilled bread and a plate heaped high with eggs and bacon.

'Mum thought you needed veg,' Steph explained when my eyes widened at the mound of fried mushrooms and tomatoes that accompanied the breakfast. 'She said you looked like death.'

'Thank you!' I said. Mary's critique of my appearance did nothing to diminish my appreciation for the extra food.

Steph grinned and Clairmont offered me a small smile when I picked up the fork and applied myself to the plate.

Everything was piping hot and fragrant, with the perfect ratio of fried surface to melting, tender insides. My hunger appeased, I started a methodical attack on the toast rack, taking up the first triangle of cold toast and scraping butter over its surface. The vampire watched me eat with the same acute attention he'd devoted to watching me make my tea.

'So why science?' I ventured, tucking the toast into my mouth so he'd have to answer.

'Why history?' His voice was dismissive, but he wasn't going to fend me off that easily.

'You first.'

'I suppose I need to know why I'm here,' he said, looking fixedly at the table. He was building a moated castle from the sugar jar and a ring of blue artificial-sweetener packets.

I froze at the similarity between his explanation and what Agatha had told me the day before about Ashmole 782. 'That's a question for philosophers, not scientists.' I sucked a drop of butter off my finger to hide my confusion.

His eyes glittered with another wave of sudden anger. 'You don't really believe that – that scientists don't care about why.'

'They used to be interested in the whys,' I conceded, keeping a wary eye on him. His sudden shifts in mood were down-right frightening. 'Now it seems all they're concerned with is the question of how – how does the body work, how do the planets move?'

Clairmont snorted. 'Not the good scientists.' The people behind him got up to leave, and he tensed, ready if they decided to rush the table.

'And you're a good scientist.'

He let my assessment pass without comment.

'Someday you'll have to explain to me the relationship between neuroscience, DNA research, animal behavior, and evolution. They don't obviously fit together.' I took another bite of toast.

Clairmont's left eyebrow rose toward his hairline. 'You've been catching up on your scientific journals,' he said sharply.

I shrugged. 'You had an unfair advantage. You knew all about my work. I was just leveling the playing field.'

He mumbled something under his breath that sounded French. 'I've had a lot of time to think,' he replied flatly in English, enlarging the moat around his castle with another ring of sweetener packets. 'There's no connection between them.'

'Liar,' I said softly.

Not surprisingly, my accusation made Clairmont furious, but the speed of the transformation still took me aback. It was a reminder that I was having breakfast with a creature who could be lethal.

'Tell me what the connection is, then,' he said through clenched teeth.

'I'm not sure,' I said truthfully. 'Something's holding them all together, a question that links your research interests and gives meaning to them. The only other explanation is that you're an intellectual magpie – which is ridiculous, given how highly regarded your work is – or maybe you get bored easily. You don't seem the type to be prone to intellectual ennui. Quite the opposite, in fact.'

Clairmont studied me until the silence grew uncomfortable. My stomach was starting to complain at the amount of food I'd expected it to absorb. I poured fresh tea and doctored it while waiting for him to speak.

'For a witch you're observant, too.' The vampire's eyes showed grudging admiration.

'Vampires aren't the only creatures who can hunt, Matthew.'

'No. We all hunt something, don't we Diana?' He lingered over my name. 'Now it's my turn. Why history?'

'You haven't answered all my questions.' And I hadn't yet asked him my most important question.

He shook his head firmly, and I redirected my energy from

ferreting out information to protecting myself from Clairmont's attempts to obtain it.

'At first it was the neatness of it, I suppose.' My voice sounded surprisingly tentative. 'The past seemed so predictable, as if nothing that happened there was surprising.'

'Spoken like someone who wasn't there,' the vampire said drily.

I gave a short laugh. 'I found that out soon enough. But in the beginning that's how it seemed. At Oxford the professors made the past a tidy story with a beginning, a middle, and an end. Everything seemed logical, inevitable. Their stories hooked me, and that was it. No other subject interested me. I became a historian and have never looked back.'

'Even though you discovered that human beings – past or present – aren't logical?'

'History only became more challenging when it became less neat. Every time I pick up a book or a document from the past, I'm in a battle with people who lived hundreds of years ago. They have their secrets and obsessions – all the things they won't or can't reveal. It's my job to discover and explain them.'

'What if you can't? What if they defy explanation?'

'That's never happened,' I said after considering his question. 'At least I don't think it has. All you have to do is be a good listener. Nobody really wants to keep secrets, not even the dead. People leave clues everywhere, and if you pay attention, you can piece them together.'

'So you're the historian as detective,' he observed.

'Yes. With far lower stakes.' I sat back in my chair, thinking the interview was over.

'Why the history of science, then?' he continued.

'The challenge of great minds, I suppose?' I tried not to sound glib, nor to let my voice rise up at the end of the sentence into a question, and failed on both counts.

Clairmont bowed his head and slowly began to take apart his moated castle.

Common sense told me to remain silent, but the knotted threads of my own secrets began to loosen. 'I wanted to know how humans came up with a view of the world that had so little magic in it,' I added abruptly. 'I needed to understand how they convinced themselves that magic wasn't important.'

The vampire's cool gray eyes lifted to mine. 'Have you found out?'

'Yes and no.' I hesitated. 'I saw the logic that they used, and the death of a thousand cuts as experimental scientists slowly chipped away at the belief that the world was an inexplicably powerful, magical place. Ultimately they failed, though. The magic never really went away. It waited, quietly, for people to return to it when they found the science wanting.'

'So alchemy,' he said.

'No,' I protested. 'Alchemy is one of the earliest forms of experimental science.'

'Perhaps. But you don't believe that alchemy is devoid of magic.' Matthew's voice was certain. 'I've read your work. Not even you can keep it away entirely.'

'Then it's science with magic. Or magic with science, if you prefer.'

'Which do you prefer?'

'I'm not sure,' I said defensively.

'Thank you.' Clairmont's look suggested he knew how difficult it was for me to talk about this.

'You're welcome. I think.' I pushed my hair back from my eyes, feeling a little shaky. 'Can I ask you something else?' His eyes were wary, but he nodded. 'Why are you interested in my work — in alchemy?'

He almost didn't answer, ready to brush the question aside, then reconsidered. I'd given him a secret. Now it was his turn.

'The alchemists wanted to know why we're here, too.' Clairmont was telling the truth — I could see that — but it got me no closer to understanding his interest in Ashmole 782. He glanced at his watch. 'If you're finished, I should get you back to college. You must want to get into warm clothes before you go to the library.'

'What I need is a shower.' I stood and stretched, twisting my neck in an effort to ease its chronic tightness. 'And I *have* to go to yoga tonight. I'm spending too much time sitting at a desk.'

The vampire's eyes glinted. 'You practice yoga?'

'Couldn't live without it,' I replied. 'I love the movement, and the meditation.'

'I'm not surprised,' he said. 'That's the way you row — a combination of movement and meditation.'

My cheeks colored. He was watching me as closely on the river as he had in the library.

Clairmont put a twenty-pound note on the table and waved at Mary. She waved back, and he touched my elbow lightly, steering me between the tables and the few remaining customers.

'Whom do you have classes with?' he asked after he opened the car door and settled me inside.

'I go to that studio on the High Street. I haven't found a teacher I like yet, but it's close, and beggars can't be choosers.' New Haven had several yoga studios, but Oxford was lagging behind.

The vampire settled himself in the car, turned the key, and neatly reversed in a nearby driveway before heading back to town.

'You won't find the class you need there,' he said confidently.

'You do yoga, too?' I was fascinated by the image of his massive body twisting itself through a practice.

'Some,' he said. 'If you want to go to yoga with me tomorrow, I could pick you up outside Hertford at six. This evening you'd have to brave the studio in town, but tomorrow you'd have a good practice.'

'Where's your studio? I'll call and see if they have a class tonight.'

Clairmont shook his head. 'They aren't open tonight. Monday, Wednesday, Friday, and Sunday evenings only.'

'Oh,' I said, disappointed. 'What's the class like?'

'You'll see. It's hard to describe.' He was trying not to smile.

To my surprise, we'd arrived at the lodge. Fred craned his neck to see who was idling inside the gates, saw the Radcliffe tag, and strolled over to see what was going on.

Clairmont let me out of the car. Outside, I gave Fred a wave, and extended my hand. 'I enjoyed breakfast. Thanks for the tea and company.'

'Anytime,' he said. 'I'll see you in the library.'

Fred whistled as Clairmont pulled away. 'Nice car, Dr Bishop. Friend of yours?' It was his job to know as much as possible about what happened in the college for safety's sake as well as to satisfy the unabashed curiosity that was part of a porter's job description.

'I suppose so,' I said thoughtfully.

In my rooms I pulled out my passport case and removed a ten-dollar bill from my stash of American currency. It took me a few minutes to find an envelope. After slipping the bill inside without a note, I addressed it to Chris, wrote *AIRMAIL* on the front in capital letters, and stuck the required postage in the upper corner.

Chris was never going to let me forget he'd won this bet. Never.

CHAPTER 8

'Honestly, that car is such a cliché.' The hair clung to my fingers, crackling and snapping as I tried to push it from my face.

Clairmont was lounging against the side of his Jaguar looking unrumpled and at ease. Even his yoga clothes, characteristically gray and black, looked bandbox fresh, though considerably less tailored than what he wore to the library.

Contemplating the sleek black car and the elegant vampire, I felt unaccountably cross. It had not been a good day. The conveyor belt broke in the library, and it took forever for them to fetch my manuscripts. My keynote address remained elusive, and I was beginning to look at the calendar with alarm, imagining a roomful of colleagues peppering me with difficult questions. It was nearly October, and the conference was in November.

'You think a subcompact would be better subterfuge?' he asked, holding out his hand for my yoga mat.

'Not really, no.' Standing in the fall twilight, he positively screamed vampire, yet the rising tide of undergraduates and dons passed him without a second glance. If they couldn't sense what he was – *see* what he was, standing in the open air – the car was immaterial. The irritation built under my skin.

'Have I done something wrong?' His gray-green eyes were wide and guileless. He opened the car door, taking a deep breath as I slid past.

My temper flared. 'Are you smelling me?' After yesterday I suspected that my body was giving him all kinds of information I didn't want him to have.

'Don't tempt me,' he murmured, shutting me inside. The hair on my neck rose slightly as the implication of his words sank in. He popped open the trunk and put my mat inside.

Night air filled the car as the vampire climbed in without any visible effort or moment of limb-bent awkwardness. His face creased into the semblance of a sympathetic frown. 'Bad day?'

I gave him a withering glance. Clairmont knew exactly how my day had been. He and Miriam had been in Duke Humfrey's again, keeping the other creatures out of my immediate environment. When we left to change for yoga, Miriam had remained to make sure we weren't followed by a train of daemons – or worse.

Clairmont started the car and headed down the Woodstock Road without further attempts at small talk. There was nothing on it but houses.

'Where are we going?' I asked suspiciously.

'To yoga,' he replied calmly. 'Based on your mood, I'd say you need it.'

'And where is yoga?' I demanded. We were headed out to the countryside in the direction of Blenheim.

'Have you changed your mind?' Matthew's voice was touched with exasperation. 'Should I take you back to the studio on the High Street?'

I shuddered at the memory of last night's uninspiring class. 'No.'

'Then relax. I'm not kidnapping you. It can be pleasant to let someone else take charge. Besides, it's a surprise.'

'Hmph,' I said. He switched on the stereo system, and classical music poured from the speakers.

'Stop thinking and listen,' he commanded. 'It's impossible to be tense around Mozart.'

Hardly recognizing myself, I settled in the seat with a sigh and shut my eyes. The Jaguar's motion was so subtle and the sounds from outside so muffled that I felt suspended above the ground, held up by invisible, musical hands.

The car slowed, and we pulled up to a set of high iron gates that even I, though practiced, couldn't have scaled. The walls on either side were warm red brick, with irregular forms and intricate woven patterns. I sat up a little straighter.

'You can't see it from here,' Clairmont said, laughing. He rolled down his window and punched a series of numbers into a polished keypad. A tone sounded, and the gates swung open.

Gravel crunched under the tires as we passed through another set of gates even older than the first. There was no scrolled ironwork here, just an archway spanning brick walls that were much lower than the ones facing the Woodstock Road. The archway had a tiny room on top, with windows on all sides like a lantern. To the left of the gate was a splendid brick gatehouse, with twisted chimneys and leaded windows. A small brass plaque with weathered edges read THE OLD LODGE.

'Beautiful,' I breathed.

'I thought you'd like it.' The vampire looked pleased.

Through the growing darkness, we passed into a park. A small herd of deer skittered off at the sound of the car, jumping into the protective shadows as the Jaguar's headlights swept the grounds. We climbed a slight hill and rounded a curve in the drive. The car slowed to a crawl as we reached the top of the rise and the headlights dipped over into blackness.

'There,' Clairmont said, pointing with his left hand.

A two-story Tudor manor house was arranged around a central courtyard. Its bricks glowed in the illumination of powerful spotlights that shone up through the branches of gnarled oak trees to light the face of the building.

I was so dumbfounded that I swore. Clairmont looked at me in shock, then chuckled.

He pulled the car in to the circular drive in front and parked behind a late-model Audi sports car. A dozen more cars were already parked there, and headlights continued to sweep down over the hill.

'Are you sure I'm going to be all right?' I'd been doing yoga for more than a decade, but that didn't mean I was any good at it. It had never occurred to me to ask whether this might be the kind of class where people balanced on one forearm with their feet suspended in midair.

'It's a mixed class,' he assured me.

'Okay.' My anxiety went up a notch in spite of his easy answer.

Clairmont took our yoga mats out of the trunk. Moving slowly as the last of the arrivals headed for the wide entry, he finally reached my door and put out his hand. *This is new*, I noted before putting my hand in his. I was still not entirely comfortable when our bodies came into contact. He was shockingly cold, and the contrast between our body temperatures took me aback.

The vampire held my hand lightly and tugged on it gently to help me out of the car. Before releasing me, he gave a soft encouraging squeeze. Surprised, I glanced at him and caught him doing the same thing. Both of us looked away in confusion.

We entered the house through another arched gate and a central courtyard. The manor was in an astonishing state of preservation. No later architects had been allowed to cut out symmetrical Georgian windows or affix fussy Victorian conservatories to it. We might have been stepping back in time.

'Unbelievable,' I murmured.

Clairmont grinned and steered me through a big wooden door propped open with an iron doorstop. I gasped. The outside was remarkable, but the inside was stunning. Miles of linenfold paneling extended in every direction, all burnished and glowing. Someone had lit a fire in the room's enormous fireplace. A single trestle table and some benches looked about as old as the house, and electric lights were the only evidence that we were in the twenty-first century.

Rows of shoes sat in front of the benches, and mounds of sweaters and coats covered their dark oak surfaces. Clairmont laid his keys on the table and removed his shoes. I kicked off my own and followed him.

'Remember I said this was a mixed class?' the vampire asked when we reached a door set into the paneling. I looked up, nodded. 'It is. But there's only one way to get into this room – you have to be one of us.'

He pulled open the door. Dozens of curious eyes nudged, tingled, and froze in my direction. The room was full of daemons, witches, and vampires. They sat on brightly colored mats – some with crossed legs, others kneeling – waiting for class to begin. Some of the daemons had headphones jammed into their ears. The witches were gossiping in a steady hum. The vampires sat quietly, their faces displaying little emotion.

My jaw dropped.

'Sorry,' Clairmont said. 'I was afraid you wouldn't come if I told you – and it really is the best class in Oxford.'

A tall witch who had short, jet-black hair and skin the color of coffee with cream walked toward us, and the rest of the room turned away, resuming their silent meditations. Clairmont, who'd tensed slightly when we entered, visibly relaxed as the witch approached us.

'Matthew.' Her husky voice was brushed with an Indian accent. 'Welcome.'

'Amira.' He nodded in greeting. 'This is the woman I told you about, Diana Bishop.'

The witch looked at me closely, her eyes taking in every detail of my face. She smiled. 'Diana. Nice to meet you. Are you new to yoga?'

'No.' My heart pounded with a fresh wave of anxiety. 'But this is my first time here.'

Her smile widened. 'Welcome to the Old Lodge.'

I wondered if anyone here knew about Ashmole 782, but there wasn't a single familiar face and the atmosphere in the room was open and easy, with none of the usual tension between creatures.

A warm, firm hand closed around my wrist, and my heart slowed immediately. I looked at Amira in astonishment. How had she done that?

She let loose my wrist, and my pulse remained steady. 'I think that you and Diana will be most comfortable here,' she told Clairmont. 'Get settled and we'll begin.'

We unrolled our mats in the back of the room, close to the door. There was no one to my immediate right, but across a small expanse of open floor two daemons sat in lotus position with their eyes closed. My shoulder tingled. I started, wondering who was looking at me. The feeling quickly disappeared.

Sorry, a guilty voice said quite distinctly within my skull.

The voice came from the front of the room, from the same direction as the tingle. Amira frowned slightly at someone in the first row before bringing the class to attention.

Out of sheer habit, my body folded obediently into a cross-legged position when she began to speak, and after a few seconds Clairmont followed suit.

'It's time to close your eyes.' Amira picked up a tiny remote control, and the soft strains of a meditative chant came out of the walls and ceiling. It sounded medieval, and one of the vampires sighed happily.

My eyes wandered, distracted by the ornate plasterwork of what must once have been the house's great hall.

'Close your eyes,' Amira suggested again gently. 'It can be hard to let go of our worries, our preoccupations, our egos. That's why we're here tonight.'

The words were familiar – I'd heard variations on this theme before, in other yoga classes – but they took on new meaning in this room.

'We're here tonight to learn to manage our energy. We spend our time striving and straining to be something that we're not. Let those desires go. Honor who you are.'

Amira took us through some gentle stretches and got us onto our knees to warm up our spines before we pushed back into downward dog. We held the posture for a few breaths before walking our hands to our feet and standing up.

'Root your feet into the earth,' she instructed, 'and take mountain pose.'

I concentrated on my feet and felt an unexpected jolt from the floor. My eyes widened.

We followed Amira as she began her *vinyasas*. We swung our arms up toward the ceiling before diving down to place our hands next to our feet. We rose halfway, spines parallel to the floor, before folding over and shooting our legs back into a pushup position. Dozens of daemons, vampires, and witches dipped and swooped their bodies into graceful, upward curves. We continued to fold and lift, sweeping our arms overhead once more before touching palms lightly together. Then Amira freed us to move at our own pace. She pushed a button on the stereo's remote, and a slow, melodic cover of Elton John's 'Rocket Man' filled the room.

The music was oddly appropriate, and I repeated the familiar movements in time to it, breathing into my tight muscles and letting the flow of the class push all thoughts from my head. After we'd started the series of poses for a third time, the energy in the room shifted.

Three witches were floating about a foot off the wooden floor-boards.

'Stay grounded,' Amira said in a neutral voice.

Two quietly returned to the floor. The third had to swan-dive to get back down, and even then his hands reached the floor before his feet.

Both the daemons and the vampires were having trouble with the pacing. Some of the daemons were moving so slowly that I wondered if they were stuck. The vampires were having the opposite problem, their powerful muscles coiling and then springing with sudden intensity.

'Gently,' Amira murmured. 'There's no need to push, no need to strain.'

Gradually the room's energy settled again. Amira moved us through a series of standing poses. Here the vampires were clearly at their best, able to sustain them for minutes without effort. Soon I was no longer concerned with who was in the room with me or whether I could keep up with the class. There was only the moment and the movement.

By the time we took to the floor for back bends and inversions, everyone in the room was dripping wet – except for the vampires, who didn't even look dewy. Some performed death-defying arm balances and handstands, but I wasn't among them. Clairmont was, however. At one point he looked to be attached to the ground by nothing more than his ear, his entire body in perfect alignment above him.

The hardest part of any practice for me was the final corpse pose – *savasana*. I found it nearly impossible to lie flat on my back without moving. The fact that everyone else seemed to find it relaxing only added to my anxiety. I lay as quietly as possible, eyes closed, trying not to twitch. A swoosh of feet moved between me and the vampire.

'Diana,' Amira whispered, 'this pose is not for you. Roll over onto your side.'

My eyes popped open. I stared into the witch's wide black eyes, mortified that she had somehow uncovered my secret.

'Curl into a ball.' Mystified, I did what she said. My body instantly relaxed. She patted me lightly on the shoulder. 'Keep your eyes open, too.'

I had turned toward Clairmont. Amira lowered the lights, but the glow of his luminous skin allowed me to see his features clearly.

In profile he looked like a medieval knight lying atop a tomb in Westminster Abbey: long legs, long torso, long arms, and a remarkably strong face. There was something ancient about his looks, even though he appeared to be only a few years older than I was. I mentally traced the line of his forehead with an imaginary finger, from where it started at his uneven hairline up slightly over his prominent brow bone with its thick, black brows. My imaginary finger crested the tip of his nose and the bowing of his lips.

I counted as he breathed. At two hundred his chest lifted. He didn't exhale for a long, long time afterward.

Finally Amira told the class it was time to rejoin the world outside. Matthew turned toward me and opened his eyes. His face softened, and my own did the same. There was movement all around us, but the socially correct had no pull on me. I stayed where I was, staring into a vampire's eyes. Matthew waited, utterly still, watching me watch him. When I sat up, the room spun at the sudden movement of blood through my body.

At last the room stopped its dizzying revolutions. Amira closed the practice with chant and rang some tiny silver bells that were attached to her fingers. Class was over.

There were gentle murmurs throughout the room as vampire greeted vampire and witch greeted witch. The daemons were more ebullient, arranging for midnight meetings at clubs around Oxford, asking where the best jazz could be found. They were following the energy, I realized with a smile, thinking back to Agatha's description of what tugged at a daemon's soul. Two investment bankers from London – both vampires – were talking about a spate of unsolved London murders. I thought of Westminster and felt a flicker of unease. Matthew scowled at them, and they began arranging lunch tomorrow instead.

Everyone had to file by us as they left. The witches nodded at us curiously. Even the daemons made eye contact, grinning and exchanging meaningful glances. The vampires studiously avoided me, but every one of them said hello to Clairmont.

Finally only Amira, Matthew, and I remained. She gathered up her mat and padded toward us. 'Good practice, Diana,' she said.

'Thank you, Amira. This was a class I'll never forget.'

'You're welcome anytime. With or without Matthew,' she added, tapping him lightly on the shoulder. 'You should have warned her.'

'I was afraid Diana wouldn't come. And I thought she'd like it, if she gave it a chance.' He looked at me shyly.

'Turn out the lights, will you, when you leave?' Amira called over her shoulder, already halfway out of the room.

My eyes traveled around the perfect jewel of a great hall. 'This was certainly a surprise,' I said drily, not yet ready to let him off the hook.

He came up behind me, swift and soundless. 'A pleasant one, I hope. You did like the class?'

I nodded slowly and turned to reply. He was disconcertingly close, and the difference in our heights meant that I had to lift my eyes so as not to be staring straight into his sternum. 'I did.'

Matthew's face split into his heart-stopping smile. 'I'm glad.' It was difficult to pull free from the undertow of his eyes. To break their spell, I bent down and began rolling up my mat. Matthew turned off the lights and grabbed his own gear. We slid our shoes on in the gallery, where the fire had burned down to embers.

He picked up his keys. 'Can I interest you in some tea before we head back to Oxford?'

'Where?'

'We'll go to the gatehouse,' Matthew said matter-of-factly.

'There's a café there?'

'No, but there's a kitchen. A place to sit down, too. I can make tea,' he teased.

'Matthew,' I said, shocked, 'is this your house?'

By that time we were standing in the doorway, looking out into the courtyard. I saw the keystone over the house's gate: 1536.

'I built it,' he said, watching me closely.

Matthew Clairmont was at least five hundred years old.

'The spoils of the Reformation,' he continued. 'Henry gave me the land, on the condition that I tear down the abbey that was here and start again. I saved what I could, but it was difficult to get away with much. The king was in a foul mood that year. There's an angel here and there, and some stonework I couldn't bear to destroy. Other than that, it's all new construction.'

'I've never heard anyone describe a house built in the early sixteenth century as "new construction" before.' I tried to see the house not only through Matthew's eyes but as a part of him. This was the house he had wanted to live in nearly five hundred years ago. In seeing it I knew him better. It was quiet and still, just as he was. More than that, it was solid and true. There was nothing unnecessary – no extra ornamentation, no distractions.

'It's beautiful,' I said simply.

'It's too big to live in now,' he replied, 'not to mention too fragile. Every time I open a window, something seems to fall off it, despite careful maintenance. I let Amira live in some of the rooms and open the house to her students a few times a week.'

'You live in the gatehouse?' I asked as we walked across the open expanse of cobbles and brick to the car.

'Part of the time. I live in Oxford during the week but come here at weekends. It's quieter.'

I thought that it must be challenging for a vampire to live surrounded by noisy undergraduates whose conversations he couldn't help overhearing.

We got back into the car and drove the short distance to the gatehouse. As the manor's onetime public face, it had slightly more frills and embellishments than the main house. I studied the twisted chimneys and the elaborate patterns in the brick.

Matthew groaned. 'I know. The chimneys were a mistake. The stonemason was dying to try his hand at them. His cousin worked for Wolsey at Hampton Court, and the man simply wouldn't take no for an answer.'

He flipped a light switch near the door, and the gatehouse's main room was bathed in a golden glow. It had serviceable flagstone floors and a big stone fireplace suitable for roasting an ox.

'Are you cold?' Matthew asked as he went to the part of the space that had been turned into a sleek, modern kitchen. It was dominated by a refrigerator rather than a stove. I tried not to think about what he might keep in it.

'A little bit.' I drew my sweater closer. It was still relatively warm in Oxford, but my drying perspiration made the night air feel chilly.

'Light the fire, then,' Matthew suggested. It was already laid, and I set it alight with a long match drawn from an antique pewter tankard.

Matthew put the kettle on, and I walked around the room, taking in the elements of his taste. It ran heavily toward brown leather and dark polished wood, which stood out handsomely against the flagstones. An old carpet in warm shades of red, blue, and ocher provided jolts of color. Over the mantel there was an enormous portrait of a dark-haired, late-seventeenth-century beauty in a yellow gown. It had certainly been painted by Sir Peter Lely.

Matthew noticed my interest. 'My sister Louisa,' he said, coming around the counter with a fully outfitted tea tray. He looked up at the canvas, his face touched with sadness. '*Dieu*, she was beautiful.'

'What happened to her?'

'She went to Barbados, intent on making herself queen of the Indies. We tried to tell her that her taste for young gentlemen was not likely to go unnoticed on a small island, but she wouldn't listen. Louisa loved plantation life. She invested in sugar – and slaves.' A shadow flitted across his face. 'During one of the island's rebellions, her fellow plantation owners, who had figured out what she was, decided to get rid of her. They sliced off Louisa's head and cut her body into pieces. Then they burned her and blamed it on the slaves.'

'I'm so sorry,' I said, knowing that words were inadequate in the face of such a loss.

He mustered a small smile. 'The death was only as terrible as the woman who suffered it. I loved my sister, but she didn't make that easy. She absorbed every vice of every age she lived through. If there was excess to be had, Louisa found it.' Matthew shook himself free from his sister's cold, beautiful face with difficulty. 'Will you pour?' he asked. He put the tray on a low, polished oak table in front of the fireplace between two overstuffed leather sofas.

I agreed, happy to lighten the mood even though I had enough questions to fill more than one evening of conversation. Louisa's huge black eyes watched me, and I made sure not to spill a drop of liquid on the shining wooden surface of the table just in case it had once been hers. Matthew had remembered the big jug of milk and the sugar, and I doctored my tea until it was precisely the right color before sinking back into the cushions with a sigh.

Matthew held his mug politely without once lifting it to his lips.

'You don't have to for my sake, you know,' I said, glancing at the cup.

'I know.' He shrugged. 'It's a habit, and comforting to go through the motions.'

'When did you start practicing yoga?' I asked, changing the subject.

'The same time that Louisa went to Barbados. I went to the other

Indies — the East Indies — and found myself in Goa during the monsoons. There wasn't a lot to do but drink too much and learn about India. The yogis were different then, more spiritual than most teachers today. I met Amira a few years ago when I was speaking at a conference in Mumbai. As soon as I heard her lead a class, it was clear to me that she had the gifts of the old yogis, and she didn't share the concerns some witches have about fraternizing with vampires.' There was a touch of bitterness in his voice.

'You invited her to come to England?'

'I explained what might be possible here, and she agreed to give it a try. It's been almost ten years now, and the class is full to capacity every week. Of course, Amira teaches private classes, too, mainly to humans.'

'I'm not used to seeing witches, vampires, and daemons sharing anything — never mind a yoga class,' I confessed. The taboos against mixing with other creatures were strong. 'If you'd told me it was possible, I wouldn't have believed you.'

'Amira is an optimist, and she loves a challenge. It wasn't easy at first. The vampires refused to be in the same room with the daemons during the early days, and of course no one trusted the witches when they started showing up.' His voice betrayed his own ingrained prejudices. 'Now most in the room accept we're more similar than different and treat one another with courtesy.'

'We may look similar,' I said, taking a gulp of tea and drawing my knees toward my chest, 'but we certainly don't feel similar.'

'What do you mean?' Matthew said, looking at me attentively.

'The way we know that someone is one of us — a creature,' I replied, confused. 'The nudges, the tingles, the cold.'

Matthew shook his head. 'No, I don't know. I'm not a witch.'

'You can't feel it when I look at you?' I asked.

'No. Can you?' His eyes were guileless and caused the familiar reaction on my skin.

I nodded.

'Tell me what it feels like.' He leaned forward. Everything seemed perfectly ordinary, but I felt that a trap was being set.

'It feels . . . cold,' I said slowly, unsure how much to divulge, 'like ice growing under my skin.'

'That sounds unpleasant.' His forehead creased slightly.

'It's not,' I replied truthfully. 'Just a little strange. The daemons are the worst – when they stare at me, it's like being kissed.' I made a face.

Matthew laughed and put his tea down on the table. He rested his elbows on his knees and kept his body angled toward mine. 'So you do use some of your witch's power.'

The trap snapped shut.

I looked at the floor, furious, my cheeks flushing. 'I wish I'd never opened Ashmole 782 or taken that damn journal off the shelf! That was only the fifth time I've used magic this year, and the washing machine shouldn't count, because if I hadn't used a spell the water would have caused a flood and wrecked the apartment downstairs.'

Both his hands came up in a gesture of surrender. 'Diana, I don't care if you use magic or not. But I'm surprised at how much you do.'

'I don't use magic or power or witchcraft or whatever you want to call it. It's not who I am.' Two red patches burned on my cheeks.

'It is who you are. It's in your blood. It's in your bones. You were born a witch, just as you were born to have blond hair and blue eyes.'

I'd never been able to explain to anyone my reasons for avoiding magic. Sarah and Em had never understood. Matthew wouldn't either. My tea grew cold, and my body remained in a tight ball as I struggled to avoid his scrutiny.

'I don't want it,' I finally said through gritted teeth, 'and never asked for it.'

'What's wrong with it? You were glad of Amira's power of empathy tonight. That's a large part of her magic. It's no better or worse to have the talents of a witch than it is to have the talent to make music or to write poetry – it's just different.'

'I don't want to be different,' I said fiercely. 'I want a simple, ordinary life . . . like humans enjoy.' *One that doesn't involve death and danger and the fear of being discovered*, I thought, my mouth closed tight against the words. 'You must wish you were normal.'

'I can tell you as a scientist, Diana, that there's no such thing as "normal".' His voice was losing its careful softness. '"Normal" is a bedtime story – a fable – that humans tell themselves to feel better when faced with overwhelming evidence that most of what's happening around them is not "normal" at all.'

Nothing he said would shake my conviction that it was dangerous to be a creature in a world dominated by humans.

'Diana, look at me.'

Against my instincts I did.

'You're trying to push your magic aside, just as you believe your scientists did hundreds of years ago. The problem is,' he continued quietly, 'it didn't work. Not even the humans among them could push the magic out of their world entirely. You said so yourself. It kept returning.'

'This is different,' I whispered. 'This is my life. I can control my life.'

'It isn't different.' His voice was calm and sure. 'You can try to keep the magic away, but it won't work, any more than it worked for Robert Hooke or Isaac Newton. They both knew there was no such thing as a world without magic. Hooke was brilliant, with his ability to think through scientific problems in three dimensions and construct instruments and experiments. But he never reached his full potential because he was so fearful of the mysteries of nature. Newton? He had the most fearless intellect I've ever known. Newton wasn't afraid of what couldn't be seen and easily explained – he embraced it all. As a historian you know that it was alchemy and his belief in invisible, powerful forces of growth and change that led him to the theory of gravity.'

'Then I'm Robert Hooke in this story,' I said. 'I don't need to be a legend like Newton.' *Like my mother*.

'Hooke's fears made him bitter and envious,' Matthew warned. 'He spent his life looking over his shoulder and designing other people's experiments. It's no way to live.'

'I'm not having magic involved in my work,' I said stubbornly.

'You're no Hooke, Diana,' Matthew said roughly. 'He was only a human, and he ruined his life trying to resist the lure of magic. You're a witch. If you do the same, it will destroy you.'

Fear began to worm its way into my thoughts, pulling me away from Matthew Clairmont. He was alluring, and he made it seem as if you could be a creature without any worries or repercussions. But he was a vampire and couldn't be trusted. And he was wrong about the magic. He had to be. If not, then my whole life had been a fruitless struggle against an imaginary enemy.

And it was my own fault I was afraid. I'd let magic into my life – against my own rules – and a vampire had crept in with it. Dozens of creatures had followed. Remembering the way that magic had contributed to the loss of my parents, I felt the beginnings of panic in shallow breath and prickling skin.

'Living without magic is the only way I know to survive, Matthew.' I breathed slowly so that the feelings wouldn't take root, but it was difficult with the ghosts of my mother and father in the room.

'You're living a lie – and an unconvincing one at that. You think you pass as a human.' Matthew's tone was matter-of-fact, almost clinical. 'You don't fool anyone except yourself. I've seen them watching you. They know you're different.'

'That's nonsense.'

'Every time you look at Sean, you reduce him to speechlessness.'

'He had a crush on me when I was a graduate student,' I said dismissively.

'Sean still has a crush on you – that's not the point. Is Mr Johnson one of your admirers, too? He's nearly as bad as Sean, trembling at your slightest change of mood and worrying because you might have to sit in a different seat. And it's not just the humans. You frightened Dom Berno nearly to death when you turned and glared at him.'

'That monk in the library?' My tone was disbelieving. '*You* frightened him, not *me*!'

'I've known Dom Berno since 1718,' Matthew said drily. 'He knows me far too well to fear me. We met at the Duke of Chandos's house party, where he was singing the role of Damon in Handel's *Acis and Galatea*. I assure you, it was your power and not mine that startled him.'

'This is a human world, Matthew, not a fairy tale. Humans outnumber and fear us. And there's nothing more powerful than human fear – not magic, not vampire strength. Nothing.'

'Fear and denial are what humans do best, Diana, but it's not a way that's open to a witch.'

'I'm not afraid.'

'Yes you are,' he said softly, rising to his feet. 'And I think it's time I took you home.'

'Look,' I said, my need for information about the manuscript pushing all other thoughts aside, 'we're both interested in Ashmole 782. A vampire and a witch can't be friends, but we should be able to work together.'

'I'm not so sure,' Matthew said impassively.

The ride back to Oxford was quiet. Humans had it all wrong when it came to vampires, I reflected. To make them frightening, humans imagined vampires as bloodthirsty. But it was Matthew's remoteness, combined with his flashes of anger and abrupt mood swings, that scared me.

When we arrived at the New College lodge, Matthew retrieved my mat from the trunk.

'Have a good weekend,' he said without emotion.

'Good night, Matthew. Thank you for taking me to yoga.' My voice was as devoid of expression as his, and I resolutely refused to look back, even though his cold eyes watched me walk away.

CHAPTER 9

Matthew crossed the river Avon, driving over the bridge's high, arched spans. He found the familiar Lanarkshire landscape of craggy hills, dark sky, and stark contrasts soothing. Little about this part of Scotland was soft or inviting, and its forbidding beauty suited his present mood. He downshifted through the lime alley that had once led to a palace and now led nowhere, an odd remnant of a grand life no one wanted to live anymore. Pulling up to what had been the back entrance of an old hunting lodge, where rough brown stone stood in sharp contrast to the creamy stuccoed front, he climbed out of his Jaguar and lifted his bags from the trunk.

The lodge's welcoming white door opened. 'You look like hell.' A wiry daemon with dark hair, twinkling brown eyes, and a hooked nose stood with his hand on the latch and inspected his best friend from head to foot.

Hamish Osborne had met Matthew Clairmont at Oxford nearly twenty years ago. Like most creatures, they'd been taught to fear each other and were uncertain how to behave. The two became inseparable once they'd realized they shared a similar sense of humor and the same passion for ideas.

Matthew's face registered anger and resignation in quick succession. 'Nice to see you, too,' he said gruffly, dropping his bags by the door. He drank in the house's cold, clear smell, with its nuances of old plaster and aging wood, and Hamish's unique aroma of lavender and peppermint. The vampire was desperate to get the smell of witch out of his nose.

Jordan, Hamish's human butler, appeared silently and brought with him the scent of lemon furniture polish and starch. It didn't drive Diana's honeysuckle and horehound entirely from Matthew's nostrils, but it helped.

'Good to see you, sir,' he said before heading for the stairs with Matthew's bags. Jordan was a butler of the old school. Even had he not been paid handsomely to keep his employer's secrets, he would never divulge to a soul that Osborne was a daemon or that he sometimes entertained vampires. It would be as unthinkable as letting slip that he was occasionally asked to serve peanut butter and banana sandwiches at breakfast.

'Thank you, Jordan.' Matthew surveyed the downstairs hall so that he wouldn't have to meet Hamish's eyes. 'You've picked up a new Hamilton, I see.' He stared raptly at the unfamiliar landscape on the far wall.

'You don't usually notice my new acquisitions.' Like Matthew's, Hamish's accent was mostly Oxbridge with a touch of something else. In his case it was the burr of Glasgow's streets.

'Speaking of new acquisitions, how is Sweet William?' William was Hamish's new lover, a human so adorable and easygoing that Matthew had nicknamed him after a spring flower. It stuck. Now Hamish used it as an endearment, and William had started bothering florists in the city for pots of it to give to friends.

'Grumpy,' Hamish said with a chuckle. 'I'd promised him a quiet weekend at home.'

'You didn't have to come, you know. I didn't expect it.' Matthew sounded grumpy, too.

'Yes, I know. But it's been awhile since we've seen each other, and Cadzow is beautiful this time of year.'

Matthew glowered at Hamish, disbelief evident on his face.

'Christ, you do need to go hunting, don't you?' was all Hamish could say.

'Badly,' the vampire replied, his voice clipped.

'Do we have time for a drink first, or do you need to get straight to it?'

'I believe I can manage a drink,' Matthew said in a withering tone.

'Excellent. I've got a bottle of wine for you and some whiskey for me.' Hamish had asked Jordan to pull some of the good wine out of the cellar shortly after he'd received Matthew's dawn call. He hated to drink alone, and Matthew refused to touch whiskey. 'Then you can tell me why you have such an urgent need to go hunting this fine September weekend.'

Hamish led the way across the gleaming floors and upstairs to his library. The warm brown paneling had been added in the nineteenth century, ruining the architect's original intention to provide an airy, spacious place for eighteenth-century ladies to wait while their husbands busied themselves with sport. The original white ceiling remained, festooned with plaster garlands and busy angels, a constant reproach to modernity.

The two men settled into the leather chairs that flanked the fireplace, where a cheerful blaze was already taking the edge off the autumn chill. Hamish showed Matthew the bottle of wine, and the vampire made an appreciative sound. 'That will do nicely.'

'I should think so. The gentlemen at Berry Brothers and Rudd assured me it was excellent.' Hamish poured the wine and pulled the stopper from his decanter. Glasses in hand, the two men sat in companionable silence.

'I'm sorry to drag you into all this,' Matthew began. 'I'm in a difficult situation. It's . . . complicated.'

Hamish chuckled. 'It always is, with you.'

Matthew had been drawn to Hamish Osborne in part because of his directness and in part because, unlike most daemons, he was levelheaded and difficult to unsettle. Over the years a number of the vampire's friends had been daemons, gifted and cursed in equal measure. Hamish was far more comfortable to be around. There were no blazing arguments, bursts of wild activity, or dangerous depressions. Time with Hamish consisted of long stretches of silence, followed by blindingly sharp conversation, all colored by his serene approach to life.

Hamish's differences extended to his work, which was not in the usual daemonic pursuits of art or music. Instead he had a gift for money — for making it and for spotting fatal weaknesses in international financial instruments and markets. He took a daemon's characteristic creativity and applied it to spreadsheets rather than sonatas, understanding the intricacies of currency exchange with such remarkable precision that he was consulted by presidents, monarchs, and prime ministers.

The daemon's uncommon predilection for the economy fascinated Matthew, as did his ease among humans. Hamish loved being around them and found their faults stimulating rather than aggravating. It was a legacy of his childhood, with an insurance broker for a father and a housewife as a mother. Having met the unflappable Osbornes, Matthew could understand Hamish's fondness.

The crackling of the fire and the smooth smell of whiskey in the air began to do their work, and the vampire found himself relaxing. Matthew sat forward, holding his wineglass lightly between his fingers, the red liquid winking in the firelight.

'I don't know where to begin,' he said shakily.

'At the end, of course. Why did you pick up the phone and call me?'

'I needed to get away from a witch.'

Hamish watched his friend for a moment, noting Matthew's obvious agitation. Somehow Hamish was certain the witch wasn't male.

'What makes this witch so special?' he asked quietly.

Matthew looked up from under his heavy brows. 'Everything.'

'Oh. You are in trouble, aren't you?' Hamish's burr deepened in sympathy and amusement.

Matthew laughed unpleasantly. 'You could say that, yes.'

'Does this witch have a name?'

'Diana. She's a historian. And American.'

'The goddess of the hunt,' Hamish said slowly. 'Apart from her ancient name, is she an ordinary witch?'

'No,' Matthew said abruptly. 'She is far from ordinary.'

'Ah. The complications.' Hamish studied his friend's face for signs that he was calming down but saw that Matthew was spoiling for a fight instead.

'She's a Bishop.' Matthew waited. He'd learned it was never a good idea to anticipate that the daemon wouldn't grasp the significance of a reference, no matter how obscure.

Hamish sifted and sorted through his mind and found what he was seeking. 'As in Salem, Massachusetts?'

Matthew nodded grimly. 'She's the last of the Bishop witches. Her father is a Proctor.'

The daemon whistled softly. 'A witch twice over, with a distinguished magical lineage. You never do things by half, do you? She must be powerful.'

'Her mother is. I don't know much about her father. Rebecca Bishop, though – that's a different story. She was doing spells at thirteen that most witches can't manage after a lifetime of study and experience. And her childhood abilities as a seer were astonishing.'

'Do you know her, Matt?' Hamish had to ask. Matthew had lived many lives and crossed paths with too many people for his friend to keep track of them all.

Matthew shook his head. 'No. There's always talk about her, though – and plenty of envy. You know how witches are,' he said, his voice taking on the slightly unpleasant tone it did whenever he referred to the species.

Hamish let the remark about witches pass and eyed Matthew over the rim of his glass.

'And Diana?'

'She claims she doesn't use magic.'

There were two threads in that brief sentence that needed pulling. Hamish tugged on the easier one first. 'What, not for anything? Finding a lost earring? Coloring her hair?' Hamish sounded doubtful.

'She's not the earrings and colored hair type. She's more the three-mile run followed by an hour on the river in a dangerously tiny boat type.'

'With her background I find it difficult to believe she never uses her power.' Hamish was a pragmatist as well as a dreamer. It was why he was so good with other people's money. 'And you don't believe it either, or you wouldn't suggest that she's lying.' There was the second thread pulled.

'She says she only uses magic occasionally – for little things.' Matthew hesitated, raked his fingers through his hair so half of it stood on end, and took a gulp of wine. 'I've been watching her, though, and she's using it more than that. I can smell it,' he said, his voice frank and open for the first time since his arrival. 'The scent is like an electrical storm about to break, or summer lightning. There are times when I can see it, too. Diana shimmers when she's angry or lost in her work.' *And when she's asleep*, he thought, frowning. 'Christ, there are times when I think I can even taste it.'

'She shimmers?'

'It's nothing you would see, though you might sense the energy some other way. The *chatoiement* – her witch's shimmer – is very faint. Even when I was a young vampire, only the most powerful witches emitted these tiny pulses of light. It's rare to see it today. Diana's unaware she's doing it, and she's oblivious to its significance.' Matthew shuddered and balled up his fist.

The daemon glanced at his watch. The day was young, but he already knew why his friend was in Scotland.

Matthew Clairmont was falling in love.

Jordan came in, his timing impeccable. 'The gillie dropped off the Jeep, sir. I told him you wouldn't need his services today.' The butler knew there was little need for a guide to track down deer when you had a vampire in the house.

'Excellent,' Hamish said, rising to his feet and draining his glass. He sorely wanted more whiskey, but it was better to keep his wits about him.

Matthew looked up. 'I'll go out by myself, Hamish. I'd rather hunt alone.' The vampire didn't like hunting with warmbloods, a category that included humans, daemons, and witches. He usually made an exception for Hamish, but today he wanted to be on his own while he got his craving for Diana Bishop under control.

'Oh, we're not going hunting,' Hamish said with a wicked glint in his eye. 'We're going stalking.' The daemon had a plan. It involved occupying his friend's mind until he let down his guard and willingly shared what was going on in Oxford rather than requiring Hamish to drag it out of him. 'Come on, it's a beautiful day. You'll have fun.'

Outside, Matthew grimly climbed into Hamish's beat-up Jeep. It was what the two of them preferred to roam around in when they were at Cadzow, even though a Land Rover was the vehicle of choice in grand Scottish hunting lodges. Matthew didn't mind that it was freezing to drive in, and Hamish found its hypermasculinity amusing.

In the hills Hamish ground the Jeep's gears – the vampire cringed at the sound each time – as he climbed to where the deer grazed. Matthew spotted a pair of stags on the next crag and told Hamish to stop. He got out of the Jeep quietly and crouched by the front tire, already mesmerized.

Hamish smiled and joined him.

The daemon had stalked deer with Matthew before and understood what he needed. The vampire did not always feed, though today Hamish was certain that, left to his own devices, Matthew would have come home sated after dark – and there would be two fewer stags on the estate. His friend was as much predator as carnivore. It was the hunt that defined vampires' identity, not their feeding or what they fed upon. Sometimes, when Matthew was restless, he just went out and tracked whatever he could chase without making a kill.

While the vampire watched the deer, the daemon watched Matthew. There was trouble in Oxford. He could feel it.

Matthew sat patiently for the next several hours, considering whether the stags were worth pursuing. Through his extraordinary senses of smell, sight, and hearing, he tracked their movements, figured out their habits, and gauged their every response to a cracking twig or a bird in flight. The vampire's attention was avid, but he never showed impatience. For Matthew the crucial moment came when his prey acknowledged that it was beaten and surrendered.

The light was dimming when he finally rose and nodded to Hamish. It was enough for the first day, and though he didn't need the light to see the deer, he knew that Hamish needed it to get back down the mountain.

By the time they reached the lodge, it was pitch black, and Jordan had turned on every lamp, which made the building look even more ridiculous, sitting on a rise in the middle of nowhere.

'This lodge never did make any sense,' Matthew said in a conversational tone that was nevertheless intended to sting. 'Robert Adam was insane to take the commission.'

'You've shared your thoughts on my little extravagance many times, Matthew,' Hamish said serenely, 'and I don't care if you understand the principles of architectural design better than I do or whether you believe that Adam was a madman to construct – what do you always call it? – an "ill-conceived folly" in the Lanarkshire wilderness. I love it, and nothing you say is going to change that.' They'd had versions of this conversation regularly since Hamish's announcement he'd purchased the lodge – complete with all its furnishings, the gillie, and Jordan – from an aristocrat who had no use for the building and no money to repair it. Matthew had been horrified. To Hamish, however, Cadzow Lodge was a sign he had risen so far above his Glasgow roots that he could spend money on something impractical that he could love for its own sake.

'Hmph,' Matthew said with a scowl.

Grumpiness was preferable to agitation, Hamish thought. He moved on to the next step of his plan.

'Dinner's at eight,' he said, 'in the dining room.'

Matthew hated the dining room, which was grand, high-ceilinged, and drafty. More important, it upset the vampire because it was gaudy and feminine. It was Hamish's favorite room.

Matthew groaned. 'I'm not hungry.'

'You're famished,' Hamish said sharply, taking in the color and texture of Matthew's skin. 'When was your last real meal?'

'Weeks ago.' Matthew shrugged with his usual disregard for the passage of time. 'I can't remember.'

'Tonight you're having wine and soup. Tomorrow – it's up to you what you eat. Do you want some time alone before dinner, or will you risk playing billiards with me?' Hamish was extremely good at billiards and even better at snooker, which he had learned to play as a teenager. He'd made his first money in Glasgow's billiards halls and could beat almost anyone. Matthew refused to play snooker with him anymore on the grounds that it was no fun to lose every time, even to a friend. The vampire had tried to teach him carambole instead, the old French game involving balls and cues, but Matthew always won those games. Billiards was the sensible compromise.

Unable to resist a battle of any sort, Matthew agreed. 'I'll change and join you.'

Hamish's felt-covered billiards table was in a room opposite the library. He was there in a sweater and trousers when Matthew arrived in a white shirt and jeans. The vampire avoided wearing white, which made him look startling and ghostly, but it was the only decent shirt he had with him. He'd packed for a hunting trip, not a dinner party.

He picked up his cue and stood at the end of the table. 'Ready?'

Hamish nodded. 'Let's say an hour of play, shall we? Then we'll go down for a drink.'

The two men bent over their cues. 'Be gentle with me, Matthew,' Hamish murmured just before they struck the balls. The vampire snorted as they shot to the far end, hit the cushion, and rebounded.

'I'll take the white,' said Matthew when the balls stopped rolling and his was closest. He palmed the other and tossed it to Hamish. The daemon put a red ball on its mark and stood back.

As in hunting, Matthew was in no rush to score points. He shot fifteen hazards in a row, putting the red ball in a different pocket each time. 'If you don't mind,' he drawled, pointing to the table. The daemon put his yellow ball on it without comment.

Matthew mixed up simple shots that took the red ball into the pockets with trickier shots known as cannons that were not his forte. Cannons involved hitting both Hamish's yellow ball and the red ball with one strike of the cue, and they required not only strength but finesse.

'Where did you find the witch?' Hamish asked casually after Matthew cannoned the yellow and red balls.

Matthew retrieved the white ball and prepared for his next shot. 'The Bodleian.'

The daemon's eyebrows rose in surprise. 'The Bodleian? Since when have you been a regular at the library?'

Matthew fouled, his white ball hopping over the cushion and onto the floor. 'Since I was at a concert and overheard two witches talking about an American who'd got her hands on a long-lost manuscript,' he said. 'I couldn't figure out why the witches would give a damn.' He stepped back from the table, annoyed at his error.

Hamish quickly played his fifteen hazards. Matthew placed his ball on the table and picked up the chalk to mark down Hamish's score.

'So you just strolled in there and struck up a conversation with her to find out?' The daemon pocketed all three balls with a single shot.

'I went looking for her, yes.' Matthew watched while Hamish moved around the table. 'I was curious.'

'Was she happy to see you?' Hamish asked mildly, making another tricky shot. He knew that vampires, witches, and daemons seldom mixed. They preferred to spend time within close-knit circles of similar creatures. His friendship with Matthew was a relative rarity, and Hamish's daemonic friends thought it was madness to let a vampire get so close. On a night like this one, he thought they might have a point.

'Not exactly. Diana was frightened at first, even though she met my eyes without flinching. Her eyes are extraordinary – blue and gold and green and gray,' Matthew mused. 'Later she wanted to hit me. She smelled so angry.'

Hamish bit back a laugh. 'Sounds like a reasonable response to being ambushed by a vampire in the Bodleian.' He decided to be kind to Matthew and save him from a reply. The daemon shot his yellow ball over the red, deliberately nicking it just enough that the red ball drifted forward and collided with it. 'Damn,' he groaned. 'A foul.'

Matthew returned to the table, shot a few hazards, and tried a cannon or two.

'Have you seen each other outside the library?' Hamish asked when the vampire had regained some of his composure.

'I don't see her much, actually, even in the library. I sit in one part and she sits in another. I've taken her to breakfast, though. And to the Old Lodge, to meet Amira.'

Hamish kept his jaw closed with difficulty. Matthew had known women for years without taking them to the Old Lodge. And what was this about sitting at opposite ends of the library?

'Wouldn't it be easier to sit next to her in the library, if you're interested in her?'

'I'm not interested in *her*!' Matthew's cue exploded into the white ball. 'I want the manuscript. I've been trying to get my hands on it for more than a hundred years. She just put in the slip and up it came from the stacks.' His voice was envious.

'What manuscript, Matt?' Hamish was doing his best to be patient, but the exchange was rapidly becoming unendurable. Matthew was giving out information like a miser parting with pennies. It was intensely aggravating for quick-minded daemons to deal with creatures who didn't consider any division of time smaller than a decade particularly important.

'An alchemical book that belonged to Elias Ashmole. Diana Bishop is a highly respected historian of alchemy.'

Matthew fouled again by striking the balls too hard. Hamish respotted the balls and continued to rack up points while his friend simmered down. Finally Jordan came to tell them that drinks were available downstairs.

'What's the score?' Hamish peered at the chalk marks. He knew he'd won, but the gentlemanly thing was to ask – or so Matthew had told him.

'You won, of course.'

Matthew stalked out of the room and pounded down the stairs at considerably more than a human pace. Jordan eyed the polished treads with concern.

'Professor Clairmont is having a difficult day, Jordan.'

'So it would seem,' the butler murmured.

'Better bring up another bottle of red. It's going to be a long night.'

They had their drinks in what had once been the lodge's reception area. Its windows looked out on the gardens, which were still kept in orderly, classical parterres despite the fact that their proportions were all wrong for a hunting lodge. They were too grand – they belonged to a palace, not a folly.

In front of the fireplace, drinks in hand, Hamish could at last press his way into the heart of the mystery. 'Tell me about this manuscript of Diana's, Matthew. It contains what, exactly? The recipe for the philosopher's stone that turns lead into gold?' Hamish's voice was lightly mocking. 'Instructions on how to concoct the elixir of life so you can transform mortal into immortal flesh?'

The daemon stopped his teasing the instant Matthew's eyes rose to meet his.

'You aren't serious,' Hamish whispered, his voice shocked. The philosopher's stone was just a legend, like the Holy Grail or Atlantis. It couldn't possibly be real. Belatedly, he realized that vampires, daemons, and witches weren't supposed to be real either.

'Do I look like I'm joking?' Matthew asked.

'No.' The daemon shuddered. Matthew had always been convinced that he could use his scientific skills to figure out what made vampires resistant to death and decay. The philosopher's stone fit neatly into those dreams.

'It's the lost book,' Matthew said grimly. 'I know it.'

Like most creatures, Hamish had heard the stories. One version suggested the witches had stolen a precious book from the vampires, a book that held the secret of immortality. Another claimed the vampires had snatched an ancient spell book from the witches and then lost it. Some whispered that it was not a spell book at all, but a primer covering the basic traits of all four humanoid species on earth.

Matthew had his own theories about what the book might contain. An explanation of why vampires were so difficult to kill and accounts of early human and creature history were only a small part of it.

'You really think this alchemical manuscript is your book?' he asked. When Matthew nodded, Hamish let out his breath with a sigh. 'No wonder the witches were gossiping. How did they discover Diana had found it?'

Matthew turned, ferocious. 'Who knows or cares? The problems began when they couldn't keep their mouths shut.'

Hamish was reminded once again that Matthew and his family really didn't like witches.

'I wasn't the only one to overhear them on Sunday. Other vampires did, too. And then the daemons sensed that something interesting was happening, and—'

'Now Oxford is crawling with creatures,' the daemon finished. 'What a mess. Isn't term about to start? The humans will be next. They're about to return in droves.'

'It gets worse.' Matthew's expression was grim. 'The manuscript wasn't simply lost. It was under a spell, and Diana broke it. Then she sent it back to the stacks and shows no interest in recalling it. And I'm not the only one waiting for her to do so.'

'Matthew,' Hamish said, voice tense, 'are you protecting her from other witches?'

'She doesn't seem to recognize her own power. It puts her at risk. I couldn't let them get to her first.' Matthew seemed suddenly, disconcertingly, vulnerable.

'Oh, Matt,' Hamish said, shaking his head. 'You shouldn't interfere between Diana and her own people. You'll only cause more trouble. Besides,' he continued, 'no witch will be openly hostile to a Bishop. Her family's too old and distinguished.'

Nowadays creatures no longer killed one another except in self-defense. Aggression was frowned on in their world. Matthew had told Hamish what it was like in the old days, when blood feuds and vendettas had raged and creatures were constantly catching human attention.

'The daemons are disorganized, and the vampires won't dare to cross me. But the witches can't be trusted.' Matthew rose, taking his wine to the fireplace.

'Let Diana Bishop be,' Hamish advised. 'Besides, if this manuscript is bewitched, you're not going to be able to examine it.'

'I will if she helps me,' Matthew said in a deceptively easy tone, staring into the fire.

'Matthew,' the daemon said in the same voice he used to let his junior partners know when they were on thin ice, 'leave the witch and the manuscript alone.'

The vampire placed his wineglass carefully on the mantel and turned away. 'I don't think I can, Hamish. I'm . . . craving her.' Even saying the word made the hunger spread. When his hunger focused, grew insistent like this, not just any blood would do. His body demanded something more specific. If only he could taste it – taste Diana – he would be satisfied and the painful longing would subside.

Hamish studied Matthew's tense shoulders. He wasn't surprised that his friend craved Diana Bishop. A vampire had to desire another creature more than anyone or anything else in order to mate, and cravings were rooted in desire. Hamish strongly suspected that Matthew – despite his previous fervent declarations that he was incapable of finding anyone who would stir that kind of feeling – was mating.

'Then the real problem you're facing at the moment is not the witches, nor Diana. And it's certainly not some ancient manuscript that may or may not hold the answers to your questions.' Hamish let his words sink in before continuing. 'You do realize you're hunting her?'

The vampire exhaled, relieved that it had been said aloud. 'I know. I climbed into her window when she was sleeping. I follow her when she's running. She resists my attempts to help her, and the more she does, the hungrier I feel.' He looked so perplexed that Hamish had to bite the inside of his lip to keep from smiling. Matthew's women didn't usually resist him. They did what he told them to do, dazzled by his good looks and charm. No wonder he was fascinated.

'But I don't need Diana's blood – not physically. I won't give in to this craving. Being around her needn't be a problem.' Matthew's face crumpled unexpectedly. 'What am I saying? We can't be near each other. We'll attract attention.'

'Not necessarily. *We've* spent a fair bit of time together, and no one has been bothered,' Hamish pointed out. In the early years of their friendship, the two had struggled to mask their differences from curious eyes. They were brilliant enough separately to attract human interest. When they were together – their dark heads bent to share a joke at dinner or sitting in the quadrangle in the early hours of the morning with empty champagne bottles at their feet – they were impossible to ignore.

'It's not the same thing, and you know it,' Matthew said impatiently.

'Oh, yes, I forgot.' Hamish's temper snapped. 'Nobody cares what daemons do. But a vampire and a witch? That's important. *You're* the creatures who really matter in this world.'

'Hamish!' Matthew protested. 'You know that's not how I feel.'

'You have the characteristic vampire contempt for daemons, Matthew. Witches, too, I might add. Think long and hard how you feel about other creatures before you take this witch to bed.'

'I have no intention of taking Diana to bed,' Matthew said, his voice acid.

'Dinner is served, sir.' Jordan had been standing in the doorway, unobserved, for some time.

'Thank God,' Hamish said with relief, getting up from his chair. The vampire was easier to manage if he was dividing his attention between the conversation and something – anything – else.

Seated in the dining room at one end of a vast table designed to feed a house party's worth of guests, Hamish tucked into the first of several courses while Matthew toyed with a soup spoon until his meal cooled. The vampire leaned over the bowl and sniffed.

'Mushrooms and sherry?' he asked.

'Yes. Jordan wanted to try something new, and since it didn't contain anything you find objectionable, I let him.'

Matthew didn't ordinarily require much in the way of supplemental sustenance at Cadzow Lodge, but Jordan was a wizard with soup, and Hamish didn't like to eat alone any more than he liked drinking alone.

'I'm sorry, Hamish,' Matthew said, watching his friend eat.

'I accept your apology, Matt,' Hamish said, the soup spoon hovering near his mouth. 'But you cannot imagine how difficult it is to accept being a daemon or a witch. With vampires it's definite and incontrovertible. You're not a vampire, and then you are. No question, no room for doubt. The rest of us have to wait, watch, and wonder. It makes your vampire superiority doubly hard to take.'

Matthew was twirling the spoon's handle in his fingers like a baton. 'Witches know they're witches. They're not like daemons at all,' he said with a frown.

Hamish put his spoon down with a clatter and topped off his wineglass. 'You know full well that having a witch for a parent is no guarantee. You can turn out perfectly ordinary. Or you can set your crib on fire. There's no telling if, when, or how your powers are going to manifest.' Unlike Matthew, Hamish had a friend who was a witch. Janine did his hair, which had never looked better, and made her own skin lotion, which was nothing short of miraculous. He suspected that witchcraft was involved.

'It's not a total surprise, though,' Matthew persisted, scooping some soup into his spoon and waving it slightly to cool it further. 'Diana has centuries of family history to rely upon. It's nothing like what you went through as a teenager.'

'I had a breeze of a time,' Hamish said, recalling some of the daemonic coming-of-age stories he'd been privy to over the years.

When Hamish was twelve, his life had gone topsy-turvy in the space of one afternoon. He had come to realize, over the long Scottish autumn, that he was far smarter than his teachers. Most children who reach twelve suspect this, but Hamish knew it with deeply upsetting certainty. He responded by feigning sickness so he could skip school and, when that no longer worked, by doing his schoolwork as rapidly as he could and abandoning all pretense of normalcy. In desperation his schoolmaster sent for someone from the university mathematics department to evaluate Hamish's troublesome ability to solve in minutes problems that occupied his schoolmates for a week or more.

Jack Watson, a young daemon from the University of Glasgow with red hair and brilliant blue eyes, took one look at elfin Hamish Osborne and suspected that he, too, was a daemon. After going through the motions of a formal evaluation, which produced the expected documentary proof that Hamish was a mathematical prodigy whose mind did not fit within normal parameters, Watson invited him to attend lectures at the university. He also explained to the headmaster that the child could not be accommodated within a normal classroom without becoming a pyromaniac or something equally destructive.

After that, Watson made a visit to the Osbornes' modest home and told an astonished family how the world worked and exactly what kinds of creatures were in it. Percy Osborne, who came from a staunch Presbyterian background, resisted the notion of multiple supernatural and preternatural creatures until his wife pointed out that he had been raised to believe in witches – why not daemons and vampires, too? Hamish wept with relief, no longer feeling utterly alone. His mother hugged him fiercely and told him that she had always known he was special.

While Watson was still sitting in front of their electric fire drinking tea with her husband and son, Jessica Osborne thought she might as well take the opportunity to broach other aspects of Hamish's life that might make him feel different. She informed her son over chocolate biscuits that she also knew he was unlikely to marry the girl next door, who was infatuated with him. Instead Hamish was drawn to the girl's elder brother, a strapping lad of fifteen who could kick a football farther than anyone else in the neighborhood. Neither Percy nor Jack seemed remotely surprised or distressed by the revelation.

'Still,' Matthew said now, after his first sip of tepid soup, 'Diana's whole family must have expected her to be a witch – and she is, whether she uses her magic or not.'

'I should think that would be every bit as bad as being among a bunch of clueless humans. Can you imagine the pressure? Not to mention the awful sense that your life didn't belong to you?' Hamish shuddered. 'I'd prefer blind ignorance.'

'What did it feel like,' Matthew asked hesitantly, 'the first day you woke up knowing you were a daemon?' The vampire didn't normally ask such personal questions.

'Like being reborn,' Hamish said. 'It was every bit as powerful and confusing as when you woke up craving blood and hearing the grass grow, blade by blade. Everything looked different. Everything felt different. Most of the time I smiled like a fool who'd won the lottery, and the rest of the time I cried in my room. But I don't think I believed it – you know, *really* believed it – until you smuggled me into the hospital.'

Matthew's first birthday present to Hamish, after they became friends, had involved a bottle of Krug and a trip to the John Radcliffe. There Matthew sent Hamish through the MRI while the vampire asked him a series of questions. Afterward they compared Hamish's scans with those of an eminent brain surgeon on the staff, both of them drinking champagne and the daemon still in a surgical gown. Hamish made Matthew play the scans back repeatedly, fascinated by the way his brain lit up like a pinball machine even when he was replying to basic questions. It remained the best birthday present he'd ever received.

'From what you've told me, Diana is where I was before that MRI,' Hamish said. 'She knows she's a witch. But she still feels she's living a lie.'

'She *is* living a lie,' Matthew growled, taking another sip of soup. 'Diana's pretending she's human.'

'Wouldn't it be interesting to know why that's the case? More important, can you be around someone like that? You don't like lies.'

Matthew looked thoughtful but didn't respond.

'There's something else,' Hamish continued. 'For someone who dislikes lies as much as you do, you keep a lot of secrets. If you need this witch, for whatever reason, you're going to have to win her trust.

And the only way to do that is by telling her things you don't want her to know. She's roused your protective instincts, and you're going to have to fight them.'

While Matthew mulled the situation over, Hamish turned the conversation to the latest catastrophes in the City and the government. The vampire calmed further, caught up in the intricacies of finance and policy.

'You've heard about the murders in Westminster, I presume,' Hamish said when Matthew was completely at ease.

'I have. Somebody needs to put a stop to it.'

'You?' Hamish asked.

'It's not my job – yet.'

Hamish knew that Matthew had a theory about the murders, one that was linked to his scientific research. 'You still think the murders are a sign that vampires are dying out?'

'Yes,' Matthew said.

Matthew was convinced that creatures were slowly becoming extinct. Hamish had dismissed his friend's hypotheses at first, but he was beginning to think Matthew might be right.

They returned to less disturbing topics of conversation and, after dinner, retreated upstairs. The daemon had divided one of the lodge's redundant reception rooms into a sitting room and a bedroom. The sitting room was dominated by a large, ancient chessboard with carved ivory and ebony pieces that by all rights should be in a museum under protective glass rather than in a drafty hunting lodge. Like the MRI, the chess set had been a present from Matthew.

Their friendship had deepened over long evenings like this one, spent playing chess and discussing their work. One night Matthew began to tell Hamish stories of his past exploits. Now there was little about Matthew Clairmont that the daemon did not know, and the vampire was the only creature Hamish had ever met who wasn't frightened of his powerful intellect.

Hamish, as was his custom, sat down behind the black pieces.

'Did we finish our last game?' Matthew asked, feigning surprise at the neatly arranged board.

'Yes. You won,' Hamish said curtly, earning one of his friend's rare, broad smiles.

The two began to move their pieces, Matthew taking his time and Hamish moving swiftly and decisively when it was his turn. There was no sound except for the crackle of the fire and the ticking of the clock.

After an hour of play, Hamish moved to the final stage of his plan.

'I have a question.' His voice was careful as he waited for his friend to make his next move. 'Do you want the witch for herself – or for her power over that manuscript?'

'I don't want her power!' Matthew exploded, making a bad decision with his rook, which Hamish quickly captured. He bowed his head, looking more than ever like a Renaissance angel focused on some celestial mystery. 'Christ, I don't know what I want.'

Hamish sat as still as possible. 'I think you do, Matt.'

Matthew moved a pawn and made no reply.

'The other creatures in Oxford,' Hamish continued, 'they'll know soon, if they don't know already, that you're interested in more than this old book. What's your endgame?'

'I don't know,' the vampire whispered.

'Love? Tasting her? Making her like you?'

Matthew snarled.

'Very impressive,' Hamish said in a bored tone.

'There's a lot I don't understand about all this, Hamish, but there are three things I do know,' Matthew said emphatically, picking up his wineglass from the floor by his feet. 'I will not give in to this craving for her blood. I do not want to control her power. And I certainly have no wish to make her a vampire.' He shuddered at the thought.

'That leaves love. You have your answer, then. You *do* know what you want.'

Matthew swallowed a gulp of wine. 'I want what I shouldn't want, and I crave someone I can never have.'

'You're not afraid you'd hurt her?' Hamish asked gently. 'You've had relationships with warm-blooded women before, and you've never harmed any of them.'

Matthew's heavy crystal wine goblet snapped in two. The bowl toppled to the floor, red wine spreading on the carpet. Hamish saw the glint of powdered glass between the vampire's index finger and thumb.

'Oh, Matt. Why didn't you tell me?' Hamish governed his features, making sure that not a particle of his shock was evident.

'How could I?' Matthew stared at his hands and ground the shards between his fingertips until they sparkled reddish black from the mixture of glass and blood. 'You always had too much faith in me, you know.'

'Who was she?'

'Her name was Eleanor.' Matthew stumbled over the name. He dashed the back of his hand across his eyes, a fruitless attempt to wipe the image of her face from his mind. 'My brother and I were fighting. Now I can't even remember what the argument was about. Back then I wanted to destroy him with my bare hands. Eleanor tried to make me see reason. She got between us and—' The vampire's voice broke. He cradled his head without bothering to clean the bloody residue from his already healed fingers. 'I loved her so much, and I killed her.'

'When was this?' Hamish whispered.

Matthew lowered his hands, turning them over to study his long, strong fingers. 'Ages ago. Yesterday. What does it matter?' he asked with a vampire's disregard for time.

'It matters enormously if you made this mistake when you were a newly minted vampire and not in control of your instincts and your hunger.'

'Ah. Then it will also matter that I killed another woman, Cecilia Martin, just over a century ago. I wasn't "a newly minted vampire" then.' Matthew got up from his chair and walked to the windows. He wanted to run into the night's blackness and disappear so he wouldn't have to see the horror in Hamish's eyes.

'Are there more?' Hamish asked sharply.

Matthew shook his head. 'Two is enough. There can't be a third. Not ever.'

'Tell me about Cecilia,' Hamish commanded, leaning forward in his chair.

'She was a banker's wife,' Matthew said reluctantly. 'I saw her at the opera and became infatuated. Everyone in Paris was infatuated with someone else's wife at the time.' His finger traced the outline of a woman's face on the pane of glass before him. 'It didn't strike me as a challenge. I only wanted a taste of her, that night I went to her house. But once I started, I couldn't stop. And yet I couldn't let her die either – she was mine, and I wouldn't give her up. I barely stopped feeding in time. *Dieu*, she hated being a vampire. Cecilia walked into a burning house before I could stop her.'

Hamish frowned. 'Then you didn't kill her, Matt. She killed herself.'

'I fed on her until she was at the brink of death, forced her to drink my blood, and turned her into a creature without her permission because I was selfish and scared,' he said furiously. 'In what way did I not kill her? I took her life, her identity, her vitality – that's death, Hamish.'

'Why did you keep this from me?' Hamish tried not to care that his best friend had done so, but it was difficult.

'Even vampires feel shame,' Matthew said tightly. 'I hate myself – and I should – for what I did to those women.'

'This is why you have to stop keeping secrets, Matt. They're going to destroy you from the inside.' Hamish thought about what he wanted to say before he continued. 'You didn't set out to kill Eleanor and Cecilia. You're not a murderer.'

Matthew rested his fingertips on the white-painted window frame and pressed his forehead against the cold panes of glass. When he spoke, his voice was flat and dead. 'No, I'm a monster. Eleanor forgave me for it. Cecilia never did.'

'You're not a monster,' Hamish said, worried by Matthew's tone.

'Maybe not, but I am dangerous.' He turned and faced Hamish.

'Especially around Diana. Not even Eleanor made me feel this way.' The mere thought of Diana brought the craving back, the tightness spreading from his heart to his abdomen. His face darkened with the effort to bring it under control.

'Come back here and finish this game,' Hamish said, his voice rough.

'I could go, Hamish,' Matthew said uncertainly. 'You don't have to share your roof with me.'

'Don't be an idiot,' Hamish replied as quick as a whip. 'You're not going anywhere.'

Matthew sat. 'I don't understand how you can know about Eleanor and Cecilia and not hate me, too,' he said after a few minutes.

'I can't conceive of what you would have to do to make me hate you, Matthew. I love you like a brother, and I will until I draw my last breath.'

'Thank you,' Matthew said, his face somber. 'I'll try to deserve it.'

'Don't try. Do it,' Hamish said gruffly. 'You're about to lose your bishop, by the way.'

The two creatures dragged their attention back to the game with difficulty, and they were still playing in the early morning when Jordan brought up coffee for Hamish and a bottle of port for Matthew. The butler picked up the ruined wineglass without comment, and Hamish sent him off to bed.

When Jordan was gone, Hamish surveyed the board and made his final move. 'Checkmate.'

Matthew let out his breath and sat back in his chair, staring at the chessboard. His queen stood encircled by his own pieces – pawns, a knight, and a rook. Across the board his king was checked by a lowly black pawn. The game was over, and he had lost.

'There's more to the game than protecting your queen,' Hamish said. 'Why do you find it so difficult to remember that it's the king who's not expendable?'

'The king just sits there, moving one square at a time. The queen can move so freely. I suppose I'd rather lose the game than forfeit her freedom.'

Hamish wondered if he was talking about chess or Diana. 'Is she worth the cost, Matt?' he asked softly.

'Yes,' Matthew said without a moment of hesitation, lifting the white queen from the board and holding it between his fingers.

'I thought so,' Hamish said. 'You don't feel this way now, but you're lucky to have found her at last.'

The vampire's eyes glittered, and his mouth twisted into a crooked smile. 'But is *she* lucky, Hamish? Is she fortunate to have a creature like me in pursuit?'

'That's entirely up to you. Just remember – no secrets. Not if you love her.'

Matthew looked into his queen's serene face, his fingers closing protectively around the small carved figure.

He was still holding it when the sun rose, long after Hamish had gone to sleep.

CHAPTER 10

Still trying to shake the ice from my shoulders left by Matthew's stare, I opened the door to my rooms. Inside, the answering machine greeted me with a flashing red '13'. There were nine additional voice-mail messages on my mobile. All of them were from Sarah and reflected an escalating concern about what her sixth sense told her was happening in Oxford.

Unable to face my all-too-prescient aunts, I turned down the volume on the answering machine, turned off the ringers on both phones, and climbed wearily into bed.

Next morning, when I passed through the porter's lodge for a run, Fred waved a stack of message slips at me.

'I'll pick them up later,' I called, and he flashed his thumb in acknowledgment.

My feet pounded on familiar dirt paths through the fields and marshes north of the city, the exercise helping to keep at bay both my guilt over not calling my aunts and the memory of Matthew's cold face.

Back in college I collected the messages and threw them into the trash. Then I staved off the inevitable call home with cherished weekend rituals: boiling an egg, brewing tea, gathering laundry, piling up the drifts of papers that littered every surface. After I'd wasted most of the morning, there was nothing left to do but call New York. It was early there, but there was no chance that anyone was still in bed.

'What do you think you're up to, Diana?' Sarah demanded in lieu of hello.

'Good morning, Sarah.' I sank into the armchair by the defunct fireplace and crossed my feet on a nearby bookshelf. This was going to take awhile.

'It is not a good morning,' Sarah said tartly. 'We've been beside ourselves. What's going on?'

Em picked up the extension.

'Hi, Em,' I said, recrossing my legs. This was going to take a *long* while.

'Is that vampire bothering you?' Em asked anxiously.

'Not exactly.'

'We know you've been spending time with vampires and daemons,' my aunt broke in impatiently. 'Have you lost your mind, or is something seriously wrong?'

'I haven't lost my mind, and nothing's wrong.' The last bit was a lie, but I crossed my fingers and hoped for the best.

'Do you really think you're going to fool us? You cannot lie to a fellow witch!' Sarah exclaimed. 'Out with it, Diana.'

So much for that plan.

'Let her speak, Sarah,' Em said. 'We trust Diana to make the right decisions, remember?'

The ensuing silence led me to believe that this had been a matter of some controversy.

Sarah drew in her breath, but Em cut her off. 'Where were you last night?'

'Yoga.' There was no way of squirming out of this inquisition, but it was to my advantage to keep all responses brief and to the point.

'Yoga?' Sarah asked, incredulous. 'Why are you doing yoga with those creatures? You know it's dangerous to mix with daemons and vampires.'

'The class was led by a witch!' I became indignant, seeing Amira's serene, lovely face before me.

'This yoga class, was it his idea?' Em asked.

'Yes. It was at Clairmont's house.'

Sarah made a disgusted sound.

'Told you it was him,' Em muttered to my aunt. She directed her next words to me. 'I see a vampire standing between you and . . . something. I'm not sure what, exactly.'

'And I keep telling you, Emily Mather, that's nonsense. Vampires don't protect witches.' Sarah's voice was crisp with certainty.

'This one does,' I said.

'What?' Em asked and Sarah shouted.

'He has been for days.' I bit my lip, unsure how to tell the story, then plunged in. 'Something happened at the library. I called up a manuscript, and it was bewitched.'

There was silence.

'A bewitched book.' Sarah's voice was keen with interest. 'Was it a grimoire?' She was an expert on grimoires, and her most cherished possession was the ancient volume of spells that had been passed down in the Bishop family.

'I don't think so,' I said. 'All that was visible were alchemical illustrations.'

'What else?' My aunt knew that the visible was only the beginning when it came to bewitched books.

'Someone's put a spell on the manuscript's text. There were faint lines of writing – layers upon layers of them – moving underneath the surface of the pages.'

In New York, Sarah put down her coffee mug with a sharp sound. 'Was this before or after Matthew Clairmont appeared?'

'Before,' I whispered.

'You didn't think this was worth mentioning when you told us you'd met a vampire?' Sarah did nothing to disguise her anger. 'By the goddess, Diana, you can be so reckless. How was this book bewitched? And don't tell me you don't know.'

'It smelled funny. It felt . . . wrong. At first I couldn't lift the book's cover. I put my palm on it.' I turned my hand over on my lap, recalling the sense of instant recognition between me and the manuscript, half expecting to see the shimmer that Matthew had mentioned.

'And?' Sarah asked.

'It tingled against my hand, then sighed and . . . relaxed. I could feel it, through the leather and the wooden boards.'

'How did you manage to unravel this spell? Did you say any words? What were you thinking?' Sarah's curiosity was now thoroughly roused.

'There was no witchcraft involved, Sarah. I needed to look at the book for my research, and I laid my palm flat on it, that's all.' I took a deep breath. 'Once it was open, I took some notes, closed it, and returned the manuscript.'

'You *returned it?*' There was a loud clatter as Sarah's phone hit the floor. I winced and held the receiver away from my head, but her colorful language was still audible.

'Diana?' Em said faintly. 'Are you there?'

'I'm here,' I said sharply.

'Diana Bishop, you know better.' Sarah's voice was reproachful. 'How could you send back a magical object you didn't fully understand?'

My aunt had taught me how to recognize enchanted and bewitched objects – and what to do with them. You were to avoid touching or moving them until you knew how their magic worked. Spells could be delicate, and many had protective mechanisms built into them.

'What was I supposed to do, Sarah?' I could hear my defensiveness. 'Refuse to leave the library until you could examine it? It was a Friday night. I wanted to go home.'

'What happened when you returned it?' Sarah said tightly.

'The air might have been a little funny,' I admitted. 'And the library might have given the impression it shrank for just a moment.'

'You sent the manuscript back and the spell reactivated,' Sarah said. She swore again. 'Few witches are adept enough to set up a spell that automatically resets when it's broken. You're not dealing with an amateur.'

'That's the energy that drew them to Oxford,' I said, suddenly understanding. 'It wasn't my opening the manuscript. It was the resetting of the spell. The creatures aren't just at yoga, Sarah. I'm surrounded by vampires and daemons in the Bodleian. Clairmont came to the library on Monday night, hoping to catch a glimpse of the manuscript after he heard two witches talking about it. By Tuesday the library was crawling with them.'

'Here we go again,' Sarah said with a sigh. 'Before the month's out, daemons will be showing up in Madison looking for you.'

'There must be witches you can rely on for help.' Em was making an effort to keep her voice level, but I could hear the concern in it.

'There are witches,' I said haltingly, 'but they're not helpful. A wizard in a brown tweed coat tried to force his way into my head. He would have succeeded, too, if not for Matthew.'

'The vampire put himself between you and another witch?' Em was horrified. 'That's not done. You never interfere in business between witches if you're not one of us.'

'You should be grateful!' I might not want to be lectured by Clairmont or have breakfast with him again, but the vampire deserved some credit. 'If he hadn't been there, I don't know what would have happened. No witch has ever been so . . . invasive with me before.'

'Maybe you should get out of Oxford for a while,' Em suggested.

'I'm not going to leave because there's a witch with no manners in town.'

Em and Sarah whispered to each other, their hands over the receivers.

'I don't like this one bit,' my aunt finally said in a tone that suggested that the world was falling apart. 'Bewitched books? Daemons following you? Vampires taking you to yoga? Witches threatening a Bishop? Witches are supposed to avoid notice, Diana. Even the humans are going to know something's going on.'

'If you stay in Oxford, you'll have to be more inconspicuous,' Em agreed. 'There's nothing wrong with coming home for a while and letting the situation cool off, if that becomes impossible. You don't have the manuscript anymore. Maybe they'll lose interest.'

None of us believed that was likely.

'I'm not running away.'

'You wouldn't be,' Em protested.

'I would.' And I wasn't going to display a shred of cowardice so long as Matthew Clairmont was around.

'He can't be with you every minute of every day, honey,' Em said sadly, hearing my unspoken thoughts.

'I should think not,' Sarah said darkly.

'I don't need Matthew Clairmont's help. I can take care of myself,' I retorted.

'Diana, that vampire isn't protecting you out of the goodness of his heart,' Em said. 'You represent something he wants. You have to figure out what it is.'

'Maybe he *is* interested in alchemy. Maybe he's just bored.'

'Vampires do not get bored,' Sarah said crisply, 'not when there's a witch's blood around.'

There was nothing to be done about my aunt's prejudices. I was tempted to tell her about yoga class, where for over an hour I'd been gloriously free from fear of other creatures. But there was no point.

'Enough.' I was firm. 'Matthew Clairmont won't get any closer, and you needn't worry about me fiddling with more bewitched manuscripts. But I'm not leaving Oxford, and that's final.'

'All right,' Sarah said. 'But there's not much we can do from here if things go wrong.'

'I know, Sarah.'

'And the next time you get handed something magical – whether you expected it or not – behave like the witch you are, not some silly human. Don't ignore it or tell yourself you're imagining things.' Willful ignorance and dismissing the supernatural were at the top of Sarah's list of human pet peeves. 'Treat it with respect, and if you don't know what to do, ask for help.'

'Promise,' I said quickly, wanting to get off the phone. But Sarah wasn't through yet.

'I never thought I'd see the day when a Bishop relied on a vampire for protection, rather than her own power,' she said. 'My mother must be turning in her grave. This is what comes from avoiding who you are, Diana. You've got a mess on your hands, and it's all because you thought you could ignore your heritage. It doesn't work that way.'

Sarah's bitterness soured the atmosphere in my room long after I'd hung up the phone.

The next morning I stretched my way through some yoga poses for half an hour and then made a pot of tea. Its vanilla and floral aromas were comforting, and it had just enough caffeine to keep me from dozing in the afternoon without keeping me awake at night. After the leaves steeped, I wrapped the white porcelain pot in a towel to hold in the heat and carried it to the chair by the fireplace reserved for my deep thinking.

Calmed by the tea's familiar scent, I pulled my knees up to my chin and reviewed my week. No matter where I started, I found myself returning to my last conversation with Matthew Clairmont. Had my efforts to prevent magic from seeping into my life and work meant nothing?

Whenever I was stuck with my research, I imagined a white table, gleaming and empty, and the evidence as a jigsaw puzzle that needed to be pieced together. It took the pressure off and felt like a game.

Now I tumbled everything from the past week onto that table – Ashmole 782, Matthew Clairmont, Agatha Wilson's wandering attention, the tweedy wizard, my tendency to walk with my eyes closed, the creatures in the Bodleian, how I'd fetched *Notes and Queries* from the shelf, Amira's yoga class. I swirled the bright pieces around, putting some together and trying to form a picture, but there were too many gaps, and no clear image emerged.

Sometimes picking up a random piece of evidence helped me figure out what was most important. Putting my imaginary fingers on the table, I drew out a shape, expecting to see Ashmole 782.

Matthew Clairmont's dark eyes looked back at me.

Why was this vampire so important?

The pieces of my puzzle started to move of their own volition, swirling in patterns that were too fast to follow. I slapped my imaginary hands on the table, and the pieces stopped their dance. My palms tingled with recognition.

This didn't seem like a game anymore. It seemed like magic. And if it was, then I'd been using it in my schoolwork, in my college courses, and now in my scholarship. But there was no room in my life for magic, and my mind closed resolutely against the possibility that I'd been violating my own rules without knowing it.

The next day I arrived in the library's cloakroom at my normal time, went up the stairs, rounded the corner near the collection desk, and braced myself to see him.

Clairmont wasn't there.

'Do you need something?' Miriam said in an irritable voice, scraping her chair against the floor as she stood.

'Where is Professor Clairmont?'

'He's hunting,' Miriam said, eyes snapping with dislike, 'in Scotland.'

Hunting. I swallowed hard. 'Oh. When will he be back?'

'I honestly don't know, Dr Bishop.' Miriam crossed her arms and put out a tiny foot.

'I was hoping he'd take me to yoga at the Old Lodge tonight,' I said faintly, trying to come up with a reasonable excuse for stopping.

Miriam turned and picked up a ball of black fluff. She tossed it at me, and I grabbed it as it flew by my hip. 'You left that in his car on Friday.'

'Thank you.' My sweater smelled of carnations and cinnamon.

'You should be more careful with your things,' Miriam muttered. 'You're a witch, Dr Bishop. Take care of *yourself* and stop putting Matthew in this impossible situation.'

I turned on my heel without comment and went to pick up my manuscripts from Sean.

'Everything all right?' he asked, eyeing Miriam with a frown.

'Perfectly.' I gave him my usual seat number and, when he still looked concerned, a warm smile.

How dare Miriam speak to me like that? I fumed while settling into my workspace.

My fingers itched as if hundreds of insects were crawling under the skin. Tiny sparks of blue-green were arcing between my fingertips, leaving traces of energy as they erupted from the edges of my body. I clenched my hands and quickly sat on top of them.

This was *not* good. Like all members of the university, I'd sworn an oath not to bring fire or flame into Bodley's Library. The last time my fingers had behaved like this, I was thirteen and the fire department had to be called to extinguish the blaze in the kitchen.

When the burning sensation abated, I looked around carefully and sighed with relief. I was alone in the Selden End. No one had witnessed my fireworks display. Pulling my hands from underneath my thighs, I scrutinized them for further signs of supernatural activity. The blue was already diminishing to a silvery gray as the power retreated from my fingertips.

I opened the first box only after ascertaining I wouldn't set fire to it and pretended that nothing unusual had happened. Still, I hesitated to touch my computer for fear that my fingers would fuse to the plastic keys.

Not surprisingly, it was difficult to concentrate, and that same manuscript was still before me at lunchtime. Maybe some tea would calm me down.

At the beginning of term, one would expect to see a handful of human readers in Duke Humfrey's medieval wing. Today there was only one: an elderly human woman examining an illuminated manuscript with a magnifying glass. She was squashed between an unfamiliar daemon and one of the female vampires from last week. Gillian Chamberlain was there, too, glowering at me along with four other witches as if I'd let down our entire species.

Hurrying past, I stopped at Miriam's desk. 'I presume you have instructions to follow me to lunch. Are you coming?'

She put down her pencil with exaggerated care. 'After you.'

Miriam was in front of me by the time I reached the back staircase. She pointed to the steps on the other side. 'Go down that way.'

'Why? What difference does it make?'

'Suit yourself.' She shrugged.

One flight down I glanced through the small window stuck into the swinging door that led to the Upper Reading Room, and I gasped.

The room was full to bursting with creatures. They had segregated themselves. One long table held nothing but daemons, conspicuous because not a single book – open or closed – sat in front of them. Vampires sat at another table, their bodies perfectly still and their eyes never blinking. The witches appeared studious, but their frowns were signs of irritation rather than concentration, since the daemons and vampires had staked out the tables closest to the staircase.

'No wonder we're not supposed to mix. No human could ignore this,' Miriam observed.

'What have I done now?' I asked in a whisper.

'Nothing. Matthew's not here,' she said matter-of-factly.

'Why are they so afraid of Matthew?'

'You'll have to ask him. Vampires don't tell tales. But don't worry,' she continued, baring her sharp, white teeth, 'these work perfectly, so you've got nothing to fear.'

Shoving my hands into my pockets, I clattered down the stairs, pushing through the tourists in the quadrangle. At Blackwell's, I swallowed a sandwich and a bottle of water. Miriam caught my eye as I passed by her on the way to the exit. She put aside a murder mystery and followed me.

'Diana,' she said quietly as we passed through the library's gates, 'what are you up to?'

'None of your business,' I snapped.

Miriam sighed.

Back in Duke Humfrey's, I located the wizard in brown tweed. Miriam watched intently from the center aisle, still as a statue.

'Are you in charge?'

He tipped his head to the side in acknowledgment.

'I'm Diana Bishop,' I said, sticking out my hand.

'Peter Knox. And I know very well who you are. You're Rebecca and Stephen's child.' He touched my fingertips lightly with his own. There was a nineteenth-century grimoire sitting in front of him, a stack of reference books at his side.

The name was familiar, though I couldn't place it, and hearing my parents' names come out of this wizard's mouth was disquieting. I swallowed, hard. 'Please clear your . . . friends out of the library. The new students arrive today, and we wouldn't want to frighten them.'

'If we could have a quiet word, Dr Bishop, I'm sure we could come to some arrangement.' He pushed his glasses up over the bridge of his nose. The closer I was to Knox, the more danger I felt. The skin under my fingernails started to prickle ominously.

'You have nothing to fear from me,' he said sorrowfully. 'That vampire, on the other hand—'

'You think I found something that belongs to the witches,' I interrupted. 'I no longer have it. If you want Ashmole 782, there are request slips on the desk in front of you.'

'You don't understand the complexity of the situation.'

'No, and I don't *want* to know. Please, leave me alone.'

'Physically you are very like your mother.' Knox's eyes swept over my face. 'But you have some of Stephen's stubbornness as well, I see.'

I felt the usual combination of envy and irritation that accompanied a witch's references to my parents or family history – as if they had an equal claim to mine.

'I'll try,' he continued, 'but I don't control those animals.' He waved across the aisle, where one of the Scary Sisters was watching Knox and me with interest. I hesitated, then crossed over to her seat.

'I'm sure you heard our conversation, and you must know I'm under the direct supervision of two vampires already,' I said. 'You're welcome to stay, if you don't trust Matthew and Miriam. But clear the others out of the Upper Reading Room.'

'Witches are hardly ever worth a moment of a vampire's time, but you are full of surprises today, Diana Bishop. Wait until I tell my sister Clarissa what she's missed.' The female vampire's words came out in a lush, unhurried drawl redolent of impeccable breeding and a fine education. She smiled, teeth gleaming in the low light of the medieval wing. 'Challenging Knox – a child like you? What a tale I'll have to tell.'

I dragged my eyes away from her flawless features and went off in search of a familiar daemonic face.

The latte-loving daemon was drifting around the computer terminals wearing headphones and humming under his breath to some unheard music as the end of the cord was swinging freely around the tops of his thighs. Once he pulled the white plastic disks from his ears, I tried to impress upon him the seriousness of the situation.

'Listen, you're welcome to keep surfing the Net up here. But we've got a problem downstairs. It's not necessary for two dozen daemons to be watching me.'

The daemon made an indulgent sound. 'You'll know soon enough.'

'Could they watch me from farther away? The Sheldonian? The White Horse?' I was trying to be helpful. 'If not, the human readers will start asking questions.'

'We're not like you,' he said dreamily.

'Does that mean you can't help or you won't?' I tried not to sound impatient.

'It's all the same thing. We need to know, too.'

This was impossible. 'Whatever you can do to take some of the pressure off the seats would be greatly appreciated.'

Miriam was still watching me. Ignoring her, I returned to my desk.

At the end of the completely unproductive day, I pinched the bridge of my nose, swore under my breath, and packed up my things.

The next morning the Bodleian was far less crowded. Miriam was scribbling furiously and didn't look up when I passed. There was still no sign of Clairmont. Even so, everybody was observing the rules that he had clearly, if silently, laid down, and they stayed out of the Selden End. Gillian was in the medieval wing, crouched over her papyri, as were both Scary Sisters and a few daemons. With the exception of Gillian, who was doing real work, the rest went through the motions with perfect respectability. And when I stuck my head around the swinging door into the Upper Reading Room after a hot cup of tea at midmorning, only a few creatures looked up. The musical, coffee-loving daemon was among them. He tipped his fingers and winked at me knowingly.

I got a reasonable amount of work done, although not enough to make up for yesterday. I began by reading alchemical poems – the trickiest of texts – that were attributed to Mary, the sister of Moses. '*Three things if you three hours attend*,' read one part of the poem, '*Are chained together in the End*.' The meaning of the verses remained a mystery, although the most likely subject was the chemical combination of silver, gold, and mercury. Could Chris produce an experiment from this poem? I wondered, noting the possible chemical processes involved.

When I turned to another, anonymous poem, entitled 'Verse on the Threefold Sophic Fire,' the similarities between its imagery and an illumination I'd seen yesterday of an alchemical mountain, riddled with mines and miners digging in the ground for precious metals and stones, were unmistakable.

> Within this Mine two Stones of old were found,
> Whence this the Ancients called Holy Ground;
> Who knew their Value, Power and Extent,
> And Nature how with Nature to Ferment
> For these if you Ferment with Natural Gold
> Or Silver, their hid Treasures they unfold.

I stifled a groan. My research would become exponentially more complicated if I had to connect not only art and science but art and poetry.

'It must be hard to concentrate on your research with vampires watching you.'

Gillian Chamberlain was standing next to me, her hazel eyes sparking with suppressed malevolence.

'What do you want, Gillian?'

'I'm just being friendly, Diana. We're sisters, remember?' Gillian's shiny black hair swung above her collar. Its smoothness suggested that she was not troubled by surges of static electricity. Her power must be regularly released. I shivered.

'I have no sisters, Gillian. I'm an only child.'

'It's a good thing, too. Your family has caused more than enough trouble. Look at what happened at Salem. It was all Bridget Bishop's fault.' Gillian's tone was vicious.

Here we go again, I thought, closing the volume before me. As usual, the Bishops were proving to be an irresistible topic of conversation.

'What are you talking about, Gillian?' My voice was sharp. 'Bridget Bishop was found guilty of witchcraft and executed. She didn't instigate the witch-hunt – she was a victim of it, just like the others. You know that, as does every other witch in this library.'

'Bridget Bishop drew human attention, first with those poppets of hers and then with her provocative clothes and immorality. The human hysteria would have passed if not for her.'

'She was found innocent of practicing witchcraft,' I retorted, bristling.

'In 1680 – but no one believed it. Not after they found the poppets in her cellar wall, pins stuck through them and the heads ripped off. Afterward Bridget did nothing to protect her fellow witches from falling under suspicion. She was so independent.' Gillian's voice dropped. 'That was your mother's fatal flaw, too.'

'Stop it, Gillian.' The air around us seemed unnaturally cold and clear.

'Your mother and father were standoffish, just like you, thinking they didn't need the Cambridge coven's support after they got married. They learned, didn't they?'

I shut my eyes, but it was impossible to block out the image I'd spent most of my life trying to forget: my mother and father lying dead in the middle of a chalk-marked circle somewhere in Nigeria, their bodies broken and bloody. My aunt wouldn't share the details of their death at the time, so I'd slipped into the public library to look them up. That's where I'd first seen the picture and the lurid headline that accompanied it. The nightmares had gone on for years afterward.

'There was nothing the Cambridge coven could do to prevent my parents' murder. They were killed on another continent by fearful humans.' I gripped the arms of my chair, hoping that she wouldn't see my white knuckles.

Gillian gave an unpleasant laugh. 'It wasn't humans, Diana. If it had been, their killers would have been caught and dealt with.' She crouched down, her face close to mine. 'Rebecca Bishop and Stephen Proctor were keeping secrets from other witches. We needed to discover them. Their deaths were unfortunate, but necessary. Your father had more power than we ever dreamed.'

'Stop talking about *my* family and *my* parents as though they belong to you,' I warned. 'They were killed by humans.' There was a roaring in my ears, and the coldness that surrounded us was intensifying.

'Are you sure?' Gillian whispered, sending a fresh chill into my bones. 'As a witch, you'd know if I was lying to you.'

I governed my features, determined not to show my confusion. What Gillian said about my parents couldn't be true, and yet there were none of the subtle alarms that typically accompanied untruths between witches — the spark of anger, an overwhelming feeling of contempt.

'Think about what happened to Bridget Bishop and your parents the next time you turn down an invitation to a coven gathering,' Gillian murmured, her lips so close to my ear that her breath swept against my skin. 'A witch shouldn't keep secrets from other witches. Bad things happen when she does.'

Gillian straightened and stared at me for a few seconds, the tingle of her glance growing uncomfortable the longer it lasted. Staring fixedly at the closed manuscript before me, I refused to meet her eyes.

After she left, the air's temperature returned to normal. When my heart stopped pounding and the roaring in my ears abated, I packed my belongings with shaking hands, badly wanting to be back in my rooms. Adrenaline was coursing through my body, and I wasn't sure how long it would be possible to fend off my panic.

I managed to get out of the library without incident, avoiding Miriam's sharp glance. If Gillian was right, it was the jealousy of fellow witches that I needed to be wary of, not human fear. And the mention of my father's hidden powers made something half remembered flit at the edges of my mind, but it eluded me when I tried to fix it in place long enough to see it clearly.

At New College, Fred hailed me from the porter's lodge with a fistful of mail. A creamy envelope, thick with a distinctive woven feeling, lay on top.

It was a note from the warden, summoning me for a drink before dinner.

In my rooms I considered calling his secretary and feigning illness to get out of the invitation. My head was reeling, and there was little chance I could keep down even a drop of sherry in my present state.

But the college had behaved handsomely when I'd requested a place to stay. The least I could do was express my thanks personally. My sense of professional obligation began to supplant the anxiety stirred up by Gillian. Holding on to my identity as a scholar like a lifeline, I resolved to make my appreciation known.

After changing, I made my way to the warden's lodgings and rang the bell. A member of the college staff opened the door and ushered me inside, leading me to the parlor.

'Hello, Dr Bishop.' Nicholas Marsh's blue eyes crinkled at the corners, and his snowy white hair and round red cheeks made him look like Santa Claus. Soothed by his warmth and armored with a sense of professional duty, I smiled.

'Professor Marsh.' I took his outstretched hand. 'Thank you for inviting me.'

'It's overdue, I'm afraid. I was in Italy, you know.'

'Yes, the bursar told me.'

'Then you have forgiven me for neglecting you for so long,' he said. 'I hope to make it up to you by introducing you to an old friend of mine who is in Oxford for a few days. He's a well-known author and writes about subjects that might interest you.'

Marsh stood aside, giving me a glimpse of a thick head of brown hair peppered with gray and the sleeve of a brown tweed jacket. I froze in confusion.

'Come and meet Peter Knox,' the warden said, taking my elbow gently. 'He's acquainted with your work.'

The wizard stood. Finally I recognized what had been eluding me. Knox's name had been in the newspaper story about vampire murders. He was the expert the police called in to examine deaths that had an occult twist. My fingers started to itch.

'Dr Bishop,' Knox said, holding out his hand. 'I've seen you in the Bodleian.'

'Yes, I believe you have.' I extended my own and was relieved to see that it was not emitting sparks. We clasped hands as briefly as possible.

His right fingertips flickered slightly, a tiny furl and a release of bones and skin that no human would have noticed. It reminded me of my childhood, when my mother's hands had flickered and furled to produce pancakes and fold laundry. Shutting my eyes, I braced for an outpouring of magic.

The phone rang.

'I must get that, I'm afraid,' Marsh apologized. 'Do sit down.'

I sat as far from Knox as possible, perched on a straight-backed wooden chair usually reserved for disgraced junior members of the college.

Knox and I remained silent while Marsh murmured and tutted into the phone. He punched a button on the console and approached me, a glass of sherry in his hand. 'That's the vice-chancellor. Two freshers have gone missing,' he said, using the university's slang term for new students. 'You two chat while I deal with this in my study. Please excuse me.'

Distant doors opened and closed, and muffled voices conferred in the hall before there was silence.

'Missing students?' I said blandly. Surely Knox had magically engineered both the crisis and the phone call that had drawn Marsh away.

'I don't understand, Dr Bishop,' Knox murmured. 'It seems unfortunate for the university to misplace two children. Besides, this gives us a chance to talk privately.'

'What do we have to talk about?' I sniffed my sherry and prayed for the warden's return.

'A great many things.'

I glanced at the door.

'Nicholas will be quite busy until we're through.'

'Let's get this over with, then, so that the warden can return to his drink.'

'As you wish,' Knox said. 'Tell me what brought you to Oxford, Dr Bishop.'

'Alchemy.' I would answer the man's questions, if only to get Marsh back into the room, but wasn't going to tell him more than was necessary.

'You must have known that Ashmole 782 was bewitched. No one with even a drop of Bishop blood in her veins could have failed to notice. Why did you send it back?' Knox's brown eyes were sharp. He wanted the manuscript as much as Matthew Clairmont did – if not more.

'I was done with it.' It was difficult to keep my voice even.

'Was there nothing about the manuscript that piqued your interest?'

'Nothing.'

Peter Knox's mouth twisted into an ugly expression. He knew I was lying. 'Have you shared your observations with the vampire?'

'I take it you mean Professor Clairmont.' When creatures refused to use proper names, it was a way of denying that those who were not like you were your equals.

Knox's fingers unwound once more. When I thought he might point them at me, he curled them around the arms of his chair instead. 'We all respect your family and what you've endured. Nevertheless, questions have been raised about your unorthodox relationship with this creature. You are betraying your ancestral lineage with this self-indulgent behavior. It must stop.'

'Professor Clairmont is a professional colleague,' I said, steering the conversation away from my family, 'and I know nothing about the manuscript. It was in my possession for a matter of minutes. Yes, I knew it was under a spell. But that was immaterial to me, since I'd requested it to study the contents.'

'The vampire has wanted that book for more than a century,' Knox said, his voice vicious. 'He mustn't be allowed to have it.'

'Why?' My voice crackled with suppressed anger. 'Because it belongs to the witches? Vampires and daemons can't enchant objects. A witch put that book under a spell, and now it's back under the same spell. What are you worried about?'

'More than you could possibly comprehend, Dr Bishop.'

'I'm confident I can keep up, *Mr* Knox,' I replied. Knox's mouth tightened with displeasure when I emphasized his position outside the academy. Every time the wizard used my title, his formality sounded like a taunt, as if he were trying to make a point that he, not I, was the real expert. I might not use my power, and I couldn't have conjured up my own lost keys, but being patronized by this wizard was intolerable.

'I am disturbed that you – a Bishop – are associating with a vampire.' He held up his hand as a protest bubbled to my lips. 'Let's not insult each other with further untruths. Instead of the natural revulsion you should feel for that animal, you feel gratitude.'

I remained silent, seething.

'And I'm concerned because we are perilously close to catching human attention,' he continued.

'I tried to get the creatures out of the library.'

'Ah, but it's not just the library, is it? A vampire is leaving drained, bloodless corpses around Westminster. The daemons are unusually restless, vulnerable as ever to their own madness and the swings of energy in the world. We can't afford to be noticed.'

'You told the reporters that there was nothing supernatural about those deaths.'

Knox looked incredulous. 'You don't expect me to tell *humans* everything?'

'I do, actually, when they're paying you.'

'You're not only self-indulgent, you're foolish. That surprises me, Dr Bishop. Your father was known for his good sense.'

'I've had a long day. Is that all?' Standing abruptly, I moved toward the door. Even in normal circumstances, it was difficult to listen to anyone but Sarah and Em talking about my parents. Now — after Gillian's revelations — there was something almost obscene about it.

'No, it is not,' said Knox unpleasantly. 'What I am most intrigued by, at present, is the question of how an ignorant witch with no training of any sort managed to break a spell that has defied the efforts of those far more adept than you will ever be.'

'So that's why you're all watching me.' I sat down, my back pressing against the chair's slats.

'Don't look so pleased with yourself,' he said curtly. 'Your success may have been a fluke — an anniversary reaction related to when the spell was first cast. The passage of time can interfere with witchcraft, and anniversaries are particularly volatile moments. You haven't tried to recall it yet, but when you do, it may not come as easily as it did the first time.'

'And what anniversary would we be celebrating?'

'The sesquicentennial.'

I had wondered why a witch would put a spell on the manuscript in the first place. Someone must have been looking for it all those years ago, too. I blanched.

We were back to Matthew Clairmont and his interest in Ashmole 782.

'You *are* managing to keep up, aren't you? The next time you see your vampire, ask him what he was doing in the autumn of 1859. I doubt he'll tell you the truth, but he might reveal enough for you to figure it out on your own.'

'I'm tired. Why don't you tell me, witch to witch, what *your* interest is in Ashmole 782?' I'd heard why the daemons wanted the manuscript. Even Matthew had given me some explanation. Knox's fascination with it was a missing piece of the puzzle.

'That manuscript belongs to us,' Knox said fiercely. 'We're the only creatures who can understand its secrets and the only creatures who can be trusted to keep them.'

'*What is in the manuscript?*' I said, temper flaring at last.

'The first spells ever constructed. Descriptions of the enchantments that bind the world together.' Knox's face grew dreamy. 'The secret of immortality. How witches made the first daemon. How vampires can be destroyed, once and for all.' His eyes pierced mine. 'It's the source of all our power, past and present. It cannot be allowed to fall into the hands of daemons or vampires – or humans.'

The events of the afternoon were catching up with me, and I had to press my knees together to keep them from shaking. 'Nobody would put all that information in a single book.'

'The first witch did,' Knox said. 'And her sons and daughters, too, down through time. It's our history, Diana. Surely you want to protect it from prying eyes.'

The warden entered the room as if he'd been waiting by the door. The tension was suffocating, but he seemed blissfully unaware of it.

'What a palaver over nothing.' Marsh shook his white head. 'The freshers illegally obtained a punt. They were located, stuck under a bridge and a little worse for wine, utterly content with their situation. A romance may result.'

'I'm so glad,' I murmured. The clocks struck forty-five minutes past the hour, and I stood. 'Is that the time? I have a dinner engagement.'

'You won't be joining us for dinner?' the warden asked with a frown. 'Peter has been looking forward to talking to you about alchemy.'

'Our paths will cross again. Soon,' Knox said smoothly. 'My visit was such a surprise, and of course the lady has better things to do than have dinner with two men our age.'

Be careful with Matthew Clairmont. Knox's voice rang in my head. *He's a killer.*

Marsh smiled. 'Yes, of course. I do hope to see you again – when the freshers have settled down.'

Ask him about 1859. See if he'll share his secrets with a witch.

It's hardly a secret if you know it. Surprise registered on Knox's face when I replied to his mental warning in kind. It was the sixth time I'd used magic this year, but these were surely extenuating circumstances.

'It would be a pleasure, Warden. And thank you again for letting me stay in college this year.' I nodded to the wizard. 'Mr Knox.'

Fleeing from the warden's lodgings, I turned toward my old refuge in the cloisters and walked among the pillars until my pulse stopped racing. My mind was occupied with only one question: what to do now that two witches – my own people – had threatened me in the space of a single afternoon. With sudden clarity I knew the answer.

In my rooms I searched my bag until my fingers found Clairmont's crumpled business card, and then I dialed the first number.

He didn't answer.

After a robotic voice indicated that it was ready to receive my message, I spoke.

'Matthew, it's Diana. I'm sorry to bother you when you're out of town.' I took a deep breath, trying to dispel some of the guilt associated with my decision not to tell Clairmont about Gillian and my parents, but only about Knox. 'We need to talk. Something has happened. It's that wizard from the library. His name is Peter Knox. If you get this message, please call me.'

I'd assured Sarah and Em that no vampire would meddle in my life. Gillian Chamberlain and Peter Knox had changed my mind. With shaking hands I lowered the shades and locked the door, wishing I'd never heard of Ashmole 782.

CHAPTER 11

That night, sleep was impossible. I sat on the sofa, then on the bed, the phone at my side. Not even a pot of tea and a raft of e-mail took my mind off the day's events. The notion that witches might have murdered my parents was beyond my comprehension. Pushing back those thoughts, I instead puzzled over the spell on Ashmole 782 and Knox's interest in it.

Still awake at dawn, I showered and changed. The idea of breakfast was uncharacteristically unappetizing. Rather than eat, I perched by the door until the Bodleian opened, then walked the short distance to the library and took my regular seat. My phone was in my pocket, set to vibrate, even though I hated it when other people's phones started buzzing and hopping in the quiet.

At half past ten, Peter Knox strolled in and sat at the opposite end of the room. On the premise of returning a manuscript, I walked back to the call desk to make sure that Miriam was still in the library. She was – and she was angry.

'Tell me that witch didn't take a seat down there.'

'He did. He keeps staring at my back while I work.'

'I wish I were larger,' Miriam said with a frown.

'Somehow I think it would take more than size to deter that creature.' I gave her a lopsided smile.

When Matthew came into the Selden End, without warning or sound, no icy patches announced his arrival. Instead there were touches of snowflakes all along my hair, shoulders, and back, as if he were checking quickly to make sure I was all in one piece.

My fingers gripped the table in front of me. For a few moments, I didn't dare turn in case it was simply Miriam. When I saw it was indeed Matthew, my heart gave a single loud thump.

But the vampire was no longer looking in my direction. He was staring at Peter Knox, his face ferocious.

'Matthew,' I called softly, rising to my feet.

He dragged his eyes from the witch and strode to my side. When I frowned uncertainly at his fierce expression, he gave me a reassuring smile. 'I understand there's been some excitement.' He was so close that the coolness of his body felt as refreshing as a breeze on a summer day.

'Nothing we couldn't handle,' I said evenly, conscious of Peter Knox.

'Can our conversation wait – just until the end of the day?' he asked. Matthew's fingers strayed up to touch a bump on his sternum that was visible under the soft fibers of his sweater. I wondered what he was wearing, close to his heart. 'We could go to yoga.'

Though I'd had no sleep, a drive to Woodstock in a moving vehicle with very good sound insulation, followed by an hour and a half of meditative movement, sounded perfect.

'That would be wonderful,' I said sincerely.

'Would you like me to work here, with you?' he asked, leaning toward me. His scent was so powerful it was dizzying.

'That's not necessary,' I said firmly.

'Let me know if you change your mind. Otherwise I'll see you outside Hertford at six.' Matthew held my eyes a few moments longer. Then he sent a look of loathing in Peter Knox's direction and returned to his seat.

When I passed his desk on the way to lunch, Matthew coughed. Miriam slammed her pencil down in irritation and joined me. Knox would not be following me to Blackwell's. Matthew would see to that.

The afternoon dragged on interminably, and it was almost impossible to stay awake. By five o'clock, I was more than ready to leave the library. Knox remained in the Selden End, along with a motley assortment of humans. Matthew walked me downstairs, and my spirits lightened as I raced back to college, changed, and picked up my yoga mat. When his car pulled up to Hertford's metal railings, I was waiting for him.

'You're early,' he observed with a smile, taking my mat and putting it into the trunk. Matthew breathed in sharply as he helped me into the car, and I wondered what messages my body had passed on to him.

'We need to talk.'

'There's no rush. Let's get out of Oxford first.' He closed the car door behind me and climbed into the driver's seat.

The traffic on the Woodstock Road was heavier due to the influx of students and dons. Matthew maneuvered deftly around the slow spots.

'How was Scotland?' I asked as we cleared the city limits, not caring what he talked about so long as he talked.

Matthew glanced at me and returned his eyes to the road. 'Fine.'

'Miriam said you were hunting.'

He exhaled softly, his fingers rising to the bump under his sweater. 'She shouldn't have.'

'Why?'

'Because some things shouldn't be discussed in mixed company,' he said with a touch of impatience. 'Do witches tell creatures who aren't witches that they've just returned from four days of casting spells and boiling bats?'

'Witches don't boil bats!' I said indignantly.

'The point remains.'

'Were you alone?' I asked.

Matthew waited a long time before answering. 'No.'

'I wasn't alone in Oxford either,' I began. 'The creatures—'

'Miriam told me.' His hands tightened on the wheel. 'If I'd known that the witch bothering you was Peter Knox, I'd never have left Oxford.'

'You were right,' I blurted, needing to make my own confession before tackling the subject of Knox. 'I've never kept the magic out of my life. I've been using it in my work, without realizing it. It's in everything. I've been fooling myself for years.' The words tumbled from my mouth. Matthew remained focused on the traffic. 'I'm frightened.'

His cold hand touched my knee. 'I know.'

'What am I going to do?' I whispered.

'We'll figure it out,' he said calmly, turning in to the Old Lodge's gates. He scrutinized my face as we crested the rise and pulled in to the circular drive. 'You're tired. Can you manage yoga?'

I nodded.

Matthew got out of the car and opened the door for me. This time he didn't help me out. Instead he fished around in the trunk, pulled out our mats, and shouldered both of them himself. Other members of the class filtered by, casting curious looks in our direction.

He waited until we were the only ones on the drive. Matthew looked down at me, wrestling with himself over something. I frowned, my head tilted back to meet his eyes. I'd just confessed to engaging in magic without realizing it. What was so awful that he couldn't tell me?

'I was in Scotland with an old friend, Hamish Osborne,' he finally said.

'The man the newspapers want to run for Parliament so he can be chancellor of the exchequer?' I said in amazement.

'Hamish will not be running for Parliament,' Matthew said drily, adjusting the strap of his yoga bag with a twitch.

'So he *is* gay!' I said, thinking back to a recent late-night news program.

Matthew gave me a withering glance. 'Yes. More important, he's a daemon.' I didn't know much about the world of creatures, but participating in human politics or religion was also forbidden.

'Oh. Finance is an odd career choice for a daemon.' I thought for a moment. 'It explains why he's so good at figuring out what to do with all that money, though.'

'He is good at figuring things out.' The silence stretched on, and Matthew made no move for the door. 'I needed to get away and hunt.'

I gave him a confused look.

'You left your sweater in my car,' he said, as if that were an explanation.

'Miriam gave it back to me already.'

'I know. I couldn't hold on to it. Do you understand why?'

When I shook my head, he sighed and then swore in French.

'My car was full of your scent, Diana. I needed to leave Oxford.'

'I still don't understand,' I admitted.

'I couldn't stop thinking about you.' He raked his hand through his hair and looked down the drive.

My heart was beating irregularly, and the reduced blood flow slowed my mental processes. Finally, though, I understood.

'You're not afraid you would hurt me?' I had a healthy fear of vampires, but Matthew seemed different.

'I can't be sure.' His eyes were wary, and his voice held a warning.

'So you didn't go because of what happened Friday night.' My breath released in sudden relief.

'No,' he said gently, 'it had nothing to do with that.'

'Are you two coming in, or are you going to practice out here on the drive?' Amira called from the doorway.

We went in to class, occasionally glancing at each other when one of us thought the other wasn't looking. Our first honest exchange of information had altered things. We were both trying to figure out what was going to happen next.

After class ended, when Matthew swung his sweater over his head, something shining and silver caught my eye. The object was tied around his neck on a thin leather cord. It was what he kept touching through his sweater, over and over, like a talisman.

'What's that?' I pointed.

'A reminder,' Matthew said shortly.

'Of what?'

'The destructive power of anger.'

Peter Knox had warned me to be careful around Matthew.

'Is it a pilgrim's badge?' The shape reminded me of one in the British Museum. It looked ancient.

He nodded and pulled the badge out by the cord. It swung freely, glinting as the light struck it. 'It's an ampulla from Bethany.' It was shaped like a coffin and just big enough to hold a few drops of holy water.

'Lazarus,' I said faintly, eyeing the coffin. Bethany was where Christ had resurrected Lazarus from the dead. And though raised a pagan, I knew why Christians went on pilgrimage. They did it to atone for their sins.

Matthew slid the ampulla back into his sweater, concealing it from the eyes of the creatures who were still filing out of the room.

We said good-bye to Amira and stood outside the Old Lodge in the crisp autumn air. It was dark, despite the floodlights that bathed the bricks of the house.

'Do you feel better?' Matthew asked, breaking into my thoughts. I nodded. 'Then tell me what's happened.'

'It's the manuscript. Knox wants it. Agatha Wilson – the creature I met in Blackwell's – said the daemons want it. You want it, too. But Ashmole 782 is under a spell.'

'I know,' he said again.

A white owl swooped down in front of us, its wings beating the air. I flinched and lifted my arms to protect myself, convinced it was going to strike me with its beak and talons. But then the owl lost interest and soared up into the oak trees along the drive.

My heart was pounding, and a sudden rush of panic swept up from my feet. Without any warning, Matthew pulled open the back door of the Jaguar and pushed me into the seat. 'Keep your head down and breathe,' he said, crouching on the gravel with his fingers resting on my knees. The bile rose – there was nothing in my stomach but water – and crawled up my throat, choking me. I covered my mouth with my hand and retched convulsively. He reached over and tucked a wayward piece of hair behind my ear, his fingers cool and soothing.

'You're safe,' he said.

'I'm so sorry.' My shaking hand passed across my mouth as the nausea subsided. 'The panic started last night after I saw Knox.'

'Do you want to walk a bit?'

'No,' I said hastily. The park seemed overly large and very black, and my legs felt like they were made of rubber bands.

Matthew inspected me with his keen eyes. 'I'm taking you home. The rest of this conversation can wait.'

He pulled me up from the backseat and held my hand loosely until he had me settled in the front of the car. I closed my eyes while he climbed in. We sat for a moment in silence, and then Matthew turned the key in the ignition. The Jaguar quickly sprang to life.

'Does this happen often?' he asked, his voice neutral.

'No, thank God,' I said. 'It happened a lot when I was a child, but it's much better now. It's just an excess of adrenaline.' Matthew's glance settled on my hands as I pushed my hair from my face.

'I know,' he said yet again, disengaging the parking brake and pulling out onto the drive.

'Can you smell it?'

He nodded. 'It's been building up in you since you told me you were using magic. Is this why you exercise so much – the running, the rowing, the yoga?'

'I don't like taking drugs. They make me feel fuzzy.'

'The exercise is probably more effective anyway.'

'It hasn't done the trick this time,' I murmured, thinking of my recently electrified hands.

Matthew pulled out of the Old Lodge's grounds and onto the road. He concentrated on his driving while the car's smooth movements rocked me gently.

'Why did you call me?' Matthew asked abruptly, interrupting my reveries.

'Because of Knox and Ashmole 782,' I said, flickers of panic returning at his sudden shift in mood.

'I know that. What I'm asking is why you called *me*. Surely you have friends – witches, humans – who could help you.'

'Not really. None of my human friends know I'm a witch. It would take days just to explain what's really happening in this world – if they stuck around long enough for me to finish, that is. I don't have friends who are witches, and I can't drag my aunts into this. It's not their fault I did something stupid and sent the manuscript back when I didn't understand it.' I bit my lip. 'Should I not have called you?'

'I don't know, Diana. On Friday you said witches and vampires couldn't be friends.'

'On Friday I told you lots of things.'

Matthew was quiet, giving his full attention to the curves in the road.

'I don't know what to think anymore.' I paused, considering my next words carefully. 'But there is one thing I know for sure. I'd rather share the library with you than with Knox.'

'Vampires are never completely trustworthy – not when they're around warmbloods.' Matthew's eyes focused on me for a single, cold moment.

'Warmbloods?' I asked with a frown.

'Humans, witches, daemons – everyone who's not a vampire.'

'I'll risk your bite before I let Knox slither into my brain to fish for information.'

'Has he tried to do that?' Matthew's voice was quiet, but there was a promise of violence in it.

'It was nothing,' I said hastily. 'He was just warning me about you.'

'So he should. Nobody can be what he's not, no matter how hard he tries. You mustn't romanticize vampires. Knox may not have your best interests at heart, but he was right about me.'

'Other people don't pick my friends – certainly not bigots like Knox.' My fingers began to prickle as my anger mounted, and I shoved them under my thighs.

'Is that what we are, then? Friends?' Matthew asked.

'I think so. Friends tell each other the truth, even when it's difficult.' Disconcerted by the seriousness of the conversation, I toyed with the ties on my sweater.

'Vampires aren't particularly good at friendship.' He sounded angry again.

'Look, if you want me to leave you alone—'

'Of course not,' Matthew interrupted. 'It's just that vampire relationships are . . . complicated. We can be protective – possessive, even. You might not like it.'

'A little protectiveness sounds pretty good to me about now.'

My answer brought a look of raw vulnerability to Matthew's eyes. 'I'll remind you of that when you start complaining,' he said, the rawness quickly replaced with wry amusement.

He pulled off Holywell Street into the arched gates of the lodge. Fred glanced at the car and grinned before looking discreetly away. I waited for Matthew to open the door, checking the car carefully to make sure that nothing of mine was left there – not even a hair elastic – so as not to drive him back to Scotland.

'But there's more to all this than Knox and the manuscript,' I said urgently when he handed me the mat. From his behavior you wouldn't think there were creatures closing in on me from every direction.

'It can wait, Diana. And don't worry. Peter Knox won't get within fifty feet of you again.' His voice was grim, and he touched the ampulla under his sweater.

We needed time together – not in the library, but alone.

'Would you like to come to dinner tomorrow?' I asked him, my voice low. 'We could talk about what happened then.'

Matthew froze, confusion flitting over his face along with something I couldn't name. His fingers flexed slightly around the pilgrim's badge before he released it.

'I'd like that,' he said slowly.

'Good.' I smiled. 'How's half past seven?'

He nodded and gave me a shy grin. I managed to walk two steps before realizing there was one matter that needed to be resolved before tomorrow night.

'What do you eat?' I whispered, my face flushing.

'I'm omnivorous,' Matthew said, his face brightening further into a smile that made my heart skip a beat.

'Half past seven, then.' I turned away, laughing and shaking my head at his unhelpful answer. 'Oh, one more thing,' I said, turning back. 'Let Miriam do her own work. I really can take care of myself.'

'So she tells me,' Matthew said, walking around to the driver's side of the car. 'I'll consider it. But you'll find me in Duke Humfrey's tomorrow, as usual.' He got into the car, and when I showed no sign of moving, he rolled down his window.

'I'm not leaving until you're out of my sight,' he said, looking at me in disapproval.

'Vampires,' I muttered, shaking my head at his old-fashioned ways.

CHAPTER 12

Nothing in my culinary experience had taught me what to feed a vampire when he came for dinner.

In the library I spent most of the day on the Internet looking for recipes that involved raw foods, my manuscripts forgotten on the desk. Matthew said he was omnivorous, but that couldn't be true. A vampire must be more likely to tolerate uncooked food if he was used to a diet of blood. But he was so civilized he would no doubt eat whatever I put in front of him.

After undertaking extensive gastronomical research, I left the library at midafternoon. Matthew had held down Fortress Bishop by himself today, which must have pleased Miriam. There was no sign of Peter Knox or Gillian Chamberlain anywhere in Duke Humfrey's, which made me happy. Even Matthew looked in good humor when I trotted down the aisle to return my manuscripts.

Passing by the dome of the Radcliffe Camera, where the undergraduates read their assigned books, and the medieval walls of Jesus College, I went shopping along the aisles of Oxford's Covered Market. List in hand, I made my first stop at the butcher for fresh venison and rabbit, and then to the fishmonger for Scottish salmon.

Did vampires eat greens?

Thanks to my mobile, I was able to reach the zoology department and inquire about the feeding habits of wolves. They asked me what kind of wolves. I'd seen gray wolves on a long-ago field trip to the Boston zoo, and it was Matthew's favorite color, so that was my answer. After rattling off a long list of tasty mammals and explaining that they were 'preferred foods,' the bored voice on the other end told me that gray wolves also ate nuts, seeds, and berries. 'But you shouldn't feed them!' the voice warned. 'They're not house pets!'

'Thanks for the advice,' I said, trying not to giggle.

The grocer apologetically sold me the last of the summer's black-currants and some fragrant wild strawberries. A bag of chestnuts found its way into my expanding shopping bag, too.

Then it was off to the wine store, where I found myself at the mercy of a viticultural evangelist who asked if 'the gentleman knew wine.' That was enough to send me into a tailspin. The clerk seized upon my confusion to sell me what ended up being remarkably few French and German bottles of wine for a king's ransom. He then tucked me into a cab to recover from the shock during the drive back to college.

In my rooms I swept all the papers off a battered eighteenth-century table that served as both desk and dining room and moved it closer to the fireplace. I set the table carefully, using the old porcelain and silver that was in my cupboards, along with heavy crystal glasses that had to be the final remainders of an Edwardian set once used in the senior common room. My loyal kitchen ladies had supplied me with stacks of crisp white linen, which were now draped over the table, folded next to the silver, and spread on the chipped wooden tray that would help me carry things the short distance from the kitchen.

Once I started making dinner, it became clear that cooking for a vampire doesn't take much time. You don't actually *cook* much of anything.

By seven o'clock the candles were lit, the food was ready except for what could be done only at the last minute, and all that was left to get ready was me.

My wardrobe contained precious little that said 'dinner with a vampire.' There was no way I was dining with Matthew in a suit or in the outfit I'd worn to meet the warden. The number of black trousers and leggings I owned was mind-boggling, all with different degrees of spandex, but most were splotched with tea, boat grease, or both. Finally I found a pair of swishy black trousers that looked a bit like pajama bottoms but with slightly more style. They'd do.

Wearing nothing but a bra and the trousers, I ran into the bathroom and dragged a comb through my shoulder-length, straw-colored hair. Not only was it tied in knots at the end, it was daring me to make it behave by lifting up from my scalp with every touch of the comb. I briefly considered resorting to the curling iron, but chances were excellent I'd get only half my head done by the time Matthew arrived. He was going to be on time. I just knew it.

While brushing my teeth, I decided the only thing to do about my hair was to pull it away from my face and twist it into a knot. This made my chin and nose look more pointed but created the illusion of cheekbones and got my hair out of my eyes, which is where it gravitated these days. I pinned it back, and one piece immediately flopped forward. I sighed.

My mother's face stared back at me from the mirror. I thought of how beautiful she'd looked when she sat down to dinner, and I wondered what she'd done to make her pale eyebrows and lashes stand out the way they did and why her wide mouth looked so different when she smiled at me or my father. The clock ruled out any idea of achieving a similar transformation cosmetically. I had only three minutes to find a shirt, or I was going to be greeting Matthew Clairmont, distinguished professor of biochemistry and neuroscience, in my underwear.

The wardrobe contained two possibilities, one black and one midnight blue. The midnight blue had the virtue of being clean, which was the determining factor in its favor. It also had a funny collar that stood up in the back and winged toward my face before descending into a V-shaped neckline. The arms were relatively snug and ended in long, stiff cuffs that flared out slightly and ended up somewhere around the middle of the back of my hand. I was sticking a pair of silver earrings through my ears when there was a knock at the door.

My chest fluttered at the sound, as if this were a date. I squashed the thought immediately.

When I pulled the door open, Matthew stood outside looking like the prince in a fairy tale, tall and straight. In a break with his usual habits, he wore unadulterated black, which only made him look more striking – and more a vampire.

He waited patiently on the landing while I examined him.

'Where are my manners? Please come in, Matthew. Will that do as a formal invitation to enter my house?' I had seen that on TV or read it in a book.

His lips curved into a smile. 'Forget most of what you think you know about vampires, Diana. This is just normal politeness. I'm not being held back by a mystical barrier standing between me and a fair maiden.' Matthew had to stoop slightly to make it through the doorframe. He cradled a bottle of wine and carried some white roses.

'For you,' he said, giving me an approving look and handing me the flowers. 'Is there somewhere I can put this until dessert?' He glanced down at the bottle.

'Thank you, I love roses. How about the windowsill?' I suggested, before heading to the kitchen to look for a vase. My other vase had turned out to be a decanter, according to the senior common room's wine steward, who had come to my rooms a few hours earlier to point it out to me when I expressed doubt that I had such an item.

'Perfect,' Matthew replied.

When I returned with the flowers, he was drifting around the room looking at the engravings.

'You know, these really aren't too bad,' he said as I set the vase on a scarred Napoleonic-era chest of drawers.

'Mostly hunting scenes, I'm afraid.'

'That had not escaped my attention,' Matthew said, his mouth curved in amusement. I flushed with embarrassment.

'Are you hungry?' I had completely forgotten the obligatory nibbles and drinks you were supposed to serve before dinner.

'I could eat,' the vampire said with a grin.

Safely back in the kitchen, I pulled two plates out of the refrigerator. The first course was smoked salmon with fresh dill sprinkled on top and a small pile of capers and gherkins arranged artistically on the side, where they could be construed as garnish if vampires didn't eat greens.

When I returned with the food, Matthew was waiting by the chair that was farthest from the kitchen. The wine was waiting in a high-sided silver coaster I'd been using to hold change but which the same helpful member of the senior common room's staff had explained was actually intended to hold wine. Matthew sat down while I extracted the cork from a bottle of German Riesling. I poured two glasses without spilling a drop and joined him.

My dinner guest was lost in concentration, holding the Riesling in front of his long, aquiline nose. I waited for him to finish whatever he was doing, wondering how many sensory receptors vampires had in their noses, as opposed to dogs.

I really didn't know the first thing about vampires.

'Very nice,' he finally said, opening his eyes and smiling at me.

'I'm not responsible for the wine,' I said quickly, snapping my napkin onto my lap. 'The man at the wine store picked everything out, so if it's no good, it's not my fault.'

'Very nice,' he said again, 'and the salmon looks wonderful.'

Matthew picked up his knife and fork and speared a piece of fish. Watching him from under my lashes to see if he could actually eat it, I piled a bit of pickle, a caper, and some salmon on the back of my own fork.

'You don't eat like an American,' he commented after he'd taken a sip of wine.

'No,' I said, looking at the fork in my left hand and the knife in my right. 'I expect I've spent too much time in England. Can you really eat this?' I blurted, unable to stand it anymore.

He laughed. 'Yes, I happen to like smoked salmon.'

'But you don't eat everything,' I insisted, turning my attention back to my plate.

'No,' he admitted, 'but I can manage a few bites of most food. It doesn't taste like much to me, though, unless it's raw.'

'That's odd, considering that vampires have such perfect senses.

I'd think that all food would taste wonderful.' My salmon tasted as clean as fresh, cold water.

He picked up his wineglass and looked into the pale, golden liquid. 'Wine tastes wonderful. Food tastes wrong to a vampire once it's been cooked to death.'

I reviewed the menu with enormous relief.

'If food doesn't taste good, why do you keep inviting me out to eat?' I asked.

Matthew's eyes flicked over my cheeks, my eyes, and lingered on my mouth. 'It's easier to be around you when you're eating. The smell of cooked food nauseates me.'

I blinked at him, still confused.

'As long as I'm nauseated, I'm not hungry,' Matthew said, his voice exasperated.

'Oh!' The pieces clicked together. I already knew he liked the way I smelled. Apparently that made him hungry.

Oh. I flushed.

'I thought you knew that about vampires,' he said more gently, 'and that's why you invited me for dinner.'

I shook my head, tucking another bundle of salmon together. 'I probably know less about vampires than most humans do. And the little my Aunt Sarah taught me has to be treated as highly suspect, given her prejudices. She was quite clear, for instance, on your diet. She said vampires will consume only blood, because it's all you need to survive. But that isn't true, is it?'

Matthew's eyes narrowed, and his tone was suddenly frosty. 'No. You need water to survive. Is that all you drink?'

'Should I not be talking about this?' My questions were making him angry. Nervously I wrapped my legs around the base of the chair and realized I'd never put on any shoes. I was entertaining in bare feet.

'You can't help being curious, I suppose,' Matthew replied after considering my question for a long moment. 'I drink wine and can eat food – preferably uncooked food, or food that's cold, so that it doesn't smell.'

'But the food and wine don't nourish you,' I guessed. 'You feed on blood – all kinds of blood.' He flinched. 'And you don't have to wait outside until I invite you into my house. What else do I have wrong about vampires?'

Matthew's face adopted an expression of long-suffering patience. He sat back in his chair, taking the wineglass with him. I stood up slightly and reached across the table to pour him some more. If I was going to ply him with questions, I could at least ply him with wine, too. Leaning over the candles, I almost set my shirt on fire. Matthew grabbed the wine bottle.

'Why don't I do that?' he suggested. He poured himself some more and topped up my glass as well before he answered. 'Most of what you know about me – about vampires – was dreamed up by humans. These legends made it possible for humans to live around us. Creatures frighten them. And I'm not talking solely about vampires.'

'Black hats, bats, brooms.' It was the unholy trinity of witchcraft lore, which burst into spectacular, ridiculous life every year on Halloween.

'Exactly.' Matthew nodded. 'Somewhere in each of these stories, there's a nugget of truth, something that frightened humans and helped them deny we were real. The strongest distinguishing characteristic of humans is their power of denial. I have strength and long life, you have supernatural abilities, daemons have awe-inspiring creativity. Humans can convince themselves up is down and black is white. It's their special gift.'

'What's the truth in the story about vampires not being allowed inside without an invitation?' Having pressed him on his diet, I focused on the entrance protocols.

'Humans are with us all the time. They just refuse to acknowledge our existence because we don't make sense in their limited world. Once they allow us in – see us for who we really are – then we're in to stay, just as someone you've invited into your home can be hard to get rid of. They can't ignore us anymore.'

'So it's like the stories of sunlight,' I said slowly. 'It's not that you can't be in sunlight, but when you are, it's harder for humans to ignore you. Rather than admit that you're walking among them, humans tell themselves you can't survive the light.'

Matthew nodded again. 'They manage to ignore us anyway, of course. We can't stay indoors until it's dark. But we make more sense to humans after twilight – and that goes for you, too. You should see the looks when you walk into a room or down the street.'

I thought about my ordinary appearance and glanced at him doubtfully. Matthew chuckled.

'You don't believe me, I know. But it's true. When humans see a creature in broad daylight, it makes them uneasy. We're too much for them – too tall, too strong, too confident, too creative, too powerful, too different. They try very hard to push our square pegs into their round holes all day long. At night it's a bit easier to dismiss us as merely odd.'

I stood up and removed the fish plates, happy to see that Matthew had eaten everything but the garnish. He poured a bit more of the German wine into his glass while I pulled two more plates out of the refrigerator. Each held neatly arranged slices of raw venison so thin that the butcher insisted you could read the *Oxford Mail* through them. Vampires didn't like greens. We'd see about root vegetables and cheese. I heaped beets in the center of each plate and shaved Parmesan on top.

A broad-bottomed decanter full of red wine went into the center of the table, where it quickly caught Matthew's attention.

'May I?' he asked, no doubt worried about my burning down the college. He reached for the plain glass container, poured a bit of wine into our glasses, then held it up to his nose.

'Côte-Rôtie,' he said with satisfaction. 'One of my favorites.'

I eyed the plain glass container. 'You can tell that just from smelling it?'

He laughed. 'Some vampire stories are true. I have an exceptional sense of smell – and excellent sight and hearing, too. But even a human could tell that this was Côte-Rôtie.' He closed his eyes again. 'Is it 2003?'

My mouth gaped open. 'Yes!' This was better than watching a

game show. There had been a little crown on the label. 'Does your nose tell you who made it?'

'Yes, but that's because I've walked the fields where the grapes were grown,' he confessed sheepishly, as if he'd been caught pulling a trick on me.

'You can smell the fields in this?' I stuck my nose in the glass, relieved that the odor of horse manure was no longer there.

'Sometimes I believe I can remember everything I've ever smelled. It's probably vanity,' he said ruefully, 'but scents bring back powerful memories. I remember the first time I smelled chocolate as if it were yesterday.'

'Really?' I pitched forward in my chair.

'It was 1615. War hadn't broken out yet, and the French king had married a Spanish princess that no one liked – especially not the king.' When I smiled, he smiled back, though his eyes were fixed on some distant image. 'She brought chocolate to Paris. It was as bitter as sin and as decadent, too. We drank the cacao straight, mixed with water and no sugar.'

I laughed. 'It sounds awful. Thank goodness someone figured out that chocolate deserved to be sweet.'

'That was a human, I'm afraid. The vampires liked it bitter and thick.'

We picked up our forks and started in on the venison. 'More Scottish food,' I said, gesturing at the meat with my knife.

Matthew chewed a piece. 'Red deer. A young Highlands stag from the taste of it.'

I shook my head in amazement.

'As I said,' he continued, 'some of the stories are true.'

'Can you fly?' I asked, already knowing the answer.

He snorted. 'Of course not. We leave that to the witches, since you can control the elements. But we're strong and fast. Vampires can run and jump, which makes humans think we can fly. We're efficient, too.'

'Efficient?' I put my fork down, unsure whether raw venison was to my liking.

'Our bodies don't waste much energy. We have a lot of it to spend on moving when we need to.'

'You don't breathe much,' I said, thinking back to yoga and taking a sip of wine.

'No,' Matthew said. 'Our hearts don't beat very often. We don't need to eat very often. We run cold, which slows down most bodily processes and helps explain why we live so long.'

'The coffin story! You don't sleep much, but when you do, you sleep like the dead.'

He grinned. 'You're getting the hang of this, I see.'

Matthew's plate was empty of everything except for the beets, and mine was empty except for the venison. I cleared away the second course and invited him to pour more wine.

The main dish was the only part of the meal that required heat, and not much of it. I had already made a bizarre biscuitlike thing from ground chestnuts. All that was left for me to do was sear some rabbit. The list of ingredients included rosemary, garlic, and celery. I decided to forgo the garlic. With his sense of smell, garlic must overpower everything else – there was the nugget of truth in *that* vampire legend. The celery was also ruled out. Vampires categorically did not like vegetables. Spices didn't seem to pose a problem, so I kept the rosemary and ground some pepper over the rabbit while it seared in the pan.

Leaving Matthew's rabbit a little underdone, I cooked mine a bit more than was required, in the hope that it would get the taste of raw venison out of my mouth. After assembling everything in an artistic pile, I delivered it to the table. 'This is cooked, I'm afraid – but barely.'

'You don't think this is a test of some sort, do you?' Matthew's face creased into a frown.

'No, no,' I said hurriedly. 'But I'm not used to entertaining vampires.'

'I'm relieved to hear it,' he murmured. He gave the rabbit a sniff. 'It smells delicious.' While he was bent over his plate, the heat from the rabbit amplified his distinctive scent of cinnamon and clove.

Matthew forked up a bit of the chestnut biscuit. As it traveled to his mouth, his eyes widened. 'Chestnuts?'

'Nothing but chestnuts, olive oil, and a bit of baking powder.'

'And salt. And water, rosemary, and pepper,' he commented calmly, taking another bite of the biscuit.

'Given your dietary restrictions, it's a good thing you can figure out exactly what you're putting in your mouth,' I grumbled jokingly.

With most of the meal behind us, I began to relax. We chatted about Oxford while I cleared the plates and brought cheese, berries, and roasted chestnuts to the table.

'Help yourself,' I said, putting an empty plate in front of him. Matthew savored the aroma of the tiny strawberries and sighed happily as he picked up a chestnut.

'These really are better warm,' he observed. He cracked the hard nut easily in his fingers and popped the meat out of the shell. The nutcracker hanging off the edge of the bowl was clearly optional equipment with a vampire at the table.

'What do I smell like?' I asked, toying with the stem of my wineglass.

For a few moments, it seemed as though he wasn't going to answer. The silence stretched thin before he turned wistful eyes on me. His lids fell, and he inhaled deeply.

'You smell of willow sap. And chamomile that's been crushed underfoot.' He sniffed again and smiled a small, sad smile. 'There's honeysuckle and fallen oak leaves, too,' he said softly, breathing out, 'along with witch hazel blooming and the first narcissus of spring. And ancient things – horehound, frankincense, lady's mantle. Scents I thought I'd forgotten.'

His eyes opened slowly, and I looked into their gray depths, afraid to breathe and break the spell his words had cast.

'What about me?' he asked, his eyes holding on to mine.

'Cinnamon.' My voice was hesitant. 'And cloves. Sometimes I think you smell of carnations – not the kind in the florist shops but the old-fashioned ones that grow in English cottage gardens.'

'Clove pinks,' Matthew said, his eyes crinkling at the corners in amusement. 'Not bad for a witch.'

I reached for a chestnut. Cupping the nut in my palms, I rolled it from one hand to the other, the warmth traveling up my suddenly chilly arms.

Matthew sat back in his chair again, surveying my face with little flicks of his eyes. 'How did you decide what to serve for dinner tonight?' He gestured at the berries and nuts that were left from the meal.

'Well, it wasn't magic. The zoology department helped a lot,' I explained.

He looked startled, then roared with laughter. 'You asked the zoology department what to make me for dinner?'

'Not exactly,' I said defensively. 'There were raw-food recipes on the Net, but I got stuck after I bought the meat. They told me what gray wolves ate.'

Matthew shook his head, but he was still smiling, and my irritation dissolved. 'Thank you,' he said simply. 'It's been a very long time since someone made me a meal.'

'You're welcome. The wine was the worst part.'

Matthew's eyes brightened. 'Speaking of wine,' he said, standing up and folding his napkin, 'I brought us something to have after dinner.'

He asked me to fetch two fresh glasses from the kitchen. An old, slightly lopsided bottle was sitting on the table when I returned. It had a faded cream label with simple lettering and a coronet. Matthew was working the corkscrew carefully into a cork that was crumbly and black with age.

His nostrils flared when he pulled it free, his face taking on the look of a cat in secure possession of a delectable canary. The wine that came out of the bottle was syrupy, its golden color glinting in the light of the candles.

'Smell it,' he commanded, handing me one of the glasses, 'and tell me what you think.'

I took a sniff and gasped. 'It smells like caramels and berries,'

I said, wondering how something so yellow could smell of something red.

Matthew was watching me closely, interested in my reactions. 'Take a sip,' he suggested.

The wine's sweet flavors exploded in my mouth. Apricots and vanilla custard from the kitchen ladies tumbled across my tongue, and my mouth tingled with them long after I'd swallowed. It was like drinking magic.

'What is this?' I finally said, after the taste of the wine had faded.

'It was made from grapes picked a long, long time ago. That summer had been hot and sunny, and the farmers worried that the rains were going to come and ruin the crop. But the weather held, and they got the grapes in just before the weather changed.'

'You can taste the sunshine,' I said, earning myself another beautiful smile.

'During the harvest a comet blazed over the vineyards. It had been visible through astronomers' telescopes for months, but in October it was so bright you could almost read by its light. The workers saw it as a sign that the grapes were blessed.'

'Was this in 1986? Was it Halley's comet?'

Matthew shook his head. 'No. It was 1811.' I stared in astonishment at the almost two-hundred-year-old wine in my glass, fearing it might evaporate before my eyes. 'Halley's comet came in 1759 and 1835.' He pronounced the name 'Hawley.'

'Where did you get it?' The wine store by the train station did not have wine like this.

'I bought it from Antoine-Marie as soon as he told me it was going to be extraordinary,' he said with amusement.

Turning the bottle, I looked at the label. Château Yquem. Even I had heard of that.

'And you've had it ever since,' I said. He'd drunk chocolate in Paris in 1615 and received a building permit from Henry VIII in 1536 – of course he was buying wine in 1811. And there was the ancient-looking ampulla he was wearing around his neck, the cord visible at his throat.

'Matthew,' I said slowly, watching him for any early warning signs of anger. 'How old are you?'

His mouth hardened, but he kept his voice light. 'I'm older than I look.'

'I know that,' I said, unable to curb my impatience.

'Why is my age important?'

'I'm a historian. If somebody tells me he remembers when chocolate was introduced into France or a comet passing overhead in 1811, it's difficult not to be curious about the other events he might have lived through. You were alive in 1536 – I've been to the house you had built. Did you know Machiavelli? Live through the Black Death? Attend the University of Paris when Abelard was teaching there?'

He remained silent. The hair on the back of my neck started to prickle.

'Your pilgrim's badge tells me you were once in the Holy Land. Did you go on crusade? See Halley's comet pass over Normandy in 1066?'

Still nothing.

'Watch Charlemagne's coronation? Survive the fall of Carthage? Help keep Attila from reaching Rome?'

Matthew held up his right index finger. 'Which fall of Carthage?'

'You tell me!'

'Damn you, Hamish Osborne,' he muttered, his hand flexing on the tablecloth. For the second time in two days, Matthew struggled over what to say. He stared into the candle, drawing his finger slowly through the flame. His flesh erupted into angry red blisters, then smoothed itself out into white, cold perfection an instant later without a flicker of pain evident on his face.

'I believe that my body is nearly thirty-seven years of age. I was born around the time Clovis converted to Christianity. My parents remembered that, or I'd have no idea. We didn't keep track of birthdays back then. It's tidier to pick the date of five hundred and be done with it.' He looked up at me, briefly, and returned his attention to the candles. 'I was reborn a vampire in 537, and with the exception of Attila – who was before my time – you've touched on most of the high and low points in the millennium between then and the year I put the keystone into my house in Woodstock. Because you're a historian, I feel obligated to tell you that Machiavelli was not nearly as impressive as you all seem to think he was. He was just a Florentine politician – and not a terribly good one at that.' A note of weariness had crept into his voice.

Matthew Clairmont was more than fifteen hundred years old.

'I shouldn't pry,' I said by way of apology, unsure of where to look and mystified as to what had led me to think that knowing the historical events this vampire had lived through would help me know him better. A line from Ben Jonson floated into my mind. It seemed to explain Matthew in a way that the coronation of Charlemagne could not. ' "*He was not of an age, but for all time*," ' I murmured.

' "*With thee conversing I forget all time*," ' he responded, traveling further into seventeenth-century literature and offering up a line from Milton.

We looked at each other for as long as we could stand it, working another fragile spell between us. I broke it.

'What were you doing in the fall of 1859?'

His face darkened. 'What has Peter Knox been telling you?'

'That you were unlikely to share your secrets with a witch.' My voice sounded calmer than I felt.

'Did he?' Matthew said softly, sounding less angry than he clearly was. I could see it in the set of his jaw and shoulders. 'In September 1859 I was looking through the manuscripts in the Ashmolean Museum.'

'Why, Matthew?' *Please tell me*, I urged silently, crossing my fingers in my lap. I'd provoked him into revealing the first part of his secret but wanted him to freely give me the rest. *No games, no riddles. Just tell me*.

'I'd recently finished reading a book manuscript that was soon going to press. It was written by a Cambridge naturalist.' Matthew put down his glass.

My hand flew to my mouth as the significance of the date

registered. '*Origin*.' Like Newton's great work of physics, the *Principia*, this was a book that did not require a full citation. Anyone who'd passed high-school biology knew Darwin's *On the Origin of Species*.

'Darwin's article the previous summer laid out his theory of natural selection, but the book was quite different. It was marvelous, the way he established easily observable changes in nature and inched you toward accepting something so revolutionary.'

'But alchemy has nothing to do with evolution.' Grabbing the bottle, I poured myself more of the precious wine, less concerned that it might vanish than that I might come unglued.

'Lamarck believed that each species descended from different ancestors and progressed independently toward higher forms of being. It's remarkably similar to what your alchemists believed – that the philosopher's stone was the elusive end product of a natural transmutation of base metals into more exalted metals like copper, silver, and gold.' Matthew reached for the wine, and I pushed it toward him.

'But Darwin disagreed with Lamarck, even if he did use the same word – "transmutation" – in his initial discussions of evolution.'

'He disagreed with linear transmutation, it's true. But Darwin's theory of natural selection can still be seen as a series of linked transmutations.'

Maybe Matthew was right and magic really was in everything. It was in Newton's theory of gravity, and it might be in Darwin's theory of evolution, too.

'There are alchemical manuscripts all over the world.' I was trying to remain moored to the details while coming to terms with the bigger picture. 'Why the Ashmole manuscripts?'

'When I read Darwin and saw how he seemed to explore the alchemical theory of transmutation through biology, I remembered stories about a mysterious book that explained the origin of our three species – daemons, witches, and vampires. I'd always dismissed them as fantastic.' He took a sip of wine. 'Most suggested that the story was concealed from human eyes in a book of alchemy. The publication of

Origin prompted me to look for it, and if such a book existed, Elias Ashmole would have bought it. He had an uncanny ability to find bizarre manuscripts.'

'You were looking for it here in Oxford, one hundred and fifty years ago?'

'Yes,' Matthew said. 'And one hundred and fifty years before you received Ashmole 782, I was told that it was missing.'

My heart sped up, and he looked at me in concern. 'Keep going,' I said, waving him on.

'I've been trying to get my hands on it ever since. Every other Ashmole manuscript was there, and none seemed promising. I've looked at manuscripts in other libraries – at the Herzog August Bibliothek in Germany, the Bibliothèque Nationale in France, the Medici Library in Florence, the Vatican, the Library of Congress.'

I blinked, thinking of a vampire wandering the hallways of the Vatican.

'The only manuscript I haven't seen is Ashmole 782. By simple process of elimination, it must be the manuscript that contains our story – if it still survives.'

'You've looked at more alchemical manuscripts than I have.'

'Perhaps,' Matthew admitted, 'but it doesn't mean I understand them as well as you do. What all the manuscripts I've seen have in common, though, is an absolute confidence that the alchemist can help one substance change into another, creating new forms of life.'

'That sounds like evolution,' I said flatly.

'Yes,' Matthew said gently, 'it does.'

We moved to the sofas, and I curled up into a ball at the end of one while Matthew sprawled in the corner of the other, his long legs stretched out in front of him. Happily, he'd brought the wine. Once we were settled, it was time for more honesty between us.

'I met a daemon, Agatha Wilson, at Blackwell's last week. According to the Internet, she's a famous designer. Agatha told me the daemons believe that Ashmole 782 is the story of all origins – even human origins. Peter Knox told me a different story. He said it was the first grimoire, the source of all witches' power. Knox believes that the manuscript contains the secret of immortality,' I said, glancing at Matthew, 'and how to destroy vampires. I've heard the daemon and witch versions of the story – now I want yours.'

'Vampires believe the lost manuscript explains our longevity and our strength,' he said. 'In the past, our fear was that this secret – if it fell into witches' hands – would lead to our extermination. Some fear that magic was involved in our making and that the witches might find a way to reverse the magic and destroy us. It seems that that part of the legend might be true.' He exhaled softly, looking worried.

'I still don't understand why you're so certain that this book of origins – whatever it may contain – is hidden inside an alchemy book.'

'An alchemy book could hide these secrets in plain sight – just like Peter Knox hides his identity as a witch under the veneer that he's an expert in the occult. I think it was vampires who learned that the book was alchemical. It's too perfect a fit to be coincidence. The human alchemists seemed to capture what it is to be a vampire when they wrote about the philosopher's stone. Becoming a vampire makes us nearly immortal, it makes most of us rich, and it gives us the chance to accrue unimaginable knowledge and learning.'

'That's the philosopher's stone, all right.' The parallels between this mythic substance and the creature sitting opposite me were striking – and chilling. 'But it's still hard to imagine such a book really exists. For one thing, all the stories contradict one another. And who would be so foolish as to put so much information in one place?'

'As with the legends about vampires and witches, there's at least a nugget of truth in all the stories about the manuscript. We just have to figure out what that nugget is and strip away the rest. Then we'll begin to understand.'

Matthew's face bore no trace of deceit or evasion. Encouraged by his use of 'we,' I decided he'd earned more information.

'You're right about Ashmole 782. The book you've been seeking is inside it.'

'Go on,' Matthew said softly, trying to control his curiosity.

'It's an alchemy book on the surface. The images contain errors, or deliberate mistakes – I still can't decide which.' I bit my lip in concentration, and his eyes fixed on the place where my teeth had drawn a tiny bead of blood to the surface.

'What do you mean "it's an alchemy book on the surface"?' Matthew held his glass closer to his nose.

'It's a palimpsest. But the ink hasn't been washed away. Magic is hiding the text. I almost missed the words, they're hidden so well. But when I turned one of the pages, the light was at just the right angle and I could see lines of writing moving underneath.'

'Could you read it?'

'No.' I shook my head. 'If Ashmole 782 contains information about who we are, how we came to be, and how we might be destroyed, it's deeply buried.'

'It's fine if it remains buried,' Matthew said grimly, 'at least for now. But the time is quickly coming when we will need that book.'

'Why? What makes it so urgent?'

'I'd rather show you than tell you. Can you come to my lab tomorrow?'

I nodded, mystified.

'We can walk there after lunch,' he said, standing up and stretching. We had emptied the bottle of wine amid all this talk of secrets and origins. 'It's late. I should go.'

Matthew reached for the doorknob and gave it a twist. It rattled, and the catch sprang open easily.

He frowned. 'Have you had trouble with your lock?'

'No,' I said, pushing the mechanism in and out, 'not that I'm aware of.'

'You should have them look at that,' he said, still jiggling the door's hardware. 'It might not close properly until you do.'

When I looked up from the door, an emotion I couldn't name flitted across his face.

'I'm sorry the evening ended on such a serious note,' he said softly. 'I did have a lovely time.'

'Was the dinner really all right?' I asked. We'd talked about the secrets of the universe, but I was more worried about how his stomach was faring.

'It was more than all right,' he assured me.

My face softened at his beautiful, ancient features. How could people walk by him on the street and not gasp? Before I could stop myself, my toes were gripping the old rug and I was stretching up to kiss him quickly on the cheek. His skin felt smooth and cold like satin, and my lips felt unusually warm against his flesh.

Why did you do that? I asked myself, coming down off my toes and gazing at the questionable doorknob to hide my confusion.

It was over in a matter of seconds, but as I knew from using magic to get *Notes and Queries* off the Bodleian's shelf, a few seconds was all it took to change your life.

Matthew studied me. When I showed no sign of hysteria or an inclination to make a run for it, he leaned toward me and kissed me slowly once, twice in the French manner. His face skimmed over mine, and he drank in my scent of willow sap and honeysuckle. When he straightened, Matthew's eyes looked smokier than usual.

'Good night, Diana,' he said with a smile.

Moments later, leaning against the closed door, I spied the blinking number one on my answering machine. Mercifully, the machine's volume was turned down.

Aunt Sarah wanted to ask the same question I'd asked myself.

I just didn't want to answer.

CHAPTER 13

Matthew came to collect me after lunch – the only creature among the human readers in the Selden End. While he walked me under the ornately painted exposed beams, he kept up a steady patter of questions about my work and what I'd been reading.

Oxford had turned resolutely cold and gray, and I pulled my collar up around my neck, shivering in the damp air. Matthew seemed not to mind and wasn't wearing a coat. The gloomy weather made him look a little less startling, but it wasn't enough to make him blend in entirely. People turned and stared in the Bodleian's central courtyard, then shook their heads.

'You've been noticed,' I told him.

'I forgot my coat. Besides, they're looking at you, not me.' He gave me a dazzling smile. A woman's jaw dropped, and she poked her friend, inclining her head in Matthew's direction.

I laughed. 'You are so wrong.'

We headed toward Keble College and the University Parks, making a right turn at Rhodes House before entering the labyrinth of modern buildings devoted to laboratory and computer space. Built in the shadow of the Museum of Natural History, the enormous redbrick Victorian cathedral to science, these were monuments of unimaginative, functional contemporary architecture.

Matthew pointed to our destination – a nondescript, low-slung building – and fished in his pocket for a plastic identity card. He swiped it through the reader at the door handle and punched in a set of codes in two different sequences. Once the door unlocked, he ushered me to the guard's station, where he signed me in as a guest and handed me a pass to clip to my sweater.

'That's a lot of security for a university laboratory,' I commented, fiddling with the badge.

The security only increased as we walked down the miles of corridors that somehow managed to fit behind the modest façade. At the end of one hallway, Matthew took a different card out of his pocket, swiped it, and put his index finger on a glass panel next to a door. The glass panel chimed, and a touch pad appeared on its surface. Matthew's fingers raced over the numbered keys. The door clicked softly open, and there was a clean, slightly antiseptic smell reminiscent of hospitals and empty professional kitchens. It derived from unbroken expanses of tile, stainless steel, and electronic equipment.

A series of glass-enclosed rooms stretched ahead of us. One held a round table for meetings, a black monolith of a monitor, and several computers. Another held an old wooden desk, a leather chair, an enormous Persian rug that must have been worth a fortune, telephones, fax machines, and still more computers and monitors. Beyond were other enclosures that held banks of file cabinets, microscopes, refrigerators, autoclaves, racks upon racks of test tubes, centrifuges, and dozens of unrecognizable devices and instruments.

The whole area seemed unoccupied, although from somewhere there came faint strains of a Bach cello concerto and something that sounded an awful lot like the latest hit recorded by the Eurovision song-contest winners.

As we passed by the two office spaces, Matthew gestured at the one with the rug. 'My office,' he explained. He then steered me into the first laboratory on the left. Every surface held some combination of computers, microscopes, and specimen containers arranged neatly in racks. File cabinets ringed the walls. One of their drawers had a label that read '<0'.

'Welcome to the history lab.' The blue light made his face look whiter, his hair blacker. 'This is where we're studying evolution. We take in physical specimens from old burial sites, excavations, fossilized remains, and living beings, and extract DNA from the samples.'

Matthew opened a different drawer and pulled out a handful of files. 'We're just one laboratory among hundreds all over the world using genetics to study problems of species origin and extinction. The difference between our lab and the rest is that humans aren't the only species we're studying.'

His words dropped, cold and clear, around me.

'You're studying vampire genetics?'

'Witches and daemons, too.' Matthew hooked a wheeled stool with his foot and gently sat me on top of it.

A vampire wearing black Converse high-tops came rocketing around the corner and squeaked to a halt, pulling on a pair of latex gloves. He was in his late twenties, with the blond hair and blue eyes of a California surfer. Standing next to Matthew, his average height and build made him look slight, but his body was wiry and energetic.

'AB-negative,' he said, studying me admiringly. 'Wow, terrific find.' He closed his eyes and inhaled deeply. 'And a witch, too!'

'Marcus Whitmore, meet Diana Bishop. She's a professor of history from Yale' – Matthew frowned at the younger vampire – 'and is here as a guest, not a pincushion.'

'Oh.' Marcus looked disappointed, then brightened. 'Would you mind if I took some of your blood anyway?'

'Yes, as a matter of fact.' I had no wish to be poked and prodded by a vampire phlebotomist.

Marcus whistled. 'That's some fight-or-flight response you have there, Dr Bishop. Smell that adrenaline.'

'What's going on?' a familiar soprano voice called out. Miriam's diminutive frame was visible a few seconds later.

'Dr Bishop is a bit overwhelmed by the laboratory, Miriam.'

'Sorry. I didn't realize it was her,' Miriam said. 'She smells different. Is it adrenaline?'

Marcus nodded. 'Yep. Are you always like this? All dressed up in adrenaline and no place to go?'

'Marcus.' Matthew could issue a bone-chilling warning in remarkably few syllables.

'Since I was seven,' I said, meeting his startling blue eyes.

Marcus whistled again. 'That explains a lot. No vampire could turn his back on that.' Marcus wasn't referring to my physical features, even though he gestured in my direction.

'What are you talking about?' I asked, curiosity overcoming my nerves.

Matthew pulled on the hair at his temples and gave Marcus a glare that would curdle milk. The younger vampire looked blasé and cracked his knuckles. I jumped at the sharp sound.

'Vampires are predators, Diana,' Matthew explained. 'We're attracted to the fight-or-flight response. When people or animals become agitated, we can smell it.'

'We can taste it, too. Adrenaline makes blood even more delicious,' Marcus said. 'Spicy, silky, and then it turns sweet. Really good stuff.'

A low rumble started in Matthew's throat. His lips curled away from his teeth, and Marcus stepped backward. Miriam placed her hand firmly on the blond vampire's forearm.

'What? I'm not hungry!' Marcus protested, shaking off Miriam's hand.

'Dr Bishop may not know that vampires don't have to be physically hungry to be sensitive to adrenaline, Marcus.' Matthew controlled himself with visible effort. 'Vampires don't always need to feed, but we always crave the hunt and the adrenaline reaction of prey to predator.'

Given my struggle to control anxiety, it was no wonder Matthew was always asking me out for a meal. It wasn't my honeysuckle scent that made him hungry – it was my excess adrenaline.

'Thank you for explaining, Matthew.' Even after last night, I was still relatively ignorant about vampires. 'I'll try to calm down.'

'There's no need,' Matthew said shortly. 'It's not your job to calm down. It's our job to exercise a modicum of courtesy and control.' He glowered at Marcus and pulled one of the files forward.

Miriam shot a worried glance in my direction. 'Maybe we should start at the beginning.'

'No. I think it's better to start at the end,' he replied, opening the file.

'Do they know about Ashmole 782?' I asked Matthew when Miriam and Marcus showed no sign of leaving. He nodded. 'And you told them what I saw?' He nodded again.

'Did you tell anyone else?' Miriam's question to me reflected centuries of suspicion.

'If you mean Peter Knox, no. Only my aunt and her partner, Emily, know.'

'Three witches and three vampires sharing a secret,' Marcus said thoughtfully, glancing at Matthew. 'Interesting.'

'Let's hope we can do a better job keeping it than we have done at hiding this.' Matthew slid the file toward me.

Three sets of vampire eyes watched me attentively as I opened it. VAMPIRE ON THE LOOSE IN LONDON, the headline screamed. My stomach flopped over, and I moved the newspaper clipping aside. Underneath was the report of another mysterious death involving a bloodless corpse. Below that was a magazine story accompanied by a picture that made its contents clear despite my inability to read Russian. The victim's throat had been ripped open from jaw to carotid artery.

There were dozens more murders, and reports in every language imaginable. Some of the deaths involved beheadings. Some involved corpses drained of blood, without a speck of blood evidence found at the scene. Others suggested an animal attack, due to the ferocity of the injuries to the neck and torso.

'We're dying,' Matthew said when I pushed the last of the stories aside.

'Humans are dying, that's for sure.' My voice was harsh.

'Not just the humans,' he said. 'Based on this evidence, vampires are exhibiting signs of species deterioration.'

'This is what you wanted to show me?' My voice shook. 'What do these have to do with the origin of creatures or Ashmole 782?' Gillian's recent warnings had stirred painful memories, and these pictures only brought them into sharper focus.

'Hear me out,' Matthew said quietly. 'Please.'

He might not be making sense, but he wasn't deliberately frightening me either. Matthew must have had a good reason for sharing this. Hugging the file folder, I sat down on my stool.

'These deaths,' he began, drawing the folder gently away from me, 'result from botched attempts to transform humans into vampires. What was once second nature to us has become difficult. Our blood is increasingly incapable of making new life out of death.'

Failure to reproduce would make any species extinct. Based on the pictures I'd just seen, however, the world didn't need more vampires.

'It's easier for those who are older – vampires such as myself who fed predominantly on human blood when we were young,' Matthew continued. 'As a vampire ages, however, we feel less compulsion to make new vampires. Younger vampires, though, are a different story. They want to start families to dispel the loneliness of their new lives. When they find a human they want to mate with, or try to make children, some discover that their blood isn't powerful enough.'

'You said *we're* all going extinct,' I reminded him evenly, my anger still simmering.

'Modern witches aren't as powerful as their ancestors were.' Miriam's voice was matter-of-fact. 'And you don't produce as many children as in times past.'

'That doesn't sound like evidence – it sounds like a subjective assessment,' I said.

'You want to see the evidence?' Miriam picked up two more file folders and tossed them across the gleaming surface so that they slid into my arms. 'There it is – though I doubt you'll understand much of it.'

One had a purple-edged label with 'Benvenguda' typed neatly on it. The other had a red-edged label, bearing the name 'Good, Beatrice.' The folders contained nothing but graphs. Those on top were hoop-shaped and brilliantly colored. Underneath, more graphs showed black and gray bars marching across white paper.

'That's not fair,' Marcus protested. 'No historian could read those.'

'These are DNA sequences,' I said, pointing to the black-and-white images. 'But what are the colored graphs?'

Matthew rested his elbows on the table next to me. 'They're also genetic test results,' he said, drawing the hoop-covered page closer. 'These tell us about the mitochondrial DNA of a woman named Benvenguda, which she inherited from her mother, and her mother's mother, and every female ancestor before her. They tell us the story of her matrilineage.'

'What about her father's genetic legacy?'

Matthew picked up the black-and-white DNA results. 'Benvenguda's human father is here, in her nuclear DNA – her genome – along with her mother, who was a witch.' He returned to the multicolored hoops. 'But the mitochondrial DNA, outside the cell's nucleus, records only her maternal ancestry.'

'Why are you studying both her genome and her mitochondrial DNA?' I had heard of the genome, but mitochondrial DNA was new territory for me.

'Your nuclear DNA tells us about you as a unique individual – how the genetic legacy of your mother and father recombined to create you. It's the mixture of your father's genes and your mother's genes that gave you blue eyes, blond hair, and freckles. Mitochondrial DNA can help us to understand the history of a whole species.'

'That means the origin and evolution of the species is recorded in every one of us,' I said slowly. 'It's in our blood and every cell in our body.'

Matthew nodded. 'But every origin story tells another tale – not of beginnings but of endings.'

'We're back to Darwin,' I said, frowning. '*Origin* wasn't entirely about where different species came from. It was about natural selection and species extinction, too.'

'Some would say *Origin* was mostly about extinction,' Marcus agreed, rolling up to the other side of the lab bench.

I looked at Benvenguda's brilliant hoops. 'Who was she?'

'A very powerful witch,' Miriam said, 'who lived in Brittany in the seventh century. She was a marvel in an age that produced many marvels. Beatrice Good is one of her last-known direct descendants.'

'Did Beatrice Good's family come from Salem?' I whispered, touching her folder. There had been Goods living there alongside the Bishops and Proctors.

'Beatrice's lineage includes Sarah and Dorothy Good of Salem,' Matthew said, confirming my hunch. He opened Beatrice's file folder and put her mitochondrial test results next to those of Benvenguda.

'But they're different,' I said. You could see it in the colors and the way they were arranged.

'Not so different,' Matthew corrected me. 'Beatrice's nuclear DNA has fewer markers common among witches. This indicates that her ancestors, as the centuries passed, relied less and less on magic and witchcraft as they struggled to survive. Those changing needs began to force mutations in her DNA – mutations that pushed the magic aside.' His message sounded perfectly scientific, but it was meant for me.

'Beatrice's ancestors pushed their magic aside, and that will eventually destroy the family?'

'It's not entirely the witches' fault. Nature is to blame, too.' Matthew's eyes were sad. 'It seems that witches, like vampires, have also felt the pressures of surviving in a world that is increasingly human. Daemons, too. They exhibit less genius – which was how we used to distinguish them from the human population – and more madness.'

'The humans aren't dying out?' I asked.

'Yes and no,' Matthew said. 'We think that the humans have – until now – proved better at adapting. Their immune systems are more responsive, and they have a stronger urge to reproduce than either vampires or witches. Once the world was divided more evenly between humans and creatures. Now humans are in the majority and creatures make up only ten percent of the world's population.'

'The world was a different place when there were as many creatures as humans.' Miriam sounded regretful that the genetic deck was no longer stacked in our favor. 'But their sensitive immune systems are going to get humans in the end.'

'How different are we – the creatures – from humans?'

'Considerably, at least on the genetic level. We appear similar, but under the surface our chromosomal makeup is distinctive.' Matthew sketched a diagram on the outside of Beatrice Good's folder. 'Humans have twenty-three chromosomal pairs in every cell nucleus, each arranged in long code sequences. Vampires and witches have twenty-four chromosome pairs.'

'More than humans, pinot noir grapes, or pigs.' Marcus winked.

'What about daemons?'

'They have the same number of chromosome pairs as humans – but they also have a single extra chromosome. As far as we can tell, it's their extra chromosome that makes them daemonic,' Matthew replied, 'and prone to instability.'

While I was studying his pencil sketch, a piece of hair fell into my eyes. I pushed at it impatiently. 'What's in the extra chromosomes?' It was as hard for me to keep up with Matthew now as it had been managing to pass college biology.

'Genetic material that distinguishes us from humans,' Matthew said, 'as well as material that regulates cell function or is what scientists call "junk DNA." '

'It's not junk, though,' Marcus said. 'All that genetic material has to be left over from previous selection, or it's waiting to be used in the next evolutionary change. We just don't know what its purpose is – yet.'

'Wait a minute,' I interjected. 'Witches and daemons are born. I was born with an extra pair of chromosomes, and your friend Hamish was born with a single extra chromosome. But vampires aren't born – you're made, from human DNA. Where do you acquire an extra chromosome pair?'

'When a human is reborn a vampire, the maker first removes all the human's blood, which causes organ failure. Before death can occur, the maker gives his or her blood to the one being reborn,' replied Matthew. 'As far as we can tell, the influx of a vampire's blood forces spontaneous genetic mutations in every cell of the body.'

Matthew had used the term 'reborn' last night, but I'd never heard the word 'maker' in connection with vampires before.

'The maker's blood floods the reborn's system, carrying new genetic information with it,' Miriam said. 'Something similar happens with human blood transfusions. But a vampire's blood causes hundreds of modifications in the DNA.'

'We started looking in the genome for evidence of such explosive change,' Matthew explained. 'We found it – mutations proving that all new vampires went through a spontaneous adaptation to survive when they absorbed their makers' blood. That's what prompts the development of an extra chromosome pair.'

'A genetic big bang. You're like a galaxy born from a dying star. In a few moments, your genes transform you into something else – something inhuman.' I looked at Matthew in wonder.

'Are you all right?' he asked. 'We can take a break.'

'Could I have some water?'

'I'll get it.' Marcus hopped up from his stool. 'There's some in the specimen fridge.'

'Humans provided the first clue that acute cellular stress from bacteria and other forms of genetic bombardment could trigger quick mutations, rather than the slower changes of natural selection.' Miriam pulled a folder out of a file drawer. Opening it, she pointed to a section of a black-and-white graph. 'This man died in 1375. He survived smallpox, but the disease forced a mutation on the third chromosome as his body quickly coped with the influx of bacteria.'

Marcus returned with my water. I took the cap off and drank thirstily.

'Vampire DNA is full of similar mutations resulting from disease resistance. Those changes might be slowly leading to our extinction.' Matthew looked worried. 'Now we're trying to focus on what it is about vampire blood that triggers the generation of new chromosomes. The answer may lie in the mitochondria.'

Miriam shook her head. 'No way. The answer's in the nuclear

DNA. When a body is assaulted by vampire blood, it must trigger a reaction that makes it possible for the body to capture and assimilate the changes.'

'Maybe, but if so, we need to look more closely at the junk DNA, too. Everything must be there to generate new chromosomes,' Marcus insisted.

While the three of them argued, I was rolling up my sleeve. When the fabric cleared my elbow and the veins in my arm were exposed to the cool air of the laboratory, they directed their freezing attention at my skin.

'Diana,' Matthew said coldly, touching his Lazarus badge, 'what are you doing?'

'Do you still have your gloves handy, Marcus?' I asked, continuing to inch my sleeve up.

Marcus grinned. 'Yeah.' He stood and pulled a pair of latex gloves out of a nearby box.

'You don't have to do this.' Matthew's voice caught in his throat.

'I know that. I want to.' My veins looked even bluer in the lab's light.

'Good veins,' Miriam said with a nod of approval, eliciting a warning purr from the tall vampire standing next to me.

'If this is going to be a problem for you, Matthew, wait outside,' I said calmly.

'Before you do this, I want you to think about it,' Matthew said, bending over me protectively as he had when Peter Knox had approached me at the Bodleian. 'We have no way of predicting what the tests will reveal. It's your whole life, and your family's history, all laid out in black and white. Are you absolutely sure you want that scrutinized?'

'What do you mean, my whole life?' The intensity of his stare made me squirm.

'These tests tell us about a lot more than the color of your eyes and your hair. They'll indicate what other traits your mother and father passed down to you. Not to mention traits from all your female ancestors.' We exchanged a long look.

'That's why I want you to take a sample from me,' I said patiently. Confusion passed over his face. 'I've wondered my whole life what the Bishop blood was doing as it pumped through my veins. Everyone who knew about my family wondered. Now we'll know.'

It seemed very simple to me. My blood could tell Matthew things I didn't want to risk discovering haphazardly. I didn't want to set fire to the furniture, or fly through the trees, or think a bad thought about someone only to have that person fall deathly ill two days later. Matthew might think giving blood was risky. To me it seemed safe as houses, all things considered.

'Besides, you told me witches are dying out. I'm the last Bishop. Maybe my blood will help you figure out why.'

We stared at each other, vampire and witch, while Miriam and Marcus waited patiently. Finally Matthew made a sound of exasperation. 'Bring me a specimen kit,' he told Marcus.

'I can do it,' Marcus said defensively, snapping the wrist on his latex gloves. Miriam tried to hold him back, but Marcus kept coming at me with a box of vials and sharps.

'Marcus,' Miriam warned.

Matthew grabbed the equipment from Marcus and stopped the younger vampire with a startling, deadly look. 'I'm sorry, Marcus. But if anyone is going to take Diana's blood, it's going to be me.'

Holding my wrist in his cold fingers, he bent my arm up and down a few times before extending it fully and resting my hand gently on the stainless surface. There was something undeniably creepy about having a vampire stick a needle into your vein. Matthew tied a piece of rubber tubing above my elbow.

'Make a fist,' he said quietly, pulling on his gloves and preparing the hollow needle and the first vial.

I did as he asked, clenching my hand and watching the veins bulge. Matthew didn't bother with the usual announcement that I would feel a prick or a sting. He just leaned down without ceremony and slid the sharp metal instrument into my arm.

'Nicely done.' I loosened my fist to get the blood flowing freely. Matthew's wide mouth tightened while he changed vials. When he was finished, he withdrew the needle and tossed it into a sealed biohazard container. Marcus collected the vials and handed them to Miriam, who labeled them in a tiny, precise script. Matthew put a square of gauze over the stick site and held it there with strong, cold fingers. With his other hand, he picked up a roll of adhesive tape and attached it securely across the pad.

'Date of birth?' Miriam asked crisply, pen poised above the test tube.

'August thirteenth, 1976.'

Miriam stared. 'August thirteenth?'

'Yes. Why?'

'Just being sure,' she murmured.

'In most cases we like to take a cheek swab, too.' Matthew opened a package and removed two white pieces of plastic. They were shaped like miniature paddles, the wide ends slightly rough.

Wordlessly I opened my mouth and let Matthew twirl first one swab, then the other, against the inside of my cheek. Each swab went into a different sealed plastic tube. 'All done.'

Looking around the lab, at the quiet serenity of stainless steel and blue lights, I was reminded of my alchemists, toiling away over charcoal fires in dim light with improvised equipment and broken clay crucibles. What they would have given for the chance to work in a place like this – with tools that might have helped them understand the mysteries of creation.

'Are you looking for the first vampire?' I asked, gesturing at the file drawers.

'Sometimes,' Matthew said slowly. 'Mostly we're tracking how food and disease affect the species, and how and when certain family lines go extinct.'

'And is it really true we're four distinct species, or do daemons, humans, vampires, and witches share a common ancestor?' I'd always wondered if Sarah's insistence that witches shared little of consequence with humans or other creatures was based on anything more than tradition and wishful thinking. In Darwin's time many thought that it was impossible for a pair of common human ancestors to have produced so many different racial types. When some white Europeans looked at black Africans, they embraced the theory of polygenism instead, which argued that the races had descended from different, unrelated ancestors.

'Daemons, humans, vampires, and witches vary considerably at the genetic level.' Matthew's eyes were piercing. He understood why I was asking, even though he refused to give me a straight answer.

'If you prove we aren't different species, but only different lineages within the same species, it will change everything,' I warned.

'In time we'll be able to figure out how – if – the four groups are related. We're still a long way from that point, though.' He stood. 'I think that's enough science for today.'

After saying good-bye to Miriam and Marcus, Matthew drove me to New College. He went to change and returned to pick me up for yoga. We rode to Woodstock in near silence, both lost in our own thoughts.

At the Old Lodge, Matthew let me out as usual, unloaded the mats from the trunk, and slung them over his shoulder.

A pair of vampires brushed by. One touched me briefly, and Matthew's hand was lightning fast as he laced his fingers through mine. The contrast between us was so striking, his skin so pale and cold, and mine so alive and warm in comparison.

Matthew held on to me until we got inside. After class we drove back to Oxford, talking first about something Amira had said, then about something one of the daemons had inadvertently done or not done that seemed to perfectly capture what it was to be a daemon. Once inside the New College gates, Matthew uncharacteristically turned off the car before he let me out.

Fred looked up from his security monitors when the vampire went to the lodge's glass partition. The porter slid it open. 'Yes?'

'I'd like to walk Dr Bishop to her rooms. Is it all right if I leave the car here, and the keys, too, in case you need to shift it?'

Fred eyed the John Radcliffe tag and nodded. Matthew tossed the keys through the window.

'Matthew,' I said urgently, 'it's just across the way. You don't have to walk me home.'

'I am, though,' he said, in a tone that inhibited further discussion. Beyond the lodge's archways and out of Fred's sight, he caught my hand again. This time the shock of his cold skin was accompanied by a disturbing lick of warmth in the pit of my stomach.

At the bottom of my staircase, I faced Matthew, still holding his hand. 'Thanks for taking me to yoga – again.'

'You're welcome.' He tucked my impossible piece of hair back behind my ear, fingers lingering on my cheek. 'Come to dinner tomorrow,' he said softly. 'My turn to cook. Can I pick you up here at half past seven?'

My heart leaped. *Say no*, I told myself sternly in spite of its sudden jump.

'I'd love to,' came out instead.

The vampire pressed his cold lips first to one cheek, then the other. '*Ma vaillante fille*,' he whispered into my ear. The dizzying, alluring smell of him filled my nose.

Upstairs, someone had tightened the doorknob as requested, and it was a struggle to turn the key in the lock. The blinking light on the answering machine greeted me, indicating there was another message from Sarah. I crossed to the window and looked down, only to see Matthew looking up. I waved. He smiled, put his hands in his pockets, and turned back to the lodge, slipping into the night's darkness as if it belonged to him.

CHAPTER 14

Matthew was waiting for me in the lodge at half past seven, immaculate as always in a monochromatic combination of dove and charcoal, his dark hair swept back from his uneven hairline. He patiently withstood the inspection of the weekend porter, who sent me off with a nod and a deliberate, 'We'll see you later, Dr Bishop.'

'You do bring out people's protective instincts,' Matthew murmured as we passed through the gates.

'Where are we going?' There was no sign of his car in the street.

'We're dining in college tonight,' he answered, gesturing down toward the Bodleian. I had fully anticipated he would take me to Woodstock, or an apartment in some Victorian pile in North Oxford. It had never occurred to me that he might live in a college.

'In hall, at high table?' I felt terribly underdressed and pulled at the hem of my silky black top.

Matthew tilted his head back and laughed. 'I avoid hall whenever possible. And I'm certainly not taking you in there, to sit in the Siege Perilous and be inspected by the fellows.'

We rounded the corner and turned toward the Radcliffe Camera. When we passed by the entrance to Hertford College without stopping, I put my hand on his arm. There was one college in Oxford notorious for its exclusivity and rigid attention to protocol.

It was the same college famous for its brilliant fellows.

'You aren't.'

Matthew stopped. 'Why does it matter what college I belong to?'

He looked away. 'If you'd rather be around other people, of course, I understand.'

'I'm not worried you're going to eat *me* for dinner, Matthew. I've just never been inside.' A pair of ornate, scrolled gates guarded his college as if it were Wonderland. Matthew made an impatient noise and caught my hand to prevent me from peering through them.

'It's just a collection of people in a set of old buildings.' His gruffness did nothing to detract from the fact that he was one of six dozen or so fellows in a college with no students. 'Besides, we're going to my rooms.'

We walked the remaining distance, Matthew relaxing into the darkness with every step as if in the company of an old friend. We passed through a low wooden door that kept the public out of his college's quiet confines. There was no one in the lodge except the porter, no undergraduates or graduates on the benches in the front quad. It was as quiet and hushed as if its members truly were the 'souls of all the faithful people deceased in the university of Oxford.'

Matthew looked down with a shy smile. 'Welcome to All Souls.'

All Souls College was a masterpiece of late Gothic architecture, resembling the love child of a wedding cake and a cathedral, with its airy spires and delicate stonework. I sighed with pleasure, unable to say much – at least not yet. But Matthew was going to have a lot of explaining to do later.

'Evening, James,' he said to the porter, who looked over his bifocals and nodded in welcome. Matthew held up his hand. An ancient key dangled off his index finger from a leather loop. 'I'll be just a moment.'

'Right, Professor Clairmont.'

Matthew took my hand again. 'Let's go. We need to continue your education.'

He was like a mischievous boy on a treasure hunt, pulling me along. We ducked through a cracked door black with age, and Matthew switched on a light. His white skin leaped out of the dark, and he looked every inch a vampire.

'It's a good thing I'm a witch,' I teased. 'The sight of you here would be enough to scare a human to death.'

At the bottom of a flight of stairs, Matthew entered a long string of numbers at a security keypad, then hit the star key. I heard a soft click, and he pulled another door open. The smell of must and age and something else that I couldn't name hit me in a wave. Blackness extended away from the stairway lights.

'This is straight out of a Gothic novel. Where are you taking me?'

'Patience, Diana. It's not much farther.' Patience, alas, was not the strong suit of Bishop women.

Matthew reached past my shoulder and flipped another switch. Suspended on wires like trapeze artists, a string of old bulbs cast pools of light over what looked like horse stalls for miniature Shetland ponies.

I stared at Matthew, a hundred questions in my eyes.

'After you,' he said with a bow.

Stepping forward, I recognized the strange smell. It was stale alcohol – like the pub on Sunday morning. 'Wine?'

'Wine.'

We passed dozens of small enclosures that contained bottles in racks, piles, and crates. Each had a small slate tag, a year scrawled on it in chalk. We wandered past bins that held wine from the First World War and the Second, as well as bottles that Florence Nightingale might have packed in her trunks for the Crimea. There were wines from the year the Berlin Wall was built and the year it came down. Deeper into the cellar, the years scrawled on the slates gave way to broad categories like 'Old Claret' and 'Vintage Port.'

Finally we reached the end of the room. A dozen small doors stood locked and silent, and Matthew opened one of them. There was no electricity here, but he picked up a candle and wedged it securely into a brass holder before lighting it.

Inside, everything was as neat and orderly as Matthew himself, but for a layer of dust. Tightly spaced wooden racks held the wine off the floor and made it possible to remove a single bottle without making the whole arrangement tumble down. There were red stains next to the jamb where wine had been spit, year after year. The smell of old grapes, corks, and a trace of mildew filled the air.

'Is this yours?' I was incredulous.

'Yes, it's mine. A few of the fellows have private cellars.'

'What can you possibly have in here that isn't already out there?' The room behind me must contain a bottle of every wine ever produced. Oxford's finest wine emporium now seemed barren and oddly sterile in comparison.

Matthew smiled mysteriously. 'All sorts of things.'

He moved quickly around the small, windowless room, happily pulling out wines here and there. He handed me a heavy, dark bottle with a gold shield for a label and a wire basket over the cork. Champagne – Dom Perignon.

The next bottle was made from dark green glass, with a simple cream label and black script. He presented it to me with a little flourish, and I saw the date: 1976.

'The year I was born!' I said.

Matthew emerged with two more bottles: one with a long, octagonal label bearing a picture of a château on it and thick red wax around the top; the other lopsided and black, bearing no label and sealed with something that looked like tar. An old manila tag was tied around the neck of the second bottle with a dirty piece of string.

'Shall we?' Matthew asked, blowing out the candle. He locked the door carefully behind him, balancing the two bottles in his other hand, and slipped the key into his pocket. We left behind the smell of wine and climbed back to ground level.

In the dusky air, Matthew seemed to shine with pleasure, his arms full of wine. 'What a wonderful night,' he said happily.

We went up to his rooms, which were grander than I had imagined in some ways and much less grand in others. They were smaller than my rooms at New College, located at the very top of one of the oldest blocks in All Souls, full of funny angles and odd slopes. Though the ceilings were tall enough to accommodate Matthew's height, the rooms still seemed too small to contain him. He had to stoop through every door, and the windowsills reached down to somewhere near his thighs.

What the rooms lacked in size they more than made up for in furnishings. A faded Aubusson rug stretched across the floors, anchored with a collection of original William Morris furniture. Somehow the fifteenth-century architecture, the eighteenth-century rug, and the nineteenth-century rough-hewn oak looked splendid together and gave the rooms the atmosphere of a select Edwardian gentlemen's club.

A vast refectory table stood at the far side of the main room, with newspapers, books, and the assorted detritus of academic life neatly arranged at one end – memos about new policies, scholarly journals, requests for letters and peer reviews. Each pile was weighted down with a different object. Matthew's paperweights included the genuine article in heavy blown glass, an old brick, a bronze medal that was no doubt some award he'd won, and a small fire poker. At the other end of the table, a soft linen cloth had been thrown over the wood, held down by the most gorgeous Georgian silver candlesticks I'd ever seen outside a museum. A full array of different-shaped wineglasses stood guard over simple white plates and more Georgian silver.

'I love it.' I looked around with delight. Not a stick of furniture or a single ornament in this room belonged to the college. It was all perfectly, quintessentially Matthew.

'Have a seat.' He rescued the two wine bottles from my slack fingers and whisked them off to what looked like a glorified closet. 'All Souls doesn't believe that fellows should eat in their rooms,' he said by way of explanation as I eyed the meager kitchen facilities, 'so we'll get by as best we can.'

What I was about to eat would equal the finest dinner in town, no doubt.

Matthew plunked the champagne into a silver bucket full of ice and joined me in one of the cozy chairs flanking his nonfunctional fireplace. 'Nobody lets you build fires in Oxford fireplaces anymore.' He motioned ruefully at the empty stone enclosure. 'When every fireplace was lit, the city smelled like a bonfire.'

'When did you first come to Oxford?' I hoped the openness of my question would assure him I wasn't prying into his past lives.

'This time it was 1989.' He stretched his long legs out with a sigh of relaxation. 'I came to Oriel as a science student and stayed on for a doctorate. When I won an All Souls Prize Fellowship, I switched over here for a few years. When my degree was completed, the university offered me a place and the members elected me a fellow.' Every time he opened his mouth, something amazing popped out. A Prize Fellow? There were only two of those a year.

'And this is your first time at All Souls?' I bit my lip, and he laughed.

'Let's get this over with,' he said, holding up his hands and beginning to tick off colleges. 'I've been a member – once – of Merton, Magdalen, and University colleges. I've been a member of New College and Oriel twice each. And this is the first time All Souls has paid any attention to me.'

Multiplying this answer by a factor of Cambridge, Paris, Padua, and Montpellier – all of which, I was sure, had once had a student on their books named Matthew Clairmont, or some variation thereof – sent a dizzying set of degrees dancing through my head. What must he have studied, all those many years, and whom had he studied with?

'Diana?' Matthew's amused voice penetrated my thoughts. 'Did you hear me?'

'I'm sorry.' I closed my eyes and tightened my hands on my thighs in an effort to keep my mind from wandering. 'It's like a disease. I can't keep the curiosity at bay when you start reminiscing.'

'I know. It's one of the difficulties a vampire faces when he spends time with a witch who's a historian.' Matthew's mouth was bent in a mock frown, but his eyes twinkled like black stars.

'If you want to avoid these difficulties in future, I suggest you avoid the Bodleian's paleography reference section,' I said tartly.

'One historian is all I can manage at the moment.' Matthew rose smoothly to his feet. 'I asked if you were hungry.'

Why he continued to do so was a mystery — when was I not hungry?

'Yes,' I said, trying to extract myself from a deep Morris chair. Matthew stuck out his hand. I grasped it, and he lifted me easily.

We stood facing each other, our bodies nearly touching. I fixed my attention on the bump of his Bethany ampulla under his sweater.

His eyes flickered over me, leaving their trail of snowflakes. 'You look lovely.' I ducked my head, and the usual piece of hair fell over my face. He reached up as he had several times recently and tucked it behind my ear. This time his fingers continued to the base of my skull. He lifted my hair away from my neck and let it fall through his fingers as if it were water. I shivered at the touch of cool air on my skin.

'I love your hair,' he murmured. 'It has every color imaginable — even strands of red and black.' I heard the sharp intake of breath that meant he had picked up a new scent.

'What do you smell?' My voice was thick, and I still hadn't dared to meet his eyes.

'You,' he breathed.

My eyes floated up to his.

'Shall we have dinner?'

After that, it was hard to concentrate on the food, but I did my best. Matthew pulled out my rush-seated chair, which had a full view of the warm, beautiful room. From a miniscule refrigerator, he removed two plates, each with six fresh oysters nestled on top of a bed of crushed ice like the rays of a star.

'Lecture One of your continuing education consists of oysters and champagne.' Matthew sat down and held up a finger like a don about to embark on a favorite subject. He reached for the wine, which was within the wingspan of his long arm, and pulled it from the bucket. With one turn he popped the cork free of the neck of the bottle.

'I usually find that more difficult,' I commented drily, looking at his strong, elegant fingers.

'I can teach you to knock the cork off with a sword if you want.' Matthew grinned. 'Of course, a knife works, too, if you don't have a sword lying around.' He poured some of the liquid into our glasses, where it fizzed and danced in the candlelight.

He raised his glass to me. '*À la tienne.*'

'*À la tienne.*' I lifted my own flute and watched the bubbles break on the surface. 'Why are the bubbles so tiny?'

'Because the wine is so old. Most champagne is drunk long before this. But I like the old wine – it reminds me of the way champagne used to taste.'

'How old is it?'

'Older than you are,' Matthew replied. He was pulling the oyster shells apart with his bare hands – something that usually required a very sharp knife and a lot of skill – and chucking the shells into a glass bowl in the center of the table. He handed one plate over to me. 'It's from 1961.'

'Please tell me this is the oldest thing we're drinking tonight,' I said, thinking back to the wine he'd brought to dinner on Thursday, the bottle from which was now holding the last of his white roses on my bedside table.

'Not by a long shot,' he said with a grin.

I tipped the contents of the first shell into my mouth. My eyes popped open as my mouth filled with the taste of the Atlantic.

'Now drink.' He picked up his own glass and watched me take a sip of the golden liquid. 'What do you taste?'

The creaminess of the wine and the oysters collided with the taste of sea salt in ways that were utterly bewitching. 'It's as if the whole ocean is in my mouth,' I answered, taking another sip.

We finished the oysters and moved on to an enormous salad. It had every expensive green known to mankind, nuts, berries, and a delicious dressing made with champagne vinegar and olive oil that Matthew whisked together at the table. The tiny slices of meat that adorned it were partridge from the Old Lodge's grounds. We sipped at what Matthew called my 'birthday wine,' which smelled like lemon floor polish and smoke and tasted like chalk and butterscotch.

The next course was a stew, with chunks of meat in a fragrant sauce. My first bite told me it was veal, fixed with apples and a bit of cream, served atop rice. Matthew watched me eat, and he smiled as I tasted the tartness of the apple for the first time. 'It's an old recipe from Normandy,' he said. 'Do you like it?'

'It's wonderful. Did you make it?'

'No,' he said. 'The chef from the Old Parsonage's restaurant made it — and provided precise instructions on how not to burn it to a crisp when I reheated it.'

'You can reheat my dinner anytime.' I let the warmth of the stew soak into my body. 'You aren't eating, though.'

'No, but I'm not hungry.' He continued to watch me eat for a few moments, then returned to the kitchen to fetch another wine. It was the bottle sealed with red wax. He sliced through the wax and pulled the cork out of the bottle. 'Perfect,' he pronounced, pouring the scarlet liquid carefully into a nearby decanter.

'Can you already smell it?' I was still unsure of the range of his olfactory powers.

'Oh, yes. This wine in particular.' Matthew poured me a bit and splashed some into his own glass. 'Are you ready to taste something miraculous?' he asked. I nodded. 'This is Château Margaux from a very great vintage. Some people consider it the finest red wine ever made.'

We picked up our glasses, and I mimicked each of Matthew's movements. He put his nose in his glass, and I in mine. The smell of violets washed over me. My first taste was like drinking velvet. Then there was milk chocolate, cherries, and a flood of flavors that made no sense and brought back memories of the long-ago smell of my father's study after he'd been smoking and of emptying the shavings from the pencil sharpener in second grade. The very last thing I noted was a spicy taste that reminded me of Matthew.

'This tastes like you!' I said.

'How so?' he asked.

'Spicy,' I said, flushing suddenly from my cheeks to my hairline. 'Just spicy?'

'No. First I thought it would taste like flowers — violets — because that's how it smelled. But then I tasted all kinds of things. What do you taste?'

This was going to be far more interesting and less embarrassing than my reaction. He sniffed, swirled, and tasted. 'Violets – I agree with you there. Those purple violets covered with sugar. Elizabeth Tudor loved candied violets, and they ruined her teeth.' He sipped again. 'Cigar smoke from good cigars, like they used to have at the Marlborough Club when the Prince of Wales stopped in. Blackberries picked wild in the hedgerows outside the Old Lodge's stables and red currants macerated in brandy.'

Watching a vampire use his sensory powers had to be one of the most surreal experiences anyone could have. It was not just that Matthew could see and hear things I could not – it was that when he did sense something, the perception was so acute and precise. It wasn't any blackberry – it was a particular blackberry, from a particular place or a particular time.

Matthew kept drinking his wine, and I finished my stew. I took up my wineglass with a contented sigh, toying with the stem so that it caught the light from the candles.

'What do you think I would taste like?' I wondered aloud, my tone playful.

Matthew shot to his feet, his face white and furious. His napkin fell, unnoticed, to the floor. A vein in his forehead pulsed once before subsiding.

I had said something wrong.

He was at my side in the time it took me to blink, pulling me up from my chair. His fingers dug into my elbows.

'There's one legend about vampires we haven't discussed, isn't there?' His eyes were strange, his face frightening. I tried to squirm out of his reach, but his fingers dug deeper. 'The one about a vampire who finds himself so bewitched by a woman that he cannot help himself.'

My mind sped over what had happened. He'd asked me what I tasted. I'd tasted him. Then he told me what he tasted and I said—

'Oh, Matthew,' I whispered.

'Do you wonder what it would be like for me to taste you?' Matthew's voice dropped from a purr toward something deeper and more dangerous. For a moment I felt revulsion.

Before that feeling could grow, he released my arms. There was no time to react or draw away. Matthew had woven his fingers through my hair, his thumbs pressing against the base of my skull. I was caught again, and a feeling of stillness came over me, spreading out from his cold touch. Was I drunk from two glasses of wine? Drugged? What else would explain the feeling that I couldn't break free?

'It's not only your scent that pleases me. I can *hear* your witch's blood as it moves through your veins.' Matthew's cold lips were against my ear, and his breath was sweet. 'Did you know that a witch's blood makes music? Like a siren who sings to the sailor, asking him to steer his ship into the rocks, the call of your blood could be my undoing – and yours.' His words were so quiet and intimate he seemed to be talking directly into my mind.

The vampire's lips began to move incrementally along my jawbone. Each place his mouth touched froze, then burned as my blood rushed back to the skin's surface.

'Matthew,' I breathed around the catch in my throat. I closed my eyes, expecting to feel teeth against my neck yet unable – unwilling – to move.

Instead Matthew's hungry lips met mine. His arms locked around me, and his fingertips cradled my head. My lips parted under his, my hands trapped between his chest and mine. Underneath my palms his heart beat, once.

With the thump of his heart, the kiss changed. Matthew was no less demanding, but the hunger in his touch turned to something bittersweet. His hands moved forward smoothly until he was cupping my face, and he pulled away reluctantly. For the first time, I heard a soft, ragged sound. It was not like human breathing. It was the sound of minute amounts of oxygen passing through a vampire's powerful lungs.

'I took advantage of your fear. I shouldn't have,' he whispered.

My eyes were closed, and I still felt intoxicated, his cinnamon and clove scent driving off the scent of violets from the wine. Restless, I stirred in his grip.

'Be still,' he said, voice harsh. 'I might not be able to control myself if you step away.'

He'd warned me in the lab about the relationship between predator and prey. Now he was trying to get me to play dead so the predator in him would lose interest in me.

But I wasn't dead.

My eyes flew open. There was no mistaking the sharp look on his face. It was avid, hungry. Matthew was a creature of instinct now. But I had instincts, too.

'I'm safe with you.' I formed the words with lips that were freezing and burning at the same time, unused to the feeling of a vampire's kiss.

'A witch – safe with a vampire? Never be sure of that. It would only take a moment. You wouldn't be able to stop me if I struck, and I wouldn't be able to stop myself.' Our eyes met and locked, neither of us blinking. Matthew made a low sound of surprise. 'How brave you are.'

'I've never been brave.'

'When you gave blood in the lab, the way you meet a vampire's eyes, how you ordered the creatures out of the library, even the fact that you go back there day after day, refusing to let people keep you from what you want to do – it's all bravery.'

'That's stubbornness.' Sarah had explained the difference a long time ago.

'I've seen courage like yours before – from women, mostly.' Matthew continued as if I hadn't spoken. 'Men don't have it. Our resolve is born out of fear. It's merely bravado.'

His glance flickered over me in snowflakes that melted into mere coolness the moment they touched me. One cold finger reached out and captured a tear from the tips of my eyelashes. His face was sad as he lowered me gently into the chair and crouched next to me, resting one hand on my knee and the other on the arm of the rush-seated chair in a protective circle. 'Promise me that you will never joke with a vampire – not even me – about blood or how you might taste.'

'I'm sorry,' I whispered, forcing myself not to look away.

He shook his head. 'You told me before that you don't know much about vampires. What you need to understand is that no vampire is immune to this temptation. Vampires with a conscience spend most of their time trying not to imagine how people would taste. If you were to meet one without a conscience – and there are plenty who fit that category – then God help you.'

'I didn't think.' I still couldn't. My mind was whirling with the memory of his kiss, his fury, and his palpable hunger.

He bowed his head, resting the crown against my shoulder. The ampulla from Bethany tumbled out of the neck of his sweater and swung like a pendulum, its tiny coffin glinting in the light from the candles.

He spoke so softly that I had to strain to hear. 'Witches and vampires aren't meant to feel this way. I'm experiencing emotions I've never—' He broke off.

'I know.' Carefully I leaned my cheek against his hair. It felt as satiny as it looked. 'I feel them, too.'

Matthew's arms had remained where he left them, one hand on my knee and the other on the arm of the chair. At my words he moved them slowly and clasped my waist. The coldness of his flesh cut through my clothing, but I didn't shiver. Instead I moved closer so that I could rest my arms on his shoulders.

A vampire evidently could have remained comfortable in that position for days. For a mere witch, however, it wasn't an option. When I shifted slightly, he looked at me in confusion, and then his face lightened in recognition.

'I forgot,' he said, rising with his swift smoothness and stepping away from me. I moved first one leg and then the other, restoring the circulation to my feet.

Matthew handed me my wine and returned to his own seat. Once he was settled, I tried to give him something to think about other than how I might taste.

'What was the fifth question you had to answer for the Prize Fellowship?' Candidates were invited to sit an exam that involved four questions combining thought-provoking breadth and depth with devilish complexity. If you survived the first four questions, you were asked the famous 'fifth question.' It was not a question at all, but a single word like 'water,' or 'absence.' It was up to the candidate to decide how to respond, and only the most brilliant answer won you a place at All Souls.

He reached across the table – without setting himself on fire – and poured some more wine into my glass. 'Desire,' he said, studiously avoiding my eyes.

So much for that diversionary plan.

'Desire? What did you write?'

'As far as I can tell, there are only two emotions that keep the world spinning, year after year.' He hesitated, then continued. 'One is fear. The other is desire. That's what I wrote about.'

Love hadn't factored into his response, I noticed. It was a brutal picture, a tug-of-war between two equal but opposing impulses. It had the ring of truth, however, which was more than could be said of the glib 'love makes the world go round.' Matthew kept hinting that his desire – for blood, chiefly – was so strong that it put everything else at risk.

But vampires weren't the only creatures who had to manage such strong impulses. Much of what qualified as magic was simply desire in action. Witchcraft was different – that took spells and rituals. But magic? A wish, a need, a hunger too strong to be denied – these could turn into deeds when they crossed a witch's mind.

And if Matthew was going to tell me his secrets, it didn't seem fair to keep mine so close.

'Magic is desire made real. It's how I pulled down *Notes and Queries* the night we met,' I said slowly. 'When a witch concentrates on something she wants, and then imagines how she might get it, she can make it happen. That's why I have to be so careful about my work.' I took a sip of wine, my hand trembling on the glass.

'Then you spend most of your time trying not to want things, just like me. For some of the same reasons, too.' Matthew's snowflake glances flickered across my cheeks.

'If you mean the fear that if I started, there would be no stopping me – yes. I don't want to look back on a life where I took everything rather than earned it.'

'So you earn everything twice over. First you earn it by not simply taking it, and then you earn it again through work and effort.' He laughed bitterly. 'The advantages of being an otherworldly creature don't amount to much, do they?'

Matthew suggested we sit by his fireless fireplace. I lounged on the sofa, and he carried some nutty biscuits over to the table by me, before disappearing into the kitchen once more. When he returned, he was carrying a small tray with the ancient black bottle on it – the cork now pulled – and two glasses of amber-colored liquid. He handed one to me.

'Close your eyes and tell me what you smell,' he instructed in his Oxford don's voice. My lids dropped obediently. The wine seemed at once old and vibrant. It smelled of flowers and nuts and candied lemons and of some other, long-past world that I had – until now – been able only to read about and imagine.

'It smells like the past. But not the dead past. It's so alive.'

'Open your eyes and take a sip.'

As the sweet, bright liquid went down my throat, something ancient and powerful entered my bloodstream. *This must be what vampire blood tastes like.* I kept my thoughts to myself.

'Are you going to tell me what it is?' I asked around the flavors in my mouth.

'Malmsey,' he replied with a grin. 'Old, old malmsey.'

'How old?' I said suspiciously. 'As old as you are?'

He laughed. 'No. You don't want to drink anything as old as I am. It's from 1795, from grapes grown on the island of Madeira. It was quite popular once, but nobody pays much attention to it now.'

'Good,' I said with greedy satisfaction. 'All the more for me.' He laughed again and sat easily in one of his Morris chairs.

We talked about his time at All Souls, about Hamish – the other Prize Fellow, it turned out – and their adventures in Oxford. I laughed at his stories of dining in hall and how he'd bolted to Woodstock after every meal to clean the taste of overcooked beef from his mouth.

'You look tired,' he finally said, standing after another glass of malmsey and another hour of conversation.

'I am tired.' Despite my fatigue, there was something I needed to tell him before he took me home. I put my glass down carefully. 'I've made a decision, Matthew. On Monday I'll be recalling Ashmole 782.'

The vampire sat down abruptly.

'I don't know how I broke the spell the first time, but I'll try to do it again. Knox doesn't have much faith that I'll succeed.' My mouth tightened. 'What does he know? He hasn't been able to break the spell once. And you might be able to see the words in the magical palimpsest that lie under the images.'

'What do you mean, you don't know what you did to break the spell?' Matthew's forehead creased with confusion. 'What words did you use? What powers did you call upon?'

'I broke the spell without realizing it,' I explained.

'Christ, Diana.' He shot to his feet again. 'Does Knox know that you didn't use witchcraft?'

'If he knows, I didn't tell him.' I shrugged. 'Besides, what does it matter?'

'It matters because if you didn't break the enchantment, then you met its conditions. Right now the creatures are waiting to observe whatever counterspell you used, copy it if they can, and get Ashmole 782 themselves. When your fellow witches discover that the spell opened for you of its own accord, they won't be so patient and well behaved.'

Gillian's angry face swam before my eyes, accompanied by a vivid recollection of the lengths she reported witches had gone to in order to pry secrets from my parents. I brushed the thoughts aside, my stomach rolling, and focused on the flaws in Matthew's argument.

'The spell was constructed more than a century before I was born. That's impossible.'

'Just because something seems impossible doesn't make it untrue,' he said grimly. 'Newton knew that. There's no telling what Knox will do when he understands your relationship to the spell.'

'I'm in danger whether I recall the manuscript or not,' I pointed out. 'Knox isn't going to let this go, is he?'

'No,' he agreed reluctantly. 'And he wouldn't hesitate to use magic against you even if every human in the Bodleian saw him do it. I might not be able to reach you in time.'

Vampires were fast, but magic was faster.

'I'll sit near the desk with you, then. We'll know as soon as the manuscript's delivered.'

'I don't like this,' Matthew said, clearly worried. 'There's a fine line between bravery and recklessness, Diana.'

'It's not reckless – I just want my life back.'

'What if this is your life?' he asked. 'What if you can't keep the magic away after all?'

'I'll keep parts of it.' Remembering his kiss, and the sudden, intense feeling of vitality that had accompanied it, I looked straight into his eyes so he would know he was included. 'But I'm not going to be bullied.'

Matthew was still worrying over my plan as he walked me home. When I turned in to New College Lane to use the back entrance, he caught my hand.

'Not on your life,' he said. 'Did you see the look that porter gave me? I want him to know you're safely in college.'

We navigated the uneven sidewalks of Holywell Street, past the entrance to the Turf pub, and through the New College gates. We strolled by the watchful porter, still hand in hand.

'Will you be rowing tomorrow?' Matthew asked at the bottom of my staircase.

I groaned. 'No, I've got a thousand letters of recommendation to write. I'm going to stay in my rooms and clear my desk.'

'I'm going to Woodstock to go hunting,' he said casually.

'Good hunting, then,' I said, equally casually.

'It doesn't bother you at all to know I'll be out culling my own deer?' Matthew sounded taken aback.

'No. Occasionally I eat partridge. Occasionally you feed on deer.' I shrugged. 'I honestly don't see the difference.'

Matthew's eyes glittered. He stretched his fingers slightly but didn't let go of my hand. Instead he lifted it to his lips and put a slow kiss on the tender flesh in the hollow of my palm.

'Off to bed,' he said, releasing my fingers. His eyes left trails of ice and snow behind as they lingered not only over my face but my body, too.

Wordlessly I looked back at him, astonished that a kiss on the palm could be so intimate.

'Good night,' I breathed out along with my next exhale. 'I'll see you Monday.'

I climbed the narrow steps to my rooms. Whoever tightened the doorknob had made a mess of the lock, and the metal hardware and the wood were covered in fresh scratches. Inside, I switched on the lights. The answering machine was blinking, of course. At the window I raised my hand to show that I was safely inside.

When I peeked out a few seconds later, Matthew was already gone.

CHAPTER 15

On Monday morning the air had that magically still quality common in autumn. The whole world felt crisp and bright, and time seemed suspended. I shot out of bed at dawn and pulled on my waiting rowing gear, eager to be outdoors.

The river was empty for the first hour. As the sun broke over the horizon, the fog burned off toward the waterline so that I was slipping through alternate bands of mist and rosy sunshine.

When I pulled up to the dock, Matthew was waiting for me on the curving steps that led to the boathouse's balcony, an ancient brown-and-bone-striped New College scarf hanging around his neck. I climbed out of the boat, put my hands on my hips, and stared at him in disbelief.

'Where did you get that thing?' I pointed at the scarf.

'You should have more respect for the old members,' he said with his mischievous grin, tossing one end of it over his shoulder. 'I think I bought it in 1920, but I can't honestly remember. After the Great War ended, certainly.'

Shaking my head, I took the oars into the boathouse. Two crews glided by the dock in perfect, powerful unison just as I was lifting my boat out of the water. My knees dipped slightly and the boat swung up and over until its weight rested on my head.

'Why don't you let me help you with that?' Matthew said, rising from his perch.

'No chance.' My steps were steady as I walked the boat inside. He grumbled something under his breath.

With the boat safely in its rack, Matthew easily talked me into breakfast at Mary and Dan's café. He was going to have to sit next to me much of the day, and I was hungry after the morning's exertions. He steered me by the elbow around the other diners, his hand firmer on my back than before. Mary greeted me like an old friend, and Steph didn't bother with a menu, just announced 'the usual' when she came by the table. There wasn't a hint of a question in her voice, and when the plate came – laden with eggs, bacon, mushrooms, and tomatoes – I was glad I hadn't insisted on something more ladylike.

After breakfast I trotted through the lodge and up to my rooms for a shower and a change of clothes. Fred peered around his window to see if it was indeed Matthew's Jaguar pulled up outside the gates. The porters were no doubt laying wagers on competing predictions regarding our oddly formal relationship. This morning was the first time I'd managed to convince my escort to simply drop me off.

'It's broad daylight, and Fred will have kittens if you clog up his gate during delivery hours,' I protested when Matthew started to get out of the car. He'd glowered but agreed that merely pulling straight across the entrance to bar possible vehicular attack was sufficient.

This morning every step of my routine needed to be slow and deliberate. My shower was long and leisurely, the hot water slipping against my tired muscles. Still in no rush, I put on comfortable black trousers, a turtleneck to keep my shoulders from seizing up in the increasingly chilly library, and a reasonably presentable midnight blue cardigan to break up the unalleviated black. My hair was caught in a low ponytail. The short piece in the front fell forward as it always did, and I grumbled and shoved it behind my ear.

In spite of my efforts, my anxiety rose as I pushed open the library's glass doors. The guard's eyes narrowed at my uncharacteristically warm smile, and he took an inordinate amount of time checking my face against the picture on my reader's card. Finally he admitted me, and I pelted up the stairs to Duke Humfrey's.

It had been no more than an hour since I'd been with Matthew, but the sight of him stretched out among the first bay of Elizabethan desks in one of the medieval wing's purgatorial chairs was welcome.

He looked up when my laptop dropped on the scarred wooden surface.

'Is he here?' I whispered, reluctant to say Knox's name.

Matthew nodded grimly. 'In the Selden End.'

'Well, he can wait down there all day as far as I'm concerned,' I said under my breath, picking up a blank request slip from the shallow rectangular tray on the desk. On it I wrote '*Ashmole MS 782*,' my name, and my reader number.

Sean was at the collection desk. 'I've got two items on reserve,' I told him with a smile. He went into the cage and returned with my manuscripts, then held out his hand for my new request. He put the slip into the worn, gray cardboard envelope that would be sent to the stacks.

'May I talk to you a minute?' Sean asked.

'Sure.' I gestured to indicate that Matthew should stay where he was and followed Sean through the swinging gate into the Arts End, which, like the Selden End, ran perpendicular to the length of the old library. We stood beneath a bank of leaded windows that let in the weak morning sunshine.

'Is he bothering you?'

'Professor Clairmont? No.'

'It's none of my business, but I don't like him.' Sean looked down the central aisle as if he expected Matthew to pop out and glare at him. 'The whole place has been full of strange ducks over the last week or so.'

Unable to disagree, I resorted to muffled noises of sympathy.

'You'd let me know if there was something wrong, wouldn't you?'

'Of course, Sean. But Professor Clairmont's okay. You don't have to worry about him.'

My old friend looked unconvinced.

'Sean may know I'm different – but it seems I'm not as different as you,' I told Matthew after returning to my seat.

'Few are,' he said darkly, picking up his reading.

I turned on my computer and tried to concentrate on my work.

It would take hours for the manuscript to appear. But thinking about alchemy was harder than ever, caught as I was between a vampire and the call desk. Every time new books emerged from the stacks, I looked up.

After several false alarms, soft steps approached from the Selden End. Matthew tensed in his chair.

Peter Knox strolled up and stopped. 'Dr Bishop,' he said coolly.

'Mr Knox.' My voice was equally chilly, and I returned my attention to the open volume before me. Knox took a step in my direction.

Matthew spoke quietly, without raising his eyes from the Needham papers. 'I'd stop there unless Dr Bishop wishes to speak with you.'

'I'm very busy.' A sense of pressure wound around my forehead, and a voice whispered in my skull. Every ounce of my energy was devoted to keeping the witch out of my thoughts. 'I said I'm busy,' I repeated stonily.

Matthew put his pencil down and pushed away from the desk.

'Mr Knox was just leaving, Matthew.' Turning to my laptop, I typed a few sentences of utter nonsense.

'I hope you understand what you're doing,' Knox spit.

Matthew growled, and I laid a hand lightly on his arm. Knox's eyes fixed on the spot where the bodies of a witch and a vampire touched.

Until that moment Knox had only suspected that Matthew and I were too close for the comfort of witches. Now he was sure.

You've told him what you know about our book. Knox's vicious voice sounded through my head, and though I tried to push against his intrusion, the wizard was too strong. When he resisted my efforts, I gasped in surprise.

Sean looked up from the call desk in alarm. Matthew's arm was vibrating, his growl subsiding into a somehow more menacing purr.

'Who's caught human attention now?' I hissed at the witch, squeezing Matthew's arm to let him know I didn't need his help.

Knox smiled unpleasantly. 'You've caught the attention of more than humans this morning, Dr Bishop. Before nightfall every witch in Oxford will know you're a traitor.'

Matthew's muscles coiled, and he reached up to the coffin he wore around his neck.

Oh, God, I thought, *he's going to kill a witch in the Bodleian.* I placed myself squarely between the two of them.

'Enough,' I told Knox quietly. 'If you don't leave, I'm going to tell Sean you're harassing me and have him call security.'

'The light in the Selden End is rather glaring today,' Knox said at last, breaking the standoff. 'I believe I'll move to this part of the library.' He strolled away.

Matthew lifted my hand from his arm and began to pack up his belongings. 'We're leaving.'

'No we're not. We are not leaving until we get that manuscript.'

'Were you listening?' Matthew said hotly. 'He threatened you! I don't need this manuscript, but I do need—' He stopped abruptly.

I pushed Matthew into his seat. Sean was still staring in our direction, his hand hovering above the phone. Smiling, I shook my head at him before returning my attention to the vampire.

'It's my fault. I shouldn't have touched you while he was standing there,' I murmured, looking down at his shoulder, where my hand still rested.

Matthew's cool fingers lifted my chin. 'Do you regret the touch – or the fact that the witch saw you?'

'Neither,' I whispered. His gray eyes went from sad to surprised in an instant. 'But you don't want me to be reckless.'

As Knox approached again, Matthew's grip on my chin tightened, his senses tuned into the witch. When Knox remained a few desks away, the vampire returned his attention to me. 'One more word from him and we're leaving – manuscript or no manuscript. I mean it, Diana.'

Thinking about alchemical illustrations proved impossible after that. Gillian's warning about what happened to witches who kept secrets from other witches, and Knox's firm pronouncement that I was a traitor, resounded through my head. When Matthew tried to get me to stop for lunch, I refused. The manuscript had still not appeared, and we couldn't be at Blackwell's when it arrived – not with Knox so close.

'Did you see what I had for breakfast?' I asked when Matthew insisted. 'I'm not hungry.'

My coffee-loving daemon drifted by shortly afterward, swinging his headset by the cord. 'Hey,' he said with a wave at Matthew and me.

Matthew looked up sharply.

'Good to see you two again. Is it okay if I check my e-mail down there since the witch is here with you?'

'What's your name?' I asked, smothering a smile.

'Timothy,' he answered, rocking back on his heels. He was wearing mismatched cowboy boots, one red and one black. His eyes were mismatched, too – one was blue and one was green.

'You're more than welcome to check your e-mail, Timothy.'

'You're the one.' He tipped his fingers at me, pivoted on the heel of the red boot, and walked away.

An hour later I stood, unable to control my impatience. 'The manuscript should have arrived by now.'

The vampire's eyes followed me across the six feet of open space to the call desk. They felt hard and crisp like ice, rather than soft as snowfall, and they clung to my shoulder blades.

'Hi, Sean. Will you check to see if the manuscript I requested this morning has been delivered?'

'Someone else must have it,' Sean said. 'Nothing's come up for you.'

'Are you sure?' Nobody else had it.

Sean riffled through the slips and found my request. Paper-clipped to it was a note. 'It's missing.'

'It's not missing. I saw it a few weeks ago.'

'Let's see.' He rounded the desk, headed for the supervisor's office. Matthew looked up from his papers and watched as Sean rapped against the open doorframe.

'Dr Bishop wants this manuscript, and it's been noted as missing,' Sean explained. He held out the slip.

Mr Johnson consulted a book on his desk, running his finger over lines scrawled by generations of reading-room supervisors. 'Ah, yes. Ashmole 782. That's been missing since 1859. We don't have a microfilm.' Matthew's chair scraped away from his desk.

'But I saw it a few *weeks* ago.'

'That's not possible, Dr Bishop. No one has seen this manuscript for one hundred and fifty years.' Mr Johnson blinked behind his thick-rimmed glasses.

'Dr Bishop, could I show you something when you have a moment?' Matthew's voice made me jump.

'Yes, of course.' I turned blindly toward him. 'Thank you,' I whispered to Mr Johnson.

'We're leaving. Now,' Matthew hissed. In the aisle an assortment of creatures was focused intently on us. I saw Knox, Timothy, the Scary Sisters, Gillian – and a few more unfamiliar faces. Above the tall bookcases, the old portraits of kings, queens, and other illustrious persons that decorated the walls of Duke Humfrey's Reading Room stared at us, too, with every bit as much sour disapproval.

'It can't be missing. I just saw it,' I repeated numbly. 'We should have them check.'

'Don't talk about it now – don't even think about it.' He gathered up my things with lightning speed, his hands a blur as he saved my work and shut down the computer.

I obediently started reciting English monarchs in my head, beginning with William the Conqueror, to rid my mind of thoughts of the missing manuscript.

Knox passed by, busily texting on his mobile. He was followed by the Scary Sisters, who looked grimmer than usual.

'Why are they all leaving?' I asked Matthew.

'You didn't recall Ashmole 782. They're regrouping.' He thrust my bag and computer at me and picked up my two manuscripts. With his free hand, he snared my elbow and moved us toward the call desk.

Timothy waved sadly from the Selden End before making a peace sign and turning away.

'Sean, Dr Bishop is going back to college with me to help solve a problem I've found in the Needham papers. She won't require these for the rest of the day. And I won't be returning either.' Matthew handed Sean the boxed manuscripts. Sean gave the vampire a dark look before thumping them into a neater pile and heading for the locked manuscript hold.

We didn't exchange a word on the way down the stairs, and by the time we pushed through the glass doors into the courtyard, I was ready to explode with questions.

Peter Knox was lounging against the iron railings surrounding the bronze statue of William Herbert. Matthew stopped abruptly and, with a fast step in front of me and a flick of his shoulder, placed me behind his considerable bulk.

'So, Dr Bishop, you didn't get it back,' Knox said maliciously. 'I told you it was a fluke. Not even a Bishop could break that spell without proper training in witchcraft. Your mother might have managed it, but you don't appear to share her talents.'

Matthew curled his lip but said nothing. He was trying not to interfere between witches, yet he wouldn't be able to resist throttling Knox indefinitely.

'It's missing. My mother was gifted, but she wasn't a bloodhound.' I bristled, and Matthew's hand rose slightly to quiet me.

'It's been missing,' Knox said. 'You found it anyway. It's a good thing you didn't manage to break the spell a second time, though.'

'Why is that?' I asked impatiently.

'Because we cannot let our history fall into the hands of animals like him. Witches and vampires don't mix, Dr Bishop. There are excellent reasons for it. Remember who you are. If you don't, you will regret it.'

A witch shouldn't keep secrets from other witches. Bad things happen when she does. Gillian's voice echoed in my head, and the walls of the Bodleian drew closer. I fought down the panic that was burbling to the surface.

'Threaten her again and I'll kill you on the spot.' Matthew's voice was calm, but a passing tourist's frozen look suggested that his face betrayed stronger emotions.

'Matthew,' I said quietly. 'Not here.'

'Killing witches now, Clairmont?' Knox sneered. 'Have you run out of vampires and humans to harm?'

'Leave her alone.' Matthew's voice remained even, but his body was poised to strike if Knox moved a muscle in my direction.

The witch's face twisted. 'There's no chance of that. She belongs to us, not you. So does the manuscript.'

'Matthew,' I repeated more urgently. A human boy of thirteen with a nose ring and a troubled complexion was now studying him with interest. 'The humans are staring.'

He reached back and grabbed my hand in his. The shock of cold skin against warm and the sensation that I was tethered to him were simultaneous. He pulled me forward, tucking me under his shoulder.

Knox laughed scornfully. 'It will take more than that to keep her safe, Clairmont. She'll get the manuscript back for us. We'll make sure of it.'

Without another word, Matthew propelled me through the quadrangle and onto the wide cobblestone path surrounding the Radcliffe Camera. He eyed All Souls' closed iron gates, swore quickly and enthusiastically, and kept me going toward the High Street.

'Not much farther,' he said, his hand gripping mine a bit more tightly.

Matthew didn't let go of me in the lodge, and he gave a curt nod to the porter on the way to his rooms. Up we climbed to his garret, which was just as warm and comfortable as it had been Saturday evening.

Matthew threw his keys onto the sideboard and deposited me unceremoniously on the sofa. He disappeared into the kitchen and returned with a glass of water. He handed it to me, and I held it without drinking until he scowled so darkly that I took a sip and almost choked.

'Why couldn't I get the manuscript a second time?' I was rattled that Knox had been proved right.

'I should have followed my instincts.' Matthew was standing by the window, clenching and unclenching his right hand and paying absolutely no attention to me. 'We don't understand your connection to the spell. You've been in grave danger since you saw Ashmole 782.'

'Knox may threaten, Matthew, but he's not going to do something stupid in front of so many witnesses.'

'You're staying at Woodstock for a few days. I want you away from Knox – no more chance meetings in college, no passing by him in the Bodleian.'

'Knox was right: I can't get the manuscript back. He won't pay any more attention to me.'

'That's wishful thinking, Diana. Knox wants to understand the secrets of Ashmole 782 as much as you or I do.' Matthew's normally impeccable appearance was suffering. He'd run his fingers through his hair until it stood up like a scarecrow's in places.

'How can you both be so certain there are secrets in the hidden text?' I wondered, moving toward the fireplace. 'It's an alchemy book. Maybe that's all it is.'

'Alchemy is the story of creation, told chemically. Creatures are chemistry, mapped onto biology.'

'But when Ashmole 782 was written, they didn't know about biology or share your sense of chemistry.'

Matthew eyes collapsed into slits. 'Diana Bishop, I'm shocked at your narrow-mindedness.' He meant it, too. 'The creatures who made the manuscript might not have known about DNA, but what proof do you have that they weren't asking the same questions about creation as a modern scientist?'

'Alchemical texts are allegories, not instruction manuals.' I redirected the fear and frustration of the past several days at him. 'They may hint at larger truths, but you can't build a reliable experiment from them.'

'I never said you could,' he replied, his eyes still dark with suppressed anger. 'But we're talking about potential readers who are witches, daemons, and vampires. A little supernatural reading, a bit of otherworldly creativity, and some long memories to fill in the blanks may give creatures information we don't want them to have.'

'Information *you* don't want them to have!' I remembered my promise to Agatha Wilson, and my voice rose. 'You're as bad as Knox. You want Ashmole 782 to satisfy your own curiosity.' My hands itched as I grabbed at my things.

'Calm down.' There was an edge to his voice that I didn't like.

'Stop telling me what to do.' The itching sensation intensified.

My fingers were brilliant blue and shooting out little arcs of fire that sputtered at the edges like the sparklers on birthday cakes. I dropped my computer and held them up.

Matthew should have been horrified. Instead he looked intrigued.

'Does that happen often?' His voice was carefully neutral.

'Oh, *no*.' I ran for the kitchen, trailing sparks.

Matthew beat me to the door. 'Not water,' he said sharply. 'They smell electrical.'

Ah. That explained the last time I set fire to the kitchen.

I stood mutely, holding my hands up between us. We watched for a few minutes while the blue left my fingertips and the sparks went out entirely, leaving behind a definite smell of bad electrical wiring.

When the fireworks ended, Matthew was lounging against the kitchen doorframe with the nonchalant air of a Renaissance aristocrat waiting to have his portrait painted.

'Well,' he said, watching me with the stillness of an eagle ready to pounce on his prey, 'that was interesting. Are you always like that when you get angry?'

'I don't do angry,' I said, turning away from him. His hand shot out and whirled me back around to face him.

'You're not getting off that easy.' Matthew's voice was soft, but the sharp edge was back. 'You do angry. I just saw it. And you left at least one hole in my carpet to prove it.'

'Let me go!' My mouth contorted into what Sarah called my 'sourpuss.' It was enough to make my students quake. Right now I hoped it would make Matthew curl up into a ball and roll away. At the very least, I wanted him to take his hand off my arm so I could get out of there.

'I warned you. Friendships with vampires are complicated. I couldn't let you go now – even if I wanted to.'

My eyes lowered deliberately to his hand. Matthew removed it with a snort of impatience, and I turned to pick up my bag.

You really shouldn't turn your back on a vampire if you've been arguing.

Matthew's arms shot around me from behind, pressing my back against his chest so hard that I could feel every flexed muscle. 'Now,' he said directly into my ear, 'we're going to talk like civilized creatures about what happened. You are not running away from this – or from me.'

'Let me go, Matthew.' I struggled in his arms.

'No.'

No man had ever refused when I asked him to stop doing something – whether it was blowing his nose in the library or trying to slip a hand up my shirt after a movie. I struggled again. Matthew's arms got tighter.

'Stop fighting me.' He sounded amused. 'You'll get tired long before I do, I assure you.'

In my women's self-defense class, they'd taught me what to do if grabbed from behind. I lifted my foot to stomp on his. Matthew moved out of the way, and it smashed into the floor instead.

'We can do this all afternoon if you want,' he murmured. 'But I honestly can't recommend it. My reflexes are much faster than yours.'

'Let me go and we can talk,' I said through clenched teeth.

He laughed softly, his spicy breath tickling the exposed skin at the base of my skull. 'That wasn't a worthy attempt at negotiation, Diana. No, we're going to talk like this. I want to know how often your fingers have turned blue.'

'Not often.' My instructor had recommended I relax if grabbed from behind and slip out of an assailant's arms. Matthew's grip on me only tightened. 'A few times, when I was a child, I set fire to things – the kitchen cabinets, but that may have been because I tried to put my hands out in the sink and the fire got worse. My bedroom curtains, once or twice. A tree outside the house – but it was just a small tree.'

'Since then?'

'It happened last week, when Miriam made me angry.'

'How did she do that?' he asked, resting his cheek against the side of my head. It was comforting, if I overlooked the fact that he was holding me against my wishes.

'She told me I needed to learn how to take care of myself and stop relying on you to protect me. She basically accused me of playing the damsel in distress.' Just the thought made my blood simmer and my fingers itch all over again.

'You are many things, Diana, but a damsel in distress is not one of them. You've had this reaction twice in less than a week.' Matthew's voice was thoughtful. 'Interesting.'

'I don't think so.'

'No, I don't imagine you do,' he said, 'but it is interesting just the same. Now let's turn to another topic.' His mouth drifted toward my ear, and I tried – unsuccessfully – to pull it away. 'What is this nonsense about my not being interested in anything but an old manuscript?'

I flushed. This was mortifying. 'Sarah and Em said you were only spending time with me because you wanted something. I assume it's Ashmole 782.'

'But that's not true, is it?' he said, running his lips and cheek gently against my hair. My blood started to sing in response. Even I could hear it. He laughed again, this time with satisfaction. 'I didn't think you believed it. I just wanted to be sure.'

My body relaxed into his. 'Matthew—' I began.

'I'm letting you go,' he said, cutting me off. 'But don't bolt for the door, understand?'

We were prey and predator once more. If I ran, his instincts would tell him to give chase. I nodded, and he slipped his arms from me, leaving me oddly unsteady.

'What am I going to do with you?' He was standing with his hands on his hips, a lopsided smile on his face. 'You are the most exasperating creature I've ever met.'

'No one has ever known what to do with me.'

'That I believe.' He surveyed me for a moment. 'We're going to Woodstock.'

'No! I'm perfectly safe in college.' He'd warned me about vampires and protectiveness. He was right – I didn't like it.

'You are not,' he said with an angry glint in his eyes. 'Someone's tried to break in to your rooms.'

'What?' I was aghast.

'The loose lock, remember?'

In fact, there were fresh scratches on the hardware. But Matthew did not need to know about that.

'You'll stay at Woodstock until Peter Knox leaves Oxford.'

My face must have betrayed my dismay.

'It won't be so bad,' he said gently. 'You'll have all the yoga you want.'

With Matthew in bodyguard mode, I didn't have much choice. And if he was right – which I suspected he was – someone had already gotten past Fred and into my rooms.

'Come,' he said, picking up my computer bag. 'I'll take you to New College and wait while you get your things. But this conversation about the connection between Ashmole 782 and your blue fingers is not over,' he continued, forcing me to meet his eyes. 'It's just beginning.'

We went down to the fellows' car park, and Matthew retrieved the Jaguar from between a modest blue Vauxhall and an old Peugeot. Given the city's restrictive traffic patterns, it took twice as long to drive as it would have to walk.

Matthew pulled in to the lodge gates. 'I'll be right back,' I said, slinging my computer bag over my shoulder as he let me out of the car.

'Dr Bishop, you have mail,' Fred called from the lodge.

I collected the contents of my pigeonhole, my head pounding with stress and anxiety, and waved my mail at Matthew before heading toward my rooms.

Inside, I kicked off my shoes, rubbed my temples, and glanced at the message machine. Mercifully, it wasn't blinking. The mail contained nothing but bills and a large brown envelope with my name typed on it. There was no stamp, indicating it came from someone within the university. I slid my finger under the flap and pulled out the contents.

A piece of ordinary paper was clipped to something smooth and shiny. Typed on the paper was a single line of text.

'*Remember?*'

Hands shaking, I pulled off the slip. The paper fluttered to the floor, revealing a familiar glossy photograph. I'd only seen it reproduced in black and white, though, in the newspapers. This was in color, and as bright and vivid as the day it had been taken, in 1983.

My mother's body lay facedown in a chalk circle, her left leg at an impossible angle. Her right arm reached toward my father, who was lying face-up, his head caved in on one side and a gash splitting his torso from throat to groin. Some of his entrails had been pulled out and were lying next to him on the ground.

A sound between a moan and a scream slipped from my mouth. I dropped to the floor, trembling but unable to tear my eyes from the image.

'Diana!' Matthew's voice sounded frantic, but he was too far away for me to care. In the distance someone jiggled the doorknob. Feet clattered up the stairs, a key scraped in the lock.

The door burst open, and I looked up into Matthew's ashen face, along with Fred's concerned one.

'Dr Bishop?' Fred asked.

Matthew moved so quickly that Fred had to know he was a vampire. He crouched in front of me. My teeth chattered with shock.

'If I give you my keys, can you move the car to All Souls for me?' Matthew asked over his shoulder. 'Dr Bishop isn't well, and she shouldn't be alone.'

'No worries, Professor Clairmont. We'll keep it here in the warden's lot,' replied Fred. Matthew threw his keys at the porter, who caught them neatly. Flashing me a worried look, Fred closed the door.

'I'm going to be sick,' I whispered.

Matthew pulled me to my feet and led me to the bathroom. Sinking next to the toilet, I threw up, dropping the picture on the floor to grip the sides of the bowl. Once my stomach was empty, the worst of the shaking subsided, but every few seconds a tremble radiated through me.

I closed the lid and reached up to flush, pushing down on the toilet for leverage. My head spun. Matthew caught me before I hit the bathroom wall.

Suddenly my feet were not on the ground. Matthew's chest was against my right shoulder and his arms underneath my knees. Moments later he laid me gently on my bed and turned the light on, angling the shade away. My wrist was in his cool fingers, and with his touch my pulse began to slow. That made it possible for me to focus on his face. It looked as calm as ever, except that the tiny dark vein in his forehead throbbed slightly every minute or so.

'I'm going to get you something to drink.' He let go of my wrist and stood.

Another wave of panic washed over me. I bolted to my feet, all my instincts telling me to run as far and as fast as possible.

Matthew grabbed me by the shoulders, trying to make eye contact. 'Stop, Diana.'

My stomach had invaded my lungs, pressing out all the air, and I struggled against his grasp, not knowing or caring what he was saying. 'Let me go,' I pleaded, pushing against his chest with both hands.

'Diana, look at me.' There was no ignoring Matthew's voice, or the moonlike pull of his eyes. 'What's wrong?'

'My parents. Gillian told me witches killed my parents.' My voice was high and tight.

Matthew said something in a language I didn't understand. 'When did this happen? Where were they? Did the witch leave a message on your phone? Did she threaten you?' His hold on me strengthened.

'Nigeria. She said the Bishops have always been trouble.'

'I'll go with you. Let me make a few phone calls first.' Matthew took in a deep, shuddering breath. 'I'm so sorry, Diana.'

'Go where?' Nothing was making any sense.

'To Africa.' Matthew sounded confused. 'Someone will have to identify the bodies.'

'My parents were killed when I was seven.'

His eyes widened with shock.

'Even though it happened so long ago, they're all the witches want to talk about these days – Gillian, Peter Knox.' Shivering as the panic escalated, I felt a scream rise up in my throat. Matthew pressed me to him before it could erupt, holding me so tightly that the outlines of his muscles and bones were sharp against my skin. The scream turned into a sob. 'Bad things happen to witches who keep secrets. Gillian said so.'

'No matter what she said, I will not let Knox or any other witch harm you. I've got you now.' Matthew's voice was fierce, and he bowed his head and rested his cheek on my hair while I cried. 'Oh, Diana. Why didn't you tell me?'

Somewhere in the center of my soul, a rusty chain began to unwind. It freed itself, link by link, from where it had rested unobserved, waiting for him. My hands, which had been balled up and pressed against his chest, unfurled with it. The chain continued to drop, to an unfathomable depth where there was nothing but darkness and Matthew. At last it snapped to its full length, anchoring me to a vampire. Despite the manuscript, despite the fact that my hands contained enough voltage to run a microwave, and despite the photograph, as long as I was connected to him, I was safe.

When my sobs quieted, Matthew drew away. 'I'm going to get

you some water, and then you're going to rest.' His tone did not invite discussion, and he was back in a matter of seconds carrying a glass of water and two tiny pills.

'Take these,' he said, handing them to me along with the water.

'What are they?'

'A sedative.' His stern look encouraged me to pop both pills into my mouth, immediately, along with a gulp of water. 'I've been carrying some since you told me you suffered from panic attacks.'

'I hate taking tranquilizers.'

'You've had a shock, and you've got too much adrenaline in your system. You need to rest.' Matthew dragged the duvet around me until I was encased in a lumpy cocoon. He sat on the bed, and his shoes thumped against the floor before he stretched out, his back propped up against the pillows. When he gathered my duvet-wrapped body against him, I sighed. Matthew reached across with his left arm and held me securely. My body, for all its wrappings, fit against him perfectly.

The drug worked its way through my bloodstream. As I was drifting off to sleep, Matthew's phone shook in his pocket, startling me into wakefulness.

'It's nothing, probably Marcus,' he said, brushing his lips against my forehead. My heartbeat settled. 'Try to rest. You aren't alone anymore.'

I could still feel the chain that anchored me to Matthew, witch to vampire.

With the links of that chain tight and shining, I slept.

CHAPTER 16

The sky was dark outside Diana's windows before Matthew could leave her side. Restless at first, she had at last fallen into deep sleep. He noted the subtle changes of scent as her shock subsided, a cold fierceness sweeping over him every time he thought of Peter Knox and Gillian Chamberlain.

Matthew couldn't remember when he'd felt so protective of another being. He felt other emotions as well, that he was reluctant to acknowledge or name.

She's a witch, he reminded himself as he watched her sleep. *She's not for you.*

The more he said it, the less it seemed to matter.

At last he gently extracted himself and crept from the room, leaving the door open a crack in case she stirred.

Alone in the hall, the vampire let surface the cold anger that had been seething inside for hours. The intensity of it almost choked him. He drew the leather cord from the neck of his sweater and touched the worn, smooth surfaces of Lazarus's silver coffin. The sound of Diana's breathing was all that kept him from leaping through the night to hunt down two witches.

The clocks of Oxford struck eight, their familiar, weary tolling reminding Matthew of the call he'd missed. He pulled his phone out of his pocket and checked the messages, quickly thumbing through the automatic notifications from the security systems at the labs and the Old Lodge. There were several messages from Marcus.

Matthew frowned and punched the number to retrieve them. Marcus was not prone to alarm. What could be so urgent?

'*Matthew.*' The familiar voice held none of its usual playful charm. '*I have Diana's DNA test results. They're . . . surprising. Call me.*'

The recorded voice was still speaking when the vampire's finger punched another single key on the phone. He raked his hair with his free hand while he waited for Marcus to pick up. It took only one ring.

'Matthew.' There was no warmth in Marcus's response, only relief. It had been hours since he'd left the messages. Marcus had even checked Matthew's favorite Oxford haunt, the Pitt Rivers Museum, where the vampire could often be found dividing his attention between the skeleton of an iguanodon and a likeness of Darwin. Miriam had finally banished him from the lab, irritated by his constant questions about where Matthew might be and with whom.

'He's with her, of course,' Miriam had said in the late afternoon, her voice full of disapproval. 'Where else? And if you're not going to do any work, go home and wait for his call there. You're in my way.'

'What did the tests show?' Matthew's voice was low, but his rage was audible.

'What's happened?' Marcus asked quickly.

A picture lying faceup on the floor of the bathroom caught Matthew's attention. Diana had been clutching it that afternoon. His eyes narrowed to slits as he took in the image. 'Where are you?' he rasped.

'Home,' Marcus answered uneasily.

Matthew picked the photo off the floor and traced its scent to where a piece of paper had slid half under the couch. He read the single word of the message, took a sharp breath. 'Bring the reports and my passport to New College. Diana's rooms are in the garden quadrangle at the top of staircase seven.'

Twenty minutes later Matthew opened the door, his hair standing on end and a ferocious look on his face. The younger vampire had to school himself not to take a step backward.

Marcus held out a manila folder with a maroon passport folded around it, every move deliberate, and patiently waited. He wasn't about to enter the witch's rooms without Matthew's permission, not when the vampire was in this state.

Permission was slow in coming, but at last Matthew took the folder and stepped aside to let Marcus enter.

While Matthew scrutinized Diana's test results, Marcus studied him. His keen nose took in the old wood and well-worn textiles, along with the smell of the witch's fear and the vampire's barely controlled emotions. His own hackles rose at the volatile combination, and a reflexive growl caught in his throat.

Over the years Marcus had come to appreciate Matthew's finer qualities – his compassion, his conscience, his patience with those he loved. He also knew his faults, anger chief among them. Typically, Matthew's rage was so destructive that once the poison was out of his system, he disappeared for months or even years to come to terms with what he'd done.

And Marcus had never seen his father so coldly furious as he was now.

Matthew Clairmont had entered Marcus's life in 1777 and changed it – forever. He had appeared in the Bennett farmhouse at the side of an improvised sling that carried the wounded Marquis de Lafayette from the killing fields at the Battle of Brandywine. Matthew towered over the other men, barking orders at everyone regardless of rank.

No one disputed his commands – not even Lafayette, who joked with his friend despite his injuries. The marquis's good humor couldn't stave off a tongue-lashing from Matthew, however. When Lafayette protested that he could manage while soldiers with more serious injuries were tended to, Clairmont released a volley of French so laced with expletives and ultimatums that his own men looked at him with awe and the marquis subsided into silence.

Marcus had listened, wide-eyed, when the French soldier railed at the head of the army's medical corps, the esteemed Dr Shippen, rejecting his treatment plan as 'barbaric.' Clairmont demanded that the doctor's second in command, John Cochran, treat Lafayette instead. Two days later Clairmont and Shippen could be heard arguing the finer points of anatomy and physiology in fluent Latin – to the delight of the medical staff and General Washington.

Matthew had killed more than his share of British soldiers before the Continental Army was defeated at Brandywine. Men brought into the hospital spun impossible tales of his fearlessness in battle. Some claimed he walked straight into enemy lines, unfazed by bullets and bayonets. When the guns stopped, Clairmont insisted that Marcus remain with the marquis as his nurse.

In the autumn, once Lafayette was able to ride again, the two of them disappeared into the forests of Pennsylvania and New York. They returned with an army of Oneida warriors. The Oneida called Lafayette 'Kayewla' for his skill with the horse. Matthew they referred to as 'atlutanu'n,' the warrior chief, because of his ability to lead men into battle.

Matthew remained with the army long after Lafayette returned to France. Marcus continued to serve, too, as a lowly surgeon's assistant. Day after day he tried to stanch the wounds of soldiers injured by musket, cannon, and sword. Clairmont always sought him out whenever one of his own men was injured. Marcus, he said, had a gift for healing.

Shortly after the Continental Army arrived in Yorktown in 1781, Marcus caught a fever. His gift for healing meant nothing then. He lay cold and shivering, tended to only when someone had the time. After four days of suffering, Marcus knew he was dying. When Clairmont came to visit some of his own stricken men, accompanied once again by Lafayette, he saw Marcus on a broken cot in the corner and smelled the scent of death.

The French officer sat at the young man's side as night turned toward day and shared his story. Marcus thought he was dreaming. A man who drank blood and found it impossible to die? After hearing that, Marcus became convinced that he was already dead and being tormented by one of the devils his father had warned him would prey on his sinful nature.

The vampire explained that Marcus could survive the fever, but there would be a price. First he would have to be reborn. Then he would have to hunt, and kill, and drink blood – even human blood. For a time his need for it would make working among the injured and sick impossible. Matthew promised to send Marcus to university while he got used to his new life.

Sometime before dawn, when the pain became excruciating, Marcus decided he wanted to live more than he feared the new life the vampire had laid out for him. Matthew carried him, limp and burning with fever, out of the hospital and into the woods, where the Oneida waited to lead them into the mountains. Matthew drained him of his blood in a remote hollow, where no one could hear his screams. Even now Marcus remembered the powerful thirst that had followed. He'd been mad with it, desperate to swallow anything cold and liquid.

Finally Matthew had slashed his own wrist with his teeth and let Marcus drink. The vampire's powerful blood brought him back to startling life.

The Oneida waited impassively at the mouth of the cave and prevented him from wreaking havoc on the nearby farms when his hunger for blood surfaced. They had recognized what Matthew was the moment he appeared in their village. He was like Dagwanoenyent, the witch who lived in the whirlwind and could not die. Why the gods had decided to give the French warrior these gifts was a mystery to the Oneida, but the gods were known for their puzzling decisions. All they could do was make sure their children knew Dagwanoenyent's legend, carefully instructing them how to kill such a creature by burning him, grinding his bones into powder, and dispersing it to the four winds so that he could not be reborn.

Thwarted, Marcus had behaved like the child he was, howling with frustration and shaking with need. When Matthew hunted down a deer to feed the young man who had been reborn as his son, Marcus quickly sucked it dry. It sated his hunger but didn't dull the thrumming in his veins as Matthew's ancient blood suffused his body.

After a week of bringing fresh kills back to their den, Matthew decided Marcus was ready to hunt for himself. Father and son tracked deer and bear through deep forests and along moonlit mountain ridges. Matthew trained him to smell the air, to watch in the shadows for the smallest hint of movement, and to feel changes in the wind that would bring fresh scents their way. And he taught the healer how to kill.

In those early days, Marcus wanted richer blood. He needed it, too, to quench his deep thirst and feed his ravenous body. But Matthew waited until Marcus could track a deer quickly, bring it down, and drain its blood without making a mess before he let him hunt humans. Women were off-limits. Too confusing for newly reborn vampires, Matthew explained, as the lines between sex and death, courtship and hunting, were too finely drawn.

First father and son fed on sick British soldiers. Some begged Marcus to spare their life, and Matthew taught him how to feed on warmbloods without killing them. Then they hunted criminals, who cried for mercy and didn't deserve it. In every case Matthew made Marcus explain why he'd picked a particular man as his prey. Marcus's ethics developed, in the halting, deliberate way that they must when a vampire comes to terms with what he needs to do in order to survive.

Matthew was widely known for his finely developed sense of right and wrong. All his mistakes in judgment could be traced back to decisions made in anger. Marcus had been told that his father was not as prone to that dangerous emotion as he'd been in the past. Perhaps so, but tonight in Oxford, Matthew's face wore the same murderous expression it had at Brandywine – and there was no battlefield to vent his rage.

'You've made a mistake.' Matthew's eyes were wild when he finished poring over the witch's DNA tests.

Marcus shook his head. 'I analyzed her blood twice. Miriam confirmed my findings with the DNA from the swab. I admit the results are surprising.'

Matthew drew in a shaky breath. 'They're preposterous.'

'Diana possesses nearly every genetic marker we've ever seen in a witch.' His mouth tightened into a grim line as he flipped to the final pages. 'But these sequences have us concerned.'

Matthew leafed quickly through the data. There were more than two dozen sequences of DNA, some short and some long, with Miriam's tiny red question marks next to them.

'Christ,' he said, tossing them back at his son. 'We already have enough to worry about. That bastard Peter Knox has threatened her. He wants the manuscript. Diana tried to recall it, but Ashmole 782 has gone back into the library and won't come out again. Happily, Knox is convinced – for now – that she first obtained it by deliberately breaking its spell.'

'She didn't?'

'No. Diana doesn't have the knowledge or control to do anything that intricate. Her power is completely undisciplined. She put a hole in my rug.' Matthew looked sour, and his son struggled not to smile. His father did love his antiques.

'Then we'll keep Knox away and give Diana a chance to come to terms with her abilities. That doesn't sound too difficult.'

'Knox is not my only concern. Diana received these in the mail today.' Matthew picked up the photograph and its accompanying slip of paper and handed them to his son. When he continued, his voice had a dangerous, flat tone. 'Her parents. I remember hearing about two American witches killed in Nigeria, but it was so long ago. I never connected them to Diana.'

'Holy God,' Marcus said softly. Staring at the picture, he tried to imagine what it would be like to receive a photo of his own father ripped to pieces and tossed into the dirt to die.

'There's more. From what I can piece together, Diana has long believed that her parents were killed by humans. That's the chief reason she's tried to keep magic from her life.'

'That won't work, will it?' muttered Marcus, thinking of the witch's DNA.

'No,' Matthew agreed, grim-faced. 'While I was in Scotland, another American witch, Gillian Chamberlain, informed her that it wasn't humans at all – but fellow witches – who murdered her parents.'

'Did they?'

'I'm not sure. But there's clearly more to this situation than a witch's discovery of Ashmole 782.' Matthew's tone turned deadly. 'I intend to find out what it is.'

Something silver glinted against his father's dusky sweater. *He's wearing Lazarus's coffin*, Marcus realized.

No one in the family talked openly about Eleanor St Leger or the events surrounding her death, for fear of driving Matthew into one of his rages. Marcus understood that his father hadn't wanted to leave Paris in 1140, where he was happily studying philosophy. But when the head of the family, Matthew's own father, Philippe, called him back to Jerusalem to help resolve the conflicts that continued to plague the Holy Land long after the conclusion of Urban II's Crusade, Matthew obeyed without question. He had met Eleanor, befriended her sprawling English family, and fallen resolutely in love.

But the St Legers and the de Clermonts were often on opposite sides in the disputes, and Matthew's older brothers – Hugh, Godfrey, and Baldwin – urged him to put the woman aside, leaving a clear path for them to destroy her family. Matthew refused. One day a squabble between Baldwin and Matthew over some petty political crisis involving the St Legers spiraled out of control. Before Philippe could be found and made to stop it, Eleanor intervened. By the time Matthew and Baldwin came to their senses, she'd lost too much blood to recover.

Marcus still didn't understand why Matthew had let Eleanor die if he'd loved her so much.

Now Matthew wore his pilgrim's badge only when he was afraid he was going to kill someone or when he was thinking of Eleanor St Leger – or both.

'That picture is a threat – and not an idle one. Hamish thought the Bishop name would make the witches more cautious, but I fear the opposite is true. No matter how great her innate talents might be, Diana can't protect herself, and she's too damn self-reliant to ask for help. I need you to stay with her for a few hours.' Matthew dragged his eyes from the picture of Rebecca Bishop and Stephen Proctor. 'I'm going to find Gillian Chamberlain.'

'You can't be sure it was Gillian who delivered that picture,' Marcus pointed out. 'There are two different scents on it.'

'The other belongs to Peter Knox.'

'But Peter Knox is a member of the Congregation!' Marcus knew that a nine-member council of daemons, witches, and vampires had been formed during the Crusades – three representatives from each species. The Congregation's job was to ensure every creature's safety by seeing to it that no one caught the attention of humans. 'If you make a move in his direction, it will be seen as a challenge to their authority. The whole family will be implicated. You aren't seriously considering endangering us just to avenge a witch?'

'You aren't questioning my loyalty, are you?' Matthew purred.

'No, I'm questioning your judgment,' Marcus said hotly, facing his father without fear. 'This ridiculous romance is bad enough. The Congregation already has one reason to take steps against you. Don't give them another.'

During Marcus's first visit to France, his vampire grandmother had explained that he was now bound by a covenant that prohibited close relationships between different orders of creatures, as well as any meddling in human religion and politics. All other interactions with humans – including affairs of the heart – were to be avoided but were permitted as long as they didn't lead to trouble. Marcus preferred spending time with vampires and always had, so the covenant's terms had mattered little to him – until now.

'Nobody cares anymore,' Matthew said defensively, his gray eyes drifting in the direction of Diana's bedroom door.

'My God, she doesn't understand about the covenant,' Marcus said contemptuously, 'and you have no intention of telling her. You damn well know you can't keep this secret from her indefinitely.'

'The Congregation isn't going to enforce a promise made nearly a thousand years ago in a very different world.' Matthew's eyes were now fixed on an antique print of the goddess Diana aiming her bow at a hunter fleeing through the forest. He remembered a passage from a book written long ago by a friend – '*for they are no longer hunters, but the hunted*' – and shivered.

'Think before you do this, Matthew.'

'I've made my decision.' He avoided his son's eyes. 'Will you check on her while I'm gone, make sure she's all right?'

Marcus nodded, unable to deny the raw appeal in his father's voice.

After the door closed behind his father, Marcus went to Diana. He lifted one of her eyelids, then the other, and picked up her wrist. He sniffed, noting the fear and shock that surrounded her. He also detected the drug that was still circulating through her veins. *Good*, he thought. At least his father had had the presence of mind to give her a sedative.

Marcus continued to probe Diana's condition, looking minutely at her skin and listening to the sound of her breath. When he was finished, he stood quietly at the witch's bedside, watching her dream. Her forehead was creased into a frown, as if she were arguing with someone.

After his examination Marcus knew two things. First, Diana would be fine. She'd had a serious shock and needed rest, but no permanent damage had been done. Second, his father's scent was all over her. He'd done it deliberately, to mark Diana so that every vampire would know to whom she belonged. That meant the situation had gone further than Marcus had believed possible. It was going to be difficult for his father to detach himself from this witch. And he would have to, if the stories that Marcus's grandmother had told him were true.

It was after midnight when Matthew reappeared. He looked even angrier than when he'd left, but he was spotless and impeccable as always. He ran his fingers through his hair and strode straight into Diana's room without a word to his son.

Marcus knew better than to question Matthew then. After he emerged from the witch's room, Marcus asked only, 'Will you discuss the DNA findings with Diana?'

'No,' Matthew said shortly, without a hint of guilt over keeping information of this magnitude from her. 'Nor am I going to share what the witches of the Congregation might do to her. She's been through enough.'

'Diana Bishop is less fragile than you think. You have no right to keep that information to yourself, if you are going to continue to spend time with her.' Marcus knew that a vampire's life was measured not in hours or years but in secrets revealed and kept. Vampires guarded their personal relationships, the names they'd adopted, and the details of the many lives they'd led. Nonetheless, his father kept more secrets than most, and his urge to hide things from his own family was intensely aggravating.

'Stay out of this, Marcus,' his father snarled. 'It's not your business.'

Marcus swore. 'Your damned secrets are going to be the family's undoing.'

Matthew had his son by the scruff of the neck before he'd finished speaking. 'My secrets have kept this family safe for many centuries, my son. Where would you be today if not for my secrets?'

'Food for worms in an unmarked Yorktown grave, I expect,' Marcus said breathlessly, his vocal cords constricted.

Over the years Marcus had tried with little success to uncover some of his father's secrets. He'd never been able to discover who tipped Matthew off that Marcus was raising hell in New Orleans after Jefferson made the Louisiana Purchase, for example. There he'd created a vampire family as boisterous and charming as himself from the city's youngest, least responsible citizens. Marcus's brood – which included an alarming number of gamblers and ne'er-do-wells – risked human discovery every time they went out after dark. The witches of New Orleans, Marcus remembered, had made it clear they wanted them to leave town.

Then Matthew had shown up, uninvited and unannounced, with a gorgeous mixed-race vampire: Juliette Durand. Matthew and Juliette had waged a campaign to bring Marcus's family to heel. Within days they'd formed an unholy alliance with a foppish young French vampire in the Garden District who had implausibly golden hair and a streak of ruthlessness as wide as the Mississippi. That was when the real trouble began.

By the end of the first fortnight, Marcus's new family was

considerably, and mysteriously, smaller. As the number of deaths and disappearances mounted, Matthew threw up his hands and murmured about the dangers of New Orleans. Juliette, whom Marcus had grown to detest in the few days he'd known her, smiled secretively and cooed encouraging words in his father's ears. She was the most manipulative creature Marcus had ever met, and he was thrilled when she and his father parted ways.

Under pressure from his remaining children, Marcus made devout assurances to behave if only Matthew and Juliette would leave.

Matthew agreed, after setting out what was expected of members of the de Clermont family in exacting detail. 'If you are determined to make me a grandfather,' his father instructed during an extremely unpleasant interview held in the presence of several of the city's oldest and most powerful vampires, 'take more care.' The memory still made Marcus blanch.

Who or what gave Matthew and Juliette the authority to act as they did remained a mystery. His father's strength, Juliette's cunning, and the luster of the de Clermont name may have helped them gain the support of the vampires. But there was more to it than that. Every creature in New Orleans – even the witches – had treated his father like royalty.

Marcus wondered if his father had been a member of the Congregation, all those years ago. It would explain a great deal.

Matthew's voice sent his son's memories flying. 'Diana may be brave, Marcus, but she doesn't need to know everything now.' He released Marcus and stepped away.

'Does she know about our family, then? Your other children?' *Does she know about your father?* Marcus didn't say the last aloud.

Matthew knew what he was thinking anyway. 'I don't tell other vampires' tales.'

'You're making a mistake,' said Marcus, shaking his head. 'Diana won't thank you for keeping things from her.'

'So you and Hamish say. When she's ready, I'll tell her everything – but not before.' His father's voice was firm. 'My only concern right now is getting Diana out of Oxford.'

'Will you drop her off in Scotland? Surely she'll be beyond anyone's reach there.' Marcus thought at once of Hamish's remote estate. 'Or will you leave her at Woodstock before you go?'

'Before I go where?' Matthew's face was puzzled.

'You had me bring your passport.' Now it was Marcus who was puzzled. That's what his father did – he got angry and went away by himself until he was under better control.

'I have no intention of leaving Diana,' Matthew said icily. 'I'm taking her to Sept-Tours.'

'You can't possibly put her under the same roof as Ysabeau!' Marcus's shocked voice rang in the small room.

'It's my home, too,' Matthew said, jaw set in a stubborn line.

'Your mother openly boasts about the witches she's killed and blames every witch she meets for what happened to Louisa and your father.'

Matthew's face crumpled, and Marcus at last understood. The photograph had reminded Matthew of Philippe's death and Ysabeau's battle with madness in the years that followed.

Matthew pressed the palms of his hands against his temples, as if desperately trying to shape a better plan from the outside in. 'Diana had nothing to do with either tragedy. Ysabeau will understand.'

'She won't – you know she won't,' Marcus said obstinately. He loved his grandmother and didn't want her hurt. And if Matthew – her favorite – brought a witch home, it was going to hurt her. Badly.

'There's nowhere as safe as Sept-Tours. The witches will think twice before tangling with Ysabeau – especially at her own home.'

'For God's sake, don't leave the two of them alone together.'

'I won't,' Matthew promised. 'I'll need you and Miriam to move into the gatehouse in hopes that will convince everyone Diana is there. They'll figure out the truth eventually, but it may win us a few days. My keys are with the porter. Come back in a few hours, when we've gone. Take the duvet from her bed – it will have her scent on it – and drive to Woodstock. Stay there until you hear from me.'

'Can you protect yourself and that witch at the same time?' Marcus asked quietly.

'I can handle it,' Matthew said with certainty.

Marcus nodded, and the two vampires gripped forearms, exchanging a meaningful look. Anything they needed to say to each other at moments like these had long since been said.

When Matthew was alone again, he sank into the sofa and cradled his head in his hands. Marcus's vehement opposition had shaken him.

He looked up and stared again at the print of the goddess of the hunt stalking her prey. Another line from the same old poem came into his mind. ' "*I saw her coming from the forest,*" ' he whispered, ' "*Huntress of myself, beloved Diana.*" '

In the bedroom, too far away for a warmblood to have heard, Diana stirred and cried out. Matthew sped to her side and gathered her into his arms. The protectiveness returned, and with it a renewed sense of purpose.

'I'm here,' he murmured against the rainbow strands of her hair. He looked down at Diana's sleeping face, her mouth puckered and a fierce frown between her eyes. It was a face he'd studied for hours and knew well, but its contradictions still fascinated him. 'Have you bewitched me?' he wondered aloud.

After tonight Matthew knew his need for her was greater than anything else. Neither his family nor his next taste of blood mattered as much as knowing that she was safe and within arm's reach. If that was what it meant to be bewitched, he was a lost man.

His arms tightened, holding Diana in sleep as he would not allow himself to do when she was awake. She sighed, nestling closer.

Were he not a vampire he wouldn't have caught her faint, murmured words as she clutched both his ampulla and the fabric of his sweater, her fist resting firmly against his heart.

'You're not lost. I found you.'

Matthew wondered fleetingly if he'd imagined it but knew that he hadn't.

She could hear his thoughts.

Not all the time, not when she was conscious – not yet. But it was only a matter of time before Diana knew everything there was to know about him. She would know his secrets, the dark and terrible things he wasn't brave enough to face.

She answered with another faint murmur. 'I'm brave enough for both of us.'

Matthew bent his head toward hers. 'You'll have to be.'

CHAPTER 17

There was a powerful taste of cloves in my mouth, and I'd been mummified in my own duvet. When I stirred in my wrappings, the bed's old springs gave slightly.

'Shh.' Matthew's lips were at my ear, and his body formed a shell against my back. We lay there like spoons in a drawer, tight against each other.

'What time is it?' My voice was hoarse.

Matthew pulled away slightly and looked at his watch. 'It's after one.'

'How long have I been asleep?'

'Since around six last night.'

Last night.

My mind shattered into words and images: the alchemical manuscript, Peter Knox's threat, my fingers turning blue with electricity, the photograph of my parents, my mother's hand frozen in a never-ending reach.

'You gave me drugs.' I pushed against the duvet, trying to work my hands free. 'I don't like taking drugs, Matthew.'

'Next time you go into shock, I'll let you suffer needlessly.' He gave a single twitch to the bed covering that was more effective than all my previous wrestling with it.

Matthew's sharp tone shook the shards of memory, and new images rose to the surface. Gillian Chamberlain's twisted face warned me about keeping secrets, and the piece of paper commanded me to remember. For a few moments, I was seven again, trying to understand how my bright, vital parents could be gone from my life.

In my rooms I reached toward Matthew, while in my mind's eye my mother's hand reached for my father across a chalk-inscribed circle. The lingering childhood desolation of their death collided with a new, adult empathy for my mother's desperate attempt to touch my father. Abruptly pulling from Matthew's arms, I lifted my knees to my chest in a tight, protective ball.

Matthew wanted to help – I could see that – but he was unsure of me, and the shadow of my own conflicted emotions fell over his face.

Knox's voice sounded again in my mind, full of poison. *Remember who you are.*

'*Remember?*' the note asked.

Without warning, I turned back toward the vampire, closing the distance between me and him in a rush. My parents were gone, but Matthew was here. Tucking my head under his chin, I listened for several minutes for the next pump of blood through his system. The leisurely rhythms of his vampire heart soon put me to sleep.

My own heart was pounding when I awoke again in the dark, kicking at the loosened duvet and swimming to a seated position. Behind me, Matthew turned on the lamp, its shade still angled away from the bed.

'What is it?' he asked.

'The magic found me. The witches did, too. I'll be killed for my magic, like my parents were killed.' The words rushed from my mouth, panic speeding their passage, and I stumbled to my feet.

'No.' Matthew rose and stood between me and the door. 'We're going to face this, Diana, whatever it is. Otherwise you'll never stop running.'

Part of me knew that what he said was true. The rest wanted to flee into the darkness. But how could I, with a vampire standing in the way?

The air began to stir around me as if trying to drive off the feeling of being trapped. Chilly wisps edged up the legs of my trousers. The air crept up my body, lifting the hair around my face in a gentle breeze. Matthew swore and stepped toward me, his arm outstretched.

The breeze increased into gusts of wind that ruffled the bedclothes and the curtains.

'It's all right.' His voice was pitched deliberately to be heard above the whirlwind and to calm me at the same time.

But it wasn't enough.

The force of the wind kept rising, and with it my arms rose, too, shaping the air into a column that enclosed me as protectively as the duvet. On the other side of the disturbance, Matthew stood, one hand still extended, eyes fixed on mine. When I opened my mouth to warn him to stay away, nothing came out but frigid air.

'It's all right,' he said again, not breaking his gaze. 'I won't move.'

I hadn't realized that was the problem until he said the words.

'I promise,' he said firmly.

The wind faltered. The cyclone surrounding me became a whirlwind, then a breeze, then disappeared entirely. I gasped and dropped to my knees.

'What is happening to me?' Every day I ran and rowed and did yoga, and my body did what I told it to. Now it was doing unimaginable things. I looked down to make sure my hands weren't sparkling with electricity and my feet weren't still being buffeted by winds.

'That was a witchwind,' Matthew explained, not moving. 'Do you know what that is?'

I'd heard of a witch in Albany who could summon storms, but no one had ever called it a 'witchwind.'

'Not really,' I confessed, still sneaking glances at my hands and feet.

'Some witches have inherited the ability to control the element of air. You're one of them,' he said.

'That wasn't control.'

'It was your first time.' Matthew was matter-of-fact. He gestured around the small bedroom: the intact curtains and sheets, all the clothing strewn on the chest of drawers and floor exactly where they'd been left that morning. 'We're both still standing, and the

room doesn't look like a tornado went through it. That's control —
for now.'

'But I didn't ask for it. Do these things just happen to witches
— electrical fires and winds they didn't summon?' I pushed the hair
out of my eyes and swayed, exhausted. Too much had happened in
the past twenty-four hours. Matthew's body inclined toward me as if
to catch me should I fall.

'Witchwinds and blue fingers are rare these days. There's magic
inside you, Diana, and it wants to get out, whether you ask for it or
not.'

'I felt trapped.'

'I shouldn't have cornered you last night.' Matthew looked
ashamed. 'Sometimes I don't know what to do with you. You're like
a perpetual-motion machine. All I wanted was for you to stand still
for a moment and listen.'

It must be even harder to cope with my incessant need to move if
you were a vampire who seldom needed to breathe. Once again the
space between Matthew and me was suddenly too large. I started to
rise.

'Am I forgiven?' he asked sincerely. I nodded. 'May I?' he asked,
gesturing at his feet. I nodded again.

He took three fast steps in the time it took me to stand up. My
body pitched into him just as it had in the Bodleian the first night I
saw him, standing aristocratic and serene in Duke Humfrey's Reading
Room. This time, however, I didn't pull away so quickly. Instead I
rested against him willingly, his skin soothingly cool rather than
frightening and cold.

We stood silent for a few moments, holding each other. My heart
quieted, and his arms remained loose, although his shuddering breath
suggested that this was not easy.

'I'm sorry, too.' My body softened into him, his sweater scratchy
on my cheek. 'I'll try to keep my energy under control.'

'There's nothing to be sorry about. And you shouldn't try so
hard to be something you're not. Would you drink tea if I made you
some?' he asked, his lips moving against the top of my head.

Outside, the night was unalleviated by any hint of sunrise. 'What time is it now?'

Matthew's hand swiveled between my shoulder blades so that he could see the face of his watch. 'Just after three.'

I groaned. 'I'm so tired, but tea sounds wonderful.'

'I'll make it, then.' He gently loosened my arms from around his waist. 'Be right back.'

Not wanting to let him out of my sight, I drifted along. He rummaged through the tins and bags of available teas.

'I told you I liked tea,' I said apologetically as he found yet another brown bag in the cupboard, tucked behind a coffee press I seldom used.

'Do you have a preference?' He gestured at the crowded shelf.

'The one in the black bag with the gold label, please.' Green tea seemed the most soothing option.

He busied himself with the kettle and pot. He poured hot water over the fragrant leaves and thrust a chipped old mug in my direction once it was ready. The aromas of green tea, vanilla, and citrus were so very different from Matthew, but comforting nevertheless.

He made himself a mug, too, his nostrils flaring in appreciation. 'That actually doesn't smell too bad,' he acknowledged, taking a small sip. It was the only time I'd seen him drink anything other than wine.

'Where shall we sit?' I asked, cradling the warm mug in my hands.

Matthew inclined his head toward the living room. 'In there. We need to talk.'

He sat in one corner of the comfortable old sofa, and I arranged myself opposite. The steam from the tea rose around my face, a gentle reminder of the witchwind.

'I need to understand why Knox thinks you've broken the spell on Ashmole 782,' Matthew said when we were settled.

I replayed the conversation in the warden's rooms. 'He said that spells become volatile around the anniversaries of their casting. Other witches – ones who know witchcraft – have tried to break it, and they've failed. He figured I was just in the right place at the right time.'

'A talented witch bound Ashmole 782, and I suspect this spell is nearly impossible to break. No one who's tried to get the manuscript before met its conditions, no matter how much witchcraft they knew or what time of year they tried.' He stared into the depths of his tea. 'You did. The question is how, and why.'

'The idea that I could fulfill the conditions of a spell cast before I was born is harder to believe than that it was just an anniversary aberration. And if I fulfilled the conditions once, why not again?' Matthew opened his mouth, and I shook my head. 'No, it's not because of you.'

'Knox knows witchcraft, and spells are complicated. I suppose it's possible that time pulls them out of shape every now and again.' He looked unconvinced.

'I wish I could see the pattern in all this.' My white table rose into view, with pieces of the puzzle laid on it. Though I moved a few pieces around – Knox, the manuscript, my parents – they refused to form an image. Matthew's voice broke through my reveries.

'Diana?'

'Hmm?'

'What are you doing?'

'Nothing,' I said, too quickly.

'You're using magic,' he said, putting his tea down. 'I can smell it. See it, too. You're shimmering.'

'It's what I do when I can't solve a puzzle – like now.' My head was bowed to hide how difficult it was to talk about this. 'I see a white table and imagine all the different pieces. They have shapes and colors, and they move around until they form a pattern. When the pattern forms, they stop moving to show I'm on the right track.'

Matthew waited a long time before he responded. 'How often do you play this game?'

'All the time,' I said reluctantly. 'While you were in Scotland, I realized that it was yet more magic, like knowing who's looking at me without turning my head.'

'There is a pattern, you know,' he said. 'You use your magic when you're not thinking.'

'What do you mean?' The puzzle pieces started dancing on the white table.

'When you're moving, you don't think – not with the rational part of your mind, at least. You're somewhere else entirely when you row, or run, or do yoga. Without your mind keeping your gifts in check, out they come.'

'But I was thinking before,' I said, 'and the witchwind came anyway.'

'Ah, but then you were feeling a powerful emotion,' he explained, leaning forward and resting his elbows on his knees. 'That always keeps the intellect at bay. It's the same thing that happened when your fingers turned blue with Miriam and then with me. This white table of yours is an exception to the general rule.'

'Moods and movement are enough to trigger these forces? Who would want to be a witch if something so simple can make all hell break loose?'

'A great many people, I would imagine.' Matthew glanced away. 'I want to ask you to do something for me,' he said. The sofa creaked as he faced me once more. 'And I want you to think about it before you answer. Will you do that?'

'Of course.' I nodded.

'I want to take you home.'

'I'm not going back to America.' It had taken me five seconds to do exactly what he'd asked me not to.

Matthew shook his head. 'Not your home. My home. You need to get out of Oxford.'

'I already told you I'd go to Woodstock.'

'The Old Lodge is my *house*, Diana,' Matthew explained patiently. 'I want to take you to my *home* – to France.'

'France?' I pushed the hair out of my face to get a clearer view of him.

'The witches are intent on getting Ashmole 782 and keeping it from the other creatures. Their theory that you broke the spell and the prominence of your family are all that's kept them at arm's length. When Knox and the others find out that you used no witchcraft to obtain the manuscript – that the spell was set to open for you – they'll want to know how and why.'

My eyes closed against the sudden, sharp image of my father and mother. 'And they won't ask nicely.'

'Probably not.' Matthew took a deep breath, and the vein in his forehead throbbed. 'I saw the photo, Diana. I want you away from Peter Knox and the library. I want you under *my* roof for a while.'

'Gillian said it was witches.' When my eyes met his, I was struck by how tiny the pupils were. Usually they were black and enormous, but something was different about Matthew tonight. His skin was less ghostly, and there was a touch more color in his normally pale lips. 'Was she right?'

'I can't know for sure, Diana. The Nigerian Hausa believe that the source of a witch's power is contained in stones in the stomach. Someone went looking for them in your father,' he said regretfully. 'Another witch is the most likely scenario.'

There was a soft click, and the light on the answering machine began to blink. I groaned.

'That's the fifth time your aunts have called,' Matthew observed.

No matter how low the volume, the vampire was going to be able to hear the message. I walked to the table near him and picked up the receiver.

'I'm here, I'm here,' I began, talking over my aunt's agitated voice.

'We thought you were dead,' Sarah said. The realization that she and I were the last remaining Bishops struck me forcefully. I could picture her sitting in the kitchen, phone to her ear and hair wild around her face. She was getting older, and despite her feistiness, the fact that I was far away and in danger had rocked her.

'I'm not dead. I'm in my rooms, and Matthew is with me.' I smiled at him weakly. He didn't smile back.

'What's going on?' Em asked from another extension. After my parents died, Em's hair had turned silver in the space of a few months.

At the time she was still a young woman – not yet thirty – but Em had always seemed more fragile after that, as if she might blow away in the next puff of wind. Like my aunt, she was clearly upset at what her sixth sense told her was happening in Oxford.

'I tried to recall the manuscript, that's all,' I said lightly, making an effort not to worry them further. Matthew stared at me disapprovingly, and I turned away. It didn't help. His glacial eyes bored into my shoulder instead. 'But this time it didn't come up from the stacks.'

'You think we're calling because of that *book*?' demanded Sarah.

Long, cold fingers grasped the phone and drew it away from my ear.

'Ms Bishop, this is Matthew Clairmont,' he said crisply. When I reached to take the receiver from him, Matthew gripped my wrist and shook his head, once, in warning. 'Diana's been threatened. By other witches. One of them is Peter Knox.'

I didn't need to be a vampire to hear the outburst on the other end of the line. He dropped my wrist and handed me the phone.

'Peter Knox!' Sarah cried. Matthew's eyes closed as if the sound hurt his eardrums. 'How long has he been hanging around?'

'Since the beginning,' I said, my voice wavering. 'He was the brown wizard who tried to push his way into my head.'

'You didn't let him get very far, did you?' Sarah sounded frightened.

'I did what I could, Sarah. I don't exactly know what I'm doing, magic-wise.'

Em intervened. 'Honey, a lot of us have problems with Peter Knox. More important, your father didn't trust him – not at all.'

'My *father*?' The floor shifted under my feet, and Matthew's arm circled my waist, keeping me steady. I wiped at my eyes but couldn't remove the sight of my father's misshapen head and gashed torso.

'Diana, what else happened?' Sarah said softly. 'Peter Knox should scare the socks off you, but there's more to it than that.'

My free hand clutched at Matthew's arm. 'Somebody sent me a picture of Mom and Dad.'

The silence stretched on the other end of the line. 'Oh, Diana,' Em murmured.

'*That* picture?' Sarah asked grimly.

'Yes,' I whispered.

Sarah swore. 'Put him back on the phone.'

'He can hear you perfectly from where he's standing,' I remarked. 'Besides, anything you have to say to him you can say to me, too.'

Matthew's hand moved from my waist to the small of my back. He began to rub it with the heel of his hand, pressing into the rigid muscles until they started to relax.

'Both of you listen to me, then. Get far, far away from Peter Knox. And that vampire had better see that you do, or I'm holding him responsible. Stephen Proctor was the most easygoing man alive. It took a lot to make him dislike someone – and he detested that wizard. Diana, you will come home *immediately*.'

'I will not, Sarah! I'm going to France with Matthew.' Sarah's far less attractive option had just convinced me.

There was silence.

'France?' Em said faintly.

Matthew held out his hand.

'Matthew would like to speak to you.' I handed him the phone before Sarah could protest.

'Ms Bishop? Do you have caller ID?'

I snorted. The brown phone hanging on the kitchen wall in Madison had a rotary dial and a cord a mile long so that Sarah could wander around while she talked. It took forever to simply dial a local number. Caller ID? Not likely.

'No? Take down these numbers, then.' Matthew slowly doled out the number to his mobile and another that presumably belonged to the house, along with detailed instructions on international dialing codes. 'Call at any time.'

Sarah then said something pointed, based on Matthew's startled expression.

'I'll make sure she's safe.' He handed me the phone.

'I'm getting off now. I love you both. Don't worry.'

'Stop telling us not to worry,' Sarah scolded. 'You're our niece. We're good and worried, Diana, and likely to stay that way.'

I sighed. 'What can I do to convince you that I'm all right?'

'Pick up the phone more often, for starters,' she said grimly.

When we'd said our good-byes, I stood next to Matthew, unwilling to meet his eyes. 'All this is my fault, just like Sarah said. I've been behaving like a clueless human.'

He turned away and walked to the end of the sofa, as far from me as he could get in the small room, and sank into the cushions. 'This bargain you made about magic and its place in your life – you made it when you were a lonely, frightened child. Now, every time you take a step, it's as though your future hinges on whether you manage to put your foot down in the right place.'

Matthew looked startled when I sat next to him and silently took his hands in mine, resisting the urge to tell him it was going to be all right.

'In France maybe you can just *be* for a few days – not trying, not worrying about making a mistake,' he continued. 'Maybe you could rest – although I've never seen you stop moving long enough. You even move in your sleep, you know.'

'I don't have time to rest, Matthew.' I was already having second thoughts about leaving Oxford. 'The alchemy conference is less than six weeks away. They're expecting me to deliver the opening lecture. I've barely started it, and without access to the Bodleian there's no chance of finishing it in time.'

Matthew's eyes narrowed speculatively. 'Your paper is on alchemical illustrations, I assume?'

'Yes, on the allegorical image tradition in England.'

'Then I don't suppose you would be interested in seeing my fourteenth-century copy of *Aurora Consurgens*. It's French, regrettably.'

My eyes widened. *Aurora Consurgens* was a baffling manuscript about the opposing forces of alchemical transformation – silver and gold, female and male, dark and light. Its illustrations were equally complex and puzzling.

'The earliest known copy of the *Aurora* is from the 1420s.'

'Mine is from 1356.'

'But a manuscript from such an early date won't be illustrated,' I pointed out. Finding an illuminated alchemical manuscript from before 1400 was as unlikely as discovering a Model-T Ford parked on the battlefield at Gettysburg.

'This one is.'

'Does it contain all thirty-eight images?'

'No. It has forty.' He smiled. 'It would seem that previous historians have been wrong about several particulars.'

Discoveries on this scale were rare. To get first crack at an unknown, fourteenth-century illustrated copy of *Aurora Consurgens* represented the opportunity of a lifetime for a historian of alchemy.

'What do the extra illustrations show? Is the text the same?'

'You'll have to come to France to find out.'

'Let's go, then,' I said promptly. After weeks of frustration, writing my keynote address suddenly seemed possible.

'You won't go for your own safety, but if there's a manuscript involved?' He shook his head ruefully. 'So much for common sense.'

'I've never been known for my common sense,' I confessed. 'When do we leave?'

'An hour?'

'An hour.' This was no spur-of-the-moment decision. He'd been planning it since I'd fallen asleep the night before.

He nodded. 'There's a plane waiting at the airstrip by the old American air force base. How long will it take you to get your things together?'

'That depends on what I need to bring with me,' I said, my head spinning.

'Nothing much. We won't be going anywhere. Pack warm clothes, and I don't imagine you'll consider leaving without your running shoes. It will be just the two of us, along with my mother and her housekeeper.'

His. Mother.

'Matthew,' I said faintly, 'I didn't know you had a mother.'

'Everybody has a mother, Diana,' he said, turning his clear gray eyes to mine. 'I've had two. The woman who gave birth to me and Ysabeau – the woman who made me a vampire.'

Matthew was one thing. A houseful of unfamiliar vampires was quite another. Caution about taking such a dangerous step pushed aside some of my eagerness to see the manuscript. My hesitation must have shown.

'I hadn't thought,' he said, his voice tinged with hurt. 'Of course you have no reason to trust Ysabeau. But she did assure me that you would be safe with her and Marthe.'

'If you trust them, then I do, too.' To my surprise, I meant it – in spite of the niggling worry that he'd had to ask them if they planned on taking a piece out of my neck.

'Thank you,' he said simply. Matthew's eyes drifted to my mouth, and my blood tingled in response. 'You pack, and I'll wash up and make a few phone calls.'

When I passed by his end of the sofa, he caught my hand in his. Once again the shock of his cold skin was counteracted by an answering warmth in my own.

'You're doing the right thing,' he murmured before he released me.

It was almost laundry day, and my bedroom was draped with dirty clothes. A rummage through the wardrobe yielded several nearly identical pairs of black pants that were clean, a few pairs of leggings, and half a dozen long-sleeved T-shirts and turtlenecks. There was a beat-up Yale duffel bag on top of it, and I jumped up and snagged the strap with one hand. The clothes all went into the old blue-and-white canvas bag, along with a few sweaters and a fleece pullover. I also chucked in sneakers, socks, and underwear, along with some old yoga clothes. I didn't own decent pajamas and could sleep in those. Remembering Matthew's French mother, I slipped in one presentable shirt and pair of trousers.

Matthew's low voice floated down the hall. He talked first to Fred, then to Marcus, and then to a cab company. With the bag's strap over my shoulder, I maneuvered myself awkwardly into the bathroom. Toothbrush, soap, shampoo, and a hairbrush all went inside, along with a hair dryer and a tube of mascara. I hardly ever wore the stuff, but on this occasion a cosmetic aid seemed a good idea.

When I was finished, I rejoined Matthew in the living room. He was thumbing through the messages on his phone, my computer case at his feet. 'Is that it?' he asked, eyeing the duffel bag with surprise.

'You told me I didn't need much.'

'Yes, but I'm not used to women listening to me when it comes to luggage. When Miriam goes away for the weekend, she packs enough to outfit the French Foreign Legion, and my mother requires multiple steamer trunks. Louisa wouldn't have crossed the street with what you're carrying, never mind leave the country.'

'Along with having no common sense, I'm not known for being high maintenance either.'

Matthew nodded appreciatively. 'Do you have your passport?'

I pointed. 'It's in my computer bag.'

'We can go, then,' Matthew said, his eyes sweeping the rooms one last time.

'Where's the photo?' It seemed wrong to just leave it.

'Marcus has it,' he said quickly.

'When was Marcus here?' I asked with a frown.

'While you were sleeping. Do you want me to get it back for you?' His finger hovered over a key on his phone.

'No.' I shook my head. There was no reason for me to look at it again.

Matthew took my bags and managed to get them and me down the stairs with no mishaps. A cab was waiting outside the college gates. Matthew stopped for a brief conversation with Fred. The vampire handed the porter a card, and the two men shook hands. Some deal had been struck, the particulars of which would never be disclosed to me. Matthew tucked me into the cab, and we drove for about thirty minutes, leaving the lights of Oxford behind us.

'Why didn't we take your car?' I asked as we headed into the countryside.

'This is better,' he explained. 'There's no need to have Marcus fetch it later.'

The sway of the cab was rocking me to sleep. Leaning against Matthew's shoulder, I dozed.

At the airport we were airborne soon after we'd had our passports checked and the pilot filed the paperwork. We sat opposite each other on couches arranged around a low table during the takeoff. I yawned every few moments, ears popping as we climbed. Once we reached cruising altitude, Matthew unsnapped his seat belt and gathered up some pillows and a blanket from a cabinet under the windows.

'We'll be in France soon.' He propped the pillows at the end of my sofa, which was about as deep as a twin bed, and held the blanket open to cover me. 'Meanwhile you should get some sleep.'

I didn't want to sleep. The truth was, I was afraid to. That photograph was etched on the inside of my eyelids.

He crouched next to me, the blanket hanging lightly from his fingers. 'What is it?'

'I don't want to close my eyes.'

Matthew tossed all the pillows except one onto the floor. 'Come here,' he said, sitting beside me and patting the fluffy white rectangle invitingly. I swung around, shimmied down the leather-covered surface, and put my head on his lap, stretching out my legs. He tossed the edge of the blanket from his right hand to his left so that it covered me in soft folds.

'Thank you,' I whispered.

'You're welcome.' He took his fingers and touched them to his lips, then to mine. I tasted salt. 'Sleep. I'll be right here.'

I did sleep, heavy and deep with no dreams, waking only when Matthew's cool fingers touched my face and he told me we were about to land.

'What time is it?' I asked, now thoroughly disoriented.

'It's about eight,' he said, looking at his watch.

'Where are we?' I swung to a seated position and rooted for my seat belt.

'Outside Lyon, in the Auvergne.'

'In the center of the country?' I asked, imagining the map of France. He nodded. 'Is that where you're from?'

'I was born and reborn nearby. My home – my family's home – is an hour or two away. We should arrive by midmorning.'

We landed in the private area of the busy regional airport and had our passports and travel documents checked by a bored-looking civil servant who snapped to attention the moment he saw Matthew's name.

'Do you always travel this way?' It was far easier than flying a commercial airline through London's Heathrow or Paris's Charles de Gaulle airport.

'Yes,' he said without apology or self-consciousness. 'The one time I'm entirely glad that I'm a vampire and have money to burn is when I travel.'

Matthew stopped behind a Range Rover the size of Connecticut and fished a set of keys out of his pocket. He opened the back door, stowing my bags inside. The Range Rover was slightly less deluxe than his Jaguar, but what it lacked in elegance it more than made up for in heft. It was like traveling in an armored personnel carrier.

'Do you really need this much car to drive in France?' I eyed the smooth roads.

Matthew laughed. 'You haven't seen my mother's house yet.'

We drove west through beautiful countryside, studded here and there with grand châteaus and steep mountains. Fields and vineyards stretched in all directions, and even under the steely sky the land seemed to blaze with the color of turning leaves. A sign indicated the direction of Clermont-Ferrand. That couldn't be a coincidence, in spite of the different spelling.

Matthew kept heading west. He slowed, turned down a narrow road, and pulled to the side. He pointed off to the distance. 'There,' he said. 'Sept-Tours.'

In the center of rolling hills was a flattened peak dominated by a crenellated hulk of buff and rose stone. Seven smaller towers surrounded it, and a turreted gatehouse stood guard in front. This was not a pretty, fairy-tale castle made for moonlit balls. Sept-Tours was a fortress.

'That's home?' I gasped.

'That's home.' Matthew took his phone out of his pocket and dialed a number. '*Maman?* We're almost there.'

Something was said on the other end, and the line went dead. Matthew smiled tightly and pulled back onto the road.

'She's expecting us?' I asked, just managing to keep the tremor out of my voice.

'She is.'

'And this is all right with her?' I didn't ask the real question – *Are you sure it's okay that you're bringing a witch home?* – but didn't need to.

Matthew's eyes remained fixed on the road. 'Ysabeau doesn't like surprises as much as I do,' he said lightly, turning on to something that looked like a goat track.

We drove between rows of chestnut trees, climbing until we reached Sept-Tours. Matthew steered the car between two of the seven towers and through to a paved courtyard in front of the entrance to the central structure. Parterres and gardens peeked out to the right and left, before the forest took over. The vampire parked the car.

'Ready?' he asked with a bright smile.

'As I'll ever be,' I replied warily.

Matthew opened my car door and helped me down. Pulling at my black jacket, I looked up at the château's imposing stone façade. The forbidding lines of the castle were nothing compared to what awaited me inside. The door swung open.

'*Courage*,' Matthew said, kissing me gently on the cheek.

CHAPTER 18

Ysabeau stood in the doorway of her enormous château, regal and icy, and glared at her vampire son as we climbed the stone stairs.

Matthew stooped a full foot to kiss her softly on both cheeks. 'Shall we come inside, or do you wish to continue our greetings out here?'

His mother stepped back to let us pass. I felt her furious gaze and smelled something reminiscent of sarsaparilla soda and caramel. We walked through a short, dark hallway, lined in a none-too-welcoming fashion with pikes that pointed directly at the visitor's head, and into a room with high ceilings and wall paintings that had clearly been done by some imaginative nineteenth-century artist to reflect a medieval past that never was. Lions, fleurs-de-lis, a snake with his tail in his mouth, and scallop shells were painted on white walls. At one end a circular set of stairs climbed to the top of one of the towers.

Indoors I faced the full force of Ysabeau's stare. Matthew's mother personified the terrifying elegance that seemed bred to the bone in Frenchwomen. Like her son – who disconcertingly appeared to be slightly older than she was – she was dressed in a monochromatic palette that minimized her uncanny paleness. Ysabeau's preferred colors ranged from cream to soft brown. Every inch of her ensemble was expensive and simple, from the tips of her soft, buff-colored leather shoes to the topazes that fluttered from her ears. Slivers of startling, cold emerald surrounded dark pupils, and the high slashes of her cheekbones kept her perfect features and dazzling white skin from sliding into mere prettiness. Her hair had the color and texture of honey, a golden pour of silk caught at the base of her skull in a heavy, low knot.

'You might have shown some consideration, Matthew.' Her accent softened his name, making it sound ancient. Like all vampires she had a seductive and melodic voice. In Ysabeau's case it sounded of distant bells, pure and deep.

'Afraid of the gossip, *Maman*? I thought you prided yourself on being a radical.' Matthew sounded both indulgent and impatient. He tossed the keys onto a nearby table. They slid across the perfect finish and landed with a clatter at the base of a Chinese porcelain bowl.

'I have never been a radical!' Ysabeau was horrified. 'Change is very much overrated.'

She turned and surveyed me from head to toe. Her perfectly formed mouth tightened.

She did not like what she saw – and it was no wonder. I tried to see myself through her eyes – the sandy hair that was neither thick nor well behaved, the dusting of freckles from being outdoors too much, the nose that was too long for the rest of my face. My eyes were my best feature, but they were unlikely to make up for my fashion sense. Next to her elegance and Matthew's perpetually unruffled self, I felt – and looked – like a gauche country mouse. I pulled at the hem of my jacket with my free hand, glad to see that there was no sign of magic at the fingertips, and hoped that there was also no sign of that phantom 'shimmering' that Matthew had mentioned.

'*Maman*, this is Diana Bishop. Diana, my mother, Ysabeau de Clermont.' The syllables rolled off his tongue.

Ysabeau's nostrils flared delicately. 'I do not like the way witches smell.' Her English was flawless, her glittering eyes fixed on mine. 'She is sweet and repulsively green, like spring.'

Matthew launched into a volley of something unintelligible that sounded like a cross between French, Spanish, and Latin. He kept his voice low, but there was no disguising the anger in it.

'*Ça suffit*,' Ysabeau retorted in recognizable French, drawing her hand across her throat. I swallowed hard and reflexively reached for the collar of my jacket.

'Diana.' Ysabeau said it with a long *e* rather than an *i* and an emphasis on the first rather than the second syllable. She extended one white, cold hand, and I took her fingers lightly in mine. Matthew grabbed my left hand in his, and for a moment we made an odd chain of vampires and a witch. '*Encantada.*'

'She's pleased to meet you,' Matthew said, translating for me and shooting a warning glance at his mother.

'Yes, yes,' Ysabeau said impatiently, turning back to her son. 'Of course she speaks only English and new French. Modern warmbloods are so poorly educated.'

A stout old woman with skin like snow and a mass of incongruously dark hair wrapped around her head in intricate braids stepped into the front hall, her arms outstretched. 'Matthew!' she cried. '*Cossí anatz?*'

'*Va plan, mercés. E tu?*' Matthew caught her in a hug, and kissed her on both cheeks.

'*Aital aital,*' she replied, grabbing her elbow and grimacing.

Matthew murmured in sympathy, and Ysabeau appealed to the ceiling for deliverance from the emotional spectacle.

'Marthe, this is my friend Diana,' he said, drawing me forward.

Marthe, too, was a vampire, one of the oldest I'd ever seen. She had to have been in her sixties when she was reborn, and though her hair was dark, there was no mistaking her age. Lines crisscrossed her face, and the joints of her hands were so gnarled that apparently not even vampiric blood could straighten them.

'Welcome, Diana,' she said in a husky voice of sand and treacle, looking deep into my eyes. She nodded at Matthew and reached for my hand. Her nostrils flared. '*Elle est une puissante sorcière,*' she said to Matthew, her voice appreciative.

'She says you're a powerful witch,' Matthew explained. His closeness somewhat diminished my instinctive concern with having a vampire sniff me.

Having no idea what the proper French response was to such a comment, I smiled weakly at Marthe and hoped that would do.

'You're exhausted,' Matthew said, his eyes flicking over my face.

He began rapidly questioning the two vampires in the unfamiliar language. This led to a great deal of pointing, eye rolling, emphatic gestures, and sighs. When Ysabeau mentioned the name Louisa, Matthew looked at his mother with renewed fury. His voice took on a flat, abrupt finality when he answered her.

Ysabeau shrugged. 'Of course, Matthew,' she murmured with patent insincerity.

'Let's get you settled.' Matthew's voice warmed as he spoke to me.

'I will bring food and wine,' Marthe said in halting English.

'Thank you,' I said. 'And thank you, Ysabeau, for having me in your home.' She sniffed and bared her teeth. I hoped it was a smile but feared it was not.

'And water, Marthe,' Matthew added. 'Oh, and food is coming this morning.'

'Some of it has already arrived,' his mother said tartly. 'Leaves. Sacks of vegetables and eggs. You were very bad to ask them to drive it down.'

'Diana needs to eat, *Maman*. I didn't imagine you had a great deal of proper food in the house.' Matthew's long ribbon of patience was fraying from the events of last evening and now his lukewarm home-coming.

'*I* need fresh blood, but I don't expect Victoire and Alain to fetch it from Paris in the middle of the night.' Ysabeau looked vastly pleased with herself as my knees swayed.

Matthew exhaled sharply, his hand under my elbow to steady me. 'Marthe,' he asked, pointedly ignoring Ysabeau, 'can you bring up eggs and toast and some tea for Diana?'

Marthe eyed Ysabeau and then Matthew as if she were at center court at Wimbledon. She cackled with laughter. '*Òc*,' she replied, with a cheerful nod.

'We'll see you two at dinner,' Matthew said calmly. I felt four icy patches on my shoulders as the women watched us depart. Marthe said something to Ysabeau that made her snort and Matthew smile broadly.

'What did Marthe say?' I whispered, remembering too late that there were few conversations, whispered or shouted, that would not be overheard by everyone in the house.

'She said we looked well together.'

'I don't want Ysabeau to be furious with me the whole time we're here.'

'Pay no attention to her,' he said serenely. 'Her bark is worse than her bite.'

We passed through a doorway into a long room with a wide assortment of chairs and tables of many different styles and periods. There were two fireplaces, and two knights in glistening armor jousted over one of them, their bright lances crossing neatly without a drop of bloodshed. The fresco had clearly been painted by the same dewy-eyed chivalric enthusiast who'd decorated the hall. A pair of doors led to another room, this one lined with bookcases.

'Is that a library?' I asked, Ysabeau's hostility momentarily forgotten. 'Can I see your copy of *Aurora Consurgens* now?'

'Later,' Matthew said firmly. 'You're going to eat something and then sleep.'

He led the way to another curving staircase, navigating through the labyrinth of ancient furniture with the ease of long experience. My own passage was more tentative, and my thighs grazed a bow-fronted chest of drawers, setting a tall porcelain vase swaying. When we finally reached the bottom of the staircase, Matthew paused.

'It's a long climb, and you're tired. Do you need me to carry you?'

'No,' I said indignantly. 'You are not going to sling me over your shoulder like a victorious medieval knight making off with the spoils of battle.'

Matthew pressed his lips together, eyes dancing.

'Don't you dare laugh at me.'

He did laugh, the sound bouncing off the stone walls as if a pack of amused vampires were standing in the stairwell. This was, after all, precisely the kind of place where knights would have carried women upstairs. But I didn't plan on being counted among them.

By the fifteenth tread, my sides were heaving with effort. The tower's worn stone steps were not made for ordinary feet and legs – they had clearly been designed for vampires like Matthew who were either over six feet tall, extremely agile, or both. I gritted my teeth and kept climbing. Around a final bend in the stairs, a room opened up suddenly.

'Oh.' My hand traveled to my mouth in amazement.

I didn't have to be told whose room this was. It was Matthew's, through and through.

We were in the château's graceful round tower – the one that still had its smooth, conical copper roof and was set on the back of the massive main building. Tall, narrow windows punctuated the walls, their leaded panes letting in slashes of light and autumn colors from the fields and trees outside.

The room was circular, and high bookcases smoothed its graceful curves into occasional straight lines. A large fireplace was set squarely into the walls that butted up against the château's central structure. This fireplace had miraculously escaped the attention of the nineteenth-century fresco painter. There were armchairs and couches, tables and hassocks, most in shades of green, brown, and gold. Despite the size of the room and the expanses of gray stone, the overall effect was of cozy warmth.

The room's most intriguing objects were those Matthew had chosen to keep from one of his many lives. A painting by Vermeer was propped up on a bookshelf next to a shell. It was unfamiliar – not one of the artist's few known canvases. The subject looked an awful lot like Matthew. A broadsword so long and heavy that no one but a vampire could have wielded it hung over the fireplace, and a Matthew-size suit of armor stood in one corner. Opposite, there was an ancient-looking human skeleton hanging from a wooden stand, the bones tied together with something resembling piano wire. On the table next to it were two microscopes, both made in the seventeenth century unless I was very much mistaken. An ornate crucifix studded with large red, green, and blue stones was tucked into a niche in the wall along with a stunning ivory carving of the Virgin.

Matthew's snowflakes drifted across my face as he watched me survey his belongings.

'It's a Matthew museum,' I said softly, knowing that every object there told a story.

'It's just my study.'

'Where did you—' I began, pointing at the microscopes.

'Later,' he said again. 'You have thirty more steps to climb.'

Matthew led me to the other side of the room and a second staircase. This one, too, curved up toward the heavens. Thirty slow steps later, I stood on the edge of another round room dominated by an enormous walnut four-poster bed complete with tester and heavy hangings. High above it were the exposed beams and supports that held the copper roof in place. A table was pushed against one wall, a fireplace was tucked into another, and a few comfortable chairs were arranged before it. Opposite, a door stood ajar, revealing an enormous bathtub.

'It's like a falcon's lair,' I said, peering out the window. Matthew had been looking at this landscape from these windows since the Middle Ages. I wondered, briefly, about the other women he'd brought here before me. I was sure I wasn't the first, but I didn't think there had been many. There was something intensely private about the château.

Matthew came up behind me and looked over my shoulder. 'Do you approve?' His breath was soft against my ear. I nodded.

'How long?' I asked, unable to help myself.

'This tower?' he asked. 'About seven hundred years.'

'And the village? Do they know about you?'

'Yes. Like witches, vampires are safer when they're part of a community who knows what they are but doesn't ask too many questions.'

Generations of Bishops had lived in Madison without anyone's making a fuss. Like Peter Knox, we were hiding in plain sight.

'Thank you for bringing me to Sept-Tours,' I said. 'It does feel safer than Oxford.' *In spite of Ysabeau.*

'Thank you for braving my mother.' Matthew chuckled as if he'd heard my unspoken words. The distinctive scent of carnations accompanied the sound. 'She's overprotective, like most parents.'

'I felt like an idiot – and underdressed, too. I didn't bring a single thing to wear that will meet with her approval.' I bit my lip, my forehead creased.

'Coco Chanel didn't meet with Ysabeau's approval. You may be aiming a bit high.'

I laughed and turned, my eyes seeking his. When they met, my breath caught. Matthew's gaze lingered on my eyes, cheeks, and finally my mouth. His hand rose to my face.

'You're so alive,' he said gruffly. 'You should be with a man much, much younger.'

I lifted to my toes. He bent his head. Before our lips touched, a tray clattered on the table.

' "*Vos etz arbres e branca*," ' Marthe sang, giving Matthew a wicked look.

He laughed and sang back in a clear baritone, ' "*On fruitz de gaug s'asazona.*" '

'What language is that?' I asked, getting down off my tiptoes and following Matthew to the fireplace.

'The old tongue,' Marthe replied.

'Occitan.' Matthew removed the silver cover from a plate of eggs. The aroma of hot food filled the room. 'Marthe decided to recite poetry before you sat down to eat.'

Marthe giggled and swatted at Matthew's wrist with a towel that she pulled from her waist. He dropped the cover and took a seat.

'Come here, come here,' she said, gesturing at the chair across from him. 'Sit, eat.' I did as I was told. Marthe poured Matthew a goblet of wine from a tall, silver-handled glass pitcher.

'*Mercés*,' he murmured, his nose going immediately to the glass in anticipation.

A similar pitcher held icy-cold water, and Marthe put this in another goblet, which she handed to me. She poured a steaming cup of tea, which I recognized immediately as coming from Mariage Frères in Paris. Apparently Matthew had raided my cupboards while

I slept last night and been quite specific with his shopping lists. Marthe poured thick cream into the cup before he could stop her, and I shot him a warning glance. At this point I needed allies. Besides, I was too thirsty to care. He leaned back in his chair meekly, sipping his wine.

Marthe pulled more items from her tray – a silver place setting, salt, pepper, butter, jam, toast, and a golden omelet flecked with fresh herbs.

'*Merci*, Marthe,' I said with heartfelt gratitude.

'Eat!' she commanded, aiming her towel at me this time.

Marthe looked satisfied with the enthusiasm of my first few bites. Then she sniffed the air. She frowned and directed an exclamation of disgust at Matthew before striding to the fireplace. A match snapped, and the dry wood began to crackle.

'Marthe,' Matthew protested, standing up with his wineglass, 'I can do that.'

'She is cold,' Marthe grumbled, clearly aggravated that he hadn't anticipated this before he sat down, 'and you are thirsty. I will make the fire.'

Within minutes there was a blaze. Though no fire would make the enormous room toasty, it took the chill from the air. Marthe brushed her hands together and stood. 'She must sleep. I can smell she has been afraid.'

'She'll sleep when she's through eating,' Matthew said, holding up his right hand in a pledge. Marthe looked at him for a long moment and shook her finger at him as though he were fifteen, and not fifteen hundred, years old. Finally his innocent expression convinced her. She left the room, her ancient feet moving surely down the challenging stairs.

'Occitan is the language of the troubadours, isn't it?' I asked, after Marthe had departed. The vampire nodded. 'I didn't realize it was spoken this far north.'

'We're not that far north,' Matthew said with a smile. 'Once, Paris was nothing more than an insignificant borderlands town. Most people spoke Occitan then. The hills kept the northerners – and their language – at a distance. Even now people here are wary of outsiders.'

'What do the words mean?' I asked.

'"*You are the tree and branch*,"' he said, fixing his eyes on the slashes of countryside visible through the nearest window, '"*where delight's fruit ripens*."' Matthew shook his head ruefully. 'Marthe will hum the song all afternoon and make Ysabeau crazy.'

The fire continued to spread its warmth through the room, and the heat made me drowsy. By the time the eggs were gone, it was difficult to keep my eyes open.

I was in the middle of a jaw-splitting yawn when Matthew drew me from the chair. He scooped me into his arms, my feet swinging in midair. I started to protest.

'Enough,' he said. 'You can barely sit up straight, never mind walk.'

He put me gently on the end of the bed and pulled the coverlet back. The snowy-white sheets looked so crisp and inviting. I dropped my head onto the mountain of down pillows arranged against the bed's intricate walnut carvings.

'Sleep.' Matthew took the bed's curtains in both hands and gave them a yank.

'I'm not sure I'll be able to,' I said, stifling another yawn. 'I'm not good at napping.'

'All appearances to the contrary,' he said drily. 'You're in France now. You're not supposed to try. I'll be downstairs. Call if you need anything.'

With one staircase leading from the hall up to his study and the other staircase leading to the bedroom from the opposite side, no one could reach this room without going past – and through – Matthew. The rooms had been designed as if he needed to protect himself from his own family.

A question rose to my lips, but he gave the curtains a final tug until they were closed, effectively silencing me. The heavy bed hangings didn't allow the light to penetrate, and they shut out the worst of the drafts as well. Relaxing into the firm mattress, my body's warmth magnified by the layers of bedding, I quickly fell asleep.

I woke up to the rustle of turning pages and sat bolt upright, trying to imagine why someone had shut me into a box made of fabric. Then I remembered.

France. Matthew. At his home.

'Matthew?' I called softly.

He parted the curtains and looked down with a smile. Behind him, candles were lit – dozens and dozens of them. Some were set into the sconces around the room, and others stood in ornate candelabras on the floor and tables.

'For someone who doesn't nap, you slept quite soundly,' he said with satisfaction. As far as he was concerned, the trip to France had already proved a success.

'What time is it?'

'I'm going to get you a watch if you don't stop asking me that.' Matthew glanced at his old Cartier. 'It's nearly two in the afternoon. Marthe will probably be here any minute with some tea. Do you want to shower and change?'

The thought of a hot shower had me eagerly pushing back the covers. 'Yes, please!'

Matthew dodged my flying limbs and helped me to the floor, which was farther away than I had expected. It was cold, too, the stone flagstones stinging against my bare feet.

'Your bag is in the bathroom, the computer is downstairs in my study, and there are fresh towels. Take your time.' He watched as I skittered into the bathroom.

'This is a palace!' I exclaimed. An enormous white, freestanding tub was tucked between two of the windows, and a long wooden bench held my dilapidated Yale duffel. In the far corner, a showerhead was set into the wall.

I started running the water, expecting to wait a long time for it to heat up. Miraculously, steam enveloped me immediately, and the honey-and-nectarine scent of my soap helped to lift the tension of the past twenty-four hours.

Once my muscles were unkinked, I slipped on jeans and a

turtleneck, along with a pair of socks. There was no outlet for my blow dryer, so I settled instead for roughly toweling my hair and dragging a comb through it before tying it back in a ponytail.

'Marthe brought up tea,' he said when I walked into the bedroom, glancing at a teapot and cup sitting on the table. 'Do you want me to pour you some?'

I sighed with pleasure as the soothing liquid went down my throat. 'When can I see the *Aurora* manuscript?'

'When I'm sure you won't get lost on your way to the library. Ready for the grand tour?'

'Yes, please.' I slid loafers on over my socks and ran back into the bathroom to get a sweater. As I raced around, Matthew waited patiently, standing near the top of the stairs.

'Should we take the teapot down?' I asked, skidding to a halt.

'No, she'd be furious if I let a guest touch a dish. Wait twenty-four hours before helping Marthe.'

Matthew slipped down the stairs as if he could handle the uneven, smooth treads blindfolded. I crept along, guiding my fingers against the stone wall.

When we reached his study, he pointed to my computer, already plugged in and resting on a table by the window, before we descended to the salon. Marthe had been there, and a warm fire was crackling in the fireplace, sending the smell of wood smoke through the room. I grabbed Matthew.

'The library,' I said. 'The tour needs to start there.'

It was another room that had been filled over the years with bric-a-brac and furniture. An Italian Savonarola folding chair was pulled up to a French Directory secretary, while a vast oak table circa 1700 held display cabinets that looked as if they'd been plucked from a Victorian museum. Despite the mismatches, the room was held together by miles of leather-bound books on walnut shelving and by an enormous Aubusson carpet in soft golds, blues, and browns.

As in most old libraries, the books were shelved by size. There were thick manuscripts in leather bindings, shelved with spines in and ornamental clasps out, the titles inked onto the fore edges of the vellum. There were tiny incunabula and pocket-size books in neat rows on one bookcase, spanning the history of print from the 1450s to the present. A number of rare modern first editions, including a run of Arthur Conan Doyle's Sherlock Holmes stories and T. H. White's *The Sword in the Stone*, were there, too. One case held nothing but large folios – botanical books, atlases, medical books. If all this was downstairs, what treasures lived in Matthew's tower study?

He let me circle the room, peering at the titles and gasping. When I returned to his side, all I could do was shake my head in disbelief.

'Imagine what you'd have if you'd been buying books for centuries,' Matthew said with a shrug that reminded me of Ysabeau. 'Things pile up. We've gotten rid of a lot over the years. We had to. Otherwise this room would be the size of the Bibliothèque Nationale.'

'So where is it?'

'You're already out of patience, I see.' He went to a shelf, his eyes darting among the volumes. He pulled out a small book with black tooled covers and presented it to me.

When I looked for a velveteen cradle to put it on, he laughed.

'Just open it, Diana. It's not going to disintegrate.'

It felt strange to hold such a manuscript in my hands, trained as I was to think of them as rare, precious objects rather than reading material. Trying not to open the covers too wide and crack the binding, I peeked inside. An explosion of bright colors, gold, and silver leaped out.

'Oh,' I breathed. The other copies I'd seen of *Aurora Consurgens* were not nearly so fine. 'It's beautiful. Do you know who did the illuminations?'

'A woman named Bourgot Le Noir. She was quite popular in Paris in the middle of the fourteenth century.' Matthew took the book from me and opened it fully. 'There. Now you can see it properly.'

The first illumination showed a queen standing on a small hill, sheltering seven small creatures inside her outspread cloak. Delicate vines framed the image, twisting and turning their way across the vellum. Here and there, buds burst into flowers, and birds sat on the branches. In the afternoon light, the queen's embroidered golden dress glowed against a brilliant vermilion background. At the bottom of the page, a man in a black robe sat atop a shield that bore a coat of arms in black and silver. The man's attention was directed at the queen, a rapt expression on his face and his hands raised in supplication.

'Nobody is going to believe this. An unknown copy of *Aurora Consurgens* — with illuminations by a *woman*?' I shook my head in amazement. 'How will I cite it?'

'I'll loan the manuscript to the Beinecke Library for a year, if that helps. Anonymously, of course. As for Bourgot, the experts will say it's her father's work. But it's all hers. We probably have the receipt for it somewhere,' Matthew said vaguely, looking around. 'I'll ask Ysabeau where Godfrey's things are.'

'Godfrey?' The unfamiliar coat of arms featured a fleur-de-lis, surrounded by a snake with its tail in its mouth.

'My brother.' The vagueness left his voice, and his face darkened. 'He died in 1668, fighting in one of Louis XIV's infernal wars.' Closing the manuscript gently, he put it on a nearby table. 'I'll take this up to my study later so you can look at it more closely. In the morning Ysabeau reads her newspapers here, but otherwise it sits empty. You're welcome to browse the shelves whenever you like.'

With that promise he moved me through the salon and into the great hall. We stood by the table with the Chinese bowl, and he pointed out features of the room, including the old minstrels' gallery, the trapdoor in the roof that had let the smoke out before the fireplaces and chimneys were constructed, and the entrance to the square watchtower overlooking the main approach to the château. That climb could wait until another day.

Matthew led me down to the lower ground floor, with its maze of storerooms, wine cellars, kitchens, servants' rooms, larders, and pantries. Marthe stepped out of one of the kitchens, flour covering her arms up to the elbows, and handed me a warm roll fresh from the oven. I munched on it as Matthew walked the corridors, pointing out the old purposes of every room – where the grain was stored, the venison hung, the cheese made.

'Vampires don't eat anything,' I said, confused.

'No, but our tenants did. Marthe loves to cook.'

I promised to keep her busy. The roll was delicious, and the eggs had been perfect.

Our next stop was the gardens. Though we had descended a flight of stairs to get to the kitchens, we left the château at ground level. The gardens were straight out of the sixteenth century, with divided beds full of herbs and autumn vegetables. Rosebushes, some with a few lonely blooms remaining, filled the borders.

But the aroma that intrigued me wasn't floral. I made a beeline for a low-slung building.

'Be careful, Diana,' he called, striding across the gravel, 'Balthasar bites.'

'Which one is Balthasar?'

He rounded the stable entrance, an anxious look on his face. 'The stallion using your spine as a scratching post,' Matthew replied tightly. I was standing with my back to a large, heavy-footed horse while a mastiff and a wolfhound circled my feet, sniffing me with interest.

'Oh, he won't bite me.' The enormous Percheron maneuvered his head so he could rub his ears on my hip. 'And who are these gentlemen?' I asked, ruffling the fur on the wolfhound's neck while the mastiff tried to put my hand in his mouth.

'The hound is Fallon, and the mastiff is Hector.' Matthew snapped his fingers, and both dogs came running to his side, where they sat obediently and watched his face for further instructions. 'Please step away from that horse.'

'Why? He's fine.' Balthasar stamped the ground in agreement and pitched an ear back to look haughtily at Matthew.

' "*If the butterfly wings its way to the sweet light that attracts it, it's only because it doesn't know that the fire can consume it,*" ' Matthew murmured under his breath. 'Balthasar is only fine until he gets bored. I'd like you to move away *before* he kicks the stall door down.'

'We're making your master nervous, and he's started reciting obscure bits of poetry written by mad Italian clerics. I'll be back tomorrow with something sweet.' I turned and kissed Balthasar on the nose. He nickered, his hooves dancing with impatience.

Matthew tried to cover his surprise. 'You recognized that?'

'Giordano Bruno. "*If the thirsty stag runs to the brook, it's only because he isn't aware of the cruel bow,*"' I continued. ' "*If the unicorn runs to its chaste nest, it's only because he doesn't see the noose prepared for him.*"'

'You know the work of the Nolan?' Matthew used the sixteenth-century mystic's own way of referring to himself.

My eyes narrowed. Good God, had he known Bruno as well as Machiavelli? Matthew seemed to have been attracted to every strange character who'd ever lived. 'He was an early supporter of Copernicus, and I'm a historian of science. How do you know Bruno's work?'

'I'm a great reader,' he said evasively.

'You knew him!' My tone was accusing. 'Was he a daemon?'

'One who crossed the madness-genius divide rather too frequently, I'm afraid.'

'I should have known. He believed in extraterrestrial life and cursed his inquisitors on the way to the stake,' I said, shaking my head.

'Nevertheless, he understood the power of desire.'

I looked sharply at the vampire. ' "*Desire urges me on, as fear bridles me.*" Did Bruno feature in your essay for All Souls?'

'A bit.' Matthew's mouth flattened into a hard line. 'Will you please come away from there? We can talk about philosophy another time.'

Other passages drifted through my mind. There was something else about Bruno's work that might make Matthew think of him. He wrote about the goddess Diana.

I stepped away from the stall.

'Balthasar isn't a pony,' Matthew warned, pulling my elbow.

'I can see that. But I could handle that horse.' Both the alchemical manuscript and the Italian philosopher vanished from my mind at the thought of such a challenge.

'You don't ride as well?' Matthew asked in disbelief.

'I grew up in the country and have ridden since I was a child — dressage, jumping, everything.' Being on a horse was even more like flying than rowing was.

'We have other horses. Balthasar stays where he is,' he said firmly.

Riding was an unforeseen bonus of coming to France, one that almost made Ysabeau's cold presence bearable. Matthew led me to the other end of the stables, where six more fine animals waited. Two of them were big and black — although not as large as Balthasar — one a fairly round chestnut mare, another a bay gelding. There were two gray Andalusians as well, with large feet and curved necks. One came to the door to see what was going on in her domain.

'This is Nar Rakasa,' he said, gently rubbing her muzzle. 'Her name means "fire dancer." We usually just call her Rakasa. She moves beautifully, but she's willful. You two should get along famously.'

I refused to take the bait, though it was charmingly offered, and let Rakasa sniff at my hair and face. 'What's her sister's name?'

'Fiddat — "silver".' Fiddat came forward when Matthew said her name, her dark eyes affectionate. 'Fiddat is Ysabeau's horse, and Rakasa is her sister.' Matthew pointed to the two blacks. 'Those are mine. Dahr and Sayad.'

'What do their names mean?' I asked, walking to their stalls.

'Dahr is Arabic for "time", and Sayad means "hunter",' Matthew explained, joining me. 'Sayad loves riding across the fields chasing game and jumping hedges. Dahr is patient and steady.'

We continued the tour, Matthew pointing out features of the mountains and orienting me to the town. He showed me where the château had been modified and how restorers had used a different kind of stone because the original was no longer available. By the time we were finished, I wasn't likely to get lost — in part due to the central keep, which was hard to misplace.

'Why am I so tired?' I yawned as we returned to the château.

'You're hopeless,' Matthew said in exasperation. 'Do you really need me to recount the events of the past thirty-six hours?'

At his urging I agreed to another nap. Leaving him in the study, I climbed the stairs and flung myself into bed, too tired to even blow out the candles.

Moments later I was dreaming of riding through a dark forest, a loose green tunic belted around my waist. There were sandals tied onto my feet, their leather fastenings crossed around my ankles and calves. Dogs bayed and hooves crashed in the underbrush behind me. A quiver of arrows nestled against my shoulder, and in one fist I held a bow. Despite the ominous sounds of my pursuers, I felt no fear.

In my dream I smiled with the knowledge I could outrun those who hunted me.

'Fly,' I commanded – and the horse did.

CHAPTER 19

The next morning my first thoughts were also of riding.

I ran a brush through my hair, rinsed my mouth out, and threw on a close-fitting pair of black leggings. They were the nearest thing to riding breeches that I had with me. Running shoes would make it impossible to keep my heels down in the stirrups, so on went my loafers instead. Not exactly proper footwear, but they'd do. A long-sleeved T-shirt and a fleece pullover completed my ensemble. Dragging my hair back into a ponytail, I returned to the bedroom.

Matthew lifted his eyebrow as I rocketed into the room, his arm barring me from going any farther. He was leaning against the wide archway that led to the stairs, well groomed as always, wearing dark gray breeches and a black sweater. 'Let's ride in the afternoon.'

I'd been expecting this. Dinner with Ysabeau had been tense at best, and afterward my sleep had been punctuated with nightmares. Matthew had climbed the stairs to check on me several times.

'I'm fine. Exercise and fresh air will be the best thing in the world for me.' When I tried to get past him again, he stopped me with only a dark look.

'If you so much as sway in the saddle, I'm bringing you home. Understood?'

'Understood.'

Downstairs, I headed for the dining room, but Matthew pulled me in the other direction. 'Let's eat in the kitchens,' he said quietly. No formal breakfast with Ysabeau staring at me over *Le Monde*. That was welcome news.

We ate in what were ostensibly the housekeeper's rooms, in front of a blazing fire at a table set for two – though I would be the only one eating Marthe's excellent, abundant food. A huge pot of tea sat on the scarred, round wooden table, wrapped in a linen towel to keep it hot. Marthe glanced at me with concern, tutting at my dark circles and pale skin.

When my fork slowed, Matthew reached for a pyramid of boxes crowned with a black-velvet-covered helmet. 'For you,' he said, putting them on the table.

The helmet was self-explanatory. It was shaped like a high-crowned baseball hat, with a fold of black grosgrain ribbon at the nape. Despite its velvet covering and ribbon, the helmet was sturdy and made expressly to keep soft human skulls from cracking if they met with the ground. I hated them, but it was a wise precaution.

'Thank you,' I said. 'What's in the boxes?'

'Open them and see.'

The first box held a pair of black breeches with suede patches inside the knees to grip the saddle. They would be far more pleasant to ride in than my thin, slippery leggings and looked like they would fit, too. Matthew must have been making more phone calls and relaying approximate measurements while I napped. I smiled at him in gratitude.

The box also held a black padded vest with a long tail and stiff metal supports sewn into the seams. It looked and would no doubt feel like a turtle's shell – uncomfortable and unwieldy.

'This isn't necessary.' I held it up, frowning.

'It is if you're going riding.' His voice didn't show the slightest hint of emotion. 'You tell me you're experienced. If so, you won't have a problem adjusting to its weight.'

My color rose and my fingertips gave a warning tingle. Matthew watched me with interest, and Marthe came to the door and gave a sniff. I breathed in and out until the tingling stopped.

'You wear a seat belt in my car,' Matthew said evenly. 'You'll wear a vest on my horse.'

We stared at each other in a standoff of wills. The thought of the fresh air defeated me, and Marthe's eyes glittered with amusement.

No doubt our negotiations were as much fun to watch as were the volleys between Matthew and Ysabeau.

I pulled the final box toward me in silent concession. It was long and heavy, and there was a sharp tang of leather when the lid lifted.

Boots. Knee-length, black boots. I'd never shown horses and had limited resources, so I had never owned a proper pair of riding boots. These were beautiful, with their curved calves and supple leather. My fingers touched their shining surfaces.

'Thank you,' I breathed, delighted with his surprise.

'I'm pretty sure they'll fit,' Matthew said, his eyes soft.

'Come, girl,' Marthe said cheerfully from the door. 'You change.'

She barely got me into the laundry room before I'd kicked off my loafers and peeled the leggings from my body. She took the worn Lycra and cotton from me while I wriggled into the breeches.

'There was a time when women didn't ride like men,' Marthe said, looking at the muscles in my legs and shaking her head.

Matthew was on his phone when I returned, sending out instructions to all the other people in his world who required his management. He looked up with approval.

'Those will be more comfortable.' He stood and picked up the boots. 'There's no jack in here. You'll have to wear your other shoes to the stables.'

'No, I want to put them on now,' I said, fingers outstretched.

'Sit down, then.' He shook his head at my impatience. 'You'll never get them on the first time without help.' Matthew picked up my chair with me in it and turned it so he had more room to maneuver. He held out the right boot, and I stuck my foot in as far as the ankle. He was right. No amount of tugging was going to get my foot around the stiff bend. He stood over my foot, grasping the heel and toe of the boot and wriggling it gently as I pulled the leather in the other direction. After several minutes of struggle, my foot worked its way into the shank. Matthew gave the sole a final, firm push, and the boot snuggled against my bones.

Once both boots were on, I held my legs out to admire. Matthew tugged and patted, sliding his cold fingers around the top rim to make sure my blood could circulate. I stood, my legs feeling unusually long, took a few stiff-ankled steps, and did a little twirl.

'Thank you.' I threw my arms around his neck, the toes of my boots grazing the floor. 'I love them.'

Matthew carried my vest and hat to the stables, much as he had carried my computer and yoga mat in Oxford. The stable doors were flung open, and there were sounds of activity.

'Georges?' Matthew called. A small, wiry man of indeterminate age – though not a vampire – came around the corner, carrying a bridle and a curry comb. When we passed Balthasar's stall, the stallion stomped angrily and tossed his head. *You promised*, he seemed to say. Inside my pocket was a tiny apple that I'd wheedled from Marthe.

'Here you go, baby,' I said, holding it out on a flat palm. Matthew watched warily as Balthasar extended his neck and reached with delicate lips to pick the fruit from my hand. Once it was in his mouth, he looked at his owner triumphantly.

'Yes, I see that you are behaving like a prince,' Matthew said drily, 'but that doesn't mean you won't behave like a devil at the first opportunity.' Balthasar's hooves struck the ground in annoyance.

We passed by the tack room. In addition to the regular saddles, bridles, and reins, there were freestanding wooden frames that held something like a small armchair with odd supports on one side.

'What are they?'

'Sidesaddles,' Matthew said, kicking off his shoes and stepping into a tall pair of well-worn boots. His foot slid down easily with a simple stamp on the heel and a tug at the top. 'Ysabeau prefers them.'

In the paddock Dahr and Rakasa turned their heads and looked with interest while Georges and Matthew began a detailed discussion of all the natural obstacles we might encounter. I held my palm out to Dahr, sorry that there were no more apples in my pocket. The gelding looked disappointed, too, once he picked up the sweet scent.

'Next time,' I promised. Ducking under his neck, I arrived at Rakasa's side. 'Hello, beauty.'

Rakasa picked up her right front foot and cocked her head toward me. I ran my hands over her neck and shoulders, getting her used to my scent and touch, and gave the saddle a tug, checking the tightness of the girth strap and making sure the blanket underneath was smooth. She reached around and gave me an inquiring smell and a snuffle, nosing at my pullover where the apple had been. She tossed her head in indignation.

'You, too,' I promised her with a laugh, placing my left hand firmly on her rump. 'Let's have a look.'

Horses like having their feet touched about as much as most witches like being dunked in water – which is to say not much. But, out of habit and superstition, I'd never ridden a horse without first checking to make sure that nothing was lodged in their soft hooves.

When I straightened, the two men were watching me closely. Georges said something that indicated I would do. Matthew nodded thoughtfully, holding out my vest and hat. The vest was snug and hard – but it wasn't as bad as I'd expected. The hat interfered with my ponytail, and I slid the elastic band lower to accommodate it before snapping the chin band together. Matthew was at my back in the time it took me to grab the reins and lift my foot to Rakasa's stirrup.

'Will you never wait until I help you?' he growled into my ear.

'I can get onto a horse myself,' I said hotly.

'But you don't need to.' Matthew's hands cupped my shin, lifting me effortlessly into the saddle. After that, he checked my stirrup length, rechecked the girth strap, and finally went to his own horse. He swung into the saddle with a practiced air that suggested he'd been on horseback for hundreds of years. Once there, he looked like a king.

Rakasa started to dance in impatience, and I pushed my heels down. She stopped, looking puzzled. 'Quiet,' I whispered. She nodded her head and stared forward, her ears working back and forth.

'Take her around the paddock while I check my saddle,' Matthew said casually, swinging his left knee onto Dahr's shoulder and fiddling with his stirrup leather. My eyes narrowed. His stirrups needed no adjustment. He was checking out my riding skills.

I walked Rakasa halfway around the paddock, to feel her gait. The Andalusian really did dance, delicately picking up her feet and putting them down firmly in a beautiful, rocking movement. When I pressed both heels into her sides, Rakasa's dancing walk turned into an equally rollicking, smooth trot. We passed Matthew, who had given up all pretense of adjusting his saddle. Georges leaned against the fence, smiling broadly.

Beautiful girl, I breathed silently. Her left ear shot back, and she picked up the pace slightly. My calf pressed into her flank, just behind the stirrup, and she broke into a canter, her feet reaching out into the air and her neck arched. How angry would Matthew be if we jumped the paddock fence?

Angry, I was sure.

Rakasa rounded the corner, and I slowed her to a trot. 'Well?' I demanded.

Georges nodded and opened the paddock gate.

'You have a good seat,' Matthew said, eyeing my backside. 'Good hands, too. You'll be all right. By the way,' he continued in a conversational tone, leaning toward me and dropping his voice, 'if you'd jumped the fence back there, today's outing would have been over.'

Once we'd cleared the gardens and passed through the old gate, the trees thickened, and Matthew scanned the forest. A few feet into the woods, he began to relax, having accounted for every creature within and discovered that none of them were of the two-legged variety.

Matthew kicked Dahr into a trot, and Rakasa obediently waited for me to kick her as well. I did, amazed all over again at how smoothly she moved.

'What kind of horse is Dahr?' I asked, noticing his equally smooth gait.

'I suppose you'd call him a destrier,' Matthew explained. That was the mount that carried knights to the Crusades. 'He was bred for speed and agility.'

'I thought destriers were enormous warhorses.' Dahr was bigger than Rakasa, but not much.

'They were large for the time. But they weren't big enough to carry any of the men in this family into battle, not once we had armor on our backs, and weapons. We trained on horses like Dahr and rode them for pleasure, but we fought on Percherons like Balthasar.'

I stared between Rakasa's ears, working up the courage to broach another subject. 'May I ask you something about your mother?'

'Of course,' Matthew said, twisting in his saddle. He put one fist on his hip and held his horse's reins lightly in the other hand. I now knew with absolute certainty how a medieval knight looked on horseback.

'Why does she hate witches so much? Vampires and witches are traditional enemies, but Ysabeau's dislike of me goes beyond that. It seems personal.'

'I suppose you want a better answer than that you smell like spring.'

'Yes, I want the real reason.'

'She's jealous.' Matthew patted Dahr's shoulder.

'What on earth is she jealous of?'

'Let's see. Your power – especially a witch's ability to see the future. Your ability to bear children and pass that power to a new generation. And the ease with which you die, I suppose,' he said, his voice reflective.

'Ysabeau had you and Louisa for children.'

'Yes, Ysabeau made both of us. But it's not quite the same as bearing a child, I think.'

'Why does she envy a witch's second sight?'

'That has to do with how Ysabeau was made. Her maker didn't ask permission first.' Matthew's face darkened. 'He wanted her for a wife, and he just took her and turned her into a vampire. She had a reputation as a seer and was young enough to still hope for children. When she became a vampire, both of those abilities were gone. She's never quite gotten over it, and witches are a constant reminder of the life she lost.'

'Why does she envy that witches die so easily?'

'Because she misses my father.' He abruptly stopped talking, and it was clear I'd pressed him enough.

The trees thinned, and Rakasa's ears shot back and forth impatiently.

'Go ahead,' he said with resignation, gesturing at the open field before us.

Rakasa leaped forward at the touch of my heels, catching the bit in her teeth. She slowed climbing the hill, and once on the crest she pranced and tossed her head, clearly enjoying the fact that Dahr was standing at the bottom while she was on top. I circled her into a fast figure eight, changing her leads on the fly to keep her from stumbling as she went around corners.

Dahr took off – not at a canter but a gallop – his black tail streaming out behind him and his hooves striking the earth with unbelievable speed. I gasped and pulled lightly on Rakasa's reins to make her stop. So that was the point of destriers. They could go from zero to sixty like a finely tuned sports car. Matthew made no effort to slow his horse as he approached, but Dahr stopped on a dime about six feet away from us, his sides bowed out slightly with the exertion.

'Show-off! You won't let me jump a fence and you put on that display?' I teased.

'Dahr doesn't get enough exercise either. This is exactly what he needs.' Matthew grinned and patted his horse on the shoulder. 'Are you interested in a race? We'll give you a head start, of course,' he said with a courtly bow.

'You're on. Where to?'

Matthew pointed to a solitary tree on the top of the ridge and watched me, alert for the first indication of movement. He'd picked something that you could shoot past without running into anything. Maybe Rakasa wasn't as good at abrupt stops as Dahr was.

There was no way I was going to surprise a vampire and no way my horse – for all her smooth gait – was going to beat Dahr up the ridge. Still, I was eager to see how well she would perform. I leaned forward and patted Rakasa on the neck, resting my chin for just a moment on her warm flesh and closing my eyes.

Fly, I encouraged her silently.

Rakasa shot forward as if she'd been slapped on the rump, and my instincts took over.

I lifted myself out of the saddle to make it easier for her to carry my weight, tying a loose knot in the reins. When her speed stabilized, I lowered myself into the saddle, clutching her warm body between my legs. My feet kicked free from the unnecessary stirrups, and my fingers wove through her mane. Matthew and Dahr thundered behind us. It was like my dream, the one where dogs and horses were chasing me. My left hand curled as if holding something, and I bent low along Rakasa's neck, eyes closed.

Fly, I repeated, but the voice in my head no longer sounded like my own. Rakasa responded with still more speed.

I felt the tree grow closer. Matthew swore in Occitan, and Rakasa swerved to the left at the last minute, slowing to a canter and then a trot. There was a tug on her reins. My eyes shot open in alarm.

'Do you always ride unfamiliar horses at top speed, with your eyes closed, no reins, and no stirrups?' Matthew's voice was coldly furious. 'You row with your eyes closed – I've seen you. And you walk with them closed, too. I always suspected that magic was involved. You must use your power to ride as well. Otherwise you'd be dead. And for what it's worth, I believe you're telling Rakasa what to do with your mind and not with your hands and legs.'

I wondered if what he said was true. Matthew made an impatient sound and dismounted by swinging his right leg high over Dahr's head, kicking his left foot out of the stirrup, and sliding down the horse's side facing front.

'Get down from there,' he said roughly, grabbing Rakasa's loose reins.

Dismounting the traditional way, I swung my right leg over Rakasa's rump. When my back was to him, Matthew reached up and scooped me off the horse. Now I knew why he preferred to face front. It kept you from being grabbed from behind and hauled off your mount. He turned me around and crushed me to his chest.

'*Dieu*,' he whispered into my hair. 'Don't do anything like that again, please.'

'You told me not to worry about what I was doing. It's why you brought me to France,' I said, confused by his reaction.

'I'm sorry,' he said earnestly. 'I'm trying not to interfere. But it's difficult to watch you using powers you don't understand – especially when you're not aware you're doing it.'

Matthew left me to tend to the horses, tying their reins so that they wouldn't step on them but giving them the freedom to nibble the sparse fall grass. When he returned, his face was somber.

'There's something I need to show you.' He led me to the tree, and we sat underneath it. I folded my legs carefully to the side so that my boots didn't cut into my legs. Matthew simply dropped, his knees on the ground and his feet curled under his thighs.

He reached into the pocket of his breeches and drew out a piece of paper with black and gray bars on a white background. It had been folded and refolded several times.

It was a DNA report. 'Mine?'

'Yours.'

'When?' My fingers traced the bars along the page.

'Marcus brought the results to New College. I didn't want to share them with you so soon after you were reminded of your parents' death.' He hesitated. 'Was I right to wait?'

When I nodded, Matthew looked relieved. 'What does it say?' I asked.

'We don't understand everything,' he replied slowly. 'But Marcus and Miriam did identify markers in your DNA that we've seen before.'

Miriam's tiny, precise handwriting marched down the left side of the page, and the bars, some circled with red pen, marched down the right. 'This is the genetic marker for precognition,' Matthew continued, pointing to the first circled smudge. His finger began slowly moving down the page. 'This one is for flight. This helps witches find things that are lost.'

Matthew kept reeling off powers and abilities one at a time until my head spun.

'This one is for talking with the dead, this is transmogrification, this is telekinesis, this is spell casting, this one is charms, this one is curses. And you've got mind reading, telepathy, and empathy – they're next to one another.'

'This can't be right.' I'd never heard of a witch with more than one or two powers. Matthew had already reached a dozen.

'I think the findings are right, Diana. These powers may never manifest, but you've inherited the genetic predisposition for them.' He flipped the page. There were more red circles and more careful annotations by Miriam. 'Here are the elemental markers. Earth is present in almost all witches, and some have either earth and air or earth and water. You've got all three, which we've never seen before. And you've also got fire. Fire is very, very rare.' Matthew pointed to the four smudges.

'What are elemental markers?' My feet were feeling uncomfortably breezy, and my fingers were tingling.

'Indications that you have the genetic predisposition to control one or more of the elements. They explain why you could raise a witchwind. Based on this, you could command witchfire and what's called witchwater as well.'

'What does earth do?'

'Herbal magic, the power to affect growing things – the basics. Combined with spell casting, cursing, and charms – or any one of them, really – it means you have not only powerful magical abilities but an innate talent for witchcraft.'

My aunt was good with spells. Emily wasn't but could fly for short distances and see the future. These were classic differences among witches – dividing those who used witchcraft, like Sarah, from those who used magic. It all boiled down to whether words shaped your power or whether you just had it and could wield it as you liked. I buried my face in my hands. The prospect of seeing the future as my mother could had been scary enough. Control of the elements? Talking with the dead?

'There is a long list of powers on that sheet. We've only seen — what? — four or five of them?' It was terrifying.

'I suspect we've seen more than that — like the way you move with your eyes closed, your ability to communicate with Rakasa, and your sparkly fingers. We just don't have names for them yet.'

'Please tell me that's all.'

Matthew hesitated. 'Not quite.' He flipped to another page. 'We can't yet identify these markers. In most cases we have to correlate accounts of a witch's activities — some of them centuries old — with DNA evidence. It can be hard to match them up.'

'Do the tests explain why my magic is emerging now?'

'We don't need a test for that. Your magic is behaving as if it's waking after a long sleep. All that inactivity has made it restless, and now it wants to have its way. Blood will out,' Matthew said lightly. He rocked gracefully to his feet and lifted me up. 'You'll catch cold sitting on the ground, and I'll have a hell of a time explaining myself to Marthe if you get sick.' He whistled to the horses. They strolled in our direction, still munching on their unexpected treat.

We rode for another hour, exploring the woods and fields around Sept-Tours. Matthew pointed out the best place to hunt rabbits and where his father had taught him to shoot a crossbow without taking out his own eye. When we turned back to the stables, my worries over the test results had been replaced with a pleasant feeling of exhaustion.

'My muscles will be sore tomorrow,' I said, groaning. 'I haven't been on a horse for years.'

'Nobody would have guessed that from the way that you rode today,' he said. We passed out of the forest and entered the château's stone gate. 'You're a good rider, Diana, but you mustn't go out by yourself. It's too easy to lose your way.'

Matthew wasn't worried I'd get lost. He was worried I'd be found.

'I won't.'

His long fingers relaxed on the reins. He'd been clutching them for the past five minutes. This vampire was used to giving orders that were obeyed instantly. He wasn't accustomed to making requests and negotiating agreements. And his usual quick temper was nowhere in evidence.

Sidling Rakasa closer to Dahr, I reached over and raised Matthew's palm to my mouth. My lips were warm against his hard, cold flesh.

His pupils dilated in surprise.

I let go and, clucking Rakasa forward, headed into the stables.

CHAPTER 20

Ysabeau was mercifully absent at lunch. Afterward I wanted to go straight to Matthew's study and start examining *Aurora Consurgens*, but he convinced me to take a bath first. It would, he promised, make the inevitable muscle stiffness more bearable. Halfway upstairs, I had to stop and rub a cramp in my leg. I was going to pay for the morning's enthusiasm.

The bath was heavenly – long, hot, and relaxing. I put on loose black trousers, a sweater, and a pair of socks and padded downstairs, where a fire was blazing. My flesh turned orange and red as I held my hands out to the flames. What would it be like to control fire? My fingers tingled in response to the question, and I slid them safely into my pockets.

Matthew looked up from his desk. 'Your manuscript is next to your computer.'

Its black covers drew me as surely as a magnet. I sat down at the table and opened them, holding the book carefully. The colors were even brighter than I remembered. After staring at the queen for several minutes, I turned the first page.

'*Incipit tractatus Aurora Consurgens intitulatus.*' The words were familiar – 'Here begins the treatise called the Rising of the Dawn' – but I still felt the shiver of pleasure associated with seeing a manuscript for the first time. '*Everything good comes to me along with her. She is known as the Wisdom of the South, who calls out in the streets, and to the multitudes,*' I read silently, translating from the Latin. It was a beautiful work, full of paraphrases from Scripture as well as other texts.

'Do you have a Bible up here?' It would be wise for me to have one handy as I made my way through the manuscript.

'Yes — but I'm not sure where it is. Do you want me to look for it?' Matthew rose slightly from his chair, but his eyes were still glued to his computer screen.

'No, I'll find it.' I got up and ran my finger down the edge of the nearest shelf. Matthew's books were arranged not by size but in a running time line. Those on the first bookshelf were so ancient that I couldn't bear to think about what they contained — the lost works of Aristotle, perhaps? Anything was possible.

Roughly half of Matthew's books were shelved spine in to protect the books' fragile edges. Many of these had identifying marks written along the edges of the pages, and thick black letters spelled out a title here, an author's name there. Halfway around the room, the books began to appear spine out, their titles and authors embossed in gold and silver.

I slid past the manuscripts with their thick and bumpy pages, some with small Greek letters on the front edge. I kept going, looking for a large, fat, printed book. My index finger froze in front of one bound in brown leather and covered with gilding.

'Matthew, please tell me "Biblia Sacra 1450" is not what I think it is.'

'Okay, it's not what you think it is,' he said automatically, fingers racing over the keys with more than human speed. He was paying little attention to what I was doing and none at all to what I was saying.

Leaving Gutenberg's Bible where it was, I continued along the shelves, hoping that it wasn't the only one available to me. My finger froze again at a book labeled *Will's Playes*. 'Were these books given to you by friends?'

'Most of them.' Matthew didn't even look up.

Like German printing, the early days of English drama were a subject for later discussion.

For the most part, Matthew's books were in pristine condition. This was not entirely surprising, given their owner. Some, though, were well worn. A slender, tall book on the bottom shelf, for instance, had corners so torn and thin you could see the wooden boards peeking through the leather. Curious to see what had made this book a favorite, I pulled it out and opened the pages. It was Vesalius's anatomy book from 1543, the first to depict dissected human bodies in exacting detail.

Now hunting for fresh insights into Matthew, I sought out the next book to show signs of heavy use. This time it was a smaller, thicker volume. Inked onto the fore edge was the title *De motu*. William Harvey's study of the circulation of the blood and his explanation of how the heart pumped must have been interesting reading for vampires when it was first published in the 1620s, though they must already have had some notion that this might be the case.

Matthew's well-worn books included works on electricity, microscopy, and physiology. But the most battered book I'd seen yet was resting on the nineteenth-century shelves: a first edition of Darwin's *On the Origin of Species*.

Sneaking a glance at Matthew, I pulled the book off the shelf with the stealth of a shoplifter. Its green cloth binding, with the title and author stamped in gold, was frayed with wear. Matthew had written his name in a beautiful copperplate script on the flyleaf.

There was a letter folded inside.

'*Dear Sir,*' it began. '*Your letter of 15 October has reached me at last. I am mortified at my slow reply. I have for many years been collecting all the facts which I could in regard to the variation and origin of species, and your approval of my reasonings comes as welcome news as my book will soon pass into the publisher's hands.*' It was signed '*C. Darwin,*' and the date was 1859.

The two men had been exchanging letters just weeks prior to *Origin*'s publication in November.

The book's pages were covered with the vampire's notes in pencil and ink, leaving hardly an inch of blank paper. Three chapters were annotated even more heavily than the rest. They were the chapters on instinct, hybridism, and the affinities between the species.

Like Harvey's treatise on the circulation of blood, Darwin's seventh chapter, on natural instincts, must have been page-turning reading for vampires. Matthew had underlined specific passages and written above and below the lines as well as in the margins as he grew more excited by Darwin's ideas. '*Hence, we may conclude, that <u>domestic instincts have been acquired</u> and <u>natural instincts have been lost partly by habit</u>, and partly by <u>man selecting and accumulating</u> during successive generations, <u>peculiar mental habits and actions</u>, which at first appeared from what we must <u>in our ignorance call an accident</u>.*' Matthew's scribbled remarks included questions about which instincts might have been acquired and whether accidents were possible in nature. '*Can it be that we have maintained as instincts what humans have given up through accident and habit?*' he asked across the bottom margin. There was no need for me to ask who was included in 'we.' He meant creatures – not just vampires, but witches and daemons, too.

In the chapter on hybridism, Matthew's interest had been caught by the problems of crossbreeding and sterility. '*First crosses between forms sufficiently distinct to be ranked as species, and their hybrids,*' Darwin wrote, '*are very generally, but <u>not universally, sterile</u>.*' A sketch of a family tree crowded the margins next to the underlined passage. There was a question mark where the roots belonged and four branches. '*Why has inbreeding not led to sterility or madness?*' Matthew wondered in the tree's trunk. At the top of the page, he had written, '*1 species or 4?*' and '*comment sont faites les dāēōs?*'

I traced the writing with my finger. This was my specialty – turning the scribbles of scientists into something sensible to everyone else. In his last note, Matthew had used a familiar technique to hide his thoughts. He'd written in a combination of French and Latin – and used an archaic abbreviation for daemons for good measure in which the consonants save the first and last had been replaced with lines over the vowels. That way no one paging through his book would see the word 'daemons' and stop for a closer look.

'How are daemons made?' Matthew had wondered in 1859. He was still looking for the answer a century and a half later.

When Darwin began discussing the affinities between species, Matthew's pen had been unable to stop racing across the page, making it nearly impossible to read the printed text. Against a passage explaining, '*From the first dawn of life, all organic beings are found to resemble each other in descending degrees, so that they can be classed in groups under groups,*' Matthew had written '*ORIGINS*' in large black letters. A few lines down, another passage had been underlined twice: '*The existence of groups would have been of simple signification, if one group had been exclusively fitted to inhabit the land, and another the water; one to feed on flesh, another on vegetable matter, and so on; but the case is widely different in nature; for it is notorious how commonly members of even the same subgroup have different habits.*'

Did Matthew believe that the vampire diet was a habit rather than a defining characteristic of the species? Reading on, I found the next clue. '*Finally, the several classes of facts which have been considered in this chapter, seem to me to proclaim so plainly, that the innumerable species, genera, and families of organic beings, with which this world is peopled, have all descended, each within its own class or group, from common parents, and have all been modified in the course of descent.*' In the margins Matthew had written '*COMMON PARENTS*' and '*ce qui explique tout.*'

The vampire believed that monogenesis explained everything – or at least he had in 1859. Matthew thought it was possible that daemons, humans, vampires, and witches shared common ancestors. Our considerable differences were matters of descent, habit, and selection. He had evaded me in his laboratory when I asked whether we were one species or four, but he couldn't do so in his library.

Matthew remained fixated on his computer. Closing the covers of *Aurora Consurgens* to protect its pages and abandoning my search for a more ordinary Bible, I carried his copy of Darwin to the fire and curled up on the sofa. I opened it, intending to try to make sense of the vampire based on the notes he'd made in his book.

He was still a mystery to me – perhaps even more so here at Sept-Tours. Matthew in France was different from Matthew in England. He'd never lost himself in his work this way. Here his shoulders weren't fiercely squared but relaxed, and he'd caught his lower lip in his slightly elongated, sharp cuspid as he typed. It was a sign of concentration, as was the crease between his eyes. Matthew was oblivious to my attention, his fingers flying over the keys, clattering on the computer with a considerable amount of force. He must go through laptops at quite a rate, given their delicate plastic parts. He reached the end of a sentence, leaned back in his chair, and stretched. Then he yawned.

I'd never seen him yawn before. Was his yawn, like his lowered shoulders, a sign of relaxation? The day after we'd first met, Matthew had told me that he liked to know his environment. Here he knew every inch of the place – every smell was familiar, as was every creature who roamed nearby. And then there was his relationship with his mother and Marthe. They were a family, this odd assortment of vampires, and they had taken me in for Matthew's sake.

I turned back to Darwin. But the bath, the warm fire, and the constant background noise of his clacking fingers lulled me to sleep. I woke up covered with a blanket, *On the Origin of Species* lying on the floor nearby, neatly closed with a slip of paper marking my place.

I flushed.

I'd been caught snooping.

'Good evening,' Matthew said from the sofa opposite. He slid a piece of paper into the book that he was reading and rested it on his knee. 'Can I interest you in some wine?'

Wine sounded very, very good. 'Yes, please.'

Matthew went to a small eighteenth-century table near the landing. There was a bottle with no label, the cork pulled and lying at its side. He poured two glasses and carried one to me before he sat down. I sniffed, anticipating his first question.

'Raspberries and rocks.'

'For a witch you're really quite good at this.' Matthew nodded in approval.

'What is it that I'm drinking?' I asked, taking a sip. 'Is it ancient? Rare?'

Matthew put his head back and laughed. 'Neither. It was probably put in the bottle about five months ago. It's local wine, from vineyards down the road. Nothing fancy, nothing special.'

It may not have been fancy or special, but it was fresh and tasted woody and earthy like the air around Sept-Tours.

'I see that you gave up your search for a Bible in favor of something more scientific. Were you enjoying Darwin?' he asked mildly after watching me drink for a few moments.

'Do you still believe that creatures and humans are descended from common parents? Is it really possible that the differences between us are merely racial?'

He made a small sound of impatience. 'I told you in the lab that I didn't know.'

'You were sure in 1859. And you thought that drinking blood might be simply a dietary habit, not a mark of differentiation.'

'Do you know how many scientific advances have taken place between Darwin's time and today? It's a scientist's prerogative to change his mind as new information comes to light.' He drank some wine and rested the glass against his knee, turning it this way and that so the firelight played on the liquid inside. 'Besides, there's no longer much scientific evidence for human notions of racial distinctions. Modern research suggests that most ideas about race are nothing more than an outmoded human method for explaining easily observable differences between themselves and someone else.'

'The question of why you're here – how we're all here – really does consume you,' I said slowly. 'I could see it on every page of Darwin's book.'

Matthew studied his wine. 'It's the only question worth asking.'

His voice was soft, but his profile was stern, with its sharp lines and heavy brow. I wanted to smooth the lines and lift his features into a smile but remained seated while the firelight danced over his white skin and dark hair. Matthew picked up his book again, cradling it in one set of long fingers while his wineglass rested in the other.

I stared at the fire as the light dimmed. When a clock on the desk struck seven, Matthew put down his book. 'Should we join Ysabeau in the salon before dinner?'

'Yes,' I replied, squaring my shoulders slightly. 'But let me change first.' My wardrobe couldn't hold a candle to Ysabeau's, but I didn't want Matthew to be completely ashamed of me. As ever, he looked ready for a boardroom or a Milan catwalk in a simple pair of black wool trousers and a fresh selection from his endless supply of sweaters. My recent close encounters with them had convinced me they were all cashmere – thick and luscious.

Upstairs, I rooted through the items in my duffel bag and selected a gray pair of trousers and a sapphire blue sweater made out of finely spun wool with a tight, funnel-shaped neck and bell-shaped sleeves. My hair had a wave in it thanks to my earlier bath and the fact that it had finished drying scrunched under my head on the sofa.

With the minimum conditions of presentability met, I slid on my loafers and started down the stairs. Matthew's keen ears had picked up the sound of my movements, and he met me on the landing. When he saw me, his eyes lit up and his smile was wide and slow.

'I like you in blue as much as I like you in black. You look beautiful,' he murmured, kissing me formally on both cheeks. The blood moved toward them as Matthew lifted my hair around my shoulders, the strands falling through his long white fingers. 'Now, don't let Ysabeau get under your skin no matter what she says.'

'I'll try,' I said with a little laugh, looking up at him uncertainly.

When we reached the salon, Marthe and Ysabeau were already there. His mother was surrounded by newspapers written in every major European language, as well as one in Hebrew and another in Arabic. Marthe, on the other hand, was reading a paperback murder mystery with a lurid cover, her black eyes darting over the lines of print with enviable speed.

'Good evening, *Maman*,' Matthew said, moving to give Ysabeau a kiss on each cold cheek. Her nostrils flared as he moved his body from one side to the other, and her cold eyes fixed on mine angrily.

I knew what had earned me such a black look.

Matthew smelled like me.

'Come, girl,' Marthe said, patting the cushion next to her and shooting Matthew's mother a warning glance. Ysabeau closed her eyes. When they opened again, the anger was gone, replaced by something like resignation.

'*Gab es einen anderen Tod*,' Ysabeau murmured to her son as Matthew picked up *Die Welt* and began scanning the headlines with a sound of disgust.

'Where?' I asked. Another bloodless corpse had been found. If Ysabeau thought she was going to shut me out of the conversation with German, she'd better think again.

'Munich,' Matthew said, his face buried in the pages. 'Christ, why doesn't someone *do* something about this?'

'We must be careful what we wish for, Matthew,' Ysabeau said. She changed the subject abruptly. 'How was your ride, Diana?'

Matthew peered warily at his mother over *Die Welt*'s headlines.

'It was wonderful. Thank you for letting me ride Rakasa,' I replied, sitting back next to Marthe and forcing myself to meet Ysabeau's eyes without blinking.

'She is too willful for my liking,' she said, shifting her attention to her son, who had the good sense to put his nose back in his paper. 'Fiddat is much more biddable. As I get older, I find that quality admirable in horses.'

In sons, too, I thought.

Marthe smiled encouragingly at me and got up to fuss at a sideboard. She carried a large goblet of wine to Ysabeau and a much smaller one to me. Marthe returned to the table and came back with another glass for Matthew. He sniffed it appreciatively.

'Thank you, *Maman*,' he said, raising his glass in tribute.

'*Hein*, it's not much,' Ysabeau said, taking a sip of the same wine.

'No, not much. Just one of my favorites. Thank you for remembering.' Matthew savored the wine's flavors before swallowing the liquid down.

'Are all vampires as fond of wine as you are?' I asked Matthew, smelling the peppery wine. 'You drink it all the time, and you never get the slightest bit tipsy.'

Matthew grinned. 'Most vampires are much fonder of it. As for getting drunk, our family has always been known for its admirable restraint, hasn't it, *Maman*?'

Ysabeau gave a most unladylike snort. 'Occasionally. With respect to wine, perhaps.'

'You should be a diplomat, Ysabeau. You're very good with a quick non-answer,' I said.

Matthew shouted with laughter. '*Dieu*, I never thought the day would come when my mother would be thought diplomatic. Especially not with her tongue. Ysabeau's always been much better with the diplomacy of the sword.'

Marthe snickered in agreement.

Ysabeau and I both looked indignant, which only made him shout again.

The atmosphere at dinner was considerably warmer than it had been last night. Matthew sat at the head of the table, with Ysabeau to his left and me at his right. Marthe traveled incessantly from kitchen to fireside to table, sitting now and again to take a sip of wine and make small contributions to the conversation.

Plates full of food came and went – everything from wild mushroom soup to quail to delicate slices of beef. I marveled aloud that someone who no longer ate cooked food could have such a deft hand with spices. Marthe blushed and dimpled, swatting at Matthew when he tried to tell stories of her more spectacular culinary disasters.

'Do you remember the live pigeon pie?' He chortled. 'No one ever explained that you had to keep the birds from eating for twenty-four hours before you baked it or the inside would resemble a birdbath.' That earned him a sharp tap on the back of his skull.

'Matthew,' Ysabeau warned, wiping the tears from her eyes after a prolonged bout of laughter, 'you shouldn't bait Marthe. You have had your share of disasters over the years, too.'

'And I have seen them all,' Marthe pronounced, carrying over a salad. Her English got stronger by the hour, as she switched into the language whenever she talked in front of me. She returned to the sideboard and fetched a bowl of nuts, which she put between Matthew and Ysabeau. 'When you flooded the castle with your idea for capturing water on the roof, for one,' she said, ticking it off on her fingers. 'When you forgot to collect the taxes, two. It was spring, you were bored, and so you got up one morning and went to Italy to make war. Your father had to beg forgiveness from the king on his knees. And then there was New York!' she shouted triumphantly.

The three vampires continued to swap reminiscences. None of them talked about Ysabeau's past, though. When something came up that touched on her, or Matthew's father, or his sister, the conversation slid gracefully away. I noticed the pattern and wondered about the reasons for it but said nothing, content to let the evening develop as they wished it to and strangely comforted to be part of a family again – even a family of vampires.

After dinner we returned to the salon, where the fire was larger and more impressive than before. The castle's chimneys were heating up with each log thrown into the grate. The fires burned hotter, and the room almost felt warm as a result. Matthew made sure that Ysabeau was comfortable, getting her yet another glass of wine, and fiddled with a nearby stereo. Marthe made me tea instead, thrusting the cup and saucer into my hands.

'Drink,' she instructed, her eyes attentive. Ysabeau watched me drink, too, and gave Marthe a long look. 'It will help you sleep.'

'Did you make this?' It tasted of herbs and flowers. Normally I didn't like herbal tea, but this one was fresh and slightly bitter.

'Yes,' she answered, turning up her chin at Ysabeau's stare. 'I have made it for a long time. My mother taught me. I will teach you as well.'

The sound of dance music filled the room, lively and rhythmic. Matthew adjusted the position of the chairs by the fireplace, clearing a spot on the floor.

'*Vòles dançar amb ieu?*' Matthew asked his mother, holding out both hands.

Ysabeau's smile was radiant, transforming her lovely, cold features into something indescribably beautiful. '*Òc,*' she said, putting her tiny hands into his. The two of them took their places in front of the fire, waiting for the next song to start.

When Matthew and his mother began to dance, they made Astaire and Rogers look clumsy. Their bodies came together and drew apart, turned in circles away from each other and then dipped and turned. The slightest touch from Matthew sent Ysabeau reeling, and the merest hint of an undulation or a hesitation from Ysabeau caused a corresponding response in him.

Ysabeau dipped into a graceful curtsy, and Matthew swept into a bow at the precise moment the music drew to its close.

'What was that?' I asked.

'It started out as a tarantella,' Matthew said, escorting his mother back to her chair, 'but *Maman* never can stick to one dance. So there were elements of the volta in the middle, and we finished with a minuet, didn't we?' Ysabeau nodded and reached up to pat him on the cheek.

'You always were a good dancer,' she said proudly.

'Ah, but not as good as you – and certainly not as good as Father was,' Matthew said, settling her in her chair. Ysabeau's eyes darkened, and a heartbreaking look of sadness crossed her face. Matthew picked up her hand and brushed his lips across her knuckles. Ysabeau managed a small smile in return.

'Now it's your turn,' he said, coming to me.

'I don't like to dance, Matthew,' I protested, holding up my hands to fend him off.

'I find that hard to believe,' he said, taking my right hand in his left and drawing me close. 'You contort your body into improbable shapes, skim across the water in a boat the width of a feather, and ride like the wind. Dancing should be second nature.'

The next song sounded like something that might have been popular in Parisian dance halls in the 1920s. Notes of trumpet and drum filled the room.

'Matthew, be careful with her,' Ysabeau warned as he moved me across the floor.

'She won't break, *Maman*.' Matthew proceeded to dance, despite my best efforts to put my feet in his way at every opportunity. With his right hand at my waist, he gently steered me into the proper steps.

I started to think about where my legs were in an effort to help the process along, but this only made things worse. My back stiffened, and Matthew clasped me tighter.

'Relax,' he murmured into my ear. 'You're trying to lead. Your job is to follow.'

'I can't,' I whispered back, gripping his shoulder as if he were a life preserver.

Matthew spun us around again. 'Yes you can. Close your eyes, stop thinking about it, and let me do the rest.'

Inside the circle of his arms, it was easy to do what he instructed. Without the whirling shapes and colors of the room coming at me from all directions, I could relax and stop worrying that we were about to crash. Gradually the movement of our bodies in the darkness became enjoyable. Soon it was possible for me to concentrate not on what I was doing but on what his legs and arms were telling me he was about to do. It felt like floating.

'Matthew.' Ysabeau's voice held a note of caution. '*Le chatoiement.*'

'I know,' he murmured. The muscles in my shoulders tensed with concern. 'Trust me,' he said quietly into my ear. 'I've got you.'

My eyes remained tightly closed, and I sighed happily. We continued to swirl together. Matthew gently released me, spinning me out to the end of his fingers, then rolled me back along his arm until I came to rest, my back tight against his chest. The music stopped.

'Open your eyes,' he said softly.

My eyelids slowly lifted. The feeling of floating remained. Dancing was better than I had expected it to be – at least it was with a partner who'd been dancing for more than a millennium and never stepped on your toes.

I tilted my face up to thank him, but his was much closer than expected.

'Look down,' Matthew said.

Turning my head in the other direction revealed that my toes were dangling several inches above the floor. Matthew released me. He wasn't holding me up.

I was holding me up.

The air was holding me up.

With that realization the weight returned to the lower half of my body. Matthew gripped both elbows to keep my feet from smashing into the floor.

From her seat by the fire, Marthe hummed a tune under her breath. Ysabeau's head whipped around, eyes narrowed. Matthew smiled at me reassuringly, while I concentrated on the uncanny feeling of the earth under my feet. Had the ground always seemed so alive? It was as if a thousand tiny hands were waiting under the soles of my shoes to catch me or give me a push.

'Was it fun?' Matthew asked as the last notes of Marthe's song faded, eyes gleaming.

'It was,' I answered, laughing, after considering his question.

'I hoped it would be. You've been practicing for years. Now maybe you'll ride with your eyes open for a change.' He caught me up in an embrace full of happiness and possibility.

Ysabeau began to sing the same song Marthe had been humming.

> '*Whoever sees her dance,*
>   *And her body move so gracefully,*
>   *Could say, in truth,*
>   *That in all the world she has no equal,*
> *our joyful queen.*
> *Go away, go away, jealous ones,*
> *Let us, let us,*
> *Dance together, together.*'

'*Go away, go away, jealous ones,*' Matthew repeated as the final echo of his mother's voice faded, '*let us dance together.*'

I laughed again. 'With you I'll dance. But until I figure out how this flying business works, there will be no other partners.'

'Properly speaking, you were floating, not flying,' Matthew corrected me.

'Floating, flying – whatever you call it, it would be best not to do it with strangers.'

'Agreed,' he said.

Marthe had vacated the sofa for a chair near Ysabeau. Matthew and I sat together, our hands still entwined.

'This was her first time?' Ysabeau asked him, her voice genuinely puzzled.

'Diana doesn't use magic, *Maman*, except for little things,' he explained.

'She is full of power, Matthew. Her witch's blood sings in her veins. She should be able to use it for big things, too.'

He frowned. 'It's hers to use or not.'

'Enough of such childishness,' she said, turning her attention to me. 'It is time for you to grow up, Diana, and accept responsibility for who you are.'

Matthew growled softly.

'Do not growl at me, Matthew de Clermont! I am saying what needs to be said.'

'You're telling her what to do. It's not your job.'

'Nor yours, my son!' Ysabeau retorted.

'Excuse me!' My sharp tone caught their attention, and the de Clermonts, mother and son, stared at me. 'It's my decision whether – and how – to use my magic. But,' I said, turning to Ysabeau, 'it can't be ignored any longer. It seems to be bubbling out of me. I need to learn how to control my power, at the very least.'

Ysabeau and Matthew continued to stare. Finally Ysabeau nodded. Matthew did, too.

We continued to sit by the fire until the logs burned down. Matthew danced with Marthe, and each of them broke into song occasionally when a piece of music reminded them of another night, by another fire. But I didn't dance again, and Matthew didn't press me.

Finally he stood. 'I am taking the only one of us who needs her sleep up to bed.'

I stood as well, smoothing my trousers against my thighs. 'Good night, Ysabeau. Good night, Marthe. Thank you both for a lovely dinner and a surprising evening.'

Marthe gave me a smile in return. Ysabeau did her best but managed only a tight grimace.

Matthew let me lead the way and put his hand gently against the small of my back as we climbed the stairs.

'I might read for a bit,' I said, turning to face him when we reached his study.

He was directly behind me, so close that the faint, ragged sound of his breath was audible. He took my face in his hands.

'What spell have you put on me?' He searched my face. 'It's not simply your eyes – though they do make it impossible for me to think straight – or the fact you smell like honey.' He buried his face in my neck, the fingers of one hand sliding into my hair while the other drifted down my back, pulling my hips toward him.

My body softened into his, as if it were meant to fit there.

'It's your fearlessness,' he murmured against my skin, 'and the way you move without thinking, and the shimmer you give off when you concentrate – or when you fly.'

My neck arched, exposing more flesh to his touch. Matthew slowly turned my face toward him, his thumb seeking out the warmth of my lips.

'Did you know that your mouth puckers when you sleep? You look as though you might be displeased with your dreams, but I prefer to think you wish to be kissed.' He sounded more French with each word that he spoke.

Aware of Ysabeau's disapproving presence downstairs, as well as her acute, vampiric hearing, I tried to pull away. It wasn't convincing, and Matthew's arms tightened.

'Matthew, your mother—'

He gave me no chance to complete my sentence. With a soft, satisfied sound, he deliberately fitted his lips to mine and kissed me, gently but thoroughly, until my entire body – not just my hands – was tingling. I kissed him back, feeling a simultaneous sense of floating and falling until I had no clear awareness of where my body ended and his began. His mouth drifted to my cheeks and eyelids. When it brushed against my ear, I gasped. Matthew's lips curved into a smile, and he pressed them once more against my own.

'Your lips are as red as poppies, and your hair is so alive,' he said when he was quite finished kissing me with an intensity that left me breathless.

'What is it with you and my hair? Why anyone with a head of hair like yours would be impressed with this,' I said, grabbing a fistful of it and pulling, 'is beyond me. Ysabeau's hair looks like satin, so does Marthe's. Mine is a mess – every color of the rainbow and badly behaved as well.'

'That's why I love it,' Matthew said, gently freeing the strands. 'It's imperfect, just like life. It's not vampire hair, all polished and flawless. I like that you're not a vampire, Diana.'

'And I like that you *are* a vampire, Matthew.'

A shadow flitted across his eyes, gone in a moment.

'I like your strength,' I said, kissing him with the same enthusiasm as he had kissed me. 'I like your intelligence. Sometimes I even like your bossiness. But most of all' – I rubbed the tip of my nose gently against his – 'I like the way you smell.'

'You do?'

'I do.' My nose went into the hollow between his collarbones, which I was fast learning was the spiciest, sweetest part of him.

'It's late. You need your rest.' He released me reluctantly.

'Come to bed with me.'

His eyes widened with surprise at the invitation, and the blood coursed to my face.

Matthew brought my hand to his heart. It beat once, powerfully. 'I will come up,' he said, 'but not to stay. We have time, Diana. You've known me for only a few weeks. There's no need to rush.'

Spoken like a vampire.

He saw my dejection and drew me closer for another lingering kiss. 'A promise,' he said, when he was finished, 'of what's to come. In time.'

It *was* time. But my lips were alternately freezing and burning, making me wonder for a fleeting second if I was as ready as I thought.

Upstairs, the room was ablaze with candles and warm from the fire. How Marthe had managed to get up here, change dozens of candles, and light them so that they would still be burning at bedtime was a mystery, but the room didn't have a single electrical outlet, so I was doubly grateful for her efforts.

Changing in the bathroom behind a partially closed door, I listened to Matthew's plans for the next day. These involved a long walk, another long ride, and more work in the study.

I agreed to all of it – provided that the work came first. The alchemical manuscript was calling to me, and I was eager to get a closer look at it.

I got into Matthew's vast four-poster, and he tightened the sheets around my body before pinching out the candles.

'Sing to me,' I said, watching his long fingers fearlessly move through the flames. 'An old song – one Marthe likes.' Her wicked fondness for love songs had not gone unnoticed.

He was quiet for a few moments while he walked through the room, snuffing the candles and trailing shadows behind him as the room fell into darkness. He began to sing in his rich baritone.

> *'Ni muer ni viu ni no guaris,*
> *Ni mal no·om sent e si l'ai gran,*
> *Quar de s'amor no suy devis,*
> *Ni no sai si ja n'aurai ni quan,*
> *Qu'en lieys es tota le mercés*
> *Que·m pot sorʒer o decaʒer.'*

The song was full of yearning, and teetered on the edge of sadness. By the time he returned to my side, the song was finished. Matthew left one candle burning next to the bed.

'What do the words mean?' I reached for his hand.

' "*Not dying nor living nor healing, there is no pain in my sickness, for I am not kept from her love.*" ' He leaned down and kissed me on the forehead. ' "*I don't know if I will ever have it, for all the mercy that makes me flourish or decay is in her power.*" '

'Who wrote that?' I asked, struck by the aptness of the words when sung by a vampire.

'My father wrote it for Ysabeau. Someone else took the credit, though,' Matthew said, his eyes gleaming and his smile bright and content. He hummed the song under his breath as he went downstairs. I lay in his bed, alone, and watched the last candle burn until it guttered out.

CHAPTER 21

A vampire holding a breakfast tray greeted me the next morning after my shower.

'I told Marthe you wanted to work this morning,' Matthew explained, lifting the cover that was keeping the food warm.

'You two are spoiling me.' I unfolded the napkin waiting on a nearby chair.

'I don't think your character is in any real danger.' Matthew stooped and gave me a lingering kiss, his eyes smoky. 'Good morning. Did you sleep well?'

'Very well.' I took the plate from his hands, my cheeks reddening at the memory of the invitation I'd extended to him last night. There was still a twinge of hurt when I recalled his gentle rebuff, but this morning's kiss confirmed that we had slipped past the limits of friendship and were moving in a new direction.

After my breakfast we headed downstairs, turned on our computers, and got to work. Matthew had left a perfectly ordinary nineteenth-century copy of an early English translation of the Vulgate Bible on the table next to his manuscript.

'Thank you,' I called over my shoulder, holding it up.

'I found it downstairs. Apparently the one I have isn't good enough for you.' He grinned.

'I absolutely refuse to treat a Gutenberg Bible as a reference book, Matthew.' My voice came out more sternly than anticipated, making me sound like a schoolmarm.

'I know the Bible backwards and forwards. If you have a question, you could just ask me,' he suggested.

'I'm not using you as a reference book either.'

'Suit yourself,' he said with a shrug and another smile.

With my computer at my side and an alchemical manuscript before me, I was soon absorbed in reading, analyzing, and recording my ideas. There was one distracting incident when I asked Matthew for something to weight down the book's pages while I typed. He rummaged around and found a bronze medal with the likeness of Louis XIV on it and a small wooden foot that he claimed came from a German angel. He wouldn't surrender the two objects without sureties for their return. Finally he was satisfied by several more kisses.

Aurora Consurgens was one of the most beautiful texts in the alchemical tradition, a meditation on the female figure of Wisdom as well as an exploration of the chemical reconciliation of opposing natural forces. The text in Matthew's copy was nearly identical to the copies I'd consulted in Zurich, Glasgow, and London. But the illustrations were quite different.

The artist, Bourgot Le Noir, had been a true master of her craft. Each illumination was precise and beautifully executed. But her talent did not lie simply in technical mastery. Her depictions of the female characters showed a different sensibility. Bourgot's Wisdom was full of strength, but there was a softness to her as well. In the first illumination, where Wisdom shielded the personification of the seven metals in her cloak, she bore an expression of fierce, maternal pride.

There were two illuminations – just as Matthew had promised – that weren't included in any known copy of *Aurora Consurgens*. Both appeared in the final parable, devoted to the chemical wedding of gold and silver. The first accompanied words spoken by the female principle in alchemical change. Often represented as a queen dressed in white with emblems of the moon to show her association with silver, she had been transformed by Bourgot into a beautiful, terrifying creature with silvery snakes instead of hair, her face shadowed like a moon eclipsed by the sun. Silently I read the accompanying text, translating the Latin into English: '*Turn to me with all your heart. Do not refuse me because I am dark and shadowed.*

The fire of the sun has altered me. The seas have encompassed me. The earth has been corrupted because of my work. Night fell over the earth when I sank into the miry deep, and my substance was hidden.'

The Moon Queen held a star in one outstretched palm. *'From the depths of the water I cried out to you, and from the depths of the earth I will call to those who pass by me,'* I continued. *'Watch for me. See me. And if you find another who is like me, I will give him the morning star.'* My lips formed the words, and Bourgot's illumination bought the text to life in the Moon Queen's expression that showed both her fear of rejection and her shy pride.

The second unique illumination came on the next page and accompanied the words spoken by the male principle, the golden Sun King. The hair on my neck rose at Bourgot's depiction of a heavy stone sarcophagus, its lid open just enough to reveal a golden body lying within. The king's eyes were closed peacefully, and there was a look of hope on his face as if he were dreaming of his release. *'I will rise now and go about the city. In its streets I will seek out a pure woman to marry,'* I read, *'her face beautiful, her body more beautiful, her raiment most beautiful. She will roll away the stone from the entrance of my tomb and give me the wings of a dove so that I might fly with her to the heavens to live forever and be at rest.'* The passage reminded me of Matthew's badge from Bethany and Lazarus's tiny silver coffin. I reached for the Bible.

'Mark 16, Psalms 55, and Deuteronomy 32, verse 40.' Matthew's voice cut through the quiet, spouting references like an automated biblical concordance.

'How did you know what I was reading?' I twisted in my chair to get a better view of him.

'Your lips were moving,' he replied, staring fixedly at his computer screen, his fingers clattering on the keys.

Pressing my lips together I returned to the text. The author had drawn on every biblical passage that fit the alchemical story of death and creation, paraphrasing and cobbling them together. I pulled the Bible across the desk. It was bound in black leather and a gold cross adorned the cover. Opening it to the Gospel of Mark, I scanned chapter 16. There it was, Mark 16:3, '*And they said one to another: Who shall roll us back the stone from the door of the sepulchre?*'

'Find it?' Matthew inquired mildly.

'Yes.'

'Good.'

The room grew silent once more.

'Where's the verse about the morning star?' Sometimes my pagan background was a serious professional liability.

'Revelation 2, verse 28.'

'Thank you.'

'My pleasure.' A smothered laugh came from the other desk. I bent my head to the manuscript and ignored it.

After two hours of reading tiny, Gothic handwriting and searching for corresponding biblical references, I was more than ready to go riding when Matthew suggested it was time for a break. As an added bonus, he promised to tell me over lunch how he knew the seventeenth-century physiologist William Harvey.

'It's not a very interesting story,' Matthew had protested.

'Maybe not to you. But to a historian of science? It's the closest thing I'll get to meeting the man who figured out that the heart is a pump.'

We hadn't seen the sun since we'd arrived at Sept-Tours, but neither of us minded. Matthew seemed more relaxed, and I was surprisingly happy to be out of Oxford. Gillian's threats, the picture of my parents, even Peter Knox – they all receded with each hour that passed.

As we walked out into the gardens, Matthew chatted animatedly about a problem at work that involved a missing strand of something that should have been present in a blood sample but wasn't. He sketched out a chromosome in the air in an effort to explain, pointing to the offending area, and I nodded even though what was at stake remained mysterious. The words continued to roll out of his mouth, and he put an arm around my shoulder, drawing me close.

We rounded a line of hedges. A man in black stood outside the gate we'd passed through yesterday on our ride. The way he leaned against a chestnut tree, with the elegance of a leopard on the prowl, suggested he was a vampire.

Matthew scooped me behind him.

The man pulled himself gracefully away from the tree's rough trunk and strolled toward us. The fact that he was a vampire was now confirmed by his unnaturally white skin and huge, dark eyes, emphasized by his black leather jacket, jeans, and boots. This vampire didn't care who knew he was different. His wolfish expression was the only imperfection in an otherwise angelic face, with symmetrical features and dark hair worn curling low onto his collar. He was smaller and slighter than Matthew, but the power he exuded was undeniable. His eyes sent coldness deep under my skin, where it spread like a stain.

'Domenico,' Matthew said calmly, though his voice was louder than usual.

'Matthew.' The glance the vampire turned on Matthew was full of hate.

'It's been years.' Matthew's casual tone suggested that the vampire's sudden appearance was an everyday occurrence.

Domenico looked thoughtful. 'When was that? In Ferrara? We were both fighting the Pope – though for different reasons, as I remember. I was trying to save Venice. You were trying to save the Templars.'

Matthew nodded slowly, his eyes fixed on the other vampire. 'I think you must be right.'

'After that, my friend, you seemed to disappear. We shared so many adventures in our youth: on the seas, in the Holy Land. Venice was always full of amusements for a vampire such as you, Matthew.' Domenico shook his head in apparent sorrow. The vampire inside the château gate did look Venetian – or like some unholy cross between an angel and a devil. 'Why did you not come and visit me when you passed between France and one of your other haunts?'

'If I caused offense, Domenico, it was surely too long ago to be of any concern to us now.'

'Perhaps, but one thing hasn't changed in all these years. Whenever there's a crisis, there's a de Clermont nearby.' He turned to me, and something avaricious bloomed on his face. 'This must be the witch I've heard so much about.'

'Diana, go back to the house,' Matthew said sharply.

The sense of danger was palpable, and I hesitated, not wanting to leave him alone.

'Go,' he said again, his voice as keen edged as a sword.

Our vampire visitor spotted something over my shoulder and smiled. An icy breeze brushed past me and a cold, hard arm linked through mine.

'Domenico,' chimed Ysabeau's musical voice. 'What an unexpected visit.'

He bowed formally. 'My lady, it is a pleasure to see you in such good health. How did you know I was here?'

'I smelled you,' Ysabeau said contemptuously. 'You come here, to my house, uninvited. What would your mother say if she knew you behaved in such a fashion?'

'If my mother was still alive, we could ask her,' Domenico said with barely concealed savagery.

'*Maman*, take Diana back to the house.'

'Of course, Matthew. We will leave the two of you to talk.' Ysabeau turned, tugging me along with her.

'I'll be gone more quickly if you let me deliver my message,' Domenico warned. 'If I have to come back, I won't be alone. Today's visit was a courtesy to you, Ysabeau.'

'She doesn't have the book,' Matthew said sharply.

'I'm not here about the witches' damned book, Matthew. Let them keep it. I've come from the Congregation.'

Ysabeau exhaled, soft and long, as if she'd been holding her breath for days. A question burbled to my lips, but she silenced it with a warning look.

'Well done, Domenico. I'm surprised you have the time to call on old friends, with all your new responsibilities.' Matthew's voice was scornful. 'Why is the Congregation wasting time paying official visits on the de Clermont family when there are vampires leaving bloodless corpses all over Europe for humans to find?'

'It's not forbidden for vampires to feed on humans – though the carelessness is regrettable. As you know, death follows vampires wherever we go.' Domenico shrugged off the brutality, and I shivered at his casual disregard for frail, warmblooded life. 'But the covenant clearly forbids any liaison between a vampire and a witch.'

I turned and stared at Domenico. '*What* did you say?'

'She can speak!' Domenico clasped his hands in mock delight. 'Why not let the witch take part in this conversation?'

Matthew reached around and drew me forward. Ysabeau remained entwined through my other arm. We stood in a short, tight line of vampire, witch, and vampire.

'Diana Bishop.' Domenico bowed low. 'It's an honor to meet a witch of such ancient, distinguished lineage. So few of the old families are still with us.' Every word he uttered – no matter how formally phrased – sounded like a threat.

'Who are you?' I asked. 'And why are you concerned with whom I spend time?'

The Venetian looked at me with interest before his head fell back and he howled with laughter. 'They said you were argumentative like your father, but I didn't believe them.'

My fingers tingled slightly, and Ysabeau's arm grew fractionally tighter.

'Have I made your witch angry?' Domenico's eyes were fixed on Ysabeau's arm.

'Say what you came to say and get off our land.' Matthew's voice was entirely conversational.

'My name is Domenico Michele. I have known Matthew since I was reborn, and Ysabeau nearly as long. I know neither of them so well as I knew the lovely Louisa, of course. But we should not speak lightly of the dead.' The Venetian crossed himself piously.

'You should try not to speak of my sister at all.' Matthew sounded calm, but Ysabeau looked murderous, her lips white.

'You still haven't answered my question,' I said, drawing Domenico's attention once more.

The Venetian's eyes glittered with frank appraisal.

'Diana,' Matthew said, unable to stop the rumble in his throat. It was as close as he'd ever been to growling at me. Marthe came out of the kitchens, a look of alarm on her face.

'She is more fiery than most of her kind, I see. Is that why you're risking everything to keep her with you? Does she amuse you? Or do you intend to feed on her until you get bored and then discard her, as you have with other warmbloods?'

Matthew's hands strayed to Lazarus's coffin, evident only as a bump under his sweater. He hadn't touched it since we'd arrived in Sept-Tours.

Domenico's keen eyes noticed the gesture, too, and his answering smile was vindictive. 'Feeling guilty?'

Furious at the way Domenico was baiting Matthew, I opened my mouth to speak.

'Diana, go back to the house immediately.' Matthew's tone suggested that we would have a serious, unpleasant talk later. He pushed me slightly in Ysabeau's direction and put himself even more squarely between his mother, me, and the dark Venetian. By that time Marthe was nearby, her arms crossed over her sturdy body in a striking imitation of Matthew.

'Not before the witch hears what I have to say. I have come to serve you with a warning, Diana Bishop. Relationships between witches and vampires are forbidden. You must leave this house and no longer associate with Matthew de Clermont or any of his family. If you don't, the Congregation will take whatever steps are necessary to preserve the covenant.'

'I don't know your Congregation, and I agreed to no such covenant,' I said, still furious. 'Besides, covenants aren't enforceable. They're voluntary.'

'Are you a lawyer as well as a historian? You modern women with your fine educations are so fascinating. But women are no good at theology,' Domenico continued sorrowfully, 'which is why we never thought it worth educating you in the first place. Do you think we adhered to the ideas of that heretic Calvin when we made these promises to one another? When the covenant was sworn, it bound all vampires, daemons, and witches – past, present, and future. This is not a path you can follow or not as you please.'

'You've delivered your warning, Domenico,' Matthew said in a voice like silk.

'That's all I have to say to the witch,' the Venetian replied. 'I have more to say to you.'

'Then Diana will return to the house. Get her out of here, *Maman*,' he said tersely.

This time his mother did what he asked immediately, and Marthe followed. 'Don't,' Ysabeau hissed when I turned to look back at Matthew.

'Where did that thing come from?' Marthe asked once we were safely inside.

'From hell, presumably,' said Ysabeau. She touched my face briefly with her fingertips, drawing them back hastily when they met the warmth of my angry cheeks. 'You are brave, girl, but what you did was reckless. You are not a vampire. Do not put yourself at risk by arguing with Domenico or any of his allies. Stay away from them.'

Ysabeau gave me no time to respond, speeding me through the kitchens, the dining room, the salon, and into the great hall. Finally she towed me toward the arch that led to the keep's most formidable tower. My calves seized up at the thought of the climb.

'We must,' she insisted. 'Matthew will be looking for us there.'

Fear and anger propelled me halfway up the stairs. The second half I conquered through sheer determination. Lifting my feet from the final tread, I found myself on a flat roof with a view for miles in every direction. A faint breeze blew, loosening my braided hair and coaxing the mist around me.

Ysabeau moved swiftly to a pole that extended another dozen feet into the sky. She raised a forked black banner adorned with a silver ouroboros. It unfurled in the gloomy light, the snake holding its shimmering tail in its mouth. I ran to the far side of the crenellated walls, and Domenico looked up.

Moments later a similar banner rose over the top of a building in the village and a bell began to toll. Men and women slowly came out of houses, bars, shops, and offices, their faces turned toward Sept-Tours, where the ancient symbol of eternity and rebirth snapped in the wind. I looked at Ysabeau, my question evident on my face.

'Our family's emblem, and a warning to the village to be on their guard,' she explained. 'We fly the banner only when others are with us. The villagers have grown too accustomed to living among vampires, and though they have nothing to fear from us, we have kept it for times such as this. The world is full of vampires who cannot be trusted, Diana. Domenico Michele is one of them.'

'You didn't need to tell me that. Who the hell is he?'

'One of Matthew's oldest friends,' Ysabeau murmured, eyes on her son, 'which makes him a very dangerous enemy.'

My attention turned to Matthew, who continued to exchange words with Domenico across a precisely drawn zone of engagement. There was a blur of black and gray movement, and the Venetian hurtled backward toward the chestnut tree he'd been leaning against when we first spotted him. A loud crack carried across the grounds.

'Well done,' Ysabeau muttered.

'Where's Marthe?' I looked over my shoulder toward the stairs.

'In the hall. Just in case.' Ysabeau's keen eyes remained fixed on her son.

'Would Domenico really come in here and rip my throat open?'

Ysabeau turned her black, glittering gaze on me. 'That would be all too easy, my dear. He would play with you first. He always plays with his prey. And Domenico loves an audience.'

I swallowed hard. 'I'm capable of taking care of myself.'

'You are, if you have as much power as Matthew believes. Witches are very good at protecting themselves, I've found, with a little effort and a drop of courage,' Ysabeau said.

'What is this Congregation that Domenico mentioned?' I asked.

'A council of nine – three from each order of daemons, witches, and vampires. It was established during the Crusades to keep us from being exposed to the humans. We were careless and became too involved in their politics and other forms of insanity.' Ysabeau's voice was bitter. 'Ambition, pride, and grasping creatures like Michele who were never content with their lot in life and always wanted more – they drove us to the covenant.'

'And you agreed to certain conditions?' It was ludicrous to think that promises made by creatures in the Middle Ages could affect Matthew and me.

Ysabeau nodded, the breeze catching a few strands of her heavy, honeyed hair and moving them around her face. 'When we mixed with one another, we were too conspicuous. When we became involved in human affairs, they grew suspicious of our cleverness. They are not quick, the poor creatures, but they are not entirely stupid either.'

'By "mixing", you don't mean dinners and dancing.'

'No dinners, no dancing – and no kissing and singing songs to each other,' Ysabeau said pointedly. 'And what comes after the dancing and the kissing was forbidden as well. We were full of arrogance before we agreed to the covenant. There were more of us, and we'd become accustomed to taking whatever we wanted, no matter the cost.'

'What else does this promise cover?'

'No politics or religion. Too many princes and popes were otherworldly creatures. It became more difficult to pass from one life to the next once humans started writing their chronicles.' Ysabeau shuddered. 'Vampires found it difficult to feign a good death and move on to a new life with humans nosing around.'

I glanced quickly at Matthew and Domenico, but they were still talking outside the château's walls. 'So,' I repeated, ticking items off my fingers. 'No mixing between different types of creatures. No careers in human politics or religion. Anything else?' Apparently my aunt's xenophobia and fierce opposition to my studying the law derived from her imperfect understanding of this long-ago agreement.

'Yes. If any creature breaks the covenant, it is the responsibility of the Congregation to see that the misconduct is stopped and the oath is upheld.'

'And if *two* creatures break the covenant?'

The silence stretched taut between us.

'To my knowledge it has never happened,' she said grimly. 'It is a very good thing, therefore, that the two of you have not done so.'

Last night I'd made a simple request that Matthew join me in my bed. But he'd known it wasn't a simple request. It wasn't me he was unsure of, or his feelings. Matthew wanted to know how far he could go before the Congregation would intervene.

The answer had come quickly. They weren't going to let us get very far at all.

My relief was quickly replaced by anger. Had no one complained, as our relationship developed, he might never have told me about the Congregation or the covenant. And his silence would have had implications for my relationship with my own family, and with his. I might have gone to my grave believing that my aunt and Ysabeau were bigots. Instead they were living up to a promise made long ago – which was less understandable but somehow more excusable.

'Your son needs to stop keeping things from me.' My temper rose, the tingling mounting in my fingertips. 'And you should worry less about the Congregation and more about what I'm going to do when I see him again.'

She snorted. 'You won't get the chance to do much before he takes you to task for questioning his authority in front of Domenico.'

'I'm not under Matthew's authority.'

'You, my dear, have a great deal to learn about vampires,' she said with a note of satisfaction.

'And you have a great deal to learn about me. So does the Congregation.'

Ysabeau took me by the shoulders, her fingers digging into the flesh of my arms. 'This is not a game, Diana! Matthew would willingly turn his back on creatures he has known for centuries to protect your right to be whatever you imagine you want to be in your fleeting life.

I'm begging you not to let him do it. They will kill him if he persists.'

'He's his own man, Ysabeau,' I said coldly. 'I don't tell Matthew what to do.'

'No, but you have the power to send him away. Tell him you refuse to break the covenant for him, for his sake – or that you feel nothing more for him than curiosity – witches are famous for it.' She flung me away. 'If you love him, you'll know what to say.'

'It is over,' Marthe called from the top of the stairs.

We both rushed to the edge of the tower. A black horse and rider streaked out of the stables and cleared the paddock fence before thundering into the forest.

CHAPTER 22

We'd been waiting in the salon, the three of us, since he'd ridden off on Balthasar in the late morning. Now the shadows were lengthening toward twilight. A human would be half dead from the prolonged effort needed to control that enormous horse in the open countryside. However, the events of the morning had reminded me that Matthew wasn't human, but a vampire – with many secrets, a complicated past, and frightening enemies.

Overhead, a door closed.

'He's back. He will go to his father's room, as he always does when he is troubled,' Ysabeau explained.

Matthew's beautiful young mother sat and stared at the fire, while I wrung my hands in my lap, refusing everything Marthe put in front of me. I hadn't eaten since breakfast, but my hollowness had nothing to do with hunger.

I felt shattered, surrounded by the broken pieces of my formerly ordered life. My degree from Oxford, my position at Yale, and my carefully researched and written books had long provided meaning and structure to my life. But none of them were of comfort to me in this strange new world of menacing vampires and threatening witches. My exposure to it had left me raw, with a new fragility linked to a vampire and the invisible, undeniable movement of a witch's blood in my veins.

At last Matthew entered the salon, clean and dressed in fresh clothes. His eyes sought me out immediately, their cold touch fluttering over me as he checked that I was unharmed. His mouth softened in relief.

It was the last hint of comforting familiarity that I detected in him.

The vampire who entered the salon was not the Matthew that I knew. He was not the elegant, charming creature who had slipped into my life with a mocking smile and invitations to breakfast. Nor was he the scientist, absorbed in his work and preoccupied with the question of why he was here. And there was no sign of the Matthew who had swung me into his arms and kissed me with such passionate intensity only the night before.

This Matthew was cold and impassive. The few soft edges he'd once possessed – around his mouth, in the delicacy of his hands, the stillness of his eyes – had been replaced by hard lines and angles. He seemed older than I remembered, a combination of weariness and careful remove reflecting every moment of his nearly fifteen hundred years of age.

A log broke in the fireplace. The sparks caught my eye, burning blood orange as they fell in the grate.

Nothing but the color red appeared at first. Then the red took on a texture, strands of red burnished here and there with gold and silver. The texture became a thing – hair, Sarah's hair. My fingers caught the strap of a backpack from my shoulder, and I dropped my lunch box on the floor of the family room with the same officious clatter as my father when he dropped his briefcase by the door.

'I'm home.' My child's voice was high and bright. 'Are there cookies?'

Sarah's head turned, red and orange, catching sparks in the late-afternoon light.

But her face was pure white.

The white overwhelmed the other colors, became silver, and assumed a texture like the scales of a fish. Chain mail clung to a familiar, muscular body. Matthew.

'I'm through.' His white hands tore at a black tunic with a silver cross on the front, rending it at the shoulders. He flung it at someone's feet, turned, and strode away.

With a single blink of my eyes, the vision was gone, replaced by the warm tones of the salon at Sept-Tours, but the startling knowledge of what had happened lingered. As with the witchwind, there had been no warning when this hidden talent of mine was released. Had my mother's visions come on so suddenly and had such clarity? I glanced around the room, but the only creature who seemed to have noticed something was odd was Marthe, who looked at me with concern.

Matthew went to Ysabeau and kissed her lightly on both of her flawless white cheeks. 'I'm so sorry, *Maman*,' he murmured.

'*Hein*, he was always a pig. It's not your fault.' Ysabeau gave her son's hand a gentle squeeze. 'I am glad you are home.'

'He's gone. There's nothing to worry about tonight,' Matthew said, his mouth tight. He drew his fingers through his hair.

'Drink.' Marthe belonged to the sustenance school of crisis management. She handed a glass of wine to Matthew and plunked yet another cup of tea next to me. It sat on the table, untouched, sending tendrils of steam into the room.

'Thank you, Marthe.' Matthew drank deeply. As he did, his eyes returned to mine, but he deliberately looked away as he swallowed. 'My phone,' he said, turning toward his study.

He descended the stairs a few moments later. 'For you.' He gave me the phone in such a way that our hands didn't need to touch.

I knew who was on the line. 'Hello, Sarah.'

'I've been calling for more than eight hours. What on earth is wrong?' Sarah knew something bad was happening – she wouldn't have called a vampire otherwise. Her tense voice conjured up the image of her white face from my vision. She'd been frightened in it, not just sad.

'There's nothing wrong,' I said, not wanting her to be scared anymore. 'I'm with Matthew.'

'Being with Matthew is what got you into this trouble in the first place.'

'Sarah, I can't talk now.' The last thing I needed was to argue with my aunt.

She drew in her breath. 'Diana, there are a few things you need to know before you decide to throw in your lot with a vampire.'

'Really?' I asked, my temper flaring. 'Do you think now is the time to tell me about the covenant? You don't by any chance know the witches who are among the current members of the Congregation, do you? I have a few things I'd like to say to them.' My fingers were burning, and the skin under my nails was becoming a vivid sky blue.

'You turned your back on your power, Diana, and refused to talk about magic. The covenant wasn't relevant to your life, nor was the Congregation.' Sarah sounded defensive.

My bitter laugh helped the blue tinge fade from my fingers. 'Justify it any way you want, Sarah. After Mom and Dad were killed, you and Em should have told me, and not just hinted at something in mysterious half-truths. But it's too late now. I need to talk to Matthew. I'll call you tomorrow.' After severing the connection and flinging the phone onto the ottoman at my feet, I closed my eyes and waited for the tingling in my fingers to subside.

All three vampires were staring at me – I could feel it.

'So,' I said into the silence, 'are we to expect more visitors from this Congregation?'

Matthew's mouth tightened. 'No.'

It was a one-word answer, but at least it was the word I wanted to hear. Over the past few days, I'd had a respite from Matthew's mood changes and had almost forgotten how alarming they could be. His next words wiped away my hope that this latest outburst would soon pass.

'There will be no visits from the Congregation because we aren't going to break the covenant. We'll stay here for a few more days, then return to Oxford. Is that all right with you, *Maman*?'

'Of course,' Ysabeau replied promptly. She sighed with relief.

'We should keep the standard flying,' Matthew continued, his voice businesslike. 'The village should know to be on its guard.'

Ysabeau nodded, and her son took a sip of his wine. I stared, first at one and then the other. Neither responded to my silent demand for more information.

'It's only been a few days since you took me *out* of Oxford,' I said after no one rose to my wordless challenge.

Matthew's eyes lifted to mine in forbidding response. 'Now you're going back,' he said evenly. 'Meanwhile there will be no walks outside the grounds. No riding on your own.' His present coldness was more frightening than anything that Domenico had said.

'And?' I pressed him.

'No more dancing,' Matthew said, his abruptness suggesting that a host of other activities were included in this category. 'We're going to abide by the Congregation's rules. If we stop aggravating them, they'll turn their attention to more important matters.'

'I see. You want me to play dead. And you'll give up your work and Ashmole 782? I don't believe that.' I stood and moved toward the door.

Matthew's hand was rough on my arm. It violated all the laws of physics that he could have reached my side so quickly.

'Sit down, Diana.' His voice was as rough as his touch, but it was oddly gratifying that he was showing any emotion at all.

'Why are you giving in?' I whispered.

'To avoid exposing us all to the humans – and to keep you alive.' He pulled me back to the sofa and pushed me onto the cushions. 'This family is not a democracy, especially not at a time like this. When I tell you to do something, you do it, without hesitation or question. Understood?' Matthew's tone indicated that the discussion was over.

'Or what?' I was deliberately provoking him, but his aloofness frightened me.

He put down his wine, and the crystal captured the light from the candles.

I felt myself falling, this time into a pool of water.

The pool became a drop, the drop a tear glistening on a white cheek.

Sarah's cheeks were covered in tears, her eyes red and swollen. Em was in the kitchen. When she joined us, it was evident that she'd been crying, too. She looked devastated.

'What?' I said, fear gripping my stomach. 'What's happened?'

Sarah wiped at her eyes, her fingers stained with the herbs and spices she used in her spell-casting.

Her fingers grew longer, the stains dissolving.

'What?' Matthew said, his eyes wild, white fingers brushing a tiny, bloodstained tear from an equally white cheek. 'What's happened?'

'Witches. They have your father,' Ysabeau said, her voice breaking.

As the vision faded, I searched for Matthew, hoping his eyes would exert their usual pull and relieve my lingering disorientation. As soon as our glances met, he came and hovered over me. But there was none of the usual comfort associated with his presence.

'I will kill you myself before I let anyone hurt you.' The words caught in his throat. 'And I don't want to kill you. So please do what I tell you.'

'So that's it?' I asked when I could manage it. 'We're going to abide by an ancient, narrow-minded agreement made almost a thousand years ago. Case closed.'

'You mustn't be under the Congregation's scrutiny. You have no control over your magic and no understanding of your relationship to Ashmole 782. At Sept-Tours you may be protected from Peter Knox, Diana, but I've told you before that you aren't safe around vampires. No warmblood is. Ever.'

'You won't hurt me.' In spite of what had happened over the past several days, on this point I was absolutely certain.

'You persist in this romantic vision of what it is to be a vampire, but despite my best efforts to curb it I have a taste for blood.'

I made a dismissive gesture. 'You've killed humans. I know this, Matthew. You're a vampire, and you've lived for hundreds of years. Do you think I imagined you survived on nothing but animals?'

Ysabeau was watching her son closely.

'Saying you know I've killed humans and understanding what that means are two different things, Diana. You have no idea what I'm capable of.' He touched his talisman from Bethany and moved away from me with swift, impatient steps.

'I know who you are.' Here was another point of absolute certainty. I wondered what made me so instinctively sure of Matthew as the evidence about the brutality of vampires – even witches – mounted.

'You don't know yourself. And three weeks ago you'd never heard of me.' Matthew's gaze was restless and his hands, like mine, were shaking. This worried me less than the fact that Ysabeau had pitched farther forward in her seat. He picked up a poker and gave the fire a vicious thrust before throwing it aside. The metal rang against the stone, gouging the hard surface as if it were butter.

'We will figure this out. Give us some time.' I tried to make my voice low and soothing.

'There's nothing to figure out.' Matthew was pacing now. 'You have too much undisciplined power. It's like a drug – a highly addictive, dangerous drug that other creatures are desperate to share. You'll never be safe so long as a witch or vampire is near you.'

My mouth opened to respond, but the place where he'd been standing was empty. Matthew's icy fingers were on my chin, lifting me to my feet.

'I'm a predator, Diana.' He said it with the seductiveness of a lover. The dark aroma of cloves made me dizzy. 'I have to hunt and kill to survive.' He turned my face away from him with a savage twist, exposing my neck. His restless eyes raked over my throat.

'Matthew, put Diana down.' Ysabeau sounded unconcerned, and my own faith in him remained unshaken. He wanted to frighten me off for some reason, but I was in no real danger – not as I had been with Domenico.

'She thinks she knows me, *Maman*,' he purred. 'But Diana doesn't know what it's like when the craving for a warmblood tightens your stomach so much that you're mad with need. She doesn't know how much we want to feel the blood of another heart pulsing through our veins. Or how difficult it is for me to stand here, so close, and not taste her.'

Ysabeau rose but remained where she was. 'Now is not the time to teach her, Matthew.'

'You see, it's not just that I could kill you outright,' he continued, ignoring his mother. His black eyes were mesmerizing. 'I could feed on you slowly, taking your blood and letting it replenish, only to begin again the next day.' His grip moved from my chin to circle my neck, and his thumb stroked the pulse at my throat as if he were gauging just where to sink his teeth into my flesh.

'Stop it,' I said sharply. His scare tactics had gone on long enough.

Matthew dropped me abruptly on the soft carpet. By the time I felt the impact, the vampire was across the room, his back to me and his head bowed.

I stared at the pattern on the rug beneath my hands and knees.

A swirl of colors, too many to distinguish, moved before my eyes.

They were leaves dancing against the sky — green, brown, blue, gold.

'It's your mom and dad,' Sarah was explaining, her voice tight. 'They've been killed. They're gone, honey.'

I dragged my eyes from the carpet to the vampire standing with his back to me.

'No.' I shook my head.

'What is it, Diana?' Matthew turned, concern momentarily pushing the predator away.

The swirl of colors captured my attention again — green, brown, blue, gold. They were leaves, caught in an eddy on a pool of water, falling onto the ground around my hands. A bow, curved and polished, rested next to a scattering of arrows and a half-empty quiver.

I reached for the bow and felt the taut string cut into my flesh.

'Matthew,' Ysabeau warned, sniffing the air delicately.

'I know, I can smell it, too,' he said grimly.

He's yours, a strange voice whispered. You mustn't let him go.

'I know,' I murmured impatiently.

'What do you know, Diana?' Matthew took a step toward me.

Marthe shot to my side. 'Leave her,' she hissed. 'The child is not in this world.'

I was nowhere, caught between the terrible ache of losing my parents and the certain knowledge that soon Matthew, too, would be gone.

Be careful, the strange voice warned.

'It's too late for that.' I raised my hand from the floor and smashed it into the bow, snapping it in two. 'Much too late.'

'What's too late?' Matthew asked.

'I've fallen in love with you.'

'You can't have,' he said numbly. The room was utterly silent, except for the crackling of the fire. 'It's too soon.'

'Why do vampires have such a strange attitude toward time?' I mused aloud, still caught in a bewildering mix of past and present. The word 'love' had sent feelings of possessiveness through me, however, drawing me to the here and now. 'Witches don't have centuries to fall in love. We do it quickly. Sarah says my mother fell in love with my father the moment she saw him. I've loved you since I decided not to hit you with an oar on the City of Oxford's dock.' The blood in my veins began to hum. Marthe looked startled, suggesting she could hear it, too.

'You don't understand.' It sounded as if Matthew, like the bow, might snap in two.

'I do. The Congregation will try to stop me, but they won't tell me who to love.' When my parents were taken from me, I was a child with no options and did what people told me. I was an adult now, and I was going to fight for Matthew.

'Domenico's overtures are nothing compared to what you can expect from Peter Knox. What happened today was an attempt at rapprochement, a diplomatic mission. You aren't ready to face the Congregation, Diana, no matter what you think. And if you did stand up to them, what then? Bringing these old animosities to the surface could spin out of control, expose us to humans. Your family might suffer.' Matthew's words were brutal, meant to make me stop and reconsider. But nothing he said outweighed what I felt for him.

'I love you, and I'm not going to stop.' Of this, too, I was certain.

'You are not in love with me.'

'I decide who I love, and how, and when. Stop telling me what to do, Matthew. My ideas about vampires may be romantic, but your attitudes toward women need a major overhaul.'

Before he could respond, his phone began to hop across the ottoman. He swore an oath in Occitan that must have been truly awe-inspiring, because even Marthe looked shocked. He reached down and snagged the phone before it could skitter onto the floor.

'What is it?' he said, his eyes fixed on me.

There were faint murmurs on the other end of the line. Marthe and Ysabeau exchanged worried glances.

'When?' Matthew's voice sounded like a gunshot. 'Did they take anything?' My forehead creased at the anger in his voice. 'Thank God. Was there damage?'

Something had happened in Oxford while we were gone, and it sounded like a robbery. I hoped it wasn't the Old Lodge.

The voice on the other end of the phone continued. Matthew passed a hand over his eyes.

'What else?' he asked, his voice rising.

There was another long silence. He turned away and walked to the fireplace, his right hand splayed flat against the mantel.

'So much for diplomacy.' Matthew swore under his breath. 'I'll be there in a few hours. Can you pick me up?'

We were going back to Oxford. I stood.

'Fine. I'll call before I land. And, Marcus? Find out who else besides Peter Knox and Domenico Michele are members of the Congregation.'

Peter Knox? The pieces of the puzzle began to click into place. No wonder Matthew had come back to Oxford so quickly when I'd told him who the brown wizard was. It explained why he was so eager to push me away now, too. We were breaking the covenant, and it was Knox's job to enforce it.

Matthew stood silently for a few moments after the line went dead, one hand clenched as if he were resisting the urge to beat the stone mantel into submission.

'That was Marcus. Someone tried to break in to the lab. I need to go back to Oxford.' He turned, his eyes dead.

'Is everything all right?' Ysabeau shot a worried look in my direction.

'They didn't make it through the security controls. Still, I need to talk to the university officials and make sure whoever it was doesn't succeed the next time.' Nothing that Matthew was saying made sense. If the burglars had failed, why wasn't he relieved? And why was he shaking his head at his mother?

'Who were they?' I asked warily.

'Marcus isn't sure.'

That was odd, given a vampire's preternaturally sharp sense of smell. 'Was it humans?'

'No.' We were back to the monosyllabic answers.

'I'll get my things.' I turned toward the stairs.

'You aren't coming. You're staying here.' Matthew's words brought me to a standstill.

'I'd rather be in Oxford,' I protested, 'with you.'

'Oxford's not safe at the moment. I'll be back when it is.'

'You just told me we should return there! Make up your mind, Matthew. Where is the danger? The manuscript and the witches? Peter Knox and the Congregation? Or Domenico Michele and the vampires?'

'Were you listening? *I* am the danger.' Matthew's voice was sharp.

'Oh, I heard you. But you're keeping something from me. It's a historian's job to uncover secrets,' I promised him softly. 'And I'm very good at it.' He opened his mouth to speak, but I stopped him. 'No more excuses or false explanations. Go to Oxford. I'll stay here.'

'Do you need anything from upstairs?' Ysabeau asked. 'You should take a coat. Humans will notice if you're wearing only a sweater.'

'Just my computer. My passport's in the bag.'

'I'll get them.' Wanting a respite from all the de Clermonts for a moment, I pelted up the stairs. In Matthew's study I looked around the room that held so much of him.

The armor's silvery surfaces winked in the firelight, holding my attention while a jumble of faces flashed through my mind, the visions as swift as comets through the sky. There was a pale woman with enormous blue eyes and a sweet smile, another woman whose firm chin and square shoulders exuded determination, a man with a hawkish nose in terrible pain. There were other faces, too, but the only one I recognized was Louisa de Clermont, holding dripping, bloody fingers in front of her face.

Resisting the vision's pull helped the faces fade, but it left my body shaking and my mind bewildered. The DNA report had indicated that visions were likely to come. But there'd been no more warning of their arrival than there had been last night when I floated in Matthew's arms. It was as if someone had pulled the stopper on a bottle and my magic – released at last – was rushing to get out.

Once I was able to jerk the cord from the socket I slid it into Matthew's bag, along with the computer. His passport was in the front pocket, as he'd said it would be.

When I returned to the salon, Matthew was alone, his keys in his hands and a suede barn jacket draped across his shoulders. Marthe muttered and paced in the great hall.

I handed him his computer and stood far away to better resist the urge to touch him once more. Matthew pocketed his keys and took the bag.

'I know this is hard.' His voice was hushed and strange. 'But you need to let me take care of it. And I need to know that you're safe while I'm doing that.'

'I'm safe with you, wherever we are.'

He shook his head. 'My name should have been enough to protect you. It wasn't.'

'Leaving me isn't the answer. I don't understand all of what's happened today, but Domenico's hatred goes beyond me. He wants to destroy your family and everything else you care about. Domenico might decide this isn't the right time to pursue his vendetta. But Peter Knox? He wants Ashmole 782, and he thinks I can get it for him. He won't be put off so easily.' I shivered.

'He'll make a deal if I offer him one.'

'A deal? What do you have to trade?'

The vampire fell silent.

'Matthew?' I insisted.

'The manuscript,' he said flatly. 'I'll leave it – and you – alone if he promises the same. Ashmole 782 has been undisturbed for a century and a half. We'll let it remain that way.'

'You can't make a deal with Knox. He can't be trusted.' I was horrified. 'Besides, you have all the time you need to wait for the manuscript. Knox doesn't. Your deal won't appeal to him.'

'Just leave Knox to me,' he said gruffly.

My eyes snapped with anger. 'Leave Domenico to you. Leave Knox to you. What do you imagine *I'm* going to do? You said I'm not a damsel in distress. So stop treating me like one.'

'I suppose I deserved that,' he said slowly, his eyes black, 'but you have a lot to learn about vampires.'

'So your mother tells me. But you may have a few things to learn about witches, too.' I pushed the hair out of my eyes and crossed my arms over my chest. 'Go to Oxford. Sort out what happened there.' *Whatever happened that you won't share with me.* 'But for God's sake, Matthew, don't negotiate with Peter Knox. Decide how *you* feel about *me* – not because of what the covenant forbids, or the Congregation wants, or even what Peter Knox and Domenico Michele make you afraid of.'

My beloved vampire, with a face that would make an angel envious, looked at me with sorrow. 'You know how I feel about you.'

I shook my head. 'No, I don't. When you're ready, you'll tell me.'

Matthew struggled with something and left it unsaid. Wordlessly he walked toward the door into the hall. When he reached it, he gave me a long look of snowflakes and frost before walking through.

Marthe met him in the hall. He kissed her softly on both cheeks and said something in rapid Occitan.

'*Compreni, compreni*,' she said, nodding vehemently and looking past him at me.

'*Mercés amb tot meu còr*,' he said quietly.

'*Al rebèire. Mèfi.*'

'*T'afortissi.*' Matthew turned to me. 'And you'll promise me the same thing — that you'll be careful. Listen to Ysabeau.'

He left without a glance or a final, reassuring touch.

I bit my lip and tried to swallow the tears, but they spilled out. After three slow steps toward the watchtower stairs, my feet began to run, tears streaming down my face. With a look of understanding, Marthe let me go.

When I came out into the cold, damp air, the de Clermont standard was snapping gently to and fro and the clouds continued to obscure the moon. Darkness pressed on me from every direction, and the one creature who kept it at bay was leaving, taking the light with him.

Peering down over the tower's ramparts, I saw Matthew standing by the Range Rover, talking furiously to Ysabeau. She looked shocked and grabbed the sleeve of his jacket as if to stop him from getting in the car.

His hand was a white blur as he pulled his arm free. His fist pounded, once, into the car's roof. I jumped. Matthew had never used his strength on anything bigger than a walnut or an oyster shell when he was around me, and the dent he'd left in the metal was alarmingly deep.

He hung his head. Ysabeau touched him lightly on the cheek, his sad features gleaming in the dim light. He climbed into the car and said a few more words. His mother nodded and looked briefly at the watchtower. I stepped back, hoping neither of them had seen me. The car turned over, and its heavy tires crunched across the gravel as Matthew pulled away.

The Range Rover's lights disappeared below the hill. With Matthew gone, I slid down the stone wall of the keep and gave in to the tears.

It was then that I discovered what witchwater was all about.

CHAPTER 23

Before I met Matthew, there didn't seem to be room in my life for a single additional element – especially not something as significant as a fifteen-hundred-year-old vampire. But he'd slipped into unexplored, empty places when I wasn't looking.

Now that he'd left, I was terribly aware of his absence. As I sat on the roof of the watchtower, my tears softened my determination to fight for him. Soon there was water everywhere. I was sitting in a puddle of it, and the level just kept rising.

It wasn't raining, despite the cloudy skies.

The water was coming out of me.

My tears fell normally but swelled as they dropped into globules the size of snowballs that hit the stone roof of the watchtower with a splash. My hair snaked over my shoulders in sheets of water that poured over the curves of my body. I opened my mouth to take a breath because the water streaming down my face was blocking my nose, and water gushed out in a torrent that tasted of the sea.

Through a film of moisture, Marthe and Ysabeau watched me. Marthe's face was grim. Ysabeau's lips were moving, but the roar of a thousand seashells made it impossible to hear her.

I stood, hoping the water would stop. It didn't. I tried to tell the two women to let the water carry me away along with my grief and the memory of Matthew – but all that produced was another gush of ocean. I reached out, thinking that would help the water drain from me. Even more water cascaded from my fingertips. The gesture reminded me of my mother's arm reaching toward my father, and the waves increased.

As the water poured forth, my control slipped further. Domenico's sudden appearance had frightened me more than I'd been willing to admit. Matthew was gone. And I had vowed to fight for him against enemies I couldn't identify and didn't understand. It was now clear that Matthew's past was not composed simply of homely elements of firelight, wine, and books. Nor had it unfolded solely within the limits of a loyal family. Domenico had alluded to something darker that was full of enmity, danger, and death.

Exhaustion overtook me, and the water pulled me under. A strange sense of exhilaration accompanied the fatigue. I was poised between mortality and something elemental that held within it the promise of a vast, incomprehensible power. If I surrendered to the undertow, there would be no more Diana Bishop. Instead I would become water – nowhere, everywhere, free of my body and the pain.

'I'm sorry, Matthew.' My words were nothing more than a burble as the water began its inexorable work.

Ysabeau stepped toward me, and a sharp crack sounded in my brain. My warning to her was lost in a roar like a tidal wave coming ashore. The winds rose around my feet, whipping the water into a hurricane. I raised my arms to the sky, water and wind shaping themselves into a funnel that encircled my body.

Marthe grabbed Ysabeau's arm, her mouth moving rapidly. Matthew's mother tried to pull away, her own mouth shaping the word 'no,' but Marthe held on, staring at her fixedly. After a few moments, Ysabeau's shoulders slumped. She turned toward me and started to sing. Haunting and yearning, her voice penetrated the water and called me back to the world.

The winds began to die down. The de Clermont standard, which had been whipping around, resumed its gentle swaying. The cascade of water from my fingertips slowed to a river, then to a trickle, and stopped entirely. The waves flowing from my hair subsided into swells, and then they, too, disappeared. At last nothing came out of my mouth but a gasp of surprise. The balls of water falling from my eyes were the last vestige of the witchwater to disappear, just as they had been the first sign of its power moving through me. The remains of my deluge sluiced toward small holes at the base of the crenellated walls. Far, far below, water splashed onto the courtyard's thick bed of gravel.

When the last of the water left me, I felt scooped out like a pumpkin, and freezing cold, too. My knees buckled, banging painfully on the stone.

'Thank God,' Ysabeau murmured. 'We almost lost her.'

I was shaking violently from exhaustion and cold. Both women flew at me and lifted me to my feet. They each gripped an elbow and supported me down the curving flight of stairs with a speed that made me shiver. Once in the hall, Marthe headed toward Matthew's rooms and Ysabeau pulled in the opposite direction.

'Mine are closer,' Matthew's mother said sharply.

'She will feel safer closer to him,' Marthe said.

With a sound of exasperation, Ysabeau conceded.

At the bottom of Matthew's staircase, Ysabeau blurted out a string of colorful phrases that sounded totally incongruous coming from her delicate mouth. 'I'll carry her,' she said when she was finished cursing her son, the forces of nature, the powers of the universe, and many other unspecified individuals of questionable parentage who'd taken part in building the tower. Ysabeau lifted my much larger body easily. 'Why he had to make these stairs so twisting – and in two separate flights – is beyond my understanding.'

Marthe tucked my wet hair into the crook of Ysabeau's elbow and shrugged. 'To make it harder, of course. He has always made things harder. For him. For everyone else, too.'

No one had thought to come up in the late afternoon to light the candles, but the fire still smoldered and the room retained some of its warmth. Marthe disappeared into the bathroom, and the sound of running water made me examine my fingers with alarm. Ysabeau threw two enormous logs onto the grate as if they were kindling, snapping a long splinter off one before it caught. She stirred the coals into flames with it and then used it to light a dozen candles in the space of a few seconds. In their warm glow, she surveyed me anxiously from head to foot.

'He will never forgive me if you become ill,' she said, picking up my hands and examining my nails. They were bluish again, but not from electricity. Now they were blue with cold and wrinkled from witchwater. She rubbed them vigorously between her palms.

Still shaking so much that my teeth were chattering, I withdrew my hands to hug myself in an attempt to conserve what little warmth was left in my body. Ysabeau picked me up again without ceremony and swept me into the bathroom.

'She needs to be in there now,' Ysabeau said brusquely. The room was full of steam, and Marthe turned from the bath to help strip off my clothes. Soon I was naked and the two of them were lifting me into the hot water, one cold, vampiric hand in each armpit. The shock of the water's heat on my frigid skin was extreme. Crying out, I struggled to pull myself from Matthew's deep bathtub.

'Shh,' Ysabeau said, holding my hair away from my face while Marthe pushed me back into the water. 'It will warm you. We must get you warm.'

Marthe stood sentinel at one end of the tub, and Ysabeau remained at the other, whispering soothing sounds and humming softly under her breath. It was a long time before the shaking stopped.

At one point Marthe murmured something in Occitan that included the name Marcus.

Ysabeau and I said no at the same moment.

'I'll be fine. Don't tell Marcus what happened. Matthew mustn't know about the magic. Not now,' I said through chattering teeth.

'We just need some time to warm you.' Ysabeau sounded calm, but she looked concerned.

Slowly the heat began to reverse the changes the witchwater had worked on my body. Marthe kept adding fresh hot water to the tub as my body cooled it down. Ysabeau grabbed a beat-up tin pitcher from under the window and dipped it into the bath, pouring hot water over my head and shoulders. Once my head was warm, she wrapped it in a towel and pushed me slightly lower in the water.

'Soak,' she commanded.

Marthe bustled between the bathroom and the bedroom, carrying clothes and towels. She tutted over my lack of pajamas and the old yoga clothes I'd brought to sleep in. None of them met her requirements for warmth.

Ysabeau felt my cheeks and the top of my head with the back of her hand. She nodded.

They let me get myself out of the tub. The water falling off my body reminded me of the watchtower roof, and I dug my toes into the floor to resist the element's insidious pull.

Marthe and Ysabeau bundled me into towels fresh from the fireside that smelled faintly of wood smoke. In the bedroom they somehow managed to dry me without ever exposing an inch of my flesh to the air, rolling me this way and that inside the towels until I could feel heat radiating from my body. Rough strokes of another towel scratched against my hair before Marthe's fingers raked through the strands and twisted them into a tight braid against my scalp. Ysabeau tossed the damp towels onto a chair near the fire as I shed them to dress, seemingly unconcerned by their contact with antique wood and fine upholstery.

Now fully clothed, I sat down and stared mindlessly at the fire. Marthe disappeared without a word into the lower regions of the château and returned with a tray of tiny sandwiches and a steaming pot of her herbal tea.

'You will eat. Now.' It was not a request but a command.

I brought one of the sandwiches to my mouth and nibbled around the edges.

Marthe's eyes narrowed at this sudden change in my eating habits. 'Eat.'

The food tasted like sawdust, but my stomach rumbled nonetheless. After I'd swallowed two of the tiny sandwiches, Marthe thrust a mug into my hands. She didn't need to tell me to drink. The hot liquid slid down my throat, carrying away the water's salty vestiges.

'Was that witchwater?' I shivered at the memory of all that water coming out of me.

Ysabeau, who had been standing by the window looking out into the darkness, walked toward the opposite sofa. 'Yes,' she said. 'It has been a long time, though, since we have seen it come forth like that.'

'Thank God that wasn't the usual way,' I said faintly, swallowing another sip of tea.

'Most witches today are not powerful enough to draw on the witchwater as you did. They can make waves on ponds and cause rain when there are clouds. They do not become the water.' Ysabeau sat across from me, studying me with evident curiosity.

I had become the water. Knowing that this was no longer common made me feel vulnerable – and even more alone.

A phone rang.

Ysabeau reached into her pocket and pulled out a small red phone that seemed uncharacteristically bright and high-tech against her pale skin and classic, buff-colored clothes.

'*Oui?* Ah, good. I am glad that you are there and safe.' She spoke English out of courtesy to me and nodded in my direction. 'Yes, she is fine. She is eating.' She stood and handed me the phone. 'Matthew would like to speak with you.'

'Diana?' Matthew was barely audible.

'Yes?' I didn't trust myself to say much for fear that more than words would tumble out.

He made a soft sound of relief. 'I just wanted to make sure you were all right.'

'Your mother and Marthe are taking good care of me.' *And I didn't flood the castle*, I thought.

'You're tired.' The distance between us was making him anxious, and he was tuned into every nuance of our exchange.

'I am. It's been a long day.'

'Sleep, then,' he said, his tone unexpectedly gentle. My eyes closed against the sudden sting of tears. There would be little sleep for me tonight. I was too worried about what he might do in some half-baked, heroic attempt to protect me.

'Have you been to the lab?'

'I'm headed there now. Marcus wants me to go over everything carefully and make sure we've taken all the necessary precautions.

Miriam's checked the security at the house as well.' He told the half-truth with smooth conviction, but I knew it for what it was. The silence stretched out until it became uncomfortable.

'Don't do it, Matthew. Please don't try to negotiate with Knox.'

'I'll make sure you're safe before you return to Oxford.'

'Then there's nothing more to say. You've decided. So have I.' I returned the phone to Ysabeau.

She frowned, her cold fingers pulling it from my grip. Ysabeau said good-bye to her son, his reply audible only as a staccato burst of unintelligible sound.

'Thank you for not telling him about the witchwater,' I said quietly after she'd disconnected the line.

'That is your tale to tell, not mine.' Ysabeau drifted toward the fireplace.

'It's no good trying to tell a story you don't understand. Why is the power coming out now? First it was the wind, then the visions, and now the water, too.' I shuddered.

'What kind of visions?' Ysabeau asked, her curiosity evident.

'Didn't Matthew tell you? My DNA has all this . . . *magic*,' I said, stumbling over the word, 'in it. The tests warned there might be visions, and they've begun.'

'Matthew would never tell me what your blood revealed — certainly not without your permission, and probably not with your permission either.'

'I've seen them here in the château.' I hesitated. 'How did you learn to control them?'

'Matthew told you that I had visions before I became a vampire.' Ysabeau shook her head. 'He should not have.'

'Were you a witch?' That might explain why she disliked me so much.

'A witch? No. Matthew wonders if I was a daemon, but I'm sure I was an ordinary human. They have their visionaries, too. It's not only creatures who are blessed and cursed in this way.'

'Did you ever manage to control your second sight and anticipate it?'

'It gets easier. There are warning signs. They can be subtle, but you will learn. Marthe helped me as well.'

It was the only piece of information I had about Marthe's past. Not for the first time, I wondered how old these two women were and what workings of fate had brought them together.

Marthe stood with her arms crossed. 'Òc,' she said, giving Ysabeau a tender, protective look. 'It is easier if you let the visions move through you without fighting.'

'I'm too shocked to fight,' I said, thinking back to the salon and the library.

'Shock is your body's way of resisting,' Ysabeau said. 'You must try to relax.'

'It's difficult to let go when you see knights in armor and the faces of women you've never met mixed up with scenes from your own past.' My jaw cracked with a yawn.

'You are too exhausted to think about this now.' Ysabeau rose to her feet.

'I'm not ready to sleep.' I smothered another yawn with the back of my hand.

She eyed me speculatively, like a beautiful falcon scrutinizing a field mouse. Ysabeau's glance turned mischievous. 'Get into bed, and I will tell you how I made Matthew.'

Her offer was too tempting to resist. I did as she told me while she pulled up a chair and Marthe busied herself with dishes and towels.

'So where do I begin?' She drew herself straighter in the chair and stared into the candles' flames. 'I cannot begin simply with my part of the story but must start with his birth, here in the village. I remember him as a baby, you know. His father and mother came when Philippe decided to build on this land back when Clovis was king. That's the only reason the village is here – it was where the farmers and craftsmen who built the church and castle lived.'

'Why did your husband pick this spot?' I leaned against the pillows, my knees folded close to my chest under the bedclothes.

'Clovis promised him the land in hopes it would encourage

Philippe to fight against the king's rivals. My husband was always playing both sides against the middle.' Ysabeau smiled wistfully. 'Very few people caught him at it, though.'

'Was Matthew's father a farmer?'

'A farmer?' Ysabeau looked surprised. 'No, he was a carpenter, as was Matthew – before he became a stonemason.'

A mason. The tower's stones all fit together so smoothly they didn't seem to require mortar. And there were the oddly ornate chimneys at the Old Lodge gatehouse that Matthew just had to let some craftsman try his hand at constructing. His long, slender fingers were strong enough to twist open an oyster shell or crack a chestnut. Another piece of Matthew fell into place, fitting perfectly next to the warrior, the scientist, and the courtier.

'And they both worked on the château?'

'Not this château,' Ysabeau said, looking around her. 'This was a present from Matthew, when I was sad over being forced to leave a place that I loved. He tore down the fortress his father had built and replaced it with a new one.' Her green-and-black eyes glittered with amusement. 'Philippe was furious. But it was time for a change. The first château was made of wood, and even though there had been stone additions over the years, it was a bit ramshackle.'

My mind tried to take in the time line of events, from the construction of the first fortress and its village in the sixth century to Matthew's tower in the thirteenth century.

Ysabeau's nose crinkled in distaste. 'Then he stuck this tower onto the back when he returned home and didn't want to live so close to the family. I never liked it – it seemed a romantic trifle – but it was his wish, and I let him.' She shrugged. 'Such a funny tower. It didn't help defend the castle. He had already built far more towers here than we needed.'

Ysabeau continued to spin her tale, seeming only partially in the twenty-first century.

'Matthew was born in the village. He was always such a bright child, so curious. He drove his father mad, following him to the château and picking up tools and sticks and stones. Children learned their trades early then, but Matthew was precocious. By the time he could hold a hatchet without injuring himself, he was put to work.'

An eight-year-old Matthew with gangly legs and gray-green eyes ran around the hills in my imagination.

'Yes.' She smiled, agreeing with my unspoken thoughts. 'He was indeed a beautiful child. A beautiful young man as well. Matthew was unusually tall for the time, though not as tall as he became once he was a vampire.

'And he had a wicked sense of humor. He was always pretending that something had gone wrong or that instructions had not been given to him regarding this roof beam or that foundation. Philippe never failed to believe the tall tales Matthew told him.' Ysabeau's voice was indulgent. 'Matthew's first father died when he was in his late teens, and his first mother had been dead for years by then. He was alone, and we worried about him finding a woman to settle down with and start a family.

'And then he met Blanca.' Ysabeau paused, her look level and without malice. 'You cannot have imagined that he was without the love of women.' It was a statement, not a question. Marthe shot Ysabeau an evil look but kept quiet.

'Of course not,' I said calmly, though my heart felt heavy.

'Blanca was new to the village, a servant to one of the master masons Philippe had brought in from Ravenna to construct the first church. She was as pale as her name suggested, with white skin, eyes the color of a spring sky, and hair that looked like spun gold.'

A pale, beautiful woman had appeared in my visions when I went to fetch Matthew's computer. Ysabeau's description of Blanca fit her perfectly.

'She had a sweet smile, didn't she?' I whispered.

Ysabeau's eyes widened. 'Yes, she did.'

'I know. I saw her when Matthew's armor caught the light in his study.'

Marthe made a warning sound, but Ysabeau continued.

'Sometimes Blanca seemed so delicate that I feared she would break when drawing water from the well or picking vegetables.

My Matthew was drawn to that delicacy, I suppose. He has always liked fragile things.' Ysabeau's eyes flicked over my far-from-fragile form. 'They were married when Matthew turned twenty-five and could support a family. Blanca was just nineteen.

'They were a beautiful couple, of course. There was such a strong contrast between Matthew's darkness and Blanca's pale prettiness. They were very much in love, and the marriage was a happy one. But they could not seem to have children. Blanca had miscarriage after miscarriage. I cannot imagine what it was like inside their house, to see so many children of your body die before they drew breath.' I wasn't sure if vampires could cry, though I remembered the bloodstained tear on Ysabeau's cheek from my earlier visions in the salon. Even without the tears, however, she looked now as though she were weeping, her face a mask of regret.

'Finally, after so many years of trying and failing, Blanca was with child. It was 531. Such a year. There was a new king to the south, and the battles had started all over again. Matthew began to look happy, as if he dared to hope this baby would survive. And it did. Lucas was born in the autumn and was baptized in the unfinished church that Matthew was helping to build. It was a hard birth for Blanca. The midwife said that he would be the last child she bore. For Matthew, though, Lucas was enough. And he was so like his father, with his black curls and pointed chin – and those long legs.'

'What happened to Blanca and Lucas?' I asked softly. We were only six years from Matthew's transformation into a vampire. Something must have happened, or he would never have let Ysabeau exchange his life for a new one.

'Matthew and Blanca watched their son grow and thrive. Matthew had learned to work in stone rather than wood, and he was in high demand among the lords from here to Paris. Then fever came to the village. Everyone fell ill. Matthew survived. Blanca and Lucas did not. That was in 536. The year before had been strange, with very little sunshine, and the winter was cold. When spring came, the sickness came, too, and carried Blanca and Lucas away.'

'Didn't the villagers wonder why you and Philippe remained healthy?'

'Of course. But there were more explanations then than there would be today. It was easier to think God was angry with the village or that the castle was cursed than to think that the manjasang were living among them.'

'*Manjasang?*' I tried to roll the syllables around my mouth as Ysabeau had.

'It is the old tongue's word for vampire – "blood eater". There were those who suspected the truth and whispered by the fireside. But in those days the return of the Ostrogoth warriors was a far more frightening prospect than a *manjasang* overlord. Philippe promised the village his protection if the raiders came back. Besides, we made it a point never to feed close to home,' she explained primly.

'What did Matthew do after Blanca and Lucas were gone?'

'He grieved. Matthew was inconsolable. He stopped eating. He looked like a skeleton, and the village came to us for help. I took him food' – Ysabeau smiled at Marthe – 'and made him eat and walked with him until he wasn't so restless. When he could not sleep, we went to church and prayed for the souls of Blanca and Lucas. Matthew was very religious in those days. We talked about heaven and hell, and he worried about where their souls were and if he would be able to find them again.'

Matthew was so gentle with me when I woke up in terror. Had the nights before he'd become a vampire been as sleepless as those that came after?

'By autumn he seemed more hopeful. But the winter was difficult. People were hungry, and the sickness continued. Death was everywhere. The spring could not lift the gloom. Philippe was anxious about the church's progress, and Matthew worked harder than ever. At the beginning of the second week in June, he was found on the floor beneath its vaulted ceiling, his legs and back broken.'

I gasped at the thought of Matthew's soft, human body plummeting to the hard stones.

'There was no way he could survive the fall, of course,' Ysabeau said softly. 'He was a dying man. Some of the masons said he'd slipped. Others said he was standing on the scaffolding one moment and gone the next. They thought Matthew had jumped and were already talking about how he could not be buried in the church because he was a suicide. I could not let him die fearing he might not be saved from hell. He was so worried about being with Blanca and Lucas – how could he go to his death wondering if he would be separated from them for all eternity?'

'You did the right thing.' It would have been impossible for me to walk away from him no matter what the state of his soul. Leaving his body broken and hurting was unthinkable. If my blood would have saved him, I would have used it.

'Did I?' Ysabeau shook her head. 'I have never been sure. Philippe told me it was my decision whether to make Matthew one of our family. I had made other vampires with my blood, and I would make others after him. But Matthew was different. I was fond of him, and I knew that the gods were giving me a chance to make him my child. It would be my responsibility to teach him how a vampire must be in the world.'

'Did Matthew resist you?' I asked, unable to stop myself.

'No,' she replied. 'He was out of his mind with pain. We told everyone to leave, saying we would fetch a priest. We didn't, of course. Philippe and I went to Matthew and explained we could make him live forever, without pain, without suffering. Much later Matthew told us that he thought we were John the Baptist and the Blessed Mother come to take him to heaven to be with his wife and child. When I offered him my blood, he thought I was the priest offering him last rites.'

The only sounds in the room were my quiet breathing and the crackle of logs in the fireplace. I wanted Ysabeau to tell me the particulars of how she had made Matthew, but I was afraid to ask in case it was something that vampires didn't talk about. Perhaps it was too private, or too painful. Ysabeau soon told me without prompting.

'He took my blood so easily, like he was born to it,' she said with a rustling sigh. 'Matthew was not one of those humans who turn their face from the scent or sight. I opened my wrist with my own teeth and told him my blood would heal him. He drank his salvation without fear.'

'And afterward?' I whispered.

'Afterward he was . . . difficult,' Ysabeau said carefully. 'All new vampires are strong and full of hunger, but Matthew was almost impossible to control. He was in a rage at being a vampire, and his need to feed was endless. Philippe and I had to hunt all day for weeks to satisfy him. And his body changed more than we expected. We all get taller, finer, stronger. I was much smaller before I became a vampire. But Matthew developed from a reed-thin human into a formidable creature. My husband was larger than my new son, but in the first flush of my blood Matthew was a handful even for Philippe.'

I forced myself not to shrink from Matthew's hunger and rage. Instead my eyes remained fixed on his mother, not closing my eyes for an instant against the knowledge of him. This was what Matthew feared, that I would come to understand who he had been – who he still was – and feel revulsion.

'What calmed him?' I asked.

'Philippe took him hunting,' Ysabeau explained, 'once he thought that Matthew would no longer kill everything in his path. The hunt engaged his mind, and the chase engaged his body. He soon craved the hunt more than the blood, which is a good sign in young vampires. It meant he was no longer a creature of pure appetite but was once again rational. After that, it was only a matter of time before his conscience returned and he began to think before he killed. Then all we had to fear were his black periods, when he felt the loss of Blanca and Lucas again and turned to humans to dull his hunger.'

'Did anything help Matthew then?'

'Sometimes I sang to him – the same song I sang to you tonight, and others as well. That often broke the spell of his grief. Other times Matthew would go away. Philippe forbade me to follow or to ask questions when he returned.' Ysabeau's eyes were black as she looked at me. Our glances confirmed what we both suspected: that Matthew had been lost with other women, seeking solace in their blood and the touch of hands that belonged to neither his mother nor his wife.

'He's so controlled,' I mused aloud, 'it's hard to imagine him like that.'

'Matthew feels deeply. It is a blessing as well as a burden to love so much that you can hurt so badly when love is gone.'

There was a threat in Ysabeau's voice. My chin went up in defiance, my fingers tingling. 'Then I'll have to make sure my love never leaves him,' I said tightly.

'And how will you do that?' Ysabeau taunted. 'Would you become a vampire, then, and join us in our hunting?' She laughed, but there was neither joy nor mirth in the sound. 'No doubt that's what Domenico suggested. One simple bite, the draining of your veins, the exchange of our blood for yours. The Congregation would have no grounds to intrude on your business then.'

'What do you mean?' I asked numbly.

'Don't you see?' Ysabeau snarled. 'If you must be with Matthew, then become one of us and put him – and yourself – out of danger. The witches may want to keep you as their own, but they cannot object to your relationship if you are a vampire, too.'

A low rumble started in Marthe's throat.

'Is that why Matthew went away? Did the Congregation order him to make me a vampire?'

'Matthew would never make you a *manjasang*,' Marthe said scornfully, her eyes snapping with fury.

'No.' Ysabeau's voice was softly malicious. 'He has always loved fragile things, as I told you.'

This was one of the secrets that Matthew was keeping. If I were a vampire, there would be no prohibitions looming over us and thus no reason to fear the Congregation. All I had to do was become something else.

I contemplated the prospect with surprisingly little panic or fear. I could be with Matthew, and I might even be taller. Ysabeau would do it. Her eyes glittered as she took in the way my hand moved to my neck.

But there were my visions to consider, not to mention the power of the wind and the water. I didn't yet understand the magical potential in my blood. And as a vampire I might never solve the mystery of Ashmole 782.

'I promised him,' Marthe said, her voice rough. 'Diana must stay as she is – a witch.'

Ysabeau bared her teeth slightly, unpleasantly, and nodded.

'Did you also promise not to tell me what really happened in Oxford?'

Matthew's mother scrutinized me closely. 'You must ask Matthew when he returns. It is not my tale to tell.'

I had other questions as well – questions that Matthew might have been too distracted to mark as off-limits.

'Can you tell me why it matters that it was a creature who tried to break in to the lab, rather than a human?'

There was silence while Ysabeau considered my words. Finally, she replied.

'Clever girl. I did not promise Matthew to remain silent about appropriate rules of conduct, after all.' She looked at me with a touch of approval. 'Such behavior is not acceptable among creatures. We must hope it was a mischievous daemon who does not realize the seriousness of what he has done. Matthew might forgive that.'

'He has always forgiven daemons,' Marthe muttered darkly.

'What if it wasn't a daemon?'

'If it was a vampire, it represents a terrible insult. We are territorial creatures. A vampire does not cross into another vampire's house or land without permission.'

'Would Matthew forgive such an insult?' Given the look on Matthew's face when he'd thrown a punch at the car, I suspected that the answer was no.

'Perhaps,' Ysabeau said doubtfully. 'Nothing was taken, nothing was harmed. But it is more likely Matthew would demand some form of retribution.'

Once more I'd been dropped into the Middle Ages, with the maintenance of honor and reputation the primary concern.

'And if it was a witch?' I asked softly.

Matthew's mother turned her face away. 'For a witch to do such a thing would be an act of aggression. No apology would be adequate.'

Alarm bells sounded.

I flung the covers aside and swung my legs out of bed. 'The break-in was meant to provoke Matthew. He went to Oxford thinking he could make a good-faith deal with Knox. We have to warn him.'

Ysabeau's hands were firm on my knees and shoulder, stopping my motion.

'He already knows, Diana.'

That information settled in my mind. 'Is that why he wouldn't take me to Oxford with him? Is he in danger?'

'Of course he is in danger,' Ysabeau said sharply. 'But he will do what he can to put an end to this.' She lifted my legs back onto the bed and tucked the covers tightly around me.

'I should be there,' I protested.

'You would be nothing but a distraction. You will stay here, as he told you.'

'Don't I get a say in this?' I asked for what seemed like the hundredth time since I came to Sept-Tours.

'No,' both women said at the same moment.

'You really do have a lot to learn about vampires,' Ysabeau said once again, but this time she sounded mildly regretful.

I had a lot to learn about vampires. This I knew.

But who was going to teach me? And when?

CHAPTER 24

' "*From afar I beheld a black cloud covering the earth. It absorbed the earth and covered my soul as the seas entered, becoming putrid and corrupted at the prospect of hell and the shadow of death. A tempest had overwhelmed me*," ' I read aloud from Matthew's copy of *Aurora Consurgens*.

Turning to my computer, I typed notes about the imagery my anonymous author had used to describe *nigredo*, one of the dangerous steps in alchemical transformation. During this part of the process, the combination of substances like mercury and lead gave off fumes that endangered the alchemist's health. Appropriately, one of Bourgot Le Noir's gargoyle-like faces pinched his nose tight shut, avoiding the cloud mentioned in the text.

'Get your riding clothes on.'

My head lifted from the pages of the manuscript.

'Matthew made me promise to take you outdoors. He said it would keep you from getting sick,' Ysabeau explained.

'You don't have to, Ysabeau. Domenico and the witchwater have depleted my adrenaline supply, if that's your concern.'

'Matthew must have told you how alluring the smell of panic is to a vampire.'

'Marcus told me,' I corrected her. 'Actually, he told me what it tastes like. What does it smell like?'

Ysabeau shrugged. 'Like it tastes. Maybe a bit more exotic — a touch of muskiness, perhaps. I was never much drawn to it. I prefer the kill to the hunt. But to each her own.'

'I'm not having as many panic attacks these days. There's no need for you to take me riding.' I turned back to my work.

'Why do you think they have gone away?' Ysabeau asked.

'I honestly don't know,' I said with a sigh, looking at Matthew's mother.

'You have been like this for a long time?'

'Since I was seven.'

'What happened then?'

'My parents were killed in Nigeria,' I replied shortly.

'This was the picture you received – the one that caused Matthew to bring you to Sept-Tours.'

When I nodded in response, Ysabeau's mouth flattened into a familiar, hard line. 'Pigs.'

There were worse things to call them, but 'pigs' did the job pretty well. And if it grouped whoever had sent me the photograph with Domenico Michele, then it was the right category.

'Panic or no panic,' Ysabeau said briskly, 'we are going to exercise as Matthew wanted.'

I powered off the computer and went upstairs to change. My riding clothes were folded neatly in the bathroom, courtesy of Marthe, though my boots were in the stables, along with my helmet and vest. I slithered into the black breeches, added a turtleneck, and slipped on loafers over a pair of warm socks, then went downstairs in search of Matthew's mother.

'I'm in here,' she called. I followed the sound to a small room painted warm terra-cotta. It was ornamented with old plates, animal horns, and an ancient dresser large enough to store an entire inn's worth of plates, cups, and cutlery. Ysabeau peered over the pages of *Le Monde*, her eyes covering every inch of me. 'Marthe tells me you slept.'

'Yes, thank you,' I shifted from one foot to the other as if waiting to see the school principal to explain my misbehavior.

Marthe saved me from further discomfort by arriving with a pot of tea. She, too, surveyed me from head to foot.

'You are better today,' she finally announced, handing me a mug. She stood there frowning until Matthew's mother put down her paper, and then she departed.

When I was finished with my tea, we went to the stables. Ysabeau had to help with my boots, since they were still too stiff to slide on and off easily, and she watched carefully while I put on my turtle shell of a vest and the helmet. Clearly safety equipment had been part of Matthew's instructions. Ysabeau, of course, wore nothing more protective than a brown quilted jacket. The relative indestructibility of vampire flesh was a boon if you were a rider.

In the paddock Fiddat and Rakasa stood side by side, mirror images right down to the armchair-style saddles on their backs.

'Ysabeau,' I protested, 'Georges put the wrong tack on Rakasa. I don't ride sidesaddle.'

'Are you afraid to try?' Matthew's mother looked at me appraisingly.

'No!' I said, tamping down my temper. 'I just prefer to ride astride.'

'How do you know?' Her emerald eyes flickered with a touch of malice.

We stood for a few moments, staring at each other. Rakasa stamped her hoof and looked over her shoulder.

Are you going to ride or talk? she seemed to be asking.

Behave, I replied brusquely, walking over and putting her fetlock against my knee.

'Georges has seen to this,' Ysabeau said in a bored tone.

'I don't ride horses I haven't checked myself.' I examined Rakasa's hooves, ran my hands over her reins, and slid my fingers under the saddle.

'Philippe never did either.' Ysabeau's voice held a note of grudging respect. With poorly concealed impatience, she watched me finish. When I was done, she led Fiddat over to a set of steps and waited for me to follow. After she'd helped me get into the strange contraption of a saddle, she hopped onto her own horse. I took one look at her and knew I was in for quite a morning. Judging from her seat, Ysabeau was a better rider than Matthew – and he was the best I'd ever seen.

'Walk around,' Ysabeau said. 'I need to make sure you won't fall off and kill yourself.'

'Show a little faith, Ysabeau.' *Don't let me fall*, I bargained with Rakasa, *and I'll make sure you get an apple a day for the rest of your life.* My mount's ears shot forward, then back, and she nickered gently. We circled the paddock twice before I drew to a gentle stop in front of Matthew's mother. 'Satisfied?'

'You're a better rider than I expected,' she admitted. 'You could probably jump, but I promised Matthew we would not.'

'He managed to wheedle a fair number of promises out of you before he left,' I muttered, hoping she wouldn't hear me.

'Indeed,' she said crisply, 'some of them harder to keep than others.'

We passed through the open paddock gate. Georges touched his cap to Ysabeau and shut the gate behind us, grinning and shaking his head.

Matthew's mother kept us on relatively flat ground while I got used to the strange saddle. The trick was to keep your body square despite how off-kilter you felt.

'This isn't too bad,' I said after about twenty minutes.

'It is better now that the saddles have two pommels,' Ysabeau said. 'Before, all sidesaddles were good for was being led around by a man.' Her disgust was audible. 'It was not until the Italian queen put a pommel and stirrup on her saddle that we could control our own horses. Her husband's mistress rode astride so she could go with him when he exercised. Catherine was always being left at home, which is most unpleasant for a wife.' She shot me a withering glance. 'Henry's whore was named after the goddess of the hunt, like you.'

'I wouldn't have crossed Catherine de' Medici.' I shook my head.

'The king's mistress, Diane de Poitiers, was the dangerous one,' Ysabeau said darkly. 'She was a witch.'

'Actually or metaphorically?' I asked with interest.

'Both,' Matthew's mother said in a tone that could strip paint. I laughed. Ysabeau looked surprised, then joined in.

We rode a bit farther. Ysabeau sniffed the air and sat taller in the saddle, her face alert.

'What is it?' I asked anxiously, keeping Rakasa under a tight rein.

'Rabbit.' She kicked Fiddat into a canter. I followed closely, reluctant to see if it was as difficult to track a witch in the forest as Matthew had suggested.

We streaked through the trees and out into the open field. Ysabeau held Fiddat back, and I pulled alongside her.

'Have you ever seen a vampire kill?' Ysabeau asked, watching my reaction carefully.

'No,' I said calmly.

'Rabbits are small. That's where we will begin. Wait here.' She swung out of the saddle and dropped lightly to the ground. Fiddat stood obediently, watching her mistress. 'Diana,' she said sharply, never taking her eyes off her prey, 'do not come near me while I'm hunting or feeding. Do you understand?'

'Yes.' My mind raced at the implications. Ysabeau was going to chase down a rabbit, kill it, and drink its blood in front of me? Staying far away seemed an excellent suggestion.

Matthew's mother darted across the grassy field, moving so fast it was impossible to keep her in focus. She slowed just as a falcon does in midair before it swoops in for the kill, then bent and grabbed a frightened rabbit by the ears. Ysabeau held it up triumphantly before sinking her teeth directly into its heart.

Rabbits may be small, but they are surprisingly bloody if you bite into them while they're still alive. It was horrifying. Ysabeau sucked the blood out of the animal, which quickly ceased struggling, then wiped her mouth clean on its fur and tossed its carcass into the grass. Three seconds later she was swinging herself back into the saddle. Her cheeks were slightly flushed, and her eyes sparkled more than usual. Once mounted, she looked at me.

'Well?' she asked. 'Shall we look for something more filling, or do you need to return to the house?'

Ysabeau de Clermont was testing me.

'After you,' I said grimly, touching Rakasa's flank with my heel.

The remainder of our ride was measured not by the movement of the sun, which was still hidden behind clouds, but by the increasing amounts of blood Ysabeau's hungry mouth drew from her kills. She was a relatively neat eater. Still, it would be some time before I was happy at the prospect of a large steak.

I was numb to the sight of blood after the rabbit, the enormous squirrel-like creature that Ysabeau told me was a marmot, the fox, and the wild goat – or so I thought. When Ysabeau gave chase to a young doe, however, something prickled inside me.

'Ysabeau,' I protested. 'You can't still be hungry. Leave it.'

'What? The goddess of the hunt objects to my pursuit of her deer?' Her voice mocked, but her eyes were curious.

'Yes,' I said promptly.

'I object to your hunting of my son. See what good that has done.' Ysabeau swung down from her horse.

My fingers itched to intervene, and it was all I could do to stay out of Ysabeau's way while she stalked her prey. After each kill, her eyes revealed that she wasn't completely in command of her emotions – or her actions.

The doe tried to escape. It almost succeeded by darting into some underbrush, but Ysabeau frightened the animal back into the open. After that, fatigue put the doe at a disadvantage. The chase touched off something visceral within me. Ysabeau killed swiftly, and the doe didn't suffer, but I had to bite my lip to keep from shouting.

'There,' she said with satisfaction, returning to Fiddat. 'We can go back to Sept-Tours.'

Wordlessly I turned Rakasa's head in the direction of the château.

Ysabeau grabbed my horse's reins. There were tiny drops of blood on her cream shirt. 'Do you think vampires are beautiful now? Do you still think it would be easy to live with my son, knowing that he must kill to survive?'

It was difficult for me to put 'Matthew' and 'killing' in the same sentence. Were I to kiss him one day, when he was just returned from hunting, there might still be the taste of blood on his lips. And days like the one I was now spending with Ysabeau would be regular occurrences.

'If you're trying to frighten me away from your son, Ysabeau, you failed,' I said resolutely. 'You're going to have to do better than this.'

'Marthe said this would not be enough to make you reconsider,' she confessed.

'She was right.' My voice was curt. 'Is the trial over? Can we go home now?'

We rode toward the trees in silence. Once we were within the forest's leafy green confines, Ysabeau turned to me. 'Do you understand why you must not question Matthew when he tells you to do something?'

I sighed. 'School is over for the day.'

'Do you think our dining habits are the only obstacle standing between you and my son?'

'Spit it out, Ysabeau. Why must I do what Matthew says?'

'Because he is the strongest vampire in the château. He is the head of the house.'

I stared at her in astonishment. 'Are you saying I have to listen to him because he's the alpha dog?'

'You think *you* are?' Ysabeau chortled.

'No,' I conceded. Ysabeau wasn't the alpha dog either. She did what Matthew told her to do. So did Marcus, Miriam, and every vampire at the Bodleian Library. Even Domenico had ultimately backed down. 'Are these the de Clermont pack rules?'

Ysabeau nodded, her green eyes glittering. 'It is for your safety – and his, and everyone else's – that you must obey. This is not a game.'

'I understand, Ysabeau.' I was losing my patience.

'No, you don't,' she said softly. 'You won't either, until you are forced to see, just as I made you see what it is for a vampire to kill. Until then these are only words. One day your willfulness will cost your life, or someone else's. Then you will know why I told you this.'

We returned to the château without further conversation. When we passed through Marthe's ground-floor domain, she came out of the kitchen, a small chicken in her hands. I blanched. Marthe took in the tiny spots of blood on Ysabeau's cuffs and gasped.

'She needs to know,' Ysabeau hissed.

Marthe said something low and foul-sounding in Occitan, then nodded at me. 'Here, girl, come with me and I will teach you to make my tea.'

Now it was Ysabeau's turn to look furious. Marthe made me something to drink and handed me a plate with a few crumbly biscuits studded with nuts. Eating chicken was out of the question.

Marthe kept me busy for hours, sorting dried herbs and spices into tiny piles and teaching me their names. By midafternoon I could identify them by smell with my eyes closed as well as by appearance.

'Parsley. Ginger. Feverfew. Rosemary. Sage. Queen Anne's lace seeds. Mugwort. Pennyroyal. Angelica. Rue. Tansy. Juniper root.' I pointed to each in turn.

'Again,' Marthe said serenely, handing me a bunch of muslin bags.

I picked the strings apart, laying them individually on the table just as she did, reciting the names back to her one more time.

'Good. Now fill the bags with a pinch of each.'

'Why don't we just mix it all together and spoon it into the bags?' I asked, taking a bit of pennyroyal between my fingers and wrinkling my nose at its minty smell.

'We might miss something. Each bag must have every single herb – all twelve.'

'Would missing a tiny seed like this really make a difference to the taste?' I held a tiny Queen Anne's lace seed between my index finger and thumb.

'One pinch of each,' Marthe repeated. 'Again.'

The vampire's experienced hands moved surely from pile to pile, neatly filling the bags and tightening their strings. After we finished, Marthe brewed me a cup of tea using a bag I'd filled myself.

'It's delicious,' I said, happily sipping my very own herbal tea.

'You will take it back to Oxford with you. One cup a day. It will keep you healthy.' She started putting bags into a tin. 'When you need more, you will know how to make it.'

'Marthe, you don't have to give me all of it,' I protested.

'You will drink this for Marthe, one cup a day. Yes?'

'Of course.' It seemed the least I could do for my sole remaining ally in the house – not to mention the person who fed me.

After my tea I went upstairs to Matthew's study and switched on my computer. All that riding had made my forearms ache, so I moved the computer and manuscript to his desk, hoping that it might be more comfortable to work there rather than at my table by the window. Unfortunately, the leather chair was made for someone Matthew's height, not mine, and my feet swung freely.

Sitting in Matthew's chair made him seem closer, however, so I remained there while waiting for my computer to boot up. My eyes fell on a dark object tucked into the tallest shelf. It blended into the wood and the books' leather bindings, which hid it from casual view. From Matthew's desk, however, you could see its outlines.

It wasn't a book but an ancient block of wood, octagonal in shape. Tiny arched windows were carved into each side. The thing was black, cracked, and misshapen with age.

With a pang of sadness, I realized it was a child's toy.

Matthew had made it for Lucas before Matthew became a vampire, while he was building the first church. He'd tucked it into the corner of a shelf where no one would notice it – except him. He couldn't fail to see it, every time he sat at his desk.

With Matthew at my side, it was all too easy to think we were the only two in the world. Not even Domenico's warnings or Ysabeau's tests had shaken my sense that our growing closeness was a matter solely between him and me.

But this little wooden tower, made with love an unimaginably long time ago, brought my illusions to an end. There were children to consider, both living and dead. There were families involved, including my own, with long and complicated genealogies and deeply ingrained prejudices, including my own. And Sarah and Em still didn't know that I was in love with a vampire. It was time to share that news.

Ysabeau was in the salon, arranging flowers in a tall vase on top of a priceless Louis XIV escritoire with impeccable provenance – and a single owner.

'Ysabeau?' My voice sounded hesitant. 'Is there a phone I could use?'

'He will call you when he wants to talk to you.' She took great care placing a twig with turning leaves still attached to it among the white and gold flowers.

'I'm not calling Matthew, Ysabeau. I need to speak to my aunt.'

'The witch who called the other night?' she asked. 'What is her name?'

'Sarah,' I said with a frown.

'And she lives with a woman – another witch, yes?' Ysabeau kept putting white roses into the vase.

'Yes. Emily. Is that a problem?'

'No,' Ysabeau said, eyeing me over the blooms. 'They are both witches. That's all that matters.'

'That and they love each other.'

'Sarah is a good name,' Ysabeau continued, as if I hadn't spoken. 'You know the legend, of course.'

I shook my head. Ysabeau's changes in conversation were almost as dizzying as her son's mood swings.

'The mother of Isaac was called Sarai – "quarrelsome" – but when she became pregnant, God changed it to Sarah, which means "princess".'

'In my aunt's case, Sarai is much more appropriate.' I waited for Ysabeau to tell me where the phone was.

'Emily is also a good name, a strong, Roman name.' Ysabeau clipped a rose stem between her sharp fingernails.

'What does Emily mean, Ysabeau?' Happily I was running out of family members.

'It means "industrious." Of course, the most interesting name belonged to your mother. Rebecca means "captivated," or "bound,"'

Ysabeau said, a frown of concentration on her face as she studied the vase from one side and then the other. 'An interesting name for a witch.'

'And what does your name mean?' I said impatiently.

'I was not always Ysabeau, but it was the name Philippe liked for me. It means "God's promise."' Ysabeau hesitated, searching my face, and made a decision. 'My full name is Geneviève Mélisande Hélène Ysabeau Aude de Clermont.'

'It's beautiful.' My patience returned as I speculated about the history behind the names.

Ysabeau gave me a small smile. 'Names are important.'

'Does Matthew have other names?' I took a white rose from the basket and handed it to her. She murmured her thanks.

'Of course. We give all of our children many names when they are reborn to us. But Matthew was the name he came to us with, and he wanted to keep it. Christianity was very new then, and Philippe thought it might be useful if our son were named after an evangelist.'

'What are his other names?'

'His full name is Matthew Gabriel Philippe Bertrand Sébastien de Clermont. He was also a very good Sébastien, and a passable Gabriel. He hates Bertrand and will not answer to Philippe.'

'What is it about Philippe that bothers him?'

'It was his father's favorite name.' Ysabeau's hands stilled for a moment. 'You must know he is dead. The Nazis caught him fighting for the Resistance.'

In the vision I'd had of Ysabeau, she'd said Matthew's father was captured by witches.

'Nazis, Ysabeau, or witches?' I asked quietly, fearing the worst.

'Did Matthew tell you?' Ysabeau looked shocked.

'No. I saw you in one of my visions yesterday. You were crying.'

'Witches and Nazis both killed Philippe,' she said after a long pause. 'The pain is recent, and sharp, but it will fade in time. For years after he was gone I hunted only in Argentina and Germany. It kept me sane.'

'Ysabeau, I'm so sorry.' The words were inadequate, but they were heartfelt. Matthew's mother must have heard my sincerity, and she gave me a hesitant smile.

'It is not your fault. You were not there.'

'What names would you give me if you had to choose?' I asked softly, handing another stem to Ysabeau.

'Matthew is right. You are only Diana,' she said, pronouncing it in the French style as she always did, with the emphasis on the first syllable. 'There are no other names for you. It is who you are.' Ysabeau pointed her white finger at the door to the library. 'The phone is inside.'

Seated at the desk in the library, I switched on the lamp and dialed New York, hoping that both Sarah and Em were home.

'Diana.' Sarah sounded relieved. 'Em said it was you.'

'I'm sorry I couldn't call back last night. A lot happened.' I picked up a pencil and began to twirl it through my fingers.

'Would you like to talk about it?' Sarah asked. I almost dropped the phone. My aunt demanded we talk about things – she never *requested*.

'Is Em there? I'd rather tell the story once.'

Em picked up the extension, her voice warm and comforting. 'Hi, Diana. Where are you?'

'With Matthew's mother near Lyon.'

'Matthew's mother?' Em was curious about genealogy. Not just her own, which was long and complicated, but everyone else's, too.

'Ysabeau de Clermont.' I did my best to pronounce it as Ysabeau did, with its long vowels and swallowed consonants. 'She's something, Em. Sometimes I think she's the reason humans are so afraid of vampires. Ysabeau's straight out of a fairy tale.'

There was a pause. 'Do you mean you're with *Mélisande* de Clermont?' Em's voice was intense. 'I didn't even think of the de Clermonts when you told me about Matthew. You're sure her name is Ysabeau?'

I frowned. 'Actually, her name is Geneviève. I think there's a Mélisande in there, too. She just prefers Ysabeau.'

'Be careful, Diana,' Em warned. 'Mélisande de Clermont is notorious. She hates witches, and she ate her way through most of Berlin after World War II.'

'She has good reason to hate witches,' I said, rubbing my temples. 'I'm surprised she let me into her house.' If the situation was reversed, and vampires were involved in my parents' death, I wouldn't be so forgiving.

'What about the water?' Sarah interjected. 'I'm more worried about the vision Em had of a tempest.'

'Oh. I started raining last night after Matthew left.' The soggy memory made me shiver.

'Witchwater,' Sarah breathed, now understanding. 'What brought it on?'

'I don't know, Sarah. I felt . . . empty. When Matthew pulled out of the driveway, the tears I'd been fighting since Domenico showed up all just poured out of me.'

'Domenico who?' Emily flipped through her mental roster of legendary creatures again.

'Michele – a Venetian vampire.' My voice filled with anger. 'And if he bothers me again, I'm going to rip his head off, vampire or not.'

'He's dangerous!' Em cried. 'That creature doesn't play by the rules.'

'I've been told that many times over, and you can rest easy knowing I'm under guard twenty-four hours a day. Don't worry.'

'We'll worry until you're no longer hanging around with vampires,' Sarah observed.

'You'll be worrying for a good long time, then,' I said stubbornly. 'I love Matthew, Sarah.'

'That's impossible, Diana. Vampires and witches—' Sarah began.

'Domenico told me about the covenant,' I interjected. 'I'm not asking anyone else to break it, and I understand that this might mean you can't or won't have anything to do with me. For me there's no choice.'

'But the Congregation will do what they must to end this relationship,' Em said urgently.

'I've been told that, too. They'll have to kill me to do it.' Until this moment I hadn't said the words out loud, but I'd been thinking them since last night. 'Matthew's harder to get rid of, but I'm a pretty easy target.'

'You can't just walk into danger that way.' Em was fighting back tears.

'Her mother did,' Sarah said quietly.

'What about my mother?' My voice broke at the mention of her, along with my composure.

'Rebecca walked straight into Stephen's arms even though people said it was a bad idea for two witches with their talents to be together. And she refused to listen when people told her to stay out of Nigeria.'

'All the more reason that Diana should listen now,' Em said. 'You've only known him for a few weeks. Come back home and see if you can forget about him.'

'*Forget* about him?' It was ridiculous. 'This isn't a crush. I've never felt this way about anyone.'

'Leave her alone, Em. We've had enough of that kind of talk in this family. I didn't forget about you, and she's not going to forget about him.' Sarah let out her breath with a sigh that carried all the way to the Auvergne. 'This may not be the life I would have chosen for you, but we all have to decide for ourselves. Your mother did. I did – and your grandmother did not have an easy time with it, by the way. Now it's your turn. But no Bishop ever turns her back on another Bishop.'

Tears stung my eyes. 'Thank you, Sarah.'

'Besides,' Sarah continued, working herself into a state, 'if the Congregation is made up of things like Domenico Michele, then they can all go to hell.'

'What does Matthew say about this?' Em asked. 'I'm surprised he would leave you once you two had decided to break with a thousand years of tradition.'

'Matthew hasn't told me how he feels yet.' I methodically unbent a paper clip.

There was dead silence on the line.

Finally Sarah spoke. 'What is he waiting for?'

I laughed out loud. 'You've done nothing but warn me to stay away from Matthew. Now you're upset because he refuses to put me in greater danger than I'm already in?'

'You want to be with him. That should be enough.'

'This isn't some kind of magical arranged marriage, Sarah. I get to make my decision. So does he.' The tiny clock with the porcelain face that was sitting on the desk indicated it had been twenty-four hours since he left.

'If you're determined to stay there, with those creatures, then be careful,' Sarah warned as we said good-bye. 'And if you need to come home, come home.'

After I hung up, the clock struck the half hour. It was already dark in Oxford.

To hell with waiting. I lifted the receiver again and dialed his number.

'Diana?' He was clearly anxious.

I laughed. 'Did you know it was me, or was it caller ID?'

'You're all right.' The anxiety was replaced with relief.

'Yes, your mother is keeping me vastly entertained.'

'I was afraid of that. What lies has she been telling you?'

The more trying parts of the day could wait. 'Only the truth,' I said. 'That her son is some diabolical combination of Lancelot and Superman.'

'That sounds like Ysabeau,' he said with a hint of laughter. 'What a relief to know that she hasn't been irreversibly changed by sleeping under the same roof as a witch.'

Distance no doubt helped me evade him with my half-truths. Distance couldn't diminish my vivid picture of him sitting in his Morris chair at All Souls, however. The room would be glowing from the lamps, and his skin would look like polished pearl. I imagined him reading, the deep crease of concentration between his brows.

'What are you drinking?' It was the only detail my imagination couldn't supply.

'Since when have you cared about wine?' He sounded genuinely surprised.

'Since I found out how much there was to know.' *Since I found out that you cared about wine, you idiot.*

'Something Spanish tonight – Vega Sicilia.'

'From when?'

'Do you mean which vintage?' Matthew teased. 'It's 1964.'

'A relative baby, then?' I teased back, relieved at the change in his mood.

'An infant,' he agreed. I didn't need a sixth sense to know that he was smiling.

'How did everything go today?'

'Fine. We've increased our security, though nothing was missing. Someone tried to hack in to the computers, but Miriam assures me there's no way anyone could break in to her system.'

'Are you coming back soon?' The words escaped before I could stop them, and the ensuing silence stretched longer than was comfortable. I told myself it was the connection.

'I don't know,' he said coolly. 'I'll be back when I can.'

'Do you want to talk to your mother? I could find her for you.' His sudden aloofness hurt, and it was a struggle to keep my voice even.

'No, you can tell her the labs are fine. The house, too.'

We said good-bye. My chest was tight, and it was difficult to inhale. When I managed to stand and turn around, Matthew's mother was waiting in the doorway.

'That was Matthew. Nothing at the lab or the house was damaged. I'm tired, Ysabeau, and not very hungry. I think I'll go to bed.' It was nearly eight, a perfectly respectable time to turn in.

'Of course.' Ysabeau stepped out of my way with glittering eyes. 'Sleep well, Diana.'

CHAPTER 25

Marthe had been up to Matthew's study while I was on the phone, and sandwiches, tea, and water were waiting for me. She'd loaded the fireplace with logs to burn through the night, and a handful of candles shed their golden glow. The same inviting light and warmth upstairs would be in the bedroom, too, but my mind would not shut off, and trying to sleep would be futile. The *Aurora* manuscript was waiting for me on Matthew's desk. Sitting down at my computer, I avoided the sight of his winking armor and switched on his space-age, minimalist desk light to read.

> '*I spoke aloud: Give me knowledge of my end and the measure of my days, so I may know my frailty. My lifetime is no longer than the width of my hand. It is only a moment, compared to yours.*'

The passage only made me think of Matthew.

Trying to concentrate on alchemy was pointless, so I decided to make a list of queries regarding what I'd already read. All that was needed was a pen and a piece of paper.

Matthew's massive mahogany desk was as dark and solid as its owner, and it exuded the same gravitas. It had drawers extending down both sides of the space left for his knees, the drawers resting on round, bun-shaped feet. Just below the writing surface, running all around the perimeter, was a thick band of carving. Acanthus leaves, tulips, scrolls, and geometrical shapes invited you to trace their outlines. Unlike the surface of my desk – which was always piled so high with papers, books, and half-drunk cups of tea that you risked disaster whenever you tried to work on it – this desk held only an Edwardian desk pad, a sword-shaped letter opener, and the lamp. Like Matthew, it was a bizarrely harmonious blend of ancient and modern.

There were, however, no office supplies in sight. I grasped the round brass pull on the top right-hand drawer. Inside, everything was neat and precisely arranged. The Montblanc pens were segregated from the Montblanc pencils, and the paper clips were arranged by size. After selecting a pen and putting it on the desk, I attempted to open the remaining drawers. They were locked. The key wasn't underneath the paper clips – I dumped them on the desk, just to be sure.

An unmarked sheet of pale green blotting paper stretched between the desk pad's leather bumpers. In lieu of a legal pad, that would have to do. Picking up my computer to clear the desk, I knocked the pen to the floor.

It had fallen under the drawers and was just out of reach. I crawled into the desk's kneehole to retrieve it. Worming my hand under the drawers, my fingers found the thick barrel just as my eyes spotted the outline of a drawer in the dark wood above.

Frowning, I wriggled out from under the desk. There was nothing in the deep carving circling the desktop that released the catch on the concealed drawer. Leave it to Matthew to stash basic supplies in a drawer that was difficult to open. It would serve him right if every inch of his blotter was covered with graffiti when he returned home.

I wrote the number 1 in thick black ink on the green paper. Then I froze.

A desk drawer that was difficult to find was designed to hide something.

Matthew kept secrets – this I knew. But we had known each other only a few weeks, and even the closest of lovers deserved privacy. Still, Matthew's tight-lipped manner was infuriating, and his secrets surrounded him like a fortress devised to keep other people – me – out.

Besides, I only needed a piece of paper. Hadn't he rifled through my belongings at the Bodleian when he was looking for Ashmole 782? We'd barely met when he pulled that stunt. And he had left me to shift for myself in France.

As I carefully recapped the pen, my conscience nevertheless prickled. But my sense of injury helped me to cast that warning aside.

Pushing and pulling at every bump and bulge, my fingers searched the carvings on the desk's front edge once more without success. Matthew's letter opener rested invitingly near my right hand. It might be possible to wedge it into the seam underneath and pry the drawer open. Given the age of the desk, the historian in me squawked – much louder than my conscience had. Violating Matthew's privacy and engaging in ethically questionable behavior might be permissible, but I wasn't going to deface an antique.

Under the desk once more, I found it was too dark to see the underside of the drawer clearly, but my fingers located something cold and hard embedded in the wood. To the left of the drawer's nearly imperceptible join was a small metal bump approximately one long vampire reach from the front of the desk. It was round and had cross-hatching in the center – to make it look like a screw or an old nail head.

There was a soft click overhead when I pushed it.

Standing, I stared into a tray about four inches deep. It was lined with black velvet, and there were three depressions in the thick padding. Each held a bronze coin or medal.

The largest one had a building's outline cut into its surface and rested in the midst of a hollow nearly four inches across. The image was surprisingly detailed and showed four steps leading up to a door flanked by two columns. Between them was a shrouded figure. The building's crisp outlines were marred by fragments of black wax. Around the edge of the coin were the words '*militie Lazari a Bethania.*'

The knights of Lazarus of Bethany.

Gripping the tray's edges to steady myself, I abruptly sat down.

The metal disks weren't coins or medals. They were seals – the kind used to close official correspondence and certify property transactions. A wax impression attached to an ordinary piece of paper could once have commanded armies to leave the field or auctioned off great estates.

Based on the residue, at least one seal had been used recently.

Fingers shaking, I pried one of the smaller disks from the tray. Its surface bore a copy of the same building. The columns and the shrouded figure of Lazarus – the man from Bethany whom Christ raised from the dead after he'd been entombed for four days – were unmistakable. Here Lazarus was depicted stepping out of a shallow coffin. But no words encircled this seal. Instead the building was surrounded by a snake, its tail in its mouth.

I couldn't close my eyes quickly enough to banish the sight of the de Clermont family standard and its silver ouroboros snapping in the breeze above Sept-Tours.

The seal lay in my palm, its bronze surfaces gleaming. I focused on the shiny metal, willing my new visionary power to shed light on the mystery. But I'd spent more than two decades ignoring the magic in my blood, and it felt no compunction to come to my aid now.

Without a vision, my mundane historical skills would have to be put to work. I examined the back of the small seal closely, taking in its details. A cross with flared edges divided the seal into quarters, similar to the one Matthew had worn on his tunic in my vision. In the upper right quadrant of the seal was a crescent moon, its horns curved upward and a six-pointed star nestled in its belly. In the lower left quadrant was a fleur-de-lis, the traditional symbol of France.

Inscribed around the edge of the seal was the date MDCI – 1601 in Roman numerals – along with the words '*secretum Lazari*' – 'the secret of Lazarus.'

It couldn't be a coincidence that Lazarus, like a vampire, had made the journey from life to death and back again. Moreover, the cross, combined with a legendary figure from the Holy Land and the mention of knights, strongly suggested that the seals in Matthew's desk drawer belonged to one of the orders of Crusader knights established in the Middle Ages. The best known were the Templars, who had mysteriously disappeared in the early fourteenth century after being accused of heresy and worse. But I'd never heard of the Knights of Lazarus.

Turning the seal this way and that to catch the light, I focused on the date 1601. It was late for a medieval chivalric order. I searched my memory for important events of that year that might shed light on the mystery. Queen Elizabeth I beheaded the Earl of Essex, and the Danish astronomer Tycho Brahe died under far less colorful circumstances. Neither of these events seemed remotely relevant.

My fingers moved lightly over the carving. The meaning of MDCI washed over me.

Matthew de Clermont.

These were letters, not Roman numerals. It was an abbreviation of Matthew's name: MDCl. I was misreading the final letter.

The two-inch disk sat in my palm, and my fingers closed firmly around it, pressing the incised surface deep into the skin.

This smaller disk must have been Matthew's private seal. The power of such seals was so great that they were usually destroyed when someone died or left office so that no one else could use them to commit fraud.

And only one knight would have both the great seal and a personal seal in his possession: the order's leader.

Why Matthew kept the seals hidden puzzled me. Who cared about or even remembered the Knights of Lazarus, never mind his onetime role in the order? My attention was captured by the black wax on the great seal.

'It's not possible,' I whispered numbly, shaking my head. Knights in shining armor belonged to the past. They weren't active today.

The Matthew-size suit of armor gleamed in the candlelight.

I dropped the metal disk into the drawer with a clatter. The flesh of my palm had poured into the impressions and now carried its image, right down to its flared cross, crescent moon and star, and fleur-de-lis.

The reason Matthew had the seals, and the reason fresh wax clung to one of them, was that they were still in use. The Knights of Lazarus were still in existence.

'Diana? Are you all right?' Ysabeau's voice echoed up from the foot of the stairs.

'Yes, Ysabeau!' I called, staring at the seal's image on my hand. 'I'm reading my e-mail and got some unexpected news, that's all!'

'Shall I send Marthe up for the tray?'

'No!' I blurted. 'I'm still eating.'

Her footsteps receded toward the salon. When there was complete silence, I let out my breath.

Moving as quickly and quietly as possible, I flipped the other seal over in its velvet-lined niche. It was nearly identical to Matthew's, except that the upper right quadrant held only the crescent moon and '*Philippus*' was inscribed around the border.

This seal had belonged to Matthew's father, which mean that the Knights of Lazarus were a de Clermont family affair.

Certain there would be no more clues about the order in the desk, I turned the seals so that Lazarus's tomb was facing me once more. The drawer made a hushed click as it slid invisibly into position underneath the desk.

I picked up the table that Matthew used to hold his afternoon wine and carried it over to the bookcases. He wouldn't mind me looking through his library – or so I told myself, kicking off my loafers. The table's burnished surface gave a warning creak when I swung my feet onto it and stood, but the wood held fast.

The wooden toy at the far right of the top shelf was at eye level now. I sucked in a deep breath and pulled out the first item from the opposite end. It was ancient – the oldest manuscript I'd ever handled. The leather cover complained when it opened, and the smell of old sheepskin rose from the pages.

'*Carmina qui quondam studio florente peregi, /Flebilis heu maestos cogor inire modos,*' read the first lines. My eyes pricked with tears. It was Boethius's sixth-century work, *The Consolation of Philosophy*, written in prison while he was awaiting death. '*To pleasant songs my work was once given, and bright were all my labors then; /But now in tears to sad refrains I must return.*' I imagined Matthew, bereft of Blanca and Lucas and bewildered by his new identity as a vampire, reading words written by a condemned man. Giving silent thanks to whoever had offered him this in hope of lessening his grief, I slid the book back into place.

The next volume was a beautifully illustrated manuscript of Genesis, the biblical story of creation. Its strong blues and reds looked as fresh as the day they had been painted. Another illustrated manuscript, this one a copy of Dioscorides' book of plants, was also on the top shelf, along with more than a dozen other biblical books, several law books, and a book in Greek.

The shelf below held more of the same – books of the Bible mostly, along with a medical book and a very early copy of a seventh-century encyclopedia. It represented Isidore of Seville's attempt to capture all of human knowledge, and it would have appealed to Matthew's endless curiosity. At the bottom of the first folio was the name '*MATHIEU*,' along with the phrase '*meus liber*' – 'my book'.

Feeling the same urge to trace the letters as when I faced Ashmole 782 in the Bodleian, my fingers faltered on their way to the surface of the vellum. Then I'd been too afraid of the reading-room supervisors and my own magic to risk it. Now it was fear of learning something unexpected about Matthew that held me back. But there was no supervisor here, and my fears became insignificant when weighed against my desire to understand the vampire's past. I traced Matthew's name. An image of him, sharp and clear, came to me without the use of stern commands or shining surfaces.

He was seated at a plain table by a window, looking just as he did now, biting his lip with concentration as he practiced his writing. Matthew's long fingers gripped a reed pen, and he was surrounded by sheets of vellum, all of which bore repeated blotchy attempts to write his own name and copy out biblical passages. Following Marthe's advice, I didn't fight the vision's arrival or departure, and the experience was not as disorienting as it had been last night.

Once my fingers had revealed all they could, I replaced the encyclopedia and continued working my way through the remaining volumes in the case. There were history books, more law books, books on medicine and optics, Greek philosophy, books of accounts, the collected works of early church notables like Bernard of Clairvaux, and chivalric romances – one involving a knight who changed into a wolf once a week. But none revealed fresh information about the Knights of Lazarus. I bit back a sound of frustration and climbed down from the table.

My knowledge of Crusader orders was sketchy. Most of them started out as military units that were renowned for bravery and discipline. The Templars were famous for being the first to enter the field of battle and the last to leave. But the orders' military efforts were not limited to the area around Jerusalem. The knights fought in Europe, too, and many answered only to the Pope rather than to kings or other secular authorities.

Nor was the power of the chivalric orders solely military. They'd built churches, schools, and leper hospitals. The military orders safeguarded Crusader interests, whether spiritual, financial, or physical. Vampires like Matthew were territorial and possessive to the last, and therefore ideally suited to the role of guardians.

But the power of the military orders led ultimately to their downfall. Monarchs and popes were jealous of their wealth and influence. In 1312 the Pope and the French king saw to it that the Templars were disbanded, ridding themselves of the threat posed by the largest, most prestigious brotherhood. Most of the other orders gradually petered out due to lack of support and interest.

There were all those conspiracy theories, of course. A vast, complex international institution is hard to dismantle overnight, and the sudden dissolution of the Knights Templar had led to all sorts of fantastic tales about rogue Crusaders and underground operations. People still searched for traces of the Templars' fabulous wealth. The fact that no one had ever found evidence of how it was disbursed only added to the intrigue.

The money. It was one of the first lessons historians learned: follow the money. I refocused my search.

The sturdy outlines of the first ledger were visible on the third shelf, tucked between Al-Hazen's *Optics* and a romantic French chanson de geste. A small Greek letter was inked on the manuscript's fore edge: α. Figuring it must be an indexing mark of some sort, I scanned the shelves and located the second account book. It, too, had a small Greek letter, β. My eyes lit on γ, δ, and ε, scattered among the shelves, too. A more careful search would locate the rest, I was sure.

Feeling like Eliot Ness waving a fistful of tax receipts in pursuit of Al Capone, I held up my hand. There was no time to waste on climbing to retrieve it. The first account book slid from its resting place and fell into my waiting palm.

Its entries were dated 1117 and were made by a number of different hands. Names and numbers danced across the pages. My fingers were busy, taking in all the information they could from the writing. A few faces bloomed out of the vellum repeatedly – Matthew, the dark man with the hawkish nose, a man with bright hair the color of burnished copper, another with warm brown eyes and a serious face.

My hands stilled over an entry for money received in 1149. '*Eleanor Regina, 40,000 marks.*' It was a staggering sum – more than half the yearly income of the kingdom of England. Why was the queen of England giving so much to a military order led by vampires? But the Middle Ages were too far outside my expertise for me to be able to answer that question or to know much about the people engaging in the transfers. I shut the book with a snap and went to the sixteenth- and seventeenth-century bookcases.

Nestled among the other books was a volume bearing the identifying mark of a Greek lambda. My eyes widened once it was open.

Based on this ledger, the Knights of Lazarus had paid – somewhat unbelievably – for a wide range of wars, goods, services, and diplomatic feats, including providing Mary Tudor's dowry when she married Philip of Spain, buying the cannon for the Battle of Lepanto, bribing the French so they'd attend the Council of Trent, and financing most of the military actions of the Lutheran Schmalkaldic

League. Apparently the brotherhood didn't allow politics or religion to get in the way of their investment decisions. In a single year, they'd bankrolled Mary Stuart's return to the Scottish throne and paid off Elizabeth I's sizable debts to the Antwerp Bourse.

I walked along the shelves looking for more books marked with Greek letters. On the nineteenth-century shelves, there was one with the forked letter psi on its faded blue buckram spine. Inside, vast sums of money were meticulously accounted for, along with property sales that made my head spin – how did one secretly purchase most of the factories in Manchester? – and familiar names belonging to royalty, aristocrats, presidents, and Civil War generals. There were also smaller payouts for school fees, clothing allowances, and books, along with entries concerning dowries paid, hospital bills settled, and past-due rents brought up to date. Next to all the unfamiliar names was the abbreviation 'MLB' or 'FMLB.'

My Latin was not as good as it should be, but I was sure the abbreviations stood for the Knights of Lazarus of Bethany – *militie Lazari a Bethania* – or for *filia militie* or *filius militie*, the daughters and sons of the knights. And if the order was still disbursing funds in the middle of the nineteenth century, the same was probably true today. Somewhere in the world, a piece of paper – a real-estate transaction, a legal agreement – bore an impression of the order's great seal in thick, black wax.

And Matthew had applied it.

Hours later I was back in the medieval section of Matthew's library and opened my last account book. This volume spanned the period from the late thirteenth century to the first half of the fourteenth century. The staggering sums were now expected, but around 1310 the number of entries increased dramatically. So, too, did the flow of money. A new annotation accompanied some of the names: a tiny red cross. In 1313, next to one of these marks, was a name I recognized: Jacques de Molay, the last grand master of the Knights Templar.

He'd been burned at the stake for heresy in 1314. A year before he was executed, he'd turned over everything he owned to the Knights of Lazarus.

There were hundreds of names marked with red crosses. Were they all Templars? If so, then the mystery of the Templars was solved. The knights and their money hadn't disappeared. Both had simply been absorbed into the order of Lazarus.

It couldn't be true. Such a thing would have taken too much planning and coordination. And no one could have kept such a grand scheme secret. The idea was as implausible as stories about—

Witches and vampires.

The Knights of Lazarus were no more or less believable than I was.

As for conspiracy theories, their chief weakness was that they were so complex. No lifetime was sufficient to gather the necessary information, build the links between all the required elements, and then set the plans in motion. Unless, of course, the conspirators were vampires. If you were a vampire – or, better yet, a family of vampires – then the passage of time would matter little. As I knew from Matthew's scholarly career, vampires had all the time they needed.

The enormity of what it meant to love a vampire struck home as I slid the account book back onto the shelf. It was not just his age that posed the difficulties, or his dining habits, or the fact that he had killed humans and would do so again. It was the secrets.

Matthew had been accumulating secrets – large ones like the Knights of Lazarus and his son Lucas, small ones like his relationships with William Harvey and Charles Darwin – for well over a millennium. My life might be too brief to hear them all, never mind understand them.

But it was not only vampires who kept secrets. All creatures learned to do so out of fear of discovery and to preserve something – anything – just for ourselves within our clannish, almost tribal, world. Matthew was not simply a hunter, a killer, a scientist, or a vampire, but a web of secrets, just as I was. For us to be together, we needed to decide which secrets to share and then let the others go.

The computer chimed in the quiet room when my finger pressed the power button. Marthe's sandwiches were dry and the tea was cold, but I nibbled so that she wouldn't think her efforts had gone unappreciated.

Finished, I sat back and stared into the fire. The Knights of Lazarus roused me as a historian, and my witch's instincts told me the brotherhood was important to understanding Matthew. But their existence was not his most important secret. Matthew was guarding himself – his innermost nature.

What a complicated, delicate business it was going to be to love him. We were the stuff of fairy tales – vampires, witches, knights in shining armor. But there was a troubling reality to face. I had been threatened, and creatures watched me in the Bodleian in hopes I'd recall a book that everyone wanted but no one understood. Matthew's laboratory had been targeted. And our relationship was destabilizing the fragile détente that had long existed among daemons, humans, vampires, and witches. This was a new world, in which creatures were pitted against creatures and a silent, secret army could be called into action by a stamp in a pool of black wax. It was no wonder that Matthew might prefer to put me aside.

I snuffed the candles and climbed the stairs to bed. Exhausted, I quickly drifted off, my dreams filled with knights, bronze seals, and endless books of accounts.

A cold, slender hand touched my shoulder, waking me instantly.

'Matthew?' I sat bolt upright.

Ysabeau's white face glimmered in the darkness. 'It's for you.' She handed me her red mobile and left the room.

'Sarah?' I was terrified that something had happened to my aunts.

'It's all right, Diana.'

Matthew.

'What's happened?' My voice shook. 'Did you make a deal with Knox?'

'No. I can't make any progress there. There's nothing left for me in Oxford. I want to be home, with you. I should be there in a few hours.' He sounded strange, his voice thick.

'Am I dreaming?'

'You're not dreaming,' Matthew said. 'And, Diana?' He hesitated. 'I love you.'

It was what I most wanted to hear. The forgotten chain inside me started to sing, quietly, in the dark.

'Come here and tell me that,' I said softly, my eyes filling with tears of relief.

'You haven't changed your mind?'

'Never,' I said fiercely.

'You'll be in danger, and your family, too. Are you willing to risk that, for my sake?'

'I made my choice.'

We said good-bye and hung up reluctantly, afraid of the silence that would follow after so much had been said.

While he was gone, I had stood at a crossroads, unable to see a way forward.

My mother had been known for her uncanny visionary abilities. Would she have been powerful enough to see what awaited us as we took our first steps, together?

CHAPTER 26

I'd been waiting for the crunch of tires on gravel since pushing the disconnect button on Ysabeau's tiny mobile phone – and since then it hadn't been out of my sight.

A fresh pot of tea and breakfast rolls were waiting for me when I emerged from the bathroom, phone in hand. I bolted the food, flung on the first clothes that my fingers touched, and flew down the stairs with wet hair. Matthew wouldn't reach Sept-Tours for hours, but I was determined to be waiting when he pulled up.

First I waited in the salon on a sofa by the fire, wondering what had happened in Oxford to make Matthew change his mind. Marthe brought me a towel and roughly dried my hair with it when I showed no inclination to use it myself.

As the time of his arrival grew nearer, pacing in the hall was preferable to sitting in the salon. Ysabeau appeared and stood with her hands on her hips. I continued, despite her forbidding presence, until Marthe brought a wooden chair to the front door. She convinced me to sit, though the chair's carving had clearly been designed to acquaint its occupants with the discomforts of hell, and Matthew's mother retreated to the library.

When the Range Rover entered the courtyard, I flew outside. For the first time in our relationship, Matthew didn't beat me to the door. He was still straightening his long legs when my arms locked around his neck, my toes barely touching the ground.

'Don't do that again,' I whispered, my eyes shut against sudden tears. 'Don't ever do that again.'

Matthew's arms went around me, and he buried his face in my

neck. We held each other without speaking. Matthew reached up and loosened my grip, gently setting me back on my feet. He cupped my face, and familiar touches of snow and frost melted on my skin. I committed new details of his features to memory, such as the tiny creases at the corners of his eyes and the precise curve of the hollow under his full lower lip.

'*Dieu*,' he whispered in wonder, 'I was wrong.'

'Wrong?' My voice was panicky.

'I thought I knew how much I missed you. But I had no idea.'

'Tell me.' I wanted to hear again the words he'd said on the phone last night.

'I love you, Diana. God help me, I tried not to.'

My face softened into his hands. 'I love you, too, Matthew, with all my heart.'

Something in his body altered subtly at my response. It wasn't his pulse, since he didn't have much of a pulse, nor his skin, which remained deliciously cool. Instead there was a sound – a catch in his throat, a murmur of longing that sent a shock of desire through me. Matthew detected it, and his face grew fierce. He bent his head, fitting his cold lips to mine.

The resulting changes in my body were neither slight nor subtle. My bones turned to fire, and my hands crept around his back and slid down. When he tried to draw away, I pulled his hips back toward me.

Not so fast, I thought.

His mouth hovered above mine in surprise. My hands slid lower, holding on to his backside possessively, and his breath caught again until it purred in his throat.

'Diana,' he began, a note of caution in his voice.

My kiss demanded he tell me what the problem was.

Matthew's only answer was to move his mouth against mine. He stroked the pulse in my neck, then floated his hand down to cup my left breast, now stroking the fabric over the sensitive skin between my arm and my heart. With his other hand at my waist, he pulled me more tightly against him.

After a long while, Matthew loosened his hold enough that he could speak. 'You are mine now.'

My lips were too numb to reply, so I nodded and kept a firm grip on his backside.

He stared down at me. 'Still no doubts?'

'None.'

'We are one, from this moment forward. Do you understand?'

'I think so.' I understood, at the very least, that no one and nothing was going to keep me from Matthew.

'She has no idea.' Ysabeau's voice rang through the courtyard. Matthew stiffened, his arms circling me protectively. 'With that kiss you have broken every rule that holds our world together and keeps us safe. Matthew, you have marked that witch as your own. And, Diana, you have offered your witch's blood – your power – to a vampire. You have turned your back on your own kind and pledged yourself to a creature who is your enemy.'

'It was a kiss,' I said, shaken.

'It was an oath. And having made this promise to each other, you are outlaws. May the gods help you both.'

'Then we are outlaws,' Matthew said quietly. 'Should we leave, Ysabeau?' There was a vulnerable child's voice behind the man's, and something inside me broke for making him choose between us.

His mother strode forward and slapped him, hard, across the face. 'How dare you ask that question?'

Mother and son both looked shocked. The mark of Ysabeau's slender hand stood out against Matthew's cheek for a split second – red, then blue – before it faded.

'You are my most beloved son,' she continued, her voice as strong as iron. 'And Diana is now my daughter – my responsibility as well as yours. Your fight is my fight, your enemies are my enemies.'

'You don't have to shelter us, *Maman*.' Matthew's voice was taut as a bowstring.

'Enough of that nonsense. You are going to be hounded to the ends of the earth because of this love you share. We fight as a family.' Ysabeau turned to me. 'As for you, daughter – you *will* fight, as you promised. You are reckless – the truly brave always are – but I cannot fault your courage. Still, you need him as much as you need the air you breathe, and he wants you as he's wanted nothing and no one since I made him. So it is done, and we will make the best of it.' Ysabeau unexpectedly pulled me toward her and pressed her cold lips to my right cheek, then my left. I'd been living under the woman's roof for days, but this was my official welcome. She looked coolly at Matthew and made her real point.

'The way we will make the best of it begins with Diana behaving like a witch and not some pathetic human. The women of the de Clermont family defend themselves.'

Matthew bristled. 'I'll see that she's safe.'

'This is why you are always losing at chess, Matthew.' Ysabeau shook her finger at him. 'Like Diana, the queen has almost unlimited power. Yet you insist on surrounding her and leaving yourself vulnerable. This is not a game, however, and her weakness puts us all at risk.'

'Stay out of this, Ysabeau,' Matthew warned. 'Nobody is going to force Diana to be something she isn't.'

His mother gave an elegant, expressive snort.

'Exactly. We are no longer going to let Diana force herself to be a human, which she is not. She is a witch. You are a vampire. If this was not true, we would not be in such a mess. Matthew, *mon cher*, if the witch is brave enough to want you, she has no reason to fear her own power. You could rip her apart if you wanted to. And so can the ones who will come for you when they realize what you have done.'

'She's right, Matthew,' I said.

'Come, we should go inside.' He kept a wary eye on his mother. 'You're cold, and we need to talk about Oxford. Then we'll tackle the subject of magic.'

'I need to tell you what happened here, too.' If this was going to work, we would have to reveal some of our secrets – such as the possibility that I might turn into running water at any moment.

'There's plenty of time for you to tell me everything,' said Matthew, leading me toward the château.

Marthe was waiting for him when he walked through the door. She gave him a fierce hug, as if he'd returned in triumph from battle, and settled us all in front of the salon's blazing fire.

Matthew positioned himself next to me and watched me drink some tea. Every few moments he put his hand on my knee, or smoothed the sweater across my shoulders, or tucked a bit of hair back into place, as if trying to make up for his brief absence. Once he'd begun to relax, the questions began. They were innocently ordinary in the beginning. Soon the conversation turned to Oxford.

'Were Marcus and Miriam in the lab when the break-in was attempted?' I asked.

'They were,' he said, taking a sip from the glass of wine Marthe had put beside him, 'but the thieves didn't get far. The two of them weren't in any real danger.'

'Thank God,' Ysabeau murmured, staring at the fire.

'What were they looking for?'

'Information. About you,' he said reluctantly. 'Someone broke in to your rooms at New College as well.'

There was one secret out in the open.

'Fred was horrified,' Matthew continued. 'He assured me they'll put new locks on your doors and a camera in your stairwell.'

'It's not Fred's fault. With the new students, all you need to get past the porters is a confident step and a university scarf. But there was nothing for them to take! Were they after my research?' The mere thought of such a thing was ridiculous. Who cared enough about the history of alchemy to engineer a break-in?

'You have your computer, with your research notes on it.' Matthew gripped my hands tighter. 'But it wasn't your work they were after. They tore apart your bedroom and the bathroom. We think they were looking for a sample of your DNA – hair, skin, fingernail clippings. When they couldn't get into the lab, they went looking in your rooms.'

My hand was shaking slightly. I tried to pull it from his grip, not wanting him to know how badly this news had jangled me. Matthew held on.

'You're not alone in this, remember?' He fixed his gaze on me.

'So it wasn't an ordinary burglar. It was a creature, someone who knows about us and about Ashmole 782.'

He nodded.

'Well, they won't find much. Not in my rooms.' When Matthew looked puzzled, I explained. 'My mother insisted that I clean my hairbrush before leaving for school each morning. It's an ingrained habit. She made me flush the hair down the toilet – my nail clippings, too.'

Matthew now appeared stunned. Ysabeau didn't look surprised at all.

'Your mother sounds more and more like someone I would have been eager to know,' Ysabeau said quietly.

'Do you remember what she told you?' Matthew asked.

'Not really.' There were faint memories of sitting on the edge of the bathtub while my mother demonstrated her morning and evening routine, but little more. I frowned with concentration, the flickering recollections growing brighter. 'I remember counting to twenty. Somewhere along the way, I twirled around and said something.'

'What could she have been thinking?' Matthew mused out loud. 'Hair and fingernails carry a lot of genetic information.'

'Who knows? My mother was famous for her premonitions. Then again, she could just have been thinking like a Bishop. We're not the sanest bunch.'

'Your mother was not mad, Diana, and not everything can be explained by your modern science, Matthew. Witches have believed for centuries that hair and fingernails had power,' said Ysabeau.

Marthe muttered in agreement and rolled her eyes at the ignorance of youth.

'Witches use them to work spells,' Ysabeau continued. 'Binding spells, love magic – they depend on such things.'

'You told me you weren't a witch, Ysabeau,' I said, astonished.

'I have known many witches over the years. Not one of them would leave a strand of her hair or scrap of her nails for fear that another witch would find them.'

'My mother never told me.' I wondered what other secrets my mother had kept.

'Sometimes it is best for a mother to reveal things slowly to her children.' Ysabeau's glance flicked from me to her son.

'Who broke in?' I remembered Ysabeau's list of possibilities.

'Vampires tried to get into the lab, but we're less sure about your rooms. Marcus thinks it was vampires and witches working together, but I think it was just witches.'

'Is this why you were so angry? Because those creatures violated my territory?'

'Yes.'

We were back to monosyllables. I waited for the rest of the answer.

'I might overlook a trespasser on my land or in my lab, Diana, but I cannot stand by while someone does it to you. It feels like a threat, and I simply . . . can't. Keeping you safe is instinctive now.' Matthew ran his white fingers through his hair, and a patch stuck out over his ear.

'I'm not a vampire, and I don't know the rules. You have to explain how this works,' I said, smoothing his hair into place. 'So it was the break-in at New College that convinced you to be with me?'

Matthew's hands moved in a flash to rest on either side of my face. 'I needed no encouragement to be with you. You say you've loved me since you resisted hitting me with an oar at the river.' His eyes were unguarded. 'I've loved you longer than that – since the moment you used magic to take a book from its shelf at the Bodleian. You looked so relieved, and then so terribly guilty.'

Ysabeau stood, uncomfortable with her son's open affection. 'We will leave you.'

Marthe started rustling at the table, preparing to depart for the kitchens, where she would doubtless begin whipping up a ten-course feast.

'No, *Maman*. You should hear the rest.'

'So you are not merely outlaws.' Ysabeau's voice was heavy. She sank back onto her chair.

'There's always been animosity between creatures – vampires and witches especially. But Diana and I have brought those tensions into the open. It's just an excuse, though. The Congregation isn't really bothered by our decision to break the covenant.'

'Stop speaking in riddles, Matthew,' Ysabeau said sharply. 'I'm out of patience with them.'

Matthew looked at me regretfully before he responded. 'The Congregation has become interested in Ashmole 782 and the mystery of how Diana acquired it. Witches have been watching the manuscript for at least as long as I have. They never foresaw that you would be the one to reclaim it. And no one imagined that I would reach you first.'

Old fears wriggled to the surface, telling me there was something wrong deep inside me.

'If not for Mabon,' Matthew continued, 'powerful witches would have been in the Bodleian, witches who knew the manuscript's importance. But they were busy with the festival and let their guard down. They left the task to that young witch, and she let you – and the manuscript – slip through her fingers.'

'Poor Gillian,' I whispered. Peter Knox must be furious with her.

'Indeed.' Matthew's mouth tightened. 'But the Congregation has been watching you, too – for reasons that go well beyond the book and have to do with your power.'

'How long?' I wasn't able to finish my sentence.

'Probably your whole life.'

'Since my parents died.' Unsettling memories from childhood floated back to me, of feeling the tingles of a witch's attention while on the swings at school and a vampire's cold stare at a friend's birthday party. 'They've been watching me since my parents died.'

Ysabeau opened her mouth to speak, saw her son's face, and thought better of it.

'If they have you, they'll have the book, too, or so they think. You're connected to Ashmole 782 in some powerful way I don't yet understand. I don't believe they do either.'

'Not even Peter Knox?'

'Marcus asked around. He's good at wheedling information out of people. As far as we can tell, Knox is still mystified.'

'I don't want Marcus to put himself at risk – not for me. He needs to stay out of this, Matthew.'

'Marcus knows how to take care of himself.'

'I have things to tell you, too.' I'd lose my nerve entirely if given a chance to reconsider.

Matthew took both my hands, and his nostrils flared slightly. 'You're tired,' he said, 'and hungry. Maybe we should wait until after lunch.'

'You can smell when I'm *hungry*?' I asked incredulously. 'That's not fair.'

Matthew's head tipped back, and he laughed. He kept my hands in his, pulling them behind me so that my arms were shaped like wings.

'This from a witch, who could, if she felt like it, read my thoughts as if they were written on ticker tape. Diana, my darling, I know when you change your mind. I know when you're thinking bad thoughts, like how much fun it would be to jump the paddock fence. And I most definitely know when you're hungry,' he said, kissing me to make his point clear.

'Speaking of my being a witch,' I said, slightly breathless when he was finished, 'we've confirmed witchwater on the list of genetic possibilities.'

'What?' Matthew looked at me with concern. 'When did that happen?'

'The moment you pulled away from Sept-Tours. I wouldn't let myself cry while you were here. Once you were gone, I cried – a lot.'

'You've cried before,' he said thoughtfully, bringing my hands forward again. He turned them over and examined my palms and fingers. 'The water came out of your hands?'

'It came out of everywhere.' I said. His eyebrows rose in alarm. 'My hands, my hair, my eyes, my feet – even my mouth. It was like there was no me left, or if there was, I was nothing but water. I thought I'd never taste anything except salt again.'

'Were you alone?' Matthew's voice turned sharp.

'No, no, of course not,' I said hurriedly. 'Marthe and your mother were there. They just couldn't get near me. There was a lot of water, Matthew. Wind, too.'

'What made it stop?' he asked.

'Ysabeau.'

Matthew gave his mother a long look.

'She sang to me.'

The vampire's heavy lids dropped, shielding his eyes. 'Once she sang all the time. Thank you, *Maman*.'

I waited for him to tell me that she used to sing to him and that Ysabeau hadn't been the same since Philippe died. But he told me none of those things. Instead he wrapped me up in a fierce hug, and I tried not to mind that he wouldn't trust me with these parts of himself.

As the day unfolded, Matthew's happiness at being home was infectious. We moved from lunch to his study. On the floor in front of the fireplace, he discovered most of the places that I was ticklish. Throughout, he never let me behind the walls he'd so carefully constructed to keep creatures away from his secrets.

Once I reached out with invisible fingers to locate a chink in Matthew's defenses. He looked up at me in surprise.

'Did you say something?' he asked.

'No,' I said, drawing hastily away.

We enjoyed a quiet dinner with Ysabeau, who followed along in Matthew's lighthearted wake. But she watched him closely, a look of sadness on her face.

Putting on my sorry excuse for pajamas after dinner, I worried about the desk drawer and whether my scent would be on the velvet that cushioned the seals, and I steeled myself to say good night before Matthew retreated, alone, to his study.

He appeared shortly afterward wearing a pair of loose, striped pajama bottoms and a faded black T-shirt, with no shoes on his long, slender feet. 'Do you want the left side or the right?' he asked casually, waiting by the bedpost with his arms crossed.

I wasn't a vampire, but I could turn my head fast enough when it was warranted.

'If it doesn't matter to you, I'd prefer the left,' he said gravely. 'It will be easier for me to relax if I'm between you and the door.'

'I . . . I don't care,' I stammered.

'Then get in and slide over.' Matthew took the bedding out of my hand, and I did as he asked. He slid under the sheets behind me with a groan of satisfaction.

'This is the most comfortable bed in the house. My mother doesn't believe we need to bother with good mattresses since we spend so little time sleeping. Her beds are purgatorial.'

'Are you going to sleep with me?' I squeaked, trying and failing to sound as nonchalant as he did.

Matthew put his right arm out and hooked me into it until my head was resting on his shoulder. 'I thought I might,' he said. 'I won't actually sleep, though.'

Snuggled against him, I placed my palm flat on his heart so that I would know every time it beat. 'What will you do?'

'Watch you, of course.' His eyes were bright. 'And when I get tired of doing that – *if* I get tired of doing that' – he dropped a kiss on each eyelid – 'I'll read. Will the candles bother you?'

'No,' I responded. 'I'm a sound sleeper. Nothing wakes me up.'

'I like a challenge,' he said softly. 'If I'm bored, I'll figure out something that will wake you up.'

'Do you bore easily?' I teased, reaching up and threading my fingers through the hair at the base of his skull.

'You'll have to wait and see,' he said with a wicked grin.

His arms were cool and soothing, and the feeling of safety in his presence was more restful than any lullaby.

'Will this ever stop?' I asked quietly.

'The Congregation?' Matthew's voice was worried. 'I don't know.'

'No.' My head rose in surprise. 'I don't care about that.'

'What do you mean, then?'

I kissed him on his quizzical mouth. 'This feeling when I'm with you – as if I'm fully alive for the first time.'

Matthew smiled, his expression uncharacteristically sweet and shy. 'I hope not.'

Sighing with contentment, I lowered my head onto his chest and fell into dreamless sleep.

CHAPTER 27

I t occurred to me the next morning that my days with Matthew, thus far, had fallen into one of two categories. Either he steered the day along, keeping me safe and making sure nothing upset his careful arrangements, or the day unfolded without rhyme or reason. Not long ago what happened in my day had been determined by carefully drawn-up lists and schedules.

Today I was going to take charge. Today Matthew was going to let me into his life as a vampire.

Unfortunately my decision was bound to ruin what promised to be a wonderful day.

It started at dawn with Matthew's physical proximity, which sent the same shock of desire through me that I'd felt yesterday in the courtyard. It was more effective than any alarm clock. His response was gratifyingly immediate as well, and he kissed me with enthusiasm.

'I thought you'd never wake up,' he grumbled between kisses. 'I feared I would have to send to the village for the town band, and the only trumpeter who knew how to sound reveille died last year.'

Lying at his side, I noticed he was not wearing the ampulla from Bethany.

'Where did your pilgrim's badge go?' It was the perfect opportunity for him to tell me about the Knights of Lazarus, but he didn't take it.

'I don't need it anymore,' he'd said, distracting me by winding a lock of my hair around his finger and then pulling it to the side so he could kiss the sensitive flesh behind my ear. 'Tell me,' I'd insisted, squirming away slightly.

'Later,' he said, lips drifting down to the place where neck met shoulder.

My body foiled any further attempts at rational conversation. We both behaved instinctually, touching through the barriers of thin clothing and noting the small changes – a shiver, an eruption of gooseflesh, a soft moan – that promised greater pleasure to come. When I became insistent, reaching to seize bare flesh, Matthew stopped me.

'No rushing. We have time.'

'Vampires,' was all I managed to say before he stopped my words with his mouth.

We were still behind the bed curtains when Marthe entered the room. She left the breakfast tray on the table with an officious clatter and threw two logs on the fire with the enthusiasm of a Scot tossing the caber. Matthew peered out, proclaimed it a perfect morning, and declared that I was ravenous.

Marthe erupted into a string of Occitan and departed, humming a song under her breath. He refused to translate on the grounds that the lyrics were too bawdy for my delicate ears.

This morning, instead of quietly watching me eat, Matthew complained that he was bored. He did it with a wicked gleam in his eyes, his fingers restless on his thighs.

'We'll go riding after breakfast,' I promised, forking some eggs into my mouth and taking a scalding sip of tea. 'My work can wait until later.'

'Riding won't fix it,' Matthew purred.

Kissing worked to drive away his ennui. My lips felt bruised, and I had a much finer understanding of the interconnectedness of my own nervous system when Matthew finally conceded it was time to go riding.

He went downstairs to change while I showered. Marthe came upstairs to retrieve the tray, and I told her my plans while braiding my hair into a thick rope. Her eyes widened at the important part, but she agreed to send a small pack of sandwiches and a bottle of water out to Georges for Rakasa's saddlebag.

After that, there was nothing left but to inform Matthew.

He was humming and sitting at his desk, clattering on his computer and occasionally reaching over to thumb through messages on his phone. He looked up and grinned.

'There you are,' he said. 'I thought I was going to have to fish you out of the water.'

Desire shot through me, and my knees went weak. The feelings were exacerbated by the knowledge that what I was about to say would wipe the smile clean off his face.

Please let this be right, I whispered to myself, resting my hands on his shoulders. Matthew tilted his head back against my chest and smiled up at me.

'Kiss me,' he commanded.

I complied without a second thought, amazed at the comfort between us. This was so different from books and movies, where love was made into something tense and difficult. Loving Matthew was much more like coming into port than heading out into a storm.

'How do you manage it?' I asked him, holding his face in my hands. 'I feel like I've known you forever.'

Matthew smiled happily and returned his attention to his computer, shutting down his various programs. While he did, I drank in his spicy scent and smoothed his hair along the curve of his skull.

'That feels wonderful,' he said, leaning back into my hand.

It was time to ruin his day. Crouching down, I rested my chin on his shoulder.

'Take me hunting.'

Every muscle in his body stiffened.

'That's not funny, Diana,' he said icily.

'I'm not trying to be.' My chin and hands remained where they were. He tried to shrug me off, but I wouldn't let him. Though I didn't have the courage to face him, he wasn't going to escape. 'You need to do this, Matthew. You need to know that you can trust me.'

He stood up explosively, leaving me no choice but to step back and let him go. Matthew strode away, and one hand strayed to the spot where his Bethany ampulla used to rest. Not a good sign.

'Vampires don't take warmbloods hunting, Diana.'

This was not a good sign either. He was lying to me.

'Yes they do,' I said softly. 'You hunt with Hamish.'

'That's different. I've known him for years, and I don't share a bed with him.' Matthew's voice was rough, and he was staring fixedly at his bookshelves.

I started toward him, slowly. 'If Hamish can hunt with you, so can I.'

'No.' The muscles in his shoulders stood out in sharp relief, their outlines visible under his sweater.

'Ysabeau took me with her.'

The silence in the room was absolute. Matthew drew in a single, ragged breath, and the muscles in his shoulder twitched. I took another step.

'Don't,' he said harshly. 'I don't want you near me when I'm angry.'

Reminding myself that he wasn't in charge today, I took my next steps at a much faster pace and stood directly behind him. That way he couldn't avoid my scent or the sound of my heartbeat, which was measured and steady.

'I didn't mean to make you angry.'

'I'm not angry with you.' He sounded bitter. 'My mother, however, has a lot to answer for. She's done a great deal to try my patience over the centuries, but taking you hunting is unforgivable.'

'Ysabeau asked me if I needed to come back to the château.'

'You shouldn't have been given the choice,' he barked, whirling around to face me. 'Vampires aren't in control when they're hunting – not entirely. My mother certainly isn't to be trusted when she smells blood. For her it's all about the kill and the feeding. If the wind had caught your scent, she would have fed on you, too, without a second thought.'

Matthew had reacted more negatively than I'd expected. With

one of my feet firmly in the fire, however, the other one might as well go in, too.

'Your mother was only protecting you. She was concerned that I didn't understand the stakes. You would have done the same for Lucas.' Once again the silence was deep and long.

'She had no right to tell you about Lucas. He belonged to me, not to her.' Matthew's voice was soft, but filled with more venom than I'd ever heard in it. His eyes flickered to the shelf that held the tower.

'To you and to Blanca,' I said, my voice equally soft.

'The life stories of a vampire are theirs to tell – and theirs alone. We may be outlaws, you and I, but my mother has broken a few rules herself in the past few days.' He reached again for the missing Bethany ampulla.

I crossed the small distance that separated us, moving quietly and surely, as if he were a nervous animal, so as to keep him from lashing out in a way he would regret later. When I was standing no more than an inch from him, I took hold of his arms.

'Ysabeau told me other things as well. We talked about your father. She told me all of your names, and which ones you don't like, and her names as well. I don't really understand their significance, but it's not something she tells everyone. And she told me how she made you. The song she sang to make my witchwater go away was the same song she sang to you when you were first a vampire.' *When you couldn't stop feeding*.

Matthew met my eyes with difficulty. They were full of pain and a vulnerability that he'd carefully hidden before now. It broke my heart.

'I can't risk it, Diana,' he said. 'I want you – more than anyone I've ever known. I want you physically, I want you emotionally. If my concentration shifts for an instant while we're out hunting, the deer's scent could get confused with yours, and my instinct to hunt an animal could cross with my desire to have you.'

'You already have me,' I said, holding on to him with my hands, my eyes, my mind, my heart. 'There's no need to hunt me. I'm yours.'

'It doesn't work that way,' he said. 'I'll never possess you completely. I'll always want more than you can give.'

'You didn't in my bed this morning.' My cheeks reddened at the memory of his latest rebuff. 'I was more than willing to give myself to you, and you said no.'

'I didn't say no – I said later.'

'Is that how you hunt, too? Seduction, delay, then surrender?'

He shuddered. It was all the answer I required.

'Show me,' I insisted.

'No.'

'Show me!'

He growled, but I stood my ground. The sound was a warning, not a threat.

'I know you're frightened. So am I.' Regret flickered in his eyes, and I made a sound of impatience. 'For the last time, I am not frightened of you. It's my own power that scares me. You didn't see the witchwater, Matthew. When the water moved within me, I could have destroyed everyone and everything and not felt a drop of remorse. You're not the only dangerous creature in this room. But we have to learn how to be with each other in spite of who we are.'

He gave a bitter laugh. 'Maybe that's why there are rules against vampires and witches being together. Maybe it's too difficult to cross these lines after all.'

'You don't believe that,' I said fiercely, taking his hand in mine and holding it to my face. The shock of cold against warm sent a delicious feeling through my bones, and my heart gave its usual thump of acknowledgment. 'What we feel for each other is not – cannot – be wrong.'

'Diana,' he began, shaking his head and drawing his fingers away.

Gripping him more tightly, I turned the palm over. His lifeline was long and smooth, and after tracing it I brought my fingers to rest on his veins. They looked black under the white skin, and Matthew shivered at my touch. There was still pain in his eyes, but he was not as furious.

'This is not wrong. You know it. Now you have to know that you can trust me, too.' I laced my fingers through his and gave him time to think. But I didn't let go.

'I'll take you hunting,' Matthew said at last, 'provided you don't come near me and don't get down from Rakasa's back. If you get so much as a hint that I'm looking at you – that I'm even thinking about you – turn around and ride straight home to Marthe.'

The decision made, Matthew stalked downstairs, waiting patiently each time he realized I was lagging behind. As he breezed past the door of the salon, Ysabeau rose from her seat.

'Come on,' he said tightly, gripping my elbow and steering me downstairs.

Ysabeau was only a few feet behind us by the time we reached the kitchens, where Marthe stood in the doorway to the cold-foods larder, eyeing Matthew and me as if watching the latest drama on afternoon television. Neither needed to be told that something was wrong.

'I don't know when we'll be back,' Matthew shot over his shoulder. His fingers didn't loosen, and he gave me no opportunity to do more than turn toward her with an apologetic face and mouth the word 'Sorry.'

'*Elle a plus de courage que j'ai pensé*,' Ysabeau murmured to Marthe.

Matthew stopped abruptly, his lip curled in an unpleasant snarl.

'Yes, Mother. Diana has more courage than we deserve, you and I. And if you ever test that again, it will be the last time you see either of us. Understood?'

'Of course, Matthew,' Ysabeau murmured. It was her favorite noncommittal response.

Matthew didn't speak to me on the way to the stables. Half a dozen times, he looked as though he were going to turn around and march us back to the château. At the stable door, he gripped my shoulders, searching my face and body for signs of fear. My chin went up in the air.

'Shall we?' I motioned toward the paddock.

He made a sound of exasperation and shouted for Georges.

Balthasar bellowed in response and caught the apple that I tossed in his direction. Mercifully, I didn't need any help getting my boots on, though it did take me longer than it took Matthew. He watched carefully as I did up the vest's fastenings and snapped the chin strap on the helmet.

'Take this,' he said, handing me a cropped whip.

'I don't need it.'

'You'll take the crop, Diana.'

I took it, resolved to ditch it in the brush at the first opportunity.

'And if you toss it aside when we enter the forest, we're coming home.'

Did he really think I would use the crop on him? I shoved it into my boot, the handle sticking out by my knee, and stomped out into the paddock.

The horses skittered nervously when we came into view. Like Ysabeau, both knew that something was wrong. Rakasa took the apple I owed her, and I ran my fingers over her flesh and spoke to her softly in an effort to soothe her. Matthew didn't bother with Dahr. He was all business, checking the horse's tack with lightning speed. When I'd finished, Matthew tossed me onto Rakasa's back. His hands were firm around my waist, but he didn't hold on a moment longer than necessary. He didn't want any more of my scent on him.

In the forest Matthew made sure the crop was still in my boot.

'Your right stirrup needs shortening,' he pointed out after we had the horses trotting. He wanted my tack in racing trim in case I needed to make a run for it. I pulled Rakasa in with a scowl and adjusted the stirrup leathers.

The now-familiar field opened up in front of me, and Matthew sniffed the air. He grabbed Rakasa's reins and brought me to a halt. He was still black with anger.

'There's a rabbit over there.' Matthew nodded to the western section of the field.

'I've done rabbit,' I said calmly. 'And marmot, and goat, and a doe.'

Matthew swore. It was concise and comprehensive, and I hoped we were out of the range of Ysabeau's keen ears.

'The phrase is "cut to the chase," is it not?'

'I don't hunt deer like my mother does, by frightening it to death and pouncing on it. I can kill a rabbit for you, or even a goat. But I'm not stalking a deer while you're with me.' Matthew's jaw was set in an obstinate line.

'Stop pretending and trust me.' I gestured at my saddlebag. 'I'm prepared for the wait.'

He shook his head. 'Not with you at my side.'

'Since I've met you,' I said quietly, 'you've shown me all the pleasant parts of being a vampire. You taste things I can't even imagine. You remember events and people that I can only read about in books. You smell when I change my mind or want to kiss you. You've woken me to a world of sensory possibilities I never dreamed existed.'

I paused for a moment, hoping I was making progress. I wasn't.

'At the same time, you've seen me throw up, set fire to your rug, and come completely unglued when I received something unexpected in the mail. You missed the waterworks, but they weren't pretty. In return I'm asking you to let me watch you feed yourself. It's a basic thing, Matthew. If you can't bear it, then we can make the Congregation happy and call it off.'

'*Dieu.* Will you never stop surprising me?' Matthew's head lifted, and he stared into the distance. His attention was caught by a young stag on the crest of the hill. The stag was cropping the grass, and the wind was blowing toward us, so he hadn't yet picked up our scent.

Thank you, I breathed silently. It was a gift from the gods for the stag to appear like that. Matthew's eyes locked on his prey, and the anger left him to make room for a preternatural awareness of his environment. I fixed my eyes on the vampire, watching for slight changes that signaled what he was thinking or feeling, but there were precious few clues.

Don't you dare move, I warned when Rakasa tensed in preparation for a fidget. She rooted her hooves into the earth and stood at attention.

Matthew smelled the wind change and took Rakasa's reins. He slowly moved both horses to the right, keeping them within the path of the downward breezes. The stag raised his head and looked down the hill, then resumed his quiet clipping of the grass. Matthew's eyes darted over the terrain, lingering momentarily on a rabbit and widening when a fox stuck his head out of a hole. A falcon swooped overhead, riding the breezes like a surfer rides the waves, and he took that in as well. I began to appreciate how he'd managed the creatures in the Bodleian. There was not a living thing in this field that he had not located, identified, and been prepared to kill after only a few minutes of observation. Matthew inched the horses toward the trees, camouflaging my presence by putting me in the midst of other animal scents and sounds.

While we moved, Matthew noted when the falcon was joined by another bird or when one rabbit disappeared down a hole and another popped up to take its place. We startled a spotted animal that looked like a cat, with a long striped tail. From the pitch of Matthew's body, it was clear he wanted to chase it, and had he been alone he would have hunted it down before turning to the stag. With difficulty he drew his eyes away from the animal's leaping form.

It took us almost an hour to make our way from the bottom of the field around the forest's edge. When we were near the top, Matthew performed his face-forward dismount. He smacked Dahr on the rump, and the horse obediently turned and headed for home.

Matthew hadn't let go of Rakasa's reins during these maneuvers, and he didn't release them now. He led her to the edge of the forest and drew in a deep breath, taking in every trace of scent. Without a sound he put us inside a small thicket of low-growing birch.

The vampire crouched, both knees bent in a position that would have been excruciating to a human after about four minutes. Matthew held it for nearly two hours. My feet fell asleep, and I woke them up by flexing my ankles in the stirrups.

Matthew had not exaggerated the difference between his way of hunting and his mother's. For Ysabeau it was primarily about filling a biological need. She needed blood, the animals had it, and she took it from them as efficiently as possible without feeling remorse that her survival required the death of another creature. For her son, however, it was clearly more complicated. He, too, needed the physical nourishment that their blood provided. But Matthew felt a kinship with his prey that reminded me of the tone of respect I'd detected in his articles about the wolves. For Matthew, hunting was primarily about strategy, about pitting his feral intelligence against something that thought and sensed the world as he did.

Remembering our play in bed that morning, my eyes closed against a sudden jolt of desire. I wanted him as badly here in the forest when he was about to kill something as I had this morning, and I began to understand what worried Matthew about hunting with me. Survival and sexuality were linked in ways I'd never appreciated until now.

He exhaled softly and left my side without warning, his body prowling through the edges of the forest. When Matthew loped across the ridge, the stag raised his head, curious to see what this strange creature was.

It took the stag only a few seconds to assess Matthew as a threat, which was longer than it would have taken me. My hair was standing on end, and I felt the same pull of concern for the stag that I had for Ysabeau's deer. The stag sprang into action, leaping down the hillside. But Matthew was faster, and he cut the animal off before it could get too close to where I was hiding. He chased it up the hill and back across the ridge. With every step, Matthew drew closer and the stag became more anxious.

I know that you're afraid, I said silently, hoping the stag could hear me. *He needs to do this. He doesn't do this for sport, or to harm you. He does it to stay alive*.

Rakasa's head swung around, and she eyed me nervously. I reached down to reassure her and kept my hand on her neck.

Be still, I urged the stag. *Stop running. Not even you are fast enough to outrun this creature*. The stag slowed, stumbling over a hole in the ground. He was running straight for me, as if he could hear my voice and was following it to its source.

Matthew reached and grabbed the stag's horns, twisting his head to one side. The stag fell on his back, his sides heaving with exertion. Matthew sank to his knees, holding its head securely, about twenty feet from the thicket. The stag tried to kick his way to his feet.

Let go, I said sadly. *It's time. This is the creature who will end your life.*

The stag gave a final kick of frustration and fear and then quieted. Matthew stared deep into the eyes of his prey, as if waiting for permission to finish the job, then moved so swiftly that there was nothing more than a blur of black and white as he battened onto the stag's neck.

As he fed, the stag's life seeped away and a surge of energy entered Matthew. There was a clean tang of iron in the air, though no drops of blood fell. When the stag's life force was gone, Matthew remained still, kneeling quietly next to the carcass with his head bowed.

I kicked Rakasa into a walk. Matthew's back stiffened at my approach. He looked up, his eyes pale gray-green and bright with satisfaction. Taking the crop out of my boot, I threw it as far as I could in the opposite direction. It sailed into the underbrush and became hopelessly entangled in the gorse. Matthew watched with interest, but the danger that he might mistake me for a doe had clearly passed.

Deliberately I took off my helmet and dismounted with my back turned. Even now I trusted him, though he didn't trust himself. Resting my hand lightly on his shoulder, I dropped to my knees and put the helmet down near the stag's staring eyes.

'I like the way you hunt better than the way Ysabeau does it. So does the deer, I think.'

'How does my mother kill, that it is so different from me?' Matthew's French accent was stronger, and his voice sounded even more fluid and hypnotic than usual. He smelled different, too.

'She hunts out of biological need,' I said simply. 'You hunt because it makes you feel wholly alive. And you two reached an agreement.' I motioned at the stag. 'He was at peace, I think, in the end.'

Matthew looked at me intently, snow turning to ice on my skin as he stared. 'Were you talking to this stag as you talk to Balthasar and Rakasa?'

'I didn't interfere, if that's what you're worried about,' I said hastily. 'The kill was yours.' Maybe such things mattered to vampires.

Matthew shuddered. 'I don't keep score.' He dragged his eyes from the stag and rose to his feet in one of those smooth movements that marked him unmistakably as a vampire. A long, slender hand reached down. 'Come. You're cold kneeling on the ground.'

I placed my hand in his and stood, wondering who would get rid of the stag's carcass. Some combination of Georges and Marthe would be involved. Rakasa was contentedly eating grass, unconcerned by the dead animal lying so close. Unaccountably, I was ravenous.

Rakasa, I called silently. She looked up and walked over.

'Do you mind if I eat?' I asked hesitantly, unsure what Matthew's reaction would be.

His mouth twitched. 'No. Given what you've seen today, the least I can do is watch you have a sandwich.'

'There's no difference, Matthew.' I undid the buckle on Rakasa's saddlebag and said a silent word of thanks. Marthe, bless her, had packed cheese sandwiches. The worst of my hunger checked, I brushed the crumbs from my hands.

Matthew was watching me like a hawk. 'Do you mind?' he asked quietly.

'Mind what?' I'd already told him I didn't mind about the deer.

'Blanca and Lucas. That I was married and had a child once, so long ago.'

I was jealous of Blanca, but Matthew wouldn't understand how or why. I gathered my thoughts and emotions and tried to sort them into something that was both true and would make sense to him.

'I don't mind one moment of love that you've shared with any creature, living or dead,' I said emphatically, 'so long as you want to be with me right at this moment.'

'Just at this moment?' he asked, his eyebrow arching up into a question mark.

'This is the only moment that matters.' It all seemed so simple. 'No one who has lived as long as you have comes without a past, Matthew. You weren't a monk, and I don't expect you to have no regrets about who you've lost along the way. How could you not have been loved before, when I love you so much?'

Matthew gathered me to his heart. I went eagerly, glad that the day's hunting had not ended in disaster and that his anger was fading. It still smoldered – it was evident in a lingering tightness in his face and shoulders – but it no longer threatened to engulf us. He cupped my chin in his long fingers and tilted my face up to his.

'Would you mind very much if I kissed you?' Matthew glanced away for a moment when he asked.

'Of course not.' I stood on tiptoes so that my mouth was closer to his. Still, he hesitated, so I reached up and clasped my hands behind his neck. 'Don't be idiotic. Kiss me.'

He did, briefly but firmly. The final traces of blood were still on his lips, but it was neither frightening nor unpleasant. It was just Matthew.

'You know there won't be any children between us,' he said while he held me close, our faces nearly touching. 'Vampires can't father children the traditional way. Do you mind that?'

'There's more than one way to make a child.' Children were not something I'd thought about before. 'Ysabeau made you, and you belong to her no less than Lucas belonged to you and Blanca. And there are a lot of children in the world who don't have parents.' I remembered the moment when Sarah and Em told me mine were gone and never coming back. 'We could take them in – a whole coven of them, if we wanted to.'

'I haven't made a vampire for years,' he said. 'I can still manage it, but I hope you don't intend that we have a large family.'

'My family has doubled in the past three weeks, with you, Marthe, and Ysabeau added. I don't know how much more family I can take.'

'You need to add one more to that number.'

My eyes widened. 'There are more of you?'

'Oh, there are always more,' he said drily. 'Vampire genealogies are much more complicated than witch genealogies, after all. We have blood relations on three sides, not just two. But this is a member of the family that you've already met.'

'Marcus?' I asked, thinking of the young American vampire and his high-tops.

Matthew nodded. 'He'll have to tell you his own story – I'm not as much of an iconoclast as my mother, despite falling in love with a witch. I made him, more than two hundred years ago. And I'm proud of him and what he's done with his life.'

'But you didn't want him to take my blood in the lab,' I said with a frown. 'He's your son. Why couldn't you trust him with me?' Parents were supposed to trust their children.

'He was made with my blood, my darling,' Matthew said, looking patient and possessive at the same time. 'If I find you so irresistible, why wouldn't he? Remember, none of us is immune to the lure of blood. I might trust him more than I would a stranger, but I'll never be completely at ease when any vampire is too close to you.'

'Not even Marthe?' I was aghast. I trusted Marthe completely.

'Not even Marthe,' he said firmly. 'You really aren't her type at all, though. She prefers her blood from far brawnier creatures.'

'You don't have to worry about Marthe, or Ysabeau either.' I was equally firm.

'Be careful with my mother,' Matthew warned. 'My father told me never to turn my back on her, and he was right. She's always been fascinated by and envious of witches. Given the right circumstances and the right mood . . . ?' He shook his head.

'And then there's what happened to Philippe.'

Matthew froze.

'I'm seeing things now, Matthew. I saw Ysabeau tell you about the witches who captured your father. She has no reason to trust me, but she let me in her house anyway. The real threat is the Congregation. And there would be no danger from them if you made me into a vampire.'

His face darkened. 'My mother and I are going to have a long talk about appropriate topics of conversation.'

'You can't keep the world of vampires – your world – away from me. I'm in it. I need to know how it works and what the rules are.' My temper flared, seething down my arms and toward my nails, where it erupted into arcs of blue fire.

Matthew's eyes widened.

'You aren't the only scary creature around, are you?' I waved my fiery hands between us until the vampire shook his head. 'So stop being all heroic and let me share your life. I don't want to be with Sir Lancelot. Be yourself – Matthew Clairmont. Complete with your sharp vampire teeth and your scary mother, your test tubes full of blood and your DNA, your infuriating bossiness and your maddening sense of smell.'

Once I had spit all that out, the blue sparks retreated from my fingertips. They waited, somewhere around my elbows, in case I needed them again.

'If I come closer,' Matthew said conversationally, as though asking for the time or the temperature, 'will you turn blue again, or is that it for now?'

'I think I'm done for the time being.'

'You think?' His eyebrow arched again.

'I'm perfectly under control,' I said with more conviction, remembering with regret the hole in his rug in Oxford.

Matthew had his arms around me in a flash.

'Oof,' I complained as he crushed my elbows into my ribs.

'And you are going to give me gray hairs – long thought impossible among vampires, by the way – with your courage, your firecracker hands, and the impossible things you say.' To make sure he was safe from the last, Matthew kissed me quite thoroughly. When he was finished, I was unlikely to say much, surprising or otherwise. My ear rested against his sternum, listening patiently for his heart to thump. When it did, I gave him a satisfied squeeze, glad not to be the only one whose heart was full.

'You win, *ma vaillante fille*,' he said, cradling me against his body. 'I will try – *try* – not to coddle you so much. And you must not under-estimate how dangerous vampires can be.'

It was hard to put 'danger' and 'vampire' into the same thought while pressed so firmly against him. Rakasa gazed at us indulgently, the grass sprouting out of both sides of her mouth.

'Are you finished?' I angled back my head to look at him.

'If you're asking if I need to hunt more, the answer is no.'

'Rakasa is going to explode. She's been eating grass for quite some time. And she can't carry both of us.' My hands took stock of Matthew's hips and buttocks.

His breath caught in his throat, making a very different kind of purring sound from the one he made when he was angry.

'You ride, and I'll walk alongside,' he suggested after another very thorough kiss.

'Let's both walk.' After hours in the saddle, I was not eager to get back up on Rakasa.

It was twilight when Matthew led us back through the château gates. Sept-Tours was ablaze, every lamp illuminated in silent greeting.

'Home,' I said, my heart lifting at the sight.

Matthew looked at me, rather than the house, and smiled. 'Home.'

CHAPTER 28

Safely back at the château, we ate in the housekeeper's room before a blazing fire.

'Where's Ysabeau?' I asked Marthe when she brought me a fresh cup of tea.

'Out.' She stalked back toward the kitchen.

'Out where?'

'Marthe,' Matthew called. 'We're trying not to keep things from Diana.'

She turned and glared. I couldn't decide if it was directed at him, his absent mother, or me. 'She went to the village to see that priest. The mayor, too.' Marthe stopped, hesitated, and started again. 'Then she was going to clean.'

'Clean what?' I wondered.

'The woods. The hills. The caves.' Marthe seemed to think this explanation was sufficient, but I looked at Matthew for clarification.

'Marthe sometimes confuses clean and clear.' The light from the fire caught the facets of his heavy goblet. He was having some of the fresh wine from down the road, but he didn't drink as much as usual. 'It would seem that *Maman* has gone out to make sure there are no vampires lurking around Sept-Tours.'

'Is she looking for anyone in particular?'

'Domenico, of course. And one of the Congregation's other vampires, Gerbert. He's also from the Auvergne, from Aurillac. She'll look in some of his hiding places just to make sure he isn't nearby.'

'Gerbert. From Aurillac? *The* Gerbert of Aurillac, the tenth-century pope who reputedly owned a brass head that spoke oracles?' The fact that Gerbert was a vampire and had once been pope was of much less interest to me than was his reputation as a student of science and magic.

'I keep forgetting how much history you know. You put even vampires to shame. Yes, *that* Gerbert. And,' he warned, 'I would like it very much if you'd stay out of his way. If you do meet him, no quizzing him about Arabic medicine or astronomy. He has always been acquisitive when it comes to witches and magic.' Matthew looked at me possessively.

'Does Ysabeau know him?'

'Oh, yes. They were thick as thieves once. If he's anywhere near here, she'll find him. But you don't have to worry he'll come to the château,' Matthew assured me. 'He knows he's not welcome here. Stay inside the walls unless one of us is with you.'

'Don't worry. I won't leave the grounds.' Gerbert of Aurillac was not someone I wanted to stumble upon unexpectedly.

'I suspect she's trying to apologize for her behavior.' Matthew's voice was neutral, but he was still angry.

'You're going to have to forgive her,' I said again. 'She didn't want you to be hurt.'

'I'm not a child, Diana, and my mother needn't protect me from my own wife.' He kept turning his glass this way and that. The word 'wife' echoed in the room for a few moments.

'Did I miss something?' I finally asked. 'When were we married?'

Matthew's eyes lifted. 'The moment I came home and said I loved you. It wouldn't stand up in court perhaps, but as far as vampires are concerned, we're wed.'

'Not when I said I loved you, and not when you said you loved me on the phone – it only happened when you came home and told me to my face?' This was something that demanded precision. I was planning on starting a new file on my computer with the title 'Phrases That Sound One Way to Witches but Mean Something Else to Vampires.'

'Vampires mate the way lions do, or wolves,' he explained, sounding like a scientist in a television documentary. 'The female selects her mate, and once the male has agreed, that's it. They're mated for life, and the rest of the community acknowledges their bond.'

'Ah,' I said faintly. We were back to the Norwegian wolves.

'I've never liked the word "mate," though. It always sounds impersonal, as if you're trying to match up socks, or shoes.' Matthew put his goblet down and crossed his arms, resting them on the scarred surface of the table. 'But you're not a vampire. Do you mind that I think of you as my wife?'

A small cyclone whipped around my brain as I tried to figure out what my love for Matthew had to do with the deadlier members of the animal kingdom and a social institution that I'd never been particularly enthusiastic about. In the whirlwind there were no warning signs or guideposts to help me find my way.

'And when two vampires mate,' I inquired, when I could manage it, 'is it expected that the female will obey the male, just like the rest of the pack?'

'I'm afraid so,' he said, looking down at his hands.

'Hmm.' I narrowed my eyes at his dark, bowed head. 'What do I get out of this arrangement?'

'Love, honor, guard, and keep,' he said, finally daring to meet my eyes.

'That sounds an awful lot like a medieval wedding service.'

'A vampire wrote that part of the liturgy. But I'm not going to make you serve me,' he assured me hastily, with a straight face. 'That was put in to make the humans happy.'

'The men, at least. I don't imagine it put a smile on the faces of the women.'

'Probably not,' he said, attempting a lopsided grin. Nerves got the better of him, and it collapsed into an anxious look instead. His gaze returned to his hands.

The past seemed gray and cold without Matthew. And the future promised to be much more interesting with him in it. No matter how brief our courtship, I certainly felt bound to him. And, given vampires' pack behavior, it wasn't going to be possible to swap obedience for something more progressive, whether he called me 'wife' or not.

'I feel I should point out, husband, that, strictly speaking, your mother was not protecting you from your wife.' The words 'husband' and 'wife' felt strange on my tongue. 'I wasn't your wife, under the terms laid out here, until you came home. Instead I was just some creature you left like a package with no forwarding address. Given that, I got off lightly.'

A smile hovered at the corners of his mouth. 'You think so? Then I suppose I should honor your wishes and forgive her.' He reached for my hand and carried it to his mouth, brushing the knuckles with his lips. 'I said you were mine. I meant it.'

'This is why Ysabeau was so upset yesterday over our kiss in the courtyard.' It explained both her anger and her abrupt surrender. 'Once you were with me, there was no going back.'

'Not for a vampire.'

'Not for a witch either.'

Matthew cut the growing thickness in the air by casting a pointed look at my empty bowl. I'd devoured three helpings of stew, insisting all the while I wasn't hungry.

'Are you finished?' he asked.

'Yes,' I grumbled, annoyed at being caught out.

It was still early, but my yawns had already begun. We found Marthe rubbing down a vast wooden table with a fragrant combination of boiling water, sea salt, and lemons, and we said good night.

'Ysabeau will return soon,' Matthew told her.

'She will be out all night,' Marthe replied darkly, looking up from her lemons. 'I will stay here.'

'As you like, Marthe.' He gripped her shoulder for a moment.

On the way upstairs to his study Matthew told me the story of where he bought his copy of Vesalius's anatomy book and what he thought when he first saw the illustrations. I dropped onto the sofa with the book in question and happily looked at pictures of flayed corpses, too tired to concentrate on *Aurora Consurgens*, while Matthew answered e-mail. The hidden drawer in his desk was firmly closed, I noted with relief.

'I'm going to take a bath,' I said an hour later, rising and stretching my stiff muscles in preparation for climbing more stairs. I needed some time alone to think through the implications of my new status as Matthew's wife. The idea of marriage was overwhelming enough. When you factored in vampire possessiveness and my own ignorance about what was happening, it seemed an ideal time for a moment of reflection.

'I'll be up shortly,' Matthew said, barely looking up from the glow of his computer screen.

The bathwater was as hot and plentiful as ever, and I sank into the tub with a groan of pleasure. Marthe had been up and had worked her magic with candles and the fire. The rooms felt cozy, if not precisely warm. I drifted through a satisfying replay of the day's accomplishments. Being in charge was better than letting random events take place.

I was still soaking in the bathtub, my hair falling over the edge in a cascade of straw, when there was a gentle knock on the door. Matthew pushed it open without waiting for me to respond. Sitting up with a start, I quickly sank back into the water when he walked in.

He grabbed one of the towels and held it out like a sail in the wind. His eyes were smoky. 'Come to bed,' he said, his voice gruff.

I sat in the water for a few heartbeats, trying to read his face. Matthew stood patiently during my examination, towel extended. After a deep breath, I stood, the water streaming over my naked body. Matthew's pupils dilated suddenly, his body still. Then he stood back to let me step out of the tub before he wrapped the towel around me.

Clutching it to my chest, I kept my eyes on him. When they didn't waver, I let the towel fall, the light from the candles glinting off damp skin. His eyes lingered over my body, their slow, cold progress sending a shiver of anticipation down my spine. He pulled me toward him without a word, his lips moving over my neck and shoulders. Matthew breathed in my scent, his long, cool fingers lifting the hair off my neck and back. I gasped when his thumb came to rest against the pulse in my throat.

'*Dieu*, you are beautiful,' he murmured, 'and so alive.'

He began to kiss me again. Pulling at his T-shirt, my warm fingers moved against his cool, smooth skin. Matthew shuddered. It was much like my reaction to his first, cold touches. I smiled against his busy mouth, and he paused with a question on his face.

'It feels nice, doesn't it, when your coldness and my warmth meet?'

Matthew laughed, and the sound was as deep and smoky as his eyes. With my help, his shirt went up and over his shoulders. I started to fold it neatly. He snatched it away, balled it up, and threw it into the corner.

'Later,' Matthew said impatiently, his hands moving once more over my body. Broad expanses of skin touched skin for the first time, warm and cold, in a meeting of opposites.

It was my turn to laugh, delighted by how perfectly our bodies fit. I traced his spine, my fingers sweeping up and down his back until they sent Matthew diving down to capture the hollow of my throat and the tips of my breasts with his lips.

My knees started to soften, and I grabbed his waist for support. More inequity. My hands traveled to the front of his soft pajama bottoms and undid the tie that kept them up. Matthew stopped kissing me long enough to give me a searching look. Without breaking his stare, I eased the loosened material over his hips and let it fall.

'There,' I said softly. 'Now we're even.'

'Not even close,' Matthew said, stepping out of the fabric.

I very nearly gasped but bit my lip at the last moment to keep the sound in. Nevertheless my eyes widened at the sight of him. The parts of him that hadn't been visible to me were just as perfect as those that had. Seeing Matthew, naked and gleaming, was like witnessing a classical sculpture brought to life.

Wordlessly he took my hand and led me toward the bed. Standing beside its curtained confines, he jerked the coverlet and sheets aside and lifted me onto the high mattress. Matthew climbed into bed after me. Once he'd joined me under the covers, he lay on his side with his head resting on his hand. Like his position at the end of yoga class, here was another pose that reminded me of the effigies of medieval knights in English churches.

I drew the sheets up to my chin, conscious of the parts of my own body that were far from perfect.

'What's wrong?' He frowned.

'A little nervous, that's all.'

'About what?'

'I've never had sex with a vampire before.'

Matthew looked genuinely shocked. 'And you're not going to tonight either.'

The sheet forgotten, I raised myself on my elbows. 'You come into my bath, watch me get out of it naked and dripping wet, let me undress you, and then tell me we are *not* going to make love tonight?'

'I keep telling you we have no reason to rush. Modern creatures are always in such a hurry,' Matthew murmured, drawing the fallen sheet down to my waist. 'Call me old-fashioned if you'd like, but I want to enjoy every moment of our courtship.'

I tried to snatch the edge of the bedding and cover myself with it, but his reflexes were quicker than mine. He inched the sheet lower, out of my reach, eyes keen.

'Courtship?' I cried indignantly. 'You've already brought me flowers and wine. Now you're my husband, or so you tell me.' I flicked the sheets off his torso. My pulse quickened once more at the sight of him.

'As a historian, you must know that scores of weddings weren't consummated immediately.' His attention lingered over my hips and thighs, making them cold, then warm, in an entirely pleasant fashion. 'Years of courtship were required in some cases.'

'Most of those *courtships* led to bloodshed and tears.' I put a slight emphasis on the word in question. Matthew grinned and stroked my breast with feather-light fingers until my gasp made him purr with satisfaction.

'I promise not to draw blood, if you promise not to weep.'

It was easier to ignore his words than his fingers. 'Prince Arthur and Catherine of Aragon!' I said triumphantly, pleased at my ability to recall relevant historical information under such distracting conditions. 'Did you know them?'

'Not Arthur. I was in Florence. But Catherine, yes. She was nearly as brave as you are. Speaking of the past,' Matthew drew the back of his hand down my arm, 'what does the distinguished historian know about bundling?'

I turned on my side and slowly extended my fingertip along his jawbone. 'I'm familiar with the custom. But you are neither Amish nor English. Are you telling me that – like wedding vows – the practice of getting two people into bed to talk all night but not have sex was dreamed up by vampires?'

'Modern creatures aren't only in a hurry, they're overly focused on the act of sexual intercourse. It's far too clinical and narrow a definition. Making love should be about intimacy, about knowing another's body as well as your own.'

'Answer my question,' I insisted, unable to think clearly now that he was kissing my shoulder. 'Did vampires invent bundling?'

'No,' he said softly, his eyes glittering as my fingertip rounded his chin. He nipped at it with his teeth. As promised, he drew no blood. 'Once upon a time, we all did it. The Dutch and then the English came up with the variation of putting boards between the intended couple. The rest of us did it the old-fashioned way – we were just wrapped in blankets, shut into a room at dusk, and let out at dawn.'

'It sounds dreadful,' I said sternly. His attention drifted down my arm and across the swell of my belly. I tried to squirm away, but his free hand clamped onto my hip, keeping me still. 'Matthew,' I protested.

'As I recall,' he said, as if I hadn't spoken, 'it was a very pleasant way to spend a long winter's night. The hard part was looking innocent the next day.'

His fingers played against my stomach, making my heart skip around inside my rib cage. I eyed Matthew's body with interest, picking my next target. My mouth landed on his collarbone while my hand snaked down along his flat stomach.

'I'm sure sleep was involved,' I said after he found it necessary to snatch my hand and hold it away for a few minutes. My hip free, I pressed the length of my body against him. His body responded, and my face showed my satisfaction at the reaction. 'No one can talk all night.'

'Ah, but vampires don't need to sleep,' he reminded me, just before he pulled back, bent his head, and planted a kiss below my breastbone.

I grabbed his head and lifted it. 'There's only one vampire in this bed. Is this how you imagine you'll keep me awake?'

'I've been imagining little else from the first moment I saw you.' Matthew's eyes shone darkly as he lowered his head. My body arched up to meet his mouth. When it did, he gently but firmly turned me onto my back, grabbing both of my wrists in his right hand and pinning them to the pillow.

Matthew shook his head. 'No rushing, remember?'

I was accustomed to the kind of sex that involved a physical release without needless delay or unnecessary emotional complications. As an athlete who spent much of my time with other athletes, I was well acquainted with my body and its needs, and there was usually someone around to help me fill them. I was never casual about sex or my choice of partners, but most of my experiences had been with men who shared my frank attitude and were content to enjoy a few ardent encounters and then return to being friends again as though nothing had happened.

Matthew was making it clear that those days and nights were over. With him there would be no more straightforward sex – and I'd had no other kind. I might as well be a virgin. My deep feelings for him were becoming inextricably bound with my body's responses, his fingers and mouth tying them together in complicated, agonizing knots.

'We have all the time we need,' he said stroking the undersides of my arms with his fingertips, weaving love and physical longing together until my body felt tight.

Matthew proceeded to study me with the rapt attention of a cartographer who found himself on the shores of a new world. I tried to keep up with him, wanting to discover his body while he was discovering mine, but he held my wrists firmly against the pillows. When I began to complain in earnest about the unfairness of this situation, he found an effective way to silence me. His cool fingers dipped between my legs and touched the only inches of my body that remained uncharted.

'Matthew,' I breathed, 'I don't think that's bundling.'

'It is in France,' he said complacently, a wicked gleam in his eye. He let go of my wrists, convinced quite rightly that there would be no attempts to squirm away now, and I caught his face in my hands. We kissed each other, long and deep, while my legs opened like the covers of a book. Matthew's fingers coaxed, teased, and danced between them until the pleasure was so intense it left me shaking.

He held me until the tremors subsided and my heart returned to its normal rhythm. When I finally mustered the energy to look at him, he had the self-satisfied look of a cat.

'What are the historian's thoughts on bundling now?' he asked.

'It's far less wholesome than it's been made out to be in the scholarly literature,' I said, touching his lips with my fingers. 'And if this is what the Amish do at night, it's no wonder they don't need television.'

Matthew chuckled, the look of contentment never leaving his face. 'Are you sleepy now?' he asked, trailing his fingers through my hair.

'Oh, no.' I pushed him over onto his back. He folded his hands beneath his head and looked up at me with another grin. 'Not in the slightest. Besides, it's my turn.'

I studied him with the same intensity that he'd lavished on me. While I was inching up his hip bone, a white shadow in the shape of a triangle caught my attention. It was deep under the surface of his smooth, perfect skin. Frowning, I looked across the expanse of his chest. There were more odd marks, some shaped like snowflakes, others in crisscrossing lines. None of them were on the skin, though. They were all deep within him.

'What is this, Matthew?' I touched a particularly large snowflake under his left collarbone.

'It's just a scar,' he said, craning his neck to see. 'That one was made by the tip of a broadsword. The Hundred Years' War, maybe? I can't remember.'

I slithered up his body to get a better look, pressing my warm skin against him, and he sighed happily.

'A scar? Turn over.'

He made little sounds of pleasure while my hands swept across his back.

'Oh, Matthew.' My worst fears were realized. There were dozens, if not hundreds, of marks. I knelt and pulled the sheet down to his feet. They were on his legs, too.

His head swiveled over his shoulder. 'What's wrong?' The sight of my face was answer enough, and he turned over and sat up. 'It's nothing, *mon coeur*. Just my vampire body, holding on to trauma.'

'There are so many of them.' There was another one, on the swell of muscles where his arm met his shoulders.

'I said vampires were difficult to kill. Creatures try their best to do so anyway.'

'Did it hurt when you were wounded?'

'You know I feel pleasure. Why not pain, too? Yes, they hurt. But they healed quickly.'

'Why haven't I seen them before?'

'The light has to be just right, and you have to look carefully. Do they bother you?' Matthew asked hesitantly.

'The scars themselves?' I shook my head. 'No, of course not. I just want to hunt down all the people who gave them to you.'

Like Ashmole 782, Matthew's body was a palimpsest, its bright surface obscuring the tale of him hinted at by all those scars. I shivered at the thought of the battles Matthew had already fought, in wars declared and undeclared.

'You've fought enough.' My voice shook with anger and remorse. 'No more.'

'It's a bit late for that, Diana. I'm a warrior.'

'No you're not,' I said fiercely. 'You're a scientist.'

'I've been a warrior longer. I'm hard to kill. Here's the proof.' He gestured at his long white body. As evidence of his indestructibility, the scars were strangely comforting. 'Besides, most creatures who wounded me are long gone. You'll have to set that desire aside.'

'Whatever will I replace it with?' I pulled the sheets over my head like a tent. Then there was silence except for an occasional gasp from Matthew, the crackle of the logs in the fireplace, and in time his own cry of pleasure. Tucking myself under his arm, I hooked my leg over his. Matthew looked down at me, one eye opened and one closed.

'Is this what they're teaching at Oxford these days?' he asked.

'It's magic. I was born knowing how to make you happy.' My hand rested on his heart, pleased that I instinctively understood where and how to touch him, when to be gentle and when to leave my passion unchecked.

'If it is magic, then I'm even more delighted to be sharing the rest of my life with a witch,' he said, sounding as content as I felt.

'You mean the rest of *my* life, not the rest of yours.'

Matthew was suspiciously quiet, and I pushed myself up to see his expression. 'Tonight I feel thirty-seven. Even more important, I believe that next year I will feel thirty-eight.'

'I don't understand,' I said uneasily.

He drew me back down and tucked my head under his chin. 'For more than a thousand years, I've stood outside of time, watching the days and years go by. Since I've been with you, I'm aware of its passage. It's easy for vampires to forget such things. It's one of the reasons Ysabeau is so obsessed with reading the newspapers – to remind herself that there's always change, even though time doesn't alter her.'

'You've never felt this way before?'

'A few times, very fleetingly. Once or twice in battle, when I feared I was about to die.'

'So it's about danger, not just love.' A cold wisp of fear moved through me at this matter-of-fact talk of war and death.

'My life now has a beginning, a middle, and an end. Everything before was preamble. Now I have you. One day you will be gone, and my life will be over.'

'Not necessarily,' I said hastily. 'I've only got another handful of decades in me – you could go on forever.' A world without Matthew was unthinkable.

'We'll see,' he said quietly, stroking my shoulder.

Suddenly his safety was of paramount concern to me. 'You will be careful?'

'No one sees as many centuries as I have without being careful. I'm always careful. Now more than ever, since I have so much more to lose.'

'I would rather have had this moment with you – just this one night – than centuries with someone else,' I whispered.

Matthew considered my words. 'I suppose if it's taken me only a few weeks to feel thirty-seven again, I might be able to reach the point where one moment with you was enough,' he said, cuddling me closer. 'But this talk is too serious for a marriage bed.'

'I thought conversation was the point of bundling,' I said primly.

'It depends on whom you ask – the bundlers or those being bundled.' He began working his mouth down from my ear to my shoulders. 'Besides, I have another part of the medieval wedding service I'd like to discuss with you.'

'You do, husband?' I bit his ear gently as it moved past.

'Don't do that,' he said, with mock severity. 'No biting in bed.' I did it again anyway. 'What I was referring to was the part of the ceremony where the obedient wife,' he said, looking at me pointedly, 'promises to be "bonny and buxom in bed and board". How do you intend to fulfill that promise?' He buried his face in my breasts as if he might find the answer there.

After several more hours discussing the medieval liturgy, I had a new appreciation for church ceremonies as well as folk customs. And being with him in this way was more intimate than I'd ever been with another creature.

Relaxed and at ease, I curled against Matthew's now-familiar body so that my head rested below his heart. His fingers ran through my hair again and again, until I fell asleep.

It was just before dawn when I awoke to a strange sound coming from the bed next to me, like gravel rolling around in a metal tube.

Matthew was sleeping – and snoring, too. He looked even more like the effigy of a knight on a tombstone now. All that was missing was the dog at his feet and the sword clasped at his waist.

I pulled the covers over him. He didn't stir. I smoothed his hair back, and he kept breathing deeply. I kissed him lightly on the mouth, and there was still no reaction. I smiled at my beautiful vampire, sleeping like the dead, and felt like the luckiest creature on the planet as I crept from under the covers.

Outside, the clouds were still hanging in the sky, but at the horizon they were thin enough to reveal faint traces of red behind the gray layers. It might actually clear today, I thought, stretching slightly and looking back at Matthew's recumbent form. He would be unconscious for hours. I, on the other hand, was feeling restless and oddly rejuvenated. I dressed quickly, wanting to go outside in the gardens and be by myself for a while.

When I finished dressing, Matthew was still lost in his rare, peaceful slumber. 'I'll be back before you know it,' I whispered, kissing him.

There was no sign of Marthe, or of Ysabeau. In the kitchen I took an apple from the bowl set aside for the horses and bit into it. The apple's crisp flesh tasted bright against my tongue.

I drifted into the garden, walking along the gravel paths, drinking in the smells of herbs and the white roses that glowed in the early-morning light. If not for my modern clothes, it could have been in the sixteenth century, with the orderly square beds and the willow fences that were supposed to keep the rabbits out – though the château's vampire occupants were no doubt a better deterrent than a scant foot of bent twigs.

Reaching down, I ran my fingers over the herbs growing at my feet. One of them was in Marthe's tea. Rue, I realized with satisfaction, pleased that the knowledge had stuck.

A gust of wind brushed past me, pulling loose the same infernal lock of hair that would not stay put. My fingers scraped it back in place, just as an arm swept me off the ground.

Ears popping, I was rocketed straight up into the sky.

The gentle tingle against my skin told me what I already knew.

When my eyes opened, I would be looking at a witch.

CHAPTER 29

My captor's eyes were bright blue, angled over high, strong cheekbones and topped by a shock of platinum hair. She was wearing a thick, hand-knit turtleneck and a pair of tight-fitting jeans. No black robes or brooms, but she was – unmistakably – a witch.

With a contemptuous flick of her fingers, she stopped the sound of my scream before it broke free. Her arm swept to the left, carrying us more horizontally than vertically for the first time since she'd plucked me from the garden at Sept-Tours.

Matthew would wake up and find me gone. He would never forgive himself for falling asleep, or me for going outside. *Idiot*, I told myself.

'Yes you are, Diana Bishop,' the witch said in a strangely accented voice.

I slammed shut the imaginary doors behind my eyes that had always kept out the casual, invasive efforts of witches and daemons.

She laughed, a silvery sound that chilled me to the bone. Frightened, and hundreds of feet above the Auvergne, I emptied my mind in hopes of leaving nothing for her to find once she breached my inadequate defenses. Then she dropped me.

As the ground flew up, my thoughts organized themselves around a single word – Matthew.

The witch caught me up in her grip at my first whiff of earth. 'You're too light to carry for one who can't fly. Why won't you, I wonder?'

Silently I recited the kings and queens of England to keep my mind blank.

She sighed. 'I'm not your enemy, Diana. We are both witches.'

The winds changed as the witch flew south and west, away from Sept-Tours. I quickly grew disoriented. The blaze of light in the distance might be Lyon, but we weren't headed toward it. Instead we were moving deeper into the mountains — and they didn't look like the peaks Matthew had pointed out to me earlier.

We descended toward something that looked like a crater set apart from the surrounding countryside by yawning ravines and overgrown forests. It proved to be the ruin of a medieval castle, with high walls and thick foundations that extended deep into the earth. Trees grew inside the husks of long-abandoned buildings huddled in the fortress's shadow. The castle didn't have a single graceful line or pleasing feature. There was only one reason for its existence — to keep out anyone who wished to enter. The poor dirt roads leading over the mountains were the castle's only link to the rest of the world. My heart sank.

The witch swung her feet down and pointed her toes, and when I didn't do the same, she forced mine down with another flick of her fingers. The tiny bones complained at the invisible stress. We slid along what remained of the gray tiled roofs without touching them, headed toward a small central courtyard. My feet flattened out suddenly and slammed into the stone paving, the shock reverberating through my legs.

'In time you'll learn to land more softly,' the witch said matter-of-factly.

It was impossible to process my change in circumstances. Just moments ago, it seemed, I had been lying, drowsy and content, in bed with Matthew. Now I was standing in a dank castle with a strange witch.

When two pale figures detached themselves from the shadows, my confusion turned to terror. One was Domenico Michele. The other was unknown to me, but the freezing touch of his eyes told me he was a vampire, too. A wave of incense and brimstone identified him: this was Gerbert of Aurillac, the vampire-pope.

Gerbert wasn't physically intimidating, but there was evil at the core of him that made me shrink instinctively. Traces of that darkness were in brown eyes that looked out from deep sockets set over cheekbones so prominent that the skin appeared to be stretched thin over them. His nose hooked slightly, pointing down to thin lips that were curled into a cruel smile. With this vampire's dark eyes pinned on me, the threat posed by Peter Knox paled in comparison.

'Thank you for this place, Gerbert,' the witch said smoothly, keeping me close by her side. 'You're right – I won't be disturbed here.'

'It was my pleasure, Satu. May I examine your witch?' Gerbert asked softly, walking slowly to the left and right as if searching for the best vantage point from which to view a prize. 'It is difficult, when she has been with de Clermont, to tell where her scents begin and his end.'

My captor glowered at the reference to Matthew. 'Diana Bishop is in my care now. There is no need for your presence here any longer.'

Gerbert's attention remained fixed on me as he took small, measured steps toward me. His exaggerated slowness only heightened his menace. 'It is a strange book, is it not, Diana? A thousand years ago, I took it from a great wizard in Toledo. When I brought it to France, it was already bound by layers of enchantment.'

'Despite your knowledge of magic, you could not discover its secrets.' The scorn in the witch's voice was unmistakable. 'The manuscript is no less bewitched now than it was then. Leave this to us.'

He continued to advance. 'I knew a witch then whose name was similar to yours – Meridiana. She didn't want to help me unlock the manuscript's secrets, of course. But my blood kept her in thrall.' He was close enough now that the cold emanating from his body chilled me. 'Each time I drank from her, small insights into her magic and fragments of her knowledge passed to me. They were frustratingly fleeting, though. I had to keep going back for more. She became weak, and easy to control.' Gerbert's finger touched my face. 'Meridiana's eyes were rather like yours, too. What did you see, Diana? Will you share it with me?'

'Enough, Gerbert.' Satu's voice crackled with warning, and Domenico snarled.

'Do not think this is the last time you will see me, Diana. First the witches will bring you to heel. Then the Congregation will decide what to do with you.' Gerbert's eyes bored into mine, and his finger moved down my cheek in a caress. 'After that, you will be mine. For now,' he said with a small bow in Satu's direction, 'she is yours.'

The vampires withdrew. Domenico looked back, reluctant to leave. Satu waited, her gaze vacant, until the sound of metal meeting up with wood and stone signaled that they were gone from the castle. Her blue eyes snapped to attention, and she fixed them on me. With a small gesture, she released her spell that had kept me silent.

'Who are you?' I croaked when it was possible to form words again.

'My name is Satu Järvinen,' she said, walking around me in a slow circle, trailing a hand behind her. It triggered a deep memory of another hand that had moved like hers. Once Sarah had walked a similar path in the backyard in Madison when she'd tried to bind a lost dog, but the hands in my mind did not belong to her.

Sarah's talents were nothing compared to those possessed by this witch. It had been evident she was powerful from the way she flew. But she was adept at spells, too. Even now she was restraining me inside gossamer filaments of magic that stretched across the courtyard without her uttering a single word. Any hope of easy escape vanished.

'Why did you kidnap me?' I asked, trying to distract her from her work.

'We tried to make you see how dangerous Clairmont was. As witches, we didn't want to go to these lengths, but you refused to listen.' Satu's words were cordial, her voice warm. 'You wouldn't join us for Mabon, you ignored Peter Knox. Every day that vampire drew closer. But you're safely beyond his reach now.'

Every instinct screamed danger.

'It's not your fault,' Satu continued, touching me lightly on the shoulder. My skin tingled, and the witch smiled. 'Vampires are so seductive, so charming. You've been caught in his thrall, just as Meridiana was caught by Gerbert. We don't blame you for this, Diana. You led such a sheltered childhood. It wasn't possible for you to see him for what he is.'

'I'm not in Matthew's thrall,' I insisted. Beyond the dictionary definition, I had no idea what it might involve, but Satu made it sound coercive.

'Are you quite sure?' she asked gently. 'You've never tasted a drop of his blood?'

'Of course not!' My childhood might have been devoid of extensive magical training, but I wasn't a complete idiot. Vampire blood was a powerful, life-altering substance.

'No memories of a taste of concentrated salt? No unusual fatigue? You've never fallen deeply asleep when he was in your presence, even though you didn't want to close your eyes?'

On the plane to France, Matthew had touched his fingers to his own lips, then to mine. I'd tasted salt then. The next thing I knew, I was in France. My certainty wavered.

'I see. So he *has* given you his blood.' Satu shook her head. 'That's not good, Diana. We thought it might be the case, after he followed you back to college on Mabon and climbed through your window.'

'What are you talking about?' My blood froze in my veins. Matthew would never give me his blood. Nor would he violate my territory. If he had done these things, there would have been a reason, and he would have shared it with me.

'The night you met, Clairmont hunted you down to your rooms. He crept through an open window and was there for hours. Didn't you wake up? If not, he must have used his blood to keep you asleep. How else can we explain it?'

My mouth had been full of the taste of cloves. I closed my eyes against the recollection, and the pain that accompanied it.

'This relationship has been nothing more than an elaborate deception, Diana. Matthew Clairmont has wanted only one thing: the lost manuscript. Everything the vampire has done and every lie he's told along the way have been a means to that end.'

'No.' It was impossible. He couldn't have been lying to me last night. Not when we lay in each other's arms.

'Yes. I'm sorry to have to tell you these things, but you left us no other choice. We tried to keep you apart, but you are so stubborn.'

Just like my father, I thought. My eyes narrowed. 'How do I know that you're not lying?'

'One witch can't lie to another witch. We're sisters, after all.'

'Sisters?' I demanded, my suspicions sharpening. 'You're just like Gillian – pretending sisterhood while gathering information and trying to poison my mind against Matthew.'

'So you know about Gillian,' Satu said regretfully.

'I know she's been watching me.'

'Do you know she's dead?' Satu's voice was suddenly vicious.

'What?' The floor seemed to tilt, and I felt myself sliding down the sudden incline.

'Clairmont killed her. It's why he took you away from Oxford so quickly. It's yet another innocent death we haven't been able to keep out of the press. What did the headlines say . . . ? Oh, yes: "Young American Scholar Dies Abroad While Doing Research."' Satu's mouth curved into a malicious smile.

'No.' I shook my head. 'Matthew wouldn't kill her.'

'I assure you he did. No doubt he questioned her first. Apparently vampires have never learned that killing the messenger is pointless.'

'The picture of my parents.' Matthew might have killed whoever sent me that photo.

'It was heavy-handed for Peter to send it to you and careless of him to let Gillian deliver it,' Satu continued. 'Clairmont's too smart to leave evidence, though. He made it look like a suicide and left her body propped up like a calling card against Peter's door at the Randolph Hotel.'

Gillian Chamberlain hadn't been a friend, but the knowledge that she would never again crouch over her glass-encased papyrus fragments was more distressing than I would have expected.

And it was Matthew who had killed her. My mind whirled. How

could Matthew say he loved me and yet keep such things from me? Secrets were one thing, but murder – even under the guise of revenge and retaliation – was something else. He kept warning me he couldn't be trusted. I'd paid no attention to him, brushing his words aside. Had that been part of his plan, too, another strategy to lure me into trusting him?

'You must let me help you.' Satu's voice was gentle once more. 'This has gone too far, and you are in terrible danger. I can teach you to use your power. Then you'll be able to protect yourself from Clairmont and other vampires, like Gerbert and Domenico. You will be a great witch one day, just like your mother. You can trust me, Diana. We're family.'

'Family,' I repeated numbly.

'Your mother and father wouldn't have wanted you to fall into a vampire's snares,' Satu explained, as if I were a child. 'They knew how important it was to preserve the bonds between witches.'

'What did you say?' There was no whirling now. Instead my mind seemed unusually sharp and my skin was tingling all over, as if a thousand witches were staring at me. There was something I was forgetting, something about my parents that made everything Satu said a lie.

A strange sound slithered into my ears. It was a hissing and creaking, like ropes being pulled over stone. Looking down, I saw thick brown roots stretching and twisting across the floor. They crawled in my direction.

Satu seemed unaware of their approach. 'Your parents would have wanted you to live up to your responsibilities as a Bishop and as a witch.'

'My parents?' I drew my attention from the floor, trying to focus on Satu's words.

'You owe your loyalty and allegiance to me and your fellow witches, not to Matthew Clairmont. Think of your mother and father. Think of what this relationship would do to them, if only they knew.'

A cold finger of foreboding traced my spine, and all my instincts told me that this witch was dangerous. The roots had reached my feet by then. As if they could sense my distress the roots abruptly changed direction, digging into the paving stones on either side of where I stood, before weaving themselves into a sturdy, invisible web beneath the castle floors.

'Gillian told me that witches killed my parents,' I said. 'Can you deny it? Tell me the truth about what happened in Nigeria.'

Satu remained silent. It was as good as a confession.

'Just as I thought,' I said bitterly.

A tiny motion of her wrist threw me onto my back, feet in the air, before invisible hands dragged me across the slick surface of the freezing courtyard and into a cavernous space with tall windows and only a portion of roof remaining.

My back was battered from its trip across the stones of the castle's old hall. Worse yet, my struggles against Satu's magic were inexperienced and futile. Ysabeau was right. My weakness – my ignorance of who I was and how to defend myself – had landed me in serious trouble.

'Once again you refuse to listen to reason. I don't want to hurt you, Diana, but I will if it's the only way to make you see the seriousness of this situation. You must give up Matthew Clairmont and show us what you did to call the manuscript.'

'I will never give up my husband, nor will I help any of you claim Ashmole 782. It doesn't belong to us.'

This remark earned me the sensation of my head splitting in two as a bloodcurdling shriek tore through the air. A cacophony of horrifying sounds followed. They were so painful I sank to my knees, and covered my head with my arms.

Satu's eyes narrowed to slits, and I found myself on my backside on the cold stone. '*Us?* You dare to think of yourself as a witch when you've come straight from the bed of a vampire?'

'I *am* a witch,' I replied sharply, surprised at how much her dismissal stung.

'You're a disgrace, just like Stephen,' Satu hissed. 'Stubborn, argumentative, independent. And so full of secrets.'

'That's right, Satu, I'm just like my father. He wouldn't have told you anything. I'm not going to either.'

'Yes you will. The only way vampires can discover a witch's secrets is drop by drop.' To show what she meant, Satu flicked her fingers in the direction of my right forearm. Another witch's hand had flicked at a long-ago cut on my knee, but that gesture had closed my wound better than any Band-Aid. This one sliced an invisible knife through my skin. Blood began to trickle from the gash. Satu watched the flow of blood, mesmerized.

My hand covered the cut, putting pressure on the wound. It was surprisingly painful, and my anxiety began to climb.

No, said a familiar, fierce voice. *You must not give in to the pain.* I struggled to bring myself under control.

'As a witch, I have other ways to uncover what you're hiding. I'm going to open you up, Diana, and locate every secret you possess,' Satu promised. 'We'll see how stubborn you are then.'

All the blood left my head, making me dizzy. The familiar voice caught my attention, whispering my name. *Who do we keep our secrets from, Diana?*

Everybody, I answered, silently and automatically, as if the question were routine. Another set of far sturdier doors banged shut behind the inadequate barriers that had been all I'd ever needed to keep a curious witch out of my head.

Satu smiled, her eyes sparkling as she detected my new defenses. 'There's one secret uncovered already. Let's see what else you have, besides the ability to protect your mind.'

The witch muttered, and my body spun around and then flattened against the floor, facedown. The impact knocked the wind out of me. A circle of fire licked up from the cold stones, the flames green and noxious.

Something white-hot seared my back. It curved from shoulder to shoulder like a shooting star, descended to the small of my back, then curved again before climbing once again to where it had started. Satu's magic held me fast, making it impossible to wriggle away. The pain was unspeakable, but before the welcoming blackness could take me, she held off. When the darkness receded, the pain began again.

It was then that I realized with a sickening lurch of my stomach that she was opening me up, just as she'd promised. She was drawing a magical circle – onto me.

You must be very, very brave.

Through the haze of pain I followed the snaking tree roots covering the floor of the hall in the direction of the familiar voice. My mother was sitting under an apple tree just outside the line of green fire.

'Mama!' I cried weakly, reaching out for her. But Satu's magic held.

My mother's eyes – darker than I remembered, but so like my own in shape – were tenacious. She put one ghostly finger to her lips in a gesture of silence. The last of my energy was expended in a nod that acknowledged her presence. My last coherent thought was of Matthew.

After that, there was nothing but pain and fear, along with a dull desire to close my eyes and go to sleep forever.

It must have been many hours before Satu tossed me across the room in frustration. My back burned from her spell, and she'd reopened my injured forearm again and again. At some point she suspended me upside down by my ankle to weaken my resistance and taunted me about my inability to fly away and escape. Despite these efforts, Satu was no closer to understanding my magic than when she started.

She roared with anger, the low heels of her boots clicking against the stones as she paced and plotted fresh assaults. I lifted myself onto my elbow to better anticipate her next move.

Hold on. Be brave. My mother was still under the apple tree, her face shining with tears. It brought back echoes of Ysabeau telling Marthe that I had more courage than she had thought, and Matthew whispering 'My brave girl' into my ear. I mustered the energy to smile, not wanting my mother to cry. My smile only made Satu more furious.

'Why won't you use your power to protect yourself? I know it's inside you!' she bellowed. Satu drew her arms together over her chest, then thrust them out with a string of words. My body rolled into a ball around a jagged pain in my abdomen. The sensation reminded me of my father's eviscerated body, the guts pulled out and lying next to him.

That's what's next. I was oddly relieved to know.

Satu's next words flung me across the floor of the ruined hall. My hands reached futilely past my head to try to stop the momentum as I skidded across the uneven stones and bumpy tree roots. My fingers flexed once as if they might reach across the Auvergne and connect to Matthew.

My mother's body had looked like this, resting inside a magic circle in Nigeria. I exhaled sharply and cried out.

Diana, you must listen to me. You will feel all alone. My mother was talking to me, and with the sound I became a child again, sitting on a swing hanging from the apple tree in the back yard of our house in Cambridge on a long-ago August afternoon. There was the smell of cut grass, fresh and green, and my mother's scent of lilies of the valley. *Can you be brave while you're alone? Can you do that for me?*

There were no soft August breezes against my skin now. Instead rough stone scraped my cheek when I nodded in reply.

Satu flipped me over, and the pointy stones cut into my back.

'We don't want to do this, sister,' she said with regret. 'But we must. You will understand, once Clairmont is forgotten, and forgive me for this.'

Not bloody likely, I thought. *If he doesn't kill you, I'll haunt you for the rest of your life once I'm gone.*

With a few whispered words Satu lifted me from the floor and propelled me with carefully directed gusts of wind out of the hall and down a flight of curving stairs that wound into the depths of the castle. She moved me through the castle's ancient dungeons. Something rustled behind me, and I craned my neck to see what it was.

Ghosts – dozens of ghosts – were filing behind us in a spectral funeral procession, their faces sad and afraid. For all Satu's powers, she seemed unable to see the dead everywhere around us, just as she had been unable to see my mother.

The witch was attempting to raise a heavy wooden slab in the floor with her hands. I closed my eyes and braced myself for a fall. Instead Satu grabbed my hair and aimed my face into a dark hole. The smell of death rose in a noxious wave, and the ghosts shifted and moaned.

'Do you know what this is, Diana?'

I shrank back and shook my head, too frightened and exhausted to speak.

'It's an oubliette.' The word rustled from ghost to ghost. A wispy woman, her face creased with age, began to weep. 'Oubliettes are places of forgetting. Humans who are dropped into oubliettes go mad and then starve to death – if they survive the impact. It's a very long way down. They can't get out without help from above, and help never comes.'

The ghost of a young man with a deep gash across his chest nodded in agreement with Satu's words. *Don't fall, girl*, he said in a sorrowful voice.

'But we won't forget you. I'm going for reinforcements. You might be stubborn in the face of one of the Congregation's witches, but not all three. We found that out with your father and mother, too.' She tightened her grip, and we sailed more than sixty feet down to the bottom of the oubliette. The rock walls changed color and consistency as we tunneled deeper into the mountain.

'Please,' I begged when Satu dropped me on the floor. 'Don't leave me down here. I don't have any secrets. I don't know how to use my magic or how to recall the manuscript.'

'You're Rebecca Bishop's daughter,' Satu said. 'You have power – I can feel it – and we'll make sure that it breaks free. If your mother were here, she would simply fly out.' Satu looked into the blackness above us, then to my ankle. 'But you're not really your mother's daughter, are you? Not in any way that matters.'

Satu bent her knees, lifted her arms, and pushed gently against the oubliette's stone floor. She soared up and became a blur of white and blue before disappearing. Far above me the wooden door closed.

Matthew would never find me down here. By now any trail would be long gone, our scents scattered to the four winds. The only way to get out, short of being retrieved by Satu, Peter Knox, and some unknown third witch, was to get myself out.

Standing with my weight on one foot, I bent my knees, lifted my arms, and pushed against the floor as Satu had. Nothing happened. Closing my eyes, I tried to focus on the way it had felt to dance in the salon, hoping it would make me float again. All it did was make me think of Matthew, and the secrets he had kept from me. My breath turned into a sob, and when the oubliette's dank air passed into my lungs, the resulting cough brought me to my knees.

I slept a bit, but it was hard to ignore the ghosts once they started chattering. At least they provided some light in the gloom. Every time they moved, a tiny bit of phosphorescence smudged the air, linking where they had just been to where they were going. A young woman in filthy rags sat opposite me, humming quietly to herself and staring in my direction with vacant eyes. In the center of the room, a monk, a knight in full armor, and a musketeer peered into an even deeper hole that emitted a feeling of such loss that I couldn't bear to go near it. The monk muttered the mass for the dead, and the musketeer kept reaching into the pit as if looking for something he had lost.

My mind slid toward oblivion, losing its struggle against the combination of fear, pain, and cold. Frowning with concentration, I remembered the last passages I'd read in the *Aurora Consurgens* and repeated them aloud in the hope it would help me remain sane.

' "*It is I who mediates the elements, bringing each into agreement,*" ' I mumbled through stiff lips. ' "*I make what is moist dry again, and what is dry I make moist. I make what is hard soft again, and soften that which is hard. As I am the end, so my lover is the beginning. I encompass the whole work of creation, and all knowledge is hidden in me.*" ' Something shimmered against the wall nearby. Here was another ghost, come to say hello, but I closed my eyes, too tired to care, and returned to my recitation.

' "*Who will dare to separate me from my love? No one, for our love is as strong as death.*" '

My mother interrupted me. *Won't you try to sleep, little witch?*

Behind my closed eyes, I saw my attic bedroom in Madison. It was only a few days before my parents' final trip to Africa, and I'd been brought to stay with Sarah while they were gone.

'I'm not sleepy,' I replied. My voice was stubborn and childlike. I opened my eyes. The ghosts were drawing closer to the shimmer in the shadows to my right.

My mother was sitting there, propped against the oubliette's damp stone walls, holding her arms open. I inched toward her, holding my breath for fear she would disappear. She smiled in welcome, her dark eyes shining with unshed tears. My mother's ghostly arms and fingers flicked this way and that as I snuggled closer to her familiar body.

Shall I tell you a story?

'It was your hands I saw when Satu worked her magic.'

Her answering laugh was gentle and made the cold stones beneath me less painful. *You were very brave.*

'I'm so tired.' I sighed.

It's time for your story, then. Once upon a time, she began, *there was a little witch named Diana. When she was very small, her fairy godmother wrapped her in invisible ribbons that were every color of the rainbow.*

I remembered this tale from my childhood, when my pajamas had been purple and pink with stars on them and my hair was braided into two long pigtails that snaked down my back. Waves of memories flooded into rooms of my mind that had sat empty and unused since my parents' death.

'Why did the fairy godmother wrap her up?' I asked in my child's voice.

Because Diana loved making magic, and she was very good at it, too. But her fairy godmother knew that other witches would be jealous of her power. 'When you are ready,' *the fairy godmother told her,* 'you will shrug off these ribbons. Until then you won't be able to fly, or make magic.'

'That's not fair,' I protested, as seven-year-olds are fond of doing. 'Punish the other witches, not me.'

The world isn't fair, is it? my mother asked.

I shook my head glumly.

No matter how hard Diana tried, she couldn't shake her ribbons off. In time she forgot all about them. And she forgot her magic, too.

'I would never forget my magic,' I insisted.

My mother frowned. *But you have*, she said in her soft whisper. Her story continued. *One day, long after, Diana met a handsome prince who lived in the shadows between sunset and moonrise.*

This had been my favorite part. Memories of other nights flooded forth. Sometimes I had asked for his name, other times I'd proclaimed my lack of interest in a stupid prince. Mostly I wondered why anyone would want to be with a useless witch.

The prince loved Diana, despite the fact that she couldn't seem to fly. He could see the ribbons binding her, though nobody else could. He wondered what they were for and what would happen if the witch took them off. But the prince didn't think it was polite to mention them, in case she felt self-conscious. I nodded my seven-year-old head, impressed with the prince's empathy, and my much older head moved against the stone walls, too. *But he did wonder why a witch wouldn't want to fly, if she could.*

Then, my mother said, smoothing my hair, *three witches came to town. They could see the ribbons, too, and suspected that Diana was more powerful than they were. So they spirited her away to a dark castle. But the ribbons wouldn't budge, even though the witches pulled and tugged. So the witches locked her in a room, hoping she'd be so afraid she'd take the ribbons off herself.*

'Was Diana all alone?'

All alone, my mother said.

'I don't think I like this story.' I pulled up my childhood bedspread, a patchwork quilt in bright colors that Sarah had bought at a Syracuse department store in anticipation of my visit, and slid down to the floor of the oubliette. My mother tucked me against the stones. 'Mama?'

Yes, Diana?

'I did what you told me to do. I kept my secrets – from everybody.'

I know it was difficult.

'Do you have any secrets?' In my mind I was running like a deer through a field, my mother chasing me.

Of course, she said, reaching out and flicking her fingers so that I soared through the air and landed in her arms.

'Will you tell me one of them?'

Yes. Her mouth was so close to my ear that it tickled. *You. You are my greatest secret.*

'But I'm right here!' I squealed, squirming free and running in the direction of the apple tree. 'How can I be a secret if I'm right here?'

My mother put her fingers to her lips and smiled.

Magic.

CHAPTER 30

'Where is she?' Matthew slammed the keys to the Range Rover onto the table.

'We will find her, Matthew.' Ysabeau was trying to be calm for her son's sake, but it had been nearly ten hours since they'd found a half-eaten apple next to a patch of rue in the garden. The two had been combing the countryside ever since, working in methodical slices of territory that Matthew divided up on a map.

After all the searching, they'd found no sign of Diana and had been unable to pick up her trail. She had simply vanished.

'It has to be a witch who took her.' Matthew ran his fingers through his hair. 'I told her she'd be safe as long as she stayed inside the château. I never thought the witches would dare to come here.'

His mother's mouth tightened. The fact that witches had kidnapped Diana did not surprise her.

Matthew started handing out orders like a general on a battlefield. 'We'll go out again. I'll drive to Brioude. Go past Aubusson, Ysabeau, and into Limousin. Marthe, wait here in case she comes back or someone calls with news.'

There would be no phone calls, Ysabeau knew. If Diana had access to a phone, she would have used it before now. And though Matthew's preferred battle strategy was to chop through obstacles until he reached his goal, it was not always the best way to proceed.

'We should wait, Matthew.'

'Wait?' Matthew snarled. 'For what?'

'For Baldwin. He was in London and left an hour ago.'

'Ysabeau, how could you tell him?' His older brother, Matthew had learned through experience, liked to destroy things. It was what he did best. Over the years he'd done it physically, mentally, and then financially, once he'd discovered that destroying people's livelihoods was almost as thrilling as flattening a village.

'When she was not in the stables or in the woods, I felt it was time. Baldwin is better at this than you are, Matthew. He can track anything.'

'Yes, Baldwin's always been good at pursuing his prey. Now finding my wife is only my first task. Then I'll have to make sure she's not his next target.' Matthew picked up his keys. 'You wait for Baldwin. I'll go out alone.'

'Once he knows that Diana belongs to you, he will not harm her. Baldwin is the head of this family. So long as this is a family matter, he has to know.'

Ysabeau's words struck him as odd. She knew how much he distrusted his older brother. Matthew shrugged their strangeness aside. 'They came into your home, *Maman*. It was an insult to you. If you want Baldwin involved, it's your right.'

'I called Baldwin for Diana's sake – not mine. She must not be left in the hands of witches, Matthew, even if she is a witch herself.'

Marthe's nose went into the air, alert to a new scent.

'Baldwin,' Ysabeau said unnecessarily, her green eyes glittering.

A heavy door slammed overhead, and angry footsteps followed. Matthew stiffened, and Marthe rolled her eyes.

'Down here,' Ysabeau said softly. Even in a crisis, she didn't raise her voice. They were vampires, after all, with no need for histrionics.

Baldwin Montclair, as he was known in the financial markets, strode down the hall of the ground floor. His copper-colored hair gleamed in the electric light, and his muscles twitched with the quick reflexes of a born athlete. Trained to wield a sword from childhood, he had been imposing before becoming a vampire, and after his rebirth few dared to cross him. The middle son in Philippe de

Clermont's brood of three male children, Baldwin had been made a vampire in Roman times and had been Philippe's favorite. They were cut from the same cloth – fond of war, women, and wine, in that order. Despite these amiable characteristics, those who faced him in combat seldom lived to recount the experience.

Now he directed his anger at Matthew. They'd taken a dislike to each other the first time they'd met, their personalities at such odds that even Philippe had given up hope of their ever being friends. His nostrils flared as he tried to detect his brother's underlying scent of cinnamon and cloves.

'Where the hell are you, Matthew?' His deep voice echoed against the glass and stone.

Matthew stepped into his brother's path. 'Here, Baldwin.'

Baldwin had him by the throat before the words were out of his mouth. Their heads close together, one dark and one bright, they rocketed to the far end of the hall. Matthew's body smashed into a wooden door, splintering it with the impact.

'How could you take up with a witch, knowing what they did to Father?'

'She wasn't even born when he was captured.' Matthew's voice was tight given the pressure on his vocal cords, but he showed no fear.

'She's a witch,' Baldwin spat. 'They're all responsible. They knew how the Nazis were torturing him and did nothing to stop it.'

'Baldwin.' Ysabeau's sharp tone caught his attention. 'Philippe left strict instructions that no revenge was to be taken if he came to harm.' Though she had told Baldwin this repeatedly, it never lessened his anger.

'The witches helped those animals capture Philippe. Once the Nazis had him, they experimented on him to determine how much damage a vampire's body could take without dying. The witches' spells made it impossible for us to find him and free him.'

'They failed to destroy Philippe's body, but they destroyed his soul.' Matthew sounded hollow. 'Christ, Baldwin. They could do the same to Diana.'

If the witches hurt her physically, Matthew knew she might recover. But she would never be the same if the witches broke her spirit. He closed his eyes against the painful thought that Diana might not return the same stubborn, willful creature.

'So what?' Baldwin tossed his brother onto the floor in disgust and pounced on him.

A copper kettle the size of a timpani drum crashed into the wall. Both brothers leaped to their feet.

Marthe stood with gnarled hands on ample hips, glaring at them.

'She is his wife,' she told Baldwin curtly.

'You *mated* with her?' Baldwin was incredulous.

'Diana is part of this family now,' Ysabeau answered. 'Marthe and I have accepted her. You must as well.'

'Never,' he said flatly. 'No witch will ever be a de Clermont, or welcome in this house. Mating is a powerful instinct, but it doesn't survive death. If the witches don't kill this Bishop woman, I will.'

Matthew lunged at his brother's throat. There was a sound of flesh tearing. Baldwin reeled back and howled, his hand on his neck.

'You bit me!'

'Threaten my wife again and I'll do more than that.' Matthew's sides were heaving and his eyes were wild.

'Enough!' Ysabeau startled them into silence. 'I have already lost my husband, a daughter, and two of my sons. I will *not* have you at each other's throats. I will *not* let witches take someone from my home without my permission.' Her last words were uttered in a low hiss. 'And I will *not* stand here and argue while my son's wife is in the hands of my enemies.'

'In 1944 you insisted that challenging the witches wouldn't solve anything. Now look at you,' Baldwin snapped, glaring at his brother.

'This is different,' Matthew said tightly.

'Oh, it's different, I grant you that. You're risking the Congregation's interference in our family's affairs just so you can bed one of them.'

'The decision to engage in open hostilities with the witches was not yours to make then. It was your father's – and he expressly forbade prolonging a world war.' Ysabeau stopped behind Baldwin and waited until he turned to face her. 'You must let this go. The power to punish such atrocities was placed in the hands of human authorities.'

Baldwin looked at her sourly. 'You took matters into your own hands, as I recall, Ysabeau. How many Nazis did you dine on before you were satisfied?' It was an unforgivable thing to say, but he had been pushed past his normal limits.

'As for Diana,' Ysabeau continued smoothly, though her eyes sparked in warning, 'if your father were alive, Lucius Sigéric Benoit Christophe Baldwin de Clermont, he would be out looking for her – witch or not. He would be ashamed of you, in here settling old scores with your brother.' Every one of the names Philippe had given him over the years sounded like a slap, and Baldwin's head jerked back when they struck.

He exhaled slowly through his nose. 'Thank you for the advice, Ysabeau, and the history lesson. Now, happily, it *is* my decision. Matthew will not indulge himself with this girl. End of discussion.' He felt better after exercising his authority and turned to stalk out of Sept-Tours.

'Then you leave me no choice.' Matthew's response stopped him in his tracks.

'Choice?' Baldwin snorted. 'You'll do what I tell you to do.'

'I may not be head of the family, but this is no longer a family matter.' Matthew had, at last, figured out the point of Ysabeau's earlier remark.

'Fine.' Baldwin shrugged. 'Go on this foolish crusade, if you must. Find your witch. Take Marthe – she seems to be as enamored of her as you are. If the two of you want to pester the witches and bring the Congregation down on your heads, that's your business. To protect the family, I'll disown you.'

He was on his way out the door again when his younger brother laid down his trump.

'I absolve the de Clermonts of any responsibility for sheltering

Diana Bishop. The Knights of Lazarus will now see to her safety, as we have done for others in the past.'

Ysabeau turned away to hide her expression of pride.

'You can't be serious,' Baldwin hissed. 'If you rally the brotherhood, it will be tantamount to a declaration of war.'

'If that's your decision, you know the consequences. I could kill you for your disobedience, but I don't have time. Your lands and possessions are forfeit. Leave this house, and surrender your seal of office. A new French master will be appointed within the week. You are beyond the protection of the order and have seven days to find yourself a new place to live.'

'Try to take Sept-Tours from me,' Baldwin growled, 'and you'll regret it.'

'Sept-Tours isn't yours. It belongs to the Knights of Lazarus. Ysabeau lives here with the brotherhood's blessing. I'll give you one more chance to be included in that arrangement.' Matthew's voice took on an indisputable tone of command. 'Baldwin de Clermont, I call upon you to fulfill your sworn oath and enter the field of battle, where you will obey my commands until I release you.'

He hadn't spoken or written the words for ages, but Matthew remembered each one perfectly. The Knights of Lazarus were in his blood, just as Diana was. Long-unused muscles flexed deep within him, and talents that had grown rusty began to sharpen.

'The Knights don't come to their master's aid because of a love affair gone wrong, Matthew. We fought at the Battle of Acre. We helped the Albigensian heretics resist the northerners. We survived the demise of the Templars and the English advances at Crécy and Agincourt. The Knights of Lazarus were on the ships that beat back the Ottoman Empire at Lepanto, and when we refused to fight any further, the Thirty Years' War came to an end. The brotherhood's purpose is to ensure that vampires survive in a world dominated by humans.'

'We started out protecting those who could not protect themselves, Baldwin. Our heroic reputation was simply an unexpected by-product of that mission.'

'Father should never have passed the order on to you when he died. You're a soldier – and an idealist – not a commander. You don't have the stomach to make the difficult decisions.' Baldwin's scorn for his brother was clear from his words, but his eyes were worried.

'Diana came to me seeking protection from her own people. I will see to it that she gets it – just as the Knights protected the citizens of Jerusalem, and Germany, and Occitania when they were under threat.'

'No one will believe that this isn't personal, any more than they would have believed it in 1944. Then you said no.'

'I was wrong.'

Baldwin looked shocked.

Matthew drew a long, shuddering breath. 'Once we would have responded immediately to such an outrage and to hell with the consequences. But a fear of divulging the family's secrets and a reluctance to raise the Congregation's ire held me back. This only encouraged our enemies to strike at this family again, and I won't make the same mistake where Diana is concerned. The witches will stop at nothing to learn about her power. They've invaded our home and snatched one of their own. It's worse than what they did to Philippe. In the witches' eyes, he was only a vampire. By taking Diana they've gone too far.'

As Baldwin considered his brother's words, Matthew's anxiety grew more acute.

'Diana.' Ysabeau brought Baldwin back to the matter at hand.

Baldwin nodded, once.

'Thank you,' Matthew said simply. 'A witch grabbed her straight up and out of the garden. Any clues there might have been about the direction they took were gone by the time we discovered she was missing.' He pulled a creased map from his pocket. 'Here is where we still need to search.'

Baldwin looked at the areas that Ysabeau and his brother had already covered and the wide swaths of countryside that remained. 'You've been searching all these places since she was taken?'

Matthew nodded. 'Of course.'

Baldwin couldn't conceal his irritation. 'Matthew, will you never learn to stop and think before you act? Show me the garden.'

Matthew and Baldwin went outdoors, leaving Marthe and Ysabeau inside so that their scents wouldn't obscure any faint traces of Diana. When the two were gone, Ysabeau began to shake from head to toe.

'It is too much, Marthe. If they have harmed her—'

'We have always known, you and I, that a day like this was coming.' Marthe put a compassionate hand on her mistress's shoulder, then walked into the kitchens, leaving Ysabeau sitting pensively by the cold hearth.

In the garden Baldwin turned his preternaturally sharp eyes to the ground, where an apple lay next to a billowing patch of rue. Ysabeau had wisely insisted that they leave the fruit where they'd found it. Its location helped Baldwin see what his brother had not. The stems on the rue were slightly bent and led to another patch of herbs with ruffled leaves, then another.

'Which way was the wind blowing?' Baldwin's imagination was caught already.

'From the west,' Matthew replied, trying to see what Baldwin was tracking. He gave up with a frustrated sigh. 'This is taking too much time. We should split up. We can cover more ground that way. I'll go through the caves again.'

'She won't be in the caves,' Baldwin said, straightening his knees and brushing the scent of herbs from his hands. 'Vampires use the caves, not witches. Besides, they went south.'

'South? There's nothing to the south.'

'Not anymore,' Baldwin agreed. 'But there must be something there, or the witch wouldn't have gone in that direction. We'll ask Ysabeau.'

One reason the de Clermont family was so long-lived was that each member had different skills in a crisis. Philippe had always been the leader of men, a charismatic figure who could convince vampires and humans and sometimes even daemons to fight for a common cause. Their brother Hugh had been the negotiator, bringing warring sides to the bargaining table and resolving even the fiercest of conflicts. Godfrey, the youngest of Philippe's three sons, had been their conscience, teasing out the ethical implications of every decision. To Baldwin fell the battle strategies, his sharp mind quick to analyze every plan for flaws and weaknesses. Louisa had been useful as bait or as a spy, depending on the situation.

Matthew, improbably enough, had been the family's fiercest warrior. His early adventures with the sword had made his father wild with their lack of discipline, but he'd changed. Now whenever Matthew held a weapon in his hand, something in him went cold and he fought his way through obstacles with a tenacity that made him unbeatable.

Then there was Ysabeau. Everyone underestimated her except for Philippe, who had called her either 'the general' or 'my secret weapon.' She missed nothing and had a longer memory than Mnemosyne.

The brothers went back into the house. Baldwin shouted for Ysabeau and strode into the kitchen, grabbing a handful of flour from an open bowl and scattering it onto Marthe's worktable. He traced the outline of the Auvergne into the flour and dug his thumb into the spot where Sept-Tours stood.

'Where would a witch take another witch that is south and west of here?' he asked.

Ysabeau's forehead creased. 'It would depend on the reason she was taken.'

Matthew and Baldwin exchanged exasperated looks. This was the only problem with their secret weapon. Ysabeau never wanted to answer the question you posed to her – she always felt there was a more pressing one that needed to be addressed first.

'Think, *Maman*,' Matthew said urgently. 'The witches want to keep Diana from me.'

'No, my child. You could be separated in so many ways. By coming into my home and taking my guest, the witches have done something unforgivable to this family. Hostilities such as these are like chess,' Ysabeau said, touching her son's cheek with a cold hand.

'The witches wanted to prove how weak we have become. You wanted Diana. Now they have taken her to make it impossible for you to ignore their challenge.'

'Please, Ysabeau. Where?'

'There is nothing but barren mountains and goat tracks between here and the Cantal,' Ysabeau said.

'The Cantal?' Baldwin snapped.

'Yes,' she whispered, her cold blood chilled by the implications.

The Cantal was where Gerbert of Aurillac had been born. It was his home territory, and if the de Clermonts trespassed, the witches would not be the only forces gathering against them.

'If this were chess, taking her to the Cantal would put us in check,' Matthew said grimly. 'It's too soon for that.'

Baldwin nodded approvingly. 'Then we're missing something, between here and there.'

'There's nothing but ruins,' Ysabeau said.

Baldwin let out a frustrated sigh. 'Why can't Matthew's witch defend herself?'

Marthe came into the room, wiping her hands on a towel. She and Ysabeau exchanged glances. '*Elle est enchantée*,' Marthe said gruffly.

'The child is spellbound,' Ysabeau agreed with reluctance. 'We are certain of it.'

'Spellbound?' Matthew frowned. Spellbinding put a witch in invisible shackles. It was as unforgivable among witches as trespassing was among vampires.

'Yes. It is not that she refuses her magic. She has been kept from it – deliberately.' Ysabeau scowled at the idea.

'Why?' her son wondered. 'It's like defanging and declawing a tiger and then returning it to the jungle. Why would you leave anyone without a way to defend herself?'

Ysabeau shrugged. 'I can think of many people who might want to do such a thing – many reasons, too – and I do not know this witch well. Call her family. Ask them.'

Matthew reached into his pocket and pulled out his phone. He had the house in Madison on speed dial, Baldwin noticed. The witches on the other end picked up on the first ring.

'Matthew?' The witch was frantic. 'Where is she? She's in terrible pain, I can feel it.'

'We know where to look for her, Sarah,' Matthew said quietly, trying to soothe her. 'But I need to ask you something first. Diana doesn't use her magic.'

'She hasn't since her mother and father died. What does that have to do with anything?' Sarah was shouting now. Ysabeau closed her eyes against the harsh sound.

'Is there a chance, Sarah — any chance at all — that Diana is spellbound?'

The silence on the other end was absolute.

'Spellbound?' Sarah finally said, aghast. 'Of course not!'

The de Clermonts heard a soft click.

'It was Rebecca,' another witch said much more softly. 'I promised her I wouldn't tell. And I don't know what she did or how she did it, so don't ask. Rebecca knew she and Stephen wouldn't be coming back from Africa. She'd seen something — knew something — that frightened her to death. All she would tell me was that she was going to keep Diana safe.'

'Safe from what?' Sarah was horrified.

'Not "safe from what." Safe *until*.' Em's voice dropped further. 'Rebecca said she would make sure Diana was safe until her daughter was with her shadowed man.'

'Her shadowed man?' Matthew repeated.

'Yes,' Em whispered. 'As soon as Diana told me she was spending time with a vampire, I wondered if you were the one Rebecca had foreseen. But it all happened so fast.'

'Do you see anything, Emily — anything at all — that might help us?' Matthew asked.

'No. There's a darkness. Diana's in it. She's not dead,' she said hastily when Matthew sucked in his breath, 'but she's in pain and somehow not entirely in this world.'

As Baldwin listened, he narrowed his eyes at Ysabeau. Her

questions, though maddening, had been most illuminating. He uncrossed his arms and reached into his pocket for his phone. He turned away, dialed, and murmured something into it. Baldwin then looked at Matthew and drew a finger across his throat.

'I'm going for her now,' Matthew said. 'When we have news, we'll call you.' He disconnected before Sarah or Em could pepper him with questions.

'Where are my keys?' Matthew shouted, heading for the door.

Baldwin was in front of him, barring the way.

'Calm down and think,' he said roughly, kicking a stool in his brother's direction. 'What were the castles between here and the Cantal? We only need to know the old castles, the ones Gerbert would be most familiar with.'

'Christ, Baldwin, I can't remember. Let me through!'

'No. You need to be smart about this. The witches wouldn't have brought her into Gerbert's territory – not if they have any sense. If Diana is spellbound, then she's a mystery to them, too. It will take them some time to solve it. They'll want privacy, and no vampires interrupting them.' It was the first time Baldwin had managed to say the witch's name. 'In the Cantal the witches would have to answer to Gerbert, so they must be somewhere near the border. Think.' Baldwin's last drop of patience evaporated. 'By the gods, Matthew, you built or designed most of them.'

Matthew's mind raced over the possibilities, discarding some because they were too close, others because they were too ruined. He looked up in shock. 'La Pierre.'

Ysabeau's mouth tightened, and Marthe looked worried. La Pierre had been the region's most forbidding castle. It was built on a foundation of basalt that couldn't be tunneled through and had walls high enough to resist any siege.

Overhead, there was a sound of air being compressed and moved.

'A helicopter,' Baldwin said. 'It was waiting in Clermont-Ferrand to take me back to Lyon. Your garden will need work, Ysabeau, but you no doubt think it's a small price to pay.'

The two vampires streaked out of the château toward the helicopter. They jumped in and were soon flying high above the Auvergne. Nothing but blackness lay below them, punctuated here and there with a soft glow of light from a farmhouse window. It took them more than thirty minutes to arrive at the castle, and even though the brothers knew where it was, the pilot located its outlines with difficulty.

'There's nowhere to land!' the pilot shouted.

Matthew pointed to an old road that stretched away from the castle. 'What about there?' he shouted back. He was already scanning the walls for signs of light or movement.

Baldwin told the pilot to put down where Matthew had indicated, and he received a dubious look in reply.

When they were still twenty feet off the ground, Matthew jumped out and set off at a dead run toward the castle's gate. Baldwin sighed and jumped after him, first directing the pilot not to move until they were both back on board.

Matthew was already inside, shouting for Diana. 'Christ, she'll be terrified,' he whispered when the echoes faded, running his fingers through his hair.

Baldwin caught up with him and grabbed his brother's arm. 'There are two ways to do this, Matthew. We can split up and search the place from top to bottom. Or you can stop for five seconds and figure out where you would hide something in La Pierre.'

'Let me go,' Matthew said, baring his teeth and trying to pull his arm from his brother's grip. Baldwin's hand only tightened.

'Think,' he commanded. 'It will be quicker, I promise you.'

Matthew went over the castle's floor plan in his mind. He started at the entrance, going up through the castle's rooms, through the tower, the sleeping apartments, the audience chambers, and the great hall. Then he worked his way from the entrance down through the kitchens, the cellars, and the dungeons. He stared at his brother in horror.

'The oubliette.' He set off in the direction of the kitchens.

Baldwin's face froze. '*Dieu*,' he whispered, watching his brother's receding back. What was it about this witch that had made her own people throw her down a sixty-foot hole?

And if she were that precious, whoever had put Diana into the oubliette would be back.

Baldwin tore after Matthew, hoping it was not already too late to stop him from giving the witches not one but two hostages.

CHAPTER 31

*D*iana, *it's time to wake up.* My mother's voice was low but insistent. Too exhausted to respond, I pulled the brightly colored patchwork quilt over my head, hoping that she wouldn't be able to find me. My body curled into a tight ball, and I wondered why everything hurt so much.

Wake up, sleepyhead. My father's blunt fingers gripped the fabric. A jolt of joy momentarily pushed the pain aside. He pretended he was a bear and growled. Squealing with happiness, I tightened my own hands and giggled, but when he pulled at the coverings, the cold air swept around me.

Something was wrong. I opened one eye, expecting to see the bright posters and stuffed animals that lined my room in Cambridge. But my bedroom didn't have wet, gray walls.

My father was smiling down at me with twinkling eyes. As usual, his hair was curled up at the ends and needed combing, and his collar was askew. I loved him anyway and tried to fling my arms around his neck, but they refused to work properly. He pulled me gently toward him instead, his insubstantial form clinging to me like a shield.

Fancy seeing you here, Miss Bishop. It was what he always said when I sneaked into his study at home or crept downstairs late at night for one more bedtime story.

'I'm so tired.' Even though his shirt was transparent, it somehow retained the smell of stale cigarette smoke and the chocolate caramels that he kept in his pockets.

I know, my father said, his eyes no longer twinkling. *But you can't sleep anymore.*

You have to wake up. My mother's hands were on me now, trying to extricate me from my father's lap.

'Tell me the rest of the story first,' I begged, 'and skip the bad parts.'

It doesn't work that way. My mother shook her head, and my father sadly handed me into her arms.

'But I don't feel well.' My child's voice wheedled for special treatment.

My mother's sigh rustled against the stone walls. *I can't skip the bad parts. You have to face them. Can you do that, little witch?*

After considering what would be required, I nodded.

Where were we? my mother asked, sitting down next to the ghostly monk in the center of the oubliette. He looked shocked and moved a few inches away. My father stifled a smile with the back of his hand, looking at my mother the same way I looked at Matthew.

I remember, she said. *Diana was locked in a dark room, all alone. She sat hour after hour and wondered how she would ever get out. Then she heard a knocking at the window. It was the prince. 'I'm trapped inside by witches!' Diana cried. The prince tried to break the window, but it was made of magic glass and he couldn't even crack it. Then the prince raced to the door and tried to open it, but it was held fast by an enchanted lock. He rattled the door in the frame, but the wood was too thick and it didn't budge.*

'Wasn't the prince strong?' I asked, slightly annoyed that he wasn't up to the task.

Very strong, said her mother solemnly, *but he was no wizard. So Diana looked around for something else for the prince to try. She spied a tiny hole in the roof. It was just big enough for a witch like her to squeeze through. Diana told the prince to fly up and lift her out. But the prince couldn't fly.*

'Because he wasn't a wizard,' I repeated. The monk crossed himself every time magic or a wizard was mentioned.

That's right, my mother said. *But Diana remembered that once upon a time she had flown. She looked down and found the edge of a silver ribbon. It was wound tightly around her, but when she tugged on the end, the ribbon came loose. Diana tossed it high above her head. Then there was nothing left for her body to do except follow it up to the sky. When she got close to the hole in the roof, she put her arms together, stretched them straight, and went through into the night air. 'I knew you could do it,' said the prince.*

'And they lived happily ever after,' I said firmly.

My mother's smile was bittersweet. *Yes, Diana.* She gave my father a long look, the kind that children don't understand until they're older.

I sighed happily, and it didn't matter so much that my back was on fire or that this was a strange place with people you could see right through.

It's time, my mother said to my father. He nodded.

Above me, heavy wood met ancient stone with a deafening crash.

'Diana?' It was Matthew. He sounded frantic. His anxiety sent a simultaneous rush of relief and adrenaline through my body.

'Matthew!' My call came out as a dull croak.

'I'm coming down.' Matthew's response, echoing down all that stone, hurt my head. It was throbbing and there was something sticky on my cheek. I rubbed some of the stickiness on to my finger, but it was too dark to see what it was.

'No,' said a deeper, rougher voice. 'You can get down there, but I won't be able to get you out. And we need to do this fast, Matthew. They'll be back for her.'

I looked up to see who was speaking, but all that was visible was a pale white ring.

'Diana, listen to me.' Matthew boomed a little less now. 'You need to fly. Can you do that?'

My mother nodded encouragingly. *It's time to wake up and be a witch. There's no need for secrets anymore.*

'I think so.' I tried to get to my feet. My right ankle gave way underneath me, and I fell hard onto my knee. 'Are you sure Satu's gone?'

'There's no one here but me and my brother, Baldwin. Fly up

and we'll get you away.' The other man muttered something, and Matthew replied angrily.

I didn't know who Baldwin was, and I had met enough strangers today. Not even Matthew felt entirely safe, after what Satu had said. I looked for somewhere to hide.

You can't hide from Matthew, my mother said, casting a rueful smile at my father. *He'll always find you, no matter what. You can trust him. He's the one we've been waiting for.*

My father's arms crept around her, and I remembered the feeling of Matthew's arms. Someone who held me like that couldn't be deceiving me.

'Diana, please try.' Matthew couldn't keep the pleading out of his voice.

In order to fly, I needed a silver ribbon. But there wasn't one wrapped around me. Uncertain of how to proceed, I searched for my parents in the gloom. They were paler than before.

Don't you want to fly? my mother asked.

Magic is in the heart, Diana, my father said. *Don't forget.*

I shut my eyes and imagined a ribbon into place. With the end securely in my fingers, I threw it toward the white ring that flickered in the darkness. The ribbon unfurled and soared through the hole, taking my body with it.

My mother was smiling, and my father looked as proud as he had when he took the training wheels off my first bicycle. Matthew peered down, along with another face that must belong to his brother. With them were a clutch of ghosts who looked amazed that anyone, after all these years, was making it out alive.

'Thank God,' Matthew breathed, stretching his long, white fingers toward me. 'Take my hand.'

The moment he had me in his grip, my body lost its weightlessness.

'My arm!' I cried out as the muscles pulled and the gash on my forearm gaped.

Matthew grabbed at my shoulder, assisted by another, unfamiliar hand. They lifted me out of the oubliette, and I was crushed for a moment against Matthew's chest. Grabbing handfuls of his sweater, I clung to him.

'I knew you could do it,' he murmured like the prince in my mother's story, his voice full of relief.

'We don't have time for this.' Matthew's brother was already running down the corridor toward the door.

Matthew gripped my shoulders and took rapid stock of my injuries. His nostrils flared at the scent of dried blood. 'Can you walk?' he asked softly.

'Pick her up and get her out of here, or you'll have more to worry about than a little blood!' the other vampire shouted.

Matthew swept me up like a sack of flour and started to run, his arm tight across my lower back. I bit my lip and closed my eyes so the floor rushing underneath me wouldn't remind me of flying with Satu. A change in the air told me we were free. As my lungs filled, I began to shake.

Matthew ran even faster, carrying me toward a helicopter that was improbably parked outside the castle walls on a dirt road. He ducked his body protectively over mine and jumped into the helicopter's open door. His brother followed, the lights from the cockpit controls glinting green against his bright copper hair.

My foot brushed against Baldwin's thigh as he sat down, and he gave me a look of hatred mingled with curiosity. His face was familiar from the visions I'd seen in Matthew's study: first in light caught in the suit of armor, then again when touching the seals of the Knights of Lazarus. 'I thought you were dead.' I shrank toward Matthew.

Baldwin's eyes widened. 'Go!' he shouted to the pilot, and we lifted into the sky.

Being airborne brought back fresh memories of Satu, and my shaking increased.

'She's gone into shock,' Matthew said. 'Can this thing move faster, Baldwin?'

'Knock her out,' Baldwin said impatiently.

'I don't have a sedative with me.'

'Yes you do.' His brother's eyes glittered. 'Do you want me to do it?'

Matthew looked down at me and tried to smile. My shaking subsided a little, but every time the helicopter dipped and swayed in the wind, it returned, along with my memories of Satu.

'By the gods, Matthew, she's terrified,' Baldwin said angrily. 'Just do it.'

Matthew bit into his lip until a drop of blood beaded up on the smooth skin. He dipped his head to kiss me.

'No.' I squirmed to avoid his mouth. 'I know what you're doing. Satu told me. You're using your blood to keep me quiet.'

'You're in shock, Diana. It's all I have. Let me help you.' His face was anguished. Reaching up, I caught the drop of blood on my fingertip.

'No. I'll do it.' There would be no more gossip among witches about my being in Matthew's control. I sucked the salty liquid from my numb fingertip. Lips and tongue tingled before the nerves in my mouth went dead.

The next thing I knew, there was cold air on my cheeks, perfumed with Marthe's herbs. We were in the garden at Sept-Tours. Matthew's arms were hard underneath my aching back, and he'd tucked my head into his neck. I stirred, looked around.

'We're home,' he whispered, striding toward the lights of the château.

'Ysabeau and Marthe,' I said, struggling to lift my head, 'are they all right?'

'Perfectly all right,' Matthew replied, cuddling me closer.

We passed into the kitchen corridor, which was ablaze with light. It hurt my eyes, and I turned away from it until the pain subsided. One of my eyes seemed smaller than the other, and I narrowed the larger one so they matched. A group of vampires came into view, standing down the corridor from Matthew and me. Baldwin looked curious, Ysabeau furious, Marthe grim and worried. Ysabeau took a step, and Matthew snarled.

'Matthew,' she began in a patient voice, her eyes fixed on me with a look of maternal concern, 'you need to call her family. Where is your phone?'

His arms tightened. My head felt too heavy for my neck. It was easier to lean it against Matthew's shoulder.

'It's in his pocket, I suppose, but he's not going to drop the witch to get it. Nor will he let you get close enough to fish it out.' Baldwin handed Ysabeau his phone. 'Use this.'

Baldwin's gaze traveled over my battered body with such close attention that it felt as if ice packs were being applied and removed, one by one. 'She certainly looks like she's been through a battle.' His voice expressed reluctant admiration.

Marthe said something in Occitan, and Matthew's brother nodded.

'*Òc*,' he said, eyeing me in appraisal.

'Not this time, Baldwin,' Matthew rumbled.

'The number, Matthew,' Ysabeau said crisply, diverting her son's attention. He rattled it off, and his mother pushed the corresponding buttons, the faint electronic tones audible.

'I'm fine,' I croaked when Sarah picked up the phone. 'Put me down, Matthew.'

'No, this is Ysabeau de Clermont. Diana is with us.'

There was more silence while Ysabeau's icicle touches swept over me. 'She is hurt, but her injuries are not life-threatening. Nevertheless, Matthew should bring her home. To you.'

'No. She'll follow me. Satu mustn't harm Sarah and Em,' I said, struggling to break free.

'Matthew,' Baldwin growled, 'let Marthe see to her or keep her quiet.'

'Stay out of this, Baldwin,' Matthew snapped. His cool lips touched my cheeks, and my pulse slowed. His voice dropped to a murmur. 'We won't do anything you don't want to do.'

'We can protect her from vampires.' Ysabeau sounded farther and farther away. 'But not from other witches. She needs to be with those who can.' The conversation faded, and a curtain of gray fog descended.

This time I came to consciousness upstairs in Matthew's tower. Every candle was lit, and the fire was roaring in the hearth. The room felt almost warm, but adrenaline and shock made me shiver. Matthew was sitting on his heels on the floor with me propped between his knees, examining my right forearm. My blood-soaked pullover had a long slit where Satu had cut me. A fresh red stain was seeping into the darker spots.

Marthe and Ysabeau stood in the doorway like a watchful pair of hawks.

'I can take care of my wife, *Maman*,' Matthew said.

'Of course, Matthew,' Ysabeau murmured in her patented subservient tone.

Matthew tore the last inch of the sleeve to fully expose my flesh, and he swore. 'Get my bag, Marthe.'

'No,' she said firmly. 'She is filthy, Matthew.'

'Let her take a bath,' Ysabeau joined in, lending Marthe her support. 'Diana is freezing, and you cannot even see her injuries. This is not helping, my child.'

'No bath,' he said decidedly.

'Why ever not?' Ysabeau asked impatiently. She gestured at the stairs, and Marthe departed.

'The water would be full of her blood,' he said tightly. 'Baldwin would smell it.'

'This is not Jerusalem, Matthew,' Ysabeau said. 'He has never set foot in this tower, not since it was built.'

'What happened in Jerusalem?' I reached for the spot where Matthew's silver coffin usually hung.

'My love, I need to look at your back.'

'Okay,' I whispered dully. My mind drifted, seeking an apple tree and my mother's voice.

'Lie on your stomach for me.'

The cold stone floors of the castle where Satu had pinned me down were all too palpable under my chest and legs. 'No, Matthew. You think I'm keeping secrets, but I don't know anything about my magic. Satu said—'

Matthew swore again. 'There's no witch here, and your magic is immaterial to me.' His cold hand gripped mine, as sure and firm as his gaze. 'Just lean forward over my hand. I'll hold you.'

Seated on his thigh, I bent from the waist, resting my chest on our clasped hands. The position stretched the skin on my back painfully, but it was better than the alternative. Underneath me, Matthew stiffened.

'Your fleece is stuck to your skin. I can't see much with it in the way. We're going to have to put you in the bath for a bit before it can be removed. Can you fill the tub, Ysabeau?'

His mother disappeared, her absence followed by the sound of running water.

'Not too hot,' he called softly after her.

'What happened in Jerusalem?' I asked again.

'Later,' he said, lifting me gently upright.

'The time for secrets has passed, Matthew. Tell her, and be quick about it.' Ysabeau spoke sharply from the bathroom door. 'She is your wife and has a right to know.'

'It must be something awful, or you wouldn't have worn Lazarus's coffin.' I pressed lightly on the empty spot above his heart.

With a desperate look, Matthew began his story. It came out of him in quick, staccato bursts. 'I killed a woman in Jerusalem. She got between Baldwin and me. There was a great deal of blood. I loved her, and she—'

He'd killed someone else, not a witch, but a human. My finger stilled his lips. 'That's enough for now. It was a long time ago.' I felt calm but was shaking again, unable to bear any more revelations.

Matthew brought my left hand to his lips and kissed me hard on the knuckles. His eyes told me what he couldn't say aloud. Finally he released both my hand and my eyes and spoke. 'If you're worried about Baldwin, we'll do it another way. We can soak the fleece off with compresses, or you could shower.'

The mere thought of water falling on my back or the application of pressure convinced me to risk Baldwin's possible thirst. 'The bath would be better.'

Matthew lowered me into the lukewarm water, fully clothed right down to my running shoes. Propped in the tub, my back drawn away from the porcelain and the water wicking slowly up my fleece pullover, I began the slow process of letting go, my legs twitching and dancing under the water. Each muscle and nerve had to be told to relax, and some refused to obey.

While I soaked, Matthew tended to my face, his fingers pressing my cheekbone. He frowned in concern and called softly for Marthe. She appeared with a huge black medical bag. Matthew took out a tiny flashlight and checked my eyes, his lips pressed tightly together.

'My face hit the floor.' I winced. 'Is it broken?'

'I don't think so, *mon coeur*, just badly bruised.'

Marthe ripped open a package, and a whiff of rubbing alcohol reached my nose. When Matthew held the pad on the sticky part of my cheek, I gripped the sides of the tub, my eyes smarting with tears. The pad came away scarlet.

'I cut it on the edge of a stone.' My voice was matter-of-fact in an attempt to quiet the memories of Satu that the pain brought back.

Matthew's cool fingers traced the stinging wound to where it disappeared under my hairline. 'It's superficial. You don't need stitches.' He reached for a jar of ointment and smoothed some onto my skin. It smelled of mint and herbs from the garden. 'Are you allergic to any medications?' he asked when he was through.

I shook my head.

He again called to Marthe, who trotted in with her arms full of towels. He rattled off a list of drugs, and Marthe nodded, jiggling a set of keys she pulled out of her pocket. Only one drug was familiar.

'Morphine?' I asked, my pulse beginning to race.

'It will alleviate the pain. The other drugs will combat swelling and infection.'

The bath had lulled some of my anxiety and lessened my shock, but the pain was getting worse. The prospect of banishing it was enticing, and I reluctantly agreed to the drug in exchange for getting out of the bath. Sitting in the rusty water was making me queasy.

Before climbing out, though, Matthew insisted on looking at my right foot. He hoisted it up and out of the water, resting the sole of my shoe against his shoulder. Even that slight pressure had me gasping.

'Ysabeau. Can you come here, please?'

Like Marthe, Ysabeau was waiting patiently in the bedroom in case her son needed help. When she came in, Matthew had her stand behind me while he snapped the water-soaked shoelaces with ease and began to pry the shoe from my foot. Ysabeau held my shoulders, keeping me from thrashing my way out of the tub.

I cried during Matthew's examination – even after he stopped trying to pull the shoe off and began to rip it apart by tearing as precisely as a dressmaker cutting into fine cloth. He tore my sock off, too, and ripped along the seam of my leggings, then peeled the fabric away to reveal the ankle. It had a ring around it as though it had been closed in a manacle that had burned through the skin, leaving it black and blistered in places with odd white patches.

Matthew looked up, his eyes angry. 'How was this done?'

'Satu hung me upside down. She wanted to see if I could fly.' I turned away uncertainly, unable to understand why so many people were furious with me over things that weren't my fault.

Ysabeau gently took my foot. Matthew knelt beside the tub, his black hair slicked back from his forehead and his clothing ruined from water and blood. He turned my face toward him, looking at me with a mixture of fierce protectiveness and pride.

'You were born in August, yes? Under the sign of Leo?' He sounded entirely French, most of the Oxbridge accent gone.

I nodded.

'Then I will have to call you my lioness now, because only she could have fought as you did. But even *la lionne* needs her protectors.' His eyes flickered toward my right arm. My gripping the tub had made the bleeding resume. 'Your ankle is sprained, but it's not serious. I'll bind it later. Now let's see to your back and your arm.'

Matthew scooped me out of the tub and set me down, instructing me to keep the weight off my right foot. Marthe and Ysabeau steadied me while he cut off my leggings and underclothes. The three vampires' premodern matter-of-factness about bodies left me strangely unconcerned at standing half naked in front of them. Matthew lifted the front hem of my soggy pullover, revealing a dark purple bruise that spread across my abdomen.

'Christ,' he said, his fingers pushing into the stained flesh above my pubic bone. 'How the hell did she do that?'

'Satu lost her temper.' My teeth chattered at the memory of flying through the air and the sharp pain in my gut. Matthew tucked the towel around my waist.

'Let's get the pullover off,' he said grimly. He went behind me, and there was a sting of cold metal against my back.

'What are you doing?' I twisted my head, desperate to see. Satu had kept me on my stomach for hours, and it was intolerable to have anyone — even Matthew — behind me. The trembling in my body intensified.

'Stop, Matthew,' Ysabeau said urgently. 'She cannot bear it.'

A pair of scissors clattered to the floor.

'It's all right.' Matthew nestled his body against mine like a protective shell. He crossed his arms over my chest, completely enfolding me. 'I'll do it from the front.'

Once the shaking subsided, he came around and resumed cutting the fabric away from my body. The cold air on my back told me that there wasn't much of it left in any case. He sliced through my bra, then got the front panel of the pullover off.

Ysabeau gasped as the last shreds fell from my back.

'*Maria, Deu maire.*' Marthe sounded stunned.

'What is it? What did she do?' The room was swinging like a chandelier in an earthquake. Matthew whipped me around to face his mother. Grief and sympathy were etched on her face.

'*La sorcière est morte,*' Matthew said softly.

He was already planning on killing another witch. Ice filled my veins, and there was blackness at the edges of my vision.

Matthew's hands held me upright. 'Stay with me, Diana.'

'Did you have to kill Gillian?' I sobbed.

'Yes.' His voice was flat and dead.

'Why did you let me hear this from someone else? Satu told me you'd been in my rooms – that you were using your blood to drug me. Why, Matthew? Why didn't you tell me?'

'Because I was afraid of losing you. You know so little about me, Diana. Secrecy, the instinct to protect – to kill if I must. This is who I am.'

I turned to face him, wearing nothing but a towel around my waist. My arms were crossed over my bare chest, and my emotions careened from fear to anger to something darker. 'So you'll kill Satu also?'

'Yes.' He made no apologies and offered no further explanation, but his eyes were full of barely controlled rage. Cold and gray, they searched my face. 'You're far braver than I am. I've told you that before. Do you want to see what she did to you?' Matthew asked, gripping my elbows.

I thought for a moment, then nodded.

Ysabeau protested in rapid Occitan, and Matthew stopped her with a hiss.

'She survived the doing of it, *Maman*. The seeing of it cannot possibly be worse.'

Ysabeau and Marthe went downstairs to fetch two mirrors while Matthew patted my torso with feather-light touches of a towel until it was barely damp.

'Stay with me,' he repeated every time I tried to slip away from the rough fabric.

The women returned with one mirror in an ornate gilt frame from the salon and a tall cheval glass that only a vampire could have carried up to the tower. Matthew positioned the larger mirror behind me, and Ysabeau and Marthe held the other in front, angling it so that I could see both my back and Matthew, too.

But it couldn't be my back. It was someone else's – someone who had been flayed and burned until her skin was red, and blue, and black. There were strange marks on it, too – circles and symbols. The memory of fire erupted along the lesions.

'Satu said she was going to open me up,' I whispered, mesmerized.

'But I kept my secrets inside, Mama, just like you wanted.'

Matthew's attempt to catch me was the last thing I saw reflected in the mirror before the blackness overtook me.

I awoke next to the bedroom fire again. My lower half was still wrapped up in a towel, and I was sitting on the edge of one damask-covered chair, bent over at the waist, with my torso draped across a stack of pillows on another damask-covered chair. All I could see was feet, and someone was applying ointment to my back. It was Marthe, her rough strength clearly distinguishable from Matthew's cool touches.

'Matthew?' I croaked, swiveling my head to the side to look for him.

His face appeared. 'Yes, my darling?'

'Where did the pain go?'

'It's magic,' he said, attempting a lopsided grin for my benefit.

'Morphine,' I said slowly, remembering the list of drugs he'd given to Marthe.

'That's what I said. Everyone who has ever been in pain knows that morphine and magic are the same. Now that you're awake, we're going to wrap you up.' He tossed a spool of gauze to Marthe, explaining that it would keep down the swelling and further protect my skin. It also had the benefit of binding my breasts, since I would not be wearing a bra in the near future.

The two of them unrolled miles of white surgical dressing around my torso. Thanks to the drugs, I underwent the process with a curious sense of detachment. It vanished, however, when Matthew began to rummage in his medical bag and talk about sutures. As a child I'd fallen and stuck a long fork used for toasting marshmallows into my thigh. It had required sutures, too, and my nightmares had lasted for months. I told Matthew my fears, but he was resolute.

'The cut on your arm is deep, Diana. It won't heal properly unless it's sutured.'

Afterward the women got me dressed while Matthew drank some wine, his fingers shaking. I didn't have anything that fastened up the front, so Marthe disappeared once more, returning with her arms full of Matthew's clothing. They slid me into one of his fine cotton shirts. It swam on me but felt silky against my skin. Marthe carefully draped a black cashmere cardigan with leather-covered buttons – also Matthew's – around my shoulders, and she and Ysabeau snaked a pair of my own stretchy black pants up my legs and over my hips. Then Matthew lowered me into a nest of pillows on the sofa.

'Change,' Marthe ordered, pushing him in the direction of the bathroom.

Matthew showered quickly and emerged from the bathroom in a fresh pair of trousers. He dried his hair roughly by the fire before pulling on the rest of his clothes.

'Will you be all right if I go downstairs for a moment?' he asked. 'Marthe and Ysabeau will stay with you.'

I suspected his trip downstairs involved his brother, and I nodded, still feeling the effects of the powerful drug.

While he was gone, Ysabeau muttered every now and again in a language that was neither Occitan nor French, and Marthe clucked and fussed. They'd removed most of the ruined clothes and bloody linen from the room by the time Matthew reappeared. Fallon and Hector were padding along at his side, their tongues hanging out.

Ysabeau's eyes narrowed. 'Your dogs do not belong in my house.'

Fallon and Hector looked from Ysabeau to Matthew with interest. Matthew clicked his fingers and pointed to the floor. The dogs sank down, their watchful faces turned to me.

'They'll stay with Diana until we leave,' he said firmly, and though his mother sighed, she didn't argue with him.

Matthew picked up my feet and slid his body underneath them, his hands lightly stroking my legs. Marthe plunked down a glass of wine in front of him, then thrust a mug of tea into my hands. She and Ysabeau withdrew, leaving us alone with the watchful dogs.

My mind drifted, soothed by the morphine and the hypnotic touch of Matthew's fingers. I sorted through my memories, trying to distinguish what was real from what I'd only imagined. Had my mother's ghost really been in the oubliette, or was that a recollection of our time together before Africa? Or was it my mind's attempt to cope with stress by fracturing off into an imaginary world? I frowned.

'What is it, *ma lionne*?' Matthew asked, his voice concerned. 'Are you in pain?'

'No. I'm just thinking.' I focused on his face, pulling myself through the fog to his safer shores. 'Where was I?'

'La Pierre. It's an old castle that no one has lived in for years.'

'I met Gerbert.' My brain was playing hopscotch, not wanting to linger in one place for too long.

Matthew's fingers stilled. 'He was there?'

'Only in the beginning. He and Domenico were waiting when we arrived, but Satu sent them away.'

'I see. Did he touch you?' Matthew's body tensed.

'On the cheek.' I shivered. 'He had the manuscript, Matthew, long, long ago. Gerbert boasted about how he'd taken it from Spain. It was under a spell even then. He kept a witch enthralled, hoping she would be able to break the enchantment.'

'Do you want to tell me what happened?'

I thought it was too soon and was about to tell him so, but the story spilled out. When I recounted Satu's attempts to open me so that she could find the magic inside, Matthew rose and replaced the pillows supporting my back with his own body, cradling the length of me between his legs.

He held me while I spoke, and when I couldn't speak, and when I cried. Whatever Matthew's emotions when I shared Satu's revelations about him, he held them firmly in check. Even when I told him about my mother sitting under an apple tree whose roots spread across La Pierre's stone floors, he never pressed for more details, though he must have had a hundred unanswered questions.

It was not the whole tale – I left out my father's presence, my vivid memories of bedtime stories, and running through the fields behind Sarah's house in Madison. But it was a start, and the rest of it would come in time.

'What do we do now?' I asked when finished. 'We can't let the Congregation harm Sarah or Em – or Marthe and Ysabeau.'

'That's up to you,' Matthew replied slowly. 'I'll understand if you've had enough.' I craned my neck to look at him, but he wouldn't meet my eyes, staring resolutely out the window into the darkness.

'You told me we were mated for life.'

'Nothing will change the way I feel about you, but you aren't a vampire. What happened to you today—' Matthew stopped, started again. 'If you've changed your mind about this – about me – I'll understand.'

'Not even Satu could change my mind. And she tried. My mother sounded so certain when she told me that you were the one I'd been waiting for. That was when I flew.' That wasn't exactly it – my mother had said that Matthew was the one *we* had been waiting for. But since it made no sense, I kept it to myself.

'You're sure?' Matthew tilted my chin up and studied my face.

'Absolutely.'

His face lost some of its anguish. He bent his head to kiss me, then drew back.

'My lips are the only part of me that doesn't hurt.' Besides, I needed to be reminded that there were creatures in the world who could touch me without causing pain.

He pressed his mouth gently against mine, his breath full of cloves and spice. It took away the memories of La Pierre, and for a few moments I could close my eyes and rest in his arms. But an urgent need to know what would happen next pulled me back to alertness.

'So . . . what now?' I asked again.

'Ysabeau is right. We should go to your family. Vampires can't help you learn about your magic, and the witches will keep pursuing you.'

'When?' After La Pierre, I was oddly content to let him do whatever he thought best.

Matthew twitched slightly underneath me, his surprise at my compliance evident. 'We'll join Baldwin and take the helicopter to Lyon. His plane is fueled and ready to leave. Satu and the Congregation's other witches won't come back here immediately, but they will be back,' he said grimly.

'Ysabeau and Marthe will be safe at Sept-Tours without you?'

Matthew's laughter rumbled under me. 'They've been in the thick of every major armed conflict in history. A pack of hunting vampires or a few inquisitive witches are unlikely to trouble them. I have something to see to, though, before we leave. Will you rest, if Marthe stays with you?'

'I'll need to get my things together.'

'Marthe will do it. Ysabeau will help, if you'll let her.'

I nodded. The idea of Ysabeau's returning to the room was surprisingly comforting.

Matthew rearranged me on the pillows, his hands tender. He called softly to Marthe and Ysabeau and gestured the dogs to the stairs, where they took up positions reminiscent of the lions at the New York Public Library.

The two women moved silently about the room, their quiet puttering and snippets of conversation providing a soothing background noise that finally lulled me to sleep. When I woke several hours later, my old duffel bag was packed and waiting by the fire and Marthe was bent over it tucking a tin inside.

'What's that?' I asked, rubbing the sleep from my eyes.

'Your tea. One cup every day. Remember?'

'Yes, Marthe.' My head fell back on the pillows. 'Thank you. For everything.'

Marthe's gnarled hands stroked my forehead. 'He loves you. You know this?' Her voice was gruffer than usual.

'I know, Marthe. I love him, too.'

Hector and Fallon turned their heads, their attention caught by a sound on the stairs that was too faint for me to hear. Matthew's dark form appeared. He came to the sofa and took stock of me and nodded with approval after he felt my pulse. Then he scooped me into his arms as if I weighed nothing, the morphine ensuring that there was no more than an unpleasant tug on my back as he carried me down the stairs. Hector and Fallon brought up the rear of our little procession as we descended.

His study was lit only by firelight, and it cast shadows on the books and objects there. His eyes flickered to the wooden tower in a silent good-bye to Lucas and Blanca.

'We'll be back – as soon as we can,' I promised.

Matthew smiled, but it never touched his eyes.

Baldwin was waiting for us in the hall. Hector and Fallon milled around Matthew's legs, keeping anyone from getting close. He called them off so Ysabeau could approach.

She put her cold hands on my shoulders. 'Be brave, daughter, but listen to Matthew,' she instructed, giving me a kiss on each check.

'I'm so sorry to have brought this trouble to your house.'

'*Hein*, this house has seen worse,' she replied before turning to Baldwin.

'Let me know if you need anything, Ysabeau.' Baldwin brushed her cheeks with his lips.

'Of course, Baldwin. Fly safely,' she murmured as he walked outside.

'There are seven letters in Father's study,' Matthew told her when his brother was gone. He spoke low and very fast. 'Alain will come to fetch them. He knows what to do.' Ysabeau nodded, her eyes bright.

'And so it begins again,' she whispered. 'Your father would be proud of you, Matthew.' She touched him on the arm and picked up his bags.

We made our way – a line of vampires, dogs, and witch – across the château's lawns. The helicopter's blades started moving slowly when we appeared. Matthew took me by the waist and lifted me into the cabin, then climbed in behind me.

We lifted off and hovered for a moment over the château's illuminated walls before heading east, where the lights of Lyon were visible in the dark morning sky.

CHAPTER 32

My eyes remained firmly closed on the way to the airport. It would be a long time before I flew without thinking of Satu.

In Lyon everything was blindingly fast and efficient. Clearly Matthew had been arranging matters from Sept-Tours and had informed the authorities that the plane was being used for medical transport. Once he'd flashed his identification and airport personnel got a good look at my face, I was whisked into a wheelchair against my objections and pushed toward the plane while an immigration officer followed behind, stamping my passport. Baldwin strode in front, and people hastily got out of our way.

The de Clermont jet was outfitted like a luxury yacht, with chairs that folded down flat to make beds, areas of upholstered seating and tables, and a small galley where a uniformed attendant waited with a bottle of red wine and some chilled mineral water. Matthew got me settled in one of the recliners, arranging pillows like bolsters to take pressure off my back. He claimed the seat nearest me. Baldwin took charge of a table large enough to hold a board meeting, where he spread out papers, logged on to two different computers, and began talking incessantly on the phone.

After takeoff Matthew ordered me to sleep. When I resisted, he threatened to give me more morphine. We were still negotiating when his phone buzzed in his pocket.

'Marcus,' he said, glancing at the screen. Baldwin looked up from his table.

Matthew pushed the green button. 'Hello, Marcus. I'm on a plane headed for New York with Baldwin and Diana.' He spoke quickly, giving Marcus no chance to reply. His son couldn't have managed more than a few words before being disconnected.

No sooner had Matthew punched the phone's red button than lines of text began to light up his screen. Text messaging must have been a godsend for vampires in need of privacy. Matthew responded, his fingers flying over the keys. The screen went dark, and he gave me a tight smile.

'Everything all right?' I asked mildly, knowing the full story would have to wait until we were away from Baldwin.

'Yes. He was just curious where we were.' This seemed doubtful, given the hour.

Drowsiness made it unnecessary for Matthew to make any further requests that I sleep. 'Thank you for finding me,' I said, my eyes drifting closed.

His only response was to bow his head and rest it silently on my shoulder.

I didn't wake until we landed at La Guardia, where we pulled in to the area reserved for private aircraft. Our arrival there and not at a busier, more crowded airport on the other side of town was yet another example of the magical efficiency and convenience of vampire travel. Matthew's identification worked still more magic, and the officials sped us through. Once we'd cleared customs and immigration, Baldwin surveyed us, me in my wheelchair and his brother standing grimly behind.

'You both look like hell,' he commented.

'*Ta gueule*,' Matthew said with a false smile, his voice acid. Even with my limited French, I knew this wasn't something you would say in front of your mother.

Baldwin smiled broadly. 'That's better, Matthew. I'm glad to see you have some fight left in you. You're going to need it.' He glanced at his watch. It was as masculine as he was, the type made for divers and fighter pilots, with multiple dials and the ability to survive negative G-force pressure. 'I have a meeting in a few hours, but I wanted to give you some advice first.'

'I've got this covered, Baldwin,' Matthew said in a dangerously silky voice.

'No, you don't. Besides, I'm not talking to you.' Baldwin crouched down, folding his massive body so he could lock his uncanny, light brown eyes on mine. 'Do you know what a gambit is, Diana?'

'Vaguely. It's from chess.'

'That's right,' he replied. 'A gambit lulls your opponent into a sense of false safety. You make a deliberate sacrifice in order to gain a greater advantage.'

Matthew growled slightly.

'I understand the basic principles,' I said.

'What happened at La Pierre feels like a gambit to me,' Baldwin continued, his eyes never wavering. 'The Congregation let you go for some reason of their own. Make your next move before they make theirs. Don't wait your turn like a good girl, and don't be duped into thinking your current freedom means you're safe. Decide what to do to survive, and do it.'

'Thanks.' He might be Matthew's brother, but Baldwin's close physical presence was unnerving. I extended my gauze-wrapped right arm to him in farewell.

'Sister, that's not how family bids each other *adieu*.' Baldwin's voice was softly mocking. He gave me no time to react but gripped my shoulders and kissed me on the cheeks. As his face passed over mine, he deliberately breathed in my scent. It felt like a threat, and I wondered if he meant it as such. He released me and stood. 'Matthew, *à bientôt*.'

'Wait.' Matthew followed his brother. Using his broad back to block my view, he handed Baldwin an envelope. The curved sliver of black wax on it was visible despite his efforts.

'You said you wouldn't obey my orders. After La Pierre you might have reconsidered.'

Baldwin stared at the white rectangle. His face twisted sourly before falling into lines of resignation. Taking the envelope, he bowed his head and said, '*Je suis à votre commande, seigneur*.'

The words were formal, motivated by protocol rather than

genuine feeling. He was a knight, and Matthew was his master. Baldwin had bowed – technically – to Matthew's authority. But just because he had followed tradition, that did not mean he liked it. He raised the envelope to his forehead in a parody of a salute.

Matthew waited until Baldwin was out of sight before returning to me. He grasped the handles of the wheelchair. 'Come, let's get the car.'

Somewhere over the Atlantic, Matthew had made advance arrangements for our arrival. We picked up a Range Rover at the terminal curb from a man in uniform who dropped the keys into Matthew's palm, stowed our bags in the trunk, and left without a word. Matthew reached into the backseat, plucked out a blue parka designed for arctic trekking rather than autumn in New York, and arranged it like a down-filled nest in the passenger seat.

Soon we were driving through early-morning city traffic and then out into the countryside. The navigation system had been programmed with the address of the house in Madison and informed us that we should arrive in a little more than four hours. I looked at the brightening sky and started worrying about how Sarah and Em would react to Matthew.

'We'll be home just after breakfast. That will be interesting.' Sarah was not at her best before coffee – copious amounts of it – had entered her bloodstream. 'We should call and let them know when to expect us.'

'They already know. I called them from Sept-Tours.'

Feeling thoroughly managed and slightly muzzy from morphine and fatigue, I settled back for the drive.

We passed hardscrabble farms and small houses with early-morning lights twinkling in kitchens and bedrooms. Upstate New York is at its best in October. Now the trees were on fire with red and gold foliage. After the leaves fell, Madison and the surrounding countryside would turn rusty gray and remain that way until the first snows blanketed the world in pristine white batting.

We turned down the rutted road leading to the Bishop house. Its late-eighteenth-century lines were boxy and generous, and it sat back from the road on a little knoll, surrounded by aged apple trees and lilac bushes. The white clapboard was in desperate need of repainting, and the old picket fence was falling down in places. Pale plumes rose in welcome from both chimneys, however, filling the air with the autumn scent of wood smoke.

Matthew pulled in to the driveway, which was pitted with ice-crusted potholes. The Range Rover rumbled its way over them, and he parked next to Sarah's beat-up, once-purple car. A new crop of bumper stickers adorned the back. MY OTHER CAR IS A BROOM, a perennial favorite, was stuck next to I'M PAGAN AND I VOTE. Another proclaimed WICCAN ARMY: WE WILL NOT GO SILENTLY INTO THE NIGHT. I sighed.

Matthew turned off the car and looked at me. 'I'm supposed to be the nervous one.'

'Aren't you?'

'Not as nervous as you are.'

'Coming home always makes me behave like a teenager. All I want to do is hog the TV remote and eat ice cream.' Though trying to be bright and cheerful for his sake, I was not looking forward to this homecoming.

'I'm sure we can arrange for that,' he said with a frown. 'Meanwhile stop pretending nothing has happened. You're not fooling me, and you won't fool your aunts either.'

He left me sitting in the car while he carried our luggage to the front door. We'd amassed a surprisingly large amount of it, including two computer bags, my disreputable Yale duffel, and an elegant leather valise that might have been mistaken for a Victorian original. There was also Matthew's medical kit, his long gray coat, my bright new parka, and a case of wine. The last was a wise precaution on Matthew's part. Sarah's taste ran to harder stuff, and Em was a teetotaler.

Matthew returned and lifted me out of the car, my legs swinging. Safely on the steps, I gingerly put weight on my right ankle. We both faced the house's red, eighteenth-century door. It was flanked by tiny windows that offered a view of the front hall. Every lamp in the house was lit to welcome us.

'I smell coffee,' he said, smiling down at me.

'They're up, then.' The catch on the worn, familiar door latch released at my touch. 'Unlocked as usual.' Before losing my nerve, I warily stepped inside. 'Em? Sarah?'

A note in Sarah's dark, decisive handwriting was taped to the staircase's newel post.

'*Out. Thought the house needed some time alone with you first. Move slowly. Matthew can stay in Em's old room. Your room is ready.*' There was a postscript, in Em's rounder scrawl. '*Both of you use your parents' room.*'

My eyes swept over the doors leading from the hall. They were all standing open, and there was no banging upstairs. Even the coffin doors into the keeping room were quiet, rather than swinging wildly on their hinges.

'That's a good sign.'

'What? That they're out of the house?' Matthew looked confused.

'No, the silence. The house has been known to misbehave with new people.'

'The house is haunted?' Matthew looked around with interest.

'We're witches — of course the house is haunted. But it's more than that. The house is . . . alive. It has its own ideas about visitors, and the more Bishops there are, the worse it acts up. That's why Em and Sarah left.'

A phosphorescent smudge moved in and out of my peripheral vision. My long-dead grandmother, whom I'd never met, was sitting by the keeping room's fireplace in an unfamiliar rocking chair. She looked as young and beautiful as in her wedding picture on the landing upstairs. When she smiled, my own lips curved in response.

'Grandma?' I said tentatively.

He's a looker, isn't he? she said with a wink, her voice rustling like waxed paper.

Another head popped around the doorframe. *I'll say*, the other ghost agreed. *Should be dead, though.*

My grandmother nodded. *Suppose so, Elizabeth, but he is what he is. We'll get used to him.*

Matthew was staring in the direction of the keeping room. 'Someone is there,' he said, full of wonder. 'I can almost smell them and hear faint sounds. But I can't see them.'

'Ghosts.' Reminded of the castle dungeons, I looked around for my mother and father.

Oh, they're not here, my grandmother said sadly.

Disappointed, I turned my attention from my dead family to my undead husband. 'Let's go upstairs and put the bags away. That will give the house a chance to know you.'

Before we could move another inch, a charcoal ball of fur rocketed out of the back of the house with a blood-chilling yowl. It stopped abruptly one foot away from me and transformed into a hissing cat. She arched her back and screeched again.

'Nice to see you too, Tabitha.' Sarah's cat detested me, and the feeling was mutual.

Tabitha lowered her spine into its proper alignment and stalked toward Matthew.

'Vampires are more comfortable with dogs, as a rule,' he commented as Tabitha wound around his ankles.

With unerring feline instincts, Tabitha latched onto Matthew's discomfort and was now determined to change his mind about her species. She butted her head against his shin, purring loudly.

'I'll be damned,' I said. For Tabitha this was an astonishing display of affection. 'She really is the most perverse cat in the history of the world.'

Tabitha hissed at me and resumed her sybaritic attention to Matthew's lower legs.

'Just ignore her,' I recommended, hobbling toward the stairs. Matthew swept up the bags and followed.

Gripping the banister, I made a slow ascent. Matthew took each step with me, his face alight with excitement and interest. He didn't seem at all alarmed that the house was giving him the once-over.

My body was rigid with anticipation, however. Pictures had fallen onto unsuspecting guests, doors and windows flapped open and closed, and lights went on and off without warning. I let out a sigh of relief when we made it to the landing without incident.

'Not many of my friends visited the house,' I explained when he raised an eyebrow. 'It was easier to see them at the mall in Syracuse.'

The upstairs rooms were arranged in a square around the central staircase. Em and Sarah's room was in the front corner, overlooking the driveway. My mother and father's room was at the back of the house, with a view of the fields and a section of the old apple orchard that gradually gave way to a deeper wood of oaks and maples. The door was open, a light on inside. I stepped hesitantly toward the welcoming, golden rectangle and over the threshold.

The room was warm and comfortable, its broad bed loaded with quilts and pillows. Nothing matched, except for the plain white curtains. The floor was constructed out of wide pine planks with gaps large enough to swallow a hairbrush. A bathroom opened up to the right, and a radiator was popping and hissing inside.

'Lily of the valley,' Matthew commented, his nostrils flaring at all the new scents.

'My mother's favorite perfume.' An ancient bottle of Diorissimo with a faded black-and-white houndstooth ribbon wrapped around the neck still stood on the bureau.

Matthew dropped the bags onto the floor. 'Is it going to bother you to be in here?' His eyes were worried. 'You could have your old room, as Sarah suggested.'

'No chance,' I said firmly. 'It's in the attic, and the bathroom is down here. Besides, there's no way we'll both fit in a single bed.'

Matthew looked away. 'I had thought we might—'

'We're not sleeping in separate beds. I'm no less your wife among witches than among vampires,' I interrupted, drawing him toward me. The house settled on its foundations with a tiny sigh, as if bracing itself for a long conversation.

'No, but it might be easier—'

'For whom?' I interrupted again.

'For you,' he finished. 'You're in pain. You'd sleep more soundly in bed alone.'

There would be no sleep for me at all without him at my side. Not wanting to worry him by saying so, I rested my hands on his chest in an attempt to distract him from the matter of sleeping arrangements. 'Kiss me.'

His mouth tightened into a no, but his eyes said yes. I pressed my body against his, and he responded with a kiss that was both sweet and gentle.

'I thought you were lost,' he murmured when we parted, resting his forehead against mine, 'forever. Now I'm afraid you might shatter into a thousand pieces because of what Satu did. If something had happened to you, I'd have gone mad.'

My scent enveloped Matthew, and he relaxed a fraction. He relaxed further when his hands slid around my hips. They were relatively unscathed, and his touch was both comforting and electrifying. My need for him had only intensified since my ordeal with Satu.

'Can you feel it?' I took his hand in mine, pressing it against the center of my chest.

'Feel what?' Matthew's face was puzzled.

Unsure what would make an impression on his preternatural senses, I concentrated on the chain that had unfurled when he'd first kissed me. When I touched it with an imaginary finger, it emitted a low, steady hum.

Matthew gasped, a look of wonder on his face. 'I can hear something. What is it?' He bent to rest his ear against my chest.

'It's you, inside me,' I said. 'You ground me — an anchor at the end of a long, silvery chain. It's why I'm so certain of you, I suppose.' My voice dropped. 'Provided I could feel you — had this connection to you — there was nothing Satu could say or do that I couldn't endure.'

'It's like the sound your blood makes when you talk to Rakasa with your mind, or when you called the witchwind. Now that I know what to listen for, it's audible.'

Ysabeau had mentioned she could hear my witch's blood singing. I tried to make the chain's music louder, its vibrations passing into the rest of my body.

Matthew lifted his head and gave me a glorious smile. 'Amazing.'

The humming grew more intense, and I lost control of the energy pulsing through me. Overhead, a score of stars burst into life and shot through the room.

'Oops.' Dozens of ghostly eyes tingled against my back. The house shut the door firmly against the inquiring looks of my ancestors, who had assembled to see the fireworks display as if it were Independence Day.

'Did you do that?' Matthew stared intently at the closed door.

'No,' I explained earnestly. 'The sparklers were mine. That was the house. It has a thing about privacy.'

'Thank God,' he murmured, pulling my hips firmly to his and kissing me again in a way that had the ghosts on the other side muttering.

The fireworks fizzled out in a stream of aquamarine light over the chest of drawers.

'I love you, Matthew Clairmont,' I said at the earliest opportunity.

'And I love you, Diana Bishop,' he replied formally. 'But your aunt and Emily must be freezing. Show me the rest of the house so that they can come inside.'

Slowly we went through the other rooms on the second floor, most unused now and filled with assorted bric-a-brac from Em's yard-sale addiction and all the junk Sarah couldn't bear to throw away for fear she might need it one day.

Matthew helped me up the stairs to the attic bedroom where I'd endured my adolescence. It still had posters of musicians tacked to the walls and sported the strong shades of purple and green that were a teenager's attempt at a sophisticated color scheme.

Downstairs, we explored the big formal rooms built to receive guests – the keeping room on one side of the front door and the office and small parlor opposite. We passed through the rarely used dining room and into the heart of the house – a family room large enough to serve as TV room and eating area, with the kitchen at the far end.

'It looks like Em's taken up needlepoint – again,' I said, picking up a half-finished canvas with a basket of flowers on it. 'And Sarah's fallen off the wagon.'

'She's a smoker?' Matthew gave the air a long sniff.

'When she's stressed. Em makes her smoke outside – but you can still smell it. Does it bother you?' I asked, acutely aware of how sensitive he might be to the odor.

'*Dieu*, Diana, I've smelled worse,' he replied.

The cavernous kitchen retained its wall of brick ovens and a gigantic walk-in fireplace. There were modern appliances, too, and old stone floors that had endured two centuries of dropped pans, wet animals, muddy shoes, and other more witchy substances. I ushered him into Sarah's adjacent workroom. Originally a freestanding summer kitchen, it was now connected to the house and still equipped with cranes for holding cauldrons of stew and spits for roasting meat. Herbs hung from the ceiling, and a storage loft held drying fruits and jars of her lotions and potions. The tour over, we returned to the kitchen.

'This room is so *brown*.' I studied the decor while flicking the porch light on and off again, the Bishops' long-standing signal that it was safe to enter. There was a brown refrigerator, brown wooden cabinets, warm red-brown brick, a brown rotary-dial phone, and tired brown-checked wallpaper. 'What it needs is a fresh coat of white paint.'

Matthew's chin lifted, and his eyes panned to the back door.

'February would be ideal for the job, if you're offering to do the work,' a throaty voice said from the mudroom. Sarah rounded the corner, wearing jeans and an oversize plaid flannel shirt. Her red hair was wild and her cheeks bright with the cold.

'Hello, Sarah,' I said, backing up toward the sink.

'Hello, Diana.' Sarah stared fixedly at the bruise under my eye. 'This is the vampire, I take it?'

'Yes.' I hobbled forward again to make the introductions. Sarah's sharp gaze turned to my ankle. 'Sarah, this is Matthew Clairmont. Matthew, my aunt, Sarah Bishop.'

Matthew extended his right hand. 'Sarah,' he said, meeting her eyes without hesitation.

Sarah pursed her lips in response. Like me, she had the Bishop chin, which was slightly too long for the rest of her face. It was now jutting out even more.

'Matthew.' When their hands met, Sarah flinched. 'Yep,' she said, turning her head slightly, 'he's definitely a vampire, Em.'

'Thanks for the help, Sarah,' Em grumbled, walking in with an armful of small logs and an impatient expression. She was taller than me or Sarah, and her shining silver cap of hair somehow made her look younger than the color would suggest. Her narrow face broke into a delighted smile when she saw us standing in the kitchen.

Matthew jumped to take the wood away from her. Tabitha, who had been absent during the first flurry of greeting, hampered his progress to the fireplace by tracing figure eights between his feet. Miraculously, the vampire made it to the other side of the room without stepping on her.

'Thank you, Matthew. And thank you for bringing her home as well. We've been so worried.' Em shook out her arms, bits of bark flying from the wool of her sweater.

'You're welcome, Emily,' he said, his voice irresistibly warm and rich. Em already looked charmed. Sarah was going to be tougher, although she was studying Tabitha's efforts to scale Matthew's arm with amazement.

I tried to retreat into the shadows before Em got a clear look at my face, but I was too late. She gasped, horrified. 'Oh, Diana.'

Sarah pulled out a stool. 'Sit,' she ordered.

Matthew crossed his arms tightly, as if resisting the temptation to interfere. His wolfish need to protect me had not diminished just because we were in Madison, and his strong dislike of creatures getting too near me was not reserved for other vampires.

My aunt's eyes traveled from my face down over my collarbones. 'Let's get the shirt off,' she said.

I reached for the buttons dutifully.

'Maybe you should examine Diana upstairs.' Em shot a worried look at Matthew.

'I don't imagine he'll get an eyeful of anything he hasn't already seen. You aren't hungry, are you?' Sarah said without a backward glance.

'No,' Matthew said drily, 'I ate on the plane.'

My aunt's eyes tingled across my neck. So did Em's.

'Sarah! Em!' I was indignant.

'Just checking,' Sarah said mildly. The shirt was off now, and she took in the gauze wrapping on my forearm, my mummified torso, and the other cuts and bruises.

'Matthew's already examined me. He's a doctor, remember?'

Her fingers probed my collarbone. I winced. 'He missed this, though. It's a hairline fracture.' She moved up to the cheekbone. I winced again. 'What's wrong with her ankle?' As usual, I hadn't been able to conceal anything from Sarah.

'A bad sprain accompanied by superficial first- and second-degree burns.' Matthew was staring at Sarah's hands, ready to haul her off if she caused me too much discomfort.

'How do you get burns and a sprain in the same place?' Sarah was treating Matthew like a first-year medical student on grand rounds.

'You get them from being hung upside down by a sadistic witch,' I answered for him, squirming slightly as Sarah continued to examine my face.

'What's under that?' Sarah demanded, as if I hadn't spoken, pointing to my arm.

'An incision deep enough to require suturing,' Matthew replied patiently.

'What have you got her on?'

'Painkillers, a diuretic to minimize swelling, and a broad-spectrum antibiotic.' There was the barest trace of annoyance in his voice.

'Why is she wrapped up like a mummy?' Em asked, chewing on her lip.

The blood drained from my face. Sarah stopped what she was doing and gave me a probing look before she spoke.

'Let's wait on that, Em. First things first. Who did this to you, Diana?'

'A witch named Satu Järvinen. I think she's Swedish.' My arms crossed protectively over my chest.

Matthew's mouth tightened, and he left my side long enough to pile more logs on the fire.

'She's not Swedish, she's Finnish,' Sarah said, 'and quite powerful. The next time I see her, though, she'll wish she'd never been born.'

'There won't be much left of her after I'm done,' Matthew murmured, 'so if you want a shot at her, you'll have to reach her before I do. And I'm known for my speed.'

Sarah gave him an appraising look. Her words were only a threat. Matthew's were something else entirely. They were a promise. 'Who treated Diana besides you?'

'My mother and her housekeeper, Marthe.'

'They know old herbal remedies. But I can do a bit more.' Sarah rolled up her sleeves.

'It's a little early in the day for witchcraft. Have you had enough coffee?' I looked at Em imploringly, silently begging her to call Sarah off.

'Let Sarah fix it, honey,' Em said, taking my hand and giving it a squeeze. 'The sooner she does, the sooner you'll be fully healed.'

Sarah's lips were already moving. Matthew edged closer, fascinated. She laid her fingertips on my face. The bone underneath tingled with electricity before the crack fused with a snap.

'Ow!' I held my cheek.

'It will only sting for a bit,' Sarah said. 'You were strong enough to withstand the injury – you should have no problem with the cure.' She studied my cheek for a moment and nodded with satisfaction before turning to my collarbone. The electrical twinge required to mend it was more powerful, no doubt because the bones were thicker.

'Get her shoe off,' she instructed Matthew, headed for the stillroom. He was the most overqualified medical assistant ever known, but he obeyed her orders without a grumble.

When Sarah returned with a pot of one of her ointments, Matthew had my foot propped up on his thigh. 'There are scissors in my bag upstairs,' he told my aunt, sniffing curiously as she unscrewed the pot's lid. 'Shall I go get them?'

'Don't need them.' Sarah muttered a few words and gestured at my ankle. The gauze began to unwind itself.

'That's handy,' Matthew said enviously.

'Show-off,' I said under my breath.

All eyes returned to my ankle when the gauze was finished rolling itself into a ball. It still looked nasty and was starting to ooze. Sarah calmly recited fresh spells, though the red spots on her cheeks hinted at her underlying fury. When she had finished, the black and white marks were gone, and though there was still an angry ring around my ankle, the joint itself was noticeably smaller in size.

'Thanks, Sarah.' I flexed my foot while she smeared fresh ointment over the skin.

'You won't be doing any yoga for a week or so – and no running for three, Diana. It needs rest and time to fully recover.' She muttered some more and beckoned to a fresh roll of gauze, which started to wind around my foot and ankle.

'Amazing,' Matthew said again, shaking his head.

'Do you mind if I look at the arm?'

'Not at all.' He sounded almost eager. 'The muscle was slightly damaged. Can you mend that, as well as the skin?'

'Probably,' Sarah said with just a hint of smugness. Fifteen minutes and a few muffled curses later, there was nothing but a thin red line running down my arm to indicate where Satu had sliced it open.

'Nice work,' Matthew said, turning my arm to admire Sarah's skill.

'You, too. That was fine stitching.' Sarah drank thirstily from a glass of water.

I reached for Matthew's shirt.

'You should see to her back as well.'

'It can wait.' I shot him an evil look. 'Sarah's tired, and so am I.'

Sarah's eyes moved from me to the vampire. 'Matthew?' she asked, relegating me to the bottom of the pecking order.

'I want you to treat her back,' he said without taking his eyes off me.

'No,' I whispered, clutching his shirt to my chest.

He crouched in front of me, hands on my knees. 'You've seen what Sarah can do. Your recovery will be faster if you let her help you.'

Recovery? No witchcraft could help me recover from La Pierre.

'Please, *mon coeur*.' Matthew gently extricated his balled-up shirt from my hands.

Reluctantly I agreed. There was a tingle of witches' glances when Em and Sarah moved around to study my back, and my instincts urged me to run. I reached blindly for Matthew instead, and he clasped both my hands in his.

'I'm here,' he assured me while Sarah muttered her first spell. The gauze wrappings parted along my spine, her words slicing through them with ease.

Em's sharp intake of breath and Sarah's silence told me when the marks were visible.

'This is an opening spell,' Sarah said angrily, staring at my back. 'You don't use this on living beings. She could have killed you.'

'She was trying to get my magic out – like I was a piñata.' With my back exposed, my emotions were swinging wildly again, and I nearly giggled at the thought of hanging from a tree while a blind-folded Satu swatted me with a stick. Matthew noticed my mounting hysteria.

'The quicker you can do this, the better, Sarah. Not to rush you, of course,' he said hastily. I could easily imagine the look he'd received. 'We can talk about Satu later.'

Every bit of witchcraft Sarah used reminded me of Satu, and having two witches stand behind me made it impossible to keep my thoughts from returning to La Pierre. I burrowed more deeply inside myself for protection and let my mind go numb. Sarah worked more magic. But I could take no more and set my soul adrift.

'Are you almost done?' Matthew said, his voice taut with concern.

'There are two marks I can't do much with. They'll leave scars. Here,' Sarah said, tracing the lines of a star between my shoulder blades, 'and here.' Her fingers moved down to my lower back, moving from rib to rib and scooping down to my waist in between.

My mind was no longer blank but seared with a picture to match Sarah's gestures.

A star hanging above a crescent moon.

'They suspect, Matthew!' I cried, frozen to the stool with terror. Matthew's drawerful of seals swam through my memories. They had been hidden so completely, I knew instinctively that the order of knights must be just as deeply concealed. But Satu knew about them, which meant the other witches of the Congregation probably did, too.

'My darling, what is it?' Matthew pulled me into his arms.

I pushed against his chest, trying to make him listen. 'When I refused to give you up, Satu marked me – with your seal.'

He turned me inside his arms, protecting as much of my exposed flesh as he could. When he'd seen what was inscribed there, Matthew went still. 'They no longer suspect. At last, they know.'

'What are you talking about?' demanded Sarah.

'May I have Diana's shirt, please?'

'I don't think the scars will be too bad,' my aunt said somewhat defensively.

'The shirt.' Matthew's voice was icy.

Em tossed it to him. Matthew pulled the sleeves gently over my arms, drawing the edges together in front. He was hiding his eyes, but the vein in his forehead was pulsing.

'I'm so sorry,' I murmured.

'You have *nothing* to be sorry for.' He took my face in his hands. 'Any vampire would know you were mine – with or without this brand on your back. Satu wanted to make sure that every other creature knew who you belonged to, as well. When I was reborn, they used to shear the hair from the heads of women who gave their bodies to the enemy. It was a crude way of exposing traitors. This is no different.' He looked away. 'Did Ysabeau tell you?'

'No. I was looking for paper and found the drawer.'

'What the hell is going on?' Sarah snapped.

'I invaded your privacy. I shouldn't have,' I whispered, clutching at his arms.

He drew away and stared at me incredulously, then crushed me to his chest without any concern for my injuries. Mercifully, Sarah's witchcraft meant that there was very little pain. 'Christ, Diana. Satu told you what I did. I followed you home and broke in to your rooms. Besides, how can I blame you for finding out on your own what I should have told you myself?'

A thunderclap echoed through the kitchen, setting the pots and pans clanging.

When the sound had faded into silence, Sarah spoke. 'If someone doesn't tell us what is going on *immediately*, all hell is going to break loose.' A spell rose to her lips.

My fingertips tingled, and winds circled my feet. 'Back off, Sarah.' The wind roared through my veins, and I stepped between Sarah and Matthew. My aunt kept muttering, and my eyes narrowed.

Em put her hand on Sarah's arm in alarm. 'Don't push her. She's not in control.'

I could see a bow in my left hand, an arrow in my right. They felt heavy, yet strangely familiar. A few steps away, Sarah was in my sights. Without hesitation, my arms rose and drew apart in preparation to shoot.

My aunt stopped muttering in midspell. 'Holy shit,' she breathed, looking at Em in amazement.

'Honey, put the fire down.' Em made a gesture of surrender.

Confused, I reexamined my hands. There was no fire in them.

'Not inside. If you want to unleash witchfire, we'll go outside,' said Em.

'Calm down, Diana.' Matthew pinned my elbows to my sides, and the heaviness associated with the bow and arrow dissolved.

'I don't like it when she threatens you.' My voice sounded echoing and strange.

'Sarah wasn't threatening me. She just wanted to know what we were talking about. We need to tell her.'

'But it's a secret,' I said, confused. We had to keep our secrets – from everyone – whether they involved my abilities or Matthew's knights.

'No more secrets,' he said firmly, his breath against my neck. 'They're not good for either of us.' When the winds died down, he spun me tightly against him.

'Is she always like that? Wild and out of control?' Sarah asked.

'Your niece did brilliantly,' Matthew retorted, continuing to hold me.

Sarah and Matthew faced off across the kitchen floor.

'I suppose,' she admitted with poor grace when their silent battle had concluded, 'though you might have told us you could control witchfire, Diana. It's not exactly a run-of-the-mill ability.'

'I can't *control* anything.' Suddenly I was exhausted and didn't want to be standing up anymore. My legs agreed and began to buckle.

'Upstairs,' he said, his tone brooking no argument. 'We'll finish this conversation there.'

In my parents' room, after giving me another dose of painkillers and antibiotics, Matthew tucked me into bed. Then he told my aunts more about Satu's mark. Tabitha condescended to sit on my feet as he did so in order to be closer to the sound of Matthew's voice.

'The mark Satu left on Diana's back belongs to an . . . organization that my family started many years ago. Most people have long forgotten it, and those who haven't think it doesn't exist anymore. We like to preserve that illusion. With the star and moon on her back, Satu marked your niece as my property and made it known that the witches had discovered my family's secret.'

'Does this secret organization have a name?' Sarah asked.

'You don't have to tell them everything, Matthew.' I reached for his hand. There was danger associated with disclosing too much about the Knights of Lazarus. I could feel it, seeping around me like a dark cloud, and I didn't want it to enfold Sarah and Em, too.

'The Knights of Lazarus of Bethany.' He said it quickly, as if afraid he'd lose his resolve. 'It's an old chivalric order.'

Sarah snorted. 'Never heard of them. Are they like the Knights of Columbus? They've got a chapter in Oneida.'

'Not really.' Matthew's mouth twitched. 'The Knights of Lazarus date back to the Crusades.'

'Didn't we watch a television program about the Crusades that had an order of knights in it?' Em asked Sarah.

'The Templars. But all those conspiracy theories are nonsense. There's no such thing as Templars now,' Sarah said decidedly.

'There aren't supposed to be witches and vampires either, Sarah,' I pointed out.

Matthew reached for my wrist, his fingers cool against my pulse.

'This conversation is over for the present,' he said firmly. 'There's plenty of time to talk about whether the Knights of Lazarus exist or not.'

Matthew ushered out a reluctant Em and Sarah. Once my aunts were in the hall, the house took matters into its own hands and shut the door. The lock scraped in the frame.

'I don't have a key for that room,' Sarah called to Matthew.

Unconcerned, Matthew climbed onto the bed, pulling me into the crook of his arm so that my head rested on his heart. Every time I tried to speak, he shushed me into silence.

'Later,' he kept repeating.

His heart pulsed once and then, several minutes later, pulsed again.

Before it could pulse a third time, I was sound asleep.

CHAPTER 33

A combination of exhaustion, medication, and the familiarity of home kept me in bed for hours. I woke on my stomach, one knee bent and arm outstretched, searching vainly for Matthew.

Too groggy to sit up, I turned my head toward the door. A large key sat in the lock, and there were low voices on the other side. As the muzziness of sleep slowly gave way to awareness, the mumbling became clearer.

'It's appalling,' Matthew snapped. 'How could you let her go on this way?'

'We didn't know about the extent of her power – not absolutely,' Sarah said, sounding equally furious. 'She was bound to be different, given her parents. I never expected witchfire, though.'

'How did you recognize she was trying to call it, Emily?' Matthew softened his voice.

'A witch on Cape Cod summoned it when I was a child. She must have been seventy,' Em said. 'I never forgot what she looked like or what it felt like to be near that kind of power.'

'Witchfire is lethal. No spell can ward it off, and no witchcraft can heal the burns. My mother taught me to recognize the signs for my own protection – the smell of sulfur, the way a witch's arms moved,' said Sarah. 'She told me that the goddess is present when witchfire is called. I thought I'd go to my grave without witnessing it, and I certainly never expected my niece to unleash it on me in my own kitchen. Witchfire – and witchwater, too?'

'I hoped the witchfire would be recessive,' Matthew confessed. 'Tell me about Stephen Proctor.' Until recently, the authoritative tone he adopted in moments like this had seemed a vestige of his past life as a soldier. Now that I knew about the Knights of Lazarus, I understood it as part of his present, too.

Sarah was not accustomed to having anyone use that tone with her, however, and she bristled. 'Stephen was private. He didn't flaunt his power.'

'No wonder the witches went digging to discover it, then.'

My eyes closed tightly against the sight of my father's body, opened up from throat to groin so that other witches could understand his magic. His fate had nearly been mine.

Matthew's bulk shifted in the hall, and the house protested at the unusual weight. 'He was an experienced wizard, but he was no match for them. Diana might have inherited his abilities – and Rebecca's, too, God help her. But she doesn't have their knowledge, and without it she's helpless. She might as well have a target painted on her.'

I continued eavesdropping shamelessly.

'She's not a transistor radio, Matthew,' Sarah said defensively. 'Diana didn't come to us with batteries and an instruction manual. We did the best we could. She became a different child after Rebecca and Stephen were killed, withdrawing so far that no one could reach her. What should we have done? Forced her to face what she was so determined to deny?'

'I don't know.' Matthew's exasperation was audible. 'But you shouldn't have left her like this. That witch held her captive for more than twelve hours.'

'We'll teach her what she needs to know.'

'For her sake, it had better not take too long.'

'It will take her whole life,' Sarah snapped. 'Magic isn't macramé. It takes time.'

'We don't have time,' Matthew hissed. The creaking of the floorboards told me Sarah had taken an instinctive step away from him. 'The Congregation has been playing cat-and-mouse games, but the mark on Diana's back indicates those days are over.'

'How dare you call what happened to my niece a game?' Sarah's voice rose.

'Shh,' Em said. 'You'll wake her.'

'What might help us understand how Diana is spellbound, Emily?' Matthew was whispering now. 'Can you remember anything about the days before Rebecca and Stephen left for Africa – small details, what they were worried about?'

Spellbound.

The word echoed in my mind as I slowly drew myself upright. Spellbinding was reserved for extreme circumstances – life-threatening danger, madness, pure and uncontrollable evil. Merely to threaten it earned you the censure of other witches.

Spellbound?

By the time I got to my feet, Matthew was at my side. He was frowning. 'What do you need?'

'I want to talk to Em.' My fingers were snapping and turning blue. So were my toes, sticking out of the bandages that protected my ankle. The gauze on my foot snagged an old nail head poking up from the floor's pine boards as I pushed past him.

Sarah and Em were waiting on the landing, trepidation on their faces.

'What's wrong with me?' I demanded.

Emily crept into the crook of Sarah's arm. 'There's nothing wrong with you.'

'You said I'm spellbound. That my own *mother* did it.' I was some kind of monster. It was the only possible explanation.

Emily heard my thoughts as if I'd spoken them aloud. 'You're not a monster, honey. Rebecca did it because she was afraid for you.'

'She was afraid *of* me, you mean.' My blue fingers provided an excellent reason for someone to be terrified. I tried to hide them but didn't want to singe Matthew's shirt, and resting them on the old wooden stair rail risked setting the whole house on fire.

Watch the rug, girl! The tall female ghost from the keeping room was peeking around Sarah and Em's door and pointing urgently at the floor. I lifted my toes slightly.

'No one is afraid of you.' Matthew stared with frosty intensity at my back, willing me to face him.

'They are.' I pointed a sparkling finger at my aunts, eyes resolutely in their direction.

So am I, confessed another dead Bishop, this one a teenage boy with slightly protruding teeth. He was carrying a berry basket and wore a pair of ripped britches.

My aunts took a step backward as I continued to glare at them.

'You have every right to be frustrated.' Matthew moved so that he was standing just behind me. The wind rose, and touches of snow from his glance glazed my thighs, too. 'Now the witchwind has come because you feel trapped.' He crept closer, and the air around my lower legs increased slightly. 'See?'

Yes, that roiling feeling might be frustration rather than anger. Distracted from the issue of spellbinding, I turned to ask him more about his theories. The color in my fingers was already fading, and the snapping sound was gone.

'You have to try to understand,' Em pleaded. 'Rebecca and Stephen went to Africa to protect you. They spellbound you for the same reason. All they wanted was for you to be safe.'

The house moaned through its timbers and held its breath, its old wooden joists creaking.

Coldness spread through me from the inside out.

'Is it my fault they died? They went to Africa and someone killed them – because of me?' I looked at Matthew in horror.

Without waiting for an answer, I made my way blindly to the stairs, unconcerned with the pain in my ankle or anything else except fleeing.

'No, Sarah. Let her go,' Matthew said sharply.

The house opened all the doors before me and slammed them behind as I went through the front hall, the dining room, the family room, and into the kitchen. A pair of Sarah's gardening boots slipped over my bare feet, their rubber surfaces cold and smooth. Once outside, I did what I'd always done when the family was too much for me and went into the woods.

My feet didn't slow until I had made it through the scraggy apple trees and into the shadows cast by the ancient white oaks and sugar maples. Out of breath and shaking with shock and exhaustion, I found myself at the foot of an enormous tree almost as wide as it was tall. Low, sprawling branches nearly touched the ground, their red and purple deeply lobed leaves standing out against the ashy bark.

All through my childhood and adolescence, I'd poured out my heartbreak and loneliness underneath its limbs. Generations of Bishops had found the same solace here and carved their initials into the tree. Mine were gouged with a penknife next to the 'RB' my mother had left before me, and I traced their curves before curling up in a ball near the rough trunk and rocking myself like a child.

There was a cool touch on my hair before the blue parka settled over my shoulders. Matthew's solid frame lowered to the ground, his back scraping against the tree's bark.

'Did they tell you what's wrong with me?' My voice was muffled against my legs.

'There's nothing wrong with you, *mon coeur*.'

'You have a lot to learn about witches.' I rested my chin on my knees but still wouldn't look at him. 'Witches don't spellbind someone without a damn good reason.'

Matthew was quiet. I slid a sidelong glance in his direction. His legs were just visible from the corner of my eye – one stretched forward and the other bent – as was a long, white hand. It was draped loosely over his knee.

'Your parents had a damn good reason. They were saving their daughter's life.' His voice was quiet and even, but there were stronger emotions underneath. 'It's what I would have done.'

'Did you know I was spellbound, too?' It wasn't possible for me to keep from sounding accusatory.

'Marthe and Ysabeau figured it out. They told me just before we left for La Pierre. Emily confirmed their suspicions. I hadn't had a chance to tell you.'

'How could Em keep this from me?' I felt betrayed and alone, just as I had when Satu told me about what Matthew had done.

'You must forgive your parents and Emily. They were doing what they thought was best – for you.'

'You don't understand, Matthew,' I said, shaking my head stubbornly. 'My mother tied me up and went to Africa as if I were an evil, deranged creature who couldn't be trusted.'

'Your parents were worried about the Congregation.'

'That's nonsense.' My fingers tingled, and I pushed the feeling back toward my elbows, trying to control my temper. 'Not everything is about the damn Congregation, Matthew.'

'No, but this is. You don't have to be a witch to see it.'

My white table appeared before me without warning, events past and present scattered on its surface. The puzzle pieces began to arrange themselves: my mother chasing after me while I clapped my hands and flew over the linoleum floor of our kitchen in Cambridge, my father shouting at Peter Knox in his study at home, a bedtime story about a fairy godmother and magical ribbons, both my parents standing over my bed saying spells and working magic while I lay quietly on top of the quilt. The pieces clicked into place, and the pattern emerged.

'My mother's bedtime stories,' I said, turning to him in amazement. 'She couldn't tell me her plans outright, so she turned it all into a story about evil witches and enchanted ribbons and a fairy godmother. Every night she told me, so that some part of me would remember.'

'And do you remember anything else?'

'Before they spellbound me, Peter Knox came to see my father.' I shuddered, hearing the doorbell ringing and seeing again the expression on my father's face when he opened the door. 'That creature was in my house. He touched my head.' Knox's hand resting on the back of my skull had produced an uncanny sensation, I recalled.

'My father sent me to my room, and the two of them fought. My mother stayed in the kitchen. It was strange that she didn't come to see what was going on. Then my father went out for a long time. My mother was frantic. She called Em that night.' The memories were coming thick and fast now.

'Emily told me Rebecca's spell was cast so that it would hold until the "shadowed man" came. Your mother thought I would be able to protect you from Knox and the Congregation.' His face darkened.

'Nobody could have protected me – except me. Satu was right. I'm a sorry excuse for a witch.' My head went back to my knees again. 'I'm not like my mother at all.'

Matthew stood, extending one hand. 'Get up,' he said abruptly.

I slid my hand into his, expecting him to comfort me with a hug. Instead he pushed my arms into the sleeves of the blue parka and stepped away.

'You are a witch. It's time you learned how to take care of yourself.'

'Not now, Matthew.'

'I wish we could let you decide, but we can't,' he said brusquely. 'The Congregation wants your power – or the knowledge of it at the very least. They want Ashmole 782, and you're the only creature in more than a century to see it.'

'They want you and the Knights of Lazarus, too.' I was desperate to make this about something besides me and my ill-understood magic.

'They could have brought down the brotherhood before. The Congregation has had plenty of chances.' Matthew was obviously sizing me up and gauging my few strengths and considerable weaknesses. It made me feel vulnerable. 'But they don't really care about that. They don't want me to have you or the manuscript.'

'But I'm surrounded by protectors. You're with me – Sarah and Em, too.'

'We can't be with you every moment, Diana. Besides, do you want Sarah and Emily to risk their lives to save yours?' It was a blunt question, and his face twisted. He backed away from me, eyes narrowed to slits.

'You're frightening me,' I said as his body lowered into a crouch. The final, lingering touches of morphine drifted through my blood, chased away by the first rush of adrenaline.

'No I'm not.' He shook his head slowly, looking every inch a wolf as his hair swayed around his face. 'I'd smell it if you were truly frightened. You're just off balance.'

A rumbling began in the back of Matthew's throat that was a far cry from the sounds he made when he felt pleasure. I took a wary step away from him.

'That's better,' he purred. 'At least you have a taste of fear now.'

'Why are you doing this?' I whispered.

He was gone without a word.

I blinked. 'Matthew?'

Two cold patches bored into the top of my skull.

Matthew was hanging like a bat between two tree limbs, his arms outstretched like wings. His feet were hooked around another branch. He watched me intently, little flickers of frost my only indication of the changes in his focus.

'I'm not a colleague you're having an argument with. This isn't an academic dispute – this is life or death.'

'Come down from there,' I said sharply. 'You've made your point.'

I didn't see him land at my side, but I felt his cold fingers at my neck and chin, twisting my head to the side and exposing my throat. 'If I were Gerbert, you'd be dead already,' he hissed.

'Stop it, Matthew.' I struggled to break free but made no progress.

'No.' His grip tightened. 'Satu tried to break you, and you want to disappear because of it. But you have to fight back.'

'I am.' I pushed against his arms to prove my point.

'Not like a human,' Matthew said contemptuously. 'Fight back like a witch.'

He vanished again. This time he wasn't in the tree, nor could I feel his cold eyes on me.

'I'm tired. I'm going back to the house.' After I'd taken only three steps in that direction, there was a whoosh. Matthew had slung me over his shoulder, and I was moving – fast – the opposite way.

'You aren't going anywhere.'

'Sarah and Em will be out here if you keep this up.' One of them was bound to sense that something was wrong. And if *they* didn't, Tabitha would surely kick up a fuss.

'No they won't.' Matthew set me on my feet deeper in the woods. 'They promised not to leave the house – not if you screamed, no matter what danger they sensed.'

I crept backward, wanting to put some distance between me and his huge black eyes. The muscles in his legs coiled to spring. When I turned to make a run for it, he was already in front of me. I turned in the opposite direction, but he was there. A breeze stirred around my feet.

'Good,' he said with satisfaction. Matthew's body lowered into the same position he'd taken stalking the stag at Sept-Tours, and the menacing growl started up again.

The breeze moved around my feet in gusts, but it didn't increase. The tingling descended from my elbows into my nails. Instead of pushing back my frustration, I let the feeling mount. Arcs of blue electricity moved between my fingers.

'Use your power,' he rasped. 'You can't fight me any other way.'

My hands waved in his direction. It didn't seem very threatening, but it was all I could think of. Matthew proved just how worthless my efforts were by pouncing on me and spinning me around before vanishing into the trees.

'You're dead – again.' His voice came from somewhere to my right.

'Whatever you're trying to do isn't working!' I shouted in his direction.

'I'm right behind you,' he purred into my ear.

My scream split the silence of the forest, and the winds rose around me in a cyclonic cocoon. 'Stay away!' I roared.

Matthew reached for me with a determined look, his hands shooting through my windy barrier. I flung mine in his direction, instinct taking over, and a rush of air knocked him back on his heels. He looked surprised, and the predator appeared in the depths of his eyes. He came at me again in another attempt to break the wind's hold. Though I concentrated on pushing him back, the air didn't respond as I wanted it to.

'Stop trying to force it,' Matthew said. He was fearless and had made his way through the cyclone, his fingers digging into my upper arms. 'Your mother spellbound you so that no one could force your magic – not even you.'

'Then how do I call it when needed and control it when it's not?'

'Figure it out.' Matthew's snowy gaze flickered over my neck and shoulders, instinctively locating my major veins and arteries.

'I can't.' A wave of panic engulfed me. 'I'm not a witch.'

'Stop saying that. It's not true, and you know it.' He dropped me abruptly. 'Close your eyes. Start walking.'

'What?'

'I've watched you for weeks, Diana.' The way he was moving was completely feral, the smell of cloves so overpowering that my throat closed. 'You need movement and sensory deprivation so that all you can do is *feel*.' He gave me a push, and I stumbled. When I turned back, he was gone.

My eyes circled the forest. The woods were eerily silent, the animals shielding themselves from the powerful predator in their midst.

Closing my eyes, I began to breathe deeply. A breeze ruffled past me, first in one direction, then in another. It was Matthew, taunting me. I focused on my breathing, trying to be as still as the rest of the creatures in the forest, then set out.

There was a tightness between my eyes. I breathed into it, too, remembering Amira's yoga instruction and Marthe's advice to let the visions pass through me. The tightness turned to tingling and the tingling to a sense of possibility as my mind's eye – a witch's third eye – opened fully for the first time.

It took in everything that was alive in the forest – the vegetation, the energy in the earth, the water moving underneath the ground – each vital force distinct in color and shade. My mind's eye saw the rabbits crouched in the hollow of a tree, their hearts thundering in fear as they smelled the vampire. It detected the barn owls, their late-afternoon naps brought to a premature end by this creature who swung from tree limbs and jumped like a panther. The rabbits and owls knew they couldn't escape him.

'King of the beasts,' I whispered.

Matthew's low chuckle sounded through the trees.

No creature in the forest could fight Matthew and win. 'Except me,' I breathed.

My mind's eye swept over the forest. A vampire is not fully alive, and it was hard to find him amid the dazzling energy that surrounded me. Finally I located his shape, a concentration of darkness like a black hole, the edges glowing red where his preternatural life force met the vitality of the world. Instinctively turning my face in his direction alerted him to my scrutiny and he slid away, fading into the shadows between the trees.

With both eyes closed and my mind's eye open, I started walking, hoping to lure him into following. Behind me his darkness detached from a maple tree in a gash of red and black amid the green. This time my face remained pointed in the opposite direction.

'I see you, Matthew,' I said softly.

'Do you, *ma lionne*? And what will you do about it?' He chuckled again but kept stalking me, the distance between us constant.

With each step my mind's eye grew brighter, its vision more acute. There was a brushy shrub to my left, and I leaned to the right. Then there was a rock in front of me, its sharp gray edges protruding from the soil. I picked up my foot to keep from tripping.

The movement of air across my chest told me there was a small clearing. It wasn't just the life of the forest that was speaking to me now. All around me the elements were sending messages to guide my way. Earth, air, fire, and water connected with me in tiny pinpricks of awareness that were distinct from the life in the forest.

Matthew's energy focused in on itself and became darker and deeper. Then his darkness – his absence of life – arced through the air in a graceful pounce that any lion would have envied. He stretched his arms to grab me.

Fly, I thought, a second before his fingers touched my skin.

The wind rose from my body in a sudden whoosh of power. The earth released me with a gentle push upward. Just as Matthew had promised, it was easy to let my body follow where my thoughts had led. It took no more effort than following an imaginary ribbon up to the sky.

Far below, Matthew somersaulted in midair and landed lightly on his feet precisely where I'd stood a few moments before.

I soared above the treetops, my eyes wide. They felt full of the sea, as vast as the horizon, and bright with sunlight and stars. My hair floated on the currents of air, the ends of each strand turning into tongues of flame that licked my face without burning. The tendrils caressed my cheeks with warmth as the cold air swept past. A raven swooped by me in flight, amazed at this strange new creature sharing her airspace.

Matthew's pale face was turned up to me, his eyes full of wonder. When our gazes connected, he smiled.

It was the most beautiful thing I'd ever seen. There was a surge of desire, strong and visceral, and a rush of pride that he was mine.

My body dove toward him, and Matthew's face turned in an instant from wonder to wariness. He snarled, unsure of me, his instincts warning that I might attack.

Pulling back on my nosedive, I descended more slowly until our eyes were level, my feet streaming behind in Sarah's rubber boots. The wind whipped a lock of my flaming hair in his direction.

Don't harm him. My every thought was focused on his safety. Air and fire obeyed me, and my third eye drank in his darkness.

'Stay away from me,' he growled, 'just for a moment.' Matthew was struggling to master his predatory instincts. He *wanted* to hunt me now. The king of beasts didn't like to be bested.

Paying no attention to his warning, I lowered my feet until they floated a few inches above the ground and held out my hand, palm upturned. My mind's eye filled with the image of my own energy: a shifting mass of silver and gold, green and blue, shimmering like a morning star. I scooped some of it up, watching as it rolled from my heart through my shoulder and arm.

A pulsing, swirling ball of sky, sea, earth, and fire sat in my palm. The ancient philosophers would have called it a microcosm – a little world that contained fragments of me as well as the larger universe.

'For you,' I said, voice hollow. My fingers tipped toward him.

Matthew caught the ball as it fell. It moved like quicksilver, molding itself to his cold flesh. My energy came to a quivering rest in the scoop of his hand.

'What is it?' he asked, distracted from his urge to hunt by the gleaming substance.

'Me,' I said simply. Matthew fixed his attention on my face, his pupils engulfing the gray-green irises in a wave of black. 'You won't hurt me. I won't hurt you either.'

The vampire cradled my microcosm carefully in his hand, afraid to spill a drop.

'I still don't know how to fight,' I said sadly. 'All I can do is fly away.'

'That's the most important lesson a warrior learns, witch.' Matthew's mouth turned what was usually a derogatory term among vampires into an endearment. 'You learn how to pick your battles and let go of those you can't win, to fight another day.'

'Are you afraid of me?' I asked, my body still hovering.

'No,' he said.

My third eye tingled. He was telling the truth. 'Even though I have that inside me?' My glance flickered to the glowing, twitching mass in his hand.

Matthew's face was guarded and careful. 'I've seen powerful witches before. We still don't know all that's inside you, though. We have to find out.'

'I never wanted to know.'

'Why, Diana? Why wouldn't you want these gifts?' He drew his hand tighter, as if my magic might be snatched away and destroyed before he understood its possibilities.

'Fear? Desire?' I said softly, touching his strong cheekbones with the tips of my fingers, shocked anew at the power of my love for him. Remembering what his daemon friend Bruno had written in the sixteenth century, I quoted it again. ' "*Desire urges me on, as fear bridles me.*" Doesn't that explain everything that happens in the world?'

'Everything but you,' he told me, his voice thick. 'There's no accounting for you.'

My feet touched the ground, and I pulled my fingers from his face, slowly unfurling them. My body seemed to know the smooth movement, though my mind was quick to register its strangeness. The piece of myself that I'd given to Matthew leaped from his hand into mine. My palm closed around it, the energy quickly reabsorbed. There was the tingle of a witch's power, and I recognized it as my own. I hung my head, frightened by the creature I was becoming.

Matthew's fingertip drew aside my curtain of hair. 'Nothing will hide you from this magic – not science, not willpower, not concentration. It will always find you. And you can't hide from me either.'

'That's what my mother said in the oubliette. She knew about us.' Frightened by the memory of La Pierre, my mind's eye closed protectively. I shivered, and Matthew drew me near. It was no warmer in his cold arms, but it felt far safer.

'Perhaps that made it easier for them, to know you wouldn't be alone,' Matthew said softly. His lips were cool and firm, and my own parted to draw him closer. He buried his face in my neck, and I heard him take in my scent with a sharp inhalation. He pulled away with reluctance, smoothing my hair and tucking the parka more closely around me.

'Will you train me to fight, like one of your knights?'

Matthew's hands stilled. 'They knew how to defend themselves long before coming to me. But I've trained warriors in the past – humans, vampires, daemons. Even Marcus, and God knows he was a challenge. Never a witch, though.'

'Let's go home.' My ankle was still throbbing, and I was ready to drop with fatigue. After a few halting steps, Matthew swung me onto his back like a child and walked through the twilight with my arms clasped around his neck. 'Thank you again for finding me,' I whispered when the house came into view. He knew this time I wasn't talking about La Pierre.

'I'd stopped looking long ago. But there you were in the Bodleian Library on Mabon. A historian. A witch, no less.' Matthew shook his head in disbelief.

'That's what makes it magic,' I said, planting a soft kiss above his collar. He was still purring when he put me down on the back porch.

Matthew went to the woodshed to get more logs for the fire, leaving me to make peace with my aunts. Both of them looked uneasy.

'I understand why you kept it secret,' I explained, giving Em a hug that made her gasp with relief, 'but Mom told me the time for secrets was over.'

'You've seen Rebecca?' Sarah said carefully, her face white.

'In La Pierre. When Satu tried to frighten me into cooperating with her.' I paused. 'Daddy, too.'

'Was she . . . were they happy?' Sarah had to choke out the words. My grandmother was standing behind her, watching with concern.

'They were together,' I said simply, looking out the window to see if Matthew was headed back to the house.

'And they were with you,' Em said firmly, her eyes full. 'That means they were more than happy.'

My aunt opened her mouth to say something, thought better of it, and closed it again.

'What, Sarah?' I said, putting a hand on her arm.

'Did Rebecca speak to you?' Her voice was hushed.

'She told me stories. The same stories she told me when I was a little girl – about witches and princes and a fairy godmother. Even though she and Daddy spellbound me, Mom tried to find a way to make me remember my magic. But I wanted to forget.'

'That last summer, before your mom and dad went to Africa, Rebecca asked me what made the most lasting impression on children. I told her it was the stories their parents read to them at night, and all the messages about hope and strength and love that were embedded in them.' Em's eyes were spilling over now, and she dashed her tears away.

'You were right,' I said softly.

Though the three witches had made amends, when Matthew came into the kitchen, his arms laden with wood, Sarah pounced on him.

'Don't ever ask me to ignore Diana's cries for help, and don't you ever threaten her again – no matter what the reason. If you do, I'll put a spell on you that will make you wish you'd never been reborn. Got that, vampire?'

'Of course, Sarah,' Matthew murmured blandly, in perfect imitation of Ysabeau.

We ate dinner at the table in the family room. Matthew and Sarah were in an uneasy state of détente, but open warfare threatened when my aunt saw that there wasn't a scrap of meat in sight.

'You're smoking like a chimney,' Em said patiently when Sarah grumbled about the lack of 'real' food. 'Your arteries will thank me.'

'You didn't do it for me,' Sarah said, shooting Matthew an accusatory glance. 'You did it so he wouldn't feel the urge to bite Diana.'

Matthew smiled mildly and pulled the cork from a bottle he'd brought in from the Range Rover. 'Wine, Sarah?'

She eyed the bottle suspiciously. 'Is that imported?'

'It's French,' he said, pouring the deep red liquid into her water tumbler.

'I don't like the French.'

'Don't believe everything you read. We're much nicer than we're made out to be,' he said, teasing her into a grudging smile. 'Trust me, we'll grow on you.' As if to prove it, Tabitha jumped onto his shoulder from the floor and sat there like a parrot for the rest of the meal.

Matthew drank his wine and chatted about the house, asking Sarah and Em about the state of the farm and the place's history. I was left with little to do but watch them – these three creatures I loved so much – and wolf down large quantities of chili and cornbread.

When at last we went up to bed, I slipped between the sheets naked, desperate to feel Matthew's cool body against mine. He joined me, drawing me toward his bare flesh.

'You're warm,' he said, snuggling more tightly against me.

'Mmm. You smell good,' I said, my nose pressed against his chest. The key turned itself in the lock. It had been there when I woke up that afternoon. 'Was the key in the bureau?'

'The house had it.' His laughter rumbled underneath me. 'It shot out of the floorboards next to the bed at an angle, hit the wall over the light switch, and slid down. When I didn't pick it up straightaway, it flew across the room and landed in my lap.'

I laughed while his fingers drifted around my waist. He studiously avoided Satu's marks.

'You have your battle scars,' I said, hoping to soothe him. 'Now I have mine.'

His lips found mine unerringly in the darkness. One hand moved to the small of my back, covering the crescent moon. The other traveled between my shoulder blades, blotting out the star. No magic was necessary to understand his pain and regret. It was everywhere evident – in his gentle touch, the words he murmured in the darkness, and his body that was so solid next to mine. Gradually he let go of the worst of his fear and anger. We touched with mouths and fingers, our initial urgency slowing to prolong the joy of reunion.

Stars burst into life at the peak of my pleasure, and a few still hung beneath the ceiling, sparkling and sputtering out the remainder of their brief lives while we lay in each other's arms and waited for the morning to find us.

CHAPTER 34

M atthew planted a kiss on my shoulder before the sun rose, and then he slipped downstairs. My muscles were tight in an uncustomary combination of stiffness and languor. At last I dragged myself out of bed and went looking for him.

I found Sarah and Em instead. They were standing by the back window, each clutching a steaming cup of coffee. Glancing over their shoulders, I went to fill the kettle. Matthew could wait — tea could not.

'What are you looking at?' I expected them to name some rare bird.

'Matthew.'

I backed up a few steps.

'He's been out there for hours. I don't think he's moved a muscle. A raven flew by. I believe she plans to perch on him,' Sarah continued, taking a sip of her coffee.

Matthew was standing with his feet rooted in the earth and his arms stretched out to the sides at shoulder level, index fingers and thumbs gently touching. In his gray T-shirt and black yoga pants, he did look like an unusually well-dressed, robust scarecrow.

'Should we be worried about him? He's got nothing on his feet.' Em stared at Matthew over the edge of her coffee cup. 'He must be freezing.'

'Vampires burn, Em. They don't freeze. He'll come in when he's ready.'

After filling the kettle, I made tea and stood with my aunts, silently watching Matthew. On my second cup, he finally lowered his arms and folded over at the waist. Sarah and Em moved hastily away from the window.

'He knows we've been watching him. He's a vampire, remember?' I laughed and pushed Sarah's boots on over my wool socks and a frayed pair of leggings and clomped outside.

'Thank you for being so patient,' Matthew said after he'd gathered me into his arms and soundly kissed me good morning.

I was still clutching my mug, which had been in danger of spilling tea down his back. 'Meditation is the only rest you get. I'm not about to disturb it. How long have you been out here?'

'Since dawn. I needed time to think.'

'The house does that to people. There are too many voices, too much going on.' It was chilly, and I snuggled inside my sweatshirt with the faded maroon bobcat on the back.

Matthew touched the dark circles under my eyes. 'You're still exhausted. Some meditation wouldn't do you any harm either, you know.'

My sleep had been fitful, full of dreams, snatches of alchemical poetry, and mumbled tirades directed at Satu. Even my grandmother had been worried. She'd been leaning against the chest of drawers with a watchful expression while Matthew soothed me back to sleep.

'I was strictly forbidden to do anything resembling yoga for a week.'

'And you obey your aunt when she sets down these rules?' Matthew's eyebrow made a question mark.

'Not usually.' I laughed, grabbing him by the sleeve to pull him back inside.

Matthew had my tea out of my hands and was lifting me out of Sarah's boots in an instant. He arranged my body and stood behind me. 'Are your eyes closed?'

'Now they are,' I said, closing my eyes and digging my toes through my socks into the cold earth. Thoughts chased around in my mind like playful kittens.

'You're thinking,' Matthew said impatiently. 'Just breathe.'

My mind and breath settled. Matthew came around and lifted my arms, pressing my thumbs to the tips of my ring fingers and pinkies.

'Now I look like a scarecrow, too,' I said. 'What am I doing with my hands?'

'Prana mudra,' Matthew explained. 'It encourages the life force and is good for healing.'

As I stood with arms outstretched and palms facing the sky, the silence and peace worked their way through my battered body. After about five minutes, the tightness between my eyes lifted and my mind's eye opened. There was a corresponding, subtle change inside me – an ebb and flow like water lapping on the shore. With each breath I took, a drop of cold, fresh water formed in my palm. My mind remained resolutely blank, unconcerned that I might be engulfed in witchwater even as the level of water in my hands slowly rose.

My mind's eye brightened, focusing on my surroundings. When it did, I saw the fields around the house as never before. Water ran beneath the ground's surface in deep blue veins. The roots of the apple trees extended into them, and finer webs of water shimmered in the leaves as they rustled in the morning breeze. Underneath my feet the water flowed toward me, trying to understand my connection to its power.

Calmly I breathed in and out. The water level in my palms rose and fell in response to the changing tides within and underneath me. When I could control the water no longer, the mudras broke open, water cascading from my flattened palms. I was left standing in the middle of the backyard, eyes open and arms outstretched, a small puddle on the ground under each hand.

My vampire stood twelve feet away from me with a proud look on his face, his arms crossed. My aunts were on the back porch, astonished.

'That was impressive,' Matthew murmured, bending to pick up the stone-cold mug of tea. 'You're going to be as good at this as you are at your research, you know. Magic's not just emotional and mental – it's physical, too.'

'Have you coached witches before?' I slid back into Sarah's boots, my stomach rumbling loudly.

'No. You're my one and only.' Matthew laughed. 'And yes, I know you're hungry. We'll talk more about this after breakfast.' He held out his hand, and we walked together toward the house.

'You can make a lot of money water witching, you know,' Sarah called as we approached. 'Everyone in town needs a new well, and old Harry was buried with his dowsing rod when he died last year.'

'I don't need a dowsing rod – I *am* a dowsing rod. And if you're thinking of digging, do it there.' I pointed to a cluster of apple trees that looked less scraggy than the rest.

Inside, Matthew boiled fresh water for my tea before turning his attention to the *Syracuse Post-Standard*. It could not compete with *Le Monde*, but he seemed content. With my vampire occupied, I ate slice after slice of bread hot from the toaster. Em and Sarah refilled their coffee cups and looked warily at my hands every time I got near the electrical appliances.

'This is going to be a three-pot morning,' Sarah announced, dumping the used grounds out of the coffeemaker. I looked at Em in alarm.

It's mostly decaf, she said without speaking, her lips pressed together in silent mirth. *I've been adulterating it for years.* Like text messaging, silent speech was useful if you wanted to have a private discussion in this house.

Smiling broadly, I returned my attention to the toaster. I scraped the last of the butter onto my toast and wondered idly if there was more.

A plastic tub appeared at my elbow.

I turned to thank Em, but she was on the other side of the kitchen. So was Sarah. Matthew looked up from his paper and stared at the refrigerator.

The door was open, and the jams and mustards were rearranging themselves on the top shelf. When they were in place, the door quietly closed.

'Was that the house?' Matthew asked casually.

'No,' Sarah replied, looking at me with interest. 'That was Diana.'

'What happened?' I gasped, looking at the butter.

'You tell us,' Sarah said crisply. 'You were fiddling with your ninth piece of toast when the refrigerator opened and the butter sailed out.'

'All I did was wonder if there was more.' I picked up the empty container.

Em clapped her hands with delight at my newest sign of power, and Sarah insisted that I try to get something else out of the refrigerator. No matter what I called, it refused to come.

'Try the cabinets,' Em suggested. 'The doors aren't as heavy.'

Matthew had been watching the activity with interest. 'You just wondered about the butter because you needed it?'

I nodded.

'And when you flew yesterday, did you command the air to cooperate?'

'I thought "Fly," and I flew. I needed to do it more than I needed the butter, though – you were about to kill me. Again.'

'Diana flew?' Sarah asked faintly.

'Is there anything you need now?' inquired Matthew.

'To sit down.' My knees felt a little shaky.

A kitchen stool traveled across the floor and parked obligingly beneath my backside.

Matthew smiled with satisfaction and picked up the paper. 'It's just as I thought,' he murmured, returning to the headlines.

Sarah tore the paper from his hands. 'Stop grinning like the Cheshire cat. What did you think?'

At the mention of another member of her species, Tabitha strutted into the house through the cat door. With a look of complete devotion, she dropped a tiny, dead field mouse at Matthew's feet.

'*Merci, ma petite*,' Matthew said gravely. 'Unfortunately, I am not hungry at present.'

Tabitha yowled in frustration and hauled her offering off to the corner, where she punished it by batting it between her paws for failing to please Matthew.

Undeterred, Sarah repeated her question. 'What do you think?'

'The spells that Rebecca and Stephen cast ensure that nobody can force the magic from Diana. Her magic is bound up in necessity. Very clever.' He smoothed out his rumpled paper and resumed reading.

'Clever and impossible,' Sarah grumbled.

'Not impossible,' he replied. 'We just have to think like her parents. Rebecca had seen what would happen at La Pierre – not every detail, but she knew that her daughter would be held captive by a witch. Rebecca also knew that she would get away. That's why the spellbinding held fast. Diana didn't need her magic.'

'How are we supposed to teach Diana how to control her power if she can't command it?' demanded my aunt.

The house gave us no chance to consider the options. There was a sound like cannon fire, followed by tap dancing.

'Oh, hell.' Sarah groaned. 'What does it want now?'

Matthew put down his paper. 'Is something wrong?'

'The house wants us. It slams the coffin doors on the keeping room and then moves the furniture around to get our attention.' I licked the butter off my fingers and padded through the family room. The lights flickered in the front hall.

'All right, all right,' Sarah said testily. 'We're coming.'

We followed my aunts into the keeping room. The house sent a wing chair careening across the floor in my direction.

'It wants Diana,' Emily said unnecessarily.

The house might have wanted me, but it didn't anticipate the interference of a protective vampire with quick reflexes. Matthew shot his foot out and stopped the chair before it hit me in the back of the knees. There was a crack of old wood on strong bones.

'Don't worry, Matthew. The house only wants me to sit down.' I did so, waiting for its next move.

'The house needs to learn some manners,' he retorted.

'Where did Mom's rocker come from? We got rid of it years

ago,' Sarah said, pursing her lips at the old chair near the front window.

'The rocking chair is back, and so is Grandma,' I said. 'She said hello when we arrived.'

'Was Elizabeth with her?' Em sat on the uncomfortable Victorian sofa. 'Tall? Serious expression?'

'Yes. I didn't get a good look, though. She was mostly behind the door.'

'The ghosts don't hang around much these days,' Sarah said. 'We think she's some distant Bishop cousin who died in the 1870s.'

A ball of green wool and two knitting needles rocketed down the chimney and rolled across the hearth.

'Does the house think I should take up knitting?' I asked.

'That's mine – I started making a sweater a few years ago, and then one day it disappeared. The house takes all sorts of things and keeps them,' Em explained to Matthew as she retrieved her project. She gestured at the sofa's hideous floral upholstery. 'Come sit with me. Sometimes it takes the house awhile to get to the point. And we're missing some photographs, a telephone book, the turkey platter, and my favorite winter coat.'

Matthew, not surprisingly, found it difficult to relax, given that a porcelain serving dish might decapitate him, but he did his best. Sarah sat in a Windsor chair nearby, looking annoyed.

'Come on, out with it,' she snapped several minutes later. 'I've got things to do.'

A thick brown envelope wormed its way through a crack in the green-painted paneling next to the fireplace. Once it had worked itself free, it shot across the keeping room and landed, faceup, in my lap.

'*Diana*' was scrawled on the front in blue ballpoint ink. My mother's small, feminine handwriting was recognizable from permission slips and birthday cards.

'It's from Mom.' I looked at Sarah, amazed. 'What is it?'

She was equally startled. 'I have no idea.'

Inside were a smaller envelope and something carefully wrapped in layers of tissue paper. The envelope was pale green, with a darker green border around the edges. My father had helped me pick it out for my mother's birthday. It had a cluster of white and green lily of the valley raised up slightly on the corner of each page. My eyes filled with tears.

'Do you want to be alone?' Matthew asked quietly, already on his feet.

'Stay. Please.'

Shaking, I tore the envelope open and unfolded the papers inside. The date underneath the lily of the valley – August 13, 1983 – caught my eye immediately.

My seventh birthday. It had fallen only days before my parents left for Nigeria.

I galloped through the first page of my mother's letter. The sheet fell from my fingers, drifted onto the floor, and came to rest at my feet.

Em's fear was palpable. 'Diana? What is it?'

Without answering, I tucked the rest of the letter next to my thigh and picked up the brown envelope the house had been hiding for my mother. Pulling at the tissue paper, I wriggled a flat, rectangular object into the open. It was heavier than it should be, and it tingled with power.

I recognized that power and had felt it before.

Matthew heard my blood begin to sing. He came to stand behind me, his hands resting lightly on my shoulders.

I unfolded the wrappings. On top, blocking Mathew's view and separated by still more tissue from what lay beneath, was a piece of ordinary white paper, the edges brown with age. There were three lines written on it in spidery script.

' "*It begins with absence and desire,*" ' I whispered around the tightness in my throat. ' "*It begins with blood and fear.*" '

' "*It begins with a discovery of witches,*" ' Matthew finished, looking over my shoulder.

After I'd delivered the note to Matthew's waiting fingers, he held it to his nose for a moment before passing it silently to Sarah. I lifted the top sheet of tissue paper.

Sitting in my lap was one of the missing pages from Ashmole 782.

'Christ,' he breathed. 'Is that what I think it is? How did your mother get it?'

'She explains in the letter,' I said numbly, staring down at the brightly colored image.

Matthew bent and picked up the dropped sheet of stationery. '*"My darling Diana,"*' he read aloud. '*"Today you are seven – a magical age for a witch, when your powers should begin to stir and take shape. But your powers have been stirring since you were born. You have always been different."*'

My knees shifted under the image's uncanny weight.

'*"That you are reading this means that your father and I succeeded. We were able to convince the Congregation that it was your father – and not you – whose power they sought. You mustn't blame yourself. It was the only decision we could possibly make. We trust that you are old enough now to understand."*' Matthew gave my shoulder a gentle squeeze before continuing.

'*"You're old enough now, too, to take up the hunt that we began when you were born – the hunt for information about you and your magic. We received the enclosed note and drawing when you were three. It came to us in an envelope with an Israeli stamp. The department secretary told us there was no return address or signature – just the note and the picture.*

'*"We've spent much of the past four years trying to make sense of it. We couldn't ask too many questions. But we think the picture shows a wedding."*'

'It is a wedding – the chemical marriage of mercury and sulfur. It's a crucial step in making the philosopher's stone.' My voice sounded harsh after Matthew's rich tones.

It was one of the most beautiful depictions of the chemical wedding I'd ever seen. A golden-haired woman in a pristine white gown held a white rose in one hand. It was an offering to her pale, dark-haired husband, a message that she was pure and worthy of him. He wore black-and-red robes and clasped her other hand. He, too, held a rose – but his was as red as fresh-spilled blood, a token of love and death. Behind the couple, chemicals and metals were personified as wedding guests, milling around in a landscape of trees and rocky hills. A whole menagerie of animals gathered to witness the ceremony: ravens, eagles, toads, green lions, peacocks, pelicans. A unicorn and a wolf stood side by side in the center background, behind the bride and groom. The whole scene was gathered within the outspread wings of a phoenix, its feathers flaming at the edges and its head curved down to watch the scene unfold.

'What does it mean?' Em asked.

'That someone has been waiting for Matthew and me to find each other for a long time.'

'How could that picture possibly be about you and Matthew?' Sarah craned her neck to inspect it more closely.

'The queen is wearing Matthew's crest.' A gleaming silver-and-gold circlet held back the bride's hair. In its midst, resting against her forehead, was a jewel in the shape of a crescent moon with a star rising above it.

Matthew reached past the picture and took up the rest of my mother's letter. 'Do you mind if I continue?' he asked gently.

I shook my head, the page from the manuscript still resting on my knees. Em and Sarah, wary of its power, were exercising proper caution in the presence of an unfamiliar bewitched object and remained where they were.

' "*We think the woman in white is meant to be you, Diana. We are less certain about the identity of the dark man. I've seen him in your dreams, but he's hard to place. He walks through your future, but he's in the past as well. He's always in shadows, never in the light. And though he's dangerous, the shadowed man doesn't pose a threat to you. Is he with you now? I hope so. I wish I could have known him. There is so much I would have liked to tell him about you.*" ' Matthew's voice stumbled over the last words.

' "*We hope the two of you will be able to discover the source of this picture. Your father thinks it's from an old book. Sometimes we see text moving on the back of the page, but then the words disappear again for weeks, even months, at a time.*" '

Sarah sprang out of her chair. 'Give me the picture.'

'It's from the book I told you about. The one in Oxford.' I handed it to her reluctantly.

'It feels so heavy,' she said, walking toward the window with a frown. She turned the picture over and angled the page this way and that. 'But I don't see any words. Of course, it's no wonder. If this page was removed from the book it belongs to, then the magic is badly damaged.'

'Is that why the words I saw were moving so fast?'

Sarah nodded. 'Probably. They were searching for this page and couldn't find it.'

'Pages.' This was a detail I hadn't told Matthew.

'What do you mean, "pages"?' Matthew came around the chair, flicking little shards of ice over my features.

'This isn't the only page that's missing from Ashmole 782.'

'How many were removed?'

'Three,' I whispered. 'Three pages were missing from the front of the manuscript. I could see the stubs. It didn't seem important at the time.'

'Three,' Matthew repeated. His voice was flat, and it sounded as though he were about to break something apart with his bare hands.

'What does it matter whether there are three pages missing or three hundred?' Sarah was still trying to detect the hidden words. 'The magic is still broken.'

'Because there are three types of otherworldly creatures.' Matthew touched my face to let me know he wasn't angry at me.

'And if we have one of the pages . . .' I started.

'Then who has the others?' Em finished.

'Damn it all to hell, why didn't Rebecca tell us about this?' Sarah, too, sounded like she wanted to destroy something. Emily took the picture from her hands and laid it carefully on an antique tea table.

Matthew continued reading. ' "*Your father says that you will have to travel far to unlock its secrets. I won't say more, for fear this note will fall into the wrong hands. But you will figure it out, I know.*" '

He handed the sheet to me and went on to the next. ' "*The house wouldn't have shared this letter if you weren't ready. That means you also know that your father and I spellbound you. Sarah will be furious, but it was the only way to protect you from the Congregation before the shadowed man was with you. He will help you with your magic. Sarah will say it's not his business because he's not a Bishop. Ignore her."'*

Sarah snorted and looked daggers at the vampire.

'"*Because you will love him as you love no one else, I tied your magic to your feelings for him. Even so, only you will have the ability to draw it into the open. I'm sorry about the panic attacks. They were the only thing I could think of. Sometimes you're too brave for your own good. Good luck learning your spells — Sarah is a perfectionist.*"'

Matthew smiled. 'There always was something odd about your anxiety.'

'Odd how?'

'After we met in the Bodleian, it was almost impossible to provoke you into panicking.'

'But I panicked when you came out of the fog by the boathouses.'

'You were startled. Your instincts should have been screaming with panic whenever I was near. Instead you came closer and closer.' Matthew dropped a kiss on my head and turned to the last page.

'"*It's hard to know how to finish this letter when there is so much in my heart. The past seven years have been the happiest of my life. I wouldn't give up a moment of our precious time with you — not for an ocean of power or a long, safe life without you. We don't know why the goddess entrusted you to us, but not a day has passed that we didn't thank her for it.*"'

I suppressed a sob but couldn't stop the tears.

'"*I cannot shield you from the challenges you will face. You will know great loss and danger, but also great joy. You may doubt your instincts in the years to come, but your feet have been walking this path since the moment you were born. We knew it when you came into the world a caulbearer. You've remained between worlds ever since. It's who you are, and your destiny. Don't let anyone keep you from it.*"'

'What's a caulbearer?' I whispered.

'Someone born with the amniotic sac still intact around them. It's a sign of luck,' Sarah explained.

Matthew's free hand cradled the back of my skull. 'Much more than luck is associated with the caul. In times past, it was thought to foretell the birth of a great seer. Some believed it was a sign you would become a vampire, a witch, or a werewolf.' He gave me a lopsided grin.

'Where is it?' Em asked Sarah.

Matthew and I swung our heads in quick unison. 'What?' we asked simultaneously.

'Cauls have enormous power. Stephen and Rebecca would have saved it.'

We all looked at the crack in the paneling. A phonebook landed in the grate with a thud, sending a cloud of ash into the room.

'How do you save a caul?' I wondered aloud. 'Do you put it in a baggie or something?'

'Traditionally, you press a piece of paper or fabric onto the baby's face and the caul sticks to it. Then you save the paper,' explained Em.

All eyes swiveled to the page from Ashmole 782. Sarah picked it up and studied it closely. She muttered a few words and stared some more.

'There's something uncanny about this picture,' she reported, 'but it doesn't have Diana's caul attached to it.'

That was a relief. It would have been one strange thing too many.

'So is that all, or does my sister have any other secrets she'd like to share with us?' Sarah asked tartly. Matthew frowned at her. 'Sorry, Diana,' she murmured.

'There's not much more. Can you manage it, *mon coeur*?'

I grabbed his free hand and nodded. He perched on one of the chair's padded arms, which creaked slightly under his weight.

' "*Try not to be too hard on yourself as you journey into the future. Keep your wits about you, and trust your instincts. It's not much in the way of advice, but it's all that a mother can give. We can scarcely bear leaving you, but the only alternative is to risk losing you forever. Forgive us. If we have wronged you, it was because we loved you so much. Mom."*'

The room was silent, and even the house was holding its breath. A sound of loss started somewhere deep within me just before a tear fell from my eye. It swelled to the size of a softball and hit the floor with a splash. My legs felt liquid.

'Here it comes,' Sarah warned.

Matthew dropped the page from the letter and swept me out of the chair and through the front door. He set me on the driveway, and my toes gripped the soil. The witchwater released harmlessly into the ground while my tears continued to flow. After a few moments, Matthew's hands slid around my waist from behind. His body shielded me from the rest of the world, and I relaxed against his chest.

'Let it all go,' he murmured, his lips against my ear.

The witchwater subsided, leaving behind an aching sense of loss that would never go away completely.

'I wish they were here,' I cried. 'My mother and father would know what to do.'

'I know you miss them. But they didn't know what to do – not really. Like all parents, they were just doing their best from moment to moment.'

'My mother saw you, and what the Congregation might do. She was a great seer.'

'And so will you be, one day. Until then we're going to have to manage without knowing what the future holds. But there are two of us. You don't have to do it by yourself.'

We went back inside, where Sarah and Em were still scrutinizing the page from the manuscript. I announced that more tea and a fresh pot of coffee were in order, and Matthew came with me into the kitchen, though his eyes lingered on the brightly colored image.

The kitchen looked like a war zone, as usual. Every surface was covered with dishes. While the kettle came to the boil and the coffee brewed, I rolled up my sleeves to do the dishes.

Matthew's phone buzzed in his pocket. He was ignoring it, intent on putting more logs into the already overloaded fireplace.

'You should get that,' I said, squirting dish liquid into the sink.

He pulled out his phone. His face revealed that this was not a call he wanted to take. '*Oui?*'

It must be Ysabeau. Something had gone wrong, someone wasn't where he or she was supposed to be – it was impossible for me to follow the particulars given their rapid exchange, but Matthew's annoyance was clear. He barked out a few orders and disconnected the phone.

'Is Ysabeau all right?' I swished my fingers through the warm water, hoping there was no new crisis.

Matthew's hands pushed my shoulders gently away from my ears, kneading the tight muscles. 'She's fine. This had nothing to do with Ysabeau. It was Alain. He was doing some business for the family and ran into an unexpected situation.'

'Business?' I picked up the sponge and started washing. 'For the Knights of Lazarus?'

'Yes,' he said shortly.

'Who is Alain?' I set the clean plate in the drainer.

'He began as my father's squire. Philippe couldn't manage without him, in war or in peace, so Marthe made him a vampire. He knows every aspect of the brotherhood's business. When my father died, Alain transferred his loyalty from Philippe to me. He called to warn me that Marcus wasn't pleased to receive my message.'

I turned to meet his eyes. 'Was it the same message you gave to Baldwin at La Guardia?'

He nodded.

'I'm nothing but trouble to your family.'

'This isn't a de Clermont family matter anymore, Diana. The Knights of Lazarus protect those who cannot protect themselves. Marcus knew that when he accepted a place among them.'

Matthew's phone buzzed again.

'And that will be Marcus,' he said grimly.

'Go talk to him in private.' I tilted my chin toward the door.

Matthew kissed my cheek before pushing the green button on his phone and heading into the backyard.

'Hello, Marcus,' he said warily, shutting the door behind him.

I continued moving the soapy water over the dishes, the repetitive motion soothing.

'Where's Matthew?' Sarah and Em were standing in the doorway, holding hands.

'Outside, talking to England,' I said, nodding again in the direction of the back door.

Sarah got another clean mug out of the cabinet – the fourth she'd used that morning, by my count – and filled it with fresh coffee. Emily picked up the newspaper. Still, their eyes tingled with curiosity. The back door opened and closed. I braced for the worst.

'How is Marcus?'

'He and Miriam are on their way to New York. They have something to discuss with you.' Matthew's face looked like a thundercloud.

'Me? What is it?'

'He wouldn't tell me.'

'Marcus didn't want you to be on your own with only witches to keep you company.' I smiled at him, and some of the tension left his face.

'They'll be here by nightfall and will check in to the inn we passed on our way through town. I'll go by and see them tonight. Whatever they need to tell you can wait until tomorrow.' Matthew's worried eyes darted to Sarah and Em.

I turned to the sink again. 'Call him back, Matthew. They should come straight here.'

'They won't want to disturb anyone,' he said smoothly. Matthew didn't want to upset Sarah and the rest of the Bishops by bringing two more vampires into the house. But my mother would never have let Marcus travel so far only to stay in a hotel.

Marcus was Matthew's son. He was my son.

My fingers prickled, and the cup I was washing slipped from my grasp. It bobbed in the water for a few moments, then sank.

'No son of mine is checking in to a hotel. He belongs in the Bishop house, with his family, and Miriam shouldn't be alone. They're both staying here, and that's final,' I said firmly.

'Son?' said Sarah faintly.

'Marcus is Matthew's son, which makes him my son, too. That makes him a Bishop, and this house belongs to him as much as it does to you, or me, or Em.' I turned to face them, grabbing the sleeves of my shirt tightly with my wet hands, which were shaking.

My grandmother drifted down the hallway to see what the fuss was about.

'Did you hear me, Grandma?' I called.

I believe we all heard you, Diana, she said in her rustly voice.

'Good. No acting up. And that goes for every Bishop in this house – living and dead.'

The house opened its front and back doors in a premature gesture of welcome, sending a gust of chilly air through the downstairs rooms.

'Where will they sleep?' Sarah grumbled.

'They don't sleep, Sarah. They're vampires.' The prickling in my fingers increased.

'Diana,' Matthew said, 'please step away from the sink. The electricity, *mon coeur*.'

I gripped my sleeves tighter. The edges of my fingers were bright blue.

'We get the message,' Sarah said hastily, eyeing my hands. 'We've already got one vampire in the house.'

'I'll get their rooms ready,' Emily said, with a smile that looked genuine. 'I'm glad we'll have a chance to meet your son, Matthew.'

Matthew, who had been leaning against an ancient wooden cupboard, pulled himself upright and walked slowly toward me. 'All right,' he said, drawing me from the sink and tucking my head under his chin. 'You've made your point. I'll call Marcus and let him know they're welcome here.'

'Don't tell Marcus I called him my son. He may not want a stepmother.'

'You two will have to sort that out,' Matthew said, trying to suppress his amusement.

'What's so funny?' I tipped my face up to look at him.

'With all that's happened this morning, the one thing you're worried about is whether Marcus wants a stepmother. You confound me.' Matthew shook his head. 'Are all witches this surprising, Sarah, or is it just Bishops?'

Sarah considered her answer. 'Just Bishops.'

I peeked around Matthew's shoulder to give her a grateful smile.

My aunts were surrounded by a mob of ghosts, all of whom were solemnly nodding in agreement.

CHAPTER 35

After the dishes were done, Matthew and I gathered up my mother's letter, the mysterious note, and the page from Ashmole 782 and carried them into the dining room. We spread the papers out on the room's vast, well-worn table. These days it was seldom used, since it made no sense for two people to sit at the end of a piece of furniture designed to easily seat twelve. My aunts joined us, steaming mugs of coffee in their hands.

Sarah and Matthew crouched over the page from the alchemical manuscript.

'Why is it so heavy?' Sarah picked the page up and weighed it carefully.

'I don't feel any special weightiness,' Matthew confessed, taking it from her hands, 'but there's something odd about the way it smells.'

Sarah gave it a long sniff. 'No, it just smells old.'

'It's more than that. I know what old smells like,' he said sardonically.

Em and I, on the other hand, were more interested in the enigmatic note.

'What do you think it means?' I asked, pulling out a chair and sitting down.

'I'm not sure.' Em hesitated. 'Blood usually signifies family, war, or death. But what about absence? Does it mean this page is absent from the book? Or did it warn your parents that they wouldn't be present as you grew up?'

'Look at the last line. Did my parents discover something in Africa?'

'Or were *you* the discovery of witches?' Em suggested gently.

'The last line must be about Diana's discovery of Ashmole 782,' Matthew chimed in, looking up from the chemical wedding.

'You believe that everything is about me and that manuscript,' I grumbled. 'The note mentions the subject of your All Souls essay – fear and desire. Don't you think that's strange?'

'No stranger than the fact that the white queen in this picture is wearing my crest.' Matthew brought the illustration over to me.

'She's the embodiment of quicksilver – the principle of volatility in alchemy,' I said.

'Quicksilver?' Matthew looked amused. 'A metallic perpetual-motion machine?'

'You could say that.' I smiled, too, thinking of the ball of energy I'd given him.

'What about the red king?'

'He's stable and grounded.' I frowned. 'But he's also supposed to be the sun, and he's not usually depicted wearing black and red. Usually he's just red.'

'So maybe the king isn't me and the queen isn't you.' He touched the white queen's face delicately with his fingertip.

'Perhaps,' I said slowly, remembering a passage from Matthew's *Aurora* manuscript. ' "*Attend to me, all people, and listen to me, all who inhabit the world: my beloved, who is red, has called to me. He sought, and found me. I am the flower of the field, a lily growing in the valley. I am the mother of true love, and of fear, and of understanding, and blessed hope.*" '

'What is that?' Matthew touched my face now. 'It sounds biblical, but the words aren't quite right.'

'It's one of the passages on the chemical wedding from the *Aurora Consurgens*.' Our eyes locked, held. When the air became heavy, I changed the subject. 'What did my father mean when he said we'd have to travel far to figure out the picture's significance?'

'The stamp came from Israel. Maybe Stephen meant we would have to return there.'

'There are a lot of alchemical manuscripts in Jerusalem at the Hebrew University. Most of them belonged to Isaac Newton.' Given Matthew's history with the place, not to mention the Knights of Lazarus, it was not a city I was eager to visit.

'Israel didn't count as "traveling far" for your father,' said Sarah, sitting opposite. Em walked around the table and joined her.

'What *did* qualify?' Matthew picked up my mother's letter and scanned the last page for further clues.

'The Australian outback. Wyoming. Mali. Those were his favorite places to timewalk.'

The word cut through me with the same intensity as 'spellbound' had only a few days before. I knew that some witches could move between past, present, and future, but I'd never thought to ask whether anyone in my own family had the ability. It was rare – almost as rare as witchfire.

'Stephen Proctor could travel in time?' Matthew's voice assumed the deliberate evenness it often did when magic was mentioned.

Sarah nodded. 'Yes. Stephen went to the past or the future at least once a year, usually after the annual anthropologists' convention in December.'

'There's something on the back of Rebecca's letter.' Em bent her neck to see underneath the page.

Matthew quickly flipped it over. 'I dropped the page to get you outside before the witchwater broke. I didn't see this. It's not your mother's handwriting,' he said, passing it to me.

The handwriting on the penciled note had elongated loops and spiky peaks. '*Remember, Diana: "The most beautiful experience we can have is the mysterious. It is the fundamental emotion that stands at the cradle of true art and true science. Whoever does not know it and can no longer wonder, no longer marvel, is as good as dead, and his eyes are dimmed."*' I'd seen that hand somewhere before. In the recesses of my memory, I flipped through images trying to locate its source but without success.

'Who would have written a quote from Albert Einstein on the back of Mom's note?' I asked Sarah and Em, angling the page to face them and struck again by its familiarity.

'That looks like your dad. He took calligraphy lessons. Rebecca poked fun at him for it. It made his handwriting look so old-fashioned.'

Slowly I turned the page over, scrutinizing the writing again. It did look nineteenth-century in style, like the handwriting of the clerks employed to compile the catalogs in the Bodleian back during Victoria's reign. I stiffened, looked more closely at the writing, shook my head.

'No, it's not possible.' There was no way my father could have been one of those clerks, no way he could have written the nineteenth-century subtitle on Ashmole 782.

But my father could timewalk. And the message from Einstein was unquestionably meant for me. I dropped the page onto the table and put my head in my hands.

Matthew sat next to me and waited. When Sarah made an impatient sound, he silenced her with a decisive gesture. Once my mind stopped spinning, I spoke.

'There were two inscriptions on the first page of the manuscript. One was in ink, written by Elias Ashmole: "*Anthropologia, or a treatis containing a short description of Man.*" The other was in a different hand, in pencil: "*in two parts: the first Anatomical, the second Psychological.*"'

'The second inscription had to be written much later,' Matthew observed. 'There was no such thing as "psychology" during Ashmole's lifetime.'

'I thought it dated from the nineteenth century.' I pulled my father's note toward me. 'But this makes me think my father wrote it.'

The room fell silent.

'Touch the words,' Sarah finally suggested. 'See what else they say.'

My fingers passed lightly over the penciled letters. Images

bloomed from the page, of my father in a dark frock coat with wide lapels and a high black cravat, crouched over a desk covered with books. There were other images, too, of him in his study at home wearing his familiar corduroy jacket, scrawling a note with a No. 2 pencil while my mother looked over his shoulder, weeping.

'It was him.' My fingers lifted from the page, shaking visibly.

Matthew took my hand in his. 'That's enough bravery for one day, *ma lionne*.'

'But your father didn't remove the chemical wedding from the book at the Bodleian,' mused Em, 'so what was he doing there?'

'Stephen Proctor was bewitching Ashmole 782 so that no one but his daughter could call it from the stacks.' Matthew sounded sure.

'So that's why the spell recognized me. But why didn't it behave the same way when I recalled it?'

'You didn't need it. Oh, you *wanted* it,' Matthew said with a wry smile when I opened my mouth to protest, 'but that's different. Remember, your parents bound your magic so that your power couldn't be forced from you. The spell on the manuscript was no different.'

'When I first called Ashmole 782, all I needed was to check the next item off my to-do list. It's hard to believe that something so insignificant could trigger such a reaction.'

'Your mother and father couldn't have foreseen everything – such as the fact that you would be a historian of alchemy and would regularly work at the Bodleian. Could Rebecca timewalk, too?' Matthew asked Sarah.

'No. It's rare, of course, and the most adept timewalkers are well versed in witchcraft as well. Without the right spells and precautions, you can easily end up somewhere you don't want to be, no matter how much power you have.'

'Yes,' Matthew said drily. 'I can think of any number of times and places you would want to avoid.'

'Rebecca went with Stephen sometimes, but he had to carry her.' Sarah smiled at Em. 'Do you remember Vienna? Stephen decided he was going to take her waltzing. He spent a full year figuring out which bonnet she should wear for the journey.'

'You need three objects from the particular time and place you want to travel back to. They keep you from getting lost,' Em continued. 'If you want to go to the future, you have to use witchcraft, because it's the only way to direct yourself.'

Sarah picked up the picture of the chemical wedding, no longer interested in timewalking. 'What's the unicorn for?'

'Forget the unicorn, Sarah,' I said impatiently. 'Daddy couldn't have wanted me to go back in the past and get the manuscript. What did he think, that I'd timewalk and snatch it before it was bewitched? What if I ran into Matthew by accident? Surely that would mess up the space–time continuum.'

'Oh, relativity.' Sarah's voice was dismissive. 'As an explanation that only goes so far.'

'Stephen always said timewalking was like changing trains,' Em said. 'You get off one train, then wait at the station until there's a place for you on a different train. When you timewalk, you depart from the here and now and you're held out of time until there's room for you sometime else.'

'That's similar to the way vampires change lives,' Matthew mused. 'We abandon one life – arrange a death, a disappearance, a change of residence – and look for another one. You'd be amazed at how easily people walk away from their homes, jobs, and families.'

'Surely someone notices that the John Smith they knew last week doesn't look the same,' I protested.

'That's even more amazing,' Matthew admitted. 'So long as you pick carefully, no one says a word. A few years in the Holy Land, a life-threatening illness, the likelihood of losing an inheritance – all provide excellent excuses for creatures and humans to turn a blind eye.'

'Well, whether it's possible or not, I can't timewalk. It wasn't on the DNA report.'

'Of course you can timewalk. You've been doing it since you were a child.' Sarah sounded smug as she discredited Matthew's scientific findings. 'The first time you were three. Your parents were scared to death, the police were called out – it was quite a scene. Four hours later they found you sitting in the kitchen high chair eating a slice of birthday cake. You must have been hungry and gone back to your own birthday party. After that, whenever you disappeared, we figured you were sometime else and you'd turn up. And you disappeared a lot.'

My alarm at the thought of a toddler traveling through time gave way to the realization that I had the power to answer any historical question. I brightened considerably.

Matthew had already figured this out and was waiting patiently for me to catch up. 'No matter what your father wanted, you aren't going back to 1859,' he said firmly, turning the chair around so I faced him. 'Time is not something you're going to meddle with. Understood?'

Even after assuring him that I would stay in the present, no one left me alone for an instant. The three of them silently passed me from one to the other in choreography worthy of Broadway. Em followed me upstairs to make sure there were towels, though I knew perfectly well where the linen closet was. When I came out of the bathroom, Matthew was lying on the bed fiddling with his phone. He stayed upstairs when I went down to make a cup of tea, knowing that Sarah and Em would be waiting for me in the family room.

Marthe's tin was in my hands, and I felt guilty for missing yesterday and breaking my promise to her. Determined to have some tea today, I filled the kettle and opened the black metal box. The smell of rue triggered a sharp recollection of being swept into the air by Satu. Gripping the lid more tightly, I focused on the other scents and happier memories of Sept-Tours. I missed its gray stone walls, the gardens, Marthe, Rakasa – even Ysabeau.

'Where did you get that, Diana?' Sarah came in the kitchen and pointed at the tin.

'Marthe and I made it.'

'That's his mother's housekeeper? The one who made the medicine for your back?'

'*Marthe* is *Ysabeau*'s housekeeper, yes.' I put a slight emphasis on their proper names. 'Vampires have names, just like witches. You need to learn them.'

Sarah sniffed. 'I would have thought you'd go to the doctor for a prescription, not depend on old herbal lore.'

'Dr Fowler will fit you in if you want something more reliable.' Em had come in, too. 'Not even Sarah is much of an advocate of herbal contraception.'

I hid my confusion by plopping a tea bag into the mug, keeping my mind blank and my face hidden. 'This is fine. There's no need to see Dr Fowler.'

'True. Not if you're sleeping with a vampire. They can't reproduce – not in any way that contraception is going to prevent. All you have to watch out for is teeth on your neck.'

'I know, Sarah.'

But I didn't. Why had Marthe taught me so carefully how to make a completely unnecessary tea? Matthew had been clear that he couldn't father children as warmbloods did. Despite my promise to Marthe, I dumped the half-steeped cup down the sink and threw the bag in the trash. The tin went on the top shelf in the cupboard, where it would be safely out of sight.

By late afternoon, in spite of many conversations about the note, the letter, and the picture, we were no closer to understanding the mystery of Ashmole 782 and my father's connection to it. My aunts started to make dinner, which meant that Em roasted a chicken while Sarah drank a glass of bourbon and criticized the quantity of vegetables being prepared. Matthew prowled around the kitchen island, uncharacteristically restless.

'Come on,' he said, grabbing my hand. 'You need some exercise.'

It was he who needed fresh air, not I, but the prospect of going outdoors was enticing. A search in the mudroom closet revealed an old pair of my running shoes. They were worn, but they fit better than Sarah's boots.

We made it as far as the first apple trees before Matthew swung me around and pressed me between his body and one of the old, gnarled trunks. The low canopy of branches shielded us from the house's sight.

Despite my being trapped, there was no answering rush of witchwind. There were plenty of other feelings, though.

'Christ, that house is crowded,' Matthew said, pausing just long enough to get the words out before refastening his lips on mine.

We'd had too little time alone since he'd returned from Oxford. It seemed a lifetime ago, but it was only days. One of his hands slid into the waistband of my jeans, his fingers cool against my bare flesh. I shivered with pleasure, and he drew me closer, his other hand locating the rounded curves of my breast. We pressed the length of our bodies against each other, but he kept looking for new ways to connect.

Finally there was only one possibility left. For a moment it seemed Matthew intended to consummate our marriage the old-fashioned way – standing up, outdoors, in a blinding rush of physical need. His control returned, however, and he pulled away.

'Not like this,' he rasped, his eyes black.

'I don't care.' I pulled him back against me.

'I do.' There was a soft, ragged expulsion of air as Matthew breathed a vampire's sigh. 'When we make love for the first time, I want you to myself – not surrounded by other people. And I'll want you for more than the few snatched moments we'd have now, believe me.'

'I want you, too,' I said, 'and I'm not known for my patience.'

His lips drew up into a smile, and he made a soft sound of agreement.

Matthew's thumb stroked the hollow in my throat, and my blood leaped. He put his lips where his thumb had been, pressing them softly against the outward sign of the vitality that pulsed beneath the surface. He traced a vein up the side of my neck toward my ear.

'I'm enjoying learning where you like to be touched. Like here.' Matthew kissed behind my ear. 'And here.' His lips moved to my eyelids, and I made a soft sound of pleasure. 'And here.' He ran his thumb over my lower lip.

'Matthew,' I whispered, my eyes pleading.

'What, *mon coeur*?' He watched, fascinated, as his touch drew fresh blood to the surface.

I didn't answer but pulled him to me, unconcerned with the cold, the growing darkness, and the rough bark beneath my sore back. We remained there until Sarah called from the porch.

'You didn't get very far, did you?' Her snort carried clear across the field. 'That hardly qualifies as exercise.'

Feeling like a schoolgirl caught necking in the driveway, I pulled my sweatshirt into the proper position and headed back to the house. Matthew chuckled and followed.

'You look pleased with yourself,' Sarah said when he stepped into the kitchen. Standing under the bright lights, he was every inch a vampire – and a self-satisfied one, at that. But his eyes were no longer restless, and for that I was grateful.

'Leave him alone.' Em's voice was uncharacteristically sharp. She handed me the salad and pointed me to the table in the family room where we usually ate. 'We saw a fair amount of that apple tree ourselves while Diana was growing up.'

'Hmph,' Sarah said. She picked up three wineglasses and waved them in Matthew's direction. 'Got any more of that wine, Casanova?'

'I'm French, Sarah, not Italian. And I'm a vampire. I always have wine,' Matthew said with a wicked smile. 'There's no danger of running out either. Marcus will bring more. He's not French – or Italian either, alas – but his education compensated for it.'

We sat around the table, and the three witches proceeded to demolish Em's roast chicken and potatoes. Tabitha sat next to Matthew, her tail swishing flirtatiously across his feet every few minutes. He kept the wine flowing into Sarah's glass, and I sipped at my own. Em asked repeatedly if he wanted to taste anything, but Matthew declined.

'I'm not hungry, Emily, but thank you.'

'Is there anything at all that you *would* eat?' Em wasn't used to people refusing her food.

'Nuts,' I said firmly. 'If you have to buy him food, get him nuts.'

Em hesitated. 'What about raw meat?'

Matthew grabbed my hand and squeezed it before I could reply. 'If you want to feed me, uncooked meat would be just fine. I like broth, too – plain, no vegetables.'

'Is that what your son and colleague eat, too, or are these just your favorite foods?'

Matthew's impatience with my earlier questions about his lifestyle and dining habits made sense to me now.

'It's pretty standard vampire fare when we're among warmbloods.' Matthew released my hand and poured himself more wine.

'You must hang out at bars a lot, what with the wine and nuts,' Sarah observed.

Em put her fork down and stared at her.

'What?' Sarah demanded.

'Sarah Bishop, if you embarrass us in front of Matthew's son, I'll never forgive you.'

My resulting fit of giggles quickly turned into full-blown laughter. Sarah was the first to join in, followed by Em. Matthew sat and smiled as if he'd been dropped into a lunatic asylum but was too polite to mention it.

When the laughter subsided, he turned to Sarah. 'I was wondering if I could borrow your stillroom to analyze the pigments used in the picture of the chemical wedding. Maybe they can tell us where and when it was made.'

'You're not going to remove anything from that picture.' The historian in me rose up in horror at the thought.

'It won't come to any harm,' Matthew said mildly. 'I do know how to analyze tiny pieces of evidence.'

'No! We should leave it alone until we know what we're dealing with.'

'Don't be so prim, Diana. Besides, it's a bit late for that when it was you who sent the book back.' Sarah stood, her eyes brightening. 'Let's see if the cookbook can help.'

'Well, well,' Em said under her breath. 'You're one of the family now, Matthew.'

Sarah disappeared into the stillroom and returned holding a leather-bound book the size of a family Bible. Within its covers was all the learning and lore of the Bishops, handed down from witch to witch for nearly four hundred years. The first name in the book was Rebecca, accompanied by the date 1617 in an ornate, round hand. Other names were sprawled down the first page in two columns, each one in a slightly different ink with a different date attached to it. The names continued onto the back of the sheet as well, with Susannahs, Elizabeths, Margarets, Rebeccas, and Sarahs dominating the list. My aunt never showed anybody this book – not even other witches. You had to be family to see her 'cookbook.'

'What is that, Sarah?' Matthew's nostrils flared at the scent of old paper, herbs, and smoke that was released as Sarah splayed its covers open.

'The Bishop grimoire.' She pointed to the first name. 'It first belonged to Rebecca Davies, Bridget Bishop's grandmother, then to her mother, Rebecca Playfer. Bridget handed the book down to her first daughter, born out of wedlock in England around 1650. Bridget was still in her teens at the time, and she named her daughter after her mother and grandmother. Unable to care for the girl, Bridget gave her up to a family in London.' Sarah made a soft sound of disgust. 'The rumors of her immorality haunted her for the rest of her life. Later her daughter Rebecca joined her and worked in her mother's tavern. Bridget was on her second husband then, and had another daughter named Christian.'

'And you're descended from Christian Bishop?' Matthew asked.

Sarah shook her head. 'Christian Oliver, you mean – Bridget's daughter from her second marriage. Edward Bishop was Bridget's third husband. No, our ancestor is Rebecca. After Bridget was executed, Rebecca legally changed her name to Bishop. Rebecca was a widow, with no husband to argue with. It was an act of defiance.'

Matthew gave me a long look. Defiance, it seemed to say, was clearly a genetic trait.

'Nobody remembers all of Bridget Bishop's many names anymore – she was married three times,' Sarah continued. 'All anyone remembers is the name she bore when she was found guilty of witchcraft and executed. Since that time the women of the family have preserved the Bishop name, regardless of marriage or of who their father was.'

'I read about Bridget's death shortly after,' Matthew said softly. 'It was a dark time for creatures. Even though the new science seemed to strip all the mystery from the world, humans were still convinced that unseen forces were all around them. They were right, of course.'

'Well, the tension between what science promised and what their common sense told them was true resulted in the deaths of hundreds of witches.' Sarah started flipping through the grimoire's pages.

'What are you looking for?' I asked, frowning. 'Was one of the Bishops a manuscript conservator? If not, you won't find much help in that spell book.'

'You don't know what is in this spell book, miss,' Sarah said serenely. 'You've never shown one bit of interest in it.'

My lips pressed into a thin line. 'Nobody is damaging that manuscript.'

'Ah, here it is.' Sarah pointed triumphantly at the grimoire. 'One of Margaret Bishop's spells from the 1780s. She was a powerful witch. "*My method for perceiving obscurities in paper or fabric.*" That's where we'll start.' She stood up, her finger marking the place.

'If you stain—' I began.

'I heard you the first two times, Diana. This is a spell for a vapor. Nothing but air will touch your precious manuscript page. Stop fussing.'

'I'll go get it,' Matthew said hastily. I shot him a filthy look.

After he returned from the dining room with the picture cradled carefully in his hands, he and Sarah went off into the stillroom together. My aunt was talking a mile a minute as Matthew listened intently.

'Who would have imagined?' said Em, shaking her head.

Em and I washed the dinner dishes and had started the process of tidying the family room, which looked like a crime scene, when a pair of headlights swept the driveway.

'They're here.' My stomach tightened.

'It'll be fine, honey. They're Matthew's family.' Em squeezed my arm encouragingly.

By the time I reached the front door, Marcus and Miriam were getting out of the car. Miriam looked awkward and out of place in a lightweight brown sweater with the sleeves rolled up to her elbows, a miniskirt, and ankle boots, her dark eyes taking in the farm and its surroundings with an attitude of disbelief. Marcus was observing the house's architecture and sniffing the breeze – which was no doubt redolent with coffee and witches – clothed in a short-sleeved T-shirt from a 1982 concert tour and a pair of jeans.

When the door swung open, Marcus's blue eyes met mine with a twinkle. 'Hi, Mom, we're home!'

'Did he tell you?' I demanded, furious with Matthew for not obeying my wishes.

'Tell me what?' Marcus's forehead creased in puzzlement.

'Nothing,' I muttered. 'Hello, Marcus. Hello, Miriam.'

'Diana.' Miriam's fine features were drawn into their familiar look of disapproval.

'Nice house.' Marcus headed up the porch stairs. He held a brown bottle in his fingers. Under the porch lights, his golden hair and polished white skin positively gleamed.

'Come in, welcome.' I hurriedly pulled him inside, hoping that no one driving by the house had glimpsed the vampire on the landing.

'How are you, Diana?' There was worry in his eyes, and his nose flared to take in my scent. Matthew had told him about La Pierre.

'I'm fine.' Upstairs, a door closed with a bang. 'No nonsense! I am deadly serious!'

'About what?' Miriam stopped in her tracks, and her flat black curls wiggled over her shoulders like snakes.

'Nothing. Don't worry about it.' Now that both vampires were safely within the walls, the house sighed.

'Nothing?' Miriam had heard the sigh, too, and her brows rose.

'The house gets a bit worried when visitors come to call, that's all.'

Miriam looked up the staircase and sniffed. 'How many residents does the house have?'

It was a simple question, for which there was no simple answer.

'Unsure,' I said shortly, lugging a duffel bag in the direction of the stairs. 'What do you have in here?'

'It's Miriam's bag. Let me.' Marcus hooked it easily with his index finger.

We went upstairs so I could show them their rooms. Em had asked Matthew outright if the two would be sharing a bed. First he'd looked shocked at the impropriety of the question, and then he'd burst into gales of laughter and assured her that if they weren't separated, there would be one dead vampire by morning. Periodically throughout the day, he'd chuckled under his breath, saying 'Marcus and Miriam. What an idea.'

Marcus was staying in the guest bedroom that used to belong to Em, and we'd put Miriam in my old attic room. Stacks of fluffy towels were waiting on their beds, and I showed each of them where the bathroom was. There wasn't much to do to get vampire guests settled – you couldn't offer them food, or a place to lie down, or much of anything in the way of creature comforts. Happily, there'd been no spectral apparitions or falling plaster to indicate the house was displeased with their presence.

Matthew certainly knew that his son and Miriam had arrived, but the stillroom was secluded enough that Sarah remained oblivious. When I led the two vampires past the keeping room, Elizabeth peeped around the door, her eyes wide as an owl's.

'Go find Grandma.' I turned to Marcus and Miriam. 'Sorry, we've got ghosts.'

Marcus covered his laugh with a cough. 'Do all of your ancestors live with you?'

Thinking of my parents, I shook my head.

'Too bad,' he murmured.

Em was waiting in the family room, her smile wide and genuine.

'You must be Marcus,' she said, getting to her feet and holding out her hand. 'I'm Emily Mather.'

'Em, this is Matthew's colleague, Miriam Shephard.'

Miriam stepped forward. Though she and Em were both fine-boned, Miriam looked like a china doll in comparison.

'Welcome, Miriam,' said Em, looking down with a smile. 'Do either of you need something to drink? Matthew opened wine.' She was entirely natural, as if vampires were always dropping by. Both Marcus and Miriam shook their heads.

'Where's Matthew?' Miriam asked, making her priorities clear. Her keen senses absorbed the details of her new environment. 'I can hear him.'

We led the two vampires toward the old wooden door that closed off Sarah's private sanctuary. Marcus and Miriam continued to take in all the scents of the Bishop house as we proceeded – the food, the clothes, the witches, the coffee, and the cat.

Tabitha came screeching out of the shadows by the fireplace, aiming straight for Miriam as if the two were deadly enemies.

Miriam hissed, and Tabitha froze in mid-hurtle. The two assessed each other, predator to predator. Tabitha was the first to avert her eyes when, after several long moments, the cat discovered an urgent need to groom herself. It was a silent acknowledgment that she was no longer the only female of consequence on the premises.

'That's Tabitha,' I said weakly. 'She's quite fond of Matthew.'

In the stillroom Matthew and Sarah were crouched over a pot of something set atop an old electric burner, rapt expressions on their faces. Bunches of dried herbs swung from the rafters, and the original colonial ovens stood ready for use, their iron hooks and cranes waiting to hold heavy cauldrons over the coals.

'The eyebright is crucial,' Sarah was explaining like a schoolmarm. 'It clears the sight.'

'That smells vile,' Miriam observed, wrinkling her tiny nose and creeping closer.

Matthew's face darkened.

'Matthew,' Marcus said evenly.

'Marcus,' his father replied.

Sarah stood and examined the newest members of the household, both of whom glowed. The stillroom's subdued light only accentuated their unnatural paleness and the startling effect of their dilated pupils. 'Goddess save us, how does anyone think you're human?'

'It's always been a mystery to me,' Miriam said, studying Sarah with equal interest. 'You're not exactly inconspicuous either, with all that red hair and the smell of henbane coming off you in waves. I'm Miriam Shephard.'

Matthew and I exchanged a long look, wondering how Miriam and Sarah were going to coexist peacefully under the same roof.

'Welcome to the Bishop house, Miriam.' Sarah's eyes narrowed, and Miriam responded in kind. My aunt turned her attention to Marcus. 'So you're his kid.' As usual, she had no patience with social niceties.

'I'm Matthew's son, yes.' Marcus, who looked like he'd seen a ghost, slowly held out a brown bottle. 'Your namesake was a healer, like you. Sarah Bishop taught me how to set a broken leg after the Battle of Bunker Hill. I still do it the way she taught me.'

Two roughly shod feet dangled over the edge of the stillroom loft.

Let's hope he's got more strength now than he did then, said a woman who was the spitting image of Sarah.

'Whiskey,' Sarah said, looking from the bottle to my son with new appreciation.

'She liked spirits. I thought you might, too.'

Both Sarah Bishops nodded.

'You thought right,' my aunt said.

'How's the potion going?' I said, trying not to sneeze in the close atmosphere.

'It needs to steep for nine hours,' Sarah said. 'Then we boil it again, draw the manuscript through the vapor, and see what we see.' She eyed the whiskey.

'Let's take a break, then. I could open that for you,' Matthew suggested, gesturing at the bottle.

'Don't mind if I do.' She took the bottle from Marcus. 'Thank you, Marcus.'

Sarah turned off the burner and clapped a lid on the pot before we all streamed into the kitchen. Matthew poured himself some wine, offered it to Miriam and Marcus, who declined again, and got Sarah some whiskey. I made myself tea – plain Lipton's from the grocery store – while Matthew asked the vampires about their trip and the state of work at the lab.

There was no trace of warmth in Matthew's voice, or any indication he was pleased by his son's arrival. Marcus shifted uneasily from one foot to the other, knowing that he wasn't welcome. I suggested we might go into the family room and sit down in hopes that some of the awkwardness would fade.

'Let's go to the dining room instead.' Sarah raised her glass to her charming great-nephew. 'We'll show them the letter. Get Diana's picture, Matthew. They should see that, too.'

'Marcus and Miriam won't be staying long,' Matthew said with quiet reproach. 'They have something to tell Diana, and then they're going back to England.'

'But they're family,' Sarah pointed out, seemingly oblivious to the tension in the room.

My aunt retrieved the picture herself while Matthew continued to glower at his son. Sarah led us to the front of the house. Matthew, Em, and I assembled on one side of the table. Miriam, Marcus, and Sarah sat on the other. Once settled, my aunt began chattering about the morning's events. Whenever she asked Matthew for some point of clarification, he bit out the answer without embellishment. Everyone in the room save Sarah seemed to understand that Matthew didn't want Miriam and Marcus to know the details of what had happened. My aunt blithely continued, finishing with a recitation of my mother's letter along with the postscript from my father. Matthew held firmly on to my hand while she did so.

Miriam took up the picture of the chemical wedding. She studied it carefully before turning her eyes to me. 'Your mother was right. This is a picture of you. Matthew, too.'

'I know,' I said, meeting her gaze. 'Do you know what it means?'

'Miriam?' Matthew said sharply.

'We can wait until tomorrow.' Marcus looked uneasy and rose to his feet. 'It's late.'

'She already knows,' Miriam said softly. 'What comes after marriage, Diana? What's the next step in alchemical transmutation after *conjunctio*?'

The room tilted, and I smelled the herbs in my tea from Sept-Tours.

'*Conceptio.*' My body turned to jelly, and I slid down the back of the chair as everything went black.

CHAPTER 36

My head was between my knees amid the utter pandemonium. Matthew's hand kept my attention glued to the pattern in the worn Oriental rug under my feet. In the background Marcus was telling Sarah that if she approached me, his father would likely rip her head off.

'It's a vampire thing,' Marcus said soothingly. 'We're very protective of our spouses.'

'When were they married?' asked Sarah, slightly dazed.

Miriam's efforts to calm Em were far less soothing. 'We call it shielding,' her bell-like soprano chimed. 'Ever seen a hawk with its prey? That's what Matthew's doing.'

'But Diana's not his prey, is she? He's not going to . . . to bite her?' Em glanced at my neck.

'I shouldn't think so,' Miriam said slowly, considering the question. 'He's not hungry, and she's not bleeding. The danger is minimal.'

'Knock it off, Miriam,' said Marcus. 'There's nothing to worry about, Emily.'

'I can sit up now,' I mumbled.

'Don't move. The blood flow to your head isn't back to normal yet.' Matthew tried not to growl at me but couldn't manage it.

Sarah made a strangled sound, her suspicions that Matthew was constantly monitoring my blood supply now confirmed.

'Do you think he'd let me walk past Diana to get her test results?' Miriam asked Marcus.

'That depends on how pissed off he is. If you'd blindsided my wife that way, I'd poleax you and then eat you for breakfast. I'd sit tight if I were you.'

Miriam's chair scraped against the floor. 'I'll risk it.' She darted past.

'Damn,' Sarah breathed.

'She's unusually quick,' Marcus reassured her, 'even for a vampire.'

Matthew maneuvered me into a sitting position. Even that gentle movement made my head feel like it was exploding and set the room whirling. I closed my eyes momentarily, and when I opened them again, Matthew's were looking back, full of concern.

'All right, *mon coeur*?'

'A little overwhelmed.'

Matthew's fingers circled my wrist to take my pulse.

'I'm sorry, Matthew,' Marcus murmured. 'I had no idea Miriam would behave like this.'

'You should be sorry,' his father said flatly, without looking up. 'Start explaining what this visit is about – quickly.' The vein throbbed in Matthew's forehead.

'Miriam—' Marcus began.

'I didn't ask Miriam. I'm asking you,' his father snapped.

'What's going on, Diana?' my aunt asked, looking wild. Marcus still had his arm around her shoulders.

'Miriam thinks the alchemical picture is about me and Matthew,' I said cautiously. 'About the stage in the making of the philosopher's stone called *conjunctio*, or marriage. The next step is *conceptio*.'

'*Conceptio*?' Sarah asked. 'Does that mean what I think it does?'

'Probably. It's Latin – for conception,' Matthew explained.

Sarah's eyes widened. 'As in children?'

But my mind was elsewhere, flipping through the pictures in Ashmole 782.

'*Conceptio* was missing, too.' I reached for Matthew. 'Someone has it, just like we have *conjunctio*.'

Miriam glided into the room with impeccable timing, carrying a sheaf of papers. 'Who do I give these to?'

After she'd gotten a look from Matthew that I hoped never to see again, Miriam's face went from white to pearl gray. She hastily handed him the reports.

'You've brought the wrong results, Miriam. These belong to a male,' said Matthew, impatiently scanning the first two pages.

'The results do belong to Diana,' Marcus said. 'She's a chimera, Matthew.'

'What's that?' Em asked. A chimera was a mythological beast that combined the body parts of a lioness, a dragon, and a goat. I looked down, half expecting to glimpse a tail between my legs.

'A person with cells that possess two or more different genetic profiles.' Matthew was staring in disbelief at the first page.

'That's impossible.' My heart gave a loud thump. Matthew circled me with his arms, holding the test results on the table in front of us.

'It's rare, but not impossible,' he said grimly, his eyes moving over the gray bars.

'My guess is VTS,' Miriam said, ignoring Marcus's warning frown. 'Those results came from her hair. There were strands of it on the quilt we took to the Old Lodge.'

'Vanishing twin syndrome,' Marcus explained, turning to Sarah. 'Did Rebecca have problems early in her pregnancy? Any bleeding or concerns about miscarriage?'

Sarah shook her head. 'No. I don't think so. But they weren't here – Stephen and Rebecca were in Africa. They didn't come back to the States until the end of her first trimester.'

Nobody had ever told me I was conceived in Africa.

'Rebecca wouldn't have known there was anything wrong.' Matthew shook his head, his mouth pressed into a hard, firm line. 'VTS happens before most women know they're pregnant.'

'So I was a twin, and Mom miscarried my sibling?'

'Your brother,' Matthew said, pointing to the test results with his free hand. 'Your twin was male. In cases like yours, the viable fetus absorbs the blood and tissues of the other. It happens quite early, and in most cases there's no evidence of the vanished twin. Does Diana's hair indicate she might possess powers that didn't show up in her other DNA results?'

'A few – timewalking, shape-shifting, divination,' his son replied. 'Diana fully absorbed most of them.'

'My brother was supposed to be the timewalker, not me,' I said slowly.

A trail of phosphorescent smudges marked my grandmother's progress as she drifted into the room, touched me lightly on the shoulder, and sat at the far end of the table.

'He would have had the genetic predisposition to control witchfire, too,' Marcus said, nodding. 'We found only the fire marker in the hair sample – no other traces of elemental magic.'

'And you don't think my mother knew about my brother?' I ran my fingertip along the bars of gray, black, and white.

'Oh, she knew.' Miriam sounded confident. 'You were born on the goddess's feast day. She named you Diana.'

'So?' I shivered, pushing aside the memory of riding through the forest in sandals and a tunic, along with the strange feeling of holding a bow and arrow that accompanied witchfire.

'The goddess of the moon had a twin – Apollo. "*This Lion maketh the Sun so soon, /To be joined to his sister, the Moon.*"' Miriam's eyes gleamed as she recited the alchemical poem. She was up to something.

'You know "The Hunting of the Green Lion."'

'I know the next verses, too: "*By way of a wedding, a wondrous thing, / This Lion should cause them to beget a king.*"'

'What is she talking about?' Sarah asked testily.

When Miriam tried to answer, Matthew shook his head. The vampire fell silent.

'The sun king and moon queen – philosophical sulfur and mercury – married and conceived a child,' I told Sarah. 'In alchemical imagery the resulting child is a hermaphrodite, to symbolize a mixed chemical substance.'

'In other words, Matthew,' Miriam interjected tartly, 'Ashmole 782 is not just about origins, nor is it just about evolution and extinction. It's about reproduction.'

I scowled. 'Nonsense.'

'You may think it's nonsense, Diana, but it's clear to me. Vampires and witches may be able to have children together after all. So might other mixed partners.' Miriam sat back in her chair triumphantly, silently inviting Matthew to explode.

'But vampires can't reproduce biologically,' Em said. 'They've never been able to. And different species can't mix like that.'

'Species change, adapting to new circumstances,' said Marcus. 'The instinct to survive through reproduction is a powerful one – certainly powerful enough to cause genetic changes.'

Sarah frowned. 'You make it sound like we're going extinct.'

'We might be.' Matthew pushed the test results into the center of the table along with the notes and the page from Ashmole 782. 'Witches are having fewer children and possess diminishing powers. Vampires are finding it harder to take a warmblood through the process of rebirth. And the daemons are more unstable than ever.'

'I still don't see why that would allow vampires and witches to share children,' Em said. 'And if there is a change, why should it begin with Diana and Matthew?'

'Miriam began to wonder while watching them in the library,' Marcus explained.

'We've seen vampires exhibit protective behavior before when they want to shield their prey or a mate. But at some point other instincts – to hunt, to feed – overwhelm the urge to protect. Matthew's protective instincts toward Diana just got stronger,' said Miriam. 'Then he started a vampire's equivalent of flashing his plumage, swooping and diving in the air to attract attention away from her.'

'That's about protecting future children,' Marcus told his father. 'Nothing else makes a predator go to those lengths.'

'Emily's right. Vampires and witches are too different. Diana and I can't have children,' Matthew said sharply, meeting Marcus's eyes.

'We don't know that. Not absolutely. Look at the spadefoot toad.' Marcus rested his elbows on the table's surface, weaving his fingers together with a loud crack of his knuckles.

'The spadefoot toad?' Sarah picked up the picture of the chemical wedding, her fingers crumpling the edge. 'Wait a minute. Is Diana the lion, the toad, or the queen in this picture?'

'She's the queen. Maybe the unicorn, too.' Marcus gently pried the page from my aunt's fingers and went back to amphibians. 'In certain situations, the female spadefoot toad will mate with a different – though not completely unrelated – species of toad. Her offspring benefit from new traits, like faster development, that help them survive.'

'Vampires and witches are not spadefoot toads, Marcus,' Matthew said coldly. 'And not all of the changes that result are positive.'

'Why are you so resistant?' Miriam asked impatiently. 'Cross-species breeding *is* the next evolutionary step.'

'Genetic supercombinations – like those that would occur if a witch and a vampire were to have children – lead to accelerated evolutionary developments. All species take such leaps. It's your own findings we're reporting back to you, Matthew,' said Marcus apologetically.

'You're both ignoring the high mortality associated with genetic supercombinations. And if you think we're going to test those odds with Diana, you are very much mistaken.' Matthew's voice was dangerously soft.

'Because she's a chimera – and AB-negative as well – she may be less likely to reject a fetus that's half vampire. She's a universal blood recipient and has already absorbed foreign DNA into her body. Like the spadefoot toad, she might have been led to you by the pressures of survival.'

'That's a hell of a lot of conjecture, Marcus.'

'Diana is different, Matthew. She's not like other witches.' Marcus's eyes flickered from Matthew to me. 'You haven't looked at her mtDNA report.'

Matthew shuffled the pages. His breath came out in a hiss.

The sheet was covered in brightly covered hoops. Miriam had written across the top in red ink '*Unknown Clan*,' accompanied by a symbol that looked like a backward *E* set at an angle with a long tail. Matthew's eyes darted over the page, and the next.

'I knew you'd question the findings, so I brought comparatives,' Miriam said quietly.

'What's a clan?' I watched Matthew carefully for a sign of what he was feeling.

'A genetic lineage. Through a witch's mitochondrial DNA, we can trace descent back to one of four women who were the female ancestors of every witch we've studied.'

'Except you,' Marcus said to me. 'You and Sarah aren't descended from any of them.'

'What does this mean?' I touched the backward *E*.

'It's an ancient glyph for *heh*, the Hebrew number five.' Matthew directed his next words to Miriam. 'How old is it?'

Miriam considered her words carefully. 'Clan Heh is old – no matter which mitochondrial-clock theory you adhere to.'

'Older than Clan Gimel?' Matthew asked, referring to the Hebrew word for the number three.

'Yes.' Miriam hesitated. 'And to answer your next question, there are two possibilities. Clan Heh could just be another line of descent from mtLilith.'

Sarah opened her mouth to ask a question, and I quieted her with a shake of my head.

'Or Clan Heh could descend from a sister of mtLilith – which would make Diana's ancestor a clan mother, but not the witches' equivalent of mtEve. In either case it's possible that without Diana's issue Clan Heh will die out in this generation.'

I slid the brown envelope from my mother in Matthew's direction. 'Could you draw a picture?' No one in the room was going to understand this without visual assistance.

Matthew's hand sped over the page, sketching out two sprawling diagrams. One looked like a snake, the other branched out like the brackets for a sports tournament. Matthew pointed to the snake. 'These are the seven known daughters of mitochondrial Eve – mtEve for short. Scientists consider them to be the most recent common matrilineal ancestors of every human of Western European descent. Each woman appears in the DNA record at a different point in history and in a different region of the globe. They once shared a common female ancestor, though.'

'That would be mtEve,' I said.

'Yes.' He pointed at the tournament bracket. 'This is what we've uncovered about the matrilineal descent of witches. There are four lines of descent, or clans. We numbered them in the order we found them, although the woman who was mother to Clan Aleph – the first clan we discovered – lived more recently than the others.'

'Define "recently," please,' Em requested.

'Aleph lived about seven thousand years ago.'

'Seven *thousand* years ago?' Sarah said incredulously. 'But the Bishops can only trace our female ancestors back to 1617.'

'Gimel lived about forty thousand years ago,' Matthew said grimly. 'So if Miriam is right, and Clan Heh is older, you'll be well beyond that.'

'Damn,' Sarah breathed again. 'Who's Lilith?'

'The first witch.' I drew Matthew's diagrams closer, remembering his cryptic response in Oxford to my asking if he was searching for the first vampire. 'Or at least the first witch from whom present-day witches can claim matrilineal descent.'

'Marcus is fond of the Pre-Raphaelites, and Miriam knows a lot of mythology. They picked the name,' Matthew said by way of explanation.

'The Pre-Raphaelites loved Lilith. Dante Gabriel Rossetti described her as the witch Adam loved before Eve.' Marcus's eyes turned dreamy. ' "*So went/Thy spell through him, and left his straight neck bent/And round his heart one strangling golden hair.*" '

'That's the Song of Songs,' Matthew observed. ' "*You have wounded my heart, my sister, my spouse, you have wounded my heart with one of your eyes, and with one hair of your neck.*" '

'The alchemists admired the same passage,' I murmured with a shake of my head. 'It's in the *Aurora Consurgens*, too.'

'Other accounts of Lilith are far less rapturous,' Miriam said in stern tones, drawing us back to the matter at hand. 'In ancient stories she was a creature of the night, goddess of the wind and the moon, and the mate of Samael, the angel of death.'

'Did the goddess of the moon and the angel of death have children?' Sarah asked, looking at us sharply. Once more the similarities between old stories, alchemical texts, and my relationship with a vampire were uncanny.

'Yes.' Matthew plucked the reports from my hands and put them into a tidy pile.

'So that's what the Congregation is worried about,' I said softly. 'They fear the birth of children that are neither vampire nor witch nor daemon, but mixed. What would they do then?'

'How many other creatures have been in the same position as you and Matthew, over the years?' wondered Marcus.

'How many are there now?' Miriam added.

'The Congregation doesn't know about these test results – and thank God for that.' Matthew slid the pile of papers back into the center of the table. 'But there's still no evidence that Diana can have my child.'

'So why did your mother's housekeeper teach Diana how to make that tea?' Sarah asked. 'She thinks it's possible.'

Oh, dear, my grandmother said sympathetically. *It's going to hit the fan now*.

Matthew stiffened, and his scent became overpoweringly spicy. 'I don't understand.'

'That tea that Diana and what's-her-name – Marthe – made in France. It's full of abortifacients and contraceptive herbs. I smelled them the moment the tin was open.'

'Did you know?' Matthew's face was white with fury.

'No,' I whispered. 'But no harm was done.'

Matthew stood. He pulled his phone from his pocket, avoiding my eyes. 'Please excuse me,' he said to Em and Sarah before striding out of the room.

'Sarah, how could you?' I cried after the front door shut behind him.

'He has a right to know – and so do you. No one should take drugs without consenting to it.'

'It's not your job to tell him.'

'No,' Miriam said with satisfaction. 'It was yours.'

'Stay out of this, Miriam.' I was spitting mad, and my hands were twitching.

'I'm already in it, Diana. Your relationship with Matthew puts every creature in this room in danger. It's going to change *everything*, whether you two have children or not. And now he's brought the Knights of Lazarus into it.' Miriam was as furious as I was. 'The more creatures who sanction your relationship, the likelier it is that there will be war.'

'Don't be ridiculous. War?' The marks Satu burned into my back prickled ominously. 'Wars break out between nations, not because a witch and a vampire love each other.'

'What Satu did to you was a challenge. Matthew responded just as they hoped he would: by calling on the brotherhood.' Miriam made a sound of disgust. 'Since you walked into the Bodleian, he's lost control of his senses. And the last time he lost his senses over a woman, my husband died.'

The room was quiet as a tomb. Even my grandmother looked startled.

Matthew wasn't a killer, or so I told myself over and over again. But he killed to feed himself, and he killed in angry, possessive rages. I knew both of these truths and loved him anyway. What did it say about me, that I could love such a creature so completely?

'Calm down, Miriam,' Marcus warned.

'No,' she snarled. 'This is my tale. Not yours, Marcus.'

'Then tell it,' I said tersely, gripping the edges of the table.

'Bertrand was Matthew's best friend. When Eleanor St Leger was killed, Jerusalem came to the brink of war. The English and the French were at each other's throats. He called on the Knights of Lazarus to resolve the conflict. We were nearly exposed to the humans as a result.' Miriam's brittle voice broke. 'Someone had to pay for Eleanor's death. The St Legers demanded justice. Eleanor died at Matthew's hands, but he was the grand master then, just as he is now. My husband took the blame – to protect

Matthew as well as the order. A Saracen executioner beheaded him.'

'I'm sorry, Miriam – truly sorry – about your husband's death. But I'm not Eleanor St Leger, and this isn't Jerusalem. It was a long time ago, and Matthew's not the same creature.'

'It seems like yesterday to me,' Miriam said simply. 'Once again Matthew de Clermont wants what he cannot have. He hasn't changed at all.'

The room fell silent. Sarah looked aghast. Miriam's story had confirmed her worst suspicions about vampires in general and Matthew in particular.

'Perhaps you'll remain true to him, even after you know him better,' Miriam continued, her voice dead. 'But how many more creatures will Matthew destroy on your behalf? Do you think Satu Järvinen will escape Gillian Chamberlain's fate?'

'What happened to Gillian?' Em asked, her voice rising.

Miriam opened her mouth to respond, and the fingers on my right hand curled instinctively into a loose ball. The index and middle fingers released in her direction with a tiny snap. She grabbed her throat and made a gurgling sound.

That wasn't very nice, Diana, my grandmother said with a shake of her finger. *You need to watch your temper, my girl*.

'Stay out of this, Grandma – and you too, Miriam.' I gave both of them withering glances and turned to Em. 'Gillian's dead. She and Peter Knox sent me the picture of Mom and Dad in Nigeria. It was a threat, and Matthew felt he had to protect me. It's instinctive in him, like breathing. Please try to forgive him.'

Em turned white. 'Matthew killed her for *delivering a picture*?'

'Not just for that,' said Marcus. 'She'd been spying on Diana for years. Gillian and Knox broke in to her rooms at New College and ransacked them. They were looking for DNA evidence so they could learn more about her power. If they'd found out what we now know—'

My fate would be far worse than death if Gillian and Knox knew what was in my test results. It was devastating that Matthew hadn't told me himself, though. I hid my thoughts, trying to close the shutters behind my eyes. My aunts didn't need to know that my husband kept things from me.

But there was no keeping my grandmother out. *Oh, Diana*, she whispered. *Are you sure you know what you're doing?*

'I want you all out of my house.' Sarah pushed her chair back. 'You, too, Diana.'

A long, slow shudder started in the house's old root cellar under the family room and spread throughout the floorboards. It climbed up the walls and shook the panes of glass in the windows. Sarah's chair shot forward, pressing her against the table. The door between the dining room and the family room slammed shut.

The house never likes it when Sarah tries to take charge, my grandmother commented.

My own chair pulled back and dumped me unceremoniously onto the floor. I used the table to haul myself up, and when I was on my feet, invisible hands spun me around and pushed me through the door toward the front entrance. The dining-room door crashed behind me, locking two witches, two vampires, and a ghost inside. There were muffled sounds of outrage.

Another ghost – one I'd never seen before – walked out of the keeping room and beckoned me forward. She wore a bodice covered with intricate embroidery atop a dark, full skirt that touched the floor. Her face was creased with age, but the stubborn chin and long nose of the Bishops was unmistakable.

Be careful, daughter. Her voice was low and husky. *You are a creature of the crossroads, neither here nor there. 'Tis a dangerous place to be.*

'Who are you?'

She looked toward the front door without answering. It opened soundlessly, its usually creaky hinges silent and smooth. *I have always known he would come – and come for you. My own mother told me so.*

I was torn between the Bishops and the de Clermonts, part of me wanting to return to the dining room, the other part needing to be with Matthew. The ghost smiled at my dilemma.

You have always been a child between, a witch apart. But there is no path forward that does not have him in it. Whichever way you go, you must choose him.

She disappeared, leaving fading traces of phosphorescence. Matthew's white face and hands were just visible through the open door, a blur of movement in the darkness at the end of the driveway. At the sight of him my decision became easy.

Outside, I drew my sleeves down over my hands to protect them from the chilly air. I picked up one foot . . . and when I put it down, Matthew was directly in front of me, his back turned. It had taken me a single step to travel the length of the driveway.

He was speaking in furiously fast Occitan. Ysabeau must be on the other end.

'Matthew.' I spoke softly, not wanting to startle him.

He whipped around with a frown. 'Diana. I didn't hear you.'

'No, you wouldn't have. May I speak to Ysabeau, please?' I reached for the phone.

'Diana, it would be better—'

Our families were locked in the dining room, and Sarah was threatening to throw us all out. We had enough problems without severing ties with Ysabeau and Marthe.

'What was it that Abraham Lincoln said about houses?'

' "*A house divided against itself cannot stand*," ' Matthew said, a puzzled look on his face.

'Exactly. Give me the phone.' Reluctantly he did so.

'Diana?' Ysabeau's voice had an uncharacteristic edge.

'No matter what Matthew has said, I'm not angry with you. No harm was done.'

'Thank you,' she breathed. 'I have been trying to tell him – it was only a feeling that we had, something half remembered from very long ago. Diana was the goddess of fertility then. Your scent reminds me of those times, and of the priestesses who helped women conceive.'

Matthew's eyes touched me through the darkness.

'You'll tell Marthe, too?'

'I will, Diana.' She paused. 'Matthew has shared your test results and Marcus's theories with me. It is a sign of how much they have startled him, that he told your tale. I do not know whether to weep with joy or sorrow at the news.'

'It's early days, Ysabeau – maybe both?'

She laughed softly. 'It will not be the first time my children have driven me to tears. But I wouldn't give up the sorrow if it meant giving up the joy as well.'

'Is everything all right at home?' The words escaped before I thought them through, and Matthew's eyes softened.

'Home?' The significance of the word was not lost on Ysabeau either. 'Yes, we are all well here. It is very . . . quiet since you both left.'

My eyes filled with tears. Despite Ysabeau's sharp edges, there was something so maternal about her. 'Witches are noisier than vampires, I'm afraid.'

'Yes. And happiness is always louder than sadness. There hasn't been enough happiness in this house.' Her voice grew brisk. 'Matthew has said everything to me that he needs to say. We must hope the worst of his anger has been spent. You will take care of each other.' Ysabeau's last sentence was a statement of fact. It was what the women in her family – my family – did for those they loved.

'Always.' I looked at my vampire, his white skin gleaming in the dark, and pushed the red button to disconnect the line. The fields on either side of the driveway were frost-covered, the ice crystals catching the faint traces of moonlight coming through the clouds.

'Did you suspect, too? Is that why you won't make love to me?' I asked Matthew.

'I told you my reasons. Making love should be about intimacy, not just physical need.' He sounded frustrated at having to repeat himself.

'If you don't want to have children with me, I *will* understand,' I said firmly, though part of me quietly protested.

His hands were rough on my arms. 'Christ, Diana, how can you think that I wouldn't want our children? But it might be dangerous — for you, for them.'

'There's always risk with pregnancy. Not even you control nature.'

'We have no idea what our children would be. What if they shared my need for blood?'

'All babies are vampires, Matthew. They're all nourished with their mother's blood.'

'It's not the same, and you know it. I gave up all hope of children long ago.' Our eyes met, searching for reassurance that nothing between us had changed. 'But it's too soon for me to imagine losing you.'

And I couldn't bear losing our children.

Matthew's unspoken words were as clear to me as an owl hooting overhead. The pain of Lucas's loss would never leave him. It cut deeper than the deaths of Blanca or Eleanor. When he lost Lucas, he lost part of himself that could never be recovered.

'So you've decided. No children. You're sure.' I rested my hands on his chest, waiting for the next beat of his heart.

'I'm not sure of anything,' Matthew said. 'We haven't had time to discuss it.'

'Then we'll take every precaution. I'll drink Marthe's tea.'

'You'll do a damn sight more than that,' he said grimly. 'That stuff is better than nothing, but it's a far cry from modern medicine. Even so, no human form of contraception may be effective when it comes to witches and vampires.'

'I'll take the pills anyway,' I assured him.

'And what about you?' he asked, his fingers on my chin to keep me from avoiding his eyes. 'Do you want to carry my children?'

'I never imagined myself a mother.' A shadow flickered across his face. 'But when I think of your children, it feels as though it was meant to be.'

He dropped my chin. We stood silently in the darkness, his arms around my waist and my head on his chest. The air felt heavy, and I recognized it as the weight of responsibility. Matthew was responsible for his family, his past, the Knights of Lazarus – and now for me.

'You're worried that you couldn't protect them,' I said, suddenly understanding.

'I can't even protect you,' he said harshly, fingers playing over the crescent moon burned into my back.

'We don't have to decide just yet. With or without children, we already have a family to keep together.' The heaviness in the air shifted, some of it settling on my shoulders. All my life I'd lived for myself alone, pushing away the obligations of family and tradition. Even now part of me wanted to return to the safety of independence and leave these new burdens behind.

His eyes traveled up the drive to the house. 'What happened after I left?'

'Oh, what you'd expect. Miriam told us about Bertrand and Jerusalem – and let slip about Gillian. Marcus told us who broke in to my rooms. And then there's the fact that we might have started some kind of war.'

'*Dieu*, why can't they keep their mouths shut?' He ran his fingers through his hair, his regret at concealing all this from me clear in his eyes. 'At first I was sure this was about the manuscript. Then I supposed it was all about you. Now I'll be damned if I can figure out *what* it's about. Some old, powerful secret is unraveling, and we're caught up in it.'

'Is Miriam right to wonder how many other creatures are tangled in it, too?' I stared at the moon as if she might answer my question. Matthew did instead.

'It's doubtful we're the first creatures to love those we should not, and we surely won't be the last.' He took my arm. 'Let's go inside. We have some explaining to do.'

On our way up the drive, Matthew observed that explanations, like medicines, go down easier when accompanied by liquid refreshment. We entered the house through the back door to pick up the necessary supplies. While I arranged a tray, Matthew's eyes rested on me.

'What?' I looked up. 'Did I forget something?'

A smile played at the corners of his mouth. 'No, *ma lionne*. I'm just trying to figure out how I acquired such a fierce wife. Even putting cups on a tray, you look formidable.'

'I'm not formidable,' I said, tightening my ponytail self-consciously.

'Yes, you are.' Matthew smiled. 'Miriam wouldn't be in such a state otherwise.'

When we reached the door between the dining room and the family room, we listened for sounds of a battle within, but there was nothing except quiet murmurs and low conversation. The house unlocked the door and opened it for us.

'We thought you might be thirsty,' I said, putting the tray on the table.

A multitude of eyes turned in our direction – vampires, witches, ghosts. My grandmother had a whole flock of Bishops at her back, all of them rustling and shifting as they tried to adjust to having vampires in the dining room.

'Whiskey, Sarah?' Matthew asked, picking up a tumbler from the tray.

She gave him a long look. 'Miriam says that by accepting your relationship we invite war. My father fought in World War II.'

'So did mine,' Matthew said, pouring the whiskey. So had he, no doubt, but he was silent on that point.

'He always said whiskey made it possible to close your eyes at night without hating yourself for everything you'd been ordered to do that day.'

'It's no guarantee, but it helps.' Matthew held out the glass.

Sarah took it. 'Would you kill your own son if you thought he was a threat to Diana?'

He nodded. 'Without hesitation.'

'That's what he said.' Sarah nodded at Marcus. 'Get him a drink, too. It can't be easy, knowing your own father could kill you.'

Matthew got Marcus his whiskey and poured Miriam a glass of wine. I made Em a cup of milky coffee. She'd been crying and looked more fragile than usual.

'I just don't know if I can handle this, Diana,' she whispered when she took the mug. 'Marcus explained what Gillian and Peter Knox had planned. But when I think of Barbara Chamberlain and what she must be feeling now that her daughter is dead—' Em shuddered to a stop.

'Gillian Chamberlain was an ambitious woman, Emily,' said Matthew. 'All she ever wanted was a seat at the Congregation's table.'

'But you didn't have to kill her,' Em insisted.

'Gillian believed absolutely that witches and vampires should remain apart. The Congregation has never been satisfied that they fully understood Stephen Proctor's power and asked her to watch Diana. She wouldn't have rested until both Ashmole 782 and Diana were in the Congregation's control.'

'But it was just a picture.' Em wiped at her eyes.

'It was a threat. The Congregation had to understand that I was not going to stand by and let them take Diana.'

'Satu took her anyway,' Em pointed out, her voice unusually sharp.

'That's enough, Em.' I reached over and covered her hand with mine.

'What about this issue of children?' Sarah asked, gesturing with her glass. 'Surely you two won't do something so risky?'

'That's enough,' I repeated, standing and banging my hand on the table. Everyone but Matthew and my grandmother jumped in surprise. 'If we are at war, we're not fighting for a bewitched alchemical manuscript, or for my safety, or for our right to marry and have children. This is about the future of all of us.' I saw that future for just a moment, its bright potential spooling away in a thousand different directions. 'If our children don't take the next evolutionary steps, it will be someone else's children. And whiskey isn't going to make it possible for me to close my eyes and forget that. No one else will go through this kind of hell because they love someone they're not supposed to love. I won't allow it.'

My grandmother gave me a slow, sweet smile. *There's my girl. Spoken like a Bishop.*

'We don't expect anyone else to fight with us. But understand this: our army has one general. Matthew. If you don't like it, don't enlist.'

In the front hall, the old case clock began to strike midnight.

The witching hour. My grandmother nodded.

Sarah looked at Em. 'Well, honey? Are we going to stand with Diana and join Matthew's army or let the devil take the hindmost?'

'I don't understand what you all mean by war. Will there be battles? Will vampires and witches come here?' Em asked Matthew in a shaky voice.

'The Congregation believes Diana holds answers to their questions. They won't stop looking for her.'

'But Matthew and I don't have to stay,' I said. 'We can be gone by morning.'

'My mother always said my life wouldn't be worth living once it was tangled up with the Bishops,' Em said with a wan smile.

'Thank you, Em,' Sarah said simply, although her face spoke volumes.

The clock tolled a final time. Its gears whirred into place, ready to strike the next hour when it came.

'Miriam?' Matthew asked. 'Are you staying here or are you going back to Oxford?'

'My place is with the de Clermonts.'

'Diana is a de Clermont now.' His tone was icy.

'I understand, Matthew.' Miriam directed a level gaze at me. 'It won't happen again.'

'How strange,' Marcus murmured, his eyes sweeping the room. 'First it was a shared secret. Now three witches and three vampires have pledged loyalty to one another. If we had a trio of daemons, we'd be a shadow Congregation.'

'We're unlikely to run into three daemons in downtown Madison,' Matthew said drily. 'And whatever happens, what we've talked about tonight remains among the six of us – understood? Diana's DNA is no one else's business.'

There were nods all around the table as Matthew's motley army fell into line behind him, ready to face an enemy we didn't know and couldn't name.

We said our good-nights and went upstairs. Matthew kept his arm around me, guiding me through the doorframe and into the bedroom when I found it impossible to navigate the turn on my own. I slid between the icy sheets, teeth chattering. When his cool body pressed against mine, the chattering ceased.

I slept heavily, waking only once. Matthew's eyes glittered in the darkness, and he pulled me back so that we lay like spoons.

'Sleep,' he said, kissing me behind the ear. 'I'm here.' His cold hand curved over my belly, already protecting children yet to be born.

CHAPTER 37

Over the next several days, Matthew's tiny army learned the first requirement of war: allies must not kill each other.

Difficult as it was for my aunts to accept vampires into their house, it was the vampires who had the real trouble adjusting. It wasn't just the ghosts and the cat. More than nuts would have to be kept in the house if vampires and warmbloods were to live in such close quarters. The very next day Marcus and Miriam had a conversation with Matthew in the driveway, then left in the Range Rover. Several hours later they returned bearing a small refrigerator marked with a red cross and enough blood and medical supplies to outfit an army field hospital. At Matthew's request, Sarah selected a corner of the stillroom to serve as the blood bank.

'It's just a precaution,' Matthew assured her.

'In case Miriam gets the munchies?' Sarah picked up a bag of O-negative blood.

'I ate before I left England,' Miriam said primly, her tiny bare feet slipping quietly over the stone floors as she put items away.

The deliveries also included a blister pack of birth-control pills inside a hideous yellow plastic case with a flower molded into the lid. Matthew presented them to me at bedtime.

'You can start them now or wait a few days until your period starts.'

'How do you know when my period is going to start?' I'd finished my last cycle the day before Mabon — the day before I'd met Matthew.

'I know when you're planning on jumping a paddock fence. You can imagine how easy it is for me to know when you're about to bleed.'

'Can you be around me while I'm menstruating?' I held the case gingerly as if it might explode.

Matthew looked surprised, then chuckled. '*Dieu*, Diana. There wouldn't be a woman alive if I couldn't.' He shook his head. 'It's not the same thing.'

I started the pills that night.

As we adjusted to the close quarters, new patterns of activity developed in the house – many of them around me. I was never alone and never more than ten feet away from the nearest vampire. It was perfect pack behavior. The vampires were closing ranks around me.

My day was divided into zones of activity punctuated by meals, which Matthew insisted I needed at regular intervals to fully recover from La Pierre. He joined me in yoga between breakfast and lunch, and after lunch Sarah and Em tried to teach me how to use my magic and perform spells. When I was tearing my hair out with frustration, Matthew would whisk me off for a long walk before dinner. We lingered around the table in the family room after the warmbloods had eaten, talking about current events and old movies. Marcus unearthed a chessboard, and he and his father often played together while Em and I cleaned up.

Sarah, Marcus, and Miriam shared a fondness for film noir, which now dominated the house's TV-viewing schedule. Sarah had discovered this happy coincidence when, during one of her habitual bouts of insomnia, she went downstairs in the middle of the night and found Miriam and Marcus watching *Out of the Past*. The three also shared a love of Scrabble and popcorn. By the time the rest of the house awoke, they'd transformed the family room into a cinema and everything had been swept off the coffee table save a game board, a cracked bowl full of lettered tiles, and two battered dictionaries.

Miriam proved to be a genius at remembering archaic seven-letter words.

' "Smoored"!' Sarah was exclaiming one morning when I came downstairs. 'What the hell kind of word is "smoored"? If you mean those campfire desserts with marshmallows and graham crackers, you've spelled it wrong.'

'It means "smothered,"' Miriam explained. 'It's what we did to fires to keep them banked overnight. We smoored them. Look it up if you don't believe me.'

Sarah grumbled and retreated to the kitchen for coffee.

'Who's winning?' I inquired.

'You need to ask?' The vampire smiled with satisfaction.

When not playing Scrabble or watching old movies, Miriam held classes covering Vampires 101. In the space of a few afternoons, she managed to teach Em the importance of names, pack behavior, possessive rituals, preternatural senses, and dining habits. Lately talk had turned to more advanced topics, such as how to slay a vampire.

'No, not even slicing our necks open is foolproof, Em,' Miriam told her patiently. The two were sitting in the family room while I made tea in the kitchen. 'You want to cause as much blood loss as possible. Go for the groin as well.'

Matthew shook his head at the exchange and took the opportunity (since everyone else was otherwise engaged) to pin me behind the refrigerator door. My shirt was askew and my hair tumbling around my ears when our son came into the room with an armload of wood.

'Did you lose something behind the refrigerator, Matthew?' Marcus's face was the picture of innocence.

'No,' Matthew purred. He buried his face in my hair so he could drink in the scent of my arousal. I swatted ineffectually at his shoulders, but he just held me tighter.

'Thanks for replenishing the firewood, Marcus,' I said breathlessly.

'Should I go get more?' One blond eyebrow arched up in perfect imitation of his father.

'Good idea. It will be cold tonight.' I twisted my head to reason with Matthew, but he mistook it as an invitation to kiss me again. Marcus and the wood supply faded into inconsequence.

When not lying in wait in dark corners, Matthew joined Sarah and Marcus in the most unholy trio of potion brewers since

Shakespeare put three witches around a cauldron. The vapor Sarah and Matthew brewed up for the picture of the chemical wedding hadn't revealed anything, but this didn't deter them. They occupied the stillroom at all hours, consulting the Bishop grimoire and making strange concoctions that smelled bad, exploded, or both. On one occasion Em and I investigated a loud bang followed by the sound of rolling thunder.

'What are you three up to?' Em asked, hands on hips. Sarah's face was covered in gray soot, and debris was falling down the chimney.

'Nothing,' Sarah grumbled. 'I was trying to cleave the air and the spell got bent out of shape, that's all.'

'Cleaving?' I looked at the mess, astonished.

Matthew and Marcus nodded solemnly.

'You'd better clean up this room before dinner, Sarah Bishop, or I'll show you cleaving!' Em sputtered.

Of course, not all encounters between residents were happy ones. Marcus and Matthew walked together at sunrise, leaving me to the tender care of Miriam, Sarah, and the teapot. They never went far. They were always visible from the kitchen window, their heads bent together in conversation. One morning Marcus turned on his heel and stormed back to the house, leaving his father alone in the old apple orchard.

'Diana,' he growled in greeting before streaking through the family room and straight out the front door. 'I'm too damn young for this!' he shouted as he left.

His engine revved – Marcus preferred sports cars to SUVs – and the tires bit into the gravel when he reversed and pulled out of the driveway.

'What's Marcus upset about?' I asked when Matthew returned, kissing his cold cheek as he reached for the paper.

'Business,' he said shortly, kissing me back.

'You didn't make him seneschal?' Miriam asked incredulously.

Matthew flipped the paper open. 'You must have a very high opinion of me, Miriam, if you think the brotherhood has functioned for all these years without a seneschal. That position is already occupied.'

'What's a seneschal?' I put two slices of bread in the beat-up toaster. It had six slots, but only two of them worked with any reliability.

'My second in command,' Matthew said briefly.

'If he's not the seneschal, why has Marcus sped out of here?' Miriam pressed.

'I appointed him marshal,' Matthew said, scanning the headlines.

'He's the least likely marshal I've ever seen,' she said severely. 'He's a physician, for God's sake. Why not Baldwin?'

Matthew looked up from his paper and cocked his eyebrow at her. 'Baldwin?'

'Okay, not Baldwin,' Miriam hastily replied. 'There must be someone else.'

'Had I two thousand knights to choose from as I once did, there might be someone else. But there are only eight knights under my command at present — one of whom is the ninth knight and not required to fight — a handful of sergeants, and a few squires. Someone has to be marshal. I was Philippe's marshal. Now it's Marcus's turn.' The terminology was so antiquated it invited giggles, but the serious look on Miriam's face kept me quiet.

'Have you told him he's to start raising banners?' Miriam and Matthew continued to speak a language of war I didn't understand.

'What's a marshal?' The toast sprang out and winged its way to the kitchen island when my stomach rumbled.

'Matthew's chief military officer.' Miriam eyed the refrigerator door, which was opening without visible assistance.

'Here.' Matthew neatly caught the butter as it passed over his shoulder and then handed it to me with a smile, his face serene in spite of his colleague's pestering. Matthew, though a vampire, was self-evidently a morning person.

'The banners, Matthew. Are you raising an army?'

'Of course I am, Miriam. You're the one who keeps bringing up war. If it breaks out, you don't imagine that Marcus, Baldwin, and I are going to fight the Congregation by ourselves?' Matthew shook his head. 'You know better than that.'

'What about Fernando? Surely he's still alive and well.'

Matthew put his paper down and glowered. 'I'm not going to discuss my strategy with you. Stop interfering and leave Marcus to me.'

Now it was Miriam's turn to bolt. She pressed her lips tightly together and stalked out the back door, headed for the woods.

I ate my toast in silence, and Matthew returned to his paper. After a few minutes, he put it down again and made a sound of exasperation.

'Out with it, Diana. I can smell you thinking, and it's impossible for me to concentrate.'

'Oh, it's nothing,' I said around a mouthful of toast. 'A vast military machine is swinging into action, the precise nature of which I don't understand. And you're unlikely to explain it to me, because it's some sort of brotherhood secret.'

'*Dieu.*' Matthew ran his fingers through his hair until it stood on end. 'Miriam causes more trouble than any creature I've ever known, with the exception of Domenico Michele and my sister Louisa. If you want to know about the Knights, I'll tell you.'

Two hours later my head was spinning with information about the brotherhood. Matthew had sketched out an organizational flowchart on the back of my DNA reports. It was awesome in its complexity – and it didn't include the military side. That part of the operation was outlined on some ancient Harvard University letterhead left by my parents that we pulled out of the sideboard. I looked over Marcus's many new responsibilities.

'No wonder he's overwhelmed,' I murmured, tracing the lines that connected Marcus to Matthew above him and to seven master knights below, and then to the troops of vampires each would be expected to gather.

'He'll adjust.' Matthew's cold hands kneaded the tight muscles in my back, his fingers lingering on the star between my shoulder blades.

'Marcus will have Baldwin and the other knights to rely upon. He can handle the responsibility, or I wouldn't have asked him.'

Maybe, but he would never be the same after taking on this job for Matthew. Every new challenge would chip away a piece of his easygoing charm. It was painful to imagine the vampire Marcus would become.

'What about this Fernando? Will he help Marcus?'

Matthew's face grew secretive. 'Fernando was my first choice for marshal, but he turned me down. It was he who recommended Marcus.'

'Why?' From the way Miriam spoke, the vampire was a respected warrior.

'Marcus reminds Fernando of Philippe. If there is war, we'll need someone with my father's charm to convince the vampires to fight not only witches but other vampires, too.' Matthew nodded thoughtfully, his eyes on the rough outlines of his empire. 'Yes, Fernando will help him. And keep him from making too many mistakes.'

When we returned to the kitchen – Matthew in search of his newspaper and me in pursuit of an early lunch – Sarah and Em were just back from the grocery store. They unpacked boxes of microwave popcorn as well as tins of mixed nuts and every berry available in October in upstate New York. I picked up a bag of cranberries.

'There you are.' Sarah's eyes gleamed. 'Time for your lessons.'

'I need more tea first, and something to eat,' I protested, pouring the cranberries from one hand to the other in their plastic bag. 'No magic on an empty stomach.'

'Give me those,' Em said, grabbing the bag. 'You're squashing them, and they're Marcus's favorite.'

'You can eat later.' Sarah pushed me in the direction of the stillroom. 'Stop being such a baby and get moving.'

I turned out to be as hopeless at spells now as when I was a teenager. Unable to remember how they started, and given my mind's tendency to wander, I garbled the order of the words with disastrous results.

Sarah set a candle on the stillroom's wide table. 'Light it,' she commanded, turning back to the indescribably stained grimoire.

It was a simple trick that even a teenage witch could manage. When the spell emerged from my mouth, however, either the candle smoked without the wick's catching light or something else burst into flames instead. This time I set a bunch of lavender on fire.

'You can't just say the words, Diana,' Sarah lectured once she'd extinguished the flames. 'You have to concentrate. Do it again.'

I did it again – over and over. Once the candle wick sputtered with a tentative flame.

'This isn't working.' My hands were tingling, the nails blue, and I was ready to scream in frustration.

'You can command witchfire and you can't light a candle.'

'My arms move in a way that reminds you of someone who *could* command witchfire. That's not the same thing, and learning about magic is more important than this stuff,' I said, gesturing at the grimoire.

'Magic is not the only answer,' Sarah said tartly. 'It's like using a chainsaw to cut bread. Sometimes a knife will do.'

'You don't have a high opinion of magic, but I have a fair amount of it in me, and it wants to come out. Someone has to teach me how to control it.'

'I can't.' Sarah's voice was tinged with regret. 'I wasn't born with the ability to summon witchfire or command witchwater. But I can damn well see to it that you can learn to light a candle with one of the simplest spells ever devised.'

Sarah was right. But it took so long to master the craft, and spells would be no help if I started to spout water again.

While I returned to my candle and mumbled words, Sarah looked through the grimoire for a new challenge.

'This is a good one,' she said, pointing to a page mottled with brown, green, and red residues. 'It's a modified apparition spell that creates what's called an echo – an exact duplicate of someone's spoken words in another location. Very useful. Let's do that next.'

'No, let's take a break.' Turning away, I picked up my foot to take a step.

The apple orchard was around me when I set it down again.

In the house Sarah was shouting. 'Diana? Where are you?'

Matthew rocketed out the door and down the porch steps. His sharp eyes found me easily, and he was at my side in a few rapid strides.

'What is this about?' His hand was on my elbow so that I couldn't disappear again.

'I needed to get away from Sarah. When I put my foot down, here I was. The same thing happened on the driveway the other night.'

'You needed an apple, too? Walking into the kitchen wouldn't have been sufficient?' The corner of Matthew's mouth twitched in amusement.

'No,' I said shortly.

'Too much all at once, *ma lionne*?'

'I'm not good at witchcraft. It's too . . .'

'Precise?' he finished.

'It takes too much patience,' I confessed.

'Witchcraft and spells may not be your weapons of choice,' he said softly, brushing my tense jaw with the back of his hand, 'but you *will* learn to use them.' The note of command was slight, but it was there. 'Let's find you something to eat. That always makes you more agreeable.'

'Are you managing me?' I asked darkly.

'You've just now noticed?' He chuckled. 'It's been my full-time job for weeks.'

Matthew continued to do so throughout the afternoon, retelling stories he'd gleaned from the paper about lost cats up trees, fire-department chili cook-offs, and impending Halloween events. By the time I'd devoured a bowl of leftovers, the food and his mindless chatter had done their work, and it was possible to face Sarah and the Bishop grimoire again. Back in the stillroom, Matthew's words came back to me whenever I threatened to abandon Sarah's detailed instructions, refocusing my attempts to conjure fire, voices, or whatever else she required.

After hours of spell casting – none of which had gone particularly well – he knocked on the stillroom door and announced it was time for our walk. In the mudroom I flung on a thick sweater, slid into my sneakers, and flew out the door. Matthew joined me at a more leisurely pace, sniffing the air appreciatively and watching the play of light on the fields around the house.

Darkness fell quickly in late October, and twilight was now my favorite time of day. Matthew might be a morning person, but his natural self-protectiveness diminished at sunset. He seemed to relax into the lengthening shadows, the fading light softening his strong bones and rendering his pale skin a touch less otherworldly.

He grabbed my hand, and we walked in companionable silence, happy to be near each other and away from our families. At the edge of the forest, Matthew sped up and I deliberately hung back, wanting to stay outdoors as long as possible.

'Come on,' he said, frustrated at having to match my slow steps.

'No!' My steps became smaller and slower. 'We're just a normal couple taking a walk before dinner.'

'We're the least normal couple in the state of New York,' Matthew said with a smile. 'And this pace won't even make you break a sweat.'

'What do you have in mind?' It had become clear during our previous walks that the wolflike part of Matthew enjoyed romping in the woods like an oversize puppy. He was always coming up with new ways to play with my power so that learning how to use it wouldn't seem like a chore. The dull, dutiful stuff he left to Sarah.

'Tag.' He shot me a mischievous look that was impossible to resist and took off in an explosion of speed and strength. 'Catch me.'

I laughed and darted behind, my feet rising from the ground and my mind trying to capture a clear image of reaching his broad shoulders and touching them. My speed increased as the vision became more precise, but my agility left a lot to be desired. Simultaneously using the powers of flight and precognition at high speed made me trip over a shrub. Before I tumbled to the ground, Matthew had scooped me up.

'You smell like fresh air and wood smoke,' he said, nuzzling my hair.

There was an anomaly in the forest, felt rather than seen. It was a bending of the fading light, a sense of momentum, an aura of dark intention. My head swiveled over my shoulder.

'Someone's here,' I said.

The wind was blowing away from us. Matthew raised his head, trying to pick up the scent. He identified it with a sharp intake of breath.

'Vampire,' he said quietly, grabbing my hand and standing. He pushed me against the trunk of a white oak.

'Friend or foe?' I asked shakily.

'Leave. *Now*.' Matthew had his phone out, pushing the single number on speed dial that connected him to Marcus. He swore at the voice-mail recording. 'Someone is tracking us, Marcus. Get here — fast.' He disconnected and pushed another button that brought up a text-message screen.

The wind changed, and the skin around his mouth tightened.

'Christ, no.' His fingers flew over the keys, typing in two words before he flung the phone into the nearby bushes.

'*SOS. Juliette*.'

He turned, grabbing my shoulders. 'Do whatever you did in the stillroom. Pick up your feet and go back to the house. *Immediately*. I'm not asking you, Diana, I'm telling you.'

My feet were frozen and refused to obey him. 'I don't know how. I can't.'

'You will.' Matthew pushed me against the tree, his arms on either side and his back to the forest. 'Gerbert introduced me to this vampire a long time ago, and she isn't to be trusted or underestimated. We spent time together in France in the eighteenth century, and in New Orleans in the nineteenth century. I'll explain everything later. Now, go.'

'I'm not leaving without you.' My voice was stubborn. 'Who is Juliette?'

'I am Juliette Durand.' The melodious voice, accented with hints of French and something else, came from above. We both looked up. 'What trouble you two have caused.'

A stunning vampire was perched on a thick branch of a nearby maple. Her skin was the color of milk with a splash of coffee, and her hair shone in a blend of brown and copper. Clad in the colors of autumn – brown, green, and gold – she looked like an extension of the tree. Wide hazel eyes sat atop slanted cheekbones, and her bones implied a delicacy that I knew misrepresented her strength.

'I've been watching you – listening, too. Your scents are all tangled up together.' She made a quiet sound of reproof.

I didn't see her leave the branch, but Matthew did. He'd angled his body so that he would be in front of me when she landed. He faced her, lips curled in warning.

Juliette ignored him. 'I have to study her.' She tilted her head to the right and lifted her chin a touch, staring at me intently.

I frowned.

She frowned back.

Matthew shivered.

I glanced at him in concern, and Juliette's eyes followed mine.

She was imitating my every move. Her chin was jutting out at precisely the same angle as mine, her head was held at exactly the same incline. It was like looking into a mirror.

Panic flooded my system, filling my mouth with bitterness. I swallowed hard, and the vampire swallowed, too. Her nostrils flared, and she laughed, sharp and hard as diamonds.

'How have you resisted her, Matthew?' She took a long, slow breath. 'The smell of her should drive you mad with hunger. Do you remember that frightened young woman we stalked in Rome? She smelled rather like this one, I think.'

Matthew remained silent, his eyes fixed on the vampire.

Juliette took a few steps to the right, forcing him to adjust his position. 'You're expecting Marcus,' she observed sadly. 'I'm afraid he's not coming. So handsome. I would have liked to see him again. The last time we met, he was so young and impressionable. It took us weeks to sort out the mess he'd made in New Orleans, didn't it?'

An abyss opened before me. Had she killed Marcus? Sarah and Em?

'He's on the phone,' she continued. 'Gerbert wanted to be sure that your son understood the risk he's taking. The Congregation's anger is directed only at the two of you — now. But if you persist, others will pay the price as well.'

Marcus wasn't dead. Despite the relief, my blood ran cold at the expression on her face.

There was still no response from Matthew.

'Why so quiet, my love?' Juliette's warm voice belied the deadness of her eyes. 'You should be glad to see me. I'm everything you want. Gerbert made sure of that.'

He still didn't answer.

'Ah. You're silent because I've surprised you,' Juliette said, her tone strangely fractured between music and malice. 'You've surprised me, too. A witch?'

She feinted left, and Matthew swiveled to meet her. She somersaulted through the empty space where his head had been and landed at my side, fingers around my throat. I froze.

'I don't understand why he wants you so much.' Juliette's voice was petulant. 'What it is that you do? What did Gerbert fail to teach me?'

'Juliette, let her be.' Matthew couldn't risk a move in my direction for fear she'd snap my neck, but his legs were rigid with the effort to stay still.

'Patience, Matthew,' she said, bending her head.

I closed my eyes, expecting to feel teeth.

Instead cold lips pressed against mine. Juliette's kiss was weirdly impersonal as she teased my mouth with her tongue, trying to get me to respond. When I didn't, she made a sound of frustration.

'That should have helped me understand, but it didn't.' Juliette flung me at Matthew but kept hold of one wrist, her razor-sharp nails poised above my veins. 'Kiss her. I have to know how she's done it.'

'Why not leave this alone, Juliette?' Matthew caught me in his cool grip.

'I must learn from my mistakes – Gerbert's been saying so since you abandoned me in New York.' Juliette focused on Matthew with an avidity that made my flesh crawl.

'That was more than a hundred years ago. If you haven't learned your mistake by now, you're not going to.' Though Matthew's anger was not directed at me, its power made me recoil nonetheless. He was simmering with it, the rage coming from him in waves.

Juliette's nails cut into my arm. 'Kiss her, Matthew, or I will make her bleed.'

Cupping my face with one careful, gentle hand, he struggled to push up the corners of his mouth into a smile. 'It will be all right, *mon coeur.*' Matthew's pupils were dots in a sea of gray-green. One thumb stroked my jaw as he bent nearer, his lips nearly touching mine. His kiss was slow and tender, a testament of feeling. Juliette stared at us coldly, drinking in the details. She crept closer as Matthew drew away from me.

'Ah.' Her voice was blank and bitter. 'You like the way she responds when you touch her. But I can't *feel* anymore.'

I'd seen Ysabeau's anger and Baldwin's ruthlessness. I'd felt Domenico's desperation and smelled the unmistakable scent of evil that hung around Gerbert. But Juliette was different. Something fundamental was broken within her.

She released my arm and sprang out of Matthew's reach. His hands squeezed my elbows, and his cold fingers touched my hips. With an infinitesimal push, Matthew gave me another silent command to leave.

But I had no intention of leaving my husband alone with a psychotic vampire. Deep within, something stirred. Though neither witchwind nor witchwater would be enough to kill Juliette, they might distract her long enough for us to get away – but both refused my unspoken commands. And any spells I had learned over the past few days, no matter how imperfectly, had flown from my mind.

'Don't worry,' Juliette said softly to Matthew, her eyes bright. 'It will be over very quickly. I would like to linger, of course, so that we could remember what we once were to each other. But none of my touches will drive her from your mind. Therefore I must kill you and take your witch to face Gerbert and the Congregation.'

'Let Diana go.' Matthew raised his hands in truce. 'This is between us, Juliette.'

She shook her head, setting her heavy, burnished hair swaying. 'I'm Gerbert's instrument, Matthew. When he made me, he left no room for my desires. I didn't want to learn philosophy or mathematics. But Gerbert insisted, so that I could please you. And I did please you, didn't I?' Juliette's attention was fixed on Matthew, and her voice was as rough as the fault lines in her broken mind.

'Yes, you pleased me.'

'I thought so. But Gerbert already owned me.' Juliette's eyes turned to me. They were brilliant, suggesting she had fed recently. 'He will possess you, too, Diana, in ways you cannot imagine. In ways only I know. You'll be his, then, and lost to everyone else.'

'No.' Matthew lunged at Juliette, but she darted past.

'This is no time for games, Matthew,' said Juliette.

She moved quickly – too quickly for my eyes to see – then pulled slowly away from him with a look of triumph. There was a ripping sound, and blood welled darkly at his throat.

'That will do for a start,' she said with satisfaction.

There was a roaring in my head. Matthew stepped between me and Juliette. Even my imperfect warmblood nose could smell the metallic tang of his blood. It was soaking into his sweater, spreading in a dark stain across his chest.

'Don't do this, Juliette. If you ever loved me, you'll let her go. She doesn't deserve Gerbert.'

Juliette answered in a blur of brown leather and muscle. Her leg swung high, and there was a crack as her foot connected with Matthew's abdomen. He bent over like a felled tree.

'I didn't *deserve* Gerbert either.' There was a hysterical edge to Juliette's voice. 'But I deserved *you*. You belong to me, Matthew.'

My hands felt heavy, and I knew without looking that they held a bow and arrow. I backed away from the two vampires, raising my arms.

'Run!' Matthew shouted.

'No,' I said in a voice that was not my own, squinting down the line of my left arm. Juliette was close to Matthew, but I could release the arrow without touching him. When my right hand flexed, Juliette would be dead. Still, I hesitated, never having killed anyone before.

That moment was all Juliette needed. Her fingers punched through Matthew's chest, nails tearing through fabric and flesh as if both were paper. He gasped at the pain, and Juliette roared in victory.

All hesitation gone, my right hand tightened and opened. A ball of fire arced from the extended tips of my left fingers. Juliette heard the explosion of flame and smelled the sulfur in the air. She turned, her nails withdrawing from the hole in Matthew's chest. Disbelief showed in her eyes before the spitting ball of black, gold, and red enveloped her. Her hair caught fire first, and she reeled in panic. But I had anticipated her, and another ball of flame was waiting. She stepped right into it.

Matthew dropped to his knees, his hands pressing the blood-soaked sweater into the spot where she had punctured the skin over his heart. Screaming, Juliette reached out, trying to draw him into the inferno.

At a flick of my wrist and a word to the wind, she was picked up and carried several feet from where Matthew was collapsing into the earth. She fell onto her back, her body alight.

I wanted to run to him but continued to watch Juliette as her vampire bones and flesh resisted the flames. Her hair was gone and her skin was black and leathery, but even then she wasn't dead. Her mouth kept moving, calling Matthew's name.

My hands remained raised, ready for her to defy the odds. She lumbered to her feet once, and I released another bolt. It hit her in the middle of the chest, went through her rib cage, and came out the other side, shattering the tough skin as it passed and turning her ribs and lungs to coal. Her mouth twisted into a rictus of horror. She was beyond recovery now, no matter the strength of her vampire blood.

I rushed to Matthew's side and dropped to the ground. He could no longer keep himself upright and was lying on his back, knees bent. There was blood everywhere, pulsing out of the hole in his chest in deep purple waves and flowing more evenly from his neck, so dark it was like pitch.

'What should I do?' I frantically pressed my fingers against his throat. His white hands were still locked around the wound in his chest, but the strength was leaching out of them with each passing moment.

'Will you hold me?' he whispered.

My back to the oak tree, I pulled him between my legs.

'I'm cold,' he said with dull amazement. 'How strange.'

'You can't leave me,' I said fiercely. 'I won't have it.'

'There's nothing to be done about that now. Death has me in his grip.' Matthew was talking in a way that had not been heard in a thousand years, his fading voice rising and falling in an ancient cadence.

'No.' I fought back my tears. 'You have to fight, Matthew.'

'I *have* fought, Diana. And you are safe. Marcus will have you away from here before the Congregation knows what has happened.'

'I won't go anywhere without you.'

'You must.' He struggled in my arms, shifting so that he could see my face.

'I can't lose you, Matthew. Please hold on until Marcus gets here.' The chain inside me swayed, its links loosening one by one. I tried to resist by keeping him tight against my heart.

'Hush,' he said softly, raising a bloody finger to touch my lips. They tingled and went numb as his freezing blood came into contact with my skin. 'Marcus and Baldwin know what to do. They will see you safe to Ysabeau. Without me the Congregation will find it harder to act against you. The vampires and witches will not like it, but you are a de Clermont now, with my family's protection as well as that of the Knights of Lazarus.'

'Stay with me, Matthew.' I bent my head and pressed my lips against his, willing him to keep breathing. He did – barely – but his eyelids had closed.

'From birth I have searched for you,' Matthew whispered with a smile, his accent strongly French. 'Since finding you I have been able to hold you in my arms, have heard your heart beat against mine. It would have been a terrible thing to die without knowing what it feels like to truly love.' Tiny shudders swept over him from head to toe and then subsided.

'Matthew!' I cried, but he could no longer respond. 'Marcus!' I screamed into the trees, praying to the goddess all the while. By the time his son reached us, I'd already thought several times that Matthew was dead.

'Holy God,' Marcus said, taking in Juliette's charred body and Matthew's bloody form.

'The bleeding won't stop,' I said. 'Where is it all coming from?'

'I need to examine him to know, Diana.' Marcus took a tentative step toward me.

Tightening my arms around my husband, I felt my eyes turn cold. The wind began to rise where I sat.

'I'm not asking you to let go of him,' Marcus said, instinctively understanding the problem, 'but I have to look at his chest.'

He crouched next to us and tore gently at his father's black sweater. With a horrible rending noise, the fabric gave way. A long gash crossed from Matthew's jugular vein to his heart. Next to the heart was a deep gouge where Juliette had tried to punch through to the aorta.

'The jugular is nearly severed, and the aorta has been damaged. Not even Matthew's blood can work fast enough to heal him in both places.' Marcus spoke quietly, but he didn't need to speak at all. Juliette had given Matthew a death blow.

My aunts were here now, Sarah puffing slightly. Miriam appeared, white-faced, behind them. After only a glance, she turned on her heel, dashing back to the house.

'It's my fault.' I sobbed, rocking Matthew like a child. 'I had a clear shot, but I hesitated. I've never killed anyone before. She wouldn't have reached his heart if I'd acted sooner.'

'Diana, baby,' Sarah whispered. 'It's not your fault. You did what you could. You're going to have to let him go.'

I made a keening sound, and my hair rose up around my face. 'No!' Fear bloomed in the eyes of vampire and witch as the forest grew quiet.

'Get away from her, Marcus!' shouted Em. He jumped backward just in time.

I'd become someone – something – who didn't care about these creatures, or that they were trying to help. It had been a mistake to hesitate before. Now the part of me that had killed Juliette was intent on only one thing: a knife. My right arm shot out toward my aunt.

Sarah always had two blades on her, one dull and black-handled, the other sharp and white-handled. At my call the white blade cut through her belt and flew at me point first. Sarah put up a hand to call it back, and I imagined a wall of blackness and fire between me and the surprised faces of my family. The white-handled knife sliced easily through the blackness and floated gently down near my bent right knee. Matthew's head lolled as I released him just enough to grasp the hilt.

Turning his face gently toward mine, I kissed his mouth long and hard. His eyes fluttered open. He looked so tired, and his skin was gray.

'Don't worry, my love. I'm going to fix it.' I raised the knife.

Two women were standing inside the barrier of flames. One was young and wore a loose tunic, with sandals on her feet and a quiver of arrows slung across her shoulders. The strap was tangled up in her hair, which was dark and thick. The other was the old lady from the keeping room, her full skirt swaying.

'Help me,' I begged.

There will be a price, the young huntress said.

'I will pay it.'

Don't make a promise to the goddess lightly, daughter, the old woman murmured with a shake of her head. *You'll have to keep it.*

'Take anything – take anyone. But leave me him.'

The huntress considered my offer and nodded. *He is yours.*

My eyes were on the two women as I raised the knife. Twisting Matthew closer to my body so that he couldn't see, I reached across and slashed the inside of my left elbow, the sharp blade cutting easily through fabric and flesh. My blood flowed, a trickle at first, then faster. I dropped the knife and tightened my left arm until it was in front of his mouth.

'Drink,' I said, steadying his head. Matthew's eyelids flickered again, and his nostrils flared. He recognized the scent of *my* blood and struggled to get away. My arms were heavy and strong as oak branches, connected to the tree at my back. I drew my open, bleeding elbow a fraction closer to his mouth. 'Drink.'

The power of the tree and the earth flowed through my veins, an unexpected offering of life to a vampire on the verge of death. I smiled in gratitude at the huntress and the ghost of the old woman, nourishing Matthew with my body. I was the mother now, the third aspect of the goddess along with the maiden and the crone. With the goddess's help, my blood would heal him.

Finally Matthew succumbed to the instinct to survive. His mouth fastened onto the soft skin of my inner arm, teeth sharp. His tongue lightly probed the ragged incision, pulling the gash in my skin wider. He drew long and hard against my veins. I felt a short, sharp burst of terror.

His skin began to lose some of its pallor, but venous blood would not be enough to heal him completely. I was hoping that a taste of me would drive him beyond his normal range of control so that he would take the next step, but I felt for the white-handled knife just in case.

Giving the huntress and the witch one last look, I returned my attention to my husband. Another shock of power ran into my body as I settled more firmly against the tree.

While he fed, I began to kiss him. My hair fell around his face, mixing my familiar scent with that of his blood and mine. He turned his eyes to me, pale green and distant, as if he weren't sure of my identity. I kissed him again, tasting my own blood on his tongue.

In two fast, smooth moves that I couldn't have stopped even had I wanted to, Matthew grabbed the hair at the nape of my neck. He tilted my head back and to the side, then lowered his mouth to my throat. There was no terror then, just surrender.

'Diana,' he said with complete satisfaction.

So this is how it happens, I thought. *This is where the legends come from*.

My spent, used blood had given him the strength to want something fresh and vital. Matthew's sharp upper teeth cut into his lower lip, and a bead formed there. His lips brushed my neck, sensuous and swift. I shivered, unexpectedly aroused at his touch. My skin went numb as his blood touched my flesh. He held my head firmly, his hands once again strong.

No mistakes, I prayed.

There were tiny pricks along my carotid arteries. My eyes opened wide in surprise when the first drawing pressure told me Matthew had reached the blood he sought.

Sarah turned away, unable to watch. Marcus reached for Em, and she went to him without hesitation, crying into his shoulder.

I pressed Matthew's body into mine, encouraging him to drink more deeply. His relish when he did so was evident. How he'd hungered for me, and how strong he'd been to resist.

Matthew settled into the rhythms of his feeding, pulling on my blood in waves.

Matthew, listen to me. Thanks to Gerbert, I knew that my blood would carry messages to him. My only worry was that they would be fleeting, and my power to communicate would be swallowed up.

He startled against my throat, then resumed his feeding.

I love you.

He gave another start of surprise.

This was my gift. I am inside you, giving you life.

Matthew shook his head as if to dislodge an annoying insect and kept drinking.

I am inside you, giving you life. It was harder to think, harder to see through the fire. I focused on Em and Sarah, tried to tell them with my eyes not to worry. I looked for Marcus, too, but couldn't move my eyes enough to find him.

I am inside you, giving you life. I repeated the mantra until it was no longer possible.

There was a slow pulsing, the sound of my heart starting to die.

Dying was nothing at all like I'd expected it to be.

There was a moment of bone-deep quiet.

A sense of parting and regret.

Then nothing.

CHAPTER 38

I n my bones there was a sudden boom as of two worlds colliding.
Something stung my right arm, accompanied by the odor of latex
and plastic, and Matthew was arguing with Marcus. There was cold
earth below me, and the tang of leaf mold replaced the other scents.
My eyes were open, but I saw nothing except blackness. With effort I
was able to pick out the half-bare branches of trees crisscrossing
above me.

'Use the left arm – it's already open,' said Matthew with
impatience.

'That arm's useless, Matthew. The tissues are full of your saliva
and won't absorb anything else. The right arm is better. Her blood
pressure is so low I'm having a hard time finding a vein, that's all.'
Marcus's voice had the unnatural quietness of the emergency-room
physician who sees death regularly.

Two thick strands of spaghetti spooled onto my face. Cold fingers
touched my nose, and I tried to shake them off, only to be held
down.

Miriam's voice came from the darkness to my right. 'Tachycardia.
I'll sedate her.'

'No,' Matthew said roughly. 'No sedatives. She's barely
conscious. They could put her into a coma.'

'Then keep her quiet.' Miriam's tone was matter-of-fact.
Tiny, cold fingers pressed against my neck with unexpected firmness.
'I can't stop her from bleeding out *and* hold her still at the same
time.'

What was happening around me was visible only in disconcerting slices — what was directly above, what could be glimpsed from the corners of my eyes, what could be tracked through the enormous effort of swiveling them in their sockets.

'Can you do anything, Sarah?' Matthew's voice was anguished.

Sarah's face swam into view. 'Witchcraft can't heal vampire bites. If it could, we'd never have had anything to fear from creatures like you.'

I began drifting to somewhere peaceful, but my progress was interrupted by Em's slipping her hand into mine, holding me firmly in my own body.

'We've got no choice, then.' Matthew sounded desperate. 'I'll do it.'

'No, Matthew,' said Miriam decidedly. 'You're not strong enough yet. Besides, I've done it hundreds of times.' There was a tearing sound. After Juliette's attack on Matthew, I recognized that it was vampire flesh.

'Are they making me a vampire?' I whispered to Em.

'No, *mon coeur*.' Matthew's voice was as decided as Miriam's had been. 'You lost — I *took* — a great deal of blood. Marcus is replacing it with human blood. Now Miriam needs to see to your neck.'

'Oh.' It was too complicated to follow. My brain was fuzzy — almost as fuzzy as my tongue and throat. 'I'm thirsty.'

'You're craving vampire blood, but you're not going to get it. Lie very still,' Matthew said firmly, holding my shoulders so tightly it was painful. Marcus's cold hands crept past my ears to my jaw, holding my mouth closed, too. 'And, Miriam—'

'Stop fussing, Matthew,' Miriam said briskly. 'I was doing this to warmbloods long before you were reborn.'

Something sharp cut into my neck, and the smell of blood filled the air.

The cutting sensation was followed by a pain that froze and burned simultaneously. The heat and cold intensified, traveling below the surface tissues of my neck to sear the bones and muscles underneath.

I wanted to escape the icy licks, but there were two vampires holding me down. My mouth was firmly closed, too, so all I could do was let out a muffled, fearful sound.

'Her artery is obscured,' Miriam said quietly. 'The wound has to be cleared.' She took a single, audible sip, drawing the blood away. The skin was numbed momentarily, but sensation returned full force when she withdrew.

The extreme pain sent adrenaline coursing through my system, and panic followed in its wake. The gray walls of La Pierre loomed around me, my inability to move putting me back within Satu's hands.

Matthew's fingers dug into my shoulders, returning me to the woods outside the Bishop house. 'Tell her what you're doing, Miriam. That Finnish witch made her afraid of what she can't see.'

'It's just drops of my blood, Diana, falling from my wrist,' Miriam said calmly. 'I know it hurts, but it's all we have. Vampire blood heals on contact. It will close your artery better than the sutures a surgeon would use. And you needn't worry. There's no chance such a small amount, applied topically, will make you one of us.'

After her description it was possible to recognize each deliberate drop falling into my open wound. There it mingled with my witch's flesh, forcing an instantaneous buildup of scar tissue. It must require enormous control, I thought, for a vampire to undertake such a procedure without giving in to hunger. At last the drops of searing coldness came to an end.

'Done,' Miriam said with a touch of relief. 'All I have to do now is sew the incision.' Her fingers flew over my neck, tugging and stitching the flesh back together. 'I tried to neaten the wound, Diana, but Matthew tore the skin with his teeth.'

'We're going to move you to the house now,' Matthew said.

He cradled my head and shoulders while Marcus supported my legs. Miriam walked alongside carrying the equipment. Someone had driven the Range Rover across the fields, and it stood waiting with its rear door open. Matthew and Miriam switched places, and he disappeared into the cargo area to ready it for me.

'Miriam,' I whispered. She bent toward me. 'If something goes wrong—' I couldn't finish, but it was imperative she understand me. I was still a witch. But I'd rather be a vampire than dead.

She stared into my eyes, searched for a moment, then nodded. 'Don't you dare die, though. He'll kill me if I do what you ask.'

Matthew talked nonstop during the bumpy ride back to the house, kissing me softly whenever I tried to sleep. Despite his gentleness, it was a wrench each time.

At the house, Sarah and Em sped around collecting cushions and pillows. They made a bed in front of the keeping room's fireplace. Sarah lit the pile of logs in the grate with a few words and a gesture. A blaze began to burn, but still I shivered uncontrollably, cold to the core.

Matthew lowered me onto the cushions and covered me with quilts while Miriam pressed a bandage onto my neck. As she worked, my husband and his son muttered in the corner.

'It's what she needs, and I do know where her lungs are,' Marcus said impatiently. 'I won't puncture anything.'

'She's strong. No central line. End of discussion. Just get rid of what's left of Juliette's body,' Matthew said, his voice quiet but commanding.

'I'll see to it,' Marcus replied. He turned on his heel, and the front door thudded behind him before the Range Rover sprang once more into life.

The ancient case clock in the front entrance ticked the minutes as they passed. The warmth soaked into my bones, making me drowsy. Matthew sat at my side, holding one hand tightly so that he could tug me back whenever I tried to escape into the welcome oblivion.

Finally Miriam said the magic word: 'stable'. Then I could give in to the blackness flitting around the edges of my consciousness. Sarah and Em kissed me and left, Miriam followed, and at last there was nothing but Matthew and the blessed quiet.

Once silence descended, however, my mind turned to Juliette.

'I killed her.' My heart raced.

'You had no choice.' His tone said no further discussion was required. 'It was self-defense.'

'No it wasn't. The witchfire . . .' It was only when he was in danger that the bow and arrow had appeared in my hands.

Matthew quieted me with a kiss. 'We can talk about that tomorrow.'

There was something that couldn't wait, something I wanted him to know now.

'I love you, Matthew.' There hadn't been a chance to tell him before Satu snatched me away from Sept-Tours. This time I wanted to be sure it was said before something else happened.

'I love you, too.' He bent his head, his lips against my ear. 'Remember our dinner in Oxford? You wanted to know how you would taste.'

I moved my head in acknowledgment.

'You taste of honey,' he murmured. 'Honey – and hope.'

My lips curved, and then I slept.

But it was not restful slumber. I was caught between waking and sleeping, Madison and La Pierre, life and death. The ghostly old woman had warned me of the danger of standing at a crossroads. There were times that death seemed to be standing patiently at my side, waiting for me to choose the road I wanted to take.

I traveled countless miles that night, fleeing from place to place, never more than a step ahead of whoever was pursuing me – Gerbert, Satu, Juliette, Peter Knox. Whenever my journey brought me back to the Bishop house, Matthew was there. Sometimes Sarah was with him. Other times it was Marcus. Most often, though, Matthew was alone.

Deep in the night, someone started humming the tune we'd danced to a lifetime ago in Ysabeau's grand salon. It wasn't Marcus or Matthew – they were talking to each other – but I was too tired to figure out where the music was coming from.

'Where did she learn that old song?' Marcus asked.

'At home. Christ, even in sleep she's trying to be brave.' Matthew's voice was desolate. 'Baldwin is right – I'm no good at strategy. I should have foreseen this.'

'Gerbert counted on your forgetting about Juliette. It had been so long. And he knew you'd be with Diana when she struck. He gloated about it on the phone.'

'Yes, he knows I'm arrogant enough to think she was safe with me at her side.'

'You've tried to protect her. But you can't – no one could. She's not the only one who needs to stop being brave.'

There was something Marcus didn't know, something Matthew was forgetting. Snatches of half-remembered conversation came back to me. The music stopped to let me speak.

'I told you before,' I said, groping for Matthew in the dark and finding only a handful of soft wool that released the scent of cloves when crushed, 'I can be brave enough for both of us.'

'Diana,' Matthew said urgently. 'Open your eyes and look at me.'

His face was inches from mine. He was cradling my head with one hand, the other cool on my lower back, where a crescent moon swept from one side of my body to the other.

'There you are,' I murmured. 'I'm afraid we're lost.'

'No, my darling, we're not lost. We're at the Bishop house. And you don't need to be brave. It's my turn.'

'Will you be able to figure out which road we need to take?'

'I'll find the way. Rest and let me take care of that.' Matthew's eyes were very green.

I drifted off once more, racing to elude Gerbert and Juliette, who were hard at my heels. Toward dawn my sleep deepened, and when I awoke, it was morning. A quick check revealed that my body was naked and tucked tightly under layers of quilts, like a patient in a British intensive-care ward. Tubing disappeared into my right arm, a bandage encased my left elbow, and something was stuck to my neck. Matthew was sitting nearby with knees bent and his back against the sofa.

'Matthew? Is everyone all right?' There was cotton wool wrapped around my tongue, and I was still fiercely thirsty.

'Everyone's fine.' Relief washed over his face as he reached for my hand and pressed his lips to my palm. Matthew's eyes flickered to my wrist, where Juliette's fingernails had left angry red crescent moons.

The sound of our voices brought the rest of the household into the room. First there were my aunts. Sarah was lost in her thoughts, dark hollows under her eyes. Em looked tired but relieved, stroking my hair and assuring me that everything was going to be all right. Marcus came next. He examined me and talked sternly about my need to rest. Finally Miriam ordered everyone else out of the room so she could change my bandages.

'How bad was it?' I asked when we were alone.

'If you mean Matthew, it was bad. The de Clermonts don't handle loss – or the threat of it – very well. Ysabeau was worse when Philippe died. It's a good thing you lived, and not just for my sake.' Miriam applied ointment to my wounds with a surprisingly delicate touch.

Her words conjured images of Matthew on a vengeful rampage. I closed my eyes to blot them out. 'Tell me about Juliette.'

Miriam emitted a low hiss of warning. 'Juliette Durand is not my tale to tell. Ask your husband.' She disconnected the IV and held out one of Sarah's old flannel shirts. After I struggled with it for a few moments, she came to my aid. Her eyes fell on the marks on my back.

'The scars don't bother me. They're just signs that I've fought and survived.' I pulled the shirt over my shoulders self-consciously nonetheless.

'They don't bother him either. Loving de Clermonts always leaves a mark. Nobody knows that better than Matthew.'

I buttoned up the shirt with shaking fingers, unwilling to meet her eyes. She handed over a pair of stretchy black leggings.

'Giving him your blood like that was unspeakably dangerous. He might not have been able to stop drinking.' A note of admiration had crept into her voice.

'Ysabeau told me the de Clermonts fight for those they love.'

'His mother will understand, but Matthew is another matter. He needs to get it out of his system – your blood, what happened last night, everything.'

Juliette. The name hung unspoken in the air between us.

Miriam reconnected the IV and adjusted its flow. 'Marcus will take him to Canada. It will be hours before Matthew finds someone he's willing to feed on, but it can't be helped.'

'Sarah and Em will be safe with both of them gone?'

'You bought us some time. The Congregation never imagined that Juliette would fail. Gerbert is as proud as Matthew, and nearly as infallible. It will take them a few days to regroup.' She froze, a guilty look on her face.

'I'd like to talk to Diana now,' Matthew said quietly from the door. He looked terrible. There was hunger in the sharpened angles of his face and the lavender smudges under his eyes.

He watched silently as Miriam walked around my makeshift bed. She shut the heavy coffin doors behind her, their catches clicking together. When he turned to me, his look was concerned.

Matthew's need for blood was at war with his protective instincts.

'When are you leaving?' I asked, hoping to make my wishes clear.

'I'm not leaving.'

'You need to regain your strength. Next time the Congregation won't send just one vampire or witch.' I wondered how many other creatures from Matthew's past were likely to come calling at the Congregation's behest, and I struggled to sit up.

'You are so experienced with war now, *ma lionne*, that you understand their strategies?' It was impossible to judge his feelings from his features, but his voice betrayed a hint of amusement.

'We've proved we can't be beaten easily.'

'Easily? You almost died.' He sat next to me on the cushions.

'So did you.'

'You used magic to save me. I could smell it – lady's mantle and ambergris.'

'It was nothing.' I didn't want him know what I'd promised in exchange for his life.

'No lies.' Matthew grabbed my chin with his fingertips. 'If you don't want to tell me, say so. Your secrets are your own. But no lies.'

'If I do keep secrets, I won't be the only one doing so in this family. Tell me about Juliette Durand.'

He let go of my chin and moved restlessly to the window. 'You know that Gerbert introduced us. He kidnapped her from a Cairo brothel, brought her to the brink of death over and over again before transforming her into a vampire, and then shaped her into someone I would find appealing. I still don't know if she was insane when Gerbert found her or if her mind broke after what he did to her.'

'Why?' I couldn't keep the incredulity from my voice.

'She was meant to worm her way into my heart and then into my family's affairs. Gerbert had always wanted to be included among the Knights of Lazarus, and my father refused him time and time again. Once Juliette had discovered the intricacies of the brotherhood and any other useful information about the de Clermonts, she was free to kill me. Gerbert trained her to be my assassin, as well as my lover.' Matthew picked at the window frame's peeling paint. 'When I first met her, she was better at hiding her illness. It took me a long time to see the signs. Baldwin and Ysabeau never trusted her, and Marcus detested her. But I— Gerbert taught her well. She reminded me of Louisa, and her emotional fragility seemed to explain her erratic behavior.'

He has always liked fragile things, Ysabeau had warned me. Matthew hadn't been just sexually attracted to Juliette. The feelings had gone deeper.

'You did love her.' I remembered Juliette's strange kiss and shuddered.

'Once. Long ago. For all the wrong reasons,' Matthew continued. 'I watched her – from a safe distance – and made sure she was cared for, since she was incapable of caring for herself. When World War I broke out, she disappeared, and I assumed she'd been killed. I never imagined she was alive somewhere.'

'And all the time you were watching her, she was watching you, too.' Juliette's attentive eyes had taken in my every movement. She must have observed Matthew with a similar keenness.

'If I'd known, she would never have been allowed to get near you.' He stared out into the pale morning light. 'But there's something else we have to discuss. You must promise me *never* to use your magic to save me. I have no wish to live longer than I'm meant to. Life and death are powerful forces. Ysabeau interfered with them on my behalf once. You aren't to do it again. And no asking Miriam – or anyone else – to make you a vampire.' His voice was startling in its coldness, and he crossed the room to my side with quick, long strides. 'No one – not even I – will transform you into something you're not.'

'You'll have to promise me something in return.'

His eyes narrowed with displeasure. 'What's that?'

'Don't ever ask me to leave you when you're in danger,' I said fiercely. 'I won't do it.'

Matthew calculated what would be required of him to keep his promise while keeping me out of harm's way. I was just as busy figuring out which of my dimly understood powers needed mastering so that I could protect him without incinerating him or drowning myself. We eyed each other warily for a few moments. Finally I touched his cheek.

'Go hunting with Marcus. We'll be fine for a few hours.' His color was all wrong. I wasn't the only one who had lost a lot of blood.

'You shouldn't be alone.'

'I have my aunts, not to mention Miriam. She told me at the Bodleian that her teeth are as sharp as yours. I believe her.' I was more knowledgeable now about vampire teeth.

'We'll be home by dark,' he said reluctantly, brushing his fingers across my cheekbone. 'Is there anything you need before I go?'

'I'd like to talk to Ysabeau.' Sarah had been distant that morning, and I wanted to hear a maternal voice.

'Of course,' he said, hiding his surprise by reaching into his pocket for his phone. Someone had taken the time to retrieve it from the bushes. He dialed Sept-Tours with a single push of his finger.

'*Maman?*' A torrent of French erupted from the phone. 'She's fine,' Matthew interrupted, his voice soothing. 'Diana wants – she's asked – to speak to you.'

There was silence, followed by a single crisp word. '*Oui.*'

Matthew handed me the phone.

'Ysabeau?' My voice cracked, and my eyes filled with sudden tears.

'I am here, Diana.' Ysabeau sounded as musical as ever.

'I almost lost him.'

'You should have obeyed him and gone as far away from Juliette as you could.' Ysabeau's tone was sharp before turning soft once more. 'But I am glad you did not.'

I cried in earnest then. Matthew stroked the hair back from my forehead, tucking my typically wayward strand behind my ear, before leaving me to my conversation.

To Ysabeau I was able to express my grief and confess my failure to kill Juliette at my first opportunity. I told her everything – about Juliette's startling appearance and her strange kiss, my terror when Matthew began to feed, about what it was like to begin to die only to return abruptly to life. Matthew's mother understood, as I'd known she would. The only time Ysabeau interrupted was during the part of my story that involved the maiden and the crone.

'So the goddess saved my son,' she murmured. 'She has a sense of justice, as well as humor. But that is too long a tale for today. When you are next at Sept-Tours, I will tell you.'

Her mention of the château caused another sharp pang of homesickness. 'I wish I were there. I'm not sure anyone in Madison can teach me all that I need to know.'

'Then we must find a different teacher. Somewhere there is a creature who can help.'

Ysabeau issued a series of firm instructions about obeying Matthew, taking care of him, taking care of myself, and returning to the château as soon as possible. I agreed to all of them with uncharacteristic alacrity and got off the phone.

A few tactful moments later, Matthew opened the door and stepped inside.

'Thank you,' I said, sniffing and holding up his phone.

He shook his head. 'Keep it. Call Marcus or Ysabeau at any time.

They're numbers two and three on speed dial. You need a new phone, as well as a watch. Yours doesn't even hold a charge.' Matthew settled me gently against the cushions and kissed my forehead. 'Miriam's working in the dining room, but she'll hear the slightest sound.'

'Sarah and Em?' I asked.

'Waiting to see you,' he said with a smile.

After visits from my aunts, I slept a few hours, until a restless yearning for Matthew had me clawing myself awake.

Em got up from my grandmother's recently returned rocker and came to me carrying a glass of water, her forehead creased in deep lines that hadn't been there a few days ago. Grandma was sitting on the sofa staring at the paneling next to the fireplace, clearly waiting for another message from the house.

'Where's Sarah?' I closed my fingers around the glass. My throat was still parched, and the water would feel divine.

'She went out for a while.' Em's delicate mouth pressed into a thin line.

'She blames this all on Matthew.'

Em dropped down to her knees on the floor until her eyes were level with mine. 'This has nothing to do with Matthew. You offered your blood to a vampire – a desperate, dying vampire.' She silenced my protests with a look. 'I know he's not just any vampire. Even so, Matthew could kill you. And Sarah's devastated that she can't teach you how to control your talents.'

'Sarah shouldn't worry about me. Did you see what I did to Juliette?'

She nodded. 'And other things as well.'

My grandmother's attention was now fixed on me instead of the paneling.

'I saw the hunger in Matthew when he fed on you,' Em continued quietly. 'I saw the maiden and the crone, too, standing on the other side of the fire.'

'Did Sarah see them?' I whispered, hoping that Miriam couldn't hear.

Em shook her head. 'No. Does Matthew know?'

'No.' I pushed my hair aside, relieved that Sarah was unaware of all that had happened last night.

'What did you promise the goddess in exchange for his life, Diana?'

'Anything she wanted.'

'Oh, honey.' Em's face crumpled. 'You shouldn't have done that. There's no telling when she'll act – or what she'll take.'

My grandmother was furiously rocking. Em eyed the chair's wild movements.

'I had to, Em. The goddess didn't seem surprised. It felt inevitable – right, somehow.'

'Have you seen the maiden and the crone before?'

I nodded. 'The maiden's been in my dreams. Sometimes it's as though I'm inside her, looking out as she rides or hunts. And the crone met me outside the keeping room.'

You're in deep water now, Diana, my grandmother rustled. *I hope you can swim.*

'You mustn't call the goddess lightly,' Em warned. 'These are powerful forces that you don't yet understand.'

'I didn't call her at all. They appeared when I decided to give Matthew my blood. They gave me their help willingly.'

Maybe it wasn't your blood to give. My grandmother continued to rock back and forth, setting the floorboards creaking. *Did you ever think of that?*

'You've known Matthew for a few weeks. Yet you follow his orders so easily, and you were willing to die for him. Surely you can see why Sarah is concerned. The Diana we've known all these years is gone.'

'I love him,' I said fiercely. 'And he loves me.' Matthew's many secrets – the Knights of Lazarus, Juliette, even Marcus – I pushed to the side, along with my knowledge of his ferocious temper and his need to control everything and everyone around him.

But Em knew what I was thinking. She shook her head. 'You can't ignore them, Diana. You tried that with your magic, and it found you. The parts of Matthew you don't like and don't understand are going to find you, too. You can't hide forever. Especially now.'

'What do you mean?'

'There are too many creatures interested in this manuscript, and in you and Matthew. I can feel them, pressing in on the Bishop house, on you. I don't know which side of this struggle they're on, but my sixth sense tells me it won't be long before we find out.'

Em tucked the quilt around me. After putting another log on the fire, she left the room.

I was awakened by my husband's distinctive, spicy scent.

'You're back,' I said, rubbing my eyes.

Matthew looked rested, and his skin had returned to its normal, pearly color.

He'd fed. On human blood.

'So are you.' Matthew brought my hand to his lips. 'Miriam said you've been sleeping for most of the day.'

'Is Sarah home?'

'Everyone's present and accounted for.' He gave me a lopsided grin. 'Even Tabitha.'

I asked to see them, and he unhooked me from my IV without argument. When my legs were too unsteady to walk to the family room, he simply swept me up and carried me.

Em and Marcus settled me into the sofa with great ceremony. I was quickly exhausted by nothing more strenuous than quiet conversation and watching the latest film noir selection on TV, and Matthew lifted me up once more.

'We're going upstairs,' he announced. 'We'll see you in the morning.'

'Do you want me to bring up Diana's IV?' Miriam asked pointedly.

'No. She doesn't need it.' His voice was brusque.

'Thank you for not hooking me up to all that stuff,' I said as he carried me through the front hall.

'Your body is still weak, but it's remarkably resilient for a warmblood,' Matthew said as he climbed the stairs. 'The reward for being a perpetual-motion machine, I imagine.'

Once he had turned off the light, I curled into his body with a contented sigh, my fingers splayed possessively across his chest. The moonlight streaming through the windows highlighted his new scars. They were already fading from pink to white.

Tired as I was, the gears of Matthew's mind were working so furiously that sleep proved impossible. It was plain from the set of his mouth and the bright glitter of his eyes that he was picking our road forward, just as he'd promised to do last night.

'Tell me,' I said when the suspense became unbearable.

'What we need is time,' he said thoughtfully.

'The Congregation isn't likely to give us that.'

'We'll take it, then.' His voice was almost inaudible. 'We'll timewalk.'

CHAPTER 39

We made it only halfway down the stairs the next morning before stopping to rest, but I was determined to get to the kitchen under my own steam. To my surprise, Matthew didn't try to dissuade me. We sat on the worn wooden treads in companionable silence. Pale, watery light seeped in through the wavy glass panes around the front door, hinting at a sunny day to come. From the family room came the click of Scrabble tiles.

'When will you tell them?' There wasn't much to divulge yet — he was still working on the basic outlines of the plan.

'Later,' he said, leaning into me. I leaned toward him, pressing our shoulders closer.

'No amount of coffee is going to keep Sarah from freaking out when she hears.' I put my hand on the banister and levered myself to my feet with a sigh. 'Let's try this again.'

In the family room, Em brought me my first cup of tea. I sipped it on the couch while Matthew and Marcus headed off for their walk with my silent blessing. They should spend as much time as possible together before we left.

After my tea Sarah made me her famous scrambled eggs. They were laden with onions, mushrooms, and cheese and topped with a spoonful of salsa. She put a steaming plate before me.

'Thanks, Sarah.' I dove in without further ceremony.

'It's not just Matthew who needs food and rest.' She glanced out the window to the orchard, where the two vampires were walking.

'I feel much better today,' I said, crunching a bite of toast.

'Your appetite seems to have recovered, at least.' There was already a sizable dent in the mountain of eggs.

When Matthew and Marcus returned, I was on my second plate of food. They both appeared grim, but Matthew shook his head at my curious look.

Apparently they hadn't been talking about our plans to timewalk. Something else had put them into a sour mood. Matthew pulled up a stool, flapped open the paper, and concentrated on the news. I ate my eggs and toast, made more tea, and bided my time while Sarah washed and put away the dishes.

At last Matthew folded his paper and set it aside.

'I'd like to go to the woods. To where Juliette died,' I announced.

He got to his feet. 'I'll pull the Range Rover to the door.'

'This is madness, Matthew. It's too soon.' Marcus turned to Sarah for support.

'Let them go,' Sarah said. 'Diana should put on warmer clothes first, though. It's chilly outside.'

Em appeared, a puzzled expression on her face. 'Are we expecting visitors? The house thinks we are.'

'You're joking!' I said. 'The house hasn't added a room since the last family reunion. Where is it?'

'Between the bathroom and the junk room.' Em pointed at the ceiling. *I told you this wasn't just about you and Matthew*, she said silently to me as we trooped upstairs to view the transformation. *My premonitions are seldom wrong*.

The newly materialized room held an ancient brass bed with enormous polished balls capping each corner, tatty red gingham curtains that Em insisted were coming down immediately, a hooked rug in clashing shades of maroon and plum, and a battered washstand with a chipped pink bowl and pitcher. None of us recognized a single item.

'Where did it all come from?' Miriam asked in amazement.

'Who knows where the house keeps this stuff?' Sarah sat on the bed and bounced on it vigorously. It responded with a series of outraged squeaks.

'The house's most legendary feats happened around my thirteenth birthday,' I remembered with a grin. 'It came up with a record four bedrooms and a Victorian parlor set.'

'And twenty-four place settings of Blue Willow china,' Em recalled. 'We've still got some of the teacups, although most of the bigger pieces disappeared again once the family left.'

After everybody had inspected the new room and the now considerably smaller storage room next door, I changed and made my halting way downstairs and into the Range Rover. When we drew close to the spot where Juliette had met her end, Matthew stopped. The heavy tires sank into the soft ground.

'Shall we walk the rest of the way?' he suggested. 'We can take it slowly.'

He was different this morning. He wasn't coddling me or telling me what to do.

'What's changed?' I asked as we approached the ancient oak tree.

'I've seen you fight,' he said quietly. 'On the battlefield the bravest men collapse in fear. They simply can't fight, even to save themselves.'

'But I froze.' My hair tumbled forward to conceal my face.

Matthew stopped in his tracks, his fingers tightening on my arm to make me stop, too. 'Of course you did. You were about to take a life. But you don't fear death.'

'No.' I'd lived with death – sometimes longed for it – since I was seven.

He swung me around to face him. 'After La Pierre, Satu left you broken and uncertain. All your life you've hidden from your fears. I wasn't sure you would be able to fight if you had to. Now all I have to do is keep you from taking unnecessary risks.' His eyes drifted to my neck.

Matthew moved forward, towing me gently along. A smudge of blackened grass told me we'd arrived at the clearing. I stiffened, and he released my arm.

The marks left by the fire led to the dead patch where Juliette had fallen. The forest was eerily quiet, without birdcalls or other sounds of life. I gathered a bit of charred wood from the ground. It crumbled to soot in my fingers.

'I didn't know Juliette, but at that moment I hated her enough to kill her.' Her brown-and-green eyes would always haunt me from shadows under the trees.

I traced the line left by the arc of conjured fire to where the maiden and the crone had agreed to help me save Matthew. I looked up into the oak tree and gasped.

'It began yesterday.' Matthew followed my gaze. 'Sarah says you pulled the life out of it.'

Above me the branches of the tree were cracked and withered. Bare limbs forked and forked again into shapes reminiscent of a stag's horns. Brown leaves swirled at my feet. Matthew had survived because I'd pushed its vitality through my veins and into his body. The oak's rough bark had exuded such permanence, yet there was nothing now but hollowness.

'Power always exacts a price,' Matthew said.

'What have I done?' The death of a tree was not going to settle my debt to the goddess. For the first time, I was afraid of the deal I'd struck.

Matthew crossed the clearing and caught me up in his arms. We hugged each other, fierce with the knowledge of all we'd almost lost.

'You promised me you would be less reckless.' There was anger in his voice.

I was angry with him, too. 'You were supposed to be indestructible.'

He rested his forehead against mine. 'I should have told you about Juliette.'

'Yes, you should have. She almost took you from me.' My pulse throbbed behind the bandage on my neck. Matthew's thumb settled against the spot where he'd bitten through flesh and muscle, his touch unexpectedly warm.

'It was far too close.' His fingers were wrapped in my hair, and his mouth was hard on mine. Then we stood, hearts pressed together, in the quiet.

'When I took Juliette's life, it made her part of mine – forever.'

Matthew stroked my hair against my skull. 'Death is its own powerful magic.'

Calm again, I said a silent word of thanks to the goddess, not only for Matthew's life but for my own.

We walked toward the Range Rover, but halfway there I stumbled with fatigue. Matthew swung me onto his back and carried me the rest of the way.

Sarah was bent over her desk in the office when we arrived at the house. She flew outside and pulled open the car door with speed a vampire might envy.

'Damn it, Matthew,' she said, looking at my exhausted face.

Together they got me inside and back onto the family-room couch, where I rested my head in Matthew's lap. I was lulled to sleep by the quiet sounds of activity all around, and the last thing I remembered clearly was the smell of vanilla and the sound of Em's battered KitchenAid mixer.

Matthew woke me for lunch, which turned out to be vegetable soup. The look on his face suggested that I would shortly need sustenance. He was about to tell our families the plan.

'Ready, *mon coeur*?' Matthew asked. I nodded, scraping up the last of my meal. Marcus's head swiveled in our direction. 'We have something to share with you,' he announced.

The new household tradition was to proceed to the dining room whenever something important needed to be discussed. Once we were assembled, all eyes turned to Matthew.

'What have you decided?' Marcus asked without preamble.

Matthew took a deliberate breath and began. 'We need to go where it won't be easy for the Congregation to follow, where Diana will have time and teachers who can help her master her magic.'

Sarah laughed under her breath. 'Where is this place, where there are powerful, patient witches who don't mind having a vampire hanging around?'

'It's not a particular place I have in mind,' Matthew said cryptically. 'We're going to hide Diana in time.'

Everyone started shouting at once. Matthew took my hand in his.

'*Courage*,' I murmured in French, repeating his advice when I met Ysabeau.

He snorted and gave me a grim smile.

I had some sympathy for their amazed disbelief. Last night, while I was lying in bed, my own reaction had been much the same. First I'd insisted that it was impossible, and then I'd asked for a thousand details about precisely when and where we were going.

He'd explained what he could – which wasn't much.

'You want to use your magic, but now it's using you. You need a teacher, one who is more adept than Sarah or Emily. It's not their fault they can't help you. Witches in the past were different. So much of their knowledge has been lost.'

'Where? When?' I'd whispered in the dark.

'Nothing too distant – though the more recent past has its own risks – but back far enough that we'll find a witch to train you. First we have to talk to Sarah about whether it can be done safely. And then we need to locate three items to steer us to the right time.'

'We?' I'd asked in surprise. 'Won't I just meet you there?'

'Not unless there's no alternative. I wasn't the same creature then, and I wouldn't entirely trust my past selves with you.'

His mouth had softened with relief after I nodded in agreement. A few days ago, he'd rejected the idea of timewalking. Apparently the risks of staying put were even worse.

'What will the others do?'

His thumb traveled slowly over the veins on the back of my hand. 'Miriam and Marcus will go back to Oxford. The Congregation will look for you here first. It would be best if Sarah and Emily went away, at least for a little while. Would they go to Ysabeau?' Matthew wondered.

On the surface it had sounded like a ridiculous idea. Sarah and Ysabeau under the same roof? The more I'd considered it, though, the less implausible it seemed.

'I don't know,' I'd mused. Then a new worry had surfaced. 'Marcus.' I didn't fully understand the intricacies of the Knights of Lazarus, but with Matthew gone he would have to shoulder even more responsibility.

'There's no other way,' Matthew had said in the darkness, quieting me with a kiss.

This was precisely the point that Em now wanted to argue.

'There must be another way,' she protested.

'I tried to think of one, Emily,' Matthew said apologetically.

'Where – or should I say *when* – are you planning on going? Diana won't exactly blend into the background. She's too tall.' Miriam looked down at her own tiny hands.

'Regardless of whether Diana could fit in, it's too dangerous,' Marcus said firmly. 'You might end up in the middle of a war. Or an epidemic.'

'Or a witch-hunt.' Miriam didn't say it maliciously, but three heads swung around in indignation nonetheless.

'Sarah, what do you think?' asked Matthew.

Of all the creatures in the room, she was the calmest. 'You'll take her to a time when she'll be with witches who will help her?'

'Yes.'

Sarah closed her eyes for a moment, then opened them. 'You two aren't safe here. Juliette Durand proved that. And if you aren't safe in Madison, you aren't safe anywhere.'

'Thank you.' Matthew opened his mouth to say something else, and Sarah held up her hand.

'Don't promise me anything,' she said, voice tight. 'You'll be careful for her sake, if not for your own.'

'Now all we have to worry about is the timewalking.' Matthew turned businesslike. 'Diana will need three items from a particular time and place in order to move safely.'

Sarah nodded.

'Do I count as a thing?' he asked her.

'Do you have a pulse? Of course you're not a thing!' It was one of the most positive statements Sarah had ever made about vampires.

'If you need old stuff to guide your way, you're welcome to these.' Marcus pulled a thin leather cord from the neck of his shirt and lifted it over his head. It was festooned with a bizarre assortment of items, including a tooth, a coin, a lump of something that shone black and gold, and a battered silver whistle. He tossed it to Matthew.

'Didn't you get this off a yellow-fever victim?' Matthew asked, fingering the tooth.

'In New Orleans,' Marcus replied. 'The epidemic of 1819.'

'New Orleans is out of the question,' Matthew said sharply.

'I suppose so.' Marcus slid a glance my way, then returned his attention to his father. 'How about Paris? One of Fanny's earbobs is on there.'

Matthew's fingers touched a tiny red stone set in gold filigree. 'Philippe and I sent you away from Paris, and Fanny, too. They called it the Terror, remember? It's no place for Diana.'

'The two of you fussed over me like old women. I'd been in one revolution already. Besides, if you're looking for a safe place in the past, you'll have a hell of a time finding one,' Marcus grumbled. His face brightened. 'Philadelphia?'

'I wasn't in Philadelphia with you, or in California,' Matthew said hastily before his son could speak. 'It would be best if we head for a time and place I know.'

'Even if you know where we're going, Matthew, I'm not sure I can pull this off.' My decision to stay clear of magic had caught up with me again.

'I think you can,' Sarah said bluntly, 'you have been doing it your whole life. When you were a baby, as a child when you played hide-and-seek with Stephen, and as an adolescent, too. Remember all those mornings we dragged you out of the woods and had to clean you up in time for school? What do you imagine you were doing then?'

'Certainly not timewalking,' I said truthfully. 'The science of this still worries me. Where does this body go when I'm somewhere else?'

'Who knows? But don't worry. It's happened to everybody. You drive to work and don't remember how you got there. Or the whole afternoon passes and you don't have a clue what you did. Whenever something like that happens, you can bet there's a timewalker nearby,' explained Sarah. She was remarkably unfazed at the prospect.

Matthew sensed my apprehension and took my hand in his. 'Einstein said that all physicists were aware that the distinctions between past, present, and future were only what he called 'a stubbornly persistent illusion.' Not only did he believe in marvels and wonders, he also believed in the elasticity of time.'

There was a tentative knock at the door.

'I didn't hear a car,' Miriam said warily, rising to her feet.

'It's just Sammy collecting the newspaper money.' Em slid from her chair.

We waited silently while she crossed the hall, the floorboards protesting under her feet. From the way their hands were pressed flat against the table's wooden surface, Matthew and Marcus were both ready to fly to the door, too.

Cold air swept into the dining room.

'Yes?' Em asked in a puzzled voice. In an instant, Marcus and Matthew rose and joined her, accompanied by Tabitha, who was intent on supporting the leader of the pack in his important business.

'Not the paperboy,' Sarah said unnecessarily, looking at the empty chair next to me.

'Are you Diana Bishop?' asked a deep male voice with a familiar foreign accent of flat vowels accompanied by a slight drawl.

'No, I'm her aunt,' Em replied.

'Is there something we can do for you?' Matthew sounded cold, though polite.

'My name is Nathaniel Wilson, and this is my wife, Sophie. We were told we might find Diana Bishop here.'

'Who told you that?' Matthew asked softly.

'His mother – Agatha.' I stood, moving to the door.

His voice reminded me of the daemon from Blackwell's, the fashion designer from Australia with the beautiful brown eyes.

Miriam tried to bar my way into the hall but stepped aside when she saw my expression. Marcus was not so easily dealt with. He grabbed my arm and held me in the shadows by the staircase.

Nathaniel's eyes nudged gently against my face. He was in his early twenties and had familiar fair hair and chocolate-colored eyes, as well as his mother's wide mouth and fine features. Where Agatha had been compact and trim, however, he was nearly as tall as Matthew, with the broad shoulders and narrow hips of a swimmer. An enormous backpack was slung over one shoulder.

'Are you Diana Bishop?' he asked.

A woman's face peeped out from Nathaniel's side. It was sweet and round, with intelligent brown eyes and a dimpled chin. She was in her early twenties as well, and the gentle, insidious pressure of her glance indicated she, too, was a daemon.

As she studied me, a long, brown braid tumbled over her shoulder. 'That's her,' the young woman said, her soft accent betraying that she was born in the South. 'She looks just as she did in my dreams.'

'It's all right, Matthew,' I said. These two daemons posed no more danger to me than did Marthe or Ysabeau.

'So you're the vampire,' Nathaniel said, giving Matthew an appraising look. 'My mother warned me about you.'

'You should listen to her,' Matthew suggested, his voice dangerously soft.

Nathaniel seemed unimpressed. 'She told me you wouldn't welcome the son of a Congregation member. But I'm not here on their behalf. I'm here because of Sophie.' He drew his wife under his arm in a protective gesture, and she shivered and crept closer. Neither was dressed for autumn in New York. Nathaniel was wearing an old barn jacket, and Sophie had on nothing warmer than a turtleneck and a hand-knit cardigan that brushed her knees.

'Are they both daemons?' Matthew asked me.

'Yes,' I replied, though something made me hesitate.

'Are you a vampire as well?' Nathaniel asked Marcus.

Marcus gave him a wolfish grin. 'Guilty.'

Sophie was still nudging me with her characteristic daemonic glance, but there was the faintest tingle on my skin. Her hand crept possessively around her belly.

'You're pregnant!' I cried.

Marcus was so surprised that he loosened his grip on me. Matthew caught me as I went by. The house, agitated by the appearance of two visitors and Matthew's sudden lunge, made its displeasure clear by banging the keeping room's doors tightly closed.

'What you feel – it's me,' Sophie said, moving an inch closer to her husband. 'My people were witches, but I came out wrong.'

Sarah came into the hall, saw the visitors, and threw up her hands. 'Here we go again. I told you daemons would be showing up in Madison before long. Still, the house usually knows our business better than we do. Now that you're here, you might as well come inside, out of the cold.'

The house groaned as if it were heartily sick of us when the daemons entered.

'Don't worry,' I said, trying to reassure them. 'The house told us you were coming, no matter what it sounds like.'

'My granny's house was just the same.' Sophie smiled. 'She lived in the old Norman place in Seven Devils. That's where I'm from. It's officially part of North Carolina, but my dad said that nobody bothered to tell the folks in town. We're kind of a nation unto ourselves.'

The keeping-room doors opened wide, revealing my grandmother and three or four more Bishops, all of whom were watching the proceedings with interest. The boy with the berry basket waved. Sophie shyly waved back.

'Granny had ghosts, too,' she said calmly.

The ghosts, combined with two unfriendly vampires and an overly expressive house, were too much for Nathaniel.

'We aren't staying longer than we have to, Sophie. You came to give something to Diana. Let's get it over with and be on our way,' Nathaniel said. Miriam chose that minute to step out of the shadows by the dining room, her arms crossed over her chest. Nathaniel took a step backward.

'First vampires. Now daemons. What next?' Sarah muttered. She turned to Sophie. 'So you're about five months along?'

'The baby quickened last week,' Sophie replied, both hands resting on her belly. 'That's when Agatha told us where we could find Diana. She didn't know about my family. I've been having dreams about you for months. And I don't know what Agatha saw that made her so scared.'

'What dreams?' Matthew said, his voice quick.

'Let's have Sophie sit down before we subject her to an inquisition.' Sarah quietly took charge. 'Em, can you bring us some of those cookies? Milk, too?'

Em headed toward the kitchen, where we could hear the distant clatter of glasses.

'They could be my dreams, or they could be hers.' Sophie gazed at her belly as Sarah led her and Nathaniel deeper into the house. She looked back over her shoulder at Matthew. 'She's a witch, you see. That's probably what worried Nathaniel's mom.'

All eyes dropped to the bump under Sophie's blue sweater.

'The dining room,' Sarah said in a tone that brooked no nonsense. 'Everybody in the dining room.'

Matthew held me back. 'There's something too convenient about their showing up right now. No mention of timewalking in front of them.'

'They're harmless.' Every instinct confirmed it.

'Nobody's harmless, and that certainly goes for Agatha Wilson's son.' Tabitha, who was sitting next to Matthew, mewled in agreement.

'Are you two joining us, or do I have to drag you into this room?' Sarah called.

'We're on our way,' Matthew said smoothly.

Sarah was at the head of the table. She pointed at the empty chairs to her right. 'Sit.'

We were facing Sophie and Nathaniel, who sat with an empty seat between them and Marcus. Matthew's son split his attention between his father and the daemons. I sat between Matthew and

Miriam, both of whom never took their eyes from Nathaniel. When Em entered, she had a tray laden with wine, milk, bowls of berries and nuts, and an enormous plate of cookies.

'God, cookies make me wish like hell I was still warmblooded,' Marcus said reverently, picking up one of the golden disks studded with chocolate and holding it to his nose. 'They smell so good, but they taste terrible.'

'Have these instead,' Em said, sliding him a bowl of walnuts. 'They're covered in vanilla and sugar. They're not cookies, but they're close.' She passed him a bottle of wine and a corkscrew, too. 'Open that and pour some for your father.'

'Thanks, Em,' Marcus said around a mouthful of sticky walnuts, already pulling the cork free from the bottle. 'You're the best.'

Sarah watched intently as Sophie drank thirstily from the glass of milk and ate a cookie. When the daemon reached for her second, my aunt turned to Nathaniel. 'Now, where's your car?' Given all that had happened, it was an odd opening question.

'We came on foot.' Nathaniel hadn't touched anything Em put in front of him.

'From where?' Marcus asked incredulously, handing Matthew a glass of wine. He'd seen enough of the surrounding countryside to know that there was nothing within walking distance.

'We rode with a friend from Durham to Washington,' Sophie explained. 'Then we caught a train from D.C. to New York. I didn't like the city much.'

'We caught the train to Albany, then went on to Syracuse. The bus took us to Cazenovia.' Nathaniel put a warning hand on Sophie's arm.

'He doesn't want me to tell you that we caught a ride from a stranger,' Sophie confided with a smile. 'The lady knew where the house was. Her kids love coming here on Halloween because you're real witches.' Sophie took another sip of milk. 'Not that we needed the directions. There's a lot of energy in this house. We couldn't have missed it.'

'Is there a reason you took such an indirect route?' Matthew asked Nathaniel.

'Somebody followed us as far as New York, but Sophie and I got back on the train for Washington and they lost interest,' Nathaniel bristled.

'Then we got off the train in New Jersey and went back to the city. The man in the station said tourists get confused all the time about which way the train is going. They didn't even charge us, did they, Nathaniel?' Sophie looked pleased at the warm reception they'd received from Amtrak.

Matthew continued with his interrogation of Nathaniel. 'Where are you staying?'

'They're staying here.' Em's voice had a sharp edge. 'They don't have a car, and the house made room for them. Besides, Sophie needs to talk to Diana.'

'I'd like that. Agatha said you'd be able to help. Something about a book for the baby,' Sophie said softly. Marcus's eyes darted to the page from Ashmole 782, the edge of which was peeking from underneath the chart laying out the Knights of Lazarus's chain of command. He hastily drew the papers into a pile, moving an innocuous-looking set of DNA results to the top.

'What book, Sophie?' I asked.

'We didn't tell Agatha my people were witches. I didn't even tell Nathaniel — not until he came home to meet my dad. We'd been together for almost four years, and my dad was sick and losing control over his magic. I didn't want Nathaniel spooked. Anyway, when we got married, we thought it was best not to cause a fuss. Agatha was on the Congregation by then and was always talking about the segregation rules and what happened when folks broke them.' Sophie shook her head. 'It never made any sense to me.'

'The book?' I repeated, gently trying to steer the conversation.

'Oh.' Sophie's forehead creased with concentration, and she fell silent.

'My mother is thrilled about the baby. She said it's going to be the best-dressed child the world has ever seen.' Nathaniel smiled tenderly at his wife. 'Then the dreams started. Sophie felt trouble was coming. She has strong premonitions for a daemon, just like my mother. In September she started seeing Diana's face and hearing her name. Sophie said people want something from you.'

Matthew's fingers touched the small of my back where Satu's scar dipped down.

'Show them her face jug, Nathaniel. It's just a picture. I wanted to bring it, but he said we couldn't carry a gallon jug from Durham to New York.'

Her husband obediently took out his phone and pulled up a picture on the screen. Nathaniel handed the phone to Sarah, who gasped.

'I'm a potter, like my mama and her mother. Granny used witchfire in her kiln, but I just do it the ordinary way. All the faces from my dreams go on my jugs. Not all of them are scary. Yours wasn't.'

Sarah passed the phone to Matthew. 'It's beautiful, Sophie,' he said sincerely.

I had to agree. Its tall, rounded shape was pale gray, and two handles curved away from its narrow spout. On the front was a face – my face, though distorted by the jug's proportions. My chin jutted out from the surface, as did my nose, my ears, and the sweep of my brow bones. Thick squiggles of clay stood in for hair. My eyes were closed, and my mouth smiled serenely, as if I were keeping a secret.

'This is for you, too.' Sophie drew a small, lumpy object out of the pocket of her cardigan. It was wrapped in oilcloth secured with string. 'When the baby quickened, I knew for sure it belonged to you. The baby knows, too. Maybe that's what made Agatha so worried. And of course we have to figure out what to do, since the baby is a witch. Nathaniel's mom thought you might have some ideas.'

We watched in silence while Sophie picked at the knots. 'Sorry,' she muttered. 'My dad tied it up. He was in the navy.'

'Can I help you?' Marcus asked, reaching for the lump.

'No, I've got it.' Sophie smiled at him sweetly and went back to her work. 'It has to be wrapped up or it turns black. And it's not supposed to be black. It's supposed to be white.'

Our collective curiosity was now thoroughly aroused, and there wasn't a sound in the house except for the lapping of Tabitha's tongue as she groomed her paws. The string fell away, followed by the oilcloth.

'There,' Sophie whispered. 'I may not be a witch, but I'm the last of the Normans. We've been keeping this for you.'

It was a small figurine no more than four inches tall and made from old silver that glowed with the softly burnished light seen in museum showcases. Sophie turned the figurine so that it faced me.

'Diana,' I said unnecessarily. The goddess was represented exactly, from the tips of the crescent moon on her brow to her sandaled feet. She was in motion, one foot striding forward while a hand reached over her shoulders to draw an arrow from her quiver. The other hand rested on the antlers of a stag.

'Where did you get that?' Matthew sounded strange, and his face had gone gray again.

Sophie shrugged. 'Nobody knows. The Normans have always had it. It's been passed down in the family from witch to witch. "When the time comes, give it to the one who has need of it." That's what my granny told my father, and my father told me. It used to be written on a little piece of paper, but that was lost a long time ago.'

'What is it, Matthew?' Marcus looked uneasy. So did Nathaniel.

'It's a chess piece,' Matthew's voice broke. 'The white queen.'

'How do you know that?' Sarah looked at the figurine critically. 'It's not like any chess piece I ever saw.'

Matthew had to force the words out from behind tight lips. 'Because it was once mine. My father gave it to me.'

'How did it end up in North Carolina?' I stretched my fingers toward the silver object, and the figurine slid across the table as if it wanted to be in my possession. The stag's antlers cut into my palm as my hand closed around it, the metal quickly warming to my touch.

'I lost it in a wager,' Matthew said quietly. 'I have no idea how it got to North Carolina.' He buried his face in his hands and murmured a single word that made no sense to me. 'Kit.'

'Do you remember when you last had it?' Sarah asked sharply.

'I remember precisely.' Matthew lifted his head. 'I was playing a game with it many years ago, on All Souls' Night. It was then that I lost my wager.'

'That's next week.' Miriam shifted in her seat so that she could meet Sarah's eyes. 'Would timewalking be easier around the feasts of All Saints and All Souls?'

'Miriam,' Matthew snarled, but it was too late.

'What's timewalking?' Nathaniel whispered to Sophie.

'Mama was a timewalker,' Sophie whispered back. 'She was good at it, too, and always came back from the 1700s with lots of ideas for pots and jugs.'

'Your mother visited the past?' Nathaniel asked faintly. He looked around the room at the motley assortment of creatures, then at his wife's belly. 'Does that run in witches' families, too, like second sight?'

Sarah answered Miriam over the daemons' whispered conversation. 'There's not much keeping the living from the dead between Halloween and All Souls. It would be easier to slip between the past and the present then.'

Nathaniel looked more anxious. 'The living and the dead? Sophie and I just came to deliver that statue or whatever it is so she can sleep through the night.'

'Will Diana be strong enough?' Marcus asked Matthew, ignoring Nathaniel.

'This time of year, it should be much easier for Diana to timewalk,' Sarah mused aloud.

Sophie looked contentedly around the table. 'This reminds me of the old days when granny and her sisters got together and gossiped. They never seemed to pay attention to one another, but they always knew what had been said.'

The room's many competing conversations stopped abruptly when the dining-room doors banged open and shut, followed by a booming sound produced by the heavier keeping-room doors. Nathaniel, Miriam, and Marcus shot to their feet.

'What the hell was that?' Marcus asked.

'The house,' I said wearily. 'I'll go see what it wants.'

Matthew scooped up the figurine and followed me.

The old woman with the embroidered bodice was waiting at the keeping room's threshold.

'Hello, ma'am.' Sophie had followed right behind and was nodding politely to the old woman. She scrutinized my features. 'The lady looks a bit like you, doesn't she?'

So you've chosen your road, the old woman said. Her voice was fainter than before.

'We have,' I said. Footsteps sounded behind me as the remaining occupants of the dining room came to see what the commotion was about.

You'll be needing something else for your journey, she replied.

The coffin doors swung open, and the press of creatures at my back was matched by the crowd of ghosts waiting by the fireplace.

This should be interesting, my grandmother said drily from her place at the head of the ghostly bunch.

There was a rumbling in the walls like bones rattling. I sat in my grandmother's rocker, my knees no longer able to hold my weight.

A crack developed in the paneling between the window and the fireplace. It stretched and widened in a diagonal slash. The old wood shuddered and squeaked. Something soft with legs and arms flew out of the gap. I flinched when it landed in my lap.

'Holy shit,' Sarah said.

That paneling will never look the same, my grandmother commented, shaking her head regretfully at the cracked wood.

Whatever flew at me was made of rough-spun fabric that had faded to an indiscriminate grayish brown. In addition to its four limbs, it had a lump where the head belonged, adorned with faded tufts of hair. Someone had stitched an X where the heart should be.

'What is it?' I reached my index finger toward the uneven, rusty stitches.

'Don't touch it!' Em cried.

'I'm already touching it,' I said, looking up in confusion. 'It's sitting on my lap.'

'I've never seen such an old poppet,' said Sophie, peering down at it.

'Poppet?' Miriam frowned. 'Didn't one of your ancestors get in trouble over a poppet?'

'Bridget Bishop.' Sarah, Em, and I said the name at the same moment.

The old woman with the embroidered bodice was now standing next to my grandmother.

'Is this yours?' I whispered.

A smile turned up one corner of Bridget's mouth. *Remember to be canny when you find yourself at a crossroads, daughter. There's no telling what secrets are buried there.*

Looking down at the poppet, I lightly touched the X on its chest. The fabric split open, revealing a stuffing made of leaves, twigs, and dried flowers and releasing the scent of herbs into the air. 'Rue,' I said, recognizing it from Marthe's tea.

'Clover, broom, knotweed, and slippery elm bark, too, from the smell of it.' Sarah gave the air a good sniff. 'That poppet was made to draw someone – Diana, presumably – but it's got a protection spell on it, too.'

You did well by her, Bridget told my grandmother with an approving nod at Sarah.

Something was gleaming through the brown. When I pulled at it gently, the poppet came apart in pieces.

And there's an end to it, Bridget said with a sigh. My grandmother put a comforting arm around her.

'It's an earring.' Its intricate golden surfaces caught the light, and an enormous, teardrop-shaped pearl shone at the end.

'How the hell did one of my mother's earrings get into Bridget Bishop's poppet?' Matthew's face was back to that pasty gray color.

'Were your mother's earrings in the same place as your chess set on that long-ago night?' Miriam asked. Both the earring and the chess piece were old – older than the poppet, older than the Bishop house.

Matthew thought a moment, then nodded. 'Yes. Is a week enough time? Can you be ready?' he asked me urgently.

'I don't know.'

'Sure you'll be ready,' Sophie crooned to her belly. 'She'll make things right for you, little witch. You'll be her godmother,' Sophie said with a radiant smile. 'She'll like that.'

'Counting the baby – and not counting the ghosts, of course,' Marcus said in a deceptively conversational tone that reminded me of the way Matthew spoke when he was stressed, 'there are nine of us in this room.'

'Four witches, three vampires, and two daemons,' Sophie said dreamily, her hands still on her belly. 'But we're short a daemon. Without one we can't be a conventicle. And once Matthew and Diana leave, we'll need another vampire, too. Is Matthew's mother still alive?'

'She's tired,' Nathaniel said apologetically, his hands tightening on his wife's shoulders. 'It makes it difficult for her to focus.'

'What did you say?' Em asked Sophie. She was struggling to keep her voice calm.

Sophie's eyes lost their dreaminess. 'A conventicle. That's what they called a gathering of dissenters in the old days. Ask them.' She inclined her head in the direction of Marcus and Miriam.

'I told you this wasn't about the Bishops or the de Clermonts,' Em said to Sarah. 'It's not even about Matthew and Diana and whether they can be together. It's about Sophie and Nathaniel, too. It's about the future, just as Diana said. This is how we'll fight the Congregation – not just as individual families but as a— What did you call it?'

'Conventicle,' Miriam answered. 'I always liked that word – so delightfully ominous.' She settled back on her heels with a satisfied smile.

Matthew turned to Nathaniel. 'It would seem your mother was right. You do belong here, with us.'

'Of course they belong here,' Sarah said briskly. 'Your bedroom is ready, Nathaniel. It's upstairs, the second door to the right.'

'Thank you,' Nathaniel said, a note of cautious relief in his voice, though he still eyed Matthew warily.

'I'm Marcus.' Matthew's son held out his hand to the daemon. Nathaniel clasped it firmly, barely reacting to the shocking coldness of vampire flesh.

'See? We didn't need to make reservations at that hotel, sweetie,' Sophie told her husband with a beatific smile. She looked for Em in the crowd. 'Are there more cookies?'

CHAPTER 40

A few days later, Sophie was sitting at the kitchen island with half a dozen pumpkins and a sharp knife when Matthew and I came in from our walk. The weather had turned colder, and there was a dreary hint of winter in the air.

'What do you think?' Sophie asked, turning the pumpkin. It had the hollow eyes, arched eyebrows, and gaping mouth of all Halloween pumpkins, but she had transformed the usual features into something remarkable. Lines pulled away from the mouth, and the forehead was creased, setting the eyes themselves slightly off-kilter. The overall effect was chilling.

'Amazing!' Matthew looked at the pumpkin with delight.

She bit her lip, regarding her work critically. 'I'm not sure the eyes are right.'

I laughed. 'At least it *has* eyes. Sometimes Sarah can't be bothered and just pokes three round holes in the side with the end of a screwdriver and calls it a day.'

'Halloween is a busy holiday for witches. We don't always have time for the finer details,' Sarah said sharply, coming out of the stillroom to inspect Sophie's work. She nodded with approval. 'But this year we'll be the envy of the neighborhood.'

Sophie smiled shyly and pulled another pumpkin toward her. 'I'll do a less scary one next. We don't want to make the little kids cry.'

With less than a week to go until Halloween, Em and Sarah were in a flurry of activity to get ready for the Madison coven's annual fall bash. There would be food, free-flowing drink (including Em's famous punch, which had at least one July birth to its credit), and enough witchy activities to keep the sugar-high children occupied and away from the bonfire after they'd been trick-or-treating. Bobbing for apples was much more challenging when the fruit in question had been put under a spell.

My aunts hinted that they would cancel their plans, but Matthew just shook his head.

'Everyone in town would wonder if you didn't show up. This is just a typical Halloween.'

We'd all looked dubious. After all, Sarah and Em weren't the only ones counting the hours to Halloween.

Last night Matthew had laid out the gradual departure of everyone in the house, starting with Nathaniel and Sophie and ending with Marcus and Miriam. It would, he believed, make our own departure less conspicuous – and it was not open to discussion.

Marcus and Nathaniel had exchanged a long look when Matthew finished his announcement, which concluded with the daemon shaking his head and pressing his lips together and the younger vampire staring fixedly at the table while a muscle in his jaw throbbed.

'But who will hand out the candy?' Em asked.

Matthew looked thoughtful. 'Diana and I will do it.'

The two young men had stormed out of the room when we broke up to go our separate ways, mumbling something about getting milk. They'd then climbed into Marcus's car and torn down the driveway.

'You've got to stop telling them what to do,' I chided Matthew, who had joined me at the front door to watch their departure. 'They're both grown men. Nathaniel has a wife, and soon he'll have a child.'

'Left to their own devices, Marcus and Nathaniel would have an army of vampires on the doorstep tomorrow.'

'You won't be here to order them around next week,' I reminded him, watching the taillights as they turned toward town. 'Your son will be in charge.'

'That's what I'm worried about.'

The real problem was that we were in the midst of an acute

outbreak of testosterone poisoning. Nathaniel and Matthew couldn't be in the same room without sparks flying, and in the increasingly crowded house it was hard for them to avoid each other.

Their next argument occurred that afternoon when a delivery arrived. It was a box with BIOHAZARD written all over the sealing tape in large red letters.

'What the hell is this?' Marcus asked, carrying the box gingerly into the family room. Nathaniel looked up from his laptop, his brown eyes widening with alarm.

'That's for me,' Matthew said smoothly, taking the box from his son.

'My wife is pregnant!' Nathaniel said furiously, snapping his laptop closed. 'How could you bring that into the house?'

'It's immunizations for Diana.' Matthew barely kept his annoyance in check.

I put aside my magazine. 'What immunizations?'

'You're not going to the past without every possible protection from disease. Come to the stillroom,' Matthew said, holding out his hand.

'Tell me what's in the box first.'

'Booster vaccines – tetanus, typhoid, polio, diphtheria – as well as some vaccines you probably haven't had, like a new one-shot rabies preventive, the latest flu shots, an immunization for cholera.' He paused, still holding out his hand. 'And a smallpox vaccine.'

'Smallpox?' They'd stopped giving smallpox vaccines to schoolchildren a few years before I was born. That meant Sophie and Nathaniel hadn't been immunized either.

Matthew reached down and hoisted me to my feet. 'Let's get started,' he said firmly.

'You aren't going to stick needles into me today.'

'Better needles today than smallpox and lockjaw tomorrow,' he countered.

'Wait a minute.' Nathaniel's voice sounded in the room like a cracking whip. 'The smallpox vaccine makes you contagious. What about Sophie and the baby?'

'Explain it to him, Marcus,' Matthew ordered, stepping aside so I could pass.

'Not contagious with smallpox, exactly.' Marcus tried to be reassuring. 'It's a different strain of the disease. Sophie will be fine, provided she doesn't touch Diana's arm or anything it comes into contact with.'

Sophie smiled at Marcus. 'Okay. I can do that.'

'Do you always do everything he tells you to do?' Nathaniel asked Marcus with contempt, unfolding from the couch. He looked down at his wife. 'Sophie, we're leaving.'

'Stop fussing, Nathaniel,' Sophie said. 'You'll upset the house – the baby, too – if you start talking about leaving. We're not going anywhere.'

Nathaniel gave Matthew an evil look and sat down.

In the stillroom Matthew had me take off my sweatshirt and turtleneck and then began swabbing my left arm with alcohol. The door creaked open.

It was Sarah. She'd stood by without comment during the exchange between Matthew and Nathaniel, though her eyes had seldom left the newly delivered box.

Matthew had already sliced open the protective tape wrapped around the molded-foam container. Seven small vials were nestled within, along with a bag of pills, something that looked like a container of salt, and a two-pronged metal instrument I'd never seen before. He'd already entered the same state of clinical detachment I'd first detected in his lab in Oxford, with no time for chatter or a warm bedside manner. Sarah was welcome moral support.

'I've got some old white shirts for you to wear.' Sarah momentarily distracted me from what Matthew was doing. 'They'll be easy to bleach. Some white towels, too. Leave your laundry upstairs and I'll take care of it.'

'Thank you, Sarah. That's one less risk of contagion to worry about.' Matthew selected one of the vials. 'We'll start with the tetanus booster.'

Each time he stuck something in my arm, I winced. By the third shot, there was a thin sheen of sweat on my forehead and my heart was pounding. 'Sarah,' I said faintly. 'Can you please not stand behind me?'

'Sorry.' Sarah moved to stand behind Matthew instead. 'I'll get you some water.' She handed me a glass of ice-cold water, the outside slippery with condensation. I took it gratefully, trying to focus on holding it steady rather than on the next vial Matthew was opening.

Another needle entered my skin, and I jumped.

'That's the last shot,' Matthew said. He opened the container that looked like it was filled with salt crystals and carefully added the contents to a bottle of liquid. After giving it a vigorous shake, he handed it to me. 'This is the cholera vaccine. It's oral. Then there's the smallpox immunization, and some pills to take after dinner for the next few nights.'

I drank it down quickly but still almost gagged at the thick texture and vile taste.

Matthew opened up the sealed pouch holding the two-pronged smallpox inoculator. 'Do you know what Thomas Jefferson wrote to Edward Jenner about this vaccine?' he asked, voice hypnotic. 'Jefferson said it was medicine's most useful discovery.' There was a cold touch of alcohol on my right arm, then pricks as the inoculator's prongs pierced the skin. 'The president dismissed Harvey's discovery of the circulation of blood as nothing more than a "beautiful addition" to medical knowledge.' Matthew moved in a circular pattern, distributing the live virus on my skin.

His diversionary tactics were working. I was too busy listening to his story to pay much attention to my arm.

'But Jefferson praised Jenner because his inoculation relegated small-pox to a disease that would be known only to historians. He'd saved the human race from one of its most deadly enemies.' Matthew dumped the empty vial and the inoculator into a sealed biohazard container. 'All done.'

'Did you know Jefferson?' I was already fantasizing about timewalking to eighteenth-century Virginia.

'I knew Washington better. He was a soldier – a man who let his actions speak for him. Jefferson was full of words. But it wasn't easy to reach the man behind the intellect. I'd never drop by his house unannounced with a bluestocking like you in tow.'

I reached for my turtleneck, but Matthew stilled my arm and carefully covered the inoculation site with a waterproof bandage. 'This is a live virus, so you have to keep it covered. Sophie and Nathaniel can't come into contact with it, or with anything that touches it.' He moved to the sink and vigorously washed his hands in steaming-hot water.

'For how long?'

'It will form a blister, and then the blister will scab over. No one should touch the site until the blister heals.'

I pulled the old, stretched-out turtleneck over my head, taking care not to dislodge the bandage.

'Now that that's done, we need to figure out how Diana is going to carry you – and herself – to some distant time by Halloween. She may have been timewalking since she was an infant, but it's still not easy,' Sarah worried, her face twisted in a frown.

Em appeared around the door. We made room for her at the table.

'I've been timewalking recently, too,' I confessed.

'When?' Matthew paused for a moment in his work of clearing up what remained from the inoculations.

'First on the driveway when you were talking to Ysabeau. Then again the day Sarah was trying to make me light a candle, when I went from the stillroom to the orchard. Both times I picked up my foot, wished myself somewhere else, and put my foot down where I wanted to be.'

'That sounds like timewalking,' Sarah said slowly. 'Of course, you didn't travel far – and you weren't carrying anything.' She sized up Matthew, her expression turning doubtful.

There was a knock at the door. 'Can I come in?' Sophie's call was muffled.

'Can she, Matthew?' Em asked.

'As long as she doesn't touch Diana.'

When Em opened the door, Sophie was moving soothing hands around her belly. 'Everything's going to be all right,' she said serenely from the threshold. 'As long as Matthew has a connection to the place they're going, he'll help Diana, not weigh her down.'

Miriam appeared behind Sophie. 'Is something interesting happening?'

'We're talking about timewalking,' I said.

'How will you practice?' Miriam stepped around Sophie and pushed her firmly back toward the door when she tried to follow.

'Diana will go back in time a few hours, then a few more. We'll increase the time involved, then the distance. Then we'll add Matthew and see what happens.' Sarah looked at Em. 'Can you help her?'

'A bit,' Em replied cautiously. 'Stephen told me how he did it. He never used spells to go back in time – his power was strong enough without them. Given Diana's early experiences with timewalking and her difficulties with witchcraft, we might want to follow his example.'

'Why don't you and Diana go to the barn and try?' Sarah suggested gently. 'She can come straight back to the stillroom.'

When Matthew started after us, Sarah put a hand out and stopped him. 'Stay here.'

Matthew's face had gone gray again. He didn't like me in a different room, never mind a different time.

The hop barn still held the sweet aroma of long-ago harvests. Em stood opposite and quietly issued instructions. 'Stand as still as possible,' she said, 'and empty your mind.'

'You sound like my yoga teacher,' I said, arranging my limbs in the familiar lines of mountain pose.

Em smiled. 'I've always thought yoga and magic had a lot in common. Now, close your eyes. Think about the stillroom you just left. You have to want to be there more than here.'

Re-creating the stillroom in my mind, I furnished it with objects, scents, people. I frowned. 'Where will you be?'

'It depends on when you arrive. If it's before we left, I'll be there. If not, I'll be here.'

'The physics of this don't make sense.' My head filled with concerns about how the universe would handle multiple Dianas and Ems – not to mention Miriams and Sarahs.

'Stop thinking about physics. What did your dad write in his note? *"Whoever can no longer wonder, no longer marvel, is as good as dead."* '

'Close enough,' I admitted reluctantly.

'It's time for you to take a big step into the mysterious, Diana. The magic and wonder that was always your birthright is waiting for you. Now, think about where you want to be.'

When my mind was brimming over with images of it, I picked up my foot.

When I put it down again, there I was in the hop barn with Em.

'It didn't work,' I said, panicking.

'You were too focused on the details of the room. Think about Matthew. Don't you want to be with him? Magic's in the heart, not the mind. It's not about words and following a procedure, like witchcraft. You have to *feel* it.'

'Desire.' I saw myself calling *Notes and Queries* from the shelf at the Bodleian, felt once more the first touch of Matthew's lips on mine in his rooms at All Souls. The barn dropped away, and Matthew was telling me the story about Thomas Jefferson and Edward Jenner.

'No,' Em said, her voice steely. 'Don't think about Jefferson. Think about Matthew.'

'Matthew.' I brought my mind back to the touch of his cool fingers against my skin, the rich sound of his voice, the sense of intense vitality when we were together.

I picked up my foot.

It landed in the corner of the stillroom, where I was squashed behind an old barrel.

'What if she gets lost?' Matthew sounded tense. 'How will we get her back?'

'We don't have to worry about that,' Sophie said, pointing in my direction. 'She's already here.'

Matthew whipped around and let out a ragged breath.

'How long have I been gone?' I felt lightheaded and disoriented, but otherwise fine.

'About ninety seconds,' Sarah said. 'More than enough time for Matthew to have a nervous breakdown.'

Matthew pulled me into his arms and tucked me under his chin. 'Thank God. How soon can she take me with her?'

'Let's not get ahead of ourselves,' Sarah warned. 'One step at a time.'

I looked around. 'Where's Em?'

'In the barn.' Sophie was beaming. 'She'll catch up.'

It took more than twenty minutes for Em to return. When she did, her cheeks were pink from concern as well as the cold, though some of the tension left her when she saw me standing with Matthew.

'You did good, Em,' Sarah said, kissing her in a rare public display of affection.

'Diana started thinking about Thomas Jefferson,' Em said. 'She might have ended up at Monticello. Then she focused on her feelings, and her body got blurry around the edges. I blinked, and she was gone.'

That afternoon, with Em's careful coaching, I took a slightly longer trip back to breakfast. Over the next few days, I went a bit farther with each timewalk. Going back in time aided by three objects was always easier than returning to the present, which required enormous concentration as well as an ability to accurately forecast where and when you wanted to arrive. Finally it was time to try carrying Matthew.

Sarah had insisted on limiting the variables to accommodate the extra effort required. 'Start out wherever you want to end up,' she advised. 'That way all you have to worry about is thinking yourself back to a particular time. The place will take care of itself.'

I took him up to the bedroom at twilight without telling him what was in store. The figure of Diana and the golden earring from Bridget Bishop's poppet were sitting on the chest of drawers in front of a photograph of my parents.

'Much as I'd like to spend a few hours with you in here – alone –

dinner is almost ready,' he protested, though there was a calculating gleam in his eyes.

'There's plenty of time. Sarah said I'm ready to take you timewalking. We're going back to our first night in the house.'

Matthew thought for a moment, and his eyes brightened further. 'Was that the night the stars came out – inside?'

I kissed him in answer.

'Oh.' He looked shyly pleased. 'What should I do?'

'Nothing.' This would be the hardest thing about timewalking for him. 'What are you always telling me? Close your eyes, relax, and let me do the rest.' I grinned wickedly.

He laced his fingers through mine. 'Witch.'

'You won't even know it's happening,' I assured him. 'It's fast. Just pick up your foot and put it down again when I tell you. And don't let go.'

'Not a chance,' Matthew said, tightening his grip.

I thought about that night, our first alone after my encounter with Satu. I remembered his touch against my back, fierce and gentle at the same time. I felt the connection, immediate and tenacious, to that shared moment in our past.

'Now,' I whispered. Our feet rose together.

But timewalking with Matthew was different. Having him along slowed us down, and for the first time I was aware of what was happening.

The past, present, and future shimmered around us in a spiderweb of light and color. Each strand in the web moved slowly, almost imperceptibly, sometimes touching another filament before moving gently away again as if caught by a breeze. Each time strands touched – and millions of strands were touching all the time – there was the soft echo of an original, inaudible sound.

Momentarily distracted by the seemingly limitless possibilities before us, we found it easy to lose sight of the twisted red-and-white strand of time we were following. I brought my concentration back to it, knowing it would take us back to our first night in Madison.

I put my foot down and felt rough floorboards against my bare skin.

'You told me it would be fast,' he said hoarsely. 'That didn't feel fast to me.'

'No, it was different,' I agreed. 'Did you see the lights?'

Matthew shook his head. 'There was nothing but blackness. I was falling, slowly, with only your hand keeping me from hitting the bottom.' He raised it to his mouth and kissed it.

There was a lingering smell of chili in the quiet house, and it was night outside. 'Can you tell who's here?'

His nostrils flared, and he closed his eyes. Then he smiled and sighed with happiness. 'Just Sarah and Em, and you and me. None of the children.'

I giggled, drawing him closer.

'If this house gets any more crowded, it's going to burst.' Matthew buried his face in my neck, then drew back. 'You still have your bandage. It means that when we go back in time, we don't stop being who we are in the present or forget what happened to us here.' His cold hands crept under the hem of my turtleneck. 'Given your rediscovered talents as a timewalker, how accurate are you at gauging the passing of time?'

Though we happily lingered in the past, we were back in the present before Emily finished making the salad.

'Timewalking agrees with you, Matthew,' Sarah said, scrutinizing his relaxed face. She rewarded him with a glass of red wine.

'Thank you, Sarah. I was in good hands.' He raised his glass to me in salute.

'Glad to hear it,' Sarah said drily, sounding like my ghostly grandmother. She threw some sliced radishes into the biggest salad bowl I'd ever seen.

'Where did that come from?' I peered into the bowl to hide my reddened lips.

'The house,' Em said, beating the salad dressing with a whisk. 'It enjoys having so many mouths to feed.'

Next morning the house let us know it was anticipating yet another addition.

Sarah, Matthew, and I were discussing whether my next timewalk should be to Oxford or to Sept-Tours when Em appeared with a load of laundry in her arms. 'Somebody is coming.'

Matthew put down his paper and stood. 'Good. I was expecting a delivery today.'

'It's not a delivery, and they're not here yet. But the house is ready for them.' She disappeared into the laundry room.

'Another room? Where did the house put this one?' Sarah shouted after her.

'Next to Marcus.' Em's reply echoed from the depths of the washing machine.

We took bets on who it would be. The guesses ranged from Agatha Wilson to Emily's friends from Cherry Valley who liked to show up unannounced for the coven's Halloween party.

Late in the morning, there was an authoritative knock on the door. It opened to a small, dark man with intelligent eyes. He was instantly recognizable from pictures taken at celebrity parties in London and television news conferences. Any remaining doubts about his identity were erased by the familiar nudges against my cheekbones.

Our mystery house guest was Matthew's friend Hamish Osborne.

'You must be Diana,' he said without pleasure or preamble, his Scottish accent lending length to the vowels. Hamish was dressed for business, in a pin-striped charcoal suit that had been tailored to fit him exactly, a pale pink shirt with heavy silver cuff links, and a fuchsia tie embroidered with tiny black flies.

'I am. Hello, Hamish. Was Matthew expecting you?' I stepped aside to let him in.

'Probably not,' Hamish said crisply, remaining on the stoop. 'Where is he?'

'Hamish.' Matthew was moving so quickly I felt the breeze behind me before hearing him approach. He extended his hand. 'This is a surprise.'

Hamish stared at the outstretched hand, then turned his eyes to its owner. 'Surprise? Let's discuss surprises. When I joined your . . . "family firm," you swore to me this would never arrive.' He brandished an envelope, its black seal broken but still clinging to the flaps.

'I did.' Matthew dropped his hand and looked at Hamish warily.

'So much for your promises, then. I'm given to understand from this letter, and from my conversation with your mother, that there's some kind of trouble.' Hamish's eyes flickered to me, then back to Matthew.

'Yes.' Matthew's lips tightened. 'But you're the ninth knight. You don't have to become involved.'

'You made a *daemon* the ninth knight?' Miriam had come through the dining room with Nathaniel.

'Who's he?' Nathaniel shook a handful of Scrabble tiles in his cupped hand while surveying the new arrival.

'Hamish Osborne. And who might you be?' Hamish asked, as if addressing an impertinent employee. The last thing we needed was more testosterone in the house.

'Oh, I'm nobody,' Nathaniel said airily, leaning against the dining-room door. He watched Marcus as he passed by.

'Hamish, why are you here?' Marcus looked confused, then saw the letter. 'Oh.'

My ancestors were congregating in the keeping room, and the house was stirring on its foundations. 'Could we continue this inside? It's the house, you see. It's a little uneasy, given you're a daemon — and angry.'

'Come, Hamish.' Matthew tried to draw him out of the doorway. 'Marcus and Sarah haven't demolished the whiskey supply yet. We'll get you a drink and sit you by the fire.'

Hamish remained where he was and kept talking.

'While visiting your mother, who was far more willing to answer my questions than you would have been, I learned that you wanted a few things from home. It seemed a shame for Alain to make such a long trip, when I was already going to come and ask you what the hell you were up to.' He lifted a bulky leather briefcase with soft sides and a formidable lock, and a smaller, hard-sided case.

'Thank you, Hamish.' The words were cordial enough, but Matthew was clearly displeased at having his arrangements altered.

'Speaking of explanations, it's a damn good thing the French don't care about the exportation of English national treasures. Have you any idea of the paperwork that would have been required to get this out of England? *If* they'd let me remove it at all, which I doubt.'

Matthew took the briefcases from Hamish's fingers, gripped him by the elbow, and pulled his friend inside. 'Later,' he said hastily. 'Marcus, take Hamish and introduce him to Diana's family while I put these away.'

'Oh, it's you,' said Sophie with delight, coming out of the dining room. The bulge of her belly showed plainly underneath a stretched University of North Carolina sweatshirt. 'You're like Nathaniel, not scatterbrained like me. Your face is on one of my pots, too.' She beamed at Hamish, who looked both charmed and startled.

'Are there more?' he asked me, with a cock of his head that made him resemble a tiny, bright-eyed bird.

'Many more,' Sophie replied happily. 'You won't see them, though.'

'Come and meet my aunts,' I said hastily.

'The witches?' It was impossible to know what Hamish was thinking. His sharp eyes missed nothing, and his face was nearly as impassive as Matthew's.

'Yes, the witches.'

Matthew disappeared upstairs while Marcus and I introduced Hamish to Em. He seemed less annoyed with her than he was with Matthew and me, and she immediately started fussing over him. Sarah met us at the stillroom door, wondering what the commotion was about.

'We're a proper conventicle now, Sarah,' Sophie observed as she reached for the pyramid of freshly baked cookies on the kitchen island. 'All nine – three witches, three daemons, and three vampires – present and accounted for.'

'Looks like it,' Sarah agreed, sizing up Hamish. She watched her partner buzzing around the kitchen like a bewildered bee. 'Em, I don't think our new guest needs tea or coffee. Is the whiskey in the dining room?'

'Diana and I call it the "war room",' Sophie confided, grabbing Hamish familiarly by the forearm, 'though it seems unlikely we could fight a war without the humans finding out. It's the only place big enough to hold us now. Some of the ghosts manage to squeeze in, too.'

'Ghosts?' Hamish reached up and loosened his tie.

'The dining room.' Sarah gripped Hamish's other elbow. 'Everybody in the dining room.'

Matthew was already there. The aroma of hot wax filled the air. When all of us had grabbed our chosen drink and found a seat, he took charge.

'Hamish has questions,' Matthew said. 'Nathaniel and Sophie, too. And I suppose this is my tale to tell – mine and Diana's.'

With that, Matthew took a deep breath and plunged in. He included everything – Ashmole 782, the Knights of Lazarus, the break-ins at Oxford, Satu and what happened at La Pierre, even Baldwin's fury. There were poppets and earrings and face jugs as well. Hamish looked at Matthew sharply when he discussed timewalking and the three objects I would need to travel back to a particular time and place.

'Matthew Clairmont,' Hamish hissed, leaning across the table. 'Is that what I brought from Sept-Tours? Does Diana know?'

'No,' Matthew confessed, looking slightly uncomfortable. 'She'll know on Halloween.'

'Well, she'd have to know on Halloween, wouldn't she?' Hamish let out an exasperated sigh.

Though the exchange between Hamish and Matthew was heated, there were only two moments when the tension threatened to escalate into outright civil war. Both of them, not surprisingly, involved Matthew and Nathaniel.

The first was when Matthew explained to Sophie what this war would be like – the unexpected attacks, the long-simmering feuds between vampires and witches that would come to a boil, the brutal deaths that were bound to occur as creature fought creature using magic, witchcraft, brute strength, speed, and preternatural cunning.

'That's not how wars are fought anymore.' Nathaniel's deep voice cut through the resulting chatter.

Matthew's eyebrow floated up, and his face took on an impatient expression. 'No?'

'Wars are fought on computers. This isn't the thirteenth century. Hand-to-hand combat isn't required.' He gestured at his laptop on the sideboard. 'With computers you can take down your enemy without ever firing a shot or shedding a drop of blood.'

'This may not be the thirteenth century, Nathaniel, but some of the combatants will have lived through those times, and they have a sentimental attachment to destroying people the old-fashioned way. Leave this to me and Marcus.' Matthew thought this was the end of the matter.

Nathaniel shook his head and stared fixedly at the table.

'Do you have something else to say?' Matthew asked, an ominous purring starting in the back of his throat.

'You've made it perfectly clear you'll do what you want in any case.' Nathaniel lifted his frank brown eyes in challenge, then shrugged. 'Suit yourself. But you're making a mistake if you think your enemies won't use more modern methods to destroy you. There are humans to consider, after all. They'll notice if vampires and witches start fighting one another in the streets.'

The second battle between Matthew and Nathaniel had to do not with war but with blood. It began innocently enough, with Matthew talking about Nathaniel's relationship to Agatha Wilson and about Sophie's witch parents.

'It's imperative that their DNA be analyzed. The baby's, too, once it's born.'

Marcus and Miriam nodded, unsurprised. The rest of us were somewhat startled.

'Nathaniel and Sophie bring into question your theory that

daemonic traits result from unpredictable mutations rather than heredity,' I said, thinking aloud.

'We have so little data.' Matthew eyed Hamish and Nathaniel with the dispassionate gaze of a scientist examining two fresh specimens. 'Our current findings might be misleading.'

'Sophie's case also raises the issue of whether daemons are more closely related to witches than we'd thought.' Miriam directed her black eyes at the daemon's belly. 'I've never heard of a witch giving birth to a daemon, never mind a daemon giving birth to a witch.'

'You think I'm going to hand over Sophie's blood – and my child's blood – to a bunch of vampires?' Nathaniel looked perilously close to losing control.

'Diana isn't the only creature in this room the Congregation will want to study, Nathaniel.' Matthew's words did nothing to soothe the daemon. 'Your mother appreciated the danger your family was facing, or she wouldn't have sent you here. One day you might discover your wife and child gone. If you do, it's highly unlikely you'll ever see them again.'

'That's enough,' Sarah said sharply. 'There's no need to threaten him.'

'Keep your hands off my family,' Nathaniel said, breathing heavily.

'I'm not a danger to them,' Matthew said. 'The danger comes from the Congregation, from the possibility of open hostility between the three species, and above all from pretending this isn't happening.'

'They'll come for us, Nathaniel. I've seen it.' Sophie's voice was purposeful, and her face had the same sudden sharpness that Agatha Wilson's had back in Oxford.

'Why didn't you tell me?' Nathaniel said.

'I started to tell Agatha, but she stopped me and ordered me not to say another word. She was so frightened. Then she gave me Diana's name and the address for the Bishop house.' Sophie's face took on its characteristic fuzzy look. 'I'm glad Matthew's mother is still alive. She'll like my pots. I'll put her face on one of them. And you can have my DNA whenever you want it, Matthew – the baby's, too.'

Sophie's announcement effectively put an end to Nathaniel's objections. When Matthew had entertained all the questions he was willing to answer, he picked up an envelope that had been sitting unnoticed at his elbow. It was sealed with black wax.

'That leaves one piece of unfinished business.' He stood and held out the letter. 'Hamish, this is for you.'

'Oh, no you don't.' Hamish crossed his arms over his chest. 'Give it to Marcus.'

'You may be the ninth knight, but you're also the seneschal of the Knights of Lazarus, and my second in command. There's a protocol we must follow,' Matthew said, tight-lipped.

'Matthew would know,' Marcus muttered. 'He's the only grand master in the history of the order who's ever resigned.'

'And now I'll be the only grand master to have resigned twice,' Matthew said, still holding out the envelope.

'To hell with protocol,' Hamish snapped, banging his fist on the table. 'Everybody out of this room except Matthew, Marcus, and Nathaniel. Please,' he added as an afterthought.

'Why do we have to leave?' Sarah asked suspiciously.

Hamish studied my aunt for a moment. 'You'd better stay, too.'

The five of them were closeted in the dining room for the rest of the day. Once an exhausted Hamish came out and requested sandwiches. The cookies, he explained, were long gone.

'Is it me, or do you also feel that the men sent us out of the room so they could smoke cigars and talk politics?' I asked, trying to distract myself from the meeting in the dining room by flipping through a jarring mix of old movies and afternoon television. Em and Sophie were both knitting, and Miriam was doing a puzzle she'd found in a book promising *Demonically Difficult Sudoku*. She chuckled now and then and made a mark in the margins.

'What are you doing, Miriam?' Sophie asked.

'Keeping score,' Miriam said, making another mark on the page.

'What are they talking about? And who's winning?' I asked, envious of her ability to hear the conversation.

'They're planning a war, Diana. As for who's winning, either Matthew or Hamish – it's too close to call,' Miriam replied. 'Marcus and Nathaniel managed to get in a few good shots, though, and Sarah's holding her own.'

It was already dark, and Em and I were making dinner when the meeting broke up. Nathaniel and Sophie were talking quietly in the family room.

'I need to catch up on a few calls,' Matthew said after he'd kissed me, his mild tone at odds with his tense face.

Seeing how tired he was, I decided my questions could wait.

'Of course,' I said, touching his cheek. 'Take your time. Dinner will be in an hour.'

Matthew kissed me again, longer and deeper, before going out the back door.

'I need a drink,' Sarah groaned, heading to the porch to sneak a cigarette.

Matthew was nothing more than a shadow through the haze of Sarah's smoke as he passed through the orchard and headed for the hop barn. Hamish came up behind me, nudging my back and neck with his eyes.

'Are you fully recovered?' he asked quietly.

'What do you think?' It had been a long day, and Hamish made no effort to hide his disapproval of me. I shook my head.

Hamish's eyes drifted away, and mine followed. We both watched as Matthew's white hands streaked through his hair before he disappeared into the barn.

' "*Tiger, tiger, burning bright / In the forests of the night,*" ' Hamish said, quoting William Blake. 'That poem has always reminded me of him.'

I rested my knife on the cutting board and faced him. 'What's on your mind, Hamish?'

'Are you certain of him, Diana?' he asked. Em wiped her hands on her apron and left the room, giving me a sad look.

'Yes.' I met his eyes, trying to make my confidence in Matthew clear.

Hamish nodded, unsurprised. 'I did wonder if you would take him on, once you knew who he was – who he still is. It would seem you're not afraid to have a tiger by the tail.'

Wordlessly I turned back to the counter and resumed my chopping.

'Be careful.' Hamish rested his hand on my forearm, forcing me to look at him. 'Matthew won't be the same man where you're going.'

'Yes he will.' I frowned. 'My Matthew is going with me. He'll be exactly the same.'

'No,' Hamish said grimly. 'He won't.'

Hamish had known Matthew far longer. And he'd pieced together where we were going based on the contents of that briefcase. I still knew nothing, except that I was headed to a time before 1976 and a place where Matthew had played chess.

Hamish joined Sarah outside, and soon two plumes of gray smoke rose into the night sky.

'Is everything all right in there?' I asked Em when she returned from the family room, where Miriam, Marcus, Nathaniel, and Sophie were talking and watching TV.

'Yes,' she replied. 'And here?'

'Just fine.' I focused on the apple trees and waited for Matthew to come in from the dark.

CHAPTER 41

The day before Halloween, a fluttery feeling developed in my stomach. Still in bed, I reached for Matthew.

'I'm nervous.'

He closed the book he was reading and drew me near. 'I know. You were nervous before you opened your eyes.'

The house was already bustling with activity. Sarah's printer was churning out page after page in the office below. The television was on, and the dryer whined faintly in the distance as it protested under another load of laundry. One sniff told me that Sarah and Em were well into the day's coffee consumption, and down the hall there was the whir of a hair dryer.

'Are we the last ones up?' I made an effort to calm my stomach.

'I think so,' he said with a smile, though there was a shadow of concern in his eyes.

Downstairs, Sarah was making eggs to order while Em pulled trays of muffins out of the oven. Nathaniel was methodically plucking one after another from the tin and popping them whole into his mouth.

'Where's Hamish?' Matthew asked.

'In my office, using the printer.' Sarah gave him a long look and returned to her pan.

Marcus left his Scrabble game and came to the kitchen to take a walk with his father. He grabbed a handful of nuts as he left, sniffing the muffins with a groan of frustrated desire.

'What's going on?' I asked quietly.

'Hamish is being a lawyer,' Sophie replied, spreading a thick layer of butter on top of a muffin. 'He says there are papers to sign.'

Hamish called us into the dining room in the late morning. We straggled in carrying wineglasses and mugs. He looked as though he hadn't slept. Neat stacks of paper were arranged across the table's expanse, along with sticks of black wax and two seals belonging to the Knights of Lazarus – one small, one large. My heart hit my stomach and bounced back into my throat.

'Should we sit?' Em asked. She'd brought in a fresh pot of coffee and topped off Hamish's mug.

'Thank you, Em,' Hamish said gratefully. Two empty chairs sat officiously at the head of the table. He gestured Matthew and me into them and picked up the first stack of papers. 'Yesterday afternoon we went over a number of practical issues related to the situation in which we now find ourselves.'

My heart sped up, and I eyed the seals again.

'A little less lawyerly, Hamish, if you please,' Matthew said, his hand tightening on my back. Hamish glowered at him and continued.

'Diana and Matthew will timewalk, as planned, on Halloween. Ignore everything else Matthew told you to do.' Hamish took an obvious pleasure in delivering this part of his message. 'We've agreed that it would be best if everyone . . . disappeared for a little while. As of this moment, your old lives are on hold.'

Hamish put a document in front of me. 'This is a power of attorney, Diana. It authorizes me – or whoever occupies the position of seneschal – to act legally on your behalf.'

The power of attorney gave the abstract idea of timewalking a new sense of finality. Matthew fished a pen from his pocket.

'Here,' he said, placing the pen before me.

The pen's nib wasn't used to the angle and pressure of my hand, and it scratched while I put my signature on the line. When I was finished, Matthew took it and dropped a warm black blob on the bottom, then reached for his personal seal and pressed it into the wax.

Hamish picked up the next stack. 'These letters are for you to sign, too. One informs your conference organizers that you cannot speak in November. The other requests a medical leave for next year. Your physician – one Dr Marcus Whitmore – has written in support. In the event you haven't returned by April, I'll send your request to Yale.'

I read the letters carefully and signed with a shaking hand, relinquishing my life in the twenty-first century.

Hamish braced his hands against the edge of the table. Clearly he was building up to something. 'There is no telling when Matthew and Diana will be back with us.' He didn't use the word 'if', but it hovered in the room nonetheless. 'Whenever any member of the firm or of the de Clermont family is preparing to take a long journey or drop out of sight for a while, it's my job to make sure their affairs are in order. Diana, you have no will.'

'No.' My mind was entirely blank. 'But I don't have any assets – not even a car.'

Hamish straightened. 'That's not entirely true, is it, Matthew?'

'Give it to me,' Matthew said reluctantly. Hamish handed him a thick document. 'This was drawn up when I was last in Oxford.'

'Before La Pierre,' I said, not touching the pages.

Matthew nodded. 'Essentially, it's our marriage agreement. It irrevocably settles a third of my personal assets on you. Even if you were to leave me, these assets would be yours.'

It was dated before he'd come home – before we were mated for life by vampire custom.

'I'll never leave you, and I don't want this.'

'You don't even know what this is,' Matthew said, putting the pages in front of me.

There was too much to absorb. Staggering sums of money, a town house on an exclusive square in London, a flat in Paris, a villa outside Rome, the Old Lodge, a house in Jerusalem, still more houses in cities like Venice and Seville, jets, cars – my mind whirled.

'I have a secure job.' I pushed the papers away. 'This is completely unnecessary.'

'It's yours nonetheless,' Matthew said gruffly.

Hamish let me gather my composure before he dropped his next bombshell. 'If Sarah were to die, you would inherit this house, too, on the condition that it would be Emily's home for as long as she wanted it. And you're Matthew's sole heir. So you do have assets — and I need to know your wishes.'

'I'm not going to talk about this.' The memories of Satu and Juliette were still fresh, and death felt all too close. I stood, ready to bolt, but Matthew grabbed my hand and held fast.

'You need to do this, *mon coeur*. We cannot leave it for Marcus and Sarah to sort out.'

I sat back down and thought quietly about what to do with the inconceivable fortune and ramshackle farmhouse that might one day be mine.

'My estate should be divided equally among our children,' I said finally. 'And that includes *all* of Matthew's children — vampire and biological, those he made himself and any that we might have together. They're to have the Bishop house, too, when Em's through with it.'

'I'll see to it,' Hamish assured me.

The only remaining documents on the table were hidden inside three envelopes. Two bore Matthew's seal. The other had black-and-silver ribbon wrapped around it, a lump of sealing wax covering the knot. Hanging from the ribbon was a thick black disk as big as a dessert plate that bore the impression of the great seal of the Knights of Lazarus.

'Finally we have the brotherhood to sort out. When Matthew's father founded the Knights of Lazarus, they were known for helping to protect those who could not protect themselves. Though most creatures have forgotten about us, we still exist. And we must continue to do so even after Matthew is gone. Tomorrow, before Marcus leaves the house, Matthew will officially give up his position in the order and appoint his son grand master.'

Hamish handed Matthew the two envelopes bearing his personal seal. He then handed the envelope with the larger seal to Nathaniel. Miriam's eyes widened.

'As soon as Marcus accepts his new position, which he will do *immediately*,' Hamish said, giving Marcus a stern look, 'he will phone Nathaniel, who has agreed to join the firm as one of the eight provincial masters. Once Nathaniel breaks the seal - on this commission, he'll be a Knight of Lazarus.'

'You can't keep making daemons like Hamish and Nathaniel members of the brotherhood! How is Nathaniel going to fight?' Miriam sounded aghast.

'With these,' Nathaniel said, wiggling his fingers in the air. 'I know computers, and I can do my part.' His voice took on a fierce edge, and he gave Sophie an equally ferocious look. 'No one is going to do to my wife or daughter what they've done to Diana.'

There was stunned silence.

'That's not all.' Hamish pulled up a chair and sat down, knitting his fingers together before him. 'Miriam believes that there will be a war. I disagree. This war has already started.'

Every eye on the room was directed at Hamish. It was clear why people wanted him to play a role in government – and why Matthew had made him his second in command. He was a born leader.

'In this room we understand why such a war might be fought. It's about Diana and the appalling lengths the Congregation will go to in an effort to understand the power she's inherited. It's about the discovery of Ashmole 782 and our fear that the book's secrets might be lost forever if it falls into the witches' hands. And it's about our common belief that no one has the right to tell two creatures that they cannot love each other – no matter what their species.'

Hamish surveyed the room to make sure no one's attention had wandered before he continued.

'It won't be long before the humans are aware of this conflict. They'll be forced to acknowledge that daemons, vampires, and witches are among them. When that happens, we'll need to be Sophie's conventicle in *fact*, not just in name. There will be casualties, hysteria, and confusion. And it will be up to us – the conventicle and the Knights of Lazarus – to help them make sense of it all and to see to it that the loss of life and destruction are minimal.'

'Ysabeau is waiting for you at Sept-Tours.' Matthew's voice was quiet and steady. 'The castle grounds may be the only territorial boundary other vampires won't dare to cross. Sarah and Emily will try to keep the witches in check. The Bishop name should help. And the Knights of Lazarus will protect Sophie and her baby.'

'So we'll scatter,' Sarah said, nodding at Matthew. 'Then reconvene at the de Clermont house. And when we do, we'll figure out how to proceed. Together.'

'Under Marcus's leadership.' Matthew raised his half-full wine-glass. 'To Marcus, Nathaniel, and Hamish. Honor and long life.'

'It's been a long time since I've heard that,' Miriam said softly.

Marcus and Nathaniel both shied away from the attention and seemed uncomfortable with their new responsibilities. Hamish merely appeared weary.

After toasting the three men – all of whom looked far too young to have to worry about a long life – Em shepherded us into the kitchen for lunch. She laid out a feast on the island, and we milled around the family room, avoiding the moment when we would have to begin our good-byes.

Finally it was time for Sophie and Nathaniel to depart. Marcus put the couple's few belongings in the trunk of his little blue sports car. Marcus and Nathaniel stood, their two blond heads close in conversation, while Sophie said good-bye to Sarah and Em. When she was finished, she turned to me. I'd been banished to the keeping room to make sure that no one inadvertently touched me.

'This isn't really good-bye,' she told me from across the hall.

My third eye opened, and in the winking of the sunlight on the banister I saw myself enveloped in one of Sophie's fierce hugs.

'No,' I said, surprised and comforted by the vision.

Sophie nodded as if she, too, had seen the glimpse of the future. 'See, I told you. Maybe the baby will be here when you get back. Remember, you'll be her godmother.'

While waiting for Sophie and Nathaniel to say their good-byes, Matthew and Miriam had positioned all the pumpkins down the driveway. With a flick of her wrist and a few mumbled words, Sarah lit them. Dusk was still hours away, but Sophie could at least get a sense of what they would look like on Halloween night. She clapped her hands and tore down the steps to fling herself into the arms of Matthew and then Miriam. Her final hug was reserved for Marcus, who exchanged a few quiet words with her before tucking her into the low-slung passenger seat.

'Thanks for the car,' Sophie said, admiring the burled wood on the dashboard. 'Nathaniel used to drive fast, but he drives like an old lady now on account of the baby.'

'No speeding,' Matthew said firmly, sounding like a father. 'Call us when you get home.'

We waved them off. When they were out of sight Sarah extinguished the pumpkins. Matthew put his arms around me as the remaining family drifted back inside.

'I'm ready for you, Diana,' Hamish said, coming out onto the porch. He'd already put on his jacket, prepared to leave for New York before returning to London.

I signed the two copies of the will, and they were witnessed by Em and Sarah. Hamish rolled up one copy and slid it into a metal cylinder. He threaded the ends of the tube with black-and-silver ribbons and sealed it with wax bearing Matthew's mark.

Matthew waited by the black rental car while Hamish said a courteous farewell to Miriam, then kissed Em and Sarah, inviting them to stay with him on their way to Sept-Tours.

'Call me if you need anything,' he told Sarah, taking her hand and giving it a single squeeze. 'You have my numbers.' He turned to me.

'Good-bye, Hamish.' I returned his kisses, first on one cheek, then the other. 'Thank you for all you did to put Matthew's mind at ease.'

'Just doing my job,' Hamish said with forced cheerfulness. His voice dropped. 'Remember what I told you. There will be no way to call for help if you need it.'

'I won't need it,' I said.

A few minutes later, the car's engine turned over and Hamish, too, was gone, red taillights blinking in the gathering darkness.

The house didn't like its new emptiness and responded by banging furniture around and moaning softly whenever anyone left or entered a room.

'I'll miss them,' Em confessed while making dinner. The house sighed sympathetically.

'Go,' Sarah said to me, taking the knife out of Em's hand. 'Take Matthew to Sept-Tours and be back here in time to make the salad.'

After much discussion we'd finally decided to timewalk to the night I'd found his copy of *Origin*.

But getting Matthew to Sept-Tours was more of a challenge than I'd expected. My arms were so full of stuff to help me steer – one of his pens and two books from his study – that Matthew had to hold on to my waist. Then we got stuck.

Invisible hands seemed to hold my foot up, refusing to let me lower it into Sept-Tours. The farther back in time we went, the thicker the strands were around my feet. And time clung to Matthew in sturdy, twining vines.

At last we made it to Matthew's study. The room was just as we'd left it, with the fire lit and an unlabeled bottle of wine waiting on the table.

I dropped the books and the pen on the sofa, shaking with fatigue.

'What's wrong?' Matthew asked.

'It was as if too many pasts were coming together, and it was impossible to wade through them. I was afraid you might let go.'

'Nothing felt different to me,' Matthew said. 'It took a bit longer than before, but I expected that, given the time and distance.'

He poured us both some wine, and we discussed the pros and cons of going downstairs. Finally, our desire to see Ysabeau and Marthe won out. Matthew remembered I'd been wearing my blue sweater. Its high neckline would hide my bandage, so I went upstairs to change.

When I came back down, his face broke into a slow, appreciative smile. 'Just as beautiful now as then,' he said, kissing me deeply. 'Maybe more so.'

'Be careful,' I warned him with a laugh. 'You hadn't decided you loved me yet.'

'Oh, I'd decided,' he said, kissing me again. 'I just hadn't told you.'

The women were sitting right where we expected them to be, Marthe with her murder mystery and Ysabeau with her newspapers. The conversation might not have been exactly the same, but it didn't seem to matter. The most difficult part of the evening was watching Matthew dance with his mother. The bittersweet expression on his face as he twirled her was new, and he definitely hadn't caught her up in a fierce bear hug when their dance was over. When he invited me to dance, I gave his hand an extra squeeze of sympathy.

'Thank you for this,' he whispered in my ear as he whirled me around. He planted a soft kiss on my neck. That definitely hadn't happened the first time.

Matthew brought the evening to a close just as he had before, by announcing that he was taking me to bed. This time we said good night knowing that it was good-bye. Our return trip was much the same, but less frightening for its familiarity. I didn't panic or lose my concentration when time resisted our passage, focusing intently on the familiar rituals of making dinner in the Bishop house. We were back in plenty of time to make the salad.

During dinner Sarah and Em regaled the vampires with tales of my adventures growing up. When my aunts ran out of stories, Matthew teased Marcus about his disastrous real-estate deals in the nineteenth century, the enormous investments he'd made in new technologies in the twentieth century that had never panned out, and his perpetual weakness for redheaded women.

'I knew I liked you.' Sarah smoothed down her own unruly red mop and poured him more whiskey.

Halloween dawned clear and bright. Snow was always a possibility in this neck of the woods, but this year the weather looked encouraging. Matthew and Marcus took a longer walk than usual, and I lingered over tea and coffee with Sarah and Em.

When the phone rang, we all jumped. Sarah answered it, and we could tell from her half of the conversation that the call was unexpected.

She hung up and joined us at the table in the family room, which was once again big enough to seat all of us. 'That was Faye. She and Janet are at the Hunters'. In their RV. They want to know if we'll join them on their fall trip. They're driving to Arizona, then up to Seattle.'

'The goddess has been busy,' Em said with a smile. The two of them had been trying for days to decide how they would extricate themselves from Madison without setting off a flurry of gossip. 'I guess that settles it. We'll hit the road, then go meet Ysabeau.'

We carried bags of food and other supplies to Sarah's beat-up old car. When it was fully loaded and you could barely see out the rearview mirror, they started issuing orders.

'The candy's on the counter,' Em instructed. 'And my costume is hanging on the back of the stillroom door. It will fit you fine. Don't forget the stockings. The kids love the stockings.'

'I won't forget them,' I assured her, 'or the hat, though it's perfectly ridiculous.'

'Of course you'll wear the hat!' Sarah said indignantly. 'It's tradition. Make sure the fire is out before you leave. Tabitha is fed at four o'clock sharp. If she isn't, she'll start barfing.'

'We've got this covered. You left a list,' I said, patting her on the shoulder.

'Can you call us at the Hunters', let us know Miriam and Marcus have left?' Em asked.

'Here. Take this,' Matthew said, handing them his phone with a lopsided smile. 'You call Marcus yourself. There won't be reception where we're going.'

'Are you sure?' Em asked doubtfully. We all thought of Matthew's phone as an extra limb, and it was strange to see it out of his hand.

'Absolutely. Most of the data has been erased, but I've left some contact numbers on it for you. If you need anything – anything at all – call someone. If you feel worried or if something strange happens, get in touch with Ysabeau or Hamish. They'll arrange for you to be picked up, no matter where you are.'

'They have helicopters,' I murmured to Em, slipping my arm through hers.

Marcus's phone rang. 'Nathaniel,' he said, looking at the screen. Then he stepped away to finish his call in a new gesture of privacy, one that was identical to what his father always did.

With a sad smile, Matthew watched his son. 'Those two will get themselves into all kinds of trouble, but at least Marcus won't feel so alone.'

'They're fine,' Marcus said, turning back to us and disconnecting the phone. He smiled and ran his fingers through his hair in another gesture reminiscent of Matthew. 'I should let Hamish know, so I'll say my good-byes and call him.'

Em held on to Marcus for a long time, her eyes spilling over. 'Call us, too,' she told him fiercely. 'We'll want to know that you're both all right.'

'Be safe.' Sarah's eyes scrunched tight as she gathered him in her arms. 'Don't doubt yourself.'

Miriam's farewell to my aunts was more composed, my own far less so.

'We're very proud of you,' Em said, cupping my face in her hands, tears now streaming down her face. 'Your parents would be, too. Take care of each other.'

'We will,' I assured her, dashing the tears away.

Sarah took my hands in hers. 'Listen to your teachers – whoever they are. Don't say no without hearing them out first.' I nodded. 'You've got more natural talent than any witch I've ever seen – maybe more than any witch who's lived for many, many years,' Sarah continued. 'I'm glad you're not going to waste it. Magic is a gift, Diana, just like love.' She turned to Matthew. 'I'm trusting you with something precious. Don't disappoint me.'

'I won't, Sarah,' Matthew promised.

She accepted our kisses, then bolted down the steps to the waiting car.

'Good-byes are hard for Sarah,' Em explained. 'We'll talk to you tomorrow, Marcus.' She climbed into the front seat, waving over her shoulder. The car spluttered to life, bumped its way across the ruts in the driveway, and turned toward town.

When we went back into the house, Miriam and Marcus were waiting in the front hall, bags at their feet.

'We thought you two should have some time alone,' Miriam said, handing her duffel bag to Marcus, 'and I hate long good-byes.' She looked around. 'Well,' she said briskly, heading down the porch stairs, 'see you when you get back.'

After shaking his head at Miriam's retreating figure, Matthew went into the dining room and returned with an envelope. 'Take it,' he said to Marcus, his voice gruff.

'I never wanted to be grand master,' Marcus said.

'You think I did? This was my father's dream. Philippe made me promise the brotherhood wouldn't fall into Baldwin's hands. I'm asking you to do the same.'

'I promise.' Marcus took the envelope. 'I wish you didn't have to go.'

'I'm sorry, Marcus.' I swallowed the lump in my throat and rested my warm fingers lightly on his cold flesh.

'For what?' His smile was bright and true. 'For making my father happy?'

'For putting you in this position and leaving behind such a mess.'

'I'm not afraid of war, if that's what you mean. It's following along in Matthew's wake that worries me.' Marcus cracked the seal. With that deceptively insignificant snap of wax, he became the grand master of the Knights of Lazarus.

'*Je suis à votre commande, seigneur,*' Matthew murmured, his head bowed. Baldwin had spoken the same words at La Guardia. They sounded so different when they were sincere.

'Then I command you to return and take back the Knights of Lazarus,' Marcus said roughly, 'before I make a complete hash of things. I'm not French, and I'm certainly no knight.'

'You have more than a drop of French blood in you, and you're the only person I trust to do the job. Besides, you can rely on your famous American charm. And it is possible you might like being grand master in the end.'

Marcus snorted and punched the number eight on his phone. 'It's done,' he said briefly to the person on the other end. There was a short exchange of words. 'Thank you.'

'Nathaniel has accepted his position,' Matthew murmured, the corners of his mouth twitching. 'His French is surprisingly good.'

Marcus scowled at his father, walked away to say a few more words to the daemon, and returned.

Between father and son there was a long look, the clasp of hand to elbow, the press of a hand on the back – a pattern of leave-taking based on hundreds of similar farewells. For me there was a gentle kiss, a murmured 'Be well,' and then Marcus, too, was gone.

I reached for Matthew's hand.

We were alone.

CHAPTER 42

'It's just us and the ghosts now.' My stomach rumbled.

'What's your favorite food?' he asked.

'Pizza,' I said promptly.

'You should have it while you can. Order some, and we'll pick it up.'

We hadn't been beyond the immediate environs of the Bishop house since our arrival, and it felt strange to be driving around the greater Madison area in a Range Rover next to a vampire. We took the back way to Hamilton, passing south over the hills into town before swinging north again to get the pizza. During the drive I pointed out where I'd gone swimming as a child and where my first real boyfriend had lived. The town was covered with Halloween decorations – black cats, witches on brooms, even trees decorated in orange and black eggs. In this part of the world, it wasn't just witches who took the celebration seriously.

When we arrived at the pizza place, Matthew climbed out with me, seemingly unconcerned that witches or humans might see us. I stretched up to kiss him, and he returned it with a laugh that was almost lighthearted.

The college student who rang us up looked at Matthew with obvious admiration when she handed him the pie.

'Good thing she isn't a witch,' I said when we got back into the car. 'She would have turned me into a newt and flown off with you on her broomstick.'

Fortified with pizza – pepperoni and mushroom – I tackled the mess left in the kitchen and the family room. Matthew brought out handfuls of paper from the dining room and burned them in the kitchen fireplace.

'What do we do with these?' he asked, holding up my mother's letter, the mysterious three-line epigram, and the page from Ashmole 782.

'Leave them in the keeping room,' I told him. 'The house will take care of them.'

I continued to putter, doing laundry and straightening up Sarah's office. It was not until I went up to put our clothes away that I noticed both computers were missing. I went pounding downstairs in a panic.

'Matthew! The computers are gone!'

'Hamish has them,' he said, catching me in his arms and smoothing my hair against the back of my head. 'It's all right. No one's been in the house.'

My shoulders sagged, heart still hammering at the idea of being surprised by another Domenico or Juliette.

He made tea, then rubbed my feet while I drank it. All the while he talked about nothing important – houses in Hamilton that had reminded him of some other place and time, his first sniff of a tomato, what he thought when he'd seen me row in Oxford – until I relaxed into the warmth and comfort.

Matthew was always different when no one else was around, but the contrast was especially marked now that our families had left. Since arriving at the Bishop house, he'd gradually taken on the responsibility for eight other lives. He'd watched over all of them, regardless of who they were or how they were related to him, with the same ferocious intensity. Now he had only one creature to manage.

'We haven't had much time to just talk,' I reflected, thinking of the whirlwind of days since we'd met. 'Not just the two of us.'

'The past weeks have been almost biblical in their tests. I think the only thing we've escaped is a plague of locusts.' He paused. 'But if the universe does want to test us the old-fashioned way, this counts as the end of our trial. It will be forty days this evening.'

So little time, for so much to have happened.

I put my empty mug on the table and reached for his hands. 'Where are we going, Matthew?'

'Can you wait a little longer, *mon coeur*?' He looked out the window. 'I want this day to last. And it will be dark soon enough.'

'You like playing house with me.' A piece of hair had fallen onto his forehead, and I brushed it back.

'I love playing house with you,' he said, capturing my hand.

We talked quietly for another half hour, before Matthew glanced outdoors again. 'Go upstairs and take a bath. Use every drop of water in the tank and take a long, hot shower, too. You may crave pizza every now and then in the days to come. But that will be nothing compared to your longing for hot water. In a few weeks, you will cheerfully commit murder for a shower.'

Matthew brought up my Halloween costume while I bathed: a calf-length black dress with a high neck, sharp-toed boots, and a pointy hat.

'What, may I ask, are these?' He brandished a pair of stockings with red and white horizontal stripes.

'Those are the stockings Em mentioned.' I groaned. 'She'll know if I don't wear them.'

'If I still had my phone, I would take a picture of you in these hideous things and blackmail you for eternity.'

'Is there anything that would ensure your silence?' I sank lower into the tub.

'I'm sure there is,' Matthew said, tossing the stockings behind him.

We were playful at first. As at dinner last night, and again at breakfast, we carefully avoided mentioning that this might be our last chance to be together. I was still a novice, but Em told me even the most experienced timewalkers respected the unpredictability of moving between past and future and recognized how easy it would be to wander indefinitely within the spiderweb of time.

Matthew sensed my changing mood and answered it first with greater gentleness, then with a fierce possessiveness that demanded I think of nothing but him.

Despite our obvious need for comfort and reassurance, we didn't consummate our marriage.

'When we're safe,' he'd murmured, kissing me along my collarbone. 'When there's more time.'

Somewhere along the way, my smallpox blister burst. Matthew examined it and pronounced that it was doing nicely – an odd description for an angry open wound the size of a dime. He removed the bandage from my neck, revealing the barest trace of Miriam's sutures, and the one from my arm as well.

'You're a fast healer,' he said approvingly, kissing the inside of my elbow where he'd drunk from my veins. His lips felt warm against my skin.

'How odd. My skin is cold there.' I touched my neck. 'Here, too.'

Matthew drew his thumb across the spot where my carotid artery passed close to the surface. I shivered at his touch. The number of nerve endings there had seemingly tripled.

'Extra sensitivity,' Matthew said, 'as if you're part vampire.' He bent and put his lips against my pulse.

'Oh,' I gasped, taken aback at the intensity of feeling.

Mindful of the time, I buttoned myself into the black dress. With a braid down my back, I might have stepped out of a photograph from the turn of the nineteenth century.

'Too bad we're not timewalking to World War I,' Matthew said, pulling at the sleeves of the dress. 'You'd make a convincing schoolmistress circa 1912 in that getup.'

'Not with these on.' I sat on the bed and started pulling on candy-striped stockings.

Matthew roared with laughter and begged me to put the hat on immediately.

'I'll set fire to myself,' I protested. 'Wait until the jack-o'-lanterns are lit.'

We went outside with matches, thinking we could light the pumpkins the human way. A breeze had kicked up, though, which made it difficult to strike the matches and impossible to keep the candles illuminated.

'Damn it,' I swore. 'Sophie's work shouldn't go to waste.'

'Can you use a spell?' Matthew said, already prepared to have another go at the matchbox.

'If not, then I have no business even pretending to be a witch on Halloween.' The mere thought of explaining my failure to Sophie made me concentrate on the task at hand, and the wick burst into life. I lit the other eleven pumpkins that were scattered down the drive, each more amazing or terrifying than the last.

At six o'clock there was a fierce pounding on the door and muffled cries of 'Trick or treat!' Matthew had never experienced an American Halloween, and he eagerly greeted our first visitors.

Whoever was outside received one of his heart-stopping smiles before Matthew grinned and beckoned me forward.

A tiny witch and a slightly larger vampire were holding hands on the front porch.

'Trick or treat,' they intoned, holding out their open pillowcases.

'I'm a vampire,' the boy said, baring his fangs at Matthew. He pointed to his sister. 'She's a witch.'

'I can see that,' Matthew said gravely, taking in the black cape and white makeup. 'I'm a vampire, too.'

The boy examined him critically. 'Your mother should have worked harder on your costume. You don't look like a vampire at all. Where's your cape?' The miniature vampire swept his arms up, a fold of his own satin cape in each fist, revealing its bat-shaped wings. 'See, you need your cape to fly. Otherwise you can't turn into a bat.'

'Ah. That is a problem. My cape is at home, and now I can't fly back and get it. Perhaps I can borrow yours.' Matthew dumped a handful of candy into each pillowcase, the eyes of both children growing large at his generosity. I peeked around the door to wave at their parents.

'You can tell she's a witch,' the girl piped up, nodding approvingly at my red-and-white-striped stockings and black boots. At their parents' urging, they shouted thank-yous as they trotted down the walk and climbed into the waiting car.

Over the next three hours, we greeted a steady stream of fairy princesses, pirates, ghosts, skeletons, mermaids, and space aliens, along with still more witches and vampires. I gently told Matthew that one piece of candy per goblin was de rigueur and that if he didn't stop distributing handfuls of goodies now, we would run out long before the trick-or-treating stopped at nine o'clock.

It was hard to criticize, however, given his obvious delight. His responses to the children who came to the door revealed a wholly new side of him. Crouching down so that he was less intimidating, he asked questions about their costumes and told every young boy purporting to be a vampire that he was the most frightening creature he'd ever beheld.

But it was his encounter with one fairy princess wearing an oversize set of wings and a gauze skirt that tugged hardest at my heart. Overwhelmed and exhausted by the occasion, she burst into tears when Matthew asked which piece of candy she wanted. Her brother, a strapping young pirate aged six, dropped her hand in horror.

'We shall ask your mother.' Matthew swept the fairy princess into his arms and grabbed the pirate by the back of his bandanna. He safely delivered both children into the waiting arms of their parents. Long before reaching them, however, the fairy princess had forgotten her tears. Instead she had one sticky hand wrapped in the collar of Matthew's sweater and was tapping him lightly on the head with her wand, repeating, 'Bippity, boppity, BOO!'

'When she grows up and thinks about Prince Charming, he'll look just like you,' I told him after he returned to the house. A shower of silver glitter fell as he dipped his head for a kiss. 'You're covered with fairy dust,' I said, laughing and brushing the last of it from his hair.

Around eight o'clock, when the tide of fairy princesses and pirates turned to Gothic teenagers wearing black lipstick and leather garments festooned with chains, Matthew handed me the basket of candy and retreated to the keeping room.

'Coward,' I teased, straightening my hat before answering the door to another gloomy bunch.

Only three minutes before it would be safe to turn out the porch light without ruining the Bishops' Halloween reputation, we heard another loud knock and a bellowed 'Trick or treat!'

'Who can that be?' I groaned, slamming my hat back on my head.

Two young wizards stood on the front steps. One was the paperboy. He was accompanied by a lanky teenager with bad skin and a pierced nose, whom I recognized dimly as belonging to the O'Neil clan. Their costumes, such as they were, consisted of torn jeans, safety-pinned T-shirts, fake blood, plastic teeth, and lengths of dog leash.

'Aren't you a bit old for this, Sammy?'

'It'th Tham now.' Sammy's voice was breaking, full of unexpected ups and downs, and his prosthetic fangs gave him a lisp.

'Hello, Sam.' There were half a dozen pieces in the bottom of the candy basket. 'You're welcome to what's left. We were just about to put out the lights. Shouldn't you be at the Hunters' house, bobbing for apples?'

'We heard your pumpkinth were really cool thith year.' Sammy shifted from one foot to the other. 'And, uh, well . . .' He flushed and took out his plastic teeth. 'Rob swore he saw a vampire here the other day. I bet him twenty bucks the Bishops wouldn't let one in the house.'

'What makes you so sure you'd recognize a vampire if you saw one?'

The vampire in question came out of the keeping room and stood behind me. 'Gentlemen,' he said quietly. Two adolescent jaws dropped.

'We'd have to be either human or really stupid not to recognize him,' said Rob, awestruck. 'He's the biggest vampire I've ever seen.'

'Cool.' Sammy grinned from ear to ear. He high-fived his friend and grabbed the candy.

'Don't forget to pay up, Sam,' I said sternly.

'And, Samuel,' Matthew said, his French accent unusually pronounced, 'could I ask you – as a favor to me – not to tell anyone else about this?'

'Ever?' Sammy was incredulous at the notion of keeping such a juicy piece of information to himself.

Matthew's mouth twitched. 'No. I see your point. Can you keep quiet until tomorrow?'

'Sure!' Sammy nodded, looking to Rob for confirmation. 'That's only three hours. We can do that. No problem.'

They got on their bikes and headed off.

'The roads are dark,' Matthew said with a frown of concern. 'We should drive them.'

'They'll be fine. They're not vampires, but they can definitely find their way to town.'

The two bikes skidded to a halt, sending up a shower of loose gravel.

'You want us to turn off the pumpkins?' Sammy shouted from the driveway.

'If you want to,' I said. 'Thanks!'

Rob O'Neil waved at the left side of the driveway and Sammy at the right, extinguishing all the jack-o'-lanterns with enviable casualness. The two boys rode off, their bikes bumping over the ruts, their progress made easier by the moon and the burgeoning sixth sense of the teenage witch.

I shut the door and leaned against it, groaning. 'My feet are killing me.' I unlaced my boots and kicked them off, tossing the hat onto the steps.

'The page from Ashmole 782 is gone,' Matthew announced quietly, leaning against the banister post.

'Mom's letter?'

'Also gone.'

'It's time, then.' I pulled myself away from the old door, and the house moaned softly.

'Make yourself some tea and meet me in the family room. I'll get the bag.'

He waited for me on the couch, the soft-sided briefcase sitting closed at his feet and the silver chess piece and gold earring lying on the coffee table. I handed him a glass of wine and sat alongside. 'That's the last of the wine.'

Matthew eyed my tea. 'And that's the last of the tea for you as well.' He ran his hands nervously through his hair and took a deep breath. 'I would have liked to go sometime closer, when there was less death and disease,' he began, sounding tentative, 'and some*where* closer, with tea and plumbing. But I think you'll like it once you get used to it.'

I still didn't know when or where 'it' was.

Matthew bent down to undo the lock. When he opened the bag and saw what was on top, he let out a sigh of relief. 'Thank God. I was afraid Ysabeau might have sent the wrong one.'

'You haven't opened the bag yet?' I was amazed at his self-control.

'No.' Matthew lifted out a book. 'I didn't want to think about it too much. Just in case.'

He handed me the book. It had black leather bindings with simple silver borders.

'It's beautiful,' I said, running my fingers over its surface.

'Open it.' Matthew looked anxious.

'Will I know where we're going once I do?' Now that the third object was in my hands, I felt strangely reluctant.

'I think so.'

The front cover creaked open, and the unmistakable scent of old paper and ink rose in the air. There were no marbled endpapers, no bookplates, no additional blank sheets such as eighteenth- and nineteenth-century collectors put in their books. And the covers were heavy, indicating that wooden boards were concealed beneath the smoothly stretched leather.

Two lines were written in thick black ink on the first page, in a tight, spiky script of the late sixteenth century.

' "*To my own sweet Matt,*" ' I read aloud. ' "*Who ever loved, that loved not at first sight?*" '

The dedication was unsigned, but it was familiar.

'Shakespeare?' I lifted my eyes to Matthew.

'Not originally,' he replied, his face tense. 'Will was something of a magpie when it came to collecting other people's words.'

I slowly turned the page.

It wasn't a printed book but a manuscript, written in the same bold hand as the inscription. I looked closer to make out the words.

> Settle thy studies, Faustus, and begin
> To sound the depth of that thou wilt profess.

'Jesus,' I said hoarsely, clapping the book shut. My hands were shaking.

'He'll laugh like a fool when he hears that was your reaction,' Matthew commented.

'Is this what I think it is?'

'Probably.'

'How did you get it?'

'Kit gave it to me.' Matthew touched the cover lightly. '*Faustus* was always my favorite.'

Every historian of alchemy knew Christopher Marlowe's play about Dr Faustus, who sold his soul to the devil in exchange for magical knowledge and power. I opened the book and ran my fingers over the inscription while Matthew continued.

'Kit and I were friends – good friends – in a dangerous time when there were few creatures you could trust. We raised a certain amount of hell and eyebrows. When Sophie pulled the chess piece I'd lost to him from her pocket, it seemed clear that England was our destination.'

The feeling my fingertips detected in the inscription was not friendship, however. This was a lover's dedication.

'Were you in love with him, too?' I asked quietly.

'No,' Matthew said shortly. 'I loved Kit, but not the way you mean, and not in the way he wanted. Left to Kit, things would have been different. But it wasn't up to him, and we were never more than friends.'

'Did he know what you are?' I hugged the book to my chest like a priceless treasure.

'Yes. We couldn't afford secrets. Besides, he was a daemon, and an unusually perceptive one at that. You'll soon discover it's pointless trying to keep anything from Kit.'

That Christopher Marlowe was a daemon made a certain sense, based on my limited knowledge of him.

'So we're going to England,' I said slowly. 'When, exactly?'

'To 1590.'

'Where?'

'Every year a group of us met at the Old Lodge for the old Catholic holidays of All Saints and All Souls. Few dared to celebrate them, but it made Kit feel daring and dangerous to commemorate them in some way. He would read us his latest draft of *Faustus* — he was always fiddling with it, never satisfied. We'd drink too much, play chess, and stay awake until dawn.' Matthew drew the manuscript from my arms. He rested it on the table and took my hands in his. 'Is this all right with you, *mon coeur*? We don't have to go. We can think of sometime else.'

But it was already too late. The historian in me had started to process the opportunities of life in Elizabethan England.

'There are alchemists in England in 1590.'

'Yes,' he said warily. 'None of them particularly pleasant to be around, given the mercury poisoning and their strange work habits. More important, Diana, there are witches — powerful witches, who can guide your magic.'

'Will you take me to the playhouses?'

'Could I keep you from them?' Matthew's brows rose.

'Probably not.' My imagination was caught by the prospect opening before us. 'Can we walk through the Royal Exchange? After they light the lamps?'

'Yes.' He drew me into his arms. 'And go to St. Paul's to hear a sermon, and to Tyburn for an execution. We'll even chat about the inmates with the clerk at Bedlam.' His body shook with suppressed laughter. 'Good Lord, Diana. I'm taking you to a time when there was plague, few comforts, no tea, and bad dentistry, and all you can think about is what Gresham's Exchange looked like at night.'

I pulled back to look at him with excitement. 'Will I meet the queen?'

'Absolutely not.' Matthew pressed me to him with a shudder.

'The mere thought of what you might say to Elizabeth Tudor – and she to you – makes my heart falter.'

'Coward,' I said for the second time that night.

'You wouldn't say so if you knew her better. She eats courtiers for breakfast.' Matthew paused. 'Besides, there's something else we can do in 1590.'

'What's that?'

'Somewhere in 1590 there's an alchemical manuscript that will one day be owned by Elias Ashmole. We might look for it.'

'The manuscript might be complete then, its magic unbroken.' I extricated myself from his arms and sat back against the cushions, staring in wonder at the three objects on the coffee table. 'We're really going to go back in time.'

'We are. Sarah told me we had to be careful not to take anything modern into the past. Marthe made you a smock and me a shirt.' Matthew reached into the briefcase again and pulled out two plain linen garments with long sleeves and strings at the neck. 'She had to sew them by hand, and she didn't have much time. They're not fancy, but at least we won't shock whomever we first meet.'

He shook them out, and a small, black velvet bag fell from their linen folds.

Matthew frowned. 'What's this?' he said, picking it up. A note was pinned to the outside. He opened it. 'From Ysabeau. "*This was an anniversary gift from your father. I thought you might like to give it to Diana. It will look old-fashioned but will suit her hand.*"'

The bag held a ring made of three separate gold bands twisted together. The two outer bands were fashioned into ornate sleeves, colored with enamel and studded with small jewels to resemble embroidery. A golden hand curved out of each sleeve, perfectly executed down to the tiny bones, slender tendons, and minute fingernails.

Clasped between the two hands, on the inner ring, was a huge stone that looked like glass. It was clear and unfaceted, set in a golden bezel with a black painted background. No jeweler would put a hunk of glass in a ring so fine. It was a diamond.

'That belongs in a museum, not on my finger.' I was mesmerized by the lifelike hands and tried not to think about the weight of the stone they held.

'My mother used to wear it all the time,' Matthew said, picking it up between his thumb and index finger. 'She called it her scribble ring because she could write on glass with the point of the diamond.' His keen eyes saw some detail of the ring that mine did not. With a twist of the golden hands, the three rings fanned out in his palm. Each band was engraved, the words twining around the flat surfaces.

We peered at the tiny writing.

'They're poesies – verses that people wrote as tokens of affection. This one says "*a ma vie de coeur entier*,"' Matthew said, the tip of his index finger touching the gold surface. 'It's old French for "my whole heart for my whole life." And this, "*mon debut et ma fin*," with an alpha and an omega.'

My French was good enough to translate that – 'my beginning and my end.'

'What's on the inner band?'

'It's engraved on both sides.' Matthew read the lines, turning the rings over as he did so. ' "*Se souvenir du passe, et qu'il y a un avenir*." "Remember the past, and that there is a future." '

'The poesies suit us perfectly.' It was eerie that Philippe had selected verses for Ysabeau so long ago that could have meaning for Matthew and me today.

'Vampires are also timewalkers of a sort.' Matthew fitted the ring together. He took my left hand and looked away, afraid of my reaction. 'Will you wear it?'

I took his chin in my fingers, turning his head toward me, and nodded, quite unable to speak. Matthew's face turned shy, and his eyes dropped to my hand, still held in his. He slid the ring over my thumb so it rested just above the knuckle.

'With this ring I thee wed, and with my body I thee honor.' Matthew's voice was quiet, and it shook just a bit. He moved the ring deliberately to my index finger, sliding it down until it met the middle joint. 'And with all my worldly goods I thee endow.'

The ring skipped over my middle finger and slid home onto the fourth finger of my left hand. 'In the name of the Father, and of the Son, and of the Holy Spirit.' He raised my hand to his mouth and his eyes to mine once more, cold lips pressing the ring into my skin. 'Amen.'

'Amen,' I repeated. 'So now we're married in the eyes of vampires and according to church law.' The ring felt heavy, but Ysabeau was right. It did suit me.

'In your eyes, too, I hope.' Matthew sounded uncertain.

'Of course we're married in my eyes.' Something of my happiness must have shown, because his answering smile was as broad and heartfelt as any I'd seen.

'Let's see if *Maman* sent more surprises.' He dove back into the briefcase and came up with a few more books. There was another note, also from Ysabeau.

' "*These were next to the manuscript you asked for,*" ' Matthew read. ' "*I sent them, too – just in case.*" '

'Are they also from 1590?'

'No,' Matthew said, his voice thoughtful, 'none of them.' He reached into the bag again. When his hand emerged, it was clutching the silver pilgrim's badge from Bethany.

There was no note to explain why it was there.

The clock in the front hall struck ten. We were due to leave – soon.

'I wish I knew why she sent these.' Matthew sounded worried.

'Maybe she thought we should carry other things that were precious to you.' I knew how strong his attachment was to the tiny silver coffin.

'Not if it makes it harder for you to concentrate on 1590.' He glanced at the ring on my left hand, and I closed my fingers. There was no way he was taking it off, whether it was from 1590 or not.

'We could call Sarah and ask her what she thinks.'

Matthew shook his head. 'No. Let's not trouble her. We know what we need to do – take three objects and nothing else from the past or present that might get in the way. We'll make an exception for the ring, now that it's on your finger.' He opened the top book and froze.

'What is it?'

'My annotations are in this book – and I don't remember putting them there.'

'It's more than four hundred years old. Maybe you forgot.' In spite of my words, a cold finger ran up my spine.

Matthew flipped through a few more pages and inhaled sharply. 'If we leave these books in the keeping room, along with the pilgrim's badge, will the house take care of them?'

'It will if we ask it to,' I said. 'Matthew, what's going on?'

'I'll tell you later. We should go. These,' he said, lifting the books and Lazarus's coffin, 'need to stay here.'

We changed in silence. I took off everything down to my bare skin, shivering as the linen smock slipped over my shoulders. The cuffs skimmed my wrists as it fell to my ankles, and the wide neck drew closed when I tugged on the string.

Matthew was out of his clothes and into his shirt quickly. It nearly reached his knees, and his long white legs stuck out below. While I collected our clothes, Matthew went to the dining room and came out with stationery and one of his favorite pens. His hand sped across the page, and he folded the single sheet and tucked it into the waiting envelope.

'A note for Sarah,' he explained. 'We'll ask the house to take care of that, too.'

We carried the extra books, the note, and the pilgrim's badge to the keeping room. Mathew put them carefully on the sofa.

'Shall we leave the lights on?' Matthew asked.

'No,' I said. 'Just the porch light, in case it's still dark when they come home.'

There was a smudge of green when we turned off the lamps. It was my grandmother, rocking in her chair.

'Good-bye, Grandma.' Neither Bridget Bishop nor Elizabeth was with her.

Good-bye, Diana.

'The house needs to take care of those.' I pointed to the pile of objects on the sofa.

Don't worry about a thing except for where you're going.

Slowly we walked the length of the house to the back door, shutting off lights as we went. In the family room, Matthew picked up *Doctor Faustus*, the earring, and the chess piece.

I looked around one last time at the familiar brown kitchen. 'Good-bye, house.'

Tabitha heard my voice and ran screeching from the stillroom. She came to an abrupt halt and stared at us without blinking.

'Good-bye, *ma petite*,' Matthew said, stooping to scratch her ears.

We'd decided to leave from the hop barn. It was quiet, with no vestiges of modern life to serve as distractions. We moved through the apple orchard and over the frost-covered grass in our bare feet, the cold quickening our steps. When Matthew pulled open the barn door, my breath was visible in the chilly air.

'It's freezing.' I drew my smock closer, teeth chattering.

'There will be a fire when we arrive at the Old Lodge,' he said, handing me the earring.

I put the thin wire through the hole in my ear and held my hand out for the goddess. Matthew dropped her into my palm.

'What else?'

'Wine, of course – red wine.' Matthew handed me the book and folded me into his arms, planting a firm kiss on my forehead.

'Where are your rooms?' I shut my eyes, remembering the Old Lodge.

'Upstairs, on the western side of the courtyard, overlooking the deer park.'

'And what will it smell like?'

'Like home,' he said. 'Wood smoke and roasted meat from the servants' dinner, beeswax from the candles, and the lavender used to keep the linens fresh.'

'Can you hear anything special?'

'Nothing at all. Just the bells from St Mary's and St Michael's, the crackle of the fires, and the dogs snoring on the stairs.'

'How do you feel when you're there?' I asked, concentrating on his words and the way they in turn made me feel.

'I've always felt . . . ordinary at the Old Lodge,' Matthew said softly. 'It's a place where I can be myself.'

A whiff of lavender swirled through the air, out of time and place in a Madison hop barn in October. I marveled at the scent and thought of my father's note. My eyes were fully open to the possibilities of magic now.

'What will we do tomorrow?'

'We'll walk in the park,' he said, his voice a murmur and his arms iron bands around my ribs. 'If the weather's fine, we'll go riding. There won't be much in the gardens this time of year. There must be a lute somewhere. I'll teach you to play, if you'd like.'

Another scent – spicy and sweet – joined with the lavender, and I saw a tree laden with heavy, golden fruit. A hand stretched up, and a diamond winked in the sunlight, but the fruit was out of reach. I felt frustration and the keen edge of desire, and I was reminded of Emily's telling me that magic was in the heart as well as the mind.

'Is there a quince in the garden?'

'Yes,' Matthew said, his mouth against my hair. 'The fruit will be ripe now.'

The tree dissolved, though the honeyed scent remained. Now I saw a shallow silver dish sitting on a long wooden table. Candles and firelight were reflected in its burnished surface. Piled inside the dish were the bright yellow quinces that were the source of the scent. My fingers flexed on the cover of the book I held in the present, but in my mind they closed on a piece of fruit in the past.

'I can smell the quinces.' Our new life in the Old Lodge was already calling to me. 'Remember, don't let go – no matter what.' With the past everywhere around me, the possibility of losing him was all that was frightening.

'Never,' he said firmly.

'And lift up your foot and then put it down again when I tell you.'

He chuckled. 'I love you, *ma lionne*.' It was an unusual response, but it was enough.

Home, I thought.

My heart tugged with longing.

An unfamiliar bell tolled the hour.

There was a warm touch of fire against my skin.

The air filled with scents of lavender, beeswax, and ripe quince.

'It's time.' Together we lifted our feet and stepped into the unknown.

CHAPTER 43

The house was unnaturally quiet.

For Sarah it wasn't just the absence of chatter or the removal of seven active minds that made it seem so empty.

It was not knowing.

They'd come home earlier than usual from the coven's gathering, claiming they needed to pack for Faye and Janet's road trip. Em had found the empty briefcase sitting by the family-room couch, and Sarah had discovered the clothes bundled up on top of the washing machine.

'They're gone,' Em had said.

Sarah went straight into her arms, her shoulders shaking.

'Are they all right?' she'd whispered.

'They're together,' Em had replied. It wasn't the answer Sarah wanted, but it was honest, just like Em.

They'd thrown their own clothes into duffel bags, paying little attention to what they were doing. Now Tabitha and Em were already in the RV, and Faye and Janet were waiting patiently for Sarah to close up the house.

Sarah and the vampire had talked for hours in the stillroom on their last night in the house, sharing a bottle of red wine. Matthew had told her something of his past and shared his fears for the future. Sarah had listened, making an effort not to show her own shock and surprise at some of the tales he told. Though she was pagan, Sarah understood he wanted to make confession and had cast her in the role of priest. She had given him the absolution she could, knowing all the while that some deeds could never be forgiven or forgotten.

But there was one secret he'd refused to share, and Sarah still knew nothing of where and when her niece had gone.

The floorboards of the Bishop house creaked a chorus of groans and wheezes as Sarah walked through the familiar, darkened rooms. She closed the keeping-room doors and turned to bid farewell to the only home she'd ever known.

The keeping-room doors opened with a sharp bang. One of the floorboards near the fireplace sprang up, revealing a small, black-bound book and a creamy envelope. It was the brightest thing in the room, and it gleamed in the moonlight.

Sarah muffled a cry and held out her hand. The cream square flew easily into it, landed with a slight smack, and flipped over. A single word was written on it.

'*Sarah.*'

She touched the letters lightly and saw Matthew's long white fingers. She tore at the paper, her heart beating fast.

'*Sarah,*' it said. '*Don't worry. We made it.*'

Her heart rate calmed.

Sarah put the single sheet of paper on her mother's rocking chair and gestured for the book. Once the house delivered it, the floorboard returned to its normal resting place with a groan of old wood and the shriek of old nails.

She flipped to the first page. *The Shadow of Night, Containing Two Poeticall Hymnes devised by G. C. Gent. 1594.* The book smelled old but not unpleasant, like incense in a dusty cathedral.

Just like Matthew, Sarah thought with a smile.

A slip of paper stuck out of the top. It led her to the dedication page. '*To my deare and most worthy friend Matthew Roydon.*' Sarah peered more closely and saw a tiny, faded drawing of a hand with a ruffled cuff pointing imperiously to the name, with the number '*29*' written underneath in ancient brown ink.

She turned obediently to page twenty-nine, struggling through tears as she read the underlined passage:

She hunters makes: and of that substance hounds

Whose mouths deafe heaven, and furrow earth with wounds,
And marvaile not a Nimphe so rich in grace
To hounds rude pursuits should be given in chase.
For she could turne her selfe to everie shape
Of swiftest beasts, and at her pleasure scape.

The words conjured up the image of Diana – clear, bright, unbidden – her face framed with gauzy wings and her throat thickly encircled with silver and diamonds. A single tear-shaped ruby quivered on her skin like a drop of blood, nestled into the notch between her collarbones.

In the stillroom, as the sun was rising, he had promised to find some way to let her know Diana was safe.

'Thank you, Matthew.' Sarah kissed the book and the note and threw them into the cavernous fireplace. She said the words to conjure a white-hot fire. The paper caught quickly, and the book's edges began to curl.

Sarah watched the fire burn for a few moments. Then she walked out the front door, leaving it unlocked, and didn't look back.

Once the door closed, a worn silver coffin shot down the chimney and landed on the burning paper. Two gobbets of blood and mercury, released from the hollow chambers inside the ampulla by the heat of the fire, chased each other around the surface of the book before falling into the grate. There they seeped into the soft old mortar of the fireplace and traveled into the heart of the house. When they reached it, the house sighed with relief and released a forgotten, forbidden scent.

Sarah drank in the cool night air as she climbed into the RV. Her senses were not sharp enough to catch the cinnamon and blackthorn, honeysuckle and chamomile dancing in the air.

'Okay?' Em asked, her voice serene.

Sarah leaned across the cat carrier that held Tabitha and squeezed Em's knee. 'Just fine.'

Faye turned the key in the ignition and pulled down the driveway and onto the county road that would take them to the interstate, chattering about where they could stop for breakfast.

The four witches were too far away to perceive the shift in atmosphere around the house as hundreds of night creatures detected the unusual aroma of commingled vampire and witch, or to see the pale green smudges of the two ghosts in the keeping-room window.

Bridget Bishop and Diana's grandmother watched the vehicle's departure.

What will we do now? Diana's grandmother asked.

What we've always done, Joanna, Bridget replied. *Remember the past – and await the future.*

ACKNOWLEDGMENTS

My greatest debt is to the friends and family who read this book, chapter by chapter, as it was written: Cara, Karen, Lisa, Margaret, and my mom, Olive. Peg and Lynn, as always, provided excellent meals, warm companionship, and wise counsel. And I am especially appreciative of the editorial work that Lisa Halttunen did to prepare the manuscript for submission.

Colleagues generously lent me their expertise as I wandered far from my own area of specialization. Philippa Levine, Andrés Reséndez, Vanessa Schwartz, and Patrick Wyman steered me in the right direction whenever I took a misstep. Any errors that remain are, of course, my own.

I will always be grateful that Sam Stoloff of the Frances Goldin Literary Agency took the news that I had written a novel, and not another work of history, with grace and good humor. He also read the early drafts with a keen eye. Additional thanks to the agency's Ellen Geiger, for her inspired choice of dinner companions!

The team at Viking has become a second family to me. My editor, Carole DeSanti, represents what every author hopes for when they are writing a book: someone who will not only appreciate what you have put on the page but can envision what story those words could tell if they were tweaked just so. Maureen Sugden, copy editor extraordinaire, polished the book in record time. Thank you also to Clare Ferraro, Leigh Butler, Hal Fessenden, and the rights group; Nancy Sheppard, Carolyn Coleburn, and the marketing and sales team; Victoria Klose, Christopher Russell and everyone who has helped transform this work from a stack of paper into a book.

Because this is a book *about* books, I consulted a substantial number of texts as I wrote. Curious readers can find some of them by consulting the Douay-Rheims translation of the Bible, Marie-Louise von Franz's critical edition and translation of *Aurora Consurgens* (Pantheon Books, 1966), and Paul Eugene Memmo's translation of Giordano Bruno's *Heroic Frenzies* (University of North Carolina Press, 1964). Those readers who do go exploring should know that the translations here are my own and therefore have their idiosyncrasies. Anyone who wants to delve further into the mind of Charles Darwin has the ideal place to start in Janet Browne's *Charles Darwin: A Biography* (2 vols., Alfred Knopf, 1995 and 2002). And for a lucid introduction to mtDNA and its application to the problems of human history consult Brian Sykes, *The Seven Daughters of Eve* (W. W. Norton, 2001).

ARE YOU READY FOR MORE?

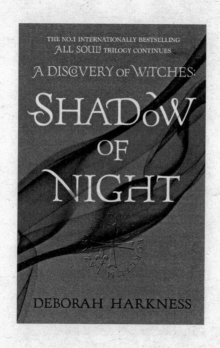

AND DON'T MISS THE SPECTACULAR
CONCLUSION TO THE ALL SOULS TRILOGY

THE BOOK OF LIFE

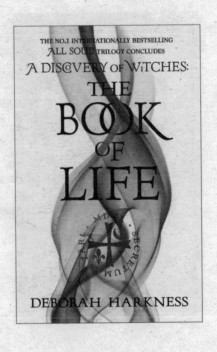

AND TIME'S CONVERT,
THE BRAND NEW NOVEL SET IN
THE ALL SOULS WORLD, IS AVAILABLE NOW